Patterns of global terrorism 1985-2005 :
REF 303.6 PAT   28424

Antioch Community High School

Antioch Community High School
Library
1133 S. Main Street
Antioch, IL 60002

DEMCO

PATTERNS of GLOBAL TERRORISM 1985–2005

U.S. DEPARTMENT OF STATE REPORTS WITH
SUPPLEMENTARY DOCUMENTS AND STATISTICS

PATTERNS of GLOBAL TERRORISM 1985–2005

U.S. DEPARTMENT OF STATE REPORTS WITH SUPPLEMENTARY DOCUMENTS AND STATISTICS

Anna Sabasteanski, Editor

www.PatternsofGlobalTerrorism.com

Volume One

BERKSHIRE PUBLISHING GROUP

Great Barrington, Massachusetts U.S.A.

Copyright © 2005 by Berkshire Publishing Group LLC

All rights reserved. No part of this book may be reproduced or utilized in any form or by any means, electronic or mechanical, including photocopying, recording, or by any information storage and retrieval system, without permission in writing from the publisher.

Most of the material included in this collection was obtained from the U.S. government. Some of the data has been retrieved from the MIPT Terrorism Knowledge Base, accessed between July and September of 2005, from the website at http://www.tkb.org. The Terrorism Knowledge Base is the property of the National Memorial Institute for the Prevention of Terrorism (MIPT) (http://www.mipt.org) and incorporates information from MIPT and third parties, which is the property of the respective copyright holders. In some cases, quotations and other material have been incorporated under "fair use" provisions of the Copyright Act.

This collection contains information compiled from sources we believe to be reliable, and we have used our best efforts to ensure accuracy of the material. However, errors may be present. Berkshire Publishing Group and its partners disclaim any liability for direct, indirect, secondary or any other damages resulting from use of this material.

Adverse mention of individuals associated with any political, social, ethnic, religious, or national group does not imply that all members of that group are terrorists.

Inclusion of web links (URLs) does not imply endorsement, nor are we responsible in any way for the content of third-party websites.

For information:
Berkshire Publishing Group LLC
314 Main Street
Great Barrington, Massachusetts 01230
www.berkshirepublishing.com

Printed in the United States of America

Library of Congress Cataloging-in-Publication Data
Patterns of global terrorism 1985–2005: U.S. Department of State reports with supplementary documents and statistics/Anna Sabasteanski, editor.
    p. cm.
    Summary: "A comprehensive reference—designed for military, government, and security professionals as well as students of politics, international relations, history, public policy, homeland security, foreign policy, emergency management, and military science—that collates the U.S. Department of State reports on terrorism, Patterns of Global Terrorism, with additional analytical and statistical material"—Provided by publisher.
    Includes index.
    ISBN 0-9743091-3-3 (alk. paper)
    1. Terrorism—Sources. 2. Terrorism—Statistics. I. Sabasteanski, Anna, 1958–
    HV6431.P3773 2005
    303.6'2509049—dc22   2005026976

Editorial and Production Staff

Project Director and Consulting Editor
David Levinson, PhD

Editorial/Production Coordinator
Marcy Ross

Editorial and Production Staff
Leslie Bateville, Julie Bourbeau, Joanne Conti, Roxanne Gawthrop, Jake Makler, and Kristin Pickford

Copyeditor
Francesca Forrest

Composition Artist
Brad Walrod

Designers
Joseph DiStefano and Brad Walrod

Graph Design
Bryan Christie

Mapmaker
XNR Productions

Proofreaders
Mary Bagg, Eileen Clawson, Robin Gold, and Elizabeth Larson

Indexer
Scott Smiley

Printers
Thomson-Shore

Contents

Reader's Guide ix

Publisher's Preface xiii

Introduction xv

Acknowledgments xxvii

About the Editors xxviii

Part 1 Counterterrorism 1

U.S. Policies in Combating Terrorism *4*
U.S. Legal Response *27*
Sanctions *35*
State Sponsors of Terrorism *52*
Terrorist Financing *111*
U.S. Military Response *135*
International Response *142*

Part 2 International Terrorist Groups 151

Part 3 Country Reports 1985–2004 203

Part 4 Chronology of Significant Terrorist Incidents 1961–2005 725

vii

Part 5 Terrorist Incidents by Country and Group 1985–2004 859

Tables of Terrorist Incidents by Country 1985–2004 *861*

Maps of Terrorist Incidents by Country 1985–2004 *883*

Tables of Terrorist Incidents by Group 1985–2005 *924*

Part 6 Trends over Time: Graphs on Terrorism 971

Incidents *974*

Casualties *979*

Targets *986*

Tactics *1009*

Index 1021

Reader's Guide

The Reader's Guide below serves as an expanded table of contents, allowing you to see in the space of four pages all the elements of Patterns of Global Terrorism *grouped by topic or, in the case of the* Country Reports *and collateral documents, by chronology.*

Introduction to *Patterns of Global Terrorism 1985–2005: U.S. Department of State Reports with Supplementary Documents and Statistics*

Part 1 Counterterrorism

Overview of Counterterrorism *Anna Sabasteanski*

U.S. Policies in Combating Terrorism
  Overview of U.S. Policies in Combating Terrorism *Anna Sabasteanski*
  Policy Developments After September 11 *Patterns of Global Terrorism 2002*
  Present U.S. Policy *George W. Bush Speech*
  Foreign Terrorist Organization Designations *Anna Sabasteanski*
  Combating Terrorism: Department of State Programs to Combat Terrorism Abroad *GAO Report*
  Terrorism and National Security: Issues and Trends *CRS Report*

U.S. Legal Response
  Overview of U.S. Legal Response *Anna Sabasteanski*
  Selections from *Patterns of Global Terrorism 1987 and 1996–2003*

Sanctions
  Overview of Sanctions *Anna Sabasteanski*
  Sanctions Lists
  Economic Sanctions to Achieve U.S. Foreign Policy Goals *CRS Report*

State Sponsors of Terrorism
  Overview of State Sponsors of Terrorism *Anna Sabasteanski*
  Collated Reports on State Sponsors of Terrorism *Patterns of Global Terrorism*
    Afghanistan, Cuba, Iran, Iraq, Libya, Nicaragua, North Korea, South Yemen, Soviet Union and Eastern Europe, Sudan, and Syria

Terrorist Financing
  Overview of Terrorist Financing *Anna Sabasteanski*
  Countering Terrorism on the Economic Front *Patterns of Global Terrorism 2002 and 2003*
  U.S. Measures Implementing the 2004 U.S.-EU Declaration on Combating Terrorism *U.S. Department of State*
  Narcoterrorism *Patterns of Global Terrorism 1989*
  Money Laundering and Terrorist Financing in the Middle East and South Asia *U.S. Department of State*
  Terrorist Financing: The 9/11 Commission Recommendation *CRS Report*
  The Financial Action Task Force: An Overview *CRS Report*

U.S. Military Response
  Overview of U.S. Military Response *Anna Sabasteanski*
  The Military Campaign in Afghanistan, 2001 *Patterns of Global Terrorism 2001*
  The Military Counterterrorism Campaign in 2002 *Patterns of Global Terrorism 2002*

The Military Counterterrorism Campaign in
2003 *Patterns of Global Terrorism 2003*
Iraq and Terrorism *Patterns of Global Terrorism 2003*
The Evolving Terrorist Threat *Patterns of Global Terrorism* 2004

International Response
Overview of International Response *Anna Sabasteanski*
International Response to September 11 *Patterns of Global Terrorism 2001*
U.N. Actions Against Terrorism *Patterns of Global Terrorism 2001*
International Counterterrorism Laws *Anna Sabasteanski*

Part 2 International Terrorist Groups

Overview of International Terrorist Groups *Anna Sabasteanski*

The "FTO List" and Congress: Sanctioning Designated Foreign Terrorist Organizations *CRS Report*

Profiles of International Terrorist Groups
Collated from *Patterns of Global Terrorism 1985–2004*

Part 3 Country Reports 1985–2004

Overview of Country Reports *Anna Sabasteanski*

Terrorism in the 1980s
Overview of Terrorism in the 1980s *Anna Sabasteanski*
Patterns of Global Terrorism 1985
Patterns of Global Terrorism 1986
Patterns of Global Terrorism 1987
Patterns of Global Terrorism 1988
Patterns of Global Terrorism 1989

Terrorism in the 1990s
Overview of Terrorism in the 1990s *Anna Sabasteanski*
Patterns of Global Terrorism 1990
Patterns of Global Terrorism 1991
Patterns of Global Terrorism 1992
Patterns of Global Terrorism 1993
Patterns of Global Terrorism 1994
Patterns of Global Terrorism 1995
Patterns of Global Terrorism 1996
Patterns of Global Terrorism 1997
Patterns of Global Terrorism 1998
Patterns of Global Terrorism 1999

Terrorism in the New Millennium
Overview of Terrorism in the New Millennium *Anna Sabasteanski*
Patterns of Global Terrorism 2000
Patterns of Global Terrorism 2001
Patterns of Global Terrorism 2002
Patterns of Global Terrorism 2003
Rollout of Patterns of Global Terrorism 2003 *Department of State Transcripts*
The Department of State's Patterns of Global Terrorism Report: Trends, State Sponsors, and Related Issues *CRS Report*
Review of the Department of State's Patterns of Global Terrorism Report 2003 *Office of the Inspector General's Report*
Proposals for Intelligence Reorganization, 1949–2004 *CRS Report*
Terrorism: Key Recommendations of the 9/11 Commission and Recent Major Commissions and Inquiries *CRS Report*
Country Reports on Terrorism 2004
Global Jihad: Evolving and Adapting *Country Reports on Terrorism 2004*
Release of Country Reports on Terrorism for 2004 *U.S. Department of State Transcripts*
Reviewing the Department of State's Annual Report on Terrorism *U.S. House of Representatives Hearing*
The National Counterterrorism Center: Implementation Challenges and Issues for Congress *CRS Report*

Part 4 Chronology of Significant Terrorist Incidents 1961–2005

Overview of Chronology of Significant Terrorist Incidents 1961–2005 *Anna Sabasteanski*

Chronology of Significant Terrorist Incidents 1961–2005

Part 5 Terrorist Incidents by Country and Group 1985–2004

Overview of Terrorist Incidents by Country 1985–2004 *Anna Sabasteanski*

Tables of Terrorist Incidents by Country 1985–2004
 Overview of Tables of Terrorist Incidents by Country 1985–2004 *Anna Sabasteanski*

Maps of Terrorist Incidents by Country 1985–2004
 Overview of Maps of Terrorist Incidents by Country 1985–2004 *Anna Sabasteanski*

Tables of Terrorist Incidents by Group 1985–2005
 Overview of Tables of Terrorist Incidents by Group 1985–2005 *Anna Sabasteanski*

Part 6 Trends over Time: Graphs on Terrorism

Overview of Trends over Time: Graphs on Terrorism *Anna Sabasteanski*

Incidents
 Overview of Incidents *Anna Sabasteanski*
 Terrorist Incidents and Incidents by Region (1981–2004)
 Anti-United States Attacks and Non-United States Attacks (1981–2004)
 Anti-United States Attacks and Non-United States Attacks as Percentages of Total Attacks (1981–2004)
 Anti-United States Attacks by Region (1981–2004)

Casualties
 Overview of Casualties *Anna Sabasteanski*
 Number of People Killed and Injured by Region (1968–2004)
 Number of Deaths by Region (1968–2004)
 Number of Injuries by Region (1968–2004)
 International Casualties by Region (1988–2004)
 Anti-United States Casualties (1988–2004)
 Anti-United States and Non-United States Casualties as Percentages of Total Casualties (1988–2004)

Targets
 Overview of Targets *Anna Sabasteanski*
 Abortion-Related—Incidents, Injuries, and Fatalities (1968–2005)
 Airports and Airlines—Incidents, Injuries, and Fatalities (1968–2005)
 Businesses—Incidents, Injuries, and Fatalities (1968–2005)
 Diplomatic—Incidents, Injuries, and Fatalities (1968–2005)
 Educational Institutions—Incidents, Injuries, and Fatalities (1968–2005)
 Food Water Supply—Incidents, Injuries, and Fatalities (1968–2005)
 Government—Incidents, Injuries, and Fatalities (1968–2005)
 Journalists and Media—Incidents, Injuries, and Fatalities (1968–2005)
 Maritime—Incidents, Injuries, and Fatalities (1968–2005)
 Military—Incidents, Injuries, and Fatalities (1968–2005)
 Non-Governmental Organizations—Incidents, Injuries, and Fatalities (1968–2005)
 Other Targets—Incidents, Injuries, and Fatalities (1968–2005)

Police-Related—Incidents, Injuries, and Fatalities (1968–2005)

Private Citizens and Property—Incidents, Injuries, and Fatalities (1968–2005)

Religious Figures or Institutions—Incidents, Injuries, and Fatalities (1968–2005)

Telecommunications—Incidents, Injuries, and Fatalities (1968–2005)

Terrorists—Incidents, Injuries, and Fatalities (1968–2005)

Tourists—Incidents, Injuries, and Fatalities (1968–2005)

Transportation—Incidents, Injuries, and Fatalities (1968–2005)

Unknown—Incidents, Injuries, and Fatalities (1968–2005)

Utilities—Incidents, Injuries, and Fatalities (1968–2005)

Number of Attacks on Business, Diplomatic, Government, Military, Other Facilities (1989–2003)

Tactics

Overview of Tactics *Anna Sabasteanski*

Armed Attacks—Incidents, Injuries, and Fatalities (1968–2005)

Arson—Incidents, Injuries, and Fatalities (1968–2005)

Assassination—Incidents, Injuries, and Fatalities (1968–2005)

Barricade/Hostage—Incidents, Injuries, and Fatalities (1968–2005)

Bombing—Incidents, Injuries, and Fatalities (1968–2005)

Hijacking—Incidents, Injuries, and Fatalities (1968–2005)

Kidnapping—Incidents, Injuries, and Fatalities (1968–2005)

Other—Incidents, Injuries, and Fatalities (1968–2005)

Unconventional Attack—Incidents, Injuries, and Fatalities (1968–2005)

Unknown Tactics—Incidents, Injuries, and Fatalities (1968–2005)

Index

Notes

Spelling conventions have varied through the years and between organizations within and outside the government. For example, within these volumes a reader will see "al-Qaeda" in one government document and "al-Qaida" in another. When possible, however, we have standardized inconsistent spellings within particular reports so that they would not appear to be typographic errors. We have listed alternate spellings in our index.

Also, the footnotes in the *Country Reports* are from the reports themselves; the pronouns "we" and "our" referred to in them relate to the State Department. However, in the early footnotes Berkshire Publishing does interject the information that the State Department's definitions of terrorist incidents can be found in Berkshire's own Introduction to this work.

Publisher's Preface

Berkshire Publishing is proud to present this compilation of *Patterns of Global Terrorism*, an enhanced collection of U.S. State Department reports published yearly from 1985 through 2004 (with additional information covering 2005) that offers readers a window into efforts to counter terrorist threats and make our world a safer place. The collection is edited by international terrorism expert Anna Sabasteanski, who has added introductory overviews, redone all the statistical tables, and supplemented the reports with additional government documents related to topics such as terrorist financing and the use of international sanctions. The resulting collection is the most complete and authoritative resource on modern terrorism around the globe.

Terrorism—violence directed against citizens, not soldiers, in order to influence public opinion and thus affect government policy—is both political and personal. It changes our perceptions of risk, trust, and allegiance in ways that have an impact on how we vote and how we interact with others in our daily lives. And of course terrorism and counterterrorist efforts have an increasingly important financial cost to taxpayers around the world.

By bringing out this collection, Berkshire Publishing makes it much easier for everyone—ordinary citizens as well as students and professionals—to understand what terrorism really is. We think it is essential that readers be able to see how the United States, the richest and most powerful country in the world, has perceived terrorism and responded to it over the course of the last twenty years.

How This Collection Came to Be

When editor Anna Sabasteanski and I met in 2002, we were surprised to find that we had both lived within a block or two of Harrods department store in London when it was bombed in 1983 by the IRA. Six people, including an American woman, lost their lives in that attack. Our work together on this project began on 21 April 2005. That morning, I made a note to call Anna to talk about possible publishing projects. Late in the day, before I'd managed to call her the phone rang. It was Anna. "Berkshire should publish *Patterns of Global Terrorism*," she said. "The State Department is canceling it, and this is the time to put the whole twenty years together." She explained that after the 1983 bombings in Lebanon, the State Department began publishing these reports on international terrorism and *Patterns* had become the premier source of authoritative information on the subject.

Many people have asked if we worried about possible repercussions from the U.S. government, given that the reports had became especially controversial after 2003. But this is not a partisan publication, and our intention is not to indict the current administration or past ones, but rather to ensure that this valuable historical information and statistical data (which we have presented in completely new charts and maps) is available and easy to use and understand. Additional background information and reports provide further detail on the history and importance of *Patterns of Global Terrorism*.

What the Reports Have to Offer

There are many things we can learn from these important documents. First, we can see changes in perspective, tone, and emphasis. For example, the African National Congress, led by Nelson Mandela (former imprisoned terrorist; today a Nobel peace prize winner), is now the respected governing party in South Africa, but when publication of *Patterns* first began, the ANC was considered a terrorist organization.

We have brought together information on state sponsors of terrorism for each year (1985–2004), so that readers can follow developments over time. Readers can see, for example, Libya's change in stance from the time of the downing of the Pan Am jet over Lockerbie, Scotland, in 1988, when it denied involvement, through its acceptance of responsibility and its abjuring of support for terrorism in the future.

Looking at the reports over the years, one can see that under President Ronald Reagan global terrorism was not well understood, that under President Bill Clinton it was not a high priority, and that since September 11, 2001 it has been overtly politicized. Changes in public policy and government attitudes to terrorism are clear. The *Patterns* of recent years often read like a school report card, assessing nations in terms of their willingness to follow the United States' lead in international affairs, and the reports have been filled with photos of President George W. Bush and leaders of nations deemed to be allies in the war on terrorism or the invasion of Iraq.

As well as showing changes in perspective, tone, and emphasis over time, the collection provides insight into the complexities of assembling statistical data and conducting global analysis. *Patterns,* as well as the many selections from other government reports and interviews, show the impressive data collection effort that has been under way and the immense amount of work that has gone on at the State Department to develop solid sources for government decision making. The confusion and missteps of recent years have also shown how vulnerable this kind of effort is to human error, budget constraints, and political expediency.

The 2003 report became controversial because it showed a slight decline in the number of terrorist attacks—suggesting that the "war on terror" was succeeding—when in fact, the number of incidents had risen, and the apparent decline was due to faulty data. Congressman Henry Waxman wrote to secretary of state Colin Powell on 17 May 2004, saying, "This manipulation may serve the Administration's political interests, but it calls into serious doubt the integrity of the report." The 2003 *Patterns* report was corrected and five specific recommendations were made for ensuring the accuracy of future reports. When Colin Powell gave a press conference on the occasion of the release of the corrected 2003 report, he said, "The report is not designed to make our efforts look better or worse, or terrorism look better or worse, but to provide the facts to the American people."

But in April 2005, the U.S. Department of State announced that it would no longer publish *Patterns.* Instead of incorporating the data, it deferred statistical reporting to the new National Counterterrorist Center (NCTC). *Patterns of Global Terrorism* is no more, and in its place, we have the yearly *Country Reports on Terrorism,* which lack the comprehensiveness and statistical information of *Patterns.*

There have been accusations on blogs and in the press that the reports were cancelled to avoid politically unattractive truths. The statistics eventually released by NCTC indeed showed that there were more significant incidents of terrorism in 2004 than ever before and that loss of life in 2004 was the second highest in thirty-five years—only the 9/11 fatalities were higher. (We have added 2005 data to most of the extensive, newly drawn charts and graphs that compose Part 6.)

Beyond the raw facts, these volumes enable us to see the impact of terrorism on people around the world. Terrorism is not new—from the time of the first human civilizations, we can find accounts of events that can reasonably be called terrorism. Innocent people have always been casualties of war, and it has long been a common form of retaliation to burn villages and murder whole families. Americans, while more conscious of terrorism today than they were prior to 9/11, remain less affected by it than virtually any other people on earth. Even with the loss of lives in the 2001 attacks in New York and Washington, more people died from terrorism elsewhere in the world that year. We Americans—and people in most other countries—are considerably more likely to be killed by lightning than by a terrorist.

The reports do reveal that terrorist attacks today are more indiscriminant than ever before, and that the number of attacks and casualties has grown enormously in recent years, including greater use of large bombs to cause mass casualties. The philosophical and cultural divide between attackers and targets seems harder than ever to bridge. Negotiation often does not seem possible—a fact that changes the tactics used by terrorists and the methods used to counter them. Terrorism is sometimes called "the war of the poor," and it does seem increasingly to terrify the rich.

Terrorism is also more varied than one would think from general media reports. It includes bombings, shootings, kidnappings, and hijackings, most of them on a relatively small scale. Terrorists are creative, often a step ahead of law enforcement, intelligence and military efforts. They have used planes as weapons, disguised bombs as pregnancies and hidden them in animal carcasses, and sent anthrax through the mail. Most are young men, but their ranks include children, the elderly and infirm, and widows. They are of all ages, ethnic groups, religions, and political persuasions.

We do not by any means believe that the U.S. Department of State has the only valuable information on terrorism. We are certain, though, that this collection is not only an unprecedented resource but that it will help researchers in other nations to understand the U.S. perspective on global terrorism. In issuing *Patterns of Global Terrorism 1985–2005,* Berkshire Publishing Group's goal is to provide students and citizens with accessible, authoritative resources that will help them understand their world, and to encourage a more thoughtful, informed approach to solving the problem of international terrorism.

Karen Christensen, 27 September 2005
CEO and Publisher
Berkshire Publishing Group LLC
Great Barrington, Massachusetts

Introduction

Anna Sabasteanski

The full story of terrorism and political violence emerges only over time. As an attack occurs, details can be confusing and contradictory, or open to interpretation. The perpetrators' identity or intent may be unclear or unknown. Injuries may turn into fatalities, and actual casualties may never be fully determined. Given the absence of a common definition of terrorism, even determining the nature of an attack is as much an art as it is a science.

Today, when the number of terrorist attacks across the globe is rising to levels never seen before, it is vital that we step back and put current events into context. This collection of major reports on global terrorism, supplemented with additional analysis, reference documents, and recent data, provides the context needed by professionals, policymakers, and citizens who open their daily newspaper to read headlines like these:

"Suicide Bomber Attacks Israeli Bus Station"

"Fear of Occupation Keeps Pyongyang on Nuclear Trail"

"Fight Continues to Make Al-Qaeda Convictions Stick"

"Armed Kurds Fomenting Unrest in Iran Pose Security Threat to Tehran"

"Killing of 2 Serbs Raises Fear of Ethnic Unrest in Kosovo"

"Afghan Parliamentary Candidate Is Killed"

"Iraq Charter a 'Recipe for Chaos'"

The core of this collection is twenty years of *Patterns of Global Terrorism* reports issued by the U.S. Department of State. Each annual report provides a chronology of global terrorism for the year, profiles of terrorist organizations, regional and nation-by-nation reviews, numeric and statistical data, and other detail relevant to that year.

This collection does not merely reproduce the reports in their original form, however. Rather, to make the reports easier to find, read, analyze, and draw conclusions from, we have taken them apart and reorganized them. In addition, we have integrated sixteen additional government reports and documents relevant to global terrorism that place the annual reports in political context and tell us what the U.S. government is doing to combat terrorism. We have also developed ninety statistical tables, graphs, and maps that show trends in global terrorism over time and across regions and nations. Finally we have added some additional information that both pre- and post-dates the reports.

Structure of Patterns of Global Terrorism, 1985–2005

This collection begins with the 1985 State Department's *Patterns of Global Terrorism* (*Patterns*) report, and includes all the subsequent reports, through the final (2003) report; it also includes the first (2004) *Country Report* and the new National Counterterrorism Center's chronology. During these two crucial decades, the world witnessed a shift from "terrorism from above" to "terrorism from below"—that is, a shift from terrorism as a tool of those in power (and so legitimizing efforts to remove them from power) to terrorism as a tool of the powerless, sometimes used against their peers.

Changes to the Original Reports

To make it easier to understand this trend, we made a number of changes and additions to the collection that are designed to make relevant information easier to find:

1. The design of the collection focuses on readability and rapid access.
2. Some information, like the definition of terrorism and the legal basis for the reports, was repeated in multiple reports. We incorporated such detail only once, using the most recent version available.
3. Information about public policy, legal issues, terrorist financing, and so on was treated differently year by year. We have gathered that information by topic; it can be found at the beginning of the collection. Similarly the annual reports on state sponsors of terrorism, terrorist groups, and chronologies have been consolidated into single sections.
4. Although the annual regional and country reports have been reproduced in full, we did consolidate some sections, as described above. We also omitted occasional tables or inserts whose contents were addressed in the body of the reports or in one of the consolidated features. For example, the U.S. hostages taken captive in Lebanon in 1985 were listed in tables in some of the early reports, although the information was also contained in the country reports and chronology.

5. Statistical data were obtained from the reports, the National Counterterrorism Center (NCTC) database, and the Memorial Institute for the Prevention of Terrorism (MIPT) Terrorism Knowledge Base. We used the most recent and comprehensive data available and have cited the relevant sources in the introduction to each section. The reports included in *Patterns* did not provide the level of detail we believe is necessary.
6. In order to maintain consistent report presentation and keep the size and cost of the collection as low as possible, we eliminated the photographs used in the original reports.
7. We have added an extensive index that permits easy cross-referencing of the materials.

Sections

Patterns of Global Terrorism, 1985–2004 is divided into six sections.

- Part 1 is a lengthy consideration and synthesis of documents about counterterrorism, with a focus on U.S. efforts to combat global terrorism. It covers U.S. policies and legal and military responses, sanctions, state sponsors of terrorism, and the financing of terrorism.
- Part 2 provides profiles of major global terrorist organizations. These are *Patterns* reports, revised and updated for inclusion here.
- Part 3, the lengthiest section of the collection, provides the regional and country reports from 1985 to 2004. These reports provide yearly summaries of each nation's experience with global terrorism as well as their efforts to combat it. The reports from 2001 onward also comment on each nation's participation in the U.S.-led "war on terrorism," and we have added other related government documents.
- Part 4 is a chronology of significant terrorist incidents from 1961 to 2005. The material from 1961 to 1984 and for 2005 has been added to the chronologies provided by the reports.
- Part 5 comprises twenty statistical tables showing the number of terrorist incidents in each nation in each year from 1985 to 2004 and twenty maps showing the same information.
- Part 6 shows trends in terrorism over time through a series of over forty graphs. The graphs, which summarize several hundred pages of information, cover number and distribution of incidents, number of people killed or injured, types of targets, tactics, and the level of activity by terrorist groups.

Using the Collection

We provide two user aids to make navigating the collection easy: the Reader's Guide and the index. The Reader's Guide at the beginning of each volume is a detailed table of contents that lists all the documents, tables, and graphs included in the work. The extensive index not only directs readers to the page on which their topic is discussed but also tells them the part of the collection in which the information is found. For example, the index entry for El Salvador shows the following:

El Salvador
  chronology of incidents (1980–1984), 729
  chronology of incidents (1985), 731, 732
  chronology of incidents (1988), 738
  chronology of incidents (1991), 742
  chronology of incidents (2000), 786
  country reports on (1985–1989), 216, 227, 237, 255, 278–279
  country reports on (1990–1994), 311, 329

This way, the reader can quickly see if the information is reported in the chronology, the country reports, or both parts of the collection.

Genesis of This Collection

This collection was first conceived after the 9/11 attacks, the first experience of international terrorism to affect many Americans personally. It seemed important to remind people that terrorism has a long history and to learn the lessons of our friends around the world who have lived with terrorism for, in some cases, millennia. After the intelligence reorganization that followed the 9/11 Commission's report on the attacks, the Department of State ceased publishing *Patterns*. We wanted to mark the end of this era with a tribute, and this collection became that tribute.

The publication of this collection marks an era of reporting on terrorism, but the U.S. documentation of terrorism predates the publication of *Patterns*. The Central Intelligence Agency (CIA) was responsible for documenting terrorism in the 1970s; some of those responsibilities were moved to the Department of State in 1982. Terrorism reporting became law in 1987, under Title 22, Chapter 38, § 2656f of the U.S. Criminal Code, as follows.:

§2656f. Annual country reports on terrorism

(a) Requirement of annual country reports on terrorism
The Secretary of State shall transmit to the Speaker of the House of Representatives and the Committee on Foreign Relations of the Senate, by April 30 of each year, a full and complete report providing—

  (1) detailed assessments with respect to each foreign country—

    (A) in which acts of international terrorism occurred which were, in the opinion of the Secretary, of major significance;

    (B) about which the Congress was notified during the preceding five years pursuant to section 2405(j) of the Appendix to title 50; and

(C) which the Secretary determines should be the subject of such report;

(2) all relevant information about the activities during the preceding year of any terrorist group, and any umbrella group under which such terrorist group falls, known to be responsible for the kidnaping or death of an American citizen during the preceding five years, any terrorist group known to be financed by countries about which Congress was notified during the preceding year pursuant to section 2405(j) of the Appendix to title 50, and any other known international terrorist group which the Secretary determines should be the subject of such report;

(3) with respect to each foreign country from which the United States Government has sought cooperation during the previous five years in the investigation or prosecution of an act of international terrorism against United States citizens or interests, information on—

   (A) the extent to which the government of the foreign country is cooperating with the United States Government in apprehending, convicting, and punishing the individual or individuals responsible for the act; and

   (B) the extent to which the government of the foreign country is cooperating in preventing further acts of terrorism against United States citizens in the foreign country; and

(4) with respect to each foreign country from which the United States Government has sought cooperation during the previous five years in the prevention of an act of international terrorism against such citizens or interests, the information described in paragraph (3)(B).

(b) Provisions to be included in report

The report required under subsection (a) of this section should to the extent feasible include (but not be limited to)—

(1) with respect to subsection (a)(1)—

   (A) a review of major counterterrorism efforts undertaken by countries which are the subject of such report, including, as appropriate, steps taken in international fora;

   (B) the response of the judicial system of each country which is the subject of such report with respect to matters relating to terrorism affecting American citizens or facilities, or which have, in the opinion of the Secretary, a significant impact on United States counterterrorism efforts, including responses to extradition requests; and

   (C) significant support, if any, for international terrorism by each country which is the subject of such report, including (but not limited to)—

      (i) political and financial support;

      (ii) diplomatic support through diplomatic recognition and use of the diplomatic pouch;

      (iii) providing sanctuary to terrorists or terrorist groups; and

      (iv) the positions (including voting records) on matters relating to terrorism in the General Assembly of the United Nations and other international bodies and fora of each country which is the subject of such report; and

(2) with respect to subsection (a)(2) of this section, any—

   (A) significant financial support provided by foreign governments to those groups directly, or provided in support of their activities;

   (B) provisions of significant military or paramilitary training or transfer of weapons by foreign governments to those groups;

   (C) provision of diplomatic recognition or privileges by foreign governments to those groups;

   (D) provision by foreign governments of sanctuary from prosecution to these groups or their members responsible for the commission, attempt, or planning of an act of international terrorism; and

   (E) efforts by the United States to eliminate international financial support provided to those groups directly or provided in support of their activities.

(c) Classification of report

(1) Except as provided in paragraph (2), the report required under subsection (a) of this section shall, to the extent practicable, be submitted in an unclassified form and may be accompanied by a classified appendix.

(2) If the Secretary of State determines that the transmittal of the information with respect to a foreign country under paragraph (3) or (4) of subsection (a) of this section in classified form would make more likely the cooperation of the government of the foreign country as specified in such paragraph, the Secretary may transmit the information under such paragraph in classified form.

(d) Definitions

As used in this section—

(1) the term "international terrorism" means terrorism involving citizens or the territory of more than 1 country;

(2) the term "terrorism" means premeditated, politically motivated violence perpetrated against noncombatant targets by subnational groups or clandestine agents; and

(3) the term "terrorist group" means any group practicing, or which has significant subgroups which practice, international terrorism.

(e) Reporting period

(1) The report required under subsection (a) of this section shall cover the events of the calendar year preceding the year in which the report is submitted.

(2) The report required by subsection (a) of this section to be submitted by March 31, 1988, may be submitted no later than August 31, 1988.[1]

Terrorism in Historical Perspective

Terrorism, even before its name emerged, has existed as long as human society. The ancient Greeks, for example, were adept in the wartime use of flamethrowers, poison gases, incendiary bombs, and biological attacks:

> It was Hercules, the greatest hero of Greek mythology, who invented the first biological weapon described in Western literature. When he dipped his arrows in serpent venom, he opened up a world not only of toxic warfare, but also of unanticipated consequences. Indeed, the deepest roots of the concept of biological weapons extend very far back in time, even before the Greek myths were written down by Homer in the eighth century B.C. Poison and arrows were deeply intertwined in the ancient Greek language itself. The word for poison in ancient Greek, *toxicon*, derived from *toxon*, arrow. And in Latin, the word for poison, *toxica*, was said to derive from *taxus*, yew, because the first poison arrows had been daubed with deadly yew-berry juice. In antiquity, then, a "toxic" substance meant "something for the bow and arrow."[2]

The Greeks appear to have terrorized their enemies as effectively with those weapons as today's armies and terrorist organizations do with more modern equipment, whether napalm or homemade explosives or land mines, chemical or nuclear devices, bicycle or truck bombs, suicide backpacks or belts, or hijacked airplanes used as weapons of mass destruction.

Terrorism from Above

Aristotle, Plato, and other ancient writers were part of a tradition that viewed despotism as the worst form of government and glorified those who spilled the blood of a tyrant. The notion of tyranny addresses what we have called terrorism from above—coercive activities undertaken by states and their surrogates—which the ancients felt merited retaliation. Aristotle wrote,

> [T]he causes of revolutions in constitutional and in royal governments must be deemed to be the same; for subjects in many cases attack monarchies because of unjust treatment and fear and contempt, and among the forms of unjust treatment most of all because of insolence, and sometimes the cause is the seizure of private properties. . . . And in some cases the attack is aimed at the person of the rulers, in others at their office. . . . And many risings have also occurred because of shameful personal indignities committed by certain monarchs.[3]

Medieval writers used Biblical sources to introduce the concept that the power of a ruler is based on an implicit contract with the people, and that a ruler who broke that contract should be removed. For example, John of Salisbury, a twelfth-century English philosopher, used the Books of Kings and Chronicles to support his case:

> For tyrants are demanded, introduced, and raised to power by sin, and are excluded, blotted out, and destroyed by repentance. And even before the time of their kings, as the book of Judges relates, the children of Israel were time without number in bondage to tyrants, being visited with affliction on many different occasions in accordance with the dispensation of God, and then often, when they cried aloud to the Lord, they were delivered. And when the allotted time of their punishment was fulfilled, they were allowed to cast off the yoke from their necks by the slaughter of their tyrants; nor is blame attached to any of those by whose valor a penitent and humbled people was thus set free, but their memory is preserved in affection by posterity as servants of the Lord.[4]

The Assassins, sometimes considered the first terrorist organization, were essentially state-sponsored terrorists, using terrorism to sustain the political influence of their brand of Islam. In 1332 the German priest Brocardus describing the hazards of traveling east during the Crusades, mentioned the Assassins:

> I name the Assassins, who are to be cursed and fled. They sell themselves, are thirsty for human blood, kill the innocent for a price, and care nothing for either life or salvation. Like the devil, they transfigure themselves into angels of light, by imitating the gestures, garments, languages, customs and acts of various nations and peoples; thus, hidden in sheep's clothing, they suffer death as soon as they are recognized.[5]

---

1 U.S. Code, Title 22, Chapter 38, Section 2656f, http://www.law.cornell.edu/uscode/html/uscode22/usc_sec_22_00002656---f000-.html

2 Adrienne Mayor, *Greek Fire, Poison Arrows, and Scorpion Bombs: Biological and Chemical Warfare in the Ancient World* (Woodstock NY: Overlook Duckworth, 2003), 368.

3 Aristotle, *Politics,* Book V. VIII. 7–11, from H. Rackham, trans., *Aristotle in Twenty-three Volumes* (Cambridge, MA: Harvard University Press, 1977), 445, 447.

4 John Salisbury, *The Statesman's Book of John of Salisbury,* John Dickinson, trans. (Englewood Cliffs, NJ: Prentice Hall, 1963), 368.

5 Bernard Lewis, *The Assassins: A Radical Sect in Islam* (New York: Oxford University Press, 1967), 1.

Wars are often seen as acts of terrorism, whether they are international conflicts, civil wars, police actions, wars of revolution or national liberation, or acts of resistance against occupants from outside. Japan's occupation of China and the Allied bombing of Dresden during World War II have both been seen as terrorist acts. Horror over the misery war causes led to the four international agreements known as the Geneva Conventions, signed in 1949 and modified in 1977.

Terrorism from Below

Terrorism from below is terrorism carried out by people outside the mainstream, who want to bring terror (fear and anxiety) to the dominant group in order to accomplish their ends. From early days, these outsiders have included religious groups, vigilantes, rioters, brigands, peasants, and dissatisfied workers or other oppressed groups. Sir Peter Ustinov described this succinctly at the beginning of the 2003 invasion of Iraq when he said on German television, "Terrorism is the war of the poor, and war is the terrorism of the rich."[6]

Among the best early examples of this phenomenon are the late medieval uprisings in Europe against serfdom. French peasants led the way in 1358 with a series of rebellions in the north, known as the Jacquerie, (from an old French name for a peasant). Similar uprisings occurred in England, Germany, and other areas of Europe. Oppression of Russian peasants for hundreds of years eventually led to the Bolshevik revolution. Peasant rebellions took place in Burma and Vietnam in the 1930s. Contemporary peasant rebellions have taken place predominantly in South America, including the Zapatista rebellion in Mexico, and in Asia, where the Khmer Rouge emerged. Maoist, or Naxalite, movements in South Asia are peasant revolts modeled after China's revolution led by Mao Zedong. Terrorist attacks today are still frequently fought over control of land and what it supports in terms of agriculture, livestock, and natural resources.

During the Industrial Revolution, worker revolts were common. The Luddites in England were a group of weavers known worldwide for their quality craft, who retaliated against the introduction of the power loom. Mechanization changed their lives drastically, from profitable cottage workers to impoverished factory laborers, and smashed looms, intimidation, and other attacks against the mills resulted. These attacks, in 1812, are just one example of the "Age of Revolution" that began with the French Revolution of 1789, continued through 1848 when Marx and Engels issued the Communist Manifesto and France constructed its first rail network,[7] and concluded with German unification in 1871. During this time, nations and nationalism emerged and capitalism became the dominant economic model. The victory of industrialization in Europe also opened the way for massive colonial expansion, even forcing open the Chinese Empire to trade and European exploitation. Multiple wars, as well as political violence and terrorism, including many anarchist movements, were part and parcel of these changes.

The notion of terrorism from below became more common after World War II, as the world experienced the "wars of national liberation" against colonial empires. The Algerian Front de Libération Nationale (FLN, National Liberation Front) led Algeria's struggle for independence from the French; Kenya's Mau Mau, South Africa's African National Congress (ANC), and Cyprus's Ethniki Organosis Kyprion Agoniston (EOKA, National Organization of Cypriot Fighters) opposed the British; and the Euskadi ta Askatasuna (ETA, Basque Fatherland and Liberty) fought for Basque independence from Spain and France. These organizations often mirrored the states they wished to destroy, with shadow cabinets ready to take over once victory was accomplished. Looking at both sides of those conflicts gives resonance to the adage "one man's terrorist is another's freedom fighter."

Throughout the centuries the motives for terrorism from below have been much the same as they are today; the biggest shift in the nature of terrorism has come from changes in technology. In *The Rebellious Century*, the Tillys summarize the beginnings of these changes this way:

> The century from 1830 to 1930, with its many revolutions, wrought fundamental changes in the whole pattern of violent protest in Europe. It was also Europe's great period of transformation from agrarian to industrial society. One can hardly avoid making the connection. *Ça saute aux yeux*, the French would say: it hits you right in the eye. If the shift in the locus and character of collective violence occurred as European countries urbanized and industrialized, the two massive sets of changes must somehow have depended on each other.[8]

Terrorists took advantage of developments in transportation that occurred during the nineteenth century. Steamships and rail travel made it possible for terrorists and their supplies to move from country to country quickly. Advances in transportation in the twentieth century made any place on the globe accessible within a day or two, while telecommunications and computers eliminated geographic barriers even more. Terrorism today mirrors the technology that supports it: it is global, decentralized, and highly effective.

Terrorism in the United States

Terrorism in the United States dates back to before the nation's independence, with European colonists and native peoples engaging in acts that today would be considered war crimes or terrorism, including treatment of the indigenous population. In 1776 and 1777 a young revolutionary known as John the Painter burned down royal navy yards across England in an effort to bring the war to England. There was a

---

6 Quoted in Ulrich Hesse, "No getting away from the Gulf conflict," *The Guardian*, March 28, 2003, http://www.guardian.co.uk/germany/article/0,2763,924274,00.html

7 Refer to Eric Hobsbawm, *The Age of Revolution 1789–1848*, London: Weidenfeld and Nicolson, 1962 for more detail.

8 Charles Tilly, Louise Tilly, and Richard Tilly, *The Rebellious Century, 1830–1930* (London: J. M. Dent, 1975), 3.

well-established anarchist movement in the United States in the nineteenth and early twentieth century. A radical left was also present in the United States during the antiwar years of the 1960s and early 1970s, when fringe leftists formed terrorist groups such as the Weathermen (later the Weather Underground) and the Symbionese Liberation Army.

It was only after the 1983 Lebanese barracks bombing that international terrorism became prominent in the eyes of the public and policy makers. That attack, in which a suicide bomber drove an explosives-laden truck into the barracks, killed 241 servicemen while they slept. The event drove the United States out of Lebanon and is cited today to demonstrate that terrorism is effective. That attack also led Congress to take measures to monitor and deter terrorism, including publication of an annual report. The following decade saw a number of terrorist attacks on U.S. civilians, government and military targets in South America, the Middle East, and elsewhere.

What Is Terrorism in the Twenty-first Century?

If, during the course of human history, so many different activities have been considered terrorism, how do we know what it is?

According to the *New Oxford American Dictionary* terrorism is "the use of violence and intimidation in the pursuit of political aims." The word derives from Late Middle English, which borrowed from the Old French *terrour*, which had come from the Latin word to frighten: *terrere*. The word first came into vogue after the French Revolution, when it was applied to Jacobin supporters and their leaders, who were responsible for the "Reign of Terror" in which any perceived threat to the Jacobin regime was ruthlessly eliminated.

Dictionary definition aside, what *is* terrorism in the twenty-first century? The changing nature of terrorism and conflicting state interests have stood in the way of adoption of an internationally accepted definition. For example, a simple definition of terrorism as attacks on nonmilitary targets was unacceptable to countries like the United States because it would not cover the 1983 bombing of a U.S. Marines barracks in Lebanon or other attacks on military installations.

An effort to define terrorism as part of an international legal framework was first attempted in 1937 at the League of Nations. This convention proposed that terrorism be defined as "all criminal acts directed against a State and intended or calculated to create a state of terror in the minds of particular persons or a group of persons or the general public."[9]

This definition, however, was never adopted. Instead, definitions of terrorism began to proliferate. Each new piece of terrorism-related legislation, whether national, regional, bilateral, or international, seemed to adopt language specific to its own circumstances.

---

9 United Nations Office on Drugs and Crime, "Definitions of Terrorism," http://www.unodc.org/unodc/terrorism_definitions.html

In 1988, Alex P. Schmid, author of *Political Terrorism* (1983) (who has served as U.N. Officer in Charge of Terrorism Prevention) proposed the following definition:

> Terrorism is an anxiety-inspiring method of repeated violent action, employed by (semi-) clandestine individual, group or state actors, for idiosyncratic, criminal or political reasons, whereby—in contrast to assassination—the direct targets of violence are not the main targets. The immediate human victims of violence are generally chosen randomly (targets of opportunity) or selectively (representative or symbolic targets) from a target population, and serve as message generators. Threat- and violence-based communication processes between terrorist (organization), (imperilled) victims, and main targets are used to manipulate the main target (audience(s)), turning it into a target of terror, a target of demands, or a target of attention, depending on whether intimidation, coercion, or propaganda is primarily sought.[10]

In 1992 Schmid suggested that terrorism is the "peacetime equivalents of war crimes."[11] Other international measures also emphasized treatment of terrorist acts as crimes. For example, the UN General Assembly Resolution 51/210 (1996):

1. Strongly condemns all acts, methods and practices of terrorism as criminal and unjustifiable, wherever and by whomsoever committed;
2. Reiterates that criminal acts intended or calculated to provoke a state of terror in the general public, a group of persons or particular persons for political purposes are in any circumstance unjustifiable, whatever the considerations of a political, philosophical, ideological, racial, ethnic, religious or other nature that may be invoked to justify them.[12]

Defining terrorism became even more difficult following the terrorist attacks of September 11 and adoption by the Bush administration of the phrase "war on terrorism,"[13] which many countries perceived as inaccurate and overly broad. Middle Eastern and African countries in particular felt that terrorism against tyranny remained acceptable and did not want to condemn national liberation movements, only acts against civilians. Here is an example of the discussion:

> "Terrorism" might be an accurate term for the September 11 attacks, but it becomes dangerously simplistic and self-serving when used by interested parties to characterize all forms of conflict, violence, and resistance to oppression.

---

10 Ibid.

11 Ibid.

12 United Nations General Assembly, "A/RES/51/210, 88th plenary meeting, 17 December 1996," http://www.un.org/documents/ga/res/51/a51r210.htm

13 Note analysis of the use of this phrase in Jeffrey Record, *Bounding the Global War on Terrorism* (Carlisle, PA: Strategic Studies Institute, U.S. Army War College, December 2003), http://carlisle-www.army.mil/ssi/pubs/2003/bounding/bounding.pdf

For that reason Amnesty International does not use the term, but speaks instead of "attacks against civilians." The indiscriminate use of the term "terrorist" allows strong parties—especially states—to define who is or is not a "terrorist," what is "legitimate" use of power and what isn't, who is "with us" and who isn't. It risks stigmatizing whole populations or religions.[14]

The Secretary-General's High-level Panel on Threats, Challenges and Change reviewed the issues in December 2004, and noted the following:

157. The United Nations' ability to develop a comprehensive strategy has been constrained by the inability of Member States to agree on an anti-terrorism convention including a definition of terrorism. This prevents the United Nations from exerting its moral authority and from sending an unequivocal message that terrorism is never an acceptable tactic, even for the most defensible of causes.

158. Since 1945, an ever stronger set of norms and laws—including the Charter of the United Nations, the Geneva Conventions and the Rome Statute for the International Criminal Court—has regulated and constrained States' decisions to use force and their conduct in war—for example in the requirement to distinguish between combatants and civilians, to use force proportionally and to live up to basic humanitarian principles. Violations of these obligations should continue to be met with widespread condemnation and war crimes should be prosecuted.

159. The norms governing the use of force by non-State actors have not kept pace with those pertaining to States. This is not so much a legal question as a political one. Legally, virtually all forms of terrorism are prohibited by one of 12 international counter-terrorism conventions, international customary law, the Geneva Conventions or the Rome Statutes. Legal scholars know this, but there is a clear difference between this scattered list of conventions and little-known provisions of other treaties and the compelling normative framework, understood by all, that should surround the question of terrorism. The United Nations must achieve the same degree of normative strength concerning non-State use of force as it has concerning State use of force. Lack of agreement on a clear and well-known definition undermines the normative and moral stance against terrorism and has stained the United Nations' image. Achieving a comprehensive convention on terrorism, including a clear definition, is a political imperative.

160. The search for an agreed definition usually stumbles on two issues. The first is the argument that any definition should include States' use of armed forces against civilians. We believe that the legal and normative framework against State violations is far stronger than in the case of non-State actors and we do not find this objection to be compelling. The second objection is that peoples under foreign occupation have a right to resistance and a definition of terrorism should not override this right. The right to resistance is contested by some. But it is not the central point: the central point is that there is nothing in the fact of occupation that justifies the targeting and killing of civilians.

161. Neither of these objections is weighty enough to contradict the argument that the strong, clear normative framework of the United Nations surrounding State use of force must be complemented by a normative framework of equal authority surrounding non-State use of force. Attacks that specifically target innocent civilians and non-combatants must be condemned clearly and unequivocally by all.[15]

That report went on to outline elements that the writers considered important to a definition of terrorism:

164. That definition of terrorism should include the following elements:

(a) Recognition, in the preamble, that State use of force against civilians is regulated by the Geneva Conventions and other instruments, and, if of sufficient scale, constitutes a war crime by the persons concerned or a crime against humanity;

(b) Restatement that acts under the 12 preceding anti-terrorism conventions are terrorism, and a declaration that they are a crime under international law; and restatement that terrorism in time of armed conflict is prohibited by the Geneva Conventions and Protocols;

(c) Reference to the definitions contained in the 1999 International Convention for the Suppression of the Financing of Terrorism and Security Council resolution 1566 (2004);

(d) Description of terrorism as "any action, in addition to actions already specified by the existing conventions on aspects of terrorism, the Geneva Conventions and Security Council resolution 1566 (2004), that is intended to cause death or serious bodily harm to civilians or non-combatants, when the purpose of such an act, by its nature or context, is to intimidate a population, or to compel a Government or an international organization to do or to abstain from doing any act."[16]

The challenge of reaching consensus on a definition of terrorism exists not only on the international level, but on the national level as well. U.S. government departments and agencies also provide a variety of definitions. President George W. Bush's *National Security Strategy of the United*

---

14 Jeff Halper, "September 11, Terrorism, and the Middle East: The Way Out," Peacework, September 2002, http://www.afsc.org/pwork/0209/020929.htm

15 Secretary-General's High-level Panel on Threats, Challenges and Change, *A More Secure World: Our Shared Responsibility* (New York: United Nations, 2004), 51–52. A complete pdf file of the report is available at http://www.un.org/secureworld/report2.pdf

16 Ibid., 52.

States of America describes terrorism as "premeditated, politically motivated violence perpetrated against innocents."[17]

Addressing the role of the Federal Bureau of Investigation, the U.S. Code of Federal Regulations offers, "Terrorism includes the unlawful use of force and violence against persons or property to intimidate or coerce a government, the civilian population, or any segment thereof, in furtherance of political or social objectives,"[18] while the Department of Defense defines terrorism as "the calculated use of unlawful violence or threat of unlawful violence to inculcate fear; intended to coerce or to intimidate governments or societies in the pursuit of goals that are generally political, religious, or ideological. See also antiterrorism; combating terrorism; counterterrorism; force protection condition; terrorist; terrorist groups."[19]

The U.S. Criminal Code, as modified by the 2001 PATRIOT Act lays out the following definition

(1) the term "international terrorism" means activities that—
  (A) involve violent acts or acts dangerous to human life that are a violation of the criminal laws of the United States or of any State, or that would be a criminal violation if committed within the jurisdiction of the United States or of any State;
  (B) appear to be intended—
    (i) to intimidate or coerce a civilian population;
    (ii) to influence the policy of a government by intimidation or coercion; or
    (iii) to affect the conduct of a government by mass destruction, assassination, or kidnapping; and
  (C) occur primarily outside the territorial jurisdiction of the United States, or transcend national boundaries in terms of the means by which they are accomplished, the persons they appear intended to intimidate or coerce, or the locale in which their perpetrators operate or seek asylum;
(2) the term "national of the United States" has the meaning given such term in section 101(a)(22) of the Immigration and Nationality Act;
(3) the term "person" means any individual or entity capable of holding a legal or beneficial interest in property;
(4) the term "act of war" means any act occurring in the course of—
  (A) declared war;
  (B) armed conflict, whether or not war has been declared, between two or more nations; or
  (C) armed conflict between military forces of any origin; and
(5) the term "domestic terrorism" means activities that—
  (A) involve acts dangerous to human life that are a violation of the criminal laws of the United States or of any State;
  (B) appear to be intended—
    (i) to intimidate or coerce a civilian population;
    (ii) to influence the policy of a government by intimidation or coercion; or
    (iii) to affect the conduct of a government by mass destruction, assassination, or kidnapping; and
  (C) occur primarily within the territorial jurisdiction of the United States.[20]

The Department of State relies on the following definitions used in Title 22 of the U.S. Code:

(1) the term "international terrorism" means terrorism involving citizens or the territory of more than 1 country;
(2) the term "terrorism" means premeditated, politically motivated violence perpetrated against noncombatant targets by subnational groups or clandestine agents; and
(3) the term "terrorist group" means any group practicing, or which has significant subgroups which practice, international terrorism.[21]

The definitions used in *Patterns of Global Terrorism* follow Title 22 as well, with additional explanation:

There are a wide variety of definitions used by experts to describe the phenomenon of terrorism, but no single one has gained universal acceptance. For purposes of recording and coding data on terrorist incidents, we have adhered to definitions that represent a middle ground within the broad range of expert opinion, both foreign and domestic. ***Terrorism*** is premeditated, politically motivated violence perpetrated against noncombatant targets by

---

17 The White House, *National Security Strategy of the United States of America* (Washington, D.C.: The White House, 2002), 5. A pdf version of the National Security Strategy is available at http://www.whitehouse.gov/nsc/nss.pdf

18 U.S. Code of Federal Regulations, "Title 28: Judicial Administration; Chapter 1: Department of Justice," http://edocket.access.gpo.gov/cfr_2004/julqtr/28cfr0.85.htm

19 Department of Defense, *DOD Dictionary of Military and Associated Terms*, "terrorism," http://www.dtic.mil/doctrine/jel/doddict/data/t/05370.html

20 U.S. Code Title 18, Part I, Chapter 113B, section 2331, http://www4.law.cornell.edu/uscode/html/uscode18/usc_sec_18_00002331----000-.html

21 U.S. Code Title 22, Chapter 38, Section 2656f(d). Cited here from U.S. Department of State, "Chapter 1: Legislative Requirements and Key Terms," in *Country Reports on Terrorism* (Washington, D.C.: U.S. Department of State, 2005), http://www.state.gov/s/ct/rls/45323.htm

subnational groups or clandestine state agents, usually intended to influence an audience. ***International terrorism*** is terrorism involving citizens or territory of more than one country.

As mentioned above, these definitions differ because each emerged in connection with particular legislation or departmental requirements. An interesting example of how this works in practice and what needs to be considered can be seen in the following example from the "Check-List for a Definition of Terrorism for the Purpose of Compensation" from the Organization for Economic Cooperation and Development (OECD):

This check-list is meant to help private sector entities as well as governments involved in terrorism compensation to define terrorist acts and criteria relevant to determine which terrorist acts can be indemnified, be it through private insurance mechanisms or through other compensation mechanisms. This check-list is illustrative, and neither binding nor exhaustive; it can be adapted by the various parties concerned to mirror specific market and regulatory frameworks or policy objectives.

The following criteria may be considered when defining terrorism acts for the purpose of compensation.

a) elements of definition of a terrorist act, which could include:[a]

Criterion 1—Means and effects
A terrorist act is:
— an act, including but not limited to the use of force or violence, causing serious[b] harm to human life, or to tangible or intangible property,
— or a threat thereof entailing serious[b] harm;

Criterion 2—Intention
A terrorist act is committed or threatened:
— with the intent to influence or destabilize any government or public entity and/or to provoke fear and insecurity in all or part of the population;
— in support of a political, religious, ethnic, ideological or similar goal.

b) factors of insurability, which could include:

(a) Certain countries may wish to take other criteria into consideration. The criterion of affiliation to a group or organisation, for instance, has been successfully used in several Member countries to define terrorism acts. Similarly, certain countries may wish not to take into account certain elements mentioned for their own definition of terrorist acts. For instance, the concept of "threat" of terrorism is not considered as a relevant element of definition of terrorism acts in certain countries.

(b) It is left to each country/entity to define the criteria more precisely, possibly quantitatively or qualitatively when relevant, according to their specific policy and technical consideration. It should however be noted that at least one OECD country has adopted a definition of terrorism based exclusively on qualitative criteria.

Criterion 3—Technical insurability,[c] including in principle:
— assessability (probability and severity of losses should be quantifiable);
— randomness (the time at which the insured event occurs should be unpredictable when the policy is underwritten, and the occurrence itself should be independent of the will of the insured);
— mutuality (numerous persons exposed to a given hazard should be able to join together to form a risk community within which the risk is shared and diversified).

Criterion 4—Economic insurability,[c] which could depend on the following elements:
— magnitude of potential losses: it should in principle not exceed the capacity of the private insurance/reinsurance market or the capacity of a mix of private and public multi-layer mechanisms when these exist. The insurability of the risk will be assessed against the maximum aggregate amount of funds made available by the various potential stakeholders (insurers, reinsurers and, possibly, pooling mechanisms allowing (inter)national spreading of risks, and governments) reflecting their respective capacity. The *quantitative segmentation of risks, i.e. the threshold/sub limits* (the *nature and* the *amount of sub-limits,* and the *basis on which they should be calculate*) should be defined ex ante;
— nature of the potential losses: to be insurable, potential losses should correspond to the lines of business that the available insurance mechanisms are able to cover. The list of business lines to be covered should be defined through an ex-ante *qualitative segmentation of risks.*
— price of cover: for the risk to be insurable, it should be possible to set an adequate and actuarially fair insurance premium;

Criterion 5—Legal/regulatory insurability:
Regulatory authorities may decide that a given risk, or type of risk (e.g. worker compensation, business interruption), is—explicitly or implicitly—defined as insurable, for instance through a certification procedure and/or if insurance against this risk is made compulsory. In this case, a risk may be labelled as insurable while other insurability criteria may not be met.

(c) It should be remembered that, unless terrorism risk insurance has been made compulsory, the determination of the insurability of a risk by private entities ultimately depends on internal analysis and appreciation of the insurance/reinsurance company(ies) at stake. A (re)insurer may decide, for commercial or strategic purposes in particular, to cover a risk that may not easily meet the theoretical criteria of insurability. It may also decide not to cover a risk, to take into account for instance concerns regarding its solvency situation or the balance of its risk portfolio at a given moment in time.

c) factors of compensability (insurance excluded), which could include:

Criterion 6—Compensability by the State: States need to decide about the possibility of compensation on the basis of their own public policy concerns. The risk should not exceed in magnitude the maximum financial involvement that the State is able or willing to supply for the compensation of losses entailed by terrorism.

Criterion 7—Compensability through non-governmental mechanisms: the technical characteristics of the risk should allow it to be covered through financial mechanisms other than insurance, for instance bonds placed on capital markets.

An inside look into the British Broadcasting Corporation's editorial policies (http://www.bbc.co.uk/guidelines/editorialguidelines) provides a fascinating perspective on how to address discussions of terrorism. The BBC's editorial guideline on the topic of terrorism states:

> We must report acts of terror quickly, accurately, fully and responsibly. Our credibility is undermined by the careless use of words which carry emotional or value judgements. The word "terrorist" itself can be a barrier rather than an aid to understanding. We should try to avoid the term, without attribution. We should let other people characterise while we report the facts as we know them.
>
> We should not adopt other people's language as our own. It is also usually inappropriate to use words like "liberate," "court martial" or "execute" in the absence of a clear judicial process. We should convey to our audience the full consequences of the act by describing what happened. We should use words which specifically describe the perpetrator such as "bomber," "attacker," "gunman," "kidnapper," "insurgent, and "militant." Our responsibility is to remain objective and report in ways that enable our audiences to make their own assessments about who is doing what to whom.

A discussion during an 11 November 2004 editorial meeting demonstrates how complex this can be in practice:

> The meeting then considered contrasting reports of the Madrid bombing, described as terrorism, with reports of acts in Israel termed suicide bombings. Stephen Whittle asked whether a label was necessary; was it informative or a barrier to understanding? He said the word terrorism may sometimes be thought of as convenient—even logical—shorthand but, mostly, it does not need to be used; it is usually sufficient to describe what has happened factually without the use of labels. Stephen reminded the meeting that the word terrorist is not used by the World Service to describe groups, to be sure that the BBC is not perceived to be taking sides. With all BBC News widely available on satellite and internet services, consistency is important to avoid the charge of either bias or censorship. When we take care to refer to Palestinian groups as militants, but readily apply the term terrorists to the perpetrators of the Madrid bombings, it has a knock on effect around the world. These issues are not easy. But we do need to think hard about what words we use and when.
>
> Considering whether it is appropriate to refer to those responsible for attacks as Islamic fundamentalists or extremists, Imran Khan said the word used by those who commit such attacks is radical. Peter Taylor said that he did not consider the word radical to be strong enough to indicate to audiences the extreme nature of their views. He said we need to find another phrase which we can be happy with. Stephen Whittle suggested there are some straightforward words that describe people by their actions, without carrying a value judgement; for example, bomber.
>
> Peter Taylor asked whether it would therefore be appropriate to describe those responsible for the Madrid attacks as Islamic bombers. Andres Ilves (Head of Persian/Pashto Service) said the answer depends on whether we are seeking to describe their actions or to focus on their religious beliefs. Imran Khan observed that there is an increasing tendency to substitute the word Islamist as an apparently acceptable alternative to Islamic. However, the word Islamist does not help in this context since it just means people who believe in the Islamic faith. The use of the word angers many British Muslims since they would also describe themselves as Islamist without ever having had a radical or extremist thought.
>
> Stephen Whittle observed that, in his report on the day of the Madrid bombings, Gavin Hewitt had avoided describing the suspected perpetrators as Islamic. Instead, he had simply said that a copy of the Koran had been found, thereby confining his reporting to what was actually known and delivering the relevant information to the audience in terms that were precise. Drawing the discussion to a close, he emphasised that the choices were rarely between right and wrong but were nuanced between what was the best solution in the circumstances. There are often many ways of negotiating the difficulties but we need to be sure to have examined all the options to ensure we proceed in the best way possible.

Most recently, there has been movement towards a simple clear statement that "maiming and killing of civilians is unacceptable regardless of one's cause." The future of a coordinated international approach to terrorism was one of the major agenda items for the United Nations in September 2005. Efforts to develop unified counterterrorism measures failed. Resolution 1624 regarding counterterrorism was unanimously adopted, but included only very general language, including a vague "definition" of "terrorism in all its forms and manifestations."[22] Updates on the situation are provided in the weekly www.terrorismcentral.com Newsletter.

---

22 U.N. Security Council Resolution 1624 (2005) http://www.un.org/Docs/journal/asp/ws.asp?m=s/res/1624(2005)

What Are the Odds?

An acceptable risk is one to which you have become accustomed. It is difficult to become accustomed to such extremely rare events as 9/11 or the Asian tsunami. These low-probability, high-consequence disasters were both predicted, but the measurable risk of such an event is so low that we round it down to zero, and plan accordingly.

Conventional risks, such as the risk of being in a car accident, are greater and involve a known range of consequences. The risk of being in a car accident can be mathematically modeled, and the consequent frequencies, probabilities, and profiles can be used to determine insurance rates. Drivers can learn ways to reduce or manage that risk.

Dealing with unconventional risks is more complex. The greater the number of variables, the more complex but more accurate the analysis. The reverse is also true. How, then, to model the risk of a terrorist attack? Among the tools available, researchers use advanced game theory to try to emulate the way people make decisions.

Because terrorism occurs so rarely it cannot be reliably predicted. In terms of daily life, it is barely worth a mention. The U.S. Centers for Disease Control and Prevention calculate the individual risk of being killed in any kind of terrorist attack at 1 in 88,000. A person is far more likely to be struck by lightning (1 in 3,000 odds) or to be killed in a lightning strike (1 in 55,928 odds). Even with the extraordinarily high fatalities of 9/11, fifteen times more Americans died in motor vehicle accidents.[23] Simply staying at home is far riskier. Among people who die at home,

- 1 in 197 are murdered
- 1 in 199 shot
- 1 in 5,330 strangled or hanged
- 1 in 10,010 fall from a ladder or scaffolding
- 1 in 10,455 die in the bathtub
- 1 in 10,605 die when their clothes catch fire

Natural disasters also dwarf the threat posed by terrorism. From 1985 to 2004, terrorist attacks killed or injured more than 8,500 people. Natural disasters, on the other hand, killed well over five million.

In 2004 alone there were around 650 natural disasters that have claimed more than 315,000 lives. The death toll in 2003 was 77,000, triple that of 2002. Record insurance losses in 2004 exceeded $40 billion and economic loss in excess of $130 billion. 2005 is on course to exceed these figures. Hurricane Katrina, one of the first in a season that is already predicted to have more than usual, will exceed the previous record set by Hurricane Andrew and losses are likely to exceed $200 billion. Terrorist attacks are also on the increase, though

---

[23] Statistics are from CDC data available at http://www.cdc.gov/ncipc/wisqars/ and http://www.cdc.gov/nchs/nvss.htm as well as from the National Safety Council (http://www.nsc.org/lrs/statstop.htm) and the National Weather Service (http://www.lightningsafety.noaa.gov/medical.htm).

Terrorism versus Natural Disasters, Casualties 1985–2004

Year	Terrorist Attacks	Natural Disasters
1985	1,904	100,578
1986	1,387	42,460
1987	1,540	30,638
1988	2,538	94,297
1989	921	53,025
1990	443	178,216
1991	411	460,001
1992	700	310,396
1993	3,146	67,269
1994	977	62,086
1995	6,989	173,040
1996	893	371,211
1997	1,112	116,466
1998	10,550	25,114
1999	3,181	154,301
2000	3,489	59,361
2001	8,538	336,335
2002	9,839	100,707
2003	4,985	293,331
2004	17,553	2,128,652

Sources: EM-DAT: The OFDA/CRED International Disaster Database, www.em-dat.net, Universite Catholique de Louvain, Brussels, Belgium; and MIPT/NCTC Terrorism Knowledge Base, http://www.tkb.org

at a lower rate. The number of terrorist attacks through August 2005 has almost matched the record set for all of 2004.

Understanding relative risk is important. The panic of the month should not dictate public policy or interfere with the way you conduct your daily life. When something unexpected happens, fear can be a legitimate response. Distance and experience provide perspective that helps moderate the initial response. People in Israel, Northern Ireland, London, Paris, Berlin, Jakarta, Madrid, and elsewhere have lived with terrorist threats for a long time. These threats no longer have the ability to interfere in daily life and, over time, the public policy responses to individual tragedies are moderated by experience.

Another useful perspective is offered by Max Bazerman and Michael Watkins in their book, *Predictable Surprises* (2004). They argue that that events such as 9/11 and the collapse of Enron are "events that take an individual or group by surprise, despite prior awareness of all of the information necessary to anticipate the events and their consequences." They cite six characteristics of such events:

- Leaders knew a problem existed and that the problem would not solve itself
- They can be expected when organizational members recognize that a problem is getting worse over time
- Fixing the problem would incur significant costs in the present, while the benefits of action would be delayed

- Measures to avoid predictable surprises require costs that constituencies will notice, and those undertaking such measures will not be recognized and rewarded for disasters that are averted
- Human tendency to maintain the status quo
- Special interest groups that benefit from the status quo will fight hard against change

Hurricane Katrina is one example that meets these criteria.

To address such problems, the international community, led by the United Nations' International Strategy for Disaster Reduction, has designed a disaster reduction framework, "Building the Resilience of Nations and Communities to Disasters" that was developed during the January 2005 World Conference on Disaster Reduction (http://www.unisdr.org/wcdr). Citing the consequences of rising disaster loss, they explain:

Disaster risk arises when hazards interact with physical, social, economic and environmental vulnerabilities. Events of hydrometeorological origin constitute the large majority of disasters. Despite the growing understanding and acceptance of the importance of disaster risk reduction and increased disaster response capacities, disasters and in particular the management and reduction of risk continue to pose a global challenge.

Areas covered in the framework include:

- Governance through institutional and policy frameworks for risk reduction, such as socioeconomic policies, effective utilization of resources, environmental policies, and sustainable development.
- Risk identification, assessment monitoring and early warning, such as forecasting and early warning; climate and environmental risk assessment; and urban risk.
- Knowledge management and education, including education for sustainable development, research agendas, and public awareness-raising tools.
- Reducing underlying risk factors, though such means as land use planning; environmental and natural resources management, and financial instruments serving as safety nets (including insurance and microfinance).
- Preparedness for effective response and recovery.
- Implementation mechanisms such as regional frameworks for risk reduction, international cooperation policy, and community partnerships and participation.

The use of microfinance as a disaster reduction strategy is the focus of discussion for the 2005 International Day for Disaster Reduction. This is a tool being considered to help people reconstruct their livelihoods in the aftermath of Hurricane Katrina. The same approaches are equally effective in addressing other asymmetric threats, including the mitigation of terrorism risk.

Putting terrorism in this context is not meant to belittle the threat. It is true that people are capable of committing acts of terrorism and political violence that dwarf nature's rage. Such events are, however, rare. Increasing levels of terrorism in the twenty-first century need to be placed in context, just as we have done with other historical events.

A Note of Thanks

I would like to express my gratitude to terrorism analysts in educational and government institutions and private organizations, journalists and other researchers around the world who have fought the struggle—and usually won—to put the facts first, ahead of political pressure or personal considerations. I would particularly like to thank the dedicated employees of the U.S. Department of State and Central Intelligence Agency. Without the expertise and dedication of all these individuals, over the course of many years, books such as this would not exist.

Acknowledgments

Patterns of Global Terrorism has been a different type of project for Berkshire. It clearly fit our mission to provide key global content in a clear, accessible format. However, our editorial process generally follows a now-routine set of steps from receiving original material written by scholars to editorial review, copy editing, finalizing, and typesetting. *Patterns* broke this mold, presenting us with the challenge of organizing what at first seemed like an unwieldy mix of government documents—that would need to be keyboarded from print text or converted from PDF or HTML documents.

From the moment Anna Sabasteanski brought us the idea of a work that would preserve and illuminate a twenty-year history of *Patterns,* she has worked tirelessly to assemble the needed documents, write cogent overviews of each topic, and compile data so that new, more accessible tables, maps, and graphs could be prepared to accompany the reports. We are deeply grateful for all her efforts.

Berkshire editor Marcy Ross assembled and supervised the editorial team needed to get the documents ready for production, shepherding the pieces of *Patterns* from a mass of files to a finished product. She and Julie Bourbeau, editorial assistant on the project, pored over hundreds of pages of government documents to make sure that we'd converted the material accurately and then formatted it for typesetting. Roxanne Gawthorp and Jake Makler did likewise with the voluminous chronology. It was a tough and sometimes tedious task that they each did with diligence, creativity, and even enthusiasm. Proofreaders Mary Bagg, Eileen Clawson, Robin Gold, and Libby Larson brought their eagle eyes to the project in its various phases. And the finished work was further enhanced by the considerable skills of senior copy editor Francesca Forrest and indexer Scott Smiley.

Our designer Joe DiStefano came up with a design that was both accessible and engaging—a tall order for government documents. Composition artist Brad Walrod was instrumental in organizing the documents into a visually coherent whole, making key recommendations every step of the way—in addition to his always-excellent composition work. Our appreciation also goes to XNR Productions for creating the maps that show the geographic face of terrorism and illustrator Bryan Christie for the many graphs that visually depict terrorism over time.

Special thanks as well to the cadre of experts—Benjamin Barber, David Martin Jones, Richard Miniter, Larry C. Johnson, Andrew Cochran, and Peter Bergen—who quickly and enthusiastically responded to our request for quotes on the importance of this project.

David Levinson

About the Editors

About the Editor

Anna Sabasteanski is president of the Asset Management Network, Inc and editor of the TerrorismCentral database and newsletter. She also edits the *AML/CFT Monitor*—which covers topics in AML/CFT (Anti-Money Laundering/Combating Financing of Terrorism)—and *Political Risk Monitor*. Previously, she held executive level positions with Tanning Technology and Macmillan and was the founder of Electronic Press. She has three decades of experience in the management, design and deployment of data acquisition, management, security and delivery systems for the financial services, media and entertainment, and healthcare industries. She and her clients have won numerous industry awards. Anna is an active participant in the local community, serves on the board of the Massachusetts Technology Leadership Association, and frequently speaks and writes on related issues. She first studied terrorism and political violence at Bates College (where she received her bachelor of arts degree) and the London School of Economics (where she received her master's degree).

About the Consulting Editor

David Levinson, president of Berkshire Publishing, is also a cultural anthropologist (PhD, State University of New York at Buffalo) and an expert on comparative cultural analysis, comparative religion, and global social issues. Prior to cofounding Berkshire Publishing he was vice-president of the Human Relations Area Files at Yale University. He is editor-in-chief of the *Encyclopedia of Crime and Punishment,* and author of the award-winning political science reference *Aggression & Conflict*.

PATTERNS of GLOBAL TERRORISM 1985–2005

U.S. DEPARTMENT OF STATE REPORTS WITH SUPPLEMENTARY DOCUMENTS AND STATISTICS

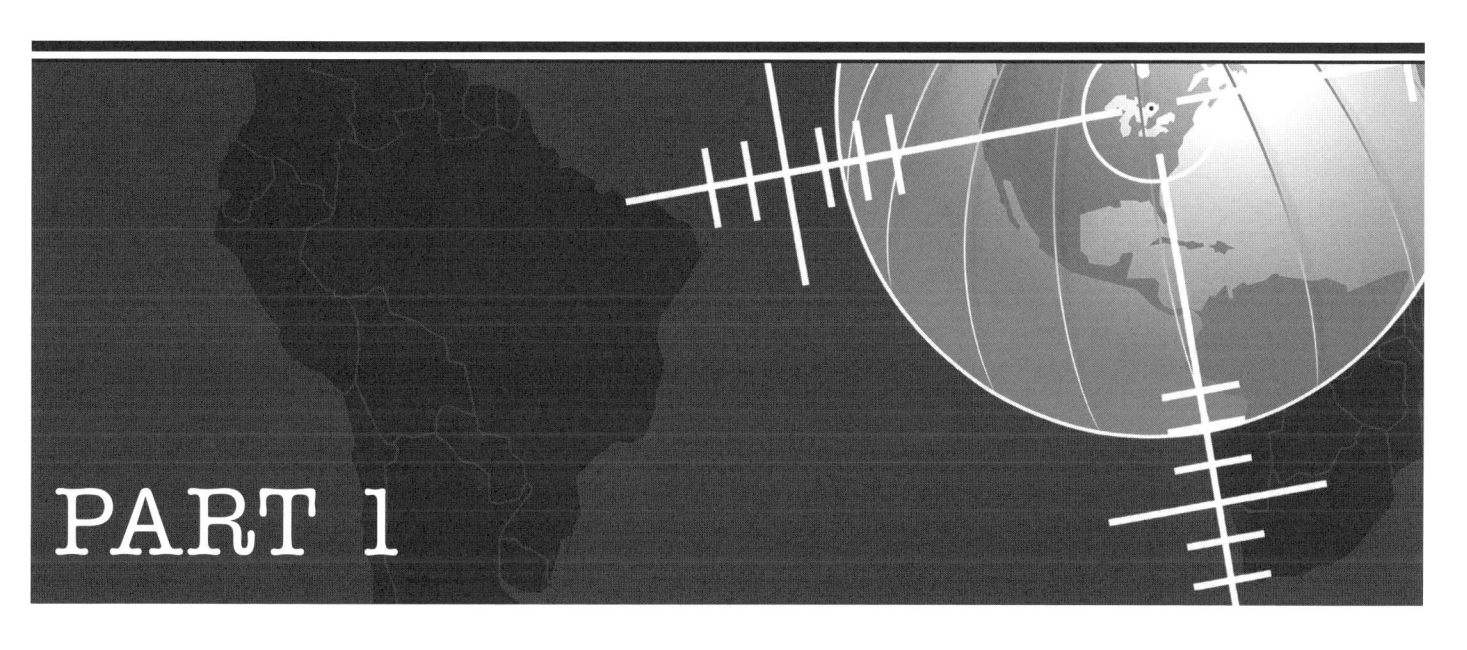

PART 1
COUNTERTERRORISM

Overview of Counterrorism

Anna Sabasteanski

Counterterrorism is a multifaceted effort that operates on domestic, regional, and international levels. The Department of State has a key role in coordinating international efforts and in collaborating with other U.S. government departments, particularly those involved in the military and international trade.

These interactions take place subject to domestic and international legislation, and are guided by these basic principles: First, make no concessions to terrorists and strike no deals; second, bring terrorists to justice for their crimes; third, isolate and put pressure on states that sponsor terrorism to force them to change their behavior; and fourth, bolster the counterterrorism capabilities of those countries that work with the United States and require assistance.

Supporting these principles requires efforts that take place in many arenas: political, diplomatic, legal, economic, military, public policy, and so forth. Programs at the Department of State range from art exhibits in embassies to interdiction of ships at sea suspected of carrying potential weapons of mass destruction. Their efforts call on finely honed diplomatic skills to manage these disparate tasks in conjunction with U.S. departments and agencies as well as governments around the world—always keeping in mind the requirements of international law and the balance that must be maintained with domestic security.

Part 1 of the collection describes the various agencies involved and how they interact, then provides more details on each of these four principles, primarily from the point of view of the U.S. Department of State, in the following seven sections:

- **U.S. Policies in Combating Terrorism** provides an overview of U.S. policy, including descriptions of current policy initiatives. This is supported by review documents from the Government Accountability Office (GAO), *Combating Terrorism: Department of State Programs to Combat Terrorism Abroad;* and the Congressional Research Service (CRS), *Terrorism and National Security: Issues and Trends.*
- **U.S. Legal Response** describes U.S. legal policy, covering both legislation and law enforcement, including relevant sections from Department of State reports.
- **Sanctions** are an important component of the legal measures available to counter terrorism. An overview of sanctions is included, along with a CRS Report, *Economic Sanctions to Achieve US Foreign Policy Goals.*
- **State Sponsors of Terrorism**—State sponsors of terrorism and terrorism financiers face particular sanctions. Designation of state sponsors and reports on designated countries, including Afghanistan, Cuba, Iran, Iraq, Libya, Nicaragua, North Korea, the Soviet Union, Sudan, Syria, and Yemen, follow.
- **Terrorist Financing**—This section deals with terrorist financing and is supported with two CRS reports on the topic: *Terrorist Financing: The 9/11 Commission Recommendation,* and *The Financial Action Task Force: An Overview*
- **U.S. Military Response** describes when the U.S. began using military force in response to terrorist attacks and includes excerpts of reports on the U.S. military campaigns in Afghanistan and Iraq.
- **International Response** reviews multinational efforts to combat terrorism. This section includes extracts on the response of the international community to the attacks of 9/11, along with a list of relevant regional and international terrorism conventions and protocols.

U.S. Policies in Combating Terrorism

Overview of U.S. Policies in Combating Terrorism

Anna Sabasteanski

U.S. counterterrorism policy includes military, political, diplomatic, economic, and public-policy measures. Prior to the 1998 bombings of U.S. embassies in Kenya and Tanzania, U.S. policy was based on a three-pronged strategy that is common to much of the international community: first, make no deals with terrorists and do not submit to blackmail; second, treat terrorists as criminals, pursue them aggressively, and apply the rule of law; and third, apply maximum pressure on states that sponsor and support terrorists by imposing economic, diplomatic, and political sanctions and by urging other states to do likewise. After the bombings, a fourth prong was added: bolster the counterterrorism capabilities of those countries that work with the United States and require assistance.

PDD-62 and PDD-63

Two important elements in U.S. counterterrorism policy are presidential decision directives (PDDs) that President Clinton signed in May 1998. The first, PDD-62, addressed the growing threat of unconventional attacks against the United States (attacks not by other states but by so-called nonstate actors —terrorists) and detailed a new, more systematic approach to fighting that threat. It codified and clarified the activities of the many U.S. agencies that participate in the battle against terrorism, activities that include apprehending and prosecuting terrorists, increasing transportation security, enhancing response capabilities, and protecting the United States' cyber infrastructure, which is critical for the functioning of the economy. PDD-62 also established the position of the National Coordinator for Security, Infrastructure Protection, and Counterterrorism to oversee the relevant policies and programs.

The second, PDD-63, was aimed at protecting the United States' telecommunications, banking and finance, energy, transportation, and essential government services infrastructures. It required the government to conduct risk assessments and begin planning to reduce the vulnerability of those infrastructures to attack, and it linked designated federal agencies with representatives in the private sector.

Active Response to the August 1998 Embassy Bombings

The U.S. response to the African embassy bombings shows well how counterterrorism efforts can embrace both military and nonmilitary tactics. With the knowledge that al-Qaeda was responsible for the embassy bombings, the U.S. government launched military strikes against terrorist targets in Afghanistan and Sudan (two countries known to harbor al-Qaeda and to permit al-Qaeda to operate training camps in their territory) on 20 August 1998. That same day, President Bill Clinton amended Executive Order 12947 to add Osama bin Laden and his key associates to the list of terrorists, thus freezing their U.S. assets (including property and bank accounts) and prohibiting all U.S. financial transactions with them. (First issued in 1995, Executive Order 12947 prohibits transactions with terrorists and contains a list of the terrorists so designated. This executive order is frequently modified to add additional names and categories.)

As a result of what the attorney general Janet Reno called the most extensive overseas criminal investigation in U.S. history, and working closely with the Kenyan and Tanzanian governments, the U.S. government indicted bin Ladin and eleven of his associates for the two bombings and other terrorist crimes. Several suspects were brought to the United States to stand trial. The Department of State announced a reward of up to $5 million for information leading to the arrest or conviction of any of the suspects anywhere in the world.

The next major changes in policy followed the terrorist attacks of September 11. *Patterns of Global Terrorism 2001* included a complete section on U.S. policy. The extracts that follow are the remarks of Secretary of State Colin Powell and of Ambassador-at-Large Francis X. Taylor (the U.S. Department of State's coordinator for counterterrorism), which served as the preface and introduction to *Patterns of Global Terrorism 2001*.

Policy Developments after September 11

Selections from Patterns of Global Terrorism 2001

From Secretary of State Colin L. Powell

In 2001, terrorism cast its lethal shadow across the globe—yet the world's resolve to defeat it has never been greater.

When the terrorists struck on September 11, their target was not just the United States, but also the values that the American people share with men and women all over the world who believe in the sanctity of human life and cherish freedom. Indeed, citizens from some 80 countries were murdered in the attacks.

Nations of every continent, culture, and creed, of every region, race, and religion, answered President Bush's call for a global coalition against terrorism. In the months since the attacks, we and our Coalition partners have taken systematic measures to break terrorism's global reach.

Country by country, region by region, we have strengthened law enforcement and intelligence cooperation and we have tightened border controls to make it harder for terrorists to move about, communicate, and plot. One by one, we are severing the financial bloodlines of terrorist organizations.

As the result of the Coalition's operations in Afghanistan, al-Qaida and Taliban leaders are now either captured, killed, or on the run. And there are fewer and fewer places they can run to—except into the long arms of Justice.

Coalition forces have lifted the yoke of oppression from the backs of the Afghan people. Afghanistan's political transformation is underway toward a government that represents citizens of every ethnic background, women as well as men. The world community already has committed an initial $4.5 billion to put the country back on its feet and its future back into the hands of its people, so that Afghanistan will never again become safe ground for terrorists.

But the campaign against international terrorism isn't only about Afghanistan and bringing the perpetrators, planners, and abettors of the September 11 attacks to account. It is also about bringing the international community's combined strengths to bear against the scourge of terrorism in its many manifestations throughout the world.

The terrorist threat is global in scope, many faceted, and determined. The world's response must be equally comprehensive, multi-dimensional, and steadfast.

We and our Coalition partners must be prepared to conduct a long, hard campaign, measured in years and fought on many fronts with every tool of statecraft—political, diplomatic, legal, economic, financial, intelligence, and when necessary, military.

In this global campaign against terrorism, no country has the luxury of remaining on the sidelines. There are no sidelines. Terrorists respect no limits, geographic or moral. The frontlines are everywhere and the stakes are high. Terrorism not only kills people. It also threatens democratic institutions, undermines economies, and destabilizes regions.

This chilling report details the very clear and present danger that terrorism poses to the world and the efforts that the United States and our partners in the international community are making to defeat it.

The cold, hard facts presented here compel the world's continued vigilance and concerted action.

From Ambassador Francis X. Taylor

History will record 2001 as a watershed year in the international fight against terrorism. On September 11, the United States suffered its bloodiest day on American soil since the Civil War, and the world experienced the most devastating international terrorist attack in recorded history. Out of the horror, we have fought back, rallying the most diverse international coalition ever assembled. The events of 9/11 galvanized civilized nations as no other event has; ironically, by their own hand, terrorists set in motion their own ultimate demise.

Early results from this unprecedented international cooperation and common resolve have been encouraging. Afghanistan has been liberated and is working to establish a government representative of its people and one that is not a threat to its neighbors. The Taliban has been overthrown, and the terrorist infrastructure it supported has been all but destroyed. Al-Qaida-linked organizations and people around the world are being pressed by aggressive intelligence and law enforcement operations that have resulted in more than 1,000 arrests/detentions since September 11.

Despite our early success in Afghanistan and against al-Qaida, we still have a long way to go to assure final victory in the global war against terrorism. But one thing is certain: If terrorists questioned our resolve to defeat them and their nefarious objectives before, they cannot question it now.

The US Government and our Coalition partners have worked countless hours to ensure that the lives of those murdered on 9/11 were not lost in vain. Since September 11, we have launched a worldwide campaign against terrorism. The Department of State has been an integral part of that effort. The Secretary and senior Department officials have traveled to every corner of the globe to develop and sustain the campaign, and officials from around the world have visited the President, the Secretary of State, the Secretary of Defense, and other government officials to demonstrate their support and offer diplomatic and material assistance to this common effort. As this annual report demonstrates, their support has been much more than rhetorical. This unprecedented Coalition of nations has sought to synchronize diplomatic, intelligence, law enforcement, economic, financial, and military power to attack terrorism globally. Indeed, the overwhelming response we have received in the wake of the September 11 tragedy is dramatic proof that people—of all nations and all faiths—understand that the murders inflicted at the Twin Towers, at the Pentagon, and in Pennsylvania, were truly an attack on the world and civilization itself.

"How will we fight and win this war? We will direct every resource at our command—every means of diplomacy, every tool of intelligence, every instrument of law enforcement, every financial influence, and every necessary weapon of war—to the disruption and to the defeat of the global terror network."—George W. Bush

The President's call to arms outlined a global campaign of unprecedented scale and complexity along multiple fronts:

Diplomatic

Diplomatic action for the campaign began within minutes of the attack.

State Department officials immediately began working with foreign officials around the world to forge a coalition to support our response. The fruits of that labor have been assessed by President Bush as having resulted in the "greatest worldwide coalition in history." Since September 11, the President has met with leaders from more than 50 nations, and Secretary Powell has met with even more foreign ministers and other representatives of our Coalition partners. Senior members of the Departments of State and Defense and the Central Intelligence Agency, as well as my staff and I, have also met with numerous foreign officials in Washington and have traveled to every continent to help fashion the diplomatic framework needed to wage the campaign to combat terrorism with a global reach. Diplomacy abroad is also the leading edge of every nation's homeland security, and the global Coalition against terrorism has required—and will continue to require—intensive and innovative effort in that arena. Since September 11, for instance, the Department of State has begun formal dialogues with China and Pakistan on terrorism, and Department officials have brought their expertise to numerous conferences around the world, such as the one hosted by Polish President Kwasniewski, designed to strengthen the capabilities of our global partners in defeating terrorism.

In addition, numerous multilateral fora such as the EU, OAS, NATO, G-7, G-8 and others have taken substantive steps to enhance information sharing, tighten border security, and combat terrorist financing. On 28 September the UN Security Council adopted Resolution 1373, which requires all states to prevent and suppress the financing of terrorist acts, including freezing funds and other financial assets. The resolution also obliges all states to improve border security, clamp down on the recruitment of terrorists, intensify information sharing and law enforcement cooperation in the international campaign against terrorism, and deny terrorists and their supporters any support or safehaven. This resolution augments the positive trend of Security Council resolutions 1267 and 1333 (passed in 1999 and 2000, respectively) which imposed targeted or "smart" sanctions against the Taliban in Afghanistan.

The existing 12 UN Conventions against terrorism represent a solid international foundation for nations to support this global struggle. In December, the United States ratified the two newest, the UN Convention for the Suppression of the Financing of Terrorism and the UN Convention for the Suppression of Terrorist Bombings. All nations should become parties to all 12 of these conventions so that terrorists can be more readily apprehended and prosecuted wherever they are located.

Public diplomacy has been an important aspect of our efforts as well. The Department of State has aggressively sought to counter distorted views of the United States overseas, to emphasize that the war on terrorism is not a war against Islam, and to underscore that terrorists are not martyrs but cowards and criminals. Senior US officials have conveyed these messages in hundreds of media interviews, and ambassadors have organized thousands of outreach activities around the world to build and maintain an international Coalition. The United States maintains Coalition Information Centers in London and Islamabad. The Department of State has an active speakers' program to explain US policies to foreign and domestic audiences. The Office of International Information Programs maintains an informative and frequently visited website featuring publications such as "The Network of Terrorism" and "Islam in the United States."

Intelligence

Cooperation among intelligence agencies around the world has expanded to unprecedented levels.

Sharing of intelligence about terrorists, their movements, and their planned attacks is an absolute prerequisite for successful interdiction. Governments in every region of the world have been able to use this information to expose the criminal netherworld in which terrorists operate. Undoubtedly, planned attacks have been prevented, and lives have been saved. Our military campaign in Afghanistan as well as law-enforcement and intelligence operations by Coalition members have yielded a wealth of intelligence that will require further exploitation for action. Such information will be extremely valuable in identifying and interdicting other terrorist cells around the world. Effective intelligence exchange allows countries to act preemptively to counter terrorists before they act. It closes an important seam that terrorists exploit to their advantage. There is room for continued improvement, but the initial results have been very encouraging.

Law Enforcement

The world's law enforcement professionals have launched a global dragnet to identify, arrest, and bring terrorists to justice.

In the United States, the FBI has led the law-enforcement engagement, working with all federal, state, and local law-enforcement agencies. More than 7000 FBI Agents and support personnel have worked diligently with their US and foreign law-enforcement partners to unravel the planning leading to the execution of the 9/11 operation, as well as to interdict other al-Qaida cells and operatives in the US and around the world. Their enhanced law-enforcement efforts, and cooperative work by officials around the world, have resulted in the apprehension of more than 1000 suspected terrorists and the breakup of al-Qaida and other terrorist cells. Many of these arrests, to include that of Zacarias Moussaoui, a suspected al-Qaida operative in the operation, are described in this report.

During 2001 and through March 2002, Secretary Powell designated or redesignated 33 groups as foreign terrorist organizations under the Immigration and Nationality Act, as amended by the Antiterrorism and Effective Death Penalty Act of 1996. The designations make it a criminal offense to provide funds or other material support to such organizations, require US financial institutions to block the funds of the groups, and make members of the groups ineligible for US visas and, if they are aliens, deportable.

On 26 October the US Congress enacted the USA PATRIOT Act, which significantly expands the ability of US law enforcement to investigate and prosecute persons who engage in terrorist acts. On 5 December, in accordance with the USA PATRIOT Act, Secretary Powell designated 39 groups as "terrorist exclusion list" organizations. The legal consequences of the designations relate to immigration, and they strengthen the US ability to exclude supporters of terrorism from entering the country or to deport them if they are found within our borders.

The United States brought to conclusion the prosecution of four al-Qaida members for the bombing of the US Embassies in Kenya and Tanzania. In May, in a courtroom within sight of the World Trade Center, guilty verdicts were handed down on all 302 counts in the trial of the bombing suspects, and all were sentenced to life in prison.

Economic

Money is like oxygen to terrorists, and it must be choked off.

When President Bush signed Executive Order 13224 on 23 September, he imposed dramatic penalties on those who provide financial support to terrorist organizations. The Order blocks the assets of designated organizations and individuals linked to global terrorism. It prohibits transactions with terrorist groups, leaders, and corporate and charitable fronts listed in the Order. It also establishes America's ability to block the US assets of, and deny access to US markets to, those foreign banks that refuse to freeze terrorist assets. As of March 2002, the Order contained the names of 189 groups, entities, and individuals. Accordingly, approximately 150 countries and independent law-enforcement jurisdictions [for example, Hong Kong, Taiwan] issued orders freezing the assets of suspected terrorists and organizations.

The US Department of Treasury has been leading the war against terrorist financing and has worked with all relevant agencies and departments to identify terrorist financing networks and to find ways to disrupt their operations.

Many nations and independent law-enforcement jurisdictions have made changes in their laws, regulations, and practices in order to suppress terrorism financing more effectively. UNSCR 1373 mandates worldwide improvements, and we are working with the UN Counter Terrorism Committee (CTC) and others to help improve the capability of countries to meet their obligations under the resolution to combat terrorist financing.

The first step has been to deny terrorists access to the world's organized financial structures; simultaneously, we have been moving to prevent the abuse of informal money-transfer systems and charities. Both lines of attack have produced results.

- President Bush launched the first offensive in the war on terrorism on 23 September by signing Executive Order 13224, freezing the US-based assets of those individuals and organizations involved with terrorism.
- All but a handful of the countries in the world have expressed their support for the financial war on terror.
- Approximately 150 countries and jurisdictions have issued orders freezing terrorist assets, and the international community was helping others improve their legal and regulatory systems so they can move effectively to block terrorist funds.
- At the end of 2001, the US had designated 158 known terrorists, terrorist organizations, and terrorist financial networks, whose assets are now subject to freezing in the US financial system.
- Between September 11 and 31 December 2001, the US blocked more than $34 million in assets of terrorist organizations. Other nations also blocked more than $33 million. The funds captured only measure the money in the pipeline at the time the accounts were shut down, which is a small fraction of the total funds disrupted by the closing of the pipeline.
- On 7 November, the US and its allies closed down operations of two major financial networks—al-Barakaat and al-Taqwa—both of which were used by al-Qaida and Usama Bin Ladin in more than 40 nations as sources of income and mechanisms to transfer funds. As part of that action, the Office of Foreign Assets Control (OFAC) was able to freeze $1,100,000 domestically in al-Barakaat-related funds. Treasury also worked closely with key officials in the Middle East to facilitate blocking of al-Barakaat's assets at its financial center of operations.
- On 4 December, President Bush froze the assets of a US-based foundation—The Holy Land Foundation for Relief and Development—that had been funneling money to the terrorist organization HAMAS. In 2000, the foundation had raised $13 million.
- International organizations are key partners in the war on financial terrorism. Since 28 September, over 100 nations have submitted reports to the United Nations on the actions they have taken to block terrorist finances, as required under United Nations Security Council resolution 1373 which calls on all nations to keep their financial systems free of terrorist funds.

- The Financial Action Task Force—a 29-nation group promoting policies to combat money laundering—adopted strict new standards to deny terrorist access to the world financial system.
- The G-20 and IMF member countries have agreed to make public the list of terrorists whose assets are subject to freezing, and the amount of assets frozen.
- For the first five months of this effort, the US identified terrorists for blocking and then sought cooperation from our allies around the world. A new stage in international cooperation was reached on 28 December 2001, when the EU took the lead and designated 6 European-based terrorists for asset blocking, on which US followed suit. Nations around the world have different information and different leads, and it is crucial that each of our allies not only blocks the terrorist financiers we identify but also develops its own leads to broaden the effort to identify and take action against those who fund terrorism.

Military

The terrorist attacks of September 11 were acts of war against the United States and a grievous affront to all humanity.

The international community has responded accordingly:

- On 12 September, the UN Security Council condemned the attacks and reiterated the inherent right of collective self defense in accordance with the UN Charter.
- On 21 September, Foreign Ministers of the OAS invoked the collective self-defense clause of the Inter-American Treaty of Reciprocal Assistance ("Rio Treaty").
- In Brussels on 5 October, NATO invoked Article 5 of the Washington Treaty, which states that an armed attack on one or more of the allies in Europe or North America shall be considered an attack against them all.
- 136 countries offered a range of military assistance.
- 89 countries granted overflight authority for US military aircraft.
- 76 countries granted landing rights for US military aircraft.
- 23 countries agreed to host US and Coalition forces involved in military operations in Afghanistan.

US Policy

President Bush has laid out the scope of the war on terrorism. Four enduring policy principles guide our counterterrorism strategy:

First, make no concessions to terrorists and strike no deals.

The US Government will make no concessions to individuals or groups holding official or private US citizens hostage. The United States will use every appropriate resource to gain the safe return of US citizens who are held hostage. At the same time, it is US Government policy to deny hostage takers the benefits of ransom, prisoner releases, policy changes, or other acts of concession.

Second, bring terrorists to justice for their crimes.

The United States will track terrorists who attack Americans, no matter how long it takes. This was demonstrated again in September 2001, when the United States arrested Zayd Hassan Abd al-Latif Masud al-Safarini, one of the chief perpetrators of the murderous hijacking in 1986 of Pan Am 73 in Karachi, Pakistan. He will stand trial in the United States for crimes committed during that brutal attack in which twenty-two persons—including two US citizens—were killed, and at least 100 persons were injured. Al-Safarini is the fourteenth international terrorist suspect arrested overseas and brought to the United States to stand trial since 1993. Others included Ramzi Yousef and Mir Aimal Kansi.

Third, isolate and apply pressure on states that sponsor terrorism to force them to change their behavior.

Libya is one of seven designated state sponsors of terrorism. Since the bombing of Pan Am 103 over Lockerbie, Scotland in 1988, the United States and Great Britain have pursued the Libyan perpetrators and sought to bring them to justice. In January 2001, a Scottish court convicted Libyan intelligence service member Abdel Basset al-Megrahi of the murder of 270 persons in connection with the Pan Am 103 attack. The court concluded that there was insufficient evidence to convict another Libyan defendant in the case. On 14 March 2002, a Scottish appellate court upheld Megrahi's conviction.

Fourth, bolster the counterterrorist capabilities of those countries that work with the United States and require assistance.

Under the Antiterrorism Assistance program, the United States provides training and related assistance to law enforcement and security services of selected friendly foreign governments. Courses cover such areas as airport security, bomb detection, hostage rescue, and crisis management. A recent component of the training targets the financial underpinnings of terrorists and criminal money launderers. Counterterrorist training and technical assistance teams are working with countries to jointly identify vulnerabilities, enhance capacities, and provide targeted assistance to address the problem of terrorist financing. At the same time special investigative teams are working with countries to identify and then dry up money used to support terrorism. We are also developing workshops to assist countries in drafting strong laws against terrorism, including terrorist financing. During the past 17 years, we have trained more than 35,000 officials from 152 countries in various aspects of counterterrorism.

A broad range of counterterrorism training resources from other US Government agencies, including military training by the Department of Defense, is being brought to bear to bolster international capabilities. We will work with the world community and seek assistance from other partner nations as well.

Our Terrorism Interdiction Program helps friendly countries stop terrorists from freely crossing international borders.

Our Rewards for Justice program offers rewards of up to $5 million for information that prevents or favorably resolves acts of international terrorism against US persons or property worldwide. Secretary Powell has authorized a reward of up to $25 million for information leading to the capture of Usama Bin Ladin and other key al-Qaida leaders.

The military phase of Operation Enduring Freedom began on 7 October 2001, destroying in weeks al-Qaida's grip on Afghanistan by driving their Taliban protectors from power. In addition to the United States, military assets were deployed from many nations, including Australia, Canada, Czech Republic, France, Germany, Italy, Japan, New Zealand, Norway, Poland, Republic of Korea, Russia, Turkey, and the United Kingdom. Forces from 55 countries augmented US forces in the overall effort, each bringing to the Coalition a unique contribution of military assets and expertise. As of March 2002, military operations continue in Afghanistan. We have also joined with our partners in Yemen, the Philippines, and Georgia to provide military training to counterterrorist forces focused on al-Qaida-related terrorist activity and groups in those countries. Such training will greatly enhance the capability of our allies to meet and defeat the threat on their soil.

Conclusion

This edition of *Patterns* is intended to place the global Coalition against terrorism into perspective. It describes results from a multifront effort, leveraging the full capability of the diplomatic, intelligence, law-enforcement, economic, and military communities in combating this international menace. In addition to our traditional country reports, we have included several new sections detailing how the activities of many different parts of the US Government and our allies have joined together to fight the scourge of Twenty-first Century terrorist groups with global reach. We also feature two case studies that emphasize the ongoing importance of global cooperation in the war on terrorism. Through effective law-enforcement and counterterrorism cooperation, the governments of Italy and Singapore have thwarted serious terrorist plots that targeted Western interests and threatened many lives. These cases—among the many that we could cite—demonstrate how the international Coalition against terrorism effectively uses the tools at its disposal to defeat the terrorist threat.

In conclusion, two points. First, I want to offer my condolences to the families, loved ones, friends, and countrymen of all the victims of terrorism in this past year. We can never replace what you have lost, but we are determined to bring to justice, however long it takes, those who were responsible and to do whatever lies in our power to see that such a tragedy will never happen again. Second, I want to recognize the true heroes of this campaign: the thousands of police, law-enforcement personnel, firefighters, intelligence professionals, military personnel, diplomats, and other government officials, and the citizens around the world who have responded so magnificently to this global menace. Like the passengers of United Airlines Flight 93 who saved many lives with their acts of heroism in the face of death, the worldwide Coalition will prevail to save countless other lives in the future. The events of this past year have truly brought the fight against terrorism to a new personal level. I'm proud to say that Americans and our allies have shown resilience and determination.

In the wake of the horror of September 11, the world has never been so focused on the threat of international terrorism nor more resolute in the need to counter this threat using the full power—diplomatic, intelligence, economic, law enforcement, financial, and military—available to the international community. Success will require patience and a continuous, relentless commitment on the part of many people in many professions, in many countries. As President Bush has said, "Ours is the cause of freedom. We've defeated freedom's enemies before, and we will defeat them again."

Present U.S. Policy

Since the issuing of Patterns of Global Terrorism 2001, *U.S. counterterrorism policy has continued to evolve. In July 2005, President George W. Bush addressed the FBI Academy in Quantico, Virginia. Part of his speech covered U.S. counterterrorism strategy and its successes. Excerpts from that speech (available online at http://www.whitehouse.gov/infocus/nationalsecurity/index.html) follow.*

America Has A Clear Strategy For Victory In The War On Terror.

- **America Must Fight The Enemy Abroad, So We Do Not Have To Face Them Here At Home.** By using every available tool to keep the enemy on the run, America's Armed Forces can ensure that terrorists spend their days trying to avoid capture, not planning their next attack.
- **The United States Must Deny Terrorists Sanctuary And The Support Of States.** By helping friendly governments control their territory and by making it clear to outlaw regimes that providing safe haven to terrorists will not be tolerated, the United States can limit the infrastructure terrorists have at their disposal to plan and carry out attacks.
- **Mass Murderers Must Not Obtain Weapons Of Mass Destruction.** The United States must prevent terrorists from obtaining nuclear, chemical, and biological weapons. This must be a global effort involving many countries.
- **Freedom And Hope Will Defeat An Ideology Of Hate.** Through the spread of democracy, the United States can help deny terrorists the ideological victories they seek. Free nations do not support terrorists or invade their neighbors. By advancing the cause of liberty across the world, we will make the world more peaceful and America more secure.

Since September 11th, America Has Made Great Strides In Winning The War On Terror.

- **The United States Has Removed Brutal Regimes In Afghanistan And Iraq That Harbored Terrorists And Threatened America.** Fifty million people were liberated in the process, and both Afghanistan and Iraq have chosen leaders in free elections.
- **Across The World, Liberty Is On The March.** In the last 18 months, we have witnessed a Purple Revolution in Iraq, an Orange Revolution in Ukraine, a Rose Revolution in Georgia, a Tulip Revolution in Kyrgyzstan, and a Cedar Revolution in Lebanon.
- **The World's Most Dangerous Nuclear Trading Network Has Been Shut Down.** The United States has launched the Proliferation Security Initiative, a global effort involving 60 countries to stop shipments of weapons of mass destruction. The black-market network that supplied nuclear weapons technology to North Korea, Libya, and Iran has been shut down, and the government of Libya has even agreed to abandon its nuclear weapons program and rejoin a community of nations.
- **In The Last Few Weeks, U.S. Forces Have Captured A Number Of Key Terrorists.** In Pakistan, one of Osama Bin Laden's senior terrorist leaders, al-Libbi, was brought to justice. Earlier this week, in Iraq, U.S. forces captured two senior operatives of the terrorist Zarqawi. America has also killed or captured hundreds of terrorists and insurgents near the Syrian border and in a series of raids throughout Baghdad.

Current Policy Initiatives

The Department of State and other departments work together to combat terrorism in the arenas of international trade, commerce, aid, and other areas. Key initiatives include the Antiterrorism Assistance Program and the Rewards for Justice Program. The following explanations of those programs is excerpted from Patterns of Global Terrorism 2003.

Antiterrorism Assistance Program

Congress authorized the Antiterrorism Assistance (ATA) Program in 1983 as part of a major initiative against international terrorism. Since that time, ATA has provided training for more than 36,000 students from 142 countries. The ATA Program provides training and related assistance to law enforcement and security services of selected friendly foreign governments. Assistance to the qualified countries focuses on the following objectives:

Enhancing the antiterrorism skills of friendly countries by providing training and equipment to deter and counter the threats of terrorism.

Strengthening the bilateral ties of the United States with friendly, foreign governments by offering concrete assistance in areas of mutual concern.

Increasing respect for human rights by sharing with civilian authorities modern, humane, and effective antiterrorism techniques.

ATA courses are developed and customized in response to terrorism trends and patterns. The training can be categorized into four functional areas: Crisis Prevention, Crisis Management, Crisis Resolution, and Investigation. Countries needing assistance are identified on the basis of the threat or actual level of terrorist activity they face.

Antiterrorism assistance and training may be conducted either in-country or within the United States. This arrangement provides flexibility to maximize the effectiveness of the program for countries of strategic importance in the global war on terrorism.

ATA programs may take the form of advisory assistance, such as police administration and management of police departments, how to train police instructors or develop a police academy, and modern interview and investigative techniques. This approach enables the program to provide a narrow focus to solutions for country-specific problems that are not resolved in the classroom-training environment. Equipment or explosive-detection trained dogs may also be included in the assistance package.

The ability of the United States to assist friendly governments to master the detection and prevention of terrorist activities will clearly enhance the mutual security of all the participating nations. Detecting and eliminating terrorist cells at the root before their violence can cross borders and oceans will ensure a safer world for all nations.

Rewards for Justice Program

The Rewards for Justice Program is one of the most valuable US Government assets in the fight against international terrorism. Established by the 1984 Act To Combat International Terrorism—Public Law 98-533—the Program is administered by the US Department of State's Bureau of Diplomatic Security.

Under the Program, The Secretary of State may offer rewards of up to $5 million for information that prevents or favorably resolves acts of international terrorism against US persons or property worldwide. Rewards may also be paid for information leading to the arrest or conviction of terrorists attempting, committing, and conspiring to commit—or aiding and abetting in the commission of—such acts.

The USA Patriot Act of 2001 authorizes the Secretary to offer or pay rewards of greater that $5 million if he determines that a greater amount is necessary to combat terrorism or to defend the United States against terrorist acts. Secretary Powell has authorized a reward of up to $25 million for the information leading to the capture of Usama Bin Ladin and other key al-Qaida leaders.

In November 2002, the State and Treasury Departments announced a $5 million rewards program that will pay for information leading to the disruption of any terrorism financing operation.

Diplomatic Security has fully supported the efforts of the

private business sector and citizens to establish a Rewards for Justice Fund, a nongovernmental, nonprofit 501 C (3) charitable organization administered by a group of private US citizens. One hundred percent of all donated funds will be used to supplement reward payments only. Diplomatic Security has forged a strong relationship with the private business and US citizen representatives of the Rewards for Justice Fund. Diplomatic Security has embarked on a much closer relationship with the US public and private businesses in the US Government's continuing efforts to bring those individuals responsible for the planning of the September 11 attacks to justice and to prevent future international terrorist attacks against the United States at home or abroad.

Since its inception, the Rewards for Justice Program has been very effective. In the past seven years, the Secretary of State has authorized payments for more than $52 million to 33 people who provided credible information that put terrorists behind bars or prevented acts of international terrorism worldwide. The program played a significant role in the arrest of international terrorist Ramzi Yousef, who was convicted in the 1993 bombing of the World Trade Center and most recently in the efforts to locate Uday and Qusay Hussein.

Foreign Terrorist Organization Designations

Anna Sabasteanski

A useful tool at the disposal of the State Department, working in conjunction with the Attorney General and the Secretary of the Treasury, is the power to designate foreign organizations as terrorist organizations. The designation "foreign terrorist organization" (FTO) is an economic means to fight terrorism. U.S. citizens and those under the jurisdiction of the United States are forbidden by law from providing material support or resources to an FTO, and U.S. financial institutions are required to freeze the funds of FTOs. By designating an organization an FTO, the United States alerts the world of its concern about the organization. The U.S. Department of State reports that as of 31 December 2004, the United States had designated a total of 397 individuals and entities as terrorists or as financiers or facilitators of terrorists.

Multilateral and Regional Cooperation

Despite the reputation for unilateralism attaching to the Bush administration, multilateral action and cooperation with regional and international partners also is an important component of U.S. antiterrorist policy. Among the organizations with whom the United States works are:

- The Counterterrorism Committee of the United Nations.
- The Egmont Group of Financial Intelligence Units. The international community has agreed to define a financial intelligence unit as "a central, national agency responsible for receiving (and, as permitted, requesting), analysing and disseminating to the competent authorities, disclosures of financial information (i) concerning suspected proceeds of crime, or (ii) required by national legislation or regulation, in order to counter money laundering" (Statement of Purpose of the Egmont Group of Financial Intelligence Units 2001, http://www1.oecd.org/fatf/pdf/EGstat-200106_en.pdf).
- The Financial Action Task Force (FATF). This is an intergovernmental body committed to the development and promotion of national and international policies to combat money laundering and terrorist financing.
- The Counterterrorism Assistance Group (CTAG), a group established by the G-8 group of nations to provide assistance to those nations that need help developing a counterterrorism capability.

Specialized multilateral organizations such as the International Civil Aviation Organization (ICAO) and the International Maritime Organization (IMO) can set international counterterrorism standards and best practices. Regional groups such as the European Union, the African Union, the Organization of American States, and so on encourage their member states to adopt these standards and best practices and help in their implementation. The United States also participates in the G-8 and the United Nations conventions and protocols in force against terrorism. (See Section on "International Response" for details.)

United States General Accounting Office,
Report to Congressional Requesters

Combating Terrorism: Department of State Programs to Combat Terrorism Abroad

Introduction

Eds. Note: This material originally appeared as an introductory letter to the report directed to the heads of the U.S. House of Representatives' Committee on International Relations and Subcommittee on National Security, Veterans Affairs, and International Relations.

Since the terrorist attacks of September 11, 2001, efforts to combat terrorism have become an increasingly important part of U.S. government activities. Such efforts have also become more important in U.S. relations with other countries and with international organizations, such as the United Nations (U.N.). The U.S. Department of State is charged with coordinating these international efforts and protecting Americans abroad; its objective is to reduce the number of terrorist attacks, especially those on U.S. citizens and interests. While countering terrorism has always been a part of State's role, it took on heightened significance in the aftermath of the 1998 al Qaeda terrorist attacks on the U.S. embassies in Tanzania and Kenya. Since the September 11 attacks on the World Trade Center in New York City and the Pentagon in Washington, D.C., State has helped direct the U.S. efforts to combat terrorism abroad by building the global coalition against terrorism, including providing diplomatic support for military operations in Afghanistan and other countries. State has also supported international law enforcement efforts to identify, arrest, and bring terrorists to justice, as well as performing other activities intended to reduce the number of terrorist attacks.

This report is intended to assist your committees in overseeing the State Department's leadership of U.S. programs to combat terrorism abroad. Specifically, this report identifies the State Department's programs and activities intended to (1) prevent terrorist attacks, (2) disrupt and destroy terrorist organizations, (3) respond to terrorist incidents, and (4) coordinate efforts to combat terrorism. Footnotes to this report identify programs and activities managed by the U.S. Agency for International Development that complement the State Department's efforts to combat terrorism abroad. This report is part of a larger effort that you jointly requested to review governmentwide programs to combat terrorism overseas. Regarding some of these programs, it is important to recognize that the State Department works in conjunction with a number of other federal agencies, including the Departments of Defense, Justice, and the Treasury, as well as the Central Intelligence Agency. As agreed with your staff, we plan to report later this year on governmentwide efforts to combat terrorism overseas.

We identified the State Department's programs and activities for combating terrorism by reviewing State documents, such as *Congressional Presentation Document, FY 2003* and *Patterns of Global Terrorism*,[1] and by conducting interviews with State officials. To identify programs and activities provided by other departments and coordinated through State, we reviewed documents and interviewed officials from the Departments of Defense, Justice, and the Treasury; the Federal Bureau of Investigation (FBI) and other law enforcement agencies; and the U.S. Agency for International Development (USAID). In addition, we conducted fieldwork at the U.S. Embassy in Athens, Greece, to observe programs and activities to combat terrorism overseas. At selected regional and functional military commands, we met with State Department Political Advisors at the U.S. Central Command at MacDill Air Force Base, Florida; the U.S. Southern Command in Miami, Florida; and the U.S. European Command in Stuttgart-Vaihingen, Germany. In addition, we conducted fieldwork at the International Law Enforcement Academy in Budapest, Hungary, to review programs to combat terrorism that the State Department manages or funds or both. We did not evaluate the effectiveness of these programs. We conducted our review from February 2002 through July 2002 in accordance with generally accepted government auditing standards.

Results in Brief

The State Department conducts multifaceted activities in its effort to prevent terrorist attacks on Americans abroad. For example, to protect U.S. officials, property, and information abroad, State operates programs that include local guards for U.S. missions, armored vehicles for embassy personnel, U.S. Marine security guards to protect sensitive information, and plans to evacuate Americans in emergencies. For Americans traveling and living abroad, State issues public travel warnings and operates warning systems to convey terrorism-

---

[1] U.S. Department of State, *Congressional Presentation Document, FY 2003* (Washington, D.C.: May 2002).

Table 1 State Department Funding to Combat Terrorism Abroad (*dollars in millions*)

	Fiscal year 2001 (actual)	Fiscal year 2002 (enacted)	Emergency Relief Fund	Fiscal year 2003 President's budget
Bureau of Administration	$ 50	$ 37	$ 0	$ 123
Bureau of Overseas Buildings Operations	1,035	1,159	105	1,286
Bureau of Consular Affairs	409	465	0	643
Bureau of Diplomatic Security	105	115	48	228.
Office of the Coordinator for Counterterrorism	35	41	50	69
Total	$1,634	$1,817	$203	$2,349

Sources: Office of Management and Budget and the Department of State (Office of the Coordinator for Counterterrorism).

related information. For U.S. businesses and universities operating overseas, State uses the Overseas Security Advisory Councils—voluntary partnerships between the State Department and the U.S. private sector—to exchange threat information. To improve the ability of foreign governments to combat terrorism, State funds several training programs that operate both in the United States and overseas.

To disrupt and destroy terrorist organizations abroad, State has numerous programs and activities that rely on military, multilateral, economic, law enforcement, intelligence, and other capabilities. For example, State's program to enhance military cooperation has resulted in 136 countries' offering a range of military assistance for Operation Enduring Freedom in Afghanistan.[2] State has supported efforts, through international organizations like the United Nations, for the global implementation of resolutions and treaties aimed at reducing terrorism. In addition, State uses extradition treaties to bring terrorists to trial in the United States and cooperates with foreign intelligence, security, and law enforcement entities to track and capture terrorists in foreign countries. If the United States has no extradition agreements with a country, then State, with the Department of Justice, can work to obtain the arrest of suspected terrorists overseas through renditions. It also provides rewards for information leading to the arrest and prosecution of designated terrorists or the thwarting of terrorist attacks.

The State Department leads the U.S. response to terrorist incidents abroad. This includes diplomatic measures to protect Americans, minimize damage, terminate terrorist attacks, and bring terrorists to justice. Once an attack has occurred, State's activities include measures to alleviate damage, protect public health, and provide emergency assistance. State also coordinates interagency exercises for combating terrorism abroad. In addition, State helps foreign governments prepare to respond to an attack by conducting multinational training exercises.

To coordinate the U.S. effort to combat terrorism internationally, State uses a variety of mechanisms to work with the Departments of Defense, Justice, and the Treasury; the intelligence agencies; the Federal Bureau of Investigation; and others. These mechanisms include interagency working groups at the headquarters level in Washington, D.C.; emergency action committees at U.S. missions overseas; and liaison exchanges with other government agencies.

Background

According to the State Department's 2002 *Annual Performance Plan*, the department's counterterrorism goals are to reduce the number of terrorist attacks, bring terrorists to justice, reduce or eliminate state-sponsored terrorist acts, delegitimize the use of terror as a political tool, enhance the U.S. response to terrorism overseas, and strengthen international cooperation and operational capabilities to combat terrorism.

The Secretary of State is responsible for coordinating all U.S. civilian departments and agencies that provide counterterrorism assistance overseas. The Secretary also is responsible for managing all U.S. bilateral and multilateral relationships intended to combat terrorism abroad.

State requested over $2.3 billion to combat terrorism in fiscal year 2003. This includes more than $1 billion for overseas embassy security and construction, as well as for counterterrorism assistance and training to countries cooperating with the global coalition against terrorism. Table 1 provides a breakdown of State's funding to combat terrorism.

By contrast, State spent about $1.6 billion in fiscal year 2001 and received about $1.8 billion to combat terrorism in fiscal year 2002. State received an additional $203 million through the Emergency Response Fund as part of the $40 billion appropriated by the Congress in response to the September 11, 2001, terrorist attacks against the United States.

The Office of Management and Budget reported that determining precise funding levels associated with activities to combat terrorism is difficult because departments may not isolate those activities from other program activities. Some activities serve multiple purposes—for example, upgrades to embassy security help protect against terrorism as well as other crimes.

---

2 Operation Enduring Freedom is the military campaign that began on October 7, 2001, against al Qaeda and Taliban forces in Afghanistan and elsewhere.

Programs and Activities to Prevent Terrorism Abroad

The State Department conducts multifaceted activities in an effort to prevent terrorist attacks on Americans abroad. For example, to protect U.S. officials, property, and information abroad, the Bureau of Diplomatic Security provides local guards for embassies and armored vehicles for embassy personnel. In addition, it provides undercover teams to detect terrorist surveillance activities. Following the 1998 embassy bombings in Africa, State upgraded security for all missions, which included strengthening building exteriors, lobby entrances, and the walls and fences at embassy perimeters.[3]

State has several programs to help warn Americans living and traveling abroad against potential threats, including those posed by terrorists. For example, to warn Americans about travel-related dangers, in fiscal year 2001 the Bureau of Consular Affairs issued 64 travel warnings, 134 public announcements, and 189 consular information sheets. In addition, missions employ a "warden system" to warn Americans registered with an embassy of threats against their security. The system varies by mission but uses telephone, E-mail, fax, and other technologies as appropriate. Finally, the Bureau of Diplomatic Security manages the Overseas Security Advisory Councils program. The councils are a voluntary, joint effort between State and the private sector to exchange threat-and security-related information. Councils currently operate in 47 countries.

In addition, State manages and funds programs to train foreign government and law enforcement officials to combat terrorism abroad. These programs include the following:

- the Antiterrorism Assistance Program, implemented by the Bureau of Diplomatic Security, to enhance the antiterrorism skills of law enforcement and security personnel in foreign countries;
- the International Law Enforcement Academies, managed by the Bureau for International Narcotics and Law Enforcement Affairs, to provide law enforcement training in four locations around the world.[4] The Departments of State, the Treasury, and Justice—including the Bureau of Diplomatic Security, Federal Bureau of Investigation, and other U.S. law enforcement agencies—provide the on-site training;
- the Department of Justice's Overseas Prosecutorial Development and Assistance Training and the International Criminal Investigation Training Assistance Program. The State Department provides policy oversight and funds this training, which is intended to build rule-of-law institutions, and includes general law enforcement and anticrime training for foreign nationals.[5]

Programs and Activities to Disrupt and Destroy Terrorist Organizations Abroad

State conducts numerous programs and activities intended to disrupt and destroy terrorist organizations. These programs and activities rely on military, multilateral, economic, law enforcement, and other capacities, as the following examples illustrate:

- The Bureau of Political-Military Affairs coordinates with Department of Defense on military cooperation with other countries. It has been State's liaison with the coalition supporting Operation Enduring Freedom, processing 72 requests for military assistance from coalition partners since September 11, 2001.
- The Bureau of International Organization Affairs helped craft and adopt United Nations Security Council Resolution 1373, obligating all member nations to fight terrorism and report on their implementation of the resolution. It also assisted with resolutions extending U.N. sanctions on al Qaeda and the Taliban and on certain African regimes, including those whose activities benefit terrorists.
- The Department of State's Office of the Coordinator for Counterterrorism, the Bureau of International Narcotics and Law Enforcement, and the Economic Bureau work with the Department of the Treasury and other agencies to stem the flow of money and other material support to terrorists. According to the State Department, since September 11, the United States has blocked $34.3 million in terrorist related assets.
- The Office of the Legal Advisor pursues extradition and mutual legal assistance treaties with foreign governments. The Office of the Legal Advisor also works with the U.N. and with other nations in drafting multilateral agreements, treaties, and conventions on counterterrorism.
- The Bureau of Diplomatic Security, working with the Department of Justice, cooperates with foreign intelligence,

---

3 The upgrades also included closed-circuit television monitors, explosive detection devices, walk-through metal detectors, and reinforced walls and security doors to provide protection inside the embassy. In addition, State plans to replace some existing embassies with buildings that meet current security standards, such as having a 100-foot setback from streets surrounding embassies. State also has programs to protect national security information discussed at meetings or stored on computers. These programs include U.S. Marine security guards controlling access to embassies, efforts to prevent foreign intelligence agencies from detecting emanations form computer equipment, and computer security programs.

4 The academies are located in Budapest, Hungary; Bangkok, Thailand; Gaborone, Botswana; and Roswell, New Mexico.

5 USAID also supports programs to train foreign law enforcement, prosecutors, and judges and to assist in rewriting legislation and criminal sentencing guidelines. USAID missions and the Bureau for Democracy, Conflict, and Humanitarian Assistance have rule-of-law and governance programs in about 60 of the 85 countries where USAID has a presence.

security, and law enforcement entities to track and capture terrorists in foreign countries, assist in their extradition to the United States, and block attempted terrorist attacks on U.S. citizens and assets abroad.
- The Office of the Coordinator for Counterterrorism, in conjunction with the Department of Justice and other agencies, coordinates State's role in facilitating the arrest of suspected terrorists through an overseas arrest, known as a rendition, when the United States lacks an extradition treaty.
- The Bureau of Diplomatic Security manages the Rewards for Justice Program. This program offers payment for information leading to the prevention of a terrorist attack or the arrest and prosecution of designated individuals involved in international terrorism. These rewards reach up to $25 million for those involved in the September 11 attacks.
- The Bureau of Intelligence and Research prepares intelligence and threat reports for the Secretary of State, high-level department officials, and ambassadors at U.S. missions. It also monitors governmentwide intelligence activities to ensure their compatibility with U.S. foreign policy objectives related to terrorism, and it seeks to expand the sharing of interagency data on known terrorist suspects.

Programs and Activities to Respond to Terrorist Incidents Abroad

The State Department is responsible for leading the U.S. response to terrorist incidents abroad. This includes measures to protect Americans, minimize incident damage, terminate terrorist attacks, and bring terrorists to trial. Once an attack has occurred, State's activities include measures to alleviate damage, protect public health, and provide emergency assistance. The Office of the Coordinator for Counterterrorism facilitates the planning and implementation of the U.S. government response to a terrorist incident overseas. In a given country, the ambassador would act as the on-scene coordinator for the response effort.

In addition, several other bureaus respond to the aftermath of a terrorist attack and help friendly governments prepare to respond to an attack by conducting joint training exercises.

- The Bureau of Political-Military Affairs is tasked with helping to prepare U.S. forces, foreign governments, and international organizations to respond to the consequences of a chemical, biological, radiological, or nuclear incident overseas. For example, the bureau is developing a database of international assets that could be used to respond to the consequences of a terrorist attack using weapons of mass destruction. It also participates in major interagency international exercises, which are led by DOD. In addition, the bureau assisted in the first operational deployment of a U.S. consequence management task force, working with the DOD regional command responsible for conducting the war in Afghanistan.
- Several bureaus and offices deploy emergency response teams to respond to terrorist attacks. For example, the Office of the Coordinator for Counterterrorism deploys multi-agency specialists in the Foreign Emergency Support Team (FEST) to assist missions in responding to ongoing terrorist attacks. For example, at the request of the Ambassador, the FEST can be dispatched rapidly to the mission. As one component of this team, the Bureau of Political-Military Affairs can deploy a Consequence Management Support Team to assist missions in managing the aftermath of terrorist attacks. In addition, the Bureau of Overseas Buildings Operations Emergency Response Team helps secure embassy grounds and restore communications following a crisis.[6]

Activities to Coordinate U.S. Efforts to Combat Terrorism Abroad

The State Department is responsible for coordinating all federal agencies' efforts to combat terrorism abroad. These include the Departments of Defense, Justice, and the Treasury; the various intelligence agencies; the FBI and other law enforcement agencies; and USAID. In addition, State coordinates U.S. efforts to combat terrorism multilaterally through international organizations and bilaterally with foreign nations. State uses a variety of methods to coordinate its efforts to combat terrorism abroad, including the following:

- In Washington, D.C., State participates in National Security Council interagency working groups, issue-specific working groups, and ad hoc working groups. For example, the Office of the Coordinator for Counterterrorism maintains policy oversight and provides leadership for the interagency Technical Support Working Group—a forum that identifies, prioritizes, and coordinates interagency and international applied research and development needs and requirements to combat terrorism.
- At U.S. embassies, State implements mission performance plans that coordinate embassy activities to combat terrorism, country team subgroups on terrorism, emergency

---

6 USAID assists in the aftermath of a terrorist incident through its Office of Foreign Disaster Assistance (OFDA). OFDA participates with other U.S. teams, deploying immediately with the Foreign Emergency Support Team. OFDA serves as an Advisor to the U.S. Chief of Mission, helping to coordinate the initial response efforts. Because of its relationships and formal agreements with both U.S. government agencies and nongovernmental organizations, OFDA can provide information on their capacities to assist a host nation in managing the consequences of a terrorist incident. OFDA is currently providing humanitarian assistance in Kabul, Afghanistan, and the United States has reestablished its mission there.

action committees to organize embassy response to terrorist threats and incidents, and ad hoc working groups. For example, selected embassies have country team subgroups dedicated to law enforcement matters, chaired by the Deputy Chief of Mission. Working with related bureaus and agencies such as the Regional Security Office, FBI Legal Attaché, and Treasury Department Financial Attaché, these subgroups coordinate efforts to combat terrorism among the various agencies overseas.

- In Washington, D.C., and elsewhere, State exchanges personnel with other agencies for liaison purposes. In Washington, D.C., for example, State personnel serve as liaisons at the CIA's Counter-Terrorism Center. The department also provides each U.S. regional military command with a Political Advisor, who helps the respective commanders coordinate with State Department Headquarters and with U.S. embassies on regional and bilateral matters, including efforts to combat terrorism.

GAO-02-1021; September 2002

CRS Issue Brief for Congress

Terrorism and National Security: Issues and Trends

Raphael Perl
Foreign Affairs, Defense, and Trade Division

Summary

International terrorism has long been recognized as a serious foreign and domestic security threat. This issue brief examines international terrorist actions and threats and the U.S. policy response. As the 9/11 Commission report released on July 19, 2004, concludes, the United States needs to use all tools at its disposal, including diplomacy, international cooperation, and constructive engagement to economic sanctions, covert action, physical security enhancement, and military force.

A modern trend in terrorism is toward loosely organized, self-financed, international networks of terrorists. Another trend is toward terrorism that is religiously—or ideologically—motivated. Radical Islamic fundamentalist groups, or groups using religion as a pretext, pose terrorist threats of varying kinds to U.S. interests and to friendly regimes. A third trend is the apparent growth of cross-national links among different terrorist organizations, which may involve combinations of military training, funding, technology transfer, or political advice.

Looming over the entire issue of international terrorism is a trend toward proliferation of weapons of mass destruction (WMD). For instance, Iran, seen as the most active state sponsor of terrorism, has been secretly conducting a longstanding uranium enrichment program, and North Korea has both admitted to having a clandestine program for uranium enrichment and claimed to have nuclear weapons. (See CRS Issue Brief IB91141, *North Korea's Nuclear Weapons Program*.) On December 19, 2003, Iran signed an agreement allowing international inspections of nuclear sites; on December 21, 2003, Libya announced similar intentions. Indications have also surfaced that Al Qaeda has attempted to acquire chemical, biological, radiological, and nuclear weapons. As a result, stakes in the war against international terrorism are increasing and margins for error in selecting appropriate policy instruments to prevent terrorist attacks are diminishing.

U.S. policy toward international terrorism contains a significant military component, reflected in the war in Iraq; U.S. operations in Afghanistan; deployment of U.S. forces around the Horn of Africa, to Djibouti, and the former Soviet Republic of Georgia; and ongoing military exercises in Colombia. Issues for Congress include whether the Administration is providing sufficient information about the long-term goals and costs of its military strategy and whether military force is necessarily an effective anti-terrorism instrument in some circumstances.

As terrorism is a global phenomenon, a major challenge facing policy makers is how to maximize international cooperation and support, without unduly compromising important U.S. national security interests. A growing issue bedeviling policymakers is how to minimize the economic and civil liberties costs of an enhanced security environment. The issue of how to combat incitement to terrorism—especially in instances where such activity is state sponsored or countenanced—perplexes policymakers as well.

On July 22, 2004, the National Commission on Terrorist Attacks upon the United States ("9/11 Commission") issued its final report. On December 17, 2004, the President signed the Intelligence Reform and Terrorism Prevention Act of 2004, establishing a National Intelligence Director and National Counterterrorism Center.

Most Recent Developments

On February 17, 2005, President Bush designated John Negroponte as the nation's first Director of National Intelligence (DNI), pending Senate confirmation. Negroponte, a seasoned diplomat, will lead and coordinate the nation's intelligence community. In testimony before Congress the previous day, CIA Director Porter Goss and other senior Administration officials expressed concern over the use of Iraq as a training ground for a new generation of terrorists; the intent of al Qaeda to conduct attacks using WMD; the potential availability of WMD material from former Russian stockpiles; and nuclear weapons and nuclear ambitions of rogue nations such as Iran and North Korea. In February 16, 2005 congressional testimony, as well, Secretary of State Condoleezza Rice was critical of Syria—"interference in Lebanese affairs" and Syrian aid to guerrillas attacking American forces in Iraq. Recently, individual Members of Congress have increasingly called for U.S. sanctions against Syria under the Syrian Accountability Act.

On December 17, 2004, President Bush signed the Intelligence Reform and Prevention Act of 2004 (S. 2845, P.L. 108-458) establishing the position of National Intelligence Director (a position separate from that of the CIA Director) to serve as the President's principal intelligence advisor, overseeing and coordinating the foreign and domestic activities of the intelligence community. Established as well is a National Counterterrorism Center designed to serve as a central knowledge bank for information about known and suspected terrorists and to coordinate and monitor counterterrorism plans and activities of all government agencies. The Center will also be responsible for preparing the daily terrorism threat report for the President.

Background And Analysis

The War on Terrorism

The Administration's response to the September 11, 2001 events was swift, wide-ranging and decisive. Administration officials attributed responsibility for the attack to Osama bin Laden and the Al Qaeda organization. One result was an announced policy shift from deterrence to preemption, generally referred to as the "Bush Doctrine." (National Security Strategy, [http://www.whitehouse.gov/nsc/nss.html].) Given the potential catastrophic consequences of terrorist attacks employing weapons of mass destruction, Administration decisionmakers felt that the nation could not afford to sit back, wait for attacks to occur, and then respond. The nation was mobilized; combating terrorism and crippling Al Qaeda became top national priorities. Preemptive use of military force against foreign terrorist groups and infrastructure gained increasing acceptance in Administration policy circles. In addition, a February 14, 2003, National Strategy for Combating Terrorism [http://www.whitehouse.gov/news/releases/2003/02/20030214-7.html] gave added emphasis to the role of international cooperation, law enforcement and economic development in countering terrorism.

A full-scale campaign was launched, using all elements of national and international power, to go after Al Qaeda and its affiliates and support structures. The campaign involved rallying the international community, especially law enforcement and intelligence components, to shut down Al Qaeda cells and financial networks. A U.S. military operation was launched in early October 2001, against the Taliban regime —which had harbored Al Qaeda since 1996—and against Al Qaeda strongholds in Afghanistan. A total of 136 countries offered a range of military assistance to the United States, including overflight and landing rights and accommodations for U.S. forces. As a result, the Taliban was removed from power, all known Al Qaeda training sites were destroyed, and some Taliban and Al Qaeda leaders were killed or detained. Since then, according to President Bush in his address to the nation on May 1, 2003, nearly half of the Al Qaeda leadership has been captured or killed. Notwithstanding, top Al Qaeda leaders Osama bin Laden and Ayman al Zawahiri as well as the Taliban leader Mullah Mohammed Omar apparently remain at large.

On March 19, 2003, after an intensive military buildup in the Persian Gulf, the United States launched the war with Iraq, one of seven nations on the State Department's sponsors of terrorism list, with an attack on a suspected meeting site of Saddam Hussein. President Bush, in his January 28, 2003 State of the Union Address, emphasized the threat posed to world security by a Saddam Hussein armed with weapons of mass destruction and stated that Iraq "aids and protects" the Al Qaeda terrorist organization. After a swift military campaign, President Bush announced on April 15, 2003, that "the regime of Saddam Hussein is no more." Saddam Hussein was arrested by U.S. personnel December 13, 2002, near his hometown of Tikrit.

In addition to U.S. troops currently in Afghanistan, U.S. forces have been dispatched to Yemen, the Philippines, and the former Soviet Republic of Georgia to train local militaries to fight terrorists. In FY2002 and FY2003, the Administration sought and received funding and permission to use such funding (subject to annual review) for U.S. military aid to Colombia to support the Colombian government's "unified campaign against narcotics trafficking, terrorist activities, and other threats to its national security." Similar authorization has granted for FY2004 and FY2005. Previously, such assistance had been restricted to supporting counterdrug operations in Colombia.

In the context of this campaign the United States has stepped up intelligence-sharing and law enforcement cooperation with other governments to root out terrorist cells. It is increasingly apparent that such cells are operating not just in places where they are welcomed or tolerated but in many other places, including Western Europe and the United States. According to *Patterns of Global Terrorism 2003 (Patterns 2003)* [http://www.state.gov/s/ct/rls/pgtrpt/2003/c12153.htm], as of January 2003 an aggressive international law enforcement effort had resulted in detention of approximately 3,000 terrorists and their supporters in more than 100 countries and in the freezing of $124 million in assets in some 600 bank accounts around the world, including $36 million in the United States alone. On June 2, 2003, the G-8 leaders publicized plans to create a Counter-Terrorism Action Group to assist nations in enhancing their anti-terrorism capabilities. Anticipated areas of activity include (1) outreach to countries in the area of counter-terrorism cooperation and (2) providing capacity building assistance to nations with insufficient capacity to fight terrorism.

An encouraging sign in the anti-terrorism struggle has been the apparent willingness of certain states to distance themselves from international terrorism and/or development of weapons of mass destruction. Libya renounced its WMD programs on December 21, 2003, and has cooperated extensively with the United States and the international community in dismantling those programs. On December 19, 2003, Iran signed an agreement allowing international inspections of its nuclear facilities. Iran has been secretly conducting a longstanding uranium enrichment program. Intensive inspections have revealed likely violations of its Nuclear Non-Proliferation Treaty (NPT) safeguards agreement, and while Iran has promised to suspend enrichment and reprocessing activities, there are indications that the suspension is not complete. Sudan, in cooperation with U.S. law enforcement and intelligence agencies, has arrested Al Qaeda members and "by and large" shut down Al Qaeda training camps on its territory. Libya has reportedly offered to share intelligence information on Al Qaeda's activities with U.S. authorities and Syria has promised to clamp down on terrorist groups on its territory and cutback overall support for terrorist groups. On June 10, 2004, press reports aired allegations, yet to be confirmed, that Libyan leader Muammar Qadhafi was involved in an plot to assassinate Saudi Crown Prince Abdullah.

Background

Increasingly, international terrorism is recognized as a threat to U.S. foreign and domestic security. Both timing and target selection by terrorists can affect U.S. interests in areas ranging from preservation of commerce to nuclear non-proliferation to the Middle East peace process. A growing number of analysts expresses concern that radical Islamic groups seek to exploit economic and political tensions in Saudi Arabia, Egypt, Indonesia, Russia, Jordan, Pakistan and other countries. Because of their avowed goal of overthrowing secular regimes in certain countries with large Moslem populations, such groups are seen as a particular threat to U.S. foreign policy objectives.

On April 29, 2004, the Department of State released its *Patterns of Global Terrorism* report *[Patterns 2003]*. *Patterns 2003* continues to list seven state sponsors of terrorism: Cuba, Iran, Iraq, Syria, North Korea, Sudan, and Libya. However the number of nations on the list was reduced to six when Iraq was removed from the list on October 20, 2004. The degree of support of, or involvement in, terrorist activities in 2003 varied dramatically from nation to nation. Of those on the U.S. terrorism list, for the year 2003, Iran continued to be characterized on one extreme as an active supporter of terrorism: a nation that uses terrorism as an instrument of policy or warfare beyond its borders. Closer to the middle of an active/passive spectrum is Syria, though not formally detected in an active role since 1986, the Assad regime reportedly uses groups in Syria and Lebanon to project power into Israel and allows groups to train in territory under its control. On the less active end of the spectrum, one might place countries such as Cuba or North Korea, which at the height of the Cold War were more active, but in recent years have seemed to settle for a more passive role of granting ongoing safe haven to previously admitted individual terrorists. Also at the less active end of the spectrum, and arguably falling off it, are Libya, and notably Sudan, which has stepped up counter-terrorism cooperation with U.S. law enforcement and intelligence. Iraq, under Saddam Hussein, would likely have been in the middle of the spectrum. *Patterns 2003* arguably implies that, of the nations on the terrorism list, Sudan is likely closest to being removed; however, the report acknowledges progress by Libya and progress, coupled with concerns, about Syria as well.

Patterns 2003, in contrast to pre "9/11" report versions, is silent about Pakistan's alleged ongoing support for Kashmiri militants and their attacks against the population of India. *Patterns 2003* also does not criticize Saudi Arabia, perceived by many analysts as a slow, unwilling, or halfhearted ally in curbing or cracking down on activities which support or spawn terrorism activities outside its borders. In contrast, *Patterns 2003* cites Saudi Arabia as "an excellent example of a nation increasingly focusing its political will to fight terrorism."

Venezuela, considered by some in the Administration to be overlooking Revolutionary Armed Forces of Colombia (FARC) rebel group activity in its territory bordering Colombia, is cited in *Patterns 2003* as a nation where cooperation is "mixed." *Patterns 2003* again is critical of efforts by the Palestinian Authority (PA) and the late Chairman Arafat to curb terrorist activity, stating, "The PA's efforts to thwart terrorist operations were minimal in 2003.... There are indications that some personnel in the security services, including several senior officers, have continued to assist terrorist operations."

In the case of North Korea, U.S. security concerns arguably focus more on the regime's weapons of mass destruction (WMD) programs than on its support for terrorist movements. North Korea announced on February 10, 2005, that it had nuclear weapons and that it would bolster its arsenal; the United States believes North Korea has a clandestine uranium enrichment program and may be producing new nuclear weapons. (See CRS Issue Brief IB91141, *North Korea's Nuclear Weapons Program*.) Although North Korea's support for international terrorism appears limited at present, given North Korea's past record of selling advanced weapons abroad indiscriminately, some see a growing danger of proliferation to terrorist states or groups.

Definitions

There is no universally accepted definition of international terrorism. One definition widely used in U.S. government circles, and incorporated into law, defines *international terrorism* as terrorism involving the citizens or property of more than one country. *Terrorism* is broadly defined as politically motivated violence perpetrated against noncombatant targets by subnational groups or clandestine agents. For example, kidnaping of U.S. birdwatchers or bombing of U.S.-owned oil pipelines by leftist guerrillas in Colombia would qualify as international terrorism. A *terrorist group* is defined as a group which practices or which has significant subgroups which practice terrorism (22 U.S.C. 2656f). One shortfall of this traditional definition is its focus on groups and its exclusion of individual ("lone wolf") terrorist activity which has recently risen in frequency and visibility. To these standard definitions which refer to violence in a traditional form must be added cyberterrorism. Analysts warn that terrorist acts will now include more sophisticated forms of destruction and extortion such as disabling a national computer infrastructure or penetrating vital commercial computer systems. Finally, the October 12, 2000 bombing of the *U.S.S. Cole*, a U.S. military vessel, raised issues of whether the standard definition would categorize this attack as terrorist, as the Cole may not qualify as a "non-combatant" (see CRS Report RS20721, *Terrorist Attack on the U.S.S. Cole)*. Though the definition of terrorism may appear essentially a political issue, it can carry significant legal implications.

Current definitions of terrorism mostly share one common element: politically motivated behavior; although religious motivation is increasingly being recognized as an important motivating factor as high-profile activities of such groups as Al Qaeda and Hamas underscore the significance of selective religious ideologies in driving terrorist violence, or at least providing a pretext. To illustrate: Osama bin Laden issued a fatwah (edict) in 1998 proclaiming in effect that all those who believe in Allah and his prophet Muhammad must kill Americans wherever they find them [http://www.ict.org.il/articles/fatwah.htm]. Moreover, the growth of international and transnational criminal organizations and the growing range and scale of such operations has resulted in a potential for widespread criminal violence with financial profit as the driving motivation. Notwithstanding, current definitions of terrorism do not include using violence for financial profit, not even in cases where mass casualties might result with entire populations "terrorized."

Complicating matters is that internationally, nations and organizations historically have been unable to agree on a definition of terrorism, since one person's terrorist is often another person's freedom fighter. To circumvent this political constraint, countries have taken the approach of enacting laws or negotiating conventions, which criminalize specific acts such as kidnaping, detonating bombs or hijacking airplanes. The 1999 International Convention for the Suppression of the Financing of Terrorism [http://untreaty.un.org/English/terrorism.asp] comes close to a consensus definition, by making it a crime to collect or provide funds with the intent of killing or injuring civilians where the purpose is to intimidate a population or coerce a government.

U.S. Policy Response

Framework

Past Administrations have employed a range of measures to combat international terrorism, from diplomacy, international cooperation, and constructive engagement to economic sanctions, covert action, protective security measures, and military force. The application of sanctions is one of the most frequently used anti-terrorist tools of U.S. policymakers. Governments supporting international terrorism are prohibited from receiving U.S. economic and military assistance. Export of munitions to such countries is foreclosed, and restrictions are imposed on exports of "dual use" equipment. Presence of a country on the "terrorism list," though, may reflect considerations—such as its pursuit of WMD or its human rights record or U.S. domestic political considerations—that are largely unrelated to support for international terrorism.

Generally, U.S. anti-terrorism policy from the late 1970s to the mid-1990s focused on deterring and punishing state sponsors as opposed to terrorist groups themselves. The passage of the Anti-Terrorism and Effective Death Penalty Act of 1996 (P.L. 104-132) signaled an important shift in policy. The act, largely initiated by the executive branch, created a legal category of Foreign Terrorist Organizations (FTOs) and banned funding, granting of visas and other material support to such organizations. The USA PATRIOT Act of 2001 (P.L. 107-56) extended and strengthened the provisions of that legislation. *Patterns 2003* lists 37 groups designated by the Secretary of State as FTOs (see also http://usinfo.state.gov/is/Archive/2004/Apr/29-636067.html).

On September 24, 2003, the White House (OMB) released its 2003 Report to Congress on Combating Terrorism, which details spending by federal agency and mission area for combating terrorism and homeland security. The report is widely considered to be an authoritative source of information on executive branch spending, program initiatives, and priority terrorism-related areas for FY2002 through FY2004 [http://www.whitehouse.gov/omb/inforeg/2003_combat_terr.pdf].

Dilemmas

In their desire to combat terrorism in a modern political context, democratic countries often face conflicting goals and courses of action: (1) providing security from terrorist acts, that is, limiting the freedom of individual terrorists, terrorist groups, and support networks to operate unimpeded in a relatively unregulated environment, versus (2) maximizing individual freedoms, democracy, and human rights. Efforts to combat terrorism are complicated by a global trend towards deregulation, open borders, and expanded commerce. In democracies such as the United States, the constitutional limits within which policy must operate are seen by some to conflict directly with a desire to secure the lives of citizens against terrorist activity more effectively. This issue has come to the fore in the post-September 11 period as the federal government has acquired broad new powers to combat internal terrorism.

Another challenge for policymakers is the need to identify the perpetrators of particular terrorist acts and those who train, fund, or otherwise support or sponsor them. As the international community increasingly demonstrates its ability to unite and apply sanctions against rogue states, states will become less likely to overtly support terrorist groups or engage in state sponsored terrorism. The possibility of covert provision of weapons, financing, and logistical support remains, and detecting such transfers will require significantly increased deployment of U.S. intelligence assets in countries and zones where terrorists operate. Particularly challenging is identification of "dual use" items—subject to U.S. export restrictions—which might creatively be adapted for military application (see CRS Report RL31669, *Terrorism: Background on Chemical, Biological, and Toxin Weapons*; CRS Report RL31780, *Trade and the 108th Congress*; CRS Report RL31826, *Protecting our Perimeter*; and CRS Report RS21422, *Dual Use Biological Equipment*).

Today, the U.S. policy focus is on terrorist organizations such as Al Qaeda and affiliated networks, and state supporters. (See also CRS Report RL32759, *Al Qaeda: Statements and Evolving Ideology*.) But in the future, it may be that new types of terrorists will emerge: individuals who are not affiliated with any established terrorist organization and who are apparently not agents of any state sponsor. The terrorist Ramzi Ahmed Yousef, who is believed to have masterminded the 1993 World Trade Center bombing, apparently did not belong to any larger, established, and previously identified group, although he may have had some ties to Al Qaeda operatives. Also, should organizational infrastructure of groups such as Al Qaeda continue to be disrupted, the threat of individual or "boutique" terrorism, or that of "spontaneous" terrorist activity, such as the bombing of bookstores in the United States after Ayatollah Khomeini's death edict against British author Salman Rushdie, may well increase. Thus, one likely profile for the terrorist of the 21st century may well be a private individual not affiliated with any established group, but drawing on other similarly-minded individuals for support. Because the U.S. international counter-terrorism policy framework has been sanctions-oriented, and has traditionally sought to pin responsibility on state sponsors, changes in policy and approaches are regularly being considered and implemented.

Another problem surfacing in the wake of a number of incidents associated with Islamic fundamentalist groups is how to condemn and combat such terrorist activity, and the extreme and violent ideology of specific radical groups, without appearing to be anti-Islamic in general. A desire to punish a state for supporting international terrorism may also conflict with other foreign policy objectives involving that nation, such as human rights concerns.

Continuing Terrorist Threats

Facing the possibility that a number of states may be rethinking their sponsorship of terrorist organizations, such organizations appear to be establishing operating bases in countries that lack functioning central governments or that do not exercise effective control over their national territory. An example is a November 17, 2003 *Washington Post* press report of Al Qaeda affiliates training Indonesian operatives in the southern Philippines. In general, gray area "terrorist activity not functionally linked to any supporting or sponsoring nation" represents an increasingly difficult challenge for U.S. policymakers.

Terrorists have been able to develop their own sources of financing, which range from NGOs and charities to illegal enterprises such as narcotics, extortion, and kidnaping. Colombia's FARC is said to make hundreds of millions annually from criminal activities, mostly from taxing or participating in the narcotics trade. Bin Laden's Al Qaeda depends on a formidable array of fundraising operations including Muslim charities and wealthy wellwishers, legitimate-seeming businesses, and banking connections in the Persian Gulf, as well as various smuggling and fraud activities. Furthermore, reports are ongoing of cross-national links among different terrorist organizations.

Looming over the entire issue of international terrorism is an apparently inexorable trend toward proliferation of weapons of mass destruction (WMD), or the means to make them. All of the seven officially designated state sponsors of terrorism, Cuba, Iran, Iraq, Libya, North Korea, Sudan, and Syria, were known or suspected to have programs for the development of nuclear, chemical, or biological weapons. (Suspicions regarding Cuba are controversial.) Three of the states —Iran, Libya, and North Korea—have nuclear weapons programs—or the potential to convert to them—at varying stages of development. This was also believed to be true of Iraq under Saddam Hussein. On December 19, 2003, Iran signed an agreement allowing international inspections of nuclear sites; on December 21, 2003 Libya announced similar intentions. Whether listed states have actually supplied terrorists with WMD wherewithal is not known with certainty; yet the possibility of covert transfers or leakages clearly exists. Furthermore terrorists have attempted to acquire WMD technology through their own resources and connections. For instance, the Aum Shinrikyo cult was able to procure technology and blueprints for producing Sarin, a deadly nerve gas, through official contacts in Russia in the early 1990s. The gas was subsequently used in an attack on the Tokyo subway in March 1995 that killed 12 people and injured 5,000.

Media reports of varying credibility suggest that Osama bin Laden has joined the WMD procurement game. A *London Daily Telegraph* dispatch (12/14/01) cites "long discussions" between bin Laden and Pakistani nuclear scientists concerning nuclear, chemical and biological weapons. The *Hindustan Times* (11/14/01) claims that a bin Laden emissary tried to buy radioactive waste from an atomic power plant in Bulgaria and cites the September 1998 arrest in Germany of an alleged bin Laden associate on charges of trying to buy reactor fuel (see also *London Times*, 10/14/01). A U.S. federal indictment handed down in 1998 charges that bin Laden operatives sought enriched uranium on various occasions. Other accounts credit Al Qaeda with attempting to purchase portable nuclear weapons or "suitcase bombs" through contacts in Chechnya and Kazakhstan. Furthermore, U.S. government sources reported discovery of a partly-constructed laboratory in Afghanistan in March 2002, in which Al Qaeda may have planned to develop biological agents, including anthrax. In April 2002, a captured Al Qaeda leader, Abu Zubaydah, told American interrogators that the organization had been working aggressively to build a dirty bomb, in which conventional explosives packaged with radioactive material are detonated to spread contamination and sow panic. BBC reports (1/30/03) cite the discovery by intelligence officials of documents indicating that Al Qaeda had built a dirty bomb near Herat in Western Afghanistan. In January 2003, British authorities reportedly disrupted a plot to use the poison ricin against personnel in England (see CRS Report RS21383, *Ricin: Technical Background and Potential Role in Terrorism*).

U.S. Policy Tools to Combat International Terrorism

Diplomacy/Constructive Engagement. Use of diplomacy to help create a global anti-terror coalition is a central component of the Bush Administration response to September 11 events. Diplomacy, for example, was a key factor leading to the composition of the U.S.-led coalition against the Taliban.

Diplomacy may not always be effective against determined terrorists or the countries that support them. However, in most cases, diplomatic measures are considered least likely to widen conflicts and therefore are usually tried first.

When responding to incidents of terrorism by subnational groups, reacting by constructive engagement is complicated by the lack of existing channels and mutually accepted rules of conduct between governmental entities and the groups in question. In some instances, legislation may specifically prohibit official contact with a terrorist organization or its members. Yet for groups that are well-entrenched in a nation's political fabric and culture, engaging the group might be preferable to trying to exterminate it. Colombia's on-again, off-again peace process with FARC is one recent example. Some observers, though, are skeptical of the value of engaging with terrorists. Former CIA director James Woolsey has noted, in a Spring, 2001, *National Strategy Forum Review* article, that increasingly, terrorists don't just want a place at the table, "they want to blow up the table and everyone who is sitting at the table."

On a different level, in the wake of the September 11 attacks, the Bush Administration explored the possibility of enlisting state sponsors of terrorism, such as Libya, Sudan, and Syria, in a broader Islamic coalition against Al Qaeda and its followers. The United States also has held discussions with Iran concerning formation of a post-Taliban coalition government in Afghanistan. To some critics, though, such initiatives detract from the imperative of taking a principled stand against international terrorism in all its guises. In mid-December 2003, both Iran and Libya announced that they would open their nuclear sites to international inspections. On June 10, 2004, press reports aired allegations that Libyan leader Muammar Qadhafi was involved in an plot, spawned in 2003, to assassinate Saudi Crown Prince Abdullah.

The media remain powerful forces in confrontations between terrorists and governments. Influencing public opinion may impact not only the actions of governments but also those of groups engaged in terrorist acts. From the terrorist perspective, media coverage is an important measure of the success of a terrorist act. In hostage-type incidents, where the media may provide the only independent means a terrorist has of knowing the chain of events set in motion, coverage can complicate rescue efforts. Public diplomacy and the media can be used to mobilize public opinion in other countries to pressure governments to take action against terrorism. An example would be to mobilize the tourist industry to pressure governments into participating in sanctions against a terrorist state.

Economic Sanctions. Sanctions regimes can be essentially unilateral—such as U.S. bans on trade and investment relations with Cuba and Iran—or multilateral, such as that mandated in response to the Pan Am 103 bombing. In the past, use of economic sanctions was usually predicated upon identification of a nation as an active supporter or sponsor of international terrorism. Yet sanctions also can be used to target assets of terrorist groups themselves. On September 23, 2001, President Bush signed Executive Order 13224 freezing the assets of 27 individuals and organizations known to be affiliated with bin Laden's network, giving the Secretary of the Treasury broad powers to impose sanctions on banks around the world that provide these entities access to the international financial system and providing for designation of additional entities as terrorist organizations. By late October 2002, according to the U.S. Treasury Department, the freeze list had expanded to include designated terrorist groups, supporters, and financiers of terror. In addition, on September 28, 2001, the U.N. Security Council adopted Resolution 1373, which requires all states to "limit the ability of terrorists and terrorist organizations to operate internationally" by freezing their assets and denying them safe haven. The Security Council also set up a Counter Terrorism Committee to oversee implementation of Resolution 1373. U.N. Security Council Resolution 1390 of January 16, 2002, obligated member states to freeze funds of "individuals, groups, undertakings, and entities" associated with the Taliban and Al Qaeda. As of September 11, 2003, in the range of $200 million in terrorist funds had been frozen worldwide as a result of these initiatives according to U.S. and U.N. financial data. [http://www.useu.be/Terrorism/ECONNews/Sept1103TreasuryTerroristFinancing.html]

The effects of these economic measures are uncertain because much of the flow of terrorist funds reportedly takes place outside of formal banking channels (in elusive "hawala" chains of money brokers). Alternatively, international banks in the Persian Gulf are reportedly used to manipulate funds through business fronts owned by Osama bin Laden. Furthermore, much of Al Qaeda's money is believed to be held not in banks but in untraceable assets such as gold and diamonds. Also, some observers have noted that lethal terrorist operations are relatively inexpensive.

With respect to nation-states, economic sanctions fall into six categories: restrictions on trading, technology transfer, foreign assistance, export credits and guarantees, foreign exchange and capital transactions, and economic access. Sanctions may include a total or partial trade embargo, an embargo on financial transactions, suspension of foreign aid, restrictions on aircraft or ship traffic, or abrogation of a friendship, commerce, and navigation treaty.

The President has a variety of laws at his disposal, but the broadest in its potential scope is the International Emergency Economic Powers Act (P.L. 95-223; 50 USC 1701, et seq.). The act permits imposition of restrictions on economic relations once the President has declared a national emergency because of a threat to U.S. national security, foreign policy, or the economy. Although the sanctions authorized must deal directly with the threat responsible for the emergency, the President can regulate imports, exports, and all types of financial transactions, such as the transfer of funds, foreign exchange, credit, and securities, between the United States and the country in question. Specific authority for the Libyan trade embargo is in Section 504 of the International Security and Development Cooperation Act of 1985 (P.L. 99-83), while Section 505 of the act (22 U.S.C. 2349aa9) authorizes the banning of imports of goods and services from any country supporting terrorism. (See also CRS Report RS20871, *The Iran-Libya Sanctions Act,* and the Iran-Libya Sanctions Act (P.L. 104-172); 50 U.S.C. 1701 note.) Other major laws that can be used against countries supporting terrorism are the Export Administration Act of 1979 (P.L. 96-72), the Arms Export Control Act (P.L. 90-629), and specific items or provisions of foreign assistance legislation. P.L. 90-629 prohibits arms sales to countries not fully cooperating with U.S. antiterrorism efforts and requires that aid be withheld to any nation providing lethal military aid to a country on the terrorism list.

The Syria Accountability and Lebanese Sovereignty Restoration Act of 2003, P.L. 108- 175, signed December 14, 2003, calls for new sanctions against Syria until the Asad regime stops providing support for terrorists groups and ceases other activities at variance with U.S. policy. Past Administrations have been critical of Syria's support for terrorism; interest in acquiring weapons of mass destruction; and military presence in Lebanon. An array of U.S. legislation currently bans aid to, and restricts commercial dealings with Syria, and P.L. 108-175 would further restrict diplomatic and commercial dealings with the Asad regime. On May 11, 2004, President Bush imposed economic sanctions against Syria, charging it had failed to take action against terrorist groups fighting Israel and failed to take action to halt the flow of foreign fighters into Iraq. As a result, most U.S. exports to Syria (which total about $200 million a year) would be banned. (See CRS Issue Brief IB92075, *Syria: U.S. Relations and Bilateral Issues.*)

Economic Inducements. Counter-terrorism initiatives might include efforts to change economic and social conditions that provide a breeding ground for terrorists. It has been noted that most terrorists worldwide are unemployed or underemployed with virtually nonexistent prospects for economic advancement. Some analysts believe that targeted assistance programs to reduce poverty and ignorance (which might also include supporting secular educational alternatives to the Madrassahs—Islamic religious schools) can make a difference in lifestyles and attitudes and diminish the appeal of extremist groups. A further rationale, they say, is to project a more positive image of the United States in terrorism-prone lands. Critics, though, argue that severe economic conditions are not the sole or even the main motivational factors driving the emergence of terrorism, stressing that resentment against a particular country or political order and religious fanaticism also are important motivations. Osama bin Laden's large personal fortune and his far-flung business empire would seem to contradict economic deprivation as explanations of his terrorism. Similarly, all of the 15 Saudi Arabian hijackers implicated in the September 11 attacks were from middle-class families or well-connected ones. The Basque Fatherland and Liberty organization (ETA) in Spain is a relatively well-heeled terrorist organization. Ambient economic conditions partly explain certain kinds of terrorist behavior in specific situations, but political factors play a significant role as well.

Covert Action. Intelligence gathering, infiltration of terrorist groups, and military operations involve a variety of clandestine or "covert" activities. Much of this activity is of a passive monitoring nature aimed at determining the strategic intentions, capabilities, and vulnerabilities of terrorist organizations. An active form of covert activity occurs during events such as a hostage crisis or hijacking when a foreign country may quietly request advice, equipment, or technical support, with no public credit to be given the providing country. Covert action may also seek to exploit vulnerabilities of terrorist organizations, for example, by spreading disinformation about leaders, encouraging defections, promoting divisions between factions, or exploiting conflicts between organizations.

Some nations have periodically resorted to unconventional methods beyond their territory for the express purpose of neutralizing individual terrorists and/or thwarting preplanned attacks. Examples of activities might run the gamut from intercepting or sabotaging delivery of funding or weapons to a terrorist group, to destroying a terrorist's embryonic WMD production facilities, to seizing and transporting a wanted terrorist to stand trial for assassination or murder. Arguably, such activity might be justified as preemptive self-defense under Article 51 of the U.N. charter. On the other hand, it could be argued that such actions violate customary international law. The Senate and House Intelligence Committees, in a December 10, 2002 report, have recommended maximizing covert action to counter terrorism [http://intelligence.senate.gov/recommendations.pdf].

Assassination is specifically prohibited by U.S. executive order (most recently, E.O. 12333), but bringing wanted criminals to the United States for trial is not. There exists an established U.S. legal doctrine that allows an individual's trial to proceed regardless of whether he is forcefully abducted from another country, international waters, or airspace.

Experts warn that bringing persons residing abroad to U.S. justice by means other than extradition or mutual agreement with the host country can vastly complicate U.S. foreign relations, sometimes jeopardizing interests far more important than "justice," deterrence, and the prosecution of a single individual. Notwithstanding the unpopularity of such abductions in nations that fail to apprehend and prosecute those accused, the "rendering" of such wanted criminals to U.S. courts is permitted under limited circumstances by a June 21, 1995, Presidential Decision Directive (PDD-39). Such conduct, however, raises prospects of other nations using similar tactics against U.S. citizens.

Rewards for Information Program. Money is a powerful motivator. Rewards for information have been instrumental in Italy in destroying the Red Brigades and in Colombia in apprehending drug cartel leaders. A State Department program is in place, supplemented by the aviation industry, usually offering rewards of up to $5 million to anyone providing information that would prevent or resolve an act of international terrorism against U.S. citizens or U.S. property, or that leads to the arrest or conviction of terrorist criminals involved in such acts. This program contributed to the 1997 arrest of Mir Amal Kansi who shot CIA personnel in Virginia, and possibly to the arrest of Ramzi Yousef, architect of the 1993 World Trade Center bombing, in 1995. The bounty for the capture of Osama bin Laden and his aide Ayman al Zawahiri has been raised to $25 million.

Extradition/Law Enforcement Cooperation. International cooperation in such areas as law enforcement, customs control, and intelligence activities is an essential pillar of the Bush Administration anti-terrorism policy. For example, the stationing of FBI agents overseas in close to 50 countries facilitates investigations of terrorist crimes and augments the flow of intelligence about terrorist group structures and membership. One law enforcement tool in combating international terrorism is extradition of terrorists. International extradition traditionally has been subject to several limitations, including the refusal of some countries to extradite for political or extraterritorial offenses or to extradite their nationals. Also, the U.S. application of the death penalty for certain crimes can impede extradition in terrorism related cases. The United States has been negotiating and concluding treaties with fewer limitations, in part as a means of facilitating the transfer of wanted terrorists. Because much terrorism involves politically motivated violence, the State Department has sought to curtail the availability of the political offense exception, found in many extradition treaties, to avoid extradition.

Military Force. Although not without difficulties, military force, particularly when wielded by a superpower such as the United States, can carry substantial clout. Proponents of selective use of military force usually emphasize the military's unique skills and specialized equipment. The April 1986 decision to bomb Libya for its alleged role in the bombing of a German discotheque exemplifies use of military force. Other examples are (1) the 1993 bombing of Iraq's military intelligence headquarters by U.S. forces in response to Iraqi efforts to assassinate former President George Bush during a visit to Kuwait; (2) the August 1998 missile attacks against bases in Afghanistan and an alleged chemical production facility, al-Shifa, in Sudan; (3) the removal of the Taliban regime in Afghanistan in 2001–2002; (4) ongoing U.S. operations in Afghanistan, and arguably (5) the Iraq war launched on March 19, 2003. Moreover, U.S. military components are currently involved in a variety of anti-terrorism related missions, exercises, and deployments in areas such as Colombia, the Horn of Africa, Djibouti, and Georgia.

Successful use of military force for preemptive or retaliatory strikes presupposes the ability to identify a terrorist perpetrator or its state sponsor, as well as the precise location of the group, information that is often unavailable from U.S. intelligence sources. Generally, terrorists possess modest physical facilities that present few high-value targets for military strikes. Some critics have observed that military action is a blunt instrument that can cause foreign civilian casualties as well as collateral damage to economic installations in the target country. According to a July 21, 2002, *New York Times* report, a "pattern of mistakes" in the U.S. bombing campaign in Afghanistan killed "as many as 400 civilians" in 11 different locations. Others argue that such action inflates terrorists' sense of importance and facilitates their recruitment efforts. A 1999 U.S. study of the sociology and psychology of terrorism states that "counterterrorist military attacks against elusive terrorists may serve only to radicalize large sectors of the Muslim population and damage the U.S. image worldwide," [http://www.loc.gov/rr/frd/pdf-files/Soc_Psych_of_Terrorism.pdf]. Other disadvantages or risks associated with the use of military force include counter-retaliation and escalation by terrorist groups or their state sponsors, failure to destroy the leaders of the organization, and the perception that the United States ignores rules of international law. In addition, the costs associated with Operation Enduring Freedom in Afghanistan have concerned some observers, as have costs of the U.S. military presence in Iraq.

International Conventions. To date, the United States has joined with the world community in developing all of the major anti-terrorism conventions. These conventions impose on their signatories an obligation either to prosecute offenders or extradite them to permit prosecution for a host of terrorism-related crimes, including hijacking vessels and aircraft, taking hostages, and harming diplomats. An important convention is the Convention for the Marking of Plastic Explosives. Implementing legislation is in P.L. 104-132. On July 26, 2002, the U.N. Convention on the Suppression of Terrorist Bombings, and the U.N. Anti-Terrorism Financing Convention both entered into force for the United States; see [http://untreaty.un.org/English/terrorism.asp].

Potential Tools

An International Court for Terrorism. Many experts have urged that an international court be established, perhaps under the U.N., to sit in permanent session to adjudicate cases against persons accused of international terrorist crimes.

Media Self-Restraint. For some, the term "media self-restraint" is an oxymoron; the sensational scoop is the golden fleece, and dull copy is to be avoided. In the past, the media have been occasionally manipulated into the role of mediator and publicist of terrorist goals. Increasingly, the media is sensitive to such charges. On October 11, 2001, five major U.S. news organizations agreed to abridge video statements by Osama bin Laden and this policy continues to date.

Policy Reform and 9/11 Commission Recommendations

Well before the September 11, 2001 events, various legislative proposals and congressionally mandated panels had called for reconfiguring the federal government's strategic planning and decision processes vis-à-vis the global terrorist threat. On November 25, 2002, the President signed the Homeland Security Act of 2002 (P.L. 107-296), consolidating at least 22 separate federal agencies, offices, and research centers comprising more than 169,000 employees into a new cabinet level Department of Homeland Security (DHS). The creation of the new department, charged with coordinating defenses and responses to terrorist attacks on U.S. soil, constitutes the most substantial reorganization of the Federal government agencies since the National Security Act of 1947 which placed the different military departments under a Secretary of Defense and created the National Security Council (NSC) and CIA. P.L. 107-296 includes provisions for an information analysis element within DHS, many of the envisioned tasks of which appear assigned to the Administration's Terrorist Threat Integration Center (TTIC) which was activated May 1, 2003.

In the 107th Congress, the USA PATRIOT Act, enacted in October 2001 (P.L.107-56), gave law enforcement increased authority to investigate suspected terrorists, including enhanced surveillance procedures such as roving wiretaps; provided for strengthened controls on international money laundering and financing of terrorism; improved measures for strengthening of defenses along the U.S. northern border, and authorized disclosure of foreign intelligence information obtained in criminal investigations to intelligence and national security officials.

On July 22, 2004, the National Commission on Terrorist Attacks upon the United States ("9/11 Commission") issued its final report [http://www.gpoaccess.gov/911/index.html]. Included are forty-one recommendations for changing the way the government is organized to combat terrorism and how it and prioritizes its efforts, many of which dovetail with elements of the Administration's February 14, 2003, National Strategy for Combating Terrorism [http://www.whitehouse.gov/news/releases/2003/02/20030214-7.html] such as diplomacy and counter-proliferation efforts, preemption, intelligence and information fusion, winning hearts and minds—including not only public diplomacy, but also policies that encourage development and more open societies, law enforcement cooperation, and defending the homeland. See also [http://usinfo.state.gov/ei/Archive/2003/Dec/31-646035.html].

Recommendations generally fall into the categories of (1) preemption (attacking terrorists and combating the growth of Islamic terrorism); (2) protecting against and preparing for attacks; (3) coordination and unity of operational planning, intelligence and sharing of information; (4) enhancing, through centralization, congressional effectiveness of intelligence and counterterrorism oversight, authorization, and appropriations; (5) centralizing congressional oversight and review of homeland security activities; and (6) beefing up FBI, DoD, and DHS capacity to assess terrorist threats and their concomitant response strategies and capabilities. The report specifically recommends confronting openly problems in the U.S.-Saudi relationship (presumably issues such as terrorist financing to include arguably the issue of ideological incitement). The report also recommends sustaining aid to Pakistan. On December 17, 2004, President Bush signed the Intelligence Reform and Terrorism Prevention Act of 2004 (S. 2845, P.L. 108-458) establishing the position of National Intelligence Director and a National Counterterrorism Center.

U.S. Interagency Coordination Framework and Program Response

The interagency framework for combating terrorism overseas is a complex web of relationships among federal organizations and agencies. Some agencies play lead roles in specific areas; others play coordination roles; yet others serve in support roles. In short, the National Security Council (NSC) advises the President on national security and foreign policy; serves as a forum for discussion among the President, presidential advisers, and cabinet officials; and is the President's mechanism for coordinating policy among government agencies on interdisciplinary issues such as terrorism. Under the NSC structure are a series of committees and working groups which address terrorism issues. Key is the Counterterrorism Security Group composed of high-level representatives from the Departments of State, Justice, Defense, and Homeland Security, and the FBI and CIA, as well as representatives of other departments or agencies as needed. A series of interagency working groups under the Counterterrorism Security Group coordinate specific efforts as needed.

The Office of Homeland Security is a homeland security council analogous to the National Security Council [http://www.dhs.gov/dhspublic/index.jsp]. Located within the Executive Office of the President, it has a number of working groups called policy coordinating committees which coordinate policy and operations across the executive departments to prevent, respond to, and recover from terrorist attacks within the United States. The Department of State, [http://www.state.gov/], is the lead agency for U.S. government efforts to combat terrorism overseas; whereas the Department of Justice, [http://www.usdoj.gov/], is the lead agency for law enforcement and criminal matters related to terrorism overseas and domestically.

On December 17, 2004, President Bush signed the Intelligence Reform and Terrorism Prevention Act of 2004 (S. 2845, P.L. 108-458) establishing the position of National Intelligence Director (a position separate from that of the CIA Director) to serve as the President's principal intelligence advisor, overseeing and coordinating the foreign and domestic activities of the intelligence community. Established as well is a National Counterterrorism Center designed to serve as a central knowledge bank for information about known and suspected terrorists and to coordinate and monitor counterterrorism plans and activities of all government agencies. The Center will also be responsible for preparing the daily terrorism threat report for the President.

Antiterrorism Assistance and Terrorism and Crime Programs

The State Department's Antiterrorism Assistance (ATA) Program is a central part of the effort to help nations develop the capacity to effectively combat terrorism. The ATA Program provides training and equipment to foreign countries to help them improve their antiterrorism capabilities. More than 35,000 individuals from 152 countries have received training since the program's inception in 1983 in such skills as crisis management, VIP protection, airport security management, and bomb detection and deactivation. The TIPOFF terrorism and crime database, maintained by the State Department Bureau of Intelligence and Research, enables the use of sensitive intelligence to detect "known persons of concern" as they apply for U.S. visas overseas, and as of mid-November 2003 had provided the names of 96,190 [sic] possible terrorists to State's Consular Lookout and Support System (CLASS). The Department of State's Terrorist Interdiction Program (TIP), initiated in FY2002, helps foreign governments improve their border control capability through software for creating an automated database watchlist for fusion of names and relevant data. A benefit of TIP is that it provides immigration officials in selected countries with a computer-based, real-time system to verify the identities of travelers presenting themselves at border crossings.

Assistance to Victims Programs
Facilitating payment of compensation to victims of terrorism by state sponsors or their agents is an ongoing area of congressional interest. P.L. 106-386, among other things, allowed victims of terrorist acts committed by Cuba and Iran to collect payment of judgments rendered from funds held by the U.S. government and clarified circumstances under which immunity from jurisdiction or attachment may not apply when victims of state-sponsored terrorism seek compensation.

Counterterrorism Research and Development Program
The State Department's Counterterrorism Research and Development Program is overseen by State's Coordinator for Counterterrorism and is managed by the Assistant Secretary of Defense for Special Operations and Low-Intensity Conflict. The program focuses on the inter-agency Technical Support Working Group (TSWG), which constitutes an R&D response to the threat posed by increasingly sophisticated equipment, explosives, and technology available to terrorist groups. Major project areas include chemical, biological, radiological, and nuclear countermeasures; explosives detection and improvised device defeat; infrastructure protection; investigative support and forensics; personnel protection; physical security; surveillance collection and operations support; and tactical operations support. State and DOD provide core funding for TSWG activities.

Diplomatic Security Program
The Diplomatic Security Program of the State Department is designed to protect U.S. personnel, information, and facilities domestically and abroad. Constructing secure facilities abroad, providing security guards, and supporting counterintelligence are some important elements of the program as is detection and investigation of passport and visa fraud.

Options for Program Enhancement
Potential areas for improvement of programs to combat terrorism include enhancing information and network security; nuclear materials safeguards; detection of nuclear, chemical, and biological weapons and conventional explosives; and critical infrastructure protection and disaster/crisis consequence management, including training of first responders. One option might include an enhanced role for the National Academies and the National Laboratories in facilitating more concerted and better coordinated involvement of the U.S. scientific community in assessing threats, developing countermeasures, and designing responses to terrorism. See [http://www.nap.edu/catalog/10415.html].

Order Code IB10119; Updated April 8, 2005

U.S. Legal Response

Overview of U.S. Legal Response

Anna Sabasteanski

There are two sides to the U.S. legal response to terrorism: legislative and enforcement. This section presents a brief overview of U.S. counterterrorism legislation, followed by the law enforcement sections included in *Patterns of Global Terrorism* and then a table of extraditions (legal transfer of suspects from one country to another) and renditions (clandestine transfer of suspects from one country to another) of terrorists to the United States from 1993 through 2001.

Legislation

USA PATRIOT Act

The best-known post-September 11 U.S. law addressing terrorism is the "Uniting and Strengthening America by Providing Appropriate Tools Required to Intercept and Obstruct Terrorism" Act, better known as the USA PATRIOT Act, which was signed into law 26 October 2001.

The PATRIOT Act grants law enforcement and international intelligence agencies new powers to track and intercept communications. It creates further border and immigration restrictions as well as new crimes, penalties, and procedures to use against terrorism. Under the PATRIOT Act, the secretary of the treasury must promulgate the following regulations:

- Securities brokers and dealers, commodity merchants, advisers, and related businesses must file Suspicious Activity Reports (SARs) when they become aware of suspicious financial activity above a certain threshold.
- Businesses that were formerly required to report aggregated transactions of more than $10,000 only to the IRS must now also file SARs, and the reporting threshold has been reduced to $5,000.

The secretary of the treasury must also:

- Impose special measures and due diligence to combat foreign money laundering.
- Prohibit correspondent accounts (accounts established by a financial institution with a foreign bank so the foreign bank can handle related transactions) for foreign shell banks (banks with no physical presence in the jurisdiction).
- Prevent customers from taking advantage of concentration account practices in which multiple individuals can move funds in a single account while concealing their identity as a means of concealing financial activities.
- Establish minimum standards for new customer identification and record keeping.
- Recommend an effective way to verify the identity of foreign customers.
- Encourage information sharing between financial institutions and law enforcement concerning possible money laundering and terrorist activities.
- Require financial institutions to maintain programs to combat money laundering; those programs must include at least a compliance officer; an employee training program; the development of internal policies, procedures, and controls; and an independent audit feature.

The PATRIOT Act also outlaws the laundering of proceeds from foreign crimes of violence or political corruption or from cyber crime. It authorizes prosecution of overseas fraud involving U.S. credit cards. It increases the penalties for counterfeiting and expands procedures of confiscation and forfeiture to include long-arm jurisdiction (reaching beyond the jurisdiction in which the crime was committed) and expands the range of crimes covered.

Other Federal Legislation and Provisions of the U.S. Code

Other federal laws that deal with terrorism include:

- Antiterrorism and Effective Death Penalty Act of 1996
- Authorization for the Use of Military Force, a Congressional Joint Resolution, September 2001
- Financial Anti-Terrorism Act of 2001 (H.R. 3004) passed in House, October 2001; portions of this bill were later incorporated into the USA Patriot Act.
- Airport and Transportation Security Act of 2001, November 2001
- Terrorism Risk Protection Act, November 2001

Provisions of the U.S. Code related to terrorism include:

- Aircraft and Motor Vehicle Crimes, Title 18, Part I, Chapter 2, which covers destruction of aircraft or aircraft facilities, destruction of motor vehicles or motor vehicle facilities, imparting or conveying false information, and violence at international airports, as well as the penalties when death occurs.
- Biological Weapons, Title 18, Part I, Chapter 10, which covers prohibitions with respect to biological weapons, requests for military assistance to enforce prohibition in certain emergencies; seizure, forfeiture, and destruction; and injunctions.
- Chemical Weapons, Title 18, Part I, Chapter 11B, which covers prohibited activities, penalties, and criminal forfeitures; destruction of weapons; individual self-defense devices; injunctions; and requests for military assistance to enforce prohibition in certain emergencies.
- Civil Disorders, Title 18, Part I, Chapter 12, which covers civil disorders and preemption (the relative authority of state or local versus federal law).
- Sabotage, Title 18, Part I, Chapter 105 deals with sabotage of fortifications, harbor defenses, or defensive sea areas; destruction of war material, war premises, or war utilities; production of defective war material, war premises, or war utilities; destruction of national-defense materials, national-defense premises, or national-defense utilities; and production of defective national-defense material, national-defense premises, or national-defense utilities.
- Wire and Electronic Communications Interception and Interception of Oral Communications, Title 18, Part I, Chapter 119 covering interception and disclosure of wire, oral, or electronic communications prohibited; manufacture, distribution, possession, and advertising of wire, oral, or electronic communication intercepting devices prohibited; confiscation of wire, oral, or electronic communication intercepting devices; prohibition of use as evidence of intercepted wire or oral communications; authorization for interception of wire, oral, or electronic communications; authorization for disclosure and use of intercepted wire, oral, or electronic communications; procedure for interception of wire, oral, or electronic communications; reports concerning intercepted wire, oral, or electronic communications; recovery of civil damages authorized, injunction against illegal interception; and enforcement of the Communications Assistance for Law Enforcement Act.
- Terrorism, Title 18, Part I, Chapter 113B covers criminal penalties for terrorism, including for use of weapons of mass destruction, acts of terrorism transcending national boundaries, and banning financial transactions with countries engaged in international terrorism; requests for military assistance in certain emergencies (arising from the use of a weapon of mass destruction); civil remedies, jurisdiction, and venue; limitation of actions and other limitations; suits against government officials; exclusive federal jurisdiction; and providing material support to terrorists or to designated foreign terrorist organizations.
- Stored Wire and Electronic Communications and Transactional Records Access, Title 18, Part I, Chapter 121 defines unlawful access to stored communications and disclosure of contents; requirements for governmental access and backup preservation; delayed notice of access; cost reimbursement; civil action; and counterintelligence access to telephone toll and transactional records.
- Rewards for Information Concerning Terrorist Acts and Espionage, Title 18, Part II, Chapter 204 covers information for which rewards are authorized, determination of entitlement to rewards, maximum amount, presidential approval, protection of identity for those who provide information, and eligibility for witness security programs, exception of governmental officials, and authorization for appropriations.
- Quarantine and Inspection, Title 42, Chapter 6A, Subchapter II, Part G contains regulations to control communicable diseases; suspension of entries and imports from designated places to prevent spread of communicable diseases; special quarantine powers in time of war; quarantine stations, grounds, and anchorages; quarantine duties of consular and other officers; bills of health; quarantine regulations governing civil air navigation and civil aircraft; and penalties for violation of quarantine laws.
- Disaster Relief, Title 42, Chapter 68, which covers federal and state disaster preparedness programs; disaster warnings; emergency support teams; performance of services; nondiscrimination in disaster assistance; use and coordination of relief organizations; insurance; procedure for declaration; general federal assistance; essential assistance; hazard mitigation; federal facilities; repair, restoration, and replacement of damaged facilities; debris removal; temporary housing assistance; minimum standards for public and private structures; unemployment assistance; individual and family grant programs; food coupons and distribution; food commodities; relocation assistance; legal services; crisis counseling assistance and training; community disaster loans; emergency communications; emergency public transportation; fire suppression grants; simplified procedure; appeals of assistance decisions; date of eligibility and expenses incurred before date of disaster; detailed functions of administration; mutual aid pacts between states and neighboring countries; contributions for personnel and administrative expenses; use of funds to prepare for and respond to hazards; and the Radiological Emergency Preparedness Fund.
- Air Commerce and Safety, Title 49, Subtitle VII, Part A, Subpart III, Chapter 449 (Security), which covers screening passengers and property, refusal to transport passengers and property, air transportation security, domestic air transportation system security, information about threats to civil aviation, foreign air carrier security programs, travel advisories and suspension of foreign assistance, pas-

senger manifests, and agreements on aircraft sabotage, aircraft hijacking, and airport security.
- War Powers Resolution, Title 50, Chapter 33, allows the president and congress to jointly declare war. It requires notification of congress each time the president involves armed forces in a potential or imminent hostile situation. It requires prior consultation before force is authorized, and lays out the legislative procedures, including formal reporting processes, for congressional approval.
- National Emergencies, Title 50, Chapter 34, which includes termination of existing declared emergencies and declarations of national emergency by the president; publication of the national emergency in the Federal Register; and accountability and reporting requirements of the president and other laws, powers, and authorities conferred thereby and actions taken thereunder.
- International Emergency Economic Powers, Title 50, Chapter 35, which covers unusual and extraordinary threats; declarations of national emergency; exercise of presidential authorities subject to congressional notification and reporting regarding specific transactions and enforcement mechanisms, including regulations necessary to exercise emergency authority.
- Foreign Intelligence Surveillance, Title 50, Chapter 36, which lays out the circumstances and procedures for electronic surveillance, including the roles of the government and communications providers permitted access to and uses of information, and penalties for abuse.
- Defense Against Weapons of Mass Destruction, Title 50, Chapter 40, which covers response to threats of terrorist use of weapons of mass destruction; emergency response assistance programs; nuclear, chemical, and biological emergency response; chemical-biological emergency response teams; testing of preparedness for emergencies involving nuclear, radiological, chemical, and biological weapons; actions to increase civilian expertise; rapid response information systems; procurement of detection equipment for United States border security; international border security; and the comprehensive preparedness program.

Certain states and local jurisdictions have implemented terrorism laws; among the states that have implemented such laws are Michigan, New Jersey, and New York.

Executive orders, decisions, and declarations cover a wide range of policy and enforcement decisions, including military orders regarding enemy combatants, declaration of a state of emergency, and sanctions. Executive orders can be found at the White House website, http://www.whitehouse.gov.

Selections from Patterns of Global Terrorism

Patterns of Global Terrorism *covered the law enforcement aspect of the U.S. response to terrorism. Relevant excerpts from 1987 and 1996–2003 are included below.*

From Patterns of Global Terrorism 1987

Successful Terrorist Prosecutions in 1987

January
- Two Montreal-resident Sikhs were given life sentences for plotting to blow up an airplane at an unnamed US airport. (Canada)
- One of two defendants suspected of involvement in the 1985 bombing of several local cafes that left 10 dead, was convicted and sentenced to death. (Kuwait)

February
- Lebanese Armed Revolutionary Faction (LARF) leader Georges Abdallah was given a life sentence for his involvement in the 1982 assassination of a US and an Israeli diplomat. (France)
- A Lebanese terrorist, arrested at Milan airport attempting to smuggle plastic explosives into Italy was sentenced to a 13-year prison term. (Italy)

May
- Two Abu Nidal terrorists were convicted and sentenced to life imprisonment for the December 1985 Vienna airport massacre. (Austria)
- A Jordanian terrorist was sentenced to 15 years in jail for the 1985 attempted rocket attack on the Jordanian Embassy in Rome. (Italy)

June
- Action Directe (AD) terrorist Regis Schleicher was sentenced to life for the 1983 Paris shooting spree in which two died. (France)
- Three Basque separatists were convicted for terrorist activities with sentences ranging to 25 years. (Spain)
- Of 16 defendants suspected of involvement in the 1986–87 oilfield bombings, 14 were convicted. Sentences ranged from two years to life imprisonment, in addition to six sentenced to death (two in absentia). (Kuwait)

July
- Prosecutions began for the five Abu Nidal terrorists involved in the attempted hijacking of a Pan Am flight in Karachi in which many passengers and crew died. [The five terrorists were sentenced to death in 1988.] (Pakistan)

October
- Neo-Nazi terrorist Odfried Hepp was sentenced to 10 and a half years for a 1982 car bombing that seriously wounded a US soldier. (West Germany)
- An Abu Musa terrorist was sentenced to 47 years for his 1986 attempt to blow up an El Al jet at Madrid airport. (Spain)

November
- An Armenian terrorist involved in the 1986 attempted bombing of the Turkish Consulate General in Melbourne was sentenced to life imprisonment. (Australia)

December
- The trial began for the sole surviving Abu Nidal terrorist involved in the December 1985 Rome airport massacre. [He received a 30-year prison sentence in early 1988, while two accomplices including Abu Nidal were sentenced in absentia to life.] (Italy)

From Patterns of Global Terrorism 1996

The Year in Review

On 19 July a US district court in Washington, DC, convicted Omar Mohammed Ali Rezaq of air piracy in connection with the 1985 terrorist hijacking of Egypt Air Flight 648. The Athens-to-Cairo flight was diverted to Malta by Rezaq and two other hijackers. On the plane, Rezaq separated US and Israeli passengers from the others and shot them in the head at point blank range. One US citizen and one Israeli died; two US citizens and one Israeli survived their wounds. When Egyptian commandos stormed the plane, dozens more died. Rezaq, the sole surviving hijacker, was tried and convicted in Malta on various charges and sentenced to 25 years in prison, but he was released after serving only seven years. With cooperation from the Governments of Nigeria and Ghana, FBI agents arrested Rezaq in Nigeria in 1993 and brought him to the United States to be tried for air piracy. Rezaq, a member of the Abu Nidal organization, claimed at his trial that he had suffered from post-traumatic stress disorder and was therefore insane at the time he hijacked the airplane. He further claimed that, because of his insanity, he could not be held criminally liable for his conduct. The jury found Rezaq guilty and rejected his claim that he was insane at the time he committed the crime. In October Rezaq was sentenced to life imprisonment.

On 5 September Ramzi Ahmed Yousef, Abdul Hakim Murad, and Wali Khan Amin Shah were convicted of a terrorist conspiracy to plant bombs aboard a number of US passenger airliners operating in East Asia. Yousef also was found guilty of placing a bomb aboard a Philippine airliner bound for Tokyo in December 1995 that exploded in midair, killing one person and injuring several others. This bombing was intended as a "trial run" for the planned multiple attacks against US aircraft, which were to take place over two days. Yousef is awaiting trial on charges that he was involved in the bombing of the World Trade Center in 1993.

On 22 September an Asian country turned over to US custody suspected Japanese Red Army terrorist Tsutomu Shirosaki to stand trial for a 1986 mortar attack against the US Embassy in Jakarta, Indonesia.

From Patterns of Global Terrorism 1997

The Year in Review

Several notable trials of international terrorist suspects in the United States also took place during the year:

On 12 November a federal jury in Manhattan convicted Ramzi Ahmed Yousef of directing and helping to carry out the World Trade Center bombing in 1993. Eyad Mahmoud Ismail Najim, who drove the truck that carried the bomb, was also found guilty. Yousef was extradited to the United States from Pakistan in February 1995; Najim was arrested in Jordan in August of that year pursuant to an extradition request from the United States, and he was returned to the United States. (In January 1998 Yousef was sentenced to 240 years in solitary confinement for his role in the World Trade Center bombing. He also received an additional sentence of life imprisonment for his previous conviction in a terrorist conspiracy to plant bombs aboard US passenger airliners operating in East Asia.)

In June 1997 US authorities arrested Mir Aimal Kansi, the suspected gunman in the attack on 25 January 1993 outside Central Intelligence Agency (CIA) Headquarters that killed two CIA employees and wounded three others. Kansi was apprehended abroad, remanded into US custody, and transported to the United States to stand trial. In November a jury in Fairfax, Virginia, found Kansi guilty of the capital murder of Frank A. Darling, the first degree murder of Lansing H. Bennett, and the malicious wounding of Nicholas Starr, Calvin R. Morgan, and Stephen E. Williams, as well as five firearms charges. [In January 1998, Kansi was sentenced to death.]

A member of the Japanese Red Army terrorist organization, Tsutomu Shirosaki, was turned over to US authorities in 1996 in an Asian country and brought to the United States to stand trial for the improvised mortar attacks against the US Embassy in Jakarta, Indonesia, on 14 May 1986. The projectiles landed on the roof and in a courtyard but failed to explode. In November a US federal court in Washington, DC, found Shirosaki guilty of all charges, including attempted murder of US Embassy personnel and attempting to harm a US Embassy. [In February 1998 Shirosaki was sentenced to a 30-year prison term.]

From Patterns of Global Terrorism 1998

Introduction: US Diplomatic Efforts

On 24 August, Secretary Albright, in an effort to bring to justice the two Libyans suspected in the Pan Am 103 bombing, announced a joint US-UK proposal to try them in the Netherlands before a Scottish court with Scottish judges applying Scottish law. The Arab League, the Organization of African Unity, the Organization of the Islamic Conference, and the Non-Aligned Movement endorsed the proposal. At yearend, however, Libya continued to defy UN Security Council resolutions by refusing to turn over the suspects for trial.

The Year In Review

On 4 November indictments were returned before the US District Court for the Southern District of New York in connection with the two US Embassy bombings in Africa. Charged in the indictment were: Usama Bin Ladin, his military commander Muhammad Atef, and al-Qaida members Wadih El Hage, Fazul Abdullah Mohammed, Mohammed Sadeek Odeh, and Mohamed Rashed Daoud al-Owhali. Two of these suspects, Odeh and al-Owhali, were turned over to US authorities in Kenya and brought to the United States to stand trial. Another suspect, Mamdouh Mahmud Salim, was arrested in Germany in September and extradited to the United States in December. On 16 December five others were indicted for their role in the Dar es Salaam Embassy bombing: Mustafa Mohammed Fadhil, Khalfan Khamis Mohamed, Ahmed Khalfan Ghailani, Fahid Mohommed Ally Msalam, and Sheikh Ahmed Salim Swedan.

In June, Mohammed Rashid was turned over to US authorities overseas and brought to the United States to stand trial on charges of planting a bomb in 1982 on a Pan Am flight from Tokyo to Honolulu that detonated, killing one passenger and wounding 15 others. Rashid had served part of a prison term in Greece in connection with the bombing until that country released him from prison early and expelled him in December 1996, in a move the United States called "incomprehensible." The nine-count US indictment against Rashid charges him with murder, sabotage, bombing, and other crimes in connection with the Pan Am explosion.

Three additional persons convicted in the bombing of the World Trade Center in 1993 were sentenced last year. Eyad Mahmoud Ismail Najim, who drove the explosive-laden van into the World Trade Center, was sentenced to 240 years in prison and ordered to pay $10 million in restitution and a $250,000 fine. Mohammad Abouhalima, who was convicted as an accessory for driving his brother to the Kennedy International Airport knowing he had participated in the bombing, was sentenced to eight years in prison. Ibrahim Ahmad Suleiman received a 10-month sentence on two counts of perjury for lying to the grand jury investigating the bombing.

In May, Abdul Hakim Murad was sentenced to life in prison without parole for his role in the failed conspiracy in January 1995 to blow up a dozen US airliners over the Pacific Ocean. Murad received an additional 60-year sentence for his role and was fined $250,000. Ramzi Ahmed Yousef, who was convicted previously in this conspiracy and for his role in the World Trade Center bombing in 1993, is serving a life prison term.

From Patterns of Global Terrorism 1999

The Year in Review: Law Enforcement

The United States brought the rule of law to bear against international terrorists in several ongoing cases throughout the year:

On 19 May the US District Court in the Southern District of New York unsealed an indictment against Ali Mohammed, charging him with conspiracy to kill U.S. nationals overseas. Ali, suspected of being a member of Usama Bin Ladin's al-Qaida terrorist organization, had been arrested in the United States in September 1998 after testifying before a grand jury concerning the U.S. Embassy bombings in East Africa.

Authorities apprehended Khalfan Khamis Mohamed in South Africa on 5 October, after a joint investigation by the Department of State's Diplomatic Security Bureau, the Federal Bureau of Investigation (FBI), and South African law enforcement authorities. U.S. officials brought him to New York to face charges in connection with the bombing of the U.S. Embassy in Dar Es Salaam, Tanzania, on 7 August 1998.

Three additional suspects in the Tanzanian and Kenyan U.S. Embassy bombings currently are in custody in the United Kingdom, pending extradition to the United States: Khalid Al-Fawwaz, Adel Mohammed Abdul Almagid Bary, and Ibrahim Hussein Abdelhadi Eidarous. Eight other suspects, including Usama Bin Ladin, remain at large. The FBI added Bin Ladin to its Ten Most Wanted Fugitives list in June. The Department of State's Rewards for Justice program pays up to $5 million for information that leads to the arrest or conviction of these and other terrorist suspects.

On 15 October, Siddig Ibrahim Siddig Ali was sentenced to 11 years in prison for his role in a plot to bomb New York City landmarks and to assassinate Egyptian President Hosni Mubarak in 1993. Siddig Ali was arrested in June 1993 on conspiracy charges and pleaded guilty in February 1995 to all charges against him. His cooperation with authorities helped prosecutors convict Shaykh Umar Abd al-Rahman and nine others for their roles in the bombing conspiracy.

In September the US Justice Department informed Hani al-Sayegh, a Saudi Arabian citizen, that he would be removed from the United States and sent to Saudi Arabia. Authorities expelled him from the United States to Saudi Arabia on 11 October, where he remains in custody. He faces charges there in connection with the attack in June 1996 on U.S. forces in Khubar, Saudi Arabia, that killed 19 U.S. citizens and wounded more than 500 others. Al-Sayegh was paroled into the United States from Canada in June 1997. After he failed to abide by an initial plea agreement with the Justice Department concerning a separate case, the State Department terminated his parole in October 1997 and placed him in removal proceedings.

From Patterns of Global Terrorism 2000

The Year in Review

In December new indictments were issued in connection with the bombings in 1998 at two US embassies in East Africa. A federal grand jury in New York charged five men—Saif Al Adel, Muhsin Musa Matwalli Atwah, Ahmed Mohamed Hamed Ali, Anas Al Liby, and Abdullah Ahmed Abdullah—in connection with the bombing attacks in Nairobi and Dar es Salaam, bringing to 22 the total number of persons charged. At the end of 2000, one suspect had pled guilty to conspiring in the attacks, five were in custody in New York awaiting trial, three were in the United Kingdom pending extradition to the United States, and 13 were fugitives, including Usama Bin Ladin.

A trial began in January 2001 in federal court in the Southern District of New York of four suspects in connection with the bombings at the US embassies in Kenya and Tanzania. Three of the four were extradited to the United States in 1999 to stand trial; the fourth was arrested in this country. The trial is expected to last through 2001.

A trial of two Libyans accused of bombing Pan Am flight 103 in 1988 began in the Netherlands on 3 May 2000. A Scottish court presided over the trial and issued its verdict on 31 January 2001. It found Abdel Basset al-Megrahi guilty of the charge of murdering 259 passengers and crew as well as 11 residents of Lockerbie, Scotland, "while acting in furtherance of the purposes of . . . Libyan Intelligence Services." Concerning the other defendant, Al-Amin Kalifa Fahima, the court concluded it had insufficient evidence to satisfy the high standard of "proof beyond reasonable doubt" that is necessary in criminal cases. The verdict of the court represents a victory for the international effort to hold terrorists accountable for their crimes.

From Patterns of Global Terrorism 2001

Introduction: Law Enforcement

The world's law-enforcement professionals have launched a global dragnet to identify, arrest, and bring terrorists to justice.

In the United States, the FBI has led the law-enforcement engagement, working with all federal, state, and local law-enforcement agencies. More than 7000 FBI Agents and support personnel have worked diligently with their US and foreign law-enforcement partners to unravel the planning leading to the execution of the 9/11 operation, as well as to interdict other al-Qaida cells and operatives in the US and around the world. Their enhanced law-enforcement efforts, and cooperative work by officials around the world, have resulted in the apprehension of more than 1000 suspected terrorists and the breakup of al-Qaida and other terrorist cells. Many of these arrests, to include that of Zacarias Moussaoui, a suspected al-Qaida operative in the operation, are described in this report.

During 2001 and through March 2002, Secretary Powell designated or redesignated 33 groups as foreign terrorist organizations under the Immigration and Nationality Act, as amended by the Antiterrorism and Effective Death Penalty Act of 1996. The designations make it a criminal offense to provide funds or other material support to such organizations, require US financial institutions to block the funds of the groups, and make members of the groups ineligible for US visas and, if they are aliens, deportable.

On 26 October the US Congress enacted the USA PATRIOT Act, which significantly expands the ability of US law enforcement to investigate and prosecute persons who engage in terrorist acts. On 5 December, in accordance with the USA PATRIOT Act, Secretary Powell designated 39 groups as "terrorist exclusion list" organizations. The legal consequences of the designations relate to immigration, and they strengthen the US ability to exclude supporters of terrorism from entering the country or to deport them if they are found within our borders.

The United States brought to conclusion the prosecution of four al-Qaida members for the bombing of the US Embassies in Kenya and Tanzania. In May, in a courtroom within sight of the World Trade Center, guilty verdicts were handed down on all 302 counts in the trial of the bombing suspects, and all were sentenced to life in prison.

Extraditions and Renditions

Table 1 below, from Patterns of Global Terrorism 2001, *details the extraditions (legal transfer of suspects from one country to another) and renditions (clandestine transfer of suspects from one country to another) of terrorists to the United States from 1993 through 2001.*

From Patterns of Global Terrorism 2002

Introduction: Law Enforcement

An impressive global dragnet has tightened around al-Qaida. Since September 11 more than 3,000 al-Qaida operatives or associates have been detained in more than 100 countries, largely as a result of cooperation among law-enforcement agencies.

Entire cells have been wrapped up in nations such as Singapore, Italy, and elsewhere. In all these cells, deadly attacks on US interests or our allies were being planned.

In the United States, the rule of law is being applied relentlessly against terrorists. For example, US Attorney General John Ashcroft called 4 October "a defining day in America's war on terrorism." On that day, the United States convicted would-be shoe bomber Richard Reid; sentenced American Taliban John Walker Lindh; and neutralized a sus-

Table 1 Extraditions and Renditions of Terrorists to the United States, 1993–2001[1]

Date	Name	Type	From
March 1993	Mahmoud Abu Halima (February 1993 World Trade Center bombing)	Extradition	Country not disclosed
July 1993	Mohammed Ali Rezaq (November 1985 hijacking of Egyptair 648)	Rendition	Nigeria
February 1995	Ramzi Ahmed Yousef (January 1995 Far East bomb plot, February 1993 World Trade Center bombing)	Extradition	Pakistan
April 1995	Abdul Hakim Murad (January 1995 Far East bomb plot)	Rendition	Philippines
August 1995	Eyad Mahmoud Ismail Najim (February 1993 World Trade Center bombing)	Extradition	Jordan
December 1995	Wali Khan Amin Shah (January 1995 Far East bomb plot)	Rendition	Country not disclosed
September 1996	Tsutomu Shirosaki (May 1986 attack on US Embassy, Jakarta)	Rendition	Country not disclosed
June 1997	Mir Aimal Kansi (January 1993 shooting outside CIA headquarters)	Rendition	Country not disclosed
June 1998	Mohammed Rashid (August 1982 Pan Am bombing)	Rendition	Country not disclosed
August 1998	Mohamed Rashed Daoud Al-Owhali (August 1998 US Embassy bombing in Kenya)	Rendition	Kenya
August 1998	Mohamed Sadeek Odeh (August 1998 US Embassy bombing in Kenya)	Rendition	Kenya
December 1998	Mamdouh Mahmud Salim (August 1998 East Africa bombings)	Extradition	Germany
October 1999	Khalfan Khamis Mohamed (August 1998 US Embassy bombing in Tanzania)	Rendition	South Africa
September 2001	Zayd Hassan Abd al-Latif Masud al-Safarini (1986 hijacking of PanAm 73 in Karachi, Pakistan)	Rendition	Country not disclosed

1 *Eds. Note:* Extradition is the surrender of an individual from one State in response to a formal demand made by another State that the individual must face prosecution or serve a sentence. Rendition is the clandestine capture and extradition of suspects to a third country for detention and interrogation. Renditions are undertaken without due process, but are legal when the countries involved agree to the exercise. Covert activities without the knowledge of the country in which the suspect resides is illegal, but takes place both in developed countries that object to the practice and in less developed countries with poor infrastructure. The distinction between a rendition and an extraordinary rendition is merely of degree, namely, knowingly sending a suspect to a country specifically so they will be tortured.

pected al-Qaida terrorist cell in Portland, Oregon. Another alleged al-Qaida cell was uncovered and its members arrested in Lackawanna, New York, during the summer.

Since the previous *Patterns of Global Terrorism* report was issued, the United States designated several additional groups as Foreign Terrorist Organizations (FTOs), including the Communist Party of the Philippines/New People's Army, Jemaah Islamiya, and Lashkar I Jhangvi. The Lashkar I Jhangvi is responsible for the kidnapping and murder of American journalist Daniel Pearl in 2002. The FTO designation carries several legal consequences: it is unlawful for US persons to knowingly provide funds and other material support to designated groups; members of these groups are ineligible for US visas; and US financial institutions must block the funds of the groups.

From Patterns of Global Terrorism 2003

Introduction: Law Enforcement

The greatly increased law enforcement cooperation among nations that followed the 9/11 attacks continued to expand throughout 2003.

Al-Qaida is no longer the organization it once was, largely due to such cooperation. Most of the group's senior leadership is dead or in custody, its membership on the run, and its capabilities sharply degraded. More than 3,400 al-Qaida suspects have been arrested or detained worldwide. In the United States, international terrorist suspects repeatedly faced the rule of law:

- In February, the Department of Justice (DOJ) announced the indictment of the alleged North American leader of the Palestine Islamic Jihad, Sami Al-Arian, and seven co-conspirators. The indictment charges them with operating a racketeering enterprise that has supported numerous violent terrorist activities since 1984. Al-Arian and three others were placed under arrest.
- In March, DOJ announced the indictment and arrest of three members of the Army for the Liberation of Rwanda for the brutal murder in 1999 of two American tourists in Uganda.
- In May, a naturalized American citizen, Iyman Faris, pled guilty to surveilling a New York City bridge for al-Qaida, and in October he was sentenced to 20 years for providing material support to that group and conspiring to give them information about possible US targets for attack.

- Also in May, the Justice Department unsealed a 50-count indictment against two Yemeni nationals for the bombing in October 2000 of the USS Cole that killed 17 American sailors and wounded more than 40.
- In November, two Yemeni suspects were extradited from Germany to the United States on federal charges of conspiring to provide material support to al-Qaida and HAMAS.
- Throughout the year, numerous members of terrorist cells that were disrupted in Detroit, Portland, Buffalo, and Seattle pled guilty to or were convicted of charges of conspiracy to provide material support to terrorists, including al-Qaida and the Taliban.

Sanctions

Overview of Sanctions

Anna Sabasteanski

Chapter 7 of the United Nations charter allows the Security Council to take measures to deal with "threats to the peace, breaches of the peace, and acts of aggression." Among those measures are economic and other sanctions, which are often a useful way to coordinate international efforts in the face of a particular threat or crisis situation. Sanctions also offer strategic guidance for foreign policies related to export, import, licensing, and similar commercial matters.

The United States imposes a variety of sanctions, some through executive order and others through legislation. Watch lists, such as those used for intelligence purposes or in connection with travel and immigration, go beyond the list of sanctioned entities to include those under suspicion and with indirect connections, such as friends and families of those on sanctions lists. In addition, a variety of sanctions control international trade and commerce. The Department of State cooperates with other agencies and is directly responsible for economic sanctions through the Office of Terrorism Finance and Economic Sanctions Policy. The State Department is also responsible for designating state sponsors of terrorism and for placing certain controls on trade and aid.

The use of sanctions in the United States has a long history. They were first used in 1773 when the colonials embargoed British tea to protest their presence and prevent tea importation. These sanctions did not prevent that war, and experience of their use since has indicated that when sanctions are broadly directed, they often have a negative impact on the general population. Having learned from experience, governments and multilateral organizations now impose sanctions more narrowly. For example, they may target a particular individual with restraints on travel and trade.

The sanctions imposed on the Taliban are a good example of "smart sanctions." *Patterns of Global Terrorism 2000* described them:

> United Nations Security Council Resolution 1333, passed in December 2000, targets the Taliban regime in Afghanistan. The Taliban ignored its obligations under UN Security Council Resolution 1267 (passed in November 1999) and has continued to provide shelter to Usama Bin Ladin. In UN Security Council Resolution 1333, the Security Council:
>
> - Demands the Taliban comply with Resolution 1267 and cease providing training and support to international terrorists.
> - Insists the Taliban turn over indicted international terrorist Usama Bin Ladin so he can be brought to justice.
> - Directs the Taliban to close all terrorist camps in Afghanistan within 30 days.
> - Until the Taliban fully complies with its obligations under this resolution and Resolution 1267, member states of the United Nations should:
> - Freeze the financial assets of Usama Bin Ladin.
> - Observe an arms embargo against the Taliban that includes a prohibition against providing military weapons, training, or advice.
> - Close all Taliban offices overseas.
> - Reduce the staff at the limited number of Taliban missions abroad.
> - Restrict travel of senior Taliban officials except for the purposes of participation in peace negotiations, compliance with the resolution, or for humanitarian reasons, including religious obligations.
> - Ban the export to Afghan territory of a precursor chemical, acetic anhydride, which is used to manufacture heroin.
> - Close all offices of Ariana Afghan Airlines and ban all nonhumanitarian assistance flights into and out of Afghanistan. Broad exemptions are given to humanitarian flights operated by, or on behalf of, nongovernmental organizations and government relief agencies providing humanitarian assistance to Afghanistan.
>
> The sanctions imposed by these two resolutions are targeted sanctions. They are not economic sanctions.
>
> - These "smart sanctions" provide for broad humanitarian exemptions to avoid harming the Afghan people.
> - They permit private-sector trade and commerce, including food, medicine, and consumer products.
> - They permit, without impediment, the work of the humanitarian organizations providing assistance to the civilian population of Afghanistan.

- They permit Afghans to travel by air for urgent humanitarian reasons and to fulfill their religious obligations, such as the hajj, including on the banned Ariana Afghan Airline. The UN Sanctions Committee already has approved about 200 flights for 13,000 Afghans in 2001 for this purpose. The Committee never has denied a request for a legitimate humanitarian waiver.
- They permit Taliban officials to travel abroad to participate in a peace process and to discuss fulfilling the demands of the Resolutions.

Additional background on the use of economic sanctions can be found in "Economic Sanctions to Achieve U.S. Foreign Policy Goals," the Congressional Research Services report found later in this section.

Sanctions Lists

The following lists deal with various types of sanctions imposed by the U.S. government. They have been instituted, by legislation or executive order, in response to particular threats —with the aim of preventing conflict, encouraging rebuilding, and intervening in commercial transactions to prevent their abuse.

Debarred List

The Department of State's Directorate of Defense Trade (DDTC) Bureau of Political-Military Affairs controls the "List of Parties Debarred for Arms Export Control Act Convictions" (the Debarred List), in accordance with laws that control defense trade exports and matters related to defense trade compliance, enforcement, and reporting.

This list contains identifying information concerning entities and individuals that have violated the Arms Export Control Act (1994) and are therefore subject to statutory debarment—arms are not to be exported to them. It does not include those who have been debarred for other export violations or who have been administratively debarred by violating a rule or regulation.

Denied Persons List

The U.S. Department of Commerce's Bureau of Industry and Security (BIS) manages the list of people whose privilege to export, or to re-export goods that had earlier been imported, has been denied.

Entity List

BIS also manages a list of foreign end users believed to pose an unacceptable risk of diverting U.S. exports, particularly those containing dual-use technology, to alternate destinations where they could be used to develop weapons of mass destruction.

Unverified List

In addition, BIS maintains what is known as the Unverified List. This list includes the names and countries of foreign persons who in the past were parties to exports and imports or for which BIS could not conduct a pre-license check or a post-shipment verification for reasons outside of the U.S. government's control. (Individual shipments are also subject to verification rules, but in small volumes these are "self-certified," by filling out the customs form and answering questions put to a person at the post office or airport. In all cases, enforcement officials have the right to question and examine the shipper. The difference is one of scale, with BIS handling commercial transactions that use a longer form to accommodate to greater scale.) People on this list are "red-flagged" for additional scrutiny when they attempt such transactions in the future.

List of Foreign Terrorist Organizations

The secretary of state designates groups as foreign terrorist organizations (FTOs) if they conduct terrorism and threaten the interests of the United States. Once a group is designated an FTO, the U.S. government can block (freeze) its assets in U.S. financial institutions, criminalize provision of material support to it, and block visas for its members without having to show that those members were involved in specific terrorist activities.

Terrorist Exclusion List

Among its many provisions, the comprehensive counterterrorism bill known as the USA PATRIOT Act (Public Law 107-56, 2001) authorized that the Secretary of State, in consultation with or at the request of the Attorney General, create a Terrorist Exclusion List (TEL) with immigration consequences for groups named therein. Aliens who provide material assistance to organizations listed on the TEL, or who solicit such assistance from others, may be denied entry to the United States or deported.

Specially Designated Nationals List

The list of Specially Designated Nationals and Blocked Persons (SDNs) is produced by the Department of the Treasury's Office of Foreign Assets Control (OFAC). The history of OFAC began before the War of 1812. During the Civil War, and the two World Wars, OFAC crafted various measures to apply economic pressures in conflicts. Today its measures extend to terrorist and other unconventional threats, as well as economic measures to encourage humanitarian reforms and other policy goals.

Organizations listed as SDNs can include front companies or parastatal entities that are owned, controlled by, or acting for or on behalf of targeted countries or groups. Individuals on the list may include terrorists or narcotics traffickers and others so designated. U.S. citizens and people under the jurisdiction of the United States are prohibited from engaging in any transactions with SDNs and must block any property in their possession or under their control in which an SDN has an interest.

An OFAC designation is very powerful and essentially blocks all transactions between the designated entity and any U.S. entity. SDNs may retain ownership of the blocked property, but they cannot exercise the powers and privileges associated with ownership without OFAC authorization. All U.S. citizens and permanent residents as well as corporations and their branches worldwide must comply with OFAC regulations, regardless of whether or not they are located inside the United States. (For more details, see the later section on "Terrorist Financing" and Part 3, "Country Reports 1985–2004").

List of State Sponsors of Terrorism

The secretary of state can designate a government as a state sponsor of terrorism if that government "has repeatedly provided support for acts of international terrorism" (U.S. Code 22, 1998, Sec. 2780). U.S. law requires the imposition of various sanctions on a state so designated. The four main categories of sanctions are bans on arms-related exports and sales; restrictions on exports of dual-use items (items that have both military and nonmilitary applications); prohibitions on official U.S. government economic assistance (except humanitarian assistance), including a requirement that the government oppose multilateral bank assistance; and imposition of miscellaneous trade and other restrictions. The six countries on the list at present are Cuba, Iran, Libya, North Korea, Sudan, and Syria. (Iraq was removed in October 2004.) For more details, see the section on "State Sponsors of Terrorism."

CRS Report for Congress

Economic Sanctions to Achieve U.S. Foreign Policy Goals: Discussion and Guide to Current Law

Dianne E. Rennack
Analyst in Foreign Policy Legislation

Robert D. Shuey
Specialist in U.S. Foreign Policy and National Defense
Foreign Affairs and National Defense Division

Abstract

This report provides background on foreign policy sanctions and the events that might necessitate their use, criteria to consider when determining if sanctions are appropriate, approaches that might be effective, and aspects of the use of sanctions that are sometimes overlooked or not considered fully. The report also provides an uncomplicated map of where sanctions policies and options currently may be found in U.S. law.

Summary

On June 4, 1998, Senator Richard Lugar circulated a "Dear Colleague" letter, stating it was his intention at the earliest opportunity to offer an amendment on the floor based on S. 1413, the "Enhancement of Trade, Security, and Human Rights through Sanctions Reform Act." S. 1413—its House counterpart is H.R. 2708, introduced by Representative Hamilton and others—seeks to clarify the use of unilateral sanctions in U.S. foreign policy imposed at the initiative of either the Administration or Congress. S. 1413/H.R. 2708 would revise procedures both branches would follow before enacting or imposing sanctions, and would require extensive reporting as to the expected costs and benefits of imposing sanctions. The measures were considered unlikely to be enacted in this Congress as freestanding bills. Senator Lugar's announcement, however, increases the odds of enactment. Press reports suggest that the National Defense Authorization Act for Fiscal Year 1999 (S. 2057), currently under Senate consideration, is the most likely legislative vehicle for such an amendment.

The 105 Congress, otherwise, currently has under consideration new sanctions legislation specifically relating to religious persecution, proliferation of weapons of mass destruction, conventional arms sales and transfers, export controls, terrorism, international narcotics control, travel restrictions, environment, workers rights (including issues of prison or forced labor and child labor), humanitarian donations of food and medicine, war crimes, torture, and human rights. Other, more routine, legislative initiatives (annual appropriations bills, for example) have become the means to target individual countries for behavior of which the United States disapproves. Economic sanctions typically include measures such as trade embargoes; restrictions on particular exports or imports; denial of foreign assistance, loans, and investments; or control of foreign assets and economic transactions that involve U.S. citizens or businesses.

Some suggest that there is a post-Cold War trend toward sanctions becoming the method of first resort in foreign policy. A recent National Association of Manufacturers report (March 1997) states that 61 U.S. laws and executive orders have been enacted in the last four years alone—targeting 35 countries—for foreign policy purposes. A frequently cited report issued by the Institute for International Economics (April 1997) concludes that U.S. unilateral sanctions may have cost U.S. businesses some $15–19 billion in 1995 alone. Others contend that sanctions, unilateral or otherwise, are a peacetime means to improving international behavior in important areas such as human rights or weapons proliferation, and should not be avoided solely for trade concerns.

This report provides background on foreign policy sanctions and the events that might necessitate their use, criteria to consider when determining if sanctions are appropriate, approaches that might be effective, and aspects of the use of sanctions that are sometimes overlooked or not considered fully.

Text of the Report

Both the Congress and the President in recent years have increasingly relied on economic sanctions as a means to establish and promote their foreign policy objectives. The 105 Congress currently has under consideration legislation relating to the procedure for drafting new sanctions regimes, as well as religious persecution, proliferation of weapons of mass destruction, conventional arms sales and transfers, export controls, terrorism, international narcotics control, travel restrictions, environment, workers rights (including issues of prison or forced labor and child labor), humanitarian donations of food and medicine, war crimes, torture, and human rights. Legislative initiatives to address particular countries' behavior—most recently Iran, Libya, Iraq, Cuba, Sudan, China, Burma, and Russia—have been debated frequently throughout government and the business community, both in the United States and in international fora. Sanctions to promote foreign policy objectives have been offered regularly during the consideration of annual appropriations bills and authorization measures.

In the fall of 1997 Representative Hamilton and Senator Lugar introduced identical bills in their respective chambers that would, in the words of the proposals' preambles, "provide a framework for consideration by the legislative and executive branches of unilateral economic sanctions." H.R. 2708/S. 1413, the "Enhancement of Trade, Security, and Human Rights through Sanctions Reform Act," seeks to clarify the use of unilateral sanctions in U.S. foreign policy imposed at the initiative of either the Administration or Congress. The bills would revise procedures both branches follow before enacting or imposing sanctions, and would require extensive reporting as to the expected costs and benefits of imposing sanctions. The measures were considered unlikely to be enacted in this Congress, until Senator Lugar, on June 4, 1998, circulated a "Dear Colleague" letter, stating it was his intention to offer an amendment on the floor based on S. 1413 at the earliest opportunity. Press reports suggest that the National Defense Authorization Act for Fiscal Year 1999 (S. 2057), currently under Senate consideration, is the most likely legislative vehicle for such an amendment.

This report provides background on the range of actions that might be termed sanctions, and a set of criteria that legislators might consider when proposing them, to help legislators judge when sanctions might be appropriate and the approach that might be the most effective. Provided as well is an uncomplicated "map" of where sanctions policies and options currently may be found in U.S. law.

Defining Economic Sanctions

Generally, economic sanctions might be defined as "coercive economic measures taken against one or more countries to force a change in policies, or at least to demonstrate a country's opinion about the other's policies."[1] The most-often quoted study on sanctions defines the term as "... the deliberate, government-inspired withdrawal, or threat of withdrawal, of customary trade or financial relations."[2] Economic sanctions typically include measures such as trade embargoes; restrictions on particular exports or imports; denial of foreign assistance, loans, and investments; or control of foreign assets and economic transactions that involve U.S. citizens or businesses. These definitions of economic sanctions would exclude diplomatic démarches, reductions in embassy staff or closing of embassies, mobilizing armed forces or going to war—tools clearly intended to change another country's behavior through other than economic means. The use of "carrots" (e.g., granting most-favored-nation status for another year or offering economic or military assistance to a country if it conforms to certain standards) would not qualify as a sanction.

Issues Related to Economic Sanctions

In any sanctions debate, one might consider the following questions to assess the benefits and/or costs of imposing sanctions against a country, company, or individual:

Why do we apply sanctions? Economic sanctions are used when one country (or alliance of countries) wants to condemn or coerce change in the behavior of another country —its government, individuals, or businesses—that violates important international standards or threatens national interests. The U.S. government might impose sanctions when other efforts to change behavior have failed, such as diplomacy, public suasion, cultural and scientific exchanges, state visits, targeted technical assistance, military training and education, or other friendly means. Sanctions might be positioned at the middle of a continuum, between the extremes of complete cooperation and agreement at one end, and to the other end open hostility, use of force, or all-out war. The United States has aimed sanctions at governments that consistently violate internationally recognized human rights; at governments that sponsor international terrorism or harbor terrorists from elsewhere; at governments, individuals or corporations that engage in the proliferation of weapons of mass destruction; at individuals or governments that traffic narcotics; at governments that conduct aggression against their neighbors, threaten regional stability, or threaten U.S. security or foreign policy interests.

What objectives does the U.S. government seek to achieve when it imposes sanctions? United States policymakers do not always state the goals or objectives they hope to accomplish through the imposition of economic sanctions [that] might be imposed when taking no action seems not enough of a response, but at the same time policymakers might resist committing to stronger measures. Generally, however, the U.S. government may choose to impose sanctions to:

- express its condemnation of a particular practice such as military aggression; human rights violations; militarization that destabilizes a country, its neighbors or the region; proliferation of nuclear, biological, or chemical weapons or missiles; political, economic, or military intimidation; terrorism; drug trafficking; or extreme national political policies contrary to basic interests or values of the United States (e.g., apartheid, communism);
- punish those engaged in objectionable behavior and deter its repetition;
- make it more expensive, difficult, or time-consuming to engage in objectionable behavior;
- block the flow of economic support that could be used by the targeted entity against the United States or U.S. interests;
- dissuade others from engaging in objectionable behavior;

---

1 Carter, Barry E., *International Economic Sanctions: Improving the Haphazard U.S. Legal Regime*. Cambridge: Cambridge University Press, 1988. P. 4.

2 Hufbauer, Gary Clyde, Jeffrey J. Schott and Kimberly Ann Elliott, *Economic Sanctions Reconsidered: History and Current Policy*. Washington, DC: Institute for International Economics, 1990 (second edition). P. 2.

- isolate a targeted country (or company or individual);
- force a change or termination of objectionable behavior; or
- coerce a change in the leadership or form of government in a targeted country.

Who imposes sanctions? The President has broad authority to impose sanctions, either pursuant to declaring a national emergency and then invoking powers vested in his office in the International Emergency Economic Powers Act, or by exercising authority stated in various Public Laws (some of which are described at the end of this report). In other instances, Congress might take the lead, either by conferring new Presidential authority to impose sanctions, or by requiring sanctions to be imposed unless the President determines and certifies that certain conditions have been met. Some sanctions are mandatory and are triggered automatically when certain conditions exist. Congress, for example, has required the imposition of sanctions when duly elected governments are overthrown by military *coup d'etat,* or when any non-nuclear weapon state explodes a nuclear device. Some behavior that would trigger the imposition of sanctions, such as proliferation or support of international terrorism, requires that the President or Secretary of State determine and certify that a violation of a standard has occurred. The Administration has considerable flexibility in making such determinations and also has the authority to waive sanctions when imposed.

What tools are available? All of the following economic policy tools have been used at one time or another, triggered by a variety of repugnant behaviors.[3]

- Foreign assistance, all or some programs, could be terminated, suspended, limited, conditioned, or prohibited. Foreign assistance to particular organizations that operate in the targeted country could be curtailed. U.S. government arms sales and transfers, military assistance, and International Military Education and Training (IMET) funding could be similarly restricted. Scientific and technological cooperation, assistance, and exchanges could be reduced or halted.
- Both public and private sector financial transactions could be restricted; assets in U.S. jurisdictions could be seized or frozen, or transactions related to travel or other forms of exchange could be limited or prohibited.
- Importation and exportation of some or all commodities could be curtailed by denying licenses, closing off shipping terminuses, or limiting related transactions.
- Government procurement contracts could be canceled or denied.
- Negative votes on loans, credits, or grants in international financial institutions could be cast, or the United States could abstain in voting.
- Trade agreements or other bilateral accords could be abrogated, made conditional, or not renewed. Beneficial trade status could be denied, withdrawn, or made conditional. Trade and import quotas for particular commodities could be lessened or eliminated altogether. The U.S. tax code could be amended to discourage commerce with a sanctioned state.
- Funding for investment, through the Overseas Private Investment Corporation, Trade and Development Agency, or Export-Import Bank, could be curtailed.
- Aviation, maritime, and surface access to the United States could be canceled or denied.
- Certain acts associated with sanctionable behavior could be made a criminal offense—making the targeted individual subject to fines or imprisonment. Additionally, sanctions could be applied against those individuals, businesses, or countries that continue to trade with or support targeted individuals, businesses, or countries.

How likely is it that sanctions will achieve the stated goal? Effectiveness is the most difficult aspect of sanctions policy to evaluate. The impact, cost and benefit of sanctions cannot be considered in a vacuum. A recent study considers geographic proximity, common language, volume of trade, a country's relative wealth, and membership in a common trading bloc all factors that might determine the success or failure of a unilaterally imposed sanctions regime.[4] One should also consider the United States' relative importance —in terms of trade, culture, scientific and intellectual exchanges, and history—to the targeted country. How important to the targeted country is our economic cooperation? Is the United States a significant trading partner, or only marginally engaged? Consider, for example, that at the time that sanctions were imposed against the former Yugoslavia, the United States took in only about 5 percent of that country's exports. The support of more substantial trading partners in Europe was needed to have any hope of having an impact. United States businesses frequently argue that U.S. sanctions that hinder their exports or imports in turn benefit their foreign competitors. Some contend that staying engaged as trading partners or investors in a problem country will have better long-term effect. The United States seeks to isolate Cuba, for example, while Cuba's European trading partners contend that full trade relations afford them opportunities to discuss human rights concerns with the island nation. Of course, relatively modest goals that do not challenge the vital interests of the targeted country or person are more likely to be achieved than are far-reaching goals, such as a change in the form of government, change in its leadership, or relinquishing territory. The smaller the goal, the more likely it can be achieved. Similarly, the lesser the cost of imposing sanctions, the more sell-

---

3 Government leaders also have a range of diplomatic, political, cultural, and military tools at their disposal to use instead of or in conjunction with economic sanctions.

4 Hufbauer, Gary Clyde and Kimberly Ann Elliott, Tess Cyrus, and Elizabeth Winston. *U.S. Economic Sanctions: Their Impact on Trade, Jobs, and Wages.* Washington, DC: Institute for International Economics, 1997. 17 p. and tables.

able and manageable the policy will be to the implementing country or alliance of countries.

What secondary consequences might sanctions have? Whether or not successful in achieving their central purpose, sanctions sometimes have undesirable—perhaps unexpected—fallout. Sanctions against former Yugoslavia, for example, were particularly hard on the economies of Serbia's neighboring states. At the same time, some analysts argue, sanctions against Serbia and Montenegro actually bolstered nationalist political movements there. In another instance, longstanding sanctions against South Africa in the 1980s, some speculate, led that nation to develop weapons manufacturing capabilities—conventional and nuclear—that remain cause for concern today. Most recently, when the United States campaigned for European friends to join in sanctions against Iran by blocking investment in Iran's oil fields in 1995, for example, nearly all of Europe declined, pointing out that they were running out of fuel sources that were not under some sanctions regime. A short while later, trading partners of Nigeria found themselves wanting to punish that country for human rights issues but were unable to restrict trade with yet another oil producer.

Other secondary—and unintended—consequences arise in nearly all cases where sanctions are applied for some duration. Analysts express concern for the impact on the nongovernmental population, particularly if food, medicine, or other basic human needs are affected. A recent study of the impact of U.S. sanctions policy on health and nutrition in Cuba concluded that U.S. restrictions on that country's ability to import food and medicine has "dramatically harmed the health and nutrition of large numbers of ordinary Cuban citizens.[5] The State Department has countered these charges, incidentally, with documentation of increased humanitarian shipments of medicine and other health-related supplies to Cuba from the United States in recent years, and with statistics that indict the Cuban government for misuse of their own treasury and inattention to its own people. Indeed, the State Department reports that the United States, since 1992, has become the largest donor of humanitarian assistance to Cuba.[6] Similar reports abound regarding Iraq and the impact of U.N.-sponsored multilateral sanctions, with those supporting sanctions and those favoring lifting the sanctions for humanitarian reasons arguing equally passionately.

Nearer to home, loss of trade, the impact on U.S. jobs, potential loss of procurement contracts or other trade relations, loss of confidence in the reliability of American suppliers subject to unilateral economic prohibitions, all need to be factored in. How do such costs compare to the benefit of achieving the stated goal?

---

[5] *Denial of Food and Medicine: The Impact of the U.S. Embargo on Health & Nutrition in Cuba,* American Association for World Health. March 1997.

[6] "The U.S. Embargo and Health Care in Cuba: Myth Versus Reality," U.S. Department of State, Press Statement, May 14, 1997.

What change is required for the sanctions to be lifted? When sanctions are imposed via enactment of public law, what is required to terminate the restrictions is usually clearly stated. If a policy is unevenly applied, however, the standard might be less clear. China, for example, as a nonmarket economy, is denied permanent most-favored-nation status on the basis of laws relating to trade, nonmarket economies, and emigration. The annual debate to renew China's MFN status, however, rarely has much to do with freedom of emigration of China's population. If sanctions are applied for a lengthy period, other problems arise, or the circumstances that triggered the sanctions at the outset might evolve. The sought after change in behavior could be redefined over time, or multilateral or domestic support for the sanctions could deteriorate. In some instances, sanctions are imposed to achieve a goal that is unclear, ever-changing, or perhaps unattainable. In such circumstances, if the sanctions are lifted or waived, it may effectively signal a friendly change of policy. If the U.S. government terminates sanctions when it appears that the targeted country has not budged at all from its sanctionable behavior, however, future attempts to achieve a standard of behavior through sanctions may be compromised. The constantly changing political landscape of the former Yugoslavia over the last seven years provides numerous incidents to demonstrate the dilemma of sending confusing signals to allies as well as the sanctioned state.

Would multilateral sanctions be more desirable and achievable? It is generally agreed that sanctions imposed by all or most of the nations on which a targeted country relies for trade and support (such as through the United Nations or other multinational organization) stand a much better chance of having an impact than unilateral restrictions or prohibitions. Consensus is difficult to reach among countries considering another country's behavior, however, and as a result multilateral sanctions are imposed infrequently. Comprehensive multilateral sanctions are even more rare. Attempts that fail to solidify international opinion against one country's objectionable behavior can actually give support to those committing the behavior (for example, [this] year the United States is condemned by the U.N. General Assembly for its unilateral sanctions regime against Cuba).

Current Law

Each sanction has its own duration, severity, and comprehensiveness or selectivity. Each section of law has its own terms for triggering the imposition, as well as reporting on, easing or tightening, waiving, and terminating the sanction. Some laws make sanctions mandatory; others provide discretionary authority to the President or his delegate to impose sanctions. Nearly all laws include some sort of waiver authority that allows the President to not impose the sanction even if an incident warrants it. Only a few laws specifically spell out what recourse Congress might take when it finds itself in disagreement with the executive branch on the imposition, waiving, or termination of a sanction.

Some laws generally authorize the Executive branch to make and carry out foreign policy and would not be considered sanctions legislation at first glance. Such authority is often cited when the President changes policy to the detriment of a targeted country. Using legislative authority to cut foreign assistance, for example, might be an administrative decision, or it might be a step taken to punish a country in violation of any number of international standards. Disallowing participation in various trade-supporting programs (such as the Overseas Private Investment Corporation or the Export-Import Bank) might be a change in policy to recognize a country's graduation from such needs, or it might be considered a punitive step taken to change the recipient country's behavior.

The following list is intended to serve only as a guide to where the authority to impose sanctions stands in the law. Careful reading of the public law text is required to determine the intent of the sanctions, what triggers their imposition, the extent of the sanction, and what is required to have the restrictions lifted. The list groups laws into broad foreign policy categories. A brief note of what form the sanction might take is included parenthetically. Many of the restrictions of foreign assistance will be found in the FY1998 foreign operations appropriations act; such a law is enacted anew each fiscal year (or, in absence of an appropriations act, a continuing resolution may extend the terms of a previous law). For specific countries, any law written specifically to address conditions in, or relations with, that country would apply, but other laws of general effect written to address an issue might apply to that country as well. This list should not be considered comprehensive but is an index of basic sanctions legislation.

General U.S. National Security or Foreign Policy Objectives

§ 621, Foreign Assistance Act of 1961 (Public Law 87-195; 22 USC 2381) (authorizes President to administer foreign assistance programs and policy; authorizes the President to prohibit foreign assistance because of illegal activities, such as fraud or corruption)

§ 633A, Foreign Assistance Act of 1961 (Public Law 87-195; 22 USC 2393a) (prohibits foreign assistance when certain informational requests are not met by recipient)

§ 3, Arms Export Control Act (Public Law 90-629; 22 USC 2753) (authorizes President to administer U.S. government arms sales and transfers with conditions and exceptions)

§ 38, Arms Export Control Act (Public Law 90-629; 22 USC 2778) (authorizes the President to limit sales and transfers in interest of world peace and security of United States. Violation of terms of section or related regulations may result in $1 million fine, 10-year imprisonment, or both)

§ 42, Arms Export Control Act (Public Law 90-629; 22 USC 2791) (authorizes the President to cancel arms sales, credits, or contracts on national security grounds)

§ 5(b), Trading with the Enemy Act (Public Law 65-91; 50 USC App. 5(b))[7] (authorizes the President to investigate, regulate, or prohibit transactions, or to freeze assets)

Title II, National Emergencies Act (Public Law 94-412; 50 USC 1621, 1622) (authorizes declaration and administration of national emergencies—required to administer authority under International Emergency Economic Powers Act)

§ 203, International Emergency Economic Powers Act (Public Law 95-223; 50 USC 1701) (authorizes control or prohibition of most financial transactions)

§ 2(b)(5)(B), Export-Import Bank Act of 1945 (Public Law 79-173; 12 USC 635(b)(5)(B)) (restricts Export-Import Bank services with country engaged in armed conflict against U.S. armed forces)

§ 5, Export Administration Act of 1979 (Public Law 96-72; 50 USC App. 2404) (imposes national security export controls)

§ 6, Export Administration Act of 1979 (Public Law 96-72; 50 USC App. 2405) (imposes foreign policy export controls)

§ 11, Export Administration Act of 1979 (Public Law 96-72; 50 USC App. 2410) (imposes penalties for violations of Act, generally)

§ 11A, Export Administration Act of 1979 (Public Law 96-72; 50 USC App. 2410a) (prohibits contracts, importation for regulations violators)

§ 233, Trade Expansion Act of 1962 (Public Law 87-794; 19 USC 1864) (authorizes President to sanction importation for violations of sec. 5 Export Administration Act national security controls)

U.S. Trade Policy Legislation Sometimes Used for Foreign Policy Objectives

§ 125, Trade Act of 1974 (Public Law 93-618; 19 USC 2135) (authorizes President to terminate or withdraw from trade agreements)

§ 126, Trade Act of 1974 (Public Law 93-618; 19 USC 2136) (authorizes President to terminate or withdraw from trade agreements where reciprocal nondiscriminatory treatment has not been upheld)

§ 604, Trade Act of 1974 (Public Law 93-618; 19 USC 2483) (authorizes President to change the Harmonized Tariff Schedules)

§ 212(b)(4), (5), Caribbean Basin Economic Recovery Act (Public Law 98-67; 19 USC 2702(b)(4), (5)) (denies beneficiary country status)

§ 232, Trade Expansion Act of 1962 (Public Law 87-794; 19 USC 1862) (authorizes President to set duties or import restrictions based on national security issues)

§ 620(d), Foreign Assistance Act of 1961 (Public Law 87-195; 22 USC 2370(d)) (prohibits foreign assistance loans)

---

7 The Trading with the Enemy Act continues to apply only to Cuba and North Korea. Presidential authority to impose similar national emergency-related sanctions may be found in the National Emergencies Act and the International Emergency Economic Powers Act.

Extradition

§ 212(b)(6) Caribbean Basin Economic Recovery Act (Public Law 98-67; 19 USC 2702(b)(6)) (denies beneficiary country status)

Proliferation, Generally

§ 620(s), Foreign Assistance Act of 1961 (Public Law 87-195; 22 USC 2370(s)) (conditions foreign assistance and loans)

§ 3(f), Arms Export Control Act (Public Law 90-629; 22 USC 2753(f)) (prohibits sales or leases to nuclear explosive device proliferators)

§ 38, Arms Export Control Act (Public Law 90-629; 22 USC 2778) (establishes penalty for violating U.S. import/export terms for defense articles and services)

§ 6(k), Export Administration Act of 1979 (Public Law 96-72; 50 USC App. 2405(k)) (restricts exportation)

§ 1211, National Defense Authorization Act for Fiscal Year 1998 (Public Law 105-85) (restricts exportation of high performance computers)

Missile Proliferation

§§ 72, 73, Arms Export Control Act (Public Law 90-629; 22 USC 2797a, 2797b) (restricts contracts, denies, export licenses, may deny importation)

§ 6(l), Export Administration Act of 1979 (Public Law 96-72; 50 USC App. 2405(l)) (restricts exportation)

§ 11B, Export Administration Act of 1979 (Public Law 96-72; 50 USC App. 2410b) (restricts contracts, denies export licenses, may deny importation)

Nuclear Proliferation

§§ 101, 102, Arms Export Control Act (Public Law 90-629; 22 USC 2799aa, 2799aa-1) (prohibits foreign or military assistance)

§ 701(b), International Financial Institutions Act (Public Law 95-118; 22 USC 262d(b)) (opposes international financial institution support)

§ 2(b)(1)(B), Export-Import Bank Act of 1945 (Public Law 79-173; 12 USC 635(b)(1)(B)) (denies Bank support where President determines in U.S. national interests related to terrorism, nuclear proliferation, environmental protection, human rights)

§ 2(b)(4), 2(b)(5)(C) Export-Import Bank Act of 1945 (Public Law 79-173; 12 USC 635(b)(4)) (prohibits Export-Import Bank support)

§ 5(b), Export Administration Act of 1979 (Public Law 96-72; 50 USC App. 2404) (restricts exports for national security reasons)

Export-Import Bank of the United States, Title I, Foreign Operations, Export Financing, and Related Programs Appropriations Act, 1998 (Public Law 105-118; 111 Stat. 2386) (prohibits Export-Import Bank funding to other than non-nuclear weapon state, if that state detonates a nuclear explosive after November 26, 1997)

§ 129, Atomic Energy Act of 1954 (Public Law 83-703; 42 USC 2158) (prohibits transfer of nuclear materials, equipment, related technology)

§ 304(b), Nuclear Non-Proliferation Act of 1978 (Public Law 95-242; 42 USC 2155a) (authorizes Department of Commerce to regulate exports significant to nuclear explosion purposes)

§ 402, Nuclear Non-Proliferation Act of 1978 (Public Law 95-242; 42 USC 2153a) (prohibits exports related to nuclear enrichment)

§ 821, Nuclear Proliferation Prevention Act of 1994 (Public Law 103-236; 22 USC 3201 note) (prohibits contracts with individuals)

§ 823, Nuclear Proliferation Prevention Act of 1994 (Public Law 103-236; 22 USC 3201 note) (opposes international financial institution support)

§ 824, Nuclear Proliferation Prevention Act of 1994 (Public Law 103-236; 22 USC 3201 note) (prohibits financial institutions from financing certain transactions)

§ 620G, Foreign Assistance Act of 1961 (Public Law 87-195; 22 USC 2378a) (prohibits foreign assistance for most sales of antitank shells containing depleted uranium penetrating component)

Chemical/Biological Weapons Proliferation

§ 81, Arms Export Control Act (Public Law 90-629; 22 USC 2798) (requires import and U.S. government procurement sanctions against CW/BW proliferators)

§ 6(m), Export Administration Act of 1979 (Public Law 96-72; 50 USC App. 2405(m)) (restricts exportation)

§ 11C, Export Administration Act of 1979 (Public Law 96-72; 50 USC App. 2410c) (requires import and U.S. government procurement sanctions against CW/BW proliferators)

§ 307, Chemical and Biological Weapons Control and Warfare Elimination Act of 1991 (Public Law 102-182; 22 USC 5605) (terminates most foreign assistance, arms sales, certain exports; may restrict international financial institution support, U.S. bank support, exports, imports, diplomatic relations, aviation access to United States)

§ 2332c, 18 USC (added by § 521, Antiterrorism and Effective Death Penalty Act of 1996) (makes use of chemical weapon in certain instances a criminal offense)

Communism (Marxist-Leninist Countries)

§ 620(f), (h), Foreign Assistance Act of 1961 (Public Law 87-195; 22 USC 2370(f), (h)) (prohibits foreign assistance)

§ 2(b)(2), Export-Import Bank Act of 1945 (Public Law 79-173; 12 USC 635(b)(2)) (prohibits Export-Import Bank transactions with Marxist-Leninist state)

§ 502(b)(1), Trade Act of 1974 (Public Law 93-618; 19 USC 2462) (denies beneficiary developing country status)

§ 5(b), Export Administration Act of 1979 (Public Law 96-72; 50 USC App. 2404) (authorizes the President to restrict exportation to Communist states, to states with policies "adverse to the national security interests of the United States")

§ 43, Bretton Woods Agreements Act (Public Law 79-171; 22 USC 286aa) (opposes international financial institution support)

§ 212(b)(1), Caribbean Basin Economic Recovery Act (Public Law 98-67; 19 USC 2702(b)(1)) (denies beneficiary country status)

Coercive Family Planning Programs (Including Abortion and Involuntary Sterilization)

§ 104(f), Foreign Assistance Act of 1961 (prohibits development assistance from being made available for coercive family planning programs)

Development Assistance, title II, Foreign Operations, Export Financing, and Related Programs Appropriations Act, 1998 (Public Law 105-118; 111 Stat. 2389) (prohibits development assistance from being made available for coercive family planning programs)

§ 518, Foreign Operations, Export Financing, and Related Programs Appropriations Act, 1998 (Public Law 105-118; 111 Stat. 2411) (prohibits development assistance from being made available for coercive family planning programs or for lobbying for or against abortion)

Human Rights

§ 116, Foreign Assistance Act of 1961 (Public Law 87-195; 22 USC 2151n) (prohibits most U.S. foreign economic assistance to any country the government of which engages in a "consistent pattern of gross violations of internationally recognized human rights")

§ 502B, Foreign Assistance Act of 1961 (Public Law 87-195; 22 USC 2304) (prohibits most U.S. security assistance to any country the government of which engages in a "consistent pattern of gross violations of internationally recognized human rights")

§ 239(i), Foreign Assistance Act of 1961 (Public Law 87-195; 22 USC 2199(i)) (requires Overseas Private Investment Corporation to consider human rights when conducting programs)

§ 660, Foreign Assistance Act of 1961 (Public Law 87-195; 22 USC 2420) (prohibits funds for police training)

§ 701(a), (b), (f) International Financial Institutions Act (Public Law 95-118; 22 USC 262d) (opposes bank loans)

§ 570, Foreign Operations, Export Financing, and Related Programs Appropriations Act, 1998 (Public Law 105-118; 111 Stat. 2429) (prohibits foreign assistance to security forces of any foreign country if Secretary of state "has credible evidence that such unit has committed gross violations of human rights")

§ 579, Foreign Operations, Export Financing, and Related Programs Appropriations Act, 1997 (§ 101(c) of title I of Public Law 104-208; 22 U.S.C. 262k-2) (opposes most international financial institution transactions for any country with a custom of female genital mutilation that has not taken steps to improve education to prevent such practices)

§ 2(b)(1)(B), Export-Import Bank Act of 1945 (Public Law 79-173; 12 USC 635(b)(1)(B)) (denies Bank support where President determines in U.S. national interests related to terrorism, nuclear proliferation, environmental protection, human rights, child labor)

War Crimes

§ 561, Foreign Operations, Export Financing, and Related Programs Appropriations Act, 1998 (Public Law 105-118; 111 Stat. 2426) (prohibits foreign assistance, transactions under the Arms Export Control Act, and international financial institution support to any country that knowingly grants sanctuary to war criminals indicted by the International Criminal Tribunal for Rwanda, those indicted by any other international tribunal in good standing under international law, or those indicted for war crimes associated with the Nazi government of Germany)

§ 573, Foreign Operations, Export Financing, and Related Programs Appropriations Act, 1998 (Public Law 105-118; 111 Stat. 2430) (prohibits foreign assistance (excluding humanitarian, democratization, or border protection assistance, U.S. Armed Forces in Bosnia-requested project support, funds to implement the Brcko Arbital Decision, Dayton Agreement-related monetary or fiscal policy support, or direct lending to a non-sanctioned entity), transactions under the Arms Export Control Act, and international financial institution support to any country, entity or canton where the Secretary of State has found and determined that authorities of that entity have failed to take necessary and significant steps to apprehend and transfer to the International Criminal Tribunal for the former Yugoslavia any indicted person)

Worker Rights

§ 231A, Foreign Assistance Act of 1961 (Public Law 87-195; 22 USC 2191a) (limits Overseas Private Investment Corporation activities)

§§ 502(b)(7), (c)(7), 504, Trade Act of 1974 (Public Law 93-618; 19 USC 2462, 2464) (authorizes the President to take into account country's worker rights record when considering beneficiary developing country status)

§ 212(b)(7) Caribbean Basin Economic Recovery Act (Public Law 98-67; 19 USC 2702(b)(7)) (denies beneficiary country status)

§ 538, Foreign Operations, Export Financing, and Related Programs Appropriations Act, 1998 (Public Law 105-118; 111 Stat. 2417) (prohibits foreign assistance to projects that contribute to the violation of internationally recognized worker rights as defined in § 502(a)(4) of the Trade Act of 1974)

Use of Forced/Prison/Convict Labor

§ 307, Tariff Act of 1930 (Public Law 71-361; 19 USC 1307) (prohibits importation of goods produced or manufactured with prison labor)

Environmental Degradation

§ 118, Foreign Assistance Act of 1961 (Public Law 87-195; 22 USC 2151p-1) (denies foreign assistance related to deforestation)

§ 2(b)(1)(B), Export-Import Bank Act of 1945 (Public

Law 79-173; 12 USC 635(b)(1)(B)) (denies Export-Import Bank support where President determines in U.S. national interests related to terrorism, nuclear proliferation, environmental protection, human rights)

§ 533, Foreign Operations, Export Financing, and Related Programs Appropriations Act, 1991 (Public Law 101-513; 22 USC 262*l*) (requires U.S. Executive Directors of multilateral development banks to promote global climate change programs—includes voting against or abstaining on loans)

§ 609(b), Sea Turtle Conservation provisions (Public Law 101-162; 16 USC 1537 note) (bans importation of shrimp and shrimp products that harvest of which adversely affects sea turtle populations, unless President determines that government of harvester documents regulatory programs and sea turtle population security)

§ 901, Dolphin Protection Consumer Information Act (Public Law 101-627; 16 USC 1835) (authorizes punitive measure against those found to have mislabeled tuna products for distribution in the United States)

Military Coups D'État

§ 508, Foreign Operations, Export Financing, and Related Programs Appropriations Act, 1998 (Public Law 105-118; 111 Stat. 2407) (prohibits foreign assistance)

Debt Arrearages, Default

§ 620(c), (q) Foreign Assistance Act of 1961 (Public Law 87-195; 22 USC 2370) (prohibits or suspends foreign assistance; for FY1998, not applicable for Nicaragua and Liberia, and for narcotics-related assistance for FY1998, not applicable for Colombia, Bolivia, and Peru)

§ 512, Foreign Operations, Export Financing, and Related Programs Appropriations Act, 1998 (Public Law 105-118; 111 Stat. 2408) (prohibits foreign assistance; for FY1998, not applicable for Nicaragua and Liberia, and for narcotics-related assistance for FY1998, not applicable for Colombia, Bolivia, and Peru)

Terrorism

§ 620A, Foreign Assistance Act of 1961 (Public Law 87-195; 22 USC 2371) (prohibits foreign assistance)

§ 620G, Foreign Assistance Act of 1961 (Public Law 87-195; 22 USC 2377) (prohibits foreign assistance)

§ 620H, Foreign Assistance Act of 1961 (Public Law 87-195; 22 USC 2378) (prohibits foreign assistance)

§ 40, Arms Export Control Act (Public Law 90-629; 22 USC 2780) (prohibits sale, transfer, lease, loan, grant, credit, foreign assistance associated with munitions items to terrorist states)

§ 40A, Arms Export Control Act (Public Law 90-629; 22 USC 2781) (prohibits sale or license for export of defense articles or defense services to country determined by President, in a fiscal year, to be not cooperating with U.S. antiterrorism efforts)

§ 505, International Security and Development Cooperation Act of 1985 (Public Law 99-83; 22 USC 2349aa-9) (authorizes the President to ban importation of goods and services from state found to support international terrorism)

§ 701(a)(2), (f), International Financial Institutions Act (Public Law 95-118; 22 USC 262d(a)(2), (f)) (opposes international financial institution loans to those offering refuge to skyjackers)

§ 1621, International Financial Institutions Act (Public Law 95-118; 22 USC 262p-4q) (opposes International financial institution loans to terrorist states)

§ 6, Bretton Woods Agreements Act Amendments, 1978 (Public Law 95-435; 22 USC 286e-11) (requires opposition to International Monetary Fund assistance)

§ 502(b)(6), Trade Act of 1974 (Public Law 93-618; 19 USC 2462)

§ 6(j), Export Administration Act of 1979 (Public Law 96-72; 50 USC App. 2405(j)) ("Fenwick amendment," requires export licenses)

§ 527, Foreign Operations, Export Financing, and Related Programs Appropriations Act, 1998 (Public Law 105-118; 111 Stat. 2413) (prohibits bilateral foreign assistance)

§ 550, Foreign Operations, Export Financing, and Related Programs Appropriations Act, 1998 (Public Law 105-118; 111 Stat. 2421) (prohibits foreign assistance to any country providing lethal military equipment to a terrorist state)

§ 2332b, 18 USC (added by § 321, Antiterrorism and Effective Death Penalty Act of 1996) (makes terrorist acts that transcend national boundaries a criminal offense)

§ 2332d, 18 USC (added by § 321, Antiterrorism and Effective Death Penalty Act of 1996) (makes financial transactions with a terrorist state a criminal offense)

§ 2339A, 18 USC (added by § 321, Antiterrorism and Effective Death Penalty Act of 1996) (makes providing material support to a terrorist or terrorist state a criminal offense)

§ 2(b)(1)(B), Export-Import Bank Act of 1945 (Public Law 79-173; 12 USC 635(b)(1)(B)) (denies Bank support where President determines in U.S. national interests related to terrorism, nuclear proliferation, environmental protection, human rights)

United Nations or Other International Organization Participation

§ 307, Foreign Assistance Act of 1961 (Public Law 87-195; 22 USC 2227) (prohibits use of U.S. foreign assistance paid in as U.S. proportionate share to international organizations when those organizations run programs in Burma, Iraq, North Korea, Syria, Libya, Iran, Cuba, or with the Palestine Liberation Organization)

§ 620(u), Foreign Assistance Act of 1961 (Public Law 87-195; 22 USC 2370(u)) (conditions foreign assistance on arrearage of UN dues)

§ 5, United Nations Participation Act of 1945 (Public Law 79-264; 22 USC 287c) (restricts economic and communications relations)

§ 516, Foreign Operations, Export Financing, and Related Programs Appropriations Act, 1998 (Public Law 105-118;

111 Stat. 2410) (prohibits foreign assistance for proportionate share payments to United Nations as stated in § 307, Foreign Assistance Act, or for Libya and Iran)

§ 534, Foreign Operations, Export Financing, and Related Programs Appropriations Act, 1998 (Public Law 105-118; 111 Stat. 2416) (prohibits foreign assistance and transactions under the Arms Export Control Act to any country not in compliance with U.N. sanctions against Iraq, Serbia and Montenegro; authorizes the President to impose importation sanctions on the same countries)

§ 582, Foreign Operations, Export Financing, and Related Programs Appropriations Act, 1998 (Public Law 105-118; 111 Stat. 2435) (reduces foreign assistance to any country not in compliance with U.N. sanctions imposed against Libya)

Emigration
§ 402, Trade Act of 1974 (Public Law 93-618; 19 USC 2432) ("Jackson-Vanik amendment," restricts commercial agreements, denies most-favored-nation status)

Diplomatic Relations (Including Action Taken When Severed)
§ 620(t), Foreign Assistance Act of 1961 (Public Law 87-195; 22 USC 2370(u)) (prohibits foreign assistance and assistance under Agricultural Trade Development and Assistance Act of 1954)

Drugs (International Narcotics Control)
§ 486, 487, 490, Foreign Assistance Act of 1961 (Public Law 87-195; 22 USC 2291e, 2291f, 2291j) (restricts foreign assistance, narcotics control assistance)

§ 13, International Development Association Act (Public Law 86-565; 22 USC 284k) (opposes international financial institution support)

§ 802, Narcotics Control Trade Act (title VIII of Public Law 93-618; 19 USC 2492) (denies preferential tariff treatment, imposes importation duty, curtails air traffic between country and United States, reduces U.S. customs staff)

§ 803, Narcotics Control Trade Act (title VIII of Public Law 93-618; 19 USC 2493) (restricts sugar quota)

Missing in Action
§ 701(b)(4), International Financial Institutions Act (Public Law 95-118; 22 USC 262d(b)(4)) (requires U.S. executive directors to international financial institutions to consider MIA issue when voting on international financial institution loans to Vietnam, Laos, Russia, independent states of former Soviet Union, and Cambodia)

§ 403, Trade Act of 1974 (Public Law 93-618; 19 USC 2433). (authorizes the President to deny nondiscriminatory trade treatment, trade-related credits and investment guarantees, or commercial agreements to countries not cooperating with U.S. efforts to account fully for MIA in Southeast Asia)

Armed Conflict (Engaging Against U.S. Armed Forces)
§ 2(b)(5), Export-Import Bank Act of 1945 (Public Law 79-173; 12 USC 635(b)(5)) (prohibits Export-Import Bank credits)

World Economy Disruption, Vital Commodities Disruption
§ 502(b)(2), (b)(3), (e)(2), Trade Act of 1974 (Public Law 93-618; 19 USC 2462) (para. (2) in part, is specifically directed at Organization of Petroleum Exporting Countries (OPEC))

§ 502(b)(5), Trade Act of 1974 (Public Law 93-618; 19 USC 2462) (conditions beneficiary developing country status)

§ 7, Export Administration Act of 1979 (Public Law 96-72; 50 USC App. 2406) (restricts exports relating to short supply)

§ 8, Export Administration Act of 1979 (Public Law 96-72; 50 USC App. 2407) (prohibits cooperating with foreign boycotts)

§ 513, Foreign Operations, Export Financing, and Related Programs Appropriations Act, 1998 (Public Law 104-208; 111 Stat. 2408) (prohibits foreign assistance)

§ 514, Foreign Operations, Export Financing, and Related Programs Appropriations Act, 1998 (Public Law 104-208; 111 Stat. 2408) (requires the Secretary of the Treasury to advise U.S. Executive Directors of international financial institutions to oppose loans where funds would be used for production or extraction of any commodity or mineral for export where commodity or mineral is in world surplus supply and its production would cause substantial injury to U.S. producers)

Parking Fines
§ 551, Foreign Operations, Export Financing, and Related Programs Appropriations Act, 1998 (Public Law 105-118; 111 Stat. 2421) (withholds foreign assistance from nations whose agents or representatives in the United States are cited as parking scofflaws)

Humanitarian Assistance Disruption
§ 620I, Foreign Assistance Act of 1961 (Public Law 87-195; 22 USC 2379) (prohibits foreign assistance)

Expropriation, Confiscation, Nationalization, Mob Action, or Other Seizure of or Threat to Property
§ 620(a), (g), (j), (l), (o), Foreign Assistance Act of 1961 (Public Law 87-195; 22 USC 2370) (prohibits foreign assistance)

§ 620(e), Foreign Assistance Act of 1961 (Public Law 87-195; 22 USC 2370(e)) (suspends foreign assistance)

§ 12, International Development Association Act (Public Law 86-565; 22 USC 284j) (opposes international financial institution support)

§ 502(b)(4), Trade Act of 1974 (Public Law 93-618; 19 USC 2462) (denies beneficiary developing country status)

§ 212(b)(2), (3), Caribbean Basin Economic Recovery Act (Public Law 98-67; 19 USC 2702(b)(2), (3)) (denies beneficiary country status)

Crime Control
§ 6(n), Export Administration Act of 1979 (Public Law 96-72; 50 USC App. 2405(n)) (restricts exports)

Palestine Liberation Organization (PLO); Palestinian Authority

§ 307, Foreign Assistance Act of 1961 (Public Law 87-195; 22 USC 2227) (prohibits use of U.S. foreign assistance paid in as U.S. proportionate share to international organizations when those organizations run programs in Burma, Iraq, North Korea, Syria, Libya, Iran, Cuba, or with the Palestine Liberation Organization)

§ 552, Foreign Operations, Export Financing and Related Programs Appropriations Act, 1998 (Public Law 105-118; 111 Stat. 2422) (prohibits foreign assistance to the PLO for the West Bank and Gaza unless the President invokes authority pursuant to § 604(a) of the Middle East Peace Facilitation Act of 1995)

§ 566, Foreign Operations, Export Financing and Related Programs Appropriations Act, 1998 (Public Law 105-118; 111 Stat. 2428) (prohibits Economic Support funds for the Palestinian Authority)

§ 114(a), State Department Authorization Act, FY1984-1985 (Public Law 98-164; 22 USC 287e note) (prohibits U.S. funds to United Nations from being used to support certain Palestinian entities (similar language in subsequent foreign relations authorization measures))

§ 414, Foreign Relations Authorization Act, FY1990-1991 (Public Law 101-246; 22 USC 287e note) (prohibits U.S. funds to United Nations if it accords the PLO status equal to that of its member states)

§ 37, Bretton Woods Agreements Act (Public Law 79-171; 22 USC 286w) (states that granting of member or observer status to PLO by the International Monetary Fund would "result in a serious diminution of United States support")

§ 1003, Anti-Terrorism Act of 1987 (Public Law 100-204; 22 USC 5202) (prohibits to receive anything of value from, expend funds from, or establish an office for, the PLO)

Current Law Related to Specific Countries

Afghanistan

§ 620D, Foreign Assistance Act of 1961 (Public Law 87-195; 22 USC 2374) (prohibits foreign assistance)

Angola

§ 2(b)(11), Export-Import Bank Act of 1945 (Public Law 79-173; 12 USC 635(b)(11)) (prohibits Export-Import Bank credits)

§ 316, National Defense Authorization Act for Fiscal Year 1987 (Public Law 99-661; 10 USC 2304 note) (prohibits Department of Defense contracts)

Azerbaijan

Assistance for the New Independent States (NIS) of the Former Soviet Union, title II, Foreign Operations, Export Financing, and Related Programs Appropriations Act, 1998 (Public Law 105-118; 111 Stat. 2397) (subsec. (n) prohibits foreign assistance to Azerbaijan until the President determines and certifies that the Government of Azerbaijan is taking demonstrable steps to cease all blockades against Armenia and Nagorno-Karabakh (excludes funds for democracy building, TDA, or the U.S. and Foreign Commercial Service))

Bosnia-Hercegovina

Assistance for Eastern Europe and the Baltic States, title II, Foreign Operations, Export Financing, and Related Programs Appropriations Act, 1998 (Public Law 105-118; 111 Stat. 2394) (withholds economic revitalization funds for Bosnia-Hercegovina until President certifies as to withdrawal of foreign forces and cessation of cooperation between Iranian and Bosnian intelligence communities)

§ 8132, Department of Defense Appropriations Act, 1998 (prohibits use of DOD funds for deployment of U.S. Armed Forces in Bosnia and Hercegovina past June 30, 1998, unless certain conditions are met)

Burma (Myanmar)

§ 138, Customs and Trade Act of 1990 (Public Law 101-382) (authorizes President to impose such economic sanctions as he determines to be appropriate)

§ 307, Foreign Assistance Act of 1961 (Public Law 87-195; 22 USC 2227) (prohibits use of U.S. foreign assistance paid in as U.S. proportionate share to international organizations when those organizations run programs in Burma, Iraq, North Korea, Syria, Libya, Iran, Cuba, or with the Palestine Liberation Organization)

§ 516, Foreign Operations, Export Financing, and Related Programs Appropriations Act, 1998 (Public Law 105-118; 111 Stat. 2410) (prohibits foreign assistance for proportionate share payments to United Nations as stated in § 307, Foreign Assistance Act, or for Libya and Iran)

§ 570, Foreign Operations, Export Financing, and Related Programs Appropriations Act, 1997 (§ 101(c) of title I of Public Law 104-208) (prohibits most foreign assistance; requires "no" votes in international financial institutions; authorizes President to restrict visas and impose investment sanctions, until such time that the President determines and certifies that Burma has made measurable and substantial progress in improving human rights and implementing democratic government)

Cambodia

§ 906, International Security and Development Cooperation Act of 1985 (Public Law 99-83) (prohibits certain aid to Khmer Rouge)

Cambodia, title II, Foreign Operations, Export Financing, and Related Programs Appropriations Act, 1998 (Public Law 105-118; 111 Stat. 2390) (prohibits most foreign assistance to Government of Cambodia (excluding humanitarian, demining, or election-related programs or activities))

§ 589, Foreign Operations, Export Financing, and Related Programs Appropriations Act, 1998 (Public Law 105-118; 111 Stat. 2438) (requires the Secretary of the Treasury to instruct U.S. executive directors of international financial institutions to oppose loans to Government of Cambodia, except loans supporting basic human needs)

Chile

§ 726, International Security and Development Cooperation Act of 1981 (Public Law 97-113) (prohibits most security and military assistance to Chile until the President certifies on certain conditions in human rights, terrorism, extraterritorial assassination)

Congo (Former Zaire)

§ 585, Foreign Operations, Export Financing, and Related Programs Appropriations Act, 1998 (Public Law 105-118; 111 Stat. 2437) (prohibits foreign assistance to the central Government of the Democratic Republic of Congo until President determines and certifies as to its cooperation with U.N. investigators in accounting for human rights violations in Congo or adjacent countries)

Cuba

§ 307, Foreign Assistance Act of 1961 (Public Law 87-195; 22 USC 2227) (prohibits use of U.S. foreign assistance paid in as U.S. proportionate share to international organizations when those organizations run programs in Burma, Iraq, North Korea, Syria, Libya, Iran, Cuba, or with the Palestine Liberation Organization)

§ 620(a), Foreign Assistance Act of 1961 (Public Law 87-195; 22 USC 2370(a)) (prohibits foreign assistance; authorizes total embargo)

§ 902(c), Food Security Act of 1985 (Public Law 99-198; 7 USC 1446 note) (prohibits sugar import quota to any country found to be importing for reexport to the United States sugar produced in Cuba)

§ 507, Foreign Operations, Export Financing, and Related Programs Appropriations Act, 1998 (Public Law 105-118; 111 Stat. 2407) (prohibits direct foreign assistance)

§ 516, Foreign Operations, Export Financing, and Related Programs Appropriations Act, 1998 (Public Law 105-118; 111 Stat. 2410) (prohibits foreign assistance for proportionate share payments to United Nations as stated in § 307, Foreign Assistance Act, or for Libya and Iran)

§ 523, Foreign Operations, Export Financing, and Related Programs Appropriations Act, 1998 (Public Law 104-208; 111 Stat. 2412) (prohibits indirect foreign assistance)

§ 1704(b), Cuban Democracy Act of 1992 (Public Law 102-484; 22 USC 6003(b)) (authorizes the prohibition of foreign assistance, arms export assistance, and debt forgiveness to any country conducting trade with Cuba)

§ 1705, Cuban Democracy Act of 1992 (Public Law 102-484; 22 USC 6004) (limits terms for donations and exportation of food and medicine to Cuba) § 1706, Cuban Democracy Act of 1992 (Public Law 102-484; 22 USC 6005) (prohibits licenses for exportation to Cuba; restricts port access to ships that have docked in Cuba; restricts remittances)

§ 102(h), Cuban Liberty and Democratic Solidarity (LIBERTAD) Act of 1996 (Public Law 104-114;22 USC 6032) (codifies 31 CFR part 515 (Cuban Assets Control Regulations) in permanent law)

§ 103, Cuban Liberty and Democratic Solidarity (LIBERTAD) Act of 1996 (Public Law 104-114;22 USC 6033) (prohibits indirect financing of any transaction involving confiscated property the claim to which is owned by a U.S. national)

§ 104, Cuban Liberty and Democratic Solidarity (LIBERTAD) Act of 1996 (Public Law 104-114;22 USC 6034) (authorizes opposition in international financial institutions to admission of Cuba; reduces U.S. contribution to any international financial institution that completes most transactions with Cuba)

§ 105, Cuban Liberty and Democratic Solidarity (LIBERTAD) Act of 1996 (Public Law 104-114;22 USC 6035) (requires continued effort to maintain suspension of Government of Cuba from Organization of American States participation)

§ 111(b), Cuban Liberty and Democratic Solidarity (LIBERTAD) Act of 1996 (Public Law 104-114;22 USC 6041(b)) (withholds assistance from any country found to be supporting the completion of Cuba's nuclear facility at Juragua, Cuba)

§ 302, Cuban Liberty and Democratic Solidarity (LIBERTAD) Act of 1996 (Public Law 104-114;22 USC 6082) (makes liable for civil claims anyone trafficking in confiscated property, to which a U.S. citizen has made a claim, in Cuba)

§ 401, Cuban Liberty and Democratic Solidarity (LIBERTAD) Act of 1996 (Public Law 104-114;22 USC 6091) (authorizes the Secretary of State to deny a visa to any alien who has trafficked in confiscated property in Cuba)

Guatemala

International Military Education and Training, title III, Foreign Operations, Export Financing, and Related Programs Appropriations Act, 1998 (Public Law 105-118; 111 Stat. 2400) (restricts International Military Education and Training funding)

Foreign Military Financing Program, title III, Foreign Operations, Export Financing, and Related Programs Appropriations Act, 1998 (Public Law 105-118; 111 Stat. 2403) (prohibits Foreign Military Finance funding)

Haiti

§ 562, Foreign Operations, Export Financing, and Related Programs Appropriations Act, 1998 (Public Law 105-118; 111 Stat. 2427) (prohibits foreign assistance, excluding humanitarian, electoral, counter-narcotics, or law enforcement assistance)

§ 621, Department of State Appropriations Act, FY1998 (Public Law 105-119; 111 Stat. 2520) (prohibits State Department funding for visa issuance to certain Haitians involved in extrajudicial and political killings, or to certain members of the Haitian High Command during 1991–1994)

Indonesia

International Military Education and Training, title III, Foreign Operations, Export Financing, and Related Programs Appropriations Act, 1998 (Public Law 105-118; 111 Stat. 2400) (restricts International Military Education and Training funding)

§ 571, Foreign Operations, Export Financing, and Related Programs Appropriations Act, 1998 (Public Law 105-118; 111 Stat. 2429) (requires any agreement for sale, transfer, or licensing of lethal equipment or helicopter for Indonesia entered into by United States to state that the United States expects that the items will not be used in East Timor)

Iran

§ 307, Foreign Assistance Act of 1961 (Public Law 87-195; 22 USC 2227) (prohibits use of U.S. foreign assistance paid in as U.S. proportionate share to international organizations when those organizations run programs in Burma, Iraq, North Korea, Syria, Libya, Iran, Cuba, or with the Palestine Liberation Organization)

§ 507, Foreign Operations, Export Financing, and Related Programs Appropriations Act, 1998 (Public Law 105-118; 111 Stat. 2407) (prohibits direct foreign assistance)

§ 516, Foreign Operations, Export Financing, and Related Programs Appropriations Act, 1998 (Public Law 105-118; 111 Stat. 2410) (prohibits foreign assistance for proportionate share payments to United Nations as stated in § 307, Foreign Assistance Act, or for Libya and Iran)

§ 523, Foreign Operations, Export Financing, and Related Programs Appropriations Act, 1998 (Public Law 105-118; 111 Stat. 2412) (prohibits indirect foreign assistance)

§ Iran Sanctions Act of 1990 (§ 586 through 586J of Public Law 101-513) (made applicable to Iran pursuant to § 1603, Public Law 102-484; see discussion under "Iraq")

§ 1604, Iran-Iraq Arms Nonproliferation Act of 1992 (Public Law 102-484; 50 USC 1701 note) (sanctions individuals for contributing to Iraq's or Iran's efforts to acquire chemical, biological, nuclear, or destabilizing numbers and types of advanced conventional weapons)

§ 1605, Iran-Iraq Arms Nonproliferation Act of 1992 (Public Law 102-484; 50 USC 1701 note) (sanctions foreign countries for contributing to Iraq's or Iran's efforts to acquire chemical, biological, nuclear, or destabilizing numbers and types of advanced conventional weapons)

§§ 5, 6, Iran and Libya Sanctions Act of 1996 (Public Law 104-172; 50 USC 1701 note) (authorizes the President to impose two or more of following sanctions on person if found to have engaged in investment in Iran: prohibit Export-Import Bank assistance, deny export licenses, prohibit U.S. financial institutions from making loans to sanctioned person, further restrict financial institutions from certain transactions, prohibit procurement contracts, restrict importation)

Iraq

§ 586C, 586F, 586G, Iraq Sanctions Act (in title V of the Foreign Operations, Export Financing, and Related Programs Appropriations Act, 1991; Public Law 101-513) (continues President's imposition of trade embargo; prohibits arms sales, foreign military financing programs, export licenses for U.S. Munitions List items, items controlled for national security or foreign policy reasons, and nuclear equipment, materials, and technology. Requires U.S. vote against international financial institution funding, prohibited Export-Import bank funding, Commodity Credit Corporation assistance, and most U.S. foreign assistance)

§ 307, Foreign Assistance Act of 1961 (Public Law 87-195; 22 USC 2227) (prohibits use of U.S. foreign assistance paid in as U.S. proportionate share to international organizations when those organizations run programs in Burma, Iraq, North Korea, Syria, Libya, Iran, Cuba, or with the Palestine Liberation Organization)

§ 507, Foreign Operations, Export Financing, and Related Programs Appropriations Act, 1998 (Public Law 105-118; 111 Stat. 2407) (prohibits direct foreign assistance)

§ 516, Foreign Operations, Export Financing, and Related Programs Appropriations Act, 1998 (Public Law 105-118; 111 Stat. 2410) (prohibits foreign assistance for proportionate share payments to United Nations as stated in § 307, Foreign Assistance Act, or for Libya and Iran)

§ 523, Foreign Operations, Export Financing, and Related Programs Appropriations Act, 1998 (Public Law 105-118; 111 Stat. 2412) (prohibits indirect foreign assistance)

§ 534, Foreign Operations, Export Financing, and Related Programs Appropriations Act, 1998 (Public Law 105-118; 111 Stat. 2416) (prohibits foreign assistance and transactions under the Arms Export Control Act to any country not in compliance with U.N. sanctions against Iraq)

§ 1604, Iran-Iraq Arms Nonproliferation Act of 1992 (Public Law 102-484; 50 USC 1701 note) (sanctions individuals for contributing to Iraq's or Iran's efforts to acquire chemical, biological, nuclear, or destabilizing numbers and types of advanced conventional weapons)

§ 1605, Iran-Iraq Arms Nonproliferation Act of 1992 (Public Law 102-484; 50 USC 1701 note) (sanctions foreign countries for contributing to Iraq's or Iran's efforts to acquire chemical, biological, nuclear, or destabilizing numbers and types of advanced conventional weapons)

Liberia

Foreign Military Financing Program, title III, Foreign Operations, Export Financing, and Related Programs Appropriations Act, 1998 (Public Law 105-118; 111 Stat. 2402) (prohibits Foreign Military Financing funding)

Libya

§ 307, Foreign Assistance Act of 1961 (Public Law 87-195; 22 USC 2227) (prohibits use of U.S. foreign assistance paid in as U.S. proportionate share to international organizations when those organizations run programs in Burma, Iraq, North Korea, Syria, Libya, Iran, Cuba, or with the Palestine Liberation Organization)

§ 504, International Security and Development Cooperation Act of 1985 (Public Law 99-83) (authorizes the President to prohibit importation and exportation of goods and services from/to Libya)

§ 507, Foreign Operations, Export Financing, and Related Programs Appropriations Act, 1998 (Public Law 105-118; 111 Stat. 2407) (prohibits direct foreign assistance)

§ 516, Foreign Operations, Export Financing, and Related Programs Appropriations Act, 1998 (Public Law 104-208;

111 Stat. 2410) (prohibits foreign assistance for proportionate share payments to United Nations as stated in § 307, Foreign Assistance Act, or for Libya and Iran)

§ 523, Foreign Operations, Export Financing, and Related Programs Appropriations Act, 1998 (Public Law 105-118; 111 Stat. 2412) (prohibits indirect foreign assistance)

§§ 5, 6, Iran and Libya Sanctions Act of 1996 (Public Law 104-172; 50 USC 1701 note) (authorizes the President to impose two or more of following sanctions on person if found to have engaged in investment in Libya: prohibit Export-Import Bank assistance, deny export licenses, prohibit U.S. financial institutions from making loans to sanctioned person, further restrict financial institutions from certain transactions, prohibit procurement contracts, restrict importation)

§ 5, Iran and Libya Sanctions Act of 1996 (Public Law 104-172; 50 USC 1701 note) (further requires mandatory sanctions as described above if person is found to have contributed to Libya's ability to acquire chemical, biological, or nuclear weapons or destabilizing numbers and types of advanced conventional weapons, or enhanced Libya' military or paramilitary capabilities; contributed to Libya's petroleum resource development; contributed to Libya's ability to maintain its aviation capabilities)

Mauritania

§ 202, Human Rights, Refugee, and Other Foreign Relations Provisions Act of 1996 (Public Law 104-319; 22 USC 2151 note) (states the President *should* prohibit economic and military assistance and arms transfers to Government of Mauritania for human rights reasons)

Nicaragua

§ 722, International Security and Development Cooperation Act of 1985 (Public Law 99-83) (prohibits foreign assistance and arms sales to paramilitary organizations and insurgent groups in Nicaragua)

North Korea

§ 307, Foreign Assistance Act of 1961 (Public Law 87-195; 22 USC 2227) (prohibits use of U.S. foreign assistance paid in as U.S. proportionate share to international organizations when those organizations run programs in Burma, Iraq, North Korea, Syria, Libya, Iran, Cuba, or with the Palestine Liberation Organization)

International Organizations and Programs, title IV, Foreign Operations, Export Financing, and Related Programs Appropriations Act, 1998 (Public Law 105-118; 111 Stat. 2405) (prohibits IO & P funding from being made available for Korean Peninsula Energy Development Organization (KEDO) programs)

§ 507, Foreign Operations, Export Financing, and Related Programs Appropriations Act, 1998 (Public Law 105-118; 111 Stat. 2407) (prohibits direct foreign assistance)

§ 516, Foreign Operations, Export Financing, and Related Programs Appropriations Act, 1998 (Public Law 105-118; 111 Stat. 2410) (prohibits foreign assistance for proportionate share payments to United Nations as stated in § 307, Foreign Assistance Act, or for Libya and Iran)

§ 523, Foreign Operations, Export Financing, and Related Programs Appropriations Act, 1998 (Public Law 104-208; 111 Stat. 2412) (prohibits indirect foreign assistance)

§ 8066, Department of Defense Appropriations Act, 1998 (Public Law 105-56) (prohibits DOD appropriations assistance)

Pakistan

§ 620E(e), Foreign Assistance Act of 1961 (Public Law 87-195; 22 USC 2375(e)) (prohibits military assistance and military sales)

Panama

§ 1302, National Defense Authorization Act, Fiscal Year 1989 (Public Law 100-456; 22 USC 2151 note) (prohibits U.S. funding for Panamanian Defense Force)

People's Republic of China

Public Law 99-183 (99 Stat. 1174) (requires certification that China is not violating sec. 129 of the Atomic Energy Act of 1954)

§ 103, International Development and Finance Act of 1989 (Public Law 101-240; 12 USC 635 note) (prohibits finance of trade with, or credits, loan, credit guarantees, insurance or reinsurance to China; waived on day it was signed into law)

§ 902, Foreign Relations Authorization Act, Fiscal Years 1990 and 1991 (Public Law 101-246; 22 USC 2151 note) (continues: suspension Overseas Private Investment Corporation insurance, reinsurance, financing or guarantees; suspension new projects by the Trade and Development Agency; suspension of exports of most defense articles on the U.S. Munitions List (USML); and nuclear trade and cooperation. Prohibits: export licenses for crime control and detection equipment; Suspends: U.S. satellite exports and liberalization of multilateral export controls)

§ 610, Departments of Commerce, Justice, and State, the Judiciary, and Related Agencies Appropriations Act, 1990 (Public Law 101-162). (prohibits State Department appropriations to be used for approving export licenses to China for launch of U.S.-built satellites; waived on case-by-case basis)

International Organizations and Programs, title IV, Foreign Operations, Export Financing, and Related Programs Appropriations Act, 1998 (Public Law 105-118; 111 Stat. 2405) (prohibits U.S. funds payable to U.N. family planning program (UNFPA) from being applied to programs in China)

§ 523, Foreign Operations, Export Financing, and Related Programs Appropriations Act, 1998 (Public Law 105-118; 111 Stat. 2412) (prohibits indirect foreign assistance)

§ 2826, National Defense Authorization Act for Fiscal Year 1998 (Public Law 105-85) (prohibits conveyance of Long Beach Naval Station property to the China Ocean Shipping Company—COSCO)

Russia (See Also [Former] Soviet Union/East Bloc)

§ 498A(b), Foreign Assistance Act of 1961 (Public Law 87-195;22 USC 2295A(b)) (states ineligibility for foreign assistance to governments of the independent states)

§ 498A(d), Foreign Assistance Act of 1961 (Public Law 87-195; 22 USC 2295A(d)) (reduces foreign assistance when Russia is found to be assisting Cuba with intelligence facilities)

Assistance for the New Independent States of the Former Soviet Union, title II, Foreign Operations, Export Financing, and Related Programs Appropriations Act, 1998 (Public Law 105-118; 111 Stat. 2395) (subsec. (b): prohibits funds under this paragraph from being made available to Russia unless that government is making progress in implementing comprehensive economic reforms, or if that government is found to be transferring such funds to support expropriation or property seizure. Subsec. (j) withholds 50 percent of funding under this paragraph until the President determines and certifies that Russia has terminated arrangements with Iran to provide that country nuclear technical expertise, training, technology, or equipment)

§ 577, Foreign Operations, Export Financing, and Related Programs Appropriations Act, 1998 (Public Law 105-118; 111 Stat. 2433) (prohibits foreign assistance to Government of the Russian Federation unless President determines and certifies that the Government of the Russian Federation "has implemented no statute, executive order, regulation or similar government action that would discriminate, or would have as its principal effect discrimination, against religious groups or religious communities...")

§ 2(b)(12), Export-Import Bank Act of 1945 (12 U.S.C. 635(b)(12)) (prohibits Export-Import Bank guarantees, insurance, credits, or other participation in connection with transactions of the Russian military if the military or government transfer or deliver an SS-N-22 missile system to China)

§ 1406, National Defense Authorization Act for Fiscal Year 1998 (Public Law 105-85) (restricts Cooperative Threat Reduction funds to Russia until President certifies on implementation of Bilateral Destruction Agreement and general national security issues)

Serbia and Montenegro

§ 1511, National Defense Authorization Act for Fiscal Year 1994 (Public Law 103-160; 50 USC 1701 note) (prohibits broad range of relations, freezes assets, travel, assistance, international financial institution support)

[Former] Soviet Union/East Bloc

§ 498A(b), Foreign Assistance Act of 1961 (Public Law 87-195; 22 USC 2295A(b)) (states ineligibility for foreign assistance to governments of the independent states)

§ 11A, Export Administration Act of 1979 (Public Law 96-72; 50 USC App. 2410a) (prohibits exports)

Assistance for the New Independent States (NIS) of the Former Soviet Union, title II, Foreign Operations, Export Financing, and Related Programs Appropriations Act, 1998 (Public Law 105-118; 111 Stat. 2395) (subsec. (c) prohibits most foreign assistance to any NIS violating another NIS's sovereignty (excludes humanitarian and refugee relief assistance. Subsec. (d) prohibits funding under this paragraph to be used for enhancing military capacity (excluding demilitarization, demining, or nonproliferation programs))

Sudan

Foreign Military Financing Program, title III, Foreign Operations, Export Financing, and Related Programs Appropriations Act, 199 (Public Law 105-118; 111 Stat. 2402) (prohibits Foreign Military Financing funding)

§ 507, Foreign Operations, Export Financing, and Related Programs Appropriations Act, 1998 (Public Law 105-118; 111 Stat. 2407) (prohibits direct foreign assistance)

Syria

§ 307, Foreign Assistance Act of 1961 (Public Law 87-195; 22 USC 2227) (prohibits use of U.S. foreign assistance paid in as U.S. proportionate share to international organizations when those organizations run programs in Burma, Iraq, North Korea, Syria, Libya, Iran, Cuba, or with the Palestine Liberation Organization)

§ 507, Foreign Operations, Export Financing, and Related Programs Appropriations Act, 1998 (Public Law 105-118; 111 Stat. 2407) (prohibits direct foreign assistance)

§ 516, Foreign Operations, Export Financing, and Related Programs Appropriations Act, 1998 (Public Law 105-118; 111 Stat. 2410) (prohibits foreign assistance for proportionate share payments to United Nations as stated in § 307, Foreign Assistance Act, or for Libya and Iran)

§ 523, Foreign Operations, Export Financing, and Related Programs Appropriations Act, 1998 (Public Law 105-118; 111 Stat. 2412) (prohibits indirect foreign assistance)

Turkey

§ 620(x), Foreign Assistance Act of 1961 (Public Law 87-195; 22 USC 2370(x)) (suspends military assistance and transactions)

§ 565, Foreign Operations, Export Financing, and Related Programs Appropriations Act, 1998 (Public Law 105-118; 111 Stat. 2428) (limits Economic Support funds)

Ukraine

Assistance for the New Independent States of the Former Soviet Union, title II, Foreign Operations, Export Financing, and Related Programs Appropriations Act, 1998 (Public Law 105-118; 111 Stat. 2395) (subsec. (k) withholds 50 percent of funding made available to Ukraine under this paragraph until the Secretary of State determines and certifies that Ukraine has made significant progress toward resolving complaints of U.S. investors)

Vietnam (Socialist Republic of)

§ 610, State Department Appropriations Act, FY1998 (Public Law 105-119; 111 Stat. 2517) (prohibits State Department funding for diplomatic or consular post until certain conditions are met)

Order 97-949F, Updated June 5, 1998

State Sponsors of Terrorism

Overview on State Sponsors of Terrorism

Anna Sabasteanski

The concept of state-sponsored terrorism was first formulated in the 1970s, when countries in the Middle East, particularly Iran, Iraq, Lebanon, Libya, and Syria, supported the Palestinian resistance against the state of Israel. This support existed across the spectrum from nonviolent to violent; from political statements to financial and operational support and training for Palestinian militants, and even to active participation in militant activities.

At around the same time, another form of state-sponsored terrorism emerged as a product of the Cold War. Both the Soviet Union and the United States became involved in proxy wars fought in Africa, Asia and South America, each superpower supporting local groups more or less aligned with its geopolitical stance. Armed by their superpower sponsors, both left- and right-wing paramilitary groups often terrorized local populations during the course of various conflicts.

Both these threads are reflected in the U.S. Department of State's reports of the time. For example, in 1985 Cuba and Nicaragua were both cited for supporting guerrilla groups internally and in the region. In the Middle East, Libya, Syria, and Iran were described as directly planning and orchestrating attacks (hijackings in particular) worldwide. As for the Soviet Union, one State Department report (*Patterns of Global Terrorism* 1985, 8) noted that it "continued to support various 'national liberation movements'—such as the PLO and the African National Congress (ANC)—with the knowledge that some of those they train later commit terrorist acts." Much of this support was through provision of arms, including items that have become perennial favorites among terrorists, including Semtex explosives and the Kalashnikov rifle.

International sanctions designed to thwart state sponsorship of terrorism had little impact compared with broader economic changes. The reduction in oil wealth (after Middle Eastern oil production began to fall in the 1970s) beginning in the 1980s reduced the ability of Middle Eastern countries to keep money flowing to the Palestinians. Economic problems in a number of Caribbean and South American countries led state sponsors of terrorism to turn to the lucrative narcotics trade, which is now responsible for financing most of the acts of terrorism and political violence in the region.

Then in 1991, the Soviet Union collapsed. The subsequent chaos created safe havens for terrorists and organized crime throughout Central Asia and Eastern Europe. In many war- and poverty-plagued parts of Africa and in Afghanistan, failed and failing states also provide safe havens.

The Legislation behind the Designation

The U.S. secretary of state is responsible for designating as state sponsors of terrorism those countries that have repeatedly supported acts of international terrorism. Three laws endow the secretary of state with that power and responsibility and provide for sanctions against offending countries; those laws are the Export Administration Act (1979), the Arms Export Control Act (1994), and the Foreign Assistance Act (1961).

The Export Administration Act

Under Section 6(j) of the Export Administration Act, the Department of State is responsible for issuing the licenses for the export of those defense articles and services that require them (items requiring licenses before they can be exported are all listed on the U.S. Munitions List). Certain items are classified as dual use: they have both military and nonmilitary applications. Such items require licenses not only from the Department of State but also from the Department of Commerce before they can be exported. The Export Administration Act of 1979 expired in 1994, was reauthorized, and expired again in 2001. Since then export controls have been issued under presidential executive orders. As might be expected, arms-related exports and sales to designated state sponsors of terrorism may be banned, and export of dual-use items may be heavily controlled. State sponsors of terrorism also face other penalties.

The Arms Export Control Act

Section 40 of the Arms Export Control Act prohibits the transfer of munitions by export, sale, lease, loan, grant, or other means to countries supporting acts of international terrorism as specified by the secretary of state pursuant to the Foreign Assistance Act.

The Foreign Assistance Act

Section 620A of the Foreign Assistance Act prohibits certain forms of aid, such as military assistance, debt relief, and other economic assistance, to countries that have repeatedly provided support for acts of international terrorism, as determined by the secretary of state.

Sanctions

Countries that have been designated as state sponsors of terrorism face sanctions that may include:

- being banned from receiving arms-related exports and sales
- having their companies prohibited from receiving U.S. Defense Department contracts above $100,000
- having their imports of dual-use items subjected to controls; for example, notification of the U.S. Congress thirty days prior to the transaction
- denial of duty-free treatment for their exports to the United States
- prohibition of economic assistance
- denial of diplomatic immunity, which makes it possible for families of terrorist victims to file civil lawsuits in U.S. courts
- financial restrictions; for example, the United States may be required to oppose loans by the World Bank and other international financial institutions to such states, or U.S. citizens may be prohibited from engaging in financial transactions with such states without a license from the Treasury Department, or companies and individuals that earn income in such states may be denied tax credits that they would otherwise receive

The Nations Designated as State Sponsors of Terrorism

For nearly two decades, Iran, Iraq, Syria, Libya, North Korea, Cuba, and Sudan were the seven nations that the secretary of state repeatedly designated as state sponsors of international terrorism. Prior to the terrorist attacks of September 11, 2001, the United States was considering adding Pakistan to this list because of reports that Pakistan supported terrorist groups and elements active in Kashmir, the Taliban in Afghanistan (which harbored al-Qaeda), the Egyptian Islamic Jihad, and the Islamic Movement of Uzbekistan. However, in the light of Pakistan's support for the post-September 11 U.S. war on terrorism, any thought of designating it a state sponsor of terrorism has been abandoned. Even the news that Abdul Qadeer Khan, the leader of Pakistan's nuclear program, had sold nuclear weapons technology to North Korea, Iran, and Libya, did not lead to sanctions. The Department of State has also been monitoring the situation in Lebanon, where a variety of terrorist groups operated and trained, but Lebanon has not been added to the list of state sponsors and is not likely to be during its current period of transition following Syria's 2005 military withdrawal.

In October 2004, following the U.S.-led invasion, Iraq was removed from the list. Libya has not been removed from the list, although in 2004 the United States lifted many sanctions after it cooperated with U.N. requirements related to the downing of Pan Am Flight 103 over Lockerbie, Scotland—a terrorist event in which it was involved—and declared that it would dismantle all of its nuclear and chemical weapons programs.

In this section, we have collated the annual reports for each country reported as a state sponsor in *Patterns of Global Terrorism*: Afghanistan (including the reports on Osama bin Laden), Cuba, Iran, Iraq, Libya, Nicaragua, North Korea, South Yemen, the Soviet Union and Eastern Europe, Sudan, and Syria. Also relevant is the previous section on "Sanctions" and the Congressional Research Report, "Terrorism and National Security: Issues and Trends" in the opening section on "U.S. Policies in Combating Terrorism."

Collated Reports on State Sponsors of Terrorism

From Patterns of Global Terrorism

Afghanistan

1987

The Afghanistan-sponsored terrorist campaign in 1987 spread beyond the North-West Frontier Province to major cities in Pakistan. The campaign is being waged by the Afghan Ministry of State Security, WAD. In addition to assassinations and bombing of civilians, the campaign included attacks against public utilities in major cities, particularly in the North-West Frontier Province. Pakistan's President Zia asserted in November that the bombings were staged "at the behest of the Soviet Union," but Moscow has vehemently denied any complicity.

In view of the close relationship WAD has with the KGB, however, we consider it likely that the Soviet Union has been cognizant of Afghan intelligence's overall operations in Pakistan.

Most of the explosive devices recovered in Pakistan during the terrorist campaign have been of Soviet manufacture. Some of the materiel can be purchased on the international black market, but the time-delay devices used in many of the bombings can be obtained only through Soviet sources.

A Pakistani Government report states that approximately 1,500 Soviet advisors work with the WAD. We expect most Soviet advisers to leave Afghanistan as their troops withdraw.

Afghan agents have also carried out terrorist operations in Iran, although details of these activities are not well known. WAD agents are widely credited with assassinating a major Mujahedin leader in Iran last year.

In their insurgency against the Kabul regime, Mujahedin guerillas generally eschew acts of violence that put civilians in jeopardy. Some bombs were detonated in Kabul, however, in areas where the likelihood of causing civilian casualties was high. The Mujahedin claimed responsibility for a car bomb blast in Jalalabad in 1987 in which there were significant civilian casualties.

The United States has registered strong concerns to the Afghan Government as well as with the Soviet Union over the WAD campaign and will continue to monitor the situation closely.

1988

Afghanistan has sponsored a bombing campaign against Pakistan since the mid-1980s in an effort to turn Pakistanis against the Afghan refugees and undermine Islamabad's support for the Afghan resistance. The bombings decreased from 128 in 1987 to 118 in 1988 but continue well above the level in 1986, when there were 22. The nature of the campaign changed in 1988:

The primary venue of bombings shifted back to the North-West Frontier Province and the Federally Administered Tribal Areas, after a number of bloody bombings in 1987 in major cities in Sind and Punjab Provinces. Bombings were renewed during the last quarter in major cities outside the border areas; probably to signal Kabul's displeasure with Islamabad's continuing support for Mujahedin operations against withdrawing Soviet troops.

The fatality rate declined by half in 1988, not only because of the shift of venue away from the main cities, but also because the terrorists have not used car bombs since December 1987.

The number of bombings also began to trail off in the second half of 1988. We attribute this to a number of factors: WAD may have had trouble infiltrating terrorists into Pakistan, as the Mujahedin controlled more Afghan territory adjacent to Pakistan; Pakistani security may have improved; and Kabul may have decided to decrease the bombings—at least against crowded Pakistani civilian areas—after the Geneva accords were signed in May.

There are also indications that WAD shifted its resources to attack Afghan rebel supply sites in Pakistan:

On 10 April a major explosion at an arms depot outside Rawalpindi killed over 100 persons and wounded approximately 1,100 others. Although the cause of the explosion was never determined, sabotage is suspected.

On 14 April an explosion in Chaman killed six persons and wounded up to 50 others. It was almost certainly caused by sabotage.

The Afghan WAD received training in 1988 by the Soviet KGB, but there is no evidence linking Soviet personnel to direct participation in terrorist operations. We consider it likely, however, that the Soviet Union has been cognizant of Afghan intelligence's overall operations in Pakistan. Pakistani sources report that physical evidence found at the sites of terrorist attacks indicates that much of the explosives and related materials are Soviet manufactured, such as specialized Soviet-made timing devices that have little utility in a military inventory.

1997

Usama Bin Ladin

Usama bin Muhammad bin Awad Bin Ladin is one of the most significant sponsors of Sunni Islamic terrorist groups. The youngest son of Saudi construction magnate Muhammad Bin Ladin, Usama joined the Afghan resistance almost immediately after the Soviet invasion in December 1979.

He played a significant role in financing, recruiting, transporting, and training Arab nationals who volunteered to fight in Afghanistan. During the war, Bin Ladin founded al-Qaida—the Base—to serve as an operational hub, predominantly for like-minded Sunni Islamic extremists. The Saudi Government revoked his citizenship in 1994 and his family officially disowned him. He had moved to Sudan in 1991, but international pressure on that government forced him to move to Afghanistan in 1996.

In August 1996, Bin Ladin issued a statement outlining his organization's goals: drive US forces from the Arabian Peninsula, overthrow the Government of Saudi Arabia, "liberate" Muslim holy sites in "Palestine," and support Islamic revolutionary groups around the world. To these ends, his organization has sent trainers throughout Afghanistan as well as to Tajikistan, Bosnia, Chechnya, Somalia, Sudan, and Yemen and has trained fighters from numerous other countries including the Philippines, Egypt, Libya, and Eritrea. Bin Ladin also has close associations with the leaders of several Islamic terrorist groups and probably has aided in creating new groups since the mid-1980s. He has trained their troops, provided safehaven and financial support, and probably helps them with other organizational matters.

Since August 1996, Bin Ladin has been very vocal in expressing his approval of and intent to use terrorism. He claimed responsibility for trying to bomb US soldiers in Yemen in late 1992 and for attacks on them in Somalia in 1993, and reports suggest his organization aided the Egyptian al-Gama'at al-Islamiyya in its assassination attempt on Egyptian President Mubarak in Ethiopia in 1995. In November 1996 he called the 1995 and 1996 bombings against US military personnel in Saudi Arabia "praiseworthy acts of terrorism" but denied having any personal participation in those bombings. At the same time, he called for further attacks against US military personnel, saying: "If someone can kill an American soldier, it is better than wasting time on other matters."

1998

Usama Bin Ladin

The bombings of the US Embassies in Nairobi, Kenya, and Dar es Salaam, Tanzania on 7 August 1998 underscored the global reach of Usama Bin Ladin—a long-time sponsor and financier of Sunni Islamic extremist causes—and his network. A series of public threats to drive the United States and its allies out of Muslim countries foreshadowed the attacks. The foremost threat was presented as a Muslim religious decree and published on 23 February 1998 by Bin Ladin and allied groups under the name "World Islamic Front for Jihad Against the Jews and Crusaders." The statement asserted that it was a religious duty for all Muslims to wage war on US citizens, military and civilian, anywhere in the world.

The 17th son of Saudi construction magnate Muhammad Bin Ladin, Usama joined the Afghan resistance almost immediately after the Soviet invasion in December 1979. He played a significant role in financing, recruiting, transporting, and training Arab nationals who volunteered to fight in Afghanistan. During the war, Bin Ladin founded al-Qaida—the "Base"—to serve as an operational hub for like-minded Sunni Islamic extremists. In 1994 the Saudi Government revoked his citizenship and his family officially disowned him. He moved to Sudan in 1991 but international pressure on Khartoum forced him to move to Afghanistan in 1996.

Bin Ladin leads a broad-based, versatile organization. Suspects named in the wake of the Embassy bombings—four Egyptians, one Comoran, one Jordanian, three Saudis, one US citizen, one or possibly two Kenyan citizens, and one Tanzanian—reflect the range of al-Qaida operatives. The diverse groups under his umbrella afford Bin Ladin resources beyond those of the people directly loyal to him. With his own inherited wealth, business interests, contributions from sympathizers in various countries, and support from close allies like the Egyptian and South Asian groups that signed his so-called fatwa, he funds, trains, and offers logistic help to extremists not directly affiliated with his organization.

Bin Ladin seeks to aid those who support his primary goal—driving US forces from the Arabian Peninsula, removing the Saudi ruling family from power, and "liberating Palestine"—or his secondary goals of removing Western military forces and overthrowing what he calls corrupt, Western-oriented governments in predominantly Muslim countries. To these ends, his organization has sent trainers throughout Afghanistan as well as to Tajikistan, Bosnia and Herzegovina, Chechnya, Somalia, Sudan, and Yemen, and has trained fighters from numerous other countries, including the Philippines, Egypt, Libya, Pakistan, and Eritrea.

Using the ties al-Qaida has developed, Bin Ladin believes he can call upon individuals and groups virtually worldwide to conduct terrorist attacks. His Egyptian and South Asian allies, for example, publicly threatened US interests in the latter half of 1998. Bin Ladin's own public remarks underscore his expanding interests, including a desire to obtain a capability to deploy weapons of mass destruction.

On 4 November indictments were returned in the US District Court for the Southern District of New York in connection with the two US Embassy bombings in Africa. Charged in the indictment were: Usama Bin Ladin, his military commander Muhammad Atef, and Wadih El Hage, Fazul Abdullah Mohammed, Mohammed Sadeek Odeh, and Mohamed Rashed Daoud al-Owhali, all members of al-Qaida. Two of these suspects, Odeh and al-Owhali, were turned over to US authorities in Kenya and brought to the United States to stand trial. Another suspect, Mamdouh Mahmud Salim, was arrested in Germany and extradited to the United States in December. On 16 December five others were indicted for their role in the Dar es Salaam Embassy bombing: Mustafa Mohammed Fadhil, Khalfan Khamis Mohamed, Ahmed Khalfan Ghailani, Fahid Mohommed Ally Msalam, and Sheikh Ahmed Salim Swedan.

Cuba

Designation date March 1, 1982

1985

The Castro regime has maintained a large and complex apparatus for subversion that supports many leftist revolutionaries and terrorists. This has ranged from arms and funding to safehaven and training—assistance that is indispensable for guerilla movements and terrorists in Latin America. Castro has given logistic assistance and financial support to thousands of guerillas and has provided them with military training.

Cuba has provided support to Salvadoran leftists and other insurgents. Many of the guerillas infiltrated into Honduras in recent years were trained in Cuba, and Havana has used Honduran territory as a transit area for material passed to Salvadoran insurgents. In addition, Colombia's M-19 has a long and well-established relationship with the Cuban government.

1986

Cuba maintains a large and complex apparatus for subversion that has substantially assisted guerilla movements and terrorists in Latin America. Cuba gives logistic assistance and financial support to thousands of regional subversives—mostly from Central America—and provides them with military training. Havana has close and long-standing relationships with terrorist groups in Chile and Colombia.

Havana is particularly close to the Colombian National Liberation Army (ELN) and the 19th of April Movement (M-19)—and has long encouraged efforts by Colombian insurgents to unite. Cuba has had a special interest in Chile since the Allende years. In August 1986, Chilean authorities discovered large arms caches north of Santiago. Available information strongly suggested the weapons had been supplied by Cuba.

1987

We were unable to trace direct sponsorship of an international terrorist attack to Cuba in 1987. Since 1959, however, Cuba has trained and supported guerillas throughout the world, including Palestinians. Such training has become increasingly specialized. Cuba has provided safehaven, weapons, and political and financial support to a wide range of leftist and insurgent organizations that use terrorism in Latin America, including groups from El Salvador, Guatemala, Ecuador, Chile, and Colombia. This support persisted in 1987. We are also aware of longstanding contacts between Cuba and Puerto Rican terrorist groups.

1988

For nearly 30 years now, Cuban President Fidel Castro has trained and supported guerillas from many parts of the world, including Palestinians, who have relied in part on terrorist operations against noncombatants to advance their political aims. Cuba has maintained a large and complex apparatus for subversion that has substantially assisted guerilla movements throughout Latin America, and many of Latin America's radical leftist organizations look to Castro for guidance and advice. Havana has particularly longstanding ties to guerilla groups in Colombia and Chile, including the FPMR, which is believed responsible for nine international terrorist incidents in Chile in 1988. In Colombia, Cuba has supported the ELN which is responsible for numerous international terrorist attacks targeting Western economic interests in 1988. In El Salvador, the FMLN, which has received support from Cuba as well as other radical countries, has publicly threatened Americans assisting the Salvadoran Government as "legitimate targets of assassination."

Because of such continuing involvement, the US Government in 1982 put Cuba on its official list of state supporters of terrorism. Although we are unable to trace direct sponsorship of an international terrorist attack in 1988 to Cuba, it continues to provide safehaven, weapons, and political and financial support to a wide range of leftist and insurgent organizations that use terrorism.

Cuba harbors terrorists wanted in the United States for their crimes. William Morales, a Puerto Rican terrorist, was granted refuge in Cuba in June 1988 after his deportation from Mexico. Morales escaped from US detention in 1987 while serving an 89-year sentence for acts of terrorism. Cuba is also believed to be harboring at least one other Puerto Rican terrorist implicated in a Wells Fargo robbery in Connecticut in 1983. Joanne Chesimard, leader of the Black Liberation Army who escaped from a US federal prison after being convicted of the murder of a New Jersey state policeman, is living in Cuba.

1989

Cuba has trained and supported radical groups from around the world, including Palestinian groups that have often used terrorism to advance their political causes. It has maintained a large and complex apparatus to support guerilla movements and extremist groups throughout Latin America. Many of Latin America's radical leftist organizations look to President Fidel Castro for guidance and advice. Havana has particularly longstanding ties to guerillas in Chile and Colombia, including the National Liberation Army—a group that has carried out more international terrorism than any other in Latin America in recent years. In El Salvador, the Farabundo Marti Liberation Movement, which receives support from Cuba as well as other radical countries, has publicly threatened Americans assisting the Salvadoran Government as "legitimate targets of assassination." Because of its continuing involvement in support to radical groups conducting terrorist actions, the US Government placed Cuba on its official list of state supporters of terrorism in 1982.

1990

Cuba continues to serve as a haven for regional revolutionaries and to provide military training, weapons, funds, and guidance to radical subversive groups that use terrorism. The island today remains a major training center and transit point for Latin subversives and some international groups.

EL Salvador's Farbundo Marti National Liberation Front (FMLN) has been the primary beneficiary of Cuba's clandestine support network over the last several years. Havana has been the point of origin for most of the weapons used by the FMLN for insurgent and terrorist operations in El Salvador. Other Central American groups, notably in Honduras and Guatemala, have also received Cuban aid. In South America, Chilean radical leftist groups have been the favored recipients of Cuban support, but their aid may have declined since Chile's peaceful transition to civilian rule in March 1990.

Several rebel organizations have offices and members stationed in Havana. Wounded rebels are often treated in Cuban hospitals. With the demise of the pro-Cuban governments in Panama and Nicaragua, Cuba's support has become even more important to radical groups.

1991

In light of its overwhelming domestic economic problems, Cuba has greatly reduced or suspended its training, arms shipments, and financial support to armed Latin American subversive groups over the past year. Havana also has downplayed political ties to many of these groups—notably in Honduras and Chile—in hopes of upgrading diplomatic and trade relations in the region. Shortly before a settlement was reached, Havana publicly backed a political settlement between the Salvadoran Government and the Farabundo Marti National Liberation Front (FMLN), a longtime beneficiary of Cuban military aid and training.

Cuba, nevertheless, reportedly continues to serve as a safehaven for some regional and international terrorist organizations. In addition, Cuba continues to provide limited political training to some leftist organizations. We have no information to confirm that Cuba has closed down its training camps for armed insurgents.

1992

Cuba's increasingly critical economic situation and continued political isolation have precluded any significant material or financial assistance to the few remaining Marxist insurgencies in Latin America. As a result, Fidel Castro has impressed upon some of the insurgent leaders the need to make peace. In the past year Castro has welcomed the peace accord in El Salvador and has publicly advised Guatemalan and Colombian insurgents to negotiate seriously to end the armed struggle.

Castro continues to allow insurgent offices such as those of the Revolutionary Armed Forces of Colombia (FARC) and the Colombian National Liberation Army (ELN) to operate in Havana. Although Cuba has adhered to UN-mandated sanctions against Libya, it has not moved to limit Libyan diplomatic representatives, as required by international law. Reports indicate that Cuba continues to host Third World leftist militants for study and political training, but military training seems to have been halted.

1993

In the past, Cuba provided significant military training, weapons, funds, and guidance to radical subversives from different parts of the world. Largely because of its steady and dramatic economic decline, Cuba has been unable to maintain support to subversive groups. Moreover, the Castro regime has minimized its ties to such groups in an attempt to upgrade diplomatic and trade relations. Although there is no evidence that Cuba directly sponsored an international terrorist attack in 1993, the island continued to serve as a safehaven for members of some regional and international terrorist organizations. Cuba has adhered to UN-mandated sanctions against Libya but has not limited Libyan diplomatic representation as required. In September, Cuban Deputy Prime Minister Pedro Miret Prieto traveled to Libya to expand bilateral cooperation.

1994

The Castro regime, which is preoccupied with its existence, is no longer able to support armed struggle actively in Latin America and other parts of the world. In years past, Havana provided significant levels of military training, weapons, funds, and guidance to leftist subversives. Currently, the regime's focus is largely on economic survival, and the government is attempting to upgrade diplomatic and trade relations within Latin America. Cuba's economy continued to deteriorate, and a large antiregime demonstration broke out for the first time in 1994.

Although there is no evidence that Cuban officials have been directly involved in sponsoring a specific act of terrorism during the past year, Havana did provide safehaven in 1994 to several terrorists in Cuba. A number of ETA Basque terrorists who sought sanctuary in Cuba several years ago continue to live on the island. Some of the more than 40 Chilean terrorists from the Manuel Rodriguez Patriotic Front (FPMR) who escaped from a Chilean prison in 1990 also probably still reside in Cuba. Colombia's two main guerrilla groups, the Revolutionary Armed Forces of Colombia (FARC) and the National Liberation Army (ELN), reportedly maintain representatives in Havana.

1995

Cuba no longer actively supports armed struggle in Latin America and other parts of the world. In earlier years, the Castro regime provided significant levels of military training, weapons, funding, and guidance to leftist extremists worldwide. Havana's focus now is to forestall an economic collapse; the government actively continued to seek the upgrading of diplomatic and trade relations with other nations.

Cuba is not known to have sponsored any international terrorist incidents in 1995. Havana, however, provided safehaven to several terrorists in Cuba during the year. A number of Basque Fatherland and Liberty (ETA) terrorists, who sought sanctuary in Cuba several years ago, still live on the island. Members of a few Latin American terrorist organizations and US fugitives also reside in Cuba.

1996

Cuba no longer actively supports armed struggle in Latin America and other parts of the world. In earlier years the Castro regime provided significant levels of military training, weapons, funding, and guidance to numerous leftist extremists. Havana's focus now is to forestall an economic collapse; the government actively continued to seek the upgrading of diplomatic and trade relations with other nations.

Although there is no current evidence that Cuban officials were directly involved in sponsoring specific acts of terrorism last year, Cuba is still a safehaven for several international terrorists, maintains close relations with other state sponsors of terrorism, and remains in contact with numerous leftist insurgent groups in Latin America.

A number of Basque Fatherland and Liberty (ETA) terrorists who sought sanctuary in Cuba several years ago continue to live on the island. Some of the more than 40 Chilean terrorists from the Manuel Rodriguez Patriotic Front (FPMR) who escaped from a Chilean prison in 1990 also probably still reside in Cuba. Colombia's two main guerrilla groups, the Revolutionary Armed Forces of Colombia (FARC) and the National Liberation Army (ELN), reportedly maintain representatives in Havana.

Cuba also provides safehaven to several nonterrorist US fugitives.

1997

Cuba no longer actively supports armed struggle in Latin America and other parts of the world. In the past, the Castro regime provided significant levels of funding, military training, arms, and guidance to various revolutionary groups across the globe. However, with the collapse of its prime sponsor—the Soviet Union—in 1989, Cuba suffered a severe economic decline. Without ready cash, Havana was forced to scale back severely its already waning support to international terrorists. To make up for this economic shortfall, the Castro government's focus in recent years has been on generating revenue through tourism. Cuba's attempts to encourage foreign investment in the hospitality industry has forced the nation to seek upgraded diplomatic and trade relations with other nations.

Although Cuba is not known to have sponsored any international terrorist incidents in 1997, it continued to give safehaven to several terrorists during the year. A number of ETA terrorists who gained sanctuary in Cuba some years ago continue to live on the island. In addition, members of a few Latin American-based international terrorist organizations and US fugitives also reside in Cuba.

Cuba also maintains close ties to other state sponsors of terrorism and remains in contact with leftist insurgent groups in Latin America. For instance, Colombia's two main terrorist groups, the FARC and the ELN, reportedly maintain representatives in Havana.

Cuba suffered from a string of small bombings targeting the island's tourism industry in 1997. At least six bombs detonated at Havana hotels and restaurants in April, July, August, and September. An Italian tourist was killed in one blast in early September, the only fatality of the bombing campaign. On 10 September, Cuban security forces announced they had arrested a Salvadoran citizen who confessed to planting the bombs. Havana charged that US-based groups were responsible for directing the bombing campaign from the United States, but it has repeatedly ignored US requests for evidence to support these charges.

1998

Cuba no longer actively supports armed struggle in Latin America or elsewhere. Previously, the Castro regime provided significant levels of funding, military training, arms, and guidance to various revolutionary groups across the globe. Since the collapse of the Soviet Union in 1991, Havana has been forced to reduce dramatically its support to leftist revolutionaries.

Cuba, nonetheless, continues to maintain close ties to other state sponsors of terrorism and leftist insurgent groups in Latin America. For instance, Colombia's two main terrorist groups, the FARC and the ELN, maintain representatives in Cuba. Moreover, Havana continues to provide safehaven to a number of international terrorists and US terrorist fugitives.

1999

Cuba continued to provide safehaven to several terrorists and U.S. fugitives in 1999. A number of Basque ETA terrorists who gained sanctuary in Cuba some years ago continued to live on the island, as did several U.S. terrorist fugitives.

Havana also maintained ties to other state sponsors of terrorism and Latin American insurgents. Colombia's two largest terrorist organizations, the Revolutionary Armed Forces of Colombia and the National Liberation Army (ELN), both maintained a permanent presence on the island. In late 1999, Cuba hosted a series of meetings between Colombian Government officials and ELN leaders.

2000

Cuba continued to provide safehaven to several terrorists and US fugitives in 2000. A number of Basque ETA terrorists who gained sanctuary in Cuba some years ago continued to live on the island, as did several US terrorist fugitives.

Havana also maintained ties to other state sponsors of terrorism and Latin American insurgents. Colombia's two largest terrorist organizations, the Revolutionary Armed Forces of Colombia and the National Liberation Army, both maintained a permanent presence on the island.

2001

Since September 11, Fidel Castro has vacillated over the war on terrorism. In October, he labeled the US-led war on terrorism "worse than the original attacks, militaristic, and fascist."

When this tactic earned ostracism rather than praise, he undertook an effort to demonstrate Cuban support for the international campaign against terrorism and signed all 12 UN counterterrorism conventions as well as the Ibero-American declaration on terrorism at the 2001 summit. Although Cuba decided not to protest the detention of suspected terrorists at the US Naval Base at Guantanamo Bay, it continued to denounce the global effort against terrorism—even by asserting that the United States was intentionally targeting Afghan children and Red Cross hospitals.

Cuba's signature of UN counterterrorism conventions notwithstanding, Castro continued to view terror as a legitimate revolutionary tactic. The Cuban Government continued to allow at least 20 Basque ETA members to reside in Cuba as privileged guests and provided some degree of safehaven and support to members of the Colombian FARC and ELN groups. In August, a Cuban spokesman revealed that Sinn Fein's official representative for Cuba and Latin America, Niall Connolly, who was one of three Irish Republican Army members arrested in Colombia on suspicion of providing explosives training to the FARC, had been based in Cuba for five years. In addition, the recent arrest in Brazil of the leader of a Chilean terrorist group, the Frente Patriotico Manuel Rodriguez (FPMR), has raised the strong possibility that in the mid-1990s, the Cuban Government harbored FPMR terrorists wanted for murder in Chile. The arrested terrorist told Brazilian authorities he had traveled through Cuba on his way to Brazil. Chilean investigators had traced calls from FPMR relatives in Chile to Cuba following an FPMR prison break in 1996, but the Cuban Government twice denied extradition requests, claiming that the wanted persons were not in Cuba and the phone numbers were incorrect.

Numerous US fugitives continued to live on the island, including Joanne Chesimard, wanted in the United States for the murder in 1973 of a New Jersey police officer and living as a guest of the Castro regime since 1979.

2002

Although Cuba signed and ratified all 12 international counterterrorism conventions in 2001, it has remained opposed to the US-led Coalition prosecuting the war on global terrorism and has been actively critical of many associated US policies and actions. On repeated occasions, for example, Cuba sent agents to US missions around the world who provided false leads designed to subvert the post-September 11 investigation. Cuba did not protest the use of the Guantanamo Bay base to house enemy combatants from the conflict in Afghanistan.

In 2002, Cuba continued to host several terrorists and US fugitives. Havana permitted up to 20 Basque Fatherland and Liberty members to reside in Cuba and provided some degree of safehaven and support to members of the Colombian Revolutionary Armed Forces of Colombia (FARC) and National Liberation Army (ELN) groups. Bogota was aware of the arrangement and apparently acquiesced; it has publicly indicated that it seeks Cuba's continued mediation with ELN agents in Cuba.

An accused Irish Republican Army (IRA) weapons expert and longtime resident of Havana went on trial in Colombia in 2002. He had been caught a year earlier in Colombia with two other IRA members and detained for allegedly training the FARC in advanced use of explosives. Some US fugitives continued to live on the island.

2003

Cuba remained opposed to the US-led Coalition prosecuting the global war on terrorism and actively condemned many associated US policies and actions throughout 2003. Government-controlled press reporting about US-led military operations in Iraq and Afghanistan were consistently critical of the United States and frequently and baselessly alleged US involvement in violations of human rights. Government propaganda claimed that those fighting for self-determination or against foreign occupation are exercising internationally recognized rights and cannot be accused of terrorism. Cuba's delegate to the UN said terrorism cannot be defined as including acts by legitimate national liberation movements— even though many such groups clearly employ tactics that intentionally target innocent civilians to advance their political, religious, or social agendas. In referring to US policy toward Cuba, the delegate asserted, "acts by states to destabilize other states is a form of terrorism."

The Cuban Government did not extradite nor request the extradition of suspected terrorists in 2003. Cuba continued to provide support to designated Foreign Terrorist Organizations, as well as to host several terrorists and dozens of fugitives from US justice. The Government refuses to return suspected terrorists to countries when it alleges that a receiving government could not provide a fair trial because the charges against the accused are "political." Cuba has publicly used this argument with respect to a number of fugitives from US justice, including Joanne Chesimard, wanted for the murder of a New Jersey State Trooper in 1973. Havana permitted up to 20 ETA members to reside in Cuba and provided some degree of safehaven and support to members of FARC and the ELN. Bogota was aware of the arrangement and apparently acquiesced; it has publicly indicated that it seeks Cuba's continued mediation with ELN agents in Cuba. A declaration issued by the Cuban Ministry of Foreign Affairs in May 2003 maintained that the presence of ETA members in Cuba arose from a request for assistance by Spain and Panama and that the issue is a bilateral matter between Cuba and Spain. The declaration similarly defended its assistance to the FARC and the ELN as contributing to a negotiated solution in Colombia.

Dozens of fugitives from US justice have taken refuge on the island. In a few cases, the Cuban Government has rendered fugitives from US justice to US authorities. The salient feature of Cuba's behavior in this arena, however, is its refusal to render to US justice any fugitive whose crime is judged by Cuba to be "political."

With respect to domestic terrorism, the Government in April 2003 executed three Cubans who attempted to hijack a ferry to the United States. The three were executed under Cuba's 2001 "Law Against Acts of Terrorism."

Cuba became a party to all 12 international conventions and protocols relating to terrorism in 2001.

2004

Throughout 2004, Cuba continued to actively oppose the US-led coalition prosecuting the global war on terrorism. Cuba continues to maintain at the UN and other fora that acts by legitimate national liberation movements cannot be defined as terrorism, and has sought to characterize as "legitimate national liberation movements" a number of groups that intentionally target innocent civilians to advance their political, religious, or social agendas. The Cuban Government claims, despite the absence of evidence, that it is a principal victim of terrorism sponsored by Cuban-Americans in the United States. The Cuban Government's actions and public statements run contrary to the spirit of the UN conventions on terrorism that it has signed.

In 2004, Cuba continued to provide limited support to designated Foreign Terrorist Organizations, as well as safehaven for terrorists. The Cuban Government refuses to turn over suspected terrorists to countries that have charged them with terrorist acts, alleging that the receiving government would not provide a fair trial on charges that are "political." Havana permitted various ETA members to reside in Cuba, despite a November 2003 public request from the Spanish Government to deny them sanctuary, and provided safehaven and some degree of support to members of the Colombian FARC and ELN guerilla groups.

Many of the over seventy fugitives from US justice that have taken refuge on the island are accused of committing violent acts in the Unites States that targeted innocents in order to advance political causes. They include Joanne Chesimard, who is wanted for the murder of a New Jersey State Trooper in 1973. On a few rare occasions the Cuban government has transferred fugitives to the United States, although it maintains that fugitives would not receive a fair trial in the United States.

Havana, Managua, and Hanoi: The Chilean Arms Cache (1986)

On 6 August 1986 security forces near Carrizal Bajo in northern Chile discovered the first of eight terrorist arms caches—which together contained the most ordnance ever found at one time in the possession of Latin American terrorists or insurgents. Their discovery presented a rare public picture of three states cooperating to abet terrorism in a fourth country.

The first cache—342 assault rifles—was found 600 meters from a small cove. Four members of the Manuel Rodriguez Patriotic Front (FPMR) arrested at the same time claimed that several illicit arms deliveries had come ashore at the cove since the beginning of the year. The terrorists led Chilean security officers to an abandoned mine 12 kilometers away in which over 200,000 rounds of rifle ammunition and 315 Soviet Bloc rocket-propelled antitank grenades were discovered.

Over the next two weeks, several other caches were found, mostly near Carrizal Bajo. They were extremely well constructed and, like the mine site, were clearly intended for the long-term storage of large quantities of arms and ammunition. Another 1,320 assault rifles, nearly 1 million rounds of ammunition, and almost 900 antitank rockets were discovered in a concrete-reinforced underground vault in an old hotel FPMR members had purchased near Vallenar. An underground training school with a firing range was found under a house in Huasco. An identical underground school was found farther south near Santiago.

The caches consisted of heretofore unheard-of quantities of some extremely lethal weapons ideal for terrorist use. Many of the recovered weapons were manufactured in the United States during the Vietnam war, including more than 3,000 M-16 rifles that had been sent to equip US forces in Vietnam. Other captured ordnance of similar origin included 167 disposable antitank rocket launchers and nearly 2 million rounds of rifle ammunition, all of which most likely was made available by Hanoi from captured stocks.

In contrast to these older US weapons, the Bloc ordnance was of recent manufacture. This included 114 RPG-7 rocket launchers and nearly 2,000 rocket rounds for them, 2,000 Soviet-style handgrenades and ignitor assemblies, 5,000 Soviet nonelectric blasting caps, and some rifle ammunition. Much of this materiel and other Bloc equipment was packed in its original shipping containers.

The size and composition of the caches and prefabricated components of the storage sites indicate state sponsorship. The cost of the weapons involved and the logistic problems associated with their delivery put an effort of this scale beyond the resources of a subnational group. Havana, which has access to both new Bloc equipment and, through its allies, to US Vietnam-vintage weapons, is the leading candidate. Havana and Managua undoubtedly hoped to gain an element of deniability by providing large quantities of US-made ordnance, but similar materiel—in smaller quantities—brokered by Cuba from Vietnam and passed through Nicaragua as an intermediary has been recovered form Cuban-backed subversives in other Latin American countries during the past few years.

The sheer volume of the materiel found in Chile—an estimated 70 tons—suggests delivery by sea, as do damp equipment and some of the seawater-corroded ammunition. That so large a quantity could be secretly delivered to terrorists in Chile indicates that other Latin American nations with long stretches of deserted coastline may also be vulnerable to Cuban subversive efforts. The discovery of similar equipment in other countries raises concerns that such operations may already be underway elsewhere in the region.

Iran

Designation date January 19, 1984

1985

The level of terrorism by Iranian-supported groups in 1985 remained high but declined from the record level of 1984. Groups with established ties to Iran carried out some 30 attacks last year, although Iran cannot be linked directly to most of these attacks. Although Iraq, France, and the United States have remained the primary targets, Persian Gulf states have faced a continuing terrorist threat that could escalate sharply should Iran choose to exercise its terrorist option.

Export of the revolution has been a central tenet of the clerical regime in Iran, with terrorism a primary instrument in advancing this objective. Iran has used its network of diplomatic and cultural missions to support terrorist operations, and many elements of the Iranian Government, including several senior officials, have been directly involved in terrorist activity. Economic constraints and the war with Iraq, however, apparently have compelled Iran increasingly to reduce its direct involvement in terrorism and pursue a more pragmatic foreign policy, putting less emphasis on the ideological use of terrorism to support the export of its Islamic revolution. Some groups that owe their inspiration and their origin to

Iran, such as the Lebanese Hizballah, have become increasingly independent of Tehran's direction, although their activities still serve Iran's foreign policy goals.

Iraq has been a primary target of Iranian-sponsored groups. Iran has trained and financed several Iraqi dissident groups, such as the Dawa Party, that are dedicated to overthrowing Iraqi President Saddam Husayn and establishing an Islamic republic in Iraq.

Lebanon has been the scene of most of the terrorism perpetrated by groups that have received Iranian support. Pro-Iranian Shi'a Muslims in Lebanon were responsible for nearly 20 international incidents last year, including eight attacks against French targets and five against US targets. Tehran apparently did not play a direct role in the majority of attacks on foreigners in Lebanon. The nature of Iran's ties to the radical Shi'as that have kidnapped foreigners and the extent to which Iran can control or direct them has remained unclear.

Tehran has maintained the capability to resume quickly terrorist activities throughout the Persian Gulf. Shi'a dissidents from several Gulf states have traveled to Iran to receive training. Iranian-backed terrorists were suspected of having planned the assassination attempt on the Amir of Kuwait in May 1985. Iran may intend to maintain its terrorist option in the region in case diplomatic initiatives fail or the war with Iraq demands more drastic measures against other Arab states.

1986

Iran in 1986 continued to view terrorism as an important instrument in its campaign to drive US and Western influence out of the Middle East, to eliminate opponents of the Khomeini regime overseas, and to intimidate the Persian Gulf states to end their support for Iraq. Although fewer international terrorist incidents were traceable to Iranian support in 1986, this does not reflect any decreased willingness to use terrorism.

In the Persian Gulf, Iran has used terrorism to promote its foreign policy goals, in particular to deter moderate Gulf states from aiding Iraq in its war effort, at times to induce these states to support OPEC oil policies favored by Iran, to further the war against Iraq, and to radicalize Shia populations in the Gulf states. Iran recruits Shias from the Gulf states, gives them religious indoctrination, paramilitary and terrorist training, and returns them to these states. Most of the Iranian-backed terrorist acts in the Gulf are conducted by such Iranian-trained and -sponsored Shia radicals. The groups promoted by Iran in 1986 included the Supreme Assembly for the Islamic Revolution in Iraq, the Islamic Front for the Liberation of Bahrain, the Islamic Dawa Party (which has local branches in Kuwait, Bahrain, and Lebanon), and the Organization for the Islamic Revolution in the Arabian Peninsula.

Iranian-backed Shia terrorists were responsible for the bombings of several oil installations in Kuwait in June 1986. Five bombs exploded near Kuwait's crude oil tank farms and at an oil well near Kuwait City.

Iran is believed to have been responsible for the attempted bombings of Saudi and Kuwaiti airlines offices in Vienna and Karachi in the past year. The attacks coincided with Tehran's warnings to Riyadh and the other Arab oil-producing states to cut production and boost oil prices.

Lebanon has been the scene of most of the terrorism perpetrated by groups that Iran supports. Tehran continues to provide significant support to the radical Shia Hizballah movement that has kidnapped foreigners and is conducting terrorist operations against Western—and particularly US and French—interests. Although Hizballah is not under Iran's complete control, Tehran has substantial influence over the group's activities and provides financial assistance as well as weapons and training.

The Revolutionary Justice Organization, believed to be a cover name used by Hizballah, abducted a four-person French television crew in March 1986. Three of the French journalists were subsequently released after France and Iran had settled bilateral issues.

The Revolutionary Justice Organization also claimed the abduction of Frank Reed, Joseph Cicippio, and Edward Tracy in September and October.

A faction of Hizballah continues to hold US hostages Terry Anderson and Thomas Sutherland, kidnapped in 1985.

Iranian-backed factions in Lebanon were probably responsible for the murder of a French military attache in Beirut in September and for the attacks against the French contingent of the UNIFIL in south Lebanon.

Tehran continues to recruit Shia dissidents from Saudi Arabia, Kuwait, Bahrain, the United Arab Emirates, and Iraq and give them military training in Iran. Iran is also trying to expand its networks in Europe, Africa, and Asia, using local Islamic communities, religious and cultural institutions, as well as its diplomatic services to bolster its capability to conduct or support terrorist activities beyond the Middle East.

1987

Of the 44 terrorist incidents in which Iran was identified as the sponsor, we recorded 25 in the Middle East, 10 in Western Europe, and nine in Asia. The preferred means were bombings (27) and armed attacks (13). Tehran uses terrorism skillfully and selectively to support its long-term objectives of ridding the Middle East of all Western influence, intimidating Iranian dissidents overseas, forcing Arab countries to end their support for Iraq, and exporting Khomeini's vision of a radical Islamic revolution to all parts of the Muslim world. We believe that most Iranian leaders agree that terrorism is an acceptable policy option, although some may disagree on specific operations.

Beginning in early January 1987, Iran stepped up its support for international terrorism when its state agents or surrogate groups:

- Attempted to put pressure on Saudi Arabia, Kuwait, and other moderate Arab states both in the Persian Gulf area and in Europe by terrorist acts.
- Allegedly ordered the kidnapping in Lebanon of US journalist Charles Glass.

- Assassinated Iranian defectors and dissidents in the United Kingdom, Switzerland, West Germany, Turkey, and Pakistan.
- Began a worldwide search to identify potential US targets for terrorist attacks.

Iran continued its policy of recruiting coreligionists from Persian Gulf states for training in Iran, where it provided them with training in subversion and terrorism. Although some of the terrorist acts in the Persian Gulf states during the year may have been conducted without Iran's explicit authorization or knowledge, Tehran most likely approved such acts in principle. Besides the Lebanese-based Hizballah, Iranian-backed factions that may have been used to conduct or support terrorism include the Supreme Assembly for the Islamic Republic of Iraq; the Organization of the Islamic Revolution in the Arabian Peninsula; the Islamic Front for the Liberation of Bahrain; and the Islamic Call Party (Dawa), which has branches in Bahrain, Kuwait, and Lebanon.

Iran has maintained its campaign against the Persian Gulf states. In June 1986, Kuwaiti Shia terrorists bombed several oil installations in Kuwait. Iran's actions in Kuwait in 1987 are described in the Kuwait section. Bahrain, too, was the target of an Iranian-inspired terrorist plot. According to press reports, Iran trained a Bahraini oil engineer to sabotage Bahrain's only oil refinery and to carry out other anti-Bahraini attacks. Bahrain authorities were able to arrest him in late December, however, shortly before the attacks were to take place.

Following the bloody Iranian-instigated clashes during the Hajj pilgrimage to Mecca in July 1987, which resulted in hundreds of Iranians being killed, Iranian leaders publicly urged the overthrow of the Saudi ruling family, revenge for the deaths of the Iranian pilgrims, and an end to Saudi control over Islamic holy places in Saudi Arabia. We suspect that pro-Iranian terrorists were responsible for the bombing of a Saudi bank in Paris in September. The terrorist threat to Saudi Arabia remains high.

Lebanon remains the major focus of Iran's support for terrorism. As in previous years, in 1987 Iran provided major assistance to Hizballah, the extremist Lebanese Shia group that regularly engages in terrorism, including the kidnapping of foreign hostages (see section on Lebanon) and other attacks on Western targets. Iran does not completely control Hizballah but retains influence over the group's activities—most notably on hostage questions—through its provision of financial support, weapons, and training. Several Iranian Revolutionary Guard units in Lebanon are colocated with Hizballah detachments. Furthermore, for extremist Shia in Lebanon, Khomeini remains the exemplar of Islamic revolutionary ideals.

Iran has made the elimination of regime opponents at home and abroad a major goal of its terrorist activities. In the past, Iranian agents have hunted down and killed dissidents in Europe, the United States, the Middle East, and Asia. In January 1987, for instance, a defector who had been chief pilot for Rafsanjani, Speaker of the Iranian Assembly, was shot dead in West Germany. All told, seven dissidents were murdered in Europe and two others threatened. Terrorist attacks against anti-Khomeini dissidents in South Asia are mentioned in the section on Pakistan.

Iran undoubtedly views terrorism as a potential major weapon in its confrontation with the United States in the Persian Gulf. Many Iranian leaders have claimed publicly that Shia terrorism against the US Marines in Beirut compelled the United States to withdraw its military forces, thus dealing the United States a humiliating defeat. In 1987, as the United States increased its military involvement in the Gulf, Iranian leaders drew parallels between events in Lebanon in 1983–84 and current developments. Although no Iranian-backed terrorist attacks were staged against specific US targets during the year, we believed that during the summer of 1987 Iran began to formulate contingency plans for anti-US terrorist operations.

1988

Iranian-sponsored terrorist incidents decreased from 45 in 1987 to 32 in 1988, with Tehran's interest shifting away from targeting Kuwaitis and Iranian dissidents to attacking Saudis. A review of individual operations indicates Tehran relies on local Iranians and Islamic fundamentalists world-wide to carry out its attacks, and the lack of arrests last year suggests they are well trained and disciplined.

After sponsoring a large number of attacks against Kuwait during 1986 and 1987 to pressure Kuwait to end support for Iraq in the Gulf War, pro-Iranian Kuwaiti Shias—possibly acting with Iranian support—probably were behind just five operations in 1988. Some elements in Iran may have provided support for the hijackings by Hizballah of Kuwait Airways Flight 422 on 5 April 1988. At a minimum, Iran provided a friendly environment at Mashhad Airport, the flight's first stop. Airport authorities apparently were expecting its arrival despite the radio silence maintained by Kuwait Airways Flight 422 throughout the course of the extended flight over wartime Iranian territory. Iranian officials may have allowed more Hizballah members and weapons to board the aircraft at Mashhad.

In 1988 most Iranian-sponsored incidents were directed at Saudi interests, in part, because of Iranian resentment over the deaths of approximately 275 Iranian pilgrims during an Iranian-instigated riot in Mecca in 1987 as well as Saudi restrictions on Iranian attendance during the 1988 pilgrimage. Iranian leaders publicly committed Iran to retaliate for the deaths of its pilgrims, to overthrow the ruling Saud family, and to end Saudi control over the Islamic holy places in Arabia. Iran and its supporters probably were responsible for a number of these anti-Saudi operations, which were primarily directed at the offices of the Saudi national airline, Saudia. Pro-Iranian terrorists also may have been behind the attempted murders of three Saudi teachers in Lagos, Nigeria, in March; the assassination of a Saudi diplomat in Ankara, Turkey, on 25 October; and an assassination attempt against another Saudi diplomat in Karachi, Pakistan, on 27 December.

Iran toned down its antidissident campaign in 1988, although Tehran continues to regard suppression of exiled regime opponents as a key focus of its terrorist activities. The only known Iranian antidissident attacks last year were an arson attack on a video store in West Germany owned by an Iranian who sold anti-Khomeini videotapes and the attempted kidnapping of a dissident in Turkey in October.

Tehran also supports—and exerts significant influence over—the extremist Shia Hizballah movement's kidnapping of Westerners in Lebanon. Iran provides Hizballah with money, weapons, and training and has approved—and in some instances may have encouraged—its seizing of some Western hostages. Tehran may have been involved in the kidnapping in Beirut of businessman Ralph Schray, a Lebanese-West German dual national, on 27 January. Iranian influence with Hizballah on foreign hostages may have been intended to produce short-term benefits for Tehran, although the continued detention of the hostages in Beirut has obstructed its acceptance as a responsible member of the international community. Tehran helped arrange the release of another German hostage. Rudolf Cordes, in September, in the hope that it might receive diplomatic and economic consideration in the future. Iran may have been involved in the kidnapping of UN officer Lt. Col. William Higgins. Higgins, a US Marine, was taken by Iran's Lebanese Shia ally, Hizballah.

1989

Iranian-sponsored terrorist incidents decreased from 32 in 1988 to 28 in 1989. Iran's extensive support for terrorism continued after the death of Ayatollah Khomeini in June. The events of 1989 indicate Tehran continued to view the selective use of terrorism as a legitimate tool to achieve specific foreign policy goals. Iranian intelligence has been used to facilitate and in some cases conduct terrorist attacks. In addition, Iran is expanding contacts with Lebanese Muslim extremists, radical Palestinian groups, and other Muslim fundamentalist groups to carry out terrorist operations against Israeli, US, Western, and moderate Arab interests. In the past year Iranian support for terrorism has included:

- Calling for the death of author Salman Rushdie and attacking publishers and distributors of *The Satanic Verses*.
- Assassinating at least five Iranian dissidents.
- Recruiting Shia to carry out attacks in Saudi Arabia during the hajj.
- Inciting radical Shia elements to attack Saudi interests in retaliation for Riyadh's execution of 16 Shia responsible for the hajj bombings.
- Probably involving itself with, if not organizing, Hizballah terrorist activities in Europe, West Africa, and elsewhere.

Ayatollah Khomeini's denunciation of Salman Rushdie's novel and calls for the author's execution had the effect of a decree, which is binding under the Shia interpretation of Islamic law. Violent demonstrations and attacks against publishers and bookstores occurred throughout Europe, Asia, and the United States. Three British Council library buildings were bombed in Pakistan, killing one local guard. At least a dozen people died and more than 120 were injured in violent street riots in Pakistan and India. President Rafsanjani's reaffirmation of the death threat rekindled anti-Western fervor and prompted renewed anti-Rushdie demonstrations and attacks. In December 1989, UK authorities arrested and expelled Iranians involved in anti-Rushdie attacks; we believe Iran is continuing to coordinate and plan attacks directed against businesses affiliated with *The Satanic Verses.*

Another indication that terrorism continues to be a feature of the Tehran regime was the public statement in May by then Parliament Speaker (now President) Rafsanjani that exhorted Palestinians to kill Americans and other Westerners in order to avenge those Palestinians killed during the uprising in the occupied West Bank and Gaza. Rafsanjani also publicly encouraged the hijacking of airplanes and the blowing up of factories.

During 1989, Tehran continued its campaign to eliminate antiregime dissidents. We believe the increase in these attacks can be attributed to the regime's fear that prominent dissident leaders presented a significant threat to Tehran during the leadership transition following the death of Ayatollah Khomeini in June. The number of attacks against dissidents increased from two in 1988 to three in 1989, resulting in five deaths—three in Austria, one in the United Arab Emirates, and one in Cyprus. These attacks appear to have been well planned and were probably carried out by Iranian intelligence officers.

Iranian-sponsored attacks directed against Saudi interests also increased during 1989. Tehran's anti-Saudi campaign can be traced to Iranian resentment over Riyadh's imposition of restrictions on the number of Iranians permitted to make the annual pilgrimage to Mecca as a result of pro-Khomeini riots during the 1987 pilgrimage. During the 1989 hajj, two bombs exploded in Mecca, killing one and wounding over 20 others; several Kuwaiti Shia confessed to the crime. During their interrogations, the Shia confessed that they had been recruited, trained, and supported by Iran. Riyadh executed 16 Kuwaitis for this attack on 21 September. Shortly after the executions, Iranian and Hizballah leaders issued numerous statements denouncing the Saudi regime and calling for revenge. As a result, attacks against Saudi interests increased:

On 14 October, a Saudi Airlines office in Lahore, Pakistan, was damaged by a bomb explosion.

On 16 October, a Saudi military attache in Ankara, Turkey, was seriously injured when a bomb exploded under the seat of his car.

On 1 November, a Saudi official in Beirut, Lebanon, was assassinated by three gunmen. Islamic Jihad—a cover name used by Hizballah terrorists—claimed responsibility for the attack that was authenticated by a photograph of a US hostage.

On 24 November, the Saudi official responsible for coordinating aid in Pakistan to the Afghan resistance movement was assassinated.

During 1989, Tehran also continued to support—and exert influence over—the radical Shia elements in Lebanon. Iran continues to provide Hizballah with money, weapons, and training and has approved—and in some cases encouraged—the kidnapping of Western citizens. Tehran also continued to develop relations with Palestinian fundamentalist groups, as well as with radical Palestinian groups such as the PFLP-GC, which has been publicly accused of complicity with Iran in the bombing of Pan Am Flight 103, as well as with Arab fundamentalist groups.

1990

Iran's extensive support for terrorism continued during 1990, although the number of terrorist acts attributed to Iranian state sponsorship dropped to 10 in 1990 from 28 in 1989.

Iran has used its intelligence services extensively to facilitate and conduct terrorist attacks, particularly against regime dissidents. Intelligence officers in embassies have used the diplomatic pouch for conveyance of weapons and finances for terrorist groups. Iran continued to strengthen its relationship with Muslim extremists throughout the world, often providing them with advice and financial assistance. Over the past year, Iranian support for terrorism has included:

- Repeating the call for the death of the author of *The Satanic Verses*, Salman Rushdie.
- Assassinations of four antiregime dissidents—in Pakistan, Switzerland, Sweden, and France.
- Supporting radical Shia attacks on Saudi interests, including the assassinations of three Saudi diplomats, in retaliation for the execution of the Hajj bombers.
- Extensive support for Hizballah, the PFLP-GC, the PIJ, and other groups, including provision of arms, funding, and training.

Iranian-backed Shia groups are believed to be in control of Western hostages in Lebanon, and most observers believe that the key to releasing the hostages rests with Iran. One such group, Hizballah, is believed to hold all the remaining American hostages. Iranian President Ali Akbar Hashemi-Rafsanjani, whose domestic political strength increased during 1990, is thought to favor a pragmatic approach to foreign policy and improved relations with the West, which would require resolution of the hostage problem. For example, *The Tehran Times*, a newspaper considered to reflect Rafsanjani's views, editorialized on 22 February that the hostages should be freed without preconditions. Two months later, US hostages Robert Polhill and Frank Reed were released. The hostages releases received some criticism from hardline elements both in Iran and within Hizballah who questioned whether Iran or the hostage holders had received any benefit for their actions in terms of a good will gesture from the West. No more hostages were freed in 1990, and press reports indicated that Iran was seeking rewards before any further movement on the hostages was possible.

Major terrorist figures, including Ahmad Jabril of the PFLP-GC and various prominent members of Hizballah, frequently visit Iran. Iran hosted a World Conference on Palestine in Tehran in December in an effort to gain increasing influence over Islamic affairs, in general, and over the Palestinian movement, in particular. Leaders of several radical Palestinian and Lebanese groups including Saiqa, HAMAS, Hizballah, and the Palestinian Islamic Jihad attended.

1991

Iran continues to be a leading state sponsor of terrorism, even though the number of terrorist acts attributed to its direct sponsorship dropped to five in 1991, down from 10 in 1990 and 28 in 1989.

Iranian intelligence services continue to facilitate and conduct terrorist attacks, particularly against regime opponents living abroad. This policy is undertaken with the approval of the highest levels of the regime, although the government routinely denies involvement in assassination of dissidents or in terrorist attacks carried out by pro-Iranian groups. Iranian diplomatic and commercial facilities are reported to be used extensively in such operations.

During the past year Iran has further strengthened its relationship with extremists who engage in acts of terrorism throughout the world, with special emphasis on the Palestinians. Tehran often provides these groups with advice and financial and material assistance, often via Iranian embassies.

Iran has not limited its assistance only to terrorists who are Islamic fundamentalist in orientation. It has also provided sanctuary and some aid to the Marxist-Leninist separatist group Turkish Kurdish Workers' Party (PKK), a group that has used terrorist tactics in a seven-year campaign to establish a separate Kurdish state in southeastern Turkey.

The outstanding example of Iranian state terrorism in 1991 was the 6 August assassination of former Iranian Prime Minister Shapur Bakhtiar and his aide in a Paris suburb. French counterterrorism investigating magistrate Jean-Louis Bruguiere has thus far arrested three Iranians and issued an international arrest warrant against Hussein Sheikhattar, a senior official in the Iranian Ministry of Telecommunications. On 31 December France requested the extradition of another suspected Iranian conspirator arrested a week earlier outside the Iranian Embassy in Bern, Switzerland. Swiss officials approved his extradition to France on 24 February 1992, subject to appeals from the suspect. A comprehensive investigation into the case continues amid press reports that Judge Bruguiere could issue additional warrants against more Iranian officials. The linking of the murder to the Iranian Government by Judge Bruguiere has had significant political repercussions for French-Iranian relations, including postponement or cancellation of visits to Iran planned by President Mitterand and Foreign Minister Dumas.

Iranian-backed Shia groups in Lebanon were involved in the continued detention of Western hostages in 1991. Iran played a key role in the UN-sponsored process that obtained the release of six American and three British hostages in 1991 and the recovery of the bodies of two Americans who died while in captivity. Iran probably helped arrange freedom for the hostages out of the belief that continuation of the crisis was detrimental to Iranian President Rafsanjani's attempt to improve relations with the West and obtain foreign assistance in modernizing Iran's economy. The hostage releases still received criticism from Iranian hardliners and elements of Hizballah. Immediately after the August release of British hostage John McCarthy, Hizballah elements opposed to the hostage releases kidnapped a French citizen. He was freed three days later only after what appeared to be significant pressure from Iran, Syria, and Lebanese figures. Iran has also reportedly offered refuge to about 40 former Hizballah hostage holders and may provide them with new identities to prevent retaliation.

Further demonstration of Iran's close involvement in hostage taking is shown by the Iranian Ambassador to Germany invoking the fate of two German relief workers in an attempt to obtain the release of the Hammadi brothers, two Hizballah terrorists jailed in Germany. Iran has indicated its willingness to help bring about the release of two German hostages believed to be held by Hizballah elements in Lebanon.

Iranian-supported groups in Turkey were believed to have been responsible for the 26 March car bombing in Ankara that injured an Iraqi diplomat and the two October car bombings that killed an American serviceman and injured an Egyptian diplomat.

Major international terrorists—including Ahmad Jabril of the PFLP-GC and various prominent members of Hizballah and factions of the PIJ—frequently visit Iran, often meeting with the regime's senior leadership. In October, representatives of these organizations and others attended a conference hosted by Iran on Palestine designed to strengthen opposition to the Middle East peace process. Tehran has in recent years focused on developing its ties to radical Palestinian groups and tried to increase its influence in the Palestinian movement as a whole.

Iran has steadfastly opposed the Middle East peace process and threatened participants. Iran's spiritual leader, Ayatollah Khamenei, declared on 30 October, "Those who take part in this treason will suffer the wrath of nations." Earlier in the month, Ayatollah Musavi-Ardabili, a senior cleric, called on Muslims to attack American lives and properties as a religious duty.

Iran has continued its death threats against author Salman Rushdie. The bounty on Mr. Rushdie was apparently increased during 1991 to a total of at least $2 million. In addition, two translators of Mr. Rushdie's works were attacked in 1991. An Italian translator was injured in an attack, and a Japanese translator was killed. Both attacks are believed to be linked to the translators' work with the writings of Salman Rushdie.

1992

Iran was the most dangerous state sponsor of terrorism in 1992, with over 20 acts in 1992 attributable to it or its surrogates. Iran's intelligence services continue to support terrorist acts—either directly or through extremist groups—aimed primarily against Iranian opponents of the regime living abroad and Israeli targets. Although Iran did not carry out direct attacks on US targets in 1992, Iranian agents regularly surveilled US missions and personnel. Tehran's leaders view terrorism as a valid tool to accomplish the regime's political objectives, and acts of terrorism are approved at the highest levels of government in Iran. Hizballah, Iran's most important client, was responsible for the deadliest act of terrorism in 1992, the bombing of the Israeli Embassy in Buenos Aires in March, which killed 29 people and wounded 242. Indications are that Iran at least had foreknowledge of this act and was probably involved.

Despite Iran's attempts to distance itself publicly from direct involvement in terrorist acts during the past year, Tehran has been tied to several bombings and assassinations in the Middle East, Europe, and Latin America.

Iranian intelligence continues to stalk members of the Iranian opposition, especially in the United States, Europe, and the Middle East. There are strong indications that Iran was responsible for the assassination of the leader of the Kurdish Democratic Party of Iran (KDPI) and three of his followers in Berlin in September. The killing closely resembled the murder of the previous head of the KDPI in Vienna in 1989. The fatal stabbing of an Iranian dissident poet in Bonn in August 1992 was reminiscent of the stabbing of former Prime Minister Bakhtiar in Paris in 1991.

In March 1992 a French court sentenced two Iranians in absentia to five years imprisonment on illegal weapons charges stemming from 1986. The two had been waiting outside the home of Abdal Rahman Barumand, an ally of former Prime Minister Bakhtiar. Barumand was assassinated in April 1991 and Bakhtiar in August 1991, both in Paris. Two Iranians were arrested in Paris in November 1992 and held for extradition to Switzerland for the murder of Mujahedin-e Khalq (MEK) leader Kazem Rajavi in 1990.

The death sentence for Salman Rushdie, British author of *The Satanic Verses*, was upheld in 1992 by both the Iranian parliament and Iran's Chief Justice, and the reward for killing him was raised to more than $2 million. The Iranian Government has tried to carry out the death threat. The United Kingdom expelled three Iranian officials who were attempting to organize Rushdie's murder.

Iran is also the world's principal sponsor of extremist Islamic and Palestinian groups, providing them with funds, weapons, and training. Turkish Islamic Jihad, believed to be backed by Iran, claimed responsibility for the March car-bomb murder of an Israeli synagogue a few days earlier. These attacks came within weeks after the killing of Hizballah chief Musawi in southern Lebanon by the Israelis. Both Iran and Hizballah had vowed revenge against Israel and the United States for his death.

Iran also supports other radical organizations that have resorted to terrorism, including the Palestine Islamic Jihad (PIJ), the Popular Front for the Liberation of Palestine—General Command (PFLP-GC), and HAMAS. In August, Iran's first vice president met with the chiefs of Hizballah and the PFLP-GC while visiting Damascus. In October, Tehran hosted a series of high-profile meetings with Hizballah and HAMAS with the stated goal of coordinating their efforts against Israel and bringing the Arab-Israeli peace talks to a halt. In the aftermath of these talks, Hizballah increased its operations against Israel, including its repeated use of rockets to attack villages in northern Israel.

Iran has become the main supporter and ally of the fundamentalist regime in Sudan. Members of Iran's Islamic Revolutionary Guard Corps provide training for the Sudanese military. The current Iranian Ambassador to Khartoum was involved in the takeover of the US Embassy in Tehran in 1979 and served as Iranian Charge in Beirut, where he played a leading role in developing the Hizballah terrorist infrastructure in the 1980s. Khartoum has become a key venue for Iranian contact with Palestinian and North African extremists of the Sunni branch of Islam.

Tehran continues to support and provide sanctuary for the Kurdistan Workers Party (PKK), which has been responsible for hundreds of deaths in Turkey this year.

1993

Iran again was the most active state sponsor of terrorism in 1993 and was implicated in terrorist attacks in Italy, Turkey, and Pakistan. Its intelligence services support terrorist acts—either directly or through extremist groups—aimed primarily against opponents of the regime living abroad. Although neither Iran nor its surrogate Hizballah has launched an attack on US interests since 1991, Iran still surveils US missions and personnel. Tehran's policymakers view terrorism as a valid tool to accomplish their political objectives, and acts of terrorism are approved at the highest levels of the Iranian Government. During the year, Iranian-sponsored terrorist attacks were less frequent in Western Europe and the Middle East, favored venues of the past, but were more frequent in other areas, especially Turkey and Pakistan.

Iranian intelligence continues to stalk members of the Iranian opposition in the United States, Europe, Asia, and the Middle East. Despite Tehran's attempts to distance itself from direct involvement in terrorist acts, Iran has been linked to several assassinations of dissidents during the past year. Iran was probably responsible for the assassination of at least four members of one opposition group, the Iraq-based Mujahedin-e-Khalq (MEK): one in Italy in March, a second in Pakistan in June in which a bystander was also killed, and two in Turkey in August. The body of a MEK member who was abducted in Istanbul at the end of 1992 has still not been found. In January, the body of another Iranian dissident who had been kidnapped in Istanbul several months before was found. All of the murders were carried out by professional assassins; no arrests have been made.

Iranian intelligence agents are under arrest in Germany and France for their links to murders of Iranian dissidents. One Iranian, identified by German prosecutors as an Iranian intelligence agent, is being tried with four Lebanese Hizballah members for their roles in the murder of three Iranian Kurdish dissidents in Berlin in September 1992. France arrested two Iranians in November 1992 for the murder of MEK leader Kazein Rajavi in Geneva in 1990; on 30 December, France expelled them to Iran, despite an extradition request from Switzerland. They had been in Europe as part of a hit team to assassinate one or more unidentified Iranian dissidents. The French Government explained that it was pursuing French national interests. A French magistrate investigating the killings of former Iranian Prime Minister Shahpur Bakhtiar and an assistant near Paris in 1991 has linked the murder to Iranian intelligence. Three men are being held in French prisons in connection with the murders, including a nephew of President Rafsanjani who was an employee of the Iranian Embassy, and a nephew of the late Ayatollah Khomeini who was an Iranian radio correspondent. French authorities have issued arrest warrants for several other men.

Iranian leaders continue to defend the late Ayatollah Khomeini's 1989 fatwa, which condemned British author Salman Rushdie for blasphemy and called for his death. In February, on the fourth anniversary of the decree, Iran's current spiritual leader, Ayatollah Ali Khamenei, declared that the death sentence must and will be carried out, no matter the consequences. To demonstrate its support, the Iranian Parliament also passed a resolution endorsing the fatwa and calling for Rushdie's death. An Iranian foundation that has offered a reward of more than $2 million for killing Rushdie has warned that Muslims will also take revenge on anyone who supports Rushdie. In Beirut, Hizballah vowed to carry out the decree. In Oslo, an unknown assailant shot and seriously wounded the Norwegian publisher of *The Satanic Verses* in October. In Turkey in July, 37 persons died in a fire set by anti-Rushdie demonstrators during a violent three-month-long campaign to prevent a Turkish magazine from publishing excerpts of Rushdie's book. At the start of the campaign, the Iranian Ambassador to Turkey proclaimed that the fatwa against Rushdie also applied in Turkey. Fundamentalists, including Turkish Hizballah groups, issued death threats to the journal's officials, distributors, and vendors and attacked printing facilities, distribution vehicles, and sales kiosks, injuring several workers. Iran is also the world's preeminent sponsor of extremist Islamic and Palestinian groups, providing funds, weapons, and training. The Lebanese Hizballah, Iran's most important client, was responsible for some of the most lethal acts of terrorism of the last decade, including the 1992 car bombing of the Israeli Embassy in Argentina. In 1993, Hizballah concentrated on guerrilla operations in southern Lebanon, including rocket attacks on civilians in northern Israel, and simultaneously boosted its political influence in the Lebanese parliament. Hizballah has also continued its efforts to develop a worldwide terrorist infrastructure.

Iran supports many other radical organizations that have resorted to terrorism, including the PIJ, the PFLP-GC, and HAMAS. Iranian leaders have worked to develop a rejectionist front, comprising Hizballah and 10 Palestinian groups based in Damascus, to counter the Middle East peace process.

An Iranian-backed Turkish group, Islamic Action—also referred to as the Islamic Movement Organization—is suspected by Turkish authorities in the car bombing of a prominent Turkish journalist in Istanbul in January and an assassination attempt on a Turkish Jewish businessman a few days later. In February, three members of an Iranian-backed radical Islamic group, possibly Islamic Action, were convicted for the bombing of an Istanbul synagogue almost a year earlier. It is unclear whether the group, some of whose members were arrested by Turkish police, were involved in the anti-Rushdie campaign in Turkey or linked to any of the several hundred murders of secular Kurdish activists in eastern Turkey that have been blamed on so-called Turkish Hizballah groups.

Tehran continues to support and provide sanctuary for the PKK, which was responsible for hundreds of deaths in Turkey during the year.

Iran has become the main supporter and ally of the fundamentalist regime in Sudan. Members of Iran's Islamic Revolutionary Guard Corps provide training for the Sudanese military. The Iranian Ambassador to Khartoum was involved in the takeover of the US Embassy in Tehran in 1979 and played a leading role in developing Hizballah in the 1980s. Khartoum has become a key venue for Iranian contact with Palestinian and North African extremists.

The opposition group MEK launched several attacks into Iran from Iraq in 1993, mostly on oil refineries and pipelines in southwestern Iran. Two guards were killed in an attack on a communications facility of the national oil company in Kermanshah in May. In December, the MEK admitted that it killed a Turkish diplomat in Baghdad, claiming he was mistaken for an Iranian official.

1994

Iran is still the most active state sponsor of international terrorism and continues to be directly involved in planning and executing terrorist acts. This year Tehran seems to have maintained its terrorist activities at the level of 1993, when there were four confirmed and two possible Iranian attacks on dissidents living outside Iran. Iranian terrorist operations concentrate on Iranian dissidents, particularly members of the Mojahedin-e Khalq (MEK) and the Kurdish Democratic Party of Iran (KDPI). Iran supports extremist Palestinian groups that have used terrorism to try to halt the Middle East peace process. Tehran also gives varying degrees of assistance to an assortment of radical Islamic and secular groups from North Africa to Central Asia.

While President Rafsanjani has tried to moderate Iran's public image to expand its economic and political ties to Western Europe and Japan, Iran continues to use terrorism as ruthlessly as it did under Khomeini. Tehran supports groups, such as its main client Hizballah, that pose a threat to Americans. Due to the continuing threat from Tehran and Hizballah, American diplomatic missions and personnel remain at risk.

Confirmed attacks on Iranian dissidents in the past year include the following: the 7 January killing of Taha Kirmeneh, a dissident who was a member of the Kurdish Democratic Party of Iran (KDPI), by gunmen in Coru, Turkey; the 10 January wounding of a member of the KDPI by a letter bomb in Stockholm, Sweden; the killing of a KDPI leader in Sulaymaniyah, Iraq, on 10 March; and the killing of two members of the Mojahedin-e Khalq (MEK) in Qabbiyah, Iraq, while driving to Baghdad on 29 May. While the MEK has been victimized by Iranian terrorism, the group has itself employed terrorist tactics. The 24 June murder of dissident Osman Muhammed Amini at his home in Copenhagen and the 12 November murder of dissident Ali Mohammed Assadi in Bucharest may also have been carried out at the Iranian Government's behest.

On 6 December, a French court handed down a decision in the trial of three Iranians accused of participating in the 1991 murder of former Iranian Prime Minister Bakhtiar and an assistant. One defendant received life imprisonment. A second, an Iranian radio correspondent who is reputed to be a nephew of the late Ayatollah Khomeini, was sentenced to 10 years in jail. The third, an employee of the Iranian Embassy in Bern, was acquitted.

Iran remains committed to implementation of the death sentence imposed on British author Salman Rushdie. When speaking to Western audiences, Iranian leaders claim that the fatwa (or religious finding) against Rushdie is a religious matter that does not involve the Government of Iran.

However, the Iranian Government continued its propaganda campaign against Rushdie. In February, the fifth anniversary of the fatwa, Tehran Radio stated that "The least punishment for (Rushdie)—is—his execution." Ayatollah Hassan Sanei, the head of a quasi-governmental foundation that has offered a $2 million reward for the murder of Rushdie, said that supporters of Rushdie who campaign for the lifting of the fatwa deserved to be "punished." A Revolutionary Guards official vowed publicly that the death sentence would be carried out. The influence of this campaign has been felt outside Iran. In September, the head of a Muslim organization in Norway threatened to kill Rushdie if he attended a conference on freedom of expression in Stavanger.

Iran is also the world's preeminent state sponsor of extremist Islamic and Palestinian groups, providing funds, weapons, and training. Hizballah, Iran's closest client, could well have been responsible for the 18 July bombing of the Argentine Israel Mutual Association that left nearly 100 persons dead. This operation was virtually identical to the one conducted in March 1992 against the Israeli Embassy in Buenos Aires, for which Hizballah claimed responsibility. Hizballah had stated that it would seek retaliation against Israel for the kidnapping of a well-known Lebanese Shia terrorist and the Israeli airstrike in June on a Hizballah camp in Lebanon that killed more than 20 militants. Iran supports many other radical organizations that have engaged in terrorism. Tehran opposes any compromise with or recognition of Israel and, as the peace process moves ahead, has worked to coordinate a rejectionist front to oppose the Israeli-PLO accords, particularly with the PIJ, the PFLP-GC, and HAMAS, as well as Hizballah.

Tehran continues to provide safehaven to the terrorist Kurdistan Workers' Party (PKK) in Iran. The PKK—seeking to establish a Kurdish state in southeastern Turkey—in 1994 conducted a violent campaign against Turkish tourism, including attacks on tourist spots frequented by foreigners, while continuing unabated the use of terrorism against Turkish citizens, including ethnic Kurds.

1995

Iran remains the premier state sponsor of international terrorism and is deeply involved in the planning and execution of terrorist acts both by its own agents and by surrogate groups. This year Tehran escalated its assassination campaign against dissidents living abroad; there were seven confirmed Iranian murders of dissidents in 1995, compared with four in 1994. Iranian antidissident operations concentrated on the regime's main opposition group, the Mojahedin-e Khalq (MEK), and the Kurdish Democratic Party of Iran (KDPI).

Leaders of Iranian dissident groups are the most frequent victims of Iranian intelligence and terrorist operations. In 1995 most antidissident attacks were conducted in Iraq, in contrast to prior years' worldwide operations. Attacks on Iranian dissidents in Iraq during the year included the shooting deaths on 17 May of two MEK members in Baghdad, the murder on 5 June of two members of the Iranian Kurdish "Toilers" Party (Komelah) in Sulaymaniyah, and the killing of three MEK members in Baghdad on 10 July. The shooting death in Paris on 17 September of Hashem Abdollahi, son of the chief witness in the trial of 1994 that convicted two Iranians for murdering former Iranian Prime Minister Bakhtiar in 1991, may have been an antidissident attack.

Sendar Hosseini, a suspect in the 1994 murder of dissident Osman Muhammad Amini in Copenhagen, Denmark, was arrested by Italian police in Bibione, Italy.

Iran provides arms, training, and money to Lebanese Hizballah and several Palestinian extremist groups that use terrorism to oppose the Middle East peace process. Tehran, which is against any compromise with or recognition of Israel, continued in 1995 to encourage Hizballah, HAMAS, the PIJ, the PFLP-GC, and other Palestinian rejectionist groups to form a coordinated front to resist Israel and the peace process through violence and terrorism.

Hizballah, Iran's closest client, remains the leading suspect in the July 1994 bombing of the Argentine-Israel Mutual Association (AMIA) in Buenos Aires that killed at least 96 persons. This operation was virtually identical to the one conducted in March 1992 against the Israeli Embassy in Buenos Aires, for which Hizballah claimed responsibility.

Iran also gives varying degrees of assistance to an assortment of radical Islamic and secular groups from North Africa to Central Asia. For example, Tehran continued to offer the Kurdistan Workers' Party (PKK) safehaven in Iran. Seeking to establish a Kurdish state in southeastern Turkey, the PKK in 1995 launched numerous attacks in Europe and continued its violent campaign against Turkish tourism, including attacks on tourist spots frequented by Westerners. Tehran also provided some support to Turkish Islamic groups that have been blamed for attacks against Turkish secular and Jewish figures.

Iranian authorities reaffirmed the validity of the death sentence imposed on British author Salman Rushdie, although some Iranian officials claimed that the Government of Iran would not implement the fatwa. Tehran, however, continued to mount a propaganda campaign against Rushdie. In February—the sixth anniversary of the judgment—Iran's official news agency IRNA reported that Deputy Foreign Minister Mahmoud Vaezi "underlined the need for the implementation of the fatwa against the author of the blasphemous book *The Satanic Verses.*" Vaezi in May declared that "the fatwa issued by the late Imam [Khomeini] could neither be revoked nor changed by anybody."

Despite increasing Iranian support for extremist groups and involvement in terrorist operations, President Rafsanjani continued to project publicly a "moderate" image of Iran to Western European countries and Japan to facilitate the expansion of its relations with them. This quest for respectability probably explains why Iran reduced its attacks in Europe last year; Tehran wants to ensure access to Western capital and markets.

Iran continued to view the United States as its principal foreign adversary, supporting groups such as Hizballah that pose a threat to US citizens. Because of Tehran's and Hizballah's deep antipathy toward the United States, US missions and personnel abroad continue to be at risk.

1996

Iran remained the premier state sponsor of terrorism in 1996. It continued to be involved in the planning and execution of terrorist acts by its own agents and by surrogates such as Lebanese Hizballah and continued to fund and train known terrorist groups.

Tehran conducted at least eight dissident assassinations outside Iran in 1996. In May 1996 Reza Mazlouman, a government official under the Shah, was murdered in Paris by an Iranian resident of Germany with alleged ties to Iran's Ministry of Intelligence and Security (MOIS). The suspect was extradited to France by Germany. Seven other dissidents were assassinated by Iran in 1996 in Turkey and northern Iraq. Iran's primary targets are members of the regime's main opposition groups, the Mujahedin-e Khalq (MEK) and the Kurdish Democratic Party of Iran (KDPI), as well as former officials of the late Shah's government who speak out against the clerical regime.

Iran continued to provide support—including money, weapons, and training—to a variety of terrorist groups, such as Hizballah, HAMAS, and the Palestine Islamic Jihad (PIJ). It continued to oppose any recognition of Israel and to encourage violent rejection of the Middle East peace process. For example, Iranian Vice President Habibi met with HAMAS leaders in Damascus and praised their successful efforts immediately following the February bombings in Israel. HAMAS claimed responsibility for two more bombings in Israel the following week.

During a routine customs inspection of an Iranian vessel in Antwerp in March, Belgian authorities discovered a disassembled mortar-like weapon hidden in a shipment of pickles. The shipment was consigned to an Iranian merchant living in Germany. Iranian dissidents claim that the mortar was intended for use in an assassination attempt against Iranian exiles in Europe.

Testimony in the three-year-long trial of an Iranian and four Lebanese for the Iran-sponsored killing of Iranian Kurdish dissidents in Berlin's Mykonos restaurant in 1992 concluded in late 1996. German authorities issued an arrest warrant in March for Ali Fallahian, Iran's Intelligence Minister. In the fall, former Iranian President Abolhassan Bani Sadr and two other witnesses testified against Iran. In final statements in late November, German prosecutors charged Iranian Supreme Leader Khamenei and Iranian President Rafsanjani with approving the operation. (Guilty verdicts for four of the accused were announced in April 1997.)

Iranian leaders have consistently denied being able to revoke the *fatwa* against Salman Rushdie's life, in effect for nearly eight years, claiming that revocation is impossible because the author of the fatwa is deceased. There is no indication that Tehran is pressuring the 15 Khordad Foundation to withdraw the $2 million reward it is offering to anyone who will kill Rushdie.

In addition, Iran provides safehaven to elements of the Kurdistan Workers' Party (PKK), a Turkish separatist group that has conducted numerous terrorist attacks in Turkey and throughout Europe. Although Turkey and Iran agreed to a joint operation in mid-October to remove the PKK from the border region, Iran reportedly failed to cooperate in a meaningful way.

Iran's terrorist network in the Persian Gulf remained active in 1996. The Government of Bahrain announced in June the discovery of a local Hizballah group of Bahraini Shiites who had been trained and sponsored by Iran in an effort to overthrow the ruling al-Khalifa family.

1997

Iran remained the most active state sponsor of terrorism in 1997. Tehran continued to be involved in the planning and execution of terrorist acts by its own agents and by surrogates such as the Lebanese Hizballah and continued to fund and train known terrorist groups throughout 1997. Although the August 1997 accession of President Khatami has resulted in more conciliatory Iranian public statements, such as public condemnations of terrorist attacks by Algerian and Egyptian groups, Iranian support for terrorism remains in place.

Tehran conducted at least 13 assassinations in 1997, the majority of which were carried out in northern Iraq. Iran's targets normally include, but are not limited to, members of the regime's main opposition groups, including the Kurdish Democratic Party of Iran (KDPI) and the Mujahedin-e Khalq (MEK). Elsewhere in Iraq, in January 1997 Iranian agents tried to attack the Baghdad headquarters of the MEK using a "supermortar" of a design similar to that discovered aboard the Iranian ship "Kolahdooz" by Belgian customs authorities in early 1996. The attack was unsuccessful, resulting in the death of one person and some damage to an Iraqi hospital building.

April 1997 witnessed the conclusion of the trial in Germany of an Iranian and four Lebanese for the 1992 killing of Iranian Kurdish dissidents, one of whom was then Secretary General of the KDPI, in Berlin's Mykonos restaurant. A German judge found the Iranian and three of the Lebanese guilty of the murders. Two defendants, Kazem Darabi and Abbas Rhayel, were sentenced to life in prison. Two others, Yousef Amin and Muhammad Atris, received sentences of 11 years and five years and three months, respectively. The fifth defendant, Aatollah Ayad, was acquitted. The court stated that the Government of Iran had followed a deliberate policy of liquidating the regime's opponents who lived outside Iran, including the opposition KDPI. The judge further stated that the Mykonos murders had been approved at the most senior levels of the Iranian Government by an extra-legal committee whose members included the Minister of Intelligence and Security, the Foreign Minister, the President, and the Supreme Leader. As a result of elections in May, however, the positions of Minister of Intelligence and Security, Foreign Minister, and President are now held by individuals other than those who were involved in the "Mykonos" murders. In March 1996 a German court had issued an arrest warrant in this case for Ali Fallahian, the former Iranian Minister of Intelligence and Security.

In September 1997, Iran's new leadership affirmed the *fatwa* on Salman Rushdie, which has been in effect since 1989, stating once again that revocation is impossible since the author of the *fatwa* is deceased. There is no indication that Tehran is pressuring the Fifteen Khordad Foundation to withdraw the $2.5 million reward it is offering for executing the *fatwa* on Rushdie.

Iran continued to provide support—in the form of training, money, and/or weapons—to a variety of terrorist groups, such as Lebanese Hizballah, HAMAS, and the PIJ. The Iranian Government continues to oppose recognition of Israel and to encourage violent rejection of the Middle East peace process. In the fall of 1997, Tehran hosted numerous representatives of terrorist groups—including HAMAS, Lebanese Hizballah, the PIJ, and the Egyptian al-Gama'at al-Islamiya —at a conference of "Liberation Movements." Participants reportedly discussed the jihad, establishing greater coordination between certain groups, and an increase in support for some groups. In October, the Algerian Government accused Tehran of training and equipping Algerian terrorists.

Iran still provides safehaven to elements of the PKK, a Turkish separatist group that has conducted numerous terrorist attacks in Turkey and on Turkish targets in Europe. Following a late 1997 Turkish incursion into northern Iran in pursuit of PKK cadres, Tehran protested the violation of its territory but in 1997 made no effort to remove the PKK from Iranian territory.

In November, Iran's Minister of Foreign Affairs, Dr. Kamal Kharrazi, publicly condemned the terrorist attack by the Egyptian al-Gama'at al-Islamiyya on tourists at Luxor, Egypt. Similarly, in early January 1998 the Foreign Ministry's official spokesman, Mahmud Mohammadi, also condemned the vicious attacks on civilians during the Muslim month of Ramadan (late December 1997 to early January 1998) "no matter who was responsible."

(President Khatemi, in a 7 January 1998 CNN interview, agreed that terrorist attacks against non-combatants, including Israeli women and children, should be condemned.)

1998

Iran in 1998 continued to be involved in the planning and execution of terrorist acts. Tehran apparently conducted fewer antidissident assassinations abroad in 1998 than in 1997. Tehran continued, however, to support a variety of groups that use terrorism to pursue their goals. Despite Iranian public statements condemning certain terrorist acts or expressing sympathy for Kenyan and Tanzanian victims of the August 1998 bombings of the US Embassies in Nairobi and Dar es Salaam, Iranian support for terrorism remains in place.

Tehran is reported to have conducted several assassinations outside Iran during 1998. In June the "League of the Followers of the Sunna" accused Iranian intelligence agents of murdering an Iranian Sunni cleric, Shaikh Nureddin Ghuraybi, in Tajikistan. In September the leaders of Sipah-e-Sahaba Pakistan, a virulently anti-Shia sectarian group, accused Iran of responsibility for the murders of two of the organization's leaders, Allama Shoaib Nadeem and Maulana Habibur Rehman Siddiqui. In late November the National Council of Resistance claimed that the Iranian regime had kidnapped and killed Reza Pirzadi in Pakistan. Pirzadi was described as a warrant officer who had been released from prison in Iran in 1996.

Members of Iran's Ministry of Security and Intelligence (MOIS) may have conducted five mysterious murders of leading writers and political activists in Iran. Late in the year, Tehran announced the discovery of an operational cell within the MOIS that it alleged operated without the knowledge of senior government officials. Tehran reportedly arrested the cell's members.

The Iranian Government stated publicly that it would take no action to enforce the *fatwa* on Salman Rushdie, a British citizen, which has been in effect since 1989. The Iranian Government's assurance led the UK Government to upgrade its diplomatic relations with Iran. Tehran stated, however, that revoking the *fatwa* is impossible since its author is deceased. Moreover, the Iranian Government has not required the Fifteen Khordad Foundation to withdraw its reward for executing the *fatwa* on Rushdie, and in November the Foundation increased its offer to $2.8 million.

Iran continued to provide support to a variety of terrorist groups, including the Lebanese Hizballah, HAMAS, and the Palestinian Islamic Jihad, which oppose the Middle East peace process through violence. Iran supports these groups with varying amounts of training, money, and/or weapons.

In March, a US district court ruled that Iran should pay $247 million to the family of Alisa Flatow, a US citizen killed in a PIJ bomb attack in Gaza in April 1995. The court ruled that Iran was responsible for her death because it provided funding to the PIJ, which claimed responsibility for the act. Palestinian sources said Iran supported the PIJ's claimed attack in Jerusalem in early November 1998, in which two suicide bombers injured some 21 persons.

Iran still provides safehaven to elements of the PKK, a Turkish separatist group that has conducted numerous terrorist attacks in Turkey and on Turkish targets in Europe.

Iran also provides support to North African groups. In an interview in April 1998, former Iranian president Bani Sadr accused Tehran of training Algerian fighters, among others.

Tehran accurately claims it also is a victim of terrorism. In 1998 several high-ranking members of the Iranian Government were attacked and at least two were killed in attacks claimed by the terrorist group Mujahedin-e Khalq (MEK). The MEK claimed responsibility for the killing on 23 August of Asadollah Lajevardi, the former director of Tehran's Evin Prison. It also claimed responsibility for the deaths in June of several persons, including Haj Hassan Salehi, allegedly a torturer at the prison, during a bombing attack on the Revolutionary Prosecutor's Office in Tehran.

Mohsen Rafiqdust, head of the Foundation for the Oppressed and Disabled, escaped an attack on his life on 13 September. He said counterrevolutionary elements had embarked on efforts to make the country insecure.

At least nine Iranian diplomatic and associated personnel died when unknown persons invaded the Iranian Consulate in Mazar-e Sharif, Afghanistan, in early August during the Taliban takeover of that city. The Taliban denied responsibility for the deaths.

1999

Although there were signs of political change in Iran in 1999, the actions of certain state institutions in support of terrorist groups made Iran the most active state sponsor of terrorism. These state institutions, notably the Revolutionary Guard Corps and the Ministry of Intelligence and Security, continued to be involved in the planning and execution of terrorist acts and continued to support a variety of groups that use terrorism to pursue their goals.

A variety of public reports indicate Iran's security forces conducted several bombings against Iranian dissidents abroad. Iranian agents, for example, were blamed for a truck bombing in early October of a Mujahedin-e Khalq (MEK) terrorist base near Basrah, Iraq, that killed several MEK members and non-MEK individuals.

Iran continued encouraging Hizballah and the Palestinian rejectionist groups—including HAMAS, the Palestinian Islamic Jihad, and Ahmad Jibril's PFLP-GC—to use violence, especially terrorist attacks, in Israel to undermine the peace process. Iran supported these groups with varying amounts of money, training, and weapons. Despite statements by the Khatami administration that Iran was not working against the peace process, Tehran stepped up its encouragement of, and support for, these groups after the election of Israeli Prime Minister Barak and the resumption of Israel-Syria peace talks. In a gesture of public support, President Khatami met with Damascus-based Palestinian rejectionist leaders during his visit to Syria in May. In addition, Iranian Supreme Leader Khamenei reflected Iran's covert actions aimed at scuttling the peace process when he sponsored a major rally in Tehran on 9 November to demonstrate Iran's opposition to Israel and peace. Hizballah and Palestinian rejectionist speakers at the rally reaffirmed their support for violent *jihad* against Israel. A Palestinian Islamic Jihad representative praised a bombing in Netanya that occurred days before and promised more such attacks.

Tehran still provided safehaven to elements of Turkey's separatist PKK that conducted numerous terrorist attacks in Turkey and against Turkish targets in Europe. One of the PKK's most senior at-large leaders, Osman Ocalan, brother of imprisoned PKK leader Abdullah Ocalan, resided at least part-time in Iran. Iran also provided support to terrorist groups in North Africa and South and Central Asia, including financial assistance and training.

Tehran accurately claimed that it also was a victim of terrorism, as the opposition Mujahedin-e Khalq conducted several terrorist attacks in Iran. On 10 April the group assassinated Brigadier General Ali Sayyad Shirazi, the Iranian Armed Forces Deputy Chief of the Joint Staff.

2000

Despite the victory for moderates in Iran's Majles elections in February, aggressive countermeasures by hardline conservatives have blocked most reform efforts. Iran remained the most active state sponsor of terrorism in 2000. Its Revolutionary Guard Corps (IRGC) and Ministry of Intelligence and Security (MOIS) continued to be involved in the planning and the execution of terrorist acts and continued to support a variety of groups that use terrorism to pursue their goals.

Iran's involvement in terrorist-related activities remained focused on support for groups opposed to Israel and peace between Israel and its neighbors. Statements by Iran's leaders demonstrated Iran's unrelenting hostility to Israel. Supreme Leader Khamenei continued to refer to Israel as a "cancerous tumor" that must be removed; President Khatami, labeling Israel an "illegal entity," called for sanctions against Israel during the intifadah; and Expediency Council Secretary Rezai said, "Iran will continue its campaign against Zionism until Israel is completely eradicated." Iran has long provided Lebanese Hizballah and the Palestinian rejectionist groups—notably HAMAS, the Palestine Islamic Jihad, and Ahmad Jibril's PFLP-GC—with varying amounts of funding, safehaven, training, and weapons. This activity continued at its already high levels following the Israeli withdrawal from southern Lebanon in May and during the intifadah in the fall. Iran continued to encourage Hizballah and the Palestinian groups to coordinate their planning and to escalate their activities against Israel. Iran also provided a lower level of support—including funding, training, and logistics assistance—to extremist groups in the Gulf, Africa, Turkey, and Central Asia.

Although the Iranian Government has taken no direct action to date to implement Ayatollah Khomeini's fatwa against Salman Rushdie, the decree has not been revoked, and the $2.8 million bounty for his assassination has not been withdrawn. Moreover, hardline Iranians continued to stress that the decree is irrevocable. On the anniversary of the fatwa in February, the IRGC released a statement that the decree remains in force, and Ayatollah Yazdi, a member of the Council of Guardians, reiterated that "the decree is irrevocable and, God willing, will be carried out."

Iran also was a victim of Mujahedin-e-Khalq (MEK)-sponsored terrorism. The Islamic Republic presented a letter to the UN Secretary General in October citing seven acts of sabotage by the MEK against Iran between January and August 2000. The United States has designated the MEK as a Foreign Terrorist Organization.

2001

Iran remained the most active state sponsor of terrorism in 2001. Iran's Islamic Revolutionary Guard Corps (IRGC) and Ministry of Intelligence and Security (MOIS) continued to be involved in the planning and support of terrorist acts and supported a variety of groups that use terrorism to pursue their goals. Although some within Iran would like to end this support, hardliners who hold the reins of power continue to thwart any efforts to moderate these policies. Since the outbreak of the intifadah, support has intensified for Palestinian groups that use violence against Israel. During the past year, however, Iran appears to have reduced its involvement in other forms of terrorist activity. There is no evidence of Iranian sponsorship or foreknowledge of the September 11 attacks in the United States. President Khatami condemned the attacks and offered condolences to the American people.

Israel claims the ship Karine-A contained 50 tons of mostly Iranian-supplied weapons for use by militants against Israelis. During 2001, Iran sought a high-profile role in encouraging anti-Israeli activity by way of increasing its support for anti-Israeli terrorist groups. Supreme Leader Khamenei continued to refer to Israel as a "cancerous tumor" that must be removed. Matching this rhetoric with action, Iran continued to provide Lebanese Hizballah and the Palestinian rejectionist groups—notably HAMAS, the Palestine Islamic Jihad, and the PFLP-GC—with varying amounts of funding, safehaven, training, and weapons. It also encouraged Hizballah and the rejectionist Palestinian groups to coordinate their planning and to escalate their activities.

In addition, Iran provided limited support to terrorist groups in the Gulf, Africa, Turkey, and Central Asia. This support is at a considerably lower level than that provided to the groups opposed to Israel and has been decreasing in recent years. The Iranian Government took no direct action in 2001 to implement Ayatollah Khomeini's fatwa against Salman Rushdie, but the decree has not been revoked nor has the $2.8 million bounty for his death been withdrawn. Moreover, on the anniversary of the fatwa in February, some hardline Iranians stressed again that the decree is irrevocable and should be carried out.

During Operation Enduring Freedom, Tehran informed the United States that, in the event US warplanes went down inside Iran, Iranian forces would assist downed air crews in accordance with international convention. Iran also worked with the United States and its allies at the Bonn Conference in late 2001 to help in the formation of the Afghan Interim Authority. Tehran pledged to close its borders with Afghanistan and Pakistan to prevent the infiltration of Taliban and al-Qaida escapees. There are, however, reports that Arab Afghans, including al-Qaida members, used Iran as a transit route to enter and leave from Afghanistan.

2002

Iran remained the most active state sponsor of terrorism in 2002. Its Islamic Revolutionary Guard Corps and Ministry of Intelligence and Security were involved in the planning of and support for terrorist acts and continued to exhort a variety of groups that use terrorism to pursue their goals.

Iran's record against al-Qaida has been mixed. While it has detained and turned over to foreign governments a number of al-Qaida members, other al-Qaida members have found virtual safehaven there and may even be receiving protection from elements of the Iranian Government. Iran's long, rugged borders are difficult to monitor, and the large number of Afghan refugees in Iran complicates efforts to locate and apprehend extremists. Nevertheless, it is unlikely that al-Qaida elements could escape the attention of Iran's formidable security services.

During 2002, Iran maintained a high-profile role in encouraging anti-Israeli activity, both rhetorically and operationally. Supreme Leader Khamenei referred to Israel as a "cancerous tumor," a sentiment echoed by other Iranian leaders in speeches and sermons. Matching this rhetoric with action, Iran provided Lebanese Hizballah and Palestinian rejectionist groups—notably HAMAS, the Palestine Islamic Jihad, and the Popular Front for the Liberation of Palestine-General Command—with funding, safehaven, training, and weapons. Tehran also encouraged Hizballah and the Palestinian rejectionist groups to coordinate their planning and to escalate their terrorist activities against Israel.

Iran also provided support to extremist groups in Central Asia, Afghanistan, and Iraq with ties to al-Qaida, though less than that provided to the groups opposed to Israel.

In 2002, Iran became party to the 1988 Protocol on the Suppression of Unlawful Acts of Violence at Airports Serving International Civil Aviation. It is party to five of the 12 international conventions and protocols relating to terrorism.

2003

Iran remained the most active state sponsor of terrorism in 2003. Its Islamic Revolutionary Guard Corps and Ministry of Intelligence and Security were involved in the planning of and support for terrorist acts and continued to exhort a variety of groups that use terrorism to pursue their goals.

Iran's record against al-Qaida remains mixed. After the fall of the Taliban regime in Afghanistan, some al-Qaida members fled to Iran where they have found virtual safehaven. Iranian officials have acknowledged that Tehran detained al-Qaida operatives during 2003, including senior members. Iran's publicized presentation of a list to the United Nations of deportees, however, was accompanied by a refusal to publicly identify senior members in Iranian custody on the grounds of "security." Iran has resisted calls to transfer custody of its al-Qaida detainees to their countries of origin or third countries for further interrogation and trial.

During 2003, Iran maintained a high-profile role in encouraging anti-Israeli activity, both rhetorically and operationally. Supreme Leader Khamenei praised Palestinian resistance operations, and President Khatami reiterated Iran's support for the "wronged people of Palestine" and their struggles. Matching this rhetoric with action, Iran provided Lebanese Hizballah and Palestinian rejectionist groups— notably HAMAS, the Palestine Islamic Jihad, and the Popular Front for the Liberation of Palestine–General Command —with funding, safehaven, training, and weapons. Iran hosted a conference in August 2003 on the Palestinian intifadah, at which an Iranian official suggested that the continued success of the Palestinian resistance depended on suicide operations.

Iran pursued a variety of policies in Iraq aimed at securing Tehran's perceived interests there, some of which ran counter to those of the Coalition. Iran has indicated support for the Iraqi Governing Council and promised to help Iraqi reconstruction.

Shortly after the fall of Saddam Hussein, individuals with ties to the Revolutionary Guard may have attempted to infiltrate southern Iraq, and elements of the Iranian Government have helped members of Ansar al-Islam transit and find safehaven in Iran. In a Friday Prayers sermon in Tehran in May, Guardian Council member Ayatollah Ahmad Jannati publicly encouraged Iraqis to follow the Palestinian model and participate in suicide operations against Coalition forces.

Iran is a party to five of the 12 international conventions and protocols relating to terrorism.

2004

Iran remained the most active state sponsor of terrorism in 2004. Its Islamic Revolutionary Guard Corps and Ministry of Intelligence and Security were involved in the planning and support of terrorist acts and continued to exhort a variety of groups to use terrorism in pursuit of their goals.

Iran continued to be unwilling to bring to justice senior al-Qaida members it detained in 2003. Iran has refused to identify publicly these senior members in its custody on "security grounds." Iran has also resisted numerous calls to transfer custody of its al-Qaida detainees to their countries of origin or third countries for interrogation and/or trial. Iranian judiciary officials claimed to have tried and convicted some Iranian supporters of al-Qaida during 2004, but refused to provide details. Iran also continued to fail to control the activities of some al Qaida members who fled to Iran following the fall of the Taliban regime in Afghanistan.

During 2004, Iran maintained a high-profile role in encouraging anti-Israeli terrorist activity, both rhetorically and operationally. Supreme Leader Khamenei praised Palestinian terrorist operations, and Iran provided Lebanese Hizballah and Palestinian terrorist groups—notably HAMAS, the Palestinian Islamic Jihad, the al-Aqsa Martyrs Brigades, and the Popular Front for the Liberation of Palestine-General Command—with funding, safe haven, training, and weapons. Iran provided an unmanned aerial vehicle that Lebanese Hizballah sent into Israeli airspace on November 7, 2004.

Iran pursued a variety of policies in Iraq during 2004, some of which appeared to be inconsistent with Iran's stated objectives regarding stability in Iraq as well as those of the Iraqi Interim Government (IIG) and the Coalition. Senior IIG officials have publicly expressed concern over Iranian interference in Iraq, and there were reports that Iran provided funding, safe transit, and arms to insurgent elements, including Muqtada al-Sadr's forces.

Iraq
1986

Baghdad has denied being a state sponsor of terrorism since 1983 when it closed down Abu Nidal's offices there, but subsequently available evidence indicates that Iraq has continued supporting some terrorist groups, particularly those opposed to Syria. Iraq sees terrorism as a useful tool for promoting its foreign policy interests. In 1986, Baghdad also permitted safehaven to some Palestinian terrorists responsible for attacks against US and Israeli targets.

Iraq justifies its support for Palestinian groups, including those engaged in terrorism, as consistent with its stated policy of assisting the struggle for a Palestinian homeland. Since the bombing of PLO headquarters in Tunis in 1985 and Yasir Arafat's difficulties in maintaining an armed presence in Lebanon, Baghdad has become a major center of PLO and Fatah political and operational activities. Iraq also views its assistance as a means of enhancing its regional prestige, refurbishing its Pan-Arab credentials, and, most important, preventing Syria from gaining control of the Palestinian movement. The Palestinians, in return, offer Baghdad political support in the war with Tehran and help it against Syria. In 1986, the following Palestinian groups were based in or had offices in Baghdad:

The Arab Liberation Front, set up by Baghdad in 1969 to counter Syrian-backed groups.

The Palestine Liberation Front, headed by Abu Abbas, which was responsible for the Achille Lauro hijacking in October 1985.

The 15 May Organization, a splinter group formed from the remnants of Wadi Haddad's PFLP Special Operations Group, and headed by Abu Ibrahim. It has claimed responsibility for a long list of operations over many years, including bombings of Israeli Embassies and El Al offices in London, Rome, Istanbul, Vienna, Athens, and Genos; the 1984 attempted assassination of the Iranian Ambassador to Damascus; and the bombings of department stores in London, Paris, and Brussels. Members of 15 May were also responsible for the 1982 bombing of a Pan Am flight over Honolulu and probably for the bombing of TWA Flight 840 over Athens in April 1986.

1987

Iraq, which previously had been on the US Government's terrorist list[1] until removed in 1982, denies any relationship to terrorist organizations. The Abu Nidal organization was expelled in 1983; since then, Iraq has striven to establish a new international image as a state abhorring terrorism. This effort is no doubt designed to engender international support as the Iran-Iraq war continues.

Certain Palestinian terrorist groups, however, such as the Palestinian Liberation Front and remnants of the May 15 Organization, are known to have received sanctuary and assistance from Iraq since 1983. Some groups may have continued to receive aid in 1987.

1988

Iraq has worked to improve its international image, beginning with the expulsion of the ANO from Iraq in 1983. This effort was, no doubt, aimed at garnering international support during the Iran-Iraq war. Iraq, nonetheless, sponsored three assassinations of exiled dissidents in the United Kingdom, Sudan, and Norway in 1988. We suspect—but cannot confirm—that the Iraqi-backed Mujahedin-e-Khalq was responsible for an attempted bombing at a Tehran bus terminal.

Iraq also continued to provide safehaven to some Palestinian groups, such as the Iraqi-created Arab Liberation Front and Abu Abbas's Palestine Liberation Front (PLF), responsible for the Achille Lauro hijacking in 1985. Baghdad views its safehaven to Palestinian groups as legitimate assistance to the struggle for a Palestinian homeland.

1990

Iraq was returned to the terrorist list in September 1990 because of its increased contact with, and support for, terrorist groups. After the formation of an international coalition against the invasion of Kuwait, Iraqi officials issued public statements endorsing terrorism as a legitimate tactic.

---

1 The "terrorism list" is a list of countries formally designated by the Secretary of State under the US Export Administration Act of 1979 as having repeatedly provided support for acts of international terrorism. Congress must be informed before goods over a certain value are exported to these countries. Iraq is included in the section of the 1987 Patterns of Global Terrorism Report dealing with state support of terrorism because it appeared on the "terrorism list" within the previous five years. Iraq will not be included in future reports unless circumstances warrant inclusion.

Following its invasion of Kuwait on 2 August, the Government of Iraq systematically seized the citizens of the United States and many other nations. This occurred in both Kuwait and Iraq and continued for several months. Many of the hostages were moved to strategic sites in Iraq, including armaments factories, weapons research facilities, and major military bases.

This mass act of hostage taking was condemned by nations throughout the world, and the United Nations Security Council adopted Resolution 664, demanding that Iraq release these hostages.

Saddam Hussein eventually released the hostages, starting with women and children. By December, all the Western hostages were freed, but many Kuwaitis remained in captivity.

Hostage taking on the scale undertaken by Iraq is unprecedented in recent history. Saddam Hussein's operation represented a cynical and futile attempt to terrorize both foreign nationals and their governments and to weaken international resolve to oppose his occupation and annexation of Kuwait.

During 1990, and particularly after 2 August, the press reported increasing movement of terrorists to Baghdad, signaling the deepening relationship between these groups and Iraq. Even before the invasion of Kuwait, Iraq provided safehaven, training, and other support to Palestinian groups with a history of terrorist actions. The Arab Liberation Front (ALF) and Abu Abbas's PLF, responsible for the 1985 Achille Lauro hijacking and the terrorist attack on Israeli beaches in May, are among these groups. The ANO is also reported to have reestablished its presence in Iraq in the first half of 1990. Abu Ibrahim, leader of the now-defunct 15 May terrorist organization and famed for his skill as a bombmaker, is also reportedly based in Baghdad.

With the end of the Iran-Iraq war, Iraq reduced its support for anti-Iranian dissident groups including the Mujahidin-e-Khalq (MEK). Speculation continues regarding increased Iraqi support for the terrorist Kurdish Worker's Party (PKK) in Turkey. This is coupled with the worsening of Turkish-Iraqi relations over Turkey's enforcement of UN mandated trade sanctions after the invasion of Kuwait and disputes over water rights.

Senior Iraqi Government officials, including Foreign Minister Tariq Aziz, made public statements justifying terrorism as a legitimate Iraqi response in the event of hostilities between Iraq and the multinational force deployed in the region. There were reports that Iraq planned to put these words into effect and that Iraqi officials, as well as Baghdad's Palestinian surrogates, conducted surveillance against various coalition targets.

1991

During 1991 Iraq was a leading state sponsor of terrorism. Iraqi agents and members of pro-Iraqi groups conducted attacks on the United States and other coalition members in a variety of locations around the world. Numerous other planned attacks were frustrated by stringent security precautions imposed by both coalition and noncoalition states in response to the threat of Iraqi-sponsored terrorism.

On 11 June Iraq agreed, in accord with United Nations Security Council Resolution 687, not to support acts of international terrorism or allow terrorists to operate in Iraq. However, Iraq reportedly continues to maintain contacts with several groups and individuals that have historically practiced terrorism. These include the Arab Liberation Front (ALF), Abu Abbas's Palestine Liberation Front (PLF), the Abu Nidal organization (ANO), and former 15 May organization leader Abu Ibrahim. Baghdad continues to make vague threats of retribution for the military defeat it suffered during Operation Desert Storm.

Iraq was linked directly to only a small number of the more than 200 war-related terrorist incidents that occurred worldwide between mid-January and the end of February 1991, a figure three times greater than the comparable period in 1990. Much of the terrorist activity associated with the Gulf war was attributed to indigenous groups such as November 17 in Greece, the Tupac Amaru Revolutionary Movement (MRTA) in Peru, the Manuel Rodriguez Patriotic Front (FPMR) in Chile, and Dev Sol in Turkey, which was responsible for the death of two US citizens. In the months before Operation Desert Storm began, Iraq reportedly trained terrorists in intelligence activities and sabotage in special camps and prepared operations against coalition targets. During Operation Desert Storm, Saddam Hussein publicly and repeatedly called upon all of his terrorist allies to attack coalition targets, frequently through announcements on Iraq's Mother of Battles radio. The massive wave of anticoalition terrorism did not come to fruition, probably because of the cooperation of several governments in arresting or expelling several hundred Iraqi operatives from their host countries, the disruption in Baghdad's communications, and increased precautions at coalition facilities during the war. The targets hit during the Gulf crisis were typically banks or commercial facilities belonging to members of the coalition; most of the attacks caused only limited property damage.

Iraq was directly involved in the 19 January attempted bombing of the US Cultural Center in Manila by two Iraqi nationals, one of whom was killed when the powerful bomb he was carrying exploded prematurely. The Philippine government expelled an Iraqi diplomat who directed the operation and his accomplices. Iraq was also responsible for an attempted bombing of the US Ambassador's residence in Indonesia during the same period.

Although Iraq reduced support for anti-Iranian dissident groups, including the Mujahedin-e-Khalq, as part of a drive to appease Iran during the war, it probably maintains contact with several of these organizations.

Iraq is also suspected of increasing support and sanctuary provided to the Kurdish Workers' party (PKK), which has staged recent large-scale raids on Turkish government facilities from Iraqi territory. This policy probably is designed to punish Turkey for supporting the coalition during the war, providing sanctuary to Kurdish refugees, enforcing UN sanctions, and being part of a longstanding dispute over water rights. Iraq has denied such involvement.

1992

Iraq has not yet fully recovered its ability to conduct international terrorist attacks since the mass expulsion of Iraqi agents from many countries during the Gulf war. Nevertheless, Baghdad conducted 39 terrorist attacks against a variety of targets in direct violation of UN Security Council Resolution 687, which required Iraq to cease support for acts of international terrorism. Iraqi intelligence has resumed sending agents abroad to track opponents of Saddam Hussein. In addition, there have been persistent reports and at least one murder that strongly suggest Iraq is training hit squads to attack Hussein's enemies in other countries. In 1992, Iraqi-sponsored terrorism has focused on Kurdish targets and on UN and Western relief organization employees stationed in northern Iraq.

The most dramatic case of an assassination committed by the Iraqis during the year occurred in December, when two Iraqis shot and killed an Iraqi nuclear scientist in Amman, Jordan, as he was preparing to defect.

There have been many casualties in the dozens of attacks aimed at driving UN and aid workers out of northern Iraq. In November, magnetic time bombs placed under UN convoy trucks exploded in Irbil; all evidence points to Iraqi Government responsibility for the attacks. In December, Iraqi authorities placed eight time bombs under UN relief convoy trucks. The bombs were set to explode in Irbil but were discovered and defused. One week later, explosions destroyed or damaged 14 relief trucks that had just passed the Iraqi checkpoint at Faydah. The trucks had crossed Iraqi-controlled territory after returning from Suleyamaniya. The houses, offices, and vehicles of UN and relief workers have been repeatedly attacked by bombs, grenades, guns, and fires.

UN Security Council Resolution 687 also requires that Iraq not allow any terrorist organization to operate within its territory. Nevertheless, Baghdad continues to maintain contacts and in some cases provide sanctuary to several groups and individuals that have practiced terrorism. Iraq hosts and supports the main Iranian opposition group, the Mujahedin-e Khalq (MEK), which carried out several violent attacks in Iran in 1992.

Saddam Hussein also supports extremist Palestinian groups including the Abu Nidal organization (ANO), the Arab Liberation Front, Abu Abbas's Palestine Liberation Front (PLF), and Abu Ibrahim, leader and master bomb maker of the now defunct 15 May organization. The 1992 conviction of Mohammed Rashid in a Greek court for bombing a Pan Am aircraft in 1982 provided clear proof of long-standing Iraqi state sponsorship of international terrorism. Baghdad is alleged to provide safehaven and support to the Kurdistan Workers Party (PKK).

1993

The attempted assassination of former President Bush in Kuwait in April was the most brazen Iraqi act of terrorism in 1993. Iraqi-sponsored terrorism has become almost commonplace in northern Iraq, where the regime has been responsible for dozens of attacks on UN and relief agency personnel and aid convoys.

Iraq has not fully recovered its ability to conduct terrorist attacks outside its borders since the mass expulsion of Iraqi agents from many countries during the Gulf war. However, Iraqi intelligence has resumed sending agents abroad to track opponents of Saddam Husayn.

Kuwaiti officials discovered the elaborate scheme to kill former President Bush with an enormous car bomb shortly before he arrived for a visit. The group arrested for the assassination attempt was also planning a bombing campaign to destabilize Kuwait. The 14 suspects—11 Iraqis and three Kuwaitis—went on trial in June. Several of the Iraqi defendants worked for Iraqi intelligence, according to testimony in the trial. Forensic evidence also clearly linked Iraq to the abortive attack.

Iraqi-backed surrogates were probably responsible for two attempts to bomb the Kuwait Airways office in Beirut and another attempt to bomb the Kuwaiti Embassy, also in Lebanon. The Iraqi regime continued its war of attrition on UN and humanitarian targets in northern Iraq aimed at driving the foreign presence out of the area and depriving the Kurdish population of relief supplies. UN and relief workers were shot at; bombs or grenades were tossed at residences and vehicles; and bombs were placed on UN trucks loaded with relief supplies. In March, a Belgian official of Handicapped International was shot and killed; a local employee of the same organization was killed and six others were injured when an aid station was bombed in December. We suspect Iraqi involvement.

On 26 September, a UN truck carrying 12 tons of medical supplies was completely destroyed by a bomb attached to the fuel tank probably by Iraqi agents at an Iraqi checkpoint. The truckdriver and 12 civilians were injured by the blast. The incident illustrates Iraqi determination to reduce aid to the Kurds.

Although the Iraqi Government agreed in 1992 to comply with UN Resolution 687, which requires that Iraq not allow any terrorist organization to operate within its territory, Baghdad still maintains contacts with or provides sanctuary to several groups and individuals that have practiced terrorism. For example, the PKK, which has killed hundreds of people in attacks inside Turkey and has mounted two separate terrorist campaigns against Turkish interests in Europe in 1993, has training camps in Iraq, according to press reports. Iraq supports an opposition group, the MEK, which carried out several violent attacks in Iran during the year from bases in Iraq. Baghdad also harbors members of several extremist Palestinian groups including the ANO, the Arab Liberation Front, and Abu Abbas's Palestine Liberation Front (PLF).

1994

Iraq continued to engage in state-sponsored internal and international terrorism in 1994. It is rebuilding its ability to mount terrorist attacks abroad, despite financial and diplomatic constraints imposed in the wake of the Gulf war. The Government of Iraq provides safehaven and logistic support to several terrorist groups and individuals, including elements of the ANO, based in Lebanon; the Mojahedin-e Khalq, which is opposed to the government in Tehran; Abu Abbas' Palestine Liberation Front (PLF); and notorious bomb-maker Abu Ibrahim. Both Abbas and Ibrahim enjoy sanctuary in Iraq.

Political killings and terrorist actions are directed against civilians, foreign relief workers, journalists, and opposition leaders. On 12 April, a prominent Iraqi expatriate oppositionist residing in Beirut, Lebanon, was assassinated. The Government of Lebanon stated that it had firm evidence linking the killing to the Government of Iraq and arrested two Iraqi diplomats in connection with the incident. Lebanon subsequently broke diplomatic relations with Iraq.

Since 1991, in violation of UN Security Council resolutions, the Government of Iraq has obstructed the international community's provision of humanitarian assistance. We believe that Iraq is responsible for more than 100 attacks on relief personnel and aid convoys over the past four years. Moreover, the Government of Iraq has offered monetary "bounties" to anyone who assassinates UN and other international relief workers.

A German journalist and her Kurdish bodyguard were shot to death on 3 April in an ambush near Suleymaniya. Kurdish authorities arrested several suspects who reportedly confessed that the government had paid them to commit the murders. Several other international personnel, including UN guards and journalists, were critically injured in bombing and shooting attacks. At least 16 such attacks were reported. On 2 January, two UN vehicles were fired on while approaching the Aski Kalak bridge between Mosul and Irbil. One vehicle was hit seven times. On 21 January a handmade device using TNT exploded in the garden of a UN residence. Two Swedish journalists were injured on 14 March near Aqrah when a bomb exploded under their car. On 24 May two vehicles carrying representatives from the NGO OXFAM were shot at while returning to Suleymaniyah from a UN-NGO meeting in Salaheddin. On 1 June handgrenades were thrown at a warehouse in Suleymaniyah belonging to the French relief group Equilibre.

In July, three members of a prominent Shi'a family, the al-Khoeis, and their driver died under suspicious circumstances in an automobile crash in southern Iraq, near Al Najaf. Evidence points to involvement by the Government of Iraq. The al-Khoei family had long been targeted for harassment and abuse by the government. On 4 June, a Kuwaiti court returned verdicts in the trial of the 14 individuals accused of participation in the plot to assassinate former President Bush during his April 1993 visit to Kuwait. Six of the 14 were sentenced to death, seven were sentenced to prison for terms ranging from six months to 12 years, and one was acquitted.

1995

During 1995 several acts of political violence in northern Iraq matched Baghdad's pattern of using terrorism against the local population and regime defectors. Although Iraq's terrorist infrastructure has not recovered from the blows it suffered during the Gulf war, Baghdad has taken measures to restore its terrorist options.

Iraq remains far from compliance with UN resolutions that require it to cease internal repression and support for terrorism. Iraqi-sponsored terrorism has been commonplace in northern Iraq, where the regime is responsible for more than 100 attacks on UN and relief agency personnel and aid convoys over the past several years. In 1995 there were a number of acts of political violence for which Baghdad is a suspect. For example, a blast on 9 November at the security office in Kurdish-controlled northern Iraq of the opposition Iraqi National Congress (INC) killed at least 25 persons. The INC has been targeted before by the regime in Baghdad.

Early in the year, a number of Iraqi oppositionists in northern Iraq were poisoned by thallium. At least one survived and was treated in a British hospital. The British Government confirmed that he was a victim of a regime assassination attempt.

In October, the British Government expelled an officer of the Iraqi Interests Section in London for engaging in "activities incompatible with his diplomatic status." The London-based Iraqi opposition reported that the official concerned was an employee of the Iraqi intelligence services who was responsible for targeting Iraqi exiles for attack.

On 20 January a US District Court in California awarded $1.5 million to Dr. Sargon Dadesho, an Iraqi oppositionist living in the United States who had brought suit against the Iraqi regime. The court concluded that the Iraqi Government was involved in a 1990 plot to assassinate Dadesho. This is the only time such a judgment on Iraq's terrorist activities has been reached in a US court. In other court action, a Kuwaiti appeals court on 20 March confirmed the death sentences against two Iraqis convicted of involvement in the plot in 1993 to assassinate President George Bush, while converting to prison terms the death sentences meted out to four others by a lower court.

Iraq continues to provide haven and training facilities for several terrorist clients. Abu Abbas' Palestine Liberation Front (PLF) maintains its headquarters in Baghdad. The Abu Nidal organization (ANO) continues to have an office in Baghdad. The Arab Liberation Front (ALF), headquartered in Baghdad, continues to receive funding from Saddam's regime. Iraq also continues to host the former head of the now-defunct 15 May organization, Abu Ibrahim, who masterminded several bombings of US aircraft. A terrorist group opposed to the current Iranian regime, the Mojahedin-e Khalq (MEK), still is based in Iraq and has carried out several violent attacks in Iran from bases in Iraq.

1996

Iraq has not managed to recover its pre-Gulf war international terrorist capabilities, but it is slowly rebuilding its intelligence network. Acts of political violence continued in northern Iraq, and intra-Kurdish fighting in August led to an increased number of operatives there under Baghdad's control. At the time of its military attack on Irbil, Iraq reportedly murdered more than 100 Iraqis associated with the dissident Iraqi National Congress (INC). Later, Baghdad renewed its threat to charge foreign relief personnel and other Iraqi staff with "espionage," a crime punishable by death.

Iraq continues to provide safehaven to a variety of Palestinian rejectionist groups, including the Abu Nidal organization (ANO), the Arab Liberation Front (ALF), and the former head of the now defunct 15 May Organization, Abu Ibrahim, who masterminded several bombings of US aircraft. The Mujahedin-e Khalq (MEK), a terrorist group that opposes the current Iranian regime, also is based in Iraq.

In mid-November a Jordanian diplomatic courier was murdered in Iraq on the road from Amman to Baghdad, and his diplomatic pouch stolen. The perpetrators of the act have yet to be identified. The diplomatic bag contained 250 new Jordanian passports, which could be used by terrorist operatives for travel under cover.

The terrorist Kurdistan Workers' Party (PKK) continues to attempt to use northern Iraq as a safehaven and base for attacks on Turkey.

1997

During 1997, Baghdad continued to rebuild its intelligence network, which had been heavily damaged during the Gulf war and which it had previously used to support international terrorism. Press reports citing oppositionist and refugee sources stated that the regime has infiltrated the UN refugee camps and Iraqi communities in Europe and the Middle East. Iraqi oppositionists have claimed publicly that the regime intends to silence them and accused Baghdad of planning to assassinate Iraqi exiles. However, there is no available evidence to indicate that Iraq's agents participated directly in terrorist attacks during 1997. The last known such attack was against former President Bush in 1993.

In October, several gunmen attacked the World Health Organization headquarters in Baghdad with handgrenades, causing property damage but no casualties. The Iraqi Government blamed the attack on Iranian agents. Iran denied any involvement. A rocket attack 2 January 1998 on the headquarters of the United Nations (UNSCOM) inspectors in Baghdad did not cause damage because the rocket did not explode. No group claimed responsibility for the attacks.

Iraq continues to provide safehaven to a variety of Palestinian terrorist groups, including the ANO, the Arab Liberation Front (ALF), and the former head of the now defunct 15 May Organization, Abu Ibrahim, who masterminded several bombings of US aircraft. Iraq also provides bases, weapons, and protection to the MEK, a terrorist group that opposes the current Iranian regime.

1998

In 1998, Baghdad continued efforts to rebuild its intelligence network, which it previously had used to support international terrorism. Press reports indicated that Iraqi intelligence agents may have been planning an attack against Radio Free Europe in Prague in October 1998. Other press reports citing "reliable diplomatic sources" in Amman claimed that Iraq had sent abroad for terrorist purposes intelligence agents who pretended to be refugees and businessmen. Iraqi oppositionists have claimed publicly that the regime intends to silence them and have accused Baghdad of planning to assassinate Iraqi exiles. There are various claims that the Iraqi intelligence service was responsible for the killings of some nine persons in Amman, but we cannot corroborate the charges.

In January 1998 an Iraqi diplomat was fired on in Amman, Jordan. Jordanian authorities arrested five persons who subsequently confessed responsibility. In a separate incident, eight persons—including an Iraqi diplomat—were murdered in the home of an Iraqi businessman. Jordanian authorities in April arrested several persons for this crime.

In southern Iraq, Ayatollah Morteza Borujerdi—a senior Shia cleric—was killed on 22 April. Oppositionists claimed the Iraqi Government assassinated Borujerdi because he refused to cease leading prayers. A second high-ranking Shia cleric, Ayatollah Ali Gharavi, was killed on 18 June. The oppositionist Supreme Assembly for the Islamic Revolution in Iraq accused Baghdad of responsibility. Both men were respected Shia clerics of Iranian origin and their murders remain unsolved.

Iraq continues to provide safehaven to a variety of Palestinian rejectionist groups, including the Abu Nidal organization, the Arab Liberation Front (ALF), and the former head of the now-defunct 15 May Organization, Abu Ibrahim, who masterminded several bombings of US aircraft. In December press reports indicated that Abu Nidal had relocated to Iraq and may be receiving medical treatment. Abu Nidal's move to Baghdad—if true—would increase the prospect that Saddam may call on the ANO to conduct anti-US attacks. Iraq also provides bases, weapons, and protection to the MEK, a terrorist group that opposes the current Iranian regime.

1999

Iraq continued to plan and sponsor international terrorism in 1999. Although Baghdad focused primarily on the anti-regime opposition both at home and abroad, it continued to provide safehaven and support to various terrorist groups.

Press reports stated that, according to a defecting Iraqi intelligence agent, the Iraqi intelligence service had planned to bomb the offices of Radio Free Europe in Prague. Radio Free Europe offices include Radio Liberty, which began broadcasting news and information to Iraq in October 1998. The plot was foiled when it became public in early 1999.

The Iraqi opposition publicly stated its fears that the Baghdad regime was planning to assassinate those opposed to Saddam Hussein. A spokesman for the Iraqi National Accord in November said that the movement's security organs had obtained information about a plan to assassinate its secretary general, Dr. Iyad 'Allawi, and a member of the movement's political bureau, as well as another Iraqi opposition leader.

Iraq continued to provide safehaven to a variety of Palestinian rejectionist groups, including the Abu Nidal organization, the Arab Liberation Front (ALF), and the former head of the now-defunct 15 May Organization, Abu Ibrahim, who masterminded several bombings of U.S. aircraft.

Iraq provided bases, weapons, and protection to the MEK, an Iranian terrorist group that opposes the current Iranian regime. In 1999, MEK cadre based in Iraq assassinated or attempted to assassinate several high-ranking Iranian Government officials, including Brigadier General Ali Sayyad Shirazi, Deputy Chief of Iran's Joint Staff, who was killed in Tehran on 10 April.

2000

Iraq planned and sponsored international terrorism in 2000. Although Baghdad focused on antidissident activity overseas, the regime continued to support various terrorist groups. The regime has not attempted an anti-Western terrorist attack since its failed plot to assassinate former President Bush in 1993 in Kuwait.

Czech police continued to provide protection to the Prague office of the US Government-funded Radio Free Europe/Radio Liberty (RFE/RL), which produces Radio Free Iraq programs and employs expatriate journalists. The police presence was augmented in 1999, following reports that the Iraqi Intelligence Service (IIS) might retaliate against RFE/RL for broadcasts critical of the Iraqi regime.

To intimidate or silence Iraqi opponents of the regime living overseas, the IIS reportedly opened several new stations in foreign capitals during 2000. Various opposition groups joined in warning Iraqi dissidents abroad against newly established "expatriates' associations," which, they asserted, are IIS front organizations. Opposition leaders in London contended that the IIS had dispatched women agents to infiltrate their ranks and was targeting dissidents for assassination. In Germany, an Iraqi opposition figure denounced the IIS for murdering his son, who had recently left Iraq to join him abroad. Dr. Ayad 'Allawi, Secretary General of the Iraqi National Accord, an opposition group, stated that relatives of dissidents living abroad are often arrested and jailed to intimidate activists overseas.

In northern Iraq, Iraqi agents reportedly killed a locally well-known religious personality who declined to echo the regime line. The regional security director in As Sulaymaniyah stated that Iraqi operatives were responsible for the car-bomb explosion that injured a score of passersby. Officials of the Iraqi Communist Party asserted that an attack on a provincial party headquarters had been thwarted when party security officers shot and wounded a terrorist employed by the IIS.

Baghdad continued to denounce and delegitimize UN personnel working in Iraq, particularly UN de-mining teams, in the wake of the killing in 1999 of an expatriate UN de-mining worker in northern Iraq under circumstances suggesting regime involvement. An Iraqi who opened fire at the UN Food and Agriculture Organization (FAO) office in Baghdad, killing two persons and wounding six, was permitted to hold a heavily publicized press conference at which he contended that his action had been motivated by the harshness of UN sanctions, which the regime regularly excoriates.

The Iraqi regime rebuffed a request from Riyadh for the extradition of two Saudis who had hijacked a Saudi Arabian Airlines flight to Baghdad, but did return promptly the passengers and the aircraft. Disregarding its obligations under international law, the regime granted political asylum to the hijackers and gave them ample opportunity to ventilate in the Iraqi Government-controlled and international media their criticisms of alleged abuses by the Saudi Arabian Government, echoing an Iraqi propaganda theme.

While the origins of the FAO attack and the hijacking were unclear, the Iraqi regime readily exploited these terrorist acts to further its policy objectives.

Several expatriate terrorist groups continued to maintain offices in Baghdad, including the Arab Liberation Front, the inactive 15 May Organization, the Palestine Liberation Front (PLF), and the Abu Nidal organization (ANO). PLF leader Abu `Abbas appeared on state-controlled television in the fall to praise Iraq's leadership in rallying Arab opposition to Israeli violence against Palestinians. The ANO threatened to attack Austrian interests unless several million dollars in a frozen ANO account in a Vienna bank were turned over to the group.

The Iraq-supported Iranian terrorist group, Mujahedin-e Khalq (MEK), regularly claimed responsibility for armed incursions into Iran that targeted police and military outposts, as well as for mortar and bomb attacks on security organization headquarters in various Iranian cities. MEK publicists reported that in March group members killed an Iranian colonel having intelligence responsibilities. A MEK claim to have wounded a general was denied by the Iranian Government. The Iraqi regime deployed MEK forces against its domestic opponents.

2001

Iraq was the only Arab-Muslim country that did not condemn the September 11 attacks against the United States. A commentary of the official Iraqi station on September 11 stated that America was ". . . reaping the fruits of [its] crimes against humanity." Subsequent commentary in a newspaper run by one of Saddam's sons expressed sympathy for Usama Bin Ladin following initial US retaliatory strikes in Afghanistan. In addition, the regime continued to provide training and political encouragement to numerous terrorist groups, although its main focus was on dissident Iraqi activity overseas.

Iraq provided bases to several terrorist groups including the Mujahedin-e-Khalq (MEK), the Kurdistan Workers' Party (PKK), the Palestine Liberation Front (PLF), and the Abu Nidal organization (ANO). In 2001, the Popular Front for the Liberation of Palestine (PFLP) raised its profile in the West Bank and Gaza Strip by carrying out successful terrorist attacks against Israeli targets. In recognition of the PFLP's growing role, an Iraqi Vice President met with former PFLP Secretary General Habbash in Baghdad in January 2001 and expressed continued Iraqi support for the intifadah. Also, in mid-September, a senior delegation from the PFLP met with an Iraqi Deputy Prime Minister. Baghdad also continued to host other Palestinian rejectionist groups, including the Arab Liberation Front, and the 15 May Organization.

Meanwhile, Czech police continued to provide protection to the Prague office of the US Government-funded Radio Free Europe/Radio Liberty (RFE/RL), which produces Radio Free Iraq programs and employs expatriate journalists. The police presence was augmented in 1999 and 2000, following reports that the Iraqi Intelligence Service might retaliate against RFE/RL for broadcasts critical of the Iraqi regime. As concerns over the facility's security mounted through 2000, the Czechs expelled an Iraqi intelligence officer in April 2001.

The Iraqi regime has not met a request from Riyadh for the extradition of two Saudis who had hijacked a Saudi Arabian Airlines flight to Baghdad in 2000. Disregarding its obligations under international law, the regime granted political asylum to the hijackers and gave them ample opportunity to voice their criticisms of alleged abuses by the Saudi Government in the Iraqi Government-controlled and international media.

2002

Iraq planned and sponsored international terrorism in 2002. Throughout the year, the Iraqi Intelligence Services (IIS) laid the groundwork for possible attacks against civilian and military targets in the United States and other Western countries. The IIS reportedly instructed its agents in early 2001 that their main mission was to obtain information about US and Israeli targets. The IIS also threatened dissidents in the Near East and Europe and stole records and computer files detailing antiregime activity. In December 2002, the press claimed Iraqi intelligence killed Walid al-Mayahi, a Shi'a Iraqi refugee in Lebanon and member of the Iraqi National Congress.

Iraq was a safehaven, transit point, and operational base for groups and individuals who direct violence against the United States, Israel, and other countries. Baghdad overtly assisted two categories of Iraqi-based terrorist organizations—Iranian dissidents devoted to toppling the Iranian Government and a variety of Palestinian groups opposed to peace with Israel. The groups include the Iranian Mujahedin-e Khalq, the Abu Nidal organization (although Iraq reportedly killed its leader), the Palestine Liberation Front (PLF), and the Arab Liberation Front (ALF). In the past year, the PLF increased its operational activity against Israel and sent its members to Iraq for training for future terrorist attacks.

Baghdad provided material assistance to other Palestinian terrorist groups that are in the forefront of the intifadah. The Popular Front for the Liberation of Palestine-General Command, HAMAS, and the Palestine Islamic Jihad are the three most important groups to whom Baghdad has extended outreach and support efforts.

Saddam paid the families of Palestinian suicide bombers to encourage Palestinian terrorism, channeling $25,000 since March through the ALF alone to families of suicide bombers in Gaza and the West Bank. Public testimonials by Palestinian civilians and officials and cancelled checks captured by Israel in the West Bank verify the transfer of a considerable amount of Iraqi money.

The presence of several hundred al-Qaida operatives fighting with the small Kurdish Islamist group Ansar al-Islam in the northeastern corner of Iraqi Kurdistan—where the IIS operates—is well documented. Iraq has an agent in the most senior levels of Ansar al-Islam as well. In addition, small numbers of highly placed al-Qaida militants were present in Baghdad and areas of Iraq that Saddam controls. It is inconceivable these groups were in Iraq without the knowledge and acquiescence of Saddam's regime. In the past year, al-Qaida operatives in northern Iraq concocted suspect chemicals under the direction of senior al-Qaida associate Abu Mus'ab al-Zarqawi and tried to smuggle them into Russia, Western Europe, and the United States for terrorist operations.

Iraq is a party to five of the 12 international conventions and protocols relating to terrorism.

2003

On 7 May 2003, President Bush suspended, with respect to Iraq, all sanctions applicable to state sponsors of terrorism, which had the practical effect of putting Iraq on a par with nonterrorist states. Although Iraq is still technically a designated state sponsor of terrorism, its name can be removed from the state sponsors list when the Secretary of State determines that it has fulfilled applicable statutory requirements, which include having a government in place that pledges not to support acts of terrorism in the future.

In 2003, Operation Iraqi Freedom removed Saddam Hussein and his Ba'athist regime from power and liberated Iraq. Since then, however, Iraq has become a central battleground in the global war on terrorism. Former regime elements, who have been conducting insurgent attacks against Coalition forces, have increasingly allied themselves tactically and operationally with foreign fighters and Islamic extremists, including some linked to Ansar al-Islam, al-Qaida, and Abu Mus'ab al-Zarqawi. The line between insurgency and terrorism has become increasingly blurred as attacks on civilian targets have become more common. By end of the year, Coalition forces had detained more than 300 suspected foreign fighters.

Extremists associated with al-Qaida claimed credit for several suicide car bombings, including attacks in October against the headquarters of the International Committee of the Red Cross and three Baghdad police stations and an attack in November against an Italian military police base in Nasiriyah. Al-Qaida associate Abu Mus'ab al-Zarqawi—accused of working with Ansar al-Islam—emerged as a key suspect in the deadly bombing of Jordan's Baghdad embassy in August.

After Coalition strikes destroyed Ansar al-Islam's base in northern Iraq in late March, Ansar al-Islam members fled across the border and regrouped in Iran. Counterterrorist operations suggest many of those fighters have since reentered

Iraq and are active in anti-Coalition activities. In September, suspected members of Ansar al-Islam were arrested in Kirkuk carrying 1,200 kilograms of TNT.

In November, Coalition forces killed two unidentified, high-ranking members of Ansar al-Islam during a raid on a terrorist hideout in Baghdad. Other terrorist groups maintained a presence in Iraq. Members of the foreign terrorist organization Mujahedin-e-Khalq—which had received military support from the regime of Saddam Hussein—were stripped of their weapons and placed under US military detention. The terrorist group KADEK—renamed the Kurdistan People's Congress (KHK) in the fall—continued to proclaim its commitment to nonviolence, while launching several attacks against Turkish targets inside Turkey. The presence of several thousand KHK members in northern Iraq underscores the group's ability to carry out terrorist operations. The KHK periodically threatens to heighten its attacks against Turkey.

Iraq has signed eight of the 12 international conventions and protocols relating to terrorism and is a party to five.

2004

The rescission of Iraq's designation on October 20, 2004 was discussed by Department Spokesman Richard Boucher at a daily press briefing on October 20, 2004. The relevant section from the Department of State website (www.state.gov/r/pa/prs/dpb/2004/37261.htm) is extracted below:

QUESTION: Yeah, today, for the second time in its history, Iraq has been taken off the State Sponsors of Terrorism list, and I'm just wondering what you have to say about that. Why the—obviously, since the President asked the Secretary to do it—

MR. BOUCHER: Why the two-stage? Yeah. Okay.

The first event that you're referring to was in April 2003 in the wake of Operation Iraqi Freedom. The President sought and the Congress approved legislation that authorized the President to make nearly all the State Sponsor of Terrorism-related sanctions inapplicable to Iraq by a presidential determination, and the President exercised that authority in May of 2003.

Existing laws provide that State Sponsor status can only be formally rescinded when the country's fundamentally changed government no longer supports international terrorism and has provided assurances that it will not support such acts in the future. That is done by a presidential certification to Congress that's followed by a determination by the Secretary of State that these legal requirements have been satisfied.

So we had to wait until the new Iraqi Government was in place and then able to provide those assurances before we could take the formal step to end the sanctions; now we've done that. So once the new Interim Iraqi Government assumed authority in June, it was possible to obtain from that government the necessary assurances and to satisfy the other legal requirements necessary for a rescission;

that's been done. And effective with the President's certification to Congress on September 24th and the Secretary's determination of October 7th, the rescission of these restrictions is effective, and that's what appeared in The Federal Register today.

Specifically, the President has certified and the Secretary then determined three basic things: First, there's been a fundamental change in leadership and policies of the Government of Iraq; second, that Iraq's Government is not supporting acts of international terrorism; and third, that Iraq's Government has provided assurances that it will not support acts of international terrorism in the future.

QUESTION: Okay, I just—this, all that is very well and good and I know that he did sign it on October 7th, but once again, I mean, it didn't take effect until its publication today in The Federal Register. So that—I just want to get that out of the way. But also, the—it is kind of unusual for a country to be—have been twice placed and twice removed from this list.

MR. BOUCHER: Well, I don't think I'd say twice removed because the initial—this is, you might say, a progressive two-step process that we had to follow in the case of Iraq because of the circumstances this time. The first was to [su]spend the restrictions in May of 2003.

QUESTION: No, no, no, Richard—

MR. BOUCHER: And then the second is actually to remove—oh, you're talking about taking them off in the '80s?

QUESTION: I'm talking their being on the list and being a charter member of this group and suddenly not—

MR. BOUCHER: Being a charter member and being taken off—

QUESTION:—being taken off in '82, and being put back on in 1990, and now being taken off again.

MR. BOUCHER: Yeah, but let's—whatever the wisdom of the step in the 1980s, I think everybody has to understand that there is a fundamentally changed situation. Iraq, unfortunately, for the Iraqi people and for the international community, Iraq had the same government throughout that period of the '70s and the '80s and the '90s, and that was Saddam Hussein. And among the many things he did was never to calculate the interest of his nation and his people, but rather to continue to try to acquire the weapons and technology that he used many times to kill his people and to attack his neighbors.

That period is over. Iraq has a fundamentally changed government. It is going to have a different relationship with the Iraqi people, and it is going to have a different relationship with the international community. So the two circumstances can be contrasted but not compared, in my opinion.

QUESTION: Well, that's fair enough, except for that my question really is that you said that these legal requirements to be made, that there has to be a fundamental change from the government and they have to renounce these kinds of—the terrorism and support for terrorism and promise not to do it in the future. And that didn't happen in 1982. In fact, Iran—I mean, Iraq, as you have noted in subsequent *Patterns of Global Terrorism* reports, continued to support this.

So, you know, you said, "Whatever the wisdom of this step in the 1980s." Well, you know, was that a mistake?

MR. BOUCHER: I'll refer you back to the briefings of the time and I'll let the historians judge whether it was a mistake or not. I'm not here to brief on a decision made in 1982.

QUESTION: It's quite relevant to today, though.

MR. BOUCHER: No, I'm saying I just explained exactly why it's not relevant at all to today because whatever, however these criteria applied in 1982, they quite clearly apply now. There is a different leader in Baghdad. There's a different set of leaders. There is a different system of government. There is a different approach to governance. And there is a different relationship of Iraq with its neighbors. And those things are so obviously different that, as I said, I think the two situations can be contrasted but not compared.

QUESTION: But, of course, they can be contrasted, which begs the question though is why they were taken off in 1982.

MR. BOUCHER: And that's a question I leave you to research and historians to judge.

QUESTION: All right. To go back in a time machine and ask the briefer in 1982?

MR. BOUCHER: No, you can just pull the transcripts off the web, I'm sure, and you'll see what the briefer said at the time.

QUESTION: Well—

MR. BOUCHER: I'm sure the briefer stands by what he said.

QUESTION: Well, check that because I'm not sure you guys have '82 on the web.

MR. BOUCHER: Well, we might not.

QUESTION: No.

MR. BOUCHER: We might not. But I—we've got it somewhere. Do I have it on CD? I can't remember.

QUESTION: I don't think—

MR. BOUCHER: I don't know how far back it goes. Anyway, it's out there somewhere. Try the National Security Archive or somewhere like that, if we don't have it. All right?

QUESTION: No.

Libya

Designation date December 29, 1979

1985

Libyan leader Muammar Qadhafi has long been the world leader most closely identified with sponsorship of terrorist groups and has made terrorism one of the primary instruments of his foreign policy. His revolutionary philosophy and anti-Western orientation lead him to aid virtually any group that opposes his perceived enemies. Tripoli has operated numerous training sites for foreign dissident groups that provide instruction in the use of explosive devices, hijacking, assassination, and various commando and guerilla techniques. It has also provided terrorist training outside Libya and has abused diplomatic privilege by storing arms and explosives at its diplomatic establishments.

In 1985 Libya was involved in fewer incidents then in the previous year—17 compared with 25—and more than half these attacks were assassination attempts against Libyan exiles during the first half of the year. In 1985 Libya sponsored five attacks against exiled Libyan dissidents in Greece, West Germany, Cyprus, Italy, and Austria. The former Libyan Ambassador to Austria survived a particularly vicious assassination attempt in February. Libya also plotted antiexile attacks in the United States. In May, for example, a Libyan diplomat at the United Nations was declared persona non grata, and other Libyans were accused when a plot to kill Libyan dissidents in several states was uncovered. The plan indicated an increased Libyan interest in embarrassing the US Government, even though the targets were not American.

Libyan support for radical Palestinian groups has continued to grow. Training for Palestinians and other radicals frequently has taken place at several locations in Libya. Qadhafi has provide safehaven, money, and arms to groups such as the Popular Front for the Liberation of Palestine—General Command (PFLP-GC), the Fatah dissidents led by Abu Musa, and the notorious Abu Nidal Group. The Abu Nidal members responsible for the attack on the El Al counter in Vienna in December 1985 used passports seized by Libya from expelled Tunisian nationals. Libya also may have been involved in the November 1985 hijacking of an Egyptian airliner. According to Libyan press reports, Sabri al-Banna (who calls himself Abu Nidal) met with Qadhafi in Libya at least twice in 1985, and, according to reliable press reports, some of the Abu Nidal Group's leadership has moved to Libya.

Tripoli has continued to support insurgents and revolutionary groups around the world. In Latin America, Libya provided support to the Colombian 19th of April Movement (M-19), a guerilla organization that frequently carries out international terrorism. Libya also provided training, guidance, and funds to a Chilean leftist terrorist group, enabling it to expand armed action against the Government of Chile. Libya also has been implicated in subversive or terrorist activity in North Africa. During 1985 Cairo captured several teams of Libyan-supported Egyptian dissidents who reported that their plan was to destabilize the Mubarak government through sabotage and inciting civil unrest. Individuals arrested after the November attempted attack on Libyan exiles in Egypt stated that Qadhafi's target list included Mubarak.

In 1985 the number of Libyan-inspired terrorist attacks in Sub-Saharan Africa declined markedly; none was directed against US personnel or facilities. Qadhafi probably calculated that his perceived political and diplomatic successes in the region reduced the need for Libyan terrorist activity there. The French withdrawal from Chad in late 1984 and the overthrow of longtime enemy President Nimeiri in Sudan eliminated two key targets of Libyan terrorism. Libya has assigned known terrorists to its facilities in Sudan, however, thereby creating a network available to resume terrorist activity at any time. Tripoli also has continued its subversive activity in Sub-Saharan Africa—providing financial, logistic, training, and material support to insurgent and terrorist groups in the region.

The level of Libyan activity in Sudan fluctuated during the course of 1985. After President Nimeiri's ouster in April, Qadhafi quickly sent in his Libyan-based Sudanese Revolutionary Committees, which provide a network for promoting pro-Libyan subversive activity. On another front, however, Tripoli ended its support to the Sudanese People's Liberation Army (SPLA), which weakened the southern insurgency. The pace of SPLA terrorist activity slowed during 1985, with only occasional kidnappings and armed attacks on Sudanese civilians and foreigners.

In Central Africa, Libya continued its subversion aimed at destabilizing local governments, as in the following examples:

- Libya continued to fund, train, and arm several hundred externally based Zairian dissidents. Tanzanian-based dissidents, possibly with Libyan support, attacked a small town in eastern Zaire in June 1985. In September Zairian officials claimed to have thwarted at least one Libyan-sponsored plot against President Mobutu. The Zairian President's effective personal security and the ineptitude of the dissidents, however, reportedly stymied the assassination plot.
- The Central African Republic was an active center for Libyan covert action. In July 1985, 15 Central Africans were arrested for conspiring with Libyan People's Bureau members.
- A large Libyan presence in Congo—including employees of the People's Bureau, economic projects, and front organizations such as the Muslim Friendship League—and frequent official travelers from Tripoli, betrayed a high level of Libyan activity.
- Libya has provided support to dissidents and students from Cameroon.

1986

Qadhafi's anti-Western attacks in 1986 focused primarily on the United States and the United Kingdom. Information in late 1985 and early 1986 indicated a greater likelihood of anti-US targeting by Tripoli, including the suspicion of Libyan involvement in the Rome and Vienna airport attacks of December 1985. This led to a largely unsuccessful effort by the United States to persuade other countries to join in peaceful economic and political measures against Libya.

Against a backdrop of tension that increased after US naval maneuvers in the central Mediterranean in January and March, Qadhafi's bellicose attitude climaxed in the Libyan-instigated attack against the La Belle discotheque in West Berlin. Libyan willingness to target US citizens directly was a dramatic new turn in Libyan terrorism. The discotheque was a nightclub popular with off-duty US servicemen. The powerful bomb that exploded there on the morning of 5 April killed three persons (including two American soldiers) and wounded more than 200 others (including more than 70 US citizens). Following the attack, the US Government announced that it had incontrovertible proof of Libyan complicity and on 15 April launched retaliatory airstrikes against Tripoli and Benghazi. Qadhafi responded with a series of terrorist attacks against the United States and also against the United Kingdom, where some of the US planes were based:

On 15 April, a US Embassy communications officer was shot in Khartoum; circumstantial evidence points to Libyan agents.

On 17 April, two British teachers and American hostage Peter Kilburn were discovered murdered in Beirut. British Foreign Secretary Howe publicly linked Libya to the murders. Another British hostage, journalist Alec Collett, was allegedly killed about the same time, but his body has not been found.

On 18 April, authorities in Ankara apprehended two Libyans with handgrenades as they approached a US officers club, where a wedding reception was being held. The pair later admitted they received the grenades from the Libyan People's Bureau (LPB).

On 25 April, a US Embassy communications officer was wounded in Sansa, North Yemen. Libya is believed to have instigated the attack.

The level of Libyan-sponsored terrorist activity fell after late April. The reduction was probably the result of several factors. Qadhafi was apparently stunned by the US air raid and probably curtailed operations, in part, to avoid further military reprisals. Libya also experienced increased internal unrest after the raid and was forced to focus temporarily on domestic matters. Qadhafi's ability to direct terrorism overseas via the LPBs was seriously damaged when more than 100 Libyan diplomats were expelled from Europe. Finally, heightened security measures taken by the United States and other Western nations undoubtedly also contributed to the lull.

Libya resumed terrorist activity in July. At least nine nationals from Togo and Benin were arrested in July for participation in a plot to attack the US Embassy and a market in

Lome. They reportedly confessed to having received a pistol, grenades, and explosive devices from the LPB in Cotonou, Benin. The suspects alleged that official Libyan facilities in Burkina and Ghana were also involved in the plot.

On 3 August, gunmen attacked the UK base at Akrotiri, Cyprus, with mortars, rocket-propelled grenades, and small arms fire. Although they did not penetrate the base's perimeter, the attackers wounded two women before withdrawing. Available information strongly links Libya to the attack, which was undoubtedly undertaken in retaliation for UK support of the US April airstrikes. Qadhafi had publicly vowed to strike back against the United kingdom after the US air raid. He claimed the base at Akrotiri had been used by US aircraft involved in the raid. In claiming responsibility for the attack, the Unified Nasserite Organization invoked the Omar al-Mukhtar Group, named after a Libyan hero who opposed colonial occupation earlier in the century. A group using a similar name claimed responsibility for a rocket attack on the British Ambassador's residence in Beirut two days after the US raid.

On September 5, four Abu Nidal organization (ANO) terrorists attempted to hijack Pan Am Flight 73 in Karachi, Pakistan. Before the incident was resolved, the terrorists had killed 21 persons, including two Americans; an additional 120 persons were wounded. The four terrorists who seized the aircraft were captured at the scene. A fifth suspect arrested later in the case has ties to Libya and probably provided logistic support to the hijackers.

Qadhafi's antidissident campaign remains one of the most consistent features of Libyan terrorism. Information suggests that all Libyan stations abroad are responsible for tracking and reporting on the exiles on Qadhafi's "hit list". During 1986, Qadhafi's worldwide pursuit of individuals he regards as dangerous to his regime resulted in the following attacks:

On 17 February, the owner of an anti-Qadhafi radio station was wounded in Rome by two suspected Libyan agents.

Masked gunmen thought to be Libyan agents shot and killed a Libyan industrialist in his home in a Paris suburb on 30 June.

Qadhafi continued his interest in provoking violence in Latin America and the Caribbean in 1986 by providing encouragement to almost any anti-US group. Qadhafi focused his efforts on the French Caribbean, because leftist groups there have been more violent than English-speaking groups. Initially disappointed by the lack of support he received after the US airstrikes, by late summer Qadhafi had renewed his efforts to collect intelligence, undermine US influence in the region, and establish his bona fides as a worldwide revolutionary leader.

Qadhafi's activities in the Western Hemisphere have not been totally successful. Tripoli provides money and some training to groups it supports, although Qadhafi frequently fails to deliver the aid he promises. Some local security forces were successful in countering terrorist plans. Local groups also resent Qadhafi's insensitivity to their problems. Cuban opposition to Libya's indiscriminate exhortations to violence has somewhat undercut Qadhafi's ability to gain influence among local radical groups.

Libyan activity in Africa reached a peak after the US airstrikes in April. Qadhafi reacted to the raid by pressuring many of the groups he had supported to mount attacks against US personnel and facilities. Libya was behind many anti-US demonstrations and threats in the region immediately after the April operation. As elsewhere, Libyan activity in Africa slowed after April, resuming in July with the aforementioned incident in Benin.

Sudan remained a hotbed of Libyan terrorist activity. Several notorious Libyan terrorists visited Sudan during 1986. One purpose of the visits was to maintain contact with the pro-Libyan Sudanese Revolutionary Committees. These committees give Tripoli a network that can be used for either subversive activities or terrorism.

1987

Although detectable Libyan involvement in terrorist activity dropped significantly in 1986 and 1987 after the US air raids in April 1986, Qadhafi shows no signs of forsaking terrorism. His desire to establish himself as an Islamic and Third World revolutionary leader causes him to establish links to or provide aid to almost any group that opposes his enemies. Qadhafi's contacts with dissident groups around the world follow no geographic pattern but simply seek alliances of opportunity. The recipients of his assistance include several international terrorist groups as well as a range of insurgent and other dissident movements.

Libyan interest in attacking French targets increased significantly in 1987, probably because of France's support for the Government of Chad in its fight against Libyan invaders.

Libya had already started to conduct surveillance against a range of potential French targets in 1986, and we suspect that Qadhafi may have been behind an attack against a government building in French Guyana in January 1987. Further attacks were staged against French Guyana in January 1987. Further attacks were staged against French interests following Qadhafi's defeats in Chad in March:

A Libyan-supported radical Palestinian terrorist group, the Popular Struggle Front, was most likely responsible for the anti-Western bombing in Djibouti in March that killed 11 persons.

Qadhafi may have had a hand in the assassination of two French gendarmes in Beirut in October. The terrorist group ASALA, which may have been responsible, has a long history of ties to Qadhafi.

We have little doubt that the US air raids on Libya in 1986 contributed heavily to Qadhafi's subsequent caution. At the same time, however, we are equally sure that he continued planning for anti-US attacks involving the use of surrogate groups to disguise Libyan responsibility. We believe that Libya also increased its surveillance of US facilities and personnel during the year, particularly in Sub-Saharan Africa.

On at least two occasions, there may have been a Libyan hand in terrorist incidents. First, the attempted murder of the three US Embassy employees in Egypt in May was carried out by the Egypt's Revolution, a group alleged to have connections to Libya (the three sons of the late Egyptian President Nasser have close ties to Qadhafi) and, second, a bomb was set off in October at the offices of the private volunteer organization World Vision in Moundou in Chad.

Qadhafi also tried to retaliate for the United Kingdom's role in the 1986 US airstrikes. In April, shortly after the first anniversary of the US air raids, two men wounded a British Army warrant officer and his companion traveling in a car near Limassol in Cyprus. Two Arabs later arrested for the attacks were identified as Libyan-supported terrorists who had previously participated in a 1986 attack on the British airbase at Akrotiri.

A spectacular French counterterrorist success in 1987 revealed Libya's deep complicity in supporting PIRA in the United Kingdom. In October, French authorities intercepted a coastal freighter, the Eksund II, off the coast of France and seized 150 tons of weapons and explosives, including surface-to-air missiles. Several known PIRA members were on board the vessel, which had been loaded in Libya. The size of the shipment has led some observers to speculate that some of the weapons may have been intended for distribution to other terrorist groups. UK authorities suspect that the Eksund II shipment may have been preceded by four others from Libya.

Libya continued to hunt down its dissidents overseas. Libyan agents murdered two exiles in 1987 and a third attempt failed:

In January, a Libyan businessman and known anti-Qadhafi activist was assassinated in a tavern in an Athens suburb. The gunmen escaped.

In May, an attacker tried but failed to kill a prominent anti-Qadhafi activist in Vienna. He dropped his Libyan passport at the scene while fleeing into the nearby Libyan People's Bureau. The attempt was the second one the dissident's life in just over two years.

In June, two assassins in Rome killed the Cairo office chief of the National Front for the Salvation of Libya, who was a well-known opponent of Qadhafi. The two men were captured and identified themselves as agents of the Libyan Revolutionary Committees.

Qadhafi has consistently offered support for radical Palestinian groups involved in terrorism. Libya has had close operational ties to the Abu Nidal organization for at least three years, and we believe that Tripoli offered sanctuary and other facilities to many ANO leaders in 1987, after the group was expelled from its headquarters in Damascus.

Qadhafi also sought with little success to establish links to anti-Western or antiregime dissidents in the Caribbean and Pacific regions. Libya suffered a setback in the Caribbean when one of its officials—a key terrorism coordinator for the area—was excluded from Suriname, Trinidad, and Venezuela. Before his exclusion, documents had been found in his possession giving details of Libyan terrorism plans for the Caribbean. In the Pacific, plans were thwarted when Libya was refused permission to open a Libyan People's Bureau in Vanuatu and its Bureau in Canberra was closed by Australian authorities.

1988

Despite a public posture of moderation in 1988, Qadhafi continued to support terrorism. Qadhafi attempted to mask his involvement in terrorism, working with and through client groups. He used his own personnel in only one known occasion in 1988. Libya has provided training, weapons, money, and other forms of support to about 30 insurgent and terrorist groups worldwide, including ASALA, the JRA, Palestinian groups such as the ANO and the Popular Struggle Front (PSF), and Latin American groups such as Colombia's M-19 and Peru's MRTA.

Circumstantial evidence links Libya to a number of attacks against US interests on the second anniversary of the US airstrikes. Qadhafi possibly offered financial incentives to client groups in return for such attacks. In 1988:

Italian police identified a JRA member as responsible for the car bombing outside a USO club in Naples on 14 April. A claim made for the attack said it was revenge for the US attack on Tripoli. A US servicewoman and four Italian citizens died in the explosion.

The M-19 group claimed the bombing of a USIS center in Colombia on 14 April.

Libyan-supported terrorists are strongly suspected in a bombing attack on 15 April against a US Air Force communications facility near Humosa, Spain.

The MRTA claimed credit for the bombing of two USIS centers in Peru on 16 April.

Libyan-supported Costa Rican terrorists are believed to be behind a bombing agent against a US-Costa Rican cultural center in San Jose on 19 April.

Libya also remained active in Sub-Saharan Africa. In February 1988, Senegalese authorities arrested two Libyans known to be terrorist operatives at Dakar Airport as they attempted to smuggle arms and explosives aboard a flight from Cotonou, Benin. The two were believed to have been planning to attack Western targets. Subsequent to the arrests, Benin expelled the head of the Libyan People's Bureau. Despite publicly recognizing the Habre government in May, 1988, Qadhafi continues to support subversion in Chad.

For the first time since 1983, there were no Libyan antidissident attacks; Qadhafi invited all exiles to return home early in the year and seemed more willing—at least temporarily—to repair relations with opponents of his regime.

Tripoli remained the ANO's primary state sponsor and was, through the provision of arms and documents, linked to an attack by the group in July in Greece. Tripoli has been the group's principal host since it was expelled from Damascus in June 1987 and has provided it with weapons and other support since the late 1970s. ANO members train in Libya, and their leader, Sabri al-Banna, lives in Tripoli. A clear indication of the ANO-Libya link emerged during investigation of the attack on the Greek day-excursion ship in July. According to Greek authorities, the ANO team leader—Samir Muhammad Khadar—traveled on a Libyan passport. Furthermore, the attackers used weapons sold to Tripoli during the 1970s. Despite Libya's extensive support of the ANO, however, we have no proof that Qadhafi ordered or participated directly in this or any of the ANO attacks in 1988.

ANO-Libyan relations are still evolving. Although Qadhafi clearly sees the value of the ANO as a surrogate, he probably calculates that ANO operations are now more directly attributable to Tripoli. As a result he may take greater precautions in providing direct Libyan support to ANO operations.

1989

Libya continued to show public signs of moderation while maintaining in its network of support for international terrorist groups. There were no terrorist incidents in 1989 that were directly attributable to Libya. A Libyan-backed group, however, the MRTA, attempted to bomb the USIS Binational Center in Peru in April to mark the third anniversary of US airstrikes against Tripoli. MRTA bombed the same facility in 1988 on the second anniversary of the air raids.

Qadhafi may have put pressure on some Libyan-backed radical Palestinian groups—the PFLP-GC and the ANC—to stand down on terrorist operations not directed against Israel or the occupied territories. Nevertheless, the Libyan leader continues to shelter the ANO's leader, Sabri Al-Banna (aka Abu Nidal), and his remaining followers.

Qadhafi continues to provide money, training, and other support to his terrorist clients, despite at least temporarily restricting their activities. The Libyans have sponsored over 30 international groups, including the Armenian Secret Army for the Liberation of Armenia (ASALA), the JRA, M-19, PIRA, and MRTA, in addition to radical Palestinian groups.

In recent speeches, Qadhafi has restated his opposition to US and Western influence in the Third World and reaffirmed Libyan willingness to support armed revolutionary struggles. Qadhafi continues to maintain Libyan contacts with subversive groups in Africa, Asia, and Latin America, possibly in hopes of cultivating surrogate agents. Qadhafi has also used front companies as conduits for financial and materiel support to international terrorist groups in order to obscure Libyan involvement.

1990

In 1990, Libya demonstrated its continued support for terrorism by supporting the Palestine Liberation Front's failed 30 May seaborne attack on crowded Israeli beaches. Tripoli helped the PLF plan, train for, supply, and carry out the seaborne operation.

Since 1986, Libyan leader Muammar Qadhafi has made public disclaimers about his support for terrorist groups. He continued to provide money, training, and other support to his terrorist clients. Qadhafi's claims of having expelled certain terrorist groups—the PLF, ANO, and PFLP-GC—remained unsubstantiated as of the end of 1990. Libya also resumed funding to the PFLP-GC, and possibly other Palestinian terrorist groups in 1990.

Libya also continues its support for a variety of terrorist/insurgent groups worldwide. In the Philippines, Libya has supported the NPA, which carried out terrorist attacks against Americans that killed five persons in 1990. Costa Rican officials believe that all 15 members of the Santamaria Patriotic Organization (OPS) arrested in Costa Rica in February for grenade attacks against US facilities had undergone terrorist training in Libya. The group that attacked the Trinidad and Tobago Parliament on 27 July in a coup attempt, which killed several persons, received training and financial support from Libya, among others.

In April, Ethiopia expelled two Libyan diplomats for alleged involvement in the 30 March bombing at the Hilton Hotel in Addis Ababa.

Throughout 1990, indications of Libya's previous involvement in acts of terrorism emerged. According to German press reports, German officials uncovered evidence in the files of the now-defunct East German secret police, the Stasi, that demonstrated Libyan responsibility for the 1986 bombing of the La Belle disco in West Berlin.

In addition, according to press reports, the investigation into the September 1989 bombing of the French UTA Flight 772—which killed 170 persons, including 7 Americans—indicates that the bomb was brought into Congo in the Libyan diplomatic pouch and delivered to three Libyan-trained Congolese terrorists by an official of the Libyan Embassy in Brazzaville. African and French press reports state that both the Congolese and Zairians are holding suspects who have implicated Libya in the bombing.

Press reports in late 1990 also laid much of the responsibility on the Libyans for the bombing in December 1988 of Pan Am Flight 103. According to American, British, and French press, investigators discovered that the detonator used in the Pan Am Flight 103 bombing was identical to one carried by two Libyan agents arrested in Dakar, Senegal, in February 1988. The official investigation into both of these cases was continuing through the end of 1990.

1991

The culmination of two important investigations in 1991 demonstrated Libya's continued responsibility for acts of international terrorism. In October, a French magistrate issued international arrest warrants charging four Libyan Government officials—including two senior officials—with the 1989 bombing of UTA 772 in which 171 persons, including seven American, died. One of those indicted is Abdullah Sanussi, Qadhafi's brother-in-law. On 14 November, simultaneous indictments were issued by US and British courts accusing two Libyan intelligence officers, Abdel Basset Ali Al-Megrahi and Lamen Khalifa Fhimah, of planting the bomb on Pan Am Flight 103 that killed 270 persons, including 189 Americans, in December 1988.

Those two cases starkly revealed Libya's direct participation in two major acts of terror. We believe that these two incidents, resulting in the murder of 441 people, were executed with the knowledge and approval of officials at the highest level of the Libyan Government.

The international reaction to the evidence indicating Libyan involvement in these two bombings has been overwhelmingly positive. Even many of those states with close political, economic, ethnic, or religious ties to Libya have recognized that the evidence clearly supports Libya's responsibility. At year's end, the United States, France, and Great Britain were building support for a United Nations Security Council resolution to require that Libya submit the accused to the appropriate legal forum and provide proof that it has ceased its support for international terrorism. (This resolution was unanimously adopted by the United Nations Security Council on 21 January 1992.)

Despite some meaningless gestures in response to international pressure following the Pan Am and UTA indictments, Libya continued its support for a variety of terrorist or insurgent groups worldwide during 1991. Radical Palestinian groups such as the PLF, the ANO, and the PFLP-GC have maintained headquarters or training facilities inside the Government of Libya. In the Philippines, Libya has supported the NPA, which has killed a number of Americans and held one American hostage at the end of 1991. Libya has also supported the MRTA in Peru, the PIRA in Ireland, the PKK in Turkey, and many other radical groups.

1992

On 21 January, the UN Security Council (UNSC) unanimously adopted Resolution 731, which endorses US, British, and French demands that Libya comply with a series of steps, including turning over for trial two Libyan intelligence agents indicted by the United States and the United Kingdom for their role in bombing Pan Am Flight 103 in 1988. The resolution also required that Libya accept responsibility for the bombing and disclose all evidence related to it, pay appropriate compensation, satisfy French demands regarding Libya's role in bombing UTS Flight 772 in 1989, and cease all forms of terrorism. On 30 March the UNSC adopted Resolution 748, imposing mandatory sanctions against Libya for its failure to meet UNSC Resolution 731 demands. Those sanctions went into effect on 15 April. The sanctions included an arms and civil aviation embargo on Libya, a demand that Libyan Arab Airlines offices be closed, and a requirement that all states reduce Libya's diplomatic presence abroad. As of the end of 1992, Tripoli has failed to comply with the Security Council resolution.

Although the Libyan regime has made some cosmetic changes to its terrorism apparatus, it retains its capability to commit terrorist acts. In addition, the regime continues to support terrorist and insurgent groups worldwide despite Tripoli's repeated offer to open to UN inspection terrorist camps—previously identified publicly by the US Government—as proof of its renunciation of terrorism. Many of these suspect camps, although they have been changed superficially, can be easily reactivated as terrorist training facilities. Members of some terrorist groups remain at other government facilities or are dispersed in Libyan cities.

Tripoli appears to have put its own terrorist operations on hold during 1992 in an effort to evade and then lift UN sanctions. However, the regime orchestrated the April mob attacks on the Venezuelan and Russian Embassies in Tripoli in retaliation for their support for UN sanctions against Libya. The attacks were staged to appear as though angry Libyan citizens had spontaneously rioted against the embassies, throwing gasoline bombs and stones.

On 4 December, German prosecutors identified two Libyan Embassy workers as having helped a Palestinian carry out the 1986 La Belle disco bombing that killed two US soldiers and a Turkish woman and wounded more than 200. The Libyans implicated in the case were working at the time at Libya's Embassy in East Germany and supplied the Palestinian with weapons and other cover support. In addition, the two Libyans had worked with the Palestinian in plotting an attack against a location where US soldiers congregated. This latest confirmation of Libyan involvement in the La Belle bombing serves as a reminder of Tripoli's traditional practice of using its diplomatic missions abroad to carry out terrorist acts.

1993

The Libyan Government took no serious measures during the year to comply fully with UN Security Council Resolution 731. The resolution demanded that Libya take steps to end its state-sponsored terrorism, including extraditing two Libyan intelligence agents indicted by the United States and the United Kingdom for their role in bombing Pan Am Flight 103 in 1988. The resolution also required that Libya accept responsibility for the bombing, disclose all evidence related to it, pay appropriate compensation, satisfy French demands regarding Libya's alleged role in bombing UTA Flight 772 in 1989, and cease all forms of terrorism. The UN Security Council adopted Resolution 748 in March 1992; it imposed an arms and civil aviation embargo on Libya, demanded that Libyan Arab Airlines offices be closed, and required that all states reduce Libya's diplomatic presence abroad. Libya's continued defiance of the resolutions led the Security Council to adopt Resolution 883 in November 1993, which imposed a limited assets freeze and oil technology embargo on Libya and significantly tightened up existing sanctions.

Although the Libyan regime made some cosmetic changes to its terrorism apparatus immediately following the adoption of Resolutions 731 and 748, it made no further attempts during the year to dismantle its broad-based terrorism network. Instead, Tripoli concentrated its efforts on extricating itself from UN sanctions by floating a number of proposals that fell short of UN demands, including offering the two suspects for trial in a "neutral" country and leaving their "surrender" up to the suspects. The Libyan regime has largely avoided association with acts of terrorism and terrorist groups while under the United Nations' watchful eye; however, its multifaceted terrorism apparatus remains intact. Qadhafi reiterated his anti-Western themes throughout the year and publicly offered support to radical Palestinian groups opposed to the PLO's Gaza-Jericho accord with Israel. In addition, Qadhafi publicly threatened to support extremist Islamic groups in neighboring Algeria and Tunisia as punishment for not having adequately supported Libya against the UN sanctions effort. Qadhafi's speeches in the fall of 1993, particularly after the mid-October uprising and subsequent crackdown, became increasingly belligerent, and he vowed to strike back against Libyan oppositionists, those who enforced sanctions against Libya, and individuals who cooperated with the United States. Qadhafi also invited notorious terrorist organizations —including the ANO and PIRA—to Libya in December. Oppositionists in exile have blamed Tripoli for the December disappearance from Cairo of prominent dissident and former Libyan Foreign Minister, Mansur Kikhia.

1994

The Libyan regime continued to defy the demands of UN Security Council Resolutions 731, 748, and 883 adopted in response to Tripoli's involvement in the bombings of Pan Am Flight 103 and UTA Flight 772. UNSCR 731 was adopted following the November 1991 indictments by British and US authorities of two Libyan intelligence agents for their role in the 1988 Pan Am bombing. The resolution incorporated US and British demands that Tripoli turn over the two suspects for trial in either a US or UK court, pay compensation to the victims, cooperate in the ongoing investigation, and cease all support for terrorism. UNSCR 731 also demanded that Tripoli cooperate with French authorities in their separate investigation of the UTA 772 bombing in 1989.

In April 1992, UNSCR 748 imposed sanctions against the Libyan regime for its refusal to comply with the demands of UNSCR 731. Those sanctions involved embargoing Libyan civil aviation and military procurement efforts, as well as requiring all states to reduce Libya's diplomatic presence. In November 1993, UNSCR 883 imposed additional sanctions to increase the pressure on Libya to comply with previous demands. The 883 sanctions added a limited assets freeze and oil technology ban and strengthened existing sanctions. By the end of 1994, Libya had taken no serious steps toward compliance with any of the UNSC demands. Instead, the Libyan regime continued to propose half measures and "compromise" solutions to the trial venue for the two suspects. Tripoli's proposals appeared disingenuous from the start, as none satisfy the demands of UNSC resolutions or meet the requirements of American or British judicial systems.

Even while Libya continued its efforts to convince international public opinion that it had abandoned terrorism, Qadhafi and his senior advisers vehemently attacked the Libyan opposition, calling them "stray dogs" and publicly threatening them. Indeed, available evidence strongly suggests Libya was behind the disappearance of prominent Libyan dissident and human rights activist, Mansour Kikhia, from his hotel room in Egypt in December 1993. Throughout 1994, Tripoli demonstrated its willingness to support groups that oppose Western interests with terrorism. Qadhafi repeatedly urged radical rejectionists of the Middle East peace process to use "whatever means" possible to oppose it. Libya opened its arms to leaders of well-known militant groups opposed to the Gaza-Jericho accord and hosted several meetings of the rejectionist groups in 1994. In addition, Libya hailed the 19 October bus-bombing attack in Tel Aviv by HAMAS as a "courageous operation." In addition, the leaders of HAMAS and the Palestinian Islamic Jihad publicly announced that Qadhafi had pledged to provide them with aid for the "liberation of Palestine."

1995

The end of 1995 marked the fourth year of the Libyan regime's refusal to comply with the demands of UN Security Council Resolution 731. This measure was adopted following the indictments in November 1991 of two Libyan intelligence agents for the bombing in 1988 of Pan Am Flight 103. UNSCR 731 endorsed US, British, and French demands that Libya turn over the two Libyan bombing suspects for trial in the United States or the United Kingdom, pay compensation to the victims, cooperate with US, UK, and French authorities in the investigations into the Pan Am 103 and UTA flight 772 bombings, and cease all support for terrorism.

UN Security Council Resolution 748 was adopted in April 1992 as a result of Libya's refusal to comply with UNSCR 731. UNSCR 748 imposed sanctions that embargoed Libya's civil aviation and military procurement efforts and required all states to reduce Libya's diplomatic presence. UNSCR 883 adopted in November 1993, imposed additional sanctions against Libya for its continued refusal to comply with UNSC demands. UNSCR 883 included a limited assets freeze and oil technology ban, and it also strengthened existing sanctions.

By the end of 1995, the Libyan regime had yet to comply in full with the UNSC demands. Although British authorities were satisfied that Libya had provided sufficient information on its past sponsorship of the Provisional Irish Republican Army (PIRA), Tripoli had failed to meet any of the other UNSC demands. Most significantly, it still refused to turn over for trial in the United States or the United Kingdom the two Libyan agents indicted for the Pan Am 103 bombing.

Throughout 1995, the Libyan regime continued to support groups violently opposed to the Middle East peace process, some of which engage in acts of international terrorism. After the murder of Palestine Islamic Jihad (PIJ) leader Fathi Shaqaqi in Malta in October 1995, it was revealed that Libya had frequently facilitated his travel. Libya also continued to sponsor meetings of the Palestinian rejectionist groups in Tripoli.

Despite the ongoing sanctions against Libya for its sponsorship of terrorism, Tripoli continued to harass and intimidate the Libyan expatriate dissident community in 1995. Libya is widely believed to be responsible for the abduction in 1993 and continued detention of prominent Libyan dissident and human rights activist Mansur Kikhia. In November 1995 a Libyan dissident resident in London was brutally murdered; the Libyan expatriate community accused Tripoli of involvement in his death. British authorities continued to investigate the case as the year ended. They also expelled the Libyan charge in London for engaging in "activities incompatible with his diplomatic status." The charge was accused of being involved in intimidation and surveillance of Libyan dissidents in the United Kingdom.

1996

The end of 1996 marked the fifth year of the Libyan regime's refusal to comply with the demands of UN Security Council Resolution 731. This measure was adopted following the indictments in November 1991 of two Libyan intelligence agents for the bombing of Pan Am Flight 103 in 1988. UNSCR 731 ordered Libya to turn over the two Libyan bombing suspects for trial in the United States or the United Kingdom, pay compensation to the victims, cooperate in the ongoing investigations into the Pan Am 103 and UTA Flight 772 bombings, and cease all support for terrorism.

UN Security Council Resolution 748 was adopted in April 1992 as a result of Libya's refusal to comply with the demands of UNSCR 731. UNSCR 748 imposed sanctions that embargoed Libya's civil aviation and military procurement efforts and required all states to reduce Libya's diplomatic presence. In November 1993 UNSCR 883 was adopted, imposing additional sanctions against Libya for its continued refusal to comply with UNSC demands. UNSCR 883 included a limited assets freeze and a ban on sales of some oil technology to Libya and strengthened existing sanctions in other ways.

By the end of 1996 Qadhafi had yet to comply in full with the UNSC demands. He did, however, allow a French magistrate to visit Libya in July to further his investigation of the 1989 bombing of UTA 772. As a result of that investigation, France has issued a total of six arrest warrants—two in 1996—for Libyan intelligence officers, who are still at large.

Tripoli continues to deny any involvement in Pan Am 103 and has made no attempt to comply with the UN resolutions. Most significantly, it still refused to turn over for trial in the United States or the United Kingdom the two Libyan agents indicted for the Pan Am bombing. In response to continued Libyan and Iranian support for terrorism, the US Congress passed the Iran and Libya Sanctions Act of 1996. This Act imposes new sanctions on companies that invest in the development of either country's petroleum resources. The law is intended to help deny revenues that could be used to finance international terrorism.

In addition to the Pan Am and UTA airliner bombings, Libya continues to be held responsible for other terrorist acts of the past that retain current interest. In October 1996 warrants were issued by German authorities for four Libyans who are suspected of initiating the 1986 Berlin discotheque bombing that killed two US citizens. The four are believed to be in Libya. Also, Libya is widely believed to be responsible for the 1993 abduction of prominent Libyan dissident and human rights activist Mansur Kikhia. The current whereabouts of Kikhia, a US green card holder, remains unknown.

Libya also continued in 1996 to provide support to a variety of Palestinian terrorist groups, including the Abu Nidal organization (ANO), the Palestine Islamic Jihad (PIJ), and Ahmed Jabril's Popular Front for the Liberation of Palestine-General Command (PFLP-GC). The ANO maintains its headquarters in Libya, where the group's leader, Sabri al-Banna (a.k.a. Abu Nidal) resides.

1997

The end of 1997 marked the sixth year of the Libyan regime's refusal to comply in full with the demands of UN Security Council Resolutions (UNSCR) 731, 748, and 883 adopted in response to Tripoli's involvement in the bombings of Pan Am Flight 103 and UTA Flight 772. The bombings claimed a total of 441 lives. UNSCR 731 was adopted following the indictments in November 1991 of two Libyan intelligence agents for the bombing of Pan Am Flight 103 in 1988. The resolution ordered Libya to turn over the two Libyan bombing suspects for trial in the United States or the United Kingdom, pay compensation, cooperate in the ongoing investigations into the Pan Am 103 and UTA 772 bombings, and cease all support for terrorism.

UNSCR 748 was adopted in April 1992 as a result of Libya's refusal to comply with UNSCR 731. UNSCR 748 imposed sanctions that embargoed Libya's civil aviation and military procurement efforts and required all states to reduce Libya's diplomatic presence. UNSCR 883, adopted in November 1993, imposed further sanctions against Libya for its continued refusal to comply with UN Security Council demands. UNSCR 883 included a limited assets freeze and an oil technology ban, and it also strengthened existing sanctions.

By the end of 1997, Qadhafi had yet to comply in full with the UN Security Council sanctions. Most significant, he continued to refuse to turn over for trial in the United States or the United Kingdom the two Libyan agents indicted for the Pan Am 103 bombing. (French officials on 29 January 1998 officially completed their investigation into the 1989 bombing of UTA 772. The officials concluded that the Libyan intelligence service was responsible, naming Qadhafi's brother-in-law, Muhammad al-Sanusi, as the mastermind of the attack. A French criminal court in 1998 or 1999 is expected to begin a trial in absentia of the six Libyan suspects, all of whom are intelligence officers and remain at large.)

Despite the ongoing sanctions against Libya for its sponsorship of terrorism, Tripoli continued to harass and intimidate Libyan expatriate dissidents in 1997. Libya is now believed to have abducted prominent Libyan dissident and human rights activist Mansur Kikhia in 1993 and to have executed him in early 1994. Kikhia, a US green cardholder, is survived by his wife and children, who are US citizens.

Libya continues to be held responsible for other past terrorist acts that retain current interest. Germany in November 1997 began the trial of five defendants in the 1986 La Belle discotheque bombing in Berlin, which killed three persons, including two US servicemen, and wounded more than 200, many of them seriously. In opening remarks, the German prosecutor said the bombing was "definitely an act of assassination commissioned by the Libyan state." German authorities have issued warrants for four other Libyan officials for their role in the case who are believed to be in Libya.

Libya also continued in 1997 to provide support to a variety of Palestinian terrorist groups, including the Abu Nidal organization (ANO), the PIJ, and the PFLP-GC. The ANO maintains its headquarters in Libya, where the group's leader, Sabri al-Banna (a.k.a. Abu Nidal), resides.

1998

Despite a joint US-UK offer to prosecute the two Libyans charged with the bombing in 1988 of Pan Am Flight 103 before a Scottish court sitting in the Netherlands, Libya remained unwilling to meet the demands of UN Security Council resolutions 731, 748, 883, and 1192. These measures call upon Libyan leader Qadhafi to cease all support to terrorism, turn over the two indicted Pan Am 103 suspects for trial, and cooperate in the investigation. (On 5 April 1999, Libya turned over the two suspects, 'Abd al Basit al-Megrahi and Lamin Kalifah Fhima, for prosecution in the Netherlands under Scottish law.)

French officials in January completed their investigation into the bombing in 1989 of UTA Flight 772. The French officials believe that the Libyan intelligence service was responsible and named Qadhafi's brother-in-law, Muhammad Sanusi, as the attack's mastermind. (Six Libyan suspects, all intelligence officers, were tried in absentia by a French court in March 1999. The suspects were convicted on 8 March 1999.)

Libya remains the primary suspect in several other past terrorist operations, including the La Belle discotheque bombing in Berlin in 1986, which killed two US servicemen, one Turkish civilian, and wounded more than 200. The trial in Germany of five defendants in the case, who are accused of "an act of assassination commissioned by the Libyan state," began in November 1997 and continued through 1998.

Despite ongoing sanctions against Libya for its sponsorship of terrorism, Tripoli in 1998 continued to harass and intimidate expatriate dissidents. Moreover, Qadhafi continued publicly and privately to support Palestinian terrorist groups, including the PIJ and the PFLP-GC. Libya has not been implicated in any international terrorist act for several years, however.

1999

In April 1999, Libya took an important step by surrendering for trial the two Libyans accused of bombing Pan Am flight 103 over Lockerbie, Scotland, in 1988. The move responded directly to the US-UK initiative; concerted efforts by the Saudi, Egyptian, and South African Governments; and the active engagement of the UN Security Council and the UN Secretary General. At yearend, however, Libya still had not complied with the remaining UN Security Council requirements: payment of appropriate compensation; acceptance of responsibility for the actions of its officials; renunciation of, and an end to, support for terrorism; and cooperation with the prosecution and trial. Libyan leader Qadhafi repeatedly stated publicly during the year that his government had adopted an antiterrorism stance, but it remained unclear whether his claims of distancing Libya from its terrorist past signified a true change in policy.

Libya also remained the primary suspect in several other past terrorist operations, including the La Belle discotheque bombing in Berlin in 1986 that killed two US servicemen and one Turkish civilian and wounded more than 200 persons. The trial in Germany of five suspects in the bombing, which began in November 1997, continued in 1999.

In 1999, Libya expelled the Abu Nidal organization and distanced itself from the Palestinian rejectionists, announcing that the Palestinian Authority was the only legitimate address for Palestinian concerns. Libya still may have retained ties to some Palestinian groups that use violence to oppose the Middle East peace process, however, including the PIJ and the PFLP-GC.

2000

In 2000, Libya continued efforts to mend its international image in the wake of its surrender in 1999 of two Libyans accused of the bombing of Pan Am flight 103 over Lockerbie, Scotland, in 1988. Trial proceedings for the two defendants began in the Netherlands in May and were ongoing at year's end. (The court issued its verdict on 31 January 2001. It found Abdel Basset al-Megrahi guilty of murder, concluding that he caused an explosive device to detonate on board the airplane resulting in the murder of the flight's 259 passengers and crew as well as 11 residents of Lockerbie, Scotland. The judges found that he acted "in furtherance of the purposes of... Libyan Intelligence Services." Concerning the other defendant, Al-Amin Kalifa Fahima, the court concluded that the Crown failed to present sufficient evidence to satisfy the high standard of "proof beyond reasonable doubt" that is necessary in criminal cases.)

In 1999, Libya paid compensation for the death of a British policewoman,[2] a move that preceded the reopening of

---

[2] In April 1984, a British policewoman was killed and 11 demonstrators were wounded when gunmen in the Libyan People's Bureau in London fired on a peaceful anti-Qadhafi demonstration outside their building.

the British Embassy. Libya also paid damages to the families of victims in the bombing of UTA flight 772. Six Libyans were convicted in absentia in that case, and the French judicial system is considering further indictments against other Libyan officials, including Libyan leader Muammar Qadhafi.

Libya played a high-profile role in negotiating the release of a group of foreign hostages seized in the Philippines by the Abu Sayyaf Group, reportedly in exchange for a ransom payment. The hostages included citizens of France, Germany, Malaysia, South Africa, Finland, the Philippines, and Lebanon. The payment of ransom to kidnappers only encourages additional hostage taking, and the Abu Sayyaf Group, emboldened by its success, did seize additional hostages—including a US citizen—later in the year. Libya's behavior and that of other parties involved in the alleged ransom arrangement served only to encourage further terrorism and to make that region far more dangerous for residents and travelers.

At year's end, Libya had yet to comply fully with the remaining UN Security Council requirements related to Pan Am 103: accepting responsibility, paying appropriate compensation, disclosing all it knows, and renouncing terrorism. The United States remains dedicated to maintaining pressure on the Libyan Government until it does so. Qadhafi stated publicly that his government had adopted an antiterrorism stance, but it remains unclear whether his claims of distancing Libya from its terrorist past signify a true change in policy.

Libya also remained the primary suspect in several other past terrorist operations, including the La Belle discotheque bombing in Berlin in 1986 that killed two US servicemen and one Turkish civilian and wounded more than 200 persons. The trial in Germany of five suspects in the bombing, which began in November 1997, continued in 2000. Although Libya expelled the Abu Nidal organization and distanced itself from the Palestinian rejectionists in 1999, it continued to have contact with groups that use violence to oppose the Middle East peace process, including the Palestine Islamic Jihad and the Popular Front for the Liberation of Palestine-General Command.

2001

Following the September 11 terrorist attacks, Libyan leader Muammar Qadhafi issued a statement condemning the attacks as horrific and gruesome and urging Libyans to donate blood for the US victims. On 16 September he declared that the United States had justification to retaliate for the attacks. Since September 11, Qadhafi has repeatedly denounced terrorism.

Libya appears to have curtailed its support for international terrorism, although it may maintain residual contacts with a few groups. Tripoli has, in recent years, sought to recast itself as a peacemaker, offering to mediate a number of conflicts such as the military standoff between India and Pakistan that began in December 2001. In October, Libya ransomed a hostage held by the Abu Sayyaf Group, although it claimed that the money was not a ransom and would be used for "humanitarian assistance."

Libya's past record of terrorist activity continued to hinder Qadhafi's efforts to shed Libya's pariah status. In January, a Scottish court found Libyan intelligence agent Abdel Basset Ali al-Megrahi guilty of murder, concluding that in 1988 he planted an explosive device on Pan Am Flight 103 whose detonation resulted in the murder of all 259 passengers and crew on board as well as 11 persons on the ground in Lockerbie, Scotland. The judges found that Megrahi had acted "in furtherance of the purposes of...Libyan Intelligence Services." His codefendant, Libyan Arab Airlines employee Al-Amin Khalifa Fhima, was acquitted on the grounds that the prosecution failed to prove his role in the bombing "beyond a reasonable doubt." At year's end, Libya had yet to comply fully with the remaining UN Security Council requirements related to Pan Am 103, including accepting responsibility for the actions of its officials, fully disclosing all that it knows about the bombing, and paying appropriate compensation to the victims' families. Libya's hesitation to do so may have reflected a hope that Meghahi's appeal would overturn his conviction. (On 14 March 2002, a Scottish appellate court upheld Megrahi's conviction.)

In November, a German court convicted four defendants in the bombing in 1986 of La Belle discotheque in West Berlin. In rendering his decision, the judge stated that Libyan Government officials had clearly orchestrated the attack. In response to the court's findings, the German Government called on Libya to accept responsibility for the attack and provide compensation to the victims. Two US servicemen and one Turkish civilian died in the bombing, and more than 200 persons were wounded.

2002

In 2002, Libyan leader Muammar Qadhafi continued the efforts he undertook following the September 11 2001 terrorist attacks to identify Libya with the war on terrorism and the struggle against Islamic extremism. In August, Qadhafi told visiting British officials that he regards Usama Bin Ladin and his Libyan followers a threat to Libya. In his 1 September speech, he declared that Libya would combat members of al-Qaida and "heretics"—a likely reference to Libyan extremists allied with al-Qaida and opposed to his regime—as doggedly as the United States did. He further claimed that all political prisoners would be released and that the Libyan Government would henceforth only hold members of al-Qaida. Libya appears to have curtailed its support for international terrorism, although it may maintain residual contacts with some of its former terrorist clients.

Libya's past record of terrorism continued to hinder Qadhafi's efforts to shed Libya's pariah status in 2002. In March, a Scottish appellate court upheld the conviction—originally returned in January 2001—of Libyan intelligence agent Abdel Basset Ali al-Megrahi for murder in connection with planting an explosive device on Pan Am Flight 103 in December 1988. The explosion killed all 259 passengers and crew on board and 11 persons on the ground in Lockerbie, Scotland. There have been reports of a proposed out-of-court settlement of a suit brought by Pan Am 103 family members against Libya, but by year's end it had not been concluded.

Despite progress toward the payment of appropriate compensation, at year's end Libya had yet to comply with the remaining UN Security Council requirements related to Pan Am Flight 103, necessary for the permanent lifting of UN sanctions, including accepting responsibility for the actions of its officials.

In October, lawyers representing the seven US citizens who died in the bombing of UTA Flight 772 in 1989—for which a French court convicted six Libyans in absentia in 1999—filed a suit against Libya and Qadhafi, reportedly seeking $3 billion in compensation. The same month, Libya reportedly pledged to French authorities to increase payments already made to victims of the UTA bombing following the French court ruling in 1999.

In 2002, Libya became a party to the 1999 Convention for the Suppression of the Financing of Terrorism and the 1991 Convention on the Marking of Plastic Explosives for the Purpose of Detection. It is a party to all the 12 international conventions and protocols relating to terrorism.

2003

In 2003, Libya held to its practice in recent years of curtailing support for international terrorism, although Tripoli continues to maintain contact with some past terrorist clients. Libyan leader Muammar Qadhafi and other Libyan officials continued their efforts to identify Tripoli with the international community in the war on terrorism. During an interview in January, Qadhafi stated that Libyan intelligence had been sharing information on al-Qaida and other Islamic extremists with Western intelligence services and characterized such cooperation as "irrevocable." In a speech marking the 34th anniversary of his revolution, he declared that Libya and the United States had a common interest in fighting al-Qaida and Islamic extremism.

Regarding its own terrorist past, Libya took long-awaited steps in 2003 to address the UN requirements arising out of the bombing of Pan Am Flight 103 but remained embroiled in efforts to settle international political and legal disputes stemming from other terrorist attacks Tripoli conducted during the 1980s.

In August, as required by the UN Security Council, the Libyan Government officially notified the UN Security Council that it accepted responsibility for the actions of its officials in connection with Pan Am Flight 103 (Abdel Basset Ali al-Meghrahi, a Libyan intelligence agent, was convicted by a Scottish court in 2001 for his role in the bombing). Libya further confirmed that it had made arrangements for the payment of appropriate compensation to the families of the victims: a total of up to $2.7 billion or $10 million for each victim. Further, Libya renounced terrorism and affirmed its adherence to a number of UN declarations and international conventions and protocols that the Libyan Government had signed in the past. Libya also pledged to cooperate in good faith with any further requests for information in connection with the Pan Am Flight 103 investigation. In response, the Security Council voted on 12 September to permanently lift sanctions that it had imposed against Libya in 1992 and suspended in 1999.

In August, the Qadhafi Foundation pledged to compensate victims wounded in the bombing in 1986 of La Belle Discotheque, a Berlin nightclub, after a German court issued its written opinion finding that the Libyan intelligence service had orchestrated the attack. The original trial had concluded in 2001 with the conviction of four individuals for carrying out the attack, in which two US servicemen and a Turkish woman were killed and 229 persons wounded. Leaders of the Qadhafi Foundation indicated, however, that their compensation was a humanitarian gesture that did not constitute Libyan acceptance of responsibility. In September, the German Government indicated that it was engaged in talks with Libyan representatives, but at the end of the year, no announcement had yet been made regarding a final compensation deal.

On 19 December, Colonel Qadhafi announced that Libya would eliminate its weapons of mass destruction programs and MTCR-class missiles and took immediate steps to implement this public commitment with the assistance of the United States, United Kingdom, and relevant international organizations. The Libyan decision to reveal its programs to the international community shed important light on the international network of proliferators intent on subverting nonproliferation regimes.

Libya is a party to all 12 international conventions and protocols relating to terrorism.

2004

Following Libya's December 19, 2003, announcement that it would eliminate its weapons of mass destruction and non-Missile Technology Control Regime class missiles, the United States, the United Kingdom, and relevant international agencies worked with Libya to eliminate these weapons in a transparent and verifiable manner. In recognition of Libya's actions, the United States and Libya began the process of improving diplomatic relations. On February 26, the United States lifted its restriction on the use of US passports for travel to Libya and eased some economic sanctions. On April 23, the United States eased more sanctions and terminated the applicability of the Iran-Libya Sanctions Act provisions to Libya. On June 28, the United States reestablished direct diplomatic relations with Libya by upgrading its Interests Section to a US Liaison Office. On September 20, the President terminated the state of emergency declared in 1986 and revoked the related executive orders. This rescinded the remaining economic sanctions against Libya under the International Emergency Economic Powers Act (IEEPA).

Libya remains designated as a state sponsor of terrorism and is still subject to the related sanctions. In 2004, Libya held to its practice in recent years of curtailing support for international terrorism, although there are outstanding questions over its residual contacts with some past terrorist clients. Libya has provided cooperation in the global war on terrorism, and Libyan leader Muammar Qadhafi continued his efforts to identify Libya with the international community in the war on terrorism. Prior to the January 30, 2005, elections in Iraq, senior Libyan officials made statements that defended insurgent attacks on US and Coalition forces; following strong US protests, Libya encouraged Iraqi participation in the elections, indicating its intent to recognize the upcoming Transitional Iraqi Government, and support reciprocal diplomatic missions with Iraq.

Following Libya's steps to eliminate its weapons of mass destruction and the September 20 revocation of US economic sanctions related to the national emergency, Libya authorized a second payment of $4 million per family to the families of the 270 victims of the 1988 Pan Am 103 bombing over Lockerbie, Scotland. This payment was part of a deal concluded in 2003 between Libya and the families in which Libya agreed to pay $10 million per family, or $2.7 billion, contingent upon the lifting of UN and US sanctions and removal of Libya from the state sponsors of terrorism list. By year's end, UN and US sanctions were lifted and the families had received a total of $8 million each, even though Libya remained designated as a state sponsor of terrorism. A remaining $2 million per family remained in a third-country escrow account, pending Libya's removal from the terrorism list.

Libya resolved two other outstanding international disputes stemming from terrorist attacks that Libya conducted during the 1980s. In January, the Qadhafi Foundation agreed to pay $170 million to the non-US families of victims of the 1989 bombing of a French UTA passenger aircraft. Separate cases for compensation filed by US victims' families are still pending in the US courts. In 2001, a German court issued a written opinion finding that the Libyan intelligence service had orchestrated the 1986 bombing of the La Belle nightclub in Berlin, in which two US servicemen and a Turkish woman were killed and 229 people were injured. The Court convicted four individuals for carrying out the attack. In August, the Qadhafi Foundation agreed to pay $35 million to compensate non-US victims of the La Belle attack. In reaching the agreement to pay compensation, Libya stressed that it was not acknowledging responsibility for the attack, but was making a humanitarian gesture. The families of the US victims are pursuing separate legal cases, and Libyan officials publicly called for compensation for their own victims of the 1986 US air strikes in Libya.

In October, Libya was instrumental in the handover of Amari Saifi, also known as Abderrazak al-Para, the number two figure in the Salafist Group for Call and Combat (GSPC), to Algeria. Al-Para, responsible for the kidnapping of 32 Western tourists in Algeria in 2003, had been held by a Chadian rebel group, the Movement for Democracy and Justice, for several months. In August, Abdulrahman Alamoudi pled guilty to one count of unlicensed travel and commerce with Libya. Alamoudi stated that he had been part of a 2003 plot to assassinate Saudi Crown Prince Abdullah at the behest of Libyan officials. The United States expressed its serious concerns about these allegations and continues to evaluate Libya's December 2003 assurances to halt all use of violence for political purposes.

In December 2004, the US designated the Libyan Islamic Fighting Group (LIFG) as a Foreign Terrorist Organization.

Nicaragua

1985

Managua has continued to provide training and support to Latin American guerilla groups, and there has been limited evidence of direct Nicaraguan involvement in specific terrorist incidents. The Sandanistas also have maintained contact with Latin American and West European groups that engage in terrorism. According to a former Italian terrorist who turned state's evidence, at least five Red Brigades leaders have become instructors in the Nicaraguan Army. Despite the publicity aroused by Western accusations, international disapproval has not discouraged the Sandinistas form pursuing terrorist ties. Several of the weapons used by Colombian M-19 terrorists during the siege of the Palace of Justice in Bogota in November 1985 were traced to Nicaragua. The PRTC, a Salvadoran insurgent group with close ties to Nicaragua, claimed responsibility for the killing of six Americans and seven other persons in downtown San Salvador on 19 June.

1986

Managua provides training and support to terrorist groups in Colombia, to Ecuador's Alfaro Vive, Carajo! (AVC), and to a variety of Latin American guerilla groups. It also provides weapons to many groups in the region and facilitates contacts among Latin American leftists, including hosting meetings between Central and South American subversives. Members of European terrorist groups, including Italy's Red Brigades and Prima Linea and Spain's Basque Fatherland and Liberty, enjoy safe haven in Managua, but there is no evidence that they stage terrorist attacks from Nicaragua or that Nicaragua supports attacks by those groups in Western Europe.

1987

Like Cuba, in 1987 Nicaragua continued to supply materiel and training to a number of terrorist and other dissident groups in Central and South America and the Caribbean. The regime maintains close ties to the M-19 insurgency in Colombia, the Alfredo Vive Carajo group in Ecuador, and the Tupac Amaru Revolutionary Movement in Peru. Nicaragua continues to provide support for the Farabundo Marti Liberation Front (FMLN) in El Salvador despite its commitment under the terms of the August 1987 Guatemala Agreement to end such assistance. In years past, Nicaragua has also provided safehaven to terrorists from Western Europe, including Italy's Red Brigades and the Basque ETA group, but we have not detected any evidence that Nicaragua has directly sponsored specific terrorist attacks by these groups.

1988

Like Cuba, Nicaragua provides training and safehaven to Latin American terrorist and guerilla groups, including the Ecuadorian Alfaro Vive, Carajo! (AVC) group, Colombia's M-19, and the MRTA of Peru. The Sandinistas also continue to support the FMLN in El Salvador despite their commitment to end such assistance. In addition to dealing with individual groups, Nicaragua occasionally acts as a coordinator for Latin American insurgents, including hosting meetings between Central and South American subversives. Nicaragua appears to have better concealed, or possibly reduced, its links to West European terrorist groups such as the Italian BR and the Basque ETA. The Nicaraguan Government also maintains diplomatic relations with all six nations currently on the US Secretary of State's terrorism list (North Korea, South Yemen, Syria, Libya, Iran, and Cuba).

North Korea

Designation date January 20, 1988

1985

Pyongyang almost certainly has continued to provide training, funds, and weapons to various foreign extremist groups, but it apparently has not been involved in any terrorist incidents since the October 1983 Rangoon bombing. North Korea has continued to obtain weapons on the gray arms market, but these probably are intended for use by North Korean agents, saboteurs, and infiltrators in operations against South Korea. Pyongyang has exported weapons to Third World governments willing to pay for them, including Iran—a country supporting international terrorism. Thus far, none of these weapons has been found at the scene of terrorist attacks or in the possession or captured terrorists.

1986

North Korea is not known to have conducted a terrorist attack since the 1983 bombing against South Korean officials in Rangoon, Burma. South Korea blames North Korea for the bombing of Seoul's Kimpo Airport on the eve of the Asian Games in September 1986, but no evidence has been found that clearly links the attack to Pyongyang.

1987

The single most lethal international terrorist attack in 1987 occurred in Asia and heralded the return of North Korea as an active agent of state terrorism for the first time since it bombed the Martyr's Memorial in Rangoon four years earlier. On 29 November, Korean Air Flight 858 disappeared en route from Abu Dhabi to Bangkok, probably over the Andaman Sea. All 115 aboard were killed. A couple who boarded the flight in Baghdad and left it in Abu Dhabi were arrested in Bahrain on 1 December for traveling on false Japanese passports as father and daughter. As they were being interrogated, they bit into cyanide capsules concealed in cigarettes. The man died, but the woman survived and was later deported to Seoul. She has since publicly confirmed that the pair were North Korean intelligence agents who had placed the bomb on the aircraft in their carry-on luggage.

According to the surviving terrorist, the KAL 858 bombing was the start of a campaign to disrupt the Olympic Games in 1988. We believe it possible that the bombing was the first in a planned series of terrorist events intended to portray South Korea as unsafe. North Korea will probably not host any Olympic events in P'yongyang or participate in the Games—a situation that might encourage it to stage further disruptive acts. On the other hand, with only a few exceptions, most Communist and Third World countries will take part in the Olympics; this participation, coupled with widespread international belief in North Korean complicity in the bombing of the airliner, might act to deter P'yongyang.

1988

North Korea continued to fund and train South Korean extremist groups and to move weapons through the gray arms market but is not known to have sponsored any international terrorist attacks in 1988. Continuing revelations throughout 1988 about North Korean complicity in the bombing of a South Korean airliner in November 1987—which may have been the opening shot in an abortive terror campaign against the South and the Olympics—possibly served to embarrass the North and dissuade it from further attempts to disrupt the Olympics through terrorist tactics.

North Korea supported at least some members of the JRA. A faction of the group, presently consisting of six members, is based in Pyongyang. Japanese police believe that Yasuhiro Shibata, a JRA member arrested in Tokyo in May, was "run" by North Korean intelligence agents. Shibata was using the identity of a former North Korean resident of Japan who had immigrated to North Korea in 1972. Japanese police have been tracking attempts by North Korean spy rings to acquire Japanese passports, some of which have been passed to the JRA in the past.

1989

North Korea was not responsible for any terrorist incidents in 1989. It has continued to provide haven to a small group of Japanese Red Army members who hijacked a JAL airliner to North Korea in 1973. North Korea also continued supplying training and possibly materiel to communist guerillas in the Philippines in 1989. North Korea remains on the list of state sponsors of terrorism because of its responsibility for the November 1987 destruction of a South Korean airliner and the 1983 terrorist attack against the Republic of Korea officials in Rangoon, Burma.

1990

North Korea is not known to have sponsored a terrorist attack since members of its intelligence service planted a bomb on a South Korean airliner in 1987. However, it continues to provide safehaven to a small group of Japanese Red Army (JRA) members who hijacked a JA airliner to North Korea in 1970. North Korea has provided some support to the New People's Army in the Philippines. It has not renounced the use of terrorism.

1991

North Korea is not known to have sponsored any international terrorist attacks since 1987. While the North Korean Government has not publicly renounced terrorism, it did agree to abandon violence against the South in the December 1991 reconciliation agreement with South Korea. North Korea has also assured the Philippines that it has broke its ties to the Communist New People's Army (NPA). Pyongyang continues to provide political asylum to a small group of Japanese Communist-League Red Army Faction members who hijacked a Japanese Airlines flight to North Korea in 1970.

1992

The Democratic People's Republic of Korea (DPRK or North Korea) is not known to have sponsored any terrorist acts since 1987, when a KAL airliner was bombed in flight. While not explicitly renouncing terrorism, the DPRK Foreign Ministry made an ambiguous condemnation of international terrorism on 26 March 1992 following the passage of a UN Security Council resolution on the bombing of Pan Am Flight 103. North Korea appears to be honoring its pledge to abandon violence against South Korea, as set out in the 1991 reconciliation agreement. North Korea also appears to be respecting a promise to the Philippine Government to suspend its support for the Communist New People's army (NPA). Normalization talks with Japan broke off in the fall of 1992, when North Korea refused to respond to questions concerning the status of a Korean resident of Japan allegedly kidnapped by North Koreans to teach Japanese to DPRK terrorists involved in the 1987 KAL bombing. Pyongyang continues to provide political sanctuary to members of the Japanese Communist League-Red Army Faction who participated in the hijacking of a Japanese airlines flight to North Korea in 1970.

1993

The Democratic People's Republic of Korea is not known to have sponsored any terrorist acts since 1987, when a KAL airliner was bombed in flight. A North Korean spokesman condemned all forms of terrorism including state terrorism after the April assassination of South African Communist Party chief Chris Hani. Pyongyang has supported the Communist Party of the Philippines/New People's Army (CPP/NPA) in the past but does not appear to be doing so at present. North Korea is believed, however, to maintain contacts with other groups that practice terrorism. Pyongyang continues to provide political sanctuary to members of the Japanese Communist League-Red Army Faction who participated in the hijacking of a Japanese airlines flight to North Korea in 1970.

1994

The Democratic People's Republic of Korea (DPRK or North Korea) is not known to have sponsored any international terrorist attacks since 1987, when it conducted the midflight bombing of a KAL airliner. A North Korean spokesman in April 1993 condemned all forms of terrorism, including state terrorism, and said his country resolutely opposed the encouragement and support of terrorism. Nevertheless, North Korea maintains contact with groups that practice terrorism and continues to provide political sanctuary to members of the Japanese Communist League-Red Army Faction who hijacked a Japan Airlines flight to North Korea in 1970.

1995

The Democratic People's Republic of Korea (DPRK or North Korea) is not known to have sponsored any international terrorist attacks since 1987, when it conducted the midflight bombing of a KAL airliner, killing all 115 persons aboard. A North Korean spokesman in November stated that the DPRK opposed "all kinds of terrorism" and "any assistance to it." North Korea, however, continued to provide political sanctuary to members of the Japanese Communist League-Red Army Faction who hijacked a Japanese Airlines flight to North Korea in 1970.

1996

North Korea has not been conclusively linked to any international terrorist attacks since 1987. North Korea is best known for its involvement in the 1987 midair bombing of KAL Flight 858 and the 1983 Rangoon bombing aimed at South Korean Government officials. A North Korean spokesman in November 1995 stated that the Democratic People's Republic of Korea (DPRK) opposed "all kinds of terrorism" and "any assistance to it."

There is no conclusive evidence the DPRK conducted any act of terrorism since 1987. The Republic of Korea, however, suspects that North Korean agents were involved in the murder of a South Korean official in Vladivostok on 1 October 1996, which shortly followed a North Korean warning that it would retaliate if Seoul did not return the bodies of several North Korean infiltrators killed in South Korea.

The DPRK provides asylum to a small group of Japanese Red Army members—the "Yodo-go" group—who hijacked a JAL airliner to North Korea in 1970. The senior surviving Yodo-go member, Yoshimi Tanaka, in late March was arrested in Cambodia on counterfeiting charges. Tanaka was captured while carrying a North Korean diplomatic passport and in the company of several North Korean diplomats. Pyongyang admitted publicly that Tanaka was a Yodo-go member, did not dispute the counterfeiting charges, and refused to take up his defense.

1997

North Korea has not been linked conclusively to any international terrorist attacks since 1987. Pyongyang may have been responsible for the February 1997 murder of a North Korean defector in South Korea and the murder of a South Korean official in Vladivostok in October 1996.

The best known case of past North Korean involvement in terrorism was the 1987 midair bombing of Korean Airlines Flight 858, which killed all 115 persons aboard. Pyongyang continues to provide sanctuary to five of the nine "Yodo-go" hijackers of a Japan Airlines jet to North Korea in 1970. Of the original nine, two have died of illness, one was arrested in Japan in the mid-1980s, and another was arrested in 1996 by Thai authorities on charges of passing counterfeit US currency.

1998

The Democratic People's Republic of Korea has not been linked solidly to the planning or execution of an international terrorist attack since 1987, when a KAL airliner was bombed in flight. North Korea continues to provide safehaven to members of the Japanese Communist League-Red Army Faction who participated in the hijacking of a Japanese Airlines flight to North Korea in 1970. In March, Pyongyang allowed members of the Japanese Diet to visit some of the hijackers.

1999

The Democratic People's Republic of Korea (DPRK) continued to provide safehaven to the Japanese Communist League-Red Army Faction members who participated in the hijacking of a Japanese Airlines flight to North Korea in 1970. Pyongyang allowed members of the Japanese Diet to visit some of the hijackers during the year. In 1999 the DPRK also attempted to kidnap in Thailand a North Korean diplomat who had defected the day before. The attempt led the North Korean Embassy to hold the former diplomat's son hostage for two weeks. Some evidence also suggests the DPRK in 1999 may have sold weapons directly or indirectly to terrorist groups.

2000

In 2000 the Democratic People's Republic of Korea (DPRK) engaged in three rounds of terrorism talks that culminated in a joint DPRK-US statement wherein the DPRK reiterated its opposition to terrorism and agreed to support international actions against such activity. The DPRK, however, continued to provide safehaven to the Japanese Communist League-Red Army Faction members who participated in the hijacking of a Japanese Airlines flight to North Korea in 1970. Some evidence also suggests the DPRK may have sold weapons directly or indirectly to terrorist groups during the year; Philippine officials publicly declared that the Moro Islamic Liberation Front had purchased weapons from North Korea with funds provided by Middle East sources.

2001

The Democratic People's Republic of Korea's (DPRK) response to international efforts to combat terrorism has been disappointing. In a statement released after the September 11 attacks, the DPRK reiterated its public policy of opposing terrorism and any support for terrorism. It also signed the UN Convention for the Suppression of the Financing of Terrorism, acceded to the Convention Against the Taking of Hostages, and indicated its willingness to sign five others. Despite the urging of the international community, however, North Korea did not take substantial steps to cooperate in efforts to combat terrorism, including responding to requests for information on how it is implementing the UN Security Council resolutions, and it did not respond to US proposals for discussions on terrorism. It did not report any efforts to search for and block financial assets as required by UN Security Council Resolution 1373. Similarly, the DPRK did not respond positively to the Republic of Korea's call to resume dialogue, where counterterrorism is an agenda item, nor to the United States in its call to undertake dialogue on improved implementation of the agreed framework. In light of President Bush's call to recognize the dangerous nexus between Weapons of Mass Destruction and terrorism, this latter failure, with its implications for nuclear development and proliferation, was especially troublesome.

In addition, Pyongyang's provision of safehaven to four remaining Japanese Communist League-Red Army Faction members who participated in the hijacking of a Japanese Airlines flight to North Korea in 1970 remained problematic in terms of support for terrorists. Moreover, some evidence suggested the DPRK may have sold limited quantities of small arms to terrorist groups during the year.

2002

The Democratic People's Republic of Korea's (DPRK) response to international efforts to combat terrorism was disappointing throughout 2002, although in a statement released after the September 11 attacks, the DPRK had reiterated its public policy of opposing terrorism and any support for terrorism. In 2001, following the September 11 attacks, it also signed the UN Convention for the Suppression of the Financing of Terrorism and became a party to the Convention Against the Taking of Hostages.

Despite the urging of the international community, however, North Korea did not take substantial steps to cooperate in efforts to combat terrorism. Its initial and supplementary reports to the UN Counterterrorism Committee on actions it had undertaken to comply with its obligations under UNSCR 1373 were largely uninformative and nonresponsive. It did not respond to previous US proposals for discussions on terrorism and did not report any efforts to freeze without delay funds and other financial assets or economic resources of persons who commit, or attempt to commit, terrorist acts that UNSCR 1373, among other things, requires all states to do.

North Korea is not known to have sponsored any terrorist acts since 1987. It has sold weapons to several terrorist groups, however, even as it reiterated its opposition to all forms of international terrorism. Pyongyang also has provided safehaven to several Japanese Red Army members who participated in the hijacking of a Japanese Airlines flight to North Korea in 1970.

Pyongyang continued to sell ballistic missile technology to countries designated by the United States as state sponsors of terrorism, including Syria and Libya.

North Korea is a party to six of the 12 international conventions and protocols relating to terrorism.

2003

The Democratic People's Republic of Korea (DPRK) is not known to have sponsored any terrorist acts since the bombing of a Korean Airlines flight in 1987.

Following the attacks of September 11, Pyongyang began laying the groundwork for a new position on terrorism by framing the issue as one of "protecting the people" and replaying language from the Joint US-DPRK Statement on International Terrorism of October 2000. It also announced to a visiting EU delegation that it planned to sign the international conventions against terrorist financing and the taking of hostages and would consider acceding to other antiterrorism agreements.

At a summit with Japanese Prime Minister Koizumi in Pyongyang in September 2002, National Defense Commission Chairman Kim Jong Il acknowledged the involvement of DPRK "special institutions" in the kidnapping of Japanese citizens and said that those responsible had already been punished. Pyongyang has allowed the return to Tokyo of five surviving abductees and is negotiating with Tokyo over the repatriation of their family members remaining in North Korea. The DPRK also has been trying to resolve the issue of harboring Japanese Red Army members involved in a jet hijacking in 1970—allowing the repatriation of several family members of the hijackers to Japan.

Although it is a party to six international conventions and protocols relating to terrorism, Pyongyang has not taken substantial steps to cooperate in efforts to combat international terrorism.

2004

The Democratic People's Republic of Korea (DPRK) is not known to have sponsored any terrorist acts since the bombing of a Korean Airlines flight in 1987.

At a summit with Japanese Prime Minister Koizumi in Pyongyang in September 2002, National Defense Commission Chairman Kim Jong Il acknowledged the involvement of DPRK "special institutions" in the kidnapping of Japanese citizens and said that those responsible had already been punished. Pyongyang in 2003 allowed the return to Japan of five surviving abductees, and in 2004 of eight family members, mostly children, of those abductees. Questions about the fate of other abductees remain the subject of ongoing negotiations between Japan and the DPRK. In November, the DPRK returned to Japan what it identified as the remains of two Japanese abductees whom the North had reported as having died in North Korea. Subsequent DNA testing in Japan indicated that the remains were not those of Megumi Yokota or Kaoru Matsuki, as Pyongyang had claimed, and the issue remained contentious at year's end. Four Japanese Red Army members remain in the DPRK following their involvement in a jet hijacking in 1970; five of their family members returned to Japan in 2004.

Although it is a party to six international conventions and protocols relating to terrorism, Pyongyang has not taken substantial steps to cooperate in efforts to combat international terrorism.

South Yemen

1985

Then South Yemeni President Hasani continued his more moderate foreign policy by curtailing Aden's direct involvement with, and support for, insurgent groups from Oman and North Yemen. South Yemen also reduced support for the Palestinians. However, Aden has continued to provide safehaven and other low-level support to groups such as the Popular Front for the Liberation of Palestine-Special Command.

1986

The People's Democratic Republic of Yemen (PDRY) continued to display a low profile in its support for groups that engage in terrorism. Aden experienced considerable domestic instability in the wake of a coup and change in government early in the year and may have curtailed its support to insurgent groups in Oman and North Yemen in an effort to improve its standing in the region. The PDRY maintains ties to some terrorist groups, and the Popular Front for the Liberation of Palestine-Special Command (PFLP-SC) is headquartered in Aden.

1987

We have detected little evidence of direct South Yemen involvement in sponsoring international terrorism since the early 1980s and believe that the new regime, which came into power following a bloody internecine conflict in January 1986, may have decided to continue its predecessor's policy of reducing close ties to terrorist groups. The regime appears preoccupied with serious domestic political and economic problems and may have been responsible for a car bomb and letter bomb explosions in Sanaa (North Yemen) in 1987, directed against supporters of the previous regime.

In 1987, South Yemen persisted in its longstanding policy of allowing Palestinian groups, including elements of the Abu Nidal organization, the Democratic Front for the Liberation of Palestine, and the Popular Struggle Front, to maintain offices in Aden. The Popular Front for the Liberation of Palestine-Special Command has its headquarters there. As long as these facilities continue to be offered, South Yemen risks being linked to overseas attacks staged by any of these groups.

1988

South Yemen has considerably reduced its support for international terrorism since the early 1980s, and we do not believe it sponsored any terrorist attacks in 1988. Aden probably was trying to project an image of moderation to encourage neighboring Arab states—and other possible aid contributors—to provide additional economic and technical assistance. The regime also appeared preoccupied with serious domestic political and economic problems.

South Yemen continued, however, to play host to a number of Palestinian groups—including the ANO, the Democratic Front for the Liberation of Palestine, the PSF, and the PFLP-SC—but no longer directly supports them with material or financial assistance. South Yemen appeared to have reconsidered—or perhaps reversed—its longstanding policy of issuing South Yemeni passports to Palestinians, although Armenian terrorist leader Hagop Hagopian was carrying a South Yemeni passport, complete with a diplomatic stamp, at the time of his death in April 1988.

1989

South Yemen has considerably reduced its support for international terrorism since the early 1980s, and we do not believe it sponsored any terrorist attacks in 1989. Aden continues to project an image of moderation in its effort to repair relations with the West and neighboring Arab states. The regime's economic problems and need for economic and technological assistance have encouraged greater pragmatism. South Yemen may have reversed its longstanding policy of issuing South Yemeni passports to Palestinians. However, it has continued to allow some radical Palestinian groups, including the ANO, to maintain a presence in South Yemen.

Soviet Union and Eastern Europe

1985

In contract to Libya, Syria, and Iran, the Soviets do not appear to directly plan or orchestrate terrorist acts by Middle Eastern, West European, or Latin American groups. Moscow has continued to support various "national liberation movements"—such as the PLO and the African National Congress (ANC)—with the knowledge that some of those they train later commit terrorist acts. The Soviets and East Europeans have provided most weapons support indirectly through the international gray arms market. Moscow's Third World clients (with Libya a leading buyer) then have resold or given the weapons to terrorists. Moscow apparently has not restricted the end use of these weapons. The Soviet Union and its East European allies also have provided arms to a variety of Palestinian groups. Some of these may ultimately be used in terrorist attacks because Palestinian terrorists routinely use light infantry weapons, such as the AK-47, that originate in the Soviet Bloc.

The Soviet's influence over their East European allies has given Moscow the leverage to elicit their support for radical and revolutionary groups. There has been extensive evidence of indirect support and scattered information about direct involvement by East European states with terrorists. At a minimum, these states have maintained surveillance on suspected terrorists and allowed them transit privileges and safehaven. A number of East European states also have trained members of African, Latin American, and Palestinian groups that use terrorist tactics.

Bulgaria has been the East European state most actively involved in terrorism. Sofia has provided weapons and political support to various Palestinian groups and has hosted terrorist-related training facilities where Palestinians, in particular, have received instruction in a variety of weapons. Materiel from Czechoslovakia has also appeared frequently in terrorist hands. A Czechoslovak-manufactured explosive material, Semtex, has been used in numerous letter bombs, as well as several recent bombings. Yugoslavia was the first state to offer initial safehaven to Muhammad Abu Abbas, the Palestine Liberation Front (PLF) leader who planned the Achille Laruo hijacking and provided the aircraft on which Abbas was flown to safety from Rome.

1986

The Soviets and various East European states provide arms and training to a broad spectrum of anti-Western groups and "national liberation movements," many of whose members commit terrorist acts. Although the Soviet Union and its allies have sold arms directly to some groups, mostly Palestinians, most Soviet weapons sold or given to terrorist groups are provided by Third World Soviet clients, such as Libya.

Various East European states provide training, equipment and/or political support to radical groups, particularly Palestinian, that commit terrorism. Polish and Bulgarian weapons have been found in possession of Abu Nidal organization terrorists and the scenes of their attacks. Many Middle Eastern groups use a Czechoslovak-manufactured explosive, Semtex-H, in their bombs. Many terrorists transit or find safehaven in East European countries, including Yugoslavia, whose geographic location, visa-free regime, and large Arab student population continue to make it an attractive area for the transit of agents and state operational uses, such as recruiting members and maintaining safehouses.

1987

As in years past, some Soviet Bloc countries continued in 1987 to provide some direct and indirect assistance to terrorist groups. Such support usually was given under the pretext of aiding "national liberation movements" and ranged from permitting transit for known terrorists to providing arms, explosives, training, funding, and political encouragement. Soviet Bloc countries also provided state sponsors of terrorism, such as Libya and Syria, with large amounts of arms and explosives, some of which were then distributed to terrorist groups. A prime example of this indirect support came to light in the French interception of the PIRA-bound Libyan arms shipment, almost all of which, we believe, was supplied by the Soviet Bloc.

Finally, according to press reports, Poland and East Germany had permitted Abu Nidal organization to operate trading offices from their territory for several years until, in the face of international concern they closed them down in 1987. Commercial agents form the Abu Nidal organization in the offices acted as brokers in several arms sales involving Poland and East Germany. Some of the weapons sold in the transactions were made in the Soviet Bloc and may have ended up with Middle East terrorist groups. The Abu Nidal organization used the profits from these ventures to finance its own activities.

The United States regularly raised its concerns regarding terrorism with the Soviets and the East Europeans, and in doing so may have persuaded Eastern Bloc countries to distance themselves somewhat from terrorism.

1988

In the past year, the Soviet Union has taken a more constructive approach to condemning terrorism than in previous years, but there is still room for improvement. The Soviets continued to provide arms, training, and materiel and diplomatic support to a range of states and groups linked to terrorism. Several countries that support terrorism—such as Libya, Syria, and North Korea—are Soviet allies. The Soviets have been reluctant thus far in taking concrete measures to discourage terrorist acts by groups or terrorism-supporting states with which Moscow has influence. For example, in the ICAO and the UN, the Soviets publicly defended North Korea against claims that it was responsible for the destruction of KAL Flight 8958, despite considerable evidence to the contrary. A Soviet Foreign Ministry spokesman in June also defended Libya against a US statement about Libyan links to terrorism.

The Soviets have, however, indicated that they maybe prepared in the future to work with others against terrorism. In public statements, the Soviets have increasingly condemned specific acts of terrorism. For example, the Soviet media denounced the holding of hostages in Beirut and the April 1988 hijacking of Kuwait Airways Flight 422. This more positive approach has also been demonstrated in practical terms. There are reports that, in the period leading up to the 1988 Summer Olympics in Seoul, the Soviets pressed P'yongyang to avoid acts that could disrupt the Games. General Secretary Gorbachev has publicly indicated Soviet interest in discussing counterterrorism issues with other interested countries.

The Soviets have also been supportive of multilateral efforts to increase airport and maritime security and have indicated their support for new legal instruments in these areas. In the UN, the Soviets have proposed a "comprehensive system of international security," which includes establishing a tribunal to investigate acts of international terrorism. This proposal, however, omits any mechanism for taking action specifically aimed at combating terrorism.

The Soviets have dealt with domestic hijacking incidents in different ways. In contrast with the handling of a domestic hijacking in March in which a Soviet assault team stormed the plane and nine civilians died, the Soviets in December allowed an Aeroflot aircraft hijacked by criminals to depart from the country without incident and then worked with the Israeli Government to secure the safe return of the plane, passengers, and the hijackers.

As for Eastern Europe, countries in this region are quick to affirm their opposition to terrorism; however, several have condoned terrorism by directly or indirectly supporting North Korea against charges of responsibility for the destruction of KAL Flight 858 in November 1987. Czechoslovakia refused to recognize North Korean responsibility, and the controlled press in Bulgaria sought to defend it against the charges. The German Democratic Republic confined its coverage in the controlled media to reporting solely North Korea's statements, and the media reporting in Romania was similarly biased. PIRA continues to use Czech-made Semtex-H explosives supplied by Libya, with deadly results in Northern Ireland. As with the Soviet Union, these East European countries maintain close relations with virtually all countries on the US Government's list of state sponsors of terrorism.

Consistent with its publicly stated policy against terrorism, in April, Bulgaria sponsored an international conference on terrorism in Druzba and supported work on counterterrorism by the Balkan foreign ministers at their conference in February. It remains to be seen what practical counterterrorism measures participants in this latter conference will adopt. The conference condemned the hijacking last April of Kuwait Airways Flight 422.

As for the matter of the Abu Nidal commercial network in Eastern Europe, which was terminated in 1987 after a US diplomatic campaign against it, there are no indications that any such relationships have resumed, although the United States continues to monitor the situation closely.

Sudan

Designation date August 12, 1993

1993

In August, the Secretary of State placed Sudan on the list of state sponsors of terrorism. Despite several warnings to cease supporting radical extremists, the Sudanese Government continued to harbor international terrorist groups in Sudan. Through the National Islamic Front (NIF), which dominates the Sudanese Government, Sudan maintained a disturbing relationship with a wide range of Islamic extremists. The list includes the ANO, the Palestinian HAMAS, the PIJ, the Lebanese Hizballah, and Egypt's al Gama'at al-Islamiyya.

The Sudanese Government also opposed the presence of the United Nations coalition in Somalia and probably provided some aid to the Somali Islamic Union and the Somali National Alliance. Egypt, Tunisia, and Algeria have complained that Sudan supports antiregime insurgents in North Africa with safehaven, weapons, passports, funds, and training. Algeria withdrew its Ambassador from Khartoum in March.

Sudan's ties to Iran, the leading state sponsor of terrorism, continued to cause concern during the past year. Sudan served as a convenient transit point, meeting site, and safehaven for Iranian-backed extremist groups. Iranian Ambassador in Khartoum Majid Kamal was involved in the 1979 takeover of the US Embassy in Tehran and guided Iranian efforts in developing the Lebanese Hizballah group while he served as Iran's top diplomat in Lebanon during the early 1980s. His presence illustrated the importance Iran places on Sudan.

Although there is no conclusive evidence linking the Government of Sudan to any specific terrorist incident during the year, five of 15 suspects arrested this summer following the New York City bomb plot are Sudanese citizens. Khartoum's anti-US rhetoric also escalated during 1993. In September, at a prominent Khartoum mosque, a radical journalist called for the murder of the US Ambassador. President Bashir dismissed the call as that of an unstable individual, but no NIF officials publicly disavowed it.

1994

The Government of Sudan provided safehaven and support for members of several international terrorist groups operating in Sudan. The regime also permitted Tehran to use Sudan as a secure transit point and meeting site for Iranian-backed extremist groups. There is no evidence that Sudan, which is dominated by the National Islamic Front (NIF), conducted or sponsored a specific act of terrorism in 1994.

The list of groups that maintain a presence or operate in Sudan is disturbing and includes some of the world's most violent organizations: the ANO, the Lebanese Hizballah, the Palestinian Islamic Resistance Movement (HAMAS), the Palestinian Islamic Jihad (PIJ), and Egypt's Islamic Group. The NIF also supports Islamic opposition groups from Algeria, Tunisia, Kenya, and Eritrea. Some of Sudan's neighbors have complained that insurgents in North Africa have received assistance from Sudan in the form of training, funds, weapons, travel documents, and indoctrination. In December, Eritrea severed diplomatic relations with Sudan for its support for subversive activities and hostile acts.

In a positive development, Sudan turned over the international terrorist "Carlos" (Ilyich Ramirez Sanchez) to France in August. Carlos—who bragged about his ties to senior government officials, carried a weapon, and flaunted Sudan's laws—had been living in Sudan since late 1993 with full knowledge and protection of senior levels of the NIF and Sudanese Government.

While the reasons for the expulsion of Carlos are not entirely clear, the regime emphasized that the affair did not signal a shift in Sudanese policy and that the fate of Carlos would not affect other terrorist elements currently harbored in Sudan. President Bashir stated publicly it was Sudan's duty to protect "mujahedin" who sought refuge. In a press interview on the suicide bus bombing in Tel Aviv by a HAMAS militant in October, which left 22 persons dead, NIF leader Hassan Turabi praised the attack, calling it "an honorable act."

The Sudanese regime regularly denied there are terrorists in Sudan, and it refused to investigate information the US Ambassador supplied in September about the training of terrorists at the Merkhiyat Popular Defense camp located northwest of Khartoum. The Foreign Minister categorically dismissed the information without even offering to look into it.

1995

Sudan continued to serve as a refuge, nexus, and training hub in 1995 for a number of international terrorist organizations, primarily of Middle Eastern origin. The Sudanese Government, which is dominated by the National Islamic Front (NIF), also condoned many of the activities of Iran and the Khartoum-based Usama Bin Ladin, a private financier of terrorism. Khartoum permitted the funneling of assistance to terrorist and radical Islamist groups operating in and transiting Sudan.

Since Sudan was placed on the US Government's official list of State Sponsors of Terrorism in August 1993, the Sudanese Government has continued to harbor members of some of the world's most violent organizations: the Abu Nidal organization (ANO), Lebanese Hizballah, the Palestine Islamic Jihad (PIJ), Egypt's al-Gama'at al-Islamiyya (Islamic Group or IG), and the Islamic Resistance Movement (HAMAS). The NIF also supports Islamic and non-Islamic opposition groups in Uganda, Tunisia, Kenya, Ethiopia, and Eritrea.

Uganda severed diplomatic relations with Sudan in April, citing the inappropriate activities of representatives of the Sudanese Embassy in Kampala. The Government of Uganda said it found these activities threatening to its security.

Both Ethiopia and Egypt accused Sudan's security services of providing direct assistance to the IG for the attempt on the life of Egyptian President Hosni Mubarak in Addis Ababa on 26 June. Three surviving assailants captured by Ethiopian police provided incriminating information about Sudan's role. Sudanese help to the IG included supplying travel documents and weapons and harboring key planners of the operation.

Despite a private plea by the Ethiopian Government, the Sudanese regime did not act on Ethiopia's request for the extradition of three Egyptian suspects involved in the Mubarak assassination attempt, claiming it was unable to locate them. Those being sought included the operation's mastermind—resident in Khartoum—his assistant, and a surviving member of the assassination team. (After the attack misfired, this last individual fled from Addis Ababa to Sudan on Sudan Airlines using a Sudanese passport.) In rare actions against a member state, the Organization of African Unity (OAU) on 11 September and again on 19 December called on Sudan to extradite the three IG suspects believed to have been involved in the assassination attempt and to stop aiding terrorism.

In an apparent attempt at damage control not long after the assassination attempt, President Bashir removed the head of Sudan's security services and proclaimed a new visa policy requiring Arab foreigners to obtain visas to enter Sudan. The policy did not apply to citizens from three state sponsors of terrorism—Iraq, Libya, and Syria—however, because of bilateral agreements.

Khartoum also permitted Usama Bin Ladin, a denaturalized Saudi citizen with mujahedin contacts, to use Sudan as a shelter for his radical Muslim followers and to finance and train militant groups. Bin Ladin, who lives in Khartoum and owns numerous business enterprises in Sudan, has been linked to numerous terrorist organizations. He directs funding and other logistic support through his companies to a number of extremist causes.

A Sudanese national, who pleaded guilty in February 1995 to various charges of complicity in the New York City bomb plots foiled by the Federal Bureau Investigation, alleged that a member of the Sudanese UN Emission had offered to facilitate access to the UN building in pursuance of the bombing plot. The Sudanese official also is said to have had full knowledge of other bombing targets.

Sudan's support to terrorist organizations has included paramilitary training, indoctrination, money, travel documentation, safe passage, and refugee in Sudan. Most of the organizations present in Sudan maintain offices or other types of representation. They use Sudan as a base to organize some of their operations and to support compatriots elsewhere. Sudan also serves as a secure transit point and meeting place for several Iranian-backed terrorist groups.

1996

Sudan in 1996 continued to serve as a refuge, nexus, and training hub for a number of international terrorist organizations, primarily of Middle East origin. The Sudanese Government also condoned many of the objectionable activities of Iran, such as funneling assistance to terrorist and radical Islamic groups operating in and transiting through Sudan.

Following the passage of three critical UN Security Council resolutions, Sudan ordered the departure of terrorist financier Usama Bin Ladin from Sudan in May. Sudan failed, however, to comply with the Security Council's demand that it cease support to terrorists and turn over the three Egyptian al-Gama'at al-Islamiyya (IG) fugitives linked to the 1995 assassination attempt of President Mubarak. Khartoum continued to deny any foreknowledge of the planning behind the Mubarak attempt and claimed not to know the whereabouts of the assailants.

Since Sudan was placed on the list of state sponsors of terrorism in August 1993, the Sudanese Government has continued to harbor members of several international terrorist and radical Islamic groups, including the Abu Nidal organization (ANO), Lebanese Hizballah, the Palestine Islamic Jihad (PIJ), the Islamic Resistance Movement (HAMAS), and the Islamic Salvation Front (FIS) of Algeria. The National Islamic Front, which is the dominant influence within the Sudanese Government, also supports opposition and insurgent groups in Uganda, Tunisia, Ethiopia, and Eritrea.

In April 1996 the Department of State expelled a Sudanese diplomat at the Sudanese UN Mission who had ties to the conspirators planning to bomb the UN building and other targets in New York in 1993. A Sudanese national, who pleaded guilty in February 1995 to various charges of complicity in the New York City bomb plots foiled by the FBI, indicated two members of the Sudanese UN Mission had offered to facilitate access to the UN building in support of the bombing plot.

1997

Sudan in 1997 continued to serve as a haven, meeting place, and training hub for a number of international terrorist organizations, primarily of Middle East origin. The Sudanese Government also condoned many of the objectionable activities of Iran, such as funneling assistance to terrorist and radical Islamic groups operating in and transiting through Sudan. The Department of State in November 1997 announced new comprehensive economic sanctions against Sudan. The sanctions convey the gravity of US concerns about Sudan's continued support for international terrorism and regional opposition groups as well as its abysmal human rights record.

Sudan has not complied with UN Security Council Resolutions 1044, 1054, and 1070 passed in 1996, despite efforts that year by the regime to distance itself somewhat from terrorism, including ordering the departure of terrorist financier Usama Bin Ladin. The Security Council's demands include that Sudan cease its support to terrorists and turn over the three Egyptian al-Gama'at fugitives linked to the 1995 attempted assassination of Egyptian President Mubarak in Ethiopia. President Bashir, consistent with Khartoum's repeated denials that its officials had any foreknowledge of the planning of the event, in October 1997 scoffed at the idea Sudan could be seen to have had anything to do with the attack.

Since Sudan was placed on the list of state sponsors of terrorism in August 1993, the Sudanese Government has continued to harbor members of several of the most violent international terrorist and radical Islamic groups. These groups include Lebanese Hizballah, the PIJ, the ANO, and HAMAS. The Sudanese Government also supports regional Islamic and non-Islamic opposition and insurgent groups in Ethiopia, Eritrea, Uganda, and Tunisia.

Sudan's support to terrorist organizations has included paramilitary training, indoctrination, money, travel documentation, safe passage, and refuge in Sudan. Most of the organizations present in Sudan maintain offices or other types of representation. They use Sudan as a base to organize some of their operations and to support compatriots elsewhere. Sudan also serves as a transit point and meeting place for several Iranian-backed terrorist groups.

1998

Sudan continued to serve as a meeting place, safehaven, and training hub for a number of international terrorist groups, particularly Usama Bin Ladin's al-Qaida organization. The Sudanese Government also condoned many of Iran's objectionable activities, such as funding terrorist and radical Islamic groups operating and transiting Sudan.

Sudan still has not complied fully with UN Security Council Resolutions 1044, 1054, and 1070, passed in 1996, despite the regime's efforts to distance itself publicly from terrorism. The UNSC demands that Sudan end all support to terrorists. It also requires Khartoum to hand over three Egyptian al-Gama'at fugitives linked to the assassination attempt in 1995 against Egyptian President Mubarak in Ethiopia. Sudanese officials continue to deny that they are harboring the three suspects and that they had a role in the attack.

Khartoum continues to provide safehaven to members of several of the world's most violent terrorist groups, including Lebanese Hizballah, the PIJ, the ANO, and HAMAS. Khartoum also supports regional Islamic and non-Islamic opposition and insurgent groups in Ethiopia, Eritrea, Uganda, and Tunisia.

Sudanese support to terrorists includes provision of paramilitary training, money, religious indoctrination, travel documents, safe passage, and refuge. Most of the organizations in Sudan maintain offices or other types of representation.

In August the United States accused Sudan of involvement in chemical weapons development. On 20 August the United States conducted military strikes against the al-Shifa pharmaceutical plant in Khartoum, which was associated with Usama Bin Ladin's terrorist network and believed to be involved in the manufacture of chemical weapons, to prevent an anti-US attack. Sudan has denied that the plant was involved in chemical weapons production and vigorously has protested the US bombing.

1999

Sudan in 1999 continued to serve as a central hub for several international terrorist groups, including Usama Bin Ladin's al-Qaida organization. The Sudanese Government also condoned Iran's assistance to terrorist and radical Islamist groups operating in and transiting through Sudan.

Khartoum served as a meeting place, safehaven, and training hub for members of the Lebanese Hizballah, Egyptian Gama'at al-Islamiyya, al-Jihad, the Palestinian Islamic Jihad, HAMAS, and Abu Nidal organization. Sudan's support to these groups included the provision of travel documentation, safe passage, and refuge. Most of the groups maintained offices and other forms of representation in the capital, using Sudan primarily as a secure base for organizing terrorist operations and assisting compatriots elsewhere.

Sudan still had not complied with UN Security Council Resolutions 1044, 1054, and 1070 passed in 1996—which demand that Sudan end all support to terrorists—despite the regime's efforts to distance itself publicly from terrorism. They also require Khartoum to hand over three Egyptian al-Gama'at fugitives linked to the assassination attempt in 1995 against Egyptian President Hosni Mubarak in Ethiopia. Sudanese officials continued to deny that they are harboring the three suspects and that they had a role in the attack.

Sudan also continued to assist several Islamist and non-Islamist rebel groups based in East Africa. Nonetheless, Sudan's relations with its neighbors appeared to improve in 1999. Ethiopia renewed previously terminated air links, while Eritrea considered reestablishing diplomatic ties. Moreover, in early December, Sudan signed a peace accord with Uganda under which both nations agreed to halt all support for any rebel groups operating on each other's soil.

2000

The United States and Sudan in mid-2000 entered into a dialogue to discuss US counterterrorism concerns. The talks, which were ongoing at the end of the year, were constructive and obtained some positive results. By the end of the year Sudan had signed all 12 international conventions for combating terrorism and had taken several other positive counterterrorism steps, including closing down the Popular Arab and Islamic Conference, which served as a forum for terrorists.

Sudan, however, continued to be used as a safehaven by members of various groups, including associates of Usama Bin Ladin's al-Qaida organization, Egyptian al-Gama'at al-Islamiyya, Egyptian Islamic Jihad, the Palestine Islamic Jihad, and HAMAS. Most groups used Sudan primarily as a secure base for assisting compatriots elsewhere.

Khartoum also still had not complied fully with UN Security Council Resolutions 1044, 1054, and 1070, passed in 1996—which demand that Sudan end all support to terrorists. They also require Khartoum to hand over three Egyptian al-Gama'at fugitives linked to the assassination attempt in 1995 against Egyptian President Hosni Mubarak in Ethiopia. Sudanese officials continued to deny that they had a role in the attack.

2001

The counterterrorism dialogue begun in mid-2000 between the US and Sudan continued and intensified during 2001. Sudan condemned the September 11 attacks and pledged its commitment to combating terrorism and fully cooperating with the United States in the campaign against terrorism. The Sudanese Government has stepped up its counterterrorism cooperation with various US agencies, and Sudanese authorities have investigated and apprehended extremists suspected of involvement in terrorist activities. In late September, the United Nations recognized Sudan's positive steps against terrorism by removing UN sanctions.

Sudan, however, remained a designated state sponsor of terrorism. A number of international terrorist groups including al-Qaida, the Egyptian Islamic Jihad, Egyptian al-Gama'at al-Islamiyya, the Palestine Islamic Jihad, and HAMAS continued to use Sudan as a safehaven, primarily for conducting logistics and other support activities. Press speculation about the extent of Sudan's cooperation with the United States probably has led some terrorist elements to depart the country. Unilateral US sanctions remained in force.

2002

Sudan was cooperating with US counterterrorism efforts before 11 September 2001, which included a close relationship with various US Government agencies to investigate and apprehend extremists suspected of involvement in terrorist activities. Sudan is a party to 11 of the 12 international conventions and protocols relating to terrorism. Sudan also has participated in regional efforts to end the civil war that has been ongoing since 1983—a US policy priority that parallels the US objective of having Sudan deny safehaven to terrorists.

While concerns remain regarding Sudanese Government support for certain terrorist groups, such as HAMAS and the Palestine Islamic Jihad, the United States is pleased with Sudan's cooperation and the progress being made in their antiterrorist activities.

2003

Sudan in 2003 deepened its cooperation with the US Government to investigate and apprehend extremists suspected of involvement in terrorist activities. Overall, Sudan's cooperation and information sharing has improved markedly, producing significant progress in combating terrorist activity, but areas of concern remain.

Domestically, Khartoum stepped up efforts to disrupt extremist activities and deter terrorists from operating in Sudan. In May, Sudanese authorities raided a probable terrorist training camp in Kurdufan State, arresting more than a dozen extremists and seizing illegal weapons. The majority of the trainees captured were Saudi citizens and were extradited to Saudi Arabia to face charges in accordance with a bilateral agreement. In June, the Sudanese Government detained several individuals linked to the publication of an alleged "hit list" attributed to the terrorist group al-Takfir wa al-Hijra. The list called for the killing of 11 prominent Sudanese Christian and leftist politicians, jurists, journalists, and others. In September, a Sudanese court convicted a Syrian engineer and two Sudanese nationals of training a group of Saudis, Palestinians, and others to carry out attacks in Iraq, Eritrea, Sudan, and Israel. A court statement said the Syrian was training others to carry out attacks against US forces in Iraq.

There were no international terrorist attacks in Sudan during 2003. Khartoum throughout the year placed a high priority on the protection of US citizens and facilities in Sudan. In November, the authorities stepped up their efforts to protect the US Embassy, which temporarily suspended operations in response to a terrorist threat that was deemed credible. Earlier in the year, Sudanese authorities closed a major Khartoum thoroughfare to enhance the Embassy's security and further upgraded security measures during Operation Iraqi Freedom.

The Sudanese Government also took steps in 2003 to strengthen its legislative and bureaucratic instruments for fighting terrorism by ratifying the International Convention for the Suppression of the Financing of Terrorism. Sudan also ratified the African Union's Convention on the Prevention and Combating of Terrorism and the Convention of the Organization of the Islamic Conference on Combating Terrorism. In June, Sudanese Minister of Justice Ali Mohamed Osman Yassin issued a decree establishing an office for combating terrorism. In 2003, Sudan signed a counterterrorism cooperation agreement with the Algerian Government, which during the 1990s accused Sudan of harboring wanted Algerian terrorists. Sudan also signed a counterterrorism agreement with Yemen and Ethiopia.

In response to ongoing US concern over the presence in Sudan of the Islamic Resistance Movement (HAMAS) and the Palestine Islamic Jihad (PIJ), Foreign Minister Mustafa Osman Ismail in June said the Sudanese Government would limit HAMAS to conducting political activities. Visiting Sudanese peace talks in Kenya in October, Secretary Powell said Sudan had yet to shut down the Khartoum offices of HAMAS and the PIJ.

President Umar al-Bashir in an interview with Al-Arabiyah television maintained that the Sudanese Government could not expel HAMAS because it has a political relationship with the group and stated there was no PIJ office in Sudan. Responding to press reports that its Sudan office had closed, HAMAS officials in Khartoum and Gaza in November said that the office remained open but that the main representative had been replaced.

Sudan also has participated in regional efforts to end its long-running civil war—a US policy priority that complements the US goal of denying terrorists safehaven in Sudan.

Sudan is a party to all 12 of the international conventions and protocols relating to terrorism.

2004

In 2004, despite serious strains in US-Sudanese relations regarding the ongoing violence in Darfur, US-Sudanese counterterrorism cooperation continued to improve. While Sudan's overall cooperation and information sharing improved markedly and produced significant progress in combating terrorist activity, areas of concern remain. In May, the US Government certified to Congress a list of countries not fully cooperating in US antiterrorism efforts. For the first time in many years, this list did not include Sudan.

Sudan increased cooperation with Ugandan authorities to diminish the capabilities of the Lord's Resistance Army (LRA), a Ugandan group which has terrorized civilians in northern Uganda and has claimed that it wants to overthrow the current Ugandan Government. The Ugandan military, with Sudanese Government cooperation, inflicted a series of defeats on the LRA at its hideouts in southern Sudan, forcing its leaders to flee into Uganda and engage in peace talks with the Ugandan Government.

Domestically, the Government of Sudan stepped up efforts to disrupt extremist activities and deter terrorists from operating in Sudan. In March 2004, a new HAMAS representative arrived in Khartoum. According to some press reports, he was received by Sudanese officials in an official capacity. In response to ongoing US concern, the Sudanese Government closed a HAMAS office in Khartoum in September. In August, Sudanese authorities arrested, prosecuted, and convicted Eritreans who had hijacked a Libyan aircraft and forced it to land in Khartoum. In October, the United States designated the Khartoum-based NGO Islamic African Relief Agency as a supporter of terrorism under EO 13224 for its support of Usama bin Ladin and al-Qaida.

The Sudanese Government also took steps in 2004 to strengthen its legislative and bureaucratic instruments for fighting terrorism. In January, Sudan co-hosted a three-day workshop on international cooperation on counterterrorism and the fight against transnational organized crime with the United Nations Office of Drug Control. Neighboring countries from the Horn of Africa and member states of the Inter-Governmental Authority on Development (IGAD) attended the workshop, which culminated in the "Khartoum Declaration on Terrorism and Transnational Organized Crime," in which IGAD member states reaffirmed their commitment to the fight against terrorism. The Khartoum Declaration also focused on the technical assistance needs of the IGAD member states with regard to implementing the 12 international conventions and protocols against terrorism.

Syria

Designation date December 29, 1979

1985

In 1985, Syria continued to use terrorist surrogates to further its Middle Eastern policy. Syrian-sponsored groups— responsible for attacks in 15 countries in the last two years —were involved in 30 terrorist attacks in 1985 against moderate Arab, US, British, Palestinian, Jordanian, and Israeli targets. Support for international terrorist groups has cost Syria little but has raised the cost to participants of any peace initiative that might exclude Damascus; it also has served to keep President Hafez Assad's regional rivals off balance.

The greater use of surrogates by Damascus in 1985 probably reflected Assad's desire to mask Syria's role in terrorist attacks. Damascus has permitted terrorist groups to use Syrian or Syrian-controlled territory for base camps, training facilities, and political headquarters, and it has provided these groups with arms, travel assistance, intelligence, and money. Palestinians who have been largely funded, trained, and armed by Syria include the PFLP-GC, Abu Musa's Fatah rebels, and Saiqa. Damascus also has supported some non-Palestinian terrorists.

The number of incidents carried out by groups operating with Syrian support increased in 1985, compared with 1984; but Syrian personnel were not directly implicated in any specific attacks. The Abu Nidal Group—despite its increased ties to Libya—remained Syria's major terrorist surrogate and was responsible for some two-thirds of the Syrian-sponsored attacks in 1985.

A key Syrian policy goal during 1985—as well as a principal Abu Nidal objective—was to disrupt tentative moves in the peace process exemplified by the February accord between King Hussein of Jordan and PLO leader Arafat. To this end, Abu Nidal conducted a series of attacks on Jordanian interests. On a single day in March, for instance, grenades were thrown at Jordanian airline offices in Rome, Athens, and Nicosia.

1986

Syria continued its role as a major sponsor of international terrorism in 1986, and, for the first time since 1982, Syrian personnel were implicated directly in terrorist operations. Damascus used terrorism as a foreign policy tool and to intimidate political opposition to the regime. In 1986, Syrian-sponsored terrorism was generally directed against pro-Arafat Palestinians, anti-Syrian Lebanese leaders, Syrian opponents of the Assad regime, and Jordanian, Turkish, Iraqi, and Israeli targets. Damascus provided several groups engaged in terrorism with base camps in Syria or in Syrian-controlled portions of Lebanon, training facilities, arms, travel assistance, intelligence, and funds. The best known groups linked to Syria are the Abu Nidal organization (ANO), the popular Front for the Liberation of Palestine (PFLP), Abu Musa's Fatah rebels, the Kurdish Workers' party (PKK), and the Armenian Secret Army for the Liberation of Armenia (ASALA).

Three major incidents in Western Europe in 1986 showed evidence of direct involvement by Syrian personnel:

On 30 March two Syrian-backed Palestinians bombed the German-Arab Friendship Union in West Berlin, injuring seven persons; the Syrian Embassy in East Berlin provided the explosive device. Evidence introduced during the trial of the two suspects also implicated Syrian Air Force Intelligence deputy Haitham Said.

On 17 April, Jordanian Nizar Hindawi had his unwitting, pregnant girlfriend carry a bomb aboard an El Al flight at Heathrow Airport. Security personnel discovered and defused the device. Among the 340 passengers were more than 220 American citizens. The investigation and trial in London implicated top Syrian officials, the Syrian airline, and Syrian Embassy personnel, including the Ambassador.

On 26 June a member of the Palestinian group known as the Fatah rebels and headed by Abu Musa attempted to have a Spaniard unwittingly carry a bomb aboard an El Al flight at Madrid airport. That device partially detonated in a baggage check area, injuring 11 persons. The suspect had a Syrian passport when he was arrested and other documents supplied by Damascus. Abu Musa's Fatah rebels are among Syria's closest Palestinian allies and are headquartered in Damascus.

Publicity about the evidence linking Syria to the March bombing of the German-Arab Friendship Union building in West Berlin and the April attempt on the El Al airliner in London during the trials of the suspects in October and November created political pressure for international action against Damascus. The United Kingdom broke relations with Syria on 24 October, and the United States and West Germany subsequently recalled their ambassadors. The EC agreed to various political and economic sanctions. In response to these moves, Syria curtailed its support to terrorist groups and attempted to curb operations by its surrogates. The Syrian support infrastructure remains largely in place, however, and may be used again.

Syria continued to provide weapons, operational bases, safehaven, and terrorist training facilities to a variety of groups, including Abu Nidal, Abu Musa, Saiqa, the PFLP, the PLFP-General Command (PFLP-GC), the Democratic Front for the Liberation of Palestine (DFLP), the Popular Struggle Front (PSF), the Syrian Social Nationalist Party (SSNP), ASALA, the PKK, and the Jordanian People's Revolutionary Party. Syrian involvement in operations by these groups during the past three years has ranged from complete control, in the case of Saiqa, to permitting the PFLP-GC to operate out of Syrian-occupied territory in Lebanon.

1987

In a radical change from Syria's previous close involvement in supporting international terrorism, we detected only one terrorist operation in 1987—a Kurdish Worker's Party (PKK) cross-border attack—in which, according to several sources, Syria was implicated, compared with six in 1986 and 34 in 1985. As part of an attempt to end Syria's diplomatic and economic isolation, President Assad, in a highly publicized move in June 1987, ousted the Abu Nidal organization from Damascus. Syria also put pressure on Iran and Hizhballah to release US journalist Charles Glass in August and claims to have tried to secure the release of other foreign hostages held in Lebanon. Nevertheless, the Abu Nidal organization and other terrorists maintain camps in Syrian-controlled areas of Lebanon, and, despite Syria's attempts to improve security, known terrorists continue to pass easily through the Syrian-controlled Beirut airport. Furthermore, Palestinians who have promoted terrorist in the past are still present in Damascus.

We believe that Syria was involved in supporting attempts by Palestinian groups to cross the border and carry out armed attacks against Israeli targets in 1987. Most of these attempts failed. Syria maintains that this support is part of its assistance for the Palestinian national liberation movement, but, unlike previous years, Syria limited such support to groups attacking only Israeli targets in the Middle East.

Syria may also bear at least partial responsibility for several cross-border terrorist attacks by the PKK, including one on a Turkish village in March during which eight persons were killed. According to press reports, Syria provides refuge and training to the PKK in its violent anti-Turkish irredentist campaign. The press also reported that Syrian support for the PKK was on the agenda during the Turkish Prime Minister's visit to Damascus in July.

Other Middle Eastern terrorist groups that, we believe, continue to receive some Syrian support include Abu Musa, the Popular Struggle Front, the Popular Front for the Liberation of Palestine, the Armenian Secret Army for the Liberation of Armenia, the Jordanian People's Revolutionary Party, the Syrian Social Nationalist Party, Saiqa, and the Japanese Red Army.

We expect that Syria will continue its sponsorship of terrorism, but that it will act circumspectly because of its keen interest in preventing the imposition of further Western political and economic sanctions, or the reimposition of those already lifted. We believe, therefore, that its involvement will be confined to the Middle East against targets not identified with West European or US interests.

1988

We did not detect direct Syrian involvement in any international terrorist incidents. Indeed, the diplomatic and economic sanctions imposed on Syria by the US and European Community in November 1986 seemed to have had a salutory effect on Syria.

Nevertheless, both Syria and the Syrian-occupied Bekaa Valley in Lebanon remain major sanctuaries for a wide variety of international groups that have engaged in terrorism. These include the ANO, Abu Musa, Hizballah, the PFLP-GC, ASALA, the PKK, the JRA, and the Syrian Social Nationalist Party. These groups continue to pose severe security threats in the region and elsewhere. For example, West German authorities in October arrested a number of members of a Damascus-based group, the PFLP-GC, which has been suspected of carrying out the bombings of US troop trains in West Germany in 1987-88. Although Syria expelled the ANO from Damascus in June 1987, the group maintains a presence in Syrian-occupied areas of the Bekaa Valley.

Syria also continues to support subversion against Turkey —despite signs of improved relations—by providing the PKK with safehaven and training. Syrian military intelligence provides the group with training facilities and probably financial support. Despite a border security agreement Assad reached with Turkish Prime Minister Ozal in July 1987, Syria still seems to be a safehaven for PKK militants operating in southeastern Turkey. Damascus probably believes the PKK gives Syria bargaining leverage on bilateral issues with Ankara.

Syria has made some efforts to improve its record as a state sponsor of terrorism. The Syrian Government has indicated its willingness to work closely with the Western governments to facilitate the release of the remaining hostages in Lebanon. Its ability to influence events at this point is seen as limited to facilitating the movement of the released hostages to Damascus and their respective embassies after they have been released. In April the Syrians denied hijacked Kuwait Airways Flight 422 permission to land in Damascus and were instrumental in a similar refusal by airport authorities at Beirut's airport. The Syrian Government has pointed to these actions as evidence of its tough stand against terrorism.

Despite Syrian statements abhorring terrorism, Syria considers Palestinian terrorist incidents directed against nocombatant targets in Israel and the occupied territories to be part of the legitimate Palestinian struggle for independence. Such terrorist incidents as the attack on a civilian bus in the Negev Desert are reported by the Syrian media in that light. Syria's ruling Ba'the party in February issued a statement in support of North Korea when the United States charged that that government was responsible for the November 1987 destruction of KAL Flight 858.

1989

There is no evidence that Syrian officials were involved in planning or executing terrorist attacks outside Lebanon since 1987, although they continue to provide support and safehaven to a number of groups that engaged in international terrorism.

Both Syria and Syrian-occupied areas of Lebanon (particularly the Bekaa Valley) remain sanctuaries for a wide variety of international groups that have engaged in terrorism, including the PFLP-GC, Hizballah, Saiqa, Abu Musa, ASALA, the PKK, the JRA, and the Syrian Social National Party. In July, JRA leader Fusako Shingenobu gave a press interview from her group's base in the Bekaa Valley. Many of these groups remain active within the region and elsewhere. Syrian support has enabled some of these groups to carry out acts of international terrorism. For example, the senior PFLP-GC official arrested in 1988 in West Germany and charged in 1989 with attempted murder in the bombing of US troop trains in 1987–88 was travelling on an official Syrian passport.

The United States has repeatedly expressed concern—both publicly and privately—about terrorist groups supported by Syria. To date, the US Government is not satisfied with the Syrian Government's responses, and we think the Syrian Government can do more.

We have discussed with the Syrians, on a number of occasions in diplomatic channels, the bombing of Pan Am Flight 103 and public accusations of PFLP-GC's involvement in that attack. We have urged Syria's full cooperation in finding those responsible. Despite Syrian statements abhorring terrorism, Syria considers Palestinian terrorist incidents directed against targets in Israel and the occupied territories to be part of the legitimate Palestinian struggle for independence.

Syria continues to support subversion against some of its neighbors. It assists the PKK insurgency against Turkey by providing the group with safehaven and safe passage in border regions, as well as sanctuary for its camps in the Bekaa Valley. The PKK insurgency escalated this year, and Turkey has publicly charged Syria with supporting armed violence in violation of the 1987 border security agreement. During 1989, Syria also allowed Iran to send arms via Damascus airport to Hizballah and the Islamic Revolutionary Guards in Lebanon.

Syria has made some effort to improve its record as a state sponsor of terrorism. The Syrian Government continued to indicate its willingness to work closely with Western governments to facilitate the release of the remaining hostages in Lebanon. Syrian President Assad has also stated publicly that Syria will punish any individual or group proved to have been involved in acts of terrorism. In early August, the Syrian Government worked closely with the Untied States following the revelation of Colonel Higgins' murder, and contributed to preventing death threats against US hostage Joseph Cicippio from being carried out. Senior Syrian officials have publicly reiterated Syria's call for the release of all hostages. In January 1989, Syria was successful in including a clause in the agreement between warring Amal and Hizballah groups in Lebanon prohibiting the taking of UN personnel hostage.

1990

There is no direct evidence of Syrian Government involvement in terrorist attacks outside Lebanon since 1987, although Syria continues to provide support and safehaven to groups that engage in international terrorism.

Syria has made some progress in moving away from support for some terrorist groups. Syria has also cooperated with Iran and others to obtain the release of Western hostages held by terrorist groups in Lebanon, including the successful release of American hostages Polhill and Reed in the spring of 1990. The government-controlled media has described the Abu Nidal organization as a terrorist organization, but the Syrian Government has failed to take concrete measures against the ANO in Syrian-controlled areas of Lebanon.

At the same time, Syria publicly supports the Palestinian right to armed struggle for their independence. President Assad has publicly defended and supported Palestinian attacks in Israel and the occupied territories. Syria continues to provide political and material support for Palestinian groups who maintain their headquarters in Damascus and who have committed terrorist acts in the past, most notably the PFLP-GC whose propaganda radio station, al Quds, broadcasts from Syrian soil. It also hosts the Abu Musa group, the Popular Struggle Front (PSF), the Popular Front for the Liberation of Palestine (PFLP), and Democratic Front for the Liberation of Palestine (DFLP). The leader of the PFLP had publicly stated that he would carry out attacks against US targets and others opposed to Iraq in the event of a military clash in the Gulf. At year's end, no such attacks had occurred.

The United States continued to express its serious concern to the Syrian Government—both publicly and privately—about terrorist groups supported by Syria. The Syrian Government has taken some positive steps, particularly since the beginning of the Gulf crisis in August 1990, to rein in terrorist groups based in Syria. They did not, however, take steps to close down these groups or expel them from Syria.

Syria has taken no steps to disband or eliminate the presence of other terrorist organizations, such as the Kurdish Worker's Party (PKK), the Armenian Secret Army for the Liberation of Armenia (ASALA), and the Japanese Red Army. A number of these groups have camps in Lebanon's Bekaa Valley, which is under the control of Syrian forces. Syria also tolerates the presence of a faction of the Palestinian Islamic Jihad that took responsibility for the massacre in February of nine Israeli civilians on a tour bus in Egypt. The PIJ statement was broadcast on the PFLP-GC-controlled radio station in southern Syria.

In 1990, and particularly since the Iraqi invasion of Kuwait, Syria has attempted to minimize its public association with terrorist activities and groups in the international arena, apparently in an attempt to improve its standing with the West. Syrian officials have said that Syria is committed to bring to justice and punish those individuals within Syria's evidence of their crimes. They have also repeated that any organization that is involved in terrorist crimes will have to bear the consequences. Following the September visit by Secretary of State James Baker, Syrian Foreign Minister Shara' stated publicly that Syria condemned all forms of terrorism, including hijacking and hostage taking. However, Syria continues to draw a distinction between "legitimate struggle against the occupation troops" and acts of terrorism—a fundamental difference between US and Syrian views.

1991

Syria continued in 1991 to provide support and safehaven to a number of groups that engage in international terrorism. However, it is not known to have sponsored any international terrorist attacks outside Lebanon since 1987. Several radical groups, including the notorious Popular Front for the Liberation of Palestine-General Command (PFLP-GC), maintain training camps or headquarters inside Syrian territory. In addition, areas of Lebanon's Bekaa Valley controlled by Syria provide sanctuary for a wide variety of groups engaged in terrorism, including factions of Hizballah, the PIJ, the ANO, the PKK, the JRA, and Dev Sol.

During Desert Shield/Desert Storm, the Syrian Government seemed to have restrained groups over which it has influence. Nevertheless, there were a number of terrorist incidents in 1991 attributed to groups based in Syria and in Syrian-controlled areas of Lebanon, particularly against Israel. Damascus tolerated the presence of active PKK and Dev Sol training camps in the Bekaa Valley and permitted the PKK to maintain its headquarters in Damascus. Dev Sol killed three Westerners, including two Americans, in terrorist attacks in 1991. The PKK was responsible for dozens of terrorist incidents in Turkey, including for the first time the kidnapping of Americans and other Westerners.

Various press sources reported that noted terrorist Ilich Ramirez (Carlos "the Jackal") lived in Damascus during most of 1991. There are unconfirmed reports that he was expelled from Syria in November, but he may have returned in December.

Syria facilitated the release of nine long-held Western hostages who were held in Lebanon.

1992

There is no evidence that Syrian officials have been directly involved in planning or executing terrorist attacks outside Lebanon since 1986, but Syria continues to provide support and safehaven to a number of groups that engage in international terrorism. Syria has at times restrained the activities of these groups.

Several radical groups maintain training camps or other facilities on Syrian territory. Ahmad Jabril's PFLP-GC, for example, has its headquarters near Damascus. In addition, areas of Lebanon's Bekaa Valley under Syria's control provide sanctuary for a wide variety of groups engaged in terrorism, including the PFLP-GC, Hizballah, the Palestinian Islamic Jihad (PIJ), the Abu Nidal organization (ANO), and the Japanese Red Army (JRA). The notorious international terrorist Carlos continues to enjoy Syrian sanctuary.

Two organizations that have engaged in terrorism in Turkey maintained training camps in the Bekaa Valley throughout much of 1992. Dev Sol killed three Westerners in Turkey, including two Americans, in terrorist attacks in 1991 and was responsible for two rocket attacks against the US Consulate in Istanbul in 1992. The Kurdistan Workers Party (PKK) is responsible for dozens of terrorist incidents in Turkey, including bombings in public places and the kidnapping of foreigners. PKK leader Ahmed Ocalan also uses Syria as his residence and base of operations, with Syrian Government knowledge and support. PKK operations are the subject of ongoing talks between Syria and Turkey, and the Turks report some progress. Press reports indicate that the Lebanese Army closed down—apparently with Syrian approval—the Dev Sol and PKK facilities in September, although ti is not clear whether the terrorist groups have left the Bekaa Valley altogether.

1993

There is no evidence that Syrian officials have been directly involved in planning or executing terrorist attacks since 1986, but Syria continues to provide support to and safehaven for several groups that engage in international terrorism. Syria has taken steps to restrain the international activities of some of these groups. In July, Damascus played an important part in cooling hostilities in southern Lebanon by inducing Hizballah to halt its rocket attacks on northern Israel. Since the signing of the Gaza-Jericho accord in September, Syria has counseled Palestinian rejectionists to refrain from violence outside the region, although it has not acted to stop rejectionist violence in southern Lebanon, or halted Iranian resupply of Hizballah via Syria.

Several radical terrorist groups maintain training camps or

other facilities on Syrian territory. Ahmad Jibril's PFLP-GC, for example, has its headquarters near Damascus. In addition, Damascus grants a wide variety of groups engaged in terrorism—including the PFLP-GC, the ANO, the PIJ, and the JRA—basing privileges or refuge in areas of Lebanon's Bekaa Valley under Syrian control. The notorious international terrorist Carlos appears to continue to enjoy Syrian sanctuary.

The Turkish PKK continues to train in the Bekaa Valley, despite earlier reports that camps had been closed. The PKK is responsible for hundreds of terrorist incidents in Turkey and across Europe, including bombings and kidnappings of foreigners. One American was held hostage by the group. PKK leader Abdullah Ocalan, who is believed to reside in Syria, made threats against Turkey and foreign tourists and residents of Turkey in press conferences in the Bekaa Valley during the year. Syrian safehaven for PKK operations was vigorously protested by Turkey and is the subject of ongoing talks between Syria and Turkey.

1994

There is no evidence that Syrian officials have been directly involved in planning or executing terrorist attacks since 1986. Damascus is publicly committed to the Middle East peace process and has taken some steps to restrain the international activities of these groups. Syria also uses its influence with Hizballah to limit outbreaks of violence on the border between Lebanon and Israel, but permits Iran to resupply Hizballah via Damascus. However, Syria continues to provide safehaven and support for several groups that engage in international terrorism; spokesmen for some of these groups have publicly claimed responsibility for attacks in Israel and the occupied territories. Several radical terrorist groups maintain training camps or other facilities on Syrian territory. Ahmad Jibril's PFLP-GC has its headquarters near Damascus. In addition, Damascus grants a wide variety of groups engaged in terrorism basing privileges or refuge in areas of Lebanon's Bekaa Valley under Syrian control: these include HAMAS, the PFLP-GC, the Palestinian Islamic Jihad (PIJ), and the Japanese Red Army (JRA).

The terrorist group PKK continues to train in the Bekaa Valley, and its leader, Abdullah Ocalan, resides at least part-time in Syria. The PKK in 1994 conducted a violent campaign against Turkish tourist spots frequented by foreigners, as well as other terrorist violence across Europe. Syrian safehaven for PKK operations was vigorously protested by Turkey and is the subject of discussions between Syria and Turkey.

1995

There is no evidence that Syrian officials have been directly involved in planning or executing terrorist attacks since 1986. Damascus continues to negotiate seriously to achieve a peace accord with Israel and has taken some steps to restrain the international activities of these groups. Syria continues to use its influence to moderate Hizballah and Palestinian rejectionist groups when tension and violence in southern Lebanon escalate. It has, however, allowed Iran to resupply Hizballah via Damascus.

At the same time, Syria provides safehaven and support for several groups that engage in international terrorism. Spokesmen for some of these groups, particularly Palestinian rejectionists, continue to claim responsibility for attacks in Israel and the occupied territories/Palestinian autonomous areas. Several radical terrorist groups maintain training camps or other facilities on Syrian territory and in Syrian-controlled areas of Lebanon, such as Ahmad Jibril's Popular Front for the Liberation of Palestine-General Command (PFLP-GC), which has its headquarters near Damascus. Syria grants basing privileges or refuge to a wide variety of groups engaged in terrorism. These include HAMAS, the PFLP-GC, the Palestine Islamic Jihad (PIJ), and the Japanese Red Army (JRA).

The terrorist group Kurdistan Workers' Party (PKK) continues to train in the Al Biqa' (Bekaa Valley), and its leader, Abdullah Ocalan, resides at least part-time in Syria. The PKK in 1995 conducted—with limited success—a violent campaign against Turkish tourist spots frequented by foreigners, as well as other terrorist violence in Europe. Syrian safehaven for PKK operations was vigorously protested by Turkey and is the subject of discussions between Syria and Turkey.

1996

There is no evidence that Syrian officials have been directly involved in planning or executing international terrorist attacks since 1986. Nevertheless, Syria continues to provide safehaven and support for several groups that engage in such attacks. Though Damascus has stated its commitment to the peace process, it has not acted to stop anti-Israeli attacks by Hizballah and Palestinian rejectionist groups in southern Lebanon. Syria also permits the resupply of arms for rejectionist groups operating in Lebanon via Damascus. On the positive side, Syria took action to prevent specific terrorist acts, continued to restrain the international activities of some terrorist groups in Syria, and has been a member of the Israel-Lebanon Monitoring Group—established by the 12 April 1996 Understanding—helping to enforce its provisions. After King Hussein of Jordan raised the issue of individuals infiltrating into Jordan from Syria with plans to attack Jordanian and Israeli targets, Damascus conducted an arrest campaign against the infiltrators' backers.

Several radical terrorist groups maintain training camps or other facilities on Syrian territory. Ahmed Jibril's PFLP-GC and the Palestine Islamic Jihad (PIJ), for example, have their headquarters near Damascus. In addition, Damascus grants basing privileges or refuge to a wide variety of groups engaged in terrorism in areas of Lebanon's Bekaa Valley under Syrian control. These include HAMAS, the PFLP-GC, the PIJ, and the Japanese Red Army (JRA). The Kurdistan Workers' Party (PKK) continues to train in Syria-controlled areas of Lebanon, and its leader, Abdullah Ocalan, resides at least part-time in Syria. In 1996 the PKK executed numerous terrorist attacks across Europe and continued—with limited success—its violent campaign against Turkish tourist spots.

Syria also suffered from several terrorist attacks in 1996, including a string of unresolved bombings in major Syrian cities.

1997

There is no evidence that Syrian officials have been directly involved in planning or executing international terrorist attacks since 1986. Syria, however, continues to provide safehaven and support for several groups that engage in such attacks. Several radical terrorist groups maintain training camps or other facilities on Syrian territory. Ahmad Jibril's PFLP-GC and the PIJ, for example, have their headquarters in Damascus. In addition, Syria grants a wide variety of terrorist groups basing privileges or refuge in areas of Lebanon's Bekaa Valley under Syrian control: these include HAMAS, the PFLP-GC, and the PIJ. The PKK also continues to train in Syrian-controlled areas of Lebanon, and its leader, Abdullah Ocalan, resides at least part-time in Syria.

Although Damascus has stated its commitment to the peace process, it has not acted to stop anti-Israeli attacks by Hizballah and Palestinian rejectionist groups in southern Lebanon. Syria also assists the resupply of Hizballah and Palestinian rejectionist groups operating in Lebanon via Damascus. Nevertheless, the Syrian Government continues to restrain the activities of some of these groups and to participate in a multi-national monitoring group to prevent attacks against civilian targets in southern Lebanon and northern Israel.

1998

There is no evidence that Syrian officials have engaged directly in planning or executing international terrorist attacks since 1986. Syria, nonetheless, continues to provide safehaven and support to several terrorist groups, allowing some to maintain training camps or other facilities on Syrian territory. Ahmad Jibril's Popular Front for the Liberation of Palestine-General Command and the Palestine Islamic Jihad, for example, have their headquarters in Damascus. In addition, Syria grants a wide variety of terrorist groups—including HAMAS, the PFLP-GC, and the PIJ—basing privileges or refuge in areas of Lebanon's Bekaa Valley under Syrian control.

In response to Turkish pressure, Damascus took several important steps against the Kurdistan Workers' Party in October. PKK leader Abdallah Ocalan departed Syria, and Damascus forced many PKK members to relocate to northern Iraq. It is unclear whether Damascus has made a long-term commitment to sever its ties to the PKK.

Although Damascus claims to be committed to the Middle East peace process, it has not acted to stop anti-Israeli attacks by Hizballah and Palestinian rejectionist groups in southern Lebanon. Syria allowed—but did not participate in—a meeting of Palestinian rejectionist groups in Damascus in December to reaffirm their public opposition to the peace process. Syria also assists the resupply of rejectionist groups operating in Lebanon via Damascus. Nonetheless, the Syrian Government continues to restrain the international activities of some groups and to participate in a multinational monitoring group to prevent attacks against civilian targets in southern Lebanon and northern Israel.

1999

Syria continued to provide safehaven and support to several terrorist groups, some of which maintained training camps or other facilities on Syrian territory. Ahmad Jibril's Popular Front Liberation of Palestinian-General Command (PFLP-GC) and the Palestinian Islamic Jihad (PIJ), for example, were headquartered in Damascus. In addition, Syria granted a wide variety of terrorist groups—including HAMAS, the PFLP-GC, and the PIJ—basing privileges or refuge in areas of Lebanon's Bekaa Valley under Syrian control. Damascus generally upheld its agreement with Ankara not to support the Kurdish PKK, however.

Syria permitted the resupply of rejectionist groups operating in Lebanon via Damascus. The Syrian Government, nonetheless, continued to restrain their international activities, instructing leaders of terrorist organizations in Damascus in August to refrain from military activities and limit their actions solely to the political realm. Syria also participated in a multinational monitoring group to prevent attacks against civilian targets in southern Lebanon and northern Israel.

2000

Syria continued to provide safehaven and support to several terrorist groups, some of which maintained training camps or other facilities on Syrian territory. Ahmad Jibril's Popular Front for the Liberation of Palestine-General Command (PFLP-GC), the Palestine Islamic Jihad (PIJ), Abu Musa's Fatah-the-Intifada, and George Habash's Popular Front for the Liberation of Palestine (PFLP) maintained their headquarters in Damascus. The Syrian Government allowed HAMAS to open a new main office in Damascus in March, although the arrangement may be temporary while HAMAS continues to seek permission to reestablish its headquarters in Jordan. In addition, Syria granted a variety of terrorist groups—including HAMAS, the PFLP-GC, and the PIJ—basing privileges or refuge in areas of Lebanon's Bekaa Valley under Syrian control. Damascus generally upheld its agreement with Ankara not to support the Kurdish PKK, however.

Although Syria claimed to be committed to the peace process, it did not act to stop Hizballah and Palestinian rejectionist groups from carrying out anti-Israeli attacks. Damascus also served as the primary transit point for terrorist operatives traveling to Lebanon and for the resupply of weapons to Hizballah. Damascus appeared to maintain its longstanding ban on attacks launched from Syrian territory or against Western targets.

2001

Syria's president, Bashar al-Asad, as well as senior Syrian officials, publicly condemned the September 11 attacks. The Syrian Government also cooperated with the United States and with other foreign governments in investigating al-Qaida and some other terrorist groups and individuals.

The Government of Syria has not been implicated directly in an act of terrorism since 1986, but it continued in 2001 to provide safehaven and logistics support to a number of terrorist groups. Ahmad Jibril's Popular Front for the Liberation of Palestine-General Command (PFLP-GC), the Palestine Islamic Jihad (PIJ), Abu Musa's Fatah-the-Intifadah, George Habash's Popular Front for the Liberation of Palestine, and HAMAS continued to maintain offices in Damascus. Syria provided Hizballah, HAMAS, PFLP-GC, the PIJ, and other terrorist organizations refuge and basing privileges in Lebanon's Bekaa Valley, under Syrian control. Damascus, however, generally upheld its September 2000 antiterrorism agreement with Ankara, honoring its 1998 pledge not to support the Kurdistan Workers' Party (PKK).

Damascus served as the primary transit point for the transfer of Iranian-supplied weapons to Hizballah. Syria continued to adhere to its longstanding policy of preventing any attacks against Israel or Western targets from Syrian territory or attacks against Western interests in Syria.

2002

The Syrian Government has continued to provide political and limited material support to a number of Palestinian groups, including allowing them to maintain headquarters or offices in Damascus. Some of these groups have committed terrorist acts, but the Syrian Government insists that their Damascus offices undertake only political and informational activities. The most notable Palestinian rejectionist groups in Syria are the Popular Front for the Liberation of Palestine (PFLP), the Popular Front for the Liberation of Palestine-General Command (PFLP-GC), the Palestine Islamic Jihad (PIJ), and the Islamic Resistance Movement (HAMAS). Syria also continued to permit Iranian resupply, via Damascus, of Hizballah in Lebanon. Nonetheless, the Syrian Government has not been implicated directly in an act of terrorism since 1986.

At the UN Security Council and in other multilateral fora, Syria has taken a leading role in espousing the view that Palestinian and Lebanese terrorist groups fighting Israel are not terrorists; it also has used its voice in the UN Security Council to encourage international support for Palestinian national aspirations and denounce Israeli actions in the Palestinian territories as "state terrorism."

The Syrian Government has repeatedly assured the United States that it will take every possible measure to protect US citizens and facilities from terrorists in Syria. In times of increased threat, it has increased police protection around the US Embassy. During the past five years, there have been no acts of terrorism against US citizens in Syria. The Government of Syria has cooperated significantly with the United States and other foreign governments against al-Qaida, the Taliban, and other terrorist organizations and individuals. It also has discouraged any signs of public support for al-Qaida, including in the media and at mosques.

In 2002, Syria became a party to the 1988 Protocol for the Suppression of Unlawful Acts of Violence at Airports Serving International Civil Aviation, making it party to five of the 12 international conventions and protocols relating to terrorism.

2003

The Syrian Government in 2003 continued to provide political and material support to Palestinian rejectionist groups. HAMAS, the PIJ, the Popular Front for the Liberation of Palestine-General Command, and the Popular Front for the Liberation of Palestine operate from Syria, although they have lowered their public profiles since May, when Damascus announced that the groups had voluntarily closed their offices. Many of these groups claimed responsibility for anti-Israeli terrorist acts in 2003; the Syrian Government insists that their Damascus offices undertake only political and informational activities. Syria also continued to permit Iran to use Damascus as a transshipment point for resupplying Hizballah in Lebanon.

Syrian officials have publicly condemned international terrorism but continue to make a distinction between terrorism and what they consider to be the legitimate armed resistance of Palestinians in the Occupied Territories and of Lebanese Hizballah. The Syrian Government has not been implicated directly in an act of terrorism since 1986.

During the past five years, there have been no acts of terrorism against US citizens in Syria. Despite tensions between the United States and Syria about the war in Iraq and Syrian support for terrorism, Damascus has repeatedly assured the United States that it will take every possible measure to protect US citizens and facilities. Damascus has cooperated with the United States and other foreign governments against al-Qaida, the Taliban, and other terrorist organizations and individuals; it also has discouraged signs of public support for al-Qaida, including in the media and at mosques.

In 2003, Syria was instrumental in returning a sought-after terrorist planner to US custody. Since the end of the war in Iraq, Syria has made efforts to tighten its borders with Iraq to limit the movement of anti-Coalition foreign fighters into Iraq, a move that has not been completely successful.

Syria is a party to seven of the 12 international conventions and protocols relating to terrorism.

2004

The Syrian Government in 2004 continued to provide political and material support to both Lebanese Hizballah and Palestinian terrorist groups. HAMAS, Palestinian Islamic

Jihad (PIJ), the Popular Front for the Liberation of Palestine (PFLP) and the Popular Front for the Liberation of Palestine-General Command (PFLP-GC), among others, continue to operate from Syria, although they have lowered their public profiles since May 2003, when Damascus announced that the groups had voluntarily closed their offices. Many of these Palestinian groups, in statements originating from both inside and outside of Syria, claimed responsibility for anti-Israeli terrorist attacks in 2004. The Syrian Government insists that these Damascus-based offices undertake only political and informational activities. Syria also continued to permit Iran to use Damascus as a transshipment point for resupplying Lebanese Hizballah in Lebanon.

Syrian officials have publicly condemned international terrorism, but make a distinction between terrorism and what they consider to be the legitimate armed resistance of Palestinians in the occupied territories and of Lebanese Hizballah. The Syrian Government has not been implicated directly in an act of terrorism since 1986, although Israeli officials accused Syria of being indirectly involved in the August 31, 2004, Beersheva bus bombings that left 16 dead.

Damascus has cooperated with the United States and other foreign governments against al-Qaida and other terrorist organizations and individuals; it also has discouraged signs of public support for al-Qaida, including in the media and at mosques.

In September 2004, Syria hosted border security discussions with the Iraqis and took a number of measures to improve the physical security of the border and establish security cooperation mechanisms. Although these and other efforts by the Syrian Government have been partly successful, more must be done in order to prevent the use of Syrian territory by those individuals and groups supporting the insurgency in Iraq.

Terrorist Financing

Overview of Terrorist Financing

Anna Sabasteanski

Terrorist attacks are not expensive. The United Nations Security Council's Analytical Support and Sanctions Monitoring Team reports:

Only the sophisticated attacks of 11 September 2001 required significant funding of over six figures. Other Al-Qaida terrorist operations have been far less expensive. The simultaneous truck bombings of the United States embassies in Kenya and the United Republic of Tanzania in August 1998 are estimated to have cost less than $50,000; the October 2000 attack on the USS Cole in Aden less than $10,000; the Bali bombings in October 2002 less than $50,000; the 2003 bombing of the Marriott Hotel in Jakarta about $30,000; the November 2003 attacks in Istanbul less than $40,000; and the March 2004 attacks in Madrid about $10,000. (U.N. Security Council, *First Report of the Analytical Support and Sanctions Monitoring Team Appointed Pursuant to Resolution 1526 (2004) Concerning Al-Qaida and the Taliban and Associated Individuals and Entities* (New York: United Nations), 12. Report S/2004/679, August 2004.)

It is easier to cut off large flows of money than small ones; because terrorist groups require relatively little capital, stopping terrorist financing is particularly difficult. The Financial Action Task Force (http://www.oecd.org/fatf/TerFinance_en.htm), which describes itself as an international policy-making body "whose purpose is the development and promotion of national and international policies to combat money laundering and terrorist financing," has developed the following special recommendations on terrorist financing:

- Take immediate steps to ratify and implement the relevant United Nations instruments.
- Criminalize the financing of terrorism, terrorist acts and terrorist organizations.
- Freeze and confiscate terrorist assets.
- Report suspicious transactions linked to terrorism.
- Provide the widest possible range of assistance to other countries' law enforcement and regulatory authorities for terrorist financing investigations.
- Impose anti-money laundering requirements on alternative remittance systems.
- Strengthen customer identification measures in international and domestic wire transfers.
- Ensure that entities, in particular non-profit organizations, cannot be misused to finance terrorism.

In the U.S. Department of State, the Office of the Coordinator for Counterterrorism, the Counterterrorism Finance Unit, and the Public Designations Unit work together and with other government agencies to try to stop financing of terrorist attacks. Each of these entities has a special focus: the Office of the Coordinator for Counterterrorism works closely with other governments to cut off the flow of money and other material support to terrorists; the Counterterrorism Finance Unit coordinates the delivery of technical assistance and training to governments around the world that seek to improve their ability to thwart terrorist financing; and the Public Designations Unit takes a leadership role working with the Department of Treasury and the Department of Justice to designate foreign terrorist organizations and their supporters.

The United States' efforts to counter the financing of terrorism are described in the excerpts from U.S. State Department documents in the pages that follow. The excerpts are followed by a description of how the United States is implementing the 2004 US-EU Declaration on Combating Terrorism and then by discussions of narcoterrorism and testimony on money laundering and terrorist financing in the Middle East and South Asia.

Countering Terrorism on the Economic Front

From Appendix F to Patterns of Global Terrorism 2002 and 2003

2002

Since the terrorist attacks of 11 September 2001, the US Government has taken a number of steps to block terrorist funding.

On 23 September 2001, for example, the President signed Executive Order (EO) 13224. In general terms, the Order provides a means to disrupt the financial-support network for terrorists and terrorist organizations. The Order authorizes the US Government to designate and block the assets of foreign individuals and entities that commit, or pose a significant risk of committing, acts of terrorism. In addition, because of the pervasiveness and expansiveness of the financial foundations of foreign terrorists, the Order authorizes the US Government to block the assets of individuals and entities that provide support, financial or other services, or assistance to, or otherwise associate with, designated terrorists and terrorist organizations. The Order also covers their subsidiaries, front organizations, agents, and associates.

The Secretary of State, in consultation with the Attorney General and the Secretary of the Treasury, has continued to designate foreign terrorist organizations (FTOs) pursuant to section 219 of the Immigration and Nationality Act, as amended. Among other consequences of such a designation, it is unlawful for US persons or any persons subject to the jurisdiction of the United States to provide funds or material support to a designated FTO. US financial institutions are also required to retain the funds of designated FTOs.

A few 2002 highlights follow:

- On 27 June, the United States designated Babbar Khalsa International responsible for the killing of 22 Americans when it bombed Air India 182.
- On 12 August, the United States added two groups and an individual (New People's Army/Communist Party of the Philippines and Jose Maria Sison) responsible for the death of Americans in the Philippines. The United States also obtained the cooperation of the European Union on this designation.
- On 23 October, the United States designated Jemaah Islamiya under both the EO and as an FTO. Jemaah Islamiya is responsible for the Bali bombings as well as plots to bomb US interests elsewhere in Southeast Asia. On the same date, 50 countries joined the United States at the United Nations in requesting that the UN Security Council Resolution (UNSCR) 1267 Sanctions Committee add this group to its consolidated list of individuals and entities associated with Usama bin Ladin, al-Qaida, or the Taliban.
- On 30 January 2003, under the authority of both the EO and FTO, the United States designated Lashkar i Jhangvi, which was involved in the killing of Wall Street Journal reporter Daniel Pearl. The UNSCR 1267 Sanctions Committee also included this group on its consolidated list.

Actions taken through January 2003 brought the total number of groups designated under EO 13224 to 250, and the total designated under the FTO authority to 36.

These steps have already achieved results. By year's end, the US Government had blocked more than $36 million in assets of the Taliban, al-Qaida, and other terrorist entities and supporters. Other nations have blocked more than $88 million in assets.

UNSCR 1373, adopted on 28 September, 2001, requires, among other things, all states to prevent and suppress the financing of terrorist acts and to deny safehaven to those who finance, plan, facilitate, or commit terrorist acts.

Since 11 September 2001, the 29-nation Financial Action Task Force (FATF) established a series of key international standards on financial regulation and best practices. It uses a variety of tools to encourage nations worldwide to adopt and implement these standards so as to deny access by terrorists to those financial institutions, formal and informal, which terrorist networks have used in the past to raise, hold, or move funds. FATF has also invited action plans from all countries to achieve full implementation of such financial standards. The G-8 and FATF have both agreed to work with the coordinating committee of the UN to provide technical assistance to countries seeking to implement UNSCR 1373.

2003

The Secretary of State, in consultation with the Attorney General and the Secretary of the Treasury, continues to designate foreign terrorist organizations (FTOs) pursuant to Section 219 of the Immigration and Nationality Act, as amended. FTO designations play a critical role in the US fight against terrorism and are an effective means of curtailing support for terrorist activities and pressuring groups to get out of the terrorism business. Among other consequences of such a designation, it is unlawful for US persons or any persons subject to the jurisdiction of the United States to provide material support or resources to a designated FTO. US financial institutions are also required to freeze the funds of designated FTOs.

EO and FTO designations support US efforts to curb financing of terrorism and encourage other nations to do the same. They stigmatize and isolate designated terrorist entities and individuals internationally. They deter donations or contributions to, and economic transactions with, named entities and individuals. They heighten public awareness and knowledge of terrorist organizations and signal to other governments US concerns about named entities and individuals.

During 2004, the United States and other UN members designated a number of individuals and entities:

- On January 16, the United States Government designated Sulaiman Jassem Sulaiman Abo Ghaith under EO 13224, and his name was added, at the request of the Kuwaiti

Government, to the UNSCR 1267 Sanctions Committee's ("Sanctions Committee") consolidated list of individuals and entities with links to the Taliban, Usama bin Ladin, or al-Qaida the same day.
- The USG designated the branch offices of the Saudi-based charity al-Haramain Islamic Foundation located in Indonesia, Kenya, Tanzania, and Pakistan on January 22 under EO 13224. At the request of the United States and Saudi Arabia, these entities were also listed by the Sanctions Committee on January 26.
- The USG designated Shaykh 'Abd al-Majid al-Zindani under EO 13224 on February 24. At the request of the United States, he was also listed by the Sanctions Committee on February 27.
- On March 15, Italy submitted 10 names to the UN 1267 Sanctions Committee, which listed them on March 17. The United States designated and froze the assets of these 10 individuals domestically on March 18.
- On May 3, the Sanctions Committee listed four names submitted by Germany. The United States designated and froze the assets of these four individuals domestically on April 30.
- On May 6, the USG designated al-Furqan, Taibah International (Bosnia), and al-Haramain & al-Masjed al-Aqsa Charity Foundation under Executive Order 13224. At the request of the United States, two of these al-Qaida-linked Bosnian charities were listed by the Sanctions Committee on May 11 and one on June 28.
- On June 2, the USG designated the al-Haramain Islamic Foundation branch offices in Afghanistan, Albania, Bangladesh, Ethiopia, and the Netherlands under EO 13224. At the request of the United States and Saudi Arabia, these additional al-Haramain branches were listed by the Sanctions Committee on July 6.
- The United States designated Hassan Abdullah Hersi al-Turki under EO 13224 on June 3. At the request of the United States, his name was listed by the Sanctions Committee on July 6.
- On June 10, the United States designated Assad Ahmad Barakat and two businesses under EO 13224.
- On June 23, the Sanctions Committee listed six names proposed by Italy, and the United States designated these six individuals under EO 13224.
- On July 13, the USG designated the Continuity Irish Republican Army (CIRA) as a Foreign Terrorist Organization (FTO) and amended the Executive Order designation of CIRA to include two aliases: Continuity Army Council and Republican Sinn Fein. The USG had designated Continuity Irish Republican Army (CIRA) under EO 13224 on December 31, 2001.
- On September 9, the United States designated al-Haramain Islamic Foundation branch offices in the United States (Ashland, Oregon and Springfield, Missouri) and a branch of the Foundation in the Comoros Islands under EO 13224. In addition, the director of the US branch of the al-Haramain Islamic Foundation, Suliman al-Buthe, was also designated. At the request of the United States, the additional al-Haramain branches and Suliman al-Buthe were listed by the UN 1267 Sanctions Committee on September 28.
- On October 13, the United States designated the Islamic African Relief Agency (IARA), its offices world wide, and five of its senior officials (Dr. Mohammed Ibrahim Sulaiman, Jaffar Ahmad Abdullah Makki, Khalid Ahmad Jumah al-Sudani, Abdul Aziz Abbabakar Muhamad, and Ibrahim Buisir) under EO 13224.
- On October 15, the United States designated Jama'at al-Tawhid wa'al-Jihad (JTJ) both as an FTO and separately under EO 13224. At the request of the United States, the United Kingdom, Jordan, and Iraq, this organization was also listed by the Sanctions Committee on October 18.
- On November 30, the USG amended the previous designation of Jama'at al-Tawhid wa'al-Jihad (JTJ), to include its new alias Tanzim Qa'idat al-Jihad fi Bilad al-Rafidayn and all its possible translations. On December 2, Japan, joined by the United Kingdom and Germany, submitted the new alias Tanzim Qa'idat al-Jihad fi Bilad al-Rafidayn and all its possible translations and transliterations to the Sanctions Committee. The USG fully supported those efforts.
- On December 17, the United States designated Khadafi Abubaker Janjalani, the leader of a major faction of the Abu Sayyaf Group, under EO 13224 and co-sponsored the submission of Janjalani to the UN 1267 Sanctions Committee with the Governments of the Philippines and Australia.
- On December 21, the United States designated Adel Abdul Jalil Batterjee and Saad Rashed Mohammad al-Faqih for providing material support to al-Qaida and Usama bin Ladin under EO 13224 and submitted both names to the UN 1267 Sanctions Committee; they were listed by the Committee on December 23.

As of December 31, 2004, the United States had designated under EO 13224 a total of 397 individuals and entities as terrorists, their financiers, or facilitators. Since September 11, 2001, the global community has frozen over $146 million in terrorist-related assets.

Throughout the year, the United States also continued to work closely with multilateral partners in numerous counterterrorist financing tracks, including the Counterterrorism Committee of the United Nations, the Egmont Group of Financial Intelligence Units, the Financial Action Task Force (FATF), and the Counterterrorism [Action] Group (CTAG), as well as in international financial institutions. In addition, in June the United States agreed with the European Union on a Declaration on Combating Terrorism that ratified a wide-ranging set of counterterrorism initiatives, including a commitment to establish a regular dialogue on terrorism finance between the European Union and the United States. Since it was launched in September 2004, the dialogue has served as the framework for ongoing exchanges to promote information-sharing and cooperation on FATF and on technical assistance issues.

Implementing the U.S.-EU Declaration

U.S. Department of State Fact Sheet, 17 June 2005

The text below outlines the measures taken to implement the U.S.-European Union Declaration on Combating Terrorism, which was issued at the U.S.-EU Summit 26 June 2004.

The June 2004 U.S.-EU Summit Declaration on Combating Terrorism renewed the Transatlantic commitment to cooperate closely and continue to work together to develop measures to maximize capacities to detect, investigate and prosecute terrorists and prevent terrorist attacks, prevent access by terrorists to financial and other economic resources, enhance information sharing and cooperation among law enforcement agencies, and improve the effectiveness of their border information systems. The following statement is keyed to the points of the Declaration [which appear in bold type]:

1. We will work together to deepen the international consensus and enhance international efforts to combat terrorism. The U.S. has worked with EU Member States to improve UN counterterrorism measures through: UN Security Council Resolution 1526 strengthening sanctions against al-Qaida and the Taliban; UNSCR 1535 establishing the Counterterrorism Executive Directorate to improve implementation of UNSCR 1373; UNSCR 1540, requiring states to take steps to prevent proliferation of weapons of mass destruction; UNSCR 1566 reaffirming that there is no justification for terrorist acts; and in the General Assembly's 6th Committee negotiations on the Nuclear Terrorism Convention, which opens for signature in September 2005. The U.S. provided funding to the Terrorism Prevention Branch (TPB) of the UN Office on Drugs and Crime (UNODC) in fiscal year 2004, and will continue contributing to TPB in fiscal 2005. The TPB has helped provide legislative drafting assistance to almost 100 countries, helping over 600 law-makers, law enforcement and other officials learn about the requirements of UNSCR 1373.

The U.S. and the European Commission have worked together in the Counterterrorism Action Group (CTAG) to facilitate universal adherence to the international counterterrorism conventions and protocols by encouraging nearly 100 countries to approve UN instruments and to meet their counterterrorism obligations under UNSCR 1373 and other UN resolutions. The U.S. and EU have also collaborated on related work in the G8 and FATF.

2. We reaffirm our total commitment to prevent access by terrorists to financial and other economic resources. The U.S. regards itself as in full compliance with the FATF Special Recommendations on Terrorist Financing (SRs), including SR IX which took effect in October 2004. SR IX calls on countries to set cross-border currency reporting requirements and confiscate funds transported in violation of such requirements, including funds related to terrorist financing and money laundering. To implement SR IX, U.S. authorities developed a list of 'red flag' indicators to aid border control authorities in detecting cash couriers, and will provide training on using the list through bilateral and multilateral workshops. The U.S. will undergo a FATF mutual evaluation at the end of 2005.

Presidential Executive Order 13224 (E.O. 13224) issued September 23, 2001, and actions taken under its authority, fulfill U.S. obligations to establish financial sanctions against terrorists, terrorist organizations, and terrorist supporters in accordance with UNSCR 1373 and the UNSCRs related to 1267. In the year since the 2004 Declaration, the United States made 20 new designations, bringing the U.S. total to 404 (172 individuals, 232 entities), of which 301 were also designated by the UN 1267 committee.

The U.S. designated four charities in the past year because of their support for terrorist activity. This brings the number of charities designated to forty-one as of June 18, 2005. Additionally, in the past year, the U.S. blocked the assets of a charity operating in the U.S. as a branch of an international charity, convicted the leader of a U.S.-based charity for terrorist financing-related offenses, and investigated other charities suspected of terrorist financing activity. The U.S. Treasury is engaged in an ongoing dialogue with the charitable sector, including charity watchdog groups, to promote use of Treasury guidelines to prevent the threat of terrorist abuse of non-profits.

The U.S. maintains a list of entities registered as Money Services Businesses (MSBs) pursuant to U.S. Bank Secrecy Act (BSA) rules. This list is updated periodically, and contains data on 23,481 registered MSBs as of April 15, 2005.

Over the past year, the U.S. participated in FATF's ongoing discussions on implementation of Special Recommendation VII on wire transfers. The U.S. has required the inclusion of wire transfer originator information on electronic funds transfers in the amount of $3,000 or more since 1996, and U.S. financial institutions are subject by regulation to certain record keeping requirements with respect to these transfers.

The U.S. endeavors to develop comprehensive identifications in connection with designation of terrorist entities to guard against attempts by designated groups to rename themselves or hide behind front organizations. The U.S. Financial Crimes Enforcement Network (FinCEN) has worked this year to further develop contacts with other FIUs to obtain additional information on specific groups and establish investigative links.

The U.S. believes private/public partnership is a key to successful implementation of national regimes to combat terrorist finance and money laundering. In the past year the U.S. and private sector partners have worked with banking associations and authorities in Tanzania and Mexico, and with the Federation of Latin American Banking Associations (FELABAN) on outreach programs to raise awareness of illicit activities and increase local expertise to address them. These activities are part of a global outreach to engage financial institutions throughout the world in "bank-to-bank" programs and training.

U.S. law contains a safe harbor provision that protects financial institutions, their directors, officers, employees, or agents from liability under U.S. federal, state or local laws or regulations, any contract or other legally enforceable agreement (including arbitration agreement), for making a voluntary disclosure of a possible Bank Secrecy Act violation to a government agency or for failure to provide notice of disclosure to the person who is the subject of the disclosure or any person identified in the disclosure.

Once the U.S. has blocked funds belonging to a designated terrorist, the U.S. Treasury's Office of Foreign Assets Control (OFAC) has an ongoing process using blocked transaction reports for enforcement follow up. These reports may be shared within the U.S. Government, including law enforcement agencies. When additional information is needed or criminal violations appear to have occurred, OFAC may refer the case to law enforcement agencies for further investigation.

The EU and U.S. established a regular dialogue on terrorism finance in September 2004. The dialogue is coordinated through an informal U.S.-EU Troika, which met most recently in May 2005, and provides a forum for review of current issues as well as a framework for cooperation involving judicial, investigatory, designation, and technical assistance issues. The Troika will meet during each EU Presidency to assess progress and provide guidance to informal expert-level groupings of judicial, technical assistance and designation professionals. Key activities since December 2004 included two joint workshops on judicial and designation issues and a joint technical assistance mission to Tanzania. The EU welcomed the participation of U.S. representatives in an EU seminar on terrorism finance with the Gulf Cooperation Council.

3. We commit to working together to develop measures to maximize our capacities to detect, investigate, and prosecute terrorists and prevent terrorist attacks. U.S.-EU efforts to enhance cyber security include providing technical assistance for drafting improved substantive and procedural cyber crime laws, promoting the G8 Critical Information Infrastructure Principles and G8 24/7 Computer Crime Network, building support for the Cybercrime Convention of the Council of Europe, and providing law enforcement officials with capacity-building training on investigations involving computer and electronic evidence.

The U.S. has proposed a conference with the EU and its Member States to encourage enactment of legislation to enable courts to receive intelligence information in criminal cases consistent with the need to protect sources and methods as well as the rights of the defendant. The U.S. has also coordinated with the EU on related work in the G8.

U.S. laws require internet service providers to preserve, upon request, specified log files, electronic mail, and other records for a limited period of time, and to disseminate that information upon court order or through statutory processes to investigators and prosecutors for use in criminal and/or terrorist cases.

U.S. efforts are underway to build a witness security program in the Balkans that could also assist in dealing with terrorism.

In March 2005, the U.S. and Europol reviewed the U.S.-Europol agreement and issued a report finding that their provisions, including those relating to personal data, were working well. The volume of information shared has continued to increase. The U.S. is working to gain access to Europol's analytical case files, and is optimistic that the Europol Convention will soon be amended to allow this. We are addressing issues related to the process for making inquiries of particular agencies on a case-by-case basis, and are looking for ways to make this cooperation more valuable from an operational perspective.

The U.S. has begun discussions with Eurojust on a formal arrangement to govern its interaction with U.S. law enforcement authorities. U.S. Counterterrorism Prosecutors met with Eurojust in March 2005, to share information on active terrorism cases of mutual interest. In the meantime, the U.S. will look for ways to work cooperatively with Eurojust on investigations, cases and issues of mutual concern, such as "recruitment," "pensions for families of suicide bombers," and other areas in which this new institution can provide value added to CT efforts.

In the past year, the U.S. has completed negotiations on bilateral instruments to implement the U.S.-EU Agreements on extradition and Mutual Legal Assistance (MLA) with nearly all of the original fifteen EU member states, and has made substantial progress towards completion with the ten new member states as well. The U.S. and the Luxembourg and UK Presidencies are committed to the completion of the protocol process during 2005 so that procedures to bring the U.S.-EU Agreements into force can proceed.

Approximately 60 USG [U.S. government] law enforcement and criminal justice officials participated in a confidence-building seminar hosted by the EU April 6–8, 2005. The seminar familiarized U.S. practitioners and policy-makers with the nature of EU judicial cooperation mechanisms and how this cooperation impacts Member States as well as third party countries such as the U.S. This is a joint program designed to educate officials on both sides of the Atlantic to each other's law enforcement and judicial systems, and a reciprocal follow-up seminar is scheduled for EU officials to learn about U.S. systems in fall 2005. The U.S. is also working to build relationships with EU Chiefs of Police, the new Police College Center (UK), and with OLAF, the EU's anti-corruption arm.

The U.S. has worked with the EU on methods for sharing sensitive information, including how the new EU-wide index of non-EU criminals will facilitate further cooperation, either through Europol or bilaterally. U.S. Counterterrorism International Initiative Prosecutors will develop ways to work cooperatively with EU counterparts on investigations, cases and issues of mutual concern. The U.S. will establish liaison with the new EU border agency in Warsaw.

4. We will seek to further protect the security of international transport and ensure effective systems of border control. The U.S.-EU Policy Dialogue on Border and Transport Security (PDBTS) has met three times including its inaugural session in April 2004. EU Troika and counterparts from the U.S. Departments of Homeland Security, State and Justice have discussed biometrics, border and visa issues, the joint initiative on lost and stolen passports, "flights of concern", cargo security, air marshals, cooperative efforts in research and development, use of advance passenger data, data protection, and other travel and trade security issues. The PDBTS has been a useful forum for information exchange, identifying potential problems and areas for further cooperation, and assigning follow-up tasks. It will continue to meet once per EU presidency and also on an ad hoc basis if circumstances warrant.

The number of ports participating in the Container Security Initiative (CSI) continued to grow over the past year, and now includes 20 EU ports in 9 countries accounting for over 80% of U.S.-bound containers from the EU. Following the April 2004 signing of the U.S.-EU Customs Cooperation Agreement, expert working groups were established to focus on security standards and customs-trade partnerships. The groups developed ten recommendations that were endorsed by the Joint Customs Cooperation Council (JCCC) in November 2004. The U.S. and EU Member States are implementing these recommendations on a bilateral-level, and the U.S. is coordinating with the EU to promote the recommendations internationally by securing adoption of the World Customs Organization (WCO) Framework of Standards to Secure and Facilitate Global Trade. If adopted at the June 2005 WCO Council, the Framework will become the primary international guidance for secure, facilitative supply chains.

The U.S. and the European Commission have worked together to develop a port security information exchange program. This program will include technical visits by EC teams to U.S. ports and U.S. teams to European ports. The first such visit will begin July 5, 2005 with an EC delegation visiting Washington D.C. and New York. The U.S. plans to visit each maritime member of the EU within the next two years. The U.S. and European Commission are also partnering to coordinate port security capacity building efforts in developing regions, especially Africa, in conjunction with efforts of the Lyon/Roma group of the G8.

The U.S.-EU Transport Security Cooperation Group (TSCG) met twice in the past year to discuss transportation security issues including legislative developments, the EU Inspection Program, U.S. Foreign Repair Station Inspections, the addition of lighters to the U.S. Prohibited Items List, and EC Third Country Requirements and Mutual Recognition. Rail security was added to the agenda for the first time. The U.S. and EU established a working group to look at improving air cargo security by better aligning air cargo security requirements on both sides of the Atlantic. The goal of the working group is to achieve mutual recognition of our respective Known Shipper System and Indirect Air Carrier (Regulated Agent) participants. Additionally, the group is evaluating cooperation on inspector training and regulatory inspection methods.

In July 2004, the U.S. and the European Commission concluded an agreement for the legal transfer of EU-origin PNR data to U.S. Customs and Border Protection. As a result of this agreement, U.S. authorities are implementing an extensive set of "Undertakings" agreed by the U.S. and Commission, including issuing Privacy Notices, filtering "sensitive data," and conducting an internal implementation review. The U.S. and EU will hold the first Joint Review to examine implementation of the Agreement and Undertakings in 2005. The U.S. has also been involved in discussions in international fora such as ICAO and the G8 on use of PNR data for passenger security.

The U.S. expects to begin issuing chip-enabled biometric passports to the American public by the end of 2005. The U.S. has played a leading role in the ICAO Technical Advisory Group on Machine Readable Travel Documents, and has been a prime mover in developing guidelines and standards to assure global interoperability of this technology. The U.S. has worked to educate and encourage other governments about the benefits of biometrics.

The U.S. delivered to Interpol, a CD containing the passport numbers of approximately 306,000 U.S. passports reported lost and stolen. The data is electronically updated on a daily basis and, as of May 2005, we have provided over 590,000 records. The next step is to make access to Interpol data more easily available to officials handling passports at ports of entry and consulates. The U.S. has been working on an automated Business to Business (B2B) process as a first step toward this goal, and will test possible solutions in 2005.

The U.S. provided a proposal to the EU to develop a system of reciprocal foreign visa lookout information exchange to ensure interoperability of travel document, visa lookout information sharing and border control databases (SIS and VIS).

5. We will work together to develop further our capabilities to deal with the consequences of a terrorist attack. The U.S. has supported discussions between NATO and the EU on four crisis management items: non-binding guidelines and minimum standards for protection of civilian populations against chemical/biological/radiological/nuclear risks; a framework agreement on the facilitation of vital cross border transport; creation of a common data base of national points of contact; and cross participation as observers in consequence management exercises.

We are proposing to engage the EU in an information exchange on characteristics and common vulnerabilities of critical infrastructure, risk analysis techniques, and risk reduction strategies.

In December 2004, the U.S. adopted the National Response Plan, including an emergency public communications protocol for coordinating Federal planning and resources during incidents of national significance. The U.S. tested the Plan during large-scale homeland security exercises in April, 2005.

The U.S. has supplied bilateral assistance as requested in investigating terrorist incidents.

6. We will work in close cooperation to diminish the underlying conditions that terrorists can seize to recruit and exploit to their advantage. By promoting democracy, development, good governance, justice, increased trade, and freedom, we can help end dictatorship and extremism that bring millions of people to misery and bring danger to our own people. The U.S. provided $500,000 in fiscal year 2004 to the UN Office of Drug Control to promote acceptance and implementation of the UN Convention against Corruption (UNCAC). We have an ongoing dialogue with the EU on terrorist recruitment and related issues in our biannual meetings with the Committee on Terrorism (COTER) Troika.

7. We will target our external relations actions towards priority Third Countries where counter-terrorist capacity or commitment to combating terrorism needs to be enhanced. The U.S. has pushed the G8 Counterterrorism Action Group (CTAG) to support the UN Counterterrorism Committee's efforts to oversee implementation of UNSCR 1373 by developing into an active forum for donors to coordinate counterterrorism cooperation and assistance with third countries.

The United States and the European Commission have worked with the UN CTC and donor states in the G8 Counterterrorism Action Group (CTAG) to coordinate diplomatic, donor cooperation, and donor assistance efforts, in order to: promote adherence to the international counterterrorism conventions; help countries comply with the FATF special recommendations on terrorist financing; coordinate assistance for improved airport security in the Western Balkans; and promoted global implementation of travel security standards developed by the G8 and promulgated to international bodies such as the ICAO and IMO. CTAG has also promoted efforts to improve document security in conformity with ICAO standards. U.S. assistance has included $2.2 million for programs managed by the International Organization for Migration in East Africa and $400,000 for assessments in the Caribbean region.

The UN Global Programme Against Money Laundering (GPML) is currently using U.S. funding to support a full-time mentor for the Eastern and Southern Africa Financial Action Task Force-style regional body, and will provide another mentor to assist Uganda, Eritrea, and Ethiopia in developing national capacities to counter money laundering and terrorist financing. In fiscal year 2004, the U.S. provided $2,900,000 for the GPML and will continue to provide support in 2005.

Narcoterrorism

From Patterns of Global Terrorism 1989

Although primarily motivated for criminal reasons, tactics of terror were increasingly adopted by narcotics traffickers in Colombia during the second half of 1989, in an attempt to pressure the government not to impede their activities. After violent attacks directed at judges, police, and governmental officials, the administration of Virgilio Barco invoked state of siege laws under the presidential decree powers. Just as the government was about to announce these tougher decrees, the narcos escalated their violence on 18 August by assassinating the leading presidential candidate. The government immediately implemented the new decrees providing for the extradition of narcofugitives and the forfeiture of narcoassets. It conducted massive raids against large narcoproperties and extradited to the United States the first of several individuals wanted here on drug-related charges.

In retaliation, the narcos further escalated their actions with terrorist bombings in major cities—over 200 bombs exploding in a three-month period—and selectively assassinated opinion makers, including leading journalists, magistrates, and one congressman. Narcos were responsible for several kidnappings, including the eldest son of one of President Barco's closest advisers.

Five narcoterrorist attacks caused both inadvertent and deliberate harm to US citizens and facilities in Colombia. Two US journalists were among several injured when a bomb went off in a Medellin restaurant in September. It is unclear whether the US reporters, who were with Colombian journalists, were the target of the attack. The restaurant is known, however, to be frequented by foreign journalists. In a suspected narco attack on 17 September, a rocket was fired at the US Embassy in Bogota, probably as a warning to US officials to stay out of the Colombian drug war.

On 6 December, the narcos detonated an 1,100-pound bomb in front of the Bogota headquarters of the security police (equivalent to the FBI) during the morning rush hour, killing 63 people and wounding several hundred. Narcos are suspected of responsibility for the midair explosion of an Avianca airliner in late November in which all 111 persons onboard perished. The narcos may have targeted the aircraft believing that a number of police informers were on board. Despite these atrocities, by yearend the Colombian Government could count some key successes against trafficker-related violence.

Just as narcotraffickers can adopt the tactics of terror, so can terrorists involve themselves in the business of narcotrafficking. In Peru, Sendero Luminoso reportedly acts as an intermediary between the peasant growers in the Upper Huallaga Valley and the drug traffickers, winning higher prices for the growers, taking a cut of the profits, and providing protection. Colombia's M-19 has cooperated with traffickers in the past to gain money and weapons, while another group, the Revolutionary Armed Forces of Colombia (FARC), has well-documented ties to drug trafficking.

In the Middle East, Hizballah allows opium to be grown in areas of the Bekaa Valley, after which it is refined into heroin and shipped out of Lebanon. Estimates of annual Hizballah profits from this activity range up to several tens of millions of dollars.

Money Laundering and Terrorist Financing in the Middle East and South Asia

U.S. Department of State

The testimony that follows was delivered before the Senate Committee on Banking, Housing, and Urban Affairs on 13 July 2005 by E. Anthony Wayne, U.S. Department of State, Assistant Secretary for Economic and Business Affairs

Thank you for the opportunity to discuss with you the contribution of the Department of State to U.S. Government efforts to combat money laundering and the financing of terrorism in the Middle East and South Asia. My colleague, Ambassador Nancy Powell, Acting Assistant Secretary for the Bureau of International Narcotics and Law Enforcement Affairs is also here, and she can answer any questions on money laundering that you may have. Combating money laundering and the financing of terrorism are vital tasks and high priorities for the Department of State. Your interest and attention to this key area is extremely valuable and much appreciated.

The main theme that you will hear throughout my presentation today is that we have made significant strides at bolstering the political will and ability of governments in the Middle East and South Asia to act against the common threat of terrorism and the financing of terrorism but that we need to do more. We face a resilient, adaptable and ruthless foe and must constantly anticipate and help the countries of these key regions prepare for the next move before it happens. This is why your hearing today is especially important.

Mr. Chairman, your letter to the Secretary noted that your committee is particularly interested in the Department of State's perspective on the interagency effort to execute this component of the war on terror. I have been working on the U.S. Government's campaign against terrorist finance since right after September 11, 2001 and agree with the 9/11 Commission's view that the current interagency structure has improved the coordination and effectiveness of our ability to block funds to terrorists. Our efforts to combat terrorist finance serve many objectives and employ many tools. My goal today is to sketch for you the role the Department of State plays in the overall interagency process that aims to strike the right balance of priorities and use the right mix of tools in our efforts to keep funds out of the hands of terrorists in the Middle East and South Asia.

Tracking Terrorist Finances

The two major policy strategies utilized by the Administration in the terror finance area are: freezing the assets of terrorist financiers and using information about terrorist financiers to disrupt the terrorist networks themselves. As terrorists largely operate internationally, a key component of the fight is to build international cooperation. To achieve this goal, our approach has been to draw as appropriate on a wide range of flexible policy tools, including:

1. Bilateral and multilateral diplomacy;
2. Law enforcement and intelligence cooperation;
3. Public designations of terrorists and their supporters for asset-freeze actions;
4. Technical assistance; and
5. Concerted international action through multilateral organizations and groups, notably the Financial Action Task Force on Money Laundering (FATF) and the United Nations.

Effective diplomacy is a key element in winning the political commitment from which cooperation in other areas flows. Our diplomats are the overseas eyes, ears and voices of the U.S. Government in dealing with foreign governments and financial institutions on terrorism finance. Our diplomats meet additional responsibilities in the many countries where we have no resident legal or Department of Treasury attaché. With enhanced cooperation, intelligence and law enforcement officers are able to follow the money trail. With international cooperation on asset-freezes (as well as travel bans and arms embargoes under UN resolutions), we force terrorists into less reliable and more costly means of moving money. Designations also chill support for terrorism—it is one thing to write a check or transfer money to terrorists when no one is looking; it is quite another to realize that such actions can bring unwanted official attention and lead to prosecution. Public identification of charitable groups that funnel some of their donations off to support terrorists has also proven a powerful tool to discourage further donations and to encourage other governments to monitor more effectively the activities of non-governmental organizations.

Since 9/11, we have ramped up our efforts and made substantial progress. We also acknowledge that much remains to be done. Since September 11, 2001, we have:

- Developed a broad and strong international coalition against terrorist financing;
- Ordered the freezing of the U.S. assets of 400 individuals and entities linked to terrorism;
- Submitted and supported the submission by other countries, including Saudi Arabia and several of our other Middle Eastern partners, over 300 al Qaida- or Taliban-linked names to the UN 1267 Sanctions Committee (also known as the al Qaida/Taliban Committee) for sanctions, including asset-freezing, thereby requiring all countries to act against these names;
- Worked closely with concerned agencies to designate three financiers of the Zarqawi network, or al Qaida in

Iraq, since the beginning of 2005 pursuant to E.O.13224. The designations of Bilal Mansur al-Hiyari on April 13, 'Ayyad al-Fadhli on February 15, and Sulayman Kahlid Darwish on January 25 are helping stem the funding of the Iraqi insurgency;
- Designated Jama'at al-Tawhid wa'al-Jihad (JTJ) both as a Foreign Terrorist Organization and separately under E.O. 13224 on October 15, 2004 for having ties to the al-Zarqawi network. At the request of the United States, the United Kingdom, Jordan, and Iraq, this organization was also listed by the UN 1267 Sanctions Committee on October 18. On November 30, the USG amended the previous designation of Jama'at al-Tawhid wa'al-Jihad (JTJ), to include its new alias Tanzim Qa'idat al-Jihad fi Bilad al-Rafidayn and all its possible translations. On December 2, Japan, joined by the United Kingdom and Germany, submitted to the Sanctions Committee the new alias Tanzim Qa'idat al-Jihad fi Bilad al-Rafidayn and all its possible translations and transliterations. The USG fully supported those efforts.
- Designated charities funding HAMAS for asset freeze; and taken action against Saudi terrorism financiers and financial support networks;
- Frozen approximately $147.4 million and seized approximately $65 million in assets located internationally, including in the United States;
- Through our embassies, formally approached world governments internationally to freeze the assets of each and every name we designate;
- Supported changing national laws, regulations and regulatory institutions around the world to better combat terrorist finance and money laundering; including working with the European Union, APEC, the Organization of American States, and the Financial Action Task Force and their Members to strengthen their counterterrorism finance regimes; and
- Made it harder for terrorists and their supporters to use both formal and informal financial systems.

Effective U.S. Government Coordination

Key to our success in tackling terrorism finance in the Middle East and worldwide is effective U.S. interagency coordination. A Policy Coordination Committee (PCC), chaired by the National Security Council, ensures that these activities are well coordinated. This strong interagency teamwork involves the intelligence agencies and the law enforcement community, led by the FBI, as well as State, Treasury, Homeland Security, Justice, and Defense collectively pursuing an understanding of the system of financial backers, facilitators and intermediaries that play a role in this shadowy financial world. As appropriate, PCC members also draw on the expertise of financial regulators. The overarching lesson I draw from my experience since 9/11 is the importance of overall direction of the terrorist finance effort by a body that can direct all of the USG participants in the process to find the right blend of instruments to use on a case-by-case basis. The NSC is ideally placed to play this coordinating role against terrorist finance, as it has traditionally done in other national security areas.

Treasury develops and coordinates financial packages that support public designations of terrorists and terrorism supporters for asset freeze action. Treasury also leads our outreach to FATF and the international financial institutions. Justice leads the investigation and prosecution in a coordinated campaign against terrorist sources of financing. And, State initiates asset-freeze designations of terrorist groups and shepherds the interagency process through which we develop and sustain the international relationships, strategies and activities to win vital international support for and cooperation with our efforts, including through UN action. These efforts include the provision of training and technical assistance in coordination with Justice, Treasury, Homeland Security and the financial regulatory agencies. The U.S. Government's task has been to identify, track and pursue terrorist financing targets and to work with the international community to take measures to thwart the ability of terrorists to raise and channel the funds they need to survive and carry out their heinous acts.

Our diplomatic posts around the world are essential partners in implementing this global strategy. They have each designated an official, generally the Deputy Chief of Mission, as the Terrorism Finance Coordination Officer (TFCO). These officers chair interagency meetings at posts on a regular basis, not only to evaluate the activities of their host governments, but also to develop and propose individual strategies on most effectively getting at specific targets in their regions. The increased level of interagency cooperation we in Washington are seeing on this front is generating new embassy initiatives focused sharply on terrorist finance. The ability of diplomats at our embassies to develop high-level and immediate contacts with host officials in these efforts has built broad responsiveness around the world to various targeting actions.

U.S. Asset Freezing (E.O. 13224) Actions

One of our tools to prevent terrorism is to starve its practitioners of financial resources. A key weapon in the effort to disrupt terrorist financing has been the President's Executive Order (E.O.) 13224, which was signed on September 23, 2001. That order, issued pursuant to the International Emergency Economic Powers Act and other authorities, provided new authorities that have been fundamental to an unprecedented effort to identify and freeze the assets of individuals and entities associated with terrorism. Under that order, the Administration has frozen the assets of 400 individuals and entities on 65 separate occasions. The agencies cooperating in this effort are in daily contact, examining and evaluating new names and targets for possible designation resulting in asset freezing. However, our actions in relation to E.O. 13224 are not taken in isolation. We consider other actions as well, including developing diplomatic initiatives with other governments to conduct audits, exchange information on records, law enforcement and intelligence efforts; and shaping new regulatory initiatives. While using E.O. 13224 to designate entities and organizations as "specially designated global terrorists" is the action that is most publicly visible, it is by no means the only action or the most important in seeking to disrupt the financing of terrorism.

Foreign Terrorist Organizations

A second tool the Secretary of State has in the war on terrorist finance is the designation of Foreign Terrorist Organizations (FTO). The Congress gave the Secretary of State this authority in 1996, and 40 organizations are currently designated as FTOs. In addition to requiring the freezing of FTO assets by U.S. financial institutions that know they control or possess FTO funds, this authority renders FTO members who are aliens inadmissible to the United States, and permits their removal under certain circumstances. Once an organization is designated as an FTO, it becomes a criminal offense to knowingly provide material support or resources to the organization. Offenders are subject to prison terms of up to fifteen years (or, if death results from the offense, life imprisonment). The designation of groups under this authority is one of the steps most widely recognized by the American public in the war on terrorism and terrorist finance.

United Nations Actions

Even before 9/11, the UN Security Council (UNSC) had taken action to address the threat of terrorism. It had adopted resolutions 1267 and 1333, which collectively imposed sanctions against the Taliban, Usama bin Laden and al Qaida. Following 9/11, the UNSC stepped up its counterterrorism efforts by adopting Resolutions 1373 and 1390. Among other things, Resolution 1373 requires all States to prevent and suppress the financing of terrorist acts and to freeze the assets of terrorists and their supporters. It also imposes travel restrictions on these individuals. Resolution 1390 (strengthened by Resolutions 1455 and 1526) expanded sanctions, including asset freezes, travel restrictions and arms embargos, against Usama bin Laden, and members of the Taliban and al Qaida and those associated with them. The UN 1267 Sanctions Committee maintains and updates a list of individuals and entities subject to these sanctions, which all States are obligated to implement.

Through these actions, the UNSC has sent a clear and strong message underscoring the global commitment against terrorists and their supporters and obligating UN Member States to implement asset freezes and other sanctions. This is extremely important, because: (1) most of the assets making their way to terrorists are not under U.S. control; and (2) when the 1267 Sanctions Committee designates individuals or entities associated with al Qaida, all 191 UN Member States are obligated to implement against those persons the applicable sanctions, which include asset freezes. The 1267 Sanctions Committee has listed over 300 persons and over 100 entities that are subject to the sanctions. With respect to South Asia, we recently convinced the UN 1267 Sanctions Committee to list Pakistani supporters of al Qaida for worldwide asset freeze and travel ban.

In January, then-Treasury Assistant Secretary Zarate and I met with the 1267 Committee to detail U.S. implementation of the resolution's asset freeze, travel ban and arms embargo provisions. At this meeting I proposed several ideas aimed at reinforcing current sanctions, including enhancing the sanctions list, promoting international standards and furthering bilateral and multilateral cooperation. The Committee is actively encouraging other members to make similar presentations. In mid-May, the UK addressed the Committee on their implementation efforts, with an emphasis on oversight of charitable organizations. In July, Dutch and Australian officials addressed the Committee on their implementation efforts. We have also begun initial discussions with other Security Council Members on further steps to strengthen the implementation and reach of these UN sanctions in the context of a new resolution that the Council will consider this month; the U.S. is taking the lead in drafting that resolution.

In those cases where the United States Government decides to propose the inclusion of a terrorist and/or the terrorist's financier on the 1267 Committee list, State plays a key role in recommending how best to gain the broadest international support. First, we need to be sure that we can make an effective public case. This is much more difficult and time-consuming than it sounds—but is crucial to the success of this approach. Often, strong cases are based heavily on classified information, and we must weigh competing priorities. If we go to the UN to propose a designation and the unclassified information standing alone is weak, other Member States will not support us. On the other hand, there are often compelling reasons not to declassify further information. The Department and our embassies help the interagency team strike the right balance by providing advice and insights on what it will require for a designation to gain international approval. Once a designation proposal is decided, the Department seeks international support in the form of potential cosponsors and must garner unanimous support from members of the UN Committee. When a new name goes onto the Committee's list, we bring it to the attention of world governments to ensure that they are able to take effective and quick action against the designee.

Improving National Laws, Regulations and Standards

In addition to advances on the UN front, we have witnessed considerable progress on the part of countries around the world to equip themselves with the instruments they need to clamp down on domestic terrorist financing. Since 9/11, about 90 countries in every region of the world, including the Middle East and South Asia, have either adopted new laws or regulations to fight terrorist financing or are in the process of doing so. This is an ongoing process with many countries refining their laws and regulations to assure they have all of the tools needed to combat terrorist financing.

To ensure that these new laws and regulations are effective, the United States has worked very closely with the Financial Action Task Force (FATF), a multinational organization whose 33 members are devoted to combating money laundering. In 2003, FATF revised its 40 Recommendations to combat money laundering to include terrorist financing provisions. These Recommendations along with the complementary Special Recommendations on Terrorist Financing, adopted in 2001, provide a framework for countries to establish a comprehensive regime to fight money laundering and terrorist financing. The two guiding principles the FATF has identified as critical to fighting terrorist finance are cooperation with the UN (respecting, ratifying and implementing anti-terrorist treaties and resolutions) and identifying, defining and criminalizing terrorist financial activity.

The FATF continues to provide critical guidance on the development of comprehensive regimes to attack the full range of financial crimes, including terrorist financing. In October 2004, the FATF added Special Recommendation IX on terrorist financing (to those approved in 2001), addressing the problem of cash couriers. It also continues its efforts to clarify and refine these Special Recommendations by publishing interpretive notes and best practices guidelines to help regulators, enforcers, financial institutions and others better understand and implement the most technical recommendations. The FATF has also worked closely with the IMF and World Bank to develop a common methodology to incorporate FATF's Recommendations into the financial sector reviews that all three entities undertake.

The FATF-Style Regional Bodies (FSRBS) worked throughout the year to adapt the Recommendations to their particular regional requirements. The FATF approved two new FSRBS in 2004, (bringing the total to eight FSRBS): the Eurasian Group (EAG) and the Middle East and North African Financial Action Task Force (MENA FATF). These two new groups filled in critical gaps in global coverage, and the U.S. is an observer in both. The EAG was inaugurated on October 6, 2004 by six member states: Belarus, China, Kazakhstan, Kyrgyz Republic, Russia and Tajikistan. Seven jurisdictions and nine international organizations were admitted as observers. EAG's second plenary was held just this past April in Shanghai, China. The fourteen founding members of MENA FATF are Algeria, Bahrain, Egypt, Jordan, Kuwait, Lebanon, Morocco, Oman, Qatar, Saudi Arabia, Syria, Tunisia, the UAE, and Yemen. The group was inaugurated on November 29, 2004, and held its inaugural plenary meeting the next day. Another plenary session was held in mid-April in Bahrain at which the MENA FATF agreed to begin the first round of mutual evaluations in 2006.

FATF is also working cooperatively with the UN Counterterrorism Committee (CTC) and the G-8-initiated Counterterrorism Action Group (CTAG) to conduct assessments of selected countries' needs for technical assistance to improve local ability to combat terrorist financing. FATF has conducted six of these assessments: Morocco, Egypt, Nigeria, Cambodia, Indonesia, and Tunisia. FATF did not conduct an assessment in Thailand as was requested because a recent IMF survey had been done, or in Cote d'Ivoire due to political instability there. The UAE did not accept a FATF assessment, indicating to the USG that a prior U.S.-conducted assessment was enough. CTAG donors have established a gaps/assistance matrix based on the counterterrorism finance needs identified in FATF's assessment. Although donors made a good start in meeting the needs of these countries, CTAG agreed that sustained assistance over time would be required to close the gaps.

We have seen substantial progress in securing countries' commitment to strengthen their anti-money laundering laws and regulations, which is inextricably linked to combating the financing of terrorism. In large part due to FATF's focus and our technical assistance and diplomatic pressure, governments pass amendments to improve their ability to combat terrorist financing. For instance, the Indonesian Parliament passed important amendments to its anti-money laundering law on September 16, 2003 that will improve the country's ability to take actions against terrorist financing. Similarly, it was FATF's efforts, in conjunction with our diplomacy and technical assistance, which led the Philippines to pass legislation in March 2003 that will significantly increase that country's ability to carry out meaningful anti-terrorist financing measures. FATF advises on whether such regulations and legislation meet international standards and are effective instruments to combat money laundering and terrorist financing.

In addition to providing countries with the guidance they need to develop effective regimes, FATF also places pressure on difficult countries via its Non-Cooperating Countries and Territories (NCCT) program, which provides for listing countries that are non-cooperative with respect to internationally accepted anti-money laundering practices. FATF's NCCT program creates an incentive for States to vigorously address their legal and regulatory environments to allow appropriate action against money laundering. Nigeria and the Philippines, for instance, in December 2002 and February 2003 respectively, took meaningful legislative steps to strengthen their anti-money laundering laws to avoid imposition of FATF measures. Our extensive efforts with the Philippines and Indonesia also played a key role in their removal from the FATF Non-Cooperative Countries and Territories list.

As we, together with others in the international community, began to look into how terrorist groups raised and moved their funds, the fact that much of this took place outside regular banking systems quickly became apparent. As a result, international efforts underway to set standards for tackling terrorist financing are also addressing how to prevent charities and not-for-profit organizations from being abused by those with malicious intentions and also how to help keep cash couriers and alternative remittance systems, such as "hawala," from being used to finance terrorism. The FATF, which has already addressed some of these issues through its Special Recommendations on terrorist financing, is now working to develop guidelines and standards on wire transfers and regulation of charities and non-governmental organizations. Setting new standards and norms in these areas is key to making our international efforts more effective.

Economic Tools

U.S. policies to counter terrorism do include economic policies that encourage development. An important tactic to stamp out terrorism is to improve the economic prosperity and employment opportunities in priority countries. Extremism and terrorism thrive in countries that lack freedom, political expression, and economic and educational opportunity. People, especially youth, who live in poverty and have no voice are more likely to be susceptible to extremist ideologies and to join terrorist organizations. To support the reforms already underway in the region, the United States and its G-8 partners joined at the 2004 Sea Island Summit to launch the Broader Middle East and North Africa (BMENA) Initiative in partnership with governments, businesses, and civil society groups from the region. BMENA includes initiatives to increase democratic participation, promote the development of civil society, fight illiteracy, and support job-creating small businesses. These reforms will allow the people of the Broader Middle East more opportunity to have a say in the direction their societies are taking and help combat extremism.

As a matter of United States policy, development is central to the President's National Security Strategy. Well-conceived and targeted aid is a potential leveraging instrument that can help countries implement sound policies, reducing any attraction that anti-Western terrorist groups may have in failing states.

The Millennium Challenge Account represents a new compact for development—a new way of doing business. It provides assistance to those countries that rule justly, invest in their people and encourage economic freedom. Good governance, which attracts investment and allows the private sector to flourish, not foreign aid, is the key to economic development. U.S. trade and investment flows to the developing world dwarf our foreign aid. Unutilized capital in developing countries, owing to weak policies and poor property rights, is estimated to be as high as $9 trillion.

Debt relief for the poorest countries is another element of our development strategy. Our long-standing support for the Heavily Indebted Poor Countries (HIPC) initiative promotes debt sustainability and enables the poorest countries to devote additional resources to reducing poverty and promoting economic growth.

Our aggressive multilateral and bilateral trade agenda to open agricultural and non-agricultural markets and liberalize financial services, transportation, telecommunications and government procurement all support development. Free trade and open markets can be drivers for greater prosperity and job opportunities, especially for the young people in these key regions who are thirsting for a stake in the future. Under the President's vision for a Middle East Free Trade Area (MEFTA) by 2013, the U.S. has concluded a bilateral free trade agreement with Jordan. Agreements with Morocco and Bahrain should go into effect in the near future; and Free Trade Agreement (FTA) talks with Oman and the United Arab Emirates have just been launched. We also have Trade and Investment Framework Agreements (TIFA), which typically serve as pre-cursors to an FTA, in place with most Arab countries. We are also aiming to conclude a TIFA with Afghanistan. The U.S. is working with countries in both the Middle East and South Asia, such as Saudi Arabia and Afghanistan, to assist them in their efforts to join the World Trade Organization and become more fully integrated into the global trading system.

Bilateral Investment Treaties (BITs) are another tool to promote the adoption of market-oriented economic policies that can promote growth and new employment opportunities. Historically, investors in many countries in the Middle East and South Asia have too often faced discrimination or otherwise been treated in a biased and nontransparent manner by host governments. As a result, foreign investors have turned elsewhere. Our bilateral investment treaties address this problem by assuring that certain core investment protections are available to investors, and by providing access to an independent, non-political mechanism for investors to enforce those protections. We have held two rounds of BIT negotiations with Pakistan since February, with a further round likely in August. Saudi Arabia has expressed interest in exploratory discussions on possible BIT negotiations, and we have also identified Algeria as a possible BIT candidate.

Capacity Building

On the technical assistance front, the interagency Terrorist Finance Working Group (TFWG), chaired by the State Department, has provided over $11.5 million in Foreign Assistance funding to provide technical assistance and training to develop and reinforce counterterrorist financing/anti-money laundering (CTF/AML) regimes of frontline states, many of which are in the Middle East and South Asia regions. To date, over twenty U.S. Government offices and agencies participating in the TFWG, which include the Justice, Treasury and Homeland Security Departments and financial regulatory agencies, have provided assistance to eighteen countries on five different continents including Saudi Arabia, the UAE, Kuwait, Qatar, Jordan and Egypt in the Middle East and Bangladesh and Pakistan in South Asia regions. These comprehensive training and technical assistance programs include legislative drafting, financial regulatory training, Financial Intelligence Unit (FIU) development, law enforcement training, and prosecutorial/judicial development.

We have provided several countries in the Gulf and South Asia with different types of training related to sound counterterrorist finance practices, including the detection of trade-based money laundering (moving money for criminal purposes by manipulation of trade documents), customs training, anti-terrorist finance techniques and case studies for bank examiners, and general financial investigative skills for law enforcement/counterterrorist officials. Our international partners have welcomed this type of training, and we plan to provide it to other vulnerable jurisdictions in other regions.

Burden sharing with our key coalition partners is an emerging success story. For instance, the Governments of Australia, New Zealand and the United Kingdom, as well as the EU, and the Asian Development Bank, have significant technical assistance initiatives underway in countries such as the Philippines, Indonesia, Pakistan, Malaysia, and Egypt. We have also funded the UN Global Program Against Money Laundering to place a yearlong mentor in the Philippines to assist with further development of its FIU. Despite its importance in the overall counterterrorism effort, and all the discussions about it, relatively few dollars are devoted to training and technical assistance for AML and CTF. Congress could strengthen this tool by fully supporting the Administration's funding request for this crucial task.

Areas of Focused Cooperation

The Administration is actively involved in combating terrorist financing through partnerships we have established throughout the Middle East and South Asia. These activities rely on the full range of tools in our toolkit.

Saudi Arabia

We are working on this approach with many countries, but I want to highlight for you the range of activities in Saudi Arabia, where we have used each of these elements in a process steered by the NSC-led Terrorist Finance PCC. We have instituted a regular high-level diplomatic effort to urge enhanced emphasis by the Saudis on combating terrorist finance. Homeland Security Advisor Frances Townsend has traveled regularly to Saudi Arabia to engage with the highest-level Saudi authorities on this issue. The U.S. Ambassador to Saudi Arabia and his staff also reinforce these messages in their daily dialogue with a wide range of Saudi officials.

We have jointly designated, with the Saudis, over a dozen Saudi-related entities and multiple individuals under UNSCR 1267.

As part of a State-led interagency assistance program, Federal banking regulators have provided specialized anti-money laundering and counterterrorist financing training to their Saudi counterparts.

Demonstrating its commitment to address systemic factors contributing to the flow of funds to terrorists, Saudi Arabia is working to establish a Charities Commission to regulate all charitable donations leaving the Kingdom. Saudi Arabia has made important changes to its banking and charity systems to help strangle the funds that support al Qaida. Saudi Arabia's new banking regulations place strict controls on accounts held by charities. Saudi Arabia has also ordered an end to the collection of donations at mosques and instructed retail establishments to remove charity collection boxes from their premises. These steps have been extremely challenging for the Saudi government, but they have been ordered because it understands that terrorists are more likely to use funds collected anonymously and without an audit trail than those that move through regular banking channels. We believe that Saudi actions have, in fact, significantly reduced the flow of cash from Saudi Arabia to al Qaida and other terrorist groups in the region.

The Saudi Government has continued to publicize counterterrorism efforts and to speak out denouncing terrorism. The declaration from the February 2005 International Counterterrorism Conference, hosted by the Saudi Government, in Riyadh stated that there can be no justification for terrorism and called for greater religious tolerance. Homeland Security Advisor Townsend led a large U.S. interagency delegation to the conference and spoke at the plenary session, emphasizing the need to block the financing of terrorism. I participated in the working group on terrorist finance. The Saudi Government plans to establish an international counterterrorism center in Riyadh which can further international efforts at curbing all aspects of terrorism, including terrorist finance. We plan to continue to work with the Saudis on ways to make this center most effective. On the issue of greater religious tolerance, the Saudi Government, on its own initiative, recently completed a comprehensive revision of textbooks to "remove objectionable language," and these new textbooks are now being used in Saudi schools. In 2005, the Saudis intensified their wide-ranging anti-terror public relations campaign. The campaign condemns terrorism and encourages moderation through statements by politicians and religious leaders. A mix of television programs, advertisements, and billboards depict the graphic results of terrorism to send a strong anti-terror message to the Saudi public. For the last four years, the State Department has sponsored special International Visitors programs for Saudi religious educators, to expose them to the nature of U.S. religious diversity and the role of religion in U.S. society. Two groups of ten had visited so far in fiscal year 2005, with another group of ten scheduled in the fall.

Saudi Arabia has been working with us for a year and a half in the context of the Joint Task Force on Terrorist Financing, led on the U.S. side by the FBI. As part of the State-led interagency counterterrorist financing assistance program, experts from the FBI and IRS have completed a training module designed to strengthen the financial investigative capabilities of the Saudi security forces, with more advanced courses to follow. The Department of Homeland Security's Bureau of Immigration and Customs Enforcement (ICE) will provide a week of cash courier-related training to Saudi customs officials starting July 16. That being said, this remains a work in progress. We have reason to believe that the new task force on terrorist financing will be effective, but we need to see results.

We believe the Saudi Arabian Government is implementing its new charity regulations, but there too, we continue to stress in our discussions with the Saudis the need for full implementation, including a fully functioning Charities Commission. Additionally, appropriate regulatory oversight of organizations headquartered in the Kingdom such as the World Muslim League, the International Islamic Relief Organization (IIRO) and the World Assembly of Muslim Youth (WAMY) is absolutely necessary. The Saudi government is working to train personnel to staff its nascent Financial Intelligence Unit (FIU) and we will encourage the Saudi FIU to join the Egmont Group in 2006. On June 19, a Ministry of Interior spokesman announced that a "special department for tracing illegal financial activities in the Kingdom" (the FIU) will be completed soon. The September 2003 FATF mutual assessment of Saudi Arabia found that the Kingdom has taken essential steps—closer bank supervision, tighter banking laws, enhanced oversight—critical to curbing terrorist financing and money laundering. On June 14, for example, the Council of Ministers adopted a recommendation that private donations to beneficiaries outside the Kingdom be channeled only through the National Commission for Relief and Charitable Work Abroad. There is more to do, and we will continue to press ahead with our efforts with the Saudi Arabian Government and with other governments in the region.

Beyond these activities, the Saudis are also continuing to fight terrorism on the ground. On June 28, Saudi Arabia issued a new list of 36 "most wanted" terrorists in the Kingdom. At least one has been killed and one has surrendered since the list was released.

Other Gulf States

The governments of the Arabian Peninsula are themselves on the front lines in the war on terrorism, and have become essential partners of the United States in countering the threat of terrorism in the region. We have developed highly cooperative and mutually beneficial relations with the Gulf States in the areas of law enforcement, intelligence sharing, and terrorist finance. However, there is still more that can be done. We will continue high-level engagement and will focus on sustaining the capacity of these governments to effectively address the terrorist threat.

Our efforts to combat the financing of terrorism are working, and now al Qaida and other terrorist groups are increasingly resorting to cash couriers to move their funds across borders to fund their terrorist activities. The USG is working with the governments in the Gulf to combat the illicit use of cash couriers, which is especially pertinent to these cash-based economies. We have recently provided training to the Saudi Customs Service to identify cash couriers. We look forward to supporting these governments as they enhance their cash courier regulations. Additionally, FATF issued Special Recommendation IX in October 2004, under which member countries should ensure that they have measures in place to detect, and appropriately sanction, those moving currency if suspected of money laundering or terrorist financing.

The Gulf States have made significant progress to improve their ability to combat terrorist financing and have worked closely with us in this area. These nations have diligently implemented UNSC sanctions.

Kuwait formed a ministerial committee to develop strategies to combat terrorism and extremism, and forbade Kuwaiti Ministries and other institutions from extending official invitations to twenty-six Saudi clerics who reportedly signed a statement in support of Jihad in Iraq. There are regular consultations between U.S. and Kuwaiti officials on ways to strengthen measures to combat money laundering and terrorist finance. During a recent visit to Kuwait by Treasury Deputy Assistant Secretary Daniel Glaser, the Kuwaitis discussed some of the additional measures they are taking to combat terrorist financing. The GOK has formed a working group to draft a new piece of legislation that would specifically criminalize terrorist finance and strengthen Kuwait's anti-money laundering/terrorist finance (AML/TF) regime. The legislation is intended to address weaknesses in Kuwait's current anti-terrorist finance legal regime (absence of a law specifically criminalizing terrorist finance; prohibition of direct information-sharing by the Financial Intelligence Unit (FIU) without prior case-by-case approval of the Public Prosecutor's Office; lack of restrictions on cash couriers). The USG has offered, and the GOK has accepted, USDOJ Office of Overseas Prosecutorial Development, Assistance, and Training (OPDAT) assistance in reviewing Kuwait's legislation. GOK officials have also indicated that they may ask the IMF and FinCEN for assistance. The Embassy is also working with the Department of Justice, the Federal Reserve and other agencies on a counterterrorism training package for the Government of Kuwait.

In November 2004, Bahrain hosted the inaugural meeting of the Middle East and North Africa (MENA) FATF, which will promote the implementation of the FATF Recommendations to combat money laundering and terrorist finance. In April 2005, Bahrain hosted a two-day plenary session of the MENAFATF followed by a two-day anti-money laundering/counterterrorist finance workshop co-hosted by the World Bank and IMF.

The UAE aggressively enforces anti-money laundering regulations and in 2004 enacted legislation criminalizing terror finance. In April, the UAE hosted the third international conference where ways to prevent use of the hawala (informal money transfer) system by terrorist financiers was discussed. We sent U.S. delegates and a speaker to this conference, and over 400 participants from 74 different countries attended. Conference attendees included representatives from financial institutions, Central Banks, law enforcement agencies, FATF, the IMF, and the World Bank, as well as other international officials involved in regulating money transfer systems. The government registers hawala dealers.

Oman has implemented a tight anti-money laundering regime that monitors unusual transactions. Financial institutions plan to verify customer identities using sophisticated biometrics technology.

Qatar has enacted laws to combat terrorist financing and to monitor all domestic and international charity activities.

Yemen routinely cooperates with U.S. law enforcement and took action against al Qaida by arresting several individuals suspected of al Qaida ties and prosecuting the perpetrators of several terrorist acts, including the 2002 attack on the USS Cole.

We have conducted Anti-Terrorism Assistance (ATA) programs with all of the Arabian Peninsula states.

Now that MENAFATF is set up, it needs to become an effective, practicing institution. Members of MENAFATF should all set up operational FIUs, conduct mutual assessments, establish best practices and meet overall FATF standards.

Jordan

The government of Jordan has cooperated with us on a wide range of terrorist finance issues, including designations at the UN. We urge passage of the new anti-money laundering legislation, which will strengthen significantly Jordan's legal basis for tackling the financing of terrorism and its international cooperation on AML and counterterrorism financing cases.

Syria

In May 2004, Treasury designated the Commercial Bank of Syria (CBS) as a "primary money laundering concern" pursuant to Section 311 of the USA PATRIOT Act and proposed to implement a special measure against the bank. Since then, we have worked with the Syrian government and the CBS to strengthen their anti-money laundering controls and their cooperation with the U.S. on money laundering and terrorist financing issues. We have not implemented the special measure, which would require U.S. financial institutions to sever their correspondent relationships with CBS, pending an assessment of Syrian progress toward resolving U.S. concerns. In addition, the Syrians joined us on the submission of Sulayman Khalid Darwish to the UN 1267 Committee.

However, the Syrian government needs to do more to address U.S. concerns about Syria's continued efforts to influence Lebanese political developments, its pursuit of WMD, and the use of Syrian territory by those supporting terrorism and the insurgency in Iraq. On June 9, the Treasury Department designated a Syrian-based entity and its two managers pursuant to EO 13315, which is aimed at blocking the property of the former Iraqi regime or those who acted for on its behalf. On June 29, the Treasury Department designated another Syrian entity pursuant to its newly-issued Executive Order on WMD Proliferation Financing. On June 30, the Treasury Department designated two Syrians for an assets freeze pursuant to the provision in EO 13338 that is aimed at financially isolating those individuals and entities contributing to the Syrian government's military and security presence in Lebanon.

South Asia

South Asia, and especially Pakistan, is a priority region for counterterrorist financing, due to the presence of al Qaida and other terrorist groups, porous borders, and cash-based economies that often operate through informal mechanisms, such as hawala. All countries in the region need to improve their terrorist financing regimes to meet international standards, including the establishment of functioning Financial Intelligence Units. Both political will and technical assistance are needed to make this region a more effective partner.

Turning to Pakistan specifically, we welcome the concrete actions it has taken to implement its obligations under UN Security Council Resolutions, including the freezing of over $10 million of al Qaida assets. Pakistan has also apprehended terrorists, including Abu Farraj Al Libbi, al Qaida's operational leader. We are encouraged by Pakistan's concern about the infiltration of terrorist groups into charitable organizations, and would welcome the opportunity to provide technical assistance to help Pakistan meet international standards on preventing abuse of its non-profit sector.

We have provided Pakistan assistance on drafting an anti-money laundering/counterterrorist financing (AML/CTF) law that meets international standards, but this legislation is still awaiting parliamentary consideration. As soon as a law that meets international standards is enacted, we will be able to accelerate training efforts, including assistance for the establishment of a Financial Intelligence Unit (FIU). In the absence of an anti-money laundering and counterterrorism financing law, the State Bank of Pakistan has introduced FATF-compliant regulations in know-your-customer policy, record retention, due diligence of correspondent banks, and reporting suspicious transactions. Also in compliance with FATF recommendations, the Securities and Exchange Commission of Pakistan has applied know-your-customer regulations to stock exchanges, trusts, and other non-bank financial institutions. All settlements exceeding Rs 50,000 ($840) must be performed by check or bank draft, as opposed to cash.

Afghanistan recently passed anti-money laundering and counterterrorist financing legislation, and many efforts are being made to strengthen police and customs forces. However, there remain few resources and little expertise to combat financial crimes, or to produce meaningful financial intelligence, and they have requested the U.S. for assistance in building capacity to do so. Arrangements are underway to send an assessment team. The most fundamental obstacles continue to be legal, cultural and historical factors that many times conflict with more Western-style proposed reforms to the financial sector generally.

In India, the Prevention of Money Laundering Act (PMLA) became effective on July 1. The Act provides the statutory basis for the Financial Intelligence Unit (FIU) to perform its functions. It criminalizes money laundering and requires banks and other financial institutions and intermediaries to report individual transactions valued over $23,000 to the FIU. Two accounts belonging to terrorist individuals/entities have been identified, but the Government of India (GOI) has not frozen any assets to date. It is aware of the UN 1267 Committee list, however, and has conducted investigations. India has indicated that it wants to join FATF. However, at a recent FATF Plenary meeting in Paris, concerns were raised regarding India's ability to provide effective international cooperation in a timely manner, and to extend mutual legal assistance. The GOI maintains tight controls over charities, which are required to register with the government. The November 2004 amendment of the 1967 Unlawful Activities (Prevention) Act criminalized terrorist financing.

Speaking generally, South Asian countries lack sophisticated tools to combat the financing of terrorism. Not one country in the region is a member of the Egmont Group of countries with operational FIUs, which is unusual given the large numbers and regional spread of Egmont's membership. Anti-money laundering programs also tend to be absent or not up to international standards. Nonetheless, there is a degree of interest in all countries of the region, and we have seen some progress.

Efforts are underway to develop and implement international AML/CTF standards bilaterally and regionally through such organizations such as the Asia Pacific Group on Money Laundering (APG). Bilaterally the U.S. has conducted training and technical assistance assessments for most countries in South Asia. We have provided AML/CTF legal drafting assistance, financial regulatory training, and FIU development support. In Bangladesh we support a Resident Legal Advisor to assist authorities in drafting and implementing AML/CTF laws as well as providing specialized training for prosecutors and other law enforcement officials.

Designations and Asset Freezes: Only Part of the Picture

The international designations and asset freeze process has helped us develop and deepen a set of invaluable long-term relationships with our interagency and international partners. Through this collaborative international effort, we have built cooperation and the political will necessary to fight terrorism, both through designations and asset freezes, as well as through operational law enforcement actions. As described above, U.S. Government agencies meet regularly to identify, track and pursue terrorist financing targets and to determine, on a case-by-case basis, which type of action is most appropriate. Designation for asset freezing should not come at the expense of taking appropriate law enforcement action. On the contrary, the two approaches frequently complement each other. There are cases where operational law enforcement action can be initiated quickly to trace, prosecute and shut down terrorists. In other cases, for instance where long-term investigations are under way, the better option may be to designate for asset freezing in order to stop the flow of money that might be used to carry out terrorist activity until law enforcement actions can be taken.

We have used multilateral asset freezes, together with technical assistance and the FATF multilateral standard setting process, as valuable devices to isolate terrorist financiers, drive them out of the formal financial system, and unite the international community through collective action. In these cases, designations are preventative, making it harder for terrorists and their supporters to operate. We continue to work together with our international partners to strengthen the multilateral designation process. By carefully working with our allies, we seek to build international consensus, thereby preventing unwanted delays in the process. We urge all foreign governments to fulfill their UN obligations to freeze assets without delay. In cases where an individual or entity assumes a new name, we initiate action to designate the alias, thwarting their efforts to simply continue "business as usual" under a new name. These actions prevent open fundraising, diminish support to illicit charities, and act as an element of diplomacy to demonstrate international resolve.

In the fight against global terrorism, the Administration must continue to use vigorously all of the tools at its disposal —including designations/asset freezing, law enforcement/intelligence cooperation, and the establishment and enforcement of international norms and standards. Given that the money that gets into the hands of terrorists flows around the world, the only way we will be successful in drying up their financial resources is through continued, active U.S. engagement with allies, friends, and other countries around the globe. We must continue to broaden and deepen our efforts worldwide. These efforts have paid off—and they will continue to do so.

The Department of State plays a pivotal role in, and adds great value to, this broadening and deepening of international cooperation. Officers in our embassies and in Washington bring their experience to bear in judging the best approach to a specific terrorist or group in a specific country or region. Their political, economic and cultural expertise allows them to weigh the pros and cons of various approaches given the other political and economic dynamics of the countries whose help we are enlisting in the war against terrorism. There are no "off-the-shelf" answers in this field. Each case is different, and the State Department is uniquely placed to help weigh options and craft tailor-made strategies to produce effective action.

CRS Report for Congress

Terrorist Financing: The 9/11 Commission Recommendation

Martin A. Weiss
Analyst in International Trade and Finance,
Foreign Affairs, Defense, and Trade

Summary

Although efforts to seize terrorist funds have met with some success, in July 2004, the 9/11 Commission asserted that the likelihood of being able to continue freezing funds may diminish as terrorists seek increasingly more informal methods of earning and moving money. The financial support of terrorism involves both earning funds, through legal and illegal means, and the illicit movement of money to terrorist groups. The Commission recommended that the U.S. government shift the focus of its efforts to counter terrorist financing from a strategy based on seizing terrorist assets to a strategy based on exploiting intelligence gathered from financial investigations. This report will be updated as events require.

Introduction

Since the September 11, 2001 attacks, there has been increasing interest in terrorist financing. Following the attacks, the administration stated its goal of "starving the terrorists of funding and shutting down the institutions that support or facilitate terrorism."[1] In the months immediately following the attacks, a significant amount of funds were frozen internationally. After this initial sweep, the freezing of terrorist assets slowed down considerably. As of November 2002, estimates indicated that of the roughly $121 million in terrorist assets frozen worldwide, more than 80% were blocked in the first three months following the attacks.[2] Over the next year and a half, an additional $80 million has been seized, bringing the current total frozen to roughly $200 million.[3]

While separating terrorist organizations from their assets will continue to be a major component of the campaign against terrorism, many have questioned the feasibility of this goal. The slowdown in the amounts frozen reflects numerous changes in how Al Qaeda and other terrorist groups finance their activities. Terrorist organizations are increasingly relying on informal methods of money transfer, and regional cells have begun independently generating funds through criminal activity.[4]

In response to these changes, the National Commission on Terrorist Attacks Upon the United States (also known as the 9/11 Commission), an independent, bipartisan commission created by congressional legislation and President Bush has recommended that the U.S. government shift the focus of its efforts to counter terrorist financing from a strategy based on seizing terrorist assets to a strategy based on exploiting intelligence gathered from financial investigations. According to the Commission, the United States should "expect less from trying to dry up terrorist money and more from following the money for intelligence, as a tool to hunt terrorists, understand their networks, and disrupt their operations."[5] According to Commission Chairman Thomas Kean, "Right now we have been spending a lot of energy in the government trying to dry up sources of funding. When it only costs $400,000 to $500,000 to pull off an operation like 9/11, we'll never dry up money. But by using the money trail, we may be able to catch some of these things [terrorist plots] and break them up." Kean further asserted, "Obviously if you can dry up money, you dry it up, but we believe one thing we didn't do effectively is follow the money. That's what we have to do."[6]

While the goals of freezing terrorist funds and tracking them for intelligence[7] are not mutually exclusive, they tend to emphasize different strategies and approaches. For example,

---

1 Statement of Secretary Paul O'Neill on Signing of Executive Order Authorizing the Treasury Department to Block Funds of Terrorists and their Associates, September 24, 2001.

2 CRS Report RL31658, *Terrorist Financing: The U.S. and International Response*; p. 1.

3 Testimony of Samuel W. Bodman, Deputy Secretary U.S. Department of the Treasury Before the Senate Committee on Banking, Housing and Urban Affairs, April 29, 2004.

4 See General Accounting Office Report GAO-040-163, *Terrorist Financing: U.S. Agencies Should Systematically Assess Terrorists' Use of Alternative Financing Mechanisms*, November, 2003.

5 Executive Summary, Final Report of the National Commission on Terrorist Attacks Upon the United States, July 2004, pp. 18–19, available at www.9-11commission.gov/report/911Report_Exec.pdf.

6 Laura Sullivan, "U.S. Split on Usefulness of Tracing Money Trails to Prevent Terrorist Plots," *The Seattle Times*, August 3, 2004.

7 In full report, the Commission embraced tracking, recommending that vigorous efforts to track terrorist financing remain front and center. In contrast, "trying to starve the terrorists of money," said the Commission, "is like trying to catch one kind of fish by draining the ocean." *Final Report of the National Commission on Terrorist Attacks Upon the United States*, July 2004, p. 382.

the FBI and other intelligence agencies have a history of gathering intelligence by monitoring financial transactions and relationships over extended periods of time, for example in its investigations of the Mafia, and then using laws against financial crimes to eventually arrest the perpetrators. The Department of the Treasury, by contrast, has traditionally favored freezing terrorist assets as soon as possible. Each strategy reflects the agency's primary skills and capabilities. According to Treasury Assistant Secretary for Terrorist Financing and Financial Crime Juan Zarate, "I think we need to do everything the commission said with respect to the money trail, but we also need to continue—and frankly be even more vigorous—on attacking the sources because that affects the long-term ability of Al-Qaeda to do all the nasty things we want to stop them from doing."[8] This tension is echoed by Jonathan Winer, a former Deputy Assistant Secretary of State for International Law Enforcement under President Bill Clinton, "There is a big ideological divide right now between the asset freezers and the people who want to follow the money as it changes hands. There's no easy answer one way or another."[9]

Effectively combating terrorist financing requires effective coordination of many different elements of national power including intelligence gathering, financial regulation, law enforcement, and building international coalitions. "There are a number of areas where jurisdiction is blurred," according to one senior official.[10] According to most analysts, interagency cooperation is imperative to successfully combat this threat.

What Is Terrorist Financing?

Earning Money

The financial support of terrorism involves both earning funds—through legal and illegal means—and the illicit movement of money to terrorist groups. It is important to note that in many cases, charities being the main example, funds transferred to terrorists are often raised legally and only acquire their relationship to terrorist financing through subsequent money laundering. In a case currently under investigation, on July 27, 2004, the Holy Land Foundation for Relief and Development, the largest Muslim charity in the United States, was indicted on charges it provided financial support to Hamas, an Islamic terrorist group.[11] Its finances had been frozen more than two years earlier, in December 2001. Many of the organization's donors reported no knowledge that their donations were being diverted to illegal activities. In addition to charities, apparently legitimate businesses whose profits go to terrorism are another means of earning funds. Finally, terrorists have engaged in criminal activity such as drug trafficking, and smuggling cigarettes or commodities as a means of raising funds.

Moving Money

For many years—especially prior to the September 11, 2001 attacks—terrorists have exploited the formal banking sector's international reach and often weak regulation. While the international system is moving towards increased regulation of international banking, there are many built-in impediments to regulatory and law enforcement cooperation. For example, domestic laws and regulations have allowed the United States to freeze large amounts of terrorist assets in banks located in U.S. jurisdictions. However, the ability of the United States to freeze funds in other jurisdictions is limited. The United States and other countries are working to make the international financial sector more secure from terrorist financing abuses. For example, the Federal Reserve Board recently fined the U.S. arm of UBS AG $100 million for funneling $5 billion to countries such as Cuba, Iran, and Libya.[12] Riggs Bank was fined $25 million in May 2004, for failing to report unusual transactions.[13] The United States is also working with the Financial Action Task Force (FATF) and other international financial institutions to create new standards and best practices for the formal financial sector.

As governments have begun to crack down on terrorist abuse of the formal banking sector, terrorists have increasingly turned to informal means in order to move money around. These services are cheaper than formal banking or money transfer arrangements, they can provide anonymity for all parties involved, and they can reach countries where there is no formal banking sector, in some cases even arranging for hand delivery of the cash. While most use these systems for legitimate purposes, their lack of documentation and anonymous, informal nature make them attractive for money laundering and/or terrorist financing purposes.

Alternative remittance systems, or more broadly informal value transfer systems (IVTS) date back hundreds of years and were originally used to finance trade in regions where traveling with gold or other forms of payment was not safe.[14] The system goes by various names including *Hue* (Vietnam), *Fei-Ch'ien* (China) *Phei Kwan* (Thailand) *Hundi* (South Asia), or *Hui Kuan* (Hong Kong). The primary current network is the *hawala* system (*hawala* means "transfer" in Arabic) in use in South Asia and the Middle East. The primary users of the *hawala* system are emigrants in Europe, the Persian Gulf, and North America who send remittances back to their family in South and East Asia, Africa, Eastern Europe, and other regions.[15] The most

---

8 Ibid.

9 Ibid.

10 Laura Shepard, "Nominees Stalled by Turf Battle," *The Hill*, June 9, 2004.

11 "Holy Land Foundation, Muslim Charity, Accused of Aiding Terror," *Bloomberg*, July 27, 2004.

---

12 See Kathleen Day and Terence O'Hara, "Obstacles Block Tracking of Terror Funding; Task Is Complex, Leadership Is Lacking, Critics Say," *The Washington Post*, July 14, 2004.

13 Ibid.

14 Mohammed El-Qorchi, "Hawala," *Finance and Development*, December 2002, p. 31.

15 Ibid.

basic *hawala* transfer would involve a migrant going to a *hawaladar* (an IVTS agent), mostly likely located through an ethnic neighborhood, and giving the agent money to send to someone abroad. The agent will call/fax/or e-mail instructions to a counterpart in the recipient country with instructions. Accounts may be settled in multiple ways. Since the *hawala* system operates on trust, and often familial networks, accounts between *hawaladars* can remain open and active for years before being settled. Settlement might occur simply with a transfer in the opposite direction, over (or under) invoicing of traded items, through occasional wire transfers, or some other bartering arrangement.

Authorities have also noted the use of cash couriers to transport sums of money between terrorist operatives. Cash couriers are particularly common in Middle Eastern and South Asian countries with predominantly cash economies. Many of these countries have weak or no formal financial system. In many countries, cross border currency transportation limits are relatively high or nonexistent.

Can Terrorist Financing Be Stopped?

As the 9/11 Commission has stressed, the cost of a terrorist attack is very small, and the impediments to freezing money are many and varied. Collaboration between local, state, national, and international actors, both private and public provides a comprehensive response that can prevent terrorists from exploiting gaps or weaknesses within the multi-layered international financial system. Going forward, action at the multilateral level may become increasingly more important.

Financial Action Task Force (FATF)

FATF is an inter-governmental body that develops and promotes policies and standards to combat money laundering (the so-called *Forty Recommendations*) and terrorist financing (*Eight Special Recommendations on Terrorist Financing*). It is housed at the Organization for Economic Cooperation and Development (OECD) in Paris. FATF currently has 33 members.[16] FATF sets minimum standards and makes recommendations for its member countries.

During 2003-2004, the IMF and the World Bank undertook a twelve-month pilot program that evaluated 33 countries and assessed their compliance with the FATF 40 + 8 recommendations. In addition, 8 countries were assessed either by FATF or one of the FATF-style regional bodies. At the G-7 meeting in Boca Raton during February 2004, finance ministers requested the IMF to make the assessments a normal component of its economic surveillance reports. In March 2004, the IMF and World Bank reviewed the pilot program and subsequently included AML/CFT assessments as part of its normal country surveillance.[17]

A concern is that of the 41 countries assessed in the Bank/Fund pilot program, only three—Jordan, Oman, and Algeria—are in the Middle East or North Africa, arguably the region of primary concern regarding terrorist financing, especially informal money transfers. An assessment of numerous Islamic countries' compliance with international counterterrorist finance standards was undertaken by the Watson Institute for International Studies at Brown University in consultation with the Council on Foreign Relations (CFR) Independent Task Force on Terrorist Financing.[18] According to the Watson Institute's report, Saudi Arabia's compliance with the guidelines established by FATF is "among the most robust in the sample."[19] A similar assessment of Saudi Arabia was reached by FATF in 2004.[20] Other Middle Eastern countries, while making strides in establishing legal and administrative frameworks, still lack effective regulatory and enforcement tools. A step in this direction is a 2004 initiative to start a FATF-style regional body for the Middle East and North Africa.

Legislation

The Intelligence Reform and Terrorism Prevention Act (P.L. 108-458) made technical corrections to Title III of the USA PATRIOT Act and included provisions that would require the Treasury Department to develop a national money laundering strategy; grant the Securities and Exchange Commission (SEC) emergency authority to respond to extraordinary market disturbances; boost the authority of the Financial Crimes Enforcement Network, the U.S. Government's financial intelligence unit; and equates the possession of counterfeiting tools with the intent to use them and the actual act of counterfeiting. The Treasury Department would also be authorized to print the currency, postage stamps, and other security documents of other nations.

A provision to crack down on illegal internet gambling by barring financial institutions from processing certain internet gambling transactions that occur via credit cards, wire transfers, or other bank instruments was also added. FinCEN was authorized an additional $35.5 million to improve technology and the SEC would be given emergency authority for up to 90 days to alter, supplement, suspend, or impose requirements or restrictions with respect to any matter or action subject to regulation by the Commission or a self-regulatory

---

16 See FATF website for a list of member countries and observer organizations available at www1.oecd.org/fatf/.

17 International Monetary Fund, "IMF Executive Board Reviews and Enhances Efforts for Anti-Money Laundering and Combating the Financing of Terrorism" Public Information Notice No. 04/33, available at www.imf.org/external/np/sec/pn/2004/pn0433.htm.

18 Council on Foreign Relations Independent Task Force on Terrorist Financing, *Update on the Global Campaign Against Terrorist Financing*, Appendix C, "A Comparative Assessment of Saudi Arabia with Other Countries of the Islamic World."

19 Ibid., p. 8.

20 See CRS Report RL 32499, *Saudi Arabia: Terrorist Financing Issues*.

organization under the securities laws, as provided for in a 2003 House-passed bill.

Congress also required the President to submit to Congress within 270 days a report evaluating and making recommendations on: (1) the effectiveness of efforts and methods to track terrorist financing; (2) ways to improve governmental cooperation; (3) ways to improve the performance of financial institutions; (4) the adequacy of agency coordination and ways to improve that coordination; and (5) recommendations for changes in law and additional resources required to improve this effort. The Administration would be required to submit an annual report on the allocation of funding within the Treasury's Office of Foreign Asset Control (OFAC).

Potential Issues for Congress

The recommendation of the 9/11 Commission to shift the U.S. strategy from one focused on freezing assets to one of exploiting terrorist financing networks for intelligence, combined with terrorist organizations' increasing shift to informal methods of money transfer point to a few challenges that may dominate future discussions on how best to counter terrorist financing. These include (1) establishing an overall U.S. strategy (seize assets vs. tracking networks), (2) establishing clear jurisdiction among the various federal departments and agencies involved in tracking terrorist financing, (3) establishing an inter-agency policy coordination mechanism, (4) increasing cooperation between law enforcement operatives, customs and border patrol authorities, and intelligence agencies, (5) establishing a congressional oversight mechanism, (6) deciding how to regulate charitable organizations and alternative remittance systems (*hawala* registration), and (7) creating a public diplomacy apparatus that can address cultural sensitivities related to increased regulation of charities and *hawala* systems.[21]

Order Code RS21902, updated February 25, 2005

---

21 April 2004, U.S. agents raided an Eritrean civic center that provided remittance services for immigrants, yet did not fully comply with Patriot Act requirements. See Allan Lengal and Mary Beth Sheridan, "Business for Fund Transfers Raided, U.S. Takes Records at Eritrean Center, *The Washington Post*, April 17, 2004.

CRS Report for Congress

The Financial Action Task Force: An Overview

James K. Jackson
Specialist in International Trade and Finance,
Foreign Affairs, Defense, and Trade Division

Summary

The National Commission on Terrorist Attacks Upon the United States, or the 9/11 Commission, recommended that tracking terrorist financing "must remain front and center in U.S. counterterrorism efforts."[1] As part of these efforts, the United States plays a leading role in the Financial Action Task Force on Money Laundering (FATF). The independent, intergovernmental policy-making body was established by the 1989 G-7 Summit in Paris as a result of growing concerns among the Summit participants about the threat posed to the international banking system by money laundering. After September 11, 2001, the body expanded its role to include identifying sources and methods of terrorist financing and adopted eight Special Recommendations on terrorist financing to track terrorists' funds. This report provides an overview of the Task Force and of its progress to date in gaining broad international support for its Recommendations. This report will be updated as warranted by events.

The Financial Action Task Force on Money Laundering is comprised of 31 member countries and territories and two international organizations[2] and was organized to develop and promote policies to combat money laundering and terrorist financing.[3] The FATF relies on a combination of annual self-assessments and periodic mutual evaluations that are completed by a team of FATF experts to provide information and to assess the compliance of its members to the FATF guidelines. FATF has no enforcement capability, but can suspend member countries that fail to comply on a timely basis with its guidelines. The FATF is housed at the headquarters of the Organization for Economic Cooperation and Development (OECD) in Paris and occasionally uses some OECD staff, but the FATF is not part of the OECD. The Presidency of the FATF is a one-year appointed position, currently held by Mr. Jean-Louis Fort of France. The FATF has operated under a five-year mandate. At the Ministerial meeting on May 14, 2004, the member countries renewed the FATF's mandate for an unprecedented eight years.

The Mandate

When it was established in 1989, the FATF was charged with examining money laundering techniques and trends, reviewing the action which had already been taken, and setting out the measures that still needed to be taken to combat money laundering. In 1990, the FATF issued a report containing a set of Forty Recommendations, which provided a comprehensive plan of action to fight against money laundering. In 2003, the FATF adopted the second revision to its original Forty Recommendations, which now apply to money laundering and terrorist financing.[4]

Since the terrorist attacks of September 11, 2001, the FATF has redirected its efforts to focus on terrorist financing. On October 31, 2001, the FATF issued a new set of guidelines

---

1 The 9/11 Commission Report: Final Report of the National Commission on Terrorist Attacks in the United States, U.S. Government Printing Office, July 2004. p. 382.

2 The FATF Members are: Argentina, Australia, Austria, Belgium, Brazil, Canada, Denmark, Finland, France, Germany, Greece, Hong Kong, Iceland, Ireland, Italy, Japan, Luxembourg, Mexico, Netherlands, New Zealand, Norway, Portugal, Russian Federation, Singapore, South Africa, Spain, Sweden, Switzerland, Turkey, United Kingdom, United States, and the two international organizations are: the European Commission, and the Gulf Cooperation Council. The following organizations have observer status: Asia/Pacific Group on Money Laundering; Caribbean Financial Action Task Force; Council of Europe Select Committee of experts on the Evaluation of Anti-Money Laundering Measures; Eastern and Southern African Anti-Money Laundering Group; Financial Action Task Force on Money Laundering in South America; other international organizations, including the African Development Bank; Asia Development Bank; European Central Bank; International Monetary Fund; Organization of American States; Organization for Economic Cooperation and Development; United Nations Office on Drug and Crime; and the World Bank.

3 To be admitted to the FATF, a country must: 1) be fully committed at the political level to implement the Forty Recommendations within a reasonable time frame (three years) and to undergo annual self-assessment exercises and two rounds of mutual evaluations; 2) be a full and active member of the relevant FATF-style regional body; 3) be a strategically important country; 4) have already made the laundering of proceeds of drug trafficking and other serious crimes a criminal offense; and, 5) have already made it mandatory for financial institutions to identify their customers and report unusual or suspicion actions.

4 For the Forty Recommendations, see www1.oecd.org/fatf/pdf/40Recs-2003_en.pdf.

and a set of eight Special Recommendations on terrorist financing.[5] At that time, the FATF indicated that it had broadened its mission beyond money laundering to focus on combating terrorist financing and that it was encouraging all countries to abide by the new set of guidelines. The FATF eight Special Recommendations are:

1. Take immediate steps to ratify and implement the 1999 United Nations International Convention for the Suppression of the Financing of Terrorism and Security Council Resolution 1373 dealing with the prevention and suppression of the financing of terrorist acts;
2. Criminalize the financing of terrorism, terrorist acts and terrorist organizations;
3. Freeze and confiscate funds or other assets of terrorists and adopt measures which allow authorities to seize and confiscate property;
4. Report funds that are believed to be linked or related to, or are to be used for terrorism, terrorist acts, or by terrorist organizations;
5. Provide the widest possible range of assistance to other countries' law enforcement and regulatory authorities in connection with criminal, civil enforcement, and administrative investigations;
6. Impose anti-money laundering requirements on alternative remittance systems;
7. Strengthen customer identification requirements on financial institutions for domestic and international wire transfers of funds;
8. Ensure that entities such as non-profit organizations cannot be misused to finance terrorism.

The FATF completed a review of its mandate and proposed changes that were adopted at the May 2004 Ministerial meeting. The new mandate provides for the following five objectives: (1) continue to establish the international standards for combating money laundering and terrorist financing; (2) support global action to combat money laundering and terrorist financing, including stronger cooperation with the IMF and the World Bank; (3) increase membership in the FATF; (4) enhance relationships between FATF and regional bodies and non-member countries and; (5) intensify its study of the techniques and trends in money laundering and terrorist financing.[6]

Progress to Date

An essential part of the FATF activities is assessing the progress of its members in complying with the FATF recommendations. As previously indicated, the FATF has attempted to accomplish this activity through assessments performed annually by the individual members and through mutual evaluations. According to the 2002-2003 assessment provided by the FATF members, two countries, France and Italy, were in full compliance, as indicated in Table 1. Only three countries, Greece, New Zealand, and Norway, were in non-compliance relative to any of the recommendations. The rest of the members were in full compliance or partial compliance of seven of the eight Special Recommendations on terrorist financing. The one Special Recommendation that is not considered in the survey relates to the performance of non-profit organizations. Part of the difficulty the FATF faces in determining how fully member countries are complying with the Special Recommendations is in reaching a mutual understanding of what the Recommendations mean and how a country should judge its performance relative to the Recommendations, since the Recommendations are periodically revised and new methodologies for analyzing money laundering and terrorist financing are adopted. In addition, a number of the Recommendations require changes in laws and other procedures that take time for member countries to implement. To assist member countries in complying with the FATF Recommendations, FATF has issued various Interpretative Notes to clarify aspects of the Recommendations and to further refine the obligations of member countries.

Between 2002 and 2003, the International Monetary Fund (IMF) and the World Bank participated in a year-long pilot program to conduct assessments on money laundering and terrorist financing in various countries[7] using the methodology developed by the FATF.[8] In March 2004, the IMF and World Bank agreed to make the program a permanent part of their activities. Over the year, the IMF and the Bank conducted assessments in 41 jurisdictions. According to these assessments, the Fund/Bank reached a number of conclusions regarding the overall compliance with the FATF 40 Recommendations and the eight Special Recommendations. In particular, they concluded that overall compliance was uneven across jurisdictions, but that jurisdictions display a higher level of compliance with the FATF 40 Recommendations than they do with the eight Special Recommendations due to shortcomings in domestic legislation. In general, the Fund/Bank concluded that compliance is higher among high and middle income countries than in low income countries. The most common weaknesses identified by the IMF and the World Bank include:

- Poor coordination among government agencies, especially among financial supervisors, financial investigators, the police, public prosecutors, and the public.
- Ineffective law enforcement due to a lack of skills, training, or resources to investigate, prosecute, and adjudicate

---

5 FATF Cracks Down on Terrorist Financing: Washington, FATF, October 31, 2001, p. 1.

6 www1.oecd.org/fatf/pdf/PR-20040514_en.pdf.

7 This group of countries is not the same as those surveyed by the FATF, although there is some overlap in coverage between the FATF and the IMF/World Bank assessments.

8 This section is based on the IMF/World Bank report: *Twelve-Month Pilot Program of Anti-Money Laundering and Combating the Financing of Terrorism (AmL/CFT) Assessments: Joint Report on the Review of the Pilot Program.* The International Monetary Fund and the World Bank, March 10, 2004.

Table 1 Country Self Assessments Relative to the FATF Special Recommendations on Terrorist Financing 2002–2003 (Special Recommendations 1–7)

Country	In Full Compliance	In Partial Compliance	Not in Compliance	Country	In Full Compliance	In Partial Compliance	Not in Compliance
Argentina	4	3	0	Japan	6	1	0
Australia	5	2	0	Luxembourg	6	1	0
Austria	6	1	0	Mexico	2	5	0
Belgium	6	1	0	Netherlands	5	2	0
Brazil	5	2	0	New Zealand	4	2	1
Canada	5	2	0	Norway	5	1	1
Denmark	6	1	0	Portugal	6	1	0
Finland	6	1	0	Singapore	6	1	0
France	7	0	0	Spain	6	1	0
Germany	6	1	0	Sweden	6	1	0
Greece	1	4	2	Switzerland	5	2	0
Hong Kong	4	3	0	Turkey	4	3	0
Iceland	6	1	0	United Kingdom	6	1	0
Ireland	4	3	0	United States	6	1	0
Italy	7	0	0				

Source: Annual Report 2002–2003, Financial Action Task Force on Money Laundering, June 20, 2003. Annex C.

money laundering cases among police, prosecutors, or the courts.

- Weak supervision by financial supervisors due to understaffed or undertrained supervisors who lacked the skills or capacity to monitor and enforce compliance with money laundering or terrorist financing requirements.
- Inadequate systems and controls among financial firms to identify and report suspicious activity, or to ensure that adequate records were being maintained.
- Shortcomings in international cooperation due to strong secrecy provisions, restrictions placed on counterpart's use of information and the inability to share information unless a criminal investigation was already underway or a formal agreement was in place.

For each of the Special Recommendations, the IMF and the World Bank offered additional conclusions:

1. Ratification and implementation of U.N. instruments. Almost one-third of the jurisdictions assessed by the IMF/World Bank failed to comply with this recommendation.
2. Criminalizing the financing of terrorism and associated money laundering. This Recommendation was one of the least observed by the jurisdictions reviewed.
3. Freezing and confiscating terrorist assets. About one third of the jurisdictions that were assessed displayed serious deficiencies complying with this Recommendation, generally because there was a lack of explicit legal provisions or other arrangements that would require the freezing of funds or assets of terrorists.
4. Reporting suspicious transactions related to terrorism. Forty percent of the assessed jurisdictions displayed a lack of legal and institutional measures that would require making a report to competent authorities when there is a suspicion that funds are linked to terrorist financing.
5. International cooperation. This recommendation, which covers mutual assistance and extradition in financing of terrorism-related cases, is one of the least observed recommendations, where almost half of the relevant countries exhibited significant deficiencies.
6. Alternative remittance systems. In most jurisdictions, such remittances were judged to be irrelevant, but of those jurisdictions that were considered, one-half were found to be deficient.
7. Wire transfers. Compliance was assessed inconsistently because there was ambiguity about whether the standard was in force. Those jurisdictions that were not in compliance generally lacked formal requirements that complete information be included in each transaction.

In February 2004, the FATF adopted a revised version of the 40 Recommendations that significantly broadens the scope and detail of the Recommendations over previous versions. Also, the FATF adopted a new methodology to track and identify money laundering and terrorist financing that applies to both the 40 Recommendations and the eight Special Recommendations. As a result of the significant length and additional detail of these new requirements, the FATF decided that it will no longer conduct self-assessment exercises based on the previous method, but will initiate follow-up reports to mutual evaluations.

Issues for Congress

Following the 9/11 attacks, Congress passed P.L. 107-56 (the USA PATRIOT Act) to expand the ability of the Treasury Department to detect, track, and prosecute those involved in money laundering and terrorist financing. In 2004, the 108th Congress adopted P.L. 108-458, which appropriated funds to combat financial crimes, made technical corrections to P.L. 107-56, and required the Treasury Department to report on the current state of U.S. efforts to curtail the international financing of terrorism. The experience of the Financial Action Task Force in tracking terrorist financing, however, indicates that there are significant national hurdles that remain to be overcome before there is a seamless flow of information shared among nations. While progress has been made, domestic legal issues and established business practices, especially those that govern the sharing of financial information across national borders, continue to hamper efforts to track certain types of financial flows across national borders. Continued progress likely will depend on the success of member countries in changing their domestic laws to allow for greater sharing of financial information, criminalizing certain types of activities, and improving efforts to identify and track terrorist-related financial accounts.

The economic implications of money laundering and terrorist financing pose another set of issues that argue for gaining greater control over this type of activity. According to the IMF, money laundering accounts for between $600 billion and $1.6 trillion in economic activity annually. Money launderers exploit differences among national anti-money laundering systems and move funds into jurisdictions with weak or ineffective laws. In such cases, organized crime can become more entrenched and create a full range of macroeconomic consequences, including unpredictable changes in money demand, risk to the soundness of financial institutions and the financial system, contamination effects on legal financial transactions and increased volatility of capital flows and exchange rates due to unprecedented cross-border transfers.[9]

Order Code RS21904, updated March 4, 2005

---

[9] The IMF and the Fight Against Money Laundering and the Financing of Terrorism. IMF Factsheet, April 2003. [http://www.imf.org/external/np/exr/facts/aml.htm]

U.S. Military Response

Overview of U.S. Military Response

Anna Sabasteanski

The first instance of a U.S. military response to terrorism occurred in 1986, when the United States launched air strikes against Libya. Libya's support for international terrorist attacks had led to dozens of U.S. casualties and put Libya at the top of the international list of state sponsors of terrorism. The strikes targeted terrorist support facilities in Libya, but also resulted in major collateral damage, including some thirty-seven civilian deaths, more than ninety injured, and damage to a hospital and the French embassy.

In the years that followed, although targeted actions were taken against other threats, the next significant action occurred in 1998, in reaction to al-Qaeda attacks on U.S. embassies in Tanzania and Kenya. *Patterns of Global Terrorism 1998* described the response to those attacks thus:

> Following the bombings of the two US Embassies in East Africa, the US Government obtained evidence implicating Usama Bin Ladin's network in the attacks. To preempt additional attacks, the United States launched military strikes against terrorist targets in Afghanistan and Sudan on 20 August. That same day, President Clinton amended Executive Order 12947 to add Usama Bin Ladin and his key associates to the list of terrorists, thus blocking their US assets—including property and bank accounts—and prohibiting all US financial transactions with them. As a result of what Attorney General Janet Reno called the most extensive overseas criminal investigation in US history, and working closely with the Kenyan and Tanzanian Governments, the US Government indicted Bin Ladin and 11 of his associates for the two bombings and other terrorist crimes. Several suspects were brought to the United States to stand trial. The Department of State announced a reward of up to $5 million for information leading to the arrest or conviction of any of the suspects anywhere in the world.
>
> In Afghanistan, U.S. missiles massively damaged buildings in four complexes that made up a terrorist training camp and bin Laden's operational base. Twenty-one people were killed and thirty injured. In Sudan, missiles struck the EL Shifa pharmaceutical factory, with at least ten casualties and the loss of most of Sudan's pharmaceutical production capacity.

Following the terrorist attacks of September 11, the United States' military response to terrorism moved into high gear. The reports from 2001 is below. Reports from 2002–2004 are on the pages that follow.

The Military Campaign in Afghanistan, 2001

From Patterns of Global Terrorism 2001

From the very moment of the September 11 attacks, suspicion turned toward al-Qaida, whose leadership and training bases were under the protection of the Taliban rulers of Afghanistan. From the outset, the US Government was faced with the need to overcome the Taliban in order to disrupt further al-Qaida activities. The President determined that this called for military action on a grand scale.

The US Central Command (CENTCOM), under the command of General Tommy Franks, set to work developing a plan and assembling forces to carry out actions in Afghanistan, which was located in the area of the world under CENTCOM's purview. First priority went to eliminating the Taliban's air defense, command and control, and mobility capabilities. On 7 October, assisted by Special Operations teams spirited into the country to identify targets, Air Force, Navy, and Marine aircraft began systematically and surgically destroying Taliban and al-Qaida warfighting equipment and positions. In a parallel effort, the United States soon began delivering the first of what was to become over two million humanitarian daily rations to alleviate the suffering of Afghans beyond reach of food supplies.

From the very beginning, the United States was joined in its war against global terrorism by other countries who saw the events of September 11 as an attack on their own way of life. Countries around the globe offered military and other assets to the growing antiterrorism Coalition. By year's end, forces from 55 countries, including some from the Muslim world, had augmented US forces in the effort to subdue al-Qaida and the Taliban. Each member brought to the Coalition a unique contribution of military assets and expertise.

The focus of the bombing campaign gradually shifted from destroying al-Qaida and Taliban equipment and facilities to disrupting the ground forces opposing the anti-Taliban Northern Alliance. On 10 November, Northern Alliance troops entered the northern city of Mazar-e-Sharif, signaling the end of Taliban control over the northern provinces. In the following days, the Taliban military forces in most of the country collapsed, many of them fleeing toward the southern city of Kandahar, where the Taliban originated. On 13 November, Northern Alliance forces entered the capital city of Kabul unopposed.

Although US Army Rangers had raided a Taliban command-and-control site near Kandahar as early as 19 October, the United States generally restricted its ground combat units to roles that did not involve assaults against fixed Taliban positions. On 26 November, US Marines established an operating base southwest of Kandahar and began conducting patrols aimed at preventing the escape of al-Qaida and Taliban leaders. Kandahar, the last city held by the Taliban, finally succumbed to pressure from incessant Coalition bombing and ground action by anti-Taliban Afghan forces on 6 December. Taliban leader Mullah Omar, however, was able to escape.

Meanwhile, Coalition and Afghan forces were searching for al-Qaida leader Usama Bin Ladin in a cave-riddled stronghold in the mountains near Tora Bora, along Afghanistan's border with Pakistan. After a tough, uphill, cave-by-cave battle, Tora Bora was finally subdued, but Bin Ladin, for the moment, also had evaded capture.

In the following weeks, anti-Taliban forces throughout Afghanistan continued to pursue the remaining Taliban and al-Qaida forces, capturing over 5,000 of them. Those identified as of special interest to the United States—key Taliban and al-Qaida leaders—were moved to US-controlled detention facilities to await further disposition.

On 26 November, representatives of numerous Afghan factions met in Bonn to negotiate a governing agreement. The resulting Afghan Interim Authority took office in Kabul on 22 December. To provide security for the nascent Afghan Government, several countries contributed forces to the British-led International Security Assistance Force established under the auspices of UN Security Council Resolution 1386 of 20 December.

The message of the successful military action in Afghanistan to persons bent on using terrorism to achieve their international objectives is clear: the United States will act swiftly and relentlessly, with worldwide reach, to pursue and eliminate them.

The Military Counterterrorism Campaign in 2002

From Patterns of Global Terrorism 2002

US military forces and allies continued their campaign to oust al-Qaida and the Taliban from Afghanistan into 2002 by completing an exhaustive search of the Tora Bora cave complex in eastern Afghanistan. Although senior al-Qaida operatives were captured in the operation, high-priority targets such as Mullah Omar and Usama Bin Ladin remained at large.

After visiting Kabul on 18 January, Secretary of State Colin Powell facilitated international efforts to rebuild Afghanistan by meeting in Tokyo with representatives from 60 nations and development organizations. Of the $4.5 billion contributed, the United States provided $297 million for 2002, the largest single pledge by any government.

Relations with Kabul's nascent government were further bolstered by the visit of interim Afghan president Hamid Karzai to Washington in late January. US forces continued to rout Taliban and al-Qaida operatives in Afghanistan as Karzai reopened his nation's embassy, met with President Bush in the oval office, and called upon State Department and Congressional officials. The abduction on 23 January, and eventual execution, of journalist Daniel Pearl in Pakistan illustrated the continued hazard to US personnel in the region.

In response to internal security concerns, Karzai's government called for additional personnel to support international peacekeeping efforts in Afghanistan. Washington renewed its commitment to train an indigenous Afghan National Army (ANA), which now comprises two brigades and will eventually grow to 18 battalions. In the regions, Provincial Reconstruction Teams (PRTs) were formed and deployed in Gardez, Bamiyan, and Konduz, beginning in December 2002. The teams will work to stabilize the regions by coordinating the reconstruction efforts of the Coalition military forces, aid organizations, nongovernmental organizations (NGOs), and the Afghan Government. Ten PRTs are planned for major regional cities in Afghanistan.

On 2 March, US-led allied forces initiated Operation Anaconda to seize the Taliban and al-Qaida–infested Shai-i-Kot valley in eastern Afghanistan. Resistance ceased after 11 days of the heaviest fighting yet seen in the campaign. Although Taliban and al-Qaida fighters were pushed out of their defensive positions during the operation, critics suggested that premature US and Canadian withdrawal from the Shai-i-Kot region on 20 March allowed many to escape through the loosely guarded Pakistani border.

Following the late March announcement by Secretary of Defense Donald Rumsfeld that training for the ANA would begin in April, US troops—in conjunction with British and Canadian allies—redeployed to seal the border between

Afghanistan and Pakistan and remove the remaining Taliban and al-Qaida strongholds in the region. Operations along the Pakistani border with Afghanistan continued despite renewed tension and the possibility of war between Pakistan and India in May and June.

As Hamid Karzai was officially sworn in as president of the Transitional State of Afghanistan (TISA) in Kabul on 19 June, US officials predicted it would take up to a year to secure Afghanistan against loyalist Taliban and al-Qaida remnants. Although grateful for the additional security provided by US forces, Afghan officials were highly critical of an incident on 1 July in which nearly 40 civilians attending a wedding celebration were reportedly killed by an AC-130 gunship responding to antiaircraft fire. Karzai's government was dealt another blow a week later in Kabul with the assassination of Vice President Abdul Qadir, who had been valued as one of the few ethnic Pashtuns in the new Afghan Government. A thwarted car-bombing attempt in Kabul the following week, as well as an assassination attempt against President Karzai in late August, dramatically illustrated the existence of continued security threats in Afghanistan.

Through the final months of 2002, efforts to destroy weapons caches and capture Taliban and al-Qaida fighters met with slow but steady success. In early November, Gen. Richard Myers, Chairman of the Joint Chiefs of Staff, stated that military operations in Afghanistan would be gradually replaced by reconstruction efforts. With the Taliban and al-Qaida presence all but removed by the end of 2002, focus shifted to implementing humanitarian development and reconstruction in Afghanistan, with cost estimates ranging from $10–15 billion over the next decade.

US counterterrorism efforts also expanded beyond the borders of Afghanistan in 2002, with operations in the Philippines, Georgia, and Yemen. Early in the year, 1,200 advisors were dispatched to the Philippines to train soldiers fighting members of the radical Islamist group Abu Sayyaf. An attempt by Philippine commandos to rescue three US citizens held by Abu Sayyaf in June resulted in the unfortunate deaths of two of the hostages. Following the conclusion of training in July, several hundred US soldiers remained in the Philippines to assist with infrastructure projects.

Washington initiated a similar, though more limited effort in the former Soviet republic of Georgia. Beginning in May, US military personnel trained 1,500 indigenous troops to clear Georgia's Pankisi Gorge region of foreign fighters that possibly included al-Qaida and Chechen separatist groups among their numbers.

The Military Counterterrorism Campaign in 2003

From Patterns of Global Terrorism 2003

Operation Iraqi Freedom

On 19 March 2003, US and Coalition forces launched Operation Iraqi Freedom (OIF). Along with freeing the Iraqi people of a vicious dictator, OIF also shut down the Salman Pak training camp, where members of al-Qaida had trained, and disrupted the Abu Musab al-Zarqawi network, which had established a poison and explosives training camp in northeastern Iraq. OIF removed the prospective threat to the international community posed by the combination of an aggressive Iraqi regime, weapons of mass destruction capabilities, and terrorists. Iraq is now the central front for the global war on terrorism.

Since the end of major combat operations, Coalition forces from 33 nations have been engaged in stability operations in Iraq, primarily against regime loyalists, remnants of Ansar al-Islam, and a number of foreign terrorists. This resistance has been responsible for such acts as the bombing of the United Nations headquarters in Baghdad on 19 August, the attack of 12 November on the Italian military police at Nasiriyah, and the coordinated attack on Bulgarian and Thai troops at Karbala on 27 December. Former regime loyalists and foreign terrorists have proved adept at adjusting their tactics to maintain attacks on Coalition forces, particularly with the use of vehicle-borne, improvised explosive devices. Coalition forces continue offensive action against these forces and, on 13 December, captured the former Iraqi dictator Saddam Hussein in Operation Red Dawn. By the end of 2003, Coalition forces had killed, captured, or taken into custody 42 of the 55 most-wanted members of the former regime of Saddam Hussein.

Coalition forces in Iraq also are training and equipping the new components of Iraq's security services, which include police, the Iraqi Civil Defense Corps, border police, the Iraqi Facility Protection Service, and a new Iraqi army. The Coalition's goal is to build the Iraqi security services to approximately 225,000 members. With the transfer of governing authority from the Coalition Provisional Authority to the Iraqi Transitional National Assembly in 2004, Iraqi security services will play an increasing role in creating a stable and united Iraq, as well as preventing foreign terrorists from establishing operations in Iraq.

Operation Enduring Freedom

US military forces continued to operate in the mountains of southern Afghanistan against al-Qaida terrorists, anti-Coalition militias, and Taliban insurgents throughout 2003.

Anti-government activity targeting Afghan security forces, civic leaders, and international aid workers continues to destabilize the southern regions of the country. These attacks resulted in the United Nations suspending operations in the southern provinces of Helmand, Oruzgan, Khandahar, and Zabol in 2003. The frequency of attacks rose steadily throughout the year, reaching peaks in September and early November and tapering off with the onset of winter.

Nevertheless, Afghanistan continued to make slow but steady progress back from 25 years of civil war and Taliban misrule. A Grand Assembly, or Loya Jirga, was formed of 502 members from around the country—including 100 women—to debate the proposed new national constitution in December. Despite efforts by anti-government forces to disrupt the proceedings, the event was successful, paving the way for UN-mandated elections in June 2004.

President Hamid Karzai worked throughout the year to replace unresponsive provincial governors and security chiefs and to centralize collection of customs revenues and taxes. Aid continued to flow into Afghanistan from around the world in 2003, funding the completion of hundreds of clinics and schools and hundreds of kilometers of irrigation projects. The United States will probably provide more than $2 billion in aid in fiscal year 2004, the largest single pledge by any government.

NATO formally assumed command of the International Security Assistance Force in August 2003, and the number of Provincial Reconstruction Teams (PRTs) planned or fielded rose to 13, including new teams to begin work in early 2004. A large German PRT took over operations in Konduz, and Great Britain and New Zealand led PRTs in Mazar-i-Sharif and Bamian, respectively. The PRTs are effective catalysts for reconstruction activity and regional security. Afghan police training is picking up speed, but efforts to build a new Afghan National Army have been hampered by problems with recruiting and retention. Approximately 5,600 men were ready for duty in the Afghan National Army at the end of 2003, including a battalion of T-62 tanks.

Afghanistan remains a security challenge. Relying on the Pashtun-dominated and largely autonomous Federally Administered Tribal Area in Pakistan as a refuge, the Taliban regrouped in 2003 and conducted a classic insurgency in the remote rural areas of the southern Pashtun tribes, using clan and family ties, propaganda, violence, and intimidation to maintain a foothold in several districts of Zabol and Oruzgan Provinces. Militant Islamic political parties openly supportive of the Taliban won landslide victories in legislative elections in 2003 in Pakistan's Baluchistan and Northwest Frontier provinces bordering Afghanistan, signaling a protracted counterinsurgency to eliminate the Taliban and other antigovernment elements.

Iraq and Terrorism

From Patterns of Global Terrorism 2002

Below is an excerpt from Secretary of State Colin L. Powell's remarks to the United Nations Security Council, 5 February 2003.

My friends, the information I have presented to you about these terrible weapons and about Iraq's continued flaunting of its obligations under Security Council Resolution 1441 links to a subject I now want to spend a little bit of time on, and that has to do with terrorism.

Our concern is not just about these illicit weapons; it's the way that these illicit weapons can be connected to terrorists and terrorist organizations that have no compunction about using such devices against innocent people around the world.

Iraq and terrorism go back decades. Baghdad trains Palestine Liberation Front members in small arms and explosives. Saddam uses the Arab Liberation Front to funnel money to the families of Palestinian suicide bombers in order to prolong the Intifadah. And it's no secret that Saddam's own intelligence service was involved in dozens of attacks or attempted assassinations in the 1990s.

But what I want to bring to your attention today is the potentially much more sinister nexus between Iraq and the al-Qaida terrorist network, a nexus that combines classic terrorist organizations and modern methods of murder. Iraq today harbors a deadly terrorist network headed by Abu Mud'ab al-Zarqawi an associate and collaborator of Usama Bin Ladin and his Al-Qaida lieutenants.

Zarqawi, Palestinian born in Jordan, fought in the Afghan war more than a decade ago. Returning to Afghanistan in 2000, he oversaw a terrorist training camp. One of his specialties, and one of the specialties of this camp, is poisons.

When our coalition ousted the Taliban, the Zarqawi network helped establish another poison and explosive training center camp, and this camp is located in northeastern Iraq. You see a picture of this camp.

The network is teaching its operatives how to produce ricin and other poisons. Let me remind you how ricin works. Less than a pinch—imagine a pinch of salt—less than a pinch of ricin, eating just this amount in your food, would cause shock, followed bycirculatory failure. Death comes within 72 hours and there is no antidote. There is no cure. It is fatal.

Those helping to run this camp are Zarqawi lieutenants operating in northern Kurdish areas outside Saddam Hussein's controlled Iraq. But Baghdad has an agent in the most senior levels of the radical organization Ansar al-Islam that controls this corner of Iraq. In 2000, this agent offered al-Qaida safehaven in the region.

After we swept al-Qaida from Afghanistan, some of those members accepted this safehaven. They remain there today.

Zarqawi's activities are not confined to this small corner of northeast Iraq. He traveled to Baghdad in May of 2002 for medical treatment, staying in the capital of Iraq for two months while he recuperated to fight another day.

During his stay, nearly two-dozen extremists converged on Baghdad and established a base of operations there. These al-Qaida affiliates based in Baghdad now coordinate the movement of people, money and supplies into and throughout Iraq for his network, and they have now been operating freely in the capital for more than eight months.

Iraqi officials deny accusations of ties with al-Qaida. These denials are simply not credible. Last year, an al-Qaida associate bragged that the situation in Iraq was "good," that Baghdad could be transited quickly.

We know these affiliates are connected to Zarqawi because they remain, even today, in regular contact with his direct subordinates, includ[ing] the poison-cell plotters. And they are involved in moving more than money and materiel. Last year, two suspected al-Qaida operatives were arrested crossing from Iraq into Saudi Arabia. They were linked to associates of the Baghdad cell and one of them received training in Afghanistan on how to use cyanide.

From his terrorist network in Iraq, Zarqawi can direct his network in the Middle East and beyond. We in the United States, all of us, the State Department and the Agency for International Development, we all lost a dear friend with the cold-blooded murder of Mr. Laurence Foley in Amman, Jordan, last October. A despicable act was committed that day, the assassination of an individual whose sole mission was to assist the people of Jordan. The captured assassin says his cell received money and weapons from Zarqawi for that murder. After the attack, an associate of the assassin left Jordan to go to Iraq to obtain weapons and explosives for further operations. Iraqi officials protest that they are not aware of the whereabouts of Zarqawi or of any of his associates. Again, these protests are not credible. We know of Zarqawi's activities in Baghdad. I described them earlier.

Now let me add one other fact. We asked a friendly security service to approach Baghdad about extraditing Zarqawi and providing information about him and his close associates. This service contacted Iraqi officials twice and we passed details that should have made it easy to find Zarqawi. The network remains in Baghdad. Zakawi [sic] still remains at large, to come and go.

As my colleagues around this table and as the citizens they represent in Europe know, Zarqawi's terrorism is not confined to the Middle East. Zarqawi and his network have plotted terrorist actions against countries including France, Britain, Spain, Italy, Germany and Russia. According to detainees Abu Atiya, who graduated from Zarqawi's terrorist camp in Afghanistan, tasked [sic] at least nine North African extremists in 2001 to travel to Europe to conduct poison and explosive attacks.

Since last year, members of this network have been apprehended in France, Britain, Spain and Italy. By our last count, 116 operatives connected to this global web have been arrested.

We know about this European network and we know about its links to Zarqawi because the detainees who provided the information about the targets also provided the names of members of the network. Three of those he identified by name were arrested in France last December. In the apartments of the terrorists, authorities found circuits for explosive devices and a list of ingredients to make toxins.

The detainee who helped piece this together says the plot also targeted Britain. Later evidence again proved him right. When the British unearthed the cell there just last month, one British police officer was murdered during the destruction of the cell.

We also know that Zarqawi's colleagues have been active in the Pankisi Gorge, Georgia, and in Chechnya, Russia. The plotting to which they are linked is not mere chatter. Members of Zarqawi's network say their goal was to kill Russians with toxins.

We are not surprised that Iraq is harboring Zarqawi and his subordinates. This understanding builds on decades-long experience with respect to ties between Iraq and al-Qaida. Going back to the early and mid-1990s when Bin Ladin was based in Sudan, an al-Qaida source tells us that Saddam and Bin Ladin reached an understanding that al-Qaida would no longer support activities against Baghdad. Early al-Qaida ties were forged by secret high-level intelligence service contacts with al-Qaida.

We know members of both organizations met repeatedly and have met at least eight times at very senior levels since the early 1990s. In 1996, a foreign security service tells us that Bin Ladin met with a senior Iraqi intelligence official in Khartoum and later met the director of the Iraqi Intelligence Service.

Saddam became more interested as he saw al-Qaida's appalling attacks. A detained al-Qaida member tells us that Saddam was more willing to assist al-Qaida after the 1998 bombings of our embassies in Kenya and Tanzania. Saddam was also impressed by al-Qaida's attacks on the USS Cole in Yemen in October 2000.

Iraqis continue to visit Bin Ladin in his new home in Afghanistan. A senior defector, one of Saddam's former intelligence chiefs in Europe, says Saddam sent his agents to Afghanistan sometime in the mid-1990s to provide training to al-Qaida members on document forgery.

From the late 1990s until 2001, the Iraqi Embassy in Pakistan played the role of liaison to the al-Qaida organization.

Some believe, some claim, these contacts do not amount to much. They say Saddam Hussein's secular tyranny and al-Qaida's religious tyranny do not mix. I am not comforted by this thought. Ambition and hatred are enough to bring Iraq and al-Qaida together, enough so al-Qaida could learn how to build more sophisticated bombs and learn how to forge documents, and enough so that al-Qaida could turn to Iraq for help in acquiring expertise on weapons of mass destruction.

And the record of Saddam Hussein's cooperation with other Islamist terrorist organizations is clear. HAMAS, for example, opened an office in Baghdad in 1999, and Iraq has hosted conferences attended by Palestine Islamic Jihad. These groups are at the forefront of sponsoring suicide attacks against Israel.

Al-Qaida continues to have a deep interest in acquiring weapons of mass destruction. As with the story of Zarqawi and his network, I can trace the story of a senior terrorist operative telling how Iraq provided training in these weapons to al-Qaida. Fortunately, this operative is now detained and he has told his story. I will relate it to you now as he, himself, described it.

This senior al-Qaida terrorist was responsible for one of al-Qaida's training camps in Afghanistan. His information comes firsthand from his personal involvement at senior levels of al-Qaida. He says Bin Ladin and his top deputy in Afghanistan, deceased al-Qaida leader Mohammed Atef, did not believe that al-Qaida labs in Afghanistan were capable enough to manufacture these chemical or biological agents. They needed to go somewhere else. They had to look outside of Afghanistan for help.

Where did they go? Where did they look? They went to Iraq. The support that the operative describes included Iraq offering chemical or biological weapons training for two al-Qaida associates beginning in December 2000. He says that a militant known as Abdullah al-Araqi had been sent to Iraq several times between 1997 and 2000 for help in acquiring poisons and gasses. Abdullah al-Araqi characterized the relationship he forged with Iraqi officials as successful.

As I said at the outset, none of this should come as a surprise to any of us. Terrorism has been a tool used by Saddam for decades. Saddam was a supporter of terrorism long before these terrorist networks had a name, and this support continues. The nexus of poisons and terror is new. The nexus of Iraq and terror is old. The combination is lethal.

With this track record, Iraqi denials of supporting terrorism take their place alongside the other Iraqi denials of weapons of mass destruction. It is all a web of lies.

When we confront a regime that harbors ambitions for regional domination, hides weapons of mass destruction, and provides haven and active support for terrorists, we are not confronting the past; we are confronting the present. And unless we act, we are confronting an even more frightening future.

The Evolving Terrorist Threat

From Country Reports on Terrorism 2004

Al-Qaida leadership was degraded through arrests and ongoing Pakistani operations to assert greater control along the border with Afghanistan where some al-Qaida leaders are believed to hide. Numerous al-Qaida and affiliated foot soldiers were captured or killed during the year.

- Pakistani authorities captured al-Qaida communications expert and Heathrow bomb plot suspect Naeem Noor Khan and US Embassy bombing suspect Ahmed Khalfan Ghailani in July 2004, and killed Amjad Farooqui, suspected in the murder of US journalist Daniel Pearl, in September 2004.
- Saudi security forces killed several top leaders of the al-Qaida organization in Saudi Arabia, including Khalid Ali al-Hajj and Abdulaziz al-Muqrin.
- Abu Bakar Ba'asyir, leader of the al-Qaida-affiliated Jemaah Islamiya remained in jail pending his early 2005 trial for involvement in the 2002 Bali bombings.
- The Filipino Antiterrorism Task Force captured seven foreigners in 2004 believed to be elements of al-Qaida and Jemaah Islamiya.
- British authorities in August 2004 arrested suspected al-Qaida-affiliated individuals who were subsequently indicted in the United States for plotting to attack financial institutions in the United States.

Many senior al-Qaida leaders remained at large, continued to plan attacks against the United States, US interests, and US partners, and sought to foment attacks by inspiring new groups of Sunni Muslim extremists to undertake violent acts in the name of jihad. In some cases, al-Qaida attempted to bring other extremist groups under its banner, while in other cases, groups claimed allegiance to al-Qaida despite little evidence of any connection with al-Qaida leaders. In still other cases, the existence of new groups only became evident following an attack.

- Al-Qaida cells continued to carry out attacks in Saudi Arabia throughout 2004.
- Al-Qaida-affiliate Jemaah Islamiya continued to plot attacks against the United States, Australian and other foreign interests in Indonesia, bombing the Australian Embassy in September 2004.
- The al-Qaida cell in East Africa, including terrorists linked to the 1998 bombings of US Embassies in Nairobi and Dar es Salaam and the 2002 attacks on a Mombasa hotel and an Israeli commercial aircraft, remained at large, and are suspected of planning new attacks.
- Notorious terrorist Abu Musab al-Zarqawi pledged the fealty of himself and his group in Iraq to bin Ladin; al-Zarqawi is now the recognized leader of al-Qaida in Iraq.
- The March 2004 bombing of commuter trains in Madrid that killed 191 innocent people was executed by a previously unknown group of jihadist terrorists (mostly Moroccan immigrants resident in Spain for years) inspired by, but without direction from, al-Qaida.
- The new leader of the GSPC in Algeria announced his affiliation with al-Qaida, but there was no evidence of assistance or direction from al-Qaida leadership.

The latter two incidents illustrate what many analysts believe is a new phase of the global war on terrorism, one in which local groups inspired by al-Qaida organize and carry out attacks with little or no support or direction from al-Qaida itself.

As al-Qaida itself weakens and local groups take on greater responsibility for planning, acquiring resources and carrying out attacks in their localities, it will be ever more important for the United States to help partners who require assistance to counter this new manifestation of the terrorist threat. Furthermore, although al-Qaida remains the primary concern regarding possible WMD threats, the number of groups expressing an interest in such materials is increasing, and WMD technology and know-how is proliferating within the jihadist community.

International Response

Overview of International Response

Anna Sabasteanski

The development of terrorism as an international phenomenon began in Europe in the 1970s, when groups such as the Irish Republican Army, Action Directe, the Red Brigades, ETA and others collaborated with one another for training, financing, and operational support, including assistance in attacks in multiple countries (described in the Country Reports and Chronology of Significant Terrorists Incidents.) National liberation groups such as the African National Congress (ANC) and various Palestinian organizations established bases in Europe from which to conduct their campaigns, including accepted political activities. In the Middle East, an increasing number of attacks connected to the unresolved Palestinian problem targeted both states supporting Israel and Palestinians willing to negotiate or attempt a peaceful resolution. International travel and international communications, while bringing the world's peoples closer together, also made possible the increasingly international and disassociated form of contemporary terrorism we see today.

The ways in which the United States interacts with the international community are described below, followed by documents detailing the international response to the September 11 attacks, U.N. action against terrorism, and international counterterrorism legislation.

U.S. Efforts

U.S. initiatives to expand international cooperation in combating terrorism were driven by the high-profile and long-running hostage takings in Iran (1979–1980) and Lebanon (during the civil war), the downing of Pan Am 103 over Lockerbie, Scotland (1988), and the East African embassy bombings (1998). The United States sought legal cooperation, international sanctions, and other diplomatic measures.

Over the years, the organizations with which the United States has cooperated in the international response to terrorism have included the following:

- African Union (formerly the Organization of African Unity, OAU)
- Arab League
- Association of Southeast Asian Nations (ASEAN)
- European Union (EU)
- Group of 8 (G-8)
- International Monetary Fund (IMF)
- Interpol
- North Atlantic Treaty Organization (NATO)
- Nonaligned Movement
- Organization of American States (OAS)
- Organization of the Islamic Conference (OIC)
- Various United Nations agencies
- World Bank

International Response to September 11

From Patterns of Global Terrorism 2001

The attacks on September 11 shocked the world and marked the first time that the international community united to condemn the atrocities. The collapse of the World Trade Center provided an indelible image of this new face of international terrorism, which was reflected in the immediate global response. Documents from Appendix H in Patterns of Global Terrorism 2001 *demonstrated this international consensus.*

NATO Press Release, 12 September 2001

On September 12th, the North Atlantic Council met again in response to the appalling attacks perpetrated yesterday against the United States.

The Council agreed that if it is determined that this attack was directed from abroad against the United States, it shall be regarded as an action covered by Article 5 of the Washington Treaty, which states that an armed attack against one or more of the Allies in Europe or North America shall be considered an attack against them all.

The commitment to collective self-defence embodied in the Washington Treaty was first entered into in circumstances very different from those that exist now, but it remains no less valid and no less essential today, in a world subject to the scourge of international terrorism. When the Heads of State and Government of NATO met in Washington in 1999, they paid tribute to the success of the Alliance in ensuring the freedom of its members during the Cold War and in making possible a Europe that was whole and free. But they also recognised the existence of a wide variety of risks to security, some of them quite unlike those that had called NATO into existence. More specifically, they condemned terrorism as a serious threat to peace and stability and reaffirmed their determination to combat it in accordance with their commitments to one another, their international commitments and national legislation.

Article 5 of the Washington Treaty stipulates that in the event of attacks falling within its purview, each Ally will assist the Party that has been attacked by taking such action as it deems necessary. Accordingly, the United States' NATO Allies stand ready to provide the assistance that may be required as a consequence of these acts of barbarism.

NATO Secretary General, Lord Robertson, 2 October 2001

This morning, the United States briefed the North Atlantic Council on the results of the investigation into who was responsible for the horrific terrorist attacks which took place on September 11.

The briefing was given by Ambassador Frank Taylor, the United States Department of State Coordinator for Counterterrorism.

This morning's briefing follows those offered by United States Deputy Secretary of State Richard Armitage and United States Deputy Secretary of Defense Paul Wolfowitz, and illustrates the commitment of the United States to maintain close cooperation with Allies.

Today's was classified briefing and so I cannot give you all the details. Briefings are also being given directly by the United States to the Allies in their capitals.

The briefing addressed the events of September 11 themselves, the results of the investigation so far, what is known about Osama bin Laden and the al-Qaida organisation and their involvement in the attacks and in previous terrorist activity, and the links between al-Qaida and the Taliban regime in Afghanistan.

The facts are clear and compelling. The information presented points conclusively to an al-Qaida role in the September 11 attacks.

We know that the individuals who carried out these attacks were part of the world-wide terrorist network of al-Qaida, headed by Osama bin Laden and his key lieutenants and protected by the Taliban.

On the basis of this briefing, it has now been determined that the attack against the United States on September 11 was directed from abroad and shall therefore be regarded as an action covered by Article 5 of the Washington Treaty, which states that an armed attack on one or more of the Allies in Europe or North America shall be considered an attack against them all.

I want to reiterate that the United States of America can rely on the full support of its 18 NATO Allies in the campaign against terrorism.

Organization of the Islamic Conference Press Release

Given the international repercussions still being felt around the world since the terrorist attacks against major facilities and buildings in the United States of America, Dr. Abdelouahed Belkeziz, Secretary-General of the Organization of the Islamic Conference (OIC), reaffirmed the OIC position announced immediately after the attacks and strongly condemning the terrorist attacks that caused the death of a great number of innocent people.

The Secretary-General stated that those acts are diametrically opposed to the religion and teachings of Islam, which proscribe the unjust taking of a human life and stress the sanctity of human life. Moreover, those acts are in clear contradiction with innumerable resolutions adopted by the Organization of the Islamic Conference which condemn terrorism in all its forms and manifestations and are also in contradiction with the Code of Conduct on Combating International Terrorism and the OIC 1998 Convention on Combating Terrorism, which makes it crystal clear that Islam repudiates and denounces terrorism and exhorts the Member States to "refrain from assisting or supporting terrorists in any way, shape or form, including the harboring of terrorists and granting them financial help or other forms of assistance." The Secretary-General also reaffirmed his support of the contents of the UN Security Council resolutions Nos. 1267, 1333, and 1368 and the UN General Assembly recommendation No. 1/56, which were all adopted unanimously. He urged the Member States to continue to respond positively to the contents of those resolutions and recommendations.

The Secretary-General further expressed his satisfaction at the positive cooperation shown by the Member States with regard to the recent campaign against international terrorism in all its forms and manifestations but also underscored the need to distinguish the terrorism practiced by groups and individuals from the national resistance of peoples for liberation from occupation and colonialism.

The Secretary-General stressed the willingness of the Organization of the Islamic Conference to participate in any effort aimed at reaching a consensus on the definition of terrorism.

Meeting of Consultation of Ministers of Foreign Affairs

Resolution adopted at the first plenary session, held on 21 September 2001:

The Twenty-Fourth Meeting of Consultation of Ministers of Foreign Affairs Acting as Organ of Consultation in Application of the Inter-American Treaty of Reciprocal Assistance,

CONSIDERING the terrorist attacks perpetrated in the

United States of America on September 11, 2001, against innocent people from many nations;

RECALLING the inherent right of states to act in the exercise of the right of individual and collective self-defense in accordance with the Charter of the United Nations and with the Inter-American Treaty of Reciprocal Assistance (Rio Treaty);

EMPHASIZING that Article 2 of the Charter of the Organization of American States (OAS) proclaims as essential purposes of the Organization to strengthen the peace and security of the continent and to provide for common action on the part of member states in the event of aggression;

CONSIDERING that the obligation of mutual assistance and common defense of the American republics is essentially related to their democratic ideals and to their will to cooperate permanently in the fulfillment of the principles and purposes of a policy of peace; and

TAKING NOTE of resolution CP/RES. 797 (1293/01), dated September 19, 2001, of the Permanent Council of the Organization of American States acting as Provisional Organ of Consultation of the Rio Treaty, which called for a Meeting of Ministers of Foreign Affairs to serve as the Organ of Consultation under the Rio Treaty, in connection with the September 11, 2001, terrorist attacks in the United States,

RESOLVES:

That these terrorist attacks against the United States of America are attacks against all American states and that in accordance with all the relevant provisions of the Inter-American Treaty of Reciprocal Assistance (Rio Treaty) and the principle of continental solidarity, all States Parties to the Rio Treaty shall provide effective reciprocal assistance to address such attacks and the threat of any similar attacks against any American state, and to maintain the peace and security of the continent.

That, if a State Party has reason to believe that persons in its territory may have been involved in or in any way assisted the September 11, 2001 attacks, are harboring the perpetrators, or may otherwise be involved in terrorist activities, such State Party shall use all legally available measures to pursue, capture, extradite, and punish those individuals.

That the States Parties shall render additional assistance and support to the United States and to each other, as appropriate, to address the September 11 attacks, and also to prevent future terrorist acts.

That the States Parties shall keep the Organ of Consultation duly informed of all measures that they take in accordance with this resolution.

That this Meeting of Foreign Ministers in its capacity as Organ of Consultation shall remain open for the purpose of ensuring the prompt and effective implementation of this resolution and, if necessary, of taking appropriate additional measures to address this matter.

That we hereby designate a committee, to be composed of the representatives to the OAS Permanent Council of each State Party to the Rio Treaty, for the purpose of engaging in additional consultations and of taking measures in furtherance of the foregoing.

That we hereby request that all of the American Governments and the Organization of American States lend their full cooperation in the implementation of this resolution.

That the Permanent Council be entrusted with taking appropriate measures for implementing resolution RC.23/doc.7/01, adopted by the Twenty-third Meeting of Consultation of Ministers of Foreign Affairs.

That the Security Council of the United Nations shall be informed promptly of the text of the present resolution and of any decisions that may be taken in connection with this matter.

2001 ASEAN Declaration on Joint Action to Counter Terrorism

We, the Heads of State/Government of the Association of Southeast Asian Nations (ASEAN) gathered in Bandar Seri Begawan for the Seventh ASEAN Summit,

Recalling the agreement among Heads of State/Government during the Second Informal Summit in December 1997 in Kuala Lumpur to take firm and stern measures to combat transnational crime,

Reaffirming our primary responsibility in ensuring the peaceful and progressive development of our respective counties and our region,

Deeply concerned over the formidable challenge posed by terrorism to regional and international peace and stability as well as to economic development,

Underlying the importance of strengthening regional and international cooperation in meeting the challenges confronting us,

Do hereby,

Unequivocally condemn in the strongest terms the horrifying terrorist attacks in New York City, Washington D.C. and Pennsylvania on September 11 2001 and consider such acts as an attack against humanity and an assault on all of us;

Extend our deepest sympathy and condolences to the people and Government of the United States of America and the families of the victims from nations all around the world, including those of our nationals;

View acts of terrorism in all its forms and manifestations, committed wherever, whenever and by whomsoever, as a profound threat to international peace and security which require concerted action to protect and defend all peoples and the peace and security of the world;

Reject any attempt to link terrorism with any religion or race;

Believe terrorism to be a direct challenge to the attainment of peace, progress and prosperity of ASEAN and the realisation of ASEAN Vision 2020;

Commit to counter, prevent and suppress all forms of terrorist acts in accordance with the charter of the United Nations and other international law, especially taking into account the importance of all relevant UN resolutions;

Ensure that, in observing the above, all cooperative efforts to combat terrorism at the regional level shall consider joint practical counter-terrorism measures in line with specific circumstances in the region and in each member country;

Recommit ourselves to pursue effective policies and strategies aimed at enhancing the well-being of our people, which will be our national contribution in the fight against terrorism;

Note that, towards this end, ASEAN had established a regional framework for fighting transnational crime and adopted an ASEAN Plan of Action that outlines a cohesive regional strategy to prevent, control and neutralise transnational crime;

Approve fully the initiatives of the Third ASEAN Ministers Meeting on Transnational Crime (AMMTC) held in October 2001 to focus on terrorism and deal effectively with the issue at all levels and endorse the convening of an Ad Hoc Experts Group Meeting and special sessions of the SOMTC and AMMTC that will focus on terrorism;

Warmly welcome Malaysia's offer to host the Special AMMTC on issues of terrorism in April 2002. This meeting would represent a significant step by ASEAN to the United Nations' call to enhance coordination of national, sub-regional and international efforts to strengthen a global response to this serious challenge and threat to international security;

In strengthening further ASEAN's counter-terrorism efforts, we task our Ministers concerned to follow-up on the implementation of this declaration to advance ASEAN's efforts to fight terrorism by undertaking the following additional practical measures:

Review and strengthen our national mechanisms to combat terrorism;

Call for the early signing/ratification of or accession to all relevant anti-terrorist conventions including the International Convention for the Suppression of the Financing of Terrorism;

Deepen cooperation among our front-line law enforcement agencies in combating terrorism and sharing "best practices";

Study relevant international conventions on terrorism with the view to integrating them with ASEAN mechanisms on combating international terrorism;

Enhance information/intelligence exchange to facilitate the flow of information, in particular on terrorists and terrorist organisations, their movement and funding, and any other information needed to protect lives, property and the security of all modes of travel;

Strengthen existing cooperation and coordination between the AMMTC and other relevant ASEAN bodes in countering, preventing and suppressing all forms of terrorists acts. Particular attention would be paid to finding ways to combat terrorist organisations, support infrastructure and funding and bringing the perpetrators to justice;

Develop regional capacity building programmes to enhance existing capabilities of ASEAN member countries to investigate, detect, monitor and report on terrorist acts;

Discuss and explore practical ideas and initiatives to increase ASEAN's role in and involvement with the international community including extra-regional partners within existing frameworks such as the ASEAN + 3, the ASEAN Dialogue Partners and the ASEAN Regional Forum (ARF), to make the fight against terrorism a truly regional and global endeavor;

Strengthen cooperation at bilateral, regional and international levels in combating terrorism in a comprehensive manner and affirm that at the international level the United Nations should play a major role in this regard.

We, the Leaders of ASEAN, pledge to remain seized with the matter, and call on other regions and countries to work with ASEAN in the global struggle against terrorism.

Adopted this Fifth Day of November 2001 in Bandar Seri Begawan, Brunei Darussalam.

OAU Mechanism for Conflict Prevention, Management and Resolution

Communique of The Seventy-Sixth Ordinary Session of The Central Organ of The OAU Mechanism for Conflict Prevention, Management and Resolution Held at The Ambassadorial Level. Addis Ababa, Ethiopia, 20 September 2001

The Central Organ of the OAU Mechanism for Conflict Prevention, Management and Resolution held its 76th Ordinary Session at Ambassadorial level in Addis Ababa, Ethiopia, on Thursday, 20 September 2001. H.E. Mr. Simataa Akapelwa, Ambassador of the Republic of Zambia to Ethiopia and Permanent Representative to the OAU, chaired the Session, which was open-ended. It was also the first meeting of the Central Organ to be attended by the new Secretary-General, H.E. Mr. Amara Essy.

The Central Organ considered the Report of the Secretary-General on the preparation of the Inter-Congolese Dialogue, scheduled to start in Addis Ababa on 15 October 2001. It was also briefed on the recent developments in the peace process in Sierra Leone and in the relations between the countries of the Mano River Union. The Central Organ was further briefed on the recent terrorist attacks in the United States of America.

On this occasion, the Secretary-General made [a] statement in which he highlighted the priorities of the General Secretariat in the upcoming months.

At the end of its deliberations, the Central Organ decided as follows:

CONDEMNS unequivocally the horrific terrorist attacks that have caused enormous loss of human life and destruction in New York, Washington DC and Pennsylvania;

EXPRESSES to the Government and people of the United States of America the full solidarity and the deepest condolence of the OAU and the entire people of Africa over this tragedy which affected not only the people of the USA, but humanity as a whole;

STRESSES the urgent need to bring to justice the perpetrators and sponsors of these terrorist attacks and CALLS ON the international community to work in a more coordinated and determined manner to prevent and combat terrorism;

RECALLS the adoption of the OAU Convention on the Prevention and Combating of Terrorism and APPEALS to all Member States that have not yet done so, to sign and ratify this instrument.

U.N. Actions Against Terrorism

From Patterns of Global Terrorism 2001

The United Nations' current strategy for countering terrorism (as reported by the United Nations Information Service, http://www.unis.unvienna.org/unis/pressrels/2005/sg2095.html), was presented in March 2005 by the Secretary-General Kofi Annan. The strategy contains five main elements: (1) dissuade disaffected groups from choosing terrorism as a tactic to achieve their goals; (2) deny terrorists the means to carry out their attacks; (3) deter States from supporting terrorists; (4) develop State capacity to prevent terrorism; and (5) defend human rights in the struggle against terrorism. The excerpt below from Appendix F of Patterns of Global Terrorism 2001 *describes the U.N. role more fully.*

U.N. Role in Fighting Terrorism

In the aftermath of 11 September, the United Nations promptly intensified its focus on terrorism, taking steps to provide a mandate for strengthened international engagement in the fight against terrorism.

The Security Council adopted three important resolutions, 1368, 1373 and 1377, which affirmed the right of self-defense, found terrorism to be a threat to international peace and security, stressed the accountability of the supporter as well as the perpetrator of terrorist acts, obliged member states to limit the ability of terrorists and terrorist organizations to operate internationally by freezing assets of terrorist-affiliated persons and organizations and denying them safehaven, among other things, and set forth a Ministerial Declaration on International Terrorism.

The Security Council also established a Counter Terrorism Committee (CTC) to oversee implementation of UNSC Resolution 1373. Member states sent reports to the CTC in December 2001 on the steps they are taking to fight terrorism in seven critical areas: legislation, financial asset controls, customs, immigration, extradition, law enforcement and arms traffic.

The General Assembly adopted two antiterrorism resolutions that condemned the "heinous acts of terrorism" in Washington, Pennsylvania, and New York. The General Assembly also continued its work on the negotiation of international terrorism conventions. Twelve such conventions have been adopted to date.

Secretary General Kofi Annan repeatedly condemned terrorism acts, as in a speech he delivered on 12 September: "All nations of the world must be united in their solidarity with the victims of terrorism, and in their determination to take action, both against the terrorists themselves and against all those who give them any kind of shelter, assistance or encouragement."

Specialized agencies of the United Nations, including, the International Civil Aviation Organization and the International Maritime Organization also adopted resolutions committing members to take measures to limit terrorists' ability to act.

The International Atomic Energy Agency, an autonomous organization affiliated with the UN, adopted a resolution addressing measures to protect against acts of nuclear terrorism and is developing a program to coordinate assistance to member states in improving security of nuclear facilities and of nuclear and radioactive materials.

U.N. Security Council Resolution 1368 (2001) September 12, 2001

The Security Council,

Reaffirming the principles and purposes of the Charter of the United Nations, Determined to combat by all means threats to international peace and security caused by terrorist acts, Recognizing the inherent right of individual or collective self-defence in accordance with the Charter,

1. Unequivocally condemns in the strongest terms the horrifying terrorist attacks which took place on September 11 2001 in New York, Washington (D.C.) and Pennsylvania and regards such acts, like any act of international terrorism, as a threat to international peace and security;
2. Expresses its deepest sympathy and condolences to the victims and their families and to the People and Government of the United States of America;
3. Calls on all States to work together urgently to bring to justice the perpetrators, organizers and sponsors of these terrorist attacks and stresses that those responsible for aiding, supporting or harbouring the perpetrators, organizers and sponsors of these acts will be held accountable;
4. Calls also on the international community to redouble their efforts to prevent and suppress terrorist acts including by increased cooperation and full implementation of the relevant international anti-terrorist conventions and Security Council resolutions, in particular resolution 1269 of 19 October 1999;
5. Expresses its readiness to take all necessary steps to respond to the terrorist attacks of September 11 2001, and to combat all forms of terrorism, in accordance with its responsibilities under the Charter of the United Nations;
6. Decides to remain seized of the matter.

United Nations Security Council Resolution 1373 (2001)

Adopted by the Security Council at its 4385th meeting, on 28 September 2001

The Security Council, Reaffirming its resolutions 1269 (1999) of 19 October 1999 and 1368 (2001) of 12 September 2001,

Reaffirming also its unequivocal condemnation of the terrorist attacks which took place in New York, Washington, D.C. and Pennsylvania on September 11 2001, and expressing its determination to prevent all such acts,

Reaffirming further that such acts, like any act of international terrorism, constitute a threat to international peace and security,

Reaffirming the inherent right of individual or collective self-defence as recognized by the Charter of the United Nations as reiterated in resolution 1368 (2001),

Reaffirming the need to combat by all means, in accordance with the Charter of the United Nations, threats to international peace and security caused by terrorist acts,

Deeply concerned by the increase, in various regions of the world, of acts of terrorism motivated by intolerance or extremism,

Calling on States to work together urgently to prevent and suppress terrorist acts, including through increased cooperation and full implementation of the relevant international conventions relating to terrorism,

Recognizing the need for States to complement international cooperation by taking additional measures to prevent and suppress, in their territories through all lawful means, the financing and preparation of any acts of terrorism,

Reaffirming the principle established by the General Assembly in its declaration of October 1970 (resolution 2625 (XXV)) and reiterated by the Security Council in its resolution 1189 (1998) of 13 August 1998, namely that every State has the duty to refrain from organizing, instigating, assisting or participating in terrorist acts in another State or acquiescing in organized activities within its territory directed towards the commission of such acts,

Acting under Chapter VII of the Charter of the United Nations,

1. Decides that all States shall:
   (a) Prevent and suppress the financing of terrorist acts;
   (b) Criminalize the wilful provision or collection, by any means, directly or indirectly, of funds by their nationals or in their territories with the intention that the funds should be used, or in the knowledge that they are to be used, in order to carry out terrorist acts;
   (c) Freeze without delay funds and other financial assets or economic resources of persons who commit, or attempt to commit, terrorist acts or participate in or facilitate the commission of terrorist acts; of entities owned or controlled directly or indirectly by such persons; and of persons and entities acting on behalf of, or at the direction of such persons and entities, including funds derived or generated from property owned or controlled directly or indirectly by such persons and associated persons and entities;
   (d) Prohibit their nationals or any persons and entities within their territories from making any funds, financial assets or economic resources or financial or other related services available, directly or indirectly, for the benefit of persons who commit or attempt to commit or facilitate or participate in the commission of terrorist acts, of entities owned or controlled, directly or indirectly, by such persons and of persons and entities acting on behalf of or at the direction of such persons;

2. Decides also that all States shall:
   (a) Refrain from providing any form of support, active or passive, to entities or persons involved in terrorist acts, including by suppressing recruitment of members of terrorist groups and eliminating the supply of weapons to terrorists;
   (b) Take the necessary steps to prevent the commission of terrorist acts, including by provision of early warning to other States by exchange of information;
   (c) Deny safe haven to those who finance, plan, support, or commit terrorist acts, or provide safe havens;
   (d) Prevent those who finance, plan, facilitate or commit terrorist acts from using their respective territories for those purposes against other States or their citizens;
   (e) Ensure that any person who participates in the financing, planning, preparation or perpetration of terrorist acts or in supporting terrorist acts is brought to justice and ensure that, in addition to any other measures against them, such terrorist acts are established as serious criminal offences in domestic laws and regulations and that the punishment duly reflects the seriousness of such terrorist acts;
   (f) Afford one another the greatest measure of assistance in connection with criminal investigations or criminal proceedings relating to the financing or support of terrorist acts, including assistance in obtaining evidence in their possession necessary for the proceedings;
   (g) Prevent the movement of terrorists or terrorist groups by effective border controls and controls on issuance of identity papers and travel documents, and through measures for preventing counterfeiting, forgery or fraudulent use of identity papers and travel documents;

3. Calls upon all States to:
   (a) Find ways of intensifying and accelerating the exchange of operational information, especially regarding actions or movements of terrorist persons or networks; forged or falsified travel documents; traffic in arms, explosives or sensitive materials; use of communications technologies by terrorist groups; and the threat posed by the possession of weapons of mass destruction by terrorist groups;
   (b) Exchange information in accordance with international and domestic law and cooperate on administrative and judicial matters to prevent the commission of terrorist acts;
   (c) Cooperate, particularly through bilateral and multilateral arrangements and agreements, to prevent and suppress terrorist attacks and take action against perpetrators of such acts;

(d) Become parties as soon as possible to the relevant international conventions and protocols relating to terrorism, including the International Convention for the Suppression of the Financing of Terrorism of 9 December 1999;

(e) Increase cooperation and fully implement the relevant international conventions and protocols relating to terrorism and Security Council resolutions 1269 (1999) and 1368 (2001);

(f) Take appropriate measures in conformity with the relevant provisions of national and international law, including international standards of human rights, before granting refugee status, for the purpose of ensuring that the asylum-seeker has not planned, facilitated or participated in the commission of terrorist acts;

(g) Ensure, in conformity with international law, that refugee status is not abused by the perpetrators, organizers or facilitators of terrorist acts, and that claims of political motivation are not recognized as grounds for refusing requests for the extradition of alleged terrorists;

4. Notes with concern the close connection between international terrorism and transnational organized crime, illicit drugs, money laundering, illegal armstrafficking, and illegal movement of nuclear, chemical, biological and other potentially deadly materials, and in this regard emphasizes the need to enhance coordination of efforts on national, subregional, regional and international levels in order to strengthen a global response to this serious challenge and threat to international security;

5. Declares that acts, methods, and practices of terrorism are contrary to the purposes and principles of the United Nations and that knowingly financing, planning and inciting terrorist acts are also contrary to the purposes and principles of the United Nations;

6. Decides to establish, in accordance with rule 28 of its provisional rules of procedure, a Committee of the Security Council, consisting of all the members of the Council, to monitor implementation of this resolution, with the assistance of appropriate expertise, and calls upon all States to report to the Committee, no later than 90 days from the date of adoption of this resolution and thereafter according to a timetable to be proposed by the Committee, on the steps they have taken to implement this resolution;

7. Directs the Committee to delineate its tasks, submit a work programme within 30 days of the adoption of this resolution, and to consider the support it requires, in consultation with the Secretary-General;

8. Expresses its determination to take all necessary steps in order to ensure the full implementation of this resolution, in accordance with its responsibilities under the Charter;

9. Decides to remain seized of this matter.

International Counterterrorism Laws

Anna Sabasteanski

The following excerpt from Chapter 4 of *Country Reports on Terrorism 2004* describes the conventions and protocols that the United Nations has promulgated to combat terrorism.

There are 12 universal conventions and protocols currently in force against terrorism that have been developed under the auspices of the United Nations and its specialized agencies and are open to participation by all member states. Various UN Security Council resolutions, including Resolution 1373, have called upon all member states to become parties to these international instruments. However, many states are not yet parties to all 12 instruments (and thus have not yet implemented them), while still other states have not fully implemented them despite becoming parties. (A thirteenth instrument, the Nuclear Terrorism Convention, was adopted by the UN General Assembly on April 13, 2005, and will be opened for signature in September 2005.)

These conventions and protocols were negotiated from 1963 to 1999. Most are penal in nature with a common format. Typically, they define a particular type of terrorist conduct as an offense under the convention, such as seizure of an aircraft in flight by threat or force; require state parties to penalize that activity in their domestic law; identify certain bases upon which the relevant state parties are required to establish jurisdiction over the defined offense, such as registration, territoriality, or nationality; and create an obligation on the state party in which an accused offender is found to establish jurisdiction over the offense and to refer the offense for prosecution if the party does not extradite pursuant to other provisions of the convention. This last element gives effect to the principle of "no safe haven for terrorists." UN Security Council Resolution 1373 particularly stresses this principle and obligates all states to "deny safe haven to those who finance, plan, support, or commit terrorist acts, or provide safe havens."

U.N. Conventions

1. Convention on the Prevention and Punishment of Crimes against Internationally Protected Persons, including Diplomatic Agents, adopted by the General Assembly of the United Nations on 14 December 1973.
2. International Convention against the Taking of Hostages, adopted by the General Assembly of the United Nations on 17 December 1979.
3. International Convention for the Suppression of the Financing of Terrorism, adopted by the General Assembly of the United Nations on 9 December 1999.

4. Convention on Offences and Certain Other Acts Committed on Board Aircraft, signed at Tokyo on 14 September 1963.
5. Convention for the Suppression of Unlawful Seizure of Aircraft, signed at the Hague on 16 December 1970.
6. Convention for the Suppression of Unlawful Acts against the Safety of Civil Aviation, signed at Montreal on 23 September 1971.
7. Convention on the Physical Protection of Nuclear Material, signed at Vienna on 3 March 1980.
8. Protocol on the Suppression of Unlawful Acts of Violence at Airports Serving International Civil Aviation, supplementary to the Convention for the Suppression of Unlawful Acts against the Safety of Civil Aviation, signed at Montreal on 24 February 1988.
9. Convention for the Suppression of Unlawful Acts against the Safety of Maritime Navigation, done at Rome on 10 March 1988.
10. Protocol for the Suppression of Unlawful Acts against the Safety of Fixed Platforms Located on the Continental Shelf, done at Rome on 10 March 1988.
11. Convention on the Marking of Plastic Explosives for the Purpose of Detection, signed at Montreal on 1 March 1991.

U.N. Security Council Resolutions Relating to Terrorism

2005
- Res.1611 Threats to international peace and security caused by terrorist acts

2004
- Res.1566 Threats to international peace and security
- Res.1540 Threats to international peace and security
- Res.1535 Threats to international peace and security caused by terrorist acts
- Res.1530 on the bomb attacks in Madrid, Spain, on 11 March 2004
- Res.1526 Threats to international peace and security caused by terrorist acts

2003
- Res.1516 on the bomb attacks in Istanbul, Turkey, on 15 November 2003 and 20 November 2003
- Res.1465 on the bomb attack in Bogota, Colombia
- Res.1456 High-level meeting of the Security Council: combating terrorism
- Res.1455 on improving implementation of measures imposed by paragraph 4 (b) of Resolution 1267 (1999), paragraph 8 (c) of Resolution 1333 (2000) and paragraphs 1 and 2 of Resolution 1390 (2002) on measures against the Taliban and Al-Qaida

2002
- Res.1452 on implementation of measures imposed by paragraph 4 (b) of Resolution 1267 (1999) and paragraph 1 and 2 (a) of Resolution 1390 (2002)
- Res.1450 on condemning the terrorist bomb attack, in Kikambala, Kenya, and the attempted missile attack on the airline departing Mombasa, Kenya, 28 November 2002
- Res.1440 on condemning the act of taking hostages in Moscow, Russian Federation, on 23 October 2002
- Res.1438 on the bomb attacks in Bali, Indonesia

2001
- Res.1377 on the adoption of declaration on the global effort to combat terrorism
- Res.1373 on international cooperation to combat threats to international peace and security caused by terrorist acts
- Res.1368 condemning the terrorist attacks of 11 September 2001 in New York, Washington, D.C. and Pennsylvania, United States of America
- Res.1363 on the establishment of a mechanism to monitor the implementation of measures imposed by resolutions 1267 (1999) and 1333 (2000)

2000
- Res.1333 on measures against the Taliban

1999
- Res.1269 on international cooperation in the fight against terrorism
- Res.1267 on measures against the Taliban

1998
- Res.1214 on the situation in Afghanistan
- Res.1189 concerning the terrorist bomb attacks of 7 Aug. 1998 in Kenya and Tanzania

1996
- Res.1054 on sanctions against the Sudan in connection with non-compliance with Security Council resolution 1044 (1996) demanding extradition to Ethiopia of the three suspects wanted in connection with assassination attempt on President Mubarak of Egypt
- Res.1044 calling upon the Sudan to extradite to Ethiopia the three suspects wanted in connection with the assassination attempt against President Mubarak of Egypt

1992
- Res.731 on the destruction of Pan American flight 103 and Union des transports aériens flights 772
- Res.748 on sanctions against the Libyan Arab Jamahiriya

1991
- Res.687 on restoration of the sovereignty, independence and territorial integrity of Kuwait

1989
- Res.635 on marking of plastic or sheet explosives for the purpose of detection

Regional Conventions on Terrorism
- OAU Convention on the Prevention and Combating of Terrorism, adopted at Algiers on 14 July 1999.
- Convention of the Organization of the Islamic Conference on Combating International Terrorism, adopted at Ouagadougou on 1 July 1999.
- Treaty on Cooperation among States Members of the Commonwealth of Independent States in Combating Terrorism, done at Minsk on 4 June 1999.
- Arab Convention on the Suppression of Terrorism, signed at a meeting held at the General Secretariat of the League of Arab States in Cairo on 22 April 1998.
- SAARC Regional Convention on Suppression of Terrorism, signed at Kathmandu on 4 November 1987.
- European Convention on the Suppression of Terrorism, concluded at Strasbourg on 27 January 1977.
- OAS Convention to Prevent and Punish Acts of Terrorism Taking the Form of Crimes against Persons and Related Extortion that are of International Significance, concluded at Washington, D.C. on 2 February 1971.

PART 2

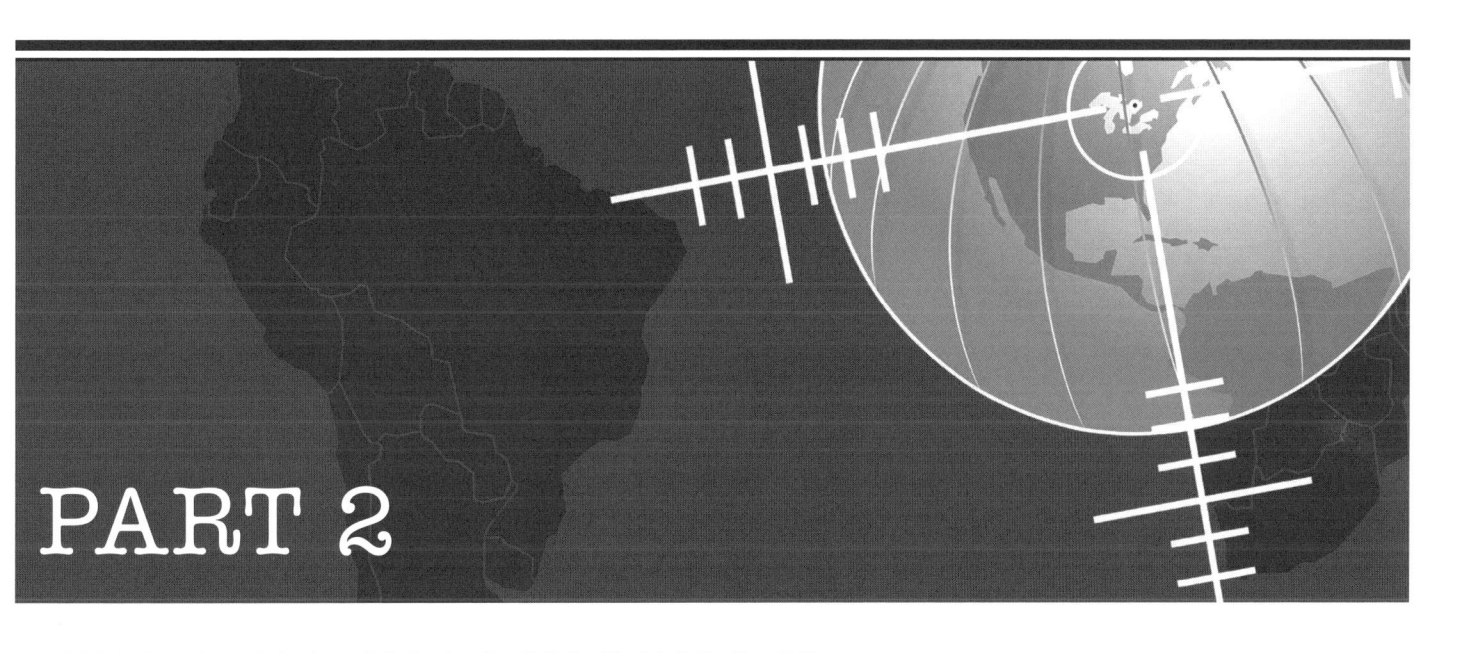

INTERNATIONAL TERRORIST GROUPS

Overview of International Terrorist Groups

Anna Sabasteanski

The U.S. State Department is required by law to include in its annual report on global terrorism information on any foreign terrorist group or umbrella organization that has been responsible for the kidnapping or death of a U.S. citizen during the previous five years. The report may also include other groups that the secretary of state deems should be included. (Because these organizations pose threats to citizens of many nations, they are also referred to as "international terrorist groups.")

To comply with this requirement, *Patterns of Global Terrorism* includes descriptions of foreign terrorist organizations (FTOs), a list of their activities, estimated strength, their location and area of operations, and whether they receive some form of external aid. Once an organization has been designated an FTO, it is unlawful for U.S. persons or any persons subject to the jurisdiction of the United States to provide that organization with financing or other material support, and U.S. financial institutions are required to block funds of the FTO and its agents and report that they are doing so to the Treasury Department. There may be additional sanctions as well; for example, members of FTOs may be denied visas or travel privileges to the United States. More detail on this is provided in the Congressional Research Service (CRS) report "The 'FTO List' and Congress: Sanctioning Designated Foreign Terrorist Organizations," which follows.

In December 2004 there were forty FTOs. The U.S. government has dozens of other terrorist lists, including screening systems used for border security, intelligence lists, and so on, but those lists are separate and distinct from the FTO designation. The only other listing that contributes data to *Patterns of Global Terrorism* is that of state sponsors of terrorism (see section on State Sponsors of Terrorism in Part 1).

In addition to discussing FTOs, *Patterns of Global Terrorism* includes information on other groups of interest. These could be organizations that, while not posing a terrorist threat, are dangerous to the United States or its allies in some way or that may pose a threat in the future, or that are particularly newsworthy or noteworthy, as determined by the Secretary of State. Both the organizations that are designated FTOs and those considered groups of interest have changed over time; observing what groups have been considered a threat over the years provides interesting insight into the ever-changing nature of terrorism.

In the 1980s, groups that are now considered forces for national liberation were reported, such as the African National Congress (ANC), which is now South Africa's governing party. Early indicators of antiglobalization are seen in descriptions of leftist European organizations that opposed the North Atlantic Treaty Organization (NATO), such as Revolutionary Organization 17 November in Greece and Action Directe in France. The list of Palestinian organizations reflects the ongoing chaos that remains part of Palestinian political reality and also shows the gradual rise of increasingly militant religious groups among Palestinian organizations. Al-Qaeda was first designated as an FTO in 1999, although it first appeared in *Patterns of Global Terrorism* in 1998. Today, it gets lengthy coverage.

In this section you will find a list of all organizations described in *Patterns of Global Terrorism* over the last twenty years. We have consolidated the full descriptions, focusing on the most recent information provided. The organizations are listed alphabetically. Use the index to cross-reference details of attacks and other mentions in the "Country Reports" (Part 3) and "Chronology" (Part 4).

CRS Report for Congress

The "FTO List" and Congress: Sanctioning Designated Foreign Terrorist Organizations

Audrey Kurth Cronin
Specialist in Terrorism—Foreign Affairs, Defense, and Trade Division

Summary

The purpose of this report is to provide Congress with an overview of the nature and status of the designated foreign terrorist organizations list, as a potential tool in overseeing the implementation and effects of U.S. legislation designed to sanction terrorists. It centers on the list of terrorist groups that are formally designated by the Secretary of State pursuant to section 219 of the Immigration and Nationality Act, as amended under the Antiterrorism and Effective Death Penalty Act of 1996 (P.L. 104-132). These groups are often collectively referred to as the "FTO list."

FTO list designations, which last for two years and must be renewed, occur after an interagency process involving the departments of State, Justice, Homeland Security, and the Treasury. Since the designations can be challenged in court, they require a detailed administrative record often based on classified information. An organization that is placed on the FTO list is subject to financial and immigration sanctions, potentially including the blocking of assets, the prosecution of supporters who provide funds, refusal of visas, and deportations of members. There have been a number of designations and changes since the list was established, but it currently includes thirty-six organizations [as of 2002].

The FTO list is often confused with some of the other "terrorist lists" that are maintained by the U.S. government. These include the "state-sponsors of terrorism" list, which is pursuant to Section 6(j) of the 1979 Export Administration Act (P.L. 96-72; 50 U.S.C. app. 2405(6)(j)); the "Specially Designated Terrorists" (SDTs) list, which is pursuant to the International Emergency Economic Powers Act (P.L. 95-223; 50 U.S.C. 1701 *et seq.*) and was initiated in 1995 under Presidential Executive Order 12947; the "Specially Designated Global Terrorists" (SDGT) list, initiated in 2001 under Presidential Executive Order 13224; and, finally, the "Specially Designated Nationals and Blocked Persons" (SDN) list, a master list that contains the other lists. All of these are summarized and maintained by the Office of Foreign Assets Control of the Treasury Department. Lastly, the "Terrorist Exclusion List" or "TEL," which relates to immigration and is pursuant to Section 411 of the USA Patriot Act of 2001 (8 U.S.C. 1182) is maintained by the State Department. Like the FTO list, the TEL includes the names of terrorist organizations, but it has a broader standard for inclusion, is subject to less stringent administrative requirements, and is not challengeable in court. There is a complicated interplay among all of these lists, and it is important to distinguish them from the better-known FTO list.

The FTO list has been of considerable interest to Congress, and there are arguments in favor and against it. It publicly stigmatizes groups and provides a clear focal point for interagency cooperation on terrorist sanctions; however, some argue that it is inflexible and misleading, since groups that are not on the list are still often subject to U.S. sanctions. The report concludes with a discussion of potential policy options for Congress, including some of the recently proposed amendments to the legislation that establishes it. It will be updated as events warrant.

Introduction

The purpose of this report is to provide Congress with an overview of the nature and status of the designated foreign terrorist organizations list (FTO list), as a potential tool in overseeing the implementation and effects of U.S. legislation designed as a basis for imposing sanctions on terrorists. The report centers on the list of terrorist groups that are formally designated by the Secretary of State pursuant to section 219 of the Immigration and Nationality Act (8 U.S.C. 1101 *et seq.*), as amended under the Antiterrorism and Effective Death Penalty Act of 1996 (P.L. 104-132). These groups are often collectively referred to as the "terrorist group list" or "FTO list."

The focus here is on the operation and effectiveness of the FTO list as a U.S. counterterrorism tool. The first part of the report provides a background on the process for designating a group, as well as the procedure used to remove a group. It describes the administration of the list and the role of the various Executive agencies involved in maintaining it. Next follows a section explaining the distinctions between the FTO list and other terrorist lists that are maintained by the U.S. government, with an emphasis on both tracing the complicated interplay among the numerous lists and untangling their confusing acronyms. The arguments in favor and against the FTO list are then discussed, with information about the practicalities of implementing it. The report concludes with a discussion of potential policy options for Congress, including some of the recently proposed amendments to the legislation that establishes it.

The potential issue for Congress is to assess, as part of its oversight responsibility, the effectiveness of the FTO list in confronting terrorist groups that are a threat to the United States. This report will be updated as events warrant.

Background

The 1996 Antiterrorism and Effective Death Penalty Act (AEDPA), which amends section 219 of the Immigration and Nationality Act (P.L. 82-414; 8 U.S.C. 1101 *et. seq.*), states that the Secretary of State is authorized to designate an organization as a "foreign terrorist organization" if three conditions are met:

1. The organization is foreign;
2. The organization engages in terrorist activity;
3. The terrorist activity threatens the security of United States citizens or the national security of the United States.[1]

If the Secretary of State decides that an organization meets these conditions, he or she may add it to the terrorist group list at any time by informing Congress and publishing a notice to that effect in the *Federal Register*. Designations last for two years, at which time they may be renewed. Groups can also be removed from the list at any time, either by the Secretary of State or by Act of Congress. The criteria for removal by the Secretary are general and are subject to interpretation: the Secretary of State may revoke a designation if he or she finds either that the circumstances that were the basis for the designation have changed, or that the national security of the United States warrants a revocation of the designation.[2] Designations normally occur after an involved interagency process; but the Secretary of State makes the ultimate decision.

Although the State Department officially designates a group and takes the lead, there are a number of agencies involved in administering the FTO list. Before the determination, the intelligence community is an important player, because the designation is based upon evidence of a group's terrorist activity. This often involves classified information and entails assembling an administrative record that will potentially stand up in court. The intelligence community also provides the information upon which decisions to renew an organization's designation are based.[3] The Justice Department weighs the legal evidence before the designation is approved, and when renewal is being considered. The Department of Homeland Security is also consulted before designations are made.

After the designation, the Treasury Department may block financial transactions involving an organization's assets and determine whether U.S. banks are complying with the law. The Justice Department determines whether or not to prosecute offenders who violate any aspect of the Treasury Department's sanctions. Judges from the Department of Justice's Executive Office of Immigration Review decide immigration cases, with appeals potentially going all the way to the Attorney General. A variety of different agencies in the Department of Homeland Security are then involved in carrying out immigration sanctions, including deportations.

Thus, from the perspective of the members of a group, the legal consequences of being designated a foreign terrorist organization are in two general areas: financing and immigration. Under the AEDPA, people who provide funds or other material support to a designated FTO are breaking the law and may be prosecuted.[4] This applies to both the members of a group and to those who may be sympathizers. If Treasury imposes sanctions, U.S. financial institutions are required to block the funds of designated FTOs and their agents and to report that blockage to the Treasury Department. This can have important consequences for a designated terrorist organization's ability to access its resources. As for immigration, members of designated FTOs can be denied visas or excluded from entering the United States, and/or they can be deported once they are in the country.

Not the Only U.S. "Terrorist List"

The FTO list is not the only so-called "terrorist list" that the U.S. government keeps.[5] There are a number of others, and it is important to clarify the distinctions among them.[6]

Probably the best known is the "state-sponsors of terrorism" list, which is pursuant to section 6(j) of the Export Administration Act of 1979 (P.L. 96-72; 50 U.S.C. app. 2405(j) (as amended)).[7] Under the terms of the act, the Secretary of State provides Congress with the list of countries that have "repeatedly provided support for acts of international terrorism."

---

1 See "Designation of foreign terrorist organizations," in the Antiterrorism and Effective Death Penalty Act, 8 U.S.C. 1189.

2 8 U.S.C. 1189 (a)(6)(A).

3 In each case, classified summaries of the administrative records gathered on each group are provided to Congress, and the unclassified descriptions of designated foreign terrorist organizations are included in the State Department's *Patterns of Global Terrorism*.

4 18 U.S.C. 2339B.

5 And there are many lists internationally. For example, the United Nations maintains its own list of individuals and entities that are sanctioned under U.N. Resolutions 1267 (1999), 1333 (2000), 1390 (2002) and 1455 (2003). See the list at [http://www.un.org/Docs/sc/committees/1267/1267ListEng.htm]. The European Union also maintains its own list.

6 All of the lists are available at the Treasury Department's Office of Foreign Assets Control web site, accessible at [http://www.treas.gov/offices/eotffc/ofac/sdn/index.html]. The Treasury Department has a compilation, in alphabetical order, of all of the persons (individuals and entities) designated under OFAC's economic sanctions regimes and includes those entities designated as FTOs by the Secretary of State. Additionally, the entire list is published as Appendix A to Chapter 5 of the CFR (See 31 CFR Ch V, App. A).

7 States may also be identified as supporters of international terrorism and sanctioned under the terms of section 40A of the Arms Export Control Act (P.L. 90-629; 22 U.S.C. 2781); and sec. 620A of the Foreign Assistance Act of 1961 (P.L. 87-195; 22 U.S.C. 2371).

There are currently seven states on the state sponsors of terrorism list: Cuba, Iran, Iraq, Libya, North Korea, Sudan, and Syria.[8] Being on the list subjects a country to a range of severe U.S. export controls, especially of dual-use technology and military weapons. The provision of U.S. foreign aid (except humanitarian assistance) is also prohibited.

The state sponsors of terrorism list has been remarkably static since its initiation in 1979, with only two states ever having been removed: South Yemen, which was removed in 1990 when it effectively ceased to exist, merging with North Yemen to form the current state of Yemen; and Iraq, which was removed from the list in 1982 (when it was allied with the United States) and was returned to the list in 1990 (after its invasion of Kuwait).[9] This list differs from the FTO list, as it is directed specifically toward states, not substate actors—like the terrorist groups that the states allegedly support. It also derives from different legislation.[10]

At least three other important U.S. "terrorist lists" are in use. The "specially designated terrorists" (SDTs) list was generated pursuant to the International Emergency Economic Powers Act (P.L. 95-223; 50 U.S.C. 1701 *et seq.*). It was initiated under Presidential Executive Order 12947 on 25 January 1995 and was specifically oriented toward persons (individuals and entities) who threaten to disrupt the Middle East Peace Process. Later, following the events of September 11, 2001, the President invoked the same emergency authorities in Presidential Executive Order 13224, to block "all property and interests in property" of certain designated terrorists and individuals and entities materially supporting them.[11] This established another, much longer list, known as the Specially Designated Global Terrorists (SDGTs) list. There are currently over three hundred persons identified as SDGTs. These two lists are especially targeted toward blocking terrorist financing, and they do not have an immigration element.

The Treasury Department maintains the so-called SDT and SDGT lists, and, unlike the FTO list, the Secretary of the Treasury takes the lead in adding individuals or organizations to the lists and then freezing the assets of persons or entities that are on them. The lists have grown to include more than 200 entities, organizations, and/or individuals. They derive from different legislation and, again, are not the same as the designated FTO list.[12]

The SDT, SDGT, state sponsors, and (as of October 2002) FTO lists were placed together in a new, larger roster called the "Specially Designated Nationals and Blocked Persons" (SDN) list maintained by the Office of Foreign Assets Control of the Treasury Department.[13] Although the individual lists retain separateness pursuant to their legislation, this comprehensive SDN list presents in one place all of the terrorist entities that are economically sanctioned through having their assets blocked. (It also includes individuals and organizations that are sanctioned by having their assets blocked for narcotics trafficking and other activities.) There are thus fourteen different sanctions programs included in the SDN list, not all of which pertain to terrorists. The list is accessible via the Internet and is frequently updated to reflect the fluid nature of U.S. economic sanctions.[14]

There is also the so-called "Terrorist Exclusion List" or "TEL," which is pursuant to Section 411 of the USA Patriot Act of 2001 (P.L. 107-56; 8 U.S.C., 1182). It authorizes the Secretary of State, in consultation with (or at the request of) the Attorney General, to designate terrorist organizations strictly for immigration purposes. Individuals associated with organizations on the TEL list are prevented from entering the United States and/or may be deported if they are already here.[15] (It is worth noting that none of these immigration sanctions has an effect on the behavior of U.S. citizens.) The TEL list expands the grounds for exclusion from the United States and has a broader standard and less detailed administrative procedure than does the FTO list. The State Department maintains the TEL list.[16]

---

8 The fact that Afghanistan was not on the list of state sponsors of terrorism before 9/11 is often cited as evidence of the negligence of pre-9/11 counterterrorist policies of the U.S. government. The explanation was that the Taliban national government was not recognized by the United States and so that state could not be named a state sponsor.

9 Paul Pillar, *Terrorism and U.S. Foreign Policy* (Washington, D.C.: Brookings Institution Press, 2001), p. 170. For more information specifically about adding and removing countries from the state sponsors of terrorism list, see CRS Report RL30613.

10 For further information on state sponsors of terrorism see CRS Report RL30613, *North Korea: Terrorism List Removal*; CRS Report RL3119, *Terrorism: Near Eastern Groups and State Sponsors, 2002*; and CRS Issue Brief IB10119, *Terrorism and National Security: Issues and Trends*. There are also individual CRS reports on each of the listed countries.

11 The President, "Blocking Property and Prohibiting Transactions to Commit or Support Terrorism." Executive Order 13224 of September 23, 2001. 66 FR 49079-49081; September 25, 2001.

12 For more information about these sanctions, see CRS Report RL31658, *Terrorist Financing: The U.S. and International Response*.

13 The National Council of Resistance for Iran is excepted from the SDN list.

14 Again, see the Office of Foreign Assets Control web site, accessible at [http://www.treas.gov/offices/eotffc/ofac/sdn/index.html]. The Treasury Department's master list, which includes SDTs, SDGTs state sponsors and FTOs and is accessible at this web site, is called the "Specially Designated Nationals and Blocked Persons" list. At the end of each entry is the acronym standing for the relevant list (SDT, SDGT, FTO, etc.) that led to the terrorist entity's inclusion on the list. (SDGTE and SDGTI stand for "Specially Designated Global Terrorist Entity" and Specially Designated Global Terrorist Individual, respectively.)

15 See Fact Sheet, Office of the Coordinator for Counterterrorism, "Terrorist Exclusion List," November 15, 2002; accessible at [http://www.state.gov/s/ct/rls/fs/2002/15222.htm]; and *Patterns of Global Terrorism 2002*, pp.151-152.

16 In addition to these lists, there are also a number of "watch lists" maintained by various agencies, currently being consolidated into the Terrorist Screening Center. For further information, see "New Terrorist Screening Center Established: Federal Government Consolidates

In sum, with respect to sanctions against terrorists, the Executive branch maintains an intricate array of lists pursuant to various legislation and Executive Orders. These lists do overlap; however, the Executive Branch implements sanctions against state sponsors of terrorism, terrorist organizations, and individual terrorists somewhat differently depending upon which legislation applies, what the purpose is, and which list is being considered. There are also international lists maintained by the United Nations and the European Union, for example, that are not considered here. This report looks in detail only at the designated FTO list and its sanctions, which the State Department takes the lead in administering and which names only specially designated terrorist organizations. The FTO list has unique importance not only because of the specific measures undertaken to thwart the activities of designated groups but also because of the symbolic, public role it plays as a tool of U.S. counterterrorism policy.

History of the FTO List

The first terrorist organizations were designated and put on the FTO list in October 1997, about eighteen months after the passage of the AEDPA. There were thirty organizations on that initial list. In October 1999, the first review and redesignation occurred. Of the 30 groups originally on the list, 27 were redesignated, three were allowed to lapse, and one more group was added.[17] Notably, the group that was added to the FTO list that year was Al Qaeda, which was designated a foreign terrorist organization especially because of its involvement in the August 1998 bombings of the U.S. embassies in Nairobi, Kenya, and Dar Es Salaam, Tanzania.

The first exercise of the Secretary of State's ability to add a group outside the usual two-year cycle occurred in 2000, when the Islamic Movement of Uzbekistan was designated on its own. Then in the regular biennial review in 2001, the State Department added two new groups, the Real Irish Republican Army (RIRA) and the United Self-Defense Forces/Group of Colombia (AUC), and combined two other groups (Kahane Chai and Kach) into one.[18] That brought the total to 28 FTOs. Since that time, the list has grown significantly. There have been eight groups added to the FTO list since October 5, 2001: the Al-Aqsa Martyrs Brigade (which is an armed wing of the Fatah movement), 'Asbat al-Ansar (a Lebanese-based group associated with Al Qaeda), the Communist Party of Philippines/New People's Army (CPP/NPA) (a Maoist group), Jaish-e-Mohammed (JEM) (an Islamic extremist group based in Pakistan), Jemaah Islamiya (JI) (a southeast Asian terrorist network connected with Al Qaeda), Lashkar-e-Tayyiba (LT) (a Pakistan-based group fighting in Kashmir), and Salafist Group for Call and Combat (GSPC) (apparent outgrowth of the Algerian GIA, active in Europe, Africa and the Middle East). There are 36 groups currently designated as foreign terrorist organizations [as of 2002].

Advantages of the FTO List

There are advantages and disadvantages for the United States in using a formal list as a mechanism for counterterrorism purposes.[19] Chief among the advantages is the fact that the FTO list brings legal clarity to efforts to identify and prosecute members of terrorist organizations and those who support them. Having the designated FTO list helps to target U.S. counterterrorist sanctions under the AEDPA because there is no ambiguity about which groups are included and which are not. If a group is on the FTO list, then the AEDPA sanctions apply; if not, they do not. Thus, being added to the list can have very substantial implications for both the organization and for U.S. counterterrorist efforts.

In practical bureaucratic terms, the FTO list also provides lucidity in the often complicated interagency process of coordinating the actions of Executive agencies, by giving them a central focal point upon which the efforts converge. U.S. counterterrorism is therefore potentially more effective. State, Treasury, Justice, Homeland Security, and other agencies all recognize that groups on the list are subject to scrutiny and sanctions. And these measures arguably make Americans more secure from terrorist attacks, for example, by cutting down on terrorist organizations' access to resources and preventing terrorist group members from entering the country. Specifically, the departments of Homeland Security and Justice have used affiliation with an FTO as grounds for deportation of aliens.[20] The Treasury Department, working with the interagency and international communities, has used the FTO list (among the other U.S. terrorist sanctions programs) in its effort reportedly to block more than $125 billion in assets worldwide.[21] And, of course, the Justice Department has

---

Terrorist Screening Into Single Comprehensive Anti-Terrorist Watchlist," White House press release, available at [http://www.whitehouse.gov/news /releases/2003/09/print/20030916-8.html].

17 The Manuel Rodriquez Patriotic Front Dissidents (FPMR/D) and the Democratic Front for the Liberation of Palestine (DFLP) were dropped "primarily because of the absence of terrorist activity, as defined by relevant law, by those groups during the past two years." The third group was the Khmer Rouge, dropped because it ceased to exist as a viable terrorist organization. See "Foreign Terrorist Organization, Designations by the Secretary of State," Released by the Office of the Coordinator for Counterterrorism, October 8, 1999; accessible at [http://www.state.gov/s/ct/rls/rpt/fto].

18 See the "2001 Report on Foreign Terrorist Organizations," Released by the Office of the Coordinator for Counterterrorism, October 5, 2001; accessible at [http://www.state.gov/s/ct/rls/rpt/fto].

19 The best single source of the arguments for and against the use of lists is Pillar, pp. 150–156. Although it was published before September 11, 2001, the book remains one of the best sources of information on this issue and was used extensively in the preparation of this section.

20 Pillar, p. 151. This is not, however, the typically preferred grounds for deportation. Other grounds are often easier to prove in deportation hearings and do not potentially require revealing sensitive intelligence sources and methods in a hearing.

21 Testimony of Juan C. Zarate, Deputy Assistant Secretary of the Executive Office of Terrorist Financing and Financial Crime, U.S.

prosecuted individuals affiliated with FTOs.[22] Having a focal point for agency coordination enhances the effectiveness of government implementation and may also serve as a deterrent to organizations that consider engaging in illegal behavior.

Likewise, the FTO list is a useful mechanism in dealing with other governments, especially those that are coordinating counterterrorism efforts with the United States. Labeling and listing terrorist organizations also opposed by other states can be an important source of convergence in bilateral national relations. There is a sense of alliance against a common enemy. Often important benefits are derived in counterterrorism or other aspects of the bilateral relationship as a result. Moreover, states that are, actually or potentially, supporting organizations on the list can be left in no doubt about U.S. policy on the issue. Clearly labeling what the United States government considers a foreign terrorist organization can have significant domestic and international foreign policy advantages. It can be a powerful diplomatic tool, residing in the State Department's Office of the Coordinator for Counterterrorism.

Another important benefit is the attention that the FTO list gives to the organizations that are on it. Drawing attention to terrorist groups aids in identifying them not only for states but for nongovernmental organizations and individuals. And likewise the terrorist organizations are fully placed on notice that someone is watching what they do. This can make it more difficult for them to operate.

The groups on the FTO list are stigmatized. Many modern terrorist organizations have a varied portfolio of activities, some of which may be ostensibly legitimate. Some who may have previously viewed an organization primarily as a charity or as a public advocacy group may reconsider supporting it. Publicizing which groups are formally designated has important legal implications: since the law punishes those who wittingly support terrorist organizations, ignorance of a listed organization's activities is less defensible. Potential donors may not necessarily be willing to contribute to an organization that is designated as "terrorist," especially if the gift may result in prosecution under U.S. law. The moral relativity that some people claim dogs the "terrorist" label is removed, at least as far as official U.S. policy is concerned.

Disadvantages of the FTO List

Although it has important legal and symbolic significance, some argue that having a "list" is overly mechanistic, restrictive and inflexible, especially in an area of foreign policy that requires flexibility. Nonstate actors such as terrorist organizations are often able to change their names and/or characteristics much more quickly than ponderous bureaucratic lists can reflect. This is a serious problem in an era when international terrorism is increasingly globalized in its reach and capabilities, with borders becoming more permeable and less relevant, in an age of Internet links and open trade areas.[23] Likewise, such lists are not very effective in dealing with ad hoc activities engaged in by "volunteers," who may not have a clear long-term relationship with an organization. This has become a particular worry with respect to Al Qaeda, for example.[24]

The statement that a group is "on the list" or "off the list" can be very misleading, and its significance is often misunderstood. It is true that the FTO list is generally considered the primary means of imposing sanctions against terrorist organizations. However, not being on the FTO list does not necessarily mean that the U.S. government has failed to recognize that a group is engaged in terrorism, is a threat, and should be subject to sanctions. Sometimes, for various reasons, groups[25] are not on the FTO list, but are on the SDT or SDGT list. They can also be on the Terrorist Exclusion List. There may be competing priorities in dealing with a group, such as a desire to engage a group in negotiations or to use the FTO naming as leverage for another foreign policy aim. Without a full appreciation of the interplay among different sanctioning lists, not to mention the interplay between competing foreign policy goals and all of the sanctioning lists, statements about whether or not a group is on a particular list may ring hollow.

It is not necessarily the case that the FTO list is the most effective or prosecutable mechanism to act against terrorist organizations, if that is the aim. Sometimes it is easier to prosecute organizations or their associates by using the Executive Orders under IEEPA. For example, it can be more difficult to prove that someone is materially supporting, or working for or on behalf of, an FTO under AEDPA than it is to prove that someone is violating the terms of Executive Order 13224. In that case, it might be to the benefit of U.S. counterterrorism

---

Department of the Treasury, testimony before the Senate Foreign Relations Committee, March 18, 2003; accessible at [http://www.treas.gov/press/releases/js139.htm]. Other estimates place the number somewhat lower; see Council on Foreign Relations, Questions and Answers, [http://www.terrorismanswers.com/responses/money2.html#Q7]; and "Terrorist Financing," *Report of an Independent Task Force Sponsored by the Council on Foreign Relations*, New York, 2002.

22 It is worth noting, however, that from the perspective of the Justice Department, the designated FTO list is only one tool for controlling or deterring the behavior of terrorist organizations that threaten the United States. Members of organizations listed as designated FTOs who engage in criminal behavior are also subject to prosecution under other criminal statutes. And often prosecution for the other crimes that terrorists typically engage in is more promising than relying upon the sanctions legislation. See Pillar, p. 151.

---

23 For more on the globalization of 21st century international terrorism, see Audrey Kurth Cronin, "Behind the Curve: Globalization and International Terrorism," *International Security*, Vol. 27, No. 3 (Winter 2002/2003), pp. 30–58.

24 See, for example, Sebastian Rotella, "Al Qaeda's Stealth Weapons; Muslim Converts Who are Drawn to Fanaticism Pose Special Dangers Well Beyond their Symbolic Impact. 'The Blue-eyed Emir' is One Example," *The Los Angeles Times*, September 20, 2003, p. A1; and *Al Qaeda after the Iraq Conflict*, CRS Report for Congress, RS 21529May 23, 2003.

25 Groups, or (to use more specific legal language) those who work for or on their behalf; are owned or controlled by them; provide material, technological, or financial support to them; or are otherwise affiliated with them, are candidates to be included on the list.

efforts to name a group a SDGT rather than an FTO. If a group is then also put on the Terrorism Exclusion List, the combined effects of the sanctions overall could be comparable to being formally named an FTO.[26] Of course, the public attention and diplomatic leverage that goes along with being on the better-known FTO list is not equalled; however, the point is that in terms of the results with respect to fighting an organization's activities, the U.S. sanctions regime is far more complicated than either being "on" the list or "off" the list would imply.

Competing foreign policy concerns often result in decisions to keep groups off the list. This is not necessarily a problem, as U.S. foreign policy considers numerous competing priorities in any given situation. The law "authorizes" but does not require the Secretary of State to make any given designation. If there are countervailing foreign policy priorities, then his or her judgment prevails. Nonetheless, inconsistencies of standards from the perspective strictly of terrorism can make the U.S. government appear hypocritical, especially in the eyes of those who see the FTO list only in black and white terms and may not appreciate the existence of other terrorist lists. Statements about organizations that are not designated regularly appear in the press, journals and academic writing, for example.[27] Having such a high-profile list can politicize and oversimplify what is actually a complex web of legal sanctions that may be in addition to, or instead of, those pursuant to the AEDPA.

Furthermore, as noted, above, the FTO list is subject to judicial review. Thus, on a number of occasions, groups have filed law suits to be removed from it. For example, the Mujahedin-e Khalq (MEK) and the Liberation Tigers of Tamil Eelam (LTTE, or Tamil Tigers) in 1999 both filed suits in the District of Columbia arguing that they had been denied due process; but they lost in court.[28] A separate legal challenge was undertaken by the LTTE and the Turkish Kurdistan Workers' Party (PKK), which argued that the FTO portion of the AEDPA was unconstitutional. The suit was brought by individuals and groups seeking to make contributions to the designated organizations. They also lost their case; however, the ability to win in court has at times evidently been an element in the initial decision whether or not to designate a group.[29] This may mean that the designation has more to do with the legalities of the evidence than with the protection of U.S. national security from a terrorist threat.

Policy Options for Congress

In the 108th Congress, a number of amendments have been offered to change the AEDPA legislation so as to improve the effectiveness and ease of implementation of the FTO list. Some have proposed that the law should be changed so that the designation does not lapse if the Secretary of State fails to renew it every two years. It is a significant bureaucratic burden to ensure that the designations are appropriately reviewed, investigated, the administrative record updated, the appropriate agencies consulted, and the public statement of renewal made every two years after the initial designation. Some might argue that the burden of proof should be placed on the terrorist organization, and that the designations should stand unless a successful appeal is placed by the organization. The requirement for renewal is one of the aspects that some believe make the FTO list less desirable than the other sanctioning tools available under IEEPA and the relevant Executive Orders.

On the other hand, opponents may point out that the powers of the federal government under the Patriot Act are already extensive, and that placing the burden of proof on designated FTOs essentially makes them guilty until they prove themselves innocent. The state sponsors of terrorism list has been largely static in part because states remain on the list until the Secretary of State is able to attest to listed states having stopped being involved in supporting terrorism. It is always difficult to prove a negative. Some might argue that the FTO list is a more flexible document with the current arrangement regarding renewals and should be kept that way. The FTO list provides a public venue for the State Department periodically to reemphasize the importance U.S. foreign policy places upon countering these organizations.

Another idea is to remove the requirement for judicial review of the FTO list. This would make it much harder for terrorist organizations to appeal their placement on the list. The arguments for and against this suggestion are similar to those presented above, since judicial review is an important mechanism available for organizations whose members believe that they have been wrongly labeled and punished. There is a precedent for trying this suggestion. The Foreign Narcotics Kingpin Designation Act (passed in December 1999) originally contained a "no judicial review provision." This caused concern among some owners of private businesses who feared that they might somehow be added to the list for unwitting business relationships with narcotics traffickers. Shortly thereafter, legislation was passed to remove the provision, and judicial review was restored.

RL32120; October 21, 2003

---

26 Another significant difference between the FTO and the SDGT list is that under the UN Sanctions regime (1390 Committee), the U.S. is obligated to designate terrorists and does so through E.O. 13224. The FTO program remains unilateral.

27 See, for instance, Gary Leech, "Good Terrorists, Bad Terrorists: How Washington Decides Who is Who," Colombia Journal Online, May 7, 2001, accessible at [http://www.colombiajournal.org/colombia62.htm].

28 See the 1999 report, "Foreign Terrorist Organization, Designations by the Secretary of State," Released by the Office of the Coordinator for Counterterrorism, October 8, 1999; accessible at [http://www.state.gov/s/ct/rls/rpt/fto].

29 Pillar, pp. 154-155. There was also an unusual recent case involving the MEK where the court held that the FTO designation decision under the AEDPA was obtained in violation of the Constitution, and that such a designation could not be a predicate for a criminal prosecution. See United States of America v. Roya Rahmani, 2097.Supp.2d 1045 (C.D. Cal. 2002).

Profiles of International Terrorist Groups

Collated from Patterns of Global Terrorism 1985–2004

15 May Organization

Description Formed in 1979 from remnants of Wadi Haddad's Popular Front for the Liberation of Palestine—Special Operations Group (PFLP-SOG). Led by Muhammad al-Umari, who is known throughout Palestinian circles as Abu Ibrahim or the bomb man. Group was never part of PLO. Reportedly disbanded in the mid-1980s when several key members joined Colonel Hawari's Special Operations Group of Fatah.

Activities Claimed responsibility for several bombings in the early-to-mid 1980s, including hotel bombing in London (1980), El Al's Rome and Istanbul offices (1981), and Israeli Embassies in Athens and Vienna (1981). Anti-US attacks include an attempted bombing of a Pan Am airliner in Rio de Janeiro and a bombing on board a Pan Am flight from Tokyo to Honolulu in August 1982. (The accused bomber in this last attack, Mohammed Rashid, is currently [1993] awaiting trial in the United States for the bombing, which killed a Japanese teenager.)

Strength 50 to 60 in the early 1980s.

Location/Area of Operation Baghdad until 1984. Before disbanding, operated in Middle East, Europe, and East Asia. Abu Ibrahim is reportedly in Iraq.

External Aid Probably received logistics and financial support from Iraq until 1984.

17 November

a.k.a. Epanastatiki Organosi 17 Noemvri, Revolutionary Organization 17 November

Designated as a Foreign Terrorist Organization

Description 17 November is a radical leftist group established in 1975 and named for the student uprising in Greece in November 1973 that protested the ruling military junta. 17 November is an anti-Greek establishment, anti-United States, anti-Turkey, and anti-NATO group that seeks the ouster of US bases from Greece, the removal of Turkish military forces from Cyprus, and the severing of Greece's ties to NATO and the European Union (EU).

Activities Initial attacks were assassinations of senior US officials and Greek public figures. They began using bombings in the 1980s. Since 1990, 17 November has expanded its targets to include EU facilities and foreign firms investing in Greece and has added improvised rocket attacks to its methods. It supported itself largely through bank robberies. A failed 17 November bombing attempt in June 2002 at the Port of Piraeus in Athens, coupled with robust detective work, led to the arrest of 19 members—the first 17 November operatives ever arrested. In December 2003, a Greek court convicted 15 members—five of whom were given multiple life terms—of hundreds of crimes. Four other alleged members were acquitted for lack of evidence. In September 2004, several jailed members serving life sentences began hunger strikes to attain better prison conditions.

Strength Unknown but presumed to be small.

Location/Area of Operation Athens, Greece.

External Aid Unknown.

Abu Nidal Organization (ANO)

a.k.a. Fatah Revolutionary Council, Arab Revolutionary Brigades, Black September, Revolutionary Organization of Socialist Muslims

Designated as a Foreign Terrorist Organization

Description The ANO international terrorist organization was founded by Sabri al-Banna (a.k.a. Abu Nidal) after splitting from the PLO in 1974. The group's previous known structure consisted of various functional committees, including political, military, and financial. In November 2002 Abu Nidal died in Baghdad; the new leadership of the organization remains unclear. First designated in October 1997.

Activities The ANO has carried out terrorist attacks in 20 countries, killing or injuring almost 900 persons. Targets include the United States, the United Kingdom, France, Israel, moderate Palestinians, the PLO, and various Arab countries. Major attacks included the Rome and Vienna airports in 1985, the Neve Shalom synagogue in Istanbul, the hijacking of Pan Am Flight 73 in Karachi in 1986, and the City of Poros day-excursion ship attack in Greece in 1988. The ANO is suspected of assassinating PLO deputy chief Abu Iyad and PLO security chief Abu Hul in Tunis in

1991. The ANO assassinated a Jordanian diplomat in Lebanon in 1994 and has been linked to the killing of the PLO representative there. The group has not staged a major attack against Western targets since the late 1980s.

Strength Few hundred plus limited overseas support structure.

Location/Area of Operation Al-Banna relocated to Iraq in December 1998 where the group maintained a presence until Operation Iraqi Freedom, but its current status in country is unknown. Known members have an operational presence in Lebanon, including in several Palestinian refugee camps. Authorities shut down the ANO's operations in Libya and Egypt in 1999. The group has demonstrated the ability to operate over a wide area, including the Middle East, Asia, and Europe. However, financial problems and internal disorganization have greatly reduced the group's activities and its ability to maintain cohesive terrorist capability.

External Aid The ANO received considerable support, including safe haven, training, logistical assistance, and financial aid from Iraq, Libya, and Syria (until 1987), in addition to close support for selected operations.

Abu Sayyaf Group (ASG)

Designated as a Foreign Terrorist Organization

Description The ASG is primarily a small, violent Muslim terrorist group operating in the southern Philippines. Some ASG leaders allegedly fought in Afghanistan during the Soviet war and are students and proponents of radical Islamic teachings. The group split from the much larger Moro National Liberation Front in the early 1990s under the leadership of Abdurajak Abubakar Janjalani, who was killed in a clash with Philippine police in December 1998. His younger brother, Khadaffy Janjalani, replaced him as the nominal leader of the group and appears to have consolidated power. First designated in October 1997.

Activities The ASG engages in kidnappings for ransom, bombings, beheadings, assassinations, and extortion. The group's stated goal is to promote an independent Islamic state in western Mindanao and the Sulu Archipelago (areas in the southern Philippines heavily populated by Muslims) but the ASG has primarily used terror for financial profit. Recent bombings may herald a return to a more radical, politicized agenda, at least among certain factions. The group's first large-scale action was a raid on the town of Ipil in Mindanao in April 1995. In April of 2000, an ASG faction kidnapped 21 persons, including 10 Western tourists, from a resort in Malaysia. On May 27, 2001, the ASG kidnapped three US citizens and 17 Filipinos from a tourist resort in Palawan, Philippines. Several of the hostages, including US citizen Guillermo Sobero, were murdered. During a Philippine military hostage rescue operation on June 7, 2002, US hostage Gracia Burnham was rescued, but her husband Martin Burnham and Filipina Deborah Yap were killed. Philippine authorities say that the ASG had a role in the bombing near a Philippine military base in Zamboanga in October 2002 that killed a US serviceman. In February 2004, Khadaffy Janjalani's faction bombed SuperFerry 14 in Manila Bay, killing approximately 132, and in March, Philippine authorities arrested an ASG cell whose bombing targets included the US Embassy in Manila.

Strength At least 1000 individuals motivated by the prospect of receiving ransom payments for foreign hostages had allegedly joined the group but membership now estimated at 200 to 500 fighters.

Location/Area of Operation The ASG was founded in Basilan Province and operates there and in the neighboring provinces of Sulu and Tawi-Tawi in the Sulu Archipelago. The group also operates on the Zamboanga peninsula, and members occasionally travel to Manila. In mid-2003, the group started operating in the major city of Cotobato and on the coast of Sultan Kudarat on Mindanao. The group expanded its operational reach to Malaysia in 2000 when it abducted foreigners from a tourist resort.

External Aid Largely self-financing through ransom and extortion; has received support from Islamic extremists in the Middle East and may receive support from regional terrorist groups. Libya publicly paid millions of dollars for the release of the foreign hostages seized from Malaysia in 2000.

Action Directe (AD)

Description Formed in 1979 as a Marxist group committed to armed struggle against "international imperialism." In 1982, split into two wings—domestic and international—of which the international wing is the more dangerous and indiscriminate. All prominent AD leaders are presently in prison.

Activities Bombings, arson, assassination, bank robberies. Targeted French Government and defense industry companies, symbolic assassinations to protest French involvement in NATO (for example, assassination of General Audran in 1985), Israeli/Jewish interests, and US interests. Claimed joint responsibility with the Red Army Faction (RAF) for bombing of the Rhein-Main Air Force Base in West Germany in 1985, in which two US citizens were killed. It has been inactive since authorities arrested the five leaders in 1987.

Strength 10 to 20.

Location/Area of Operation France, may have operated in West Germany.

External Aid Had links to several domestic terrorist groups in Western Europe, especially the RAF, and may share logistic facilities with them. In January 1985, for instance, issued a joint "anti-imperialist" communique with the RAF. Also had ties to at least one Middle Eastern group, LARF.

African National Congress (ANC)

Description Origins go back to 1912, when its forerunner, the South African Native National Congress, was set up to protect black rights. The South African Communist Party started to play a role in the pre-World War II period. In 1949 the ANC adopted a militant "Action Program." Banned in 1961; formed a guerilla wing called Umknonta Sizwe (Spear of the Nation). Remained in exile, although the South African Government announced the unbanning of the ANC in early 1990 on the grounds that there had been important shifts of emphasis in the ANC's point of view, which indicated "a new approach and a preference for peaceful solutions."

Activities Chiefly a political organization, but in past years has been involved in bombings of energy and transportation targets, government officials, and security targets, sometimes resulting in the death of civilians. Has not attacked US interests.

Strength Estimated 12,000 to 15,000 members outside South Africa, and probably minimum of several million sympathizers inside the country.

Location/Area of Operation Main installations in Zambia and Tanzania. Offices in numerous European, Asian, and African capitals.

External Aid Has received military supplies from the Soviet Bloc; financial support is offered by the Organization of African Unity and by governments and private contributors in the West. In the past, ANC members may have received training in PLO camps in Lebanon.

Al-Aqsa Martyrs Brigade (al-Aqsa)

a.k.a. al-Aqsa Martyrs Battalion
Designated as a Foreign Terrorist Organization

Description The al-Aqsa Martyrs Brigade consists of an unknown number of small cells of terrorists associated with the Palestinian Fatah organization. Al-Aqsa emerged at the outset of the 2000 Palestinian *intifadah* to attack Israeli targets with the aim of driving the Israeli military and settlers from the West Bank, Gaza Strip, and Jerusalem, and to establish a Palestinian state. First designated in March 2002.

Activities Al-Aqsa has carried out shootings and suicide operations against Israeli civilians and military personnel in Israel and the Palestinian territories, rocket and mortar attacks against Israel and Israeli settlements from the Gaza Strip, and the killing of Palestinians suspected of collaborating with Israel. Al-Aqsa has killed a number of US citizens, the majority of them dual US-Israeli citizens, in its attacks. In January 2002, al-Aqsa was the first Palestinian terrorist group to use a female suicide bomber in this region.

Strength Unknown.

Location/Area of Operation Al-Aqsa operates in Israel, the West Bank, and Gaza Strip, and has only claimed attacks inside these three areas. It may have followers in Palestinian refugee camps in southern Lebanon.

External Aid In the last year, numerous public accusations suggest Iran and Hizballah are providing support to al-Aqsa elements, but the extent of external influence on al-Aqsa as a whole is not clear.

Al Badhr Mujahedin (al-Badr)

Description The Al Badhr Mujahedin split from Hizbul-Mujahedin (HM) in 1998. Traces its origins to 1971, when a group named Al Badr attacked Bengalis in East Pakistan. Later operated as part of Gulbuddin Hekmatyar's Hizb-I Islami (HIG) in Afghanistan and, from 1990, as a unit of HM in Kashmir. The group was relatively inactive until 2000. Since then, it has increasingly claimed responsibility for attacks against Indian military targets.

Activities Has conducted a number of operations against Indian military targets in Jammu and Kashmir.

Strength Perhaps several hundred.

Location/Area of Operation Jammu and Kashmir, Pakistan, and Afghanistan.

External Aid Unknown.

Alex Boncayao Brigade (ABB)

Description The ABB, the breakaway urban hit squad of the Communist Party of the Philippines/New People's Army, was formed in the mid-1980s. The ABB was added to the Terrorist Exclusion list in December 2001.

Activities Responsible for more than 100 murders, including the murder in 1989 of US Army Col. James Rowe in the Philippines. In March 1997, the group announced it had formed an alliance with another armed group, the Revolutionary Proletarian Army (RPA). In March 2000, the group claimed credit for a rifle grenade attack against the Department of Energy building in Manila and strafed Shell Oil offices in the central Philippines to protest rising oil prices.

Strength Approximately 500.

Location/Area of Operation The largest RPA/ABB groups are on the Philippine islands of Luzon, Negros, and the Visayas.

External Aid Unknown.

Al-Fatah

a.k.a. Al-Asifa

Description Headed by Yasser Arafat, Fatah joined the PLO in 1968 and won the leadership role in 1969. Its commanders were expelled from Jordan following violent confrontations with Jordanian forces during the period 1970-71, beginning with Black September in 1970. The Israeli invasion of Lebanon in 1982 led to the group's dispersal to several Middle Eastern countries, including Tunisia, Yemen, Algeria, Iraq, and others. Maintains several military and intelligence wings that have carried out terrorist attacks, including Force 17 and the Hawari Special Operations Group. Two of its leaders, Abu Jihad and Abu Iyad, were assassinated in recent years.

Activities In the 1960s and the 1970s, Fatah offered training to a wide range of European, Middle Eastern, Asian, and African terrorist and insurgent groups. Carried out numerous acts of international terrorism in Western Europe and Middle East in the early-to-mid-1970s.

Strength 6,000 to 8,000.

Location/Area of Operation Headquartered in Tunisia with bases in Lebanon and other Middle Eastern countries.

External Aid Has had close, longstanding political and financial ties to Saudi Arabia, Kuwait, and other moderate Persian Gulf states. These relations were disrupted by the Gulf crisis of 1990-91. Also has had links to Jordan. Received weapons, explosives, and training from the former USSR and the former Communist regimes of East European states. China and North Korea have reportedly provided some weapons.

Al-Ittihad al-Islami (AIAI)

a.k.a. Islamic Union

Description AIAI rose to prominence in the Horn of Africa in the early 1990s, following the downfall of the Siad Barre regime and the subsequent collapse of the Somali nation state into anarchy. AIAI was not internally cohesive and suffered divisions between factions supporting moderate Islam and more puritanical Islamic ideology. Following military defeats in 1996 and 1997, AIAI evolved into a loose network of highly compartmentalized cells, factions, and individuals with no central control or coordination. AIAI elements pursue a variety of agendas ranging from social services and education to insurgency activities in the Ogaden. Some AIAI-associated sheikhs espouse a radical fundamentalist version of Islam, with particular emphasis on a strict adherence to Sharia (Islamic law), a view often at odds with Somali emphasis on clan identity. A small number of AIAI-associated individuals have provided logistical support to and maintain ties with al-Qaida; however, the network's central focus remains the establishment of an Islamic government in Somalia.

Activities Elements of AIAI may have been responsible for the kidnapping and murder of relief workers in Somalia and Somaliland in 2003 and 2004, and during the late 1990s. Factions of AIAI may also have been responsible for a series of bomb attacks in public places in Addis Ababa in 1996 and 1997. Most AIAI factions have recently concentrated on broadening their religious base, renewed emphasis on building businesses, and undertaking "hearts and minds" actions, such as sponsoring orphanages and schools and providing security that uses an Islamic legal structure in the areas where it is active.

Strength The actual membership strength is unknown, but has been estimated at 2,000 plus reserve militias.

Location/Area of Operations Primarily in Somalia, with a presence in the Ogaden region of Ethiopia, Kenya, and possibly Djibouti.

External Aid Receives funds from Middle East financiers and Somali diaspora communities in Europe, North America, and the Arabian Peninsula. May maintain ties to al-Qaida. Past weapons deliveries from Sudan.

Al-Jihad (AJ)

a.k.a. Jihad Group, Egyptian Islamic Jihad, EIJ

Designated as a Foreign Terrorist Organization

Description This Egyptian Islamic extremist group merged with Usama Bin Ladin's al-Qaida organization in 2001. Usama Bin Ladin's deputy, Ayman al-Zawahiri, was the former head of AJ. Active since the 1970s, AJ's primary goal has been the overthrow of the Egyptian Government and the establishment of an Islamic state. The group's primary targets, historically, have been high-level Egyptian Government officials as well as US and Israeli interests in Egypt and abroad. Regular Egyptian crackdowns on extremists, including on AJ, have greatly reduced AJ capabilities in Egypt.

Activities The original AJ was responsible for the 1981 assassination of Egyptian President Anwar Sadat. It claimed responsibility for the attempted assassinations of Interior Minister Hassan al-Alfi in August 1993 and Prime Minister Atef Sedky in November 1993. AJ has not conducted an attack inside Egypt since 1993 and has never successfully targeted foreign tourists there. The group was responsible for the Egyptian Embassy bombing in Islamabad in 1995 and a disrupted plot against the US Embassy in Albania in 1998.

Strength Unknown, but probably has several hundred hard-core members inside and outside of Egypt.

Location/Area of Operation Historically AJ operated in the Cairo area. Most AJ members today are outside Egypt in countries such as Afghanistan, Pakistan, Lebanon, the United Kingdom, and Yemen. AJ activities have been centered outside Egypt for several years under the auspices of al-Qaida.

External Aid Unknown. Since 1998 AJ received most of its funding from al-Qaida, and these close ties culminated in the eventual merger of the groups. Some funding may come from various Islamic non-governmental organizations, cover businesses, and criminal acts.

Allied Democratic Forces (ADF)

Description A diverse coalition of former members of the National Army for the Liberation of Uganda (NALU), Islamists from the Salaf Tabliq group, Hutu militiamen, and fighters from ousted regimes in Congo. The conglomeration of fighters formed in 1995 in opposition to the government of Ugandan President Yoweri Museveni.

Activities The ADF seeks to use the kidnapping and murder of civilians to create fear in the local population and undermine confidence in the Government. The group is suspected to be responsible for dozens of bombings in public areas. A Ugandan military offensive in 2000 destroyed several ADF camps, but ADF attacks continued in Kampala in 2001.

Strength A few hundred fighters.

Location/Area of Operation Western Uganda and eastern Congo.

External Aid Received past funding, supplies, and training from the Government of Sudan. Some funding suspected from sympathetic Hutu groups.

Al-Qaida

a.k.a. The Base, Qa'idat al-Jihad, Maktab al-Khidamat, International Islamic Front for Jihad Against Jews and Crusaders, Al-Jabhah al-Islamiyyah al-'Alamiyyah li-Qital al-Yahud wal-Salibiyyin, Group for the Preservation of Holy Sites, Islamic Army of the Liberation of Holy Places, Islamic Army for the Liberation of Holy Shrines, Islamic Sal, Usama Bin Ladin Organization

Designated as a Foreign Terrorist Organization

Description Al-Qaida was established by Usama Bin Ladin in 1988 with Arabs who fought in Afghanistan against the Soviet Union. Helped finance, recruit, transport, and train Sunni Islamic extremists for the Afghan resistance. Goal is to unite Muslims to fight the United States as a means of defeating Israel, overthrowing regimes it deems "non-Islamic," and expelling Westerners and non-Muslims from Muslim countries. Eventual goal would be establishment of a pan-Islamic caliphate throughout the world. Issued statement in February 1998 under the banner of "The World Islamic Front for Jihad Against the Jews and Crusaders" saying it was the duty of all Muslims to kill US citizens, civilian and military, and their allies everywhere.

Merged with al-Jihad (Egyptian Islamic Jihad) in June 2001, renaming itself "Qa'idat al-Jihad." Merged with Abu Mus'ab al-Zarqawi's organization in Iraq in late 2004, with al-Zarqawi's group changing its name to "Qa'idat al-Jihad fi Bilad al-Rafidayn" (al-Qaida in the Land of the Two Rivers).

Activities In 2004, the Saudi-based al-Qaida network and associated extremists launched at least 11 attacks, killing over 60 people, including six Americans, and wounding more than 225 in Saudi Arabia. Focused on targets associated with US and Western presence and Saudi security forces in Riyadh, Yanbu, Jeddah, and Dhahran. Attacks consisted of vehicle bombs, infantry assaults, kidnappings, targeted shootings, bombings, and beheadings. Other al-Qaida networks have been involved in attacks in Afghanistan and Iraq.

In 2003, carried out the assault and bombing on May 12 of three expatriate housing complexes in Riyadh, Saudi Arabia, that killed 30 and injured 216. Backed attacks on May 16 in Casablanca, Morocco, of a Jewish center, restaurant, nightclub, and hotel that killed 33 and injured 101. Probably supported the bombing of the J.W. Marriott Hotel in Jakarta, Indonesia, on August 5, that killed 12 and injured 149. Responsible for the assault and bombing on November 9 of a housing complex in Riyadh, Saudi Arabia, that killed 17 and injured 122. The suicide bombers and others associated with the bombings of two synagogues in Istanbul, Turkey, on November 15 that killed 20 and injured 300 and the bombings in Istanbul of the British Consulate and HSBC Bank on November 20 that resulted in 41 dead and 555 injured had strong links to al-Qaida. Conducted two assassination attempts against Pakistani President Musharraf in December 2003. Was involved in some attacks in Afghanistan and Iraq.

In 2002, carried out bombing on November 28 of a hotel in Mombasa, Kenya, killing 15 and injuring 40. Probably supported a nightclub bombing in Bali, Indonesia, on October 12 by Jemaah Islamiya that killed more than 200. Responsible for an attack on US military personnel in Kuwait on October 8 that killed one US soldier and injured another. Directed a suicide attack on the tanker M/V Limburg off the coast of Yemen on October 6 that killed one and injured four. Carried out a firebombing of a synagogue in Tunisia on April 11 that killed 19 and injured 22. On September 11, 2001, 19 al-Qaida suicide attackers hijacked and crashed four US commercial jets—two into the World Trade Center in New York City, one into the Pentagon near Washington, DC, and a fourth into a field in Shanksville, Pennsylvania—leaving nearly 3,000 individuals dead or missing. Directed the attack on the USS Cole in the port of Aden, Yemen, on October 12, 2000, killing 17 US Navy sailors and injuring another 39.

Conducted the bombings in August 1998 of the US Embassies in Nairobi, Kenya, and Dar es Salaam, Tanzania, that killed at least 301 individuals and injured more than 5,000 others. Claims to have shot down US helicopters and killed US servicemen in Somalia in 1993 and to have conducted three bombings that targeted US troops in Aden, Yemen, in December 1992.

Al-Qaida is linked to the following plans that were disrupted or not carried out: to bomb in mid-air a dozen US trans-Pacific flights in 1995, and to set off a bomb at Los Angeles International Airport in 1999. Also plotted to carry out terrorist operations against US and Israeli tourists visiting Jordan for millennial celebrations in late 1999 (Jordanian authorities thwarted the planned attacks and put 28 suspects on trial). In December 2001, suspected al-Qaida associate Richard Colvin Reid attempted to ignite a shoe bomb on a trans-Atlantic flight from Paris to Miami. Attempted to shoot down an Israeli chartered plane with a surface-to-air missile as it departed the Mombasa, Kenya, airport in November 2002.

Strength Al-Qaida's organizational strength is difficult to determine in the aftermath of extensive counterterrorist efforts since 9/11. However, the group probably has several thousand extremists and associates worldwide inspired by the group's ideology. The arrest and deaths of mid-level and senior al-Qaida operatives have disrupted some communication, financial, and facilitation nodes and interrupted some terrorist plots. Al-Qaida also serves as a focal point or umbrella organization for a worldwide network that includes many Sunni Islamic extremist groups, including some members of Gama'a al-Islamiyya, the Islamic Movement of Uzbekistan, and the Harakat ul-Mujahidin.

Location/Area of Operation Al-Qaida has cells worldwide and is reinforced by its ties to Sunni extremist networks. It was based in Afghanistan until Coalition forces removed the Taliban from power in late 2001. Al-Qaida has dispersed in small groups across South Asia, Southeast Asia, the Middle East and Africa, and probably will attempt to carry out future attacks against US interests.

External Aid Al-Qaida maintains moneymaking front businesses, solicits donations from like-minded supporters, and illicitly siphons funds from donations to Muslim charitable organizations. US and international efforts to block al-Qaida funding have hampered the group's ability to obtain money.

Al Ummah

Description Radical Indian Muslim group founded in 1992 by S. A. Basha.

Activities Believed responsible for the Coimbatore bombings in Southern India in February 1998. Basha and 30 of his followers were arrested and await trial for those bombings.

Strength Unknown. No estimate available.

Location/Area of Operation Southern India.

External Aid Unknown.

Ansar al-Islam (AI)

a.k.a. Ansar al-Sunnah Partisans of Islam, Helpers of Islam, Supporters of Islam, Jund al-Islam, Jaish Ansar al-Sunna, Kurdish Taliban

Designated as a Foreign Terrorist Organization

Description Ansar al-Islam (AI) is a radical Islamist group of Iraqi Kurds and Arabs who have vowed to establish an independent Islamic state in Iraq. The group was formed in December 2001. In the fall of 2003, a statement was issued calling all jihadists in Iraq to unite under the name Ansar al-Sunnah (AS). Since that time, it is likely that AI has posted all claims of attack under the name AS. AI is closely allied with al-Qaida and Abu Mus'ab al-Zarqawi's group, Tanzim Qa'idat al-Jihad fi Bilad al-Rafidayn (QJBR) in Iraq. Some members of AI trained in al-Qaida camps in Afghanistan, and the group provided safe haven to al-Qaida fighters before Operation Iraqi Freedom (OIF). Since OIF, AI has become one of the leading groups engaged in anti-Coalition attacks in Iraq and has developed a robust propaganda campaign. (Ansar al-Islam was designated on 20 February 2003, under E. O. 13224. The UNSCR 1267 Committee designated Ansar al-Islam pursuant to UNSCRs 1267, 1390, and 1455 on 27 February 2003.) First designated in March 2004.

Activities AI continues to conduct attacks against Coalition forces, Iraqi Government officials and security forces, and ethnic Iraqi groups and political parties. AI members have been implicated in assassinations and assassination attempts against Patriotic Union of Kurdistan (PUK) officials and Coalition forces, and also work closely with both al-Qaida operatives and associates in QJBR. AI has also claimed responsibility for many high profile attacks, including the simultaneous suicide bombings of the PUK and Kurdistan Democratic Party (KDP) party offices in Ibril on February 1, 2004, and the bombing of the US military dining facility in Mosul on December 21, 2004. Before OIF, some AI members claimed to have produced cyanide-based toxins, ricin, and alfatoxin.

Strength Approximately 500 to 1,000 members.

Location/Area of Operation Primarily central and northern Iraq.

External Aid The group receives funding, training, equipment, and combat support from al-Qaida, QJBR, and other international jihadist backers throughout the world. AI also has operational and logistic support cells in Europe.

Anti-Imperialist Territorial Nuclei (NTA)

a.k.a. Anti-Imperialist Territorial Units

Description The NTA is a clandestine leftist extremist group that first appeared in Italy's Friuli region in 1995.

Adopted the class struggle ideology of the Red Brigades of the 1970s and 1980s and a similar logo—an encircled five-point star—for their declarations. Seeks the formation of an "anti-imperialist fighting front" with other Italian leftist terrorist groups, including Revolutionary Proletarian Initiative Nuclei and the New Red Brigades. Opposes what it perceives as US and NATO imperialism and condemns Italy's foreign and labor polices. In a leaflet dated January 2002, NTA identified experts in four Italian Government sectors—federalism, privatizations, justice reform, and jobs and pensions—as potential targets.

Activities To date, NTA has conducted attacks only against property. During the NATO intervention in Kosovo in 1999, NTA members threw gasoline bombs at the Venice and Rome headquarters of the then-ruling party, Democrats of the Left. NTA claimed responsibility for a bomb attack in September 2000 against the Central European Initiative office in Trieste and a bomb attack in August 2001 against the Venice Tribunal building. In January 2002, police thwarted an attempt by four NTA members to enter the Rivolto Military Air Base. In 2003, NTA claimed responsibility for the arson attacks against three vehicles belonging to US troops serving at the Ederle and Aviano bases in Italy. There has been no reported activity by the group since the arrest in January 2004 of NTA's founder and leader.

Strength Accounts vary from one to approximately 20 members.

Location/Area of Operation Primarily northeastern Italy and near US military installations in northern Italy.

External Aid None evident.

Armed Islamic Group (GIA)

Designated as a Foreign Terrorist Organization

Description An Islamist extremist group, the GIA aims to overthrow the Algerian regime and replace it with a fundamentalist Islamic state. The GIA began its violent activity in 1992 after the military government suspended legislative elections in anticipation of an overwhelming victory by the Islamic Salvation Front, the largest Islamic opposition party. First designated in October 1997.

Activities The GIA has engaged in attacks against civilians and government workers. Starting in 1992, the GIA conducted a terrorist campaign of civilian massacres, sometimes wiping out entire villages in its area of operation, and killing tens of thousands of Algerians. GIA's brutal attacks on civilians alienated them from the Algerian populace. Since announcing its campaign against foreigners living in Algeria in 1992, the GIA has killed more than 100 expatriate men and women, mostly Europeans, in the country. The group uses assassinations and bombings, including car bombs, and it is known to favor kidnaping victims and slitting their throats. The GIA hijacked an Air France flight to Algiers in December 1994. In late 1999 a French court convicted several GIA members for conducting a series of bombings in France in 1995. In 2002, a French court sentenced two GIA members to life in prison for conducting a series of bombings in France in 1995. Many of the GIA's members have joined other Islamist groups or been killed or captured by the Algerian Government. The GIA's most recent significant attacks were in August, 2001.

Strength Precise numbers are unknown, but probably fewer than 100.

Location/Area of Operation Algeria, Sahel (i.e. northern Mali, northern Mauritania, and northern Niger), and Europe.

External Aid Algerian expatriates, some of whom reside in Western Europe, provide some financial and logistic support. In addition, the Algerian Government has accused Iran and Sudan of supporting Algerian extremists.

Armed Liberation Forces Zarate Willka (FAL)

a.k.a. Zarate Willka

Description Formed probably two years ago [1987] by various leftist extremists, some of whom may be students at the University of San Andres in La Paz. The group is urban based and anti-US.

Activities Exploded bomb along route of US Secretary of State Shultz's motorcade in La Paz in August 1988 and assassinated two Mormon missionaries in May 1989. Claimed responsibility for bombing on 20 December 1989 at US Embassy after the US military action in Panama. Claims to fight for the rights of the poor and against perceived US interventionism in Bolivia.

Strength Unknown, probably relatively small.

Location/Area of Operation Bolivia/La Paz.

External Aid Unknown.

Armenian Secret Army for the Liberation of Armenia (ASALA)

a.k.a. The Orly Group, 3rd October Organization

Description Marxist-Leninist Armenian terrorist group formed in 1975 with stated intention to compel the Turkish Government to acknowledge publicly its alleged responsibility for the deaths of 1.5 million Armenians in 1915, pay reparations, and cede territory for an Armenian homeland. Led by Hagop Hagopian until he was assassinated in Athens in April 1988.

Activities Initial bombings and assassination attacks directed against Turkish targets. Later attacked French and Swiss targets to force release of imprisoned comrades.

Made several minor bombing attacks against US airline offices in Western Europe in early 1980s. Bombing of Turkish airline counter at Orly International Airport in Paris in 1983, in which eight persons were killed and 55 were wounded, led to split in group over rationale for causing indiscriminate casualties. Suffering from internal schisms, the group has been relatively inactive.

Strength Unknown; may have hundreds of members, plus supporters.

Location/Area of Operation Operates primarily in the Basque autonomous regions of northern Spain and southwestern France but also has bombed Spanish interests in Italy and Germany and French interests in Italy.

External Aid Has received training at various times in Libya, Lebanon, and Nicaragua. Also appears to have close ties to PIRA.

Asbat al-Ansar

Designated as a Foreign Terrorist Organization

Description Asbat al-Ansar, the League of the Followers or Partisans' League, is a Lebanon-based Sunni extremist group, composed primarily of Palestinians with links to Usama Bin Ladin's al-Qaida organization and other Sunni extremist groups. The group follows an extremist interpretation of Islam that justifies violence against civilian targets to achieve political ends. Some of the group's goals include overthrowing the Lebanese Government and thwarting perceived anti-Islamic and pro-Western influences in the country. First designated in March 2002.

Activities Asbat al-Ansar has carried out multiple terrorist attacks in Lebanon since it first emerged in the early 1990s. The group assassinated Lebanese religious leaders and bombed nightclubs, theaters, and liquor stores in the mid- 1990s. The group raised its operational profile in 2000 with two attacks against Lebanese and international targets. It was involved in clashes in northern Lebanon in December 1999 and carried out a rocket-propelled grenade attack on the Russian Embassy in Beirut in January 2000. Asbat al-Ansar's leader, Abu Muhjin, remains at large despite being sentenced to death in absentia for the 1994 murder of a Muslim cleric.

Suspected Asbat al-Ansar elements were responsible for an attempt in April 2003 to use a car bomb against a McDonald's in a Beirut suburb. By October, Lebanese security forces arrested Ibn al-Shahid, who is believed to be associated with Asbat al-Ansar, and charged him with masterminding the bombing of three fast food restaurants in 2002 and the attempted attack on a McDonald's in 2003. Asbat forces were involved in other violence in Lebanon in 2003, including clashes with members of Yassir Arafat's Fatah movement in the 'Ayn al-Hilwah refugee camp and a rocket attack in June on the Future TV building in Beirut.

In 2004, no successful terrorist attacks were attributed to Asbat al-Ansar. However, in September, operatives with links to the group were believed to be involved in a planned terrorist operation targeting the Italian Embassy, the Ukrainian Consulate General, and Lebanese Government offices. The plot, which reportedly also involved other Lebanese Sunni extremists, was thwarted by Italian, Lebanese, and Syrian security agencies. In 2004, Asbat al-Ansar remained vocal in its condemnation of the United States' presence in Iraq, and in April the group urged Iraqi insurgents to kill US and other hostages to avenge the death of HAMAS leaders Abdul Aziz Rantisi and Sheikh Ahmed Yassin. In October, Mahir al-Sa'di, a member of Asbat al-Ansar, was sentenced in absentia to life imprisonment for plotting to assassinate former US Ambassador to Lebanon David Satterfield in 2000. Until his death in March 2003, al-Sa'di worked in cooperation with Abu Muhammad al-Masri, the head of al-Qaida at the 'Ayn al-Hilwah refugee camp, where fighting has occurred between Asbat al-Ansar and Fatah elements.

Strength The group commands about 300 fighters in Lebanon.

Location/Area of Operation The group's primary base of operations is the 'Ayn al- Hilwah Palestinian refugee camp near Sidon in southern Lebanon.

External Aid Probably receives money through international Sunni extremist networks and possibly Usama Bin Ladin's al-Qaida network.

Aum Shinrikyo (Aum)

a.k.a. Aum Supreme Truth, Aleph

Designated as a Foreign Terrorist Organization

Description A cult established in 1987 by Shoko Asahara, the Aum aimed to take over Japan and then the world. Approved as a religious entity in 1989 under Japanese law, the group ran candidates in a Japanese parliamentary election in 1990. Over time, the cult began to emphasize the imminence of the end of the world and stated that the United States would initiate Armageddon by starting World War III with Japan. The Japanese Government revoked its recognition of the Aum as a religious organization in October 1995, but in 1997 a Government panel decided not to invoke the Anti-Subversive Law against the group, which would have outlawed it. A 1999 law continues to give the Japanese Government authorization to maintain police surveillance of the group due to concerns that the Aum might launch future terrorist attacks. Under the leadership of Fumihiro Joyu, the Aum changed its name to Aleph in January 2000 and tried to distance itself from the violent and apocalyptic teachings of its founder. However, in late 2003, Joyu stepped down, pressured by members who wanted to return fully to the worship of Asahara. First designated in October 1997.

Activities On March 20, 1995, Aum members simultaneously released the chemical nerve agent sarin on several Tokyo subway trains, killing 12 persons and injuring up to 1,500. The group was responsible for other mysterious events involving chemical incidents in Japan in 1994. Its efforts to conduct attacks using biological agents have been unsuccessful. Japanese police arrested Asahara in May 1995, and authorities sentenced him in February 2004 to death for his role in the attacks of 1995. Since 1997, the cult has continued to recruit new members, engage in commercial enterprise, and acquire property, although it scaled back these activities significantly in 2001 in response to public outcry. In July 2001, Russian authorities arrested a group of Russian Aum followers who had planned to set off bombs near the Imperial Palace in Tokyo as part of an operation to free Asahara from jail and smuggle him to Russia.

Strength The Aum's current membership in Japan is estimated to be about 1,650 persons. At the time of the Tokyo subway attack, the group claimed to have 9,000 members in Japan and as many as 40,000 worldwide.

Location/Area of Operation The Aum's principal membership is located in Japan, but a residual branch comprising about 300 followers has surfaced in Russia.

External Aid None.

Basque Fatherland and Liberty (ETA)

a.k.a. Euzkadi Ta Askatasuna, Batasuna

Designated as a Foreign Terrorist Organization

Description ETA was founded in 1959 with the aim of establishing an independent homeland based on Marxist principles and encompassing the Spanish Basque provinces of Vizcaya, Guipuzcoa, and Alava, as well as the autonomous region of Navarra and the southwestern French Departments of Labourd, Basse-Navarra, and Soule. Spanish and French counterterrorism initiatives since 2000 have hampered the group's operational capabilities. Spanish police arrested scores of ETA members and accomplices in Spain in 2004, and dozens were apprehended in France, including two key group leaders. These arrests included the capture in October of two key ETA leaders in southwestern France. ETA's political wing, Batasuna, remains banned in Spain. Spanish and French prisons are estimated to hold over 700 ETA members. First designated in October 1997.

Activities Primarily involved in bombings and assassinations of Spanish Government officials, security and military forces, politicians, and judicial figures, but has also targeted journalists and tourist areas. Security service scrutiny and a public outcry after the Islamic extremist train bombing on March 11, 2004, in Madrid limited ETA's capabilities and willingness to inflict casualties. ETA conducted no fatal attacks in 2004, but did mount several low-level bombings in Spanish tourist areas during the summer and 11 bombings in early December, each preceded by a warning call. The group has killed more than 850 persons and injured hundreds of others since it began lethal attacks in the 1960s. ETA finances its activities primarily through extortion and robbery.

Strength Unknown; hundreds of members plus supporters.

Location/Area of Operation Operates primarily in the Basque autonomous regions of northern Spain and southwestern France, but also has attacked Spanish and French interests elsewhere.

External Aid Has received training at various times in the past in Libya, Lebanon, and Nicaragua. Some ETA members allegedly fled to Cuba and Mexico while others reside in South America. ETA members have operated and been arrested in other European countries, including Belgium, The Netherlands, and Germany.

Cambodian Freedom Fighters (CFF)

a.k.a. Cholana Kangtoap Serei Cheat Kampouchea

Description The Cambodian Freedom Fighters (CFF) emerged in November 1998 in the wake of political violence that saw many influential Cambodian leaders flee and the Cambodian People's Party assume power. With an avowed aim of overthrowing the Government, the group is led by a Cambodian-American, a former member of the opposition Sam Rainsy Party. The CFF's membership reportedly includes Cambodian-Americans based in Thailand and the United States, and former soldiers from the Khmer Rouge, Royal Cambodian Armed Forces, and various political factions.

Activities The Cambodian Government arrested seven CFF members who were reportedly planning an unspecified terrorist attack in southwestern Cambodia in late 2003, but there were no successful CFF attacks that year. Cambodian courts in February and March 2002 prosecuted 38 CFF members suspected of staging an attack in Cambodia in 2000. The courts convicted 19 members, including one US citizen, of "terrorism" and/or "membership in an armed group" and sentenced them to terms of five years to life imprisonment. The group claimed responsibility for an attack in late November 2000 on several Government installations that killed at least eight persons and wounded more than a dozen. In April 1999, five CFF members were arrested for plotting to blow up a fuel depot outside Phnom Penh with anti-tank weapons.

Strength Exact strength is unknown, but totals probably never have exceeded 100 armed fighters.

Location/Area of Operation Northeastern Cambodia near the Thai border, and the United States.

External Aid US-based leadership collects funds from the Cambodian-American community.

Central American Revolutionary Worker's Party (PRTC)

Description Marxist-Leninist, was formed in 1976 as a regional insurgency organization, of which the El Salvador group is the largest and most important. PRTC joined the El Salvador guerilla umbrella group Farabundo Marti National Liberation Front in 1980 and, although the smallest member of the guerilla alliance, has been responsible for some of the most violent acts committed by the coalition. An urban group, called the Mardoqueo Cruz Urban Commando Detachment, was created in 1984.

Activities Carried out several terrorist attacks against US Marines and businessmen in San Salvador in June 1985. Since 1985, the group has been badly damaged by government countermeasures.

Strength Several hundred

Location/Area of Operation El Salvador, branches in Costa Rica, Honduras, Guatemala, and Nicaragua.

External Aid Receives training in Cuba, Eastern Bloc countries, Vietnam, and Nicaragua. May have received arms from Libya.

Chukaku-Ha

a.k.a. Nucleus or Middle Core Faction

Description An ultra leftist/radical group with origins in the fragmentation of the Japanese Communist Party in 1957. Largest domestic militant group; has political arm plus small covert action wing called Kansai Revolutionary Army. Funding derived from membership dues, sales of its newspapers, and fundraising campaigns.

Activities Participates in mass street demonstrations and commits sporadic attacks using crude rockets and incendiary devices usually designed to cause property damage rather than casualties. Protests Japan's imperial system, Western "imperialism," and events like the Gulf war and the expansion of Tokyo's Narita airport. Launched four rockets at the US army base at Camp Zama, near Tokyo, at the start of the G-7 Summit in July 1993.

Strength 3,500 in 1994.

Location/Area of Operation Japan.

External Aid None known.

Clara Elizabeth Ramirez Front (CERF)

Description San Salvador-based urban terrorist group that shares revolutionary ideology of other leftist groups in El Salvador but operates independently.

Activities Most active during the period 1983-85 and was probably responsible for assassination in May 1983 of the deputy commander of US Military Advisory Group in San Salvador. Has been quiet since then because of arrests and defections of leaders.

Strength Unknown.

Location/Area of Operation El Salvador.

External Aid None known.

Communist Combatant Cells (CCC)

Description Founded in 1984, is revolutionary, anti-United States, and anti-NATO. Had organizational ties to the AD and the RAF.

Activities In 1984-85 carried out more than 30 bombing attacks against NATO and other defense-related targets; has also attacked domestic targets, such as banks. Leaders Pierre Carette and three associates were arrested in December 1985; since then, group has been inactive.

Strength Fewer than 10 hardcore members.

Location/Area of Operation Belgium.

External Aid Probably received aid from other terrorist groups in Western Europe, such as the AD and the RAF.

Communist Party of India (Maoist)

Formerly Maoist Communist Center of India (MCCI) and People's War (PW)

Description The Indian groups known as the Maoist Communist Center of India and People's War (a.k.a. People's War Group) joined together in September 2004 to form the Communist Party of India (Maoist), or CPI (Maoist). The MCCI was originally formed in the early 1970s, while People's War was founded in 1975. Both groups are referred to as Naxalites, after the West Bengal village where a revolutionary radical Left movement originated in 1967. The new organization continues to employ violence to achieve its goals—peasant revolution, abolition of class hierarchies, and expansion of Maoist-controlled "liberated zones," eventually leading to the creation of an independent "Maoist" state. The CPI (Maoist) reportedly has a significant cadre of women. Important leaders include Ganapati (the PW leader from Andhra Pradesh), Pramod Mishra, Uma Shankar, and P.N.G. (alias Nathuni Mistry, arrested by Jharkhand police in 2002).

Activities Prior to its consolidation with the PW, the MCCI ran a virtual parallel government in remote areas, where it collected a "tax" from the villagers and, in turn, provided infrastructure improvements such as building hospitals, schools, and irrigation projects. It ran a parallel court system wherein allegedly corrupt block development officials and landlords—frequent MCCI targets—had been punished by amputation and even death. People's War conducted a low-intensity insurgency that included attempted political assassination, theft of weapons from police stations, kidnapping police officers, assaulting civilians, extorting money from construction firms, and vandalizing the property of multinational corporations. Together the two groups were reportedly responsible for the deaths of up to 170 civilians and police a year.

Strength Although difficult to assess with any accuracy, media reports and local authorities suggest the CPI (Maoist)'s membership may be as high as 31,000, including both hard-core militants and dedicated sympathizers.

Location/Area of Operations The CPI (Maoist), believed to be enlarging the scope of its influence, operates in the Indian states of Andhra Pradesh, Orissa, Jharkhand, Bihar, Chhattisgarh, and parts of West Bengal. It also has a presence on the Bihar-Nepal border.

External Aid The CPI (Maoist) has loose links to other Maoist groups in the region, including the Communist Party of Nepal (Maoists). The MCCI was a founding member of the Coordination Committee of Maoist Parties and Organizations of South Asia (CCOMPOSA).

Communist Party of Nepal (Maoist)

a.k.a CPN/M

Description The Communist Party of Nepal (Maoist) insurgency grew out of the radicalization and fragmentation of left-wing parties following Nepal's transition to democracy in 1990. The United People's Front—a coalition of left-wing parties—participated in the elections of 1991, but the Maoist wing failed to win the required minimum number of votes, leading to its exclusion from voter lists in the elections of 1994 and prompting the group to launch the insurgency in 1996. The CPN/M's ultimate objective is the overthrow of the Nepalese Government and the establishment of a Maoist state. In 2003, the United States designated Nepal's Maoists under Executive Order (EO) 13224 as a supporter of terrorist activity.

Activities The Maoists have utilized traditional guerrilla warfare tactics and engage in murder, torture, arson, sabotage, extortion, child conscription, kidnapping, bombings, and assassinations to intimidate and coerce the populace. In 2002, Maoists claimed responsibility for assassinating two Nepalese US Embassy guards, citing anti-Maoist spying, and in a press statement threatened foreign embassies, including the US mission, to deter foreign support for the Nepalese Government. Maoists are suspected in the September 2004 bombing at the American Cultural Center in Kathmandu. The attack, which caused no injuries and only minor damage, marked the first time the Maoists had damaged US Government property.

Strength Probably several thousand full-time cadres.

Location/Area of Operation Operations are conducted throughout Nepal. Press reports indicate some Maoist leaders reside in India.

External Aid None.

Communist Party of Philippines/ New People's Army (CPP/NPA)

Designated as a Foreign Terrorist Organization.

Description The military wing of the Communist Party of the Philippines (CPP), the NPA is a Maoist group formed in March 1969 with the aim of overthrowing the Government through protracted guerrilla warfare. The chairman of the CPP's Central Committee and the NPA's founder, Jose Maria Sison, reportedly directs CPP and NPA activity from The Netherlands, where he lives in self-imposed exile. Fellow Central Committee member and director of the CPP's overt political wing, the National Democratic Front (NDF), Luis Jalandoni also lives in The Netherlands and has become a Dutch citizen. Although primarily a rural-based guerrilla group, the NPA has an active urban infrastructure to support its terrorist activities and uses city-based assassination squads. The rebels have claimed that the FTO designation has made it difficult to obtain foreign funding and forced them to step up extortion of businesses and politicians in the Philippines.

Activities The NPA primarily targets Philippine security forces, politicians, judges, government informers, former rebels who wish to leave the NPA, rival splinter groups, alleged criminals, Philippine infrastructure, and businesses that refuse to pay extortion, or "revolutionary taxes." The NPA opposes any US military presence in the Philippines and attacked US military interests, killing several US service personnel, before the US base closures in 1992. Press reports in 1999 and in late 2001 indicated the NPA was again targeting US troops participating in joint military exercises, as well as US Embassy personnel. The NPA has claimed responsibility for the assassination of two congressmen from Quezon in May 2001 and Cagayan in June 2001 and for many other killings. In January 2002, the NPA publicly expressed its intent to target US personnel if discovered in NPA operating areas.

Strength Estimated at less than 9,000, a number significantly lower than its peak strength of around 25,000 in the 1980s.

Location/Area of Operations Operates in rural Luzon, Visayas, and parts of Mindanao. Has cells in Manila and other metropolitan centers.

External Aid Unknown.

Continuity Irish Republican Army (CIRA)

a.k.a. Continuity Army Council, Republican Sinn Fein

Designated as a Foreign Terrorist Organization.

Description CIRA is a terrorist splinter group formed in the mid-1990s as the clandestine armed wing of Republican Sinn Fein, which split from Sinn Fein in 1986. "Continuity" refers to the group's belief that it is carrying on the original Irish Republican Army's (IRA) goal of forcing the British out of Northern Ireland. CIRA's aliases, Continuity Army Council and Republican Sinn Fein, were also designated as FTOs. CIRA cooperates with the larger Real IRA.

Activities CIRA has been active in Belfast and the border areas of Northern Ireland, where it has carried out bombings, assassinations, kidnappings, hijackings, extortion, and robberies. On occasion, it has provided advance warning to police of its attacks. Targets include British military, Northern Ireland security forces, and Loyalist paramilitary groups. Unlike the Provisional IRA, CIRA is not observing a cease-fire. CIRA has continued its activities with a series of hoax bomb threats, low-level improvised explosive device attacks, kidnapping, intimidation, and so-called "punishment beatings."

Strength Membership is small, with possibly fewer than 50 hardcore activists. Police counterterrorist operations have reduced the group's strength, but CIRA continues to recruit, train, and plan operations.

Location/Area of Operation Northern Ireland, Irish Republic. Does not have an established presence in Great Britain.

External Aid Suspected of receiving funds and arms from sympathizers in the United States. May have acquired arms and materiel from the Balkans in cooperation with the Real IRA.

Democratic Forces for the Liberation of Rwanda (FDLR)

a.k.a. Army for the Liberation of Rwanda (ALIR), Former Armed Forces (Ex-FAR), Interahamwe

Description The Democratic Forces for the Liberation of Rwanda (FDLR) in 2001 supplanted the Army for the Liberation of Rwanda (ALIR), which is the armed branch of the PALIR, or the Party for the Liberation of Rwanda. ALIR was formed from the merger of the Armed Forces of Rwanda (FAR), the army of the ethnic Hutu-dominated Rwandan regime that orchestrated the genocide of 500,000 or more Tutsis and regime opponents in 1994, and Interahamwe, the civilian militia force that carried out much of the killing, after the two groups were forced from Rwanda into the Democratic Republic of Congo (DRC-then Zaire) that year. Though directly descended from those who organized and carried out the genocide, identified FDLR leaders are not thought to have played a role in the killing. They have worked to build bridges to other opponents of the Kigali regime, including ethnic Tutsis.

Activities ALIR sought to topple Rwanda's Tutsi-dominated Government, reinstitute Hutu domination, and, possibly, complete the genocide. In 1996, a message—allegedly from the ALIR—threatened to kill the US ambassador to Rwanda and other US citizens. In 1999, ALIR guerrillas critical of US-UK support for the Rwandan regime kidnapped and killed eight foreign tourists, including two US citizens, in a game park on the Democratic Republic of Congo-Uganda border. Three suspects in the attack are in US custody awaiting trial. In the 1998-2002 Congolese war, the ALIR/FDLR was allied with Kinshasa against the Rwandan invaders. FDLR's political wing mainly has sought to topple the Kigali regime via an alliance with Tutsi regime opponents. It established the ADRN Igihango alliance in 2002, but it has not resonated politically in Rwanda.

Strength Exact strength is unknown, but several thousand FDLR guerrillas operate in the eastern DRC close to the Rwandan border. In 2003, the United Nations, with Rwandan assistance, repatriated close to 1,500 FDLR combatants from the DRC. The senior FDLR military commander returned to Rwanda in November 2003 and has been working with Kigali to encourage the return of his comrades.

Location/Area of Operation Mostly in the eastern Democratic Republic of the Congo.

External Support The Government of the Democratic Republic of the Congo provided training, arms, and supplies to ALIR forces to combat Rwandan armed forces that invaded the DRC in 1998. Kinshasa halted that support in 2002, though allegations persist of continued support from several local Congolese warlords and militias (including the Mai Mai).

Democratic Front for the Liberation of Palestine (DFLP)

Description Marxist group that split from the PFLP in 1969. Believes Palestinian national goals can be achieved only through revolution of the masses. In early 1980s, occupied political stance midway between Arafat and the more radical rejectionists. Split into two factions in 1991, one pro-Arafat and another more hardline faction headed by Nayif Hawatmah.

Activities In the seventies, carried out numerous small bombings and minor assaults and some more spectacular operations in Israel and the occupied territories, concentrating on Israeli targets such as the 1974 massacre in Ma'alot in which 27 Israelis were killed and over 100 wounded. Involved only in border raids since 1988.

Strength Estimated at 500 (total for both factions).

Location/Area of Operation Syria, Lebanon, and the Israeli-occupied territories; attacks have taken place entirely in Israel and the occupied territories.

External Aid Receives financial and military aid from Syria and Libya.

East Turkistan Islamic Movement (ETIM)

Description The East Turkistan Islamic Movement (ETIM) is a small Islamic extremist group based in China's western Xinjiang Province. It is the most militant of the ethnic Uighur separatist groups pursuing an independent "Eastern Turkistan," an area that would include Turkey, Kazakhstan, Kyrgyzstan, Uzbekistan, Pakistan, Afghanistan, and the Xinjiang Uighur Autonomous Region of China. ETIM is linked to al-Qaida and the international mujahedin movement. In September 2002 the group was designated under EO 13224 as a supporter of terrorist activity.

Activities ETIM militants fought alongside al-Qaida and Taliban forces in Afghanistan during Operation Enduring Freedom. In October 2003, Pakistani soldiers killed ETIM leader Hassan Makhsum during raids on al-Qaida–associated compounds in western Pakistan. US and Chinese Government information suggests ETIM is responsible for various terrorist acts inside and outside China. In May 2002, two ETIM members were deported to China from Kyrgyzstan for plotting to attack the US Embassy in Kyrgyzstan as well as other US interests abroad.

Strength Unknown. Only a small minority of ethnic Uighurs supports the Xinjiang independence movement or the formation of an Eastern Turkistan.

Location/Area of Operation Xinjiang Province and neighboring countries in the region.

External Aid ETIM has received training and financial assistance from al-Qaida.

Farabundo Marti National Liberation Front (FMLN)

Description Formed in 1980 with Cuban backing, the guerilla umbrella organization is composed of five leftist groups: Central American Workers' Revolutionary Party (PRTC), People's Revolutionary Army (ERP), Farabundo Marti Popular Liberation Forces (FPL), Armed Forces of National Resistance (FARN), and the Communist Party of El Salvador's Armed Forces of Liberation (FAL). The group reached a peace agreement with the Government of El Salvador on 31 December 1991.

Activities Bombings, assassinations, economic sabotage, arson, among other rural and urban operations. Since 1988 the FMLN increased urban terrorism in the capital.

Strength 6,000 to 7,000 combatants.

Location/Area of Operation El Salvador, limited activity in Honduras.

External Aid Has received direct support from Cuba and receives support form the Sandinistas in Nicaragua, where it maintains an office. The FMLN also receives significant financial support from front groups and sympathetic organizations in the United States and Europe.

First of October Antifascist Resistance Group (GRAPO) Grupo de Resistencia Anti-Fascista Primero de Octubre

Description GRAPO was formed in 1975 as the armed wing of the illegal Communist Party of Spain during the Franco era. Advocates the overthrow of the Spanish Government and its replacement with a Marxist-Leninist regime. GRAPO is vehemently anti-American, seeks the removal of all US military forces from Spanish territory, and has conducted and attempted several attacks against US targets since 1977. The group issued a communiqué following the September 11, 2001, attacks in the United States, expressing its satisfaction that "symbols of imperialist power" were decimated and affirming that "the war" has only just begun. Designated under EO 13224 in December 2001.

Activities GRAPO did not mount a successful terrorist operation in 2004, marking the third consecutive year without an attack. The group suffered more setbacks in 2004, with several members and sympathizers arrested and sentences upheld or handed down in April in the appellate case for GRAPO militants arrested in Paris in 2000. GRAPO has killed more than 90 persons and injured more than 200 since its formation. The group's operations traditionally have been designed to cause material damage and gain publicity rather than inflict casualties, but the terrorists have conducted lethal bombings and close range assassinations. In May 2000, the group killed two security guards during a botched armed robbery attempt of an armored truck carrying an estimated $2 million, and in November 2000, members assassinated a Spanish policeman in a possible reprisal for the arrest that month of several GRAPO leaders in France.

Strength Fewer than two dozen activists remain. Police have made periodic large-scale arrests of GRAPO members, crippling the organization and forcing it into lengthy rebuilding periods. In 2002, Spanish and French authorities arrested 22 suspected members, including some of the group's reconstituted leadership. More members were arrested throughout 2003 and 2004.

Location/Area of Operation Spain.

External Aid None.

Force 17

Description Formed in early 1970s as a personal security force for Arafat and other PLO leaders.

Activities According to press sources, in 1985 expanded operations to include terrorist attacks against Israeli targets. No confirmed terrorist activity outside Israel and the occupied territories since September 1985, when it claimed responsibility for killing three Israelis in Cyprus, an incident that was followed by Israeli air raids on PLO bases in Tunisia.

Strength Unknown.

Location/Area of Operation Based in Beirut before 1982. Since then, dispersed in several Arab countries. Now [1993] operating in Lebanon, other Middle East countries, and Europe.

External Aid PLO is main source of support.

Gama'a al-Islamiyya (IG)

a.k.a. Islamic Group, al-Gama'at
Designated as a Foreign Terrorist Organization

Description The IG, Egypt's largest militant group, has been active since the late 1970s, and is a loosely organized network. It has an external wing with supporters in several countries. The group's issuance of a cease-fire in 1997 led to a split into two factions: one, led by Mustafa Hamza, supported the cease-fire; the other, led by Rifa'i Taha Musa, called for a return to armed operations. The IG issued another ceasefire in March 1999, but its spiritual leader, Shaykh Umar Abd al-Rahman, sentenced to life in prison in January 1996 for his involvement in the 1993 World Trade Center bombing and incarcerated in the United States, rescinded his support for the cease-fire in June 2000. IG has not conducted an attack inside Egypt since the Luxor attack in 1997, which killed 58 tourists and four Egyptians and wounded dozens more. In February 1998, a senior member signed Usama Bin Ladin's fatwa calling for attacks against the United States.

In early 2001, Taha Musa published a book in which he attempted to justify terrorist attacks that would cause mass casualties. Taha Musa disappeared several months thereafter, and there is no information as to his current whereabouts. In March 2002, members of the group's historic leadership in Egypt declared use of violence misguided and renounced its future use, prompting denunciations by much of the leadership abroad. The Egyptian Government continues to release IG members from prison, including approximately 900 in 2003; likewise, most of the 700 persons released in 2004 at the end of the Muslim holy month of Ramadan were IG members.

For IG members still dedicated to violent jihad, their primary goal is to overthrow the Egyptian Government and replace it with an Islamic state. Disaffected IG members, such as those inspired by Taha Musa or Abd al-Rahman, may be interested in carrying out attacks against US interests.

Activities IG conducted armed attacks against Egyptian security and other Government officials, Coptic Christians, and Egyptian opponents of Islamic extremism before the cease-fire. After the 1997 cease-fire, the faction led by Taha Musa launched attacks on tourists in Egypt, most notably the attack in November 1997 at Luxor. IG also claimed responsibility for the attempt in June 1995 to assassinate Egyptian President Hosni Mubarak in Addis Ababa, Ethiopia.

Strength Unknown. At its peak IG probably commanded several thousand hard-core members and a like number of sympathizers. The 1999 cease-fire, security crackdowns following the attack in Luxor in 1997 and, more recently, security efforts following September 11 probably have resulted in a substantial decrease in the group's numbers.

Location/Area of Operation Operates mainly in the al-Minya, Asyut, Qina, and Sohaj Governorates of southern Egypt. Also appears to have support in Cairo, Alexandria, and other urban locations, particularly among unemployed graduates and students. Has a worldwide presence, including in the United Kingdom, Afghanistan, Yemen, and various locations in Europe.

External Aid Unknown. There is some evidence that Usama bin Ladin and Afghan militant groups support the organization. IG also may obtain some funding through various Islamic non-governmental organizations (NGOs).

HAMAS

a.k.a. Islamic Resistance Movement
Designated as a Foreign Terrorist Organization

Description HAMAS was formed in late 1987 as an outgrowth of the Palestinian branch of the Muslim Brotherhood. Various HAMAS elements have used both violent and political means, including terrorism, to pursue the goal of establishing an Islamic Palestinian state in Israel. It is loosely structured, with some elements working clandestinely and others operating openly through mosques and social service institutions to recruit members, raise money, organize activities, and distribute propaganda. HAMAS' strength is concentrated in the Gaza Strip and the West Bank. Also has engaged in political activity, such as running candidates in West Bank Chamber of Commerce elections.

Activities HAMAS terrorists, especially those in the Izz al-Din al-Qassam Brigades, have conducted many attacks, including large-scale suicide bombings, against Israeli civilian and military targets. HAMAS maintained the pace of its operational activity in 2004, claiming numerous attacks against Israeli interests. HAMAS has not yet directly targeted US interests, although the group makes little or no effort to avoid targets frequented by foreigners. HAMAS continues to confine its attacks to Israelis inside Israel and the occupied territories.

Strength Unknown number of official members; tens of thousands of supporters and sympathizers.

Location/Area of Operation HAMAS currently limits its terrorist operations to Israeli military and civilian targets in the West Bank, Gaza Strip, and Israel. Two of the group's most senior leaders in the Gaza Strip, Shaykh Ahmad Yasin and Abd al Aziz al Rantisi, were killed in Israeli air strikes in 2004. The group retains a cadre of senior leaders spread throughout the Gaza Strip, Syria, Lebanon, Iran, and the Gulf States.

External Aid Receives some funding from Iran but primarily relies on donations from Palestinian expatriates around the world and private benefactors in Saudi Arabia and other Arab states. Some fundraising and propaganda activity take place in Western Europe and North America.

Harakat ul-Jihad-I-Islami (HUJI) (Movement of Islamic Holy War)

Description HUJI, a Sunni extremist group that follows the Deobandi tradition of Islam, was founded in 1980 in Afghanistan to fight in the jihad against the Soviets. It also is affiliated with the Jamiat Ulema-i-Islam's Fazlur Rehman faction (JUI-F) of the extremist religious party Jamiat Ulema-I-Islam (JUI). The group, led by Qari Saifullah Akhtar and chief commander Amin Rabbani, is made up primarily of Pakistanis and foreign Islamists who are fighting for the liberation of Jammu and Kashmir and its accession to Pakistan. The group has links to al-Qaida. At present, Akhtar remains in detention in Pakistan after his August 2004 arrest and extradition from Dubai.

Activities Has conducted a number of operations against Indian military targets in Jammu and Kashmir. Linked to the Kashmiri militant group al-Faran that kidnapped five Western tourists in Jammu and Kashmir in July 1995; one was killed in August 1995, and the other four reportedly were killed in December of the same year.

Strength Exact numbers are unknown, but there may be several hundred members in Kashmir.

Location/Area of Operation Pakistan and Kashmir. Trained members in Afghanistan until autumn of 2001.

External Aid Specific sources of external aid are unknown.

Harakat ul-Jihad-I-Islami/ Bangladesh (HUJI-B)

Description The mission of HUJI-B, led by Shauqat Osman, is to establish Islamic rule in Bangladesh. HUJI-B has connections to the Pakistani militant groups Harakat ul-Jihad-I-Islami (HUJI) and Harakat ul-Mujahidin (HUM), which advocate similar objectives in Pakistan and Jammu and Kashmir. These groups all maintain contacts with the al-Qaida network in Afghanistan. The leaders of HUJI-B and HUM both signed the February 1998 fatwa sponsored by Usama bin Ladin that declared American civilians to be legitimate targets for attack.

Activities HUJI-B was accused of stabbing a senior Bangladeshi journalist in November 2000 for making a documentary on the plight of Hindus in Bangladesh. HUJI-B was suspected in the assassination attempt in July 2000 of Bangladeshi Prime Minister Sheikh Hasina. The group may also have been responsible for indiscriminate attacks using improvised explosive devices against cultural gatherings in Dhaka in January and April 2001.

Strength Unknown; some estimates of HUJI-B cadre strength suggest several thousand members.

Location/Area of Operation The group operates and trains members in Bangladesh, where it maintains at least six camps.

External Aid Funding of the HUJI-B comes primarily from madrassas in Bangladesh. The group also has ties to militants in Pakistan that may provide another funding source.

Harakat ul-Mujahidin (HUM)

a.k.a. Harakat ul-Ansar

Designated as a Foreign Terrorist Organization

Description HUM is an Islamist militant group based in Pakistan that operates primarily in Kashmir. It is politically aligned with the radical political party Jamiat Ulema-i-Islam's Fazlur Rehman faction (JUI-F). The long-time leader of the group, Fazlur Rehman Khalil, in mid-February 2000 stepped down as HUM emir, turning the reins over to the popular Kashmiri commander and his second-in-command, Farooqi Kashmiri. Khalil, who has been linked to Usama Bin Ladin and signed his fatwa in February 1998 calling for attacks on US and Western interests, assumed the position of HUM Secretary General. HUM operated terrorist training camps in eastern Afghanistan until Coalition air strikes destroyed them during fall 2001. Khalil was detained by the Pakistanis in mid-2004 and subsequently released in late December. In 2003, HUM began using the name Jamiat ul-Ansar (JUA), and Pakistan banned JUA in November 2003.

Activities Has conducted a number of operations against Indian troops and civilian targets in Kashmir. Linked to the Kashmiri militant group al-Faran that kidnapped five Western tourists in Kashmir in July 1995; one was killed in August 1995, and the other four reportedly were killed in December of the same year. HUM was responsible for the hijacking of an Indian airliner on December 24, 1999, which resulted in the release of Masood Azhar. Azhar, an important leader in the former Harakat ul-Ansar, was imprisoned by the Indians in 1994 and founded Jaish-e-Muhammad after his release. Also released in 1999 was Ahmed Omar Sheik, who was convicted of the abduction/murder in January-February 2002 of US journalist Daniel Pearl.

Strength Has several hundred armed supporters located in Azad Kashmir, Pakistan, and India's southern Kashmir and Doda regions and in the Kashmir valley. Supporters are mostly Pakistanis and Kashmiris and also include Afghans and Arab veterans of the Afghan war. Uses light and heavy machineguns, assault rifles, mortars, explosives, and rockets. HUM lost a significant share of its membership in defections to the Jaish-e-Mohammed (JEM) in 2000.

Location/Area of Operation Based in Muzaffarabad, Rawalpindi, and several other towns in Pakistan, but members conduct insurgent and terrorist activities primarily in Kashmir. HUM trained its militants in Afghanistan and Pakistan.

External Aid Collects donations from Saudi Arabia, other Gulf and Islamic states, Pakistanis and Kashmiris. HUM's financial collection methods also include soliciting donations in magazine ads and pamphlets. The sources and amount of HUM's military funding are unknown. In anticipation of asset seizures in 2001 by the Pakistani Government, the HUM withdrew funds from bank accounts and invested in legal businesses, such as commodity trading, real estate, and production of consumer goods. Its fundraising in Pakistan has been constrained since the Government clampdown on extremist groups and freezing of terrorist assets.

Hawari Group

a.k.a. Fatah Special Operations Group, Martyrs of Tal Al Za'atar, Amn Araissi

Description Part of Yasser Arafat's Fatah apparatus, the group is named after its leader commonly known as Colonel Hawari, who died in an automobile crash in May 1991 while traveling from Baghdad to Jordan. The group has ties historically to Iraq. Membership includes former members of the radical Palestinian 15 May organization.

Activities Carried out several attacks in 1985 and 1986, mainly in Europe and usually against Syrian targets. Has also targeted Americans, most notably in the April 1986 bombing of TWA Flight 840 over Greece in which four Americans were killed. Future of group uncertain following Hawari's death.

Strength Unknown.

Location/Area of Operation Middle Eastern countries and Europe.

External Aid PLO is main source of support.

Hizballah

a.k.a. Party of God, Islamic Jihad, Revolutionary Justice Organization, Organization of the Oppressed on Earth, Islamic Jihad for the Liberation of Palestine

Designated as a Foreign Terrorist Organization

Description Formed in 1982 in response to the Israeli invasion of Lebanon, this Lebanon-based radical Shia group takes its ideological inspiration from the Iranian revolution and the teachings of the late Ayatollah Khomeini. The Majlis al-Shura, or Consultative Council, is the group's highest governing body and is led by Secretary General Hasan Nasrallah. Hizballah is dedicated to liberating Jerusalem and eliminating Israel, and has formally advocated ultimate establishment of Islamic rule in Lebanon. Nonetheless, Hizballah has actively participated in Lebanon's political system since 1992. Hizballah is closely allied with, and often directed by, Iran but has the capability and willingness to act independently. Though Hizballah does not share the Syrian regime's secular orientation, the group has been a strong ally in helping Syria advance its political objectives in the region.

Activities Known or suspected to have been involved in numerous anti-US and anti-Israeli terrorist attacks, including the suicide truck bombings of the US Embassy and US Marine barracks in Beirut in 1983 and the US Embassy annex in Beirut in 1984. Three members of Hizballah, 'Imad Mughniyah, Hasan Izz-al-Din, and Ali Atwa, are on the FBI's list of 22 Most Wanted Terrorists for the 1985 hijacking of TWA Flight 847 during which a US Navy diver was murdered. Elements of the group were responsible for the kidnapping and detention of Americans and other Westerners in Lebanon in the 1980s. Hizballah also attacked the Israeli Embassy in Argentina in 1992 and the Israeli cultural center in Buenos Aires in 1994. In 2000, Hizballah operatives captured three Israeli soldiers in the Shab'a Farms and kidnapped an Israeli noncombatant. Hizballah also provides guidance and financial and operational support for Palestinian extremist groups engaged in terrorist operations in Israel and the occupied territories. In 2004, Hizballah launched an unmanned aerial vehicle (UAV) that left Lebanese airspace and flew over the Israeli town of Nahariya before crashing into Lebanese territorial waters. Ten days prior to the event, the Hizballah Secretary General said Hizballah would come up with new measures to counter Israeli Air Force violations of Lebanese airspace. Hizballah also continued launching small scale attacks across the Israeli border, resulting in the deaths of several Israeli soldiers. In March 2004, Hizballah and HAMAS signed an agreement to increase joint efforts to perpetrate attacks against Israel. In late 2004, Hizballah's al-Manar television station, based in Beirut with an estimated ten million viewers worldwide, was prohibited from broadcasting in France. Al-Manar was placed on the Terrorist Exclusion List (TEL) in the United States, which led to its removal from the program offerings of its main cable service provider, and made it more difficult for al-Manar associates and affiliates to operate in the United States.

Strength Several thousand supporters and a few hundred terrorist operatives.

Location/Area of Operation Operates in the southern suburbs of Beirut, the Beka'a Valley, and southern Lebanon. Has established cells in Europe, Africa, South America, North America, and Asia.

External Aid Receives financial, training, weapons, explosives, political, diplomatic, and organizational aid from Iran, and diplomatic, political, and logistical support from Syria. Hizballah also receives funding from charitable donations and business interests.

Hizb-I Islami Gulbuddin (HIG)

Description Gulbuddin Hikmatyar founded Hizb-I Islami Gulbuddin (HIG) as a faction of the Hizb-I Islami party in 1977, and it was one of the major mujahedin groups in the war against the Soviets. HIG has long-established links with Usama Bin Ladin. In the early 1990s, Hikmatyar ran several terrorist training camps in Afghanistan and was a pioneer in sending mercenary fighters to other Islamic conflicts. Hikmatyar offered to shelter Bin Ladin after the latter fled Sudan in 1996. In a late 2004 press release, Hikmatyar reiterated his commitment to fight US and Coalition forces.

Activities HIG has staged small attacks in its attempt to force US troops to withdraw from Afghanistan, overthrow the Afghan Transitional Administration, and establish an Islamic fundamentalist state. In 2004, several US soldiers were killed in attacks in Konar, Afghanistan, the area in which HIG is most active.

Strength Unknown, but possibly could have hundreds of veteran fighters on which to call.

Location/Area of Operation Eastern Afghanistan (particularly Konar and Nurestan Provinces) and adjacent areas of Pakistan's tribal areas.

External Aid Unknown.

Hizbul-Mujahedin (HM)

Description Hizbul-Mujahedin (HM), the largest Kashmiri militant group, was founded in 1989 and officially supports the liberation of Jammu and Kashmir and its accession to Pakistan, although some cadres favor independence. The group is the militant wing of Pakistan's largest Islamic political party, the Jamaat-i-Islami, and targets Indian security forces, politicians and civilians in Jammu and Kashmir. It reportedly operated in Afghanistan in the mid-1990s and trained with the Afghan Hizb-I Islami Gulbuddin (HIG) in Afghanistan until the Taliban takeover. The group, led by Syed Salahuddin, is comprised primarily of ethnic Kashmiris.

Activities HM has conducted a number of operations against Indian military targets in Jammu and Kashmir. The group also occasionally strikes at civilian targets, but has not engaged in terrorist acts outside India. HM claimed responsibility for numerous attacks within Kashmir in 2004.

Strength Exact numbers are unknown, but estimates range from several hundred to possibly as many as 1,000 members in Jammu and Kashmir and Pakistan.

Location/Area of Operation Jammu and Kashmir and Pakistan.

External Aid Specific sources of external aid are unknown.

Irish National Liberation Army (INLA)

Description The INLA is a terrorist group formed in 1975 as the military wing of the Irish Republican Socialist Party (IRSP), which split from the Official IRA (OIRA) because of OIRA's cease-fire in 1972. The group's primary aim is to end British rule in Northern Ireland, force British troops out of the province, and unite Ireland's 32 counties into a Marxist-Leninist revolutionary state. Responsible for some of the most notorious killings of "The Troubles," including the bombing of a Ballykelly pub that killed 17 people in 1982. Bloody internal feuding has repeatedly torn the INLA. The INLA announced a cease-fire in August 1998 but continues to carry out occasional attacks and punishment beatings.

Activities The INLA has been active in Belfast and the border areas of Northern Ireland, where it has conducted bombings, assassinations, kidnappings, hijackings, extortion, and robberies. It is also involved in drug trafficking. On occasion, it has provided advance warning to police of its attacks. Targets include the British military, Northern Ireland security forces, and Loyalist paramilitary groups. The INLA continues to observe a cease-fire, because—in the words of its leadership in 2003—a return to armed struggle is "not a viable option at this time." However, members of the group were accused of involvement in a robbery and kidnapping in December 2004, which the group denies.

Strength Unclear, but probably fewer than 50 hard-core activists. Police counterterrorist operations and internal feuding have reduced the group's strength and capabilities.

Location/Area of Operation Northern Ireland, Irish Republic. Does not have a significant established presence on the UK mainland.

External Aid Suspected in the past of receiving funds and arms from sympathizers in the United States.

Irish Republican Army (IRA)

a.k.a. Provisional Irish Republican Army (PIRA), the Provos

Description Formed in 1969 as the clandestine armed wing of the political movement Sinn Fein, the IRA is devoted both to removing British forces from Northern Ireland and to unifying Ireland. The IRA conducted attacks until its cease-fire in 1997 and agreed to disarm as a part of the 1998 Belfast Agreement, which established the basis for peace in Northern Ireland. Dissension within the IRA over support for the Northern Ireland peace process resulted in the formation of two more radical splinter groups: Continuity IRA (CIRA), and the Real IRA (RIRA) in mid to late 1990s. The IRA, sometimes referred to as the PIRA to distinguish it from RIRA and CIRA, is organized into small, tightly-knit cells under the leadership of the Army Council.

Activities Traditional IRA activities have included bombings, assassinations, kidnappings, punishment beatings, extortion, smuggling, and robberies. Before the cease-fire in 1997, the group had conducted bombing campaigns on various targets in Northern Ireland and Great Britain, including senior British Government officials, civilians, police, and British military targets. The group's refusal in late 2004 to allow photographic documentation of its decommissioning process was an obstacle to progress in implementing the Belfast Agreement and stalled talks. The group previously had disposed of light, medium, and heavy weapons, ammunition, and explosives in three rounds of decommissioning. However, the IRA is believed to retain the ability to conduct paramilitary operations. The group's extensive criminal activities reportedly provide the IRA and the political party Sinn Fein with millions of dollars each year; the IRA was implicated in two significant robberies in 2004, one involving almost $50 million.

Strength Several hundred members and several thousand sympathizers despite the defection of some members to RIRA and CIRA.

Location/Area of Operation Northern Ireland, Irish Republic, Great Britain, and Europe.

External Aid In the past, the IRA has received aid from a variety of groups and countries and considerable training and arms from Libya and the PLO. Is suspected of receiving funds, arms, and other terrorist-related materiel from sympathizers in the United States. Similarities in operations suggest links to ETA and the FARC. In August 2002, three suspected IRA members were arrested in Colombia on charges of helping the FARC improve its explosives capabilities.

Islamic Army of Aden (IAA)

a.k.a. Aden-Abyan Islamic Army (AAIA)

Description The Islamic Army of Aden (IAA) emerged publicly in mid-1998 when the group released a series of communiqués that expressed support for Usama Bin Ladin, appealed for the overthrow of the Yemeni Government, and called for operations against US and other Western interests in Yemen. IAA was first designated under EO 13224 in September 2001.

Activities IAA has engaged in small-scale operations such as bombings, kidnappings, and small arms attacks to promote its goals. The group reportedly was behind an attack in June 2003 against a medical assistance convoy in the Abyan Governorate. Yemeni authorities responded with a raid on a suspected IAA facility, killing several individuals and capturing others, including Khalid al-Nabi al-Yazidi, the group's leader. Before that attack, the group had not conducted operations since the bombing of the British Embassy in Sanaa in October 2000. In 2001, Yemeni authorities found an IAA member and three associates responsible for that attack. In December 1998, the group kidnapped 16 British, American, and Australian tourists near Mudiyah in southern Yemen. Although Yemeni officials previously have claimed that the group is operationally defunct, their recent attribution of the attack in 2003 against the medical convoy and reports that al-Yazidi was released from prison in mid-October 2003 suggest that the IAA, or at least elements of the group, have resumed activity. Speculation after the attack on the USS Cole pointed to the involvement of the IAA, and the group later claimed responsibility for the attack. The IAA has been affiliated with al-Qaida. IAA members are known to have trained and served in Afghanistan under the leadership of seasoned mujahedin.

Strength Not known.

Location/Area of Operation Operates in the southern governorates of Yemen—primarily Aden and Abyan.

External Aid Not known.

Islamic Great East Raiders–Front (IBDA-C)

Description The Islamic Great East Raiders–Front (IBDA-C) is a Sunni Salafist group that supports Islamic rule in Turkey and believes that Turkey's present secular leadership is "illegal." It has been known to cooperate with various opposition elements in Turkey in attempts to destabilize the country's political structure. The group supports the establishment of a "pure Islamic" state, to replace the present "corrupt" Turkish regime that is cooperating with the West. Its primary goal is the establishment of a "Federative Islamic State," a goal backed by armed terrorist attacks primarily against civilian targets. It has been active since the mid-1970s.

Activities IBDA-C has engaged in activities such as bombings, throwing Molotov cocktails, and sabotage. The group has announced its actions and targets in publications to its members, who are free to launch independent attacks. IBDA-C typically has attacked civilian targets, including churches, charities, minority-affiliated targets, television transmitters, newspapers, pro-secular journalists, Ataturk statues, taverns, banks, clubs, and tobacco shops. In May 2004, Turkish police indicted seven members of the group for the assassination of retired Colonel Ihsan Guven, the alleged leader of the "Dost" (Friend) sect, and his wife. One of IBDA-C's more renowned attacks was the killing of 37 people in a firebomb attack in July 1993 on a hotel in Sivas. Turkish police believe that IBDA-C has also claimed responsibility for attacks carried out by other groups to elevate its image.

Strength Unknown.

Location/Area of Operation Turkey.

External Aid Not known.

Islamic International Peacekeeping Brigade (IIPB)

Description The IIPB is a terrorist group affiliated with the Chechen separatist movement demanding a single Islamic state in the North Caucasus. Chechen extremist leader Shamil Basayev established the IIPB—consisting of Chechens, Arabs, and other foreign fighters—in 1998, which he led with Saudi-born mujahedin leader Ibn al-Khattab until the latter's death in March 2002. The IIPB was one of three groups affiliated with Chechen guerrillas that seized Moscow's Dubrovka Theater and took more than 700 hostages in October 2002. While this group has not been identified as conducting attacks since their designation two years ago, those Arab mujahedin still operating in Chechnya now fall under the command of Abu Hafs al-Urduni, who assumed the leadership in April 2004 after the death of Khattab's successor, Abu al-Walid. Designated under EO 13224 in February 2003.

Activities Involved in terrorist and guerilla operations against Russian forces, pro-Russian Chechen forces, and Chechen non-combatants.

Strength Up to 400 fighters, including as many as 100 Arabs and other foreign fighters.

Location/Area of Operation Primarily in Russia and adjacent areas of the North Caucasus, particularly in the mountainous south of Chechnya, with major logistical activities in Georgia, Azerbaijan, and Turkey.

External Aid The IIPB and its Arab leaders appear to be a primary conduit for Islamic funding of the Chechen guerrillas, in part through links to al-Qaida-related financiers on the Arabian Peninsula.

Islamic Jihad Group (IJG)

Description The Islamic Jihad Group (IJG), probably founded by former members of the Islamic Movement of Uzbekistan, made its first appearance in early April 2004 when it claimed responsibility for a string of events—including shootouts and terrorist attacks—in Uzbekistan in late March and early April that killed approximately 47 people, including 33 terrorists. The claim of responsibility, which was posted to multiple militant Islamic websites, raged against the leadership of Uzbekistan. In late July 2004, the group struck again with near-simultaneous suicide bombings of the US and Israeli Embassies and the Uzbek Prosecutor General's office in Tashkent. The IJG again claimed responsibility via an Islamic website and stated that martyrdom operations by the group would continue. The statement also indicated the attacks were done in support of their Palestinian, Iraqi, and Afghan brothers in the global jihad.

Activities The IJG claimed responsibility for multiple attacks in 2004 against Uzbekistani, American, and Israeli entities. The attackers in the March and April 2004 attacks, some of whom were female suicide bombers, targeted the local government offices of the Uzbekistani and Bukhara police, killing approximately 47 people, including 33 terrorists. These attacks marked the first use of female suicide bombers in Central Asia. On July 30, 2004, the group launched a set of same-day attacks against the US and Israeli Embassies and the Uzbek Prosecutor General's office. These attacks left four Uzbekistanis and three suicide operatives dead. The date of the latter attack corresponds to the start of a trial for individuals arrested for their participation in earlier attacks.

Strength Unknown.

Location/Area of Operation Militants are scattered throughout Central Asia and probably parts of South Asia.

External Aid Unknown.

Islamic Movement of Uzbekistan (IMU)

Description The Islamic Movement of Uzbekistan (IMU) is a group of Islamic militants from Uzbekistan and other Central Asian states. The IMU is closely affiliated with al-Qaida and, under the leadership of Tohir Yoldashev, has embraced Usama Bin Ladin's anti-US, anti-Western agenda. The IMU also remains committed to its original goals of overthrowing Uzbekistani President Karimov and establishing an Islamic state in Uzbekistan.

Activities The IMU in recent years has participated in attacks on US and Coalition soldiers in Afghanistan and Pakistan, and plotted attacks on US diplomatic facilities in Central Asia. In November 2004, the IMU was blamed for an explosion in the southern Kyrgyzstani city of Osh that killed one police officer and one terrorist. In May 2003, Kyrgyzstani security forces disrupted an IMU cell that was seeking to bomb the US Embassy and a nearby hotel in Bishkek, Kyrgyzstan. The IMU was also responsible for explosions in Bishkek in December 2002 and Osh in May 2003 that killed eight people. The IMU primarily targeted Uzbekistani interests before October 2001 and is believed to have been responsible for five car bombs in Tashkent in February 1999. IMU militants also took foreigners hostage in 1999 and 2000, including four US citizens who were mountain climbing in August 2000 and four Japanese geologists and eight Kyrgyzstani soldiers in August 1999.

Strength Probably fewer than 500.

Location/Area of Operation IMU militants are scattered throughout South Asia, Tajikistan, and Iran. The area of operations includes Afghanistan, Iran, Kyrgyzstan, Pakistan, Tajikistan, Kazakhstan, and Uzbekistan.

External Aid The IMU receives support from other Islamic extremist groups and patrons in the Middle East and Central and South Asia. IMU leadership have broadcast statements over Iranian radio.

Jaish-e-Mohammed (JEM)

a.k.a. Army of Mohammed Tehrik ul-Furqaan, Khuddamul-Islam

Designated as a Foreign Terrorist Organization

Description The Jaish-e-Mohammed is an Islamic extremist group based in Pakistan that was formed in early 2000 by Masood Azhar upon his release from prison in India. The group's aim is to unite Kashmir with Pakistan. It is politically aligned with the radical political party Jamiat Ulema-i-Islam's Fazlur Rehman faction (JUI-F). By 2003, JEM had splintered into Khuddam ul-Islam (KUI), headed by Azhar, and Jamaat ul-Furqan (JUF), led by Abdul Jabbar, who was released in August 2004 from Pakistani custody after being detained for suspected involvement in the December 2003 assassination attempts against President Musharraf. Pakistan banned KUI and JUF in November 2003. Elements of JEM and Lashkar e-Tayyiba combined with other groups to mount attacks as "The Save Kashmir Movement."

Activities The JEM's leader, Masood Azhar, was released from Indian imprisonment in December 1999 in exchange for 155 hijacked Indian Airlines hostages. The Harakat-ul-Ansar (HUA) kidnappings in 1994 of US and British nationals by Omar Sheik in New Delhi and the HUA/al-Faran kidnappings in July 1995 of Westerners in Kashmir were two of several previous HUA efforts to free Azhar. On October 1, 2001, JEM claimed responsibility for a suicide attack on the Jammu and Kashmir legislative assembly building in Srinagar that killed at least 31 persons but later denied the claim. The Indian Government has publicly implicated JEM, along with Lashkar e-Tayyiba, for the December 13, 2001, attack on the Indian Parliament that killed nine and injured 18. Pakistani authorities suspect that perpetrators of fatal anti-Christian attacks in Islamabad, Murree, and Taxila during 2002 were affiliated with JEM. The Pakistanis have implicated elements of JEM in the assassination attempts against President Musharraf in December 2003.

Strength Has several hundred armed supporters located in Pakistan and in India's southern Kashmir and Doda regions and in the Kashmir valley, including a large cadre of former HUM members. Supporters are mostly Pakistanis and Kashmiris and also include Afghans and Arab veterans of the Afghan war.

Location/Area of Operation Pakistan. JEM maintained training camps in Afghanistan until the fall of 2001.

External Aid Most of JEM's cadre and material resources have been drawn from the militant groups Harakat ul-Jihad-i-Islami (HUJI) and the Harakat ul-Mujahidin (HUM). JEM had close ties to Afghan Arabs and the Taliban. Usama bin Ladin is suspected of giving funding to JEM. JEM also collects funds through donation requests in magazines and pamphlets. In anticipation of asset seizures by the Pakistani Government, JEM withdrew funds from bank accounts and invested in legal businesses, such as commodity trading, real estate, and production of consumer goods.

Jamaat ul-Fuqra

Description Islamic sect that seeks to purify Islam through violence. Led by Pakistani cleric Shaykh Mubarik Ali Gilani, who established the organization in the early 1980s. Gilani now resides in Pakistan, but most cells are located in North America and the Caribbean. Members have purchased isolated rural compounds in North America to live communally, practice their faith, and insulate themselves from Western culture.

Activities Fuqra members have attacked a variety of targets that they view as enemies of Islam, including Muslims they regard as heretics and Hindus. Attacks during the 1980s included assassinations and firebombings across the United States. Fuqra members in the United States have been convicted of crimes, including murder and fraud.

Strength Unknown.

Location/Area of Operation North America; Pakistan.

External Aid None.

Jamiat ul-Mujahedin (JUM)

Description The JUM is a small, pro-Pakistan militant group formed in Jammu and Kashmir in 1990. Followers are mostly Kashmiris, but the group includes some Pakistanis.

Activities Has conducted a number of operations against Indian military and political targets in Jammu and Kashmir, including two grenade attacks against political targets in 2004.

Strength Unknown.

Location/Area of Operation Jammu and Kashmir and Pakistan.

External Aid Unknown.

Japanese Red Army (JRA)

a.k.a. Anti-Imperialist International Brigade (AIIB)

Description The JRA is an international terrorist group formed around 1970 after breaking away from the Japanese Communist League–Red Army Faction. The JRA's historical goal has been to overthrow the Japanese Government and monarchy and to help foment world revolution. JRA's leader, Fusako Shigenobu, claimed that the forefront of the battle against international imperialism was in Palestine, so in the early 1970s she led her small group to the Middle East to support the Palestinian struggle against Israel and the West. After her arrest in November 2000, Shigenobu announced she intended to pursue her goals using a legitimate political party rather than revolutionary violence, and the group announced it would disband in April 2001.

Activities During the 1970s, JRA carried out a series of attacks around the world, including the massacre in 1972 at Lod Airport in Israel, two Japanese airliner hijackings, and an attempted takeover of the US Embassy in Kuala Lumpur. During the late 1980s, JRA began to single out American targets and used car bombs and rockets in attempted attacks on US Embassies in Jakarta, Rome, and Madrid. In April 1988, JRA operative Yu Kikumura was arrested with explosives on the New Jersey Turnpike, apparently planning an attack to coincide with the bombing of a USO club in Naples, a suspected JRA operation that killed five, including a US servicewoman. He was convicted of the charges and is serving a lengthy prison sentence in the United States. Tsutomu Shirosaki, captured in 1996, is also jailed in the United States. In 2000, Lebanon deported to Japan four members it arrested in 1997, but granted a fifth operative, Kozo Okamoto, political asylum. Longtime leader Shigenobu was arrested in November 2000 and faces charges of terrorism and passport fraud. Four JRA members remain in North Korea following their involvement in a hijacking in 1970; five of their family members returned to Japan in 2004.

Strength About six hard-core members; undetermined number of sympathizers. At its peak, the group claimed to have 30 to 40 members.

Location/Area of Operation Location unknown, but possibly in Asia and/or Syrian-controlled areas of Lebanon.

External Aid Unknown.

Jemaah Islamiya Organization (JI)

Designated as a Foreign Terrorist Organization

Description Jemaah Islamiya is a Southeast Asian–based terrorist network with links to al-Qaida. The network recruited and trained extremists in the late 1990s, following the stated goal of creating an Islamic state comprising Brunei, Indonesia, Malaysia, Singapore, the southern Philippines, and southern Thailand.

Activities Jemaah Islamiya Organization is responsible for numerous high-profile bombings, including the bombing of the J. W. Marriott Hotel in Jakarta on August 5, 2003, and the Bali bombings on October 12, 2002. Members of the group have also been implicated in the September 9, 2004, attack outside the Australian Embassy in Jakarta. The Bali attack, which left more than 200 dead, was reportedly the final outcome of meetings in early 2002 in Thailand, where attacks in Singapore and against soft targets such as tourist spots were also considered. In June 2003, authorities disrupted a JI plan to attack several Western embassies and tourist sites in Thailand. In December 2001, Singaporean authorities uncovered a JI plot to attack the US and Israeli Embassies and British and Australian diplomatic buildings in Singapore. JI is also responsible for the coordinated bombings of numerous Christian churches in Indonesia on Christmas Eve 2000 and was involved in the bombings of several targets in Manila on December 31, 2000. The capture in August 2003 of Indonesian Riduan bin Isomoddin (a.k.a. Hambali), JI leader and al-Qaida Southeast Asia operations chief, damaged the JI, but the group maintains its ability to target Western interests in the region and to recruit new members through a network of radical Islamic schools based primarily in Indonesia. The emir, or spiritual leader, of JI, Abu Bakar Ba'asyir, was on trial at year's end on charges of conspiracy to commit terrorist acts, and for his links to the Bali and Jakarta Marriott bombings and to a cache of arms and explosives found in central Java.

Strength Exact numbers are unknown, but Southeast Asian authorities continue to uncover and arrest JI elements. Estimates of total JI members vary widely from the hundreds to the thousands.

Location/Area of Operation JI is believed to have cells spanning Indonesia, Malaysia, and the Philippines.

External Aid Investigations indicate that JI is fully capable of its own fundraising, although it also receives financial, ideological, and logistical support from Middle Eastern and South Asian contacts, non-governmental organizations, and other groups.

Justice Commandos of the Armenian Genocide (JCAG)

a.k.a. Armenian Revolutionary Army

Description Rightwing Armenian nationalist group founded in 1975, probably to counter influence of leftist ASALA. Goals are similar to ASALA's, but ideological differences preclude working together.

Activities Operations limited to attacks against Turkish targets, chiefly diplomats. Later operations conducted in name of ARA, inactive since last attack in 1985.

Strength Unknown.

Location/Area of Operation Unknown. Operates in Western Europe, United States, Canada, and Middle East.

External Aid Received aid from rightwing segments of Armenian community worldwide.

Kahane Chai (Kach)

Designated as a Foreign Terrorist Organization

Description Kach's stated goal is to restore the biblical state of Israel. Kach, founded by radical Israeli-American rabbi Meir Kahane, and its offshoot Kahane Chai, (translation: "Kahane Lives"), founded by Meir Kahane's son Binyamin following his father's 1990 assassination in the United States, were declared to be terrorist organizations in 1994 by the Israeli Cabinet under its 1948 Terrorism Law. This followed the groups' statements in support of Dr. Baruch Goldstein's attack in February 1994 on the al-Ibrahimi Mosque (Goldstein was affiliated with Kach) and their verbal attacks on the Israeli Government. Palestinian gunmen killed Binyamin Kahane and his wife in a drive-by shooting in December 2000 in the West Bank.

Activities The group has organized protests against the Israeli Government. Kach has harassed and threatened Arabs, Palestinians, and Israeli Government officials, and has vowed revenge for the death of Binyamin Kahane and his wife. Kach is suspected of involvement in a number of low-level attacks since the start of the al-Aqsa intifadah in 2000. Known Kach sympathizers are becoming more vocal and active against the planned Israeli withdrawal from the Gaza Strip in mid-2005.

Strength Unknown.

Location/Area of Operation Israel and West Bank settlements, particularly Qiryat Arba' in Hebron.

External Aid Receives support from sympathizers in the United States and Europe.

Khmer Rouge

a.k.a. The Party of Democratic Kampuchea

Description The Khmer Rouge (KR) Communist insurgency ended in 1999 after a series of defections, military defeats, and the capture of group leader Ta Mok. The US State Department removed the group from the list of designated foreign terrorist organizations in 1999. The Cambodian Government has been working with the United Nations to establish a court to try former KR for the deaths of up to 2 million persons in Cambodia during the 1975–79 period.

Activities Former KR may engage in criminal-type activities, especially against Vietnamese nationals.

Strength At its height up to 2,000. Currently inactive; last attack April 27, 1997.

Location/Area of Operation Cambodia, mainly in outlying provinces along the Thai border.

External Aid Received support from Vietnam in the 1950s and China in the 1980s. In the 1990s they were involved in timber sales to Thailand. No external aid currently received.

Kongra-Gel (KGK)

a.k.a. Kurdistan Workers' Party, PKK, Kurdistan Freedom and Democracy Congress, KADEK, Kurdistan People's Congress, Freedom and Democracy Congress of Kurdistan

Designated as a Foreign Terrorist Organization

Description Founded by Abdullah Ocalan in 1974 as a Marxist-Leninist separatist organization and formally named the Kurdistan Workers' Party (PKK) in 1978. The group, composed primarily of Turkish Kurds, began its campaign of armed violence in 1984, which has resulted in some 30,000 casualties. The PKK's goal has been to establish an independent, democratic Kurdish state in southeast Turkey, northern Iraq, and parts of Iran and Syria. In the early 1990s, the PKK moved beyond rural-based insurgent activities to include urban terrorism. Turkish authorities captured Ocalan in Kenya in early 1999, and the Turkish State Security Court subsequently sentenced him to death. In August 1999, Ocalan announced a "peace initiative," ordering members to refrain from violence and requesting dialogue with Ankara on Kurdish issues. At a

PKK Congress in January 2000, members supported Ocalan's initiative and claimed the group now would use only political means to achieve its public goal of improved rights for Kurds in Turkey. In April 2002 at its 8th Party Congress, the PKK changed its name to the Kurdistan Freedom and Democracy Congress (KADEK) and proclaimed a commitment to non-violent activities in support of Kurdish rights. In late 2003, the group sought to engineer another political face-lift, renaming itself Kongra-Gel (KGK) and promoting its "peaceful" intentions while continuing to conduct attacks in "self-defense" and to refuse disarmament. After five years, the group's hardline militant wing, the People's Defense Force (HPG), renounced its self-imposed cease-fire on June 1, 2004. Over the course of the cease-fire, the group had divided into two factions—politically-minded reformists, and hardliners who advocated a return to violence. The hardliners took control of the group in February 2004.

Activities Primary targets have been Turkish Government security forces, local Turkish officials, and villagers who oppose the organization in Turkey. It conducted attacks on Turkish diplomatic and commercial facilities in dozens of West European cities in 1993 and again in spring 1995. In an attempt to damage Turkey's tourist industry, the then-PKK bombed tourist sites and hotels and kidnapped foreign tourists in the early-to-mid-1990s. While most of the group's violence in 2004 was directed toward Turkish security forces, KGK was likely responsible for an unsuccessful July car bomb attack against the governor of Van Province, although it publicly denied responsibility, and may have played a role in the August bombings of two Istanbul hotels and a gas complex in which two people died.

Strength Approximately 4,000 to 5,000, 3,000 to 3,500 of whom currently are located in northern Iraq. The group has thousands of sympathizers in Turkey and Europe. In November, Dutch police raided a suspected KGK training camp in The Netherlands, arresting roughly 30 suspected members.

Location/Area of Operation Operates primarily in Turkey, Iraq, Europe, and the Middle East.

External Aid Has received safe haven and modest aid from Syria, Iraq, and Iran. Syria and Iran appear to cooperate with Turkey against KGK in a limited fashion when it serves their immediate interests. KGK uses Europe for fundraising and conducting political propaganda.

Kumpulan Mujahidin Malaysia (KMM)

Description Kumpulan Mujahidin Malaysia (KMM) favors the overthrow of the Malaysian Government and the creation of an Islamic state comprising Malaysia, Indonesia, and the southern Philippines. Malaysian authorities believe an extremist wing of the KMM has engaged in terrorist acts and has close ties to the regional terrorist organization Jemaah Islamiya (JI). Key JI leaders, including the group's spiritual head, Abu Bakar Ba'asyir, and JI operational leader Hambali, reportedly had great influence over KMM members. The Government of Singapore asserts that a Singaporean JI member assisted the KMM in buying a boat to support jihad activities in Indonesia.

Activities Malaysia is holding a number of KMM members under the Internal Security Act (ISA) for activities deemed threatening to Malaysia's national security, including planning to wage jihad, possession of weaponry, bombings and robberies, the murder of a former state assemblyman, and planning attacks on foreigners, including US citizens. A number of those detained are also believed to be members of Jemaah Islamiya. Several of the arrested KMM militants have reportedly undergone military training in Afghanistan, and some fought with the Afghan mujahedin during the war against the former Soviet Union. Some members are alleged to have ties to Islamic extremist organizations in Indonesia and the Philippines. In September 2003, alleged KMM leader Nik Adli Nik Abdul Aziz's detention was extended for another two years. In March 2004, Aziz and other suspected KMM members went on a hunger strike as part of an unsuccessful bid for freedom, but the Malaysian court rejected their applications for a writ of habeas corpus in September. One alleged KMM member was sentenced to 10 years in prison for unlawful possession of firearms, explosives, and ammunition, but eight other alleged members in detention since 2001 were released in July and in November. The Malaysian Government is confident that the arrests of KMM leaders have crippled the organization and rendered it incapable of engaging in militant activities. Malaysian officials in May 2004 denied Thailand's charge that the KMM was involved in the Muslim separatist movement in southern Thailand.

Strength KMM's current membership is unknown, but Malaysian police previously assessed membership at 70 to 80. Malaysian press reports suggest police track about 200 suspected militants.

Location/Area of Operation The KMM is reported to have networks in the Malaysian states of Perak, Johor, Kedah, Selangor, Terengganu, and Kelantan. They also operate in Kuala Lumpur. According to press reports, the KMM has ties to radical Indonesian Islamic groups and has sent members to Ambon, Indonesia, to fight against Christians and to the southern Philippines for operational training.

External Aid Largely unknown, probably self-financing.

Lashkar e-Tayyiba (LT)

a.k.a. Army of the Righteous, Lashkar-e-Toiba, al Monsooreen, al-Mansoorian, Army of the Pure, Army of the Righteous, Army of the Pure and Righteous

Designated as a Foreign Terrorist Organization

Description LT is the armed wing of the Pakistan-based religious organization, Markaz-ud-Dawa-wal-Irshad (MDI), an anti-US Sunni missionary organization formed in 1989. LT is led by Hafiz Muhammad Saeed and is one of the three largest and best trained groups fighting in Kashmir against India. It is not connected to any political party. The Pakistani Government banned the group and froze its assets in January 2002. Elements of LT and Jaish-e-Mohammed combined with other groups to mount attacks as "The Save Kashmir Movement."

Activities LT has conducted a number of operations against Indian troops and civilian targets in Jammu and Kashmir since 1993. LT claimed responsibility for numerous attacks in 2001, including an attack in January on Srinagar airport that killed five Indians; an attack on a police station in Srinagar that killed at least eight officers and wounded several others; and an attack in April against Indian border security forces that left at least four dead. The Indian Government publicly implicated LT, along with JEM, for the attack on December 13, 2001, on the Indian Parliament building, although concrete evidence is lacking. LT is also suspected of involvement in the attack on May 14, 2002, on an Indian Army base in Kaluchak that left 36 dead. Senior al-Qaida lieutenant Abu Zubaydah was captured at an LT safe house in Faisalabad in March 2002, suggesting some members are facilitating the movement of al-Qaida members in Pakistan.

Strength Has several thousand members in Azad Kashmir, Pakistan, in the southern Jammu and Kashmir and Doda regions, and in the Kashmir valley. Almost all LT members are Pakistanis from madrassas across Pakistan or Afghan veterans of the Afghan wars.

Location/Area of Operation Based in Muridke (near Lahore) and Muzaffarabad.

External Aid Collects donations from the Pakistani community in the Persian Gulf and United Kingdom, Islamic NGOs, and Pakistani and other Kashmiri business people. LT also maintains a Web site (under the name Jamaat ud-Daawa), through which it solicits funds and provides information on the group's activities. The amount of LT funding is unknown. LT maintains ties to religious/militant groups around the world, ranging from the Philippines to the Middle East and Chechnya through the fraternal network of its parent organization Jamaat ud-Dawa (formerly Markaz Dawa ul-Irshad). In anticipation of asset seizures by the Pakistani Government, the LT withdrew funds from bank accounts and invested in legal businesses, such as commodity trading, real estate, and production of consumer goods.

Lashkar i Jhangvi (LJ)

Designated as a Foreign Terrorist Organization

Description Lashkar i Jhangvi (LJ) is the militant offshoot of the Sunni sectarian group Sipah-i-Sahaba Pakistan. LJ focuses primarily on anti-Shia attacks and was banned by Pakistani President Musharraf in August 2001 as part of an effort to rein in sectarian violence. Many of its members then sought refuge in Afghanistan with the Taliban, with whom they had existing ties. After the collapse of the Taliban, LJ members became active in aiding other terrorists with safe houses, false identities, and protection in Pakistani cities, including Karachi, Peshawar, and Rawalpindi. In January 2003, the United States added LJ to the list of Foreign Terrorist Organizations.

Activities LJ specializes in armed attacks and bombings. The group attempted to assassinate former Prime Minister Nawaz Sharif and his brother Shabaz Sharif, Chief Minister of Punjab Province, in January 1999. Pakistani authorities have publicly linked LJ members to the kidnap and murder of US journalist Daniel Pearl in early 2002. Police officials initially suspected LJ members were involved in the two suicide car bombings in Karachi in 2002 against a French shuttle bus in May and the US Consulate in June, but their subsequent investigations have not led to any LJ members being charged in the attacks. Similarly, press reports have linked LJ to attacks on Christian targets in Pakistan, including a grenade assault on the Protestant International Church in Islamabad in March 2002 that killed two US citizens, but no formal charges have been filed against the group. Pakistani authorities believe LJ was responsible for the bombing in July 2003 of a Shiite mosque in Quetta, Pakistan. Authorities have also implicated LJ in several sectarian incidents in 2004, including the May and June bombings of two Shiite mosques in Karachi that killed over 40 people.

Strength Probably fewer than 100.

Location/Area of Operation LJ is active primarily in Punjab and Karachi. Some members travel between Pakistan and Afghanistan.

External Aid Unknown.

Lautaro Youth Movement (MJL)

a.k.a. The Lautaro faction of the United Popular Action Movement (MAPU/L) or Lautaro Popular Rebel Forces (FRPL)

Description Violent, anti-US extremist group that advocated the overthrow of the Chilean Government. Leadership largely from leftist elements but includes criminals and alienated youths. Became active in late 1980s, but has been seriously weakened by government counterterrorist successes in recent years.

Activities Has been linked to assassinations of policemen, bank robberies, and attacks on Mormon churches.

Strength Unknown.

Location/Area of Operation Chile; mainly Santiago.

External Aid None.

Lebanese Armed Revolutionary Faction (LARF)

a.k.a. Faction Armee Revolutionaire Libanaise (FARL)

Description Marxist-Leninist terrorist group formed about 1990 by George Ibrahim Abdallah, a pro-Palestinian Christian from northern Lebanon. Anti-"US imperialist," anti-Israel. Members recruited from two villages in northern Lebanon; many are related to each other. Some previously were members of the pro-Syrian Socialist Nationalist Party or the PFLP.

Activities Selected assassination and bombing attacks against Western targets, including attempted murder of US charge in Paris (1981), murder of US military attaché in Paris (1982), suspected involvement in murder of US head of Sinai Multinational Force and Observers in Rome (1984), and attempted murder of US Consul General in Strasbourg (1984). George Abdallah was arrested in France in 1984 and is currently serving a life sentence there.

Strength 20 to 30.

Location/Area of Operation Northern Lebanon, operated in Lebanon and Western Europe.

External Aid Press source claims that LARF had received both funding and direction from Syria and had links to several terrorist groups in Western Europe, including Action Directe, the Red Brigades, and the Red Army Faction.

Liberation Tigers of Tamil Eelam (LTTE)

a.k.a. The Tamil Tigers, The Ellalan Force
Other known front organizations: World Tamil Association (WTA), World Tamil Movement (WTM), the Federation of Associations of Canadian Tamils (FACT), the Ellalan Force, and the Sangilian Force.

Designated as a Foreign Terrorist Organization

Description Founded in 1976, the LTTE is the most powerful Tamil group in Sri Lanka. It began its insurgency against the Sri Lankan Government in 1983 and has relied on a guerrilla strategy that includes the use of terrorist tactics. The LTTE currently is observing a cease-fire agreement with the Sri Lankan Government.

Activities The LTTE has integrated a battlefield insurgent strategy with a terrorist program that targets key personnel in the countryside and senior Sri Lankan political and military leaders in Colombo and other urban centers. The LTTE is most notorious for its cadre of suicide bombers, the Black Tigers. Political assassinations and bombings were commonplace tactics prior to the cease-fire.

Strength Exact strength is unknown, but the LTTE is estimated to have 8,000 to 10,000 armed combatants in Sri Lanka, with a core of 3,000 to 6,000 trained fighters. The LTTE also has a significant overseas support structure for fundraising, weapons procurement, and propaganda activities.

Location/Area of Operations The LTTE controls most of the northern and eastern coastal areas of Sri Lanka but has conducted operations throughout the island. Headquartered in northern Sri Lanka, LTTE leader Velupillai Prabhakaran has established an extensive network of checkpoints and informants to keep track of any outsiders who enter the group's area of control.

External Aid The LTTE's overt organizations support Tamil separatism by lobbying foreign governments and the United Nations. The LTTE also uses its international contacts and the large Tamil diaspora in North America, Europe, and Asia to procure weapons, communications, funding, and other needed supplies.

Libyan Islamic Fighting Group (LIFG)

a.k.a. Al-Jama'a al-Islamiyyah al-Muqatilah bi-Libya, Fighting Islamic Group, Libyan Fighting Group, Libyan Islamic Group

Designated as a Foreign Terrorist Organization

Description The Libyan Islamic Fighting Group (LIFG) emerged in the early 1990s among Libyans who had fought against Soviet forces in Afghanistan and against the Qadhafi regime in Libya. The LIFG declared the Government of Libyan leader Muammar Qadhafi un-Islamic and pledged to overthrow it. Some members maintain a strictly anti-Qadhafi focus and organize against Libyan Government interests, but others are aligned with Usama Bin Ladin and believed to be part of al-Qaida's leadership structure or active in the international terrorist network.

Activities Libyans associated with the LIFG are part of the broader international jihadist movement. The LIFG is one of the groups believed to have planned the Casablanca suicide bombings in May 2003. The LIFG claimed responsibility for a failed assassination attempt against Qadhafi in 1996 and engaged Libyan security forces in armed clashes during the 1990s. It continues to target Libyan interests and may engage in sporadic clashes with Libyan security forces.

Strength Not known, but probably has several hundred active members or supporters.

Location/Area of Operation Probably maintains a clandestine presence in Libya, but since the late 1990s many members have fled to various Asian, Persian Gulf, African, and European countries, particularly the United Kingdom.

External Aid Not known. May obtain some funding through private donations, various Islamic non-governmental organizations, and criminal acts.

Lord's Resistance Army (LRA)

Description The LRA was formally established in 1994, succeeding the ethnic Acholi-dominated Holy Spirit Movement and other insurgent groups. LRA leader Joseph Kony has called for the overthrow of the Ugandan Government and its replacement with a regime run on the basis of the Ten Commandments. More frequently, however, he has spoken of the liberation and honor of the Acholi people, whom he sees as oppressed by the "foreign" Government of Ugandan President Museveni. Kony is the LRA's undisputed leader. He claims to have supernatural powers and to receive messages from spirits, which he uses to formulate the LRA's strategy.

Activities The Acholi people, whom Kony claims to be fighting to liberate, are the ones who suffer most from his actions. Since the early 1990's, the LRA has kidnapped some 20,000 Ugandan children, mostly ethnic Acholi, to replenish its ranks. Kony despises Acholi elders for having given up the fight against Museveni and relies on abducted children who can be brutally indoctrinated to fight for the LRA. The LRA forces kidnapped children and adult civilians to become soldiers, porters, and "wives" for LRA leaders. The LRA prefers to attack camps for internally displaced persons and other civilian targets, avoiding direct engagement with the Ugandan military. Victims of LRA attacks sometimes have their hands, fingers, ears, noses, or other extremities cut off. The LRA stepped up its activities from 2002 to 2004 after the Ugandan army, with the Sudanese Government's permission, attacked LRA positions inside Sudan. By late 2003, the number of internally displaced had doubled to 1.4 million, and the LRA had pushed deep into non-Acholi areas where it had never previously operated. During 2004, a combination of military pressure, offers of amnesty, and several rounds of negotiation markedly degraded LRA capabilities due to death, desertion, and defection of senior commanders.

Strength Estimated in early 2004 at between 500 and 1,000 fighters, 85 percent of whom are abducted children and civilians, but numbers have since declined significantly.

Location/Area of Operation Northern Uganda and southern Sudan.

External Aid Although the LRA has been supported by the Government of Sudan in the past, the Sudanese now appear to be cooperating with the Government of Uganda in a campaign to eliminate LRA sanctuaries in Sudan.

Loyalist Volunteer Force (LVF)

Description An extreme Loyalist group formed in 1996 as a faction of the Ulster Volunteer Force (UVF), the LVF did not emerge publicly until 1997. Composed largely of UVF hardliners who have sought to prevent a political settlement with Irish nationalists in Northern Ireland by attacking Catholic politicians, civilians, and Protestant politicians who endorse the Northern Ireland peace process. LVF occasionally uses the Red Hand Defenders as a cover name for its actions but has also called for the group's disbandment. In October 2001, the British Government ruled that the LVF had broken the cease-fire it declared in 1998 after linking the group to the murder of a journalist. According to the Independent International Commission on Decommissioning, the LVF decommissioned a small amount of weapons in December 1998, but it has not repeated this gesture. Designated under EO 13224 in December 2001.

Activities Bombings, kidnappings, and close-quarter shooting attacks. Finances its activities with drug money and other criminal activities. LVF attacks have been particularly vicious; the group has murdered numerous Catholic civilians with no political or paramilitary affiliations, including an 18-year-old Catholic girl in July 1997 because she had a Protestant boyfriend. The terrorists also have conducted successful attacks against Irish targets in Irish border towns. From 2000 to 2004, the LVF has been engaged in a violent feud with other Loyalists, which has left several men dead.

Strength Small, perhaps dozens of active members.

Location/Area of Operation Northern Ireland and Ireland.

External Aid None.

Manuel Rodriquez Patriotic Front (FPMR)

Description Founded in 1983 as the armed wing of the Chilean Communist Party and named for the hero of Chile's war of independence against Spain. Splintered into two factions in the late 1980s and one faction became a political party in 1991. The dissident wing FPMR/D is Chile's only remaining active terrorist group.

Activities FPMR/D attacks civilians and international targets, including US businesses and Mormon churches. In 1993, FPMR/D bombed two McDonald's restaurants and attempted to bomb a Kentucky Fried Chicken restaurant. Successful government counterterrorist operations have undercut the organizations significantly. Four FPMR/D members escaped from prison using a helicopter in December 1996. One of them, Patricio Ortiz Montenegro, fled to Switzerland where he requested political asylum. Chile requested Ortiz's extradition, but the Swiss Government—fearing Chile would not safeguard Ortiz's physical and psychological well-being—denied the request. Chilean authorities continued to pursue the whereabouts of the three others who escaped with Ortiz.

Strength In 1998 estimated 50 to 100 members.

Location/Area of Operation Chile.

External Aid None.

Moroccan Islamic Combatant Group (GICM)

Description The goals of the Moroccan Islamic Combatant Group (GICM) include establishing an Islamic state in Morocco and supporting al-Qaida's jihad against the West. The group appears to have emerged in the 1990s and is comprised of Moroccan recruits who trained in armed camps in Afghanistan and some who fought in the Afghan resistance against Soviet occupation. GICM members interact with other North African extremists, particularly in Europe. On November 22, 2002, the United States designated the GICM for asset freeze under EO 13224 following the group's submission to the UNSCR 1267 Sanctions Committee.

Activities Moroccans associated with the GICM are part of the broader international jihadist movement. GICM is one of the groups believed to be involved in planning the May 2003 Casablanca suicide bombings, and has been involved in other plots. Members work with other North African extremists, engage in trafficking falsified documents, and possibly arms smuggling. The group in the past has issued communiqués and statements against the Moroccan Government. In the last year, a number of arrests in Belgium, France, and Spain have disrupted the group's ability to operate, though cells and key members still remain throughout Europe. Although the Abu Hafs al-Masri Brigades, among others, claimed responsibility on behalf of al-Qaida, Spanish authorities are investigating the possibility that GICM was involved in the March 11, 2004, Madrid train bombings.

Strength Unknown.

Location/Area of Operation Morocco, Western Europe, Afghanistan, and Canada.

External Aid Unknown, but believed to include criminal activity abroad.

Morazanist Patriotic Front (FPM)

Description A radical, leftist terrorist group that first appeared in the late 1980s. Attacks made to protest US intervention in Honduran economic and political affairs.

Activities Attacks on US, mainly military, personnel in Honduras. Claimed responsibility for attack on a bus in March 1990 that wounded seven US servicemen. Claimed bombing of Peace Corps office in December 1988; bus bombing that wounded three US servicemen in February 1989; attack on US convoy in April 1989; and grenade attack that wounded seven US soldiers in La Ceiba in July 1989.

Strength Unknown, probably relatively small.

Location/Area of Operation Honduras.

External Aid External ties to former Government of Nicaragua and possibly Cuba.

Movement of the Revolutionary Left (MIR)

Description Formed as a political party/movement in 1965. While the leadership is middle class, the group seeks to establish a Marxist-Leninist regime led by workers and peasants. Some Cuban-trained leadership reinfiltrated Chile, having fled after fall of Allende regime.

Activities Relatively inactive in terrorist arena because of effective government countermeasures in early 1980s and also because it has split into at least two competing factions.

Strength 300 to 400 (estimated).

Location/Area of Operation Chile.

External Aid Over the years has received training and other support from several countries, especially Cuba, but also from Nicaragua, Libya, and the Eastern Bloc.

Movement of 19 April (M-19)

Description Formed in 1974, terrorist/guerilla organization takes its name from date of 1970 election defeat of then Colombian president, a military general. Led by Carlos Pizarro. Ideology is a mix of Marxism-Leninism, nationalism, and populism. Rhetoric focuses on "liberation" from ruling oligarchy, regional solidarity. In the past, it got strongest support from urban areas, especially university and professional leftists.

Activities Robberies, kidnapping for ransom, and selected assassinations. M-19 responsible for a number of terrorist attacks in recent years on international and domestic targets. Group also has cooperated with drug traffickers to gain money and weapons. In 1989, it entered into peace talks with the government leading to demobilization and entry into legitimate political activity.

Strength About 700.

Location/Area of Operation Colombia.

External Aid Has received funding, training, and arms form Cuba; may also have received aid from Libya and Nicaragua. Member of so-called America Battalion, a regional guerilla organization, which included some Peruvian MRTA and Ecuadorian AVC guerillas.

Mozambican National Resistance

a.k.a. Resistencia Nacional Mocambicana, or RENAMO

Description Established in 1976 by the Rhodesian security services, primarily to operate against anti-Rhodesian guerillas based in Mozambique. South Africa subsequently developed RENAMO into an insurgent group opposing the Front for the Liberation of Mozambique (FRELIMO).

Activities Operates as a guerilla insurgency against Mozambican Government and civilian targets; frequently and increasingly runs cross-border operations into Zimbabwe, Malawi, and Zambia, where it has murdered and kidnapped numerous civilians and destroyed property.

Strength 20,000 guerillas.

Location/Area of Operation Mozambique; border areas of Zimbabwe, Malawi, and Zambia.

External Aid Assistance previously received from South Africa as well as from private individuals and groups in Europe and elsewhere.

Mujahedin-e Khalq Organization (MEK)

a.k.a. The National Liberation Army of Iran, The People's Mujahedin Organization of Iran (PMOI), National Council of Resistance (NCR), The National Council of Resistance of Iran (NCRI), Muslim Iranian Students' Society

Designated as a Foreign Terrorist Organization

Description The MEK philosophy mixes Marxism and Islam. Formed in the 1960s, the organization was expelled from Iran after the Islamic Revolution in 1979, and its primary support came from the former Iraqi regime of Saddam Hussein starting in the late 1980s. The MEK conducted anti-Western attacks prior to the Islamic Revolution. Since then, it has conducted terrorist attacks against the interests of the clerical regime in Iran and abroad. The MEK advocates the overthrow of the Iranian regime and its replacement with the group's own leadership.

Activities The group's worldwide campaign against the Iranian Government stresses propaganda and occasionally uses terrorism. During the 1970s, the MEK killed US military personnel and US civilians working on defense projects in Tehran and supported the takeover in 1979 of the US Embassy in Tehran. In 1981, the MEK detonated bombs in the head office of the Islamic Republic Party and the Premier's office, killing some 70 high-ranking Iranian officials, including Chief Justice Ayatollah Mohammad Beheshti, President Mohammad-Ali Rajaei, and Premier Mohammad-Javad Bahonar. Near the end of the 1980-1988 war with Iran, Baghdad armed the MEK with military equipment and sent it into action against Iranian forces. In 1991, the MEK assisted the Government of Iraq in suppressing the Shia and Kurdish uprisings in southern Iraq and the Kurdish uprisings in the north. In April 1992, the MEK conducted near-simultaneous attacks on Iranian embassies and installations in 13 countries, demonstrating the group's ability to mount large-scale operations overseas. In April 1999, the MEK targeted key military officers and assassinated the deputy chief of the Iranian Armed Forces General Staff. In April 2000, the MEK attempted to assassinate the commander of the Nasr Headquarters, Tehran's interagency board responsible for coordinating policies on Iraq. The normal pace of anti-Iranian operations increased during "Operation Great Bahman" in February 2000, when the group launched a dozen attacks against Iran. One of those attacks included a mortar attack against the leadership complex in Tehran that housed the offices of the Supreme Leader and the President. In 2000 and 2001, the MEK was involved regularly in mortar attacks and hit-and-run raids on Iranian military and law enforcement units and Government buildings near the Iran-Iraq border, although MEK terrorism in Iran declined toward the end of 2001. After Coalition aircraft bombed MEK bases at the outset of Operation Iraqi Freedom, the MEK leadership ordered its members not to resist Coalition forces, and a formal cease-fire arrangement was reached in May 2003.

Strength Over 3,000 MEK members are currently confined to Camp Ashraf, the MEK's main compound north of Baghdad, where they remain under the Geneva Convention's "protected person" status and Coalition control. As a condition of the cease-fire agreement, the group relinquished its weapons, including tanks, armored vehicles, and heavy artillery. A significant number of MEK personnel have "defected" from the Ashraf group, and several dozen of them have been voluntarily repatriated to Iran.

Location/Area of Operation In the 1980s, the MEK's leaders were forced by Iranian security forces to flee to France. On resettling in Iraq in 1987, almost all of its armed units were stationed in fortified bases near the border with Iran. Since Operation Iraqi Freedom, the bulk of the group is limited to Camp Ashraf, although an overseas support structure remains with associates and supporters scattered throughout Europe and North America.

External Aid Before Operation Iraqi Freedom, the group received all of its military assistance, and most of its financial support, from the former Iraqi regime. The MEK also has used front organizations to solicit contributions from expatriate Iranian communities.

National Liberation Army (ELN)—Bolivia

Includes Nestor Paz Zamora Commission (CNPZ)

Description ELN claims to be resuscitation of group established by Che Guevara in 1960s. Includes numerous small factions of indigenous subversive groups, including CNPZ, which is largely inactive today.

CNPZ is a radical leftist terrorist organization that first appeared in October 1990. Named after deceased brother of President Paz Zamora. Violent, extremely anti-US, Marxist-Leninist organization.

Activities CNPZ attacked the US Embassy Marine guardhouse on 10 October 1990 with automatic weapons and a bomb. One Bolivian policeman was killed and another seriously injured in the attack. ELN and CNPZ have attacked US interests in past years but focused almost exclusively on Bolivian domestic targets in 1993.

Strength Unknown, probably fewer than 100.

Location/Area of Operation Bolivia.

External Aid None.

National Liberation Army (ELN)

Designated as a Foreign Terrorist Organization

Description The ELN is a Colombian Marxist insurgent group formed in 1965 by urban intellectuals inspired by Fidel Castro and Che Guevara. It is primarily rural-based, although it possesses several urban units. In May 2004, Colombian President Uribe proposed a renewal of peace talks, but by the end of the year talks had not commenced.

Activities Kidnapping, hijacking, bombing, and extortion. Minimal conventional military capability. Annually conducts hundreds of kidnappings for ransom, often targeting foreign employees of large corporations, especially in the petroleum industry. Derives some revenue from taxation of the illegal narcotics industry. Frequently assaults energy infrastructure and has inflicted major damage on pipelines and the electric distribution network.

Strength Approximately 3,000 armed combatants and an unknown number of active supporters.

Location/Area of Operation Mostly in rural and mountainous areas of northern, northeastern, and southwestern Colombia, and Venezuelan border regions.

External Aid Cuba provides some medical care and political consultation. Venezuela continues to provide a hospitable environment.

New Red Brigades/Communist Combatant Party (BR/PCC)

a.k.a. Brigate Rosse/Partito Comunista Combattente

Description This Marxist-Leninist group is a successor to the Red Brigades, active in the 1970s and 1980s. In addition to ideology, both groups share the same symbol, a five-pointed star inside a circle. The group is opposed to Italy's foreign and labor policies and to NATO.

Activities In 2004, the BR/PCC continued to suffer setbacks, with their leadership in prison and other members under pressure from the Italian Government. The BR/PCC did not claim responsibility for a blast at an employment agency in Milan in late October, although the police suspect remnants of the group are responsible. In 2003, Italian authorities captured at least seven members of the BR/PCC, dealing the terrorist group a severe blow to its operational effectiveness. Some of those arrested are suspects in the assassination in 1999 of Labor Ministry adviser Massimo D'Antona, and authorities are hoping to link them to the assassination in 2002 of Labor Ministry advisor Marco Biagi. The arrests in October came on the heels of a clash in March 2003 involving Italian Railway Police and two BR/PCC members, which resulted in the deaths of one of the operatives and an Italian security officer. The BR/PCC has financed its activities through armed robberies.

Strength Fewer than 20.

Location/Area of Operation Italy.

External Aid Unknown.

October 1st Antifascist Resistance Group (GRAPO)

Description Small, Maoist urban terrorist group that recruited members form the Spanish Communist Party—Reconstituted. Seeks to remove US military forces from Spain and set up a revolutionary regime.

Activities Carried out small-scale bombing attacks on US and NATO facilities in early 1980s. Since then some of the members arrested in January 1985 have been released from jail and have returned to action, with several armed attacks against Spanish targets in 1988-89.

Strength Unknown.

Location/Area of Operation Spain.

External Aid Reported to have ties to the French AD and the Italian BR; aid received from these groups, if any, is not known.

Orange Volunteers (OV)

Description Terrorist group that appeared about 1998–99 and is comprised largely of disgruntled loyalist hardliners who split from groups observing the cease-fire. OV seeks to prevent a political settlement with Irish nationalists by attacking Catholic civilian interests in Northern Ireland.

Activities The group has been linked to pipe-bomb attacks and sporadic assaults on Catholics. Following a successful security crackdown at the end of 1999, the OV declared a cease-fire in September 2000 and has remained quiet since 2001.

Strength Up to 20 hardcore members, some of whom are experienced in terrorist tactics and bombmaking.

Location/Area of Operations Northern Ireland.

External Aid None.

Palestinian Islamic Jihad (PIJ)

a.k.a. Palestine Islamic Jihad, Islamic Jihad of Palestine, PIJ-Shaqaqi Faction, PIJ-Shalla Faction, Al-Quds Brigades

Designated as a Foreign Terrorist Organization

Description Formed by militant Palestinians in the Gaza Strip during the 1970s, the Palestinian Islamic Jihad (PIJ) is committed to the creation of an Islamic Palestinian state and the destruction of Israel through attacks against Israeli military and civilian targets inside Israel and the Palestinian territories.

Activities PIJ militants have conducted many attacks, including large-scale suicide bombings, against Israeli civilian and military targets. The group maintained operational activity in 2004, claiming numerous attacks against Israeli interests. PIJ has not yet directly targeted US interests; it continues to direct attacks against Israelis inside Israel and the territories, although US citizens have died in attacks mounted by the PIJ.

Strength Unknown.

Location/Area of Operation Primarily Israel, the West Bank, and the Gaza Strip. The group's primary leadership resides in Syria, though other leadership elements reside in Lebanon, as well as other parts of the Middle East.

External Aid Receives financial assistance from Iran and limited logistical assistance from Syria.

Palestine Liberation Front (PLF)

a.k.a. PLF-Abu Abbas Faction

Designated as a Foreign Terrorist Organization

Description The Palestine Liberation Front (PLF) broke away from the PFLP-GC in the late 1970s and later split again into pro-PLO, pro-Syrian, and pro-Libyan factions. The pro- PLO faction was led by Muhammad Abbas (a.k.a. Abu Abbas) and was based in Baghdad prior to Operation Iraqi Freedom.

Activities Abbas' group was responsible for the attack in 1985 on the Italian cruise ship Achille Lauro and the murder of US citizen Leon Klinghoffer. Abu Abbas died of natural causes in April 2004 while in US custody in Iraq. Current leadership and membership of the relatively small PLF appears to be based in Lebanon and the Palestinian territories. The PLF has become more active since the start of the al-Aqsa intifadah and several PLF members have been arrested by Israeli authorities for planning attacks in Israel and the West Bank.

Strength Unknown.

Location/Area of Operation PLO faction based in Tunisia until Achille Lauro attack. Based in Iraq since 1990. Has a presence in Lebanon and the West Bank.

External Aid Received support mainly from Iraq; has received support from Libya in the past.

Palestine Liberation Organization (PLO)

Description Founded in 1964 as a Palestinian nationalist umbrella organization dedicated to the establishment of an independent Palestinian state. After the 1967 Arab-Israeli war, control devolved to the leadership of the various fedayeen militia groups, the most dominant of which was Yasser Arafat's Al-Fatah. In 1969, Arafat became chairman of the PLO's Executive Committee, a position he still holds [1992]. In the early 1980s, PLO became fragmented into several contending groups but remains the preeminent Palestinian organization. The United States considers the PLO an umbrella organization that includes several constituent groups and individuals holding differing views on terrorism. At the same time, US police accepts that elements of the PLO have advocated, carried out, or accepted responsibility for acts of terrorism. PLO Chairman Arafat publicly renounced terrorism in December 1988 on behalf of the PLO. The United States considers that all PLO groups, including Al-Fatah, Force 17, Hawari Group, PLF, and PFLP, are bound by Arafat's renunciation of terrorism. The US-PLO dialogue was suspended after the PLO failed to condemn the 30 May 1990 PLF attack on Israeli beaches. PLF head Abu Abbas left the PLO Executive Committee in September 1991; his seat was filled by another PLF member.

On 9 September 1993, in letters to Israeli Prime Minister Rabin and Norwegian Foreign Minister Holst, PLO Chairman Arafat committed the PLO to cease all violence and terrorism. On 13 September 1993, the Declaration of Principles between the Israelis and Palestinians was signed in Washington, DC. We have no information that any PLO element under Arafat's control was involved in terrorism from that time through 1995. (There were two incidents in 1993 in which the responsible individuals apparently acted independently.) One group under the PLO umbrella, the Popular Front for the Liberation of Palestine (PFLP), suspended its participation in the PLO in protest of the agreement and continues its sporadic campaign of violence. The US Government continues to monitor closely PLO compliance with its commitment to abandon terrorism and violence.

Activities In the early 1970s, several groups affiliated with the PLO carried out numerous international terrorist attacks. By the mid-1970s, under international pressure, the PLO claimed it would restrict attacks to Israel and the occupied territories. Several terrorist attacks were later carried out by groups affiliated with the PLO/Fatah, including the Hawari Group, the Palestine Liberation Front, and Force 17, against targets inside and outside Israel.

Strength See numbers for affiliated groups.

Location/Area of Operation Tunis, other bases in various countries in the Middle East.

External Aid See affiliated groups. Accurate public information on financial support for the PLO by Arab governments is difficult to obtain.

People Against Gangsterism and Drugs (PAGAD)

Description People Against Gangsterism and Drugs (PAGAD) and its ally Qibla (an Islamic fundamentalist group that favors political Islam and takes an anti-US and anti-Israel stance) view the South African Government as a threat to Islamic values. The two groups work to promote a greater political voice for South African Muslims. PAGAD has used front names such as Muslims Against Global Oppression and Muslims Against Illegitimate Leaders when launching anti-Western protests and campaigns.

Activities PAGAD formed in November 1995 as a vigilante group in reaction to crime in some neighborhoods of Cape Town. In September 1996, a change in the group's leadership resulted in a change in the group's goal, and it began to support a violent jihad to establish an Islamic state. Between 1996 and 2000, PAGAD conducted a total of 189 bomb attacks, including nine bombings in the Western Cape that caused serious injuries. PAGAD's targets included South African authorities, moderate Muslims, synagogues, gay nightclubs, tourist attractions, and Western-associated restaurants. PAGAD is believed to have masterminded the bombing on August 25, 1998, of the Cape Town Planet Hollywood. Since 2001, PAGAD's violent activities have been severely curtailed by law enforcement and prosecutorial efforts against leading members of the organization. Qibla leadership has organized demonstrations against visiting US dignitaries and other protests, but the extent of PAGAD's involvement is uncertain.

Strength Early estimates were several hundred members. Current operational strength is unknown, but probably vastly diminished.

Location/Area of Operation Operates mainly in the Cape Town area.

External Aid May have ties to international Islamic extremists.

People's Liberation Army (EPL)

Description Formed in 1967 as military wing of pro-Beijing group, Colombian Communist Party/Marxist-Leninist.

Activities Extortion, robberies, kidnappings for ransom, and assassination. Kidnapped two US citizens—one later released, one died of heart attack while in captivity—in December 1985.

Strength 750 to 1,000.

Location/Area of Operation Colombia.

External Aid May have received aid from Cuba and Nicaragua.

Popular Forces of 25 April (FP-25)

Description A Marxist terrorist group that takes its name form the April 1974 coup that ousted the military dictatorship in Portugal. Proclaimed goal is to create a revolutionary workers' army to overthrow current regime.

Activities In the early 1980s, carried out bombings, bank robberies, and armed attacks against domestic businessmen and property. In 1984, began to attack US interests, including rocket and mortar attacks against the US Embassy in Lisbon in 1984 and mortar attacks against NATO and US military targets in 1985 and 1986.

Strength Unknown.

Location/Area of Operation Portugal.

External Aid Has received training and financial support from Libya. Also is believed to have cooperated with terrorist groups in Western Europe, including the ETA and the RAF.

Popular Front for the Liberation of Palestine (PFLP)

Designated as a Foreign Terrorist Organization

Description Formerly a part of the PLO, the Marxist-Leninist PFLP was founded by George Habash when it broke away from the Arab Nationalist Movement in 1967. The PFLP does not view the Palestinian struggle as religious, seeing it instead as a broader revolution against Western imperialism. The group earned a reputation for spectacular international attacks, including airline hijackings, that have killed at least 20 US citizens.

Activities The PFLP committed numerous international terrorist attacks during the 1970s. Since 1978, the group has conducted attacks against Israeli or moderate Arab targets, including killing a settler and her son in December 1996. The PFLP has stepped up its operational activity since the start of the current intifadah, highlighted by at least two suicide bombings since 2003, multiple joint operations with other Palestinian terrorist groups, and assassination of the Israeli Tourism Minster in 2001 to avenge Israel's killing of the PFLP Secretary General earlier that year.

Strength Unknown, previously estimated at 800.

Location/Area of Operation Syria, Lebanon, Israel, the West Bank, and the Gaza Strip.

External Aid Receives safe haven and some logistical assistance from Syria.

Popular Front for the Liberation of Palestine–General Command (PFLP-GC)

Designated as a Foreign Terrorist Organization

Description The PFLP-GC split from the PFLP in 1968, claiming it wanted to focus more on fighting and less on politics. Originally it was violently opposed to the Arafat-led PLO. The group is led by Ahmad Jabril, a former captain in the Syrian Army, whose son Jihad was killed by a car bomb in May 2002. The PFLP-GC is closely tied to both Syria and Iran.

Activities Carried out dozens of attacks in Europe and the Middle East during the 1970s and 1980s. Known for cross-border terrorist attacks into Israel using unusual means, such as hot-air balloons and motorized hang gliders. Primary focus is now on guerrilla operations in southern Lebanon and small-scale attacks in Israel, the West Bank, and the Gaza Strip.

Strength Several hundred.

Location/Area of Operation Headquartered in Damascus with bases in Lebanon.

External Aid Receives logistical and military support from Syria and financial support from Iran.

Popular Front for the Liberation of Palestine–Special Command (PFLP-SC)

Description Marxist-Leninist group formed by Abu Salim in 1979 after breaking away from the now defunct PFLP-Special Operations Group.

Activities Has claimed responsibility for several notorious international terrorist attacks in Western Europe, including the bombing of a restaurant frequented by US servicemen in Torrejon, Spain, in April 1985. Eighteen Spanish civilians were killed in the attack.

Strength 50.

Location/Area of Operation Operates out of southern Lebanon, in various areas of the Middle East, and in Western Europe.

External Aid Probably receives financial and military support from Syria, Libya, and Iraq.

Popular Revolutionary Forces–Lorenzo Zelaya (FRP-LZ)

Description Once active revolutionary terrorist group.

Activities Claimed responsibility for numerous bombings in Tegucigalpa in the early 1980s, including attacks on US military and business targets. Activities were substantially reduced following arrest of leader in 1983 and of two other leaders in 1987.

Strength Unknown; probably fewer than 300.

Location/Area of Operation Honduras.

External Aid Receives training and other support from Cuba and Nicaragua.

Popular Struggle Front (PSF)

Description Radical Palestinian terrorist group once closely involved in the Syrian-dominated Palestinian National Salvation Front. Led by Dr. Samir Ghosheh. Rejoined the PLO in September 1991. Group is internally divided over the Declaration of Principles signed in 1993.

Activities Terrorist attacks against Israeli, moderate Arab, and PLO targets.

Strength Fewer than 200 in 1995.

Location/Area of Operation Mainly Suria and Lebanon and elsewhere in the Middle East.

External Aid Received support from Syria and may receive aid from the PLO.

Puka Inti

a.k.a. Sol Rojo, Red Sun

Description Small but violent subversive group probably formed from dissident members of AVC guerilla organization, which made peace with the Ecuadorian Government in 1989. Believed to be anti-US.

Activities Series of bombings of government buildings have been attributed to Puka Inti, but group appears to lack resources to expand much beyond current strength.

Strength Very small, perhaps fewer than 100.

Location/Area of Operation Ecuador.

External Aid None.

Real IRA (RIRA)

a.k.a. 32-County Sovereignty Committee, True IRA
Designated as a Foreign Terrorist Organization

Description RIRA was formed in the late 1990s as the clandestine armed wing of the 32-County Sovereignty

Movement, a "political pressure group" dedicated to removing British forces from Northern Ireland and unifying Ireland. The RIRA also seeks to disrupt the Northern Ireland peace process. The 32-County Sovereignty Movement opposed Sinn Fein's adoption in September 1997 of the Mitchell principles of democracy and non-violence; it also opposed the amendment in December 1999 of Articles 2 and 3 of the Irish Constitution, which had claimed the territory of Northern Ireland. Despite internal rifts and calls by some jailed members—including the group's founder Michael "Mickey" McKevitt—for a ceasefire and disbandment, RIRA has pledged additional violence and continues to conduct attacks.

Activities Bombings, assassinations, and robberies. Many Real IRA members are former Provisional Irish Republican Army members who left that organization after the Provisional IRA renewed its cease-fire in 1997. These members brought a wealth of experience in terrorist tactics and bomb making to RIRA. Targets have included civilians (most notoriously in the Omagh bombing in August 1998), British security forces, police in Northern Ireland, and local Protestant communities. RIRA's most recent fatal attack was in August 2002 at a London army base that killed a construction worker. In 2004, RIRA conducted several postal bomb attacks and made threats against prison officers, people involved in the new policing arrangements, and senior politicians. RIRA also planted incendiary devices in Belfast shopping areas and conducted a serious shooting attack against a Police Service of Northern Ireland station in September. The organization reportedly wants to improve its intelligence-gathering ability, engineering capacity, and access to weaponry; it also trains members in the use of guns and explosives. RIRA continues to attract new members, and its senior members are committed to launching attacks on security forces. Arrests in the spring led to the discovery of incendiary and explosive devices at a RIRA bomb making facility in Limerick. The group also engaged in smuggling and other non-terrorist crime in Ireland.

Strength The number of activists may have fallen to less than 100. The organization may receive limited support from IRA hardliners and Republican sympathizers dissatisfied with the IRA's continuing cease-fire and Sinn Fein's involvement in the peace process. Approximately 40 RIRA members are in Irish jails.

Location/Area of Operation Northern Ireland, Great Britain, and Irish Republic.

External Aid Suspected of receiving funds from sympathizers in the United States and of attempting to buy weapons from US gun dealers. RIRA also is reported to have purchased sophisticated weapons from the Balkans, and to have taken materials from Provisional IRA arms dumps in the later 1990s.

Red Army Faction

Description The tightly knit and disciplined RAF is the successor to the Baader-Meinhof Gang, which originated in the student protest movement in the 1960s. Ideology is an obscure mix of Marxism and Maoism; committed to armed struggle. Organized into hardcore cadres that carry out terrorist attacks and a network of supporters who provide logistic and propaganda support. Has survived despite numerous arrests of top leaders over the years.

Activities Bombings, kidnappings, assassinations, and robberies. Targets West German Government and private sector and US interests. Among the latter, attempted assassination in Belgium of NATO Commander (1979); bombing of NATO Air Force headquarters at Ramstein (1981); rocket attack of USAREUR Commander in Heidelberg (1981); bombing, with AD, of Rhein-Main Air Force Base (1985); and assassination of Deutsche Bank Chairman Alfred Herrhausen in November 1989.

Strength 10 to 20, plus several hundred supporters.

Location/Area of Operation Mainly in West Germany.

External Aid In Baader-Meinhof period, received support form Middle Eastern terrorist groups; some loose ties may still exist. Had close ties to the ADF in France and the CCC in Belgium before those groups were wrapped up by police.

Red Army for the Liberation of Catalonia (ERCA)

Description A small terrorist group whose origin is obscure; ideology is a mix of Catalonian separatism and Marxist-Leninism. May be radical offshoot of the Terra Lilure.

Activities Implicated in 1967 in a series of bombing attacks in Barcelona against US interests, including a grenade attack on a USO facility that killed a US sailor, an attack on the US Consulate, and, probably, bombing attacks against US businesses.

Strength Unknown.

Location/Area of Operation Spain.

External Aid None known.

Red Brigades (BR)

Description Formed in 1969, the Marxist-Leninist BR seeks to create a revolutionary state through armed struggle and to separate Italy from the Western Alliance. In 1984 split into two factions: the Communist Combatant Party (BR-PCC) and the Union of Combatant Communists (BR-UCC)

Activities Original group concentrated on assassination and kidnapping of Italian Government and private-sector targets; it murdered former Prime Minister Aldo Moro in 1978. Extreme leftist sympathizers have carried out several small-scale terrorist attacks to protest the presence and foreign policies of both the United States and NATO; it kidnapped US Army Brig. Gen. James Dozier in 1981 and claimed responsibility for murdering Leamon Hunt, US chief of the Sinai Multinational Force and Observer Group, in 1984. With limited resources and followers to carry out major terrorist acts, the group is mostly out of business.

Strength Probably fewer than 50, plus an unknown number of supporters.

Location/Area of Operation Based and operated in Italy. Some members probably living clandestinely in other European countries.

External Aid Currently unknown; original group apparently was self-sustaining but probably received weapons from other West European terrorist groups and from the PLO.

Red Hand Defenders (RHD)

Description The RHD is an extremist terrorist group formed in 1998 and composed largely of Protestant hardliners from Loyalist groups observing a cease-fire. RHD seeks to prevent a political settlement with Irish nationalists by attacking Catholic civilian interests in Northern Ireland. In January 2002, the group announced all staff at Catholic schools in Belfast and Catholic postal workers were legitimate targets. Despite calls in February 2002 by the Ulster Defense Association (UDA), Ulster Freedom Fighters (UFF), and Loyalist Volunteer Force (LVF) to announce its disbandment, RHD continued to make threats and issue claims of responsibility. RHD is a cover name often used by elements of the banned UDA and LVF. Designated under EO 13224 in December 2001.

Activities In early 2003, the RHD claimed responsibility for killing two UDA members as a result of what is described as Loyalist internecine warfare. It also claimed responsibility for a bomb that was left in the offices of Republican Sinn Fein in West Belfast, although the device was defused and no one was injured. In recent years, the group has carried out numerous pipe bombings and arson attacks against "soft" civilian targets such as homes, churches, and private businesses. In January 2002, the group bombed the home of a prison official in North Belfast. Twice in 2002 the group claimed responsibility for attacks—the murder of a Catholic postman and a Catholic teenager—that were later claimed by the UDAUFF, further blurring distinctions between the groups. In 2001, RHD claimed responsibility for killing five persons. The RHD has claimed responsibility for hoax bomb devices, and recently has set off petrol bombs and made death threats against local politicians.

Strength Up to 20 members, some of whom have experience in terrorist tactics and bomb making. Police arrested one member in June 2001 for making a hoax bomb threat.

Location/Area of Operation Northern Ireland.

External Aid None.

Revolutionary Armed Forces of Colombia (FARC)

Designated as a Foreign Terrorist Organization

Description Established in 1964 as the military wing of the Colombian Communist Party, the FARC is Latin America's oldest, largest, most capable, and best-equipped insurgency of Marxist origin. Although only nominally fighting in support of Marxist goals today, the FARC is governed by a general secretariat led by long-time leader Manuel Marulanda (a.k.a. "Tirofijo") and six others, including senior military commander Jorge Briceno (a.k.a. "Mono Jojoy"). Organized along military lines but includes some specialized urban fighting units. A Colombian military offensive targeting FARC fighters in their former safe haven in southern Colombia has experienced some success, with several FARC mid-level leaders killed or captured. On December 31, 2004, FARC leader Simon Trinidad, the highest-ranking FARC leader ever captured, was extradited to the United States on drug charges.

Activities Bombings, murder, mortar attacks, kidnapping, extortion, and hijacking, as well as guerrilla and conventional military action against Colombian political, military, and economic targets. In March 1999, the FARC executed three US indigenous rights activists on Venezuelan territory after it kidnapped them in Colombia. In February 2003, the FARC captured and continues to hold three US contractors and killed one other American when their plane crashed in Florencia. Foreign citizens often are targets of FARC kidnapping for ransom. The FARC has well-documented ties to the full range of narcotics trafficking activities, including taxation, cultivation, and distribution.

Strength Approximately 9,000 to 12,000 armed combatants and several thousand more supporters, mostly in rural areas.

Location/Area of Operation Primarily in Colombia with some activities—extortion, kidnapping, weapons sourcing, logistics, and R&R—suspected in neighboring Brazil, Venezuela, Panama, Peru, and Ecuador.

External Aid Cuba provides some medical care, safe haven, and political consultation. In December 2004, a Colombian Appeals Court declared three members of the Irish Republican Army—arrested in Colombia in 2001 upon exiting the former FARC-controlled demilitarized zone (despeje)—guilty of providing advanced explosives training to the FARC. The FARC often uses the Colombia/Venezuela border area for cross-border incursions and considers Venezuelan territory as a safe haven.

Revolutionary Nuclei (RN)

a.k.a. Revolutionary Cells, Revolutionary Popular Struggle, ELA

Designated as a Foreign Terrorist Organization

Description Revolutionary Nuclei (RN) emerged from a broad range of antiestablishment and anti-US/NATO/EU leftist groups active in Greece between 1995 and 1998. The group is believed to be the successor to or offshoot of Greece's most prolific terrorist group, Revolutionary People's Struggle (ELA), which has not claimed an attack since January 1995. Indeed, RN appeared to fill the void left by ELA, particularly as lesser groups faded from the scene. RN's few communiqués show strong similarities in rhetoric, tone, and theme to ELA proclamations. RN has not claimed an attack since November 2000, nor has it announced its disbandment.

Activities Since it began operations in January 1995, the group has claimed responsibility for some two dozen arson attacks and low-level bombings against a range of US, Greek, and other European targets in Greece. In its most infamous and lethal attack to date, the group claimed responsibility for a bomb it detonated at the Intercontinental Hotel in April 1999 that resulted in the death of a Greek woman and injured a Greek man. Its modus operandi includes warning calls of impending attacks, attacks targeting property instead of individuals, use of rudimentary timing devices, and strikes during the late-evening to early-morning hours. RN may have been responsible for two attacks in July 2003 against a US insurance company and a local bank in Athens. RN's last confirmed attacks against US interests in Greece came in November 2000, with two separate bombings against the Athens offices of Citigroup and the studio of a Greek-American sculptor. Greek targets have included judicial and other Government office buildings, private vehicles, and the offices of Greek firms involved in NATO-related defense contracts in Greece. Similarly, the group has attacked European interests in Athens. The group did not conduct an attack in 2004.

Strength Group membership is believed to be small, probably drawing from the Greek militant leftist or anarchist milieu.

Location/Area of Operation Primary area of operation is in the Athens metropolitan area.

External Aid Unknown but believed to be self-sustaining.

Revolutionary People's Liberation Party/Front (DHKP/C)

a.k.a. Devrimci Sol, Dev Sol, Revolutionary Left

Designated as a Foreign Terrorist Organization

Description This group originally formed in Turkey in 1978 as Devrimci Sol, or Dev Sol, a splinter faction of Dev Genc (Revolutionary Youth). Renamed in 1994 after factional infighting. "Party" refers to the group's political activities, while "Front" is a reference to the group's militant operations. The group espouses a Marxist-Leninist ideology and is vehemently anti-US, anti-NATO, and anti-Turkish establishment. Its goals are the establishment of a socialist state and the abolition of one- to three-man prison cells, called F-type prisons. DHKP/C finances its activities chiefly through donations and extortion.

Activities Since the late 1980s the group has targeted primarily current and retired Turkish security and military officials. It began a new campaign against foreign interests in 1990, which included attacks against US military and diplomatic personnel and facilities. To protest perceived US imperialism during the Gulf War, Dev Sol assassinated two US military contractors, wounded an Air Force officer, and bombed more than 20 US and NATO military, commercial, and cultural facilities. In its first significant terrorist act as DHKP/C in 1996, the group assassinated a prominent Turkish businessman and two others. DHKP/C added suicide bombings to its repertoire in 2001, with successful attacks against Turkish police in January and September. Since the end of 2001, DHKP/C has typically used improvised explosive devices against official Turkish targets and soft US targets of opportunity; attacks against US targets beginning in 2003 probably came in response to Operation Iraqi Freedom. Operations and arrests against the group have weakened its capabilities. DHKP/C did not conduct any major terrorist attacks in 2003, but on June 24, 2004—just days before the NATO summit—an explosive device detonated, apparently prematurely, aboard a passenger bus in Istanbul while a DHKP/C operative was transporting it to another location, killing the operative and three other persons.

Strength Probably several dozen terrorist operatives inside Turkey, with a large support network throughout Europe. On April 1, 2004, authorities arrested more than 40 suspected DHKP/C members in coordinated raids across Turkey and Europe. In October, 10 alleged members of the group were sentenced to life imprisonment, while charges were dropped against 20 other defendants because of a statute of limitations.

Location/Area of Operation Turkey, primarily Istanbul, Ankara, Izmir, and Adana. Raises funds in Europe.

External Aid Widely believed to have training facilities or offices in Lebanon and Syria.

Revolutionary People's Struggle (ELA)

Description Formed in 1971 to oppose the military junta; is a self-described leftwing revolutionary, anti-capitalist, anti-imperialist group. Organization is unclear, but probably consists of a loose coalition of several very small and violent groups or affiliates, possibly including 17 November.

Activities Before 1974, was nonviolent; turned to terrorism after removal of junta. Has targeted US military and business facilities and, since 1986, stepped up attacks on Greek Government and commercial interests; primary method has been bombings of buildings, apparently without intent to endanger life.

Strength Unknown, perhaps up to 20 or 30, plus supporters.

Location/Area of Operation Greece.

External Aid None known.

Revolutionary Proletarian Initiative Nuclei (NIPR)

Description The NIPR is a clandestine leftist extremist group that appeared in Rome in 2000. Adopted the logo of the Red Brigades of the 1970s and 1980s—an encircled five point star—for its declarations. Opposes Italy's foreign and labor policies. Has targeted property interests rather than personnel in its attacks.

Activities The NIPR has not claimed responsibility for any attacks since an April 2001 bomb attack on a building housing a US-Italian relations association and an international affairs institute in Rome's historic center. The NIPR claimed to have carried out a bombing in May 2000 in Rome at an oversight committee facility for implementation of the law on strikes in public services. The group also claimed responsibility for an explosion in February 2002 on Via Palermo adjacent to the Interior Ministry in Rome.

Strength Possibly 12 members.

Location/Area of Operations Mainly in Rome, Milan, Lazio, and Tuscany.

External Aid None evident.

Revolutionary Struggle (RS)

Description RS is a radical leftist group that is anti-Greek establishment and ideologically aligns itself with the organization 17 November. Although the group is not specifically anti-US, its anti-imperialist rhetoric suggests it may become so.

Activities First became known when the group conducted a bombing in September 2003 against the courthouse at which the trials of alleged 17 November members were ongoing. In May 2004, the group detonated four improvised explosive devices at a police station in Athens. These two attacks were notable for their apparent attempts to target and kill first responders—the first time a Greek terrorist group had used this tactic. RS is widely regarded as the most dangerous indigenous Greek terrorist group at this time.

Strength Likely less than 50 members.

Location/Area of Operation Athens, Greece.

External Aid Unknown.

Revolutionary United Front (RUF)

Description The RUF was a loosely organized guerrilla force seeking to retain control of the lucrative diamond-producing regions of the country that has been broken apart since the end of the civil war and capture of key leaders, including Foday Sankoh who died in custody. The group funds itself largely through the extraction and sale of diamonds obtained in areas of Sierra Leone that it controls.

Activities Sporadic incidents still occur, but during 2001, reports of serious abuses by the RUF declined significantly. The resumption of the Government's Disarmament, Demobilization, and Reintegration program in May was largely responsible. From 1991-2000, the group used guerrilla, criminal, and terror tactics, such as murder, torture, and mutilation, to fight the government, intimidate civilians, and keep UN peacekeeping units in check. In 2000 they held hundreds of UN peacekeepers hostage until their release was negotiated, in part, by the RUF's chief sponsor, Liberian President Charles Taylor. The group also has been accused of attacks in Guinea at the behest of President Taylor.

Strength Unknown but previously estimated at several thousand supporters and sympathizers.

Location/Area of Operation Sierra Leone, Liberia, Guinea.

External Aid A UN experts panel report on Sierra Leone said President Charles Taylor of Liberia provides support and leadership to the RUF. The UN has identified Libya, Gambia, and Burkina Faso as conduits for weapons and other materiel for the RUF.

Riyadus-Salikhin Reconnaissance and Sabotage Battalion of Chechen Martyrs (RSRSBCM)

Description Riyadus-Salikhin Reconnaissance and Sabotage Battalion of Chechen Martyrs (RSRSBCM), led by Chechen extremist leader Shamil Basayev, uses terrorism as part of an effort to secure an independent Muslim state in the North Caucasus. Basayev claimed the group was responsible for the Beslan school hostage crisis of September 1-3, 2004, which culminated in the deaths of about 330 people; simultaneous suicide bombings aboard two Russian civilian airliners in late August 2004; and a third suicide bombing outside a Moscow subway that same month. The RSRSBCM, whose name translates into English as "Requirements for Getting into Paradise," was not known to Western observers before October 2002, when it participated in the seizure of the Dubrovka Theater in Moscow. Designated under EO 13224 in February 2003.

Activities Primarily terrorist and guerilla operations against Russian forces, pro-Russian Chechen forces, and Russian and Chechen non-combatants.

Strength Probably no more than 50 fighters at any given time.

Location/Area of Operations Primarily Russia.

External Aid May receive some external assistance from foreign mujahedin.

Salafist Group for Call and Combat (GSPC)

a.k.a. Salafist Group for Preaching and Combat, Le Groupe Salafiste pour la Predication et le Combat

Designated as a Foreign Terrorist Organization

Description The Salafist Group for Call and Combat (GSPC), a splinter group of the Armed Islamic Group (GIA), seeks to overthrow the Algerian Government with the goal of installing an Islamic regime. GSPC eclipsed the GIA in approximately 1998, and is currently the most effective and largest armed group inside Algeria. In contrast to the GIA, the GSPC pledged to avoid civilian attacks inside Algeria.

Activities The GSPC continues to conduct operations aimed at Algerian Government and military targets, primarily in rural areas, although civilians are sometimes killed. The Government of Algeria scored major counterterrorism successes against GSPC in 2004, significantly weakening the organization, which also has been plagued with internal divisions. Algerian military forces killed GSPC leader Nabil Sahraoui and one of his top lieutenants, Abbi Abdelaziz, in June 2004 in the mountainous area east of Algiers. In October, the Algerian Government took custody of Abderazak al-Para, who led a GSPC faction that held 32 European tourists hostage in 2003. According to press reporting, some GSPC members in Europe and the Middle East maintain contact with other North African extremists sympathetic to al-Qaida. In late 2003, the GSPC leader issued a communiqué announcing the group's support of a number of jihadist causes and movements, including al-Qaida.

Strength Several hundred fighters with an unknown number of facilitators outside Algeria.

Location/Area of Operation Algeria, the Sahel (i.e. northern Mali, northern Mauritania, and northern Niger), Canada, and Western Europe.

External Aid Algerian expatriates and GSPC members abroad, many residing in Western Europe, provide financial and logistical support. GSPC members also engage in criminal activity.

Shining Path (SL)

a.k.a. Sendero Luminoso People's Liberation Army

Designated as a Foreign Terrorist Organization

Description Former university professor Abimael Guzman formed SL in Peru in the late 1960s, and his teachings created the foundation of SL's militant Maoist doctrine. In the 1980s, SL became one of the most ruthless terrorist groups in the Western Hemisphere. Approximately 30,000 persons have died since Shining Path took up arms in 1980. The Peruvian Government made dramatic gains against SL during the 1990s, but reports of recent SL involvement in narco-trafficking and kidnapping for ransom indicate it may be developing new sources of support.

In 2001, the Peruvian National Police thwarted an SL attack against "an American objective", possibly the US Embassy, when they arrested two Lima SL cell members. Additionally, Government authorities continued to arrest and prosecute active SL members, including, Ruller Mazombite, a.k.a. "Camarada Cayo", chief of the protection team of SL leader Macario Ala, a.k.a. "Artemio", and Evorcio Ascencios, a.k.a. "Camarada Canale", logistics chief of the Huallaga Regional Committee. Counterterrorist operations targeted pockets of terrorist activity in the Upper Huallaga River Valley and the Apurimac/Ene River Valley, where SL columns continued to conduct periodic attacks.

SL's stated goal is to destroy existing Peruvian institutions and replace them with a communist peasant revolutionary regime. It also opposes any influence by foreign governments. Peruvian Courts in 2003 granted approximately 1,900 members the right to request retrials in a civilian court, including the imprisoned top leadership. The trial of Guzman, who was arrested in 1992, was scheduled for November 5, 2004, but was postponed after the first day, when chaos erupted in the courtroom.

Activities Conducted indiscriminate bombing campaigns and selective assassinations.

Strength Unknown but estimated to be some 300 armed militants.

Location/Area of Operation Peru, with most activity in rural areas.

External Aid None.

Sikh Terrorism

Description Sikh terrorism is sponsored by expatriate and Indian Sikh groups who want to carve out an independent Sikh state called Khalistan (Land of the Pure) from Indian territory. Active groups include Babbar Khalsa, International Sikh Youth Federation, Dal Khalsa, Bhinderanwala Tiger Force, and the Saheed Khalsa Force.

Activities Attacks in India are mounted against Indian officials and facilities, other Sikhs, and Hindus; they include assassinations, bombings, and kidnappings. Sikh extremists probably bombed the Air India jet downed over the Irish Sea in June 1985, killing 329 passengers and crew. On the same day, a bomb planted by Sikhs on an Air India flight from Vancouver exploded in Tokyo's Narita Airport, killing two Japanese baggage handlers. In 1991, Sikh terrorists attempted to assassinate the Indian Ambassador in Romania once India's senior police officer in Punjab from 1986 to 1989 and kidnapped and held the Romanian Charge in New Delhi for seven weeks. In January 1993, Indian police arrested Sikhs in New Delhi as they were conspiring to detonate a bomb to disrupt India's Republic Day, and, in September 1993, Sikh militants attempted to assassinate the Sikh chief of the ruling Congress Party's youth wing with a bomb.

Sikh attacks in India, ranging from kidnappings and assassinations to remote-controlled bombings, have dropped markedly since mid-1992, as Indian security forces have killed or captured numerous senior Sikh militant leaders and have conducted successful Army, paramilitary and police operations. Total civilian deaths in Punjab have declined more than 95 percent since more than 3,300 civilians died in 1991. Many low-intensity bombings that might be attributable to Sikh extremists now occur without claims of credit.

Strength Unknown.

Location/Area of Operation Northern India, Western Europe, Southeast Asia, and North America.

External Aid Militant cells are active internationally, and extremists gather funds from overseas Sikh communities. Sikh expatriates have formed a variety of international organizations that lobby for the Sikh cause overseas. Most prominent are the World Sikh Organization and the International Sikh Youth Federation.

Sipah-i-Sahaba/Pakistan (SSP)

Description The Sipah-I-Sahaba/Pakistan (SSP) is a Sunni sectarian group that follows the Deobandi school. Violently anti-Shia, the SSP emerged in central Punjab in the mid-1980s as a response to the Iranian Revolution. Pakistani President Musharraf banned the SSP in January 2002. In August 2002, the SSP renamed itself Millat-i-Islami Pakistan, and Musharraf re-banned the group under its new name in November 2003. The SSP also has operated as a political party, winning seats in Pakistan's National Assembly.

Activities The group's activities range from organizing political rallies calling for Shia to be declared non-Muslims to assassinating prominent Shia leaders. The group was responsible for attacks on Shia worshippers in May 2004, when at least 50 people were killed.

Strength The SSP may have approximately 3,000 to 6,000 trained activists who carry out various kinds of sectarian activities.

Location/Area of Operation The SSP has influence in all four provinces of Pakistan. It is considered to be one of the most powerful sectarian groups in the country.

External Aid The SSP reportedly receives significant funding from Saudi Arabia through wealthy private donors in Pakistan. Funds also are acquired from other sources, including other Sunni extremist groups, madrassas, and contributions by political groups.

Special Purpose Islamic Regiment (SPIR)

Description The SPIR is one of three terrorist groups affiliated with Chechen guerrillas that furnished personnel to carry out the seizure of the Dubrovka Theater in Moscow in October 2002. The SPIR has had at least seven commanders since it was founded in the late 1990s. Movsar Barayev, who led and was killed during the theater standoff, was the first publicly identified leader. The group continues to conduct guerrilla operations in Chechnya under the leadership of the current leader, Amir Aslan, whose true identity is not known. Designated under EO 13224 in February 2003.

Activities Primarily guerrilla operations against Russian forces. Has also been involved in various hostage and ransom operations, including the execution of ethnic Chechens who have collaborated with Russian authorities.

Strength Probably no more than 100 fighters at any given time.

Location/Area of Operations Primarily Russia.

External Aid May receive some external assistance from foreign mujahedin.

Tanzim Qa'idat al-Jihad fi Bilad al-Rafidayn (QJBR)

a.k.a. Al-Zarqawi Network, Al-Qaida in Iraq, Al-Qaida of Jihad Organization in the Land of The Two Rivers, Jama'at al-Tawhid wa'al-Jihad

Designated as a Foreign Terrorist Organization

Description The Jordanian Palestinian Abu Mus'ab al-Zarqawi (Ahmad Fadhil Nazzal al-Khalaylah, a.k.a. Abu Ahmad, Abu Azraq) established cells in Iraq soon after the commencement of Operation Iraqi Freedom (OIF), formalizing his group in April 2004 to bring together jihadists and other insurgents in Iraq fighting against US and Coalition forces. Zarqawi initially called his group "Unity and Jihad" (Jama'at al- Tawhid wa'al-Jihad, or JTJ). Zarqawi and his group helped finance, recruit, transport, and train Sunni Islamic extremists for the Iraqi resistance. The group adopted its current name after its October 2004 merger with Usama Bin Ladin's al-Qaida. The immediate goal of QJBR is to expel the Coalition—through a campaign of bombings, kidnappings, assassinations, and intimidation—and establish an Islamic state in Iraq. QJBR's longer-term goal is to proliferate jihad from Iraq into "Greater Syria," that is, Syria, Lebanon, Israel, and Jordan.

Activities In August 2003, Zarqawi's group carried out a major international terrorist attack in Iraq when it bombed the Jordanian Embassy in Baghdad, followed 12 days later by a suicide vehicle-borne improvised explosive device (VBIED) attack against the UN Headquarters in Baghdad, killing 23, including the Secretary-General's Special Representative for Iraq, Sergio Vieira de Mello. Also in August the group conducted a VBIED attack against Shi'a worshipers outside the Imam Ali Mosque in Al Najaf, killing 85—including the leader of the Supreme Council for the Islamic Revolution in Iraq (SCIRI). It kept up its attack pace throughout 2003, striking numerous Iraqi, Coalition, and relief agency targets such as the Red Cross. Zarqawi's group conducted VBIED attacks against US military personnel and Iraqi infrastructure throughout 2004, including suicide attacks inside the Green Zone perimeter in Baghdad. The group successfully penetrated the Green Zone in the October bombing of a popular café and market. Zarqawi's group fulfilled a pledge to target Shi'a; its March attacks on Shi'a celebrating the religious holiday of Ashura, killing over 180, was its most lethal attack to date. The group also killed key Iraqi political figures in 2004, most notably the head of Iraq's Governing Council. The group has claimed responsibility for the videotaped execution by beheading of Americans Nicholas Berg (May 8, 2004), Jack Armstrong (September 20, 2004), and Jack Hensley (September 21, 2004). The group may have been involved in other hostage incidents as well. Zarqawi's group has been active in the Levant since its involvement in the failed Millennium plot directed against US, Western, and Jordanian targets in Jordan in late 1999. The group assassinated USAID official Laurence Foley in 2002, but the Jordanian Government has successfully disrupted further plots against US and Western interests in Jordan, including a major arrest of Zarqawi associates in 2004 planning to attack Jordanian security targets.

Strength QJBR's numerical strength is unknown, though the group has attracted new recruits to replace key leaders and other members killed or captured by Coalition forces. Zarqawi's increased stature from his formal relationship with al- Qa'ida could attract additional recruits to QJBR.

Location/Area of Operation QJBR's operations are predominately Iraq-based, but the group maintains an extensive logistical network throughout the Middle East, North Africa, and Europe.

External Aid QJBR probably receives funds from donors in the Middle East and Europe, local sympathizers in Iraq, and a variety of businesses and criminal activities. In many cases, QJBR's donors are probably motivated by support for jihad rather than affiliation with any specific terrorist group.

Terre Lilure (TL)

a.k.a. Free Land

Description Leftwing Catalonian separatist terrorist group formed in the 1970s with the goal of establishing an independent Marxist state in the Spanish Provinces of Catalonia and Valencia. Leadership announced in July 1991 that the group had ceased terrorist operations, but hardcore members may remain active.

Activities Mainly small-scale bombing attacks against property in northeastern Spain. Targets include foreign banks and travel agencies. Reportedly renounced terrorism in July 1991.

Strength Unknown.

Location/Area of Operation Spain.

External Aid None known.

Tunisian Combatant Group (TCG)

Description The Tunisian Combatant Group (TCG), also known as the Jama'a Combattante Tunisienne, seeks to establish an Islamic regime in Tunisia and has targeted US and Western interests. The group is an offshoot of the banned Tunisian Islamist movement, an-Nahda. Founded around 2000 by Tarek Maaroufi and Saifallah Ben Hassine, the TCG has drawn members from the Tunisian diaspora in Europe and elsewhere. It has lost some of its leadership, but may still exist, particularly in Western Europe. Belgian authorities arrested Maaroufi in late 2001 and sentenced him to six years in prison in 2003 for his role in the assassination of anti-Taliban commander Ahmad Shah Massoud two days before 9/11. The TCG was designated under EO 13224 in October 2002. Historically, the group has been associated with al-Qaida as well. Members also have ties to other North African extremist groups. The TCG was designated for sanctions under UNSCR 1333 in December 2000.

Activities Tunisians associated with the TCG are part of the support network of the broader international jihadist movement. According to European press reports, TCG members or affiliates in the past have engaged in trafficking falsified documents and recruiting for terror training camps in Afghanistan. Some TCG associates were suspected of planning an attack against the US, Algerian, and Tunisian diplomatic missions in Rome in April 2001. Some members reportedly maintain ties to the Algerian Salafist Group for Call and Combat.

Strength Unknown.

Location/Area of Operation Western Europe and Afghanistan.

External Aid Unknown.

Tupac Amaru Revolutionary Movement (MRTA)

Description MRTA is a traditional Marxist-Leninist revolutionary movement formed in 1983 from remnants of the Movement of the Revolutionary Left, a Peruvian insurgent group active in the 1960s. It aims to establish a Marxist regime and to rid Peru of all imperialist elements (primarily US and Japanese influence). Peru's counterterrorist program has diminished the group's ability to conduct terrorist attacks, and the MRTA has suffered from infighting, the imprisonment or deaths of senior leaders, and the loss of leftist support.

Activities Previously conducted bombings, kidnappings, ambushes, and assassinations, but recent activity has fallen drastically. In December 1996, 14 MRTA members occupied the Japanese Ambassador's residence in Lima and held 72 hostages for more than four months. Peruvian forces stormed the residence in April 1997, rescuing all but one of the remaining hostages and killing all 14 group members, including the remaining leaders. The group has not conducted a significant terrorist operation since and appears more focused on obtaining the release of imprisoned MRTA members, although there are reports of low-level rebuilding efforts.

Strength Believed to be no more than 100 members, consisting largely of young fighters who lack leadership skills and experience.

Location/Area of Operation Peru, with supporters throughout Latin America and Western Europe. Controls no territory.

External Aid None.

Tupac Katari Guerilla Army (EGTK)

Description Indigenous, anti-Western Bolivian subversive organization.

Activities Frequently attacks small, unprotected targets, such as power pylons, oil pipelines, and government offices. Has targeted Mormon churches with firebombings and attacked USAID motorpool in 1993.

Strength Fewer than 100.

Location/Area of Operation Bolivia, primarily the Chapare region, near the Peru border, and the Altiplano.

External Aid None.

Turkish Hizballah

Description Turkish Hizballah is a Kurdish Sunni Islamic terrorist organization that arose in the early 1980s in response to the Kurdistan Workers' Party (PKK)'s secularist approach of establishing an independent Kurdistan. Turkish Hizballah spent its first 10 years fighting the PKK, accusing the group of atrocities against Muslims in southeastern Turkey, where Turkish Hizballah seeks to establish an independent Islamic state.

Activities Beginning in the mid-1990s, Turkish Hizballah, which is unrelated to Lebanese Hizballah, expanded its target base and modus operandi from killing PKK militants to conducting low-level bombings against liquor stores, bordellos, and other establishments the organization considered "anti-Islamic." In January 2000, Turkish security forces killed Huseyin Velioglu, the leader of Turkish Hizballah, in a shootout at a safe house in Istanbul. The incident sparked a year-long series of counterterrorist operations against the group that resulted in the detention of some 2,000 individuals; authorities arrested several hundred of those on criminal charges. At the same time, police recovered nearly 70 bodies of Turkish and Kurdish businessmen and journalists that Turkish Hizballah had tortured and brutally murdered during the mid-to-late 1990s. The group began targeting official Turkish interests in January 2001, when its operatives assassinated the Diyarbakir police chief in the group's most sophisticated operation to date. Turkish Hizballah did not conduct a major operation in 2003 or 2004 and probably is focusing on recruitment, fundraising, and reorganization.

Strength Possibly a few hundred members and several thousand supporters.

Location/Area of Operation Primarily the Diyarbakir region of southeastern Turkey.

External Aid It is widely believed that Turkey's security apparatus originally backed Turkish Hizballah to help the Turkish Government combat the PKK. Alternative views are that the Turkish Government turned a blind eye to Turkish Hizballah's activities because its primary targets were

PKK members and supporters, or that the Government simply had to prioritize scarce resources and was unable to wage war on both groups simultaneously. Allegations of collusion have never been laid to rest, and the Government of Turkey continues to issue denials. Turkish Hizballah also is suspected of having ties with Iran, although there is not sufficient evidence to establish a link.

Ulster Defense Association/ Ulster Freedom Fighters (UDA/UFF)

Description The Ulster Defense Association (UDA), the largest Loyalist paramilitary group in Northern Ireland, was formed in 1971 as an umbrella organization for Loyalist paramilitary groups such as the Ulster Freedom Fighters (UFF). Today, the UFF constitutes almost the entire UDA membership. The UDA/UFF declared a series of cease-fires between 1994 and 1998. In September 2001, the UDA/UFF's Inner Council withdrew its support for Northern Ireland's Good Friday Agreement. The following month, after a series of murders, bombings, and street violence, the British Government ruled the UDA/UFF's cease-fire defunct. The dissolution of the organization's political wing, the Ulster Democratic Party, soon followed. In January 2002, however, the UDA created the Ulster Political Research Group to serve in a similar capacity. Designated under EO 13224 in December 2001.

Activities The UDA/UFF has evolved into a criminal organization deeply involved in drug trafficking and other moneymaking criminal activities through six largely independent "brigades." It has also been involved in murder, shootings, arson, and assaults. According to the International Monitoring Commission, "the UDA has the capacity to launch serious, if crude, attacks." Some UDA activities have been of a sectarian nature directed at the Catholic community, aimed at what are sometimes described as 'soft' targets, and often have taken place at the interface between the Protestant and Catholic communities, especially in Belfast. The organization continues to be involved in targeting individual Catholics and has undertaken attacks against retired and serving prison officers. The group has also been involved in a violent internecine war with other Loyalist paramilitary groups for the past several years. In February 2003, the UDA/UFF declared a 12-month ceasefire, but refused to decommission its arsenal until Republican groups did likewise and emphasized its continued disagreement with the Good Friday accords. The cease-fire has been extended. Even though numerous attacks on Catholics were blamed on the group, the UDA/ UFF did not claim credit for any attacks, and in August 2003 reiterated its intention to remain militarily inactive.

Strength Estimates vary from 2,000 to 5,000 members, with several hundred active in paramilitary operations.

Location/Area of Operation Northern Ireland.

External Aid Unknown.

Ulster Volunteer Force (UVF)

Description The UVF is a Loyalist terrorist group formed in 1966 to oppose liberal reforms in Northern Ireland that members feared would lead to unification of Ireland. The group adopted the name of an earlier organization formed in 1912 to combat Home Rule for Ireland. The UVF's goal is to maintain Northern Ireland's status as part of the UK; to that end it has killed some 550 persons since 1966. The UVF and its offshoots have been responsible for some of the most vicious attacks of "The Troubles," including horrific sectarian killings like those perpetrated in the 1970s by the UVF-affiliated "Shankill Butchers." In October 1994, the Combined Loyalist Military Command, which included the UVF, declared a cease-fire, and the UVF's political wing, the Progressive Unionist Party, has played an active role in the peace process. Despite the cease-fire, the organization has been involved in a series of bloody feuds with other Loyalist paramilitary organizations. The Red Hand Commando is linked to the UVF.

Activities The UVF has been active in Belfast and the border areas of Northern Ireland, where it has carried out bombings, assassinations, kidnappings, hijackings, extortion, and robberies. UVF members have been linked to recent racial attacks on minorities; however, these assaults were reportedly not authorized by the UVF leadership. On occasion, it has provided advance warning to police of its attacks. Targets include nationalist civilians, Republican paramilitary groups, and, on occasion, rival Loyalist paramilitary groups. The UVF is a relatively disciplined organization with a centralized command. The UVF leadership continues to observe a cease-fire.

Strength Unclear, but probably several hundred supporters, with a smaller number of hard-core activists. Police counterterrorist operations and internal feuding have reduced the group's strength and capabilities.

Location/Area of Operation Northern Ireland. Some support on the UK mainland.

External Aid Suspected in the past of receiving funds and arms from sympathizers overseas.

United Liberation Front of Assam (ULFA)

Description Northeast India's most prominent insurgent group, ULFA—an ethnic secessionist organization in the Indian state of Assam, bordering Bangladesh and Bhutan—was founded on April 7, 1979 at Rang Ghar, during agitation organized by the state's powerful students' union. The group's objective is an independent Assam, reflected in its ideology of "Oikya, Biplab, Mukti" ("Unity, Revolution, Freedom"). ULFA enjoyed widespread support in upper Assam in its initial years, especially in 1985-1992. ULFA's kidnappings, killings and extortion led New Delhi to ban the group and start a military offensive against it in 1990, which forced it to go underground. ULFA began to lose popularity in the late 1990s after it increasingly targeted civilians, including a prominent NGO activist. It lost further support for its anti-Indian stand during the 1999 Kargil War.

Activities ULFA trains, finances and equips cadres for a "liberation struggle" while extortion helps finance military training and weapons purchases. ULFA conducts hit and run operations on security forces in Assam, selective assassinations, and explosions in public places. During the 1980s-1990s ULFA undertook a series of abductions and murders, particularly of businessmen. In 2000, ULFA assassinated an Assam state minister. In 2003, ULFA killed more than 60 "outsiders" in Assam, mainly residents of the bordering state of Bihar. Following the December 2003 Bhutanese Army's attack on ULFA camps in Bhutan, the group is believed to have suffered a setback. Some important ULFA functionaries surrendered in Assam, but incidents of violence, though of a lesser magnitude than in the past, continue. On August 14, one civilian was killed and 18 others injured when ULFA militants triggered a grenade blast inside a cinema hall at Gauripur in Dhubri district. The next day, at an Indian Independence Day event, a bomb blast in Dhemaji killed an estimated 13 people, including 6 children, and injured 21.

Strength ULFA's earlier numbers (3,000 plus) dropped following the December 2003 attack on its camps in Bhutan. Total cadre strength now is estimated at 700.

Location/Area of Operations ULFA is active in the state of Assam, and its workers are believed to transit (and sometimes conduct operations in) parts of neighboring Arunachal Pradesh, Meghalaya and Nagaland. All ULFA camps in Bhutan are reportedly demolished. The group may have linkages with other ethnic insurgent groups active in neighboring states.

External Aid ULFA reportedly procures and trades in arms with other Northeast Indian groups, and receives aid from unknown external sources.

United Self-Defense Forces/ Group of Colombia (AUC)

a.k.a. Autodefensas Unidas de Colombia

Designated as a Foreign Terrorist Organization

Description The AUC, commonly referred to as "the paramilitaries," is an umbrella organization formed in April 1997 to coordinate the activities of local paramilitary groups and develop a cohesive paramilitary effort to combat insurgents. The AUC is supported by economic elites, drug traffickers, and local communities lacking effective Government security, and claims its primary objective is to protect its sponsors from Marxist insurgents. The AUC's affiliate groups and other paramilitary units are in negotiations with the Government of Colombia and in the midst of the largest demobilization in modern Colombian history. To date, approximately 3,600 AUC-affiliated fighters have demobilized since November 2003.

Activities AUC operations vary from assassinating suspected insurgent supporters to engaging guerrilla combat units. As much as 70 percent of the AUC's operational costs are financed with drug-related earnings, with the rest coming from "donations" from its sponsors. The AUC generally avoids actions against US personnel or interests.

Strength Estimated 8,000 to 11,000, with an unknown number of active supporters.

Location/Area of Operation AUC forces are strongest in the northwest of Colombia in Antioquia, Cordoba, Sucre, Atlantico, Magdelena, Cesar, La Guajira, and Bolivar Departments, with affiliate groups in the coffee region, Valle del Cauca, and in Meta Department.

External Aid None.

Zviadists

Description Extremist supporters of deceased former Georgian President Zviad Gamsakhurdia. Launched a revolt against his successor, Eduard Shevardnadze, which was suppressed in late 1993. Some Gamsakhurdia sympathizers formed a weak legal opposition in Georgia, but others remain opposed to Shevardnadze's rule and seek to overthrow him. Some Gamsakhurdia government officials fled to Russia following Gamsakhurdia's ouster in 1991 and were using Russia as a base of operations to bankroll anti-Shevardnadze activities.

Activities Conducted bombings and kidnappings. Attempted two assassinations against Shevardnadze, in August 1995 and in February 1998. Took UN personnel hostage following the attempt in February 1998 but released the hostages unharmed. Zviadists conducted no violent activity in 1999.

Strength Unknown.

Location/Area of Operation Georgia, especially Mingrelia and Russia.

External Aid May have received support and training in Chechen terrorist training camps. Chechen mercenaries participated in the assassination attempt against Shevardnadze in February 1998.

PART 3

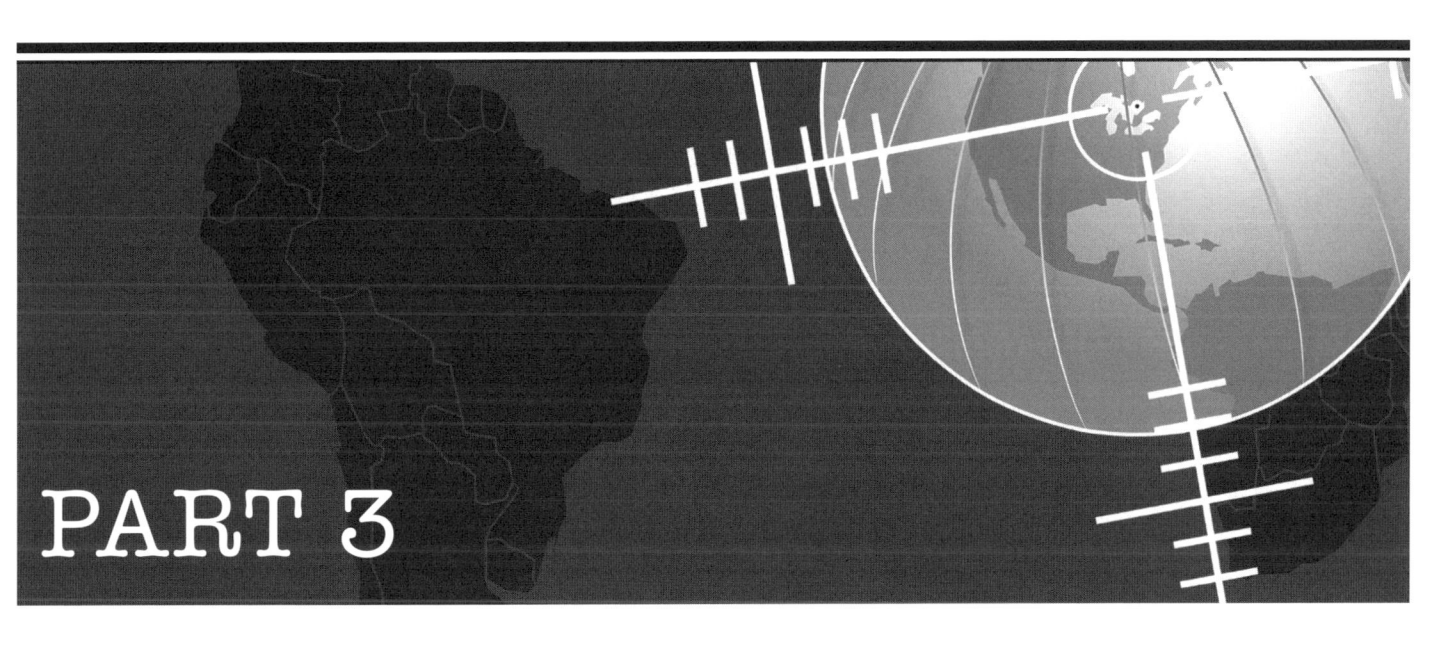

COUNTRY REPORTS 1985-2004

Overview of Country Reports on Terrorism

Anna Sabasteanski

From the precursor reports in the 1970s until *Patterns of Global Terrorism 2004*, reports on terrorism by region and country were included in the overall report along with chronological and statistical data. The intelligence reorganization that followed the attacks of September 11, 2001, established the National Counterterrorism Center (NCTC) that became responsible for coordinating terrorism data.

Transition from "Patterns" to "Country Reports"

In 2005 Secretary of State Condoleezza Rice oversaw a revision of the structure of the State Department's yearly report on terrorism. In its new format, the report excluded statistical information, which became the responsibility of the NCTC. The name of the report changed from *Patterns of Global Terrorism* to *Country Reports on Terrorism*. This part of the collection includes all the country reports from 1985 to 2004 and offers an overview of each of the three decades covered. The chronologies are collected in Part 4, and the statistics—including the 2004 data from NCTC—are in Part 6, "Trends over Time."

Other State Department Reports

Country Reports on Terrorism is just one of a wide variety of country reports and other documents that are produced by the Department of State. Others include the *Country Reports on Human Rights Practices*, lists of sovereign states and dependencies of the world, background notes on the countries of the world, and profiles of those countries.

Country Reports on Human Rights Practices

The Bureau of Democracy, Human Rights and Labor submits this annual report to Congress in compliance with sections 116(d) and 502B(b) of the Foreign Assistance Act (FAA) of 1961, as amended, and section 504 of the Trade Act of 1974, as amended. This report is delivered to the Speaker of the House of Representatives and the Committee on Foreign Relations of the Senate by February 25. It provides "a full and complete report regarding the status of internationally recognized human rights, within the meaning of subsection (A) in countries that receive assistance under this part, and (B) in all other foreign countries which are members of the United Nations and which are not otherwise the subject of a human rights report under this Act" (quoted from section 116(d)(1) of the FAA). Other countries are included at the discretion of the secretary of state. *Country Reports on Human Rights Practices* can be accessed at http://www.state.gov/g/drl/rls/hrrpt.

Lists of Independent States and Dependencies

The Bureau of Intelligence and Research maintains two lists, "Independent States in the World" and "Dependencies and Areas of Special Sovereignty." These lists provide both the commonly used and official names of the countries, two-letter country codes, and the countries' or dependencies' capitals or administrative centers. The independent states list also indicates whether the state has diplomatic relations with the United States and whether it is a member of the United Nations, while the list of dependencies shows what state has sovereignty over the dependency. These lists can be accessed at http://www.state.gov/s/inr/states.

Background Notes

The Electronic Information and Publications Office of the Bureau of Public Affairs updates and revises *Background Notes*, publications that the State Department's regional bureaus develop to provide facts about the land, people, history, government, political conditions, economy, and foreign relations of independent states and some dependencies and areas of special sovereignty. Each country's edition of *Background Notes* incorporates a link to the State Department's country page for that country, which can be accessed by clicking on the country name. *Background Notes* can be accessed at http://www.state.gov/r/pa/ei/bgn.

Country Pages

The State Department's under secretary for political affairs manages regional and bilateral policy issues, which are divided into six bureaus that cover Africa, East Asia and the Pacific, Europe and Eurasia, the Near East, South Asia, and the

Western Hemisphere. Each of these bureaus provides country pages as well as information about regional and country programs and policies. The *CIA World Factbook*, produced by the Central Intelligence Agency, provides additional country profiles that complement the State Department's offerings. These are available online at http://www.cia.gov/cia/publications/factbook/index.html.

The State Department also provides country travel information, including travel warnings, consular information sheets, and public announcements. These are available online at http://www.travel.state.gov. An example appears below.

U.S. Department of State Travel Warning for Afghanistan

The Department of State strongly warns U.S. citizens against travel to Afghanistan. There is an ongoing threat to kidnap and assassinate U.S. citizens and Non-Governmental Organization (NGO) workers throughout the country. The ability of Afghan authorities to maintain order and ensure the security of citizens and visitors is limited. Remnants of the former Taliban regime and the terrorist al-Qaida network, and other groups hostile to the government, remain active. U.S.-led military operations continue. Travel in all areas of Afghanistan, including the capital Kabul, is unsafe due to military operations, landmines, banditry, armed rivalry among political and tribal groups, and the possibility of terrorist attacks, including attacks using vehicular or other Improvised Explosive Devices (IEDs), and kidnapping. The security environment remains volatile and unpredictable. Parliamentary elections are scheduled for September 18, 2005. There is a potential risk for violence during the election period.

A number of attacks on international organizations, international aid workers, and foreign interests have occurred throughout the country since the beginning of 2005. Foreigners in Kabul and elsewhere throughout the country were targeted for violent attacks and kidnappings. In March, a Canadian diplomatic vehicle was damaged by an improvised explosive device (IED) while traveling on a main highway outside Kabul. That month a British NGO worker was shot to death in downtown Kabul after leaving a restaurant known to be popular with foreigners. In April a U.S. citizen was kidnapped in Kabul for a short time but managed to escape from his abductors.

The month of May witnessed several attempted kidnappings of foreigners in Kabul, including a group of World Bank employees. Kidnappers were successful in abducting an Italian citizen working for CARE International from her car in a downtown Kabul neighborhood popular with foreign residents. A foreign UN worker was injured in a grenade attack on an Internet café in downtown Kabul at the beginning of the month. Violent demonstrations in multiple locations throughout Afghanistan resulted in significant damage to the offices of international organizations and other foreign interests, and the death of 19 Afghans. Attacks on Afghan workers affiliated with international organizations occurred throughout the country, sometimes resulting in fatalities. There have been multiple rocket attacks in Kabul and elsewhere in Afghanistan, including a rocket that hit the International Security Assistance Forces (ISAF) compound near the Embassy in late May.

Family members of official Americans assigned to the U.S. Embassy in Kabul are not allowed to reside in Afghanistan. In addition, unofficial travel to Afghanistan by U.S. Government employees and their family members requires prior approval by the Department of State. From time to time, the U.S. Embassy places areas frequented by foreigners off limits to its personnel depending on current security conditions. Potential target areas include key national or international government establishments, international organizations and other locations with expatriate personnel, and public areas popular with the expatriate community. Private U.S. citizens are strongly urged to heed these restrictions as well and may obtain the latest information by calling the U.S. Embassy in Kabul or consulting the embassy website below. Terrorist actions may include, but are not limited to, suicide operations, bombings, assassinations, carjackings, rocket attacks, assaults or kidnappings. Possible threats include conventional weapons such as explosive devices or non-conventional weapons, including chemical or biological agents.

The United States Embassy cannot provide visa services, and its ability to provide emergency consular services to U.S. citizens in Afghanistan is limited. Afghan authorities also can provide only limited assistance to U.S. citizens facing difficulties.

June 09, 2005

Terrorism in the 1980s

Overview of Terrorism in the 1980s

Anna Sabasteanski

Worldwide Terrorist Attacks, 1985–1989

1985 782 attacks
1986 774 attacks
1987 832 attacks
1988 856 attacks
1989 528 attacks

The 1983 bombing of a U.S. army barracks in Lebanon marked the first international terrorist attack directed against U.S. interests. Although Americans had been horrified by terrorism in the 1972 Munich Olympic games and by hijackings in the 1970s, attacks directed specifically against Americans raised U.S. consciousness of terrorism to new levels. In 1985, Western hostages held captive for several years in Lebanon received intense media coverage that maintained public awareness of this new threat. *Patterns of Global Terrorism 1985* documented these events to an international audience and began two seminal decades of reports that presented the changing face of international terrorism to the world, in the context of U.S. public policy objectives.

During the 1980s, military and government targets tightened their security, making it more difficult for terrorists to succeed in an attack. As a consequence, terrorists turned to softer targets, such as business interests. Civilians, particularly international travelers, became casualties of the new tactic.

Terrorist attacks also became less focused and discriminating during the 1980s. For example, assassinations against targeted individuals or facilities declined, while the number of bombings, particularly car bombings, increased. By the end of the decade, bombings were responsible for about half of all terrorism-related attacks.

During the 1980s, the number of countries affected by terrorism ranged from a low of seventy-six to a high of eighty-seven. Middle Eastern terrorism spreading across borders was responsible for some of this increase. The State Department called this phenomenon "terrorist spillover" and attributed it primarily to Palestinian groups targeting their foes in new locales, most often in Europe. The 1985 seizure of the Italian cruise ship *Achille Lauro* is just one example of such attacks.

The State Department identified a number of reasons why Middle Eastern terrorists were increasingly active in Europe:

- Several dozen Middle East terrorists were jailed in West European prisons. This has spurred a number of Middle Eastern groups to attack West European targets seeking to pressure those governments into releasing group members.
- Large numbers of Middle Easterners—many of whom comprise expatriate and student communities—live and travel in Western Europe and provide cover, shelter, and potential recruits.
- Western Europe has fewer travel restrictions between its countries than is the case with many other regions, and some countries also have arrangements with some Middle Eastern states to facilitate guest workers. A number of West European governments recognize this vulnerability and are considering measures to tighten controls.
- Abundant accessible targets exist in Western Europe, in contract to the Middle East where formidable security measures surround most Western installations.
- Worldwide publicity accompanies international terrorist attacks in Western Europe, but in countries such as Lebanon the level of violence is so high it all but masks other than the most spectacular terrorist events.
- The open nature of West European society makes it operationally easy to function, free of the restrictions on personal freedoms prevalent elsewhere.
- A number of West European countries host exile groups and former leaders that are attractive targets for regimes, such as those in Libya and Iran, that wish to silence vocal opponents. Likewise, there are numerous targets for retaliation against such attacks, including official representatives of incumbent regimes.
- The phenomenon of Middle Eastern spillover has been abetted by the diplomatic structure of countries, such as Libya and Iran, whose diplomatic personnel have been implicated in terrorist attacks.
- Certain West European countries have offered passive support to terrorist groups or, by their rhetoric, have created environments that appear sympathetic to terrorists.

In some cases, states apparently have struck deals with terrorists—making concessions in exchange for agreements that terrorists will refrain from conducting attacks on their territory.

European nations addressed many of these vulnerabilities during the decade, and international measures were taken to better secure air travel. For their part, terrorists responded by building infrastructure to support future attacks. Their development efforts meant they had less time to launch attacks.

At the same time, the end of the Iran-Iraq war (1988), Palestine Liberation Organization (PLO) leader Yasser Arafat's renunciation of terrorism (1988), and the withdrawal of Soviet troops from Afghanistan (1989) reduced state financing of terrorism and weakened some of the most active groups, notably the Abu Nidal organization (a PLO breakaway group), which also helped reduce terrorist violence.

This combination of improved security and conflict resolution meant that the number of terrorist attacks had fallen by the end of the decade. These positive signs may have diverted attention away from the ominous trend toward bombings and indiscriminate killing that would become more significant in the future.

In the following pages we have included the country reports from *Patterns of Global Terrorism*, beginning with *Patterns of Global Terrorism 1985*. This report opened with the statement, "International terrorists had a banner year in 1985." That year, the number of terrorist incidents increased by 30 percent from the previous year to 782, with the increase largely due to 329 fatalities resulting from the bombing of an Air India plane. Of these attacks, 20 percent involved U.S. citizens or property.

The number of attacks decreased slightly in 1986 to 774. Three attempted airline bombings failed; if they had been successful, up to 800 more people might have died. However, of the 774 incidents, the number of attacks involving U.S. targets (most involving U.S. property or persons in Latin America) rose slightly, to 26 percent of the total.

The year 1987 saw a 7 percent increase in terrorist attacks, to 832 incidents, led by a wave of high-casualty bombings in Pakistan carried out by the Soviet-trained and -organized Afghan intelligence service. Those attacks were intended to deter Pakistan from aiding the anti-Soviet Afghan resistance in the Soviet-Afghan war. Improved security and cooperation in the Middle East was credited with a fall in incidents in that region that, if the bombings in Pakistan had been excluded, would have contributed to a nearly 10 percent reduction in attacks. The percentage of attacks aimed at U.S. targets dropped slightly to 24 percent.

There was little change in 1988. The number of incidents rose by 3 percent, to 856. Although this marked another record, the numbers of attacks were constrained by improved security and cooperation, some reduction in state support of terrorism, and the end of the Iran-Iraq war. During the year terrorists were responsible for three "spectacular" attacks: the hijacking of a Kuwaiti airliner in April, the attack on a Greek day-excursion ship off the coast of Greece in July, and the bombing of Pan Am Flight 103 over Scotland in December. (The Pan AM Flight 103 bombing was not included in the statistics, however, because at the time of publication terrorism had not been unequivocally established as the cause of the disaster.)

In 1989 the number of terrorist attacks dropped sharply to 528, a decline of nearly 38 percent. U.S. interests were targeted most frequently, followed by Israeli interests. There was one spectacular operation during the year—the bombing of a French airline, UTA Flight 772, over Niger on 19 September, in which 171 people were killed.

Patterns of Global Terrorism: 1985

The Year in Review

International terrorists had a banner year in 1985.[1] They carried out more attacks than in any year since the decade began; caused more casualties—especially fatalities—over that same period (329 alone occurred when an Air India jetliner was blown up in June); conducted a host of spectacular, publicity-grabbing events that ultimately ended in cold-blooded murder; increasingly turned to business and more accessible public targets as security at official and military installations was strengthened against terrorism, and, in so doing, counted among their victims a record number of innocent bystanders; and finally, gave pause to international travelers worldwide who feared the increasingly indiscriminate nature of international terrorism.

In 1985, 782 international terrorist incidents occurred, a 30-percent increase over 1984. One-third of these incidents resulted in casualties; more than 800 persons were killed and over 1,200 were wounded.

A comparison by region of the 1985 data with those of

---

1 Our statistics cover only international terrorist incidents [as defined in the Introduction], but for many countries they represent only a small fraction of the politically motivated violence. Where appropriate, therefore, the text and chronology include references to indigenous terrorism and other types of political violence. For illustrative purposes, consider the following: if a member of the French terrorist group Action Directe (AD) attacks a Frenchman in France, the incident is classified as an instance of indigenous terrorism. Should that same terrorist attack a US or other foreign national in France—or an individual or facility belonging to any nationality located outside France—the event is recorded as international terrorism. Thus, the annual statistics that we cite would include the latter incident, but not the former. Our information base on indigenous terrorism, while sizable, is not comprehensive enough to permit us to provide statistical data with the same degree of confidence as we do on international terrorism. As a result, only international terrorist incidents are included in the statistical sections.

1984 reveals no consistent pattern; international terrorist attacks increased in some places but declined in others. Last year more international terrorist incidents—more than 350—were recorded in the Middle East than in any other part of the world. If the number of attacks conducted by Middle Eastern terrorists elsewhere is also included, Middle East terrorism accounted for 441, or nearly 60 percent, of the total international terrorist incidents in 1985. For the first time in a decade, Western Europe dropped from first to second place as a venue for international terrorism, with 218 incidents. Most attacks by West European terrorists were designed to avoid casualties, but most of those by Middle Eastern terrorists were intended to cause maximum casualties. In 1985 Middle Eastern terrorists worldwide killed more than 230 persons and injured more than 820.

Citizens and property of at least 84 countries were victims or targets of international terrorist attacks in 1985, compared with 76 in 1984. International terrorist incidents took place in at least 72 countries. Attacks against business interests increased over 1984—from 165 to 227. Attacks against diplomatic personnel or facilities dropped from 133 to 91, but attacks against other official and military targets increased from 84 to 92, and from 53 to 67, respectively.

Certain categories of incidents increased markedly. Arson attacks jumped from 57 in 1984 to 102 in 1985, bombings rose from 302 to 399, and the number of kidnapings increased from 47 to 87. Attacks against US citizens or property rose from 133 in 1984 to 170 in 1985. About 45 percent of the 1985 incidents involving US targets occurred in Latin America; more than one-third took place in Western Europe. Of the 17 anti-US terrorist incidents that occurred in the Middle East, 13 were in Lebanon.

Last year saw a substantial increase in the number of indiscriminate casualties. In 1985 most victims were random targets, such as tourists or passers-by. The number of incidents against victims such as nonofficial public figures and others not expressly affiliated with business, government, or the military increased from 280 in 1984 to 479 in 1985.

Sovereign states continued to be active in supporting terrorism last year. In 1985, 93 incidents (12 percent of all international terrorist incidents), one-third of which occurred in Western Europe, bore indications of state support. More than 90 percent of state-supported terrorist incidents were conducted by groups or agents supported by Middle Eastern states—most notably Libya, Syria, and Iran. Libya moved toward closer ties to the radical Palestinian Abu Nidal Group, and Syria's role as a patron of international terrorism reached a new high. Iranian-backed groups, such as the fundamentalist Shia Hizballah in Lebanon, kidnaped nearly a dozen Westerners in Lebanon in 1985, although these kidnapings probably did not occur as a result of Iranian direction.

International terrorism of Middle East origin increased substantially in 1985. Nearly six out of every 10 attacks either occurred in the region or were conducted by Middle Easterners elsewhere. Palestinian groups—whether considered politically moderate or radical—increased their level of international terrorism by nearly 200 percent, accounting for 256 incidents, or one-third of the total.

Middle Eastern terrorists increased their level of activity outside the region, especially in Western Europe. In 1985, 74 acts of terrorism by Middle Eastern terrorists occurred in Western Europe, compared with 61 in 1984.[2] During the period from 1981 to 1983, the average annual number of such incidents was 35. The highest levels of Middle East-origin activity occurred in Greece, Cyprus, and Italy. Among these "spillover" incidents were some of the most dramatic, and lethal, attacks of the year: the hijacking in June of a TWA jetliner flying from Athens to Rome; the seizure of the Italian cruise ship Achille Lauro in October as it departed Alexandria, Egypt; the hijacking in November of an Egyptian jetliner from Athens to Malta; and near-simultaneous machinegun and grenade massacres at the Rome and Vienna airports in December.

In Israel and the occupied territories, international terrorism increased markedly in 1985.[3] Of 357 international terrorist incidents that occurred in the Middle East, more than 220 took place in Israel, the West Bank, and Gaza Strip—up nearly 200 percent from the previous year. Much of the increase was the result of the activity of various Palestinian groups, both inside and outside the Palestine Liberation Organization (PLO), against Israeli and Arab targets—partly in competition with, or opposition to, each other and partly to demonstrate that they still constitute a force to be feared.

Western Europe experienced a slightly reduced overall level of international terrorist incidents in 1985 because decreased activity by West European terrorists offset increased Middle East terrorism there. Indigenous terrorist groups remained dangerous, however, and they continued their campaign against NATO targets that began in late 1984. Concern about cooperation among several West European groups was heightened by a joint communique issued in January by the West German Red Army Faction (RAF) and the French Action Directe (AD) that called for a "common anti-imperialist front" in Western Europe and a joint claim of responsibility for the car-bombing in August at Rhein-Main airbase in West Germany.

In Latin America, international terrorism increased by about 45 percent over 1984, totaling 119 incidents. Chile and Colombia showed the greatest increase. Terrorism against US targets made up the largest portion of international terrorist activity in Latin America last year. Perhaps the most vicious anti-US attack was the June massacre of 13 persons by a component of the Central American Revolutionary Workers' Party (PRTC)—including four off-duty US Marines and two US businessmen—in a San Salvador café. Most of the

---

2 Attacks by Armenian terrorist groups are not included.

3 It should be noted that virtually all acts of political violence in the West Bank and Gaza Strip are coded here as international terrorism because of the special status of those territories. Of the 220-some incidents that took place in Israel and the occupied territories last year, 139—or 60 percent—occurred in the West Bank.

political violence in the region, however, continues to result from local insurgencies, not international terrorism.

Asia and Sub-Saharan Africa each accounted for 5 percent of all international terrorist activity last year. Asia witnessed an increase from the previous year, but activity in Sub-Saharan Africa declined somewhat. Sikh terrorists, who carried out their first international attacks in 1985, probably were responsible for the most lethal single incident of the year—the bombing of an Air India Jetliner over the North Atlantic.

In 1985, 20 percent of all international terrorist activity involved US citizens or property. Most anti-US attacks—45 percent—occurred in Latin America, primarily in Chile and Colombia. Another one-third took place in Western Europe, with West Germany a favorite location. Altogether, last year 38 US citizens were killed, and 157 were wounded, compared with 12 and 33, respectively, during the previous year. Business interests were the most frequently attacked US targets in 1985.

Terrorist Spillover From the Middle East

Growing Problem

The number of international terrorist attacks conducted by Middle Eastern groups outside the region continued to rise in 1985. As in previous years, Western Europe was the principal venue for this spillover problem, and terrorism of Middle Eastern origin accounted for a markedly increased share of the total number of international terrorist incidents in Western Europe in 1985. In 1985, 74 incidents of Middle East spillover activity occurred there, 13 more than the previous year and double the annual average for the period from 1980 to 1983. In the past, Western victims were generally people caught in the crossfire, but in 1985 they increasingly were the specific target.

In 1985 Middle Eastern terrorism spread to five West European countries—Belgium, Denmark, Malta, Sweden, and Switzerland—that had not experienced the problem in 1984. Most Middle East-origin attacks occurred in countries bordering the Mediterranean, with Greece, Cyprus, and Italy accounting for half the total. The level of spillover activity declined in a few West European states, the most dramatic example being the United Kingdom where the number of incidents dropped from 13 to two.

Middle East spillover activity accounted for much of the drama of terrorism in Western Europe in 1985 as well as the dramatic rise in the number of casualties there. Middle Eastern terrorists operating in Western Europe killed 109 people and wounded 540. Incidents included the brutal murders of Americans and other tourists on aircraft, at crowded airports, and aboard a cruise ship. Such attacks illustrate the growing disregard for innocent bystanders and the increasing tendency of Middle Eastern terrorists to attack unprotected targets in public places. Business targets suffered about a third of the Middle East-origin attacks. These terrorists also were responsible for carrying out five hijackings last year—more than the combined total of hijackings by Middle Easterners in Western Europe for the preceding four years. The victims of Middle Eastern terrorists in Western Europe were fairly equally divided between Middle Eastern and West European or North American nationalities.

For the most part, such terrorist activity in Western Europe resulted from Middle Eastern terrorists targeting fellow Middle Easterners—including Palestinians, Israelis, Jordanians, Syrians, Libyans, and Iranians. Diplomatic personnel and facilities of moderate Arab states, such as Jordan; officials of various Palestinian groups; and emigre opponents of Middle Eastern regimes were frequent targets.

Palestinian terrorists were the major contributors to the spillover violence, conducting nearly 60 percent of the incidents in 1985 and some 40 percent of all Middle East-origin attacks in Western Europe during 1980–85. This rise in Palestinian terrorism in 1985 included the resumption by pro-Arafat Palestinians of terrorist attacks outside of Israel and the occupied territories after a 10-year hiatus. Fatah, the group led by PLO head Arafat, is believed responsible for some 10 attacks in Western Europe in 1985, including the murder last September of three Israelis in Cyprus. Most Fatah attacks in Western Europe were against Syrian targets, probably in retaliation for Syrian-backed attacks against Fatah officials.

Much of the Palestinian terrorist activity in Western Europe continued to be carried out by anti-Arafat groups, who staunchly oppose a negotiated settlement with Israel and refuse to recognize Israel's right to exist. The Abu Nidal Group was one of the most active—and ruthless—of these organizations. It staged some two dozen incidents in 1985, over half of them in Western Europe. The Abu Nidal attacks in Western Europe caused 73 deaths and wounded 251 persons. Thirty-six of the victims were US citizens. Among the more dramatic Middle Eastern terrorist attacks in Western Europe in 1985 were the following:

- **Spain.** On 12 April the El Descanso restaurant outside Madrid was bombed, killing 18 Spaniards and wounding another 82 persons, including 15 Americans. Individuals claiming to represent several terrorist groups—including some West European ones—claimed responsibility, but Middle Eastern terrorists are among the prime suspects.
- **Greece/Lebanon.** On 14 June Lebanese Shia gunmen hijacked TWA flight 847 flying from Athens to Rome and forced it to land in Beirut. The hijackers released the hostages 17 days later but killed US Navy diver Robert Stethem during the early stages of the incident.
- **Greece.** On 3 September two grenades were thrown into the lobby of a Greek hotel in Glyfada, wounding 19 Britons. A caller to an Athens newspaper stated that the Palestinian Black September organization—a name used by the Abu Nidal Group—would stage numerous attacks in Athens if Greek authorities did not release one of its imprisoned members.

- **Italy.** On 16 September terrorists lobbed grenades into the Cafe de Paris restaurant in Rome, wounding 38 tourists, including nine Americans. The Revolutionary Organization of Socialist Muslims, a covername used by the Abu Nidal Group, claimed responsibility.
- **Mediterranean Sea.** On 7 October the Italian cruise ship Achille Lauro was seized by the PLF as it departed Alexandria, Egypt, for Port Said. Before surrendering to Egyptian authorities on 9 October, the terrorists killed US tourist Leon Klinghoffer.
- **Greece/Malta.** On 23 November an Egyptian jetliner was hijacked from Athens to Malta. The terrorists murdered several persons, including American Scarlett Rogencamp, and wounded the other Americans aboard before Egyptian commandos stormed the plane, killing some 60 remaining persons. The Arab Revolutionary Brigades, another covername used by the Abu Nidal Group, claimed responsibility for the hijacking jointly with the Egyptian Revolution.[4]
- **Italy and Austria.** On 27 December near-simultaneous machinegun and grenade attacks at the Rome and Vienna airports left more than 20 persons dead, including five Americans, and some 120 wounded, including 20 Americans. The Abu Nidal Group carried out both attacks.

Why Western Europe?

Middle Eastern terrorist groups operated with growing frequency in Western Europe for a number of reasons:

- Several dozen Middle Eastern terrorists were jailed in West European prisons. This has spurred a number of Middle Eastern groups—including the Lebanese Armed Revolutionary Faction and the Abu Nidal Group—to attack West European targets seeking to pressure those governments into releasing group members. Countries holding Abu Nidal members in prison are at particular risk. In December 1985 there were 21 known or suspected Abu Nidal members imprisoned in eight West European countries: Austria (five); United Kingdom (three); Italy (four); Greece (three); Spain (two); France (two); Portugal (one); and Malta (one). Some of these were released in 1986. Other Arabs being held in West European jails may also be Abu Nidal members.
- Large numbers of Middle Easterners—many of whom comprise expatriate and student communities—live and travel in Western Europe and provide cover, shelter, and potential recruits.
- Western Europe has fewer travel restrictions between its countries than is the case with many other regions, and some countries also have arrangements with some Middle Eastern states to facilitate guest workers. A number of West European governments recognize this vulnerability and are considering measures to tighten controls.
- Abundant accessible targets exist in Western Europe, in contrast to the Middle East where formidable security measures surround most Western installations.
- Worldwide publicity accompanies international terrorist attacks in Western Europe, but in countries such as Lebanon the level of violence is so high it all but masks other than the most spectacular terrorist events.
- The open nature of West European society makes it operationally easy to function, free of the restrictions on personal freedoms prevalent elsewhere.
- A number of West European countries host exile groups and former leaders that are attractive targets for regimes, such as those in Libya and Iran, that wish to silence vocal opponents. Likewise, there are numerous targets for retaliation against such attacks, including official representatives of incumbent regimes.
- The phenomenon of Middle Eastern spillover has been abetted by the diplomatic structures of countries, such as Libya and Iran, whose diplomatic personnel have been implicated in terrorist attacks.
- Certain West European countries have offered passive support to terrorist groups or, by their rhetoric, have created environments that appear sympathetic to terrorists. In some cases, states apparently have struck deals with terrorists—making concessions in exchange for agreements that terrorists will refrain from conducting attacks on their territory.

Target USA

Of the 782 international terrorist incidents in 1985, 170—or 22 percent—involved US citizens or property. US interests were second only to Israeli ones as favorite terrorist targets. Almost half the international terrorist incidents involving US citizens or property occurred in Latin America, primarily in Chile and Colombia. Over a third took place in Western Europe, with West Germany a favored location. Businesses were the most frequently attacked US targets.

Casualties

Twenty-one of the anti-US incidents resulted in American casualties, 10 in fatalities. Altogether, 38 US citizens were killed and 157 were wounded, compared with 12 and 33, respectively, during 1984. The 1985 US casualty figures were the second highest since 1980. The highest total occurred in 1983 because of two mass casualty-producing incidents—the April bombing of the US Embassy and the October bombing of the Marine barracks in Lebanon. In 1985, as in 1984, many of the US dead and wounded were incidental casualties —unlucky bystanders at incidents in which persons or facilities of other nationalities were the principal targets.

The US fatalities occurred in the following 10 incidents:

- Philippines, 12 May. An American of Filipino descent was assassinated by seven members of the New People's Army (NPA) when he rebuffed their attempts at extortion.

---

[4] It is not known if "Egyptian Revolution" is an Abu Nidal sobriquet or the name of a distinct Egyptian dissident group.

- Greece/Lebanon, 14 June. Two Shia gunmen, who hijacked TWA flight 847 en route from Athens to Rome, murdered US Navy diver Robert Stethem after the plane touched down in Beirut for the second time.
- El Salvador, 19 June. Several gunmen armed with submachine guns and automatic weapons attacked a cafe in San Salvador, killing four off-duty US Marines and two US businessmen, along with seven other persons. The Mardoqueo Cruz Urban Commandos of the PRTC claimed responsibility.
- North Atlantic, 23 June. Nineteen Americans were among the 329 passengers and crewmembers killed—probably by Sikh extremists—when a bomb exploded aboard a Shannon-bound Air India flight from Toronto.
- West Germany, 8 August. The RAF murdered US Army soldier Edward Pimental in a wooded area in Wiesbaden, evidently to obtain his identification card in order to gain entry into Rhein-Main airbase.
- West Germany, 8 August. A car bomb exploded at Rhein-Main airbase killing two US citizens—one military and one civilian—and wounding 17 other persons. The bombing was jointly claimed by the RAF and the French AD.
- Spain, 9 September. A car bomb exploded in a residential area injuring 19 persons, including a US businessman who died two days later. The American was jogging past the target—a bus transporting Spanish Civil Guards. Basque Fatherland and Liberty (ETA) claimed responsibility.
- Mediterranean Sea, 7 October. PLF terrorists who seized the Italian cruise ship Achille Lauro killed US tourist Leon Klinghoffer before surrendering to Egyptian authorities on 9 October.
- Greece/Malta, 23 November. Terrorists who hijacked an Egyptian airliner from Athens to Malta murdered American Scarlett Rogencamp, as well as four other people, and wounded the other Americans aboard. The Arab Revolutionary Brigades, an Abu Nidal covername, claimed responsibility jointly with the Egyptian Revolution.
- Italy, 27 December. Abu Nidal terrorists armed with AK-47 rifles and handgrenades attacked the El Al ticket counter at Rome airport, killing five Americans, and 10 other persons, and wounding 15 Americans and nearly 60 others.

Hostages

In 1985 some 60 US citizens were kidnaped, hijacked, or otherwise taken hostage. There were 13 kidnapings of US citizens and, by year's end, six of the victims were still being held hostage—four in Lebanon and two in Colombia.

Other Anti-US Violence

There were other manifestations of anti-US violence in 1985, some of which resulted in US casualties. A number of these occurred in Mexico, presumably by individuals connected with narcotics trafficking. In early February four gunmen kidnaped US Drug Enforcement Administration (DEA) agent Enrique Camarena Salazar as he was leaving his office in Guadalajara. Authorities discovered his body in March, along with that of a Mexican pilot who sometimes flew DEA missions. In late January another American, John Walker, also disappeared in Guadalajara, along with a Cuban companion. The two men—whose bodies were found five months later—were last seen alive in a restaurant patronized by elements of the narcotics underworld.

Regional Patterns: The Middle East

In 1985, 45 percent of all international terrorist attacks occurred in the Middle East. The inclusion of Middle East–origin events that took place elsewhere—principally in Western Europe—brings the total of Middle East–related attacks to more than half of all incidents worldwide. Last year Middle Eastern terrorists showed growing disregard for the safety of innocent bystanders and conducted an increasing number of attacks against public places. Terrorism sponsored by Middle Eastern states declined slightly but was more than offset by a nearly 200-percent increase in terrorism conducted by Palestinians.

Iran and Lebanon

The number of Iranian-sponsored attacks declined from the record level of 1984. Iran backs groups in Lebanon, Iraq, and throughout the Persian Gulf that aim to promote a Khomeini-style revolution. Their activities serve Iran's foreign policy goals, even if the groups do not formally coordinate their plans with Tehran. The fundamentalist Shia faction Hizballah in Lebanon and the Dawa Party in Kuwait and Iraq are among the most active Iranian-backed groups that conducted international terrorism in 1985.

Radical Shia terrorists were active primarily in Lebanon and the Persian Gulf. Hizballah factions kidnaped nearly a dozen Westerners in Lebanon in 1985, although two Americans—Jeremy Levin and the Reverend Benjamin Weir, both seized in 1984—escaped or were released. Two other US citizens seized in 1984—William Buckley and Peter Kilburn—continued to be held in 1985. Islamic Jihad claimed that it had murdered Buckley in early October 1985, following an Israeli raid on the PLO headquarters in Tunis. There has been no independent corroboration of his death. At year's end, Kilburn remained in captivity. Three additional Americans—the Associated Press bureau chief and a dean and an administrator from the American University of Beirut—were kidnaped in the spring. Radical Shias kidnaped four French citizens in 1985; four others—members of the French observer force—were killed early in the year. In the Persian Gulf, pro-Iranian Shias attempted to crash an explosives-laden car into the motorcade of the Amir of Kuwait in May.

One of the year's most dramatic incidents—in which an American naval enlisted man was beaten and killed—occurred in mid-June when two Shia gunmen hijacked TWA flight 847 carrying 153 passengers and crew, mostly Americans, en route from Athens to Rome. After two round trips from Beirut to Algiers, the aircraft settled in Beirut for the rest of the 17-day-long incident. The remaining 39 passengers and crew were taken to undisclosed locations in Beirut and turned over to elements of Hizballah and the Shia Amal militia. The hijackers demanded the release of 700 Shia prisoners being held by Israel. During the incident, Israel freed 31 of the prisoners, but the crisis ended only after Syria intervened and helped obtain the release of the passengers.

International terrorism in Lebanon was not limited to US and other Western targets. In late September, four Soviet diplomats were abducted in West Beirut during a period of heavy fighting in Tripoli between pro-Syrian Lebanese militias and Sunni fundamentalists sympathetic to the Islamic Unification Movement. One of the Soviets was killed and his body dumped in West Beirut two days after the kidnaping. The Islamic Liberation Organization claimed responsibility for the kidnapings and threatened to execute the remaining Soviets unless an immediate cease-fire was imposed.

A cease-fire took effect on 4 October. However, the kidnapers continued to hold the Soviets hostage, and other demands were made, including the withdrawal of Soviet troops from Afghanistan. Several weeks later, however, the three Soviets were released unharmed in a Sunni area of West Beirut. Their kidnapers, who said the release was a goodwill gesture and a warning to stop harassing Sunni fundamentalists in Tripoli, undoubtedly faced intense pressure from the Syrian-backed militias that dominate West Beirut.

In 1985, during its 10th year of civil war, violence continued to be a fact of life in Lebanon as factional militias—all of which have used terrorist tactics—continued to wage war throughout most of the country. Even though more international terrorist incidents (76) occurred in Lebanon than in any other country in the world in 1985, international terrorist activity accounted for only a fraction of that country's political violence.

Israel and the Palestinians

International terrorism motivated by the Israeli–Palestinian dispute increased dramatically in 1985 and accounted for much of the increase in Middle Eastern terrorism overall. Attacks on Jewish targets inside Israel and the occupied territories skyrocketed to 170 from a total of 50 in 1984. Of the 139 attacks that took place on the West Bank, 97 were directed at Israeli targets. Outside the Middle East, symbolic Jewish targets, such as synagogues and Jewish-owned stores, were attacked some 18 times.

Although many of the incidents on the West Bank consisted of small-scale incendiary bombings against property, Israeli citizens were killed or wounded in a number of attacks. The Democratic Front for the Liberation of Palestine claimed responsibility for the fatal shooting of an Israeli occupation official in Al-Birah in late March, as well as for the kidnaping and subsequent murder of an off-duty Israeli soldier in mid-April. Abu Musa's Fatah dissidents claimed responsibility for the killing of a civilian Israeli Defense Force worker in Nablus. A pro-Arafat wing of the PLO, Fatah Force 17, also stepped up its activity, claiming responsibility for several attacks in the West Bank and occupied territories during 1985.

Israeli extremists carried out several attacks against Arab targets in a continuing cycle of retaliation. In late April, for example, an Arab cabdriver was murdered near an area where an Israeli cabdriver had been murdered four days earlier. Israeli extremists also may have been responsible for attacks on two mayors of Palestinian refugee camps near Jerusalem.

Attacks carried out worldwide by Palestinians more than doubled, with the Abu Nidal Group alone accounting for 10 percent of these incidents. The PLO ended its self-imposed 1974 ban on violence outside Israel and the occupied territories; pro-Arafat terrorists murdered three Israelis aboard a yacht in Larnaca, Cyprus, in September. Following the slayings, the terrorists surrendered to authorities and remained in a Cypriot prison pending trial. Within a week of the shootings, Israeli jets attacked PLO headquarters in Tunis, indicating that Israel, at least, did not believe Arafat's protestations of innocence. Three days later, the pro-Iranian Islamic Jihad claimed to have executed US political officer William Buckley in retaliation for the raid. (Buckley was taken hostage in West Beirut in March 1984.)

Wings of the PLO loyal to Arafat also participated in terrorism outside the Middle East. The hijacking in October of the cruise ship Achille Lauro by the PLF was the most dramatic example, although the terrorists subsequently claimed that they originally had intended to stay aboard the ship until it reached Israel and conduct a terrorist attack there.

In 1985 radical Palestinians continued to assassinate more moderate Palestinians. In early December, for example, a prominent Palestinian lawyer who favored negotiations with Israel was stabbed to death outside his home in Ramallah on the West Bank. Radical Palestinians are believed responsible.

Kuwait

In 1985 Kuwait continued to be a target of international terrorists seeking the release of 17 Shia terrorists jailed there in connection with a series of bombings against the US and French Embassies in Kuwait in December 1983. Other motivations include a desire to punish Kuwait because of its support for Iraq in Baghdad's war with Iran and to intimidate Kuwait into providing more political and financial support to hardline Arab states. In late May 1985, members of the Iranian-backed Dawa Party carried out a car-bombing on the motorcade of the Amir of Kuwait. Six people died in the explosion and ensuing melee, and 12 were injured. The Amir suffered minor injuries. Islamic Jihad claimed responsibility for the attack, stating it was conducted in response to Kuwait's failure to release the imprisoned Shia terrorists.

The Arab Revolutionary Brigades, a covername used by the Abu Nidal Group when attacking interests of Persian Gulf states, claimed responsibility for a number of anti-Kuwaiti attacks in 1985, including near-simultaneous bombings in mid-July of two crowded outdoor cafes in Kuwait. The explosions killed eight persons and injured some 90 others.

Kuwaiti security forces detonated a third bomb found in yet another cafe.

Jordan

In 1985, a handful of international terrorist incidents took place in Jordan. Elsewhere, Jordanian interests—principally in Western Europe—were attacked some 10 times. The Palestine National Council meeting in Amman in November 1984 and the PLO–Jordan accord of February 1985 stimulated almost double the number of attacks against Jordanian targets by Syrian-supported groups in 1985, compared with 1984. Most of the anti-Jordanian attacks in Western Europe were claimed by the Black September Organization, a covername used by the Syrian-supported Abu Nidal Group when it targets Jordanian interests. Among the group's attacks in 1985 were the near-simultaneous grenade attacks in March against Jordanian airline offices in Athens, Rome, and Nicosia, a rocket attack in April against a Jordanian airliner in Athens, and the assassination in July of a Jordanian diplomat in Ankara. In mid-1985 Amman made overtures to Damascus in hopes of improving their strained relations. These led to discussions between President Assad and King Hussein in Damascus in December. Despite the lack of major bilateral agreements, the near-term threat that Syrian-backed groups posed to Jordanian security has been reduced significantly since the dialogue began.

Syria

In 1985, 14 incidents of international terrorism occurred in Syria. Another eight attacks were conducted against Syrian personnel or property abroad. In late May 1985, in Rabat, Morocco, a vehicle registered to the Syrian Embassy—and parked in front of the Syrian Ambassador's residence—was destroyed by an explosion. Though, for the most part, claims of responsibility are not made in connection with anti-Syrian terrorism, pro-Arafat Palestinians are prime suspects in anti-Syrian activity outside of Syria. Within Syria, likely perpetrators include pro-Arafat Palestinians, pro-Iraqi dissidents, Lebanese Christians, the Muslim Brotherhood, and other disaffected elements.

Regional Patterns: Western Europe

In Western Europe the number of international terrorist incidents in 1985 declined somewhat from that of the previous year—from 232 to 218. Of these, nearly 150 were conducted by West European terrorist groups. Terrorism by European groups remained a major concern because of the so-called Euroterrorist campaign. Three terrorist groups—West Germany's RAF, France's AD, and Belgium's Communist Combatant Cells (CCC)—began a series of anti-NATO attacks in their respective countries in late 1984 causing speculation that the groups had joined forces and were coordinating their attacks. A joint communique issued by the RAF and AD in January 1985 calling for a "common anti-imperialist front" in Western Europe fueled this concern as did their joint claims of responsibility in August for a terrorist attack in West Germany. In Brussels, the CCC cited solidarity with RAF hunger strikers in January as the reason for its car-bombing of the NATO Support Facility there.

Several West European security services made significant advances against local terrorist groups. In Belgium, for example, authorities arrested several leading members of the CCC, and discovered numerous safehouses. Declining activity by some established groups—such as the Spanish First of October Anti-Fascist Resistance (GRAPO) and the Italian Red Brigades (BR)—was offset somewhat by the appearance of new ones, such as the Revolutionary Front for Proletarian Action (FRAP) in Belgium.

West Germany

In January, imprisoned RAF terrorists continued a hunger strike begun in December 1984 while the RAF periphery of part-time terrorists carried out numerous attacks against US and NATO-related installations. The RAF hardcore may have participated in the January assassination by AD in Paris of General Rene Audran—a French Defense Ministry official. The first confirmed attack in 1985 by the RAF hardcore was the assassination of West German industrialist Ernst Zimmermann in Munich on 1 February.

There were indications that the RAF was changing tactics, showing more inclination to engage in random violence than previously when its targets were carefully chosen for their high symbolic value. This was particularly evident in August when the RAF murdered a low-ranking US serviceman, claiming it did so to obtain his identification card. The group used the card the next day to gain access to Rhein-Main airbase where it detonated a car bomb that killed two Americans and wounded many others. The RAF and AD claimed responsibility jointly; the actual extent, if any, of AD involvement is still under investigation.

France

The indigenous anarchist group AD was responsible for 17 attacks in 1985. Nearly all of these were directed at domestic political targets, including the attempted assassination of Gen. Henri Blandin in June.

As in previous years, France was the stage for anti-Basque terrorism in 1985. The violent Antiterrorist Liberation Group (GAL) carried out 11 attacks in France against exiles belonging to the Spanish separatist ETA, killing 10 persons and wounding eight others. ETA retaliated by attacking French targets in Spain, thus contributing to a cycle of violence.

Numerous terrorist attacks against French interests were carried out by separatist groups attempting to win independence from France. In particular, the National Front for the Liberation of Corsica (FLNC) accounted for 96 of the 142 indigenous incidents in France in 1985. The FLNC typically set off multiple property bombs simultaneously during the night, causing few, if any, casualties. The total number of FLNC attacks declined for the fourth consecutive year, partly because of a self-imposed moratorium initiated in July. Other separatist movements such as Iparretarak, the French counterpart to Spain's Basque separatist organization, were responsible for numerous incidents, most of which were property bombings.

Belgium

The CCC continued to target US and NATO facilities in 1985, although by the end of the year domestic commercial and political installations had become increasingly favored targets. In January, two US military personnel barely escaped serious injury when the CCC detonated a car bomb outside the NATO Support Facility in Brussels. Previous CCC attacks had been limited to property damage, but, in a communique following this bombing, the group claimed that US military personnel were appropriate terrorist targets. In May the CCC caused its first fatalities when two firemen were killed trying to defuse a car bomb set by the group. The CCC received so much negative publicity following the deaths of the firemen that it later claimed that the police were actually responsible because they had not arrived at the scene quickly enough. To emphasize the point, the CCC bombed the gendarmarie administrative offices in Brussels a few days later. In December 1985 Belgian police arrested several leading CCC members and subsequently discovered CCC safehouses.

In April a previously unknown group—FRAP—surfaced. It claimed responsibility for several attacks, including the bombing in April of a building housing the North Atlantic Assembly. By the end of the summer, Belgian police had located a FRAP safehouse and later in the year discovered others.

Spain

The Military Wing of the Basque separatist organization ETA (ETA-M) remained the most serious terrorist problem in 1985, despite counterterrorist successes by Spanish and French police and continued murders of suspected ETA members by the rightwing GAL. ETA-M conducted a series of bombings against tourist targets during the spring and summer but caused only two injuries and limited property damage. The group also carried out an offensive against Spanish police and military officials that left 29 dead and several dozen wounded. Although all of ETA-M's attacks in 1985 were directed at Spanish targets, an American passer-by was killed in an attack on the Civil Guard in September. There was a lull in ETA-M attacks between mid-September and mid-November, while the group's leadership apparently discussed with Madrid its demands for unification of the Basque regions and amnesty for Basque prisoners and exiles.

Spain's other major indigenous terrorist organization, GRAPO, suffered a major setback in January when Spanish police arrested 18 of its leading members and seized large quantities of arms and ammunition. Although GRAPO was relatively inactive throughout the year, in April it claimed credit for the bombing of the El Descanso restaurant near Torrejon Airbase that killed 18 Spaniards and wounded 82 others, including 15 Americans. The bombing also was claimed by several other terrorist groups, including ETA, Islamic Jihad, and the Armed Organization of the Jewish People. Some officials believed the bombing was the work of Middle Eastern terrorists, while others attributed it to GRAPO.

Iraultza, the small, violent, anti-US wing of the Basque Communist Party, claimed responsibility for at least four bombings against US businesses in 1985. Its attacks continued to be characterized by low-yield explosives placed near buildings.

Portugal

The leftist Portuguese group Popular Forces of 25 April (FP-25) continued to attack US and NATO-related interests, which the group had begun targeting in late 1984. A mortar attack against NATO warships in January was followed by the bombing of 18 automobiles belonging to West German servicemen at Beja the following month. Although FP-25 claimed that these attacks were part of the West European "campaign" against NATO, they probably were "copycat" attacks patterned on RAF and AD activities and aimed at attaining publicity for FP-25.

FP-25 terrorist acts during the remainder of the year were directed mainly at indigenous targets and included two assassinations. In July a key witness in the scheduled trial of FP-25 members arrested in 1984 was killed. Two months later, 10 alleged group members escaped from prison and, in so doing, forced a delay in the trial of 50 other FP-25 defendants. The trial, which finally began in October, continued into 1986.

Italy

Following at least 13 months of inactivity, the BR returned to action in March with its only attack of 1985—the murder in Rome of Enzo Tarantelli, a prominent labor economist. Despite expectations of some security officials that the BR would join the other major West European terrorist groups in attacking NATO, it did not participate. The organization suffered setbacks during the year as Italian police arrested numerous members, including Barbara Balzarani, the most wanted group leader. In addition to the arrests, group activity was limited by a second year of factional struggle.

Greece

The level of terrorist activity in Greece remained high as both indigenous and Middle East-origin terrorism continued to cause concern. One-third of the international incidents that occurred there last year were directed against US targets, many in the form of arson and bombing attacks against vehicles belonging to US military personnel in Athens. The Revolutionary People's Struggle and the virulently anti-US 17 November Revolutionary Organization continued to pose high threats to US personnel in Greece. In late February, members of 17 November murdered a Greek publisher whom it identified as pro-American. Earlier that month, a bomb exploded at a bar in the Athens suburb of Glyfada, which was frequented by US servicemen. Responsibility for the attack has not been established, but American customers (59 of whom were wounded in the attack) may have been the intended victims. Greece continued to provide easy access and transit for Middle Eastern terrorists, as evidenced by the TWA hijacking in June in which Flight 847 from Athens to Rome was diverted to Beirut.

Northern Ireland

The Provisional Irish Republican Army (PIRA) detonated its first bomb in downtown Belfast in two years and exploded another bomb outside a crowded shopping center in Londonderry—both in October 1985. Throughout the year, the PIRA continued to attack businessmen and laborers who performed contract work for police stations of the Royal Ulster Constabulary. The November agreement between the United Kingdom and the Irish Republic—giving the latter a greater voice in the affairs of Northern Ireland—had no apparent impact on the level of PIRA violence. Protestant extremists, however, vented their dissatisfaction by staging demonstrations that, at least in 1985, were nonviolent.

Luxembourg

Unknown persons carried out 13 bombings against domestic targets in 1985. All of the attacks were directed against property, rather than people.

Regional Patterns: Latin America

In 1985, 119 international terrorist incidents occurred in Latin America, a 45-percent increase over the previous year and the second highest total for the region since the beginning of the decade. As a venue for international incidents, however, Latin America continued to rank third, trailing the Middle East and Western Europe. Terrorism against US targets comprised the largest portion of international terrorist activity in Latin America last year.

International terrorism represents only a small percentage of the politically inspired violence in Latin America. Most terrorism is related to local insurgencies. In El Salvador, Colombia, and Peru, leftwing, rural-based insurgencies used terrorist tactics, as did several leftwing urban groups both in those countries and in Chile and Ecuador. Government-sponsored violence in Chile continued unabated, although rightwing terrorism in El Salvador declined.

El Salvador

In 1985 elements of the leftist Farabundo Marti National Liberation Front began to increase their urban operations and upgrade their metropolitan front groups in an apparent change in tactics wrought by military setbacks in the field. In late June the killing of 13 persons, including four off-duty US Marines and two US businessmen, in a San Salvador cafe was the most ominous sign of this return to the cities. The Mardoqueo Cruz Urban Commandos, the urban terrorist element affiliated with the PRTC, took credit for the murders. In a message delivered to a foreign news agency, the group claimed that the attack was part of an operation that it called Yankee Aggressor, Another Vietnam Awaits You. The message hinted at further strikes against US military and diplomatic personnel. These killings were the first to involve official US personnel since May 1983, when Lt. Comdr. Albert Schaufelberger, deputy chief of the US military group, was shot to death in his car by radical members of the Popular Forces of Liberation insurgent group.

In mid-September, Inez Duarte Duran, the daughter of President Duarte, was kidnaped by leftist guerrillas of the "Pedro Pablo Castillo Command." She was held for nearly two months before being released in a prisoner swap involving approximately two dozen captured guerrillas.

Many Salvadoran officials believed that the Duarte kidnaping signaled the return of the guerrillas to a campaign of urban terrorism, but few significant terrorist incidents occurred during the remainder of the year. Many of the urban terrorist groups experienced heavy losses late in the year as a result of the increased effectiveness of the local security services.

Colombia

As in the past, most of the political violence that erupted in Colombia in 1985 was indigenous, generally involving skirmishes between insurgent groups and the military or guerrilla attacks on civilians and property. Even so, international terrorism in Colombia increased by approximately 60 percent—to 30 incidents—over 1984. The United States was most often the target of this increased international terrorist activity, with much of the violence consisting of low-level bombings against US businesses and binational centers. Nevertheless, there were several instances in which US business personnel were taken captive. In mid-August the M-19 claimed responsibility for the kidnaping in Bogota of an American oil company executive. The captive, an employee of a Tenneco subsidiary, was released in late December. In early December approximately 60 guerrillas of the People's Liberation Army attacked a Bechtel Corporation construction site in northern Colombia and kidnaped two US engineers. The captors demanded $6 million for their release. One of the Americans died in captivity in early 1986; the other was released shortly thereafter.

Two of the three major Colombian insurgent organizations that had signed a truce with the Betancur government in 1984 repudiated it in 1985. Only the Revolutionary

Armed Forces of Colombia (FARC), the largest of these groups, continued to adhere to the truce; it also entered the legitimate political arena. The Ricardo Franco Front, a splinter group of the FARC, staged a number of terrorist attacks during the year, but infighting sharply curtailed the level of its terrorist activity. An internal massacre in late 1985 so depleted the ranks of the organization as to all but eliminate it as a significant threat.

One of the most dramatic terrorist attacks ever recorded in Colombia occurred in Bogota in early November when a group of well-armed M-19 members seized the Palace of Justice and held Supreme Court judges and other persons hostage for nearly 30 hours. The incident ended when units of the Colombian military and security forces stormed the building and killed all the guerrillas. Although some dozen justices and dozens of employees and visitors were killed in the storming and President Betancur was criticized by some opposition leaders for using force, the public largely supported the action. The outcome demoralized the M-19 and restricted its capability to operate in Bogota. The group subsequently shifted its operations to rural southwestern Colombia, where it continued to attack villages and engage military forces while it probably seeks to rebuild its urban infrastructure.

In late 1985, the M-19, together with elements of the Ecuadoran leftist group Alfaro Vive, Carajo! (AVC), and possibly other South American terrorist organizations, formed a regional insurgent group known as the America Battalion. The M-19 has long sought to unify several insurgent groups in the region into a front to undermine what it calls imperialist influences. However, the battalion restricted its activities in 1985 to guerrilla confrontations with the Colombian military.

Chile

More than 850 bombings occurred in Chile in 1985, the largest number of terrorist incidents recorded anywhere. The Manuel Rodriguez Patriotic Front carried out most of these attacks, which were directed against Chilean targets—mainly public utilities, police, and other security facilities. International terrorist incidents there increased by approximately 60 percent over 1984. Although the number of attacks against US installations and businesses rose in 1985, anti-US terrorism—consisting principally of noncasualty-producing, low-level attacks directed against US commercial establishments and financial institutions—continued to account for a small percentage of such violence in Chile.

Peru

The Sendero Luminoso (SL), a brutal Maoist insurgent group composed mainly of Andean Indians, began its "armed struggle" in 1980 and, since then, has established a stronghold in the highlands of south-central Peru. Throughout 1985, elements of the group increased the number and intensity of terrorist attacks in the cities, especially in Lima, where SL members conducted dozens of bombings and carried out an array of sabotage activities. SL guerrillas have been implicated in the slaughter of uncooperative peasants and murders of village officials who collaborated with the government.

In 1985 the leftist terrorist group Tupac Amaru Revolutionary Movement (MRTA) continued to threaten Peruvian interests. The MRTA surfaced as an urban guerrilla group in 1984, when it claimed responsibility for several terrorist incidents in Lima. Most of the group's activities last year, however, were propaganda oriented. A number of them involved the seizure of radio stations or low-level harrassment bombings intended to underscore MRTA's anti-US and anti-imperialist ideology. In mid-1985, however, MRTA carried out its first car-bombing—against a US bank. The group suspended armed attacks against the government for three months following the inauguration in late July of President Alan Garcia; but, by early November, MRTA had resumed its activities, carrying out low-level attacks against the US and Colombian Embassies, as well as various government and business offices.

Ecuador

The leftist subversive group AVC, which espouses many of the antioligarchic, anti-US, and anti-imperialist views held by radical leftist groups in several Latin American countries, became increasingly active in 1985. In March approximately 25 AVC members broke into a police arsenal and stole several hundred firearms. In early August, the group kidnaped a wealthy local businessman and held him for about a month before security forces stormed the apartment in which he was held. The raid resulted in the deaths of the hostage and several terrorists.

Regional Patterns: Asia

In 1985 Asia accounted for 5 percent of the international terrorist activity worldwide. The number of international terrorist attacks in the region rose from 27 in 1984 to 41 in 1985, but overall terrorism in Asia remained predominantly domestic in nature, with Sikh violence a notable exception. Several groups identified in late 1984 as potentially explosive—including Sri Lanka's Tamils, Pakistan's Al-Zulfikar, and Japan's Chukaku-ha—were, for the most part, quiescent during 1985. Isolated acts of terrorism occurred last year in such previously violence-free areas as Nepal and Singapore, but terrorist violence in places such as the Philippines, Indonesia, and New Caledonia did not rise to expected levels.

Sikh Extremists

In 1985 Sikh extremists conducted their first international terrorist attacks. They are believed responsible for last year's most spectacular act of international terrorism—the June bombing over the North Atlantic of an Air India jetliner with 329 people aboard. The Sikh Student Federation, 10th Regiment—a militant Sikh group responsible for many acts of terrorism and communal violence within India since 1981—claimed responsibility. At about the same time, another bomb exploded in the baggage handling area of Tokyo's Narita Airport, killing two Japanese workers. The bomb probably was intended to go off aboard an Air India jet bound for India. Both Air India incidents are believed to be the work of Canada-based Sikh extremists.

Sikh radicals also caused other problems in 1985. In early April, US authorities arrested five Sikhs on charges of conspiring to assassinate Prime Minister Rajiv Gandhi during his June visit to the United States. The group also planned to attack another Indian official while he underwent medical treatment in New Orleans in May. In the United Kingdom, Sikh extremists wishing to control temple management committees have attacked several Sikh moderates there since last November.

Sikh political violence within India in 1985 returned to the high level of early 1984, reaching its greatest intensity in mid-May when Sikh terrorists carried out a series of bombings that left more than 85 persons dead and more than 150 wounded in New Delhi and other cities in northern India. These attacks occurred just before the scheduled trial of three Sikhs accused of murdering former Prime Minister Indira Gandhi in October 1984. Sikh terrorism continued throughout the summer as radicals assassinated moderate Sikh leader Harchand Singh Longowal and other important Sikh and Hindu political figures.

Sri Lanka

In contrast with 1984, Tamil insurgents did not attack foreigners in 1985. Most of the five major Tamil groups restricted their attacks to police and military forces. A notable exception was the machinegun massacre of some 150 persons at the Buddhist shrine of Anuradhapura in mid-May—one of the bloodiest terrorist attacks on record. Among the victims were women, children, and Buddhist monks and nuns. No group claimed responsibility for the slaughter—which was condemned by nearly all of the Sri Lankan guerrilla groups—but the Liberation Tigers of Tamil Eelam, the most lethal of the separatist groups, was probably responsible. In the wake of the massacre, the government arranged a cease-fire to prevent other such acts from occurring.

Japan

The most dangerous group, Chukaku-ha (Nucleus Faction), mounted more domestic terrorist attacks in 1985 than in most previous years, but nearly all of them were small scale and directed against property—principally the long-favored target, Narita Airport, and other transportation facilities. In November, Chukaku-ha demonstrated its ability to conduct guerrilla-type operations with a massive, well-executed assault on the National Railway—cutting railroad communications cables, firebombing a railway station, and burning a transformer facility—that paralyzed rail traffic throughout Japan. The only attack against foreigners was an early morning rocket attack on the US Consulate General in Kobe on 1 January, when the building was unoccupied. Although that attack caused neither damage nor casualties, at least one of the three rocket warheads contained antipersonnel shrapnel. Overall, the number of international terrorist incidents in Japan declined in 1985, compared with 1984.

In 1985 the best-known Asian terrorist group, the Japanese Red Army, surfaced to receive its released member, Kozo Okamoto, who had been held by the Israelis since the Lod Airport massacre in 1972. The group—apparently inactive since 1977—continues to reside in the Bekaa Valley in southern Lebanon along with its longtime patron, the Popular Front for the Liberation of Palestine.

The Philippines

The two major Filipino insurgent groups—the NPA and the Moro National Liberation Front (MNLF)—continued their attacks against the government infrastructure and the civilian population in 1985, but, as in previous years, acts of international terrorism were rare.

The NPA used terrorist tactics in provincial capitals but did not move its violence into Manila. The NPA assassinated governors and mayors and frequently murdered ordinary citizens. Although the group has a policy of not attacking Americans, the organization was responsible for the death in May of an American of Philippine descent. The NPA may have been unaware of his citizenship, or it was irrelevant; guerrillas shot him as they had other farmers who refused to pay protection money.

The MNLF conducted only one act of international terrorism in 1985, when it kidnaped a Japanese photographer in January; he was released in April 1986. The group had been holding an American and a West German since November 1984 but released them in December 1985. The MNLF has continued to conduct guerrilla warfare on the island of Mindanao and—though it seizes foreign hostages from time to time—it remains an insurgent group that makes only occasional forays into domestic and international terrorism.

Pakistan

The Pakistani group Al-Zulfikar has been inactive since its last unsuccessful international terrorist attack two years ago. Al-Zulfikar apparently has never recovered from its attempt in July 1984 to seize foreign hostages in Vienna; during that incident nine operatives were taken into Austrian custody. In July 1985 it received yet another severe blow when one of its key leaders, Shahnawaz Bhutto, died in France. The current inability of Al-Zulfikar to recruit and operate at home appears to stem from the successes of Pakistani security forces, the lifting of martial law in late 1985, and the presence in India of a new government disinclined to support the group's activities against the Pakistani regime.

New Caledonia

Terrorist bombings and other political violence that began in New Caledonia in late 1984 persisted during 1985. Both anti-independence French settlers and members of the proindependence Kanak National Socialist Liberation Front are responsible for these actions. Although there have been no fatalities attributable to acts of terrorism, mob violence has claimed several lives, and Noumea's main courthouse was damaged by a bomb.

New Venues for Terrorism

Significant terrorist incidents occurred in 1985 in two Asian countries that were previously free of the terrorism problem. These attacks apparently were isolated and not necessarily indicative of new trends toward violence. In mid-March, a bomb exploded in front of a building housing the Israeli and Canadian Embassies in Singapore—the first terrorist incident there in this decade. In late June, a series of bombings in Kathmandu and other nearby towns in Nepal killed several persons and wounded a dozen others. The attacks apparently were committed by an antimonarchist group based in India. Although Nepalese authorities evidently have made no arrests, no other terrorist incidents occurred in the country in 1985.

Other Areas

Some countries that appeared to have developing terrorist problems in 1984 did not experience significant problems in 1985. In Indonesia, for example, conservative Islamic groups that were upset over the government's secular policies conducted a series of bombings and arson attacks in late 1984 and early 1985. Indonesian authorities made a number of arrests in 1985—followed up with prosecution and stiff sentences. The level of significant incidents in the country for the remainder of the year fell off sharply.

Regional Patterns: Sub-Saharan Africa

In 1985, as in previous years, international terrorism was not a serious problem in most of Sub-Saharan Africa. The total number of international terrorist incidents there fell slightly in 1985—down to 41 from the 1984 total of 45—largely because of a decline in the number of Libyan-sponsored attacks in Central Africa. In contrast to the downward trend that marked the region as a whole, Mozambique experienced a sharp increase in the number of international terrorist incidents. Indigenous Mozambican terrorism also occurred with greater frequency and increased lethality. Despite the announced intentions of some Sub-Saharan African insurgent groups to begin attacking Westerners, US personnel and facilities in the region were seldom directly targeted—more often they were incidental targets. US interests were attacked three times in 1985, as compared with nine the previous year.

Mozambique

In 1985 Mozambique was the venue for 16 international terrorist attacks—double the number in 1984. This increase was mostly the result of the high level of activity by the Mozambique National Resistance (RENAMO) insurgency, which, in its 10-year history, has exacted a casualty toll that numbers in the thousands. In April, RENAMO staged two ambushes of civilian convoys, resulting in the deaths of more than 200 civilians. RENAMO also killed 33 persons in an August attack on a funeral cortege. In some incidents, foreign aid workers and employees of foreign companies have been deliberately targeted. In April, for example, a UNICEF relief site was attacked, and the only official present was killed.

Ambushes such as the brutal incidents in April continued to be a favored tactic of the group, but kidnapings—of Mozambicans as well as foreigners—occurred with greater frequency than in past years. RENAMO evidently abducted thousands of Mozambican rural villagers in 1985, only some of whom were released by year's end. Among the foreign victims were Portuguese and Italian nuns, priests, tourists, and technicians. In June, RENAMO announced that it would negotiate only with Lisbon the release of some Portuguese prisoners. This policy probably was intended to gain recognition for the insurgency and to exert pressure on the Portuguese Government to assist in this effort. The new strategy apparently won the release in September of 27 foreign hostages, although many other foreign kidnap victims—including two Soviet scientists seized in 1983—are presumed dead.

South African Government support for RENAMO was supposed to have ceased following the Nkomati Accord—an agreement signed by Presidents Botha and Machel in early 1984. Public revelations in 1985 of continued South African contact with RENAMO, however, confirmed Maputo's suspicions and fueled charges of continuing South African military and other assistance to the insurgent movement.

South Africa

Attacks in South Africa by the outlawed ANC increased by as much as 200 percent in 1985. Much of the activity occurred late in the year, in the wake of the Pretoria-imposed state of emergency. The ANC began to employ bombs more indiscriminately in 1985—displaying a growing shift toward attacks on civilians. Many attacks—such as the planting of landmines in farm areas—apparently were designed to intensify unrest and shake white confidence. A narrowly averted bombing attempt of the Johannesburg Army Medical Center in May would have resulted in numerous casualties had the explosive detonated, as scheduled, during working hours.

A two-month lull in ANC bombings followed President Botha's imposition of a state of emergency in July, but in September the ANC struck back. An ANC radiobroadcast urged nonwhites for the first time to shift the violence to white areas. Two days later, nonwhites attacked houses in white residential areas of Cape Province. Several more attacks occurred later that month and during the next month. A dramatic daytime bombing in a Durban shopping center in December 1985 killed five whites, including children. Six whites were killed in a series of landmine attacks on white farms in rural Transvaal Province near the border of Zimbabwe and Botswana.

Namibia

The Namibian insurgent group South-West Africa People's Organization (SWAPO) displayed disorganization and low morale in 1985, largely because of its military impotence, tribal squabbles, and stalled international negotiations. In 1985 the SWAPO "rainy season offensive" was even less successful than those of previous years. Small bombings of such civilian targets as schools, shops, telephone lines, and service stations were standard fare, while military camps and nearby residential areas were hit by mortar attacks.

Angola

In 1985 the National Union for the Total Independence of Angola (UNITA) continued to attack Angolan economic and military facilities. Its level of international terrorist activity declined over that of the previous year—from 13 to eight incidents—and, as in the past, involved mostly foreign technicians and aid workers. Eastern Bloc representatives were frequently targeted in an attempt to pressure those governments to reduce aid to Luanda. UNITA claimed that a March attack on a hotel and a Soviet housing area resulted in the deaths of 75 Bulgarians, Cubans, and Angolans. In November a Soviet residence in Huambo was bombed, resulting in many casualties.

Westerners also have fallen victim to UNITA attacks. In May two priests were killed on their way to mass; UNITA claimed responsibility and indicated that they were targeted because they traveled with a military convoy. In another case, a Red Cross worker was killed and his plane damaged by a mine when he landed at an airport that serviced Red Cross aircraft exclusively. The crowd that gathered on the runway suffered injuries from the explosion of a second mine. Brazilian and Angolan missionaries were killed and others kidnaped in yet another attack in December.

Chad

International terrorist activity occurred infrequently in Chad in 1985. In February and November, however, a total of five US employees of a US oil company were kidnaped. In both cases, Chadian security forces recovered the hostages without incident. Southern Chadian rebels were believed to be behind both kidnapings and, by targeting US citizens, were trying to embarrass Chadian President Habre.

Patterns of Global Terrorism: 1986

The Year in Review

The level of international terrorist activity remained high in 1986, despite a slight decline in the total number of incidents.[1] This halts, at least temporarily, the dramatic upward trend in the number of incidents experienced in the previous two years. In the first part of 1986, terrorism continued to rise, but increased counter-terrorist cooperation among Western nations undoubtedly played an important role in checking the escalation of terrorism for the rest of the year. US military action against Libya in April and subsequent European diplomatic and security actions against Libya and Syria for their involvement in some of the year's major attacks helped to curb activities by terrorists supported by those countries after midyear. Nevertheless, the overall high level of activity combined with the continuing increase in attacks aimed at innocent bystanders and intended to cause mass casualties keep international terrorism as a priority item for concern.

In 1986, we recorded some 774 international terrorist incidents, a very slight decrease from the record level of 782 incidents in 1985. More than a quarter of these incidents resulted in casualties. Fewer persons were killed in international terrorist incidents in 1986 than in 1985 (576 and 825 persons, respectively), and more were wounded—1,708 versus 1,217—yielding a slightly greater total number of casualties in 1986. The decline in number of deaths is deceptive without looking behind the figures. The difference between 1985 and 1986 represents one incident—329 deaths from the Air India bombing. Moreover, 1986 could have included as many as 800 more deaths if several attempted aircraft bombings had succeeded.

Although there were fewer international attacks in 1986, a greater number were conducted against US targets—204 versus 170 in 1985—increasing the share to 26 percent in 1986 versus 22 percent in 1985. Total US casualties fell almost 43 percent, however, and US deaths alone fell 68 percent, returning to the levels of earlier in the decade. The totals would have been much greater, however, if the bombing of TWA Flight 840 had caused the plane to crash and if two attempted bombings of El Al aircraft had succeeded.

About 55 percent of the 1986 incidents involving US targets occurred in Latin America, an increase over the previous year's 45 percent. Although only about a quarter of anti-US attacks took place in Western Europe (a decline from one-third in 1985), the majority of US casualties last year stemmed from attacks there, most as a result of attacks by Middle Eastern rather than European terrorists. Slightly more anti-US attacks were registered in the Middle East (21 versus 17) last year, but the number of such attacks in Lebanon dropped in terms of both absolute numbers (10) and as a percentage (50 percent) of anti-US attacks in the Middle East—versus 13 and nearly 80 percent, respectively, in 1985.

A region-by-region comparison of the 1986 data with

---

1 Our statistics cover only international terrorist incidents [as defined in the Introduction]. Our information data base on domestic terrorism is sizable but is not comprehensive enough to permit us to provide statistical data with the same degree of confidence as we do on international terrorism.

those of 1985 reveals no worldwide pattern, but rather the interplay of local conditions. In 1986 more international terrorist incidents—360—were recorded in the Middle East than in any other part of the world, virtually unchanged from the 1985 figure of 357. If the number of attacks conducted by Middle Eastern terrorists elsewhere in the world is included, Middle Eastern terrorism accounted for 404, or about 52 percent of all international incidents, down slightly from 441 and 56 percent in 1985. Latin America, with 159 attacks and the bulk of the anti-American incidents, was the second most frequent venue for international terrorist attacks in 1986, slightly more than Western Europe, where the number of incidents continued to drop, down to 156 attacks in 1986.

In 1986 attacks by Middle Eastern terrorists world-wide killed more than 450 persons—nearly double the number in 1985—and injured nearly 1,120 others. This continues the pattern of the previous year. Attacks by West European and other terrorists tend to be designed to avoid casualties, whereas most of those by Middle Eastern terrorists are intended to cause maximum casualties.

The citizens and property of 78 countries were the victims or targets of international terrorist attacks in 1986, slightly fewer than the 84 recorded the previous year. International incidents also took place in fewer countries in 1986—65 as opposed to 72. More than half of all international attacks continue to target businessmen, tourists, and other unprotected "soft" targets. The number of attacks against diplomatic, military, and other official targets remained virtually unchanged.

The number of attacks by type varied by comparison with 1985. Arson attacks climbed slightly from 102 to 117, but kidnapings declined from 87 to 52. Bombings continued to account for more than half of all international attacks with 438 incidents in 1986, as compared with 399 in 1985.

Certain governments continued to facilitate international terrorist activity, although the number of attacks in which such support could be identified declined. Libya, Syria, or Iran was responsible for most state-sponsored terrorist attacks and the decline probably reflects their efforts to distance themselves from terrorist groups and to disguise their involvement. In 1986, Libyan and Syrian terrorist activities were publicly exposed in two major incidents in Western Europe that led to a combination of military, political, and economic sanctions against them by the United States, Canada, and West European governments.

The level of international terrorist attacks of Middle Eastern origin declined only slightly in 1986. The number of attacks occurring in the Middle East itself remained largely unchanged from 1985, but "spillover" attacks into Western Europe declined nearly 50 percent—from 74 in 1985 to 39. Several factors probably contributed: the breakdown of the Hussein-Arafat accord resulted in fewer attacks by radical Palestinians on Jordanian and PLO targets; the record levels of Middle Eastern attacks in Western Europe in 1985 led to enhanced local security measures; and the most prominent state sponsors—Syria and Libya—curtailed their levels of activity after disclosure of their involvement in two terrorist operations in April. The EC nations took a number of political and economic actions against Libya—including expelling more than 100 Libyan so-called diplomats—following the US bombing of Libya in April.

International terrorism in Israel and the occupied territories declined slightly from the record level of 1985 but still formed the majority of all international attacks recorded in the Middle East.[2] Of the 360 international incidents that occurred in the Middle East, 195 took place in Israel, the West Bank, and the Gaza Strip, down 11 percent from the previous year. Most of these were low-level attacks—isolated shootings or stabbings and many fire bombings—but some incidents, such as the bombing of a crowd of soldiers and civilians at Jerusalem's Western Wall in October, were more serious.

There was a 28-percent decrease in the overall level of international terrorist incidents in Western Europe in 1986, primarily a result of the nearly 50-percent drop in incidents of Middle Eastern origin. International attacks by West European terrorists also declined, but such groups continued to pose a threat. During the year, the West German Red Army Faction (RAF) began a campaign against nuclear-related targets. The "nationalist" wing of the French Action Directe (AD) began for the first time to engage in attacks producing deliberate fatalities, but anti-French attacks by the Basque group Fatherland and Liberty (ETA) accounted for much of the dramatic rise in incidents involving French interests. The 1985 phenomenon of "Euroterrorism"—much publicized cooperation between the RAF, AD, and other European terrorist groups—was less in evidence in those groups' activities in 1986 but remained a cause for concern among West European security forces.

International terrorism in Latin America showed another dramatic upsurge in 1986, increasing by one-third, with more than half of the 159 total incidents against US targets. As in previous years, international incidents constituted only a small part of all the political violence in the hemisphere. About 70 percent of the attacks—113 total—were against American targets, a marked increase over previous years. Most such attacks tended to be bombings of unoccupied offices or other facilities of US companies. The most prominent increases in international attacks last year occurred in Peru (59 in 1986 versus 16 in 1985) and in Colombia (50 versus 30). Chile, the leading regional venue for international attacks in 1985, experienced 25 percent fewer incidents in 1986.

Terrorist incidents in Asia and Sub-Saharan Africa, taken together, amounted to only 13 percent of all international attacks in 1986. For the second straight year, attacks in Asia rose while those recorded in Africa declined. Most terrorist

---

2 We include virtually all acts of political violence in the West Bank and Gaza Strip as international terrorism because of the special status of those territories. Of the incidents that took place in Israel and the occupied territories, 123—almost 63 percent—occurred in the West Bank.

violence in Asia continued to be the work of Tamil and Sikh separatists and Communist insurgents, but the year was also marked by increased terrorist violence in Pakistan, including a number of bombings thought to be the work of Afghan state agents. Twenty international attacks occurred in Africa, down from 41 the previous year.

Terrorist Spillover From the Middle East

After substantial increases in the previous two years, the number of terrorist attacks committed in Western Europe by Middle Eastern groups or states declined in 1986. Middle East-related attacks in Europe averaged 35 per year from 1980 to 1983, climbed to 61 in 1984, and reached 74 in 1985. In 1986 the number returned to the earlier level, declining almost 50 percent to 39. Most of the decline occurred in Mediterranean littoral states: Greece saw five Middle East-related terrorist incidents, as opposed to 14 the year before; Italy experienced only two after 11 the previous year; and only one such attack occurred in Cyprus in 1986 after 12 in 1985. France, by contrast, suffered a significant increase—from six to 16—accounting for 40 percent of all such attacks, nearly twice the percentage previously recorded for any West European country.

The 1986 terrorist attacks in Europe with a Middle Eastern connection that captured the most attention were those involving Libya and Syria. Libyan involvement in early 1986 was a continuation of Libya's actions in late 1985 when Tripoli provided Tunisian passports to the Abu Nidal organization terrorists responsible for the 27 December 1985 attack on the El Al counter at Vienna airport. In 1986, Libya is known or suspected to have been behind five incidents aimed at US or British targets in Europe: the April bombing of a West Berlin discotheque; the April attempted grenade attack on a US officers' club in Ankara, Turkey; an April bombing in London that damaged offices of British Airways and American Express; a May attempted bombing of the Bank of America office in Madrid; and the August attack by three teams of gunmen against the British base at Akrotiri, Cyprus.

Also included among the Middle Eastern spillover incidents in Europe were attacks by Libyan operatives against Qadhafi's Libyan opponents—a radio station owner in Rome and a businessman in a Paris suburb.

Libya was implicated in the most violent Middle East-related event to occur in Asia in 1986—the 5 September attempted hijacking of Pan Am Flight 73 in Karachi that left 21 persons dead, two of them Americans.

Syria's support of Middle Eastern terrorist groups that operate in Europe, including radical Palestinian factions, has long been a contributor to the Middle Eastern spillover problem there. In 1986, Syrian personnel were implicated directly in three events in Western Europe—the April attempt to bomb an El Al jetliner in London; the March bombing of the German-Arab Friendship Union building in West Berlin; and the June attempt against El Al in Madrid. Like Libya, Syria curtailed its operations in Europe during the second half of 1986, contributing to the decline in Middle Eastern terrorism there.

Iran traditionally has been circumspect in sponsoring terrorist attacks in Western Europe, and its surrogates have not been implicated in the kind of spectacular, mass casualty attacks in Europe associated with Arab and Palestinian terrorism. French police believe, however, that Hizballah-linked terrorists were involved in a series of bombing attacks in Paris in September 1986. The Khomeini regime continued its attacks against Iranian dissidents in 1986, making an abortive attempt to assassinate former Admiral Madani in Paris in January, bombing the Paris home of exile leader Masud Rajavi in April, and murdering an Iranian dissident former Army colonel in Istanbul in October. No suspects were arrested in any of these attacks.

Palestinian Activity

Palestinian terrorist groups were responsible for fewer terrorist attacks in Western Europe in 1986 than in 1985. The breakdown of the Arafat-Hussein peace initiative virtually ended the round of anti-Jordanian and anti-PLSS terrorism—much of it by the Abu Nidal organization—in Europe and elsewhere that was an important feature of the scene in 1985. Two high-ranking Palestinian officials were assassinated by unknown assailants in Athens in June and October, but the most significant Palestinian attacks in Europe were those noted above that were undertaken with assistance from Libya or Syria. The anti-Arafat Abu Musa group, which is backed by Syria, committed its first attack in Western Europe last year, the previously mentioned attempt to bomb an El Al airliner in Madrid in June.[3]

The Abu Nidal organization (ANO), which conducted more than a dozen attacks in Europe in 1985, was known to be responsible for only one there in 1986. On 6 September, just hours after the resolution of the Karachi Pan Am hijacking attempt, a suicide team attacked an Istanbul synagogue with submachineguns and handgrenades, killing 22 persons and wounding six, before blowing themselves up.

Several factors may have contributed to the decline in ANO attacks:

- The dissolution of the Hussein-Arafat accord removed the motivation for ANO attacks against Jordanian and pro-Arafat Palestinians, the focus of many of the group's attacks since late 1984.
- The pressure on ANO's key state sponsors, Libya and Syria.
- Virtually all ANO members who carried out attacks in Western Europe since mid-1985 were arrested or killed.

---

3 Altogether, eight of the 39 Middle Eastern terrorist attacks in Western Europe in 1986 were directed at airports, aircraft, or airline offices and could have killed more than 800 persons. The actual casualty for those eight attacks was four killed and 18 wounded.

Despite concerns that the June trial in Rome of Palestine Liberation Front (PLF) members charged with the 1985 hijacking of the Achille Lauro would spawn a wave of terrorism, the trial was marked only by two small bombs at Italian facilities in Athens on 19 June. All four defendants were convicted, as was PLF leader Abu Abbas (in absentia), but no terrorist retaliation occurred.

One or more members of the radical Palestinian 15 May Organization, which had been presumed inactive since 1984, are believed to be involved in the bombing of TWA Flight 840 in April. Evidence suggests that on 2 April, May Mansour, a Lebanese Christian woman, smuggled a bomb aboard the plane bound for Rome and Athens. She disembarked at an earlier stop, leaving the device, reminiscent of those placed on airliners in the early 1980s by the 15 May Organization. The bomb exploded over Greece, killing four American citizens—one an infant—who were sucked out of the aircraft through the hole created by the blast. The pilot managed to land the damaged aircraft with no further loss of life, but if the plane had been at a higher altitude when the bomb detonated, it most likely would have crashed, killing everyone aboard.

Other Middle Eastern Terrorism

The only substantial increase registered in Middle Eastern terrorist attacks in Western Europe in 1986 occurred in France. Following on the heels of two department store bombings in Paris in December 1985, Middle Eastern terrorists were responsible for 13 bombings or attempted bombings during 1986 in two separate campaigns, in February-March and in September. The bombers called for the release of three Middle Eastern terrorists—George Abdallah, leader of the Lebanese Armed Revolutionary Faction (LARF), a Marxist Christian group; a Palestinian convicted in the 1981 attempt to kill former Iranian Prime Minister Bakhtier; and a member of the Armenian Secret Army for the Liberation of Armenia (ASALA) convicted in the 1983 bombing of Orly Airport. Almost all of the 1986 attacks were claimed in the name of the "Committee for Solidarity With Arab and Middle Eastern Political Prisoners" (CSPPA), which is believed to be a covername for some combination of LARF members, Palestinians, and Armenians. Some French authorities have recently said that Iran may have been involved in at least some of these bombings through supporters of the Lebanese Hizballah militia arrested in Paris in 1987. France has been a major supplier of aircraft and missiles to Iraq in the Gulf War.

The six September bombings, which virtually paralyzed Paris that month, were intended to pressure the French into releasing Abdallah, then awaiting trial for complicity in attacks on US and Israeli diplomats between 1982 and 1984. The campaign had the opposite effect, and in February 1987, Abdallah received a life sentence.

Target USA

Over one-quarter of the international terrorist incidents in 1986, 204 of 774 or 26 percent, involved US citizens or property; these figures are higher than those of 1985—170 of 782 or 22 percent. In contrast with 1985, US interests were attacked slightly more often in 1986 than Israeli ones, usually the most frequent target. For the first time, more than half the international terrorist incidents involving US citizens or property occurred in Latin America, primarily in Chile, Colombia, and Peru. Only a quarter took place in Western Europe, with West Germany and Spain the favored locations. Businesses continued to be the most frequently attacked US targets, with such attacks increasing by about 50 percent from the previous year. Attacks on US diplomatic targets doubled, but incidents involving military targets and "other" targets, such as tourists, private citizens, and passersby, declined from the 1985 levels.

Casualties

Although the number of anti-US attacks rose in 1986, casualties declined dramatically. Eleven of the 204 anti-US incidents resulted in American casualties and six in fatalities, with totals of 12 persons killed and 100 others wounded. In contrast, in 1985, 21 of the 170 anti-US attacks resulted in American casualties, 10 in fatalities, for a total of 38 US citizens killed and 157 wounded. Half of the American deaths in 1985 were caused by a single terrorist incident: an Air India aircraft exploded and crashed in the North Atlantic in June of that year, killing all 329 persons aboard, including 19 US citizens. The decline in lethality was also because of the decline in Middle Eastern terrorist attacks in Western Europe. Even so, some two-thirds of the US casualties occurred in incidents in Europe, mostly at the hands of Middle Eastern terrorists. In Latin America, which accounted for more anti-US incidents, the most common type of attack is bombings against property, usually at times when few potential victims are present.

The US fatalities occurred in the following six incidents:

- Greece, 2 April. The bombing of TWA Flight 850 on its Rome-to-Athens leg; four US citizens were killed.
- West Berlin, 5 April. The bombing of the La Belle discotheque; two American servicemen were among the three fatalities.
- Lebanon, 17 April. Peter Kilburn, an employee of the American University in Beirut who had been kidnaped in November 1984, was discovered murdered.
- Peru, 25 June. A bomb exploded on a crowded tourist train bound for the Inca tourist site of Machu Picchu. Two Americans, one a little girl, were among the seven foreigners killed.
- Colombia, 11 August. The body of Bechtel employee Edward Sohl was found. He had been kidnaped in December 1985 by the People's Liberation Army (EPL) and may have died in captivity as early as May.

- Pakistan, 5 September. The attempted hijacking of a Pan Am jet in Karachi. Two Americans were among the 21 persons killed.

Hostages

During 1986, six US citizens were kidnaped. Two Americans were kidnaped in southern Philippines, but were soon released. Four more Americans were kidnaped in Beirut. Although two hostages taken there in 1985 were released during 1986, a total of six Americans was being held prisoner in Lebanon when the year ended.

Regional Patterns: The Middle East

For the second consecutive year, the Middle East was the principal venue for international terrorist attacks, accounting for approximately half of all international incidents for 1986. In Lebanon, Westerners continued to be at high risk of kidnaping—18 more were taken during the year and, although eight of them were released, two were known killed and eight were still being held at the end of the year. Warring militias—Palestinians and rival Lebanese Christian and Muslim groups—waged bloody internecine battles; many Middle Eastern terrorist groups participated in this "war of the camps" in Beirut.

Lebanon: The Kidnapings Continue

In Lebanon, the violence between warring militias continued throughout the year. In many cases, neither the perpetrator nor the target of a bombing attack could be conclusively established, as, for example, in the case of a series of bombings in July and August in East and West Beirut in which 76 persons were killed and hundreds wounded.

Westerners were not the primary victims of the violence in Lebanon, but they remained an important target. In the fall, the French contingent of the UN peacekeeping force in South Lebanon suffered several attacks, and the French military attaché was assassinated as he entered the Embassy in East Beirut. Westerners in Beirut were particularly attractive targets for politically motivated kidnapings. Elements of Hizballah—using a variety of cover names—probably were responsible for most of the kidnapings, although in some cases, "freelance" terrorists initially may have taken hostages in order to sell them to the highest bidder. Four members of a French television crew were kidnaped in March; three were eventually released. Another French citizen kidnaped in February was released toward the end of the year.

Two Americans, Father Lawrence Jenco and David Jacobsen, were released in July and November, respectively, but three more—Frank Reed, Joseph Cicippio, and Edward Tracy—were kidnaped in the fall. At the end of the year, they were believed still in the custody of Hizballah, along with two other Americans seized in March and June of 1985. Another American, Peter Kilburn, who was taken hostage in 1984, was murdered in April 1986, as were two British citizens kidnaped just the month before. The killings occurred following the US airstrikes on Tripoli and Benghazi in April, and Libya is thought to have been involved. Another kidnaped American, of Armenian descent, is believed to have fallen victim to Armenian factional struggles.

A third British journalist taken hostage in April was allegedly also murdered at the same time as the other two British hostages, but his body has not been found. A South Korean diplomat was kidnaped in January, but his status remains unknown. Two Cypriot students taken in April were released in June.

Iran continues to be the most influential party with the hostage holders in Lebanon. Tehran gives financial and logistic support to the extremist Hizballah factions implicated in most of the kidnapings, and Iranian Revolutionary Guard Corps units in Lebanon may well support the continued detention of Western hostages.

Iranian involvement in or influence over at least some of the hostage holding is demonstrated in the case of the French hostages who were members of the Antenne-2 TV crew. Taken in March by the Revolutionary Justice Organization, which is believed to be a cover name used by Hizballah elements, their fate appears to be directly linked to bilateral talks between Paris and Tehran. Three were released upon satisfactory conclusion of negotiations between France and Iran over debts from the pre-Khomeini era. Hizballah leaders in public statements have emphasized that Tehran is the key party in any hostage negotiations.

Israel and the Palestinians

International terrorist attacks arising from the Israeli-Palestinian dispute decreased somewhat in 1986, but even so in 1986, as in 1985, about one international attack in every four was conducted in Israel, the West Bank, or the Gaza Strip. Most of the incidents on the West Bank and in the Gaza Strip consisted of small-scale incendiary bombings against property, but Israeli citizens were killed or wounded in several attacks.

In October, Palestinian assailants hurled grenades at Israeli soldiers and their families near Jerusalem's Western Wall, killing one person and injuring 69 others. The attack—the bloodiest in Jerusalem since 1984—was claimed by several groups, including Fatah, the Abu Nidal organization, the Democratic Front for the Liberation of Palestine, and a previously unknown group, the Islamic Front for the Liberation of Palestine. In March, an American tourist—who was probably mistaken for an Israeli—was shot and wounded by unidentified terrorists in Jerusalem.

As in 1985, Palestinian operatives made several attempts to infiltrate the Israeli coast by sea from Lebanon. In July, a joint Popular Front for the Liberation of Palestine-Syrian Social Nationalist Party squad attempted a raid on an Israeli resort town, but was intercepted offshore. In the clash that ensued between the Israeli Defense Forces and the terrorist unit, two Israeli soldiers were killed and nine were injured. All four terrorists, identified as Palestinians, were killed.

Israeli security forces uncovered a number of suspected terrorist cells inside Israel and the occupied territories during 1986. For example, on 29 April Jerusalem police arrested 20 suspected terrorists reportedly connected to the radical Palestinian Abu Musa faction. Authorities announced that the cell was responsible for several terrorist attacks in Jerusalem, including the 13 April murder of a British tourist.

Israeli extremists conducted about a dozen retaliatory attacks against Arabs in the West Bank and the Gaza Strip. Ethnic tensions mounted near the end of 1986, following the murder of a Jewish religious student in the Old City of Jerusalem.

In 1986 radical Palestinians continued to murder more moderate Palestinians. In early March the Israeli-appointed mayor of Nablus was killed outside city hall by a lone gunman. The Popular Front for the Liberation of Palestine—a radical, Damascus-based Palestinian organization—is believed responsible. The PFLP waged an intense campaign of terror throughout most of 1986, which probably inhibited the development of moderate Palestinian leadership in the occupied territories. The murder of the Nablus mayor—who had been appointed by Israel and tacitly approved by the PLO—underscored the PFLP's intolerance for Palestinian cooperation with Israel. Besides the Nablus killing, the PFLP was responsible for some of the most important attacks in Israel and the occupied territories last year, including:

- The 12 January murder of an Israeli policeman in Galilee.
- The 10 July attempt with the Syrian Socialist National Party (SSNP) to raid an Israeli resort town from the sea.
- The 15 November stabbing of the Israeli student in Old Jerusalem.

Persian Gulf

As part of an Iranian campaign to pressure Persian Gulf oil producers into cutting their production, Iranian-backed terrorists bombed several important Kuwaiti oil installations just before the 19 July OPEC meeting. Tehran probably also believed such attacks served a parallel purpose of pressuring Kuwait to reduce its support for Iraq in the Gulf war. The five nearly simultaneous explosions caused extensive damage that crimped Kuwaiti oil production for weeks.

The attacks were apparently carefully planned and coordinated by persons with access to the sites, and Iran was known to have assets among the native Shias and foreign worker communities. Some of them probably worked in the Defense or Oil Ministries or in the oil industry. Kuwaiti authorities arrested nearly a dozen suspects in early 1987 for those bombings and others in January; virtually all of them were Kuwaiti Shias, some from the country's most prominent families and with ethnic ties to Iran. Police also recovered Israeli, US, and Soviet arms and explosives.

These arrests may affect somewhat Iran's subversive capability in Kuwait, but Tehran still has important assets in the Eastern Province of Saudi Arabia and other Gulf states. In Bahrain, for example, the Iranian-backed Islamic Front for the Liberation of Bahrain (IFLB) remains committed to the overthrow of the ruling family and has used terrorist tactics in the past. A few dozen IFLB members were arrested in mid-1986. The group may have as many as 1,000 members, and it has overseas branches. The IFLB has not conducted a successful terrorist attack in a few years but remains a potential destabilizing force available to the Khomeini regime.

Other Significant Attacks

The third most frequent venue for international terrorism in the Middle East in 1986—after Israel and the occupied territories, and Lebanon—was Syria. Most of the 22 international attacks recorded there were bombings in Damascus; a few of them among the most lethal attacks of 1986. On 13 March, a powerful bomb that went off in a refrigerated truck under a bridge in a Damascus suburb may have killed 60 or wounded as many as 100 persons. Syrian leaders publicly blamed Iraq for the attack. On 16 April, bombs exploded on a military bus and two civilian buses in the town of Hims, killing and injuring perhaps another 100 persons. Another bomb went off shortly thereafter aboard the Latakia-Aleppo train. Militant Lebanese Christians may also have been responsible for the March and April bombings as retaliation for Syrian military moves in Lebanon.

One of the two terrorist hijackings that occurred in 1986 was of an Iraqi airliner on Christmas Day. (The other was the attempt against Pan Am in Karachi.) In circumstances that are still not entirely clear, the Iraqi plane crashed in Saudi Arabia, killing at least 62 of the 107 persons aboard, including two of the four hijackers. Several terrorist groups, including "Islamic Jihad," claimed credit, but the actual perpetrators are still unknown. The operation may have been timed to coincide with a conference of Iraqi opposition groups that met in Tehran from 24 to 28 December; Iran denied involvement.

Regional Patterns: Latin America

Politically motivated violence continued unabated in Latin America throughout 1986, and international terrorist incidents increased some 34 percent from 1985 levels to a total of 159—the highest total for the region since the beginning of the decade. Latin America replaced Western Europe as the second-most-active arena for international terrorist incidents, with Peru, Colombia, and Chile accounting for much of the activity. More than half of all international incidents that involved US citizens or property in 1986 occurred in Latin America. Almost all of these were property bombings in Colombia, Peru, and Chile, with local branches of US-based multinational banks and the facilities of US-affiliated petroleum companies the most popular targets. Much of the terrorism in the region continues to be the outgrowth of domestic rural and urban insurgencies that are not primarily anti-American.

The increase in international attacks in the region occurred in the context of an overall increase in violence against vulnerable components of local governments' economies or highly visible symbols of multinational intervention in those governments. Oil company pipeline facilities were attacked in Colombia, for example, as much because of their visibility and vulnerability as because of the companies' affiliation with the United States. In Peru, attacks were not focused solely on US interests but on other governments' personnel and facilities as well. As of early 1987, for example, Soviet, Indian, West German, Chinese, Argentine, Spanish, North Korean, and Japanese interests had been attacked there.

Peru

International terrorism increased from 16 incidents in 1985 to a record high 59 incidents in 1986, making Peru by itself the third-most-active venue worldwide for such attacks (following only Israel/West Bank/Gaza Strip and Lebanon). Many of these incidents—mostly low-level bombings that caused little damage—were directed against local branches of US-based international financial institutions, which may symbolize international imperialism to one or both of the two main subversive groups, the Sendero Luminoso (SL) and the Revolutionary Movement Tupac Amaru (MRTA).

The Peruvian security forces' suppression of SL-inspired prison riots in Lima in June—during which more than 200 SL prisoners were killed—seemed to have no long-term effect on that group's determination or capabilities. It subsequently increased operations against unprotected economic and foreign targets. Continued economic sabotage probably costs Peru significant amounts annually in repairs to damaged infrastructure (bridges, electrical power grids, and buildings) and counterinsurgency costs. Losses from tourism or business investments discouraged by terrorist activities are more difficult to determine, however.

Expanded SL activity in Lima in 1986 further stretched the capabilities of Peruvian security forces, making it difficult for the government to adequately protect foreign diplomatic missions in Lima. Urban attacks seem to be part of a broader SL strategy to hit valuable, highly visible targets in the capital that attract more attention to its cause than operations confined to its traditional rural heartland in Ayacucho Province. SL leaders have just begun to appreciate the publicity value of such attacks; they apparently consolidated their highly compartmented apparatus in Lima to conduct more attacks in the city than in any other department in Peru. Nearly 300 confirmed terrorist incidents—mostly domestic—have occurred over the last two years in the Lima metropolitan area, giving it one of the highest rates of terrorism for any city in the world. However, as neither the SL nor the MRTA consistently claimed credit for such attacks, it is difficult to determine exactly how many of the unclaimed incidents were conducted by each group.

Part of the steady rise of violence in Lima in 1986 was attributable to MRTA activity. In contrast to Sendero Luminoso, the MRTA is almost exclusively urban based, generally targets property rather than people to attract attention to its cause, and attacks both foreign and domestic targets.

For the most part, MRTA attacks against US interests have involved throwing bombs at night from car windows at US diplomatic, commercial, and cultural facilities in Lima. In late 1986, the group carried out seven such attacks within a three-day period. MRTA attacks so far have caused relatively minor damage, but increased MRTA activity raises the possibility of incidental casualties, especially if it uses more powerful car bombs.

Colombia

International terrorist incidents in Colombia increased from 30 in 1985 to 50 in 1986, with many attacks directed against US-affiliated business interests. Rebel leaders also emphasized legal political activity throughout the year, as well as the penetration of organized labor and other interest groups. Despite this political maneuvering, the level of political violence was as high as during the civil war of the 1950s. The new president took office in August and inherited a tenuous truce with the largest insurgent group, the Revolutionary Armed Forces of Colombia (FARC), but the other three major guerrilla groups—all of which have terrorist components or occasionally resort to terrorist tactics—are in open conflict with the government.

The National Liberation Army (ELN), the 19th of April Movement (M-19), and the People's Liberation Army (EPL) — which together contain an estimated 2,500 armed combatants —are members of a loose alliance known as the National Guerrilla Coordinator (CNG). The CNG was formed in 1985 by the M-19 organization but has grown in strength under ELN influence since mid-1986. The ELN has abandoned its former isolation and appears to have forced the M-19—seriously weakened following government strikes and the losses of key leaders—out of its original role as head of the guerrilla alliance. The various CNG leaders still squabble over ideology and tactics, but the coalition was responsible for better coordination of attacks and improved propaganda efforts last year.

Colombian terrorists changed their targeting strategy in 1986, showing less interest in high-profile attacks undertaken solely for publicity value and staging more attacks on electrical pylons, transmission substations, and other economic infrastructure targets. Terrorist use of robberies, kidnapings, and extortion against both foreign and domestic businesses inflicted substantial damage on commercial activity. However, as in Peru, actual losses from tourism and business investments discouraged by terrorist attacks are difficult to measure. Narcotics traffickers continued to employ terrorist-like tactics against opponents in 1986.

Chile

Terrorist groups have exploited the continuing high level of opposition to the Pinochet regime. In 1986 terrorist incidents declined overall, although Chile was still the seventh leading venue for international terrorist attacks. Significant attacks included the bombing of the US Ambassador's residence in

April. Of the two main terrorist groups—the Manuel Rodriguez Patriotic Front (FPMR) and the Movement of the Revolutionary Left (MIR)—the FPMR was by far the most active. Although most of its operations consisted of relatively minor bombings of Chilean Government facilities, elements of the FPMR attempted to assassinate President Augusto Pinochet last September. A new development last year was the threat from extreme rightwing groups such as the 11 September Command and the National Combat Force. Little is known about these groups but their capacity for terrorist violence may be equal to that demonstrated by the extreme left.

Ecuador

No international terrorist incidents were recorded in Ecuador in 1986. The fortunes of the country's only terrorist group, Alfaro Vive, Carajo! (AVC), declined substantially after the arrests or deaths of several key leaders during the year. The AVC at the end of 1986 was in a state of disarray, with most of its leadership in prison or dead. Some active cells remained, however, and could stage limited operations.

El Salvador

There was a decline in international terrorist activity in El Salvador in 1986, reflecting the insurgents' reluctance to stage high-risk urban terrorist operations and the steadily improving capabilities of the Salvadoran security services. Despite some minor terrorist attacks in San Salvador, an expected campaign of sustained urban violence by mainline guerrilla organizations did not materialize. The security forces raided numerous safehouses, arrested more than 50 urban guerrillas, and broke up terrorist support cells. Salvadoran security has arrested most of the urban terrorist component of the Clara Elizabeth Ramirez Front, which was responsible for several assassinations in 1984 and 1985, including the slaying of six Americans in a single attack.

Regional Patterns: Western Europe

Terrorists staged 156 international attacks in Western Europe last year, a decline of 28 percent from the record high of 218 in 1985. Part of the decline stemmed from the decrease in attacks of Middle Eastern origin. (For detailed treatment of this issue, see the section on Middle Eastern spillover). The pattern of terrorism in Europe shifted in 1986. Spain became a principal location of international attacks in the region (mainly to attacks by Basque terrorists against French interests), with France and Germany in second and third place. In attacks conducted within Western Europe, French interests were most often targeted, followed by American and, less often, Spanish. Although most anti-US attacks occurred in Latin America, Western Europe remained the most dangerous region for Americans abroad, largely the result of actions by Middle Eastern rather than West European groups.

Most West European groups continued in 1986 to concentrate their attacks against domestic government facilities, the police and security forces, and businesses. The Military Wing of the Basque group Fatherland and Liberty (ETA-M) committed the most international attacks in 1986, generally harassment bombings of French businesses and privately-owned French automobiles in Spain. Such attacks, intended to pressure the French Government to reduce its cooperation with Madrid, became increasingly lethal in the course of the year.

West Germany

"Euroterrorism," which captured headlines in 1985, was less evident in 1986, although the rhetoric continued. The Red Army Faction (RAF)—the key proponent of a united terrorist front—was inactive until midyear, and none of its attacks bore the marks of involvement by non-RAF elements. The RAF issued some documents in the name of the "anti-imperialist front"—and the French group Action Directe (AD) echoed some of this rhetoric—but there was no evidence that the groups coordinated any of their 1986 operations.

RAF tactics in 1986 included the use of a remotely controlled ambush bomb, the selection of a victim because of his connections to the nuclear issue and the US Strategic Defense Initiative, and the assassination at pointblank range of a senior Foreign Ministry official. The reinvigorated RAF "illegal militant" cadre bombed at least 10 targets following the general theme of the attacks conducted by the "hardcore" members.

At a conference of terrorist support groups in February 1986, the RAF acknowledged it had erred in conducting a car bomb attack against Rhein-Main Airbase in 1985 and killing an American serviceman for his identity documents. During the year, the group used tactics designed to avoid unintended casualties. The illegal militants, for example, carried out their bombings at night and provided warnings. The RAF also concentrated its efforts on attacking West German interests and largely ignored US and NATO targets.

France

Action Directe remained divided into two operating groups—"nationalist" and "internationalist" wings—a split that occurred in 1982, partly over the issue of cooperating with the RAF. The internationalist wing attempted to assassinate an industrialist in April and killed the chairman of Renault in November, in an attack reminiscent of the RAF murder of the Foreign Ministry official the previous month. This wing maintains ties to other European groups; shares weapons, explosives and possibly accommodations; conducts symbolic assassinations; and is more likely to attack US and NATO targets.

In contrast, the nationalist wing generally operates independently, conducts bombings of unoccupied buildings, and restricts itself to French targets, especially ones it labels the "organs of repression." This wing became more lethal after its leader was arrested in March 1986. It was probably responsible for bombing a police station, which killed one senior officer, and for attempting to murder the prominent rightist mayor of Provins, which killed a municipal employee. The nationalists also carried out bombings of firms doing business with South Africa early in the year and may be linked to the shadowy "Black War" group that bombed similar targets.

Spain

The most important development in terrorism in Spain in 1986 was the attacks on French interests by the Basque separatist group ETA-M. Those attacks began in earnest after France began expelling wanted Basques to Spain or to third countries. Initially, ETA-M limited itself to firebombing unoccupied French private vehicles but by the end of the year had progressed to bombing French business interests, often without regard for inadvertent casualties. This pattern of increasing lethality differed markedly from the group's prior operating style, in which casualties usually were restricted to specific targets—most often Spanish security forces. The group continued to use the same techniques, however: bombings comprised more than two-thirds of its attacks, and arson and selective armed attacks remained important.

Other indigenous groups in Spain were generally less active in 1986, although Iraultza, a small anti-NATO terrorist group composed of radical elements of the extremist Spanish Basque Communist movement, conducted eight bombings in 1986, up from four the year before. Iraultza primarily targeted American companies in the Basque region near Bilbao, setting off small bombs late at night that caused only property damage. The Maoist urban group GRAPO (First of October Antifascist Resistance Group) remained virtually inactive for the second straight year after suffering massive arrests in January 1985. Known for its attacks on US and NATO facilities, in 1986 the group claimed responsibility only for attempting to bomb a Ford auto dealership in Oviedo, stealing a taxi in Redondela, and robbing a bank in Zaragoza. None of these actions resulted in casualties.

Portugal

The Popular Forces of 25 April (FP-25) claimed responsibility for only two international attacks in 1986, compared with 10 the previous year. One of the attacks it claimed—the explosion of a car bomb at the US Embassy on 18 February—was the only attack on US diplomatic facilities in Western Europe in 1986. On 17 May, the group took credit for firing a single 60-mm mortar round at the Iberian Atlantic Command facility. Neither incident caused any casualties.

Italy

By all accounts, 1986 was the quietest year for terrorism in Italy since 1969. The best-known group, the Red Brigades (BR), in decline since the Aldo Moro murder and the Dozier kidnaping, conducted only two attacks, one a successful murder of the former mayor of Florence, and the other a crudely bungled attempt on the life of a government adviser. Hundreds of old-line BR members—including leaders like Barbara Balzarani and Giovanni Senzani—were convicted in 1986 for crimes committed earlier in the decade.

Greece

Radical leftist terrorists expressed their growing disapproval of the Papandreou government's domestic and foreign policies with more attacks on government targets in 1986. By and large, however, Greek groups did not target foreign interests as often as in previous years. Greek terrorists attacked US citizens less often in 1986.

Turkey

The most serious new development in anti-Turkish terrorism last year was the escalating violence of the separatist Kurdish Workers' Party (PKK) after Ankara retaliated for a bloody PKK attack that killed 13 Turkish soldiers in August by launching an airstrike against the group's camps in Iraq that same month. In October, the PKK expanded its list of targets to include NATO, attacking a radar site in the southeast with rockets and automatic weapons. The group also targeted Turkish officials. Elsewhere in Western Europe:

- A young PKK member was arrested in West Germany in August as he opened a train station locker containing explosives, weapons, and ammunition. He was apparently planning to attack the Turkish Consulate General in Hamburg but was later released for lack of evidence.
- Dutch officials apprehended in late August a PKK activist who planned to attack a Turkish consulate in The Netherlands. He was carrying weapons and explosives at the time of his arrest.

Northern Ireland

The Provisional Irish Republican Army (PIRA) continued its campaign of 1985 against businesses and individuals—both Catholic and Protestant—that provided goods or services to the security forces. There were 62 deaths from domestic sectarian violence in Northern Ireland in 1986, up slightly from 1985. Most of those who died were civilians, but 24 members of the security forces also were killed. Extremist groups on both sides railed against the year-old Anglo–Irish Accord on power-sharing, but none of the statements claiming responsibility for attacks linked those actions to the agreement.

Belgium

Fewer attacks occurred in 1986 than in 1985. Arrests of virtually the entire infrastructure of the Communist Combatant Cells (CCC) in December 1985 and the discovery of several of the group's safehouses in January 1986 effectively halted the CCC's 15-month terrorist campaign.

The Netherlands

Among the 10 international terrorist attacks that occurred in the Netherlands in 1986, most were by previously unknown groups opposed to doing business with South Africa. At least two bombings occurred against Dutch construction companies that were mistakenly believed to be working on cruise missile-related projects.

Scandinavia

No indigenous terrorist groups exist in Scandinavia, but Prime Minister Olaf Palme's murder in February 1986 heightened the sense of vulnerability in the region to such attacks. Although Palme's assassination has not been firmly linked to a terrorist group, Stockholm police have aggressively pursued the possible involvement of the Kurdish Workers' Party. Otherwise, the region experienced only a few instances of Middle Eastern-sponsored terrorism.

Regional Patterns: Asia

International terrorist incidents in Asia during 1986 nearly doubled over the previous year—from 41 in 1985 to 77 in 1986. Despite the increase, international terrorist attacks occur in Asia at a rate far below the levels of such activity in other regions of the world; only Pakistan experienced a marked increase in activity. Most political violence in Asia is domestic rather than international and occurs mainly in the context of insurgencies.

Pakistan

Incidents in Pakistan accounted for much of the year's increased activity. Twice as many international attacks occurred there as in 1985; these 47 incidents represented more than half of Asia's total and made Pakistan the sixth most dangerous country for international attacks last year. Most of the attacks occurred in the North-West Frontier Province, where Afghan and Soviet-sponsored operatives conducted a terror campaign against refugees and civilians. Agents thought to be working for the Afghan secret police bombed bridges, railways, power transmission lines, shops, restaurants, and hospitals in an effort both to erode Islamabad's support for Afghan insurgents and to sow dissension between Afghan refugees and Pakistani civilians.

The most daring terrorist attack in Asia in 1986 occurred on 5 September, when four ANO gunmen stormed a Pan Am 747 in Karachi. The attack eventually left 21 persons dead and nearly 100 others wounded. After initially killing one American, the hijackers threatened to kill a passenger every 10 minutes unless they were provided a flightcrew to fly the plane to Cyprus. Two deadlines passed without further incident before the airplane's lighting failed and the gunmen opened fire on the passengers. The four gunmen, along with a fifth conspirator arrested afterwards in Islamabad, were taken into Pakistani custody.

Karachi was also the scene of other airline-related international terrorist attacks. In May, a series of four bombs exploded in a 15-minute period at four separate locations, killing a local security guard and wounding two other persons. The targets included the cargo office of Pan Am and three offices of Saudia Airlines. No group claimed credit for the blasts, but police suspected Iranian involvement.

Sri Lanka

Two spectacular attacks in 1986 represented a new level of violence for the Tamil insurgency in Sri Lanka. In early May, a bomb blew the tail off an Air Lanka passenger jet preparing to take off from Colombo for the Maldives, killing 16 persons (most of them foreigners) and injuring another 41. The bomb probably was intended to go off shortly after takeoff while the plane was over Sri Lankan territory. If the plane had been airborne, as many as 150 persons could have been killed. The leading suspect is the Tamil Eelam Army, a group thought to be responsible for an aborted 1984 bombing of another Air Lanka jet. A few days later, a large bomb demolished Colombo's Central Telegraph Office, killing at least nine persons and wounding some 50 others. No group claimed credit in the telegraph office bombing, but the Liberation Tigers of Tamil Eelam—the most lethal and hardline insurgent group—probably was responsible. Both bombings came just after an Indian Government delegation had arrived in Colombo to explore ways of restarting stalled peace talks between Colombo and Tamil moderates; the attacks probably were intended to torpedo the Indian-brokered peace talks.

Japan

Radical leftist groups mounted several operations in opposition to the Western Economic Summit held in Tokyo in May. The groups staged low-level incidents prior to and during the summit designed to obtain maximum publicity and to embarrass the Nakasone government. In the boldest such attack, the Chukaku-ha (Nucleus Faction) group fired five homemade rockets at the State Guest House as the heads of government were arriving. All the projectiles missed their targets and struck the street, sidewalks, and a building near the Canadian Embassy. There were no casualties and damage was minimal. In three separate attacks in March also designed to disrupt the summit, Senki-ha, Chukaku-ha, and Hazama-ha fired rockets against the US Embassy, the Imperial Palace, Osaka Police Headquarters, Yokota Air Base, and the State Guest House. These attacks also caused little damage and resulted in no casualties. In addition to attempts to disrupt the Summit, radical groups continued their campaign against Narita Airport, the railway system, and Japanese Government buildings, causing disruption and minor damage but few injuries.

Indonesia

An incident in Jakarta, Indonesia, just after the Tokyo summit, led to speculation that the Japanese Red Army (JRA) may have become active after nearly nine years. On 14 May homemade projectiles were fired at the US and Japanese Embassies but failed to explode. An hour later a car bomb exploded in the parking lot of an office building housing the Canadian Embassy and destroyed at least six cars. The previously unknown "Anti-Imperialist International Brigade" claimed responsibility for the attacks in retaliation for the antiterrorism declaration of the summit. Fingerprints found in a hotel room from which the projectiles were launched were identified as those of convicted JRA member Tsutomu Shirosaki. The JRA made no claim concerning the Jakarta attacks, and it is not certain whether Shirosaki acted independently, was part of a breakaway faction, or represented a return to terrorist attacks by this highly lethal group.

The Philippines

Insurgents in the Philippines continued to engage in terrorism —primarily domestic—to undermine the Aquino government and win support for their causes. The New People's Army (NPA) of the Communist Party of the Philippines stated that it will not target US and other foreign facilities and personnel unless they become actively involved in Manila's counterinsurgency effort. In March, NPA guerrillas in Kalinga-Apayao Province briefly held hostage nine US servicemen who had entered NPA territory inadvertently; they were interrogated, held overnight, and then released unharmed.

The Muslim insurgency heated up slightly in 1986, but most attacks were conducted against the police, Army, and local political targets. The Moro National Liberation Front— the largest Muslim insurgent faction—may have been involved in a series of incidents in June and July in which an American, 10 Filipino nuns, a Filipino-American, a Swiss businessman, and his Filipino companion were kidnaped. Ransom was allegedly paid in several cases and all were released unharmed.

India

Sikh militants proved throughout the year they intend to use terrorism to press their case for an independent state. They continued to target Prime Minister Rajiv Gandhi, Sikh moderates, Hindus, and government security forces, but unlike 1985 when Sikh terrorists bombed an Air India jet killing 329 persons, in 1986 they undertook no attacks that affected foreigners.

Thailand

A small time bomb packed with nails exploded near the entrance of the Erawan Hotel in Bangkok in April shortly before Secretary of Defense Caspar Weinberger was to attend a banquet hosted by the Thai Prime Minister. One Thai was killed and two others wounded. There was no claim of responsibility, but the incident was generally believed to have been related to Thai political feuding. A few weeks later, a bomb thrown from a passing car exploded inside the US Consulate compound in Songkhla, causing minor property damage and no casualties. Although no group claimed credit, Muslim separatist sympathizers may have been responsible. The small Pattani United Liberation Organization, a Muslim separatist group, has received funds from Libya, but it has been largely inactive in recent years.

South Korea

On the eve of the Asian Games in September, a bomb exploded near a crowded arrival terminal at Seoul's Kimpo Airport, killing five Koreans and injuring another 29. An anonymous caller told police that radical South Korean students were responsible. Seoul has claimed the explosion was a North Korean-engineered attempt to disrupt the Asian Games, but no evidence has come to light to link Pyongyang to the incident.

Australia

Australia experienced a rare international terrorist attack when a car bomb exploded underneath the building housing the Turkish Consulate in December, killing the bomber and injuring a bystander. It destroyed the entire floor where the Consulate offices were located. Police arrested a member of the rightwing Armenian terrorist group that had assassinated the Turkish Consul General in Sydney in 1980 but had been inactive since 1985.

Regional Patterns: Sub-Saharan Africa

As in previous years, there were few international terrorist incidents in Sub-Saharan Africa in 1986 and the number of attacks recorded in the region dropped for the second consecutive year. We recorded only 20 international attacks —compared with 41 in 1985 and 45 the year before. Several factors probably contributed to the decline: a reduction in Libyan-sponsored attacks, a more difficult operational climate for the African National Congress (ANC) and the South-West Africa People's Organization (SWAPO) as a result of aggressive South African countermeasures, and revised strategies pursued by the National Union for the Total Independence of Angola (UNITA) and the Mozambican National Resistance Movement (RENAMO).

There were four recorded attacks against US interests in the region during 1986 compared with three the year before. Most terrorism in Africa—except for that sponsored by Libya —is associated with local insurgencies. As a result, US interests have most often been incidental rather than direct targets of terrorist acts. In each of the recorded attacks in 1986, there were no American casualties and damage to US property was minimal.

The number of Libyan-backed terrorist incidents in Sub-Saharan Africa declined for the second straight year, with a direct link to Qadhafi being found in one instance. In July, Togolese security forces apprehended nine individuals who reportedly confessed to receiving explosives from the Libyan People's Bureau in Benin to attack the US Embassy and the market area in Lome. This incident indicates that Tripoli continues to support dissidents who oppose pro-Western governments in West Africa. As in similar incidents elsewhere, Qadhafi hoped to assure plausible denial through the use of surrogates—in this case Beninese and Togolese nationals—to distance Tripoli from actual attacks, so that government-to-government relations would not be jeopardized.

Southern Africa

Most international and domestic violence in southern Africa occurs in the context of insurgencies directed at incumbent governments or in the context of the anti-apartheid struggle in South Africa. Some groups occasionally resort to terrorist tactics to further their causes.

The African National Congress (ANC) openly advocates the overthrow of the South African Government, and in 1986 turned increasingly toward violent tactics to achieve this aim. The year was marked by a series of landmine blasts in the Transvaal traced to the ANC and to a limited number of bombings of military and civilian targets in South Africa's urban centers. While the ANC leadership insists that all targets were installations involved with the administration of apartheid, it is not clear that the ANC headquarters in Lusaka, Zambia, has been able or willing to impose this strategy upon all its operatives inside South Africa.

The South African Government has sought to suppress the ANC through harsh security measures in South Africa and through raids on suspected ANC targets in neighboring countries. Its tactics have included commando raids on suspected ANC hideouts and bombings. Neighboring countries continued to attempt to restrict ANC movement across the South African border.

In Mozambique, the Mozambique National Resistance (RENAMO) launched a new military offensive in September 1986. As in the past, RENAMO made direct attacks on population centers, coupling these with attempts to intimidate and/or recruit the civilian populace to its cause. The Mozambican Government regularly charged RENAMO with atrocities against the civilian population, while RENAMO spokesmen routinely insisted that the Mozambican Army was in fact guilty of these acts. RENAMO previously has been noted for its brutal attacks against civilians and foreigners, but in 1986 it released more than 60 hostages unharmed. The change of tactics probably was designed to improve the group's international image.

Patterns of Global Terrorism: 1987

The Year in Review

The level of international terrorist activity worldwide in 1987 rose by more then 7 percent over 1986, or 832 incidents compared with 774. This increase resulted from a wave of high-casualty bombings in Pakistan carried out by agents of the Soviet-trained and -organized Afghan intelligence service known as WAD. The campaign is designed to deter the Government of Pakistan from aiding resistance fighters in Afghanistan. When the Pakistani numbers are subtracted, the number of incidents in the rest of the world declined by almost 10 percent from the 1986 statistics.

The absence of terrorist "spectaculars" perpetrated by Middle Eastern groups was also noteworthy in 1987. Several factors contributed:

- Physical security at potential official and nonofficial targets around the world, especially in Europe and the Middle East, helped frustrate terrorist planning.
- Enhanced counterterrorist cooperation between Western nations and others kept terrorists off balance. Many more international terrorists from the Middle East are in prison in the West than in previous years.
- Well-publicized revelations of its complicity in sponsoring terrorism, combined with a badly deteriorating economy, compelled Syria to diminish its support for international terrorist groups to restore its international image and attract new financial credit. In June, for instance, Syria ousted the Abu Nidal organization headquarters from Damascus, temporarily disrupting its activities. Reflecting international pressure, only one instance of Syrian-supported international terrorism occurred in 1987.
- Libya maintained the caution it exercised in 1986 following US air raids and other US and European pressure.
- Events in Lebanon—such as the camp wars and the Syrian military move into Beirut early in the year—diverted the attention and resources of international terrorist groups operating in and out of Lebanon, thus limiting their ability to carry out attacks overseas.

Nevertheless, the potential for terrorist activity remains high. Several political developments are capable of generating new outbreaks of terror: violence in the Gaza Strip and the West Bank; the Iran-Iraq war; the US military presence in the Persian Gulf; Iran's ambitions to export its Islamic revolution; the groundswell of Islamic fundamentalism throughout the Middle East; an uncertain future for Afghanistan following the Soviet withdrawal; the apparent resurgence of the Japanese Red Army; and continuing insurgencies in countries such as Peru, Colombia, and the Philippines, where urban terrorism is increasingly used as a revolutionary instrument.

The 832 international terrorist incidents recorded in 1987 resulted in 633 persons killed and 2,272 wounded, including casualties to terrorists themselves. Terrorism in the Middle East and its spillover into Western Europe accounted for a major part of the total casualties: 295 killed and 770 wounded. These numbers are down substantially from the 450 killed and 1,125 wounded in 1986. Because of events in Pakistan, the casualty figures for Asia increased significantly, with 240 killed and 1,220 wounded, compared with 104 and 450, respectively, in 1986.

The United States remained a major target for international terrorists, despite the decline in the number of anti-US incidents from 204 in 1986 to 149 in 1987. US casualty figures also dropped from 12 killed and 100 wounded in 1986 to seven killed and 47 wounded in 1987. Some 47 percent of anti-US incidents took place in Latin America (55 percent in 1986), 24 percent in Western Europe (23 percent in 1986), 16 percent in Asia (7 percent in 1986), 9 percent in the Middle East (10 percent in 1986), and 4 percent in Africa (5 percent in 1986). These numbers do not represent any dramatic fluctuation geographically. The United States undoubtedly will remain a prime target, and we fear that the incidence of anti-US attacks may increase as terrorist groups adjust to newly instituted counterterrorist measures.

Regional statistics show that the Middle East again had the highest incidence, incurring 371 attacks, or 45 percent of the total worldwide. When Middle Eastern spillover attacks in Western Europe are added, Middle Eastern-inspired terrorist events rise to 50 percent, down only slightly from the 1985 and 1986 totals. Asia took second place, with 170 incidents, or 20 percent; Western Europe stayed in third, with 152 incidents, or 18 percent; and Latin America, with 108 incidents, or 13 percent, was relegated to the fourth position. Africa, as in the past, remained a distant fifth, with 30 incidents, or 4 percent. Also recorded was one incident in Eastern Europe.

The citizens and property of 84 nations were attacked by international terrorists in a total of 75 countries. As in previous years, terrorists carried out most of their attacks—75 percent of the total worldwide—against businesses, tourists, and other nonofficial and frequently unprotected targets. Attacks against government, diplomatic, and military targets decreased slightly from 27 percent of the total in 1986 to 25 percent in 1987.

The number of attacks by type varied little in comparison with the previous year. Bombing attacks remained the preferred means (57 percent of the total). Arson came next (18 percent), followed by armed attacks (16 percent). Kidnapings remained at 6 percent; over half of them (30 of 53 incidents) occurred in the Middle East, as they did in 1986 (29 of 51 incidents). We detected no signs that terrorists were using new technology in their operations.

State support for international terrorism persisted. Countries that sponsor terrorism try to hide their involvement through use of proxies and other means. Incidents that we are able to attribute to state sponsorship rose from 70 attacks in 1986 to 189 in 1987, an upsurge of more than 170 percent. As in other categories we recorded, the most significant change occurred in Pakistan, where the level of international terrorist attacks sponsored by Afghanistan rose from 29 in 1986 to 127 in 1987—an increase of 338 percent. Another important increase was in Iranian-sponsored terrorism: 44 incidents representing a 30-percent jump over 1986.

Conversely, we believe that international terrorism sponsored by the two countries most subjected to international pressure, Libya and Syria, declined significantly: Libyan-sponsored terrorism dropped from 19 attacks in 1986 to only seven in 1987, and we recorded only one for Syria in 1987. Of the 14 recorded state-sponsored attacks in Western Europe in 1987, 10 were against Libyan or Iranian dissidents, whereas in 1986 only one of 11 state-sponsored attacks was against a Middle Eastern dissident—a change in targets perhaps necessitated by the stronger security measures imposed by West European governments.

The venue for international terrorist attacks remained much the same. In both 1986 and 1987 the same 10 countries were the sites of 77 percent of the total number of incidents. In order of numerical precedence for 1987, they are Israel, the Gaza Strip and the West Bank, (24 percent combined); Pakistan (17 percent); Lebanon (13 percent); Spain (6 percent); Peru (5 percent), France (3 percent); West Germany (3 percent); and the Philippines, Colombia, and Chile (each at 2 percent).

Regional Assessments: The Middle East

The total number of incidents in the Middle East has remained fairly constant over the past three years. In 1987 we detected a drop in international terrorism overseas by radical Palestinian groups, but this decrease was countered by a rise in attacks against targets in Israel and the occupied territories. This does not mean that the 1987 figures reflect a permanent trend. Indeed, information suggests that radical Palestinian groups opposed to a negotiated solution to the Arab-Israeli dispute may be planning renewed terrorist campaigns against Israeli, moderate Arab, and US targets worldwide.

Continued legal pressure on terrorists in Europe during 1987 probably contributed to the decline in Middle East terrorism spillover there.

- In February, the head of the Lebanese Armed Revolutionary Faction, Georges Ibrahim Abdallah, was sentenced to life imprisonment in France for his involvement in the assassinations of a US and an Israeli diplomat in 1982.
- In May, an Italian appeals court upheld the sentences of the Palestine Liberation Front (PLF) terrorists convicted in the October 1985 Achille Lauro hijacking and sentenced PLF leader Abu Abbas in absentia to life imprisonment.
- Also in May, a Vienna court sentenced two Abu Nidal organization (ANO) terrorists to life imprisonment for the Vienna airport attack of December 1985.
- In July, an Italian court sentenced an ANO terrorist to a 17-year jail term for the September 1985 grenade attack on the Cafe de Paris in Rome.
- In October, a Spanish court sentenced a self-proclaimed Abu Musa terrorist—a radical Palestinian group that is anti-Arafat and pro-Syrian—to 47 years' imprisonment for the attempted bombing of an El Al airliner at Madrid airport in June 1986.
- The trial of ANO terrorists responsible for the September 1986 hijacking of the Pan Am airliner in Karachi started in November.
- The trial of the sole surviving terrorist from the ANO attack on the Rome airport in December 1985 started in December 1987 in Italy. (The accused received a 30-year prison sentence in February 1988).

- The case against the surviving ANO terrorist responsible for the hijacking of the Egyptair airliner in November 1985 may soon come to trial in Malta.

The lull in terrorism by Armenian groups of both the extreme left and extreme right, first noted in 1984, continued in 1987. The Marxist-Leninist Armenian Secret Army for the Liberation of Armenia (ASALA), however, may have been responsible for a machinegun attack in East Beirut on three French soldiers, two of whom were killed and the other wounded. A telephone caller in Beirut claimed credit on behalf of ASALA, but another alleged spokesman subsequently denied that the group was involved. The rightwing Armenian terrorist group, the Justice Commandos of the Armenian Genocide/Armenian Revolutionary Army, staged no attacks in 1987. We attribute the continuing quiescence in Armenian terrorism to a lessening of Syrian support for ASALA, effective countermeasures taken by Turkey and other governments, and perhaps reduced support in the Armenian community for terrorist violence.

Iran's involvement in Middle Eastern terrorism, including its support for the Lebanese Hizballah group, was substantial in 1987. Its role, together with those of Libya and Syria, is discussed in the section that addresses the problem of state-sponsored terrorism.

Israel

Israel remained the primary target of Palestinian terrorists in 1987. Effective Israeli security limited terrorist ability to conduct a consistent campaign of attacks against Israel and the occupied territories, but several cross-border attacks were attempted.

- In mid-April, on the eve of the Palestine National Council meeting in Algiers, terrorists linked to Fatah staged an attack into northern Israel. The group apparently planned to take Israeli hostages to be exchanged for Arab prisoners held in Israel. In a brief firefight just inside the Israeli border, three terrorists and two Israeli soldiers were killed.
- In July, Israeli forces intercepted three terrorists in the security zone across the northern border. Two of the three were members of Saiqa, a Palestinian group controlled by Syria.
- In late December in an attempt probably designed to exploit international sympathy created by the Gaza Strip and West Bank protests, three terrorists from Abu Abbas's Palestine Liberation Front penetrated Israel from Jordan. The three were captured shortly after their incursion.

In response to Palestinian acts of terrorism as well as cross-border raids, Israel has developed a highly sophisticated countermeasure capability. It also has one of the most efficient organizations in the world to deal with bombs found in populated areas. Its security efforts at airports and on airlines are extensive.

The extradition case of naturalized US citizen Mahmoud El Abed Ahmad (Atta) remained pending before US courts at year's end. Ahmad is wanted in Israel on charges of murder associated with the April 1986 firebombing of a bus en route to Jerusalem.

In March, life sentences were reduced for three Jewish settlers convicted of murdering Arabs in the West Bank. In October, a bill was defeated in Parliament that would have pardoned seven members of a group called Jewish Underground who had previously been convicted of terrorist crimes against Arabs.

Lebanon

Lebanon once again experienced well over 100 incidents of international terrorism. The known perpetrators ranged from Iranian-backed Hizballah Shia extremists—who regularly used kidnaping to contest the Western presence—to Palestinian organizations. The majority (61 percent) of the attacks were unclaimed, making it difficult to assess trends and patterns. The targets included Westerners, members of Lebanese confessional groups, Palestinians, and Syrians.

The large number of incidents and the indiscriminate nature of the 50 bombing attacks resulted in 48 persons killed and 218 wounded. For the West, hostage taking remained the most serious problem.

- Two West Germans were abducted in Beirut in January in response to the arrest by the Federal Republic of Germany of Mohammed Hamadei, an indicted Hizballah terrorist who is accused of trying to smuggle liquid explosives through the Frankfurt airport and of participating in the hijacking of TWA Flight 847 in Beirut in June 1985 and the murder of a US Navy diver. West German officials believe Mohammed Hamadei's family, including a brother who was also arrested in West Germany in January, were responsible for the kinapings.
- A French journalist, Roger Auque, was abducted in Beirut on 13 January.
- Terry Waite, the Church of England envoy who had been closely involved in negotiating with the holders of the Western hostages, was himself kidnapped on 20 January.
- On 24 January terrorists seized four professors—three of whom are US citizens—from the Beirut University College.
- American journalist Charles Glass was taken hostage on 17 June in an operation believed instigated by the Government of Iran. Glass's kidnapping in an area under Syrian control apparently motivated Syria to put pressure on Iran and Hizballah. Glass managed to escape although we do not know whether Syrian efforts played any role in this. Syrian attempts to free other hostages have evidently had no effect.
- Terrorists continued to hold five other Americans as well as hostages of other nationalities in 1987. Among the Americans are Terry Anderson and Thomas Sutherland, who have been held for more than three years.

Although responsibility for some of these kidnappings was either unclaimed or concealed, we believe that all of the hostages are held by Lebanese Shia extremists associated with the Hizballah. Later in the year, one South Korean, one West German, and two French hostages were released, reported in the press to be as a consequence of political or financial concessions. False rumors circulated in December that other hostages were to be released. The stories probably were circulated to pressure the governments concerned in the hope of arranging political or economic deals. Other motives for holding the hostages include to force the release of Shia terrorists imprisoned outside Lebanon, to exact high ransom payments, to inhibit Syrian or other forces from attacking Shia strongholds, or to be used as bargaining chips in Iran's confrontation with the West.

Preoccupied as it is with questions of internal disorder, and because of internal weaknesses such as a cabinet boycott of its President, Lebanon's Government has been unable to undertake any major counterterrorism actions for many years, including 1987.

The Lebanese Government is also unable to curb the actions of a large number of terrorist groups that operate in Lebanon. The Lebanese people themselves often suffer greatly from terrorism and hostage taking.

Hizballah, the Abu Nidal organization, ASALA, and many smaller terrorist groups are known to operate more or less freely in the Al Biqa Valley, in Beirut's southern suburbs, and in the various Palestinian refugee camps scattered throughout the country.

Egypt

In 1987, Egypt witnessed terrorist attacks from rightwing religious extremists and from a leftwing Nasserite group. Islamic fundamentalists were responsible for three terrorist attacks in 1987 against Egyptian targets. In addition, an unsuccessful attack was made by three gunmen from a self-proclaimed Nasserite group, Egypt's Revolution, against three US Embassy officials in May. The gunmen slightly wounded two of the US officials. In September, Egyptian authorities carried out a series of arrests that devastated the organization. Twenty members of the group have been indicted so far.

Egypt has a strong antiterrorism policy and has called for greater international cooperation in fighting terrorism. Egyptian authorities support the creation of a special international tribunal to handle extradition requests.

In the aftermath of the 1985 Achille Lauro hijacking, Egypt cosponsored with Italy and Austria a resolution before the International Maritime Organization calling for a convention dealing with terrorist crimes on the high seas. (The treaty was signed in Rome in March 1988. It is the first international convention against acts of terrorism at sea.) The Egyptians have worked with the United States and other countries to improve their counterterrorism and hostage-rescue capabilities.

Kuwait

International terrorism in Kuwait rose sharply from only three incidents in 1986 to 17 in 1987. We believe most of these incidents were instigated by Iran as part of its continuing campaign to destabilize moderate Arab regimes in the Persian Gulf region and intimidate them because of their support of Iraq and US naval activities in the Gulf.

In January 1987, Shia terrorists claiming to be members of a previously unknown group, the Prophet Mohammed's Forces in Kuwait-Revolutionary Organization, carried out a series of bombings at Kuwaiti oil installations. Their immediate objective appeared to be to force postponement of the organization of Islamic States summit conference. Additional bombings occurred in April and May, coinciding with the US policy to reflag and escort Kuwaiti oil tankers. In July, two Kuwaiti Shia brothers, apparently trained in sabotage in Iran, blew themselves up while attempting to bomb the Air France ticket office. In September, arsonists set a fire at the science facility at Kuwait University, and in the following two months terrorist bombs exploded at the Pan Am ticket office, the Ministry of the Interior, and an American insurance company.

Two major terrorism trials took place before the State Security Court in 1987. In the January trial, one Jordanian defendant was sentenced to death for the July 1985 cafe bombings that had left 10 dead and 80 wounded. Three other defendants tried in absentia were also convicted.

In a June trial of 16 Kuwaiti Shias (four in absentia) charged with oilfield bombings in 1986 and early 1987, all but two were convicted. The sentences ranged from two years in prison to the death penalty. The death sentences stemming from the two trials have not been carried out.

Despite continuing threats from extremist Islamic Jihad and Hizballah groups, the Kuwaiti authorities remained steadfast in their refusal to release 17 Dawa party members convicted of the 1983 bombings of the US and French Embassies and other sites in which many were killed and injured. In its continuing efforts to upgrade the capabilities of security and law enforcement personnel, the Kuwaiti Government sent police representatives to the United States for antiterrorism training in 1987.

Bahrain

In December, Bahraini authorities arrested a pro-Iranian Bahraini Shia who allegedly was planning to bomb a petroleum facility. An antiregime Shia organization, the Islamic Front for the Liberation of Bahrain, tried to recruit and mobilize Bahraini Shias for terrorist-type activities throughout 1987, but with only limited success.

The regime has countered the growing terrorist threat by improving the quality of training and equipment of its security forces, which has been largely responsible for the development of an effective counterterrorism apparatus in Bahrain. The relatively small size of the Bahraini population has also contributed to the overall effectiveness of the government's counterterrorism measures.

Saudi Arabia

The Saudi Arabian Government has worked diligently to prevent terrorism on its territory. In addition to rigorous border controls, it has trained and equipped special security forces.

There were several oilfield fires and explosions in Saudi

Arabia during 1987. Although the Iranian-backed Hizballah in Lebanon claimed responsibility for these incidents citing political motives, Saudi authorities attributed the incidents to electrical and other technical faults.

Tunisia

Although Tunisia is not normally a venue for incidents of international terrorism, three bombing attacks staged there in 1987 were deliberately aimed at foreign tourists. The attacks, which injured 33 persons including an American, were directed at a tourist bus in July and at four tourist hotels in Sousse and Monastir in August. A number of members of the Islamic Tendency Movement, which has strong Fundamentalist leanings, were arrested and sentenced to prison for the attack. We believe that the bombings were specifically related to fundamentalist unhappiness with some of the policies pursued by President Bourguiba. No incidents have taken place since the November change of government, and the fundamentalist resentment that had fueled the terrorist attacks seems to have abated.

Tunisia broke diplomatic relations with Iran in March, following the dismantling of an Iranian-backed terrorist network by French authorities in Paris. Not only had several Tunisians been implicated in that network, but the Iranian Embassy in Tunis, according to government authorities, had also recruited and trained Tunisian fundamentalists to engage in terrorist activities. The Tunisian Government has also tightened passport procedures after discovering that stolen Tunisian passports had been used in terrorist incidents.

The PLO has had its headquarters in Tunis following its US-negotiated departure from Beirut in 1982. Force 17, whose mission is to protect PLO officials, is also reportedly in Tunis and has been linked to anti-Israel terrorist operations.

Regional Assessments: Latin America

The incidence of international terrorism in Latin America dropped by 32 percent in 1987, down from 159 incidents in 1986 to 108 in 1987. The United States remained a major target. Out of the 108 incidents, 71 were directed against US interests, a figure that represented 48 percent of all anti-US attacks throughout the world. Bombings accounted for 70 percent of these attacks; the remainder consisted of arson, armed attacks, sabotage, and other types of low-level violence. Although the attacks resulted in substantial property damage, they caused no deaths of US citizens and injured only seven.

The attacks against foreigners generally were carried out by indigenous insurgent groups seeking to overthrow established regimes. The United States has become a major target because of its substantial economic presence and political influence in Latin America and its symbolic position as the engine of capitalism. The United States attracted terrorist attacks even in the religious field. Twenty Mormon churches in the Dominican Republic and Chile were firebombed because of their alleged role in spreading US political and economic influence.

As in the past two years, Peru, Colombia, and Chile incurred the greatest number of international terrorist attacks, with 70 of the 108 attacks in Latin America. The year also saw a sharp, if numerically small, increase in attacks resulting in minor damage in the Dominican Republic. Two minor attacks occurred in El Salvador and four in Honduras; none occurred in Guatemala.

In general, we believe that the decrease in the number of attacks in Latin America against US and other foreign targets may only be temporary and most likely reflects improved security measures by governments and private companies, as well as changes in the tactics of some insurgent groups involved in terrorism.

Chile

Like other countries in Latin America, Chile experienced a sharp decline in international terrorist attacks during the year, from 28 attacks in 1986 to 15 in 1987. Ten of the attacks were directed at US targets, compared with 23 such incidents in 1986. We believe that the extreme leftist Manuel Rodriguez Patriotic Front (FPMR) was the chief instigator of the attacks. The group's activities were inhibited by intensified police and security service pressure that continued throughout 1987. The FPMR remained a potent organization, however, as it demonstrated in September by holding a Chilean police colonel hostage for three months before releasing him in Sao Paulo, Brazil. The FPMR was especially active in the second half of the year, perpetrating a wave of domestic terrorist attacks against police and military targets.

The attacks against US interests were minor and did not cause serious casualties. They included one molotov cocktail thrown at the US Consulate in Santiago and eight firebombings of Mormon churches.

During 1987, a special military prosecutor continued investigations into several terrorist actions that took place the previous year, including the August 1986 discovery of large caches of military arms apparently smuggled from Cuba in support of the FPMR, and the September 1986 assassination attempt on President Pinochet. Although these investigations resulted in the arrests of significant numbers of people, the investigations have also been marred by questionable legal procedures on the part of the military prosecutor.

Rightwing terrorist groups, such as the Chilean Anti-Communist Action Group (ACHA), the September 11 Command, and the Nationalist Combat Front (FNC), operate with apparent impunity. The failure to apprehend any of the members of these groups involved in terrorist actions has led to speculation that the actions may be unofficially sanctioned by some officials in the security forces.

During 1987 the US Government, in a series of diplomatic notes, urged the Chilean Government to bring to justice two former high-ranking Chilean Army officers indicted by a US federal grand jury in connection with the Letelier-Moffitt murders committed in Washington, D.C., in 1976. The Chilean Government refused and the two indicted men remain free and at large in Chile.

Peru

The decline in international terrorism in Peru—down from 59 attacks in 1986 to 41 in 1987—does not reflect the true level of considerable violence there. Certainly the danger to US interests remained high: 23 of the international incidents were directed against US diplomatic or business personnel or facilities. Although the number of domestic terrorist incidents in Peru rose only slightly over the 1986 figure, more than 600 people were killed in the violence.

Although many international terrorist attacks in 1987 went unclaimed, two groups in particular remain of major concern. Sendero Luminoso (SL) expanded its activities into new operational areas during 1987 and, of particular concern to the international community, continued to build a dedicated infrastructure in Lima to support terrorism. While primarily focused on Peruvian targets, SL continued to attack foreign interests, especially transnational corporations, as part of its campaign to attract more publicity to its cause, drive away tourists, discourage foreign investment, and otherwise disrupt the economy.

The largely urban-based Tupac Amaru Revolutionary Movement (MRTA), although much smaller than the SL, concentrates its attacks on foreign targets, especially the United States. It generally conducts its attacks on holidays or at night to minimize casualties. This group has received training in Cuba.

The government has responded to these terrorist threats primarily through enforcement measures Several important arrests were made, including those of high-ranking members of MRTA.

The authorities were unable to weaken the SL, however, and it appears to have expanded its area of influence into coca-producing regions as well as other areas.

Judicial efforts against terrorism moved slowly, among other reasons because of a large backlog of cases pending before the courts. In 1987, fewer than 50 persons were convicted of terrorism.

Fifteen persons accused of the June 1986 bombing of the Cuzco train station, in which two Americans were killed and several wounded, were being tried at the end of 1987.

Colombia

The institutions of the democratic government of Colombia are under attack by four major guerrilla groups, all of which use terrorism and have received training and arms from Cuba and aid from Nicaragua and reportedly from Libya. Narcotics traffickers also employ terrorist tactics against anyone who threatens their interests.

Despite considerable domestic terrorism, insurgency, and narcotics-related violence, Colombia saw a major decline in the number of international terrorist attacks in 1987—19 as compared with 50 in 1986. Nearly all these attacks were committed against multinational oil company facilities—most with US affiliation—by the National Liberation Army (ELN), one of Colombia's four main insurgent groups. ELN's aim, like that of the Sendero Luminoso in Peru, is to undermine foreign investment and otherwise erode the country's economy.

In October, Colombia's main insurgent groups formed a new alliance, the Simon Bolivar Guerrilla Coordinator, under the leadership of the Revolutionary Armed Forces of Colombia. The coalition was established to provide a unified political and guerrilla front and we are concerned that it might be used to coordinate terrorist attacks against foreign interests.

Although in early 1988 the government moved to implement a new antiterrorist law under state-of-siege powers, in 1987 its response was largely reactive and piecemeal. In certain areas, the government had ceded freedom to the guerrillas and for the most part failed to deliver any significant blow against guerrilla or terrorist groups. In June, the Colombian Supreme Court struck down the implementing legislation for the 1979 bilateral extradition treaty with the United States.

Colombia has received US military as well as antiterrorism training and equipment.

Ecuador

The Ecuadorian Government has taken a strong public stand against terrorism and, with US and other foreign assistance, has successfully contained a small urban terrorist group, "Alfaro Vive, Carajo" (AVC), which first surfaced in 1983. AVC has received support from Colombia's M-19 and from Cuba.

Although weakened, the AVC is still capable of violent and coordinated action. The government's counterterrorist capabilities have been strengthened through increasingly sophisticated police techniques and training. During 1987, the government took advantage of several US antiterrorism training opportunities.

Panama

Panama's geographical position has made it a crossroads for travel and a site for transactions for various terrorist and insurgent groups.

Much of this activity is facilitated by the Cuban and Nicaraguan Embassies and the Libyan Peoples' Bureau in Panama. It is mainly transient and is not supported or condoned by the Panamanian Government. Congressional testimony, however, implicated some Panamanian officials, including General Noriega, the chief of the Panamanian Defense Forces, in the shipment of arms to such groups as Colombia's M-19 guerrillas and El Salvador's Farabundo Marti National Liberation Front (FMLN).

The leader of the FMLN's political arm has resided in Panama for a number of years and has carried out activities there in support of the FMLN, apparently with the acquiescence of the Panamanian Government.

Honduras

Various armed guerrilla groups, most trained and armed by the Sandinista regime in Nicaragua, carried out violent subversive and terrorist actions in Honduras in 1987.

Four international terrorist attacks took place in Honduras —one of them an attack against US interests—as opposed to none in 1986. The most serious incident was the bombing of a restaurant in Comayagua that was known to be frequented by US servicemen stationed at Honduras's Palmerola Airbase. Five US servicemen, a US civilian contractor, and six Hondurans were injured. No group claimed responsibility for the attack, but Honduran leftists are suspected.

Honduran authorities arrested five suspects shortly after the restaurant bombing. The five retracted their confessions in court, however, and were released due to lack of evidence. A sixth suspect found asylum in the Mexican Embassy in Tegucigalpa and, despite repeated US objections, eventually departed for Mexico.

In order to upgrade its counterterrorism capabilities, the Honduran armed forces have participated in the US antiterrorism assistance program.

El Salvador

The Farabundo Marti National Liberation Front (FMLN), comprised of five predominantly Marxist-Leninist insurgent groups, continues to employ terror tactics against Salvadorans as part of its overall strategy. The government's response has primarily been through military and police measures.

In October 1987, the government enacted a law designed to promote national reconciliation, which provided amnesty to those convicted or charged with "political crimes." Because of the broad definition given to such crimes, however, the law resulted in the courts' releasing individuals convicted of death squad crimes as well as several hundred suspected members of the FMLN who were either convicted of or pending prosecution for terrorist crimes—including the three accused gunmen responsible for the June 1985 killing of four members of the US Embassy's Marine Guard contingent at a sidewalk cafe in San Salvador.

At year's end, the Salvadoran Government planned to appeal several of the amnesty rulings made by the courts.[1]

Mexico

Some neighboring countries have criticized Mexico for giving asylum or sanctuary to insurgents and alleged terrorists. Mexico insists, however, that individuals given political asylum must abide by international norms.

Mexico has allowed the Salvadoran Farabundo Marti National Liberation Front (FMLN) and the Revolutionary Democratic Front (FDR) to establish an information office in Mexico City. The El Salvador Government has charged that these groups are using Mexico as an operational base. Mexico responded that it follows a policy of nonintervention in the affairs of other countries and that the FMLN-FDR members remain in Mexico as political asylees.

In 1987, Mexico granted asylum to approximately 10 Hondurans, most of them members of the Popular Revolutionary Forces-Lorenzo Zelaya. One was allegedly involved in a restaurant bombing in Honduras in which several US servicemen were injured. Although the United States objected, the Mexicans argued that he had not been charged in Honduras and that there was insufficient evidence to deny him asylum.

Mexico justifies this granting of asylum by citing the Central American-wide amnesty decree that is a part of the Guatemalan peace accord.

In December 1987, Mexico signed and its Congress ratified a Mutual Legal Assistance Treaty with the United States. Following US Senate ratification and entry into force of the Treaty, Mexico and the United States will be obligated to cooperate in the prosecution of transborder criminals, including terrorists, through information sharing, taking of testimony of witnesses, and other measures.

The Dominican Republic

In April 1987, an unknown group, the Maximilio Gomez Revolutionary Brigade, claimed responsibility for several crude bomb attacks against Mormon church buildings. This group also claimed responsibility for throwing a crude bomb at the Peace Corps office on 30 April, resulting in superficial damage. The group said the attacks were to commemorate the anniversary of the US military intervention in the Dominican Republic in 1965.

Haiti

The Haitian Liberation Organization (OLH), a group that believes in the use of terrorism, first surfaced in February. OLH did not commit any international terrorist attacks in 1987, but is believed to be associated with a leftist political party, the Parti National Democratique Progressiste D'Haiti. Both have ties to Cuba and the OLH may receive other outside support.

Regional Assessments: Europe and North America

In Western Europe, domestic and Middle Eastern groups staged 152 international terrorist attacks in 1987—a slight drop from the 1986 figure of 156 attacks. Eighteen percent of all attacks worldwide took place in Western Europe, compared with 20 percent in 1986. The preferred means of attack remained roughly the same: 63 percent were bombings, 22 percent were armed attacks, and 10 percent were arson attacks. Thirty-six attacks, or 24 percent, were staged against US interests, and, of these, 24 were bombings. US casualty figures in Western Europe were low: one person killed and 36

---

[1] The appeals were heard in 1988, but were unsuccessful. In the case of the Marines, however, it was determined that as Embassy employees they had been covered under an international treaty regarding crimes against internationally protected persons, which superceded domestic law. That decision, however, is being appealed by the defendants.

wounded. A breakdown of the 152 international terrorist incidents shows that 44 went unclaimed, 43 resulted from Middle East spillover, and the rest were committed by a variety of European-based ideological or separatist groups. Separatist terrorism remained by far the most persistent and dangerous. Given the intensity of emotions and at least some community support from the ethnic communities from which the terrorists come, separatist terrorism undoubtedly will continue and may well increase.

The leveling off in the number of incidents in Western Europe can be attributed to a combination of factors: caution exercised by state sponsors of terrorism, leading to a major decrease in Middle Eastern spillover terrorism; enhanced physical security; successes by law enforcement and security agencies; and increased cooperation among counterterrorism officials in Western Europe.

Canada

Although no major incidents of international terrorism occurred in 1987, Canada has taken steps to combat domestic terrorism, particularly following incidents in the mid-1980s involving Sikhs and Armenians. The British Colombia Provincial Supreme Court in February 1987, for example, found guilty the four Sikhs accused of the 1986 assassination attempt of a visiting Indian official.

Canada cooperated actively with the US and other countries during 1987 to prevent terrorism at the Winter Olympics in Calgary. The US and Canada signed an agreement in January 1988 to formalize bilateral counterterrorism efforts. Canada decided not to open an embassy in Libya and declined to accept a Libyan diplomatic presence in Ottawa. It also applied strict limitations on Libyan trade.

The United Kingdom

Four international terrorist attacks took place in the United Kingdom in 1987, the same as in 1986. None was directed against US interests, and three of the four involved attacks against Middle Eastern exiles.

Domestic terrorism by Northern Ireland organizations remained the most lethal. Sectarian violence in Northern Ireland claimed 93 lives in 1987, up from 62 in 1986, but deaths among the terrorists themselves accounted for most of the increase. The Provisional Irish Republic Army (PIRA) lost 22 operatives, including eight killed in a failed attack on a police station and two killed when the bomb they were carrying exploded. An internecine feud in the Irish National Liberation Army resulted in 10 deaths. Twenty-seven members of the security forces were killed, and 283 civilians and security personnel were wounded.

The image of PIRA as a deadly terrorist group unconcerned about innocent bystanders was reinforced in November when one of its units detonated a bomb during a British veteran's day ceremony in Enniskillen, killing 11 persons and wounding 70. The bombing received wide international condemnation, but a PIRA spokesman told the press later that the incident would not hinder PIRA's plans to increase its attacks against British targets during 1988.

As part of the effort to control the sectarian violence and terrorism in Northern Ireland, the United Kingdom and the Republic of Ireland continued to improve security cooperation, which had been augmented by the 1985 Anglo-Irish agreement. UK authorities also concluded new arrangements with the Republic of Ireland for extradition.

Significant quantities of illegal arms destined for Northern Ireland terrorists were seized during the year. In October, French authorities seized a ship carrying 150 tons of Libyan-supplied arms destined for the IRA, although four earlier shipments had apparently slipped through during the previous two years. UK police and military also seized quantities of arms destined for Protestant paramilitary organizations in Northern Ireland.

Some members of the large immigrant communities of Palestinians, Iranians, Sikhs, Iraqis, Tamils, and others have been involved in, or have been targets of, acts of terrorism. UK authorities have handled these problems through both normal police and judicial efforts, as well as through programs of cooperation with other countries to identify and apprehend terrorists and their supporters.

In 1987, legal proceedings continued against an American citizen extradited by the United States to the United Kingdom on charges stemming from involvement in IRA terrorist attacks. He was subsequently convicted of murder.

The United Kingdom grants no concessions to terrorists, and has been critical of other nations that have bargained with hostage takers and other terrorists. It works actively to enhance international counterterrorist cooperation through the Trevi group of interior ministers, the economic Summit Seven nations, and various groups within the UN. The United Kingdom has a strong bilateral relationship with the United States on counterterrorism measures and it continued in 1987 to offer assistance to other countries to help improve their capabilities.

Spain

The 47 international terrorist attacks in Spain in 1987, two less than in 1986, represented the highest total in Western Europe and the fourth highest in the world. The extent of terrorism in Spain reflects the abiding strength of radical separatist sentiment among Basques and Catalans. The First of October Antifascist Resistance Movement (GRAPO), an extreme leftist terrorist group implicated in past attacks on US and NATO facilities, remained inactive for the third straight year.

The Basque Fatherland and Liberty group (ETA) staged 21 of the 1987 attacks, 15 fewer than in 1986. As in 1986, most of ETA's international attacks consisted of bombing French-owned businesses in Spain, especially car dealerships. The attacks reflected ETA's anger at French authorities for denying ETA sanctuary and for cooperating with the Spanish

Government. Several of the bombings caused casualties in addition to property damage. Three persons were killed, including two Spanish policemen. In the past, most ETA attacks took place in small Basque cities and towns, but in 1987 the group expanded its activities into Catalonia, including Barcelona.

ETA's domestic terrorist attacks showed a new propensity for causing indiscriminate casualties. A hardline Marxist-Leninist faction took control of ETA following the death of the former leader in February. Since then, ETA has demonstrated a disregard for the safety of innocent civilians. For example, in June ETA staged its most lethal bombing attack, killing 21 shoppers in a crowded Barcelona supermarket, and in December it bombed the residences of several civil guard families, killing 11 persons, including women and children. An ETA bombing in June at a large petrochemical plant in Catalonia caused $10 million in damage and forced the evacuation of local citizens. We believe that Basque support for ETA dropped appreciably because of this campaign of indiscriminate violence.

Catalonian separatist groups turned increasingly to violence in 1987. One group of particular concern, the Catalan Red Liberation Army (ERCA), emerged in May with an ideology based on separatism and Marxist-Leninism. Its origins remain obscure; it may be a radical offshoot of Terra Lliure, another Catalonian terrorist group that has been active since 1981. Unlike other Catalonian groups, ERCA has deliberately attacked US interests and was probably responsible for bombings of the General Electric and Hewlett-Packard offices in Barcelona in May and June, respectively. In October, it claimed credit for bombing the US Consulate in Barcelona, which injured eight Spanish nationals, including two Consulate employees. Finally, ERCA was responsible for the only killing of a US citizen—a serviceman—by terrorists in Europe in 1987; the death occurred in a grenade attack on a USO facility in Barcelona over Christmas.

Terra Lliure increased its international terrorist attacks from three in 1986 to six in 1987. Most were low-grade bombings of foreign banks and travel agencies that caused only light property damage.

Iraultza, a small anti-NATO group composed of elements from the Basque Communist movement in Spain, carried out six international terrorist attacks in 1986, but staged only one in 1987—a bombing at the offices of the US-owned National Cash Register Company, which caused only minor damage.

On 15 April four crude and ineffective rockets were fired at US Embassy facilities in Madrid. All either malfunctioned or fell short of the intended target, causing only slight damage and no injuries. A caller claimed responsibility in the name of the International Front Against Imperialism in retaliation for the US air raids on Libya exactly one year earlier. The rockets used in the attacks were similar to those used in the Rome incidents in June and to those fired at the US Embassy in Madrid in February. We assume that the same group, the Japanese Red Army-linked Anti-Imperialist International Brigade, was responsible in each case.

Spain has developed a counterterrorism policy that includes efficient police enforcement, rehabilitation of terrorists not wanted for "blood crimes" who voluntarily turn themselves in, and increased multilateral and bilateral cooperation to fight terrorism.

Since the 1970s, many ETA militants have sought refuge and a base of operations in France for attacks in Spain. Following greater cooperation between the two countries within the past few years, however, France has expelled many of these individuals, who were subsequently prosecuted in Spain.

In 1987 alone, over 150 suspected Basque terrorists were expelled from France, including several reputed top leaders. In December 1987, the two governments announced the formation of a permanent police liaison office to further strengthen antiterrorist cooperation.

Spanish police action in 1987 put out of action 12 of ETA's major operational units (commandos). Police scored a further success in the April arrests in Barcelona of five members of the Italian Red Brigades.

In addition, the government sponsored a domestic antiterrorism pact that was signed by all major Spanish political parties in November.

During 1987, Spain's tough antiterrorism law was challenged in the courts on constitutional grounds. The Spanish Government has announced it will repeal the law, but will incorporate most of its provisions into the ordinary criminal code.

Also in 1987, Spanish authorities expelled two Libyans for their involvement in the Movement for the Liberation of the Canary Islands and two Syrian nationals believed to have been involved with the Abu Musa terrorist organization.

France

Nowhere in Europe was the contrast between 1987 and the previous year sharper than in France. International terrorist attacks dropped from 28 to 11, and anti-US incidents declined from three to one. Both domestic and Middle Eastern terrorist groups experienced major setbacks. Twice during the year, French authorities achieved major successes against the country's bloodiest domestic terrorist group, Action Directe (AD), which had been responsible for a series of international and domestic attacks from 1983 through 1986 and which has ties to West Germany's Red Army Faction. In February, police arrested the four leaders of AD's international wing in a farmhouse near Orleans and charged them with the 1986 murder of Renault President Georges Besse. In November, the police arrested AD's bomb expert Max Frerot, the last major suspect known to have been at large and a member of AD's so-called nationalist wing. Frerot allegedly was the instigator of at least two attacks in 1986, for which he is expected to be tried in 1988. AD, which was crippled by these arrests, committed no international terrorist attacks during 1987.

In the Middle East terrorist arena, French authorities in March seized several Tunisians with Iranian links who had been tasked with transporting and storing weapons and explosives for use by Lebanese Shia terrorists. As reported in the press, French police claimed that the group had been responsible for a terrorist bombing campaign in Paris in 1986. In November, the group's ringleader was charged with seven of the 11 attacks in the campaign; other members may be tried in 1988. Corsican National Liberation Front terrorists —who we believe have adopted a more radical political program and a more lethal terrorist strategy—carried out five small-scale bombings against foreign-owned vacation homes on Corsica. The group also was responsible for more than 70 domestic attacks against French business and government targets on Corsica and in Paris and Marseilles.

Over 150 suspected Basque terrorists, most of them members of the Spanish terrorist group ETA, were expelled or extradited to Spanish authorities during 1987. The expulsions of suspected terrorists, which also included fugitive Italian, German, and Irish terrorists, was accomplished by reactivating a 1945 emergency procedure permitting expulsions without hearings when the public order is threatened.

France's determination to prevent terrorists from using its territory to ship arms was demonstrated by the October 1987 seizure of a cargo vessel carrying over 150 tons of Libyan-supplied weapons to the Provisional Irish Republican Army.

The French courts in 1987 dealt sternly with terrorists, partially because of new legislation centralizing all terrorism cases in the Paris state prosecutor's office and creating a special court for terrorist trials.

In an important case in February, the head of the Lebanese Armed Revolutionary Faction (LARF), Georges Ibrahim Abdallah, was sentenced to life imprisonment for his involvement in the assassination of two US and Israeli diplomats in 1982, and the attempted assassination of a US Consulate official in 1984. The United States participated in the case as a "partie civile."

France's successful counterterrorism record in 1987 was blemished, however, at the conclusion of the so-called "Embassy War" in which an Iranian Embassy employee was suspected of aiding the terrorists responsible for the 1986 Paris bombing campaign. The suspect took refuge in the Iranian Embassy in Paris and the Iranian Government retaliated by blockading the French Embassy in Tehran.

A five-month standoff ended when France and Iran arranged for the departure of the Iranian employee and the French diplomats. Before the departure, a French Embassy official, despite his diplomatic immunity, appeared before a revolutionary tribunal in Tehran while the Iranian, who did not have immunity, appeared before a judge in Paris.

Shortly thereafter, in November—although French officials have denied any link—pro-Iranian terrorists in Lebanon released two French hostages. The French Government also scheduled for repayment a portion of a multimillion-dollar debt owed to prerevolutionary Iran that had been disputed by the two countries for several years. It expelled Iranian dissidents living in France, although they were allowed to return following domestic pressure. In addition, persistent rumors of arms sales to Iran led to criticism of France for having made concessions to terrorists.

Belgium

Following a mid-1980s' bombing campaign by the indigenous Euroterrorist group, the Communist Combatant Cells (CCC), Belgian law enforcement and antiterrorism procedures were restructured to meet the threat. Since the late 1985 arrests of the major CCC leaders, terrorism has markedly declined.

Two terrorist incidents were directed at the official Syrian presence in Belgium during 1987: an attempted bombing of the Embassy in February and the assassination of one of their diplomats in October. The so-called People's Mujahedin claimed responsibility for the latter incident.

As president of the European Community during the first half of 1987, Belgium helped improve antiterrorist information sharing and cooperation among the community members.

West Germany

The number of international terrorist attacks in West Germany in 1987 was 24, one less than in 1986. The attacks were perpetrated by a variety of groups. Nine attacks were by Kurds against Turks or other Kurds, with the Kurdish Worker's Party (PKK) the chief culprit. Three were aimed at Iranian dissidents, presumably by Iranian Government agents or proxies, and one involved an attack by Iranian dissidents against an Iranian Government facility. Six attacks were staged against US targets, compared with 16 for 1986. Although several of the anti-US attacks went unclaimed, we believe that most were the work of leftwing terrorist groups; one attack may have been carried out by a neo-Nazi group.

No US casualties resulted from the attacks, although there were several near misses. In August, for instance, a bomb was detonated underneath a German freight train near the town of Hademlenden, causing damage but no injuries. The bomb was probably intended for a US troop train that was scheduled to pass over the track at the time of the explosion. Similarly, in December a local Bremen commuter train was slightly damaged when it collided with a barrier on the track. This crude attempt at derailment was probably directed at a US military train that had stopped on a parallel track at the same time.

Another illustration of the wide range of international terrorist attacks in West Germany occurred in March with the explosion of a large car bomb outside the officers' club at a British Army base at Rheindahlen. Although they were not the intended victims, 27 West German military officers and their wives were wounded in the attack. The Provisional Irish Republican Army claimed responsibility for the bombing, which demonstrated the group's ability to operate outside the United Kingdom and Ireland and its willingness to risk incidental victims.

International attacks by domestic terrorist groups declined significantly in 1987. The Red Army Faction (RAF) was inactive in 1987. We believe that RAF operational plans were disrupted by the arrest of the leaders of the Action Directe (AD) group in France in February. Documents seized by French authorities during the arrest revealed that the AD and the RAF had been planning coordinated attacks for 1987, possibly similar in scope to the so-called anti-imperialist campaign of 1984-85. Despite its recent inactivity, the RAF remains dangerous.

The other important domestic group is the Revolutionary Cells (RZ). Together with an affiliated feminist group called Rote Zora, RZ staged a series of terrorist attacks during 1987, most of which were low-grade bombing and arson attacks against official and nonofficial targets.

In January 1987, German authorities at Frankfurt airport apprehended Mohammed Hamadei, one of the alleged participants in the 1985 TWA hijacking in which a US Navy diver was murdered. As the United States was requesting Hamadei's extradition, terrorists in Lebanon kidnaped two German citizens in an attempt to extort West Germany to release Hamadei or, at a minimum, not to extradite him to the United States.

West Germany in June decided not to extradite but to try Hamadei, as permitted under the terms of our extradition treaty. The German authorities have given assurances Hamadei will be prosecuted to the full extent of German law. The court case is expected to begin in mid-1988. In September, one of the two German hostages held in Beirut was released, reportedly after a German company had paid ransom for him. The second German kidnap victim remained a hostage in Lebanon at the end of the year.

In late 1987, German authorities began the prosecution of Abbas Hamadei, the brother of Mohammed, who was arrested in a separate incident in January 1987. Abbas was charged with bringing explosives into the country and seeking to coerce the federal government into releasing his brother Mohammed by participating in the hostage taking in Beirut. Abbas was subsequently convicted in 1988 and sentenced to 13 years in prison.

In 1987, West Germany granted *agrement* to Mehdi Ahari Mostafavi, then Iranian Ambassador to Austria, as Tehran's new Ambassador to Bonn. The United States, which did not learn of the pending appointment until after West Germany's formal acceptance of Mostafavi, then expressed strong concerns about the decision, providing West Germany with information pointing to Mostafavi's involvement in the holding of American diplomats hostage in Tehran during 1979-80. West Germany, however, did not reverse its decision to accept Mostafavi as Iranian Ambassador.

A Frankfurt court in late 1987 sentenced a neo-Nazi terrorist, accused of conspiracy in the 1982 car bombing that seriously injured a US soldier, to a ten-and-a-half-year prison term.

In 1987 the United States, the United Kingdom, and France—the Western Allied Powers in Berlin—actively exercised the public security responsibilities they have maintained in that city since the end of World War II. The allies issued expulsion orders against a total of 19 individuals associated with either the Iranian Consulate General in the US sector of Berlin or the Iranian Embassy in the Soviet sector. This move effectively closed down the Iranian Consulate General in Berlin (West).

Berlin prosecutors have continued their investigations into the April 1986 La Belle disco bombing in which two people died, including one US serviceman.

Switzerland

Although the Swiss Government generally supports increased international counterterrorism cooperation, Switzerland's situation as an international diplomatic, financial, business, and transportation center with relatively relaxed entry controls, makes it easy for terrorists to transit the country. Major terrorist groups may also use Swiss banks and medical facilities.

In July, the Swiss released a suspected Lebanese terrorist wanted by France in connection with a 1986 Paris bombing. The extradition request had been rejected because the French offense of belonging to a criminal group does not exist under Swiss law.

The Lebanese hijacker of a July 1987 Air Afrique flight that had made an unscheduled landing in Geneva remained in detention. The hijacker, who killed a French citizen before being overpowered by the crew and arrested by Swiss authorities, will be tried by a special federal court for air piracy and murder.

The head of the Iranian Embassy in Bern, Seyed Mohammad Hossein Malaek, has been identified as a leader of the participants in the 1979-81 occupation of the US Embassy in Tehran. The Swiss Government in early 1988 accepted Malaek's accreditation as Ambassador even though the United States had expressed deep concern about the accreditation.

In November 1987, Swiss authorities expelled three Libyans believed to be plotting the assassination of anti-Qadhafi dissidents. Despite an extensive manhunt in August, police were unable to apprehend the assassins of a former Iranian pilot who had been living in exile in Geneva.

Italy

Italy experienced six international terrorist incidents in 1987, compared with four such attacks in 1986. During 1987 Italy achieved substantial success against its major domestic terrorist group, the Red Brigades (BR). Once the largest and most dangerous group in continental Europe, the BR has not attacked a foreign target since the assassination in 1984 of Leamon R. Hunt, the US chief of the Sinai Multinational Force and Observer Group. Nevertheless, the BR—now split into two groups—remains capable of carrying out terrorist attacks. In February, the BR's Fighting Communist Party (BR-PCC) faction killed three policemen while robbing a postal van of almost $1 million. The other faction, the Union of Communist Combatants (BR-UCC), assassinated Italian Gen. Licio Giorgieri, who was involved in defense procurement.

The murder of General Giorgieri heightened cooperation among West European police and security services. By June the murderers and almost 60 other members of the BR-UCC had been arrested in Italy, Spain, and France, severely damaging the group's operating capabilities. We believe that the BR's total membership is at its lowest since the group was formed in the late 1960s.

Three almost simultaneous attacks in Rome in June were the most significant international terrorist incidents, although they caused only superficial damage. They consisted of a car bombing and two crude rocket attacks against the US and British Embassies. The attacks were probably designed to gain publicity before the Summit Seven international conference in Venice. A group calling itself the Anti-Imperialist International Brigade (AIIB) claimed responsibility. The AIIB first surfaced in two attacks against the US and Canadian Embassies in Jakarta in 1986, and we believe that it is a front for, or has close links to, the Japanese Red Army. US investigators, working under the terms of a bilateral mutual legal assistance treaty, were able to collect evidence on the US Embassy attack.

As a counterterrorism measure, Italy successfully tightened the security of its borders. In January, Lebanese national Bashir Khodr was arrested at Milan's airport while attempting to smuggle plastic explosives and detonators into the country. One month later, he was tried and sentenced to a 13-year prison term.

In December, the surviving Abu Nidal organization terrorist who had participated in the December 1985 airport massacre in Rome was brought before the courts. The trial, which was not completed until early 1988, ended with the terrorist being sentenced to 30 years in prison. Abu Nidal (Sabri al-Banna) and a third accomplice also received life sentences in absentia.

Throughout 1987, Italy sustained sanctions against Libya agreed upon by the European Community the previous year. It also joined in cooperative measures against Syria for that nation's connection to terrorism.

Motivated in part by the 1985 Achille Lauro hijacking, the Italian Government pressed for the drafting of a new "Convention for the Suppression of Unlawful Acts Against the Safety of Maritime Navigation" under the auspices of the International Maritime Organization. This agreement was signed in February 1988.

Austria

In May 1987, Austria responded through the courts to the December 1985 Abu Nidal organization attack on Vienna airport in which three died and 39 were injured. The two surviving terrorists were convicted and sentenced to life imprisonment, the maximum sentence.

The would-be assassin in a May 1987 attack on a former Libyan Ambassador and Qadhafi critic was facing trial at the end of the year. Although the assassin apparently had been supported by the Libyan People's Bureau in Vienna, the Austrian Government took no action in limiting or closing that office after its involvement became known. In early 1988, however, the assailant was convicted and sentenced to a 10-year prison term.

In 1987, the Austrian Government negotiated an anti-terrorism pact with the Saudi Arabian Government. It also established an antiterrorism unit directly subordinated to the Ministry of Interior.

Malta

The trial of the surviving terrorist in the November 1985 Egyptair 648 hijacking, Ali Rezak, is expected to begin by late summer 1988. The Maltese Government remains publicly committed to the trial. A US citizen was killed and two wounded in the hijacking.

The police are responsible for border control, but immigration procedures are limited. Citizens of several countries, including Libya, do not need visas to enter Malta. Moreover, in a recent agreement, Libyans can enter Malta by showing a Libyan identification card in lieu of a passport. A large number of Libyans visited in 1987.

Malta has an active commercial relationship with Libya, including several resident joint Libyan-Maltese commercial and other ventures that could be exploited for terrorist purposes. As an example, the Eksund II, a freighter captured by French authorities in October 1987 with over 150 tons of arms destined for the Provisional Irish Republican Army (PIRA), underwent extensive refurbishing in Malta before sailing to Libya. Although Maltese authorities say they had no prior knowledge of Libyan intentions for the Eksund, and the ship left empty, no complaint appeared to have been made about Libyan misuse of Maltese territory.

The pro-Western government, elected in May 1987, on the heels of 16 years of rule by overtly pro-Libyan Labor governments, has said that it strongly opposes terrorism and will not make its foreign policy "congruent" with that of any other government.

Greece

Eleven international terrorist attacks were staged in Greece in 1987, the same number as in 1986. Six were directed at US interests, one less than 1986. Most anti-US attacks were undertaken by extreme leftist organizations protesting the presence in Greece of US military bases. The Revolutionary People's Struggle (ELA) staged two bombings of US interests in Athens, causing only property damage: one against a Union Carbide office in April and the other against a US military commissary in September. The 17 November Revolutionary Organization staged two bombing attacks against buses transporting US military personnel in April and August, respectively, injuring a total of 17 persons. The two attacks obviously were intended to cause substantial US casualties and represent a change in tactics, which had consisted largely of selective assassinations of US officials and prominent Greek officials and businessmen.

Leftist terrorist groups also stepped up their attacks against Greek Government targets. One bombing attack against the Greek Chamber of Commerce building in Athens, for instance, clearly was designed to cause large numbers of official casualties. Greek police, as did their colleagues in

France and Italy, had some successes against domestic terrorist groups, killing one and capturing two suspected Greek terrorists in October. The police then seized several safehouses and weapons caches and unearthed evidence showing possible ties between ELA, 17 November, and other extreme left-wing groups. Greek authorities have continued efforts to improve security at airports and seaports, improve surveillance of suspected terrorists, and enhance capabilities of the antiterrorist police.

The Greek Government condemns state-sponsored terrorism generally, but is alone among the 12 members of the European Community in refusing to condemn by name specific states that sponsor terrorism. In publicly spelling out its unified approach to such terrorism issues, the Greek Government spokesman stated that Greece will insist on tangible and convincing evidence of a country's "guilt," not participate in making up a list of "terrorist countries" as long as such a list would constitute a prelude to actions that would undermine Greece's relations with those countries, and not give up its sovereign right to decide for itself what specific measures it should take whenever measures against a "terrorist country" are decided.

Throughout 1987, the United States and Greece maintained an active official dialogue on all aspects of terrorism-related issues, including a well-publicized exchange concerning Abu Nidal organization activities. As part of the continuing dialogue, the United States seeks to assist, where appropriate, the Greek Government in its technical counterterrorism efforts. A Greek Government delegation visited the United States in October for consultations on antiterrorism assistance. In its dialogue with Greece the US Government has conveyed the depth of its concern on terrorism issues whereas the United States has been made aware of Greek sensitivities.

Turkey

Eighteen international terrorist attacks were staged in Turkey in 1987, an increase of 13 over 1986. Three were against US targets. At least three were committed by the Kurdish Worker's Party (PKK) as part of its continuing campaign to establish an autonomous Kurdish state in southeastern Turkey. In 1987, the PKK expanded the range of its attacks, normally directed at the Turkish security forces, to include civilians and economic targets. Attacks on several Turkish villages in southeastern Turkey, some probably staged from PKK strongholds in neighboring Iraq and Syria, were designed both to discourage the Turkish villagers from participating in government security programs and to encourage Kurdish community support for the group. The arrest of a group of PKK members in Istanbul in November suggests that the PKK may have been planning to establish an urban terrorist infrastructure.

Turkey has instituted strong police countermeasures and has scored successes against the PKK, as well as against various other terrorist groups.

In March, several Islamic Jihad activists were arrested for attempting to bring over 200 pounds of explosives into the country to use against US and other interests.

Although Syrian and Turkish leaders signed a new border control agreement in July in which Syrian support for anti-Turkish Kurdish terrorism was to be stopped, Turkish authorities subsequently intercepted several terrorists trying to enter Turkey from Syria.

In 1987, the courts actively pursued terrorist cases. A naturalized Turk of Iranian origin was convicted of treason for working with the Abu Nidal terrorist group. A Jordanian Embassy employee was implicated in the case, but later released because of diplomatic immunity. A Syrian diplomat was implicated in another case involving Abu Nidal terrorists, but left the country before the trial began. The Turk has been charged with attempting to set up a Shia liberated zone in southeastern Turkey. An Iranian consular official was asked to leave the country in connection with this case.

Turkish authorities have instituted procedures—protested by some governments—for examining unclassified diplomatic pouches in order to stop shipment of weapons and other terrorist materials into the country.

Cyprus

Its location between Europe and the Middle East makes Cyprus a regular transit point for terrorists. Cypriot authorities have a consistent record of investigating terrorist crimes and prosecuting those involved. A swift investigation, for example, followed the attempted ambush in April of a British Army jeep in which a serviceman and a dependent were injured. Three Arab suspects were arraigned in May. Two were convicted in January 1988 and were sentenced to seven- and nine-year prison terms respectively, while the third was ordered deported.

The Cypriot Government has responded favorably to offers of antiterrorism training and technical assistance.

Yugoslavia

Yugoslavia's location between the Middle East and Western Europe, open frontiers, heavy cross-border traffic, large Arab student population, and relatively open society have made it an attractive safehaven and transit point for terrorists.

Yugoslavia has reciprocal arrangements with 55 countries, allowing visa-free entry. Some of these countries, including Iran, have been identified as supporters of terrorism. The large foreign student population in Yugoslavia includes 15,000 from Middle Eastern countries. Some of these are believed to be members of terrorist groups, including the Abu Nidal organization. They reportedly use their student status as a cover to maintain safehouses and provide operational support for transiting terrorists.

The Yugoslav Government is aware of the misuse of Yugoslav territory by some terrorist groups and is currently considering measures to tighten control over the entry and stay of foreigners. These measures include the possible reintroduction of visa requirements for some countries, tightening of entry procedures, additional training for security officers, and stricter control over the activities of foreign students.

The most serious misuse of Yugoslavian territory occurred in November, when the North Korean terrorists responsible for the destruction of Korean Air Lines Flight 858 received the bomb used to destroy the aircraft from another North Korean agent in Belgrade.

Reports in the press in 1987 claimed that Khalid Abdel Nasser, whom Egyptian authorities have charged with terrorist activities, and Middle Eastern terrorist leader "Colonel" Hawari, as well as members of his organization, were living in Yugoslavia. Later reports suggested that the government was no longer prepared to tolerate the presence of the latter group.

Yugoslavia has a military sales relationship with some countries that are identified as supporters of terrorism, such as Libya and Iran. There is no evidence, however, that Yugoslavia knows that such weapons are to be used for terrorist purposes.

Regional Assessments: Asia

The number of international incidents in Asia in 1987 (170) grew by 121 percent over that of 1986 (77). Virtually all of the increase occurred in Pakistan. Developments elsewhere in Asia pose concern for 1988, such as: the insurgencies in the Philippines, India, and Sri Lanka; the apparent reemergence of the Japanese Red Army; the terrorist activities of North Korean Government agents; and the tempting target represented by the 1988 Olympic Games in Seoul.

Pakistan

Most of the 138 international terrorist attacks recorded in 1987 in Pakistan were bombings directed against Afghan refugees and Pakistani civilians. The campaign was waged by the Afghan intelligence service, WAD, which is organized and advised by the Soviet Union. The 127 attacks conducted by WAD in 1987 represent the highest total attributable to a single state sponsor of terrorist group in any single year. Pakistan suffered the second highest total of attacks in 1987 after the Israel–Gaza Strip–West Bank area. Although casualties in other regions of the world were down substantially from the previous year, WAD attacks killed 234 persons and wounded 1,200—about half of all deaths and injuries from terrorist attacks worldwide.

The campaign started in 1985 with attacks directed against Afghan resistance and refugee camps in the border area. In 1986, the campaign expanded to include attacks on Pakistani civilians and, in 1987, spread beyond the border area to Lahore, Rawalpindi, Islamabad, and Karachi. The most brutal attack took place in July, when two car bombs in a crowded market in Karachi killed 70 persons and wounded more than 200 others.

Three of the WAD attacks were apparently aimed at US targets, but no US citizen was hurt and no property was damaged. The campaign generally has not been aimed at foreign interests, but the intensity and indiscriminate nature of the bombings, should they continue, represent a growing risk.

A handful of international terrorist attacks were also conducted by Iranian agents or local supporters of the Khomeini regime. Exiled Iranian dissidents and anti-Khomeini Pakistani religious and political figures were the target of several assassination attempts. In July, for instance, Iranian agents using automatic weapons and rocket launchers attacked Iranian dissidents in four separate houses in Karachi and one in Quetta. Some of the attackers were arrested; their disclosure of Iran's intentions probably deterred Tehran from carrying out further attacks in 1987.

Pakistani authorities have initiated tough police enforcement measures against terrorism. According to Pakistani statistics, over 300 individuals were arrested in 1987 for subversive activities, including bombings and possession of explosives.

In mid-1987, a tightly guarded special court began the trial of five suspected Abu Nidal organization terrorists involved in the September 1986 hijacking attempt in Karachi of Pan Am Flight 73. More than 20 people died in this terrorist incident. The trial continued through the remainder of the year and into 1988. The five were subsequently convicted and sentenced to death in July 1988.

The Pakistani Government participates in the US antiterrorism assistance program. In 1987, nearly 100 students receive training.

India

Only two relatively minor international terrorist incidents took place in India during 1987. The first was a crude bomb attack on the United States Information Service (USIS) center in Calcutta by demonstrating radical members of the Congress (I) Party in August, and the other was an attempted bombing in September of the Nepalese Consulate General in Calcutta by the Bengal Liberation Army, in which the bomber was killed when the device exploded prematurely.

Sikh domestic violence, as in previous years, continued to pose the greatest terrorist threat. In 1987, the Sikhs carried out numerous armed attacks against government officials, Hindu civilians, and moderate Sikhs, but none against foreign targets.

The Sikhs did not stage any attacks overseas during the year, confining their activities to attempts to seize political control of temple complexes in Canada, the United Kingdom, and the United States. Where they were successful, Sikh militants used the temple organizations to raise money for and otherwise support their coreligionists in the Punjab. Whether their terrorist activities overseas become intensified will depend largely on the way the Indian Government is able to reconcile Sikh political demands with the overall need to maintain national stability.

The Indian Government's response to domestic incidents of terror has focused on maintaining law and order. In the Punjab, extremists have been detained by the police using the extraordinary powers allowed by special legislation passed in 1987. The whole of the Punjab was also put under "President's Rule" in 1987, placing all state enforcement authority under the central government.

In bilateral relations, Indian and Pakistani officials have met to discuss problems of controlling terrorism and smuggling along their long common border.

Two Sikh separatists charged with murder in India were being held in a US jail at the end of the year pending hearings on an Indian Government request for extradition.

Sri Lanka

Although no international terrorist attacks took place in Sri Lanka during 1987, the level of violence remained high. Insurgent attacks, including terrorist operations, by the Liberation Tigers of Tamil Eelam (LTTE) continued throughout the year, even after the signing of the India-Sri Lanka peace accord in July. Under this agreement, at least 50,000 Indian troops were deployed to Sri Lanka. The LTTE guerrillas battled the Indian Peacekeeping Force as well as the Sri Lankan Government and Sinhalese civilians.

According to press reports, the Tamil separatists in Sri Lanka had previously received support—political, financial, and logistic—from elements within the Indian state of Tamil Nadu. Under the July accord, India committed itself to ensure that Indian territory is not used for anti-Sri Lankan activities.

During 1987, another group, the previously proscribed Marxist Janatha Vimukhti Peramuna (JVP, or the People's Liberation Front), added to the violence. Relatively nonviolent since its insurrection attempt in 1971, the JVP reemerged and started assassinating and kidnaping Sri Lankan Government officials, attacking police and military posts, and instigating student demonstrations. We believe that the JVP may have been responsible for the attempted assassination of President Jayewardene at a Cabinet meeting in August, an incident in which a junior minister was killed and several other senior officials were injured. The JVP has not staged any international terrorist incidents since it tried to bomb the US Embassy in 1971.

South Korea

In the past years, the Republic of Korea has been the victim of several terrorist incidents instigated by North Korea. The November 1987 destruction of the South Korean airliner by a confessed North Korean agent in which 115 people were killed has heightened the concern of the South Korean Government about terrorism, especially in view of the coming 1988 Summer Olympics.

Bilateral consultations on counterterrorism held in Washington in September between the South Korean Government and the United States reinforced the arrangements for information sharing, training, and military preparedness. The United States has publicly stated its support for a safe and secure Olympics. The South Korean Government has also established a joint bimonthly committee with Japan to coordinate antiterrorism cooperation related to the Olympics.

Following the downing of the Korean airliner, South Korea stimulated a debate on North Korean terrorism in the UN Security Council and successfully moved a condemnatory resolution in the International Civil Aviation Organization (ICAO) in early 1988.

Japan

No international terrorist attacks were staged in Japan in 1987. We are greatly concerned, however, over indications of a resurgence of the Japanese Red Army (JRA) as an active terrorist group. In May 1986, a group calling itself the Anti-Imperialist International Brigade (AIIB), which we believe is closely linked to, if not part of, the JRA, staged crude rocket and car bomb attacks against the US, Canadian, and Japanese Embassies in Jakarta. In 1987, as described in the section on Western Europe, the same group claimed responsibility for similar attacks against Western embassies in Madrid and Rome.

None of the perpetrators of these attacks was captured, but in November 1987 Japanese police arrested Osamu Maruoka, a top JRA leader, at the Tokyo airport. According to his travel documents, Maruoka had been in and out of Japan several times in 1987 and had also visited Hong Kong and the Philippines. He was carrying a substantial amount of money, which suggests that he might have been establishing or servicing JRA cells in Asia. According to Japanese press reports, while in the Philippines Maruoka met with other JRA members and with members of the Communist New People's Army. Even more worrisome, Maruoka possessed an airline ticket for a flight to Seoul on 7 December. He may have intended to set up a new cell there or to work with one already in existence to stage terrorist attacks in South Korea in conjunction with the Olympic Games in 1988. JRA terrorists might also mount attacks such as aircraft hijackings or the seizing of hostages to gain the release of Maruoka and other imprisoned JRA members.

The Chukaku-Ha (Middle Core Faction) and other radical leftist groups within Japan committed small-scale, politically motivated acts of sabotage, arson, and rocket-firing during the year but caused few casualties and little damage. The authorities have responded with efficient police enforcement measures.

The Japanese Government has taken a strong public stand against terrorism. It is a signatory of the Bonn declaration, an active participant in the annual deliberations at the economic summit of the major industrial nations, and consults with the United States in countering terrorism.

Following the destruction of the Korean airliner in November by two North Korean terrorists traveling on fraudulent Japanese passports, the Japanese Government joined the Republic of Korea and the United States in condemning North Korea. Japan also said it would establish a bilateral commission on counterterrorism cooperation with the Republic of Korea to focus on threats posed to the 1988 Olympics by terrorists based in Japan, using Japanese soil or posing as Japanese nationals. The decision reflects both governments' concern about the possible threat posed by the Chosen Soren, a pro-North Korean ethnic Korean association in Japan, as well as the Japanese Red Army.

The Philippines

Nineteen international terrorist attacks occurred in the Philippines in 1987, as opposed to only nine in 1986. Thirteen of the attacks were aimed at US targets, causing three deaths.

The potential for international terrorism directed at US interests in the Philippines, however, is greater than the 1987 statistics indicate. The insurgency waged by the New People's Army (NPA), the guerilla wing of the Communist Party of the Philippines, entered a new phase in 1987 with the increased use of assassinations by Communist terror units called sparrows.

The most serious instance involving Americans took place on 26 October when, within the space of 15 minutes, teams of assassins killed two US servicemen, a former US serviceman, and a Filipino bystander in a series of attacks near Clark Airbase. After first issuing contradictory claims and denials, the NPA eventually took responsibility and then threatened further attacks on any American deemed involved in the government's counterinsurgency effort.

On another front, dissatisfaction with the Manila Government over perceived failure to meet Filipino Muslim political demands could give both Libya and Iran an opportunity to exploit the situation by recruiting local Muslims to support possible terrorist activities, some of which might involved targeting US citizens or their property. Finally, members of the Abu Nidal organization and the Japanese Red Army were active during the year trying to form support cells among resident Middle Easterners and Japanese, respectively.

To date, the Philippine Government's response to terrorism, both domestic and international, has predominantly been through enforcement measures. The government has increased police forces in urban areas where political assassinations have most often taken place and, with US assistance, undertaken a counterterrorism program at Manila's international airport. The Philippine Government is planning an integrated counterinsurgency strategy involving civilian and military components that should reduce, over time, the threat from the Communist insurgency.

Australia

Although there are no known terrorist groups in Australia, the government has consistently taken strong stands against international terrorist acts:

- In May, it expelled the Libyan People's Bureau in Canberra, following concerns about Libyan activities in Australia and in the South Pacific.
- In November, the government prosecuted an Armenian terrorist involved in the November 1986 bombing of the Turkish Consulate General in Melbourne. The terrorist was convicted of murder and sentenced to life imprisonment.

Regional Assessments: Sub-Saharan Africa

Once again the total of international terrorist incidents in Sub-Saharan Africa remained by far the lowest in the world. Sub-Saharan Africa accounted for less than 4 percent of the attacks worldwide, 8 percent of the deaths (49 persons), and 6 percent of the wounded (136 persons). Despite an increase in the number of attacks from 20 in 1986 to 30 in 1987, we detected no significant trend in terrorism patterns. The 30 attacks occurred in 14 countries, and only Zimbabwe, Ethiopia, Sudan, and Mozambique had three or more attacks. As in previous years, almost all international attacks in the region were committed by local insurgents. Foreigners, although sometimes deliberately selected as targets, were usually inadvertent victims or targets of opportunity.

Five terrorist attacks affected US interests in 1987, but only one of them—a Libyan-sponsored bombing in Chad in October—appeared to be deliberately targeted against US interests. In other attacks involving Americans, two missionaries were killed in a massacre in Zimbabwe, a tourist was wounded in a landmine explosion along the South African border, and four persons were kidnapped in two separate incidents in Mozambique and Sudan, although they were released unharmed within a few months.

Overall, the preferred types of international terrorist attack consisted of bombings, armed attacks, and kidnappings, in roughly equal proportions. The percentage of kidnappings was unusually high in comparison with other regions. Seven different insurgent groups kidnapped foreigners to gain publicity or extract ransom; most victims were released.

State-sponsored international terrorist attacks accounted for approximately one-third of all incidents. Terrorist sponsors in the region included Libya, which was responsible for three attacks. Four attacks, mainly bombings, were directed at suspected members or supporters of the African National Congress. Strong evidence points to a South African Government role in some of these incidents.

Djibouti

The March bombing of a restaurant frequented by French civilians and military was the most spectacular anti-Western Palestinian attack of the year. The bombing, which was probably perpetrated by terrorists from the Popular Struggle Front (PSF) with Libyan backing, killed 11 persons, including five French soldiers. The choice of a target in eastern Africa involving Westerners suggests that Palestinian terrorists may look for new operating venues outside the Middle East and Western Europe. One terrorist, a Tunisian, was apprehended by Djiboutian authorities and awaits prosecution.

Chad

Chad has long been the target of terrorist activities carried out or sponsored by Libya.

The only two terrorist incidents in 1987 had little success, however. A bridge in N'Djamena was slightly damaged in a bombing (the bomber himself was killed), and a building owned by a US relief agency in a provincial city was damaged in a bombing believed to be connected to Libya.

Chad's success against Libyan terrorism has primarily resulted from the efforts of its security services, which have foiled several attempts to smuggle arms and explosives into the country.

The Central African Republic

The only aircraft hijacking during 1987 occurred on a flight that had originated in the Central African Republic. In July, a lone Lebanese Shia hijacker, who demanded freedom for a number of imprisoned Hizballan members and who may himself have belonged to the Hizballah, boarded an Air Afrique flight in Bangui armed with a pistol. After takeoff from Rome, the hijacker diverted the plane to Geneva and demanded that it be refueled and flown to Beirut. While the aircraft was grounded in Geneva, the hijacker shot and killed a French passenger before being overpowered. The hijacker may have received some support from Lebanese Shia living in the Central African Republic before he boarded the plane. The incident demonstrates that countries in western and central Africa, with their substantial Lebanese populations, lax security precautions, and an abundance of Western targets, may represent an attractive environment for terrorist groups —such as Hizballah—in search of new locales in which to carry out attacks against the West.

Central African Republic authorities with French help have attempted to improve airport security following the July 1987 hijacking. The government also has sent 29 participants to a terrorism analysis course funded by the US anti-terrorism assistance program.

Two suspects were detained in 1987 during an attempt to bring explosive devices into the country. Government authorities suspect that the two received the devices from the Libyan People's Bureau in Cotonou, Benin.

Mozambique

During 1987, Mozambique suffered from major terrorism perpetrated by the Mozambique National Resistance (RENAMO). An April 1988 State Department report covering 1987 activities documents large-scale employment of terrorist violence against noncombatant civilian populations in an apparently coordinated pattern. In a widely publicized incident at Homoine in July 1987, for example, over 400 civilians were reportedly killed. In addition, RENAMO kidnaped scores of people in cross-border raids into Zimbabwe, Malawi, and Zambia. Some of them were released after being forced to serve as porters, but others were reportedly killed or kept in captivity.

RENAMO insurgents kidnaped Western missionaries and aid workers on five separate occasions. One group of seven missionaries taken in May and released in August included a US citizen. At least four of the captives taken during 1987 remained in RENAMO hands as of May 1988.

Mozambique's response to RENAMO has been political as well as military. Its government has allowed the International Committee of the Red Cross to make arrangements for the release of persons kidnaped by RENAMO. Zimbabwe, Tanzania, and Malawi have assisted by stationing troops in Mozambique.

South Africa remains the principal supporter of RENAMO, although there is no evidence that the South African Government has a witting accomplice in the perpetration of massacres and the targeting of civilians. South Africa has also attacked suspected African National Congress (ANC) targets in Mozambique. In a South African commando raid on Maputo in May, three Mozambicans unconnected with the ANC were killed.

Zambia

During 1987, Zambia experienced several incursions by RENAMO insurgents. South African commandos carried out attacks in April against alleged ANC facilities in the border town of Livingstone, killing four people.

Eleven bombing incidents occurred in Lusaka in 1987, including a parcel bomb explosion in September in which two postal workers were killed. Although no claim of responsibility was made, Zambian officials blamed it on agents of South Africa. Two other bombings were directed against the ANC, which has its external Headquarters in Lusaka.

Zambia has attempted to respond to these incidents by aggressively deploying its security forces.

Zimbabwe

There were three distinct forms of violence with an international dimension in Zimbabwe in 1987:

- Bombing attacks against South African exiles included a car bombing in a Harare shopping center apparently aimed at a South African couple. Some of these attacks were apparently staged by groups or individuals associated with South Africa, ostensibly acting in retaliation for attacks launched against South Africa from Zimbabwean territory, which took place despite genuine efforts by the Zimbabwe Government to control such activity.
- Numerous murders, mutilations, and kidnapings of Zimbabwean citizens were carried out by RENAMO near the Mozambican border, in response to which Zimbabwe increased its military presence there.
- Local armed dissidents occasionally turned on foreign victims, including a massacre of 16 missionaries (two of whom were US citizens) and their family members in November, and the murder of two West German tourists in June. The merger of the two largest political parties in December and an amnesty announced in April 1988 may reduce violence from this source.

Botswana

Despite efforts by the Botswana Government to deny access to its territory, South African dissident groups occasionally pass through Botswana to carry out anti-South African operations. South Africa has at times used these activities as the rationale for raids against the ostensible perpetrators.

In January, an attack on a house near the South African

border killed an elderly woman. A soldier investigating the incident was killed and four others were wounded when a grenade left at the scene exploded. In April, a car bomb exploded in Gaborone, killing three Botswana citizens; the Botswana Government, after a two-month investigation, blamed South Africa. In May, a UK citizen claiming to work for South African intelligence tried but failed to assassinate a prominent South African athlete and antiapartheid activist; he was tried and sentenced to five years imprisonment on weapons-possession charges. One person was injured in grenade attacks, apparently of South African origin, at four houses and a bookstore in December.

Namibia

Despite South African and Namibian attempts to curtail infiltration, the South-West African People's Organization (SWAPO) continued to operate sporadically in northern Namibia during the year. Five bomb incidents occurred, three in Windhoek and two in Walvis Bay. Property damage was extensive, but personal injuries were slight.

South Africa

Although the struggle against apartheid has been largely nonviolent, especially since imposition of a State of Emergency in 1986, it has also generated a cycle of violent repression by the government and violent resistance by the black opposition, which have resulted in some terrorist actions.

The leadership of the African National Congress, the leading externally based liberation group, disavows a strategy that deliberately targets civilians. Nevertheless, civilians have been victims of incidents claimed by or attributed to the ANC. In two such incidents—bombings near a magistrate's court in Johannesburg in May and near the Army headquarters in central Johannesburg in July—scores of civilians were injured. A number of other bombing attacks caused property damage only.

The South African Government has responded to efforts by domestic groups to oppose apartheid by virtually banning all such groups and repressing their activities. While blacks continue to be killed by the police and military, the number has gone down sharply since imposition of the State of Emergency.

The South African Government's response to externally originated violence as been to attack suspected sources of the acts in neighboring countries. Attacks on alleged ANC installations and operatives in Mozambique and Zambia were carried out in 1987, killing three and four people, respectively. At least four incidents of bombing and murder in Botswana were attributed to South African agents. In Zimbabwe a bomb also attributed to South African agents was set off in a Harare shopping center, gravely injuring an exiled South African couple.

South Africa has provided logistic and other support to RENAMO insurgents in Mozambique who continue to target civilians.

Patterns of Global Terrorism: 1988

The Year in Review

The level of international terrorist activity worldwide was almost unchanged in 1988, rising by 3 percent with 856 incidents[1] compared with 832 for 1987. The Middle East again had the highest incidence of international terrorism, incurring 313 attacks—36 percent of the total worldwide. When Middle East spillover attacks are added, Middle East-inspired terrorist incidents account for 41 percent of the total (down 15 percent from 1987). Asia, primarily due to terrorist attacks by Afghanistan against targets in Pakistan, again held second place with 194 incidents, or 22 percent; Western Europe remained in third place with 150 incidents; Latin America, with 146 incidents, was fourth in 1988. Africa remained in fifth place—far down in the number of incidents, with 52 attacks, or 6 percent. No international events were recorded in Eastern Europe during 1988.

Terrorists were responsible for three "spectaculars" in 1988—the hijacking of a Kuwaiti airliner in April, the attack on a Greek day-excursion ship off the coast of Greece in July, and were most likely responsible for the bombing of Pan Am Flight 103 over Scotland in December. The trend in major operations from 1987, however, continued downward. Key factors restraining the growth in international terrorism in 1988 were:

- Continuing improvements in physical security at both official and nonofficial facilities frustrated terrorist targeting.
- Western and other nations built on counter-terrorist cooperation of the last several years and have imprisoned additional terrorists.
- Some state sponsors of terrorism, for example Syria and Iraq, appear to have substantially reduced their direct involvement in terrorism in 1988, although both continue to provide safe haven and training to terrorist organizations.
- Militia activities in Lebanon continued to have a diversionary influence on the capabilities of international terrorist groups to conduct overseas operations.
- Iran's decision to end the war with Iraq and expand its ties to the West lessened Iranian involvement in terrorism at least temporarily, although Tehran continues to include terrorism among its policy tools—possibly including exercising significant influence over those who hold US hostages in Lebanon. We cannot rule out, however, an increase in Iranian-supported terrorism in an attempt to

---

1 The bombing of Pan Am Flight 103 on 21 December 1988 has been included in these statistics because all evidence to date suggests that it was a terrorist act. However, criminal sabotage has not been ruled out. The investigation is continuing, and no definitive conclusions have been reached. The bombing killed 270 persons, including 189 Americans.

promote its revolutionary image overseas in the face of its setback in the Gulf War.

Even so, terrorists set a record for the number of attacks in 1988 and have the potential to continue the pace and deadliness of their activities. Moreover, the likely terrorist attack on Pan Am 103 vividly demonstrated the terrorists' capability to overcome security precautions with careful preparations. Disputes among rivals in the Middle East—many of whom have used international terrorism in the past as a policy instrument against their neighbors—could spark a resurgence of violence. The Provisional Irish Republican Army (PIRA) remained one of the most active separatist groups. West European separatist groups show no signs of slackening their use of terrorism, although their capabilities have been seriously curtailed by effective law enforcement actions. Other West European organizations such as the West German Red Army Faction (RAF) and the Italian Red Brigades (BR) have continued to pose a threat, while the 17 November group in Greece escalated its activity, including the assassination of the US defense attaché. Insurgents in Latin America and the Far East are turning increasingly to urban terrorism. And Afghanistan appears willing to continue to use terrorism against Pakistanis.

The 856 international terrorist incidents recorded in 1988 resulted in 658 persons killed and 1,131 wounded, including casualties to terrorists themselves. This is an increase in fatalities from 633 in 1987, with most of the increase resulting from the bombing of Pan Am Flight 103. The number of persons wounded, however, decreased from 2,272 injured in 1987. Excluding the Pan Am disaster, casualties were down, reflecting a decrease in attacks by Middle Eastern terrorists and Afghan-sponsored attacks in Pakistan. Although accounting for a small portion of the overall numbers, Africa experienced one of the greatest increases in the number of casualties—almost 60 percent over the total for 1987, from 163 to 259 dead and wounded. Terrorism in the Middle East and its spillover into the rest of the world accounted for 356 persons killed and 319 injured.

The United States suffered a substantial increase in terrorist attacks and casualties abroad during 1988, indicating that it remains a primary target for international terrorists. The number of anti-US incidents increased in all regions, rising from 149 in 1987 to 185, resulting in 192 persons killed and 40 wounded. In 1987, seven Americans were killed and 47 wounded. As in 1987, Latin America was the locus of the largest percent of incidents against US citizens and property —60 percent. About 20 percent of the anti-US incidents took place in Asia; 10 percent in the Middle East; and 9 percent in Western Europe. Also recorded is one attack in Africa.

The citizens and property of 79 nations were attacked by international terrorists in a total of 68 countries. Terrorists continued to carry out most of their attacks—77 percent of the total worldwide—against the least protected targets such as businesses and tourists. Attacks against government and other official targets decreased only slightly—from 25 percent of the total in 1987 to 23 percent in 1988. Many of the attacks were against individuals, indicating the necessity for constant awareness of personal security measures. Terrorists hit noncombatant military targets[2] less frequently—38 times in 1988, down from 88 in 1987—partly due to greatly enhanced security precautions and also reflecting changes in many groups' ideological concerns that decreased their interest in such targets.

The number of attacks by type varied little in comparison with 1987. Terrorists relied most often on bombings (48 percent); arson came next (28 percent), followed by armed attacks (15 percent). Terrorists decreased their use of kidnapping as a tool in 1988, accounting for 4 percent of the total; most kidnappings (12 of 32 kidnapping incidents worldwide) took place in Latin America, a change from 1987 when it was most prevalent in the Middle East (30 of 53 incidents).

State support for international terrorism remained substantial but dropped slightly in 1988. Some key Middle Eastern countries that most extensively facilitate terrorist group activities have attempted to hide their involvement through the use of proxies and other means. Incidents we are able to attribute to state sponsorship fell from 189 in 1987 to 177 in 1988, a decrease of 7 percent. International terrorist attacks sponsored by Afghanistan accounted for the largest portion, with 124 in 1988, compared with 125 in 1987 and 29 in 1986.

We believe that international terrorist incidents sponsored by three countries that were most subjected to international pressure—Iran, Libya, and Syria—declined. Iran was linked to 32 incidents in 1988, down from 45 in 1987, primarily because of the end of the war with Iraq and subsequent moves to obtain Western economic assistance. Libya is suspected of involvement in six attacks in 1988, and it continued to support dissident and terrorist groups. There was no evidence available to tie Syrian officials directly to any attacks during the year. We do not yet know what role, if any, state sponsors had in the downing of Pan Am Flight 103.

Ten countries were the venue for roughly 75 percent of the total number of incidents in 1988. In order of numerical precedence in 1988, they are: Israel, the Gaza Strip, and the West Bank (29 percent combined), Pakistan (15 percent); Colombia (10 percent); Spain (7 percent); Lebanon (3 percent); West Germany (3 percent); and Zimbabwe, South Korea, Peru and France (each at 2 percent).

The number of attacks of Middle East origin outside that region fell in 1988 to 45 from 50 in 1987—but if the Pan Am Flight 103 bombing is proved to have been caused by a Middle Eastern source, the number of casualties will have increased. Thirty of the attacks took place in Western Europe.

---

2 These are terrorist attacks, because the military personnel or facilities attacked are not functioning in any combat role. Such examples would include the assassination of US defense attaché Capt. William Nordeen in Athens in June 1988; the bombing outside a US Air Force communications facility in Spain in April 1988; and the killing of four off-duty US Marine guards at an outdoor café in San Salvador in June 1985.

Most of the attacks were in countries where Middle Eastern groups have been active for a number of years. Eight of the attacks were in Turkey; four each in Cyprus, France, and West Germany; three in the United Kingdom, and one each in Switzerland, Denmark, Greece, Italy, Norway, Spain, and Portugal. The attacks in Western Europe resulted in 291 persons being killed—including the 189 US citizens aboard Pan Am Flight 103—and 147 wounded. In 1987, 19 persons were killed and 47 wounded in the region by Middle Eastern terrorists. Four attacks in Latin America coincided with the second anniversary of the US air strikes on Libya. The prime suspects have received Libyan support in the past.

Middle East Overview

The total number of terrorist incidents in the Middle East fell from 371 in 1987 to 313. Of the total that occurred in 1988, 250 reflected violence in Israel and the occupied territories. The year 1988 also saw a violent resurgence in terrorism by two of the most dangerous Middle Eastern groups—the Abu Nidal organization (ANO) and the Iranian-backed Hizballah in Lebanon. Both groups conducted spectacular operations against Arab and Western targets. In addition, Iran encouraged a campaign of violence against Saudi Arabia in retaliation for the deaths of several hundred Iranians during the 1987 pilgrimage to Mecca.

On 14 December, Yasser Arafat, speaking in Geneva as Chairman of the Palestine Liberation Organization (PLO), accepted UN Security Council Resolutions 242 and 338, recognized Israel's right to exist, and renounced terrorism. This represents a fundamental change in PLO positions, fulfilling longstanding US conditions for the start of a substantive dialogue with that organization. We have stated that we will not be able to sustain a dialogue if PLO terrorism continues.

Three major terrorist attacks occurred in 1988. All the attacks appear to be "classic" operations—kidnapping, hijacking, bombing—by groups seeking vengeance or release of friends and family members in prison abroad. These major operations were:

- Hizballah terrorists, probably directed by Imad Mughniyah, a Hizballah security chief, hijacked a Kuwaiti airliner seeking the release of 17 Shia terrorists imprisoned in Kuwait. Although the terrorists failed to obtain release of any prisoners and killed two Kuwaitis, the operation was in some respects technically impressive. The terrorists —in suspected complicity with Iran—showed themselves to be skilled professionals in their ability to manage the incident, equip themselves, secure the airliner from rescue, and escape when an end to the incident had been negotiated. Kuwait released two of the imprisoned terrorists in late 1988 on completion of their sentences.
- The ANO in July capped a series of attacks marking its return to international terrorism with a machinegun and grenade attack on a Greek day-excursion ship, The City of Poros, killing nine persons and injuring almost 100 others. While the objective of the operation is not known, the ANO may have planned the attack to press the Greek Government to release ANO terrorists from jail.
- Pan Am Flight 103 exploded in midair in late December. While the investigation of the crash continues, and culpability has not yet been established, likely suspects could include several Middle East terrorists and governments that have supported terrorism in the past.

Egypt

Three terrorist incidents—two bombings and one attempted bombing, all unclaimed—were recorded in Egypt in 1988, and increase of one over 1987. On 10 January a small bomb exploded in an alley next to the US Consulate in Alexandria, causing damage but no casualties. Sixteen days later another small bomb exploded in a bookshop in the Nile Hilton Hotel annex in Cairo, injuring one person. The similarities in the two attacks—no claims and low-order explosives probably meant to make a political statement rather than cause casualties—led to speculation that they were related, perhaps to ongoing legal proceedings against members of the Nasserist terrorist group, Egypt's Revolution. In what appears to be an unrelated event, on 4 April a bomb was discovered at the US pavilion of the Cairo International Fair shortly before it would have exploded.

Egyptian authorities in 1988 broke up several clandestine groups suspected of terrorist actions or intentions. Twenty members of the group Egypt's Revolution were indicted and charged with attacks on US and Israeli diplomats. The prosecutor asked for death sentences for 10 and life sentences for the others. The trial, which began in November, was not completed at yearend.

Egypt has taken a firm counter-terrorism stand and has called for stronger international cooperation to combat terrorism, including improved sharing of terrorism-related information; strengthened international protocols dealing with arrest, extradition, and prosecution of terrorists; and increased international assistance to less wealthy nations for use in developing counter-terrorism programs. In January, the Egyptian Foreign Ministry, in conjunction with the University of Illinois at Chicago, sponsored an international conference on terrorism that attracted representatives from 30 countries.

In cooperation with the United States and others, Egypt has taken steps to strengthen its counter-terrorism capabilities. These include increased training and education for police officials involved in counter-terrorism, improved counter-terrorist procedures and safeguards at Cairo's international airport, and upgrading the counter-terrorism reaction forces. Egypt has also worked closely with Israeli authorities in helping to secure the border against infiltrators.

In recent months, the Egyptian Government has engaged in an extensive dialogue to encourage PLO moderation. Egypt has urged it to explicitly renounce terrorism, recognize the Israeli's right to exist and accept UN Security Council Resolutions 242 and 338. By so doing, Egypt probably contributed to the conciliatory statement in Geneva in December by PLO leader Yasser Arafat, which led to the initiation of a dialogue with the United States.

Israel

Israel remained the primary target of Palestinian terrorists during 1988. Although effective Israeli countermeasures continue to limit terrorists' abilities to orchestrate large-scale attacks against Israel and the occupied territories, several operations resulting in significant casualties took place inside Israel in 1988:

- On 7 March, three Palestinian terrorists hijacked a bus near Beersheba, in southern Israel. The terrorists—reportedly members of Force 17 or another Fatah element—and three Israeli civilians died in the attack.
- On 27 April, two Palestinian terrorists crossed into Israel from Lebanon and attacked a civilian truck. The operatives opened fire with automatic weapons and threw hand grenades, wounding the driver.
- On 21 August, terrorists, reportedly Bedouins enlisted by Fatah, launched a grenade attack against a crowded pedestrian mall in Haifa, injuring 25 civilians. The PLO issued a claim for the attack, attempting to legitimize the operation by alleging that the victims had been Israeli intelligence agents.

In addition, Israeli interests outside the Middle East were targeted in 1988. The following were among the year's incidents:

- On 14 April, Turkish national police defused a time bomb found in front of the El Al airlines office in Istanbul.
- On 11 May, suspected ANO terrorists attempted a car bomb attack against the Israeli Embassy in Nicosia, Cyprus. The driver of the explosives-laden car attempted to park near the Israeli Embassy compound several times but was turned away by security officials. The car bomb subsequently detonated, killing three persons and wounding 17.

The Israeli Government conducts a large, efficient, and comprehensive counter-terrorism effort. This effort includes providing significant resources to counter-terrorism military units, developing a massive counter-terrorist intelligence collection effort, funding research and development into new equipment and techniques, and using aggressive counter-terrorist procedures to protect Israeli citizens and visitors. Among the latter are special protection techniques for El Al and the training of citizens, including school children, in counter-terrorist tactics such as bomb recognition and reaction.

In 1988, the Israeli Government employed a variety of measures to limit terrorists' efforts to attack Israel. The armed forces carried out preemptive attacks—usually air strikes, although occasionally ground operations were employed—against locations in Lebanon that Israeli intelligence had identified as terrorist camps and places of refuge. Israeli intelligence has been successful in limiting internal terrorist activities. In December, the authorities arrested a 13-person terrorist cell in Haifa consisting of Israeli Bedouin Arabs, two of whom were on active duty with the Israeli Defense Force. The cell is believed responsible for the bombing of a Haifa shopping mall in August. Also in December, the government announced that other terrorist cells had been uncovered in the preceding two months, most of which were located in the occupied territories. The cells were reportedly linked to many terrorist incidents, including the firebombing of a civilian bus that killed a mother and her three children in October.

The Governments of the United States and Israel are seeking extradition of terrorists held in their respective countries. The United States is seeking extradition from Israel of a dual national who is wanted for a mail bombing in the United States in 1980. Israel is seeking extradition from the United States of a naturalized American citizen of Arab descent wanted for murder in a 1986 firebombing of a bus en route to Jerusalem. (In early 1989, a federal judge agreed to his extradition.)

Israel has been accused of carrying out several assassinations in 1988, including the assassination in Tunis of Khalil al Wazir, also known as Abu Jihad, the second-ranking individual in the PLO, who murder sparked a UN Security Council debate. The PLO has accused Israel of being responsible for the bombing of a car in February, which killed three PLO leaders in Limassol, Cyprus.

Jordan

Jordan, which has been the victim of past terrorist attacks both at home and abroad, experienced two minor bomb blasts in Amman in April. The two attacks were claimed by Black September, a cover name for the ANO.

As part of its efforts to combat terrorism, the Jordanian Government has initiated a multimillion-dollar project to increase police communications capabilities; has increased tenfold the size of the Desert Police Force, which interdicts drug and gun smuggling; and has cooperated in international counter-terrorism forums by sharing information and resources. The Public Security Directorate's Special Police Force has participated in bomb-detection training programs for dogs and their handlers offered by the Department of State's Anti-Terrorism Assistance Program, and groundwork for greater program participation has been laid.

Kuwait

Terrorist attacks in Kuwait in 1988 focused on foreign targets. International incidents decreased to five last year, compared to 17 attacks in 1987. As in previous years, pro-Iranian Kuwaiti Shias probably were behind most of these incidents, although press reports indicate an Iranian citizen was arrested along with two non-Kuwaiti Arabs in connection with the bombings of an Avis rental car office in May and a Saudia Airlines office in April. Efforts by Iran to improve its relations with neighboring states and the West following Tehran's decision to adopt the UN cease-fire resolution in July probably contributed to the drop in attacks in Kuwait.

The most significant attack against Kuwaiti interests in 1988 was the seizure in April of Kuwait Airways Flight 422.

The Kuwaiti Government maintained a hard line policy against dealing with the hijackers, despite the murder of two of its citizens during the 16-day ordeal and the presence of three Royal Family members among the hostages. Kuwait steadfastly refused to meet the hijackers' demand for the release of the convicted Hizballah terrorists.

Kuwait handed down sentences in trials of terrorists in 1988. On 6 June, several Kuwaiti Shias were sentenced for their part in the June 1986 and January 1987 oilfield bombings. Six were given death sentences, eight, prison sentences ranging from two years to life, and two were acquitted.

Kuwait is involved in a number of international counterterrorism efforts. In November, the Kuwaiti Cabinet endorsed three terrorism-related international conventions and set them to the Amiri Diwan for signature. The conventions deal with crimes against diplomats, the taking of hostages, and acts of violence at civil airports. Kuwait has participated in the State Department's Anti-Terrorism Training Assistance program, with training provided in VIP protection, port security, and SWAT team response.

Lebanon

The number of international terrorist incidents in Lebanon declined from 112 in 1987 to 28 in 1988, possibly because of interdiction of violence by Syrian military forces, who continued to occupy West Beirut and expanded their presence to the southern suburbs as well. Responsibility for most of these attacks (about 60 percent) went unclaimed; the groups undertaking them may have included Palestinian factions, Lebanese Christian militias, and Lebanese Shia and Sunni fundamentalists.

Kidnappings of foreigners as well as kidnappings of Lebanese nationals continued: eight foreigners were seized in 1988, including US Marine Corps Lt. Col. William Richard Higgins, who was detailed to UN peacekeeping duties with the UN Observer Group Lebanon. At yearend, 20 foreigners are believed to remain hostage:

- Hizballah terrorists in February abducted Lieutenant Colonel Higgins in southern Lebanon. Groups claiming responsibility for the attack—the Islamic Revolutionary Brigades and the Organization of the Oppressed on Earth—claimed that Higgins, who was commander of the United Nations Truce Supervisory Organization observer unit for Lebanon, was a spy and would be tried for his activities.
- The pro-Iranian radical Shia Hizballah also was probably behind the kidnapping of a West German/Lebanese dual national and the brief detentions of two Swedish journalists. Most Hizballah kidnappings have been intended to force the release of Hizballah operatives imprisoned abroad—primarily the 15 remaining terrorists held in Kuwait and Muhammad Hammadi who was on trial in West Germany.
- Radical Palestinians probably were involved in the seizure in Lebanon of a Norwegian and a Swede employed by the United Nations Relief Works Agency, a Belgian doctor working for a Norwegian aid organization, and a Swiss Red Cross official. PLO officials have publicly accused the ANO of conducting several of these kidnappings, which may have been intended to embarrass PLO Chairman Yasser Arafat and/or obtain ransom for the hostages.

Several foreign hostages were freed during the year—in some cases amid allegations of concessions or ransom paid to the kidnappers. They included the following:

- Three French hostages—diplomats Marcel Carton and Marcel Fontaine and journalist Jean-Paul Kauffman—were released on 4 May; the release occurred in the context of press reports that claimed Paris agreed to restore diplomatic relations with Tehran and to repay the balance on an Iranian loan made under the Shah.
- Syrian pressure on Hizballah may have led to the release on 3 March of West German/Lebanese dual national Ralph Schray, who had been kidnapped in January; the remaining West German hostage, Rudolf Cordes, was freed on 12 September with assistance from Iran.
- The kidnappers of Beirut University College Professor Mithileshwar Singh, an Indian citizen with US resident alien status, in a statement accompanying his release on 3 October, claimed they were freeing him as a goodwill gesture toward the United States.
- The ANO on 29 December freed two young girls it had held since capturing the French private boat Silco in the eastern Mediterranean in November 1987; the girls' mother, her newborn child, and six other French and Belgian nationals who were on the yacht continue to be held.

At yearend, the list of foreign hostages remaining in Lebanon included nine Americans—among them journalist Terry Anderson and American University of Beirut Dean Thomas Sutherland, currently in their fourth year of captivity.

In addition to its kidnappings, Hizballah terrorists, possibly from the group led by Imad Mughniyah, mounted their most ambitious hijacking to date: the takeover, possibly with Iranian assistance or at least its acquiescence, of Kuwait Airways Flight 422 on 5 April. As with previous Hizballah hijackings, the group demanded freedom for 17 Iraqi Da'wa members imprisoned in Kuwait for a series of bombings there in 1983, one of whom is Mughniyah's brother-in-law. During the 16-day ordeal—the longest lasting hijacking to date—the aircraft, which was seized out of Bangkok, Thailand, flew to Mashhad, Iran. It landed at Larnaca, Cyprus, after local officials blocked the runway at Beirut International Airport, and terminated in Algiers, Algeria. The hijackers killed two Kuwaiti hostages—the first time the group had singled out Muslims for execution—during the four days spent in Larnaca, and threatened the lives of three Kuwaiti Royal Family members on board throughout the ordeal. Kuwait refused to release any of the Da'wa 17; the incident ended on 20 April after Algiers agreed to provide safe passage to the hijackers.

Saudi Arabia

The number of attacks in and against Saudi Arabia doubled in 1988 over 1987. The rise in anti-Saudi attacks probably was a result of resentment by Iran and its sympathizers over Riyadh's imposition of restrictions on Iranian attendance at the annual Muslim pilgrimage after the Iranian-staged riots in the 1987 Hajj. Several Saudi Shias were tried and executed in September for their role in the bombings of Saudi oil facilities during the spring. Saudi interests—primarily offices of the national airline, Saudia—in Africa, Europe, Asia and the Middle East fell victim to the attacks overseas; by yearend there had been 22 such incidents. Although most of these attacks consisted of low-level bombings that caused no casualties, assassins also attempted to kill three Saudi teachers in Nigeria in March, murdered a Saudi diplomat in October in Turkey, and attempted to kill another Saudi diplomat in Karachi, Pakistan, in December. A group calling itself the Hizballah of the Hijaz—possibly composed of Saudi Shias—took credit for the assassination of the diplomat in Turkey, claiming revenge for the execution of the Saudi Shias on 30 September. A group calling itself Soldiers of the Night claimed responsibility for the attack in Karachi and accused the victim of working for the United States and Israel.

Saudi Arabia has continued a strong emphasis on upgrading its counterterrorism capabilities. Western governments including the United States provided training to the newly created special counterterrorism unit of the Saudi Special Forces, and the United States provided some training on hostage situations. Industrial security was considerably tightened following the bombings in March and April at two petroleum facilities at Ra's Tannurah and Al Jubayl in the Eastern Province. The Ulema, the nation's highest judicial authority, issued a religious decree in August declaring sabotage, to include hijacking and airplane bombing, as a major crime punishable by death.

The Saudi Government moved quickly against the three men suspected in the oilfield bombings. They were arrested in August after a gun battle in which a police officer was killed. The three, plus an accomplice, were charged with terrorism, sabotage, and conspiring with Iran; two were also charged with murder. The four were tried in closed session and sentenced to death in September. Despite threats from Hizballah of the Hijaz, they were executed after their sentences were reviewed by the King.

Tunisia

In what has been condemned by the US Government as an act of political assassination, Abu Jihad, the PLO military chief, was gunned down at his home in Tunis on 16 April, along with two Palestinian bodyguards and a Tunisian gardener. Tunisia brought a resolution before the UN Security Council condemning the killing of Abu Jihad as aggression against the country. Israel, which neither confirmed nor denied the allegation, was widely alleged to have been responsible for the Abu Jihad assassination.

Members of Force 17, the security arm of the Tunis-headquartered PLO, reportedly reside in Tunis. Although its principal responsibility is providing security for PLO leaders, Force 17 is known to have engaged in terrorist attacks, primarily in Israel and the occupied territories.

Tunisian authorities arrested an Italian terrorist leader in July and turned him over to Italian authorities.

Latin America Overview

There were 146 international terrorist attacks in Latin America during 1988, up from 108 in 1987. This increase was primarily because of a sharp rise in the number of terrorist attacks in Colombia—up from 19 in 1987 to 88 in 1988. The majority of these were bombings directed against segments of Colombia's oil pipeline system in which multinational oil companies participate as joint-venture partners. Peru and El Salvador were second and third, with Peru's total dropping from 41 international incidents in 1987 to 15 in 1988. International terrorist attacks in El Salvador increased from just two in 1987 to 13 in 1988. Chile, traditionally third among Latin American countries in the number of international terrorist attacks, dropped to fourth place with nine such attacks, down from 15 in 1987. Despite decreases in the number of international terrorist incidents in Chile and Peru, domestic terrorism continued at a high rate in both countries. Bolivia also experienced an increase in international terrorist incidents last year. Attacks there increased from three in 1987 to six in 1988, including the attempted bombing of Secretary of State Shultz's motorcade in August.

Of the 146 international terrorist attacks in Latin America during 1988, 73 percent, 110 of 146, of the incidents involved US personnel or facilities. During 1987, 66 percent—71 of the 108 attacks on international targets—involved US personnel or facilities. Nearly all international as well as domestic terrorist actions in Latin America were carried out by indigenous guerrilla or radical movements. In one terrorist incident, however, a group calling itself the Palestine Command detonated an explosive device against a Jewish target in Bolivia. Origins of this group remain unclear.

Bolivia

International terrorist incidents in Bolivia increased in 1988 to six, up from three in 1987. Among the attacks was the attempted bombing of US Secretary of State Shultz's motorcade, as it traveled from the airport outside of La Paz into the capital city on 8 August. Two groups claimed responsibility for the attempted bombing—the Simon Bolivar Guerrilla Commando and the Pablo Zarate Wilca National Indigenous Force. The attack on Secretary Shultz's motorcade was the second claimed by the Simon Bolivar Guerrilla Commando against a US target; in 1987, it claimed responsibility for the bombing of Citibank in downtown La Paz. Police investigators have developed few leads in the attack on the motorcade or the bombing of the US Embassy's commissary that took place on the same day but believe that the attacks probably were the work of the Simon Bolivar Guerrilla Commando.

In December, the assassination of a Peruvian naval attaché in La Paz raised new speculation that the activities of Peru's Sendero Luminoso (SL) might be spilling over into neighboring Bolivia. Although an unknown group claimed responsibility for the attack, wording of the claim note and the victim's reputation as a counter-insurgency expert suggest that, at the least, a group sympathetic to SL—if not SL itself—carried out the action.

Chile

In Chile, nine international terrorist incidents occurred in 1988—down from 15 the previous year. Although most of these actions remain unclaimed, they were probably conducted by members of the Manuel Rodriguez Patriotic Front (FPMR), a Marxist-Leninist group with strong ties to Cuba. Despite a slowdown of both international and domestic terrorism—just before and after the October 1988 presidential plebescite—domestic terrorism increased by about one-third over 1987 figures, up from 164 to 223.

Chile's long and porous border with Argentina has made it difficult for either side to impede the flow of arms and personnel from leftist groups there. Cooperation between the two countries has improved and Argentinian authorities have captured a number of people alleged to be directly supporting terrorists in Chile. Weapons have also been smuggled into the country via Chile's vulnerable coastline.

Even through Chile and Argentina do not have a bilateral extradition treaty, the Chilean Government has requested extraditions of FFMR suspects under the broader Montevideo extradition treaty of 1933. An extradition request in November, however, was turned down by an Argentinian judge on technical grounds, and another request in December is still pending.

The Chilean Government maintains a strong and active counter-terrorism force in response to the constant threat of the foreign-supported FPMR. Investigations by the authorities, however, sometimes violate basic human rights, according to most human rights monitors. Prison terms for those convicted under the arms control and counter-terrorism laws are generally lengthy.

Virtually all of Chile's terrorism prosecutions have been against leftists, and incidents of rightwing terrorism have rarely been followed with arrests. The failure of security forces to apprehend any members of rightwing extremists groups such as the Chilean Anti-Communist Action Group and the National Combat Front leads to speculation that the actions of these groups may be unofficially sanctioned by some officials in the security forces.

The United States has a continuing interest in the Letelier murder case, in which former Chilean Ambassador and Pinochet critic Letelier and an American associate were killed by Chilean agents in a car bombing in Washington, DC, in 1976. The most recent US attempts, however, to reopen the investigation or seek compensation for the Letelier family have been rebuffed by the Chilean Government. (In January 1989, the US Government invoked a 1914 bilateral dispute settlement treaty, which provides for an international commission to investigate the case.)

Colombia

International terrorist incidents in Colombia increased sharply in 1988, up from 19 in 1987 to 88 in 1988. The National Liberation Army (ELN) was responsible for most of the international terrorist activity in Colombia—as it was in 1987. The ELN carried out about 78 attacks on international targets, including 58 bombings of the Cano Limon–Covenas pipeline—jointly owned by Colombia and a consortium of US and other Western oil companies. In 1987, only 15 attacks on internationally owned oil facilities occurred, with the ELN responsible for 14 of them. The group has made no secret of its desire to drive foreign investment out of Colombia and has caused the country hundreds of millions of dollars in lost oil revenues. Pipeline bombings slowed significantly, however, during the last six months of 1988.

Other types of international terrorist activities in Colombia—aside from the pipeline bombings—also increased, from four in 1987 to 30 in 1988. The ELN increased its kidnappings from one in 1987 to about 14 in 1988, including a US businessman who was held for four months. ELN urban terrorism also expanded, with several bombing attacks on foreign interests. In late September, the group attempted to assassinate a US oil company executive by blowing up his car near his home in Bogotá. The 19th of April Movement (M-19)—another leftist guerrilla group in Colombia with ties to Cuba, Nicaragua, and Libya—carried out nine attacks on international targets. Many of its actions appear to have been carried out to show solidarity with causes beyond the borders of Colombia. In late March, the group fired a rocket at the US Embassy in Bogotá to protest US troop maneuvers in Central America. In mid-April, coincidentally about the second anniversary of the US air strikes in Libya, the group bombed the Colombian-US Bi-national Center in Medellin. Although there exists no evidence of direct Libyan involvement in this attack, the fact that M-19 has received training and money from Libya leads us to suspect a Libyan link. The M-19, which has also received training and other support from Cuba, carried out attacks during the same time frame on three US commercial targets, a British company, and a French bank. Tripoli in the past has encouraged its clients to attack British and French targets. At a minimum, we consider it likely that even in the absence of direct Libyan encouragement, these attacks were carried out to curry Libya's favor and support.

Colombia is a democratic country whose institutions are also threatened from attacks by narcotraffickers. Narcotics-connected violence is frequently designed to intimidate government officials and institutions to ensure the unhindered pursuit of the narcotics trade. The narcotraffickers have been successful in making prosecution or extradition of major narcotics traffickers too dangerous for most officials. Several judges and officials who took forceful action against narcotraffickers have been forced to leave the country. Although the insurgent violence is primarily domestic in character and is increasingly directed at economic targets, it does spill over into neighboring Venezuela, where kidnapping and extortion schemes are carried out.

The government enacted sweeping counter-terrorist decrees and issued state-of-siege decrees in January 1988 in response to the narcotics traffickers' killing of Attorney General Carlos Mauro Hoyos. The decrees expanded the definition of terrorism, enhanced the arrest, search, and confiscation powers of the police, and provided strict rules for the use of habeas corpus. The Supreme Court, however, subsequently overturned those powers that allowed the police and military to make arrests and searches without warrants based upon suspicion, and required registration of property and inhabitants in areas deemed to be used by terrorists.

In late November, the Colombian President issued modifications to the January decrees in response to the growing terrorist activity, including the assassination attempt on the Defense Minister. The decrees, which will be reviewed by the Supreme Court, mandate automatic life sentences for members of illegal armed groups found guilty of murder, prohibit bail for those suspected of terrorist crimes, and provide for immediate suspension of sentences for those who turn state's evidence. In addition, juries will be eliminated in all terrorist murder trials.

El Salvador

In El Salvador, a sharp increase in urban terrorism—particularly in the last half of 1988—pushed up the number of international terrorist incidents from two in 1987 to 13 in 1988. In declarations made in late 1988, elements of the Farabundo Marti National Liberation Front (FMLN) stated their intention to increase terrorism—both domestic and international—in the capital. The guerrillas warned on several occasions that US personnel would also be targeted. Among the international terrorist actions were a number of gunfire attacks on US Embassy vehicles, rocket attacks on both USAID offices and the Sheraton Hotel, and the kidnapping of a local employee of a USAID-funded private volunteer organization. The hotel attack occurred just before the arrival of representatives of the Organization of American States who were meeting at the hotel in San Salvador for the organization's 18th General Assembly. The increasing urban terrorism creates a high threat to Americans. In February, the clandestine FMLN radio station "Radio Venceremos" announced openly from Nicaragua the "legitimate targeting for assassination" of US military and civilian employees.

Along with demonstrating an ability to carry out large-scale military attacks, the FMLN turned increasingly to terrorism and economic sabotage to undermine the legitimately elected government of El Salvador.

In 1988, Salvadoran security forces organized a Joint Intelligence Operations Center (COCI), whose mission is to collect, integrate, and analyze intelligence relating to terrorist activities in metropolitan San Salvador and the surrounding area. The work of the COCI has led to more raids on safehouses, the capture of more than 40 terrorists and collaborators, and the seizure of hundreds of FMLN documents.

The Salvadoran judicial system in 1988 remained plagued by antiquated laws, untrained or incompetent personnel, corruption, and intimidation. As a result, some FMLN suspects turned over to the courts by the police were released without being tried, and many killings remained uninvestigated. Judges often avoided controversial cases because of corruption or intimidation. The police seldom presented evidence other than the accused's confessions obtained during detention. The number of unexplained murders, many similar to the rightwing "death squad" terrorist killings of the early 1980s, also rose in 1988, and few have received judicial scrutiny.

The legislative assembly failed to renew the State of Exception, which had expired in early 1987, although a proposal for renewal had been pending for some time. It was the State of Exception which had brought into effect the provisions of the special counterterrorism law, without which terrorism cases are prosecuted under normal criminal provisions of the penal codes, which are inadequate. Changes to these codes, proposed over a year ago to improve the handling of cases involving violent crime, have not been enacted.

The Salvadoran President's decision in April denying amnesty to the three FMLN suspects in the 1985 murder of four off-duty US Marine guards remained under appeal to the Supreme Court at yearend. (The 1987 amnesty, designed to promote national unity, was broadly worded in its provisions and led to the release of suspected FMLN members convicted of or pending prosecution for terrorist crimes, as well as convicted death-squad members.)

Honduras

A number of leftist guerrilla groups—most trained, armed, and logistically supported by Cuba and Nicaragua's Sandinista regime, and assisted by guerrilla insurgents in El Salvador—were active in Honduras in 1988. There was a perceptible increase in terrorist incidents over the previous year. Salvadoran guerrillas continued to use several refugee camps in Honduras for logistic support and recruitment. These guerrillas were responsible for the politically motivated killings of two Honduran farmers suspected of reporting on their movements to the military.

An investigation has failed to yield the identities of those responsible for a machinegun and grenade attack in July against off-duty US military personnel in which five were injured outside a discotheque. The incident was claimed by the leftwing Popular Liberation Movement-Cinchoneros. Fourteen individuals suspected of having participated in planning the April attack on the US Embassy and burning of the consulate building in Tegucigalpa were subsequently released provisionally from prison at the President's request. The investigation continues into the December bombing of the US Peace Corps headquarters, which has been claimed by a group calling itself the Patriotic Morazanista Liberation Front—the same group that claimed responsibility for the October killing of an American businessman and longtime resident in Honduras. Origins of this group remain unclear.

Several Hondurans believed to have been engaged in terrorist activities received asylum in Mexico. The Honduran Armed Forces carried out special counter-terrorist sweeps in areas of known subversive activity and monitored the activities of radical organizations. The Armed Forces, which have received training under the US counter-terrorism assistance program, set up a special counter-terrorist corps. Honduras also maintains a system of border inspections intended to interdict the transfer of arms and other logistics to regional terrorist and insurgent organizations.

Mexico

The US Government strongly criticized Mexico's decision in 1988 to release Puerto Rican terrorist William Guillermo Morales—jailed for killing a policeman—and deport him to Cuba. In deporting Morales, Mexico rejected a US extradition request, despite the fact that a Mexican court had earlier found Morales extraditable. Morales, a convicted Puerto Rican terrorist, had escaped a prison hospital in 1979 while serving a sentence of more than 100 years on explosive and weapons charges and was implicated in over 50 bombings by a Puerto Rican separatist group in the late 1970s. In its rejection, the Mexican Government stated that the US request charged Morales solely with possession of arms and explosives and not with terrorist activities.

In responding to Mexico's action, Washington recalled its Ambassador from Mexico City, after which a dialogue at the presidential level was initiated. The United States also expressed anger over the initial Mexican characterization of Morales as a "political fighter." A senior Mexican official later stated that Mexico did not condone the use of violence for political ends, nor did it endorse the notion that Morales was a "political fighter."

Despite Mexico's official policy of nonintervention in the affairs of other nations, the Salvadoran insurgent FMLN and Revolutionary Democratic Front are permitted to maintain offices in Mexico City.

Panama

Panama's geographical position and role as a trade and banking center makes it a crossroads for the travel and transactions of various terrorist and insurgent groups. Some of this activity is facilitated by the Cuban and Nicaraguan Embassies and the Libyan people's Bureau in Panama City. This activity is transient in nature, not involving direct participation by the Panamanian Government.

Congressional testimony and published accounts, however, implicate some Panamanian officials, including General Noriega, in the shipment of arms to such groups as El Salvador's FMLN and Colombia's M-19. The existence of a prior relationship between Noriega and M-19 was, in part, confirmed in July when M-19 asked Noriega to intercede with the Colombian Government regarding the kidnapping of the Conservative Party's president, Alvaro Gomez Hurtado, whom M-19 held hostage.

Panama in 1988 made concerted efforts, both in private and in public, to improve relations with Libya. It has also taken some small steps toward establishing trading relations with North Korea, and it has also reequipped its army using Cuban help.

Peru

In Peru, the number of international terrorist incidents fell for the second year in a row. During 1988, there were 15 international terrorist actions, down from 41 in 1987. Attacks on US interests were also down, from 23 in 1987 to five in 1988. The sharp decline in international terrorist actions is partly because of arrests of SL cell members in Lima. In some cases, these arrests appear to have disrupted planned operations against international targets. Attacks by members of the Marxist-Leninist Tupac Amaru Revolutionary Movement (MRTA)—primarily a Lima-based organization—also were down, particularly in the last six months of 1988. Although the reasons for the decline in MRTA attacks on international targets remain unclear, it is possible that the SL arrests caused the MRTA to be more cautious. The decline in international terrorism does not, however, reflect the true level of terrorist violence in Peru. Domestic terrorism continued to rise—with nearly 2,000 persons killed in 1988, according to Peruvian defense ministry statistics, more than twice as many as in 1987—because of increased SL actions against domestic targets, particularly in rural areas. In addition, a potentially dangerous terrorist situation was averted when police uncovered an ANO cell in Lima.

The major terrorist organizations operating in Peru, with the exception of the rightwing Rodrigo Franco Command, have suffered important losses through arrest by Peruvian security forces. The arrest and conviction of Osman Morote, reputedly the number-two SL leader, was among the more notable cases in 1988. While these arrests crippled the group's urban activities, its actions in rural Peru increased significantly during the same period. Three of the group's seven attacks on international targets took place in rural Peru, resulting in the deaths of one American and two Frenchmen. In June, SL guerrillas ambushed and killed an American working as a USAID contract employee on an agricultural project. In December, two French engineers working on a rural assistance project, were publicly executed by SL guerrillas, along with two Peruvians, and there was also an attack on a development project run by the European Economic Community.

The smaller, Cuban-linked MRTA, a group that had focused primarily on attacks against foreign interests, continued to pose a threat. During the first half of 1988, in addition to attacks on several foreign—including US—firms and attacks on two US-Peruvian Bi-National Centers, the group fired three mortar rounds at the residence of the US Ambassador in Lima.

In July, police arrested three suspected members of the ANO in Lima. The three were in possession of documents describing the US and Israeli Embassies and other national and international organizations, indicating that the ANO members may have been planning to target them for terrorist attacks. The ANO members remain under detention in Lima.

In the Peruvian criminal court system, terrorist prosecutions remain the single largest docket item, accounting for nearly 60 percent of all cases brought to trial. Of those, only 20 percent of the defendants are convicted, because of the lack of investigative capacity on the part of the police prosecutors, inadequate or contradictory counter-terrorist statutes, and conflicting jurisdictions over terrorist cases between various government ministries.

In November, however, the Peruvian legislature approved amendments to the existing counter-terrorism statutes. The new bill defines additional criminal acts not prosecutable under the old statutes, including criminal liability for "supporting, approving, or praising terrorist acts." The legislation also lengthened minimum prison terms for most terrorist convictions.

A state of emergency exists in 43 of the country's 181 provinces, where the military has the primary anti-subversive responsibility. In all other areas, including the cities of Lima and Callao, which are also under declared states of emergency, the civilian police have exclusive counter-terrorist enforcement responsibilities.

Venezuela

The police investigation of an April grenade attack on the US Embassy did not lead to legal action. In February, Venezuelan Government authorities clandestinely placed Cuban exile and alleged aircraft-bomber Orlando Bosch on a US-bound plane. Bosch, who has been accused of blowing up a Cuban aircraft in 1976 but was exonerated of the charge by a Venezuelan tribunal after having been held in jail for 11 years, was placed in detention following arrival in the United States and faces possible US deportation proceedings.

During the summer, American citizen and suspected Palestinian terrorist Mahmud Ahmed Atta challenged in a New York court his May 1987 extradition from Venezuela as illegal. (In early 1989, a US Court decided to accede to an Israeli extradition request that he stand trial there for a 1986 machinegun and firebomb attack on a bus in which one person died and three were wounded.)

Venezuela established a special security force along the border with Colombia in 1988 to deal with border attacks and kidnappings of Venezuelan ranchers by suspected Colombian guerrillas. The kidnappings have diminished since the unit's formation and in an incident in June, the force killed three members of the Colombian guerrilla alliance, Simon Bolivar Coordinator.

Europe and North America Overview

In Western Europe, domestic and Middle Eastern groups staged 150 international terrorist attacks in 1988, a slight decrease from 152 in 1987. Western Europe ranked third in the number of attacks worldwide, with 17 percent occurring there. Of these, 18 were against US targets, resulting in 191 deaths and 11 injured, compared to no deaths and 38 wounded in 1987. Pan Am Flight 103 accounted for 189 of the fatalities to US citizens. Thirty of the international incidents resulted from Middle Eastern spillover, 81 were conducted by indigenous groups, and 39 attacks could not be attributed to a specific group. Indigenous groups operating against domestic targets accounted for most of the terrorist attacks, indicating they remain a major problem despite their generally less spectacular nature.

Continued counter-terrorism efforts throughout the region and a sharp decline in Middle Eastern spillover—a result of caution by state sponsors and the apparent decision by some Palestinian groups to focus operations in the Middle East—contributed to another year of little change in the number of incidents in Western Europe. Authorities in Italy, Spain, and France cooperated in several notable successes against indigenous groups, including the arrests of numerous members of groups like ETA and the BR; West German authorities broke up a major network of the PFLP-GC. Attacks associated with the spillover of Middle Eastern violence declined by approximately 30 percent in Western Europe in 1988. In contrast, Greece experienced an increase in terrorist activity in 1988.

Austria

In January 1988, Mahamed Salim Elhag was convicted of the assassination attempt in May 1987 that wounded a former Libyan Ambassador to Austria, who had become an opponent of Libyan ruler Qadhafi. Elhag received a 10-year sentence for the attempt. Although the assassin had been supported by the Libyan People's Bureau in Vienna and had sought refuge there, the Austrian Government took no action to limit or close the bureau after its involvement became known.

Belgium

The number of international terrorist incidents in Belgium increased from two in 1987 to four in 1988, but no Belgian interests were attacked. Northern Irish terrorists brought their violence to Belgium in August when they killed a British soldier. Unidentified terrorists attacked the ANC office in Brussels twice in 1988, firing shots into the office and placing a bomb outside the building housing the office. In February, several supporters of the French terrorists on trial in Paris briefly occupied the French Press Agency office in Brussels.

Belgium undertook several significant counter-terrorism measures during 1988. In January, it negotiated a Mutual Legal Assistance Treaty with the United States that provides more expeditious cooperation in areas such as sharing legal and police information, locating suspects and witnesses, confiscating illegal gains, and serving warrants. Awaiting ratification, this treaty, which further reinforces cooperation between the United States and Belgium, follows other bilateral agreements, such as the 1986 treaty dealing with terrorism, and the 1987 extradition treaty.

Belgium has also continued efforts to reach agreement concerning standardized policies on visa controls, information sharing, and extradition matters with neighboring France, the Netherlands, Luxembourg, and West Germany. It has also agreed in principle with the International Civil Aviation Organization (ICAO) Council's June 1988 statement that hijacked aircraft, once on the ground, should not be allowed to refuel and take off again for another destination.

In September, four members of the indigenous Euroterrorist group Communist Combatant Cells (CCC) and two members of the Revolutionary Front for Proletarian Action (FRAP), an offshoot of CCC, were tried for various terrorist crimes, including attacks on NATO and US military facilities. The two FRAP members received five-year sentences, and the CCC members were sentenced to life imprisonment.

Belgian authorities began developing a response to the presence of Northern Irish terrorists. Following the fatal attacks by suspected PIRA sympathizers on British soldiers in Belgium and West Germany, Belgian authorities sent forensic experts to West Germany to help in the investigation of the two suspects who had been arrested for the attacks. Belgian police in June arrested suspected PIRA member Patrick Ryan in Brussels for possession of false documents and possible involvement in terrorist activities. The Belgian Government denied a British request for extradition, stating that the British conspiracy charges were excessively vague and did not correspond to statutory offenses under Belgian law. Belgian authorities transported Ryan by military transport to Ireland, a decision that was publicly criticized by the United Kingdom.

Canada

Although not the victim of terrorist activities in 1988, Canada sought to strengthen and apply the rule of law in dealing with terrorism through its national and international cooperative efforts. In January, Canada and the United States signed a Joint Declaration on Counter-terrorism, which created a bilateral consultative group for cooperation. This group exchanges information on terrorism, coordinates counter-terrorism exercises and measures for managing transborder incidents, examines areas for joint counter-terrorism research and development, and cooperates on counter-terrorism programs for third countries.

As 1988 chair of the Summit Seven Terrorism Experts meetings, Canada contributed to the further study of developments and trends in international terrorism and pushed for more progress in the area of civil aviation security. It joined with the United States in issuing the US/Canadian No-Takeoff Declaration in November, which established guidelines for dealing with hijacked airplanes. Canada cooperated with other countries in developing counter-terrorism measures for the Calgary Winter Olympics in February and for the Toronto economic summit in June.

Canada sought the extradition from the United Kingdom of a former Sikh resident of British Columbia who is accused of planting a bomb in June 1985 on an airliner departing from Canada, which killed two baggage handlers in Tokyo's Narita Airport. (The extradition request was approved in early 1989 by a British court, although it is under appeal.)

Seventeen-year-old Sikh terrorist Harkirat Singh Bagga was convicted and sentenced to 14 years' imprisonment for attempting to murder the Canadian Sikh publisher of a Canada-based Punjabi language newspaper.

A decision by Canadian immigration authorities to deport a previously convicted Palestinian terrorist from Canada is also under appeal. The terrorist, Mahmoud Mohammed Issa Mohammed, had concealed on his Canadian immigration application a conviction in Greece for participation in a 1968 attack on an El Al aircraft at Athens airport in which one person died.

Cyprus

Spillover of terrorism from the Middle East accounted for four of the five international incidents in Cyprus in 1988. Most of the attacks were directed against Palestinians. In February three PLO officials were killed when a bomb exploded in their car, and a ship slated to carry Palestinian deportees to Israel was bombed at its dock in Limassol. Four other Palestinians were killed by a car bomb in Larnaca in September. The ANO is suspected in an attempt to bomb the Israeli Embassy on the island in May, but the bomb exploded away from the Embassy, killing one of the terrorists and two Cypriots. In May, Cyprus was caught up in the hijacking of Kuwait Airways Flight 422 when it landed at Larnaca airport.

There were two successful prosecutions of international terrorists in Cypriot courts. In January two of three suspects in the April 1987 Libyan-supported attack on a British warrant officer and his companion near Limassol were convicted and sentenced to seven and nine years, respectively. In July suspected ANO terrorists Omar Hawillo was convicted and sentenced to 15 years in prison for his role in the explosion near the Israeli Embassy in Nicosia.

To find a way to prevent terrorists from coming to Cyprus, the government has been reviewing its visa and immigrations policies. Even so, Palestinian terrorist groups continue to have a presence on Cyprus and regularly transit the island to other destinations, particularly Eastern Europe.

During the Kuwait Airways hijacking incident in April, Cypriot authorities permitted the hijackers to refuel the airplane and leave after five days at Larnaca airport, during which time two hostages were killed. The US Government expressed its belief that the plane should have been kept in Cyprus and regretted the decision to allow it to leave as it probably prolonged the incident.

France

France experienced a slight increase in international terrorist attacks in 1988 over 1987, 15 compared with 11. Unlike previous years, however, no attacks were directed against US interests. Violence connected to various ethnic conflicts involving Kurdish radicals and opponents of North African immigration accounted for many of the recorded attacks. With the apparent demise of the Action Directe (AD) terrorist group and weakening of French Basque separatists, the Corsican National Liberation Front (FLNC) has become the most active French terrorist organization.

Kurdish radicals were involved in four of the international incidents in 1988. On 4 January, a West German consular employee was found shot to death in Paris. Although police found a leaflet in his coat pocket signed by the National Front for the Liberation of Kurdistan, the group denied responsibility for the murder and there were reports that his murder was a criminal, not a terrorist, attack.

France also experienced a spillover of violence from South Africa during the year. In March, the African National Congress (ANC) representative for France, Switzerland, and Luxembourg was murdered in her Paris office by an unidentified assailant. There was widespread press speculation that South Africa was behind her killing. The following day suspected terrorists from the ANC fired shotguns at the South African Consulate in Marseille. The ANC did not claim responsibility for the attack; graffiti found at the scene implied that the attack was in retaliation for the ANC representative's murder. Despite an active investigation, no arrests have been made.

Since the arrests of key AD members in 1987 and of all of the known members of the French Basque group Iparretarrak in 1988, operations by French terrorists have reflected more local concerns. Businesses owned by North Africans and hotels used by North African workers in France were the targets of several attacks that indicated a growing discontent with the large number of immigrants from the region. A beer distributor in Toulon, a restaurant in Cannes, and hostels for immigrant workers in Cannes and Nice were bombed. A Romanian citizen was killed and 12 other persons were injured by the bombing in Nice in December. Corsican separatists shifted to the use of more sophisticated and lethal tactics in 1988 in their pursuit for independence from France. In addition to low-level bombings of businesses, government buildings, and non-Corsican French police, the FLNC carried out six attacks against Corsican policemen, wounding five in a single attack with a remotely controlled bomb. The group also expanded its operations to French soil, setting off 10 bombs in Marseille during March and April. The leftist anarchist group Black War claimed four attacks in 1988, including the bombing of the offices of the Paris court bailiff association, which seriously injured two persons. The group has carried out attacks on French businesses, offices of rightwing French groups, and a civilian association that fights terrorism.

Both the center-right Chirac government and the successor Socialist Rocard government have continued the general thrust of a strong counter-terrorism policy established in 1987, and French police scored a number of successes during 1988. Early in the year, police in Corsica arrested Jean-Andre Orsoni, who is believed to be one of the top leaders of the FLNC. The FLNC itself declared a four-month truce in April and indefinitely extended it in October. In February the police arrested Phillipe Bidart, the leader of Iparretarrak, in addition to several other of its members, but others may be hiding in Spain. Authorities have also cracked down on the more powerful and lethal Spanish Basque Fatherland and Liberty Organization (ETA), arresting in February approximately 12 individuals accused of participating in ETA's logistic support network in southern France. A Paris court on 10 December convicted them of criminal conspiracy to aid and abet the activities of ETA.

Although AD was largely dismantled in 1987, French authorities apprehended several of the group's supporters in November. In September the police arrested an alleged member of the Italian Red Brigades (BR), Giovanni Alimonti, accused of murdering Italian senator Alberto Rufilli in 1987. Alimonti is awaiting extradition to Italy.

France continues working with other European countries to counter terrorism. French and Spanish border police coordinate efforts to thwart Basque ETA terrorists from using France as a safe-haven, and French security authorities exchange information with their Belgian, West German, Spanish, and British counterparts, among others. France has also hosted a seminar for the chiefs of hostage rescue and special action teams.

The Rocard government, which came to power in May, retained the counter-terrorism judicial structure of the previous Chirac government. These reforms centralized in a specialized section of the Paris Prosecutor's Office the investigation and prosecution of terrorist crimes, replaced jurors with a panel of professional magistrates for terrorism cases, and increased the amount of time terrorist suspects could be held incommunicado.

The conviction in October in absentia of Colonel Hawari —the head of the terrorist Special Operations Group of Yasser Arafat's Fatah—was a major international terrorist prosecution in France during 1988. Hawari was sentenced to 10 years' imprisonment for criminal association and for complicity in transporting arms, ammunition, and explosives. Two other Hawari operatives, including one also sentenced in absentia, were given prison terms. In other trials, a French court in February convicted 19 operatives of AD for criminal association.

The Rocard government altered the handling of ETA suspects who, under the former government, would have been expelled to Spain under an emergency expulsion mechanism, which has been little used before 1986. These expulsions, which numbered nearly 200 over the previous two years, were halted in favor of employing regular judicial procedures to expel or extradite suspected ETA sympathizers to Spain. To demonstrate that it will not tolerate ETA activities emanating from France, authorities have revoked the political refugee status previously held by several ETA suspects, including longtime ETA leader Santi Potros.

The release in early 1988 of three French hostages held in Lebanon had been preceded by the release from a French jail of Mohammed Muhadjer, a Lebanese Hizballah member suspected of participating in the wave of Hizballah-organized bombings in Paris in 1986. Speculation increased that the

Chirac government had arranged a "deal" with Iran on the hostages when France resumed diplomatic relations with Iran and repaid a portion of a large loan that had been in contention for a number of years. The French Government denied any deal had been made. The US Government publicly stated it would be sensitive to any action seen as rewarding the taking of hostages. In July the United States expressed concern to France that the Iranian appointed as Ambassador to Paris was believed by the US Government to have been associated with those who held US Embassy personnel hostage in Tehran during the period 1979-81.

Greece

Domestic and international terrorist organizations increased their activities in Greece, using more lethal means against a growing number of targets. US officials were particularly at hazard, and one US Embassy officer was assassinated. There were no significant counter-terrorist successes by the Greek Government. In addition, justice ministers twice overturned Greek court decisions to extradite terrorists wanted by Italy.

Domestic groups were responsible for three attacks against US personnel in 1988. In January, the Revolutionary Organization 17 November—the most lethal and anti-American of the Greek terrorist groups and the only major West European group against which there have been no successes—attempted to kill a US Drug Enforcement Administration official in Athens. On 28 June the group carried out a second attack, killing the US defense attaché, Navy Capt. William Nordeen, with a powerful car bomb as he was leaving his home for work. Since it first surfaced in 1975, 17 November has killed three US officials and 10 Greeks. No member of the group has ever been arrested in connection with any of its attacks. In August, 17 November demonstrated its sophistication and daring in a daylight raid of an Athens police station that netted it automatic weapons. The Revolutionary People's Solidarity, a lesser known organization that had last carried out an attack in 1983, exploded a black-powder bomb in an Athens discotheque in March that wounded five US soldiers, four British citizens, and five Greeks. A caller claimed the attack was intended to show solidarity with the Palestinians and Nicaraguan Sandinistas.

Domestic terrorists also targeted Greek and Turkish interests. The Revolutionary Popular Struggle (ELA) attacked an Athens police station because it alleged the officers were protecting local drug dealers. It also bombed several private and government offices to protest the EEC meetings held in Greece during December. A new group, Social Resistance, expressed disapproval of the Greek Government's handling of a major financial scandal by bombing offices of the two leading political parties. Also, in protest of the Athens visit of the Turkish Prime Minister, 17 November attacked Turkish interests in 1988 for the first time. On 23 May its bombs destroyed two Turkish diplomatic cars, while bombs under two other cars failed to detonate.

Transnational groups were responsible for six of the nine international incidents in Greece during the year, including one of the "spectacular" terrorist attacks carried out by Middle Eastern terrorists in 1988. On 11 July an undetermined number of terrorists, believed to be ANO members, began firing at passengers and throwing grenades that started fires on The City of Poros day-excursion ship as it was sailing toward its port near Athens. The attack left nine persons from several West European countries dead and nearly 100 wounded, none American. Earlier that day, at the ship's pier, a bomb exploded prematurely in a parked car, killing the two occupants, who were apparently connected to the ship attack. No group claimed responsibility for the attack, but the subsequent investigation pointed to the ANO as the attacker. Libya has been linked to the 11 July incidents. For example, a submachinegun recovered from the ship and another from the bomb-damaged car, were purchased by Libya in 1976. According to Greek officials, a known ANO member linked to the attacks used a Libyan passport to enter Greece.

While the Greek Government has issued statements condemning terrorism, it refused in February to extradite an Italian BR terrorist, and, in December, also refused Italy's extradition request for an ANO member held in Greece in connection with a 1982 attack on a Jewish synagogue in Rome. According to press reports, the ANO terrorist was flown out of the country to Libya. This action by Greece could encourage the ANO to press Greece and other governments to release other jailed ANO prisoners. In both of these extradition cases, the then justice minister cited the supposedly "political" character of the crimes as the basis for overruling the courts. Following the al-Zomar release, the US Secretary of State expressed his sense of disappointment and outrage over the decision. In carrying out the attack on The City of Poros, the ANO may have been attempting to pressure Greece to release three ANO members in Greek jails. In December a Greek court released two suspected members of ELA, who had been detained during an investigation of a terrorist killed in a shootout with Greek police in 1987. Greece remained reluctant to criticize directly other nations that are responsible for terrorist acts.

The government has reportedly increased the resources and priority it assigns to combating terrorism, and Greek ship owners have been in the forefront internationally in proposing and implementing improved security measures on passenger vessels. However, in 1988 there was only one arrest and conviction of a suspected terrorist—that of an Arab with West German citizenship who was found with explosives secreted in his car on an Israeli-bound ferry, and he was sentenced to three years in prison—the detention of another, and no extraditions.

In May 1988 the Greek Government detained terrorist Mohammed Rashid, a member of the PLO's Hawari Group, wanted in the United States for the 1982 bombing of a Pan American airliner over the Pacific in which a Japanese youth was killed. (Rashid was at the time a member of the anti-PLO 15 May group.) In October an Athens court found Rashid extraditable. At yearend, the case was on appeal before the Greek Supreme Court, with the final decision ultimately rest-ing with the Greek Minister of Justice. The United States considers the Rashid extradition case to be a significant bilateral issue and an important indication of Greece's commitment in fighting terrorism.

During the second half of 1988, Greece chaired the activities of the Trevi Group, a coordinating body of law enforcement officials of the European Community, and hosted its semiannual ministerial meeting in Rhodes in December. This meeting, which focused on counter-terrorism coordination, was clouded by the al-Zomar release on the eve of the meeting and by a series of bombings by Greek terrorist groups to protest the European Community's Rhodes Summit.

Ireland

Although Irish courts dismissed a few British extradition requests for suspected PIRA members on legal technicalities, a number of convicted PIRA terrorists have been extradited to the United Kingdom. British Prime Minister Margaret Thatcher in late November criticized both the Irish and Belgian Governments for failing to extradite to Britain suspected PIRA member Patrick Ryan, whom London was attempting to extradite for conspiracy to murder because of his alleged involvement in various bombing plots. In December, Dublin rejected the British extradition request but retains the option to prosecute Ryan in Ireland. A Dublin court in April sentenced members of the O'Hare kidnap gang to prison terms of seven to 40 years. The gang, led by renegade Irish National Liberation Army figure Dessie O'Hare, had kidnapped Belfast dentist John O'Grady.

Italy

Incidents of international terrorism in Italy declined from six in 1987 to three in 1988, fewer even than in 1986, which had four. The most significant of the attacks was directed against the USO club in Naples on 14 April. A car bomb exploded outside the club, killing a US Navy enlisted woman and four Italian citizens and wounding 14 others. The Organization of Jihad Brigades—believed to be associated with the JRA—claimed responsibility for the attack. The attack was one of several around the world that probably were intended to protest the bombing of Libya in 1986.

Italy continued to make significant inroads against its primary domestic terrorist threat, the BR. The BR struck once in 1988 before Italian authorities countered with damaging arrests of members of the Fighting Communist Party (PCC) wing of the group, part of a continuing string of successes against the BR since 1987. On 16 April the PCC murdered Christian Democratic Senator Roberto Ruffilli, a close associate of the Italian Prime Minister, in his home. An intensive investigation by the police led, in June and September, to the arrests of 20 PCC terrorists in Milan and Rome, some of whom were accused of killing Ruffilli. These arrests were among approximately 75 made of BR members throughout Europe in 1988, bringing to about 200 the arrests of Italian terrorists in the last two years. Although the arrests probably have disrupted the group's operations, a communiqué in December from one of the BR cells indicated it is rebuilding.

Italy achieved unprecedented cooperation from some other West European governments in its fight against the BR. Many of the terrorists were arrested in Spain—particularly in the Barcelona area—and France and extradited to Italy. The Greek Government, however, denied the Italian extradition request for an Italian BR terrorist, Maurizio Folini, who was subsequently released from prison following completion of his Greek sentence.

The Italian judiciary continued to maintain a firm line against terrorism in 1988. In March, the court of appeals upheld the convictions on weapons charges of two Lebanese Armed Revolutionary Faction (LARF) terrorists and sentenced them to an additional three years. Italy's highest court in May upheld the sentences of the terrorists responsible for the 1985 Achille Lauro cruise ship hijacking. An appeals court in November upheld the conviction of the sole surviving ANO terrorist involved in the 1985 Rome airport massacre and the *in absentia* conviction of Abu Nidal for organizing the attack. In December, Italian authorities, along with other governments including the United States, strongly protested the Greek decision denying the extradition of ANO terrorist Abdel Osama al-Zomar, wanted for the grenade and machinegun attack on a Rome synagogue in 1982. This attack resulted in the death of a two-year-old boy and the wounding of more than 35 others.

In other cases, an Italian court in June sentenced Muhammad Hamdan to 17 years for his role in attempting to place a bomb in front of the Syrian Embassy in London in 1984. In July a court in Bologna sentenced to life four rightwing extremists for their role in the bombing in August 1980 of Bologna's railroad station, which had killed more than 80 people. In October an Italian court sentenced 26 BR terrorists to life imprisonment for a series of killings, including that of former Prime Minister Aldo Moro in 1978. Another 128 BR members and sympathizers received prison sentences ranging from two to 30 years. At the end of the year, a trial was under way for those accused of participation in a neofascist bombing of the Naples-Milan passenger train in 1984.

Italy has actively promoted international cooperation against terrorism in many international forums, including the European Community's Trevi Group (the Community's Organization of Interiors, Public Order, and Justice Ministers), the International Maritime Organization, the World Tourism Organization, and the Economic Summit Seven. It has also sought to promote better bilateral cooperation with its neighbors and with the United States and to draw states along the North African littoral, particularly Egypt, into closer cooperation against terrorism and narcotics trafficking. To contain a domestic sectarian terrorist bombing campaign in the Alto Adige region along its northern border with Austria, Italy sought the aid of Austrian authorities, who subsequently arrested several extremists resident in the Austrian Tyrol region believed to have assisted in this terrorist activity.

Malta

There were no terrorist attacks in Malta in 1988. The trial of the surviving ANO terrorist in the 1985 Egyptair Flight 648 hijacking, Omar Mohammed Ali Rezak, was held in November. Rezak pled guilty to the hijacking and the willful homicide of one US citizen. He was sentenced to 25 years—the maximum under the law. (An appeal of the term of the sentence was pending at yearend.) The US Government publicly applauded the trial results. Malta has important commercial ties to nearby Libya and hosts a sizable Libyan population, both resident and visitors.

Netherlands

PIRA carried out two attacks against British soldiers in the Netherlands in 1988, accounting for all of the country's international incidents for the year. On 1 May gunmen killed one soldier and wounded two other soldiers outside a bar near the border with West Germany. Thirty minutes later, outside another nightclub, PIRA detonated a bomb that killed two British airmen and wounded a third. PIRA uses the Netherlands as a staging ground for many of its operations in Western Europe because it can find sanctuary/support among the large number of Irish workers living there. An attack against a NATO officers club in West Germany in 1987 was launched from the Netherlands. The Dutch Government collaborated closely with Britain and West Germany in investigating the incidents and taking measures to prevent future attacks.

The Dutch Government confronted some domestic terrorist problems during the year. It continued efforts to bring to justice members of the radical Revolutionary Anti-Racist Action Group (RARA) who had resorted to acts of violence, including bombings against commercial property, in their effort to force Dutch corporations to stop doing business with South Africa. Eight RARA suspects were arrested in April; one was later convicted while the others were released because of insufficient evidence. (The convicted RARA suspect, however, was released by an appellate court in January 1989 because of a technicality.)

Spain

Spain suffered the largest number of terrorist attacks in Western Europe again in 1988 and was fourth highest in the world, with 56 incidents compared with 47 in 1987. Five Spanish Basque and Catalan separatist groups were responsible for the largest share of the international incidents in Spain, with most directed against French business interests. Several of the groups, however, also attacked US interests.

ETA claimed responsibility for most of the international attacks in Spain. The targets and tactics utilized by the group varied; the majority of attacks were bombings and arsons of French car dealerships to protest Paris's cooperation with Spain's counter-terrorist efforts against the group. ETA probably was responsible for several incidents in which French-made vehicles were set afire.

ETA maintained its reputation for staging bold operations and causing indiscriminate casualties in its attacks on Spanish targets. It bombed the Civil Guard headquarters in Madrid, killing two persons and wounding 45 passers-by; fired rocket-propelled grenades at a Civil Guard barracks in Llodio; and murdered a retired Spanish Air Force general and several policemen.

Lesser known domestic groups also operate in Spain and carry out attacks against US interests; however, they were less active in 1988. Terra Lliure, for example, scaled back its attacks from six in 1987 to one in 1988 but has continued to target the Spanish Government and police with numerous bombings of office buildings and police barracks. Iraultza, a small anti-NATO group composed of elements from the Basque Communist movement in Spain, targeted a Ford automobile showroom in its one international attack for the year. The Asemblia Izquierda Tudelana, another leftist group opposed to US military presence in Spain, chose a US Air Force vehicle as the target for its one attack in 1988. The Catalan Red Liberation Army may have been responsible for only one attack in 1988, the bombing of the British Consulate in Barcelona. In 1987—when the group first appeared—it was responsible for four bombings, including attacks on the US Consulate and a USO club in Barcelona that killed one US citizen and wounded several Spanish nationals.

The First of October Anti-Fascist Group (GRAPO), which has occasionally attacked US targets in Spain and was seemingly dormant for a few years, appears to be resurfacing as a terrorist threat. GRAPO launched two attacks in 1988, both directed against domestic targets. It assassinated a Spanish businessman and killed one policeman and wounded another in a raid on a government office in Madrid to steal identity cards.

US interests also were the targets for several attacks in Spain during 1988, apparently by transnational groups. On 15 April, a bomb exploded and a second was discovered at a US Air Force communications facility near Humosa. No group claimed responsibility, but the timing on the second anniversary of the US air strikes against Libya in 1986 suggests the possibility of involvement by Libyan sympathizers. West German terrorists were connected to two operations apparently targeted against US citizens. In March, a bomb attached to a moped exploded on a Madrid street corner where US Air Force flight crews catch a bus to the Torrejon Airbase; however, no US citizens were injured. In June, a bomb attached to another moped exploded prematurely while being armed by three terrorists outside a discotheque in Rota that US servicemen frequent. After a short gunfight with a local policeman, the terrorists escaped but left behind evidence indicating that they were members of the West German Red Army Faction terrorist group. The Anti-Imperialist International Brigade (AIIB)—a group connected to the Japanese Red Army—continued to operate in Spain, taking responsibility for a failed attack on the US Embassy on 4 July.

Spain took several steps on the legal front against terrorism in 1988. The United States and Spain are preparing the groundwork for negotiations toward a treaty of mutual legal assistance. The Spanish Government announced in December a $380 million plan to modernize the police, including the strengthening of counter-terrorist programs.

During 1988, Spain repealed its tough counter-terrorism law following a 1987 court ruling that certain sections were unconstitutional. Most of the provisions of that law have since been incorporated into the country's ordinary penal code. The new provisions permit terrorist suspects to be held up to five days before charges are filed.

Spanish courts continued to mete out strong sentences to convicted ETA terrorists. In March, four ETA members were sentenced to 74 years each in prison on arms and explosives possession charges and for destruction of property. Also in March, an ETA militant was sentenced to 50 years for murder, attempted murder, and other offenses. The Spanish Government rejected in January and November truce offers from ETA.

The Spanish Government has held intermittent talks with ETA in Algeria over the last two years in an attempt to end the violence. These talks were terminated after ETA kidnapped a prominent businessman, and the government has stated that there will be no more contacts so long as the attacks continue. (The businessman was freed, and in January 1989 the Spanish Government resumed talks with ETA in Algeria designed to end the violence without acceding to ETA's political demands.)

Since 1987, there has been close and effective cooperation between the Spanish and French Governments in the fight against ETA. The close level of cooperation is expected to continue as the new French Government reformulates its policies regarding asylum, extradition, and other activities of foreign political dissidents residing in France.

Switzerland

Switzerland suffered four international terrorist attacks in 1988, compared with one in 1987. Police in Bern defused a bomb discovered on the grounds of the Yugoslav Embassy in March, and, in November, a bomb injured five passersby, including two vacationing US citizens, in downtown Geneva. The bomb exploded outside a building housing an Aeroflot office and two Middle Eastern banks and was claimed by a previously unknown group, the Socialist-Nationalist Front.

In 1988, Switzerland participated in several international counter-terrorist initiatives. It signed two international conventions dealing with counter-terrorism, the Protocol to the Montreal Convention of 1971 for Combating Illegal Acts Directed Against the Safety of Ships at Sea, which it signed in February, and the Convention on Combating Illegal Acts Directed Against the Safety of Ships at Sea, which it signed in March. Switzerland joined with other members of the Council of Europe in establishing an expert's committee on applying criminal law to terrorist acts and worked to include counter-terrorism language in the final act of the Vienna CSCE meeting.

At the end of 1988, Hussein Ali Muhammad Hariri, the accused hijacker of an Air Afrique aircraft in July 1987, remained in custody pending trial. (In late February 1989, he was given a life sentence.) In November, when a Swiss national of the Red Cross was taken hostage in Lebanon and the abduction appeared to be designed to pressure Switzerland for Hariri's release, the government publicly declared it would not submit to such pressure.

Swiss legal statutes prevented extradition of one terrorist following the arrest in June of a former member of Italy's Red Brigades. Switzerland denied a request for his extradition to Italy because the suspect held Swiss citizenship, which, under Swiss law, precluded extradition. The suspect remains in custody while Swiss authorities work with Italian investigative agencies to assemble evidence to try him in Switzerland for the terrorist offenses of which he is accused.

Switzerland's situation as an international diplomatic, financial, business, and transportation center with relaxed entry controls makes it susceptible to unsanctioned use by terrorist states, groups, and individuals as a base or transit point. Major terrorist groups are able to obtain access to Swiss banking and medical facilities. Switzerland assisted US authorities in their investigation of Japanese Red Army (JRA) member Yu Kikumura, who had been arrested in New Jersey with antipersonnel bombs. In response to a US Government request under the Mutual Legal Assistance Treaty, the Swiss made Kikumura's banking records available. In April 1988, the Swiss Government was publicly criticized by Swiss media when it became known that Seyed Mohammad Hossein Malaek, whom it had accepted as Iran's Ambassador in Bern, had been identified as one of the Tehran Embassy hostage-takers during the period 1979-81. The United States expressed its disappointment over this matter to the Swiss.

Turkey

Twelve international terrorist attacks were staged in Turkey in 1988, a decrease of five from 1987. The Kurdish Worker's Party (PKK) was responsible for numerous attacks against Turkish Government officials, police, and soldiers. The group also continued to attack civilian and economic targets, particularly in the villages in southeastern Turkey. Large-scale arrests of radical leftists by Turkish security authorities in 1981 have hindered the activities of domestic groups such as Dev Sol and Dev Yol, but they may be attempting to rebuild. During 1988 the groups engaged in numerous low-level bombings to protest the trials of accused terrorists. Turkish security measures probably also are responsible for the PKK and other Kurdish groups choosing venues elsewhere in Western Europe for their attacks against Turkish interests.

There were a number of counter-terrorism prosecutions in Turkey in 1988, including the Kirikkale munitions plant bombing trial, in which eight individuals were sentenced to 30 years for placing a bomb that killed eight persons. The ANO was involved in this plot, and a Jordanian diplomat originally indicted was released because of diplomatic immunity and returned to Jordan. (The case was thrown out of court on appeal in early 1989.) Two Libyans convicted of attempting to blow up the NATO officers club in Ankara appealed their case. (The appeals court upheld the conviction in early 1989.) At yearend, the trial was continuing for a Hizballah member who had brought 100 kilograms of explosives into Turkey in 1987 to use against interests of the United States and other countries. Going on also was the trial of individuals associated with the group Muslim Brotherhood; they were accused of involvement in importing explosives from Iraq to Syria through Turkey. Two Iranian diplomats accredited to Ankara were expelled, while two other Iranian diplomats not accredited in Turkey plus two other Iranian nationals will go on trial for the attempted kidnapping of an anti-Khomeini activist. (They were tried and sentenced in February 1989.)

Twenty-six persons were arrested in November for an alleged plot to kill a former Ankara martial law commander. A splinter group, the Turkish Communist Party, is implicated in this plot. Investigations continue into the murder in October of a Saudi diplomat in Ankara (Iranian-associated interests are suspected of attacks on this and other Saudi diplomats elsewhere) and into the low-level bombing attempts in Istanbul and the attempt to place a bomb in an American teacher's car in Izmir.

United Kingdom

The United Kingdom was the scene of what is probably the most devastating and deadly terrorist incident of 1988—the downing of Pan Am Flight 103 on 21 December, which resulted in 270 deaths. This was one of four international attacks that took place in the United Kingdom during the year, compared with four in 1987 and 1986. Ninety-three deaths resulted from the conflict in Northern Ireland, the same as in 1987. More than 40 of these were civilian deaths. PIRA was responsible for a substantial increase in the number of casualties to British Army personnel, both in Northern Ireland and in Western Europe, and to Northern Ireland's security forces. Thirty-nine soldiers and policemen were killed in 1988, compared with 27 in 1987. PIRA lost 12 of its members to various causes, including clashes with the security forces and premature detonation of bombs. Many of the explosives used by PIRA probably were supplied to the group by Libya.

PIRA appeared to be embarking on a wider campaign against nonofficial British targets at the end of the year, while stating that military personnel would continue to be key targets. Several bombs were detonated in housing areas in Northern Ireland assigned to families of British servicemen on duty there, and a PIRA bomb factory was discovered in London in December.

In 1988, the United Kingdom maintained its longstanding policy of not granting concessions to terrorists. Britain continues to be an active participant in international and regional bodies working against terrorism. There was a close cooperative and consultative relationship between the United Kingdom and the United States on counter-terrorism matters. The United Kingdom continued in 1988 to provide training and other assistance to several countries to improve their capabilities to combat terrorism.

UK authorities are still investigating the poisoning in January of a man of Iraqi origin who died shortly after dining with other Iraqis in London. Before he died, the victim told police that the other Iraqis had poisoned him. The authorities have confirmed that two of the other diners had been sent to Britain by the Iraqi Government and left immediately after the incident.

Sectarian tensions in Northern Ireland have generated a spiral of violence and terrorism by both Protestants and Catholics although most terrorist incidents were perpetrated by PIRA. British authorities worked with their counterparts in West Germany, the Netherlands, and Belgium following PIRA attacks on British soldiers in those countries in 1988. Later in the year, German police arrested two suspected PIRA members believed to have been involved in several of these incidents. The United Kingdom also worked closely with Spanish authorities in February in tracking three PIRA members who were planning to detonate a large bomb at a public square in Gibraltar, a British dependent territory. The British thwarted the attack, killing those involved.

In December, the British Parliament approved legislation strengthening existing laws to combat terrorism. It renewed and made permanent the 1984 Prevention of Terrorism Act, gave the government new powers to seize terrorist funds, to combat racketeering as a means of raising terrorist funds, and to prevent the laundering of money intended for terrorist groups. For Northern Ireland only, it reduced the remission of sentences allowed for convicted terrorists from one-half to one-third.

The legislation also renewed the authority of the government to detain suspected terrorists for up to seven days without formal charges or arraignment. Because the European Court of Human Rights had declared this practice illegal in November, Great Britain invoked the provisions of the European convention on human rights, which allow it to cite "special circumstances" and thus maintain the practice.

In February, British police arrested a Sikh wanted in Canada for suspicion of involvement in the 1985 explosion at Japan's Narita Airport in which two baggage handlers were killed. Canada requested the suspect's extradition since the bomb-rigged baggage was taken from a flight that had originated from Toronto. A British court ordered his extradition, but that decision is being appealed.

West Germany

International terrorist attacks increased marginally in 1988 from 1987, with 25 incidents compared with 24, and the number of Middle Eastern spillover incidents increased from three in 1987 to four in 1988. Only two relatively minor incidents were against US targets. The number of domestic terrorist incidents declined by 40 percent, suggesting that West German counter-terrorist efforts have been successful and that there may be ideological disarray among radical West German leftists.

A variety of groups were responsible for the international attacks. Leftwing West German groups carried out six attacks against French official and business interests in order to show solidarity with a hunger strike by AD terrorists on trial in France. PIRA carried out three attacks on British military forces stationed in West Germany. Bombs damaged two barracks, injuring 12 British soldiers and a West German civilian. In the third incident, an alert British serviceman discovered a bomb under his car before it detonated. Kurdish separatists kidnapped a former member of their group, who escaped after being beaten.

Middle Eastern terrorists were responsible for at least four of the attacks in 1988. Islamic fundamentalists or Palestinian radicals may have carried out attacks in Frankfurt against the Jewish Community Center and a Saudia Airlines ticket office in April, and a video store owned by an Iranian businessman was bombed in June. West German authorities developed evidence, after they arrested 14 members of the Damascus-based PFLP-GC in October, that the Palestinian cell may have been responsible for two bombings in West Germany of US military trains en route to West Berlin. Among the armaments seized were an antitank grenade launcher, six submachine guns, explosives, and a bomb triggered by a barometric switch. Although only two of the Palestinians remained in detention at yearend, having been charged with criminal conspiracy and illegal arms possession, the arrests may have prevented a major terrorist incident.

Domestic terrorists focused their energies in 1988 against the International Monetary Fund/World Bank Conference held in West Berlin in September. The RAF failed in its first attack since October 1986, when it attempted to murder a senior Finance Ministry official. The attack, coming one week before the Berlin IMF conference, was probably an attempt to intimidate the participants. Other elements in the RAF that usually follow up such attacks with their own operations failed to do so in this instance, suggesting there may be a rift within the organization. The RAF issued a communiqué after the attack that contained a joint statement with the Red Brigades. The statement indicated that the two groups had forged an ideological alliance, presumably to supplant the relationship with AD that was disrupted in 1987 by the arrests of the AD members. West Germany's other significant terrorist group, the Revolutionary Cells, apparently continued to suffer from the arrests of some of its members in 1987 and was virtually inactive during 1988.

The trial of Lebanese national Mohammad Hammadi began in July in a heavily guarded Frankfurt courtroom. Hammadi is being tried for air piracy and the murder of US Navy diver Robert Stethem during the June 1985 hijacking of TWA Flight 847 to Beirut. The US Government had requested Hammadi's extradition, but the West German Government decided to try him instead. A verdict is expected in April 1989. To the extent that Hammadi's group, Hizballah, has targeted West German interests in Lebanon in the past, it is conceivable that they may target West Germany after the end of the trial. Abbas Hammadi, Mohammad's brother, was convicted in April in Dusseldorf for complicity in the kidnapping of two German citizens in Lebanon, which he had engineered in an attempt to get his brother released following his arrest. Abbas was sentenced to a 14-year prison term.

Two RAF terrorists were pardoned in 1988 by the Rheinland Palatinate minister-president after having served 16 to 17 years of their life sentences for murder. In announcing the pardons, the minister-president stated that both had renounced their terrorist views. RAF member Eva Haule-Frimpong, formerly on West Germany's most-wanted list, plus two other RAF members were sentenced to prison terms in June. Haule-Frimpong was sentenced to 15 years for attempting to blow up a NATO school in Oberammergau in 1984 and for membership in the outlawed RAF. her codefendants were sentenced to 10 year and four year prison terms for another bombing attack and for RAF membership.

Police in August arrested two alleged PIRA members whose involvement is suspected in attacks on British soldiers in Belgium and in West Germany. A major effort remains under way to apprehend those involved in the attempted assassination of a Finance Ministry official, Hans Tietmeyer, in September.

Following the release in September of Rudolf Cordes, the last German hostage held in Beirut, the West German Government stated it had made no concession to gain his release.

Yugoslavia

The Yugoslav Government continues to publicly oppose terrorism and to implement measures aimed at establishing greater controls over the entry and stay of foreigners to prevent the misuse of its territory. It has also evidenced a greater willingness to seriously cooperate with other countries in investigating terrorist incidents. Yugoslavia has generally been more responsive in securing its borders against terrorists, but there still is room for improvement.

Yugoslavia's geographic position, the large numbers of visiting foreign tourists, and the approximately 15,000 students there from Middle Eastern countries continue to limit the government's ability to prevent the transit of potential terrorists across its territory. Yugoslavia maintains good relations with countries such as Libya, Iran, and North Korea, which are supporters of international terrorism. The government has denied, as has the United States, the assertion of Libyan ruler Qadhafi, carried in a US newspaper, that notorious Palestinian terrorist Abu Nidal was living in Yugoslavia.

Yugoslavia, however, continues to appear on the itineraries of suspected, arrested, and convicted terrorists. For example, Mohammed Rashid, a member of the PLO's Hawari Group, was arrested as he arrived in Greece from Yugoslavia, and a member of the PFLP-GC team rounded up in October in West Germany was arrested at a West German airport after a flight from Yugoslavia. Some of the suspected ANO team that attacked The City of Poros day-excursion ship had also reportedly come from Yugoslavia. On the other hand, we believe that the Yugoslav Government may be prepared to expel terrorists operating in its country. An apparent exception is Khalid Abdel Nasser, whom the Yugoslav press has acknowledged is living in the country. Nasser, the son of former Egyptian President Nasser, is being tried in absentia in Egypt on charges of membership in an organization that engages in terrorism. The organization, Egypt's Revolution, has conducted terrorist acts, including the targeting of US diplomats.

Asia Overview

International terrorism in Asia rose in 1988, up from 170 incidents in 1987, to 194. Sixty-five percent of the incidents occurred in Pakistan. As in 1987, most of the attacks were the work of the state-sponsored Afghan Ministry of State Security (WAD). About 10 percent of Asian incidents occurred in the Republic of Korea. In 1987 we recorded two international incidents in South Korea; however, in 1988 student unrest led to 21, mostly minor, attacks against US interests, including four against the American Cultural Center and one against the US Embassy. International terrorist acts in the Philippines made up 6 percent of the total for Asia and included the kidnapping of an American couple by alleged members of a Muslim separatist splinter group. There were four incidents in India, most notably the bombing of a Citibank office in New Delhi and an armed attack on an Alitalia air crew in Bombay. Separatists in both India and Sri Lanka continued to employ terrorist tactics, but against domestic targets.

Australia

Australia was the site of four international incidents, all protesting South Africa's racial policies and conducted by two Australian citizens. Two of the attacks wee directed at US Embassy officials. A car used by the defense attaché and two belonging to the Embassy's First Secretary sustained minor burn damage, and a South African diplomat's car was destroyed by the two Australians.

Australia, a staunch supporter of efforts to end terrorism, encouraged other members of the South Pacific Forum to increase intelligence and police liaison to deter terrorist incidents in the South Pacific.

India

Four international terrorist incidents took place in India during 1988 compared with two the previous year. In March a watchman discovered grenades and bottles of flammable liquid at the Saudi Arabian Consulate in Bombay. Police found no evidence to establish a motive or identify suspects. Later that month, a lone gunman fired shots and hurled grenades at an Alitalia Airlines crew aboard an airport bus and wounded the captain. A previously unknown group, the Organization of Arab Fedayeen Cells, claimed responsibility, but the ANO is believed to have conducted the attack. In April police arrested a Sri Lankan Tamil militant suspected of detonating a powerful bomb at a television relay center in Madura, Tamil Nadu. The explosion killed one person and seriously injured another. In early May, a powerful bomb exploded at a Citibank branch in New Delhi, killing one person and wounding at least 13 others. No group claimed responsibility, but Indian authorities believe a non-Indian group, possibly the JRA using the AIIB cover name, conducted the attack.

Sikh violence rose dramatically in 1988. Sikh extremists in the Punjab were responsible for the deaths of Congress (I) and other political party officials, religious leaders, Hindu villagers, and moderate Sikhs. They also staged attacks in the Punjab's neighboring states of Jammu and Kashmir, and Haryana. In Jammu and Kashmir, Muslim separatists stepped up their campaign of violence that culminated in a series of bomb blasts in late October. The Indian Government claimed Pakistani-trained terrorists operating out of Kashmir were responsible.

Throughout 1988, New Delhi continued to pursue its "law and order" policy as its key response to Sikh terrorism. In November, the Indian Parliament extended President's Rule in the Punjab through April 1989, leaving all state enforcement authority in the hands of the central government. Indian and Pakistani officials pursued their discussions aimed at controlling terrorism and smuggling along their borders, and the new government in Pakistan pledged closer cooperation with India to control Sikh terrorist activities.

Judicial proceedings are under way against several accused terrorists, while others are detained pending charges. An ANO terrorist believed responsible for the March attack on an Alitalia Airlines crew in Bombay is in Indian custody awaiting trial. In November, Indian courts heard the final appeals of the two convicted assassins of Prime Minister Indira Gandhi. (They were executed in January 1989.) The Indian request to the United States to extradite two Sikhs reportedly involved in the 1986 assassination of a retired Indian Army chief of staff is still before the US courts.

Japan

Two international terrorist attacks took place in Japan in 1988. In both cases, domestic organizations not known to operate outside Japan were responsible. In early March occupants in a passing car fired a single shot through a window of the Chinese Consulate General in Fukuoka but caused no injuries. Police suspect a rightist group, Mizoshita. In the second attack in late March, a bomb blast shattered the front window of the Saudia Airlines office, located in a building housing a company engaged in construction projects for the new Tokyo international airport at Narita. Police suspect the radical leftist group Chukaku-ha because of the group's violent opposition to Narita. They believe the airline office was not the intended target.

JRA activists continued to pose a dangerous international terrorist threat during 1988, using cover names such as the Anti-Imperialist International Brigade and the Jihad Brigade. JRA attacks in 1988 included the bombing in April of a USO club in Naples, Italy, and possible involvement in the bombing of a US Air Force communications facility near Humosa, Spain. The JRA also is suspected of participation in the bombing of the Citibank branch in New Delhi in May. The arrest in April of Yu Kikumura by New Jersey authorities may have thwarted a JRA bomb attack in the United States, the first known indication that the JRA could conduct an operation in North America. Kikumura pled guilty to all charges and received a 30-year prison sentence. However, the JRA staged no attacks during the Toronto economic summit in June or the Seoul Olympics in late summer, as feared, possibly because of the arrests of Kikumura and two other important JRA members.

During 1988, the JRA maintained its worldwide operations, including sustaining links to Libya and North Korea. The timing of JRA attacks or intended attacks in 1988 suggested that Libya probably continued to support the JRA. In addition, the JRA, the majority of whose members are located in Lebanon's Bekaa Valley, may have reestablished links to the original Japanese Red Army Faction, now based in North Korea. JRA members continued to travel in or through Western and eastern Europe, Southeast and Northeast Asia, and North America to stage operations and maintain links to other terrorist groups. For example, they reportedly have transited Yugoslavia, Hungary, and Greece for travel outside their base in Lebanon. In addition, their travels revealed JRA efforts to establish an international support network through a series of cells, called the Anti-War Democratic Front (ADF). Japanese authorities have identified ADF cells in the Philippines, Hong Kong, and Japan.

In the aftermath of the Korean Airlines (KAL) Flight 858 bombing, in which the two North Korean perpetrators used fraudulent Japanese identity documents, the Japanese Government issued a strongly worded public indictment of North Korean complicity and initiated trade and other sanctions against Pyongyang. Both US and Japanese sanctions were partially lifted in late 1988. Japan also cooperated in assuring security for the Seoul Olympic Games.

Japan and Korea closely coordinated their respective security policies for the Olympics as part of this cooperation, Japan provided protection for foreign athletes who trained in Japan before the Seoul Games. Japan also organized an Asian regional conference in June dealing with crime, narcotics, and terrorism, at which it was agreed to step up counter-terrorism cooperation in preparation for the Seoul Olympics.

Japanese authorities were particularly active in developing and implementing a strategy against the JRA, which included discussions with several governments. The year saw a series of successes against the JRA that, including the arrest in 1987 of Osamu Maruoka, resulted in a major—though probably not permanent—setback to the terrorist group. In May, Yasuhiro Shibata, one of the original Yodo-Go hijackers of a JAL aircraft in 1970 who had been living in North Korea, was arrested in Tokyo. In June, Hiroshi Sensui was arrested in the Philippines, where he was probably attempting to establish a JRA network, and extradited to Tokyo. Japanese authorities cooperated with US authorities in the criminal investigation of JRA terrorist Yu Kikumura. Japanese assistance made it possible to positively identify Kikumura and to establish his JRA links.

Reflecting the growing firmness of the Japanese Government's position on terrorism, the Justice Minister stated in June that, in the event of a terrorist incident, Japan would refuse to comply with terrorist demands.

Pakistan

International terrorist incidents for Pakistan in 1988 held at about the same level as 1987: 127 incidents, compared to 136. As in the past, almost all the attacks appeared attributable to the Soviet-backed WAD. The North-West Frontier Province (NWFP), on the border with Afghanistan, continued to be the primary venue for terrorist attacks, with encampments of Afghan refugees and anti-regime fighters the main targets. Pakistani courts have aided the government's counter-terrorist efforts by sentencing terrorists to lengthy prison sentences. Following a particularly vicious bombing in June in Peshawar that killed 14 people, the Pakistani Government denounced Soviet-backed Afghanistan for training operatives for subversion in its country and gave a UN group based in Islamabad a list of camps in Afghanistan that it alleged were involved.

WAD bombings in 1988 also extended to major population centers outside the NWFP, approximately 1987's range of terrorist operations to again include Islamabad, Karachi, Lahore, Rawalpindi, and Quetta. Typically, these attacks took place at transportation terminals with a high potential for casualties, areas frequented by Pakistani civilians and, in some cases, foreigners. Foreigners do not appear to have been the primary targets of the WAD bombings; rather, the attacks probably were meant as a warning to the Government of Pakistan for its support to the Afghan resistance. None of the attacks caused casualties at the level of the 1987 bombing of a crowded Karachi market that claimed 70 lives.

A bombing lull in March probably was intended to influence negotiations between Pakistan and Afghanistan in Geneva. Conversely, the resumption of bombings in Islamabad in October, the first significant terrorist operations in the capital in 1988, probably was meant to show displeasure over the continuation of Mujahedin military pressure within Afghanistan after the Soviet agreement to withdraw. Neither of these terrorist campaigns appears to have influenced Pakistani Government policy. As the fortunes of the Kabul regime weaken, the prospects of terrorism from this source will probably decrease.

Mujahedin actions in Afghanistan have been directed against military targets of the Soviet forces and Kabul regime. Although the Mujahedin groups have attempted to avoid civilian casualties, their rocket attacks this year against military installations in major Afghan cities have resulted in a large number of civilian deaths and injuries.

As in 1987, there were a few attacks attributable to Iranians or local Shia supporters of the Khomeini regime. The principal targets of the attacks were domestic opponents of the Shias and representatives of governments deemed hostile to Iran. In one such possible instance, the Saudia Airlines office in Karachi was blown up without loss of life in April.

The five ANO terrorists responsible for the Pan Am hijacking in Karachi in September 1986 were convicted in July and sentenced to death. The hijacking attempt left more than 20 persons dead, including two US citizens. The five terrorists were tried and convicted by a special court constituted by the federal government in 1987. Four of the hijackers were also given 10 consecutive life sentences for the murder of the passengers. The death sentences were commuted to life imprisonment as part of Prime Minister Bhutto's December judicial relief order.

The Pakistani Government participates in the State Department's Anti-Terrorism Assistance Program, most recently in a training program dealing with interdepartmental coordination, organization, and training. Other Western governments also provide counter-terrorism training to Pakistan.

Philippines

In the Philippines, the number of international terrorist attacks for the year declined by about 40 percent from 1987, with 12 incidents noted. Attacks against US targets also declined, and no American casualties were incurred. The threat to US personnel, nevertheless, remains high as the Communist Party of the Philippines (CPP) New People's Army (NPA) "sparrow" assassination units continue to monitor the activities of US officials.

The general reluctance of terrorist teams to attack Americans over the past year can be ascribed to a range of possible underlying motives, but their abeyance may be a result of high-level CPP/NPA directives. The negative public reaction to the killing of US servicemen outside Clark Airbase in 1987 may have dissuaded the NPA from repeating such seemingly indiscriminate "hits" and led to concentrating on finding more politically justifiable targets. Alternatively, party leaders may have assessed that the time was not yet right to open an active anti-American front. Successes in 1988 by the Philippine Government's counter-insurgency program—such as the arrest of numerous highly placed Communist figures—may also have heightened operational caution. The hardening of US military facilities and the protective measures taken by US personnel in view of the high threat are additional factors impeding terrorist action.

International terrorism in the Philippines in 1988 tended to be intertwined with financial motives, as was the case with attacks against multinational corporations—probably for nonpayment of protection money to guerrillas.

Some terrorist attacks that took place in 1988, nevertheless, suggest that reprisals were being taken against foreign nationals perceived to be involved in counter-insurgency activities, a pattern that probably will persist. An Australian national was killed, probably by NPA guerrillas, because he was believed to be assisting the Philippine military. A small bomb was set off in the building housing the Israeli Embassy—with minimal damage—by suspected NPA agents after the organization had publicly denounced Israel for aiding the government's counterinsurgency program.

The Philippine Government took a number of practical measures in 1988 to deal with terrorism spawned by the Communist insurgency, including stepped-up raids of suspected safe houses. It augmented its security forces in Manila, with increases in personnel, vehicles, and radios. The authorities also arrested a considerable number of Communist leaders during the year. Despite the authorities' success in capturing NPA leader Romulo Kinntanar in March, he escaped from prison eight months later. Criminal charges were filed against several soldiers in connection with the prison escape.

In June, authorities arrested JRA leader Hiroshi Sensui and deported him to Japan. It is believed that Sensui was setting up a terrorist base in Manila. A Philippine immigrations official later stated that JRA members were using Manila as a "transit point" while awaiting orders for terrorist attacks.

South Korea

Members of radical student and dissident organizations perpetrated 21, mostly low-level, attacks against US interests in South Korea; in 1987 two such events were recorded. Demonstrations culminating in firebomb attacks on US military and diplomatic facilities—with four incidents at the American Cultural Center in Seoul—caused minimal damage and no US casualties.

South Korean concern about international terrorism heightened considerably in anticipation of the September 1988 Summer Olympic Games in Seoul, especially after the November 1987 destruction of KAL Flight 858 by North Korean agents. That act of state-sponsored terrorism stimulated a debate on North Korean terrorism in the UN Security Council in February, and South Korea successfully moved a condemnatory resolution in the ICAO.

The security of the Olympics, in large part, was the result of protective measures carried out by the Korean Government, in cooperation with other governments and countries such as Japan that provided logistic and transportation support for the Games. Another important factor undoubtedly was the pressure on North Korea from both the Soviet Union and China to let the Olympics—in which they participated—proceed without incident. South Korean officials periodically met with their counterparts in the United States and other countries to discuss practical cooperation to prevent terrorist incidents before and during the Olympics.

South Korea co-hosted with the United States an Asia-Pacific Regional Aviation Security Conference in June that included representatives from eight nations, the International Federation of Airline Pilots Associations (IFALPA) and ICAO. The conference promoted cooperation between the airlines and airport authorities and planned for aviation security during the Olympics.

At yearend, government authorities initiated prosecution of Kim Hyon Hui, the confessed North Korean agent responsible for the KAL Flight 858 destruction. Press reports suggest that after a trial, Kim may be pardoned for her cooperation in exposing North Korean culpability. Although South Korea has a longstanding policy of lenient treatment for North Korean agents who renounce their previous activities and allegiances, the country's responsibilities under the terms of the Montreal Convention obligate it to prosecute Kim.

Sri Lanka

The Liberation Tigers of Tamil Eelam (LTTE) is believed to have been responsible for the only international terrorist incident to occur in Sri Lanka in 1988. In August, LTTE guerrillas reportedly killed an Indian Red Cross official and his driver and wounded another official when their jeep blew up in a landmine explosion.

The level of violence rose in Sri Lanka during 1988 despite continued efforts to quell LTTE insurgents and to control the resurgence of Sinhalese extremism. Despite numerous sweeps that resulted in the capture of many Tamil insurgents and their weapons, the Indian Peace Keeping Force (IPKF) has been unable to suppress the militants completely. While the IPKF directed operations against the LTTE, Sri Lankan security forces attempted to control the spread of Sinhalese violence in the south. The major radical Sinhalese group, the Marxist Janatha Vimukthi Peramuna (JVP, or People's Liberation Front), encouraged by Sinhalese resentment over the presence of Indian troops in Sri Lanka, escalated its antigovernment, anti-accord campaign of violence in 1988. Despite government efforts to address JVP grievances and bring the JVP into the political mainstream, JVP members attacked ruling United National party and other political party meetings, assassinated politicians, attacked military posts and police stations, called strikes and curfews, and attempted to disrupt elections by attacking voters.

The Sri Lankan Government enacted laws in 1988 giving its security forces broad new powers to combat the JVP. In addition, the Prevention of Terrorism Act and the Emergency Regulations remained if effect throughout 1988.

Several court cases in Sri Lanka were in process during 1988 that stem from two ongoing insurgencies. Charges against four accused suspects in the August 1987 grenade attack in Parliament were expected to be filed at yearend. Two persons died in that attack. The court case against three Tamils accused of the May 1986 bombing of an Air Lanka plane continued in 1988. Twenty-eight persons died in that bombing.

Large numbers of suspected Tamil militants were unconditionally released in 1988 in a program begun in 1987 following the signing of the Indo-Sri Lanka Accord. A total of nearly 4,000 such suspects, previously held under the Prevention of Terrorism Act and Emergency Regulations, have been released.

All members (India, Pakistan, Sri Lanka, Nepal, Bangladesh, Bhutan, and the Maldives) ratified the convention of the South Asian Association on Regional Cooperation (SAARC) on suppression of terrorism in 1988. This convention categorizes offenses under the 1970 Hague Convention for the Suppression of Unlawful Seizure of Aircraft, the 1971 Montreal Convention for the Suppression of Unlawful Acts against the Safety of Civilian Aviation, and the 1973 New York Convention on the Prevention and Punishment of Crimes Against Internationally Protected Persons as Acts of Terrorism. The SAARC convention provides for extradition among member states and recommends cooperation against terrorism through such measures as consultations, intelligence, and other exchanges.

Taiwan

The Taipei district court in October sentenced two hijackers to three and one-half years in prison on air piracy charges, even though the public prosecutor in the case had recommended suspended sentences. The two defectors from the People's Republic of China, claiming to be "freedom seekers," had hijacked a civilian airliner in May to Taiwan using a toy gun and fake explosives. Immediately following the hijacking, the US Government publicly urged Taiwan to live up to its international obligations by ensuring that the hijackers were brought to justice. The two were convicted in October and sentenced to three years in prison, although in December the district prosecutor filed an appeal for leniency in the High Court.

Thailand

The Kuwait Airways flight hijacked in April en route to Kuwait originally departed from Bangkok International Airport. The hijackers may have received logistic support from the Iranian Embassy in Bangkok, possibly with the assistance of a local criminal organization comprised primarily of non-Thais. Separate investigations by three Thai government agencies could not determine whether or how the hijackers were able to bring weapons on board the aircraft. It is possible, however, that because of the lateness of the hour, a thorough secondary inspection of passengers and hand-carried luggage had not taken place before boarding.

The Royal Thai Government cooperates informally with several countries on international counter-terrorism matters and has held discussions with the United States on counter-terrorism assistance.

Sub-Saharan Africa

Sub-Saharan Africa continued to trail other regions in total numbers of international terrorist incidents, but experienced an increase from 30 for 1987, to 52 in 1988. The increase came largely from a fivefold acceleration of cross-border raids on Zimbabwean villages by the Mozambique National Resistance Movement (RENAMO). Armed attacks and kidnappings rose proportionately because of the increase in RENAMO raids. Most other international attacks were committed by local insurgents, as in previous years. When involved, Europeans—aid workers or missionaries—tended to be targets of opportunity caught up in insurgent operations. There were no American deaths as a result of international terrorism but five injuries.

Suspected South African Government agents continued bombing attacks against ANC facilities in countries bordering South Africa. South African attacks may well have extended outside the region; an assassination attempt occurred in February against an ANC representative in Brussels, and in March, the ANC representative in Paris was killed by an unidentified assailant.

Benin

Benin-based Libyan diplomats have used the country in the past as a staging area for subversive and terrorist operations in West Africa. After the disclosure of a Libyan-sponsored terrorist operation in February uncovered in Dakar, Senegal, the Government of Benin initiated steps to limit Libyan activities. In June, the Libyan Ambassador, who has been implicated in the Dakar incident, abruptly left Cotonou.

Steps taken by the Benin Government to control Libyan movement into and out of the country included stricter visa controls. Benin also clamped down on Libyan activities at the capital's airport following reports that Libyan diplomats had used their status to gain access to the tarmac and other restricted areas. The authorities also monitored the activities of a commercial company in Cotonou that had reportedly been used to store Libyan weapons and explosives. In conjunction with the clampdown on Libyan activities, the government reassessed its counter-terrorism capabilities and has since sought Western counter-terrorism training and assistance.

Djibouti

Djiboutian authorities in 1988 continued their investigation of the previous year's bombing of the Café L'Historil, in which 11 persons were killed, including five French soldiers. An indictment against the self-confessed terrorist, now imprisoned in Djibouti, is expected.

Ivory Coast

A Hizballah arms cache discovered in August in the Ivorian capital of Abidjan pointedly reminded West African security officials that their countries continue to attract the interest of Middle Eastern terrorists. Although the target of the group that was to have used the cache remains unknown, the incident demonstrates Hizballah's abiding interest in developing an overseas infrastructure to support future terrorist operations.

Lesotho

During the papal visit in September, a splinter group of the outlawed Lesotho Liberation Army (LLA) crossed the border and seized a busload of pilgrims who were traveling to Maseru for the papal visit. After 36 hours, the hostage drama ended when Lesotho and South African security forces stormed the bus, during which three of the four hijackers and three pilgrims were killed. A fourth hijacker later died of wounds received during the assault. Following that incident, Lesotho formally requested US hostage negotiation training.

Mozambique

In 1988, Mozambique continued to suffer from domestic attacks conducted by RENAMO insurgents. International programs remained RENAMO targets of opportunity, with Italian agricultural projects coming under attack in two instances. Virtually all incidents involved looting. Despite assistance by troops from Zimbabwe, Tanzania, and Malawi, the Government of Mozambique has made few inroads toward neutralizing the RENAMO threat.

The Mozambican Government claims that support for RENAMO comes from South Africa. The US Government has maintained there is a pattern of support and communication between South Africa and RENAMO. In 1988, however, the Nkomati Peace Accords—signed in 1984 between South Africa and Mozambique pledging to end assistance to RENAMO and the ANC—were formally reactivated after a summit between South African President Botha and Mozambican President Chissano. The two countries established a joint security commission to investigate violations of the Nkomati accords.

South African concern about the ANC presence in Mozambique has led to raids against alleged ANC targets in the Maputo area. In April, Albie Sachs, a human rights lawyer and ANC member, was crippled by a bomb planted in his private automobile. South African complicity in this attack is suspect.

Senegal

Two known Libyan terrorists along with a Senegalese national were arrested on 20 February 1988 at Dakar Airport for possession of weapons and explosives. The two Libyans had come from Cotonou, Benin. Following a detention of four months, the Senegalese Government released the Libyans without trial, citing lack of evidence. The United States, both publicly and through official channels, expressed its extreme disappointment at Senegal's release of the terrorists, and stated that the action raised "questions about the country's commitment to the struggle against international terrorism."

Despite this setback, Senegal continued to upgrade security at its ports of entry. Fifteen Senegalese security personnel received counter-terrorism training in the United States under a State Department–Federal Aviation Agency program. The Senegalese also maintain a close relationship with French counter-terrorism and security agencies, receiving training and participating in regular information exchanges.

South Africa

The struggle against apartheid, although largely nonviolent, has generated a cycle of violent repression by the government and violent resistance by the black opposition, which has resulted in some acts of terrorism. The leadership of the ANC, while disavowing a strategy of deliberately targeting civilians, has not punished any of its members for violating this publicly stated policy. The US Government has strongly counseled the ANC against further acts of violence of this nature.

The increasing implantation of minilimpet mines in crowded urban settings where high casualties must be anticipated, however, suggests a possible shift in tactics or, perhaps, an inability of the ANC to exert central control.

The South African Government has attacked ANC facilities in neighboring countries, such as the March commando raid in Gaborone, Botswana, in which four persons were killed. Some of these countries have also accused South Africa of launching terrorist attacks, such as the car bombing in early January outside a house used by the ANC in Bulawayo, Zimbabwe, in which two persons died and three were injured, and at least two bombings in Zambia directed against the ANC, which has its headquarters in Lusaka.

Despite denials, South African involvement is widely suspected in the murder of ANC Paris representative Dulcie September in March, and the assassination attempt on ANC member Albie Sachs by car bomb in Maputo in April. The US Government has expressed serious and repeated concern to the South African Government about the incidents of cross-border violence.

In the South African court system, opposition activists are frequently charged with terrorism rather than political offenses. According to the South African Human Rights Commission, the courts in the first nine months of 1988 passed judgment on 60 people for "terrorism," convicting 34. In the widely publicized Delmas treason trial in November, eight opposition activists wee charged with and convicted of "terrorism."

Sudan

In October, the Khartoum high court found guilty and sentenced to death the five terrorists accused of the 15 May machinegun and explosives attacks at the Acropole Hotel and the Sudan Club, in which eight persons died and more than 20—including three Americans—were wounded. The terrorists, who had confessed to being ANO members, are appealing the sentences.

A Sudanese Government statement in July implicated an Iraqi diplomat in the assassination of Iraqi Shia opposition leader Mahdi Al-Hakim, who was killed in a hotel lobby in Khartoum while attending an Islamic political party conference in January. The investigation of the assassination ended when the Iraqi diplomat departed from the country after a Sudanese request that his diplomatic immunity be lifted for questioning was denied.

Zambia

As external political headquarters of the ANC, Zambia continues to be a venue of South African reprisals. Two instances in 1988 of bombings directed against the ANC were the likely work of South African agents. A facility associated with the South-West African People's Organization also was bombed by unidentified agents. The past year was also marked by an upsurge in RENAMO attacks in Zambia similar to those conducted into Zimbabwe.

Zimbabwe

Almost all international terrorist incidents reported in 1988 for Zimbabwe involved cross-border REMANO incursions from Mozambique. Killings of civilians during these raids appear indiscriminate and on the increase, up from 37 in 1987 to at least 55 in 1988. Typically, RENAMO raids were made against remote villages by armed guerrilla groups of fewer than 20 persons. Villagers routinely were kidnapped to act as porters for carrying off booty. Attacks were primarily to punish Harare for its support of the Chissano regime and to acquire food and supplies.

In a downturn from last year, local dissidents were responsible for only one attack against foreigners in which one missionary was killed.

Six alleged South African agents, accused of participating in a string of bombing attacks against suspected ANC targets in Harare and Bulawayo, were charged before Zimbabwean courts in 1988. In July one of the defendants was convicted and sentenced to seven years in prison. Three others were convicted in November and sentenced to death, although the sentences are being appealed. Two others await trial. The south African Government has charged that the ANC launches attacks from Zimbabwe, but the Zimbabwean Government counters that it has made concerted efforts to control ANC activity within its borders.

A Mozambican accused of being a RENAMO terrorist was convicted in November for murder, armed robbery, and possession of arms, stemming from an attack in April 1987. This was the first trial in Zimbabwean courts of an alleged RENAMO terrorist.

Domestic dissident violence and civilian attacks in Matabeleland effectively ended after the amnesty was declared in April by the Zimbabwean Government and the unity agreement reached between two opposing political groups. More than 100 dissidents previously involved in violent activity—including the rebel leader involved in the November 1987 massacre of white missionaries—turned themselves in during the period of the amnesty.

Patterns of Global Terrorism: 1989

The Year in Review

The level of international terrorism worldwide in 1989 declined sharply from that of 1988, dropping by almost 38 percent from 856 incidents in 1988 to 528.[1] The Middle East

---

[1] In past years, serious violence by Palestinians against other Palestinians in the Occupied Territories was included as international terrorism in the database of worldwide incidents because Palestinians are considered stateless persons. This resulted in such incidents being treated differently from intra-ethnic violence in other parts of the world. As a result of further review of the nature of Intra-Palestinian

continued to experience the largest number of incidents of international terrorism, incurring 193 attacks—37 percent of the total worldwide. The proportion of international terrorism connected with the Middle East increases to 45 percent, however, when Middle East spillover attacks into other regions are added. These compare to statistics of 36 percent and 41 percent, respectively, in 1988. With 131 attacks, or 25 percent of the total, Latin America ranked second. Western Europe was third with 96 incidents. With the reduction of Afghan-sponsored attacks in Pakistan, Asia dropped to fourth with 55 incidents. Africa was fifth with 48 attacks. Four international terrorist attacks took place in North America. One incident was recorded in Eastern Europe during the year, although Soviet and Eastern European interests were attacked in other parts of the world.

Several factors were responsible for the major decrease in international terrorism:

- The Afghan Government curtailed its terrorist campaign in Pakistan after Soviet troops were withdrawn.
- Yasser Arafat's renunciation of terrorism resulted in a sharp decline in operations by groups affiliated with the PLO.
- Dissension within the Abu Nidal organization (ANO)—previously one of the most active and deadly terrorist groups—and its focus on Lebanese militia matters decreased the group's operations.
- A number of states involved in terrorism, including Libya and Syria, remained wary of getting caught sponsoring terrorists and reduced their support. Iran was a notable exception to the trend.
- Partly in response to internal problems and enhanced counterterrorist measures, many terrorist groups focused on building their infrastructure throughout the world to support attacks in the future.
- Counterterrorist capabilities continued to improve in most parts of the world, and cooperation among governments increased.

There was only one "spectacular" international terrorist operation in 1989—the bombing of UTA Flight 772 over Niger on 19 September. That attack accounted for 171 deaths, the greatest number associated with a single attack during the year. Investigators have not determined who was responsible. Terrorist "spectaculars" may well be becoming more rare as there seems to be a growing perception among terrorists that they have not achieved their goals with operations such as airline hijackings and that such attacks are increasingly difficult to conduct. Moreover, some of the groups most capable of carrying out such operations have focused their energies elsewhere.

The depiction of the alleged execution of US Marine Corps Col. William R. Higgins on 31 July captured headlines and brought worldwide condemnation of the Iranian-backed terrorists responsible. Elsewhere, narcotraffickers in Colombia are believed responsible for several horrific attacks using terrorist methods to achieve their criminal goals. This likely includes the late November bombing of a domestic Avianca flight out of Bogotá in which all 111 on board perished.

The 528 international terrorist incidents recorded in 1989 resulted in 390 victims killed and 397 wounded. Fourteen terrorists were killed and 23 wounded. Reflecting the decline in the number of incidents, this represents a drop from 1988 when 638 victims were killed and 1,125 wounded. In 1988, 22 terrorists were killed and six wounded. The downing of UTA Flight 772 emphasized the continuing growth of casualties in Africa, from a total of 125 killed and 130 wounded in 1988 to 269 killed and 39 wounded in 1989. Asia experienced the most significant decline in casualties with the reduction in the Afghan campaign in Pakistan, dropping from 156 killed and 599 wounded in 1988 to 57 killed and 153 wounded in 1989. International terrorism in the Middle East accounted for 29 persons killed and 111 injured. Twenty-one persons were killed and 73 wounded in Latin America. In Western Europe, there were 14 victims killed and 21 wounded in international terrorists attacks.

The number of terrorist attacks and casualties suffered by the United States declined in 1989 from 1988, but US interests continued to be the most frequently targeted by international terrorists. In 1988, 193 attacks were directed against the United States, compared with 165 in 1989, a decline of 15 percent. Casualties among US citizens also declined, from 192 killed and 40 wounded in 1988 to 16 killed and 19 injured in 1989. The drop reflects, for the most part, the absence of a major incident that caused a large number of casualties, such as the bombing of Pan Am Flight 103 in 1988. The largest share of the attacks, or 64 percent, took place in Latin America, with bombings of oil pipelines partly owned by US companies accounting for most of the incidents. Almost 14 percent of the anti-US incidents took place in Asia, 13 percent in Western Europe, 5 percent in the Middle East, and 1 percent in Africa.

International terrorists attacked the citizens and property of 74 countries in a total of 60 countries. The United States was the most frequently targeted, followed by Israel. With the continuing increase in security for official interests, terrorist again carried out most the attacks—75 percent of the total worldwide—against businesses, tourists, and other nonofficial targets. Attacks against international organizations and governments targets decreased to 19 percent of the total. Attacks on noncombatant military targets increased marginally, to 41 from 38 in 1988; there were 88 in 1987.

The number of attacks by type followed a well-established pattern. Terrorists relied most frequently on bombings (44 percent of the total); arson was second (28 percent). Terrorists used firearms and other types of handheld weapons in 14 percent of the attacks. The incidence of kidnappings declined slightly but occurred in about 5 percent of the attacks. Ap-

---

violence, such violence is no longer included in the US Government's statistical database on international terrorism. This new refinement in the 1989 statistical database ensures its continuing accuracy and reliability. Intra-Palestinian violence, however, remains a serious concern.

proximately 44 percent of the kidnappings occurred in Latin America, with 19 percent in the Middle East.

The number of terrorist incidents that could be attributed to state sponsors declined in 1989. Evidence indicated 58 incidents involved state sponsors in 1989, a drop of 67 percent from 1988 when 176 such attacks were noted. The decrease was partly due to the ability of a number of states that have aided terrorist groups to effectively mask their involvement. The greatest portion of the drop resulted from Kabul's apparent curtailment of its bombing campaign in Pakistan following the removal of Soviet military forces. Iran's involvement in terrorism was not detected as frequently in 1989, but we suspect an upturn in its support during the second half of the year reflects a return to a greater pace of operations. Libya and Syria were not directly tied to any attacks in 1989, but they continue to provide various forms of support for several terrorist groups.

The spillover of Middle Eastern terrorism outside that region accounted for 43 attacks in 1989, down from 45 in 1988. The attacks in 1989 resulted in 181 persons killed and 15 wounded. Thirty-one incidents took place in Western Europe. Ten incidents took place in the United Kingdom and mostly were attacks on bookstores and businesses connected with Salman Rushdie's *The Satanic Verses*. Of the remainder, six were in Turkey; four in Pakistan and Belgium, and three in the United States; two each in Austria, France, and the Netherlands; and one each in Afghanistan, Canada, Cyprus, Greece, Italy, Niger, Senegal, Sweden, Thailand, and West Germany.

Despite the decline in international attacks in 1989, terrorists retain the potential for resuming a greater level of violence, particularly against the United States. Terrorists in the Philippines appear more likely to broaden their targeting of US citizens to increase pressure on the United States to withdraw, and rebel soldiers may retaliate for US support to the Aquino government during the failed coup attempt in December. In Latin America, US interests in Panama may be targeted by diehard supporters of General Noriega, and other radicals in the region and in other parts of the world may use Washington's military action in Panama as a pretext for stepped-up targeting. Other developments worldwide could spark increased terrorist operations; rivalries among Middle Eastern governments—particularly between Iran and Saudi Arabia, which has already generated a campaign of violence by Iran—and emerging alliances among Middle Eastern sponsors and groups, such as between Iran and the Popular Front for the Liberation of Palestine-General Command (PFLP-GC) and other radical Palestinian groups, are of special concern. Ethnic groups in Caucasus, Moldavia, and other areas of the Soviet Union may resort to terrorism to achieve their goals, as could some of the numerous factions throughout Eastern Europe. Émigré communities in Western Europe and the United States could be drawn into supporting the violence. West European terrorist groups remain a major threat. Basque and Northern Ireland terrorists are unlikely to reduce the pace of their attacks, and other groups, like the Red Arm Faction (RAF) in West Germany and the Revolutionary Organization 17 November in Greece, have increased their technical capabilities. In Turkey, domestic problems seem to be fostering an increase of violence by long-dormant groups.

The Middle East Overview

The total number of terrorist incidents in the Middle East fell from 313 in 1988 to 193. The incidence of Middle East spillover into other parts of the world declined from 45 to 43. The Iranian campaign against *The Satanic Verses* author Salman Rushdie accounted for a major portion of the attacks of Middle East origin in Western Europe. Of the total terrorist incidents that occurred in the Middle East in 1989, 155 —or just over 80 percent—reflected violence in Israel and the occupied territories, compared with 250 in 1988. Of the 1989 total, 117 were in the West Bank and Gaza, a decrease from 205 in 1988. Although no longer counted in the data base as international terrorist incidents because of their intra-ethnic character, there was an upsurge in intra-Palestinian violence; with the killing of many alleged "collaborators."

A number of factors contributed to the drop in terrorist incidents in the Middle East in 1989. Continuation of the year-long US dialogue with the PLO is conditional on Yasser Arafat's pledge to discontinue PLO terrorism. Since the beginning of the dialogue on 15 December 1988, moreover, we have not been able to independently confirm any act of international terrorism authorized by the PLO's leadership, although some hard-line PLO elements, apparently acted independently, claimed responsibility for several cross-border attacks aimed at Israeli civilian targets.

Another factor is the apparent internal political schism inside one of the most dangerous Middle Eastern terrorist groups—the Abu Nidal organization. The ANO was responsible for a number of attacks in 1988 that resulted in the deaths of nine persons. The group's activities in 1989 however, were disrupted by a serious internal power struggle in which hundreds of ANO members were apparently killed in a dispute over the group's terrorist agenda and its leader's dictatorial style.

The one major terrorist attack that occurred in 1989—the bombing of UTA Flight 772 over Niger on 19 September in which 171 persons were killed—may have been perpetrated by Middle Eastern terrorists. Two statements attributed to the Islamic Jihad organization—a name used by the radical pro-Iranian Hizballah organization—were issued, claiming responsibility for the bombing. Culpability for the bombing has not yet been established and the investigation continues.

Kidnappings and hostage takings also occurred during the year and a US military officer held hostage was murdered by his kidnappers. Five Westerners were taken hostage; a lone Western hostage was released. Hizballah elements and the ANO are the likely suspects in the kidnappings. The July abduction of Sheik Abdul Karim Obeid, a prominent Lebanese cleric, by Israeli forces led to a number of threats against the remaining eight US hostages in Lebanon. The Hizballah group, Organization of the Oppressed of the Earth, claimed in a communiqué that it had executed US hostage Col. William R. Higgins in retaliation for Obeid's abduction.

Although the statistics on incidents perpetrated by Middle Eastern groups reflect a downturn, there are strong indications that the risk to Western and moderate Arab interests remains as high as ever. Iran continues to actively use terrorist tactics to advance its revolutionary goals. The Palestinian issue remains unresolved, and the course of the intifada will affect the operational agenda of several Middle Eastern groups vying to influence its direction. The Middle East peace process may result in greater violence by anti-Arafat groups if perceived as a success or in fragmentation or radicalization of the PLO is perceived as a failure.

Perhaps the greatest potential terrorist threat exists from the growing ties among Iran, its surrogate Hizballah organization in Lebanon, and radical Palestinian groups. Links between Iran and radical Palestinian groups—a relationship that augments Tehran's ties to Hizballah—may have been responsible, according to some press reports, for the bombing of Pan Am Flight 103.

Algeria

The Algerian Government has condemned terrorism in international forums including the United Nations. The Higher Islamic Council in Algiers has strongly denounced Iranian death threats against author Salman Rushdie. Although Algeria condemns terrorism, it has stated that national liberation groups can legitimately resort to violence to accomplish their ends.

After talks in Algiers between the Government of Spain and the Basque separatist group ETA broke down in April, the Government of Algeria cancelled its provision of good offices and expelled some two dozen ETA members. The Algerian Government also attempted to mediate the release of US, Israeli, European, and other hostages in Lebanon last August, but its efforts failed after Hizballah refused to continue the talks.

There is no extradition agreement between the United States and Algeria, and the government has not acted on our requests for assistance in pursuing terrorist cases. As part of a longstanding policy, Algerian has permitted radical groups, some of whom engage in terrorism, to maintain representation in Algiers. The ANO continues to maintain a presence in Algiers. However, reflecting its growing concern over terrorism, the Algerian Government has taken steps to expand the capabilities of counterterrorism units in the police and security apparatus. We have seen over the past year a more pragmatic stance on terrorism issue.

Egypt

The Egyptian Government has waged a campaign to limit the potential terrorist threat posed by radical Moslem fundamentalists and by Egyptian nationalist groups. Twenty members of Egypt's Revolution—a radical group espousing the militant nationalism of former Egyptian President Nasser—have been on trial for the May 1987 attack on US Embassy personnel and for earlier attacks on Israeli diplomats in which two people were killed. The Egyptian prosecution has requested the death penalty for 10 members of the group and life sentences for the rest. There is no conclusive evidence that the sizable Palestinian and Libyan presence in Egypt poses a major terrorist threat, and the activities of expatriates are closely monitored by Egyptian authorities.

There were no terrorist attacks against US personnel in Egypt during 1989, but a number of bomb threats were made against US and UK interests. At least four telephone threats were made during the year against US and British diplomatic and commercial targets, and in June explosive devises were discovered at the US and British cultural centers in Cairo. An explosive device also was discovered at the Giza pyramids along a road traveled by Western tourists. None of the devices exploded.

Egypt has a strong counterterrorism policy and has publicly branded terrorist acts as criminal. It cooperates with the US and other countries in counterterrorism programs and has taken steps to strengthen its own capabilities across the board. It has called for stronger international cooperation in combating terrorism, including improved sharing of intelligence data, strengthened counterterrorism protocols, and increased assistance to less wealthy nations for use in developing counterterrorism programs.

Iraq

Iraq was removed from the US list of state sponsors of terrorism in 1982. Since the expulsion of the ANO in 1983, Iraq has continued working to improve its international image. Iraq did not sponsor any known acts of international terrorism in 1989. Iraq has continued, however, to provide safe haven to some Palestinian groups, including the Iraqi-created Arab Liberation Front and Abu Abbess's Palestine Liberation Front, responsible for the 1985 Achille Lauro hijacking and killing of an American passenger. In addition, press reports indicate that Abu Ibrahim, the former leader of the now defunct 15 May terrorist organization, has returned to Iraq. Abu Ibrahim is known for the skill with which he built highly sophisticated and lethal suitcase bombs. Iraq continues to support anti-Iranian dissident groups including Mujaheddin-e-Khalq (MEK).

There have been questions in the Turkish media about possible Iraqi support for the terrorist Kurdish Worker's Party (PKK). The Iraqi Government maintains it works effectively with the Turkish Government at the local level on the border as well as on a government to government basis to significantly reduce PKK violence. A major failure was the December 1989 PKK massacre of Turkish villagers near the Iraqi border.

Several terrorist attacks including bombings, apparently targeting foreigners, have taken place in Baghdad beginning in July. The perpetrators are unknown although one attack, a bombing at the New British Club which injured 230 people, was claimed by the United Organization of the Halabjah Martyrs, a suspected radical Kurdish group. An afternoon bombing in mid-December on a main business street killed and wounded many passers-by.

The Iraqi authorities are working with the FAA in improve security at Baghdad's airport.

Israel

Israel remained the primary target of Palestinian terrorist attacks during 1989. Indicative of such attacks:

- On 6 July, a 23-year-old Palestinian seeking revenge against Israel forced a crowded bus into a ravine along the Jerusalem-Tel Aviv highway. Sixteen people were killed, including an American and two Canadian tourists; over 20 were injured. This was the single bloodiest attack directed at civilians in Israel in many years.

- There were a number of fatal attacks by Palestinians against Israeli civilians in Israel:
  —On 21 March, a Palestinian stabbed and killed two Israelis and wounded two others in Tel Aviv.
  —On 3 May, a Palestinian stabbed and killed two Israelis in West Jerusalem and injured an 80-year-old woman and two men.
  —On 9 September, a Palestinian stabbed a bus driver on the Jerusalem-Tel Aviv highway and later admitted to murdering another Israeli at a worksite.

- There were also terrorist attacks by a Jewish extremist group, the Sicarii, and by Israeli settlers. Indicative of such attacks:
  —On 10 April, the Sicarii killed two Palestinians and wounded two others near the Jaffe Gate in Jerusalem. The perpetrators claimed the attack was in retaliation for the stoning of Jewish worshippers earlier in the week. This was the first acknowledged attack by the Sicarii against Palestinians. Previously, Sicarii had claimed credit for attacks on Jewish peace activists.
  —On 7 December, Sicarii claimed responsibility for burning the car of a Hebrew University professor; a second firebomb damaged his apartment.
  —On 15 December at a village near Nablus, five Israeli settlers fired weapons at the homes and vehicles of several Palestinians and at a mosque. The firing punctured water tanks, broke windows, and caused other damage.

PLO hardliners and Syrian-backed Palestinian groups outside the PLO attempted more than a dozen cross-border attacks on Israel from Lebanon, Jordan, and Egypt during the year; no Israeli civilians died as a result of these operations. While the precise target of most of the attacks is unclear, hard-line elements in the PLO claimed responsibility for at least three attacks directed at Israeli towns.

Israel has consistently taken a strong position against terrorism and had devoted significant resources to antiterrorism planning and training. Private sector and government-sponsored research is conducted into developing new equipment and techniques, as well as measuring terrorism trends. A massive counterterrorism effort covers neighboring countries known to harbor terrorists or that have failed to inhibit their activities.

Israel uses aggressive measures to protect its citizens and visitors, the best known of which deals with protecting its national air carrier El Al at home and abroad. Ordinary citizens are also trained in counterterrorism tactics, and even school children receive instruction in bomb detection.

Israeli forces have launched preemptive and retaliatory air and commando raids against suspected terrorist installations in neighboring Lebanon. In July, Israeli forces abducted Sheik Abdul Karim Obeid, a leading Hizballah figure in South Lebanon, apparently to obtain information about the whereabouts of Israeli hostages. Arab and other groups branded the abduction terrorist, while Israel defended the action as necessary in view of the threat it faces.

During the past year, Israelis have become increasingly concerned that the Palestinian uprising in the occupied territories will result in more violence within pre-1967 Israel. The police and reserve forces have been expanded and surveillance has been heightened. To enhance control over part of the Arab population, Israeli authorities compelled residents of the Gaza to obtain magnetically coded identity cards. These measures have met with limited success, however, given the relative ease of travel between the occupied territories and Israel.

Israeli courts generally hand down strict prison sentences to those convicted of terrorist and other attacks. During 1989, the courts initiated several prosecutions of suspected terrorists. In October, an Israeli court sentenced the Palestinian responsible for the July bus attack to 16 life prison terms, one life sentence for each of the victims killed in the attack.

The Israeli President in June, however, upon the recommendation of the Justice Minister, reduced the life sentence of three convicted members of the Jewish Underground to 10 years. The three had been convicted of murdering three Arab students in Hebron, wounding over 30 others, and planting explosives. They had already served five years of their life sentences.

Kuwait

There were no terrorist incidents in Kuwait in 1989; however, Iran continued actively recruiting members of the Kuwaiti Shia community to carry out acts of terrorism. The leader of the group responsible for several explosions in Saudi Arabia during the hajj confessed that officials from the Iranian Embassy in Kuwait recruited and trained the cell. According to confessions by members of the group, the explosives used in the attack were acquired from the Iranian Embassy.

The Kuwaiti State Security Court handed down sentences against several Shia in 1989. Two Shia received suspended two year sentences for possession of detonators. The detonators belonged to two of their family members who were killed in a car explosion in 1987. Authorities concluded that the two victims were planning to plant a bomb but that it exploded prematurely. In June, 22 Shia defendants—of Kuwaiti,

Iraqi, Iranian, and Lebanese origin—were sentenced to prison terms ranging from 5 to 15 years for conspiring to overthrow the Kuwaiti Government.

Lebanon

Lebanon was the scene of several acts of international terrorism, in addition to the violence associated with the fifteen-year-old bloody civil war, which has been characterized by frequent use of terrorist tactics. The most significant international attacks were the assassinations of the last remaining Saudi official in West Beirut and of Yasser Arafat's personal representative, which brought the total number of international incidents to 16 for 1989, a decrease from 28 in 1988. Random explosions and attacks on Israeli targets made up the remaining incidents, most of which went unclaimed. The groups undertaking them may have included Palestinian factions, Lebanese leftist and nationalist groups, and Moslem fundamentalist groups, both Sunni and Shia.

Kidnappings of foreigners as well as of Lebanese nationals continued to plague Lebanon. Five foreigners were kidnapped in 1989—one British citizen, two Swiss Red Cross workers, and two West German relief workers. A prominent Lebanese cleric, Sheikh Obeid, was seized by Israeli forces. At yearend as many as 24 foreigners were believed to remain hostage:

- On 31 July, pro-Iranian Hizballah terrorists released a videotape of the hanging of Col. William R. Higgins, which it claimed was in retaliation for the abduction of Sheik Obeid by Israeli Defense Forces on 28 July. Higgins, who was abducted in February 1988, was commander of the United Nations Truce Supervisory Organization observer unit for Lebanon and had been accused of spying by his captors. Higgins had probably been dead for some time when Obeid's abduction provided the Hizballah leadership with a convenient occasion to make the death public. The terrorists also threatened to kill American hostages Joseph Cicippio and Edward Tracy if Obeid was not released, but these threats were not carried out, probably because of international pressure. Obeid remains in jail in Israel.
- Radical Palestinians were probably responsible for taking hostage two Swill International Red Cross workers outside Sidon in October, and two West German relief workers in May. PLO officials have publicly accused the ANO of conducting these kidnappings, which may have been intended to embarrass PLO Chairman Arafat or to obtain ransom for the hostages.

Hizballah terrorists have also been active in attempting to smuggle weapons and explosives into Africa and Europe, undoubtedly to support future terrorist operations, possibly at Iran's behest. Cypriot authorities acting on a tip seized a shipment of jam bound for Monrovia, Liberia, and discovered that it contained explosives, grenades, and detonators. On 23 November in Valencia, Spanish authorities arrested eight radical—including three confessed Hizballah members—before they were able to accept a shipment of foodstuffs that contained additional explosives, grenades and detonators. Both shipments originated in Sidon. These and other discoveries indicate that Iran may be using Hizballah to reestablish its terrorist network in Europe.

Morocco

In September, a lone hijacker, believed to be of Western Saharan origin, hijacked a Royal Air Maroc passenger aircraft to Spain's Canary Islands in the Atlantic Ocean. The aircraft had been on a domestic flight in Morocco. The hijacker was taken into police custody by Spanish authorities upon landing. No one was injured in the incident.

In early 1989, Morocco and the United States signed an agreement on joint cooperation in fighting international terrorism, organized crime and the illicit production, trafficking, and abuse of drugs. In accord with the terms of this agreement, the United States has enjoyed excellent cooperation with the Moroccan Government in countering terrorism. A Mutual Legal Assistance Treaty negotiated in 1983 remains unsigned. The treaty includes extradition provisions.

Saudi Arabia

The Saudi Arabian Government continued to work to prevent terrorism on its territory in 1989. Despite these efforts, the hajj was once again the site of terrorist activity. We believe two explosions—which resulted in one death—were sponsored by Tehran and stemmed from resentment by Iran and radical Shia elements over Riyadh's imposition of restrictions on Iranian attendance of the hajj following pro-Khomeini riots in 1987. In the aftermath of these bombings, Saudi security forces detained a large number of people; however, most were quickly released after interrogation. The persons finally arrested were tried without publicity and according to Sharia law—the customary legal procedure in Saudi Arabia. On 21 September, after review of the sentences by two different appeals boards and the King, 16 Kuwaiti Shia were beheaded. The Saudis also televised pictures of the bombing sites and confessions of the Kuwaiti Shia. The group's leader confessed that the cell members had been recruited and trained by officials from the Iranian Embassy in Kuwait.

After Riyadh's execution of the 16 Kuwaitis, senior Iranian and Hizballah leaders issued statements threatening to avenge the "murders," prompting Saudi security agencies to intensify the internal controls, especially in airports and around Riyadh. Several months after the execution, police were continuing to set up roadblocks and carry out random identification checks. Despite heightened security measures, radical Shia elements carried out several retaliatory attacks against Saudi interests:

- On 14 October, a Saudia Airlines office was severely damaged by an explosion in Lahore, Pakistan.
- On 16 October, a Saudi diplomat in Ankara, Turkey, was seriously injured when a bomb exploded in his car.

- On 1 November, a Saudi official in Beirut was assassinated by members of the Islamic Jihad.

In the area of antiterrorism training, the Saudi Ministry of Interior announced that the antiterrorism unit of the Saudi Special Forces—which began training in 1988—was being disbanded and its West German trainers repatriated. Following a number of terrorist acts and threats against Saudi diplomatic personnel abroad, the Ministry of Foreign Affairs initiated a program aimed at setting up an embassy guard service and a system of regional security offices.

Latin America Overview

There were 131 international terrorist attacks in Latin America during 1989, down from 146 in 1988. This decrease is primarily because of reductions in oil pipeline attacks in Colombia. Elsewhere in the region, the number of international terrorist attacks in 1989 remained essentially the same as last year. Although the number of international terrorist attacks decreased in Colombia, it still led all Latin American countries with 46. Although not counted in the international terrorism statistics because of their essentially domestic nature and criminal motivation, indiscriminate narcoterrorist attacks increased significantly in Colombia, and caused many civilian deaths. Chile was second with 23 international incidents in 1989. Peru had 21, and Honduras and the Dominican Republic each had eight. As in past years, anti-US attacks comprised the majority—about 80 percent—of all international terrorist actions. US personnel of facilities were the targets of 106 of the international terrorist incidents in the region. The most violent anti-US attack was the murder of two American missionaries in Bolivia.

Bolivia

International terrorist incidents in Bolivia numbered five in 1989, down slightly from six in 1988. Attacks this year were focused on US targets, and the Forces of Liberation Zarate Willka was probably responsible for all five actions. The group conducted its most lethal terrorist action in May when it killed two American Mormon missionaries in La Paz. The two probably were killed because they were easier targets than official US personnel or facilities. A message left at the murder scene suggested that the missionaries were attacked to protest alleged US interventionism in Bolivia. In December the group claimed responsibility for a bombing at the US Embassy in retaliation for US military actions in Panama.

Bolivia's judicial system initially responded slowly to the Mormon murders. Several judges assigned to hear the case resigned in the face of threats. The police were also short of resources needed to carry out an extensive investigation. The authorities, however, have since cooperated closely with the FBI agents sent on temporary assignment to assist in the investigation. Several alleged members of Zarate Willka are expected to go to trial in 1990.

According to press reports, Peruvian guerrillas occasionally use Bolivian territory for rest and relaxation, and have shown increasing interest in assisting indigenous terrorist groups in recruitment and training activities. Peruvian guerrillas do not appear to have carried out any terrorist attacks in Bolivia in 1989. The country also is facing a growing threat from narcotraffickers, especially those from Colombia, who are seen it Bolivia with increasing frequency since the Barco government there launched its offensive against them. Immigration authorities lack sufficient intelligence on foreign terrorists and other criminals, and given the long stretches of unguarded frontier; they do not have the means for denying entry to such people.

Chile

In Chile, 23 international terrorist attacks occurred in 1989, more than double last year's total. All the attacks were anti-US actions. Many were against Mormon churches which are often targeted by leftist radicals in Chile and elsewhere in the region as easily identifiable US targets. Not all attacks this year were conducted by the Manuel Rodriguez Patriotic Front (FPMR), Chile's largest and most active radical leftist group. The Arnoldo Camu Command claimed responsibility for a bomb that detonated across the street from the US Embassy in September. The Lautaro Youth Movement conducted an attack on a Mormon chapel where an American citizen was singled out and mistreated in July, and another Lautaro group, the Lautaro Popular Rebel Forces, left leaflets at a Mormon chapel that was set on fire. In December, the Lautaro Commando claimed one of several bombings at Mormon churches in Chile, scrawling "Yankees out of Panama" on the wall of one chapel. That same week, the USIS Binational Center in Santiago was bombed by unidentified terrorists.

Because of the indigenous terrorist threat, the Pinochet government maintained a strong and active antiterrorist force comprised of army units, the Carabineros, the Investigations Police (roughly equivalent to the FBI), and the National Information Center (CNI), all of which are well trained. At times, however, their investigations and suspect interrogations violated basic human rights, according to most human rights monitors, although there was marked improvement in their performance over the previous years.

Significant quantities of weapons have been smuggled to leftist groups in the country via the porous border with Argentina and the extensive coastline.

Terrorist prosecutions in the courts have virtually been only against leftists, while incidents of rightwing terrorism have rarely been followed by arrests. The failure to apprehend any rightwing extremists has led to speculation that their activities may be unofficially sanctioned by some members of the security forces. Those terrorists arrested usually are tried by military courts and receive lengthy prison terms.

In June the Chilean Government publicly expressed disappointment over a US decision not to extradite a FPMR member who was being held in preventive custody in Alaska. The FPMR member had been en route to Sweden after being deported from Australia, but was taken off the airliner when it landed for refueling. After considering the Chilean case against him, the US authorities determined the charges of importing weapons into Chile were not extraditable offenses under the term of the US-Chilean Extradition Treaty. The FPMR member was released and put on a flight to Sweden where he maintained a residence.

In March, the Chilean Government blamed terrorists and communists for the cyanide fruit scare that threatened one of the country's most lucrative exporting industries. In the United States, the FDA had temporarily banned Chilean fruit after finding cyanide traces in Chilean grapes in Philadelphia.

The United States has a continuing interest in resolving the 1976 murders of former Chilean Ambassador and Pinochet-critic Orlando Letelier and American associate Ronni Moffitt in Washington, D.C. After being rebuffed in other legal efforts, the US Government in January invoked a 1914 Bilateral Dispute Settlement treaty to resolve the case. At yearend, the Chilean Government had yet to agree to the members or the mandate of the international commission called for in the treaty.

Colombia

Colombia is a country under attack by three leftist guerrilla groups, narcotraffickers, and rightwing paramilitary groups. Its democratic institutions are under direct threat. Cuba provides some training to all major guerrilla groups, and an undetermined number of Colombians travel their each year for training.

International terrorist incidents in Colombia during 1989 remained high, despite a decline from the year before. Amidst spiraling domestic violence, the guerrillas have targeted foreign personnel and property. The decrease in pipeline bombings in 1989 accounted for the sharp downturn in the number of attacks on international targets. Twenty-three pipeline attacks occurred in 1989, down from 58 in 1988. This decline in pipeline sabotage attacks—counted as anti-US actions as well as international terrorist actions because of US companies' involvement in the oil consortium there—probably came about as a result of aggressive counterinsurgency measures by the Colombian Government that kept the pipeline saboteurs—the National Liberation Army (ELN)—off guard.

The ELN was probably responsible for all other guerrilla-sponsored international terrorism in Colombia as well, although not every incident was claimed by the group. ELN kidnapped 11 foreigners in six separate incidents. Ten of the kidnap victims were foreign engineers working in jobs related to the oil industry. The eleventh victim was a Colombian ranch owner who holds dual US-Colombian citizenship.

The military, following reorganization by President Barco, initiated increasingly aggressive tactics against the guerrillas in 1989, culminating in a November offensive that resulted in the highest number of subversive casualties on record. The government also engaged the M-19 in peace talks that appeared close to success by yearend, as M-19 agreed to demobilize and become a legal political party.

Dominican Republic

The Dominican Republic was the scene of eight international terrorist attacks this year, all of which were directed against US targets. In February, an attempted bomb attack against the USIS Binational Center failed. In April, another bomb exploded at the Binational Center, killing a Dominican baby and wounding its mother. Bombs also exploded in April at a restaurant and on a street in Santo Domingo's business section. In December, several more anti-US attacks occurred in the wake of the US military action in Panama. In one of these attacks, a Mormon missionary was shot in the leg in Santo Domingo. Also in December, a caller claimed two attacks on a US telephone company subsidiary in the Dominican Republic in the name of the Revolutionary Army of the People.

Two suspects were charged for the April bombing on the Binational Center, although one was later released and allowed to travel to Cuba for medical treatment, where he died. The remaining suspect, believed to have planted the bomb that killed the infant, remains in custody. He reportedly received Libyan terrorist training.

In response to FAA concerns, the Dominican Government tightened security measures at Santo Domingo's international airport, and airport officials are receiving additional training at FAA facilities.

In April, the Dominican Government, with the concurrence of the Spanish Government, accepted six Basque Fatherland and Liberty (ETA) members who were being deported from Algeria. Subsequently Spain requested that two of the six be extradited to face terrorist charges. Although this request is under formal consideration, the President has indicated they will not be extradited.

Ecuador

Despite the terrorism in neighboring countries, there were no significant terrorist acts in Ecuador in 1989. Substantial reconciliation was reached with the domestic terrorist group Alfaro Vive Carajo (AVC). In March, government officials and AVC representatives signed an accord under which the AVC agreed to give up armed actions and to enter into legitimate political activities.

In October, five AVC members who had been held without formal charges in the 1985 kidnapping-murder of a local businessman were released from prison. Two other AVC members, who have been formally charged, are awaiting prosecution. In October, the government allowed the AVC to host a conference entitled "Forum on Latin American Democracy." Reportedly, representatives of several Latin American terrorist or former terrorist groups were among the attendees. Another terrorist group, the Monteneros Patria Libre (MPL), remains sworn to destroy the government.

El Salvador

In El Salvador, the number of terrorist actions involving foreign persons or property decreased in 1989, from 13 in 1988 to nine. One person with dual US-Salvadoran citizenship was killed by the FMLN as a result of his political beliefs. Two US and Canadian citizens were injured when a bomb went off in a village where they were working for the Lutheran Church. In November, Farabundo Marti Liberation Front (FMLN) guerillas launched a major offensive in San Salvador, jeopardizing civilians and targeting foreign personnel to gain international attention. Despite claims to the contrary, the guerillas' choice of a luxury hotel as a staging ground for battle with Salvadoran troops indicates that they planned to exploit the presence of foreigners for propaganda purposes, thereby endangering civilians. Several foreigners, including an American, were injured during the offensive.

FMLN-associated terrorists were responsible for the assassinations of two high-level government officials—killing the Attorney General in April and the Minister of the Presidency in June. They also killed prominent political figures, including nine mayors, the national fire chief, the former president of the supreme court, as well as numerous civilians. The FMLN also began targeting family members of military personnel and, in October, urban terrorists killed the 23-year-old daughter of an armed forces colonel. The FMLN conducted other acts of domestic terrorism such as a bus attack in August in which the driver was killed and a woman passenger severely injured, a bombing in the capital's central marketplace in June in which three died and 25 were wounded, and an earlier bus attack in May in which seven were killed and eight wounded. Following the May incident, the FMLN in a communiqué publicly accepted responsibility for the attack and laid out new "rules of engagement" intended to minimize civilian injuries. In all, during the FMLN's campaign against the transportation system, approximately 80 buses were destroyed or damaged. The FMLN also launched an economic sabotage campaign in which it inflicted losses on the coffee, cotton, sugar, and cattle industries. In November, the government suspended diplomatic relations to Managua after an aircraft originating from Nicaragua and loaded with surface-to-air missiles destined for the FMLN crashed in El Salvador.

To limit terrorist activities, the Salvadoran military and security forces conducted preemptive raids of terrorist safe houses, hideouts and support areas. Over 1,200 weapons were seized across the country. The legislature sought, starting in June, to strengthen the country's terrorism laws. In December, it passed a modified version, but the president returned the proposed law, asking that several portions be dropped or amended as he considered them restrictive of individual rights. The judicial system remains inadequate and is incapable of processing and investigating the large number of terrorism-related detainees and crimes. The courts are hampered by inadequate resources, lack of competent workers, corruption, intimidation, and antiquated laws.

There continued to be bombing incidents and killing which appear attributable to the rightwing. Individual members of the armed forces may also be involved in this violence. The Salvadoran Government announced in early 1990 that several members of the military were responsible for the 16 November murders of six Jesuit priests, their housekeeper, and her daughter. The government continues its investigation into this important human rights concern.

Guatemala

Although there were few incidents of international terrorism in Guatemala in 1989, there was a sharp increase in domestic terrorism in the capital. Terrorism took the form of bombings at shopping malls and other public locations, grenade attacks, and attacks on economic targets. There continues to be frequent cases of murder, kidnapping, disappearances and torture, some of it due to far-right elements and dissidents within the military. Although some attempts have been made by the government and various other institutions in the country to address this problem, there appears to be a general lack of social or political will to find and prosecute those responsible. In 1989, there was an increase in guerrilla activity, particularly in urban areas. These guerrillas receive support from Cuba, Nicaragua, and other communist and leftist countries and organizations.

Guatemala has sought increased cooperation with its neighbors to restrict the movement of terrorist and insurgent groups across its borders.

Honduras

The number of international terrorist incidents in Honduras increased markedly in 1989, up from two in 1988 to eight in 1989. All actions were directed at US personnel or facilities in Honduras. In the past few years, leftists have primarily targeted US military personnel. In 1989, a variety of US targets were hit, including three attacks that resulted in injuries to 10 US soldiers. Other US interests targeted included the Peace Corps, USAID, and Standard Fruit Company. The Morazanist Patriotic Front is suspected of several anti-US attacks, including an April assault on a convoy of US and Honduran soldiers.

Other leftist guerrilla groups that have resorted to terrorist tactics in the past are the Popular Liberation Movement-Cinchoneros (MPL-Cinchoneros) and the Popular Revolutionary Forces-Lorenzo Zelaya (MPF-LZ). Both receive significant logistic, training, and financial support from Nicaragua and Cuba, with key personnel maintaining their headquarters in Nicaragua.

Efforts toward increased collaboration among Honduran guerilla organizations, the FMLN in El Salvador, and the Sandinista army and intelligence organizations have been reported. The FMLN likely uses Salvadoran refugee camps in Honduras for infiltrating its guerrillas into El Salvador. The Honduran armed forces interdicted two major arms shipments transiting from Nicaragua to the Salvadoran guerrillas in 1989.

The Honduran Armed Forces continued their antiterrorist operations and monitoring of radical organizations during the year. They conducted sweeps of known guerrilla operating areas, raids on unsuspected safe houses, and border searches of vehicles for possible arms shipments. Three Hondurans believed sought for questioning for involvement with armed leftist organizations surfaced in Mexico, where they were given asylum. One of the two surviving terrorists who attempted to bomb a US Embassy warehouse in April has received a preliminary hearing and is in custody awaiting trial.

Nicaragua

Nicaragua, like Cuba, also provides training and safe haven to Latin American and other terrorist and guerrilla groups. It continues to support Salvadoran guerrillas despite a commitment to end such assistance. In Honduras, the Nicaraguan regime provides support to the Cinchoneros Popular Liberation Movement and the Popular Revolutionary Forces-Lorenzo Zelaya, and is believed to have ties to the Morazanist Patriotic Front. Managua also frequently acts as a coordinator and provides a venue for radical groups from many parts of the world as well as those from Central and South America. In recent years, Nicaragua has better concealed its links to West European terrorists. Managua maintains diplomatic relations with all six countries presently on the US list of terrorism-supporting countries.

Panama

During 1989, there were reports that the Panama Defense Forces of the Manuel Noriega regime and the paramilitary "Dignity Battalions," which were used primarily to intimidate opposition figures, had made contingency plans to seize US citizens as hostages in case of US action against Noriega. Shortly after the US invasion in December, an American teacher was taken hostage by pro-Noriega gunmen was killed. Regime agents were also suspected of being behind the February bombing of an opposition television station in an effort to destabilize the political situation prior to the national elections.

During 1989, the Noriega regime made a concerted effort to improve relations with Libya and to a lesser extent with Iran. It also took steps to establish relations with North Korea and improve its ties to Cuba.

Panama's geographical position and role as a trade and banking center made it a crossroads for the travel and transactions of various terrorist and insurgent groups, including Colombian narcoterrorists. Some of this activity was facilitated by the Cuban and Nicaraguan Embassies and the Libyan People's Bureau in Panama. Noriega and several political associates were publicly implicated in the shipment of arms to such groups as El Salvador's FMLN and Colombia's M-19 and FARC. In the later part of the year, a high-ranking FMLN leader announced his group was establishing a press center in Panama that would be issuing "war bulletins."

Peru

International terrorist attacks in Peru reached 21 in 1989, up from last year's total of 15. This number of international incidents does not reveal the true extent of violence in the country where nearly 3,200 people died in terrorism-related violence, the vast majority of which was attributed to Sendero Luminoso (SL). SL continued the trend it started late in 1988 of attacking foreigners in rural areas. Although their attacks traditionally go unclaimed, we believe the group was responsible for the death of a British tourist, an Australian, a New Zealander, an Austrian, and a German couple. All these attacks occurred in the countryside. In Lima, SL attacked a busload of touring Soviet fishermen in July and carried out simultaneous attacks later in the year at the Chinese and Soviet Embassies and the US Marine residence. Local police also suspect the group was behind an attack on the US Embassy in February. At that time, an explosive device was tossed from a passing vehicle at the front of the Embassy. SL's involvement with the drug trade may have motivated an attack on a Drug Enforcement Administration helicopter, also early in 1989.

Peru's smaller, pro-Cuban guerrilla group, the Tupac Amaru Revolutionary Movement (MRTA), probably conducted seven of the 21 international attacks in Peru in 1989. In mid-April, the group tossed an explosive device over the wall of the USIS Binational Center in the suburbs of Lima. The timing of this attack suggests that it many have been meant to mark the anniversary of the US air strikes on Libya in 1986. The MRTA has conducted other such attacks to mark the event in previous years. The group also claimed responsibility for the bombing of two Mormon churches and a Binational Center in rural Peru during December in protest of US actions in Panama.

During 1989, the Peruvian Government attempted to initiate several strategies against the domestic terrorist threat, primarily dealing with enforcement. In April, a new political-military commander was assigned to the Upper Huallaga Valley, a principal staging area for SL and MRTA activities. He was given wider latitude for dealing with these groups and was initially assigned additional resources. At yearend, eight of Peru's 24 departments had been designated emergency zones, as well as parts of the department of Lima. Such designation permits direct military involvement in antiterrorist actions.

To counter the public relations efforts of pro-Sendero support elements abroad, the Peruvian Government has attempted through international forums, including the UN and the OAS, to call attention to Sendero's antidemocratic and terrorist campaign in the country. In this effort, Peruvian Government officials have been joined by members of opposition and leftist parties.

Approximately 2,000 people are under detention in Peruvian prisons charged with terrorist crimes, three times as many as were being held just years ago. Prosecution through the courts moves slowly. The trial of Osman Morote, who was captured in 1988 and is suspected of being the second-highest-ranking SL leader, is in his third retrial. By the end of the year, the trial of Victor Polay, suspected of being number two in MRTA, had concluded and was awaiting the court's decision. Three suspected members of the Abu Nidal organization, arrested in 1988, remain under detention.

Europe and North America Overview

In Western Europe, domestic and Middle Eastern groups staged 96 international terrorist attacks in 1989, a substantial decrease from 150 in 1988. Western Europe ranked third in the number of attacks worldwide, with 18 percent occurring there. Of these, 22 were against US targets, resulting in one death, compared with 191 deaths and 11 wounded in 1988. Thirty-one of the international incidents resulted from Middle Eastern spillover. Indigenous groups operating against domestic targets accounted for most of the terrorist attacks in Western Europe, indicating they remain a major problem despite their generally less spectacular nature.

Continued counterterrorism efforts throughout the region, and a continuation of the low-level of Middle Eastern spillover—a result of caution by state sponsors and the apparent decision by Palestinian groups to focus operations elsewhere—contributed to the decline in the number of incidents in Western Europe. Multilateral cooperation among West European authorities resulted in several notable arrests of indigenous group members, including Red Brigades (BR) in Spain, France, and Switzerland, Provision Irish Republican Army (PIRA) in France and the Federal Republic of Germany, and Basque Fatherland and Liberty (ETA) in France. In addition, authorities discovered several weapons caches apparently linked to Middle Eastern groups in Denmark, Cyprus, and Spain.

Austria

There were just two international terrorist incidents in Austria in 1989. The more significant of these took place in July when three Kurdish activists, including the leader of the Iranian Kurdish Democratic Party, were assassinated in Vienna during a meeting with three Iranian officials. The government was slow to respond to these murders despite strong evidence of official Iranian complicity. After public and press complaints about the slow response, as well as accusations that the government had succumbed to Iranian threats against the lives of Austrians in Iran, the investigation was intensified and, in November, warrants were issued for the three Iranian officials on suspicion of murder. One of the officials, who was injured during the shooting, was not originally considered a suspect and had been allowed to leave the country. The second fled Austria immediately after the killings, and the third took refuge in the Iranian Embassy in Vienna.

Austrian authorities have sought Interpol's assistance in finding the fugitives and have stepped up surveillance against the Iranian Embassy in Vienna to prevent the escape of the one individual still suspected of being there.

Five Middle Eastern terrorists are imprisoned in Austria for attacks that took place in 1981 and 1985. In June, an Innsbruck court sentenced a terrorist sympathetic to the South Tyrol cause to five and a half years for crimes, including the unsuccessful attempt to derail a train in October 1988.

Austria values its role as an international center for negotiation and conciliation, and persons of all political persuasions are allowed to operate inside the country. Austria has traditionally close relations with many Arab states. The United States has noted an improvement in the policy level dialogue on counterterrorism since the November visit to Washington of the new Austrian Interior Minister.

Belgium

There were five international terrorist attacks in Belgium in 1989—one more than in 1988. In March the Saudi Arabian Sunni Imam of Brussels' largest mosque and his Tunisian librarian were killed by a gunman, probably in reaction to the Iman's public opposition to Ayatollah Khomeini's demand for the execution of author Salman Rushdie. In June an unknown gunman killed an Egyptian who worked as a driver at the Saudi Embassy in Brussels; the attack may have been linked to Saudi Arabia's refusal to allow Iran to participate in the annual Islamic pilgrimage to Mecca and Medina in July. In March, unknown assailants threw two Molotov cocktails through a window of a Yugoslav travel agency in Brussels, causing minor damage but no injuries. No group claimed responsibility, but the incident probably resulted from ethnic Albanian conflicts in the Yugoslav Province of Kosovo. In December, a Syrian diplomat escaped an attempted assassination when two grenades were discovered attached to the undercarriage of his car.

Authorities continue investigations into the October killing of Belgian Jewish leader Joseph Wybran as well as the other attacks. A little known group, Soldiers of the Right, claimed credit for the attack on Wybran as well as the March attack in Brussels on the Saudi Imam. While Belgian authorities have drawn no firm conclusions concerning the identities of the killers or reasons for the attacks, some press reports have linked Soldiers of the Right to the Abu Nidal organization, possibly working in the pay of Iran.

Belgian hostage Dr. Jan Cools was released in Lebanon in May while the Belgian trade minister was on a visit to Libya. Although the trade minister initially indicated he discussed Dr. Cools' release with Qadhafi, the Belgian Government stated the minister's visit was to discuss trade relations with Libya and was unrelated to the Lebanese hostage issue. Dr. Cools' abduction had also been claimed by the same group that claimed the Wybran and Saudi Imam's killings, Soldiers of the Right.

Belgium continued efforts in 1989 to reach agreement on border security—including visa controls, information sharing and extradition matters—with the cosignatories of the Schengen agreement (Holland, Luxembourg, France, and West Germany).

Canada and the United States

Canada was the scene of one international terrorist incident in 1989. On 7 April, a Lebanese immigrant living in Montreal hijacked a US-bound passenger bus and ordered it to

Ottawa. The hijacker claimed he was a member of the Lebanese Liberation Front and demanded that Syrian forces withdraw from Lebanon. He surrendered after releasing his hostages. No one was injured in the incident, but Canadian interests suffered from terrorist attacks in other areas of the world. One Canadian citizen was killed the bombing of UTA Flight 772 over Niger and another was wounded in a bombing in El Salvador in January.

Canada successfully sought the extradition from the United Kingdom of a former Sikh resident of Canada. He was wanted on charges of participating in the bombing that killed two baggage handlers in Tokyo's Narita Airport in 1985. The baggage handlers died when a bomb exploded in luggage bound for an Air India flight which they were removing from an arriving Canadian flight. The suspected terrorist was extradited to Canada in December.

At yearend, convicted Palestinian terrorist Mahmoud Mohammed Issa Mohammed was still contesting deportation efforts by the Canadian Government. Mohammed, a former member of the Popular Front for the Liberation of Palestine (PFLP), is accused of having lied on his immigration application by concealing a conviction in Greece for participation in a 1968 attack on an El Al airliner. One Israeli was killed in that attack. A Canadian immigration panel is still deciding Issa's claim to refugee status.

Canada participates with the US in a bilateral consultative group on counterterrorism cooperation. In 1989, it participated in a joint counterterrorism exercise, exchanged information on terrorism, discussed measures for managing transborder incidents, examined areas for joint research and development, and coordinated counterterrorism programs of third [world] countries.

The United States experienced three likely incidents of international terrorism is 1989. Bookstores in New York and California selling *The Satanic Verses* were bombed. Iran is believed to be behind the series of attacks around the world protesting the book.

Cyprus

Spillover of terrorism from the Middle East accounted for the lone terrorist incident in Cyprus in 1989. On 28 August two Iranian Kurdish dissidents—one of whom had published anti-Khomeini articles in Sweden—were shot and one killed in Larnaca as they were returning to their hotel. Authorities speculated that the murders were carried out by pro-Iranian supporters, but the investigation remains at a standstill.

In the court prosecution following the May discovery of SA-7 missiles believed to be planned for use in assassinating visiting Lebanese Christian leader General Michael Aoun, five of the six Lebanese suspects were convicted and each sentenced to a variable term of one to eight years in prison. The sixth, because of mental disorder, was sentenced to a term of one to five years. According to news reports, the six pleaded guilty to charges of illegal importation, possession and transportation of arms and explosives, in return for the government dropping the more serious charge of conspiracy to commit murder. The authorities proceeded with the trial despite repeated warning from groups sympathetic to the arrestees that Cyprus would suffer retribution should the six be prosecuted.

In June, the Cypriot Supreme Court reviewed the sentences that a lower court had imposed the previous January on two suspected Arab terrorists. The two were convicted of involvement in a 1987 ambush in which a British soldier and young female British dependent were wounded. While the Supreme Court upheld one conviction, it overturned the other, stating that the defendant's complicity had not been proved beyond "every reasonable doubt."

In October, a cache of explosives, grenades, and detonators believed to belong to Hizballah operatives was discovered in Larnaca in foodstuffs being shipped from Lebanon to Liberia. Authorities investigated the contents of the shipment after being tipped that it contained drugs. A second, related shipment was discovered in Valencia, Spain one month later. There are indications that both the Cyprus and Valencia arms and explosives were likely to be used against Western and moderate Arab targets.

Denmark

Denmark experienced no acts of international terrorism in 1989. Two cases related to terrorism, however, captured public attention. Danish police in May discovered a Copenhagen apartment filled with antitank rockets, explosives, and other military ordnance. Although it is not known to what purpose these weapons were to be put, the group involved, dubbed the "Appel gang," has been implicated in the planning of two kidnapping attempts in Europe and is suspected of involvement in several bank robberies. Seven gang members are currently imprisoned. The Danish group has been linked to the Middle East's PFLP and may have been gathering information on Jewish interests for the PFLP as well as sending them money from the robberies. The second terrorism-related case concerned the arrest and interrogation of a Danish schoolteacher in Israel in July. The schoolteacher claimed that she traveled to Israel to meet the family of her Palestinian activist boyfriend and to learn about events on the West Bank. Israeli police claim she was part of a plot to place a bomb at the Jewish Olympics and blow up the Danish delegation, which included the chief rabbi of Copenhagen. The schoolteacher maintained her innocence and returned to Denmark upon her release from jail.

In January, the Foreign Ministry indicated that relations with Libya were being upgraded when it announced that an ambassador was being assigned to replace its charge d'affaires in Tripoli. Although the Danish Foreign Ministry intended the move only as a personnel action to accommodate the rotation of its personnel, criticism immediately followed, as this move appeared to break ranks with Denmark's Western allies on how to handle relations with Libya. The Foreign Ministry subsequently withdrew the appointment and the Danish mission in Tripoli has been maintained at the charge level.

Denmark is a favorite destination of Middle Eastern asylum seekers and approximately 99 percent of all Palestinian applicants receive asylum. It is believed that most major Middle Eastern terrorist groups have taken advantage of this liberal policy to place "sleeper agents" in Denmark.

Federal Republic of Germany

International terrorist attacks decreased in 1989 from 1988, with 17 incidents as compared to 25, and the number of Middle Eastern spillover incidents decreased from four in 1988 to one in 1989. Five relatively minor incidents were against US targets. The number of domestic incidents continued to decline, suggesting that West German counterterrorist efforts have been successful and that there may be ideological disarray among radical West German leftists.

A variety of groups were responsible for the international attacks. Northern Ireland's PIRA intensified its campaign against British military forces stationed in West Germany, conducting seven attacks that killed four persons and injured eight. Leftwing German groups are suspected in six international attacks conducted in solidarity with a hunger strike by imprisoned members of the Red Army Faction. The six were: three against Shell gas stations that also protested Shell investments in South Africa, and three arson attacks against a US automobile dealership, a US hotel, and a French automobile dealership. In June, several Serbians assassinated a Kosovo Albanian in Stuttgart. The PKK is suspected in the attempted assassination of a Turkish Kurd in Celle in April.

Middle Eastern terrorists are suspected in a bombing at Cologne University that injured two persons in February. A meeting of Iranian student groups commemorating the 10th anniversary of the Iranian Revolution was taking place on the campus at the time of the explosion.

On the domestic front, the RAF claimed responsibility for the technically sophisticated bombing attack that killed Deutsche Bank Chairman Alfred Herrhausen and injured the driver of his armored car in November. The assassination was the first RAF attack since the group's failed attack against a senior Finance Ministry official in September 1988. West German authorities are undertaking one of the biggest law enforcement efforts in recent years to find the persons who planted the bomb. Efforts are still under way to identify those responsible for the 1988 attempted assassination of Finance Ministry State Secretary Hans Tietmeyer. The RAF claimed responsibility for both attacks.

In May, imprisoned RAF terrorists ended a 100-day hunger strike that failed to achieve the primary goal of collocation of RAF prisoners. At one point, up to 50 prisoners in 18 prisons throughout West Germany participated in the strike. Supporters staged dozens of arson attacks and demonstrations in an expression of solidarity with the hunger strikers.

Several counterterrorist prosecutions took place in West German courts in 1989. In May, the Hesse State Supreme Court convicted Lebanese national Muhammad Ali Hammadi and sentenced him to life imprisonment for his role in the June 1985 hijacking of TWA Flight 847 to Beirut, the murder of US Navy diver Robert Stethem, and the possession of explosives. The kidnapping of two West German relief workers in Lebanon just days before the Hammadi verdict may have been an unsuccessful attempt to influence the court in its decision. The two relief workers continue to be held. Bassam Makki, a Lebanese terrorist arrested in June 1989, received a two-year sentence for conspiracy to carry out bomb attacks against US and Israeli interests in Munich and Frankfurt. The trial of 20 PKK members for murder and other serious charges began in November 1989 in Düsseldorf. Also in Düsseldorf in June, the court sentenced a woman journalist to five years in prison for her involvement in a 1986 bombing of Lufthansa's headquarters in Cologne by the domestic terrorist group Revolutionary Cells.

German authorities are expected to begin several other counterterrorism trials early in 1990. Two suspected PIRA members are charged with the bombings of British Army barracks in Duisburg and Ratigen during the summer of 1988. In addition, the West German Government has requested the extradition from France and Ireland of five suspected PIRA members accused of participation in bombing and shooting attacks against other British targets in Germany. Hafiz Dalkamoni, a ranking official of the PFLP-GC, and another group member have been held in custody since October 1988. They will be tried for two failed attacks against US military duty trains in 1987 and 1988. Press reports have also mentioned Dalkamoni as a suspect in the Pan Am Flight 103 bombing, in view of the similarities in the bombs found in his group's possession and the one that destroyed the airliner.

The Federal Republic of Germany's policies toward asylum seekers have resulted in the presence in the country of persons from terrorist supporting states or groups. Some terrorist organizations have established a support infrastructure within the country. In addition, since German border controls are minimal and Germany is a transportation center, it is likely that some wanted terrorists have passed through the country without knowledge of the authorities.

German authorities continue to work closely with US, British, and other authorities to identify the individuals responsible for the bombing of Pan Am Flight 103 in December 1988 over Lockerbie, Scotland. West Germany actively participates with other members of groups such as Summit Seven, Interpol, the Trevi Group, and the United Nations and its specialized agencies such as ICAO and the IMO, to strengthen antiterrorism cooperation efforts. It continued efforts in 1989 to reach agreement on border security—including visa controls, information sharing, and extradition matters—with the other signatories of the Schengen agreement.

France

The number of international terrorist attacks in France declined to five in 1989 from 15 in 1988. Most of the incidents were unclaimed and involved bombs that caused property damage and no casualties. In March, a small bomb exploded on a window ledge outside the Moroccan Consulate in Lyon.

A car bomb exploded outside the Commerce Office of the People's Republic of China diplomatic mission in September. In October, a bomb damaged a publishing firm that printed the French version of *The Satanic Verses*; no injuries resulted. The French Government launched a major investigation to determine the group responsible for bombing a French UTA passenger jet in Central Africa, killing 171 persons aboard.

French police scored a number of successes against international terrorist groups in 1989. The French Government continued its fight against the Spanish Basque group ETA, which has traditionally used southwestern France as a staging ground for its operations. The Socialist government of Michel Rocard has maintained its policy of pursuing major ETA leaders living clandestinely in France, rather than expelling hundreds of minor suspected ETA terrorists or supporters as was practiced during the Chirac government during 1986/88. The action against ETA has been waged with a scrupulous regard for French laws, resulting in the occasional release of suspected Basque terrorists for lack of evidence or refusal to extradite them to Spain for procedural reasons.

In January 1989, French police arrested Jose Urruticoechea (aka Josu Ternera), considered to be among the top three ETA leaders, along with nine other ETA members. In May and June, French authorities arrested one of ETA's founders and treasurer. In December, police uncovered the largest ETA arms cache ever discovered in France.

Other international terrorist groups affected by French police actions include the Italian Red Brigades and PIRA. In September, French authorities, acting in close coordination with Italian security services, arrested five members of a Parisian cell of the Red Brigades-Fight Communist Party faction. The following month French police arrested three members of the Red Brigades' Union of Communist Combatants faction. French police worked closely with British and Irish authorities to arrest three important PIRA militants—including Patrick Murray, reputed to be one the group's most deadly members—in eastern France in July. The PIRA members were allegedly preparing for a terrorist attack against British military targets in West Germany.

French counterterrorism policies were not uniformly applied to the challenge of dealing with domestic regionalist or nationalist terrorism. Paris maintained a tough stance with the small French Basque Iparretarrak (IK) separatist movement, as well as the Breton Revolutionary Alliance (ARB). The French Government took a more conciliatory approach, however, toward the Corsican National Liberation Front (FLNC) and the small Guadeloupe-based Caribbean Revolutionary Alliance (ARC).

IK maintained a low level of violence throughout 1989. The group failed in its attack on a French Government building in Biarritz in January, but successfully bombed an empty regional French tax office in Bayonne in June, and, in its potentially most deadly act, timed a bomb to derail the Paris-Madrid express—an operation that might have killed dozens had the train not been delayed on the Spanish side of the border. Police in Bayonne arrested the group's chief ideologue in March.

The ARB carried out a nuisance campaign in 1989, targeting French public buildings in Brittany. French authorities arrested a half dozen members, and by yearend the group appeared inactive, if only temporarily.

Local police destroyed the ARC's small terrorist network in Guadeloupe during 1987, and by 1989 the group no longer presented a serious threat. Responding to protests from a variety of political forces in Guadeloupe, the French Government included a dozen ARC members in the traditional Bastille Day amnesty in July 1989. At the time of the amnesty declaration, French counterterrorism magistrates were on the verge of trying the ARC members for a variety of terrorist acts.

The French Government policy toward the Corsican FLNC has been to lure it away from violence and to convince the group to abide by the truce declared with the central government in May 1988. In addition to formulating reforms designed to grant Corsica greater political and economic autonomy, the French Government released approximately 50 suspected FLNC terrorists in French prisons, and later extended the Bastille Day amnesty to include all convicted Corsican terrorists. The FLNC appears to have used the truce to rebuild its clandestine military apparatus. In November the group blew up two tourist apartment complexes in Corsica and destroyed a French Ministry of Agriculture building in Ajaccio. No casualties resulted from the attacks.

France was active in several multilateral organizations in 1989. President Mitterrand, acting in his capacity as leader of the Group of Seven leading industrial Western countries, reacted to the December 1988 bombing of Pan Am Flight 103 by calling an emergency meeting of the Summit Seven terrorism experts group, which met in Paris in January. The French Government convened a second meeting of the group in June to discuss counterterrorism language for the July Summit communiqué. In its role as European Community President during the last half of the year, France chaired the community's Trevi Group, which manages police and security cooperation among the twelve members. Under French leadership, Trevi continue to work on the challenges stemming from the EC's 1992 open borders project and began devising security measures to compensate for the abolition of the community's internal frontiers. France was also active in multilateral efforts within ICAO and other venues to establish an international regime to tag plastic explosives.

France has one of Europe's most experienced cadres of specialized counterterrorist magistrates, and the courts convicted substantial numbers of terrorists during 1989. These included the ringleaders of the leftwing Action Directe group and several mid-level Basque terrorists from ETA and Iparretarrak. In December 1989 a Paris court convicted a member of the now-defunct Palestinian terrorist group, 15 May Organization, and sentenced him to life imprisonment for his role in a series of bombings in London and Paris between 1983 and 1985 against Marks and Spencer department stores and Bank Leumi. The former 15 May leader, Abu Ibrahim, will be tried in absentia in early 1990.

Greece

The number of international incidents declined in Greece, from nine in 1988 to five in 1989, but domestic terrorism remained a major problem. The Greek terrorist group Revolutionary Popular Struggle (ELA) bombed four cars belonging to US civilian employees at the Hellenikon Air Base—a tactic it used in its anti-US campaign in the 1970s. Another attack directed at foreigners was the bombing of a French bank to protest the convictions of French terrorists.

Greek domestic groups remained among the most active in Europe during 1989. The groups focused their attacks on targets associated with the Koskotas financial scandal, deliberations on the extradition of Mohammed Rashid, and the Parliamentary elections. The Revolutionary Organization 17 November in separate attacks killed one prosecutor and a prominent member of Parliament, Pavlos Bakoyiannis, who was the son-in-law of the leader of the conservative New Democracy party. 17 November is believed responsible for wounding a Supreme Court prosecutor and a Member of Parliament, George Petsos, who was a former Minister of Public Order. Greek authorities also believe the group was responsible for a bank robbery in June. The Revolutionary Organization 1 May claimed responsibility for killing another prosecutor and bombed the homes of a Supreme Court justice and the Greek police chief. ELA bombed a variety of domestic targets, including Greek Government buildings, a police precinct station and a European Community office, and it sent letter bombs to two journalists. Several local offices of Greek political parties were bombed before the elections in November, but no groups claimed responsibility.

The domestic terrorist attacks struck at the heart of the rule of law in Greece, targeting senior figures in the judiciary and members of Parliament. Despite repeated government declarations of actions against the terrorists in 1989, no key terrorist suspects were arrested.

In response to the shooting of the three judicial figures in January, the government of then Prime Minister Papandreou announced an eight-point counterterrorism program to increase the manpower and resources devoted to protecting potential targets and to identify and apprehend the terrorists. In the wake of the Bakoyiannis killing, the government of successor Prime Minister Tzannetakis pledged an enhanced counterterrorism effort, to include an offer of more that $1 million for information leading to the assassin's capture. Neither of these efforts, however, has yet borne fruit. Meanwhile, two accused members of the "Anti-State Struggle" group implicated in an October 1987 shootout were released on bail and their trial indefinitely postponed.

The US request for extradition of Mohammed Rashid progressed to the top of the Greek judicial system. Rashid is a suspected Palestinian terrorist believed to have been involved in the 1982 bombing aboard a Pan Am aircraft over the Pacific in which one Japanese youth was killed. In May 1989, the Supreme Court upheld a lower court's decision in favor Rashid's extradition to the US. The case has since been awaiting a final decision, which, according to the Greek Constitution, rests with the Minister of Justice. Successive justice ministers have announced that the decision would be deferred pending the outcome of two separate rounds of parliamentary elections. In neither round did any single party receive sufficient votes to form a government.

Rashid remains in detention pending the outcome of a third round of elections set for April 1990. The Greek Government has said it has grounds to hold Rashid until September 1990. The United States considers Rashid's extradition a key bilateral issue and an important indicator of Greece's commitment to the fight against international terrorism.

Ireland

There we no significant international incidents in Ireland in 1989.

The major forum for the Irish Government's counterterrorism efforts during the year remained the Intergovernmental Conference of the Anglo-Irish Agreement. British requests for extradition of convicted IRA terrorists have been pursued through Irish courts. One British request, however—for suspected PIRA paymaster Father Patrick Ryan—was unsuccessful. The Irish Director of Public Prosecutions decided subsequently that there was insufficient evidence to try Ryan in Ireland.

Italy

Terrorism remained an important item on the Italian national agenda in 1989. Despite a widespread perception in Italy that the level of politically motivated terrorist activity has declined, the authorities and the public are determined that there not be any resurgence. Consequently, the Italian police forces, with public support, have continued to take an active, aggressive approach to dealing with the problem of terrorism.

Italy experienced five minor international terrorist attacks in 1989—up from three in 1988. In March, arsonists partially destroyed a bookshop owned by Salman Rushdie's Italian publisher. In April, the small leftwing Autonomia group claimed responsibility for two arson attacks against vehicles belonging to US servicemen.

Italian police scored considerable successes against factions of the Red Brigades. In September, the French police, in coordination with Italian authorities, arrested five members of a BR cell wanted for the 1988 murder of Italian Christian Democratic Senator Ruffilli and two earlier killings. Four more members linked to the Parisian cell were picked up in Italy. Along with the four Italian terrorists, police arrested a Jordanian reportedly connected to the Abu Nidal organization but later released him for lack of evidence. The arrests followed the previous month's capture on the French-Swiss border of another fugitive BR member who was subsequently expelled to Italy. French police arrested three members of another faction in October.

In September, Italian authorities announced a series of operations aimed at disrupting the infrastructure of a suspected arms supply relationship between a Palestinian group, the Popular Struggle Front (PSF), and organized crime elements in Calabria. Raids in various Italian cities led to an ongoing investigation of possible arrangements to ship arms and explosives into Italy.

Italy continued to be very active in 1989 in cooperating with the United States and other countries in counterterrorism matters. Italy was an important participant in the counterterrorism efforts of the EC, the UN General Assembly, the IMO, the ICAO, and the Group of Seven.

Italy also joined with the United States and Spain in assisting countries in South America in dealing with narcotics-related terrorism. This assistance will include the provision of equipment to police forces in those countries and the training of police officials and magistrates.

On the judicial front, prosecutions and appeals dating from the late 1970s and 1980s continued to work their way through the court system. In February, a court in Florence sentenced five reported rightwing extremists to life in prison for the 1984 bombing of a Milan-Naples train; others involved received lesser sentences. In May, a court rejected the final appeals of the ANO members convicted for the 1985 attack on Fiumicino Airport and upheld the sentences imposed by lower courts. The sentences in absentia of Abu Nidal and another ANO official were thus confirmed, as was the 30-year sentence given to the one surviving terrorist in custody. Also in May, an Italian court sentenced, in absentia, ANO terrorist al-Zomar to life in prison for the 1982 synagogue attack in Rome.

At the close of the year, Italy adopted a new judicial code, similar in many respects to the adversarial trial system in the United States. It is expected that the new procedures, when fully implemented, will speed the course of justice.

Malta

There were no significant international incidents in Malta in 1989. During the year, a Maltese appeals court upheld the 25-year sentence of Abu Nidal terrorist Omar Mohammed Ali Rezak, convicted in 1988 for the 1985 hijacking of an Egyptair flight in which one American was killed. In 1988, Libyans became eligible to enter Malta with only an ID card, which may make it easier for any terrorists from Libya to visit or transit the country.

The Netherlands

Incidents of international terrorism in the Netherlands increased from two in 1988 to seven in 1989. Among the most significant attacks: in June, two unidentified gunmen wounded two prominent members of the PKK. The attack may have been the result of a power struggle within the group. In October, unidentified persons attacked Spanish targets on three separate occasions: a car bomb destroyed the Spanish Consulate General's private vehicle parked near his residence in The Hague; two bombs also exploded at the Spanish trade and labor offices in The Hague. In mid-November, the Spanish separatist group ETA claimed it carried out the attacks in retaliation for the deportation of four ETA members to Spain from the Netherlands in 1979, but this claim has not been confirmed. In December, ETA claimed responsibility for launching two rockets at the Spanish Ambassador's residence; damage was minimal and no injuries resulted.

In April, an Amsterdam appeals court sentenced a member of the Dutch radical group Radical Anti-Racist Group (RARA) to 18 months imprisonment, with six months suspended, for attempted arson in connection with RARA's terrorist campaign to force the Dutch owner of a chain of retail stores to give up business interests in South Africa.

Founder and current leader of the Communist Party of the Philippines (CPP), Jose Maria Sison, resides in the Netherlands where he provides the CPP with support activities, including fundraising. Sison is reportedly seeking asylum status in the Netherlands. The CPP's armed wing in the Philippines, the New People's Army, is believe responsible for assassinating three Americans in 1989.

Portugal

Portugal suffered no terrorist attacks in 1989. In October, a Portuguese court ruled that five alleged members of the Antiterrorist Groups of Liberation (GAL) were not guilty of death squad activities against Basque exiles in France in 1986. The four Portuguese and one French national had been accused of six counts of terrorism and attempted homicide and had been convicted in 1987 for membership in a terrorist organization in connection with the attacks. In May, Otelo Saraiva de Carvalho and 27 other convicted members of the Popular Front of the 25th of April group (FP-25) were released from prison on constitutional and procedural grounds. In September, however, an appeals court reaffirmed their convictions for membership in a terrorist organization. Otelo and the other defendants remain at liberty pending a ruling by the Supreme Court.

Spain

The number of international terrorist incidents in Spain declined significantly from 56 in 1988 to 22 in 1989. Although the highest number of international terrorist attacks in Western Europe occurred in Spain, all but two were low-level attacks conducted by the separatist group ETA against French targets—primarily automobile dealerships—in order to protest French arrest and extradition ETA members. Although the attacks were designed to avoid casualties, in May three policemen were killed while trying to dismantle a bomb at a Peugot dealership. In June, the smaller Basque terrorist group Iraultza, which is anti-NATO and is composed of elements from the Basque Communist movement, claimed responsibility for the bombing of a Citibank office in San Sebastian—that caused considerable damage but no casualties. In December, Iraultza bombed a Ford car dealership in Vitoria, causing minor damage and no injuries. It also claimed six other bombings against domestic targets that injured two people.

Several domestic terrorist groups maintained or returned to terrorist activity in Spain in 1989. After the collapse of talks with the Spanish Government in April, ETA abrogated its cease-fire with dozens of bombings, shooting, and rocket grenade attacks against the government, military, and judiciary targets, killing approximately 18 persons and injuring almost 3 dozen. The Catalan separatist group Terra Lliure is believed responsible for six bombings against government and civilian targets that injured two people. The First of October Anti-Fascist Group (GRAPO), which has occasionally attacked US targets in Spain and was seemingly dormant for a few years, resurfaced in 1989 as a terrorist threat. GRAPO attempted two bank robberies and launched three attacks in 1989, all directed against domestic targets, which resulted in five deaths and two injuries.

In a coordinated action in Madrid and Valencia in November, police arrested eight suspected members of the radical Shia group Hizballah and seized a large quantity of plastic explosives, electric detonators, and hand grenades. A Spanish judge released one of the suspects after he made a statement. According to Spanish police, the detainees intended to use Spain as a base from which to mount attacks against US, French, Israeli, Kuwaiti, and Saudi Arabian targets—principally airports and airlines—in Western Europe.

During 1989, Spanish courts continued to deal sternly with domestic terrorist cases. The Spanish Government regularly prosecutes members of ETA and other domestic terrorist groups for terrorist acts committed in Spain. Government prosecutors generally seek and often obtain stiff prison terms. For example, in October a Madrid court convicted two ETA members of the bombing of a Barcelona department store in June 1987 in which 21 people died and 41 were wounded. The court sentenced the two individuals to prison terms of 794 years each. Such stern penalties appear to be becoming the norm; however, the national constitution limits actual time in prison to a maximum of 30 years. This limitation makes the lengthy prison terms of only symbolic importance, but they are indicative of the general lack of sympathy of terrorism among the Spanish public and within the country's judicial system.

In October, the Spanish Government initiated extradition procedures against two prominent ETA members to have them returned from the Dominican Republic. The ETA members were exiled to that country from Algeria following the breakdown of talks between ETA and representatives of the Spanish Government in Algiers earlier in 1989. Madrid is also requesting the extradition of an ETA leader currently being held in France.

Spain is an active participant in the EC's Trevi Group and was Trevi president for the first six months of 1989. The Spanish Government also cooperates in antiterrorist operations on a bilateral basis—most notably, with France in cases involving members of ETA. France and Spain maintain a police liaison office to strengthen counterterrorist cooperation.

Sweden

Sweden was spared from international terrorist attacks in 1989. Several radical Palestinian and Kurdish groups, however, are believed to have used Sweden as a base for terrorist acts abroad. In December 1989, a Stockholm court tried four Palestinians believed linked to the PSF who were charged with bombings in Stockholm, Copenhagen, and Amsterdam in 1985 and 1986. Two of the Palestinians received life imprisonment, the remaining two received sentences of one and six years. Several Kurds who have served prison terms in Sweden for terrorist-related crimes were sentenced to deportation. Because the Kurds risk execution or persecution in their home countries, Swedish law prohibits their actual deportation. They have been allowed to remain in Sweden, but with limited freedom of movement, and they are required to report regularly to the police.

In 1989, the Swedish Government submitted to Parliament for ratification the 1988 Protocol to the 1971 Montreal Convention for the Suppression of Unlawful Acts Against the Safety of Civil Aviation and the 1988 Convention for the Suppression of Unlawful Acts Against the Safety of Maritime Navigations, both of which Sweden had signed in 1988.

Swedish authorities are seeking ways to stop the flow of Middle Eastern and other refugees and asylum seekers into the country who arrive without proper identification.

Stockholm was the site in March of an antiterrorism conference with participation by experts from the United States, Great Britain, Belgium, France, and Israel.

Switzerland

Switzerland was the scene of one international terrorist incident in 1989. An unidentified person hurled a grenade at the home of an Albanian family in Geneva. The grenade rolled under a car where it exploded without causing casualties.

Two Swiss employees of the International Red Cross (ICRC) were kidnapped in Lebanon in October—perhaps in retaliation for the sentencing of a Lebanese national earlier in the year. After the ICRC failed to resolve the kidnapping through its own contacts, the Swiss Foreign Ministry announced it would approach governments that could be of help in locating and freeing the hostages. The Swiss Government also issued an international public appeal for the release of the two Swiss Citizens.

Swiss courts prosecuted several counterterrorist trials in 1989. In February, a Lebanese national linked to Hizballah, who had hijacked an Air Afrique airliner to Geneva in 1987, killing a French passenger in the process, received a life sentence on charges of murder, hostage taking and five lesser offenses. In November, a Swiss court sentenced a member of the Italian Red Brigades terrorist group to life imprisonment for participating in the assassination of an Italian judge in 1978. The Swiss Government had earlier declined to extradite the Red Brigades member to Italy because he had acquired Swiss citizenship and could not be extradited under Swiss law.

Switzerland continued in 1989 its function as protecting power for US interests in Iran. This role included passing communications to and from Iran regarding terrorism issues, notably the holding of American hostages in Lebanon in the summer of 1989. The Swiss provided legal assistance to US authorities helpful for the pending prosecution of suspected Palestinian terrorist Mohammed Rashid and two others for the 1982 bombing on board a Pan American airliner in which one person was killed.

Turkey

Turkey experienced 12 international terrorist incidents in 1989, the same as 1988. The number of anti-US incidents, however, increased from two in 1988 to six in 1989. In September, a woman threw a pipe bomb over the wall of the Consulate General compound in Istanbul. The attacker was apprehended at the scene by Turkish police and is in custody awaiting legal proceedings. The US Air Force commissary in Izmir was bombed November, and in December, a Turkish group, the 16 June Organization, claimed responsibility for bombing a boat belonging to the US Consulate. British, Israeli, and Saudi interests were also the targets of attacks in Turkey during the year. In October, the automobile of a Saudi Arabian embassy administrative official in Ankara was blown up, severely injuring the driver, who lost both legs. In an anonymous call to a news agency, the Islamic Jihad claimed responsibility, saying the attack was in retaliation for the Saudi execution of Islamic Jihad members following the hajj bombings.

Violence by PKK separatists continued through the year. Many Turks believe that the PKK receives direct support from Syria and Iran and indirect support from Iraq and the Soviet Union. Turkish security forces mounted numerous operations against the PKK in the summer and fall. The November murder of 28 villagers, mostly women and children, in Ikiyaka on the Iraqi border was the worst terrorist incident since 1987. The PKK terrorists reportedly fled to Iraq after the attack.

Other radical Turkish groups increased the level of their operations in 1989, despite several counterterrorist successes by Turkish authorities. Dev Sol, Dev Yol, the Turkish Workers and Peasants Liberation Army (TIKKO), and the Marxist-Leninist Armed Propaganda Unit (MLAPU) were the most active, bombing several private businesses, key government office buildings, courts, and police stations. Domestic groups also were responsible for all of the anti-US incidents in Turkey during the year. The groups maintained the pace of their attacks in the face of arrests. In March, for example, the police arrested at least 50 suspected members of Dev Sol and, in May, 39 Dev Yol members were arrested. The continuing high level of operations in spite of the arrests suggests the groups a large base of potential recruits—possibly among university students, according to Turkish press reports—but have not developed a high degree of internal security.

The press reported in February that the Ankara Appeals Court reversed on technical grounds the State Security Court conviction of eight individuals accused of the 1986 munitions factory bombing in Kirikkale. Seven persons died and 24 were wounded in that incident. About September, the two Libyans previously convicted of the 1986 bombing of a US officers club were released and deported. Apparently the two terrorists had completed two-thirds of their original five-year prison terms, after which reduction is automatic under Turkish law. In late November, the press reported that the two Iranian kidnappers, who attempted to smuggle an anti-Khomeini dissident back to Iran in the trunk of their car in October 1988, were released and sent back to Iran. The two had served about one year in prison. (Two Iranian diplomats also involved in this kidnap attempt were not prosecuted because of diplomatic immunity, but they were expelled.)

United Kingdom

International incidents increased in the United Kingdom to 10 in 1989 from four in 1988, with attacks against bookstores selling Salman Rushdie's *The Satanic Verses* accounting for most of the increase. Salman Rushdie was given round-the-clock protection by British police, and government officials made it clear that the United Kingdom held Iran directly responsible for any action taken against British nationals or others as a result of Iran's threats against Rushdie.

Twenty-three Iranians were arrested and deported from the United Kingdom on national security grounds in 1989. In August, a man was killed in his London hotel room while apparently priming a bomb for use against a bookstore. Several attacks against British interests in Pakistan, Turkey, and Egypt may also have been protests of Salman Rushdie's book. British interests also were attacked in Peru, Iraq, West Germany, and Lebanon

Northern Ireland terrorists continued a high level of operations in 1989, carrying out attacks that killed 62 people. PIRA remained the most active nationalist group, and the most significant single terrorist threat to the United Kingdom, but the Irish National Liberation Army (INLA) and its offshoot, the Irish Peoples Liberation Organization (IPLO), also carried out attacks.

British authorities discovered several PIRA weapons and explosives caches that the group had prepared to support operations outside Northern Ireland. Some of the munitions were provided by Libya, and the United Kingdom has demanded information from Libya on what support it has given to PIRA. PIRA intensified its campaign against British military forces in the United Kingdom and on the Continent, bombing barracks in the United Kingdom and West Germany. British soldiers and their dependents were also the victims of several car bombings and shooting in West Germany; the wife of a British soldier and the 6-month-old child of another were killed by PIRA in separate attacks. Bombs were also set off in British housing areas in Northern Ireland and West Germany, indicating the group is intentionally targeting dependents.

Throughout the year, Nationalist and Loyalist groups engaged in an escalating series of retaliatory murders. Also, several members of the Northern Ireland security services were arrested for allegedly providing police files on suspected Nationalist group members to Loyalist paramilitary groups. In April, members of the Protestant Ulster Defense Association were accused of offering to supply South Africa with Blowpipe missiles in return for weapons.

The judicial response to Northern Ireland terrorist organizations, under the auspices of the 1984 Prevention of Terrorism Act, continued to be strong in 1989. The Act enables special courts to carry out terrorist trials in Northern Ireland despite the persistent threat of PIRA terrorism against judges and juries. Cooperative international efforts to arrange the extradition of wanted PIRA members from several West European countries as well as the United States also continued in 1989.

The United Kingdom was a leader in international efforts to combat terrorism in 1989. It provided significant assistance to other countries seeking to improve their counterterrorist capability. As the international investigation into the bombing of Pan Am 103 progressed, the United Kingdom took a leading position in the movement toward new international agreements on aviation security, control of explosives, and the sharing of information and technology to combat terrorist threats to civil aviation. The British Government is also an active leader of efforts in the UN, EC, and other international forums to penalize countries that support terrorism.

Yugoslavia

International terrorists continued to use Yugoslavia as a transit route and safe haven. The number of terrorist attacks against Yugoslav targets increased during 1989, including bombings in Baghdad that injured several Yugoslavs, and the firebombing of a Yugoslav travel agency in Brussels. Inside the country there were several bomb explosions that were apparently terrorist related, including the bombing of a bookstore belonging to a firm that had announced its intention to publish *The Satanic Verses* in Serbo-Croatian.

The Yugoslav Government continued in 1989 to publicly oppose terrorism and to implement measures aimed at establishing greater controls over the entry and stay of foreigners to prevent misuse of its territory. It has also evidenced a willingness to cooperate more seriously with other countries in investigating terrorist incidents.

Yugoslavia's geographic position, the large numbers of visiting foreign tourists, the nearly 15,000 students from Middle Eastern countries and financial stringencies, however, continue to limit the government's ability to prevent the transit of potential terrorists across its territory, although it has taken measures making such transit more difficult.

In June, Yugoslavia hosted a meeting of experts from five Balkan nations intended to increase cooperation against terrorism, drug trafficking, and other criminal activity.

The Soviet Union and Eastern Europe Overview

In 1989, Moscow and the other East European governments provided military and economic support to several radical regimes involved in terrorism that indirectly fostered continued terrorist activities. In addition, Middle Eastern and Japanese terrorists maintained a variety of support operations in Eastern Europe. The United States maintained various levels of dialogue on counterterrorism with the previous regimes in Eastern Europe. The counterterrorist dialogue is expected to improve with the coming to power of more representative governments in the region.

At the same time, international terrorist increased their targeting of Soviet and East European interests in 1989. In February, the Soviet Embassy in Beirut was the target of a rocket attack. One South African national was convicted in the hijacking of a Soviet cargo plane carrying 174 members of the African National Congress after the aircraft took off from Luanda for Dar es Salaam. Security agents on board the aircraft subdued the hijackers. Peruvian terrorists dynamited a bus carrying Soviet seamen and their wives in July, injuring 33, and bombed the Soviet Embassy in Lima in October. Sendero Luminoso probably carried out both attacks. Bulgarian, Hungarian, and Polish interests were attacked in a series of shooting and bombings in Baghdad. In one of the most serious attacks, three Poles were killed and several wounded by a car bomb outside a camp for Polish workers in Iraq.

Incidents of domestic violence and terrorism were on the rise in the Soviet Union—particularly in the Caucasus between Armenians and Azeris—in 1989. According to Soviet press reports, violence between the two groups has resulted in several hundred casualties. In September, for example, a bomb exploded on a bus traveling from Soviet Georgia to Azerbaijan, killing five people and wounding 27. Authorities claim to have confiscated thousands of firearms—including automatic weapons, allegedly smuggled into the country and stolen from the police and Soviet armed forces—and explosives from both communities in the region. In addition, Soviet officials reported at least three aircraft hijackings during the year and discovery of two bombs in the Moscow subway. Authorities stated that the incident in the subway was reminiscent of bombing of the subway system in 1977 and 1985 that they believed were carried out by Armenians.

Although the Soviet Union continued to maintain cordial relations with several state sponsors of terrorism, it took a number of specific actions against terrorism domestically and internationally in 1989, including offering cooperation with the United States and others investigating the Pan Am Flight 103 bombing.

Counterterrorism issues have become a regular topic of discussion in the ongoing US-Soviet dialogue. The Soviets have also become more active in denouncing terrorist acts. The Soviet Union ratified the Montreal Protocol in April dealing with combating violence at international airports and had supported efforts within ICAO to further enhance the security of civil aviation.

While expanding a counterterrorism dialogue with the West, the Soviets continue their preference for broader, less concrete multilateral efforts against terrorism. This likely reflects reluctance to take concrete actions against state sponsors with whom they maintain advantageous diplomatic relations, such as Syria, North Korea, Libya, Cuba, and South Yemen. The Soviets apparently have also subordinated counterterrorism in their effort to improve relations with Iran. The Soviet foreign minister visited Tehran in February immediately after Iran issued the Salman Rushdie death threat.

The United States raised its concerns to the authorities of the German Democratic Republic about questionable activities of certain accredited diplomatic missions in East Berlin, such as the Libyan People's Bureau. The previous Polish regime expressed in bilateral talks their desire to cooperate on counterterrorism matters, and the Solidarity government that replaced it is expected to demonstrate greater determination.

In Czechoslovakia, despite strong public counterterrorism stands, there were indications that the country was allowed to be used as a transit point by terrorist groups traveling between the Middle East and Europe and that terrorists may have visited Czech resorts for rest and recreation. Possibly in reaction to media charges that the Czech plastic explosive Semtex may have been used in the downing of Pan Am Flight 103, the government worked with the British to produce a UN resolution for the international control of plastic explosives.

The Bulgarian Government in August ratified the 1963 Tokyo Convention on air piracy and was accepted in November as a member of Interpol, the international police body, which should allow for greater cooperation on counterterrorism as well as other criminal matters. The controlled press under the previous Bulgarian regime never explicitly condemned the killing of Colonel Higgins in July, although it did express concern over the February Iranian death threats against Salman Rushdie.

Asia Overview

The number of international incidents in Asia dropped in 1989, down from 194 incidents in 1988, to 55. The reduction stems largely from a decrease in bombing attacks in Pakistan carried out by the Afghan Ministry of State Security (WAD). In the Philippines, the Communist New People's Army (NPA) launched several attacks against Americans, including the assassinations of US Army Colonel Rowe in April and two Department of Defense contractors in September. We believe the NPA will continue to pose a major threat to US personnel and facilities. In South Korea, students carried out several acts of arson against US facilities. Developments elsewhere in Asia that pose concern for 1990 include the insurgencies in India and Sri Lanka, the continued existence of the JRA, and North Korea's support for terrorism.

Afghanistan

The number of bombings in Pakistan sponsored by the WAD declined noticeably in 1989, following the withdrawal of Soviet forces from Afghanistan. There were 16 terrorist bombings and two armed attacks attributable to WAD in 1989, reflecting a downward trend in WAD operations inside Pakistan since the second half of 1988. There were 128 bombings attributed to WAD in 1987—the peak of Afghan-sponsored terrorist operations against Pakistan—and 118 in 1988. The pullout of Soviet forces from Afghanistan probably has forced the Kabul regime to redirect WAD manpower away from external operations to counter the insurgency inside Afghanistan. The withdrawal of regime forces into heavily defended urban areas just before the Soviet pullout also allowed the insurgents to close down border infiltration routes into Pakistan used by Afghan agents. WAD also probably lost Soviet logistic support for its external operations, although it is unlikely the Soviets participated directly in WAD operations inside Pakistan.

WAD nevertheless retains the capability to conduct terrorist operations against Afghan targets inside Pakistan. WAD agents probably contributed to an upsurge of terrorist activity in Pakistan during the second half of 1989. At least four of more than a dozen bombings that took place in northwestern Pakistan between July and November were directed against Afghan refugees. In at least two incidents, including the 10 October bombing of a Rawalpindi bus terminal, the perpetrator used a Soviet-made detonator, a trademark of past WAD bombing attacks. A large number of bombings in northwestern Pakistan probably are a result of internal domestic unrest rather than external state sponsorship, but WAD may have been able to enlist the support of Pakistani dissidents to plant bombs.

Australia

There were no international terrorist incidents in Australia although the wife of the former Pan Africanist Congress representative is awaiting trial for the 1988 fire bombings of several vehicles owned by US Embassy personnel. Canberra has continued to take a strong stand against international terrorist acts:

- In February, at an ICAO conference, Australia strongly endorsed measures to make plastic explosives susceptible to detection.
- Throughout the year, it dispatched experts on airport safety to other nations in the Pacific and South Asia. It also has shared expertise and information on terrorism with other Pacific countries.

- In May, the Australian Parliament passed the Hostages Act, implementing legislation related to the International Convention against the taking of hostages.
- The Australian Government continued to implement a 1988 Pacific Forum initiative to combat terrorism through the sharing of expertise and information on the subject.

India

Although no international attacks took place in India during 1989, the level of violence remained high. Sikh extremists continued their campaign of assassination against moderate Sikh leaders and Hindus. Major incidents included the killing of 26 members of a rightwing Hindu group, the National Volunteer Group, by Sikh militants in June. Sikh extremists were thought to be responsible for two major bombings. In June, a powerful explosion ripped through a New Delhi railway station during the morning rush hour, killing seven persons and injuring 50. In August, a bomb exploded on a bus en route from Punjab to New Delhi, killing 17 persons and injuring 30. No one has been charged in either case.

Prior to the November parliamentary elections, the Indian Government's response to domestic incidents of terror focused on maintaining law and order. In January, the two Sikh extremists convicted of the 1984 assassination of then Prime Minister Indira Gandhi were executed after all appeals were exhausted. The November elections resulted in Sikh radicals winning 10 of Punjab's 13 seats. Within days of being sworn in, the new national government began a campaign to establish rapport with the alienated Sikh community. The Prime Minister replaced the Punjab governor with a person more acceptable to the Sikhs. The new Sikh parliamentarians supported him during the first critical vote of confidence. At the end of the year, the parliament voted in favor of a government proposal to repeal a constitutional amendment that was offensive to the Sikhs. This action prevents the government from continuing central rule of Punjab beyond May 1990 without another constitutional amendment.

The government's gestures, however, did not have a noticeable effect in deterring extremist Sikh violence, which continued unabated during December. Nevertheless, the new government showed a willingness to negotiate the return of state government to locally elected officials and a political solution to the Punjab crisis.

The Indian Government continued to seek the extradition from the United States of two Sikhs alleged to have been involved in the 1986 assassination of a retired Indian Army Chief of Staff. Sikh militants in North America and the United Kingdom concentrated on wresting political control of Sikh temples to raise money for their compatriots in India.

Kashmiri terrorists opposed to the central government's influences increased their campaign of violence in 1989. Police suspect that they were responsible for the May bombing of a bus in Kashmir that killed one person and injured six and for a July attack on a police station in Srinigar, the region's summer capital. In December, Kashmiri separatists bombed an Indian Airlines office in Kashmir Valley. The same month, the Jammu and Kashmir Liberation Front (JKLF), the most prominent of the militant Muslim groups, kidnapped and held for five days the daughter of the new union home minister, himself a Kashmiri Muslim. In exchange for her release, the Jammu and Kashmir government freed five jailed JKLF members. By the end of the year, popular support for independence from India, a goal of the militants, had grown to the point that the central government began deploying Army forces to the Valley to restore order.

Although denied by Pakistan authorities, the Indian Government continued to claim that both Sikh and Kashmiri extremists were receiving training, arms, and sanctuary from Pakistan.

Japan

Two minor international terrorist incidents took place in Japan in 1989. A low-level bombing took place near Yokosuka for which no group claimed responsibility, and a bomb was found on the Burmese Embassy compound in December. Although not classified as terrorist because of the personal motivation involved, a CAAC aircraft on a domestic flight in China was hijacked to Fukuoka in mid-December. The aircraft with all passengers and crew was returned to China, and the hijacker is in a Japanese jail awaiting extradition. JRA terrorists did not carry out any attacks in 1989, but they remain a serious terrorist threat and can conduct worldwide operations. JRA members continued to travel in or through Western and Eastern Europe and Southeast and Northeast Asia to maintain links to other terrorist groups as well as North Korea and possibly with Libya. The cases of JRA members Osamu Maruoka and Hiroshi Sensui, arrested in 1987 and 1988 respectively, are still under adjudication.

The Chukaku-ha (Middle Core Faction) and other radical leftist groups within Japan committed a number of small-scale, politically motivated attacks of arson and sabotage. On several occasions, timed incendiary devices set by the Chukaku-ha destroyed the property of construction companies and government officials involved in the second-phase construction of the new Tokyo International Airport. In late February, a bomb exploded along the route of the motorcade of the Emperor's funeral but caused no injuries. The Kakurokyo, or Revolutionary Workers Association, claimed responsibility. The Kakurokyo is thought to be responsible for the February time bomb attack on the shrine of Togo Heihachiro, an admiral in the Japanese Imperial Navy.

In May 1989, the Ministry of Foreign Affairs established a Division for the Prevention of Terrorism. This office will analyze counterterrorism information, formulate policies, and coordinate cooperation in international fora. Also in May, the National Police established the Second Foreign Affairs Division, responsible for strengthening counterterrorism measures with special reference to the Japanese Red Army.

Japan continued to endorse international efforts to combat terrorism, supporting resolutions in the United Nations and the ICAO. Tokyo also cooperates with US authorities in investigations of criminal matters. Reflecting the high-level attention accorded to such matters, the Japanese Prime Minister joined the US President in a communiqué in September following their Washington summit that included agreement to cooperate in counterterrorism matters.

Pakistan

The number of international terrorist incidents reported in Pakistan dropped from 127 in 1988 to 25 in 1989, resulting from a decrease in the number of bombings against Pakistani-based Afghan resistance fighters and refugees by WAD. The bombings typically occurred in places frequented by large crowds—bus depots and train stations—in order to inflict high casualties. The 4 July bombing of a minibus in Peshawar killed 10 people. Pakistani authorities blame WAD for more than a dozen bombings in Rawalpindi, Peshawar, and Lahore, but in some cases the bombings probably were the work of Pakistani dissident groups. WAD retains the capability to stage terrorist operations inside Pakistan and probably was behind the 10 October bombing of a Rawalpindi bus terminal. WAD-sponsored terrorist acts are likely to continue inside Pakistan as long as Islamabad continues to support the Afghan mujahidin.

Iran recently stepped up attacks against Saudi interests in Pakistan, reflecting Tehran's displeasure with Riyadh's decision to execute 16 Kuwaiti Shia implicated in the 1989 Mecca bombings. Iranian agents or Shia sympathizers inside Pakistan probably were behind the 14 October bombing of a Saudia ticket office in Lahore. Iranian agents also may have assassinated Abdullah Azzam on 24 November. Azzam was considered the focal point of Saudi aid to the Afghan resistance movement. Terrorist attacks against Saudi targets inside Pakistan may increase as a result of intensifying Saudi-Iranian competition for influence with the Afghan resistance movement.

Iranian agents or Shia sympathizers probably were behind three bombings in 1989 directed against British targets in Pakistan to protest publication of *The Satanic Verses*. In February and March 1989, bombs damaged the British Council libraries in Islamabad, Peshawar, and Karachi. The bombings took place after business hours; in one incident a Pakistani security guard was killed.

None of the terrorist incidents in 1989 appear to have been directed against the United States, but the limited capabilities of Pakistan's counterterrorist forces leave US personnel vulnerable to terrorist attacks. Cooperation among government security agencies is often ineffective, and their performance has been hindered by rivalries between central and local law enforcement agencies. The Pakistani Government has attempted on a continuing basis to enhance its antiterrorist and law enforcement capabilities. Pakistan participates in the State Department's Antiterrorism Assistance Program.

The ANO terrorists convicted of the 1986 Pan Am hijacking in Karachi remain in jail while their appeals are pending before the courts.

Philippines

In the Philippines, although total incidents of terrorism against foreign targets decreased from 12 in 1988 to nine in 1989, the nature of these cases was far more serious than in previous years. In contrast to 1988, when no American casualties were incurred, attacks against US targets resulted in three fatalities. The threat to US citizens increased as CPP New People's Army (NPA) guerrillas and "sparrow" urban assassination units began to monitor the activities of a broadening range of US citizens.

The willingness of terrorist teams to attack Americans over the past year is probably the result of high-level CPP/NPA directives based on a decision to open an active anti-American front. In particular, the Communists may wish to send a strong message during preliminary US-Philippine base agreement renegotiations. Increased security at US military facilities and the protective measures taken by high-profile US officials who are priority targets, however, appear to be motivating CPP/NPA terrorists toward less selective targeting.

NPA terrorist operations in April ended a hiatus in anti-US attacks since 1987, when one retiree and two off-duty US enlisted servicemen were killed outside Clark Airbase. The recent operations against US interests have been:

- An aborted mission on 6 April to mine a road outside Clark used by US personnel to gain access to a firing range.
- The bombing on 9 April of a joint US-Philippines communications site on Mt. Cabuyao guarded by Philippine forces.
- The assassination on 21 April of US Army Col. James Rowe en route to his office in Manila.
- The killing of two US civilian Department of Defense contractors in their vehicle north of Clark on 26 September, apparently timed to coincide with the arrival of Vice President Quayle in Manila.
- A probable NPA attack on 14 December against the US Embassy's Seafront compound in Manila; two antipersonnel rifle grenades evidently intended to inflict indiscriminate casualties were launched, fortuitously resulting only in minor damage.
- The after-hours machinegun strafing on 24 December of a USIS building in Davao City in the southern Philippines.

These attacks and continuing threats against American official and military personnel indicate an active international terrorist campaign with possible links to Libya and other terrorist organizations. The CPP/NPA is also believed to obtain financial and material support from Communist and leftist sources abroad. The founder of the CPP now lives and maintains an office in the Netherlands from which he conducts public relations, fundraising, and other support activities.

During 1989, nearly 100 Philippine Government and security officials have been assassinated, the vast majority by the NPA. Besides the threat from the CPP/NPA, the Moro National Liberation Front (MNLF), a Muslim secessionist group, also seeks to attain its objectives through violent means. In addition, disgruntled participants in the Reform the Armed Forces Movement (RAM) December coup attempt have threatened to perpetrate terrorist attacks against both the Aquino government and US forces seen to have supported the government.

The Government of the Philippines has issued public statements condemning domestic terrorism and has urged security forces and the public to take measures to combat it. The government has launched a reward program for information leading to the arrest of major Communist figures in the Philippines and abroad. Despite limitations on available resources and the pressures of active Communist and Muslim insurgencies, Manila has devoted manpower and attention to the protection of US interests and the investigation of the killings of Americans. To date, these efforts have resulted in the arrest and arraignment of two suspects in the Rowe murder case. Their trial, originally expected to begin in late 1989, has been delayed until April 1990. The investigation continues into the killing of the two Defense Department civilian employees. Complaints have been filed against several suspects who remain at large. The two suspected terrorists charged in the 1987 killings of US military personnel escaped from police custody while en route to trial. Despite their escape, the trial has continued and a verdict is expected sometime in 1990.

The Government of the Philippines continues to be a willing participant in programs of bilateral cooperation with and training in the United States on counterterrorism issues.

South Korea

In 1989, there were 14 relatively minor attacks against US interests—down from 21 in 1988—by radical students and other Korean dissidents. A US military truck at Camp Henry was slightly damaged in January by student-thrown molotov cocktails. On two occasions students attacked the American Cultural Center in Kwangju with molotov cocktails, rocks, steel pipes, and sledge hammers, causing minor damage but no injuries. In March, in two separate incidents, student demonstrators hurled molotov cocktails at a US military housing area in Seoul causing slight damage but no injuries. In late July, a handful of university students unsuccessfully attempted to break into the US Cultural Center in Seoul.

In April, a South Korean court sentenced ex-North Korean agent Kim Hyon-Hui to death for planting a bomb on the November 1987 KAL Flight 858, which resulted in the death of 115 people. Kim is appealing her sentence, and it is expected that the government eventually will commute it.

Throughout the year, the Republic of Korea demonstrated a strong concern about international terrorism, maintained a close liaison relationship with the United States, and worked to improve its counterterrorist capability.

Sri Lanka

In 1989, political violence in Sri Lanka reached postindependence highs, with over 8,500 persons killed, the majority civilians. There were, however, no reported acts of international terrorism.

Tamil militant factions, including the separatist Liberation Tigers of Tamil Eelam (LTTE), and the Maoist Janatha Vimukhti Perumana (JVP), a Sinhalese extremist group, were reportedly responsible for acts of domestic terrorism during 1989. In addition, vigilante groups, in some cases credibly linked to Sri Lankan security forces, were responsible for the deaths of many JVP suspects. By the end of the year, a government crackdown on the JVP had led to the capture and death of much of the JVP leadership.

The government dropped all charges in January 1990 against a group of LTTE suspects accused of bombing an Air Lanka plane on the ground on Colombo in May 1986. Twenty-eight persons, including foreigners (but no Americans), were killed in the attack. The LTTE's relations with the government improved dramatically in 1989 and, by the end of the year, the LTTE had formed a political party to contest elections in Tamil-majority areas likely to occur in 1990.

Sub-Saharan Africa Overview

In 1989, Africa ranked fifth in incidents of international terrorism. The number of incidents classified as international terrorist acts decreased slightly from 52 to 48. The most significant terrorist act occurred on 19 September when a bomb destroyed a French UTA airliner that crashed in Niger, killing 171 people—including seven US citizens. The case remains unsolved. Armed attacks and kidnappings carried out by local insurgent groups in South and Central Africa account for the majority of international incidents. Cross-border raids into Zimbabwe by the Mozambican National Resistance Movement (RENAMO) account for more than a third of insurgent related violence. When involved, Europeans—missionaries and foreign workers—tended to be random targets caught up in insurgent operations. Americans apparently were not the primary targets of terrorist incidents.

South Africa continued to be suspected of sponsoring bombing attacks against African National Congress dissidents in neighboring African states. The South African police also have been linked publicly to "death squad" killings of two prominent antiregime activists in 1989. Libya continued to cultivate ties to subversive groups in Sub-Saharan Africa, while trying to improve Libyan relations with moderate African leaders. In April 1989, Burundi expelled the Libyan diplomatic mission, claiming the Libyan People's Bureau there was involved in an attempt to overthrow the government. Libyan diplomats were expelled from Benin in 1988 for the same reason.

There were no state-sponsored acts of terrorism against US interests in Africa during 1989, but Americans living or traveling in this region are highly vulnerable to terrorist operations. Africa provides an ideal operating environment for terrorist groups because of the limited counterterrorist capabilities of most regional states and inadequate security procedures at most African airports.

Chad

There were no international terrorist incidents in Chad during 1989, although security at N'Djamena airport has been tightened in the wake of the UTA Flight 772 bombing. That flight, originating from the Congo, had stopped in Chad before exploding over Niger.

People's Republic of the Congo

The September 1989 destruction of the UTA flight originating in Brazzaville provoked renewed interest in the government's antiterrorism measures. Forty-nine Congolese citizens were on board. Airport security procedures in Brazzaville have been increased, although new measures are limited by the country's economic crisis.

Of the six countries on the US terrorism list, four—Cuba, Iran, Libya, and North Korea—maintain diplomatic missions in Brazzaville. The Congo has long maintained a policy of offering refuge to citizens of other countries.

Djibouti

The Tunisian national charged in connection with the 1987 bombing of the Cafe [L']Historil in which 11 persons were killed remains in jail awaiting trial. In a unique development, the entire Djiboutian bar was appointed joint defense council. Since the authorities plan to interview every available witness before bringing the case to trial, it is unlikely the case will come before the courts in the foreseeable future.

Mozambique

RENAMO violence has been directed against nationals in neighboring Zimbabwe and Zambia, but in March 1989, RENAMO guerrillas killed three Italian priests and captured a fourth during an attack surrounding a mission in the central province of Zambezia. Although there have been no attacks so far against foreign aid workers in Mozambique, according to press reports, RENAMO said in November that it would no longer guarantee the safety of aid workers.

Throughout its 15-year insurgency, RENAMO has continued to direct terrorist attacks against the local population. The insurgents frequently attack soft targets such as villages, schools, factories, and relief convoys, with civilians killed daily, while others are deliberately mutilated or pressed into service as porters. There were several massacres of civilians in 1989. One in a communal village in Gaza Province took 54 lives; another 80 died in the border town of Ressano Garcia.

The government has adopted a two-pronged strategy against the insurgents: the 1987 amnesty law intended to weaken RENAMO by encouraging its members to lay down their arms and reenter civilian life; and the government's attempt to reach a negotiated settlement through the peace process mediated by Kenya and Zimbabwe. The authorities claim that several thousand RENAMO members have sought amnesty, although these figures may also include unarmed civilians living in RENAMO-controlled areas. In August, the authorities released 100 prisoners, most suspected guerrillas, who had been held on national security charges.

The South African Government states that it no longer supports the RENAMO insurgency, but some private entities within the country may be providing some assistance. Mozambique has asked that Pretoria do more to halt this aid.

Niger

Niger was the site of the deadliest terrorist incident in 1989—the in-flight destruction of UTA flight 772 by a bomb on 19 September, which killed 171, including seven Americans. The French airliner was destroyed during the second leg of a Brazzaville, Congo-N'Djamena, Chad-Paris flight. The plane's wreckage was recovered in the remote Niger desert. Two claims of responsibility for the bombing have been made so far—an anonymous caller allegedly speaking in the name of Hizballah and a previously unheard of Chadian group opposed to French support for Chadian President Habre's government. French authorities have been unable to find conclusive evidence to implicate any particular terrorist group in the bombing.

The government expended a significant portion of its limited military resources to assist in the investigation. Niger allowed France to take the lead in a comprehensive investigation and extended appropriate courtesies to US experts who were assisting the French in the initial phases of the investigation. Although the UTA flight never stopped over at Niamey airport, the government authorities have made attempts to upgrade security there following the tragedy.

South Africa

The cycle of violent repression by the South African Government and violent resistance by the black opposition abated during 1989. The political climate improved after newly installed President de Klerk began allowing peaceful political protest and initiated feelers to the ANC that may lead to formal negotiations. Senior ANC leader Walter Sisulu and others were released and allowed to function publicly as ANC leaders. The South African Government formally unbanned the organization in early 1990. The efforts to reach political accommodation, however, do no completely eliminate the possibility of further violence by ANC militants, South African extremists, or vigilante groups.

The military wings of the ANC, or its local supporters, probably were responsible for setting off limpet mine explosions in South African townships in 1989. South Africa was linked to an increased number of attacks, climbing from eight in 1988 to 11 in 1989. Its agents were allegedly responsible for bombings against ANC targets neighboring Botswana, Swaziland, and Zambia.

South African agents also are alleged to be responsible for the murder of three ANC members in Swaziland in February 1989. At least seven current or former South African policemen have been arrested for their alleged involvement in a death squad that was responsible for the murder of antiapartheid activist David Webster on 1 May in Johannesburg. The death squad also has been linked to the 10 September assassination of white SWAPO official Anton Lubowski in Namibia. Upon assuming office, the new de Klerk government stated it would not support the use of such tactics. In early 1990, Pretoria launched an independent judicial investigation into the death squad allegations.

The ANC leadership disavows a strategy that deliberately targets civilians and may be debating the wisdom of continuing the "armed struggle," as evidenced by the reduced number of attacks in 1989. Although some armed attacks may have been perpetrated by the ANC, others were possibly carried out by supporters without the approval of the ANC leadership or were unconnected at all to the ANC.

South African courts continue to pass sentences on people charged with terrorism, and nearly 71 were convicted during the first 10 months of the year. These convictions do no accurately reflect the country's counterterrorism commitment, however, as the definition of "terrorism" used by the courts includes a wide variety of antigovernment activities. In December, the Supreme Court overturned on a technicality the treason and terrorism convictions of all eight defendants in the widely publicized 1988 Delmas treason trial, where some defendants had been convicted of "terrorism."

Although South Africa in the past has provided support to RENAMO insurgents in Mozambique who target civilians, the new de Klerk government has emphatically claimed to have cut off all support.

Sudan

There were no confirmed international terrorist incidents in Sudan in 1989. Five ANO terrorists sentenced to death last year for the 1988 bombings at the Acropole Hotel and the Sudan Club have appealed their sentences. The Sudanese courts have ruled that relatives of the victims, who included five British nationals, have the option to select from several punishments, including financial compensation from the defendants in exchange for reduced sentences. This last option would allow the convicted terrorists to escape execution.

Tanzania

There was only one instance of international terrorism in 1989, the unsuccessful attempt on 18 May to hijack an unscheduled Aeroflot flight that was ferrying ANC soldiers from Luanda to Dar es Salaam. Tanzanian courts imposed a 15-year sentence on the hijacker, Bradley Richard Stacey, a white South African. Tanzania has not improved its counterterrorist capability since a Tanzanian airliner was hijacked in February 1988.

Zambia

South African agents probably were behind a series of bombings directed against facilities operated by the ANC, which has its external political headquarters in Zambia. In one instance, however, Zambian security officials concluded ANC factionalism was the motive. In mid-June, bombs destroyed or damaged at least three ANC facilities in Lusaka. Mozambican-based RENAMO insurgents conducted at least three violent cross-border raids into eastern Zambia in search of food and supplies, similar to RENAMO forays into Zimbabwe. Zambian security forces have a policy of hot pursuit in response to these incursions.

Zimbabwe

RENAMO guerrillas continued to conduct a large number of cross-border raids into Zimbabwe. Typically, small bands of RENAMO personnel would raid a village for food and supplies and kidnap the local villagers to carry the booty back to RENAMO bases in Mozambique. RENAMO attacks are characterized by ruthless and indiscriminate violence. At least 71 Zimbabweans were killed in RENAMO attacks this year as compared with 55 last year. The Zimbabwean Government has deployed troops along the eastern border and into Mozambique to combat RENAMO. Because of RENAMO atrocities, the authorities have resettled local residents into protectd villages away from the affected border areas.

There were three noteworthy court cases involving terrorism in 1989. South African agent Charles Beahan was convicted of infiltrating Zimbabwe from Botswana as part of the abortive June 1988 attempt to free six suspected South African agents who were in prison awaiting trial. Three alleged South African agents sentenced to death for their participation in the 1986 bombing of ANC targets in Harare are appealing their sentences. A Zimbabwean national who was involved in a plot to murder ANC members received an 18-year prison sentence.

Terrorism in the 1990s

Overview of Terrorism in the 1990s

Anna Sabasteanski

Worldwide Terrorist Attacks, 1990–1999

1990   455 attacks
1991   557 attacks
1992   361 attacks
1993   427 attacks
1994   321 attacks
1995   440 attacks
1996   296 attacks
1997   304 attacks
1998   273 attacks
1999   392 attacks

This section of the encyclopedia presents *Patterns of Global Terrorism*'s country reports on terrorism from the 1990s.

The decline in terrorist attacks seen in 1989 continued into 1990, with attacks dropping to 455. There were no spectacular incidents, but Iraq invaded Kuwait on 2 August, garnering support from a number of Palestinian groups. With the fall of the Berlin Wall and the opening of Eastern Europe, terrorists lost another source of support and safe haven.

The 1990 Gulf War that followed Iraq's invasion of Kuwait led to a 22 percent increase in terrorist attacks, from 455 in 1990 to 557 in 1991. Half those attacks occurred in January and February, while Operation Desert Storm was under way. Libya garnered special attention in 1991 after it was linked to the 1988 downing of Pan Am Flight 103 over Lockerbie, Scotland, and to the 1989 bombing of a French airline, UTA Flight 772, in Niger.

In 1992 there was a dramatic decrease in attacks, which declined more than one-third to 361. Nearly 40 percent of these attacks were directed against U.S. property or civilians. The one spectacular attack of the year was the bombing of the Israeli embassy in Argentina, which accounted for about 40 percent of those wounded.

In 1993 the Kurdistan Workers Party (PKK), a group fighting for an independent Kurdistan, increased the intensity of their anti-Turkish campaign, staging 150 attacks, most taking place over the course of two days in western Europe. This campaign was responsible for an increase in the total number of terrorist incidents to 427. The one spectacular attack of the year was the bombing of the World Trade Center in New York City on 26 February. Six people were killed in that attack and a thousand injured. We now know this was an announcement of al-Qaeda's intentions and a precursor of what was to come.

There were 321 international terrorist attacks in 1994, a 25 percent decline from 1993. The incident with the highest number of casualties was the July bombing of a Jewish cultural center in Buenos Aires, Argentina, that killed nearly a hundred people and wounded more than two hundred.

PKK attacks in Germany and Turkey contributed to an increase in attacks in 1995 to 440. The number of people wounded increased by a factor of ten, due to more than 5,000 people being injured when the Aum Shinrikyo religious sect released sarin gas (a nerve gas) on a Tokyo subway line. Had dispersion been more effective, the number dead could have been far higher.

In 1996 the number of attacks dropped to 296, but mass attacks against civilians and the use of more powerful bombs increased the casualty rates to their highest to that point. The deadliest attack in 1996 was in Colombo, Sri Lanka, when the Liberation Tigers of Tamil Eelam (LTTE, commonly known as the Tamil Tigers), a separatist group, rammed a truck full of explosives into the Central Bank, killing 90 and wounding more than 1,400.

The number of attacks in 1997 changed little from the year before. Colombian rebels, primarily associated with the Revolutionary Armed Forces of Colombia (FARC), repeatedly attacked oil pipelines in that country. Those attacks accounted for one-third of 1997's 304 international terrorist attacks. The deadliest attack was at the Hatshepsut Temple in Luxor, Egypt, in which fifty-eight foreign tourists were methodically shot dead or knifed, as well as two Egyptian policemen and an Egyptian tour guide. All six gunmen were killed as they fled the scene.

For many Americans and East Africans, terrorism in 1998 was defined by the bombings of the U.S. embassies in Kenya and Tanzania in August. Five thousand people were injured in Nairobi, Kenya, and 291 killed. In Dar es Salaam, Tanzania, ten were killed and seventy-seven wounded. Osama bin Laden and al-Qaeda, who claimed responsibility, began to be viewed as serious threats. In terms of overall numbers of attacks, 1998 saw a reduction to 273.

The number of casualties in 1999 declined because there were no massive attacks. However, the number of attacks increased by 43 percent to 392. The increase was attributed to protests against the NATO bombing campaign in Serbia, reaction to the arrest of PKK leader Abdullah Ocalan, and the kidnapping for ransom of foreign oil workers in Nigeria. Oil interests in Colombia were also frequently targeted.

Patterns of Global Terrorism: 1990

The Year in Review

The year 1990 was one of the few in recent times in which there were no "spectacular" terrorist incidents resulting in the death or injury of a large number of victims. Despite this fact, there were a number or major terrorist developments, including a heightened international terrorist threat owing to Iraq's renewed association with terrorist groups worldwide.

Perhaps the most significant development occurred in the wake of the 2 August Iraqi invasion of Kuwait. A number of Palestinian groups, including the Palestine Liberation Front (PFL), the Palestinian Islamic Jihad (PIJ), the Popular Front for the Liberation of Palestine (PFLP), and the Popular Front for the Liberation of Palestine-General Command (PLFP-GC), pledged their support for Saddam Hussein, and most threatened terrorist attacks against the West, Israel, and moderate Arab targets in the event of war. Although by year's end no such attacks had taken place, the threat remained high.

Another significant development was the abortive 30 May attack on Israeli beaches by the PFL. The PFL is a member of the Palestine Liberation Organization (PLO) and is therefore subject to the PLO's "renunciation" of terrorism. Following the PLO's refusal to condemn the attack, the United States suspended its dialogue with the PLO, pending action by the PLO demonstrating that it abides by the conditions it accepted in December 1988.

Both of these events highlight the continuing importance of states that support terrorists and sponsor terrorist attacks. The PLF attack on Israel was planned and executed from Libya. In 1990 Iraq, which provides support for a growing number of terrorist allies, was returned to the US Governments list of state sponsors of terrorism. The other countries on that list—Cuba, Iran, Libya, North Korea, and Syria—continued to provide varying degrees of support—safehaven, travel documents, arms, training, and technical expertise—to terrorists.

Latin America emerged in 1990 as the most frequent site for terrorist attacks against US interests. Most of these attacks took place in Chile, Peru, and Colombia. Latin American radical or guerrilla groups engaging in terrorism tended to attack domestic, rather than foreign, targets. Thus, although the number of international terrorist incidents was high, the escalating domestic political violence had an even greater impact on the region.

There was a marked increase in international terrorism in Asia in 1990, primarily because of increased activity by the Communist New People's Army (NPA) in the Philippines. At the same time, South Asia suffered from a notable upsurge in terrorism, particularly in Pakistan where the Afghan secret service was responsible for a rash of terrorist attacks.

There were several positive developments regarding terrorism in 1990. Eight Western hostages held in the Middle East —including Americans Robert Polhill and Frank Reed— were released from captivity. Furthermore, no Westerners were taken hostage in Lebanon during 1990. Another positive development was the marked decline in terrorism in the Middle East and a reduction in Middle Eastern "spillover" terrorism in other regions.

The advent of democracy in Eastern Europe bought a change in East European states' attitudes toward terrorism. The new East European governments were eager to expose the support previous regimes had provided to terrorists, such as East German safehaven for Red Army Faction (RAF) terrorists and Czechoslovak sales of Semtex plastic explosive. Terrorists no longer find official support or safehaven in the emerging democracies of Eastern Europe.

The trend toward multinational cooperation on counter-terrorist issues continued during the year. Following major terrorist attacks such as the Pan Am 103 and UTA 772 bombings, the United Nations directed the International Civil Aviation Organization (ICAO) to develop a method of "marking" plastic explosives for preblast detection. Substantial work was completed by ICAO members on a convention requiring all manufactures of plastic explosives to add chemicals to the explosives that would make them easier to detect. An agreement, called the Convention on the Marking of Plastic Explosives for the Purpose of Detection, was signed in early 1991.

Continuing the trend of previous years, a number of important terrorist trials took place in 1990, as governments continued to impose the rule of law on terrorists.

African Regional Overview

There were 52 international terrorist incidents in Africa in 1990, just slightly more than in the previous year. The most significant of these incidents occurred in Djibouti in September, when hand grenades thrown into two downtown cafés killed a child and wounded 17 persons. As in previous years, most acts of terrorism in Africa were conducted by local insurgents. In Liberia, Mozambique, and Somalia, for example, while a few international terrorists incidents took place in the context of bitter struggles against those governments, there were many more incidents of domestic terrorism. When foreigners were involved, they were usually targets of opportunity.

Angola

On 27 April, the Front for the Liberation of the Enclave of Cabinda (FLEC), an Angolan separatist group, kidnapped 13 French nationals and a number of Congolese citizens at a

French oil-prospecting company's site near the Congolese border with Cabinda. Cabinda is an Angolan enclave separated from the rest of the country by a narrow strip of Zaire. Nine French nationalists and some of the Congolese were released within a few hours; and the remaining hostages were released on 10 May. Two Portuguese aid workers were kidnapped by FLEC in September and released approximately two months later.

In October, an American was kidnapped in Cabinda Province by a different Cabindan separatist group, the Front for the Liberation of the Enclave of Cabinda-Military Position (FLEC-PM). He was released in December.

Both the Angolan Government and the National Union for the Total Independence of Angola (UNITA) have publicly and repeatedly accused each other of practicing terrorism against their opponents, including the kidnapping, killing, torturing, or maiming of civilians, but few of these allegations could be independently verified. However, UNITA leader Jonas Savimbi publicly acknowledged that a French national captured by UNITA in a war zone had died while being marched to the Zairean border, where he was to have been released.

Djibouti

There was one act of international terrorism in Djibouti in 1990. On 27 September, several grenades were thrown from a passing taxi into the Café de Paris, a sidewalk café in the capital, killing a 10-year-old French boy and injuring 17 other persons. Grenades also were thrown at the Café L'Historil, but they failed to explode. A previously unknown group, the Djiboutian Youth Movement, claimed responsibility for the attacks. Four Djibouti youths were arrested and charged in early October. During arraignment, they recanted their earlier confessions, saying they had been tortured. Djibouti authorities are continuing their investigations.

The Tunisian national charged in the 1987 bombing of the Café L'Historil, in which 11 persons were killed, remains imprisoned awaiting trial.

Ethiopia

On 30 March, a bomb exploded at the Hilton Hotel in Addis Ababa, causing damage to one room. The following day the Ethiopian Government expelled two Libyans, apparently for their alleged involvement. An Israeli diplomat staying in the hotel may have been the intended target.

Liberia

During much of 1990, Liberia was torn by a bitter civil war between the Armed Forces of Liberia (AFL), loyal to President Samuel Doe, and two factions—the national Patriotic Front of Liberia (NPFL), led by Charles Taylor, and the Independent National Patriotic Front of Liberia (INPFL), led by Prince Johnson. The battlelines were also drawn between ethnic groups, as members of rival groups sought out and massacred each other. A cease-fire has been in effect since 2 December.

In August, an American missionary was kidnapped by members of the Armed Forces of Liberia. Beaten and shot in the legs, he later died. His body was returned at the same time that another kidnapped American was released.

The NPFL ambushed a train and kidnapped two passengers—a British journalist and a Liberian national. The Englishman was released five days later. The NPFL has been accused of direct responsibility for the deaths of several Economic Community of West African States (ECOWAS) members, including two Nigerian journalists.

Prince Johnson's INPFL kidnapped a number of foreigners, including one American, ostensibly to force ECOWAS to intervene in the Liberian civil war. All of the hostages were released a few days later.

Mozambique

The Mozambican National Resistance (RENAMO) movement continued its 16-year-old insurgency in 1990, conducting terrorist attacks mostly against peasants who refused to cooperate with them. Soft targets, such as schools and villages, continued to be attacked frequently, and as many as several thousand Mozambicans were killed by the group. In February, RENAMO kidnapped a Zimbabwean businessman and a British professor; the two were rescued by a joint Zimbabwean-Mozambican military operation. In June, the group kidnapped two Swiss Red Cross workers and held them for four days. There were indications in late 1990 that RENAMO leaders were attempting to reduce the number of attacks on civilians.

In addition to RENAMO, bandits and undisciplined government troops continued to raid and loot villages. Indiscriminate violence on both sides had led to near anarchy in much of the countryside. Under these conditions, apprehension and prosecution of domestic terrorists are not feasible.

Direct talks between the Government of Mozambique and RENAMO produced an agreement in late 1990 to designate two land transport routes as "peace corridors," which would not be attacked. These talks are expected to continue. Previous government offers of amnesty to RENAMO supporters were ineffective.

Somalia

Antiregime elements were probably responsible for a series of bombing attacks throughout the year. Numerous attacks were carried out against Somali targets in an attempt to oust the government of President Siad Barre. Among the non-Somali targets were the mission of the European Community (EC) and the Libyan, Iraqi, and Chinese Embassies. The bombings caused only superficial damage to the three embassy buildings. A guard at the EC mission was injured by the blast. In May, a grenade exploded on the US Embassy compound in Mogadishu. No one claimed responsibility for the attack.

South Africa

In 1990, the South African Government began preparations for a transition to nonracial democracy by lifting the ban on opposition organizations, releasing political prisoners—including Nelson Mandela—and entering into talks with the African National Congress (ANC). In August, the ANC agreed to suspend its armed struggle against the government.

These developments led to a virtual end to violent repression by the government and violent resistance by the opposition. There was, however, a major escalation in black factional violence. More than a thousand people were killed in this fighting. Some human rights observers alleged that rightwing extremist elements of the security forces were contributing to the factional violence.

White extremists, in protest against apartheid reforms, carried out a series of terrorist attacks against both domestic and foreign elements. On 4 February, shots were fired at the British Embassy in Pretoria. A previously unknown group, the Order of the Boer People, claimed responsibility. Later in the year, the same group was responsible for the homemade bomb that exploded at the residence of US Ambassador William Swing, damaging a gatepost and a guardhouse. Three people were arrested in connection with this incident. On 6 July, an explosion at a crowded taxi and bus terminal used by black commuters in Johannesburg injured 23 people and damaged eight vehicles. The White Liberation Army—also previously unknown—claimed responsibility. On 12 September, a bomb exploded at the ruling National Party offices in Pretoria. A supporter of rightwing extremist Piet "Skiet" Rudolph claimed responsibility.

In November, the government released the findings of the Harms Commission investigation into charges of government-directed terrorism. The Commission concluded that the Civil Cooperation Bureau (CCB)—a covert element of the South African Defense Force—was involved in the murder of at least two people and conspired to kill at least three others. The CCB was found to have been responsible for at least one bombing as well. Antiapartheid activists criticized the Harms Commission report, particularly the narrow scope of its investigation and the Commission's inability to gain access to key witnesses and records. Many killings that have been linked to CCB "hit squads" remained unsolved, including the murders in 1989 of anti apartheid activist David Webster in Johannesburg and South-West Africa People's Organization (SWAPO) official Anton Lubowski in Namibia. In mid-1990 the government announced that the CCB would be disbanded.

Sudan

The five Abu Nidal organization (ANO) terrorists tried and convicted for their roles in the bombings in 1988 at the Acropole Hotel and the Sudan Club remained imprisoned at year's end, but they were released in January 1991. The Sudanese courts had sentenced the five to death but later ruled that the families of the victims, who were all British or Sudanese, had the option of accepting cash payments as compensation—in which case the terrorists would not be executed. The British families refused to accept payment of "blood money" but also opposed the death penalty.

Khartoum has a close relationship with Iraq and increasingly warm ties to Iran. In 1990, Sudan signed an "integration agreement" with Libya that, among other things, permits the Libyans much easer access to Sudan.

Asian Regional Overview

The number of international terrorist incidents in Asia increased dramatically in 1990, from 56 incidents in 1989 to 96. This increase was primarily due to greater activity by Afghan agents in Pakistan and Communist guerrillas in the Philippines. The greatest threat to Americans in the region remains in the Philippines, where Communist insurgents launched attacks against US facilities and killed five Americans. In South Korea, radical students conducted several attacks against US facilities. Domestic political violence including sectarian and communal violence in India, particularly in Kashmir and Punjab, and the festering insurgency in Sri Lanka were also of concern in 1990.

Afghanistan

The number of international terrorist incidents reported in Pakistan increased sharply in 1990 because of a renewed bombing campaign by the Afghan secret police, WAD. The WAD is believed responsible for 35 of the 45 international terrorist incidents recorded in Pakistan. Dozens of people were killed and many more injured in WAD attacks. Although WAD attacks are ostensibly against Pakistan-based Afghan resistance fighters and refugees, the targeting of markets, movie theaters, train stations, and other public gathering places suggests the goal is to intimidate and undermine the Pakistani Government's willingness to host the Afghan refugees.

India

Sectarian and ethnic conflicts within India resulted in the deaths of several thousand civilians at the hands of terrorist groups. Sikh extremists in Punjab continued to use terrorist tactics to advance their political agenda. Nearly 5,000 civilians died in the state, mostly as a result of indiscriminate violence by Sikh extremists. Although a majority of the victims were Sikhs, machinegun attacks on crowded markets in predominately Hindu towns and bombings of busses and trains were commonplace. Central government rule, imposed in 1987, remained in effect at year's end.

In Kashmir, separatist groups capitalized on the popular perception among the state's Muslims that New Delhi has discriminated against them politically and economically.

Separatist groups stepped up their campaign of violence, bombing schools and other public buildings. By year's end, some 2,300 people had died in Kashmir as a result of the violence. On 6 April, the Jammu and Kashmir Liberation Front (JKLF), the most prominent separatist group, kidnapped the vice chancellor of Kashmiri University, his secretary, and an official of the state-run Hindustan Machine Tools. Several days later, the three were murdered after the government refused to swap jailed militants for them. In July, the JKLF kidnapped the son of a Kashmiri government official and held him for three days.

Other Kashmiri separatist groups also conducted acts of terrorism. The Mujahidin Kashmir claimed responsibility for the 12 April bombing of a passenger train in Bombay, which injured 30 people. The Allah Tigers claimed responsibility for killing an Indian intelligence officer in early September.

The United Liberation Front of Assam (ULFA), which was banned by the government in November, has conducted assassinations and extortions as part of its drive for an independent Assamese state. Other tribal-based groups employed terrorism in their separatist struggles.

The Indian Government charges that Sikh and Kashmiri extremists have received training, arms, and sanctuary from Pakistan—charges denied by Pakistani authorities.

The ineffectiveness of local security services has hampered Indian attempts to counter domestic terrorism in areas of secessionist and communal violence. The Government of India frequently deploys paramilitary or military forces to restore basic law and order in terrorist-afflicted areas. In 1990, the government announced the creation of a paramilitary group called the National Rifles, whose task is to assist the security services in tumultuous areas like Punjab and Assam.

Japan

In November, Chukaku-ha, Japan's most active ultraleftist group, threw two small homemade grenades over the wall of the US Consul General's home in Osaka, causing minor damage. This incident was part of a rash of relatively minor violence surrounding the enthronement ceremonies for the Emperor.

Throughout the year, ultraleftists opposed to the imperial system carried out a series of attacks against Japanese targets. In early January, homemade rockets caused minor damage to the Tokyo residence of Prince Hitachi, the Emperor's younger brother, and struck the Kyoto Imperial Palace but caused no damage. In late January, Chukaku-ha set fires on seven trains in several prefectures; there were no injuries and only minor damage.

Ultraleftist groups carried out approximately 40 attacks with homemade mortars and incendiary devices to protest the 12 November enthronement of Emperor Akihito. The radicals fired rockets at four Self-Defense Force facilities in Tokyo and neighboring prefectures but caused no damage or casualties. Rockets that veered off course hit several buildings in Tokyo, causing minor damage. The groups also set fire to several railway lines and Shinto shrines in and around Tokyo. Before the enthronement, the Kakurokyo Hazama-ha bombed a police dormitory in Tokyo, killing one officer and injuring six others.

The Japanese Red Army (JRA) did not conduct any terrorist operations in 1990. Its leadership remains based in the Bekaa Valley of Lebanon. The cases of JRA members Osamu Maruoka and Hiroshi Sensui—arrested in 1987 and 1988, respectively—are still under adjudication in Japan.

Radical rightwing groups carried out only one incident in 1990. A member of the minuscule Seikijuku (Righteous Spiritual School) shot and wounded the mayor of Nagasaki on 18 January.

Papua New Guinea

The Free Papua Movement (OPM) kidnapped an American missionary, a New Zealand missionary, three Filipinos, and a Papua New Guinean near the Indonesian–New Guinean border in November. The OPM, which has been fighting for the independence of Iran Jaya since it was annexed by Indonesia in 1961, demanded that talks be arranged with officials of the Papua New Guinean Government. The captives were released in good condition after 12 days.

Philippines

In the Philippines, the New People's Army (NPA), the military wing of the Communist Party of the Philippines (CPP), continued to target US personnel and installations as part of its campaign against US military bases:

- In January, a bomb exploded outside the United States Information Service (USIS) office in Davao, causing minor damage.
- In late February, the NPA killed an American geologist, his Filipino wife, and his father-in-law in an ambush in Bohol Province. The father-in-law, a prominent local official, is believed to have been the target of this attack.
- In early March, a US rancher in southern Luzon was slain by the NPA for refusing to pay Communist taxes.
- The NPA was responsible for the slaying of two US airmen near Clark Airbase on 13 May and may have been responsible for the assassination of a Marine sergeant on 4 May.
- On 18 May, two rifle grenades were fired at the USIS office in Manila; one exploded, causing minor damage.
- A US Peace Corps volunteer (PCV) was kidnapped and held by the NPA on Negros Island from mid-June until 2 August, when he was released unharmed. The volunteer's disappearance was not made known until two weeks after his abduction. By that time, the US Government had already decided to withdraw all PCV's from the Philippines because of the NPA threat. A Japanese aid worker, also kidnapped by the NPA, was released 2 August.
- Small-arms fire caused minor damage to the USIS building in Davao on 2 July.
- Communists bombed the Voice of America transmitter tower in Concepcion (Tarlac) on 17 September, causing limited damage.
- An American businessman was reportedly kidnapped by the NPA on 19 October in the northern Province of Cagayan. No claim of responsibility or demands were received, and he was still missing at the end of the year.

- Two rifle grenades were fired at the US Embassy on 10 November, but caused no damage or injuries.

The Aquino administration continues to press its international campaign against supporters of the Communists. The Philippines successfully lobbied the Dutch Government to reject CPP founder Jose Maria Sison's application for political asylum. Manila also continues to publicize the diversion of funds by the Communists' National Democratic front to the CPP/NPA.

In April, the government arrested NPA Deputy Chief of Staff Antonio Cabardo upon his return from Hong Kong; Cabardo was involved in an international scheme to launder counterfeit money. In June and again in October, the government raided NPA safehouses in Manila and arrested additional members of the NPA leadership.

Manila has issued public statements condemning domestic terrorism and maintains a reward program for information leading to the arrest of key figures in the CPP/NPA apparatus in the Philippines and abroad. A verdict was expected in early 1991 in the trial of two NPA assassins accused of murdering US Army Col. James Rowe in April 1989. Reynaldo Bernardo, a senior official of the Alex Boncayao Brigade—the Communists' premier assassination squad in Manila—was arrested in early November. Bernardo is a suspect in the Rowe slaying and may be tried for that crime.

Dissident military officers were responsible for a bombing campaign against both Philippine and foreign businesses in Manila in August and September. The bombings, which caused no fatalities, apparently were designed to demonstrate President Aquino's inability to maintain law and order. The government has offered rewards for the capture of rebel military leaders, some of whom are accused of complicity in random bombing attacks. Several dissident military officers were captured in 1990.

The Government of the Philippines continues to be a willing participant in programs of bilateral cooperation with, and training in, the United States on counterterrorism issues.

South Korea

In 1990, there was a handful of relatively minor attacks against US interests by radical students and other dissidents. In February, approximately 100 youths attempted to attack the residence of the head of the American Cultural Center in Kwangju. On 12 June, about 300 students attacked the US Cultural Center in Kwangju with firebombs; there were no injuries or damage. In August, radicals threw more than 50 firebombs at the rear door of a US Army office in Seoul, causing minor damage. On 18 October, 11 students attacked the US Embassy with firebombs and small explosive devices but caused no injuries or property damage.

In April, South Korean President Roh granted a special amnesty to Kim Hyun-Hui, the 28-year-old North Korean agent convicted of planting a bomb on a Korean Airlines flight in November 1987. Kim received the death penalty for the attack, in which 115 were killed, but she was pardoned because she confessed her crime and admitted to acting on behalf of North Korea. At her trial, Kim asserted that she had been told the bombing was directly ordered by Kim Chong-Il, son of North Korean President Kim Il-song.

Sri Lanka

Domestic terrorism continued to wrack the nation. The Liberation Tigers of Tamil Eelam (LTTE) broke off talks with the government in June and launched a campaign of violence. On 22 July, government forces discovered a series of mass graves containing the bodies of up to 200 policemen near the village of Tirrukkovil in eastern Sri Lanka. The policemen, many of whom had been blindfolded and shot in the back of the head, had been captured by the LTTE in mid-June. The LTTE reportedly was responsible for a series of massacres of Moslems near the Batticaloa region in the first half of August. The LTTE also was responsible for the murder of rival Tamil politicians throughout the northeast.

The radical Sinhalese group Janatha Vimukhi Perumana (JVP) was crippled by the deaths and arrests of most of its senior leadership in 1989. As a result, it was capable of conducting only limited operations in 1990. The group's most notable attack occurred in July, when it seized and executed 15 members of a village committee in southern Matara who had been cooperating with the police. The government continues to arrest suspected JVP members, and at least 15,000 are in custody. The government intends to prosecute those believed responsible for acts of terrorism and will provide vocational rehabilitation for others.

In 1990, three individuals accused in the May 1986 bombing of an Air Lanka aircraft, which killed 28, were acquitted. Five persons accused in the August 1987 grenade attack on Parliament, which killed two officials, also were found to be innocent. The government is appealing the acquittal of the five, and they remain in custody.

European Regional Overview

Two trends emerge in examining terrorist statistics for Western Europe in 1990. The first is the sharp decline in "spillover" terrorism from the Middle East as compared with previous years (in 1988 there were 29 such incidents, 31 in 1989, and only 8 in 1990). The second is the persistence—and violence—of autonomist groups such as the Provisional Irish Republican Army (PIRA), Basque Fatherland and Liberty (ETA), and Corsican nationalists.

An alarming phenomenon is the continued attacks on Iranian political dissidents residing in Europe by official Iranian hit squads. Swiss authorities confirm official Iranian involvement in the murder of an Iranian dissident in Switzerland, and French authorities suspect that the November murder of an Iranian-American dissident in Paris was the work of Iranian hit men.

In Greece, domestic terrorist groups were responsible for several attacks on US and other targets. In September, Greece declined a US extradition request against Palestinian terrorist

Muhammad Rashid, charged with involvement in the 1982 bombing of a Pan Am aircraft. Rashid will be prosecuted in Greece.

US interests continued to be targets of terrorism in Turkey, where domestic terrorism also increased during the year.

Perhaps the most dramatic changes in the last year have come in Eastern Europe, where the fall of Communist regimes has undermined the active or passive government support that terrorists had previously enjoyed in that region.

Belgium

In February, Enver Hadri, a leader of the local Albanian Committee for the Defense of Human Rights in Kosovo, was assassinated by two unidentified gunmen in Brussels. Hadri's colleagues have accused the Yugoslav intelligence service of his murder.

Belgium authorities scored several successes against the PIRA in 1990. Four suspected PIRA members were arrested in June. One of the four, Donna Maguire, was extradited to the Netherlands for her alleged role in the murder in Holland of two Australian citizens in May. In early December, the Belgian security forces arrested three alleged PIRA commandos during a raid on a safehouse in Antwerp. The suspects are scheduled to be tried in early 1991.

In April, the Belgian Government sent a special envoy to Beirut to seek information on Belgian citizens who had been seized from the yacht Silco in the Mediterranean and held by members of the Abu Nidal organization (ANO) since 1987. One of these hostages, along with his French girlfriend and their baby, was released in April. The four remaining Belgian hostages were freed in January 1991 in an arrangement that included the release of an ANO terrorist jailed in Belgium, who had served 10 years of his life sentence.

Cyprus

There were no international terrorist incidents in Cyprus in 1990.

In January, the Government of Cyprus hosted a two-man delegation from the Kurdish Worker's Party (PKK), which was sponsored by the Cypriot Committee for Solidarity with Kurdistan. The PKK, known for its terrorist attacks in Turkey, met with senior Greek Cypriot legislators, and the Cypriot Government arranged for a PKK press conference. This meeting was followed by the equally controversial November visit of four Greek Cypriot legislators to the Bekaa Valley in Lebanon for meetings with PKK leaders.

Eastern Europe

Since the fall of the Communist regimes in 1989, the policy of many East European countries has shifted from tolerance of, or even support for, terrorist groups to active cooperation with the West on counterterrorist issues. An example of the new openness evident in the region is Czechoslovak President Havel's revelation in April that the former government had exported 1,000 tons of the plastic explosive Semtex to Libya. This was the first official acknowledgement that sales of such magnitude had taken place. In Hungary, the new government denounced he former regime's support for Illych Ramirez Sanchez, the international terrorist known as Carlos, and initiated investigations into the assistance previously offered to him and to members of the Baader-Meinhof group.

Ironically, democratization, the concomitant loosening of government control on society, and the resulting changes in government security structures may make some of the countries of the region more vulnerable to the threat of domestic terrorism. These countries may also, for the first time, find themselves targeted by international terrorists. Support for the international coalition aligned against the Iraqi invasion of Kuwait, the establishment of diplomatic relations with Israel, facilitating the transport of emigrating Soviet Jews to Israel, and the cessation of support for terrorist groups may make these new democracies the targets of terrorist attacks. The United States and other governments of the West are taking steps to help these countries deal with this challenge.

In June, a group calling itself the December 13 Independent Group claimed responsibility for an attempted firebombing against the Soviet Consulate in Gdansk, Poland. The group, named for the date in 1981 on which President Wojciech Jaruzelski declared martial law, claimed that the attack was in protest against Poland's role in the movement of Soviet Jews to Israel. The attack resulted in minor property damage and no casualties.

In October, an explosion destroyed the offices of the rights and Freedoms movement, a political movement of ethnic Turks and Pomaks, in Shumen, Bulgaria. No injuries were reported. Unrest among ethnic Turks in Bulgaria is a continuing concern.

Terrorism in Yugoslavia and the former German Democratic Republic is discussed separately.

France

In 1990, international terrorist incidents in France were largely limited to activities connected with separatist movements in Corsica and the Basque area. France maintains an active antiterrorist stance and cooperates bilaterally with the United States and with many other nations in the fight against terrorism.

In 1990, France continued its cooperation with Spain in the fight against Basque terrorism and scored several counterterrorist successes. In April, French police dismantled an alleged ETA commando unit of 10 French nationals living in France. The group, believed to be headed by Henri Parot, has been charged with participating in criminal conspiracy on behalf of ETA. The group had reportedly been operating in Spain since the late 1970s. This roundup was the first large-scale arrest of French citizens charged with terrorist activities in Spain. A large cache of arms and explosives was also uncovered in connection with the arrest.

In September, alleged ETA leader Jose Zabaleta-Elosegui (alias Waldo), reputedly the second in command of ETA's military branch, was arrested in Biarritz on terrorist-related charges. In November, French police rounded up a four-man ETA cell in southwestern France and later that month arrested a three-man ETA cell in northern France.

The French Government's conciliatory approach toward the Corsican National Liberation Front (FLNC) appears to have generated a schism within the movement between hardliners and those seeking political concessions from Paris without resorting to violence. The truce declared in May 1988 between FLNC and the government has been broken by a new faction, the Corsican National Liberation Army (ALNC), which claimed responsibility for several bombings in the summer and fall of 1990 directed principally against properties owned by foreigners. Despite Interior Minister Joxe's program of attempting to co-opt the dissidents by granting more political autonomy to Corsica, some hardliners appear determined to continue to use terrorism in the fight for complete autonomy.

The French investigation into the terrorist bombing of UTA Flight 772 over Niger in September 1989 received wide press coverage during the latter part of 1990. According to press accounts, two probable Congolese nationals—one detained in Brazzaville, Congo, and the other in Kinshasa, Zaire—suspected of being active participants in the bombing, have been interviewed by French authorities. No charges have been filed in the case.

French authorities also continue their investigation into the bombings in the last three months of 1990 against US and French targets by the leftwing anarchist group Gracchus Babeuf. The bombings, which resulted in minor property damage and no injuries, were carried out in protest against the deployment of US Forces in the Persian Gulf.

France has one of Europe's most experienced cadre of specialized counterterrorist magistrates, and during 1990 the courts handed down stiff sentences to international terrorists responsible for attacks dating back to 1982. In March, the French Correctional Court sentenced Fouad Saleh and eight other members of a Hizballah terrorist cell to sentences ranging from five to 20 years for their roles in a series of bombings in 1986. In addition, the court convicted eight other Lebanese Hizballah militants in absentia. The convictions and sentences of the Saleh group were confirmed by the court of Appeals in October. In 1991, members of the Saleh group will be tried by the Criminal Court for the actual bombings.

In June, a French court condemned Lebanese Armed Revolutionary Faction member Jacqueline Esber in absentia to life imprisonment for her role in the slaying of an Israeli diplomat in 1982 and the attempted murder of a US consul in 1984. French authorities believe Esber is hiding in Libya. In June, the court also condemned an Iraqi, Haysayn Humary, in absentia to life imprisonment for taking part in the bombing of the Marks and Spencer department store in Paris in 1985. Humary, whose whereabouts are unknown, was a member of the Palestinian terrorist group 15 May Organization, which has now disbanded. Another member of the same group, Habib Maamar, was sentenced in absentia on similar charges to 20 years' imprisonment.

French courts sentenced a number of ETA terrorists including Arrospide-Sarasola (alias Santi-Potros), who is considered to be one of the group's top leaders. Santi-Potros will probably be extradited to Spain before completing his 10-year sentence in France. Another leading ETA member, Jose-Antonio Urriticoechea (alias Ternera), was sentenced to 10 years in prison for terrorist conspiracy and illegal possession of arms. In January, a member of the Basque terrorist organization Iparretarrak was sentenced to two years in prison.

In May, France extradited the Spaniard Jose Ramon Martinez de la Fuente to Spain on charges of committing ETA-sponsored terrorist activities. The French Council of State confirmed that two other suspected ETA members, Carmelo Garcia Merchan and Jose Felix Perez, can legally be extradited; their actual extradition awaits a final decision of the French Government. In early March, a French court approved the extradition of suspected Provisional Irish Republican Army members Patrick Murray, Donagh O'Kane, and Pauline Drumm to Germany, where they were wanted for assaults against British military installations, including a bombing that killed a British military officer. The three were captured in July 1989 while reportedly preparing to attack British interests in France.

At the same time, the French Government took controversial measures in its dealings with state sponsors of terrorism. In April, the government obtained the release of the last of the French hostages—Jacqueline Valente, her Belgian companion, and their young daughter—who had been held by the Abu Nidal organization. The French Government was criticized by several Western nations for praising the role of Libyan leader Qadhafi in obtaining the hostages' release. French press reports say they had been held in Libya.

On 27 July, French President Mitterrand pardoned pro-Iranian Lebanese terrorist Anis Naccache and four of his accomplices. Naccache had been sentenced to life imprisonment in 1982 for killing a French policeman and a passer-by and for wounding three others during a failed attempt to assassinate former Iranian Prime Minister Shahpur Bakhtiar. The government expelled all five terrorists after their release from prison. According to press reports, the French had made a deal with Iran to release the prisoners in exchange for the release of French hostages in Lebanon. Foreign Minister Dumas asserted that the Naccache release was part of France's efforts to obtain freedom for the remaining Western hostages in Lebanon.

Germany

International terrorist attacks decreased from 19 incidents in 1989 to 13 in 1990. None of these incidents [were] directed against US targets. The number of domestic terrorist incidents increased, however, following the onset of a new Red Army Faction (RAF) offensive that began in late 1989.

On 3 October, the German Democratic Republic (GDR) merged with West Germany. Thus, West German law and authority were extended into the territory of the former GDR. The former Communist East German regime had maintained good relations with Libya and several terrorist groups. Information released from the files of the Stasi, the former East German secret police, and German press reports make clear the extent of East German support for German and international terrorist groups. Among the revelations:

- The Stasi, through monitoring of Libyans in East Germany, knew in advance of plans for the 1986 La Belle disco bombing in which two American servicemen were killed.
- Stasi officials provided training to Palestinian and Libyan terrorists. The Stasi also provided weapons to the Palestine Liberation Organization (PLO) in exchange for information on West German intelligence activities in Beirut.
- East Germany gave safehaven to Abu Daoud and Abu Hisham—two members of the PLO's Fatah organization who masterminded the murders at the 1972 Munich Olympics—and the notorious terrorist Illych Ramirez Sanchez, also known as Carlos.
- An East German foreign trade organization was involved in arms trading with the Abu Nidal organization.
- A number of Red Army Faction members were given new identities and safehaven by the East German Government.

The indulgent attitudes toward terrorism that characterized the Honecker regime were replaced by efforts to take a firm counterterrorist stand. In June, the GDR Government arrested 10 former RAF terrorists, most of whom voluntarily agreed to be turned over to West German authorities. Two of the suspects were released because the West German warrants for their arrest had expired. The other eight suspects—Susanne Albrecht, Inge Viett, Werner Lotze, Sigrid Sternebeck, Silke Maier-Witt, Henning Beer, Monika Helbing, and Ralf-Babtiste Friedrich—remain in custody awaiting prosecution. Press reports indicate that these suspects have provided investigators with extensive information on RAF activities between 1977 and 1981, including the 1977 assassinations of Federal Prosecutor Siegfried Buback, Dresdener Bank Chief Juergen Ponto, and Employers' Association President Hans-Martin Schleyer.

The arrests of former RAF members in East Germany have had only limited impact on the activities of the current RAF hardcore. The group continued the terrorist offensive begun in November 1989 with a technically sophisticated bombing attack that killed Deutsche Bank Chairman Alfred Herhausen and injured the driver of his armored car. The RAF aborted an attack against West German Agriculture Minister Ignatz Kiechie in April. The RAF claimed responsibility for the attempted assassination of Interior Ministry State Secretary Hans Neusel in July. The RAF also carried out arson attacks and vandalism against several Spanish automobile dealerships in Germany in support of the Spanish October 1st Antifascist resistance Group (GRAPO).

There were several international terrorist attacks in Germany during 1990. The Provisional Irish Republican Army claimed responsibility for attempted bomb attacks in May against British military installations in Hannover and Muensterm, for the assassination of a British Army officer in Dortmund and for the bombing in June of a military training facility in Hamein.

Several counterterrorist prosecutions took place in German courts in 1990. The trial of Popular Front for the Liberation of Palestine-General Command (PLFP-GC) members Hafiz Kassem Dalkamoni, a ranking official of the organization, and Abdel Fattah Ghandanfar for the failed attacks against US military duty trains in 1987 and 1988 began in October. Dalkamoni was also indicted in April on charges of "manslaughter as a result of negligence," stemming from an explosion that killed one German bomb-disposal technician and severely injured another in April 1989.

Ali Cetiner, a leading Kurdish Workers' Party member, was convicted in March of murdering another Kurd. In the first application of a new law that allows prosecution witnesses in certain terrorist cases to receive reduced sentences in exchange for testimony, Cetiner was sentenced to only five years' imprisonment, instead of the usual life term. Trials for murder and other serious crimes against 17 other alleged PKK members continued at year's end.

Suspected Provisional Irish Republican Army operatives Gerard McGeough and Gerard Hanratty were on trial in Duesseldorf at year's end. Both are implicated in the attempted bomb attacks during the summer of 1988 against British Army Barracks in Duisburg. In addition, McGeough is charged in the March 1987 bombing of a British officers' mess in Rhein Dahlem that injured dozens of Germans.

There are no legal provisions that allow German citizens to be extradited. Moreover, since Germany does not have the death penalty, foreigners charged with capital offenses are unlikely to be extradited. The German Government's policy is that individuals not extradited for terrorist crimes will be tried in Germany, regardless of where the crime was committed.

The German press has noted police complaints that a number of legal safeguards hinder investigations. Generous provisions allowing asylum seekers and refugees to remain in Germany pending resolution of their cases have enabled some persons suspected of terrorist acts to remain in Germany. For instance, Bassim Makki, a Lebanese convicted in December 1989 of conspiracy to carry out bomb attacks against US and Israeli interests in Munich and Frankfurt, was released and deported to Syria in July. Makki agreed to drop his application for political asylum and to consent to deportation in exchange for an early release.

German officials continue to work closely with US, British, and other authorities to identify the individuals responsible for the bombing of Pan Am Flight 103 in 1988.

Greece

There were four international terrorist incidents in Greece in 1990. The most notable of these were the bombings in March of 11 vehicles belonging to non-Western embassies by the terrorist organization Social Resistance and the bazooka attack in June against the offices of the US firm Proctor and Gamble by the Revolutionary Organization 17 November. A lesser known group, the Anticapitalist, Antiestablishment

Struggle Organization, claimed responsibility for a February firebombing of a US Air Force vehicle in Patras. Greece also experienced a rash of anarchist and extreme leftist violence against government and political offices, as well as police stations. The Greek police believe a number of individuals suspected of past terrorist activity were involved in these attacks.

Greek terrorist groups focused the bulk of their attacks on domestic targets, in part a reflection of Greece's economic problems and political unrest during a period of national elections. These targets included government officials, prominent Greeks, and institutions. In addition to the bazooka attack on Proctor and Gamble, 17 November carried out a daring daylight theft of two bazookas from the National Military Museum in February, detonated some 23 incendiary devices in affluent neighborhoods of Athens, attempted to assassinate Greek shipping magnate Vardis Vardinogiannis, and attacked EC offices in downtown Athens with rockets in late December. In all but the incendiary attacks and the museum robbery, 17 November made use of a variety of military explosives and rockets it had stolen from a Greek military weapons depot in Larissa in December 1989.

The level of violence by Revolutionary People's Struggle (ELA) continued apace, as the organization conducted numerous independent bombings. In April, ELA carried out its first joint attacks, with the terrorist group 1 May, against Greek Government and labor offices in Athens and Thessaloniki. In early November, suspected terrorist Kyriakos Mazokopos inadvertently directed Greek police to a suspected ELA–1 May safehouse in a downtown Athens warehouse, when a device he was assembling in the warehouse exploded prematurely. Police later uncovered a large cache of military equipment, explosives, and original proclamations of ELA, 1 May, and Revolutionary Solidarity. Revolutionary Solidarity was responsible for the February 1990 murder of Greek prison psychiatrist Mario Manatos. Fingerprints of three suspects in the murder were found on different items in the warehouse. Mazokopos and others have been charged in the warehouse case, and investigations are continuing.

In 1990, the Greek Government decided to try suspected Palestinian terrorist Mohammad Rashid in Greece for his role in the 1982 bombing of a Pan Am aircraft, rather than extradite him to the United States.

At the same time, the Greek Parliament passed a new counterterrorist law that appears to expand the investigative authority of the security services in cases of terrorism, narcotics, and organized crime. The move is seen as part of Prime Minister Mitsotakis's growing commitment to combating international and domestic terrorism. The new government has taken significant steps to improve the training, equipment, and morale of the police. The government has also initiated a terrorist-tip hotline and passed legislation allowing a ban on the publication of communiqués issued by terrorist organizations.

In August, Greek authorities detained in port the ship Tiny Star, which was used by Libyan-sponsored terrorists to launch an attack on Israel in May. The ship was later stripped of its registry by Panamanian authorities.

Ireland

Anglo-Irish counterterrorist relations faltered early in the year after the Irish Supreme Court upheld an appeal against the extradition of two PIRA members who had participated in the 1983 mass escape from Northern Ireland's Maze Prison. The two escapees had argued that, if they were returned, they would be subjected to assault by British prison officials. Dublin did, however, extradite PIRA member Desmond Ellis to the United Kingdom in November. Ellis was wanted in Britain on charges of possession of explosives with the intent to endanger life.

Irish-British dual national Brian Keenan, held hostage in Lebanon since April 1986, was released in August.

Italy

In 1990, there was only one international terrorist incident in Italy, as compared to five such incidents in 1989. There were three noteworthy terrorist-related developments in Italy during the year:

- In March, two well-known Red Brigades terrorists were formally charged with involvement in the 1984 assassination of Director General of Multinational Force and Observers (MFO) Leamon Hunt. The court later dismissed the charges because of lack of evidence.
- In July, Italian authorities issued an arrest warrant for Michael Rouphael and Waddud Al Turk, both reportedly members of the Abu Nidal organization, for their involvement in a 1984 attack in Rome in which a United Arab Emirates diplomat was wounded and his companion was killed.
- In October, the trial of four former Italian Intelligence Service officials began. They are charged with thwarting the investigation of a Palestine Liberation Organization arms shipment to Italy in 1979 that, in part, was destined for the Red Brigades.

The Italian courts presided over a number of other cases in 1990, some of which dealt with domestic terrorist incidents dating to 1980. As a result of several Italian court rulings, some 400 accused terrorist group members, including some Red Brigades cadres charged with armed insurrection against the state, were acquitted. Despite their acquittal, many of these individuals remained in prison for other offenses. In one case, 19 rightwing terrorists who had been accused in the 1980 bombing of the Bologna railroad station, in which 85 people died and 200 were wounded, were either acquitted or had their sentences reduced by an appeals court. Although the courts decided that the state's case was insufficient, the case is still under review appeal.

In February, Switzerland acceded to an Italian request to extradite Red Brigades terrorist Antonio De Luca. De Luca, who was apprehended in 1988, went through an extensive series of legal maneuvers in an unsuccessful attempt to obtain political asylum in Switzerland. In September, a second Italian request for the extradition from Greece of Red Brigades terrorist Maurizio Folini was rejected by an Athens court on the grounds of insufficient evidence. Folini has been convicted in absentia of various terrorist crimes.

The Italian Government continues to improve the effectiveness of its antiterrorist forces. Worries over Persian Gulf–related attacks prompted increased security measures at high visibility targets such as key embassies and Fiumicino International Airport. The United States and Italy have worked together on a series of cooperative investigations involving the Japanese Red Army, Hizballah, and the Abu Nidal organization.

Netherlands

Incidents of international terrorism in the Netherlands decreased from eight in 1989 to three in 1990. In May, the Provisional Irish Republican Army claimed responsibility for the murder of two Australian tourists in Roermond, stating that it had mistaken the men for off-duty British soldiers. The Basque Fatherland and Liberty Organization claimed credit for two bombings against Spanish targets in Amsterdam in 1990. In June the group bombed a building housing the Iberia Airlines office, and in July it bombed the branch office of a Spanish bank; four passers-by were slightly injured in the second attack.

The trial of four suspects in the Roermond attack—Gerard Harte, Sean Hick, Paul Hughes, and Donna Maguire—was scheduled to begin in February 1991. Although charges against the four are pending in Belgium, the Netherlands decided to prosecute them first. In a separate case, the Netherlands extradited alleged Irish People's Liberation Organization member Anthony Kerr to Belgium on 8 June. Tried in late 1990 for the December 1989 shooting in Antwerp in which a policeman was wounded, Kerr was sentenced to four and a half years in prison.

The Dutch Government continues to work actively to enhance international efforts to fight terrorism and has promoted EC-wide counterterrorist cooperation. The Netherlands has been one of the strongest voices in the EC for taking a tough stand against state supporters of terrorism.

Soviet Union

In 1990, the Soviet Union increased its efforts to combat international and domestic terrorism, both of which have become sources of increasing concern for Soviet authorities.

As in 1989, incidents of domestic violence and terrorism continued to rise in the USSR, especially in the Caucasus, Moldavia, and the Central Asian republics. In 1990, Soviet nationals also attempted at least 27 airplane hijackings, nine of which landed in Finland, Sweden, and Pakistan.

In general, Soviet authorities have made vigorous attempts to investigate incidents of violence and terrorism and to prosecute the individuals involved. The Soviets have requested and obtained the extradition of several hijackers, and several other extradition requests are pending. Moscow has also sought to disband and disarm paramilitary groups, particularly in the Caucasus. In November 1990, Soviet authorities arrested and charged a man with attempted terrorism after he allegedly fired two shots on Red Square during the Revolution Day Parade.

Soviet authorities continue to participate in bilateral exchanges with the United States and several West European governments on a broad range of counterterrorist issues. Moscow has taken an increasingly firm stand against terrorism in recent years.

Although the Soviet Union has publicly condemned terrorism, it has continued to provide military and economic assistance to several radical governments involved in terrorist activities, including Cuba, Libya, North Korea, Syria, and, until recently, Iraq. Soviet relations with these countries are not, however uniformly cordial, due to changes in the Soviet Union's foreign policy orientation and to differences over economic assistance and ideological matters. In many cases, the Soviets have found that their traditional relationships with these radical governments are inconsistent with their new emphasis on increased economic and political ties to the West.

Nevertheless, the Soviets have exhibited a reluctance to confront some of these state sponsors regarding their support for terrorism. This reluctance is no doubt due in part to the advantageous economic relations that the Soviet Union continues to maintain with some of these countries. Perhaps because of this reluctance to disturb these bilateral relationships, the Soviet Union continues to exhibit a preference for broader multilateral approaches to the terrorist problem.

Spain

Spain experienced an increase in international terrorist incidents in the past year—from 22 incidents in 1989 to 28 incidents in 1990. This is more than twice the number in any other European country. Terrorism in Spain resulted in at least 25 deaths and many more injuries. Most of these incidents were committed by either the Basque Fatherland and Liberty terrorist organization or the smaller, October 1st Antifascist Resistance Group. Spanish terrorism also spilled over into other parts of Europe. For example, ETA claimed responsibility for several terrorist attacks against Spanish installations in the Netherlands.

Spain's smaller terrorist groups were also active in 1990. These groups include Terra Lliure, which is a Catalan separatist group, and the Guerrilla Army of the Free Galician People.

The ETA organization suffered a setback in 1990 when a hitherto unknown ETA network in France called the Itinerant Command was uncovered. This group had operated for 12 years and was responsible for some 40 terrorist bombings and assassinations in Spain. The discovery led to several arrests. The network began to unravel with the apprehension in April of a French Basque, Henri Parot, in Seville before a planned ETA attack on the local headquarters of the National Police. Working together, French and Spanish security forces later rounded up other Itinerant Command terrorists in France. Parot was convicted of eight offenses—ranging from carrying out injurious attacks to possession of false identification—and in December was sentenced to prison terms totaling 86 years.

Although the Spanish courts continued to deal sternly with terrorist cases, few major prosecutions of international or domestic terrorists were concluded during 1990. As of September 1990, some 470 members of ETA were in prison in Spain awaiting trial. Madrid has also taken action against rightwing terrorists. Several persons, including a national police officer, are in preventive detention, pending prosecution for the Madrid assassination of a pro-ETA Basque legislator in late 1989; two other national police officers are awaiting trial on charges of organizing an extreme rightwing death squad that operated in southern France from 1983 to 1986. Authorities obtained court orders in July to extend their preventive detention period for two years. Spain is also pursuing the prosecution of three Hizballah terrorists arrested in November 1989 in Madrid and Valencia, despite reported warnings by Hizballah supporters in Lebanon of possible terrorist retaliation against Spanish targets. Following these arrests, Spain sponsored an international conference to discuss the Hizballah terrorist organization.

During 1990, Spain vigorously pursued efforts to extradite ETA terrorists from abroad. ETA terrorists reside in many countries including Cape Verde, Cuba, the Dominican Republic, Ecuador, France, Sao Tome and Principe, and Venezuela. French courts ordered the extradition of several ETA members to Spain.

In early 1990, Madrid instituted an intense domestic campaign for citizen assistance in apprehending six GRAPO members primarily responsible for the increased terrorist activity in late 1989 and early 1990. The government also dispersed ETA prisoners throughout the Spanish prison system in an effort to isolate them from each other and to deny them mutual support. The Spanish Government has offered a limited immunity program for terrorist prisoners who renounce the use of force. This so-called reinsertion program is designed not only to convince individual terrorists to renounce terrorism as a political tool but also to divide loyalties within the terrorist groups. Madrid passed a law in 1990 making it illegal for families and employers of kidnapped victims to "collaborate" with terrorists by paying a ransom. Several persons who acted as middlemen in the payment of ransom demands to ETA were charged with this offense in 1990.

Domestic counterterrorism, aimed primarily at ETA and GRAPO, is a high-priority effort. With the 1992 Olympic Games to be held in Barcelona and the World's Fair in Seville, Spain is increasingly concerned about the risk of terrorist attacks. In 1990, ETA threatened to disrupt the World's Fair and sent a package bomb to the executive offices of the Fair in Seville. In December, ETA set off a car bomb near the Olympic soccer stadium outside Barcelona, killing six policemen and two civilian bystanders.

Sweden

In September, an Iranian Kurdish woman was killed by a letter bomb apparently intended for her husband, the chairman of the Kurdish Independence Party in Sweden. Swedish authorities have not officially determined responsibility for the attack. Before the bombing, the dead woman's husband had reportedly told the Swedish police that he was under constant threat from Iran. Other members of the local Kurdish community have also accused Iran of the assault.

In early 1990, Swedish courts upheld the December 1989 convictions of four Palestinians believed linked to the Popular Struggle Front (PSF) who were found guilty of involvement in bombings in Stockholm, Copenhagen, and Amsterdam in 1985 and 1986. Two of the Palestinians had received life sentences; the remaining two had received sentences of one year and six years. In June, Swedish police arrested 11 Palestinians, all of whom were relatives of the four alleged PSF members, on suspicion of ties to terrorist groups. Evidence was insufficient for prosecution, but the 11 Palestinians were expelled from Sweden or departed the country voluntarily because of immigration irregularities.

Although relatively few terrorist incidents have occurred in Sweden, in the past, members of radical Palestinian and Kurdish groups have used the country as a base for terrorist operations abroad. This remains an area of continuing concern for Swedish authorities. The Swedish National Police Board reported in July that there are about 30,000 refugees and asylum seekers residing in the country who arrived without identification papers. During certain periods, as many as 80 percent of refugees arriving in Sweden have no passports or identification documents. Swedish authorities are attempting to stop the influx.

Switzerland

The lone international terrorist incident in Switzerland was the assassination of Kazem Radjavi, an Iranian dissident and brother of Iranian Mojahedin leader Massoud Radjavi. The investigating judge concluded in his report that evidence pointed to the direct involvement of one or more official Iranian services in the murder. He identified 13 suspects, all of whom had traveled to Switzerland on official Iranian passports. Most had traveled together, and their passports, as well as their airplane tickets, had been obtained at the same time. The Swiss Government condemned the assassination and summoned an Iranian Embassy officer in Bern to express its strong concern over the investigation findings. In October, the examining magistrate formally requested Iranian cooperation in investigating the assassination and submitted a series of questions regarding the case to judicial authorities in Tehran. There has been no known response. However, the Iranian Embassy has filed a complaint against the newspaper *La Suisse* under Article 296 of the Swiss Penal Code, which prohibits "insults (to) a foreign state in the person of its chief executive, diplomatic representative, or its government." The Iranian Government objected to the way the publication had reported the murder and the implications of official Iranian involvement.

Two Swiss employees of the International Committee of the Red Cross (ICRC), who had been kidnapped in Lebanon in October 1989, were freed in August. Emmanual Christen was released in Beirut on 8 August, and his colleague Elio Erriquez was freed five days later. The Swiss Government had approached a number of governments in an effort to secure the release of its citizens, as did the ICRC. Upon the hostages' return to Switzerland, the Swiss Government expressed thanks to the Governments of Libya, Algeria, Syria, and Iran, as well as the Palestine Liberation Organization, for their assistance in gaining the release of the two captives. The Swiss Government declared that it did not negotiate with the kidnappers and that it paid no ransom or other favors in exchange for their release. The identity of the kidnappers remains unclear.

Aluaro Baragiola-Lojacano, a Red Brigades terrorist who was sentenced to life imprisonment in November 1989 for the assassination of an Italian judge, appealed his case to a higher court in April. The Ticino Cantonal Court of Appeals upheld the conviction but reduced his sentence to 17 years.

In October, the Swiss Federal Council issued a report and suggested specific measures that broaden the concept of national security to include nonmilitary threats such as terrorism. It is still unclear how this report will affect Switzerland's approach to counterterrorist issues.

Turkey

Terrorism in Turkey escalated in 1990 with more than a dozen major political assassinations as well as robberies and bombings associated with terrorist organizations. Most of these were domestic incidents directed against Turkish targets. All 12 international terrorist incidents were directed against US interests. Dev Sol, the separatist Kurdish Workers' Party (PKK), the Turkish Workers and Peasant Liberation Army (TIKKO), and other terrorist groups remain active throughout Turkey.

The terrorist organization Dev Sol, the most active of these groups, claimed responsibility for a number of terrorist attacks on Western and pro-Western interests, as well as domestic security officials. The most senior victim was the retired Deputy Chief of the National Intelligence Service, Hiram Abbas, murdered in Istanbul on 26 September. In early November, Dev Sol assassinated an Istanbul public prosecutor. Member discipline in Dev Sol, fostered by the threat of retribution against those who cooperate with the authorities, has hindered government efforts to prosecute terrorists. In October, Binbir Pembgul, a young woman who threw a pipe bomb at the US Consulate in Istanbul in 1989, was set free by a military court after the prosecutor claimed the military had no jurisdiction in the case. Charges against her are still pending in civil courts.

Radical Islamic fundamentalists are believed responsible for a number of murders in Turkey. Targets have included prominent defenders of Turkey's secularism, including Prof. Muammer Aksoy in January, in Ankara; journalist Cetin Emec in March, in Istanbul; and former deputy of the Turkish Parliament Bahriye Ucok in October, in Ankara. These murders have been claimed by several Islamic groups, including the so-called Islamic Movement Organization, of which little is known.

Terrorist activity by separatists, particularly by the PKK, continued in Turkey's southeastern region, with acts of murder, arson, and destruction against both officials and civilians. The PKK claims it is targeting government interests because of a lack of government response to continuing social and economic problems plaguing Kurds in the south-central provinces. PKK insurgency, abetted by Turkey's Middle Eastern neighbors, continues to present a significant challenge to government security forces. The PKK received safehaven in Iran, Iraq, and Syria.

The surge in terrorist activity resulted in a series of government measures designed to combat terrorism. Government forces mounted numerous offensive operations against the PKK resulting in significant numbers of arrests and casualties. New counterterrorist measures went into effect in April following a summit involving the leaders of all parliamentary political parties. These comprehensive measures include doubling sentences for those convicted of cooperating with separatists and an expansion of the regional governor's powers to expel suspected terrorists from the region.

United Kingdom

International terrorist incidents decreased in the United Kingdom from 10 attacks in 1989 to only one in 1990. However, deadly acts of domestic terrorism by the PIRA continued in the United Kingdom, especially in Northern Ireland.

In 1990, 76 lives were lost in sectarian and political violence in Northern Ireland, compared with 61 in 1989. More than 50 were killed in PIRA attacks, including six in England and on the European Continent. As a measure of PIRA ruthlessness, in several incidents this year, PIRA forced men to drive car bombs into military checkpoints by holding their families hostage and threatening to kill them.

PIRA conducted 19 attacks in mainland Britain in 1990, including the car-bomb assassination of Conservative Party member of Parliament Ian Gow and other attacks on current and former government figures. Several attacks in the United Kingdom and continental Europe demonstrated an increasing PIRA tendency toward indiscriminate violence. In June, PIRA claimed credit for a bomb attack against the Carlton Club in downtown London, a popular haunt of Conservative Party members of Parliament. Two people were seriously wounded, and several passers-by, including two Americans, were injured. In July, PIRA claimed responsibility for a bomb attack against the London Stock Exchange.

Semtex is the explosive of choice in bombings in Britain. PIRA is believed to have received large quantities of the Czechoslovak-made plastic explosive from Libya in the 1980s. Other explosives—including some "homemade" from agricultural chemicals—are also used in Northern Ireland.

"Loyalist" or "Unionist" paramilitary groups in Northern Ireland also continued to commit terrorist acts. Nineteen deaths were attributed to Protestant paramilitaries in 1990.

Britain renewed diplomatic relations with the governments of Iran and Syria in 1990. The United Kingdom broke diplomatic relations with Iran in 1989 after Iran's death threat against author Salman Rushdie. Relations with Syria were severed after an April 1986 attempt to bomb an El Al aircraft, with the involvement of Syrian intelligence agents.

An Iranian student named Mehrdad Kokabi is under arrest and has been charged in connection with at least one of the several 1989 bookstore bombings in the United Kingdom related to the Salman Rushdie affair. Several others were deported from the United Kingdom in 1990 for their involvement in attempts to find and kill Rushdie.

In 1990, British investigators and their US and German counterparts continued the intensive investigation of the December 1988 bombing of Pan Am Flight 103 over Lockerbie, Scotland. British legal authorities continue to cooperate with their counterparts in Germany, Belgium, and the Netherlands in investigations of PIRA terrorist incidents there. Similarly, British officials continued to follow the investigation and the trial in France of the crew of the Eskund, a ship captured while en route to deliver Libyan arms to the PIRA in Ireland.

Yugoslavia

Yugoslav Government condemns international terrorism and has played a positive role within the UN and the Nonaligned Movement in issues relating to terrorism. In 1990, Yugoslavia continued to take a more active stance against international terrorism. This is due in part to a growing recognition that international terrorism represents a danger to Yugoslavia itself.

Yugoslavia has long suffered from sporadic and generally minor outbreaks of terrorism, mainly perpetrated by extremist émigré groups hostile to the Communist regime.

Although there were no significant terrorist acts in Yugoslavia in 1990 by such groups, Yugoslav interests abroad were attacked. Offices of Yugoslav Airlines in Brussels and Sydney and Yugoslav diplomatic missions in Germany and Belgium suffered bomb attacks. The perpetrators remain unknown, but Yugoslav officials charged that these actions were carried out by extremist émigré groups.

A new development in Yugoslavia in 1990 has been the appearance of armed groups, often connected with the tensions that are rampant among the various national groups in the country. The most conspicuous of these armed groups appeared in areas of Croatia that are primarily inhabited by Serbs. Armed bands of civilians established roadblocks, disrupted traffic, and on some occasions fired at or harassed travelers. Bomb explosions damaged some railroad lines. On two occasions persons were killed by gunfire in what appeared to be politically motivated violence. In one of these instances a police patrol car was ambushed by unknown persons; one police officer was killed and another wounded. Yugoslav authorities have charged that terrorist actions are being carried out or prepared in the Yugoslav Province of Kosovo, whose population is 90 percent Albanian. There are no indications that any terrorist actions took place in Kosovo in 1990, although press accounts suggest significant quantities of arms have been smuggled into the province.

In the Yugoslav Republic of Macedonia, a political party called the Internal Macedonian Revolutionary Organization (IMRO), which claims to trace its origins back to a notorious turn-of-the-century terrorist group, won the most seats in the first multiparty election in Macedonia since World War II. IMRO states that it has renounced terrorism, but it has made a number of extreme statements. Some IMRO members, according to press reports, have made "death threats" against politicians associated with other groups.

In the past, Yugoslavia's political ties to the Middle East have led it to take a tolerant stand toward the prosecution or extradition of international terrorists found on its soil, most notoriously in 1985 when it allowed Palestine Liberation Front leader Abu Abbas to leave Yugoslavia, following his role in the hijacking of the cruise ship Achille Lauro, in which an American citizen was murdered.

In more recent years, however, the Yugoslav authorities have become more aware of the threat posed by international terrorism, and they now appear to be more willing to act against international terrorists operating in or transiting Yugoslav territory. The Yugoslav security services act to prevent terrorism, and they have cooperated fully and actively in international terrorist investigations. Within the limits imposed by serious financial constraints, the decline of central authority in the country, and the large number of international visitors, the Yugoslav authorities have acted to reduce the abuse of Yugoslav territory by terrorists.

Latin American Regional Overview

The number of international terrorist incidents in Latin America rose to 162 in 1990, higher than any other region. Even so, these figures represent only a small percentage of the total number of terrorist acts committed in Central and South America. In most Latin American countries, the primary targets of guerrillas, narcotics traffickers, and others who engage in terrorism have been domestic—government and law enforcement officials, opinionmakers, and politicians. This was especially true in Colombia, Peru, and El Salvador where the levels of violence have been extremely high. In Peru, for example, of the more than 3,400 terrorist-related deaths in 1990 only six were of foreigners.

Roughly two-thirds of all anti-US attacks worldwide took place in Latin America, where US citizens and interests were the principal foreign targets of terrorist groups. Various groups have been operating for years in Central and South America and share a radical leftist ideology that, combined with a visible US presence in the region and historical antipathy toward the United States, contributes to the large number of attacks against Americans. Two Americans were killed in 1990—one in Peru and one in Panama—and 31 were wounded. Chile was the most common site of anti-American attacks in Latin America. The number of anti-US attacks there increased from 21 in 1989 to 61 in 1990. Most of these were bombings of Mormon Church facilities in Santiago and other parts of the country.

Although narcoterrorist and guerrilla violence continued to plague Colombia, the number of anti-American incidents fell from 39 in 1989 to 25 in 1990. In Peru, with two murderous insurgent groups—Sendero Luminoso and the Tupac Amaru Revolutionary Movement (MRTA)—there were 22 anti-American incidents in 1990.

Bolivia

Five of six international terrorist incidents in Bolivia were directed against US interests. Although the investigation continues, virtually no progress was made in the prosecution of Zarate Willka members charged with the 1989 murder of two US Mormon missionaries or the 1988 attack on then Secretary of State George Shultz. The government changed prosecutors five times and had not named a judge to hear the case by year's end.

The Nestor Paz Zamora Commission (CNPZ), a new Bolivian group named after the deceased brother of President Jaime Paz Zamora, conducted its first terrorist attacks in La Paz during 1990. The CNPZ claims to be part of a renovated National Liberation Army (ELN), the group led by Che Guevara during the 1960s. The CNPZ began with the abduction of Bolivian Coca-Cola President Jorge Lonsdale in June, later murdering him in December just as the Bolivian security forces were mounting a rescue attempt. The CNPZ also claimed responsibility for an assault in October on the US Marine house in La Paz that killed one Bolivian guard and wounded another. The group also took credit for a second bomb attack on the same day that destroyed a monument honoring John F. Kennedy.

During 1990 more evidence surfaced pointing to cooperation between Peruvian and Bolivian terrorist groups. The investigation of the Marine house assault revealed that Peru's Tupac Amaru Revolutionary Movement provided financial support and at least one member to counsel the Bolivian CNPZ terrorists in their operations. Two Sendero Luminoso members were captured in August near the border with Peru.

Chile

Terrorism in Chile increased significantly in 1990, notably since the March inauguration of the country's first democratically elected government in 16 years. International terrorist incidents rose from 23 in 1989 to 64 in 1990. Despite the democratic transition, radical leftist Chilean splinter groups remain committed to armed struggle and have been responsible for virtually all of the incidents. The dissident faction of the Communist-affiliated Manuel Rodriguez Patriotic Front (FPMR) and the Lautaro Youth Movement (MJL) have been the primary assailants.

Chile topped the list of nations worldwide where anti-US attacks have occurred, with 61 incidents in 1990. Although most of these have been directed against US-related property, such as Mormon churches and US-Chilean binational centers, two incidents appear to have been intended to cause US casualties. The November bombing of an organized softball game killed a Canadian citizen and severely wounded a US Embassy officer. The bombing of a restaurant during the same month in the coastal city of Vina del Mar seriously injured three US sailors and five other people, including one British tourist. Both incidents were claimed by the dissident faction FPMR/D of the FPMR.

Despite the new government's efforts to address the issue of the repressive policies of the Pinochet regime, leftist Chilean terrorists conducted lethal assaults against former officers in the military government as part of their own campaign. Terrorists received a major boost in January when more than 40 suspected members of the FPMR and FPMR/D staged a mass jail break. Several of the escapees had been involved in the 1986 attempt against Pinochet and presumably have access to arms caches.

The FPMR conducted several acts of domestic terrorism in 1990, including the attempted assassination of former military junta member Gustavo Leigh and another general; the murder of a retired Carabinero colonel; and the daytime shooting of an Army officer assigned to General Pinochet's security detail. The MJL continued to conduct armed robberies that, on several occasions, resulted in the deaths of security personnel. In November, Lautaro killed four security personnel in an attack on a hospital aimed at freeing one of their comrades.

The disruption of the internal intelligence apparatus resulting from the democratic transition has hindered the new government's attempts to control terrorism. The National Information Center (CNI), which was responsible for investigating terrorism under the military regime, was disbanded by President Pinochet before he left office.

Under President Aylwin, the civilian investigative police have been hampered by an outgoing reorganization aimed at rooting out corrupt elements. To compensate for the disruption in intelligence gathering, the Aylwin government sought to enhance the intelligence capability of the national uniformed police (Carabineros).

As part of its effort to combat terrorism, the new government sought a comprehensive package of legal reforms. These would address the alleged human rights abuses associated with the military jurisdiction and penalties for those accused of terrorist crimes under Pinochet. The government also requested the appointment of special judges to investigate the MJL and the more dramatic acts of terrorism.

The Chilean Government is cooperating with the US Government to resolve the murder of former Chilean Foreign Minister and Pinochet-critic Orlando Letelier and an American Associate, Ronni Moffitt, who were killed in a car bombing in Washington, DC, in 1976. Legislation that permits the transfer of jurisdiction of the case from military to civilian courts was passed by the Chilean Congress in December 1990 and went into effect in February 1991.

Colombia

Colombia's democratic government faces opposition from active leftist guerrilla groups, well-financed narcotics trafficking organizations, and rightwing paramilitary groups. All three use terrorism, primarily against domestic targets.

International terrorist incidents in Colombia declined for the second consecutive year, down from 46 in 1989 to 27 in 1990.

The most significant terrorist attacks in Colombia during 1990 were committed by the loose conglomerate of narcotics traffickers known as the Medellin Cartel. The Cartel and other traffickers, primarily criminally motivated, continued their use of terrorist tactics to hamper government attempts to impede their activities. In August 1989, following a string of political assassinations attributed to the Cartel, the government launched a crackdown. The narcotics traffickers responded with a violent campaign of bombings and assassinations of political figures and policemen that continued until mid-1990, when the traffickers declared a truce.

Suspected narcoterrorists assassinated the two leading leftist presidential candidates in March and April 1990. In May, narcotics traffickers began a campaign to kill policemen in Medellin, inflicting more than 400 police deaths. Following the August inauguration of President Gaviria, narcotics traffickers focused on kidnapping prominent Colombians, many of whom were journalists. An abducted German journalist was released in late 1990 but, by year's end, the traffickers still held nearly a dozen hostages. One of them, the daughter of former Colombian President Julio Cesar Turbay, was killed in January 1991 during a police attempt to rescue her.

The leftist National Liberation Army (ELN) conducted virtually all of the attacks against US interests in Columbia. To protest President Bush's visit to the Cartagena Summit in February, the ELN kidnapped three US citizens living in Columbia but released them shortly thereafter. Three US petroleum engineers abducted in November in northern Colombia were still in captivity by year's end. The ELN also crossed the border into Venezuela to conduct operations, including the kidnapping of a Venezuelan farmer in January.

The Colombian Government enjoyed significant success during 1990 by continuing its firm policy toward the insurgents, demanding they demobilize before they could participate in the political process. A former M-19 leader, whose rebel group turned in its weapons in March 1990, finished third in the balloting during the nation's Presidential election. Another group, the Popular Liberation Army (EPL), agreed to refrain from military operations and to begin demobilization.

The Colombian armed forces maintained pressure on the two rebel groups—the Revolutionary Armed Forces of Colombia (FARC), Colombia's largest guerrilla group, and the ELN—that rejected the government's offer to disarm and join the political process. For the first time the military conducted a major assault on the FARC headquarters. In 1990, the Colombian Government also began implementing a judicial reform program it hopes will strengthen the government's ability to convict terrorists.

El Salvador

The number of international terrorist incidents in El Salvador declined from nine in 1989 to two in 1990. This decline is more indicative of terrorist targeting—the Farabundo Marti National Liberation Front (FMLN) has deliberately refrained from targeting foreigners—than of a decrease in overt political violence in the country.

The FMLN generally adhered to its pledge to halt attacks on civilian officials and the public transportation and telephone systems between March and October 1990. But in the last months of the year, during the rebels' so-called national maneuver, the FMLN consistently caused civilian casualties in attacks on Salvadoran armed forces positions. The group also attacked or sabotaged numerous economic targets of no military significance. The FMLN's indiscriminate use of firepower resulted in more than 100 civilian casualties.

The FMLN carried out numerous attacks on important economic targets. In November, the FMLN conducted more than 100 attacks on the electrical power grid and two on major hydroelectric plants. Terrorist attacks on the electrical power system alone caused more than $10 million in damage. In December, terrorist attacks disabled 10 percent of the country's telephone system.

The FMLN also attacked off-duty military personnel and military targets near civilian areas. Significant FMLN terrorist attacks include a drive-by attack on the home of an Army battalion commander; the assassination of an Army major as he returned from a class at the national university; and a mortar attack on the presidential office complex. In November, the FMLN hurled a bomb at a group of soldiers in San Salvador's crowded central market, wounding nine civilians—among them four children—and two soldiers.

Chronic and profound deficiencies in the country's judicial system continued to impede an effective counterterrorist policy during 1990. The government is hard pressed to effectively prosecute any case, whether it be an FMLN terrorist attack—such as the Zona Rosa killings in 1985—military abuses, or even non political crimes.

The case of Army officers and troops accused of murdering six Jesuit priests and two civilians in 1989 was remanded to trial. Although extrajudicial violence directed against suspected FMLN sympathizers by members of the military acting without official sanction is much less common than in the early 1980s, evidence indicates that such activity has not disappeared.

Military and public security forces kept up their efforts to preempt terrorist and insurgent activity by the FMLN. The armed forces captured more than 1,000 weapons and routinely provided security for many potential terrorist targets. The government also maintained a special counterterrorist unit for dealing with hostage rescue and other terrorist incidents.

Guatemala

Although the incidence of international terrorism rose, from four attacks in 1989 to seven in 1990, it was the escalating domestic political violence that continued to have the most impact on conditions in Guatemala. The three major Guatemalan guerrilla groups struck at many economic and nonmilitary targets, such as policemen, bridges, powerlines, government road repair facilities, telephone equipment, missionary medical facilities, and private farms. Guerrillas attacked an American missionary family living in the countryside, vandalized their home, and stole most of their personal property. Fortunately, none of the family members were injured.

Terrorism by rightwing extremists and members of the security forces also took many victims over the past year. Leftist politicians, students, unionists, journalists, members of human rights groups, and above all, indigenous rural people suspected of proguerrilla sympathies were assassinated or disappeared. The nation's human rights ombudsman claims security forces were the main perpetrators of this violence. Security forces were suspected of involvement in the murder of a prominent leftwing Salvadoran politician who was visiting Guatemala in May. The government's investigation into the murder reached no credible conclusions.

The military continued its ongoing battle against the guerrillas, losing about 100 soldiers and civil defense members. The government also sought to end guerrilla access to sanctuaries by working more closely with its neighbor, Mexico. In an effort to end the domestic conflict, the government supported informal peace talks between representatives of the guerrillas and various political, economic, and social sectors.

Honduras

Although the number of international terrorist incidents declined in Honduras from eight in 1989 to two in 1990, the attacks were no less serious. In recent years these incidents have been directed against US interests, often US servicemen. In the most serious attack during 1990, the leftist Morazanist Patriotic Front (FPM) claimed responsibility for the ambush of a US Air Force bus in March that wounded eight airmen, two of them seriously.

The Cubans, Nicaraguan Sandinstas, and Salvadoran FMLN guerrillas continue to support the Honduran Popular Liberation Movement—Cinchoneros. The FPM is also suspected of receiving Cuban assistance. The FMLN probably continues to use Salvadoran refugee camps in Honduras for infiltrating its guerrillas into El Salvador.

The Honduran Armed Forces conducted sweeps of known guerrilla operating areas during the year. In August, an interdiction team discovered a van carrying concealed weapons at the Nicaraguan border. The van was driven by a French citizen, and the contents of the van indicated that the arms and documents were destined for the FMLN in El Salvador. During the same month, nine Cinchoneros members attempting to rob a bank were killed in an ambush by the Armed Forces. The security forces suffered four fatalities in the firefight.

Nicaragua

There were no international terrorist incidents in Nicaragua during 1990. The Sandinista government, which turned over power to the democratically elected government of Violeta Chamorro in April 1990, had supported a number of international terrorist groups during its 10 years in power. This support ranged from public statements in support of specific terrorist actions to allowing Nicaraguan territory to be used as a weapons transshipment route. Nicaragua was also used as a training and organization base for a variety of international terrorist groups. Despite the election of a new government, the Salvadoran FMLN, Basque ETA, and various other groups that have engaged in international terrorism continued to operate in Nicaragua. These organizations established a presence in Nicaragua during the former Sandinista regime and appear to continue to rely on contacts with the Sandinistas, who retain full control of the police and armed forces.

The Chamorro government secured passage of tough legislation forbidding the use of Nicaraguan territory for the purposes of support for foreign subversion. Investigations of reported FMLN support bases in Nicaragua are a sign of government resolve to carry out this policy. However, President Chamorro allowed the FMLN to operate a political office in Managua, and supplies for Salvadoran insurgents continued to originate from or pass through Nicaraguan territory. The Sandinista-controlled military publicly admitted that four of its officers sold surface-to-air missiles to the FMLN without Nicaraguan Government approval.

Panama

Since the ouster of General Noriega, most acts of violence in Panama have been attributed to a shadowy M-20 organiztion, purportedly dedicated to destabilizing the Panamanian Government. There were four international terrorist incidents in 1990. Domestic terrorism has tended to consist of low-level assaults and has included bank robberies, bombings, and threats against government officials.

In the most serious international incident in Panama during 1990, an unidentified individual threw a grenade into a crowded disco in Panama City in March that killed a US service member and injured 15 others. Fourteen Panamanians were also injured in the attack. M-20 claimed responsibility for this attack and for the drive-by shootings at the US Embassy and Marine security guard residence in June. In October, a grenade attack caused some property damage at the Austrian Consulate; the motive and perpetrators remain unknown.

The government has taken steps to end the support provided by the Noriega regime to the Colombian FARC and Salvadoran FMLN. Despite these efforts, FARC reportedly continues to operate in areas where the government has little control, especially near the Colombian border. The government continued to study increased security measures at regional airports in response to the hijacking in mid-1990 of two Panamanian aircraft, allegedly by Colombian narcotics traffickers.

When an investigation revealed that a ship registered in Panama, the Tiny Star, was used to launch the Palestine Liberation Front's abortive attack on Israel in May, Panamanian authorities withdrew the ship's registration.

Peru

The number of international terrorist incidents increased in Peru from 21 in 1989 to 28 in 1990. An even greater cause for concern, the number of politically related deaths in 1990 climbed to more than 3,400—surpassing the nearly 3,200 deaths recorded in 1989. Peru also topped the list for foreign fatalities in the region in 1990. As many as six foreigners visiting Peru may have been killed by Sendero Luminoso (SL) during the year. In January, two French tourists traveling in the southern Sierra were taken off a bus and shot by SL. An American was shot near the city of Cuzco in February; his body showed signs of torture. Two British ornithologists were apparently kidnapped and killed by Sendero Luminoso in the northern coca producing Upper Huallaga Valley in June. In November, a Japanese citizen and five other people were killed in Lima's neighboring Junin department, an increasingly dangerous area.

Both Sendero Luminoso and the Tupac Amaru Revolutionary Movement (MRTA) conducted terrorist attacks against US interests, mostly property bombings designed to gain publicity. During 1990, SL detonated explosives at the US, Soviet, Chinese, German, and Japanese Embassies. In December, Sendero Lumioso was responsible for a driverless car with a bomb inside that rolled to a stop 100 yards from the US Embassy in Lima and exploded. No injuries or damage resulted.

The leftist MRTA carried out most of the anti-US incidents in 1990 with 11 attacks. It commemorated the group's anniversary in November by conducting a campaign against US targets that included bombings of US businesses, the US Consulate, and a US-Peruvian binational center. The MRTA also detonated a bomb in the park adjacent to the US Ambassador's residence. Immediately after the explosion, five rounds of gunfire struck the residence from a passing vehicle.

Insurgent violence in 1990 continued to expand throughout the country, mostly in rural areas, marking the most violent year since Sendero Luminoso launched its armed struggle in 1980. Terrorist gunmen killed the former Defense, Labor, and Social Security Ministers in Lima. There also was an upsurge in kidnappings of prominent Peruvians by Peru's smaller terrorist group, MRTA.

To combat the wave of political violence, the government expanded the territory under emergency zone status. Constitutional rights are suspended in these zones, and the military is responsible for internal security. Eleven of Peru's 24 departments were under state-of-emergency status during some part of 1990. However, both the military and the police suffer from a lack of adequate supplies, security training, and the coordination necessary to conduct effective counterterrorist operations.

President Fujimori, inaugurated in July, promised new reforms that include speedier trials of terrorist suspects. In December, the President sought a constitutional amendment to permit the trial of accused terrorists in military courts. Prosecution through the civilian courts moves slowly, and both prosecutors and judges have been threatened by terrorist organizations. Between 50 and 75 percent of all accused terrorists in Peruvian prisons have not yet been brought to trial.

After more than two years in court, Osman Morote, SL's number-two leader, was sentenced to 20 years in prison on terrorist charges. He is the most senior terrorist figure to be charged and convicted in Peru since Sendero Luminoso embarked on its violent campaign in 1980. Four other codefendants were sentenced to lesser, but lengthy, prison terms. The trial of MRTA leader Victor Polay was suspended in July when he and more than 40 other suspected MRTA members escaped from jail.

Trinidad and Tobago

Although there were no international terrorist incidents in Trinidad and Tobago during 1990, the government successfully suppressed a coup attempt that included the taking of hostages, including Prime Minister Robinson, in the Parliament and state television facilities. The government is prosecuting 114 members of the Jamaat Al Muslimeen (JAM), a local Muslim group, on charges of treason and murder for its 27 July–1 August attempt to overthrow the government. Several JAM members including its leader, Yasin Abu Bakr, had traveled on several occasions to Libya, one of several sources of funding for the JAM.

Middle Eastern Regional Overview

The number of international terrorist incidents in the Middle East dropped sharply, from 193 in 1989 to 63 in 1990. The incidence of Middle Eastern terrorist "spillover" into other parts of the world also declined from 43 to 21 attacks.

International terrorism by Palestinians declined. Although Iraq encouraged many of the Palestinian terrorist groups to conduct operations against the international coalition opposing Baghdad's invasion of Kuwait, at year's end no such attacks had been carried out.

Following the abortive 30 May Palestine Liberation Front (PLF) attack on the beaches at Tel Aviv, President Bush announced his decision to suspend the 18-month-old dialogue between the United States and the Palestine Liberation Organization (PLO). The dialogue began in December 1988, after PLO Chairman Yasser Arafat publicly renounced terrorism, accepted UN Security Council resolutions 242 and 338, and affirmed Israel's right to exist.

The PLF is a constituent group of the PLO, and its leader, Abu Abbas, is a member o the PLO Executive Committee. After the attempted 30 May raid, the PLO refused US calls to condemn the attack, disassociate itself from the PLF, and take steps to discipline Abu Abbas.

A number of Palestinian groups, including the PLF and other members of the PLO, have made public statements supporting Iraq and opposing the multinational forces deployed to enforce the UN resolutions regarding Iraq's invasion of Kuwait. Saddam Hussein has attempted to portray his aggression against Kuwait as part of the struggle for a Palestinian homeland. Iraq's belligerence and promise of support have attracted those groups long favoring the use of force to solve the Arab-Israeli conflict. The United States rejects the linkage of these two issues. The PLF, Palestinian Islamic Jihad (PIJ), and the Palestinian Front for the Liberation of Palestine (PFLP) are among those who have threatened terrorist attacks against Western, Israeli, and moderate Arab targets in connection with the Gulf crisis.

No new Western hostages were kidnapped this year. Eight Western hostages—including two Americans, Robert Polhill and Frank Reed—were released. Although these are positive developments, Iranian-supported Hizballah members in Lebanon continue to hold some 14 Western hostages, six of them American citizens. Three of these hostages (Englishman Alec Collett, Italian Alberto Molinari, and American Lt. Col. William R. Higgins) are feared dead.

Despite the decline in the number of international terrorist incidents undertaken by Middle Eastern groups, domestic terrorism continued in Israel, the occupied territories and Lebanon. The 8 October Temple Mount (Haram al-Sharif) incident claimed the lives of 17 Arab civilians, killed by Israeli security forces. Internecine conflicts within and between Palestinian and Lebanese terrorist groups added to the violence.

Iraq's sponsorship of Palestinian terrorist groups (discussed in detail in the section on State-Sponsored Terrorism) poses a great threat. Iran's links to Hizballah, other Islamic fundamentalist groups, and the Palestinians strengthened during the year, increasing the potential that these groups will continue to use terrorism to advance their political goals. The competition for influence in politically unstable Lebanon could also spawn terrorist attacks.

Algeria

There were no acts of international terrorism in Algeria in 1990. As a longstanding policy, Algeria has permitted radical groups, some of whom engage in terrorism, to live and work in Algeria. Algeria draws a distinction between terrorism, which it condemns, and violence on the part of national liberation movements, which it believes can be legitimate. The ANO, for example, was allowed to keep a representative in Algiers even after Algerian officials condemned an attempt to kidnap an ANO defector. Algiers also allowed representatives of two terrorist groups—the Palestinian Islamic Jihad and Abu Abbas's Palestine Liberation Front—to appear on national television to rally popular support for Iraq.

Algerian officials are increasingly concerned that domestic groups may resort to terrorism. That concern has grown since August when Iraq's Saddam Hussein invaded Kuwait and since Islamic fundamentalist groups gained a majority of seats in local elections. However, at year's end no such incidents had been reported.

Egypt

The most significant terrorist incident of 1990 was the assassination of Dr. Rifat al Mahgoub, Speaker of the People's Assembly, on 12 October. Dr. Mahgoub's assassins are believed to be associated with radical Islamic elements linked to the assassination of President Anwar Sadat.

There were no terrorist attacks against US personnel in Egypt in 1990, but two attacks were carried out against Israeli citizens. In the first, an Israeli tour bus was ambushed on 4 February between Cairo and Ismailiya, Egypt. The attack, claimed by members of the PIJ, left 11 people, including nine Israelis, dead and 17 others injured. The second terrorist incident occurred 25 November when a lone gunman dressed in an Egyptian paramilitary uniform crossed the Egyptian-Israeli border near Eilat and opened fire on a bus and three vehicles carrying Israeli soldiers and workers. Four Israelis were killed, and 27 were wounded. The perpetrator fled back across the border where he was immediately arrested by Egyptian authorities. Egyptian officials also report the arrests of several suspects in the Mahgoub assassination and Israeli tour bus attack. Egypt has no specific laws dealing with terrorism as a separate issue, although the state of emergency dating from the assassination of President Sadat remains in effect.

The Egyptian Government has waged a campaign to limit the terrorist threat posed by Islamic extremists, Egyptian nationalist groups, and radical Palestinians. Twenty members of Egypt's Revolution—a radical group espousing the militant nationalism of former Egyptian President Nasser—are on trial for the May 1987 attack on US Embassy personnel and for earlier attacks on Israeli diplomats. The Egyptian prosecution has requested the death penalty for 10 members of the group and life sentences for the rest.

Khaled Abdel Naser, son of the late president, returned to Egypt from Yugoslavia after three years in exile. He has been identified as the head of the Egypt's Revolution organization. He too is on trial for masterminding the group's attacks on US and Israeli interests.

Israel

Israel remained the prime target of Palestinian terrorist attacks during 1990. Escalating tensions resulted in a number of serious incidents during the year.

On 30 May, Israeli forces foiled an attempted seaborne assault against the Tel Aviv beachfront. Four terrorists were killed and 12 captured. The attack was carried out by the Palestine Liberation Front, led by Abu Abbas, with substantial assistance from Libya. PLO Chairman Arafat's failure to take concrete actions against the PLF, a constituent PLO member, led to the suspension of US dialogue with the PLO.

Other terrorist attacks against Israel in 1990 include:

- A series of letter bombs addressed to Jewish and Christian community leaders were discovered at Tel Aviv's central post office in early January.
- Nine Israelis were killed and 17 wounded in Egypt on 4 February when their tour bus was ambushed by Arab terrorists. The Palestine Islamic Jihad claimed responsibility for the attack.
- On 28 May, one person was killed and nine others wounded when a pipe bomb exploded in a crowded Jerusalem market. Separate unconfirmed claims of responsibility were made by the Palestine Islamic Jihad, the Abu Musa group, and the General Command of Fatah's Al-Asifah Forces.
- On 23 June, a pipe bomb exploded on the beach in Tel Aviv, killing a Canadian tourist and injuring 20 other people.
- On 21 October, a Palestinian stabbed and killed three Israelis and wounded another in Jerusalem. The attack was claimed by two anonymous callers, one claiming to be a member of the Palestinian Islamic Jihad and another claiming to represent Fatah's Force 17 organization.

In early January, a Jewish extremist group known as the Sicarii claimed responsibility for planting a dummy grenade under the car of the wife of Israeli Deputy Prime Minister Peres. The Sicarii also threatened attacks on four Israeli members of Parliament because of their support for a Palestinian peace demonstration. Israeli authorities arrested a suspected leader of the group in June. Israeli peace activists and prominent Palestinian figures received a number of death threats from supporters of Israeli extremist leader Meir Kahane following his assassination on 5 November in New York.

Palestinian groups—both PLO hardliners and Syrian-backed factions outside the PLO—attempted more than a dozen cross-border raids from Lebanon, Jordan, and Egypt. In most cases, the precise targets of the attacks are unclear. Some border infiltrations were the work of disgruntled individuals acting alone or with a few colleagues, but with no discernible connection to any organized group. On 25 November, an Egyptian policeman, believed to have acted alone, ambushed a tour bus of Israelis near the Egyptian border and killed four Israelis.

Israel has consistently taken a strong stand against terrorism and has devoted significant resources to anti-terrorist planning and training.

Israel places strong emphasis on security measures designed to protect its citizens and visitors, the best known of which deal with protection for the Israeli national air carrier El Al at home and abroad. Public awareness of the terrorist threat is also stressed. Ordinary citizens are trained in counterterrorist tactics, and even schoolchildren receive instruction in bomb detection.

Israel also uses more forceful measures to thwart or deter attacks. Israeli military forces have launched preemptive and retaliatory air strikes and commando raids against suspected terrorist installations in neighboring Lebanon. Israel continued to hold Sheikh Abdul Karim Obeid, a prominent Hizballah cleric from South Lebanon, whom Israeli forces abducted in July 1989, apparently in an effort to exchange him for Israeli hostages and POW's held by Lebanese and other groups.

A number of violent incidents in Israel in 1990, such as the 2 December stabbing of three Israelis on a bus near Tel Aviv, increased Israeli fears that the Palestinian uprising in the occupied territories is spilling over into Israel. During 1990, the West Bank and Gaza were sealed off from Israel on several occasions when the threat was deemed to be especially high. In December, Israeli authorities issued identity cards to a large number of Palestinian activists on the West Bank, barring them from entering Israel. Israel also issued deportation orders for four Arabs accused of being activists in the Islamic group Hamas.

Israeli courts generally hand out strict prison sentences to those convicted of terrorist attacks. The captured terrorists from the failed 30 May seaborne assault near Tel Aviv received 30-year prison sentences in December. In October, Mahmud Abed Atta, a US citizen who is a member of the Abu Nidal organization (ANO), was extradited from the United States to Israel where he will face trial for a 1984 attack on a civilian bus.

In December, an Israeli prison review panel released three convicted members of the Jewish Underground after they had served six years of their 10-year sentences. The three had been convicted of murdering three Arab students, wounding over 30 others, and planting explosives. They were originally given life sentences in 1985, but Israeli President Chaim Herzog commuted the sentences to 10 years in 1989.

Jordan

Over the course of the year, a Jordan-based leader of the Palestine Islamic Jihad claimed responsibility for several attacks against Israel and repeatedly threatened US and Israeli interests. Jordanian authorities briefly detained five PIJ members in June. The PIJ has threatened Western interests and has targeted US and other officials for assassination.

Escalating Arab-Israeli tensions throughout 1990 raised concerns that the Palestinian uprising in the Israeli-occupied territories might spill over into Jordan. The number of armed infiltrations across the demarcation boundary with Israel increased in 1990. These infiltrations were carried out mainly by individuals with no known connection to any political organization. In July, Jordanian authorities intercepted an armed Palestinian guerrilla squad attempting to infiltrate from Syria.

The Jordanian Government is committed to the fight against terrorism. Jordan has increased security along its borders to prevent infiltrations and has cooperated in international counterterrorist efforts.

Kuwait

The Kuwaiti Government has opposed terrorism and has cooperated with other governments, including the United States, in this regard, both before and after the 2 August invasion. Despite pressure from terrorist groups in Lebanon, the Amir consistently refused to pardon 15 pro-Iranian Shia terrorists imprisoned in Kuwait for the December 1983 wave of bombings in which the US Embassy was attacked. After the Iraqi invasion, the prisoners, all members of the Dawa Party, either escaped or were released, according to press reports.

Before the Iraqi invasion, Kuwait was concerned about a terrorist threat from Iran, largely via Tehran's manipulation of Kuwaiti Shia. In May, four pro-Iranian Kuwaiti Shia were tried in Kuwait's State Security Court for numerous subversive acts, including attempting to blow up a Kuwait Airways building in 1988 and complicity in a failed bombing attempt in 1987. One of the accused was implicated in the 1989 Hajj bombing in Mecca. The defendants were acquitted on all counts on 18 June 1990. Iran had severely criticized the trial. Earlier in the year, a large number of Iranians, termed infiltrators by the Kuwaiti press, entered Kuwait illegally by sea. Most were captured within days of their entry.

Lebanon

While the number of international terrorist incidents in Lebanon fell to nine in 1990, from 16 in 1989 and 28 in 1988, and the local security situation improved somewhat later in 1990, the country remains deeply fractured, as it has for most of the past 16 years.

Until the 13 October ouster of dissident Gen. Michel Awn, the Lebanese central government controlled only a small part of the country. The bulk of Lebanon came under the control of Syria, Israel, and militias owing allegiance to particular individuals, including General Awn. Many domestic terrorist incidents occurred in 1990, mainly as a result of internecine struggles between the Lebanese factions.

Iran, Iraq, Syria, and Libya continue to support radical groups who engage in terrorism in Lebanon. These countries offer varying degrees of financial, military, and other support to such groups.

In its efforts to rebuild the country, the Lebanese Government has attempted to disband militias, increased pressure on Israel to withdraw from the south, and tried to expand its control southward, but it has had only limited success. The government has not been able to apprehend or prosecute terrorists but has frequently condemned terrorist incidents and called for the release of foreign hostages.

Several international terrorist groups including radical Palestinians, the Japanese Red Army, the Kurdish Worker's Party, the Abu Nidal organization, and the Armenian Secret Army for the Liberation of Armenian (ASALA), maintain training facilities on Lebanese soil, chiefly in the Syrian-garrisoned Bekaa Valley. Hizballah continues to hold a number of Western hostages, including six Americans. All have been maltreated by their captors, and some were reportedly exposed to poisonous substances such as arsenic. Others were kept chained for long periods of time. The United States continues to urge countries with influence over the hostage holders to use that influence to effect the hostages' unconditional release and to secure an accounting of all hostages who may have died while in captivity.

An American who, with his wife, ran an orphanage in the Israeli self-declared security zone in South Lebanon, was assassinated by individuals believed to be local inhabitants, who apparently thought he was aiding the resettlement of East European Jews.

No Westerners were taken hostage in 1990. In fact, two Swiss hostages, Irish-British dual national Keenan, US hostages Polhill and Reed, one Belgian hostage, and two French hostages were released.

Saudi Arabia

Saudi Government concern regarding terrorism deepened in the face of continued attacks from Iran and new threats from Iraq at the onset of the Gulf crisis. Pro-Iranian radical Shia terrorists were believed responsible for the assassination of three Saudi diplomats in Bangkok on 1 February and serious injury to another in the bombing of a Saudi Embassy vehicle in Ankara in January—undertaken in reaction to the Saudi execution of 16 Kuwaiti Shia in 1989 for their involvement in the Hajj bombings of that same year. Later in 1990, Iraq threatened to attack targets within the country, Saudi interests elsewhere in the Middle East and Europe, and Saudi officials and members of the royal family.

Terrorist acts are capital crimes under Saudi law. In addition to strong statements condemning several attacks Saudis abroad, the Foreign Ministry published a rebuttal in April of Iranian accusations against Saudi Arabia, including a list of Iran's misdeeds over the past three years and specifically pinning responsibility for the 1989 Mecca bombings on the Iranian Government.

Saudi security officials continue to cooperate with US security agencies on information exchange and training programs. In March, the Saudis took steps to identify illegal residents and to either regularize their status or deport them. This process was accelerated during the Gulf crisis. The Saudis also put additional security measures in effect during the 1990 Hajj, which passed without a terrorist incident.

Yemen

On 22 May 1990, the People's Democratic Republic of Yemen (PDRY) united with the Yemen Arab Republic (YAR) to form the Republic of Yemen (ROY).

The PDRY remained on the US Government's list of state sponsors of terrorism until unification. The new unified government was not placed on the terrorist list. However, regular discussions between the United States and Yemen, to ensure that the ROY provides no support to international terrorist groups, have continued since unification.

To address these concerns, the ROY put in place tighter procedures for issuing passports, particularly diplomatic passports, to non-Yemenis, including Palestinians. The government also stated that military training facilities would no longer be available to non-Yemenis. In the past, Palestinians were regularly issued PDRY passports and used a camp outside Aden for military training.

Patterns of Global Terrorism: 1991

The Year in Review

The number of international terrorist incidents rose in 1991 as a result of the Persian Gulf war, when terrorists in many regions of the world attacked targets belonging to the international coalition opposed to Saddam Hussein. Most of these were minor incidents, resulting only in property damage. War-related attacks brought the total number of international terrorist incidents in 1991 to 557, up from 456 in 1990. Fully half of the incidents in 1991 occurred during January and February, while Operation Desert Storm was under way. After the war, however, the number of terrorist incidents dropped sharply and actually fell below 1990 levels.

Several events in 1991 revealed the threat and extent of state-sponsored terrorism, particularly as practiced by Iraq, Libya, and Iran.

In the months following Iraq's invasion of Kuwait, Iraq issued repeated exhortations to terrorists to strike at coalition targets worldwide. Terrorists of many stripes embraced Saddam Hussein and publicly vowed to launch attacks in the event of war. During Operation Desert Storm, we recorded 275 terrorist incidents. Most of these attacks, however, were sporadic, uncoordinated, and low-level incidents. Only a small percentage resulted in deaths, significant injuries or property damage. The Iraqi Government was directly involved in several incidents, but the threatened massive wave of Middle Eastern terrorism that Saddam promised did not materialize; the numerous terrorist groups that had sworn allegiance to Saddam failed to act.

After an extensive investigation of worldwide scope, US and British authorities developed evidence that conclusively linked Libya to the 1988 terrorist bombing of Pan Am Flight 103. On 14 November 1991 both governments issued indictments for two Libyan agents, Abdel Basset Ali Al-Megrahi and Lamen Khalifa Fhimah, charged with carrying out the bombing. In addition, French authorities issued warrants for four Libyan agents in connection with the 1989 bombing of UTA Flight 772 that killed 171 people, including seven Americans.

Nine long-held Western hostages were freed from captivity in Lebanon last year, including six Americans, and the remains of William F. Buckley and Col. William R. Higgins were recovered and returned to the United States. The hostages, including the two who died while in captivity, had been held by elements of the Iranian-supported terrorist group Hizballah, which receives substantial amounts of financing, training, and political direction from Tehran. The release of the hostages was achieved largely through the efforts of UN Secretary General Javier Perez de Cuellar and his special envoy Giandomenico Picco. The releases apparently reflected a belief held by both the Government of Iran and the hostage holders themselves that the continued detention of the hostages served no purpose. The United States made no concessions to gain the hostages' release.

At year's end, two German hostages, Thomas Kemptner and Heinrich Surubig, remained captive in Lebanon. We continue to call for the immediate, safe, and unconditional release of all persons held outside the legal system in the region as well as an accounting of all those who may have died while in captivity.

During 1991 Iran continued to build closer ties to Palestinian terrorist groups and Islamic militant organizations. Iran has used conferences like "*Intifadah* and the Islamic World"—held in Iran during the period 19–22 October—to maintain contact with numerous terrorist groups. Subsequent to this conference, some such groups issued threats to participants in the Middle East peace talks.

Iran also continued its practice of assassinating dissidents; Iranian agents are the prime suspects in the murder of former Prime Minister Shapour Bakhtiar in Paris last August, and the French Government has issued an international arrest warrant for an Iranian official suspected of supporting the operation.

Seven Americans died during 1991 in terrorist attacks:

- On 2 January in El Salvador, the Farabundo Marti National Liberation Front (FMLN) downed a US helicopter carrying three US military advisers who were en route to Honduras. Two of them, Lt. Col. David Pickett and crew chief PFC Earnest Dawson, were brutally executed after surviving the crash. The third, CWO Daniel Scott, died of injuries suffered in the shootdown. (The incident is considered terrorism because the three advisers provided administrative/logistic support from Honduras to US military personnel assigned to El Salvador and were thus noncombatants.)
- The Turkish terrorist group Devrimci Sol (Revolutionary Left or Dev Sol) murdered two Americans last year. On 7 February in Adana, Bobbie Eugene Mozelle, an American contract employee of the Department of Defense, was shot as he left his apartment on the way to his car. On 22 March in Istanbul, another American contract employee of the Department of Defense, John Gandy, was murdered when three gunmen entered his office, separated him from the other employees, and shot him in the head.
- On 12 March in Glyfada, Greece, US Air Force Sgt. Ronald Odell Stewart was killed by a bomb explosion outside his residence. The Greek terrorist group 17 November was responsible.
- US S. Sgt. Victor D. Marvick was killed in a car bombing in Ankara, Turkey on 28 October. The Turkish-based Islamic Jihad claimed responsibility for the attack.

Attacks against US targets increased sharply in 1991 because of the Persian Gulf war (308 last year [versus] 193 in

1990.) The United States was a target in 55 percent of attacks last year as compared with 42 percent in 1990. Most of these attacks were low-level bombings that caused few casualties and little damage. US businesses such as banks and restaurants were most frequently targeted. Anti-US attacks in Western Europe numbered 93 last year, up sharply from 17 in 1990; most of these occurred in Turkey, Italy, and Greece. Numerous anti-US attacks also occurred in Peru and Colombia.

Terrorism decreased sharply in Asia (47 last year [versus] 92 in 1990) and in Africa (3 last year [versus] 53 the previous year).

There were far fewer terrorist casualties in 1991. Eighty-seven people died, as compared with 200 in 1990, and 233 were wounded, as compared with 677 in 1990.

African Overview

There were only three international terrorist incidents in Africa in 1991, strikingly fewer than the 53 reported in 1990. This is largely explained by the partial or complete settlement of several insurgencies that had produced high levels of terrorism and domestic unrest. A successful peace accord was reached in Angola, negotiations moved forward in Mozambique, and the Marxist Ethiopian Government was overthrown. The number of incidents in several other countries was down considerably, though the total collapse of the Somali and Liberian Governments leaves the long-term status of those nations in doubt. Negotiations on a transition to majority rule in South Africa were accompanied by a continued high level of violence, particularly among competing black groups, but with rightwing white groups presenting a growing threat of violence. The most disturbing development was the apparent presence in Sudan of many different international terrorist organizations, with the tacit support of the National Islamic Front–dominated government.

Sudan

In the past year Sudan has enhanced its relations with international terrorist groups, including the Abu Nidal organization (ANO). Sudan has maintained ties to state sponsors of terrorism such as Libya and Iraq and has improved its relations with Iran. The National Islamic Front (NIF), under the leadership of Hassan al-Turabi, has intensified its domination of the government of Sudanese President General Bashir and has been the main advocate of closer relations with radical groups and their sponsors. The NIF has organized its own militia, the People's Defense Force, modeled after the Iranian Revolutionary Guards Corps. Sudan was one of the few states to support Iraq in he Persian Gulf war. Ties to Libya and Iran also were maintained, as evidenced by the visit to Sudan last June by Colonel Qadhafi and the visit last December by Iranian President Rafsanjani to Khartoum.

Terrorist and militant Moslem groups also have increased their presence in Sudan. The government reportedly has allowed terrorist groups to train on its territory and has offered Sudan as a sanctuary to terrorist organizations. In October, the government of Tunisia recalled its Ambassador from Khartoum to protest Sudanese renewal of a diplomatic passport for the leader of Tunisia's An Nahda party, a group that Tunisia considers a terrorist organization. Sudan also played host to members of radical groups, such as the Islamic Resistance Movement (HAMAS), and allowed them to hold public meetings in Sudan.

Zimbabwe

There was one probable act of international terrorism in Zimbabwe in 1991. A bomb exploded at the Sheraton Hotel in Harare on 20 July, causing extensive damage to one floor and slightly injuring several people. The following day a previously unknown group, the Red Friday Liberation Movement, claimed responsibility, but the government's investigation has not determined who planted the bomb or their motives.

During the Persian Gulf war, Zimbabwe assigned additional security personnel to Western embassies, including the American Embassy. Two Iraqis suspected of plotting a terrorist operation against the US Embassy were deported in January 1991.

Asian Overview

The number of international terrorist incidents in Asia decreased from 92 incidents in 1990 to 47 in 1991, partly because of the Philippine Government successes against the Communist New People's Army. The death toll from attacks by Sikh, Kashmiri, Assamese, and other militant groups in India continued to rise, with foreigners increasingly targeted or caught in the crossfire. Sri Lankan terrorists carried out several fatal attacks in the capital of Colombo and elsewhere and are believed responsible for the assassination of Congress-I party leader Rajiv Gandhi in India. There was an increased number of attacks against Western aid workers and moderate Afghans in northwestern Pakistan attributed to militant Afghan fundamentalist groups. Also, Iraqi terrorists and their surrogates attempted or planned attacks in several Asian countries, none of which resulted in serious injuries or death to any but the terrorists themselves.

Afghanistan

Four international acts of terrorism occurred in Afghanistan in 1991, all directed at Western humanitarian organizations operating in the midst of civil strife. In January, a commander affiliated with the Afghan resistance group Hezb-I Islami kidnapped and briefly held four International Committee of the Red Cross (ICRC) workers. On 6 August, a Swiss employee of the ICRC was kidnapped by a member of an unidentified faction of the Afghan resistance about 60 kilometers north of Kabul; he was released 12 days later. Two Americans working for a British aid organization were seized by Afghan insurgents on 7 July in the Ghazni province of Afghanistan; one was released in October and the other in December. A French national working on a US AID project in Zabol province was kidnapped on 4 July and released on 16 July.

India

The level of indigenous terrorism was high throughout 1991, as Punjabi, Kashmiri, and Assamese separatists conducted attacks in a bid to win independence for their states. Violence related to separatist movements claimed at least 5,500 lives in Punjab and over 1,500 lives in Kashmir.

The separatists regularly assassinated civil servants, political candidates, and presumed government informers. Last spring in the Punjab, Sikh terrorists killed 23 candidates running for state and national office. Sikh terrorists also carried out random attacks and bombings, which included massacres of people aboard trains and busses. In Assam, the United Liberation Front of Assam (ULFA) was responsible for a spate of terrorist operations, particularly kidnappings. One such kidnapping targeted a Soviet technician, who was killed, as were several Indian kidnap victims. Kashmiri militants routinely planted bombs in and around bridges and communications targets and extorted money from local businessmen. They also kidnapped relatives of prominent officials and several foreigners.

Separatists also have stepped up attacks against journalists. In January, Sikh extremists declared war on the press in Punjab and forced reporters to stop calling them terrorists. Newsmen critical of Sikh terrorist tactics received death threats. Kashmiri groups also assassinated journalists, including the editor of the Urdu daily *Al-Safa* in April.

Although Assamese and Kashmiri terrorists limited their operations to their respective states. Sikh terrorists expanded their operations outside Punjab. In late January, Sikh terrorists bombed a movie theater in New Delhi injuring six people. Sikh extremists probably also were responsible for a bombing in New Delhi in late April that killed three people and wounded eight. In mid-October, a Sikh bomb killed at least 55 people and wounded 125 others at a Hindu festival in Uttar Pradesh, near the Nepalese border. In late August, four members of the Khalistan Liberation Front unsuccessfully attempted to assassinate the Indian Ambassador to Romania in Bucharest; Romanian antiterrorist experts killed one person and captured the other three. This was the first Sikh terrorist operation outside India since 1987. Separatists also conducted a spate of kidnappings of foreigners in a bid to attract international attention to their cause:

- On 31 March in western Kashmir, the Muslim Janbaz Force (MJF) kidnapped two Swedish engineers working at a hydroelectric project. The MJF had pledged o hold the pair until the United Nations or Amnesty International investigated alleged human rights abuses in Kashmir. On 5 July, however, the engineers escaped when they were left unguarded.
- On 26 June an obscure Kashmiri group, Pasdaran-I-Inquilab-e-Islam, kidnapped seven Israelis and a Dutch woman who were visiting Kashmir. The Dutch national was freed shortly after captured. One of the Israelis was killed and two others injured when the Israeli prisoners jumped the kidnappers. One Israeli who did not escape was freed in early July.
- On 1 July, the ULFA seized a Russian mining engineer and 14 Indian nationals; the Russian later was killed as were several of the Indians.
- On 9 October Sikh terrorists kidnapped he Romanian Charge in New Delhi shortly after he left his home for work. The Khalistan Liberation Front claimed responsibility and demanded the release of three imprisoned Sikh terrorists. The diplomat was released on 26 November without the conditions being met.
- On 14 October the Kashmiri separatist group Al-Fateh kidnapped a French engineer in Kashmir. He was freed in early 1992.

The Sri Lankan separatist group, the Liberation Tigers of Tamil Eelam (LTTE), is believed responsible for the 21 May assassination of Congress-I party president Rajiv Gandhi in southern India. Seventeen others also died in the bombing, which occurred while Gandhi was campaigning. The terrorist detonated explosives strapped to her waist as she approached and greeted Gandhi. The attack may have been conducted to avenge Gandhi's decision in 1987, when he was Prime Minister, to dispatch more than 50,000 troops to Sri Lanka to quell the Tamil separatist campaign. Numerous LTTE members suspected of involvement in the operation have committed suicide to avoid capture by Indian authorities.

Iraqi terrorists or their surrogates probably were responsible for the bombing of the American Airlines Travel Agency, and Indian-owned agent of American Airlines, in New Delhi on 16 January. The blast caused extensive damage but no casualties. New Delhi plans to either extradite or prosecute two Burmese students who hijacked a Thai airliner to Calcutta in 1991; however, the Communist-led state government in West Bengal says the pair are "freedom fighters" and is resisting New Delhi's efforts. India also has cracked down on LTTE elements in southern India following the assassination of Rajiv Gandhi.

Pakistan

Westerners and moderate Afghans in northwestern Pakistan, particularly Peshawar, have increasingly become the targets of terrorist attacks. Although the sponsors of these attacks are not known, radical Afghan fundamentalist groups are suspected:

- On 24 February, a bomb blast in Peshawar at the office of the Swedish Relief Committee—a private voluntary organization (PVO) involved in cross-border work in Afghanistan—seriously injured an Afghan-Australian national who later died from the wounds.
- On 13 August, an Afghan-American USAID contractor was wounded in a shooting attack in Peshawar.
- On 30 October, an Afghan working for an Austrian PVO in Peshawar was shot and wounded.

- On 25 November, the Afghan director of the English language program of the International Rescue Committee, and American private voluntary agency, was shot and killed by unidentified assailants.

There were also numerous bombings in Pakistan's major cities throughout the year. The Pakistani Government frequently attributed these attacks and other acts of violence to the intelligence services of India and Afghanistan. The United States is unable, however, to determine if the incidents were carried out by terrorists or criminals, or if there was external involvement.

Several terrorist attacks related to the Persian Gulf war and probably organized by Iraq or Iraqi sympathizers occurred in Pakistan in 1991. In January, gunmen fired at the Saudia Airlines office in Karachi, shattering windows but causing no casualties. In February a bomb exploded as it was thrown over the wall of the residence of the Saudi Consul General in Karachi, injuring a security guard. Later in the month a British-sponsored humanitarian organization in Peshawar was bombed.

During the Persian Gulf war, Pakistani authorities actively sought to counter possible terrorist threats. At least one Iraqi diplomat was declared persona non grata and two other Iraqis were arrested and expelled for their questionable activities. Pakistan has also cooperated with the US investigation of an additional suspect in the 1986 hijacking of Pan American flight 73.

There were continuing credible reports throughout 1991 of official Pakistani support for Kashmiri militant groups engaged in terrorism in Indian-controlled Kashmir, as well as support to Sikh militant groups engaged in terrorism in Indian Punjab. This support allegedly includes provision of weapons and training.

Philippines

The Philippine Government made major strides in its counterterrorist efforts in 1991, arresting over 80 middle-and high-level members of the Communist Party of the Philippines (CPP) and its military arm, he New People's Army (NPA). Those arrested include Romulo Kintanar, chief of the NPA's General Command, and most of the other members of the General Command. The government also successfully prosecuted two NPA operatives for the murder of US Army Col. James Rowe in April 1989. Both were sentenced in February to life imprisonment.

Primarily because of the arrests, the Communists were able to conduct only sporadic terrorist operations. The only attack against US interests occurred early in the year on 31 January, when the NPA planted bombs at the Voice of America (VOA) transmitter in Tinang; the devices were successfully disarmed. Communists in northern Luzon, however, continue to hold an American, Arvey Drown, who was kidnapped there in October 1990. They demanded the suspension of Philippine Government military operations in the region and the release of captured NPA members.

CPP leader Jose Maria Sison continues to reside in exile in the Netherlands. We believe that he is involved in raising money for his movement, mostly from sympathetic European leftist groups.

Philippine authorities aggressively worked against terrorists during the Persian Gulf war, particularly Iraqis who planned to conduct operations against Western targets in Manila. On 19 January, a bomb exploded close to the Thomas Jefferson Cultural Center in Manila, killing the man carrying the device—an Iraqi national—and seriously injuring his partner, also an Iraqi. Following the attempted bombing, the Consul General of the Iraqi Embassy was expelled. Manila also rejected the credentials of an arriving Iraqi diplomat and forced him to depart. Two Iraqi students were also expelled.

Singapore

One act of international terrorism ended in Singapore in 1991. On 26 March, four Pakistanis claiming to be members of the Pakistani People's Party (PPP) hijacked a Singapore Airlines flight shortly after takeoff from Kuala Lumpir, Malaysia and demanded the release of several people reportedly imprisoned in Pakistan. The PPP denied any involvement in the operation. The plane landed in Singapore, and local counterterrorist forces stormed the plane after six hours of negotiations proved futile. The hijackers were killed; all passengers and crew were unharmed.

Sri Lanka

Although the separatist group Liberation Tigers of Tamil Eelam (LTTE) suffered a series of setbacks on the battlefield in 1991, it continued to pose a terrorist threat.

In March 1991, the LTTE returned to urban terrorism with the car-bomb assassination of Deputy Defense Minister Ranjan Wijeratne in Colombo. Scores of innocent bystanders were killed or injured. A second car-bomb attack in June devastated the government's Military Operations Headquarters, again taking many civilian lives. Interrogation of LTTE suspects reportedly revealed that future targets included government figures and major public utilities.

In India, a Madras court indicted the leader of the LTTE and his intelligence chief in connection with the 21 May assassination of former Prime Minister Rajiv Gandhi. Seventeen others also died in this bombing, which occurred while Gandhi was campaigning. Numerous LTTE suspects tracked by Indian police committed suicide to avoid capture.

The LTTE also continued to assassinate rival Tamil politicians in Sri Lanka and India. In rural areas, the Tigers massacred hundreds of Sinhalese and Muslim villagers to drive them from areas deemed part of a "Tamil Homeland."

Western European Overview

1991 saw a marked resurgence of European leftwing terrorist groups, especially through attacks during the Persian Gulf war. Four Americans were killed in terrorist attacks in Europe this year—three were victims of indigenous leftist groups—as compared with none in 1990.

A particular concern was a surge in terrorist attacks against US, Western, and other interests in Greece and Turkey in 1991 by indigenous groups. The deadly 17 November organization carried out several bombing attacks in Greece and assassinated a US serviceman during the first quarter of 1991. In Turkey, the Turkish Revolutionary Left (Dev Sol) and the Kurdish Workers' Party (PKK) were both involved in terrorist activities such as assassinations, bombings, and kidnappings. Two Americans died in such attacks. A third American was killed in a fundamentalist-related murder.

Looking to the future, Western Europe may experience a growth in rightwing terrorism as European integration progresses and international migration into Europe increases.

Belgium

In January 1991, Belgium won the release of the last four Belgian hostages held by the Abu Nidal organization (ANO). However, the revelation that ANO spokesman and negotiator Walid Khaled, as part of the hostage settlement, had traveled to Brussels on the eve of the Persian Gulf war generated an intense domestic political reaction resulting in the reassignment for three senior aides to the Belgian Foreign Minister. According to several news reports, in exchange for the hostages who had been seized from the Silco yacht in 1987, Belgium also expelled convicted ANO terrorist Said Nasser after he had served his required minimum sentence, agreed to contribute more than $5 million in aid to Palestinian refugees, and provided two scholarships in Belgium to Palestinians.

During the Persian Gulf war itself, Belgium expelled seven Iraqi diplomats and increased security around foreign missions. There were no terrorist incidents in Belgium directly related to the Persian Gulf war.

Brussels was the scene of several incidents perpetrated by Turkish expatriates in 1991. To protest raids in Turkey against their organization, Dev Sol terrorists firebombed a Turkish bank and airlines office in July. Radical Kurds attacked a Turkish airlines office in August and a Turkish bank in December. In an unrelated development, the Belgian Parliament in March passed a motion calling for Turkey to grant full cultural and political rights for Kurds.

Three Irish suspects, who were arrested in an Antwerp safehouse in December 1990, were convicted of conspiracy against the British Government and possession of weapons and false papers in April. They were sentenced to one- (suspended), two-, and three-year terms. At least one of the three is suspected of being a member of the Provisional Irish Republican Army (PIRA). In another case, Belgium requested the extradition from the Netherlands, expected in 1992, of Irishman Peter McNally, suspected of being a member of a PIRA splinter group and involved in the wounding in 1989 of an Antwerp policeman.

Several apparent political killings in Belgium that occurred before 1991 (Jewish leader Joseph Wybrand, Muslim Imam Abdullah al-Ahdal, Canadian "supergun" inventor Gerard Bull, and ethnic Albanian leader Enver Hadri) remained unsolved.

France

While international terrorist incidents were relatively few in France, in 1991 French authorities played a significant role in calling to account state sponsors of terrorism.

At the beginning of the Persian Gulf war in January 1991, France expelled 14 Iraqi diplomats and Embassy employees and 18 others suspected of planning terrorism or sabotage. This followed an earlier expulsion in September 1990 when France expelled 11 officials from the Iraqi Embassy in Paris after Iraqi soldiers sacked the French defense attache's house in Kuwait. The government also implemented an ambitious antiterrorist plan during the Gulf crisis which provided augmented security for potential targets. There were only a few relatively minor bombings in France related to the war.

In August former Iranian Prime Minister Shapur Bakhtiar and his personal secretary were brutally murdered in Paris in an apparent act of state-sponsored terrorism. Four Iranians were arrested in France and Switzerland in connection with the assassination. In October, a French investigating magistrate issued an international arrest warrant for Hussein Sheikhattar, a high-ranking Iranian official, for his alleged role in the crime. The French investigation led also to the arrests in Turkey of several Iranians and Turks thought to be connected to the case. Both President Mitterrand and Foreign Minister Dumas postponed planned trips to Iran because of publicity linking the Iranian government to the murders.

The same French investigating magistrate also brought formal charges in October 1991 against four Libyan officials, including Colonel Qadhafi's brother-in-law, for the terrorist bombing in September 1989 of a French UTA airliner over Niger that killed 171 passengers and crew. He also issued material witness warrants for two other high-ranking Libyan officials.

The French Government joined the United States and Britain, which had issued indictments against two Libyan officials for the bombing in 1988 of Pan Am Flight 103, in formally pressing Libya to renounce terrorism and cooperate with the investigations. The case against Libya for these two terrorist attacks effectively stalled an upturn in Franco-Libyan relations.

Basque terrorism continued to create problems in France. Within France itself, Basque terrorism in 1991 resulted in a score of property bombings aimed at developers (real estate offices and Spanish bank branches) and public buildings, all claimed by the French Basque organization Iparretarrak (IK). More than a dozen IK members, including its presumed leader, were sentenced to prison terms in 1991 for criminal associations. Some of them still face charges for murder and attempted murder of police officers.

Cooperation with Spain resulted in important setbacks for ETA Basque separatists operating out of France. During

1991 there were several Franco-Spanish ministerial meetings and summits where bilateral coordination against Basque terrorists was discussed. Many, if not most, ETA terrorists are thought to be French nationals or hiding in France. French authorities arrested nearly 40 of them in 1991—about half of them in December—including several recognized ETA cadres.

One Spanish ETA member was given a 17-year sentence in June after his trial in France. A Portuguese member of the Antiterrorist Liberation Group (GAL), a clandestine rightwing Spanish organization that hunted down suspected Basque terrorists in France during the 1980s, was sentenced to 15 years in France.

Various factions of the separatist Corsican National Liberation Front accounted for the plurality of terrorist attacks in France in 1991, mainly bombings of governmental and economic targets in Corsica and the French mainland. Corsican terrorism continued despite increased autonomy accorded the island in late 1990; in May 1991 the French Constitutional Council reversed a provision of the autonomy legislation that recognized a distinct Corsican people. At least some of the violence on Corsica may actually be another manifestation of organized crime.

Four IRA gunrunners were tried in 1991. Their vessel, the Eksund, and its cargo of Libyan guns and explosives had been seized by the French in 1987. The four were sentenced by the French court to prison terms of five to seven years. The ship's captain, who had fled to Ireland in 1990, was sentenced in absentia in March 1991 to seven years.

Germany

Germany experienced few incidents of international terrorism in 1991, and its prosecution of numerous international terrorist suspects continued. Rapid political evolution in Eastern and Central Europe, as well as the continued assimilation of the former German Democratic Republic (GDR), contributed to a significant increase in rightwing extremism and violence, especially against immigrants. German leftwing radical elements pursued their traditional anticapitalist and anti-imperialist agenda.

In its first lethal attack in more than a year, the radical leftist Red Army Faction (RAF) killed Detlev Rohwedder in his Dusseldorf home in April 1991. Rohwedder was the head of the government agency responsible for privatizing or closing thousands of state-owned companies in the former GDR and symbolized for the RAF the spread of capitalism to the former Communist states. In June, a Berlin housing official was killed by a letter bomb, possibly by pro-RAF militants protesting the elimination of cheap public housing in the united city.

To protest the Persian Gulf war, the RAF strafed the American Embassy in Bonn with approximately 250 rounds of automatic rifle fire in February. Only minor property damage resulted. Militants associated with the RAF and other leftwing radical groups, such as the Revolutionary Cells, mounted 10 other attacks during the war, such as firebombings against stores in Frankfurt and IBM and Coca-Cola targets in Freiburg. In March, a NATO pipeline was blown up by the Revolutionary Cells in yet another protest against the war.

None of the current generation of the RAF commando echelon has been captured. German authorities, however, did prosecute several RAF commandos, all but one of whom were arrested in 1990 after hiding for nearly 10 years in the GDR. In 1991, five were sentenced to prison terms and three were charged for terrorist crimes committed between 1977 and 1981. A renewed campaign by RAF prisoners to press authorities to collocate themselves generated relatively little outside support, possibly indicating weaker coordination and commitment among RAF prisoners, militants, and supporters.

Evidence linking the former East German secret police, or Stasi, to currently active members of the Red Army Faction did not emerge in 1991. Arrest warrants were issued in March for several former Stasi officers familiar with previous RAF activities.

There were no attacks by the Provisional Irish Republican Army (PIRA) against British military targets in Germany in 1991. Several PIRA suspects were, however, extradited to Germany from the Netherlands in July and October to stand trial for anti-British attacks carried out there in the late 1980s. Two other suspected PIRA operatives were acquitted in Dusseldorf of an attempted bombing in 1988 of British army barracks in Duisburg; however, they will be tried on other charges.

Trials continued in 1991 for nearly 20 alleged members of the Kurdish Workers' Party (PKK) on charges ranging from membership in a terrorist organization to murder. Turkish, including Kurdish, radicals remained active in Germany in support of terrorist organizations operating in Turkey. Several were arrested when demonstrations against Turkish diplomatic or consular posts in Germany turned violent. Turkish airlines and bank offices in Germany were frequent targets of firebombings and violent protests as well. Ten German tourists were abducted by the PKK in Turkey for a week in August.

Two German relief workers were the final remaining Western hostages held in Lebanon at the end of 1991. For their release, the abductors demanded clemency for two Hizballah members jailed in Germany: Mohamed Ali Hamadi, the hijacker of a TWA flight in 1985 who is serving a life sentence for murder, and his brother Abbas Hamadi who was sentenced to 13 years by a German court for related crimes. The German Government has refused to make such concessions to the hostage takers.

Popular Front for the Liberation of Palestine-General Command (PFLP-GC) members Hafiz Dalkamoni and Abdel Fattah Ghadanfar were sentenced in June to 15 and 12 years respectively, by a German court for attempted murder in failed attacks against US military duty trains in 1987 and 1988. Dalkamoni's trial for manslaughter in the death of a German bomb-disposal technician also began in 1991. The bomb technician was killed while examining a bomb prepared for use by the PFLP-GC in its planned campaign in the fall of

1988 against civil aviation. That campaign was thwarted by arrests made by German authorities in October 1988. Charges against Daher Faour, a suspect in the 1986 bombing of the La Belle disco in Berlin, were dropped for lack of evidence.

Germany expelled nearly 30 Iraqi diplomats, including all those assigned to the Berlin office, as part of a European campaign to deny Iraq the opportunity to foment terrorist attacks against Western targets during the Persian Gulf war.

Greece

Greece experienced 29 international terrorist incidents in 1991, compared with four in 1990. All but one of these were committed by Greek terrorists.

Four terrorist attacks resulted in fatalities. In March, the Revolutionary Organization 17 November killed a US Air Force sergeant with a remote-controlled bomb. In April, a bomb intended for use against the British Consulate in Patras exploded prematurely, killing the Palestinian bomb handler and six Greek bystanders. The perpetrators in both cases were believed to be targeting symbols of the allied coalition in the Persian Gulf war. In October, 17 November killed a Turkish diplomat to protest Turkey's Cypriot policies; the same group killed a policeman in November.

These fatal attacks drew on three themes repeated in numerous other, nonfatal incidents. First, as a result of the Persian Gulf war there were more than a dozen terrorist attacks in Greece. Most were bomb or rocket attacks against material targets such as American and British corporate interests. 17 November alone committed seven of these in January. Similar attacks were mounted by the tandem of Revolutionary People's Struggle (ELA) and the 1 May group during the Persian Gulf war.

A second theme is inspired by strong nationalist/Hellenist and anti-Turkish sentiments over Cyprus. 17 November's shooting of the Turkish diplomat in October was preceded in July by a car-bomb attack that nearly killed the Turkish Charge in Athens. The latter occurred just before President Bush's visits to Greece and Turkey, during which the Cyprus issue was discussed. ELA and 1 May joined with 17 November at that time to exhort Turkish terrorist organizations in their attacks against the Turkish Government. 17 November even linked its killing of the US airman to Turkish "occupation" of northern Cyprus. The visit of four Greek members of Parliament to a Kurdish Worker's Party (PKK) training camp in Lebanon was seen as an expression of anti-Turkish solidarity with the Kurdish terrorist group.

Most of the terrorist attacks in Greece in 1991 drew on the third theme: the government's economic austerity program. Greek terrorist organizations attacked the government for its policy of reducing the size of the public sector to conform with EC standards, viewed as endangering jobs. One policeman lost his life in such an attack by 17 November, and five policemen were injured in June by an ELA/1 May bomb intended for them. Targets of the anti-EC campaign in 1991 included private European corporations—such as Siemns, Lowenbrau, and Ciment Francrais—which were portrayed as exploiting Greece's economically troubled public sector.

The Greek Government sought to increase counterterrorist cooperation with the United States and requested increased training and other assistance n 1991. During the Persian Gulf war, the Greek Government expelled several potential terrorists and supporters, including a number of Iraqi diplomats, and mounted an effective campaign to protect possible targets in Athens. In the wake of the fatal bombing in Patras after the war, 25 Palestinians were expelled including six PLO representatives. Five Palestinians were indicted for that bombing and are awaiting trial.

Greek authorities in March arrested Abdelrahim Khaled, wanted in Italy for the 1985 Achille Lauro hijacking. Italy's extradition request has been approved, but Khaled will first serve a lengthy jail sentence in Greece for narcotics trafficking crimes committed there. The trial of Palestinian Mohammad Rashid, accused in the 1982 bombing of a Pan Am aircraft, began in Athens in October and resulted in a conviction and lengthy jail term in early 1992.

Under provisions of the new antiterrorist legislation, the government invoked a ban on he publication of communiqués issued by terrorist organizations and prosecuted newspaper editors who defied the ban.

Ireland

Irish authorities continued to work closely with Britain's counterterrorist efforts. For Example, in April they uncovered a cache of PIRA guns and ammunition supplied by Libya and hidden in a farm north of Dublin. In July an Irish court sentenced Adrian Hopkins to eight years (of which five were suspended) after he pleaded guilty to running 150 tons of Libyan weapons and explosives for the PIRA as captain of the Eksund. Hopkins had fled to Ireland in 1990 from France where his vessel was seized in 1987. Caches of Libyan-supplied Semtex explosives, presumably hidden by PIRA in Ireland, have not been found, hoverer. Irish police did intercept a massive truck bomb in County Donegal on 8 July as it headed for the Ulster border. PIRA assembled its largest known vehicle bomb ever—nearly 4 tons of fertilizer and Semtex—in Ireland but abandoned it when it bogged down in a wet field in September.

Italy

International terrorist incidents increased in Italy from only one in 1990 to 32 in 1991. Most of these were attributed to the Spanish Basque separatist group ETA that, for the first time, attacked more than a dozen Spanish targets in Rome, Milan, and Florence. Some of the other incidents were because of Italy's participation in the coalition forces during the Persian Gulf war. In July an Iranian-inspired knifing wounded the Italian translator of Salman Rushdie's *Satanic Verses* in Milan.

To protest the Persian Gulf war, at least five firebombings in January occurred at a Pan Am office, a Ford dealership, a

Coca-Cola warehouse, a British school, and an international bookstore. War-related vandalism was directed against a US-affiliated bank and vehicles owned by US Air Force personnel. Italian Autonomous Workers radicals may have been responsible for at least some of the firebomb attacks. There were no deaths or injuries as a result of these.

Like other European countries, Italy ordered home many diplomats and staff of the Iraqi Embassy and expelled other potential saboteurs and terrorists during the Persian Gulf war.

At the outset of the war, Italian authorities at the Rome airport arrested Khalid Duhan al-Jawary, who is wanted in the United States for attempted bombings of Israeli targets in New York City in 1973. A final decision on a US request for his extradition will be made in 1992.

Italy has definitively emerged from the difficult period (1976–84) during which domestic terrorism was prevalent. Nevertheless, President Cossiga had to abandon his proposal to pardon Renato Curcio, the founder of the Red Brigades, to symbolize that transition following the domestic protest it provoked.

Clemency and liberal parole were, moreover, invoked for several other incarcerated foreign terrorists in 1991. In January, two Palestinians who played supporting roles in the1985 hijacking of the cruise ship Achille Lauro and were close o completing their terms, left Italy because of a blanket clemency act which reduced most sentences by two years. A juvenile participant in that hijacking, Bassam Al Ashker, serving a 17-year sentence, was accorded conditional freedom in June.

Greece gave final approval in December to Italy's request for the extradition of Abdelrahim Khaled, arrested in March, who was already convicted in absentia and sentenced to life in prison by a Genoa court for his role in the Achille Lauro affair.

Netherlands

The trial and appeal of four PIRA suspects concluded in July 1991. All were acquitted in the 1990 murder of two Australian tourists, mistaken for off-duty British soldiers, in Roermond.

The Netherlands, like other West European countries, was the scene of violence by expatriate Turks. Dev Sol members or sympathizers are believed responsible for the firebombing in July of a Turkish bank and travel agency in Amsterdam. Turks rioted at a Turkish Consulate in July, and Turkish Kurds claimed responsibility for an August attack on a Turkish bank in The Hague.

There were no terrorist incidents in the Netherlands directly attributed to the Gulf crisis. Several Iraqi diplomats were expelled after the war began. The investigation into the murder of a Dutch diplomat in Tunisia in February 1991 remained inconclusive.

In November, the extremist Radical Anti-Racist Action (RARA) group set off powerful bombs at the Interior Ministry and at the house of a junior justice minister to protest Dutch political asylum policy. This was apparently RARA's first attack since the late 1980s when its arson attacks, especially against Shell Oil, were intended to protest apartheid in South Africa.

Former Soviet Union

With the progressive dissolution of the Soviet Union, Soviet authorities were largely preoccupied with internal dynamics in 1991. Consequently, there was uncertainty about institutional responsibility for counterterrorism, particularly with the paring of the KGB. Nevertheless, Soviet authorities continued bilateral consultations with Western countries on terrorism, their concern sharpened by a perception of increased vulnerability to domestic political instability.

Political violence in certain areas of the former Soviet Union continued at a high level in 1991. Interethnic civil strife intensified between Armenians and Azerbaijanis as central authority weakened in the Caucasus. In April, a Soviet colonel responsible for logistics in the Caucausus was assassinated in Rostov, Russia. Soviet authorities subsequently arrested several Armenians in connection with the attack. Nearly 50 civilians were killed in attacks on trains and a bus in the Caucausus between May and August. A train proceeding through the Nakhichevan autonomous region of Azerbaijan en route to Armenia was hijacked in September; no casualties were reported. Several press reports describe an attempted bombing in Kiev's only synagogue in December by unknown assailants using grenades and artillery shells. A black market of military weapons is growing with the further demobilization of many former Soviet military personnel, and this may contribute to the arsenals of dissident groups.

Incidents of airplane hijackings in the former Soviet Union decreased, however, from about 30 attempts in 1990 to about 10 in 1991. One notable hijacking, to Turkey in November, was a political gesture prompted by Russian President Yeltsin's attempt to impose a state of emergency in the Checheno-Ingushetia Autonomous Republic. The Chechen president threatened Russia with terrorist retaliation, including attacks on atomic power stations.

In 1991 the Soviet Union maintained its relations with most state sponsors of terrorism—Syria, Iran, Libya, North Korea, and Cuba—although at lower levels. However, its military and economic dealings with these countries were increasingly commercialized. (Iraq was the exception; Soviet dealings with that country were governed by the various UN Security Council sanctions adopted in 1990 and 1991.) Economic and budgetary constraints, as well as the overall preoccupation with domestic matters, added impetus to the reevaluation, begun in the mid-1980s, of these ties. The announced intent to withdraw the Soviet brigade in Cuba and to sharply reduce arms deliveries to that country were perhaps the most dramatic evidence of this trend in 1991. With the final breakup of the USSR, the newly independent states exhibited little support for the former regime's alliances with state sponsors. In October, Russian President Yel'tsin outlined an agenda for Russia strictly commercial relations with former client states, including Syria, Iran, and Cuba.

Spain

International terrorist incidents in Spain decreased to 10 in 1991 from 28 in 1990. Domestic terrorism in Spain, however, increased last year, in terms of the number of incidents and casualties. The Basque Fatherland and Liberty (ETA) separatist terrorist organization accounted for the vast majority of these, resulting in 45 fatalities, as opposed to 25 the previous year. As in the past, most victims were members of the Civil Guard, National Police, military, and their families. The group appeared particularly intent on demonstrating its continued capabilities as Spain prepared to host the Barcelona Olympics, a World's Fair, and several other major international events in 1992.

One of Spain's smaller terrorist organizations, the Catalonian separatist group Terra Lliure (Free Land), renounced the use of violence. The First of October Anti-Fascist Group (GRAPO), a Marxist and anti-US organization, mounted only one confirmed attack and had two of its members arrested in 1991. More than 20 GRAPO prisoners officially ended an ineffective hunger strike in February. Iraultza, an anti-US Marxist Basque group, attempted three small bombings in March and April, but three of its members were killed in a premature explosion. A Galician separatist group was responsible for the destruction of about 10 high-tension towers; about 10 of its members, however, including the EGPGC leader, were arrested. A suspected EGPGC safehouse was discovered in Sao Martinho do Porto, Portugal.

The government directed most of its counterterrorism efforts against ETA with considerable effectiveness. Raids in Catalonia and the Basque provinces resulted in more than 40 arrests and six ETA members killed. Approximately 40 ETA members, both Spanish and French, were arrested in France in 1991, the result of increased cooperation between French and Spanish authorities. The autonomous Basque police, Ertzaintza, accounted for one ETA member killed and one arrested. The government's success may have obliged ETA to strike less professionally at softer targets, accounting for the increase in civilian casualties. Seven children of police officials were killed by ETA bombs during the year, five in one explosion in May at a Civil Guard apartment building near Barcelona, which killed a total of nine and wounded more than 50.

ETA chose many material targets associated with Spain's tourist industry in 1991. As in previous years, ETA mounted a summer campaign designed to disrupt railroad travel in Spain. ETA issued an exceptional warning to travel agencies in Europe to alert tourists to the hazards of travel to Spain. Spanish consulates, beach resorts, banks, travel agencies, airline ticket offices, tour buses, and educational institutes were targeted more than a dozen times in Italy and three times in Germany from May to August. These were ETA's first attacks in Italy and Germany.

During 1991 Spain had very limited success in winning extradition of ETA suspects from abroad. Only a few low-level members were extradited from France, with Mexico and the Dominican Republic demurring.

Henri Parot, a prominent French Basque member of ETA's Itinerant Command who was arrested in Seville in 1990 was given an additional extended sentence in 1991 for six murders.

Two members of a Spanish rightwing terrorist organization known as GAL were tried and sentenced to lengthy prison terms in 1991 for attempted murder. GAL killed more than a score of suspected ETA members and supporters in France during the 1980s.

Sweden

In October, the Swedish Security Police arrested a suspected Palestinian terrorist for his alleged involvement in the 1971 murder in Cairo of the Jordanian Prime Minister. The suspect had been living in a refugee camp in southern Sweden. Jordan's request for extradition was turned over to Swedish judicial authorities for review.

An amended Terrorist Act became effective 1 July. The new act strengthens the ability of the Security Police and the courts to expel suspected foreign terrorists. It also eliminated the municipal arrest provision under which foreign terrorists who could not be expelled from Sweden were required to limit their movements to their local community absent specific permission for broader travel. Such individuals will, however, still be required to report regularly to local authorities and may be subject to surveillance.

A neo-Nazi group demanding the release of two supporters incarcerated for bank robbery claimed responsibility for the 20 December bombing of a pizzeria outside Stockholm, threatening more incidents if its demands were not met. Another bomb, possibly planted by neo-Nazi extremists, exploded in Stockholm's main train station on 30 December, injuring a police officer. The bombing sparked a series of bomb threats in Stockholm and other cities.

Turkey

The number of international terrorist incidents in Turkey rose from 12 in 1990 to 75 in 1991, the highest number for any country. Propelling much of this dramatic rise was the renewed emphasis placed on US targets by the leftist Turkish terrorist organization Devrimci Sol (Revolutionary Left or Dev Sol).

Many of Dev Sol's anti-US targets—some 30 property bombings during the first quarter of 1991 alone—were part of a larger protest against Turkey's strategic role in the international coalition against Iraq. During that time Dev Sol also killed two American civilian Defense Department contractors: Bobbie Eugene Mozelle in Adana in February and John Gandy in Istanbul in March. Dev Sol gunmen also seriously wounded an active US military officer in Izmir in February.

In August, Dev Sol also assassinated a British businessman in Istanbul.

Since its reemergence in 1989, Dev Sol has focused most of its lethal attacks against the Turkish security establishment. In 1991, the organization killed nearly 30 policemen in Istanbul, including the deputy police chief. Dev Sol also killed four active or retired general officers. The Turkish Peasants' and Workers' Liberation Army (TIKKO), another leftist terrorist organization, is suspected in the deaths of five Istanbul policemen in 1991.

The Turkish Government responded vigorously against Dev Sol. In April, new antiterrorism legislation was enacted providing, among other things, for longer sentences for terrorists and restrictions on the publication of terrorists' statements. Police raids in July in Istanbul and Ankara killed a dozen Dev Sol members and resulted in many arrests. These raids apparently preempted several anti-US and antigovernment attacks the organization had been planning for President Bush's visit to Turkey later that month.

Despite government efforts, Dev Sol proved resilient because of its relatively large number of adherents in Turkey, thought to be more than 1,000 and the discipline of its core operatives. Dev Sol also reportedly tried to intimidate police, prison guards, and members of the judiciary. Sympathizers within Turkey's large expatriate community in Western Europe raise funds and provide other logistic support for Dev Sol. A Dev Sol training camp in the Syrian-controlled Bekaa Valley in Lebanon has also been useful as an offshore haven and for upgrading Dev Sol's paramilitary skills.

A third American, US S. Sgt. Victor D. Marvick, was killed in Ankara in October 1991 in a car bombing claimed by an Islamic Jihad cell in Turkey to protest the Middle East peace conference in Madrid. The terrorists, thought to be supported by Iran, also seriously wounded an Egyptian diplomat the same day.

Despite the significant increase in the activity of Dev Sol, the preoccupying security concern for the Turkish Government in 1991 was the continuing separatist insurgency of the Kurdish Workers' Party, or PKK, which accounted for over 900 deaths in the predominantly Kurdish region of southeastern Turkey. The plight of Kurdish refugees from Iraq after the Persian Gulf war heightened the world's awareness of Kurds in general while creating an uncertain security situation in northern Iraq. The PKK exploited this circumstance to step up its military operations in the Kurdish region of southeast Turkey. From camps in Syria, Iraq, and Iran, as well as inside Turkey, the PKK mobilized large units against Turkish military and police outposts. Lethal attacks against civilians, ranging from women and children to a provincial subgovernor in 1991, diminished beginning in April in an apparent effort to increase PKK support among ordinary Kurds. PKK gunmen struck for the first time, however, at mainly military targets outside the southeast region, killing four and wounding more than a dozen in Adana, Istanbul, and Izmir. Turkish incursions against PKK camps in northern Iraq contributed to the military escalation in Southeast Turkey.

Another departure for the PKK in 1991 was the taking of Western hostages. Propagandizing its jurisdiction over a self-proclaimed Turkish Kurdistan, the PKK kidnapped 10 German tourists in August; shortly after their release, the PKK seized a team of Biblical archeologists—three Americans and an Australian—and a British tourist, releasing them unharmed after three weeks.

Like Dev Sol, the PKK also has members and supporters among the expatriate Turkish community in Western Europe, some of whom, in the case of PKK, raise funds by drug trafficking.

United Kingdom

There were no incidents of international terrorism in the United Kingdom in 1991. Sectarian violence in Northern Ireland increased, however, though still short of levels seen in the 1970s. The Provisional Irish Republican Army (PIRA) again extended its terrorist campaign to the British mainland but was largely quiescent on the European Continent. Loyalist or Unionist paramilitary commandos in Northern Ireland significantly increased their attacks against Catholics in Ulster and mounted several terrorist operations in Ireland.

In 1991, 94 people lost their lives in the sectarian "troubles" in Northern Ireland, as compared with 76 in 1990 and some 60 in 1989. The increase is attributable to attacks by Protestant Loyalists who doubled the number of their victims in 1991. The Loyalists observed a cease-fire during the so-called Strand talks aimed at achieving some accommodation between the Protestant and Catholic communities in Northern Ireland, but they sharply increased their attacks when those talks broke down in July.

Outside Northern Ireland, PIRA mounted several attacks in England, including a mortar attack there that nearly hit a Cabinet meeting at 10 Downing Street in February. Two powerful bombs were aimed at military band concerts near London but resulted in the deaths of two PIRA bomb handlers instead. One civilian, however, was killed by a PIRA bomb on a London subway train in February. He was PIRA's only fatal victim outside Ulster in 1991, as compared with six killed by PIRA outside Ulster in 1990. Loyalist terrorists from Ulster were responsible for more than a dozen firebombings in Dublin in 1991 and killed a pro-PIRA Sinn Fein Counselor in Ireland in May. Throughout the year, but particularly in December, PIRA planted scores of incendiary devices in commercial establishments and subway trains in London and other English cities—and threatened other assaults—in a campaign to cause damage and economic disruption during the busy pre-Christmas shopping period.

Convictions brought in 1976 in English courts against seven members of the Maguire family for a PIRA bombing campaign were overturned in June owing to serious procedural errors. In March, the Birmingham Six, also PIRA suspects, were released from prison, as had been the Guilford four in October 1990. The Home Secretary appointed a royal commission to review the legal system in light of these false imprisonments. PIRA member Desmond Ellis, extradited from Ireland in 1990 to stand trial for a 1981 PIRA bombing campaign in Britain, was acquitted of all charges.

John McCarthy, Jackie Mann, and Terry Waite, held hostage in Lebanon, were released in 1991. For the most part, author Salman Rushdie remained in hiding in Britain, however, as Iran's death threats against him continued in force. Rushdie did travel to New York City in December to deliver a speech at Columbia University; this was his first international travel since the death threats were made in 1989.

At the start of the Persian Gulf war, Britain detained about 90 Iraqis and Palestinians as a security precaution, deporting many of them.

On 14 November the Lord Advocate of Scotland brought formal charges against two Libyan intelligence officers, Abdel Basset Ali Al-Megrahi and Lamen Khalifa Fhimah, for the bombing in 1988 of Pan American Flight 103 over Lockerbie, Scotland. Britain, along with the United States, formally demanded their surrender by Libya.

Eastern European Overview

Cooperation between the countries of Eastern Europe and the West on counterterrorist issues began in earnest with the fall of Communist regimes in 1989 and continued unabated in 1991. This cooperation was strengthened during the Persian Gulf crisis, as East European governments closed borders to suspected terrorists, monitored or expelled suspect alien residents, and took steps to protect US and other coalition government interests on their territories. Official procoalition stances by East European governments during the war increased the risk in several of these countries, as evidenced by numerous terrorist threats. However, only in Yugoslavia was there a war-related attack: a failed firebombing in February of a US Information Service office in Sarajevo by unknown assailants.

Incidents of international terrorism remained relatively few in Eastern Europe for the rest of the year as well. In Hungary, a caller claiming to represent "The Movement for the Protection of Jerusalem" said that the group set off a bomb in December near a bus containing Jews emigrating from the former Soviet Union to Israel. Two Hungarian policemen in an escort vehicle were severely injured in the blast. Several days before, a terrorist failed in his attempt to assassinate the Turkish Ambassador in Budapest. An anonymous caller claiming to represent the Armenian Secret Army for the Liberation of Armenia (ASALA) claimed responsibility for that attack. In August, Sikh militants in Bucharest attempted to assassinate the Indian Ambassador to Romania, who had previously served as Director-General of Police in Punjab. Sikh extremists later kidnapped a Romanian diplomat in India, demanding the release of both the two assailants held by the Romanian authorities in the attack on the Indian Ambassador and three Sikh militants held by Indian authorities for other crimes. Although none of those demands was met, the Romanian diplomat was released seven weeks later. A Soviet commercial airliner was hijacked in January to Bulgaria, where the lone Soviet hijacker was arrested.

Soviet Consulates in Poland were the targets of firebombs after the Soviet crackdown in Lithuania and Latvia in January 1991. In Latvia, Estonia, and Lithuania more than a dozen bombings were aimed at political party offices and security installations, especially during the first quarter of 1991. In July, seven Lithuanian border guards were shot dead execution style. Reactionary elements were probably responsible for the incidents in the Baltics.

The civil war that consumed Yugoslavia in 1991, however, generated serious concern that combatants or their sympathizers abroad would resort to international terrorism to continue the fight on other fronts. To discourage diplomatic recognition of Croatia, for example, Serbian extremist groups made threats against German and Austrian officials and interests abroad. Actual terrorist incidents were few, however, and included the firebombing, probably by Serb nationalists, of a Croatian church near Munich and the attempted firebombing, most likely by Croat nationalists, in November of Yugoslav diplomatic missions in Canada and Germany.

For political and budgetary reasons, police presence in the East European countries continued to decline in 1991, possibly reducing the control authorities wielded over the activities of potential terrorists. The United States and others sponsored training programs in antiterrorist techniques for law enforcement and other officials of several countries in the region. Police cooperation was the subject of several bilateral agreements between Eastern and Western European countries. All states in the region except Albania are members of Interpol. Czechoslovakia, which joined Interpol in 1991, also ratified the International Civil Aviation Organization Convention on the Marking of Plastic Explosives for the Purpose of Detection. (Semtex, a plastic explosive used in several terrorist incidents, including the bombing of Pan Am Flight 103, is a product of Czechoslovakia.)

There were no prosecutions in Eastern Europe of suspects of international terrorism in 1991. Hungary did, however, extradite to Greece a suspected Greek terrorist in August.

Bulgaria cooperated with Western countries in investigating the alleged involvement of its former Communist government in the assassination in London in 1978 of dissident writer Georgi Markov and the attempted assassination of the Pope in 1981.

Latin American Overview

A record number of international incidents occurred in Latin America during 1991, most in South America, while Central America and the Caribbean experienced only a handful of attacks against foreign interests. A considerable number of attacks in the Latin American region were inspired by the US role in the Persian Gulf war. Latin American terrorist groups conducted 224 attacks on foreign interests, continuing the upward trend of the past four years. It should be noted, however, that this figure represents only a small percentage of the total number of terrorist incidents in the region. In most countries with a terrorist problem, the primary targets of guerrillas and narcotraffickers have been domestic institutions—government employees, law enforcement personnel, politicians, and media representatives. Most of the attacks occurred in Peru, Chile, and Colombia. At least 30 people died—three were US citizens—and 62 people were injured in international incidents over the course of the year. Anti-US terrorism rose to 174 attacks—up from 131 in 1990. While the Persian Gulf war clearly was a factor in the large number of attacks in early 1991, 116 international incidents occurred after the end of Operation Desert Storm.

Bolivia

Bolivian terrorists hit power pylons belonging to a US-owned power company three times in 1991, all low-level bombing incidents. Domestic terrorism, however, increased almost sevenfold. More than 40 bombing incidents occurred. Among the targets were Bolivian Government buildings near the US Embassy. Five bombs detonated at the La Paz International Airport. The Nestor Paz Zamora Commission (CNPZ), part of the refurbished National Liberation Army (ELN), and several previously unknown terrorist groups claimed responsibility for a handful of the attacks, but most went unclaimed. The new groups included the Tupac Katari Guerrilla Army (EGTK) and the Thomas Katari Communal Army (ECTK). Both advocate the return of Bolivia to precolonial forms of government and indigenous Indian culture.

The Bolivian Government initiated improvements in its domestic and regional counterterrorism programs, while publicly downplaying the increase in terrorist incidents. The government established various crisis management mechanisms and began developing a national counterterrorism strategy. The Bolivian police held high-level meetings with their counterparts from Chile, Peru, and Brazil to help improve coordination against cross-border terrorism. While these steps demonstrated greater political willingness to deal with terrorism than in past years, a severe lack of resources and investigative and judicial weaknesses continued to hamper the government's ability to counter the growing terrorist problem. Nonetheless, eight members of the Zarate Willka Armed Forces of Liberation (FALZW) received stiff sentences for their role in the 1988 attack on Secretary Shultz's motorcade and the murder of two US Mormon missionaries in 1989. At the close of 1991, a trial was also under way for CNPZ terrorists who attacked the US Marine guard-house in La Paz in October 1990.

Chile

Since the end of the Pinochet regime in March 1990, several far-left groups, including the Communist Party of Chile (PCCH), have moved away from terrorist tactics, but other, more extreme organizations continue to use armed actions in pursuit of their political goals. Chilean terrorist organizations, which had targeted US interests in record numbers in 1990 and early 1991, were somewhat less active during the remainder of the year. There were 52 anti-US attacks in Chile in 1991, down from 61 in 1990. Of these attacks, more than half were conducted after the end of the Persian Gulf war. After a brief lull following the war, sporadic anti-US attacks resumed in May and became more numerous during the last quarter of the year. Attacks against Mormon churches increased in intensity toward the end of the year, involving more powerful bombs or bombs containing shrapnel clearly designed to cause serious injury and substantial damage. Three Chilean children were injured in one attack against a Mormon church in November. Two terrorist organizations, the dissident faction of the Manuel Rodriguez Patriotic Front (FPMR/D) and elements of the Lautaro Youth Movement (MJL), were responsible for most of the political violence. Two previously unknown groups surfaced during the year—the Guerrilla Army of the People-Free Fatherland and the Joaquin Murieta Extremist Movement. During October, the Guerrilla Army of the People carried out several low-level domestic bombings and an armed occupation of the French News Agency. Several of its leaders were subsequently arrested.

Several significant anti-US and domestic incidents occurred in 1991. On 16 February, the FPMR/D fired a light antitank weapon rocket at a US Marine guard van, but it failed to detonate. Ensuing gunfire by the terrorists injured one Marine. Some domestic incidents were pegged to the release of the National Truth and National Reconciliation Commission Report (Rettig Report) which detailed human rights violations during the Pinochet regime. The FPMR/D assassinated a retired Army medical doctor and his wife the day before the release of the report. The assassination of Senator Jaime Guzman on 1 April was probably carried out by the FPMR/D, although the investigation is continuing. The MJL claimed responsibility for the murder of investigations police chief Hector Sarmiento Hidalgo in Concepcion on 15 March.

The Chilean Government is focusing more attention on Chile's terrorism problem. Increased training and efforts by members of the police have improved their counterterrorism capabilities in the past year. During 1991, the police uncovered several safehouses and training sites used by Chilean terrorists and arrested several leaders and members of each of the country's main terrorist organizations. Immediately after the Guzman murder, the Chilean Government created the Public Security Coordinating Council, an advisory group whose function is to unite the counterterrorism efforts of government agencies. In its first report to President Aylwin, submitted in September, the Council recommended the establishment of a permanent intelligence organization to coordinate the government's counterterrorism effort. In December, President Aylwin announced a plan to set up an Under Secretariat for Public Security and Intelligence at the Interior Ministry to coordinate police efforts to combat crime and delinquency as well as terrorism. Implementing legislation will be taken up during the next session of Congress. The government has also appointed special investigating judges to try the more serious cases, such as the Guzman murder.

Colombia

Terrorist incidents in Colombia continue to be perpetrated by three leftist insurgent groups loosely affiliated under the umbrella group Simon Bolivar Guerrilla Coordinator (CGSB), by narcotics traffickers, and by rightwing para-military groups.

There were 62 international terrorist incidents in Colombia in 1991, up from 28 in 1990 and 46 in 1989. While most of the violence in the country was domestic, the two main CGSB terrorist groups, the National Liberation Army (ELN) and Revolutionary Armed Forces of Colombia (FARC), continued to target foreign workers for kidnapping. Three French and two Japanese engineers were kidnapped and held for ransom by the FARC during 1991. Three US engineers held since November 1990 by the ELN were released a year later. The majority of the international attacks in Colombia in 1991 were bombings of Colombia's oil pipelines, particularly the Cano-Limon Covenas pipeline in northern Colombia, jointly owned by Ecopetrol and a consortium of US and West European companies.

The surrender of Pablo Escobar, the head of the Medellin drug cartel, and many other members of his narcotics ring resulted in a sharp decrease in narcotics-related violence in Colombia. As a result, several paramilitary groups publicly demobilized, claiming that with Escobar behind bars the battle they had been fighting was over.

Peace talks between the Colombian Government and the CGSB continued in 1991, with little success. The end of the fifth round of talks in November prompted an increase in guerrilla attacks, primarily directed at domestic targets, as the terrorist groups sought to strengthen their negotiating position.

The Colombian Government made efforts toward improving the nation's judicial system in the past year by forming special courts to handle terrorist and narcotics cases and approving a new antiterrorist statute that strengthens sanctions for terrorist crimes. The Colombian Government also imposed a new tax to fund counterinsurgency efforts.

Ecuador

The Government of Ecuador continued its policy of negotiating with the Alfaro Vive Carajo (AVC), a small, Marxist-Leninist extremist group, to encourage its participation in the legitimate political process. This effort resulted in a ceremony in February at which a handful of AVC members turned in 65 guns. In October, some of the members publicly announced their desire to join President Borja's Democratic Left Party, while a dissident faction denounced the move to abandon clandestine terrorist activities. AVC members occupied the French Consulate in Guayaquil in January 1991 and the British Embassy in Quito in September 1991. The Ecuadorian Government chose not to prosecute those who seized the facilities, although one AVC member was charged with illegal possession of explosives in connection with an attempted bombing of the Social Welfare Ministry in May. Other minuscule extremist groups carried out five low-level attacks against foreign interests in Ecuador during 1991, four during the Gulf war.

El Salvador

The leftist Farabundo Marti National Liberation Front (FMLN) signed a cease-fire agreement on 31 December with the Government of El Salvador, ending the decade-long civil war. Before the cease-fire agreement, there were three international terrorist incidents in El Salvador in 1991. One of the incidents, notably, claimed the lives of the only three Americans to die as a result of terrorist activity in Latin America in 1991. On 2 January, the FMLN downed a US helicopter carrying three US military advisers who were enroute to Honduras. Two of them, Lt. Col. David Pickett and crew chief PFC Earnest Dawson, were brutally executed after surviving the crash. The third, Chief Warrant Officer Daniel Scott, died of injuries suffered in the shootdown. The FMLN has refused to turn over the two individuals responsible. In July, a US Embassy security vehicle was fired on in San Salvador by suspected FMLN members.

A significant development in Salvadoran justice was the September conviction of two military officers for the 1989 murder of six Jesuit priests, marking the first time a military officer has been convicted for rightwing terrorism.

Guatemala

Leftist insurgent groups under the umbrella group Guatemalan National Revolutionary Unit (URNG) accounted for much of the terrorist violence in the country in 1991. There were seven incidents of international terrorism, the same figure as in 1990.

The Gulf war prompted the most significant international terrorist incidents in Guatemala in 1991. Attempted bombings and shootings were directed against the Uruguayan, British, and Canadian Embassies, as well as the residence of the Japanese Ambassador in February. Four armed men fired shots at the US-affiliated Covenant House in July 1991. A series of threats against foreign media in Guatemala prompted representatives of several international news agencies to leave Guatemala City in August 1991.

The Guatemalan Government, with the support of the military, made some progress in direct talks with the leaders of the URNG during 1991. But the country's ineffective criminal justice system and the intransigence of the URNG have proved to be major impediments to effective counterterrorist strategies.

Mexico

Mexico, which had not experienced international terrorist incidents in the past several years, had five terrorist bombing attacks during August, apparently timed to coincide with midterm national elections. (The Government of Mexico considers the group that claimed responsibility for carrying out the bombings to be a criminal rather than terrorist organization.)

Targets included US-owned banks and other commercial interests and a Japanese automobile dealership. No other attacks were perpetrated in 1991 against foreign interests.

The Clandestine Worker's Revolutionary Party, Union of the Poor (PROCUP), a leftist extremist organization, claimed responsibility for all five attacks. PROCUP has been periodically active since its formation in 1970, but the Government of Mexico has, for the most part, effectively monitored and controlled its activities.

Peru

Terrorist activities of Peru's two insurgencies, Sendero Luminoso (SL) and the Tupac Amaru Revolutionary Movement (MRTA), have made Peru a dangerous country for foreigners. Of the 59 international attacks in Peru, 34 were against US interests. Most were probably perpetrated by the MRTA, although SL also claimed two attacks against US facilities. Violent terrorist attacks, which occurred on a nearly daily basis, were spread over much of Peru but were most heavily concentrated in Lima itself, where more than 600 terrorist attacks caused about 350 deaths. At least 2,800 people died during the year in an unknown number of terrorist attacks in the country; a record 422 people were killed in October alone. SL continued its campaign of assassinating teachers, clergy, engineers, development and human rights workers, Indian peasants, and political candidates, as well as government, police, and political party officials. SL killed at least 10 foreigners, none of them US citizens. Nine of the foreigners were missionaries, clergy, or economic assistance workers.

Despite extensive security precautions, President Alberto Fujimori was the target of two terrorist attacks in November by the MRTA. A letter bomb campaign directed against domestic targets occurred in Lima, the first of its kind in South America, resulting in the death of one pro-MRTA journalist and serious injuries to three other Peruvians. It is not clear which group, or groups, is responsible for the letter bombs. On 3 November, 17 persons were killed in the Barrios Altos neighborhood of Lima by a group of armed men. Those responsible have not been identified, but local human rights groups attribute the act to a paramilitary group.

The troubled Peruvian justice system has proved ineffective in the fight against terrorism. In 1991 the Government of Peru prosecuted no cases involving international terrorism and few cases of domestic terrorism. A chronic lack of basic resources plagues the judicial system. Severe staffing and morale problems pervade the judicial and law enforcement communities because of meager salaries. Constant terrorist actions have left hundreds of policemen, soldiers, prosecutors, and judges dead, injured, or co-opted. The lack of properly trained personnel, a failure to employ modern investigative methods, and professional rivalries between the police and prosecutors are further impediments to terrorist prosecutions. Use of criminal forensics is inadequate, and the Peruvians lack an effective witness protection program. Imprisoned terrorists largely control the facilities where they are incarcerated.

The Government of Peru, nonetheless, has taken steps to strengthen its hand against terrorism. In November, the administration issued a series of legislative decrees designed to strengthen the government's counterterrorism capabilities. Among these decrees, which were subject to review by the Peruvian Congress, are measures to reduce sentences in exchange for information, to increase the powers of military commanders in areas outside emergency zones, and to reorganize the police and intelligence services.

Middle Eastern Overview

The number of international terrorist incidents in the Middle East increased from 65 in 1990 to 79 in 1991, largely because of a spate of attacks in Lebanon during the Persian Gulf war.

International terrorism by Palestinians again decreased from 41 in 1990 to 19 last year. Although many of the Palestinian groups threatened to conduct terrorist operations against the international coalition opposing Baghdad's invasion of Kuwait, few such attacks actually occurred. Most incidents recorded during the Persian Gulf war were bombing attacks outside the Middle East region, and most of these were against commercial property belonging to coalition countries' firms. Few of these attacks were carried out against civilians.

There are several reasons why Palestinian terrorists did not carry out attacks in support of Saddam Hussein:

- Military operations disrupted the command and control links between Baghdad and the terrorist networks it had established.
- Enhanced security measures were widely implemented in most regions of the world.
- Coalition countries expelled Iraqi diplomats and intelligence operatives.
- The rapidity of the coalition advance into Iraq sealed Iraq's defeat before operations could be coordinated.

Several Palestinian groups that threatened terrorism during the Gulf war were weakened during 1991. Abu Abbas, the leader of the Palestine Liberation Front (PLF), left the Palestine Liberation Organization (PLO) Executive Committee in September, although the PLF itself is still represented on the Committee. The PLF also failed to follow through on the terrorist threats it issued from Baghdad during the war. The Hawari organization, which was based in Baghdad, was seriously damaged by the death of its leader, Colonel Hawari, in a car accident on the road between Baghdad and the Jordanian border immediately after the war.

During 1991, nine long-held foreign hostages—six Americans and three British citizens—and the remains of Col. William R. Higgins and William F. Buckley were released by Iranian-supported Hizballah members in Lebanon. At year's end, UN special negotiator Giandomenico Picco continued his efforts to secure the release of two German aid workers held in Lebanon and to negotiate an exchange of Lebanese and Palestinian prisoners for missing Israeli servicemen in Lebanon.

Despite the decline in international incidents undertaken by Middle Eastern groups, domestic terrorism continued in Israel, the occupied territories, and Lebanon. The attacks appeared to be carried out by rejectionist groups and coincided with positive developments in the Middle East peace process. Internecine conflicts within and between Palestinian and Lebanese terrorist groups once again added to the violence.

Iran's success in building closer ties to Palestinian terrorist groups poses a potential threat to international peace and security. Iran hosted a conference in October on the Palestinian problem, which generated a large amount of rhetorical protest against the Middle East peace talks.

A rocket attack was launched against the American Embassy in Beirut during the Madrid peace conference, and a bomb attack damaged several buildings at the American University of Beirut shortly thereafter.

Algeria

Algeria has condemned international terrorism but considers some acts of violence by movements of national liberation to be legitimate. As an expression of this position, Algeria has refused to sign numerous international agreements intended to counter acts of terrorism. The Algerian Government permits a number of radical groups, including some that have been involved in terrorism, to maintain a presence in Algeria. This has occasionally led to security incidents (for example, the April 1990 attack by the Abu Nidal organization (ANO) on an ANO dissident and a bomb explosion at a PLO office in Algiers in the spring of 1991.) Palestine Liberation Front (PLF) leader Abu Abbas and a few other Palestinians affiliated with terrorist organizations attended the September 1991 meeting of the Palestine National Council in Algiers, but the Algerian Government made it clear that it would not tolerate terrorist activities on its territory.

In March a lone armed hijacker took over an Air Algerie flight on the ground in Algiers, holding its 44 passengers and six crewmembers hostage. The hostages were released unharmed a few hours later. In October an Algerian court handed down 10-year prison sentences to two men responsible for a similar hijacking in late December 1990.

Algeria was thrown into and internal political crisis in late December 1991 when Muslim fundamentalists won an overwhelming victory in the first round of National Assembly elections and were poised to win the second round and gain a majority in the Assembly. Since President Bendjedid's resignation, the suspension of the second round of elections, and the crackdown on the Islamic Salvation Front (FIS) by the military, there has been a serious upsurge in violent clashes between Islamist elements and the security forces.

Egypt

There were no terrorist attacks against Americans or US interests in Egypt in 1991, despite concerns of such attacks in support of Operation Desert Shield/Desert Storm.

US and Egyptian security services cooperated closely on security and antiterrorism matters. During the Persian Gulf war, Egyptian security forces reported several apparent terrorist threats against US interests in Egypt. Egyptian security agents arrested a number of individuals suspected of planning terrorist acts against Egyptian or Western targets.

In early September, Egyptian authorities arrested armed agents of the Palestinian Islamic Jihad (PIJ) who had entered Egypt with the intention of committing terrorist acts. In November, Israeli security forces intercepted four armed Palestinians who had entered the Israeli Negev from the Sinai. It is quite likely that these terrorists entered Egypt from a third country with the intention of infiltrating into Israel for future terrorist attacks. There are unconfirmed reports that two bodies found on a Gaza beach in December were terrorists who drowned while attempting an attack that may have been launched from Egyptian territory.

The radical Islamic group Al-Gama'a Al-Islamiyaa is believed responsible for a number of armed robberies of local Egyptian merchants in 1991 but has conducted no major terrorist incident since the October 1990 assassination of assembly speaker al-Mahgoub. This group seeks the violent overthrow of the Government of Egypt but is not known to have attacked US or other Western targets. More important, it receives support from Iran and has established networks with several counterparts in the Arab world and elsewhere.

Israel and the Occupied Territories

There were numerous attacks and attempted attacks in Israel and the occupied territories in connection with the Palestinian *intifadah* and the Arab-Israeli conflict, several of which coincided with key developments in the Middle East peace process.

Many small bombs exploded or were discovered and defused by Israeli authorities in the course of the year. There were several firebomb or arson attacks on coalition interests in the occupied territories early in the year, probably in reaction to the Persian Gulf war. On 12 April, a bomb exploded in East Jerusalem at the Damascus Gate just before a visit to Israel by Secretary of State Baker. In a similar incident on 16 September, two people were injured when a bomb exploded at an outdoor market in Beersheba.

Stabbing incidents in Israel and on the West Bank occurred throughout 1991. While some of the attacks were probably carried out by organized groups, others appeared to be the work of lone individuals. On 18 May, an apparent Islamic zealot stabbed and wounded three Israelis in West Jerusalem; a faction of the Palestinian Islamic Jihad (PIJ) claimed responsibility. Several European tourists were also the victims of stabbings.

In 7 July, the Popular Front for the Liberation of Palestine (PFLP) claimed responsibility for shooting and seriously wounding an Israeli who was transporting Palestinian workers to Israel from the Gaza strip. The Democratic Front for the Liberation of Palestine (DFLP) claimed responsibility for a similar attack the following day, also in Gaza.

On 28 October, just days before the opening of the Madrid

peace conference, gunmen opened fire on a busload of Israeli settlers on the West Bank north of Jerusalem. Two Israelis were killed and at least six wounded, including five children. Both the PFLP and a PIJ faction claimed responsibility.

On numerous occasions in 1991, Jewish settlers in the occupied territories attacked Palestinian civilians and property, often in response to Palestinian attacks. In late October, the son of slain Jewish extremist leader Rabbi Meir Kahane publicly threatened to "blow up" the Madrid peace conference. He was later arrested in Madrid along with two associates while distributing leaflets critical of Israel's participation in the conference. Slogans from Kahane's group Kach were found painted on the walls of the American Cultural Center in Jerusalem after a firebombing there on 28 October.

Israeli security forces intercepted over 20 attempted guerrilla infiltrations into Israel from Lebanon, Jordan, and Egypt in 1991. Several of the attempted cross-border attacks were conducted by Lebanese groups and Palestinian fighters from factions both within and outside the PLO. Others appear to be the work of disgruntled individuals acting alone or with a few colleagues but with no discernible ties to any known terrorist group. In most cases, the infiltrators failed to penetrate the Israeli border, and the precise targets of the attacks were not clear.

In late-January, Palestinians fired several rockets over a three-day period at Israel from Lebanon. The rockets landed in the Israeli-controlled south Lebanon security zone. PLO Forces are suspected of perpetrating these rocket attacks in order to show support for Iraq.

On 13 September, a Swedish officer with the UN peacekeeping force (UNIFIL) in south Lebanon was killed and five other officers wounded in a gun battle between Israeli troops and their Lebanese allies and a group of Palestinian guerrillas attempting to infiltrate Israel by sea. The Palestinians landed in small boats in south Lebanon and took the UNIFIL officers hostage after failing to reach Israel, where they apparently intended to conduct a terrorist attack. One of the captured guerrillas admitted he was a member of Arafat's Fatah faction of the PLO.

On 11 November, four heavily armed Palestinians were killed by Israeli forces in the Negev desert as they attempted to infiltrate Israel from Egypt.

The Lebanese Shia group Hizballah conducted several dozen attacks on Israeli soldiers in Israel's self-proclaimed security zone in south Lebanon, which continued to be the site of numerous incidents.

Israel takes a strong stand against terrorism and terrorist state sponsors. The Israeli Government has made fighting terrorism a high priority and devotes a considerable proportion of its internal and external security resources to this effort. Israeli police and military forces are involved in planning and training to meet the terrorist threat.

Israeli counterterrorist efforts continue to target countries aiding, harboring, or failing to inhibit terrorists. Israeli military forces have launched preemptive and retaliatory airstrikes against suspected terrorist installations in neighboring Lebanon and have occasionally detained Lebanese nationals in an attempt to thwart attacks. At year's end, Israel continued to hold outside the legal process Sheikh Abdul Karim Obeid, a Hizballah cleric from south Lebanon whom Israeli forces abducted in July 1989, apparently in an effort to exchange him for Israeli military personnel held by Lebanese and other groups.

Israel uses curfews and other restrictive measures to control violence in the occupied territories. The West Bank and Gaza Strip were sealed off from Israel on several occasions in 1991 when the threat was considered to be especially high, most notably during the Gulf war and during sessions of the Middle East peace talks. Israel has also responded to violent incidents by deporting to neighboring countries Palestinian activists who are deemed to be of security risks or accused of anti-Israeli offenses. The United States strongly opposes deportations as a violation of the Fourth Geneva Convention.

Israeli courts generally hand down strict prison sentences to those convicted of terrorist attacks. In May, a former member of the 15 May Organization and the Hawari Special Operations Group was sentenced to 25 years in prison for a failed attempt to blow up an El Al airliner in 1984. Mahmud Atta, a member of the Abu Nidal organization who was extradited to Israel from the United States in 1991, was sentenced to life in prison in October for a machinegun attack on an Israel bus on the West Bank in 1986. Later that month, Sheikh Ahmad Yassin, founder of the Palestinian fundamentalist group Hamas, received a life sentence plus 15 years after admitting to Israeli charges, including plotting the murder of two off-duty Israeli soldiers.

Militant Jewish extremist Rabbi Moshe Levinger was sentenced in January to four months in prison for assaulting a Palestinian family in Hebron. The sentence was later reduced for good behavior. In June an Israeli court approved the extradition to the United States of an American-born Israeli couple suspected of sending a letter bomb that killed an American woman in California in 1980. One of the two is also a suspect in the murder of an Arab-American activist in 1985. The extradition case was appealed to the Israeli Supreme Court in December.

Jordan

Despite additional security measures provided by Jordanian authorities, tensions stemming from the Persian Gulf war led to a spate of attacks in early 1991 against business and diplomatic targets associated with countries taking part in the coalition against Iraq. Most such incidents were minor attacks apparently intended to cause property damage rather than casualties.

At least some of the attacks were apparently the work of a group of Islamic extremists known as Muhammad's Army. In July, Jordanian authorities arrested dozens of persons suspected of belonging to the group, 18 of whom went on trial in October. In open court, the defendants admitted to conducting a series of attacks on Jordanian and Western interests, including two car bombings that seriously wounded the daughter of a local cleric in January and a Jordanian intelligence officer in July. They also confessed to planning attacks against US and other Western diplomatic facilities. Eight defendants, including two in absentia, were found guilty and sentenced to death. In December King Hussein commuted the death sentences for six defendants to varying prison terms; he let stay the death sentences on the two tried in absentia.

A variety of Palestinian factions maintain a presence in Jordan, including elements of the PLO and more radical Islamic fundamentalist groups like Hamas and the Palestinian Islamic Jihad (PIJ). Prominent members of the PIJ in Jordan publicly threatened attacks on US interests during the Gulf war.

There were a number of armed infiltration attempts across the Jordanian boundary with Israel in 1991. Some, such as an 8 February attack claimed by Muhammad's Army, appeared to have been carried out by an organized group; others were most likely conducted by zealous individuals with no connection to any known political organization. One Israeli farmer was killed and three others wounded in a cross-border attack in April. A decline in cross-border raids in he latter half of the year may have been because of Jordan's efforts to enforce tighter border security.

Kuwait

Kuwait has historically been a target of international terrorism and has had to cope with hijackings, bombings, and assassination attempts. It has been aggressive in bringing terrorists to justice. Before the 2 August 1990 Iraqi invasion, and consistent with its no concessions policy on terrorism, the Amir resisted pressure to pardon members of the pro-Iranian fundamentalist Dawa terrorist group imprisoned in Kuwait for a series of 1983 bombing attacks against US, French, and Kuwaiti interests. The Dawa terrorists either escaped or were freed during the Iraqi occupation.

During 1991 there were no significant acts of domestic terrorism in Kuwait. The government closed down offices of the PLO and all other Palestinian groups, including some associated with terrorism. The Palestinian groups, including some associated with terrorism. The Palestinian population in Kuwait also shrunk during the Persian Gulf war and its aftermath from approximately 350,000 to about 40,000, thus severely reducing the ability of these groups to operate in Kuwait.

Lebanon

The number of international terrorist incidents in Lebanon in 1991 rose to a high of 32, up from 10 in 1990 and 16 in 1989. Much of the increase reflected a low-level bombing campaign against foreign targets, largely French-owned banks, during the Persian Gulf war. These incidents caused only minor damage and few casualties. There also were a number of domestic terrorist incidents related to struggles between various Lebanese factions.

During much of 1991, the central government extended its control into south Lebanon. The Lebanese Government, however, has been unable to fully implement the Taif Accords, which provide for the extension of its authority nation wide. It has yet to move into the Bekaa Valley or east Lebanon or to expand into portions of the south dominated by Hizballah or the South Lebanon Army (SLA).

Syria, however, continues to maintain a sizable military presence in Lebanon, exercising control over portions of the north and the east. Israel and its client Lebanese militia, the SLA, control a region along the Israeli border.

Terrorism continues to plague Lebanon, and the year saw many violent attacks. Eight people died in a 20 March car bombing believed to have been an attempt on the live of the Defense Minister, the first such incident since the central government's assumption of authority in Beirut. The year closed with a 30 December Beirut car-bombing incident in which at least 30 were reported killed and 120 injured. The year also saw a rocket attack on 29 October on the US Embassy and the 8 November bombing that destroyed buildings of the American University of Beirut. Both attacks are believed to have been protests against the opening of the Middle East peace talks. A French aid worker was abducted on 8 August to protest the release of British hostage John McCarthy. The Frenchman was freed three days later after Syrian troops and Lebanese armed forces exerted pressure on Hizballah strongholds in Beirut.

Iran, Iraq, Syria, and Libya continued to provide varying degrees of financial, military, and logistic support to radical groups engaging in terrorism in Lebanon. Several international groups including radical Palestinians, such as the Popular Front for the Liberation of Palestine-General Command (PFLP-GC), the Palestinian Islamic Jihad (PIJ), the Democratic Front for the Liberation of Palestine (DFLP), the Abu Nidal organization (ANO), and Abu Musa, as well as non-Palestinian groups, such as the Japanese Red Army (JRA), the Kurdish Workers' Party (PKK), Turkey's Revolutionary Left (Dev Sol), and the Armenian Secret Army for the Liberation of Armenia (ASALA), maintain training facilities in Lebanon, chiefly in the Syrian-garrisoned Bekaa Valley.

The Lebanese Government frequently has condemned terrorist acts and has repeatedly called for the release of foreign hostages but has been unable to rein in terrorists.

One bright spot over the past year was the winding down of the hostage problem in Lebanon. Iranian-backed elements of Hizballah freed six American and three British hostages and returned the remains of US hostages Col. William Higgins and William Buckley at the end of 1991 following a UN-orchestrated process involving frequent contact with Iran, Syria, the Lebanese Shia, Israel, and others. In return, many Lebanese held by Israel and the SLA were freed, but several hundred remain in captivity. Israel received through the UN conclusive information from Hizballah that two of its six missing soldiers were dead. The remains of another Israeli soldier killed in fighting in Lebanon in the mid-1980s were returned by the Democratic Front for the Liberation of Palestine (DFLP).

At the end of 1991, two German relief workers who are also held by Hizballah—Heinrich Struebig and Thomas

Kemptner—remained in captivity; their release has been linked to freedom for two Lebanese terrorists jailed in Germany. There had also not yet been a full accounting of all those held hostage who may have died while in captivity.

Saudi Arabia

The defining event concerning terrorism in Saudi Arabia in 1991 was Operation Desert Storm and its aftermath. Throughout the Desert Shield/Desert Storm period, Saudi Arabia shared information on possible terrorist acts with other governments and made every effort to assist the international community in countering and preventing terrorism. The Saudi Government expelled Iraqi diplomats and attaches and closed its borders with Jordan and Yemen, countries it viewed as aligned with Iraq. It also tightened visa requirements for foreign workers from countries opposing the international coalition. Many foreign workers were expelled from Saudi Arabia, and others were transferred or fired from sensitive government positions. Saudi Arabia also employed additional security measures on Saudi Airline flights.

Despite the huge US military presence in Saudi Arabia, there was only one act of terrorism directed against US forces. On 3 February 1991, two US airmen and a Saudi guard were wounded in an attack on a military bus in Jeddah. Four Palestinians (one a naturalized Saudi) and two Yemenis were arrested. The incident is still under investigation, and the four Palestinians remain in custody.

The Saudi Government is still closely following the investigation of the February 1990 killing of three Saudi diplomats in Bangkok, Thailand. The Thai Government has publicly blamed a non-Thai terrorist no longer in Thailand.

Thanks to the intensive but largely unobtrusive security precautions taken by Saudi security forces, the annual Mecca pilgrimage (*hajj*) passed without incident.

Saudi Arabia has repeatedly spoken out and voted against terrorist acts in international fora. It has raised terrorism issues in bilateral discussion with governments it considers to be state sponsors of terrorism. Saudi Arabia decries acts of terrorism allegedly committed in the name of the Palestinian cause; it considers this cause to be a legitimate movement of national liberation and resistance to military occupation. Saudi Arabia suspended financial and political support for the PLO in late 1990 because of that group's strong pro-Iraqi stance but then reportedly resumed transfer to the PLO of revenue from a tax on Palestinians working in the kingdom in late 1991.

Yemen

The Republic of Yemen (ROY) is committed to cutting all ties to terrorist groups. A few groups, however, continue to maintain a presence in ROY territory, typically with the assistance of ROY officials who were previous officials of the former People's Democratic Republic of Yemen (PDRY). The PDRY was on the US Government's list of state sponsors of terrorism until its unification with the Yemen Arab Republic (YAR) to form the ROY in 1990.

The ROY is reportedly narrowing criteria and tightening procedures for issuing passports to non-Yemenis, including Palestinians, and has denied press reports that international terrorist Carlos was granted refuge in Yemen.

During the past year several incidents of international terrorism occurred in Yemeni territory, especially during the Persian Gulf war when Yemen was a strong supporter of Iraq. In January, during the Gulf crisis, the embassies of the US, Turkey, and Japan were attacked by unknown persons. The ROY condemned these attacks and increased protection of citizens and property of coalition member countries. In October unknown persons attacked the German and US Embassies in what was probably part of a wave of attacks that also included ROY government targets.

Patterns of Global Terrorism: 1992

The Year in Review

One of the largest one-year decreases in the number of international terrorist incidents since the United States began keeping such statistics in 1968 occurred in 1992. International terrorist attacks declined during 1992 to 361, the lowest level in 17 years. This is roughly 35 percent fewer than the 567 incidents recorded in 1991, a figure that was inflated by a spate of low-level incidents at the time of the Gulf war. During 1992, US citizens and property remained the principal targets throughout the world; nearly 40 percent of the 361 International terrorist attacks during the year were directed at US targets.

US casualties from acts of terrorism were the lowest ever. Two Americans were killed,[1] and one was wounded during 1992, as opposed to seven dead and 14 wounded the previous year:

- On 8 January 1992 naturalized US citizen Jose Lopez was kidnapped by members of the National Liberation Army in Colombia and subsequently killed.
- On 10 June, Sgt. Owell Hernandez was killed in Panama when the US Army vehicle he was driving was raked by automatic gunfire from a passing car. Another American serviceman in the vehicle was wounded. No group claimed responsibility. This attack occurred just before the visit of President Bush to Panama.

The one "spectacular" international terrorist attack during the year occurred on 17 March when a powerful truck bomb destroyed the Israeli Embassy in Buenos Aires, Argentina. The

---

1 Five American missionary nuns were brutally murdered in Liberia in two separate attacks during 1992. We have not included these murders as terrorist attacks because a political motivation appears to be lacking.

blast leveled the Embassy and severely damaged a nearby church, school and retirement home. Twenty-nine persons were killed and 242 wounded. Islamic Jihad, a cover name for the Iranian-sponsored group Hizballah, publicly claimed responsibility for the attack and, to authenticate the claim, released a videotape of the Israeli Embassy taken during surveillance before the bombing. There is mounting evidence of Iranian Government responsibility for this act of terrorism.

As was the case during the preceding three years, Latin America saw more terrorism in 1992 than any other region. Antiforeign attacks in that region were predominantly against American targets. Leftwing terrorism, particularly in Europe, is in decline but ethnic and separatist groups in Europe, Latin America, South Asia, and the Middle East remained active last year.

The deadly Peruvian terrorist group Sendero Luminoso was dealt a major blow in September when security forces in Lima captured the group's founder, Abimael Guzman, and many of its high command. Guzman was subsequently sentenced to life imprisonment for his terrorist crimes.

None of the traditional state sponsors of terrorism has completely abandoned the terrorist option, especially against dissidents, nor severed ties to terrorist surrogates. Iraq's international terrorist infrastructure was largely destroyed by the Coalition's counterterrorist actions during that war. Since Operation Desert Storm, however, Saddam has used terrorism to punish regime opponents and to intimidate UN and private humanitarian workers. The Iranian regime has practiced state terrorism since it took power in 1979; it is currently the deadliest state sponsor and has achieved a worldwide reach.

There were fewer deaths caused by international terrorism during 1992, 93 [versus] 102 in 1991, but many more persons were wounded, 636 [versus] 242. The single bombing of the Israeli Embassy in Argentina accounted for about 40 percent of all those wounded in terrorist attacks in 1992.

African Overview

Ten international terrorist incidents occurred in Africa in 1992, up from the three incidents in 1991. However, political violence in Sub-Saharan Africa continued to be a major problem. A promising outlook in Angola seemed ready to dissipate at year's end, as government and its main rival, the National Union for the Total Independence of Angola (UNITA), fell out over the results of presidential elections. Civil war in Liberia and violent anarchy in Somalia spilled over into neighboring countries. The Government of Sudan persisted in harboring representatives of Mideast terrorist groups.

Angola

Four terrorist incidents occurred in 1992 in the oil-producing Angolan enclave of Cabinda. In the most serious incident, three Angolan local employees of Chevron oil were killed in December by insurgents of the Front for the Liberation of the Enclave of Cabinda (FLEC). FLEC had earlier attacked and set on fire buses used by Chevron to transport employees. FLEC factions also were responsible for the separate kidnappings of three Portuguese construction workers and two French citizens and their Angolan guides. FLEC seeks independence for Cabinda and has targeted Western oil companies because of commercial relations with the Luanda government.

Sudan

In 1992 the Government of Sudan continued a disturbing pattern of relationships with international terrorist groups. Sudan's increasing support for radical Arab terrorist groups is directly related to the extension of National Islamic Front (NIF) influence over the Government of Sudan. Elements of the Abu Nidal organization (ANO), the Palestinian Islamic Movement (HAMAS), and the Palestinian Islamic Jihad (PIJ) terrorist organizations continue to find refuge in Sudan.

There is no evidence that the Government of Sudan conducted or sponsored a specific terrorist attack in the past year, and the government denies supporting any form of terrorist activity. Increasing NIF criticism of the West and Sudanese Government actions, however, such as the execution of two Sudanese US Government employees in the southern city of Juba, indicate a hardening of Sudanese attitudes that may reflect mounting sympathy to Islamic radicals and terrorists and disregard for US concerns.

Sudan continues to strengthen its ties to Iran, a leading state sponsor of terrorism. Following Iranian President Rafsanjani's December 1991 visit to Khartoum, a high-level Sudanese military delegation visited Tehran during the summer of 1992 to seek increased support for the government's campaign against insurgents in the south. Iranian Revolutionary Guard Corps personnel are involved in training the NIF-controlled national militia, the Peoples Defense Forces (PDF), which is used as an adjunct to the Sudanese Armed Forces.

Asian Overview

Incidents of international terrorism in Asia continued to decline from 48 in 1991 to 13 in 1992. This decrease was primarily a result of the improving political climate in the Philippines. Acts of international terrorism in Thailand, Malaysia, Japan, and South Korea have been infrequent when compared to the level of attacks in many Latin American and European countries. North Korea remains on the list of nations that sponsor terrorism but appears disinclined to pursue a terrorist agenda. As witnessed during the Gulf war, Middle Eastern state sponsors of terrorism—particularly Iran, Iraq, and Libya—may consider Asia an increasingly attractive region as other areas, particularly Europe, intensify their security efforts.

Internal violence and terrorism by Sikh and Kashmiri separatists in India and Tamil insurgents in Sri Lanka continued in 1992, resulting in death and injury to thousands of civilians and potentially placing Americans at risk as targets of opportunity, convenience, or mischance.

Afghanistan

Although widespread violence occurred throughout Afghanistan in 1992, there was only one act of international terrorism there, directed at the International Committee of the Red Cross (ICRC). In April a Red Cross employee from Iceland en route to the ICRC field post at Sheikhabad was shot in the back. The assailant was captured and claimed that he had been directed by his "mullah" to kill non-Muslims. In late November, Gulbuddin Hekmatyar's Islamic opposition party, Hezb-I-Islami, threatened to execute ex-Soviet POW's held by the Hezb-I-Islami and to attack Russian citizens, claiming that Moscow was continuing to interfere in Afghanistan.

The Governments of Algeria, Egypt, and Tunisa have repeatedly claimed that members of Islamic opposition groups received training in Afghanistan while fighting with mujahedin, and may continue to receive some support. These governments claim that these fundamentalists are now using their acquired skills to undertake terrorist attacks in their own countries.

India

The level of internal violence and terrorism continued at a high rate throughout 1992, as Kasmiri, Punjabi, and Assamese separatists conducted attacks as part of their ongoing efforts to win independence for their states.

Jammu and Kashmir and the Punjab are the two areas hardest hit by terrorist violence. More than 4,000 civilians are believed to have died in 1992 as result of the violence in these two areas. Kashmiri and Sikh militants carried out repeated attacks against civilian targets, such as buses, trains, and marketplaces. In one of the deadliest attacks, a bomb exploded on a bus in Jammu in September, killing 11 passengers. In addition, these militants kidnapped and attacked security officials and their families. Some 3,500 militants and security officials also have been killed. There are credible reports of support by the Government of Pakistan for Kashmiri militants and some reports of support for Sikh separatists.

In Assam, the Bodo Security Force (BSF) stepped up its violent campaign, and the United Liberation Front of Assam (ULFA) resorted to kidnappings and extortion. The ULFA threatened a French multinational corporation, demanding either $1.7 million or the company's departure.

In addition to numerous incidents of domestic terrorism, three attacks on India in 1992 involved foreign nationals:

- On 31 March an unidentified assailant threw a grenade while inside a British Broadcasting Corporation office. There was some damage to the office, but no injuries.
- On 23 April a bomb exploded in a New Delhi hotel, injuring 13 foreign tourists. No claim was made by any group for the attack.
- On 5 May two assailants attempted to assassinate a Kuwaiti diplomat in New Delhi.

Indian security captured two top Sikh leaders in July, including the notorious Manjit Singh, alias Lal Singh, allegedly involved in the 1985 downing of an Air India 747 that killed 329 people. Lal Singh was wanted also in the United States, the United Kingdom, and Canada for his role in supporting Sikh terrorism overseas.

Japan

Japan's largest indigenous radical leftist organization, the 3,500-man Chukaku-ha (middle-Core Faction), carried out low-level attacks throughout 1992. The group's operations were designed to win publicity for its policy positions and, generally, not to cause casualties. Chukaku-ha is opposed to the imperial system and Japan's more active foreign policy in Asia, especially Tokyo's deployment of military forces overseas.

Chukaku-ha was particularly active in September and October, when it carried out a series of rocket attacks and bombings to protest the dispatch of Japanese peacekeeping troops to Cambodia and to declare its opposition to the Emperor's visit to China in late October. The group's attacks included the firing of improvised rockets at the home of Defense Agency Director General Miyashita. Chukaku-ha also claimed responsibility for explosions near the house of Japanese parliamentarian Takashi Inoue, the Chairman of the Upper House Steering Committee. The committee had approved a law allowing Japanese Self-Defense Forces to be deployed overseas. There were no injuries and only minor damage in these incidents.

Regarding rightwing terrorism, on 8 January an incendiary device was discovered outside an apartment on the US Embassy housing compound in Tokyo at the time of the incident. The vociferously anti-American extremist group Issuikai (One Water Society) may have been responsible. It had branded Bush a "war criminal," and, in December 1991, threatened to attack the US Embassy. On 25 August, another rightwing group set fire to a truck outside Prime Minister Kiichi Miyazawa's official residence.

The Japanese Red Army (JRA) remained dormant in 1992. In March an Italian court sentenced in absentia JRA member Junzo Okudaira to life imprisonment for the 14 April 1988 bombing of the USO Club in Naples. An American servicewoman and four Italians were killed in that attack. The court cleared JRA leader Fusako Shigenobu of charges related to the bombing. On 10 November the Tokyo High Court upheld the conviction of JRA member Hiroshi Sensui on charges of illegally obtaining a counterfeit passport. He is imprisoned in Japan.

Pakistan

Since the fall of the Najibullah regime in Kabul in the spring of 1992, the level of violent incidents in Pakistan related to Afghan activities has dropped markedly. Assassinations and disappearances of Afghans, however, including personnel employed by US Agency for International Development-funded programs and US private organizations, continued to occur in the North-West Frontier Province in 1992:

- On 9 January an Afghan working for the UN's Operation Salam mine awareness program was shot and killed outside his home in Peshawar.
- On 14 June a Japanese engineer working for the United Nations was killed in Peshawar.

There were numerous domestic terrorist incidents in Pakistan throughout 1992, mostly bombings.

The Government of Pakistan acknowledges that it continues to give moral, political, and diplomatic support to Kashmiri militants but denies allegations of other assistance. However, there were credible reports in 1992 of official Pakistani support for Kashmiri militants who undertake acts of terrorism in Indian-controlled Kashmir, as well as some reports of support to Sikh militants engaged in terrorism in Indian Punjab.

Philippines

There were no terrorist attacks by the Communist Party of the Philippines (CPP) and its military wing, the New People's Army (NPA), against US interests in 1992. In September, Manila legalized the CPP, which over the past several years had carried out assassinations of both US and Philippine officials.

Moreover, American hostages held by the Communists were freed during the year. In late June, the NPA unconditionally released Arvey Drown, who was abducted in Cagayan Province in October 1990. The NPA previously had demanded a government cease-fire in the province as a precondition for the release of Drown.

After his inauguration in June, President Ramos took a series of steps to end the Philippine Communists' 23-year-old insurrection. The government legalized the CPP, repealed the antisubversive act—which made membership in the CPP a crime—and released ranking imprisoned Communists, including Romulo Kintanar, the chief of the NPA. Ongoing trials of NPA detainees were also suspended. At year's end, government efforts to reconcile with the Communists were continuing.

Some Communists, however, continued to threaten American interests. In November, Felipe Marcial, an official of the Communists' National Democratic Front, said that the American military personnel remaining in the Philippines after 31 December would be treated as "occupation troops" and targeted by "revolutionary forces."

Dissident Communists also posed a threat to foreign interests in the Philippines. The Red Scorpion Group (RSG)—a gang composed of some former New People's Army members and criminal elements—kidnapped American businessman Michael Barnes in Manila on 17 January. The group demanded a $20 million ransom. On 18 March, Barnes was rescued when Philippine police launched multiple raids on the RSG's safehouses. In November, RSG leader Alfredo de Leon publicly threatened to bomb embassies in Manila.

In the southern Philippines, American missionary Augustine Fraszczak was kidnapped in October on Basilan Island and freed in late December. Two other American missionaries were kidnapped and subsequently freed in March. The motives for these kidnappings remain uncertain. While there are many criminal bands operating in this area of the Philippines, the separatist Muslim Moro National Liberation Front (MNLF) also remains active. The MNLF denied involvement in these kidnappings.

Sri Lanka

Sri Lanka continues to be the scene of widespread violence. The separatist group Liberation Tigers of Tamil Eelam (LTTE) continued to conduct terrorist acts throughout 1992. Its campaign included targeting civilians, government figures, and public utilities. The LTTE also continued to massacre hundreds of Sinhalese and Muslim villagers in the north and east to drive them from what it calls the Tamil Homeland.

In November an LTTE suicide guerrilla assassinated Sri Lanka's Navy commander by riding his motorcycle close to the officer's car and blowing it up with a powerful bomb.

The Sri Lankan Government has been unable to respond to India's request that it extradite LTTE leader V. Prabhakaran, accused of ordering the May 1991 assassination of former Indian Prime Minister Rajiv Gandhi. Prabhakaran remains at large. However, Sri Lankan officials continued to cooperate with Indian requests for assistance in the investigation. Two senior LTTE officials were indicted by India for their involvement in the assassination.

Thailand

Two serious attacks occurred in Thailand in 1992:

- On 13 August a bomb blast at the Hat Yai railway station in southern Thailand killed three people and wounded over 70 others. Although an unsigned letter bearing the logo of the separatist Pattani United Liberation Organization (PULO) was found on the scene, the group denied involvement and blamed a dissident faction for the attack. Some observers claim the attack was aimed at an antimilitary politician, who spoke at the site later the same day.
- On 18 October a bomb exploded on the compound of the Burmese Embassy in Bangkok. The bomb, containing a half pound of TNT, caused minimal property damage and no injuries. Although Burmese student dissidents may have been responsible—the Burmese Embassy in Bangkok was bombed by dissidents in July and October 1990—some Thai politicians suggested the attack may have been an attempt by regime opponents to embarrass the government.

European Overview

European countries experienced a relatively low level of international terrorism during 1992. The major events in Europe this year—the Olympics in Albertville and Barcelona, the

World's Fair in Seville, and ceremonies marking the 500th anniversary of Columbus's voyage to America—passed virtually without incident. Leftwing terrorist groups, with the exception of Dev Sol in Turkey, were relatively quiet, and Germany's Red Army Faction renounced terrorism altogether, although it my be premature to write the group's obituary. Separatist groups, particularly the Kurdistan Workers Party (PKK) in Turkey and the Provisional Irish Republican Army (PIRA), intensified their attacks on government targets, however, and showed increasing disregard for civilian casualties.

There is a danger that ethnic violence could turn to terrorism in Western and Eastern Europe and in the former Soviet republics as ethnic conflicts and rivalries emerge. European police and security services have taken measures to try to reduce the chances for terrorist organizations or their state sponsors to move agents, weapons, and funds from one country to another as a result of EC 92 initiatives to produce a borderless Europe. Violence against foreigners, which increased dramatically in some countries in 1992, particularly Germany, suggests that Western Europe may increasingly experience rightwing terrorism as European integration and international migration expand.

No Americans died as a result of terrorist attacks in Europe this year, as compared to four in 1991.

Germany

Germany had 28 incidents of international terrorism in 1992, one fewer than in 1991. Those that occurred involved third-country nationals such as the September assassinations of four Kurdish dissidents in Berlin and probably the August murder of a dissident Iranian poet in Bonn.

The Red Army Faction (RAF) in Germany has not adapted its leftist ideology to the post–Cold War world and has essentially abandoned its commitment to violent attacks against the German state and economy. The group has apparently not been able to recruit replacements for its aging, imprisoned members. It has not launched an attack since firing on the US Embassy in Bonn in February 1991. In April 1992, RAF leaders announced a cease-fire, demanding in return the release of imprisoned terrorists, improved treatment for remaining RAF inmates, and German Government flexibility on a variety of social issues.

Two German relief workers (Kemptner and Struebig), the last of the Western hostages held in Lebanon, were released on 17 June 1992 after three years of captivity.

Their abductors continue to press for release from German prisons of fellow Hizballah members Mohammed Ali Hammadi and his brother Abbas Ali Hammadi. Mohammed Ali Hammadi, imprisoned for the murder of an American, air piracy, hostage taking, aggravated battery, illegal importation of explosives, and forgery, is serving a life sentence. Abbas Ali Hammadi was sentenced to 13 years of imprisonment for plotting the kidnapping of two West Germans in the hope of forcing the release of his brother. The German Government has refused to yield to terrorist demands.

Rightwing sentiment increased in Western Europe during 1992. The greatest risk of rightwing violence resembling terrorism in 1992 was in Germany, where skinheads and neo-Nazis committed more than 2,000 attacks on foreigners; these included firebombings and brutal assaults resulting in the deaths of at least 17 people. Extreme rightwing leaders have capitalized on dissatisfaction with mainstream political parties, high unemployment rates, the arrival of hundreds of thousands of immigrants from Eastern Europe and the Third World, and latent xenophobia. Thus far, neither the skinheads nor the neo-Nazis have organized beyond the local level, and they have not joined forces with nationally organized far-right political parties. They have apparently had some contact with members of hate groups such as the Ku Klux Klan.

Greece

Although it did not attack any US target in 1992, the Greek Revolutionary Organization 17 November still poses a serious threat to US citizens. Its operations during 1992 were more reckless and less well planned than in the past, increasing the risk of incidental injury. In July, for the first time, the group killed a bystander in the course of a rocket attack in downtown Athens on the Greek Finance Minister. In late November, authorities arrested one of Greece's most wanted terrorists—a suspected member of the "Anti-State Struggle" organization who may be linked to 17 November. The group continued to attack official Greek targets, including the shooting in December of a Greek parliamentarian and the bombings of tax offices.

Spain

Incidents of international terrorism in Spain fell sharply. Neither of the country's major terrorist groups—Basque Fatherland and Liberty (ETA) or the First October Antifascist Resistance Group (GRAPO)—mounted attacks in Spain during the Barcelona Olympics or the Seville World's Fair.

ETA suffered a severe setback early in 1992 when Spanish and French police arrested three of its top leaders and more than 100 terrorists and collaborators, thereby disrupting its financial and logistic infrastructure. Midlevel leaders and several experienced terrorists remain at large, however, and ETA claimed responsibility for several attacks against Spanish officials and against Spanish and French interests in France and Italy. The preferred ETA targets continue to be Spanish business interests, National Police Guardia Civil, and the military, but not foreign nationals.

GRAPO carried out several low-level bombings against Spanish targets this year. Fernando Silva Sande, one of its key leaders, escaped from prison in March and remains at large. Although GRAPO is opposed to Spanish membership in NATO and to the US military presence in Spain, it did not attack US or NATO targets in 1992. In December paramilitary police arrested Laureano Ortega Ortega, leader of the group's last known operational cell in Spain.

Turkey

Among European groups, the Turkish revolutionary leftist group Dev Sol remains the major terrorist threat to Americans. US military personnel and commercial facilities are prime targets. The group tried to assassinate a US religious hospital administrator with a car bomb in Istanbul in July and also attacked the US Consulate General in Istanbul twice, in April and July. Dev Sol currently is recovering from the arrests of a number of its leaders and raids on several safehouses in the spring and summer of 1992.

The Kurdistan Workers Party (PKK) poses a growing threat to US personnel and facilities in Turkey, even though the group is not targeting Americans directly. It started as a rural-based insurgency but over the last year has increased operations in major cities such as Istanbul, Adana, and Izmir as well as in the Anatolia tourist region. In the summer and fall of 1992, the PKK launched six attacks on Turkish/Western joint–venture oil facilities in southeastern Turkey, fire bombed several commuter ferries, burned three passenger trains and derailed a fourth, and probably was responsible for firing at a Turkish airliner departing from Adana. Although no deaths resulted, such attacks markedly increase the chances of random injury to US citizens. The Turkish military campaign against the PKK in Iraq and Turkey killed hundreds of guerillas but did not deal a fatal blow to the group.

The shadowy Turkish Islamic Jihad remains a threat to US interests in Turkey. The group has claimed responsibility for eight operations since 1985, including car-bomb attacks that killed a US serviceman in October 1991 and an Israeli diplomat in March 1992. The group appears to be comprised of local fundamentalists sympathetic to Tehran. All of its targets have been external enemies of the Iranian regime.

United Kingdom

In 1992, as in 1991, there were no incidents of international terrorism in the United Kingdom. Sectarian violence, however, produced 84 terrorist-related deaths, only slightly fewer than the 94 in 1991. For the first time in the 24-year-old conflict, victims (38) of Protestant loyalist attacks exceeded those (34) of the Provisional Irish Republican Army (PIRA). There have been 3,029 sectarian terrorist-related deaths since 1969.

The Strand talks aimed at bringing together all parties on the Northern Ireland question ended in November with the fall of the Irish Government. Nevertheless, while the talks have not provided any major breakthroughs, all parties appear interested in pursuing them.

The PIRA remains by far the most active and lethal terrorist group in Western Europe. In April, following the British election, it exploded a van bomb—the largest ever detonated on the British mainland—in London's financial district, killing three people and wounding more than 90 others, including one American. The amount of property damage caused by this single attack is estimated to be $1.5 billion. The PIRA launched a bombing spree in London against train stations, hotels, and shopping areas in the autumn of 1992—16 attacks in October alone—that resembled its terror campaign of the mid-1970s. The latest round would have been even more devastating had police not found and defused three bombs loaded in abandoned vans; two of the three contained over 1 ton of explosives each. British insurance companies announced at the end of the year that terrorism riders on building insurance would be dropped because of the large costs of bomb damage.

Former Yugoslavia

During 1992 regions of the former Yugoslavia were convulsed by ethnic and religious conflict. The death toll in this violence was great, and the range of human rights abuses, horrific crimes, and atrocities against civilians was more extensive than any similar situation in Europe since World War II. The US Government has consistently condemned this violence and kept under close scrutiny the possible international terrorist dimension of the situation.

Former Soviet Union

In the newly independent states of the former Soviet Union, there were activities traditionally associated with terrorism—such as bombings, kidnappings, and hijackings. They generally have been related to civil wars and have not been directed against foreign interests. The potential for ethnic-based terrorism is growing as national groups assert themselves following decades of Communist-imposed "peaceful coexistence." Moreover, the Central Asian region in particular offers potentially fertile ground for some Middle Eastern groups, particularly Iran-supported Hizballah, to operate or seek recruits.

Latin American Overview

Although Latin America was again the leading region for International terrorist incidents, with 142 attacks reported against foreign interests, this number was far below the record 230 attacks in 1991. The bombing of Israel's Embassy in Buenos Aires was a troubling intrusion of Middle Eastern violence and the single most lethal terrorist event of the year. As in previous years, however, international incidents comprised only a small percentage of the total number of terrorist operations. In Peru and Colombia, where problems are greatest, terrorist insurgents and narcotraffickers focused their operations on domestic targets—government institutions and personnel, economic infrastructure, and security forces. The great majority of international incidents occurred in South America, with only a few isolated attacks in Central America and the Caribbean. The only two American deaths during 1992 in acts of international terrorism occurred in Latin America.

There have been notable counterterrorism successes in Latin America in 1992, particularly in Peru and Bolivia, where insurgent groups suffered major blows with the capture of top leaders. Insurgent groups have steadily become more isolated politically in Colombia, as a violence-weary public supported stronger counterterrorism measures. Virtually all Latin American terrorist groups had plans for violent protest of the 500th anniversary of Columbus's voyage to the New World. Increased security and low-key commemorations in many countries, however, resulted in relatively few, mostly symbolic, incidents. Spanish-affiliated banks, businesses, and diplomatic premises were the most frequently targeted during the commemorative period.

Argentina

Relatively free of terrorist problems in recent years, Argentina was the site of the single most destructive terrorist act in Latin America in 1992. On 17 March a car bomb virtually destroyed the Israeli Embassy in Buenos Aires, killing 29 people and injuring 242. The Islamic Jihad organization, an arm of the Lebanese Hizballah, took responsibility for the attack, claiming it was in retaliation for the Israeli attack that killed Hizballah leader Sheikh Musawi in February. When the authenticity of this claim was questioned, the group responded by releasing a videotape of the Israeli Embassy taken during surveillance before the bombing. The bombing focused attention on Hizballah activity in Latin America, where communities of recent Shiite Muslim émigrés in the remote border areas of Argentina, Brazil, and Paraguay could provide cover for international terrorists.

Bolivia

Several relatively unsophisticated terrorist groups continue to operate in Bolivia. However, the Bolivian Government's improvements in counterterrorism programs over the past two years resulted in significant successes in the effort to counter these.

Government counterterrorist forces captured the current leaders of the Tupac Katari Guerrilla Army (EGTK), one of Bolivia's indigenous Indian-based terrorist groups, severely affecting the organization. Also apprehended was one of the remaining perpetrators of the Zarate Willka Liberation Armed Forces (FALZW) attacks on Secretary of State Shultz's La Paz motorcade in 1988 and of the murder of two Mormon missionaries in 1989. The captured terrorist's testimony assisted government prosecutors in deflating attempts to overturn the lengthy sentences for those FALZW members already in prison. The government also moved forward with the trial of the Commission Nestor Paz Zamora (CNPZ) terrorists who attacked the US Marine House in 1990.

The National Liberation Army (ELN), thought to contain elements of several Bolivian radical groups, resurfaced and claimed responsibility for several minor bombings of government buildings and power pylons. Two attacks on Mormon churches were claimed by the EGTK.

Reports of increased cooperation between Peruvian terrorists and the EGTK and ELN in the border regions raised concerns in both countries, and the Bolivian and Peruvian Governments pledged cooperation in combating terrorism. Terrorist groups have attempted to exploit public resentment at the US role in counternarcotics efforts, but there is only fragmentary evidence of cooperation between Bolivian guerrillas and narcotraffickers.

Chile

While terrorist organizations have steadily lost their popular appeal as Chile solidifies its return to democracy, some old-line leftwing groups remain active and continue to present a limited terrorist threat. There were 39 international terrorist incidents in Chile in 1992, down from 52 in 1991, with the Manuel Rodriguez Patriot Front (FPMR) and the Latauro Youth Movement (MJL) the groups deemed responsible for these and the vast majority of domestic terrorist attacks. Virtually all of these attacks were minor, resulting almost exclusively in property damages only.

The Communist-affiliated FPMR generally sought to attack Chilean targets, particularly government buildings and banks, as well as politicians and members of the uniformed national police, the Carabineros. The MJL claimed responsibility for 27 attacks throughout Chile, as well as bank robberies and extortions of local businesses. Virtually all the attacks on Mormon churches were small-scale bombings that caused minor property damage and no serious physical injuries. Both groups carried out low-level, largely symbolic bombings of foreign interests to protest the Columbus anniversary celebrations in October, including the bombing of the Abraham Lincoln memorial near the US Embassy.

Colombia

There were 68 international terrorist incidents in Colombia in 1992, five more than in 1991. This is the largest number of terrorist incidents in any nation. Even with this large number of incidents, international terrorism was overshadowed by the marked increase in domestic violence in the latter half of the year. Continued terrorism by the Colombian guerrilla organizations, the Revolutionary Armed Forces of Colombia (FARC), the National Liberation Army (ELN), and the umbrella group the Simon Bolivar Guerrilla Coordinator (CGSB) was compounded by narcotraffickers seeking to prevent the recapture of Medellin narcotics kingpin Pablo Escobar, who escaped from prison in July.

The wave of terrorism began in earnest in October and showed no signs of abating as the year ended. Most disturbing was evidence that the ELN, possibly assisted by narcoterrorists, had developed sufficient urban infrastructure to carry out a sustained terrorist offensive in Bogota. In December a series of hotel bombings, including some tourist hotels frequented by foreigners, raised concerns that foreign visitors would become victims of random violence.

In addition to the largely symbolic foreign targets attacked during the Columbus anniversary in October, there were nearly 50 attacks on the oil pipeline jointly owned by Ecopetrol of Colombia and a consortium of US and West European countries, a traditional Colombian guerilla target. There were also six reported cases of international kidnapping. Two kidnap victims, one US and one British citizen were killed by their captors. The American, naturalized US citizen Jose Lopez, was kidnapped on 8 January by members of the National Liberation Army at his place of work. He was subsequently killed, although his kidnappers withheld this information until after the family had paid ransom.

Peace talks convened in Mexico between the guerrillas, and the government of President Cesar Gaviria foundered in May on Gaviria's demand of a universal cease-fire before negotiations could progress. After the ELN admitted that a kidnapped senior Colombian politician had died even before formal negotiations began, the government suspended peace talks indefinitely. The guerrillas, slipping drastically in public opinion, reverted to violence and economic sabotage and demanded regional cease-fires that would permit them freedom of action. President Gaviria chose to press the guerrillas militarily and ruled out an early return to negotiations without some concrete sign that the guerrillas would negotiate in good faith.

President Gaviria's task was complicated by an increase in narcotics-related violence in late 1992 as the government heightened efforts to recapture Escobar. Narcotrafficker assassinations of Colombian National Police personnel increased dramatically, especially in October and November. As the hunt continued, President Gaviria expressed concern that Escobar had attempted an alliance with the guerrillas, particularly the ELN. Although there is no evidence of a formal alliance, traffickers and guerrillas may be exchanging information and occasionally supporting one another's attacks. At a minimum, guerrillas have used government preoccupation with Escobar to expand their own operations.

President Gaviria used the public's antipathy toward violence as a strong mandate to exert force against both guerrillas and traffickers. The president has publicly insisted on unconditional surrender for Escobar and has refused any concessions to guerrillas as long as violence continues unabated. However, both Colombian military and police resources have been stretched by the requirements of the two-front war. Judicial reforms, such as the July decree establishing "faceless judges" for terrorist and narcotics offenses, may eventually prove effective. In September, however, one such jurist in Medellin was gunned down in broad daylight by narcotraffickers.

Panama

One of two American fatalities from terrorism in Latin America in 1992 occurred in Panama just before a visit by President Bush in June. On 10 June, Sgt. Owell Hernandez was killed in Panama when the US Army vehicle he was driving was raked by automatic gunfire from a passing car. Anti-US forces associated with the former Noriega regime have attacked US interests and are believed responsible for the fatal shooting, as well as two other low-level bombings at American military installations in Panama in 1992.

Terrorists operate under a variety of names in Panama, and it is likely that the so-called M-20 group that has claimed many of the bombings is actually made up of adherents of various terrorist groups. Although small and lacking widespread popular support, these groups contain a high proportion of trained ex-military personnel. Access to arms and explosives in Panama makes these groups potential threats to US interests.

Peru

Guerrillas of the Maoist Peruvian Communist Party, commonly known as Sendero Luminoso (SL), and the Cuban-style Tupac Amaru Revolutionary Movement (MRTA) continued to make Peru the most dangerous country in South America in 1992. Peruvians suffered by far the most, with a large number of terrorist attacks of various origins claiming many civilian lives. There were 13 attacks against foreign interests in Peru, chiefly in Lima, down from 59 in 1991. Targets included embassies, banks and international businesses. SL was responsible for most of the incidents, as the group mounted its most serious threat yet to the government. In well-planned urban campaigns in February, May, and July, Sendero used "armed strikes" against public transportation, assassinations, and car bombings to sap public morale and give weight to its claim of having reached a position of strategic equally with the government. In one of its boldest attacks, SL terrorists set off a massive car bomb at the American Ambassador's residence in February. The blast killed three Peruvian policemen and caused extensive damage to the residence.

During 1992 two foreign deaths were attributed to SL, an Italian priest killed in August and a Yugoslav engineer in September. These were the first terrorism-related deaths of foreigners in over a year.

President Alberto Fujimori's decision to suspend constitutional government in Peru on 5 April was in large part a result of frustration with the government's difficulty in countering terrorist successes. The President quickly proceeded with a number of stiff antiterrorism measures, including new judicial procedures and a revamping of intelligence on terrorist groups. Human rights abuses by government counterterrorist and counternarcotics forces continue, albeit less frequently. A series of government successes, including the shutting down of SL's newspaper, the recapture of terrorist-controlled Canto Grande prison in Lima, and the capture of some key Sendero urban operatives, was countered by renewed SL car-bomb onslaughts in late May and mid-July, when a bomb in the upscale Miraflores district of Lima killed at least 18 Peruvians and injured more than 100.

Peru's counterterrorist forces responded on 12 September with the stunning capture in Lima of Sendero founder and leader Abimael Guzman. Many members of SL's high command were captured with Guzman or in the wake of his arrest. Quick trials and convictions of Guzman and other terrorist leaders boosted the morale of both the security forces and the public. Throughout the last quarter of 1992,

Peruvian counterterrorism forces kept the pressure on SL, netting more leaders and hundreds of rank-and-file cadres. Sendero's efforts to disrupt elections for a new constituent assembly in November were largely thwarted.

The capture of Guzman and most of the leadership dealt Sendero's prospects for victory a major blow. Although SL has lost some of its ability to intimidate and destabilize, it has continued car bombings and assassinations throughout the country. Guzman's exhortation after his capture for a renewed war against imperialism was interpreted by some as a call for SL to intensify attacks on foreign targets. In late December, Sendero attacked several foreign embassies, hitting the Chinese twice, to mark the centenary of the birth of Mao Tse-Tung. In the countryside, government counterinsurgency forces are stretched thin, and SL units continue to operate freely in many areas. Sendero has a relatively secure base area in the coca-growing region of the Huallaga River Valley and exploits the drug trade in various ways to finance group operations.

The government has had even greater success in combating MRTA, which had been weakened by internal splits and the declining appeal of Cuban-style Marxism. In June security forces recaptured MRTA leader Victor Polay, who had escaped prison in July of 1991. MRTA urban terrorists, who in the past were considered more dangerous to foreign interests than SL, operated at a greatly reduced level in 1992. In 1991 the group was suspected in the majority of the 34 attacks against US interests, but in 1992 it attempted only two low-level attacks. An October mortar attack on the US Ambassador's residence and a November attack on a US Embassy warehouse caused little damage and no casualties.

Middle Eastern Overview

There were 79 international terrorist incidents in the Middle East during 1992, the same number of incidents that occurred the previous year. Most of the 1991 incidents were low-level attacks in Lebanon and elsewhere; many of these were related to the Gulf war and the Israeli self-declared security zone on southern Lebanon. The bulk of attacks in 1992 were Iraqi-sponsored attacks against UN personnel working in Iraq.

Iran's ongoing state sponsorship of terrorism, including its efforts to build closer ties to non-Shia terrorist groups, poses significant threats in the Middle East, Europe, Africa, and Latin America. Iranian-backed Lebanese militants claimed responsibility for one of the year's terrorist "spectaculars"—the March 1992 car-bombing of the Israeli Embassy in Buenos Aires, in which 29 people died and 242 were injured. Hizballah was responsible for several rocket attacks into areas near Israel's northern border. The trial in Amman of two Jordanian parliamentarians brought forth charges that Iran was supporting sedition against the terrorism aimed at disrupting the Arab-Israeli peace process.

Continued sanctions and international isolation of Iraq hampered Saddam's regime's ability to conduct acts of international terrorism during 1992. Nevertheless, the Iraqis were able to carry out the brazen murder of a defecting Iraqi nuclear scientist on the streets of Amman late in the year. Iraq continued to provide its traditional support and safehaven to terrorist Palestinian elements such as Palestine Liberation Front leader Abu Abbas. In addition to its support for international terrorism, the Iraqi regime was also responsible for numerous attacks on UN and humanitarian relief personnel working in Iraq pursuant to the Security Council resolutions.

There has been no evidence of direct Syrian Government involvement in terrorist acts since 1986, but Syria continues to provide support and safehaven to Arab and non-Arab terrorist organizations in Syria and in parts of Lebanon in which Syrian troops are deployed.

In defiance of UN resolutions demanding that support cease, Libya continued to sponsor international terrorism during 1992. Tripoli has defied international demands that those believed responsible for the bombings of Pan Am Flight 103 and UTA Flight 772 be handed over for trial. Qaddafi's regime made partial moves to close some terrorist training camps but still provides support and safehaven to such notorious terrorists as Abu Nidal.

The year saw a marked increase in domestic terrorism in Egypt, as Islamic radical elements expanded their antigovernment campaign by targeting foreign tourists in addition to Egyptian Coptic Christians and security officials. Among the most serious incidents was an attack in October on a tourist bus, which left a British woman dead and two other people injured; a similar attack on a bus of German tourists wounded five. The Egyptian Government cited support offered the radicals by Iran and Sudan as a contributing factor in the violence.

The terrorism picture in North Africa is mixed; the overall situation in Tunisia improved, but Algeria suffered from a rash of terrorist attacks, including the bloody 26 August explosion at Algiers Airport that resulted in 12 deaths. Lesser bomb attacks were directed against the offices of foreign airlines. In both countries, the governments contend that Sudan and Iran are providing support to organizations responsible for the attacks.

International terrorism by Palestinian groups decreased from 17 incidents in 1991 to three incidents in 1992. Much of the decrease can be attributed to restrictions placed on the activities of these groups by Syria and Libya. However, internecine struggles between Palestinian groups—particularly in Lebanon between PLO elements and the Abu Nidal organization (ANO)—generated significant violence.

The year also witnessed a considerable upsurge in violence carried out by the Islamic Resistance Movement (HAMAS). In addition to a number of lethal attacks against Israeli military targets, elements of the group were also responsible for the terrorist abduction and murder of an off-duty Israeli border policeman near Tel Aviv and have claimed responsibility for the murder of an Israeli merchant in Gaza. Over the course of the year, HAMAS's antimilitary and terrorist operations displayed a new daring and sophistication.

Yemen witnessed an upsurge of terrorism in 1992, as a spate of bombs that the Government of Yemen believes were planted by an Islamic extremist group were aimed at both Yemeni and foreign targets. Bombings at a hotel and a hotel parking lot in Aden in December killed one person and injured several others.

Algeria

Political violence in Algeria increased rapidly after the Algerian Government suspended in January 1992 the second round of elections, which the fundamentalist Islamic Salvation Front (FIS) was poised to win. The FIS was outlawed as a political party in March 1992. The fundamentalists' attacks have focused primarily on official and military targets, but some have also been directed at civilian and Western interests. President Boudiaf was assassinated in June 1992 by a security official whom the official inquiry described as having Islamist sympathies. The Government of Algeria has consistently attributed terrorist violence to the FIS and prosecuted alleged FIS members for terrorist activity. Regime repression has split the FIS into a number of militant independent cells that have gone underground, become more violent, and generally do not appear to be operating under any central command and control structure. The growing popular discontent with the government and the economy is broadening the appeal of these militants. Algerian officials, including Prime Minister Belaid Abdesselam, have pointed to a "foreign hand" behind terrorist activity but have offered no evidence. Algeria ordered Tehran to reduce its diplomatic staff to "symbolic" levels in November because of its belief that Tehran supported Algerian fundamentalists.

The number and sophistication of terrorist attacks in Algeria gradually increased during 1992, moving from primitive black-powder explosives to more complex devices such as car bombs. In January, bombs that were thrown at the US Embassy and French Consulate in Algiers were improvised, low-yield devises. By contrast, a timer-triggered, high-explosive device was used in the bombing of Boumedienne International Airport in August, which resulted in 12 deaths. Militant elements of the FIS as well as other Islamic opposition groups have also shown an improving capability to coordinate their attacks nationwide. For example, they attempted to bomb two Western airline offices at virtually the same time as the Boumedienne Airport bombing. The first use of a car bomb occurred on 31 October near an Algiers shopping area and resulted in at least three injuries.

The Algerian Government's response to the challenge to its authority in 1992 included a number of military-style operations, launched in May and June, against armed extremist groups operating southeast of Algiers and the creation in September of elite military units specifically charged with antiterrorist responsibilities. In October, Algiers promulgated a strict antiterrorist law that sharply increased the penalties for "terrorist" crimes and expanded the number of special antiterrorist courts. In the new law, Algiers has defined terrorism in very broad terms that cover most antiregime activity. Despite these measures—which also included mass arrests and the creation of detention camps for detainees—the number of attacks against regime targets had not diminished by year's end.

In 1992, the government continued to allow radical Palestinian groups that have been associated with terrorism to maintain a presence in Algeria. In April, the regime issued a statement condemning terrorism but questioned the legality of the sanctions imposed on Libya under UN Security Council Resolutions 731 and 748. The government has abided by most provisions of Resolution 748 but has not reduced the level of Libyan diplomatic representation, as required by the resolution.

Egypt

Egypt suffered a marked increase in terrorism in 1992, although there were no terrorist attacks against Americans or US interests. In May, Islamic extremists added foreign tourists to their other targets—Egyptian officials, Egyptian Coptic Christians, and secularist Egyptian Muslims—in a campaign of attacks against the Mubarak government. Most attacks have occurred in central and southern Egypt. Among the most serious incidents were the 21 October shooting attack on a tourist bus near Dayrut, which killed one British tourist and wounded two others; the 2 November shooting attack on a bus carrying 55 Egyptian Coptic Christians near Al Minya, which wounded 10 people; and the 12 November attack on another tourist bus near Qena, which wounded five German tourists and one Egyptian. In addition, Dr. Fara Foda, a prominent Egyptian politician and a strong opponent of Islamic extremism, was assassinated on 8 June in Cairo by Islamic extremists.

Most of the attacks in 1992 were perpetrated by the al-Gama'a al-Islamiyya extremist group, which was also responsible for the assassination of People's Assembly speaker al-Mahgoub in October 1990. This group seeks the violent overthrow of the Egyptian government and has targeted the tourist industry, Egypt's second-largest earner of foreign exchange, as well as Egyptian officials and Christians. Sheikh Omar Abdurrahman, a senior leader in the al-Gama'a al-Islamiyya movement, has been in the United States since 1990. US authorities are moving expeditiously with the aim of ensuing the Sheikh's departure from this country. Al-Gama'a al-Islamiyya is basically indigenous but receives support from Sudan and possibly Iran and has established ties to other militant Islamic movements.

The Egyptian Government has responded to the upsurge in terrorism with a series of tough law-and-order measures. After the assassination of Farag Foda, Egypt's People's Assembly in July passed wide-ranging, antiterrorist amendments to the penal code, including instituting the death penalty or life imprisonment for convicted terrorists and expanding police detention powers. The government has used these new laws to launch a massive security crackdown, primarily in southern Egypt and parts of Cairo, resulting in the detention of hundreds of suspected members of al-Gama'a al-Islamiyya and other extremist organizations. On 3 December, moreover, an Egyptian military court handed down death sentences to eight Muslim extremists, seven of whom were sentenced in absentia, for plotting the violent overthrow of the government. The court also gave prison sentences ranging from one year to life imprisonment to 31 other extremists.

The Egyptian Government cooperates with the United States and other countries in counterterrorism programs and has taken steps to strengthen its capabilities. It has publicly supported broader international efforts to combat terrorism, including improved intelligence sharing, strengthened counterterrorism protocols, and increased counterterrorism assistance to developing countries. Although there has been no reduction of Libya's diplomatic presence in Egypt, or vice versa, as mandated by UN sanctions in effect against Libya as of December, Cairo had not designated an ambassador to Libya as of December 1992 and has observed the civil air and arms sanctions.

Israel and the Occupied Territories

There was a sharp increase in terrorism and violence in Israel and the occupied territories at the end of 1992. The kidnapping and murder of an off-duty Israeli border guard by HAMAS—the Islamic Resistance Movement in the occupied territories—from a Tel Aviv suburb in mid-December resulted in a crackdown on Palestinian Islamic extremists, which included the deportation of over 400 suspected members and sympathizers of HAMAS and the Palestinian Islamic Jihad (PIJ) to a remote hillside in southern Lebanon. The slaying of the border guard was part of a larger overall trend by HAMAS militants toward increasingly bold operations against Israeli security forces, which included ambushes of military units in Gaza and Hebron in early December that killed four soldiers. Many such operations, including the murder of an elderly merchant in the Gaza Strip in May, were attributed to the military arm of HAMAS, the Izz ad-Din al-Qassam Forces.

In 1992, Israel carried out major counterterrrorist operations against Hizballah and the Popular Front for the Liberation of Palestine (PFLP). In February, an Israeli Defense Forces (IDF) helicopter unit killed Hizballah's leader, Abbas Musawi, his wife, and six-year-old child in southern Lebanon. In mid-September, Shin Bet—the internal security service—and the IDF captured the reputed head of the PFLP in the occupied territories, Ahmad Qattamash and seized the group's regional archives. Qattamash has been charged with "providing services to an illegal organization" but not with terrorist activity. In addition to the deportations to Lebanon, during 1992 Shin Bet and the IDF detained more than 1,000 people accused of being members of HAMAS, the PIJ, the Democratic Front for the Liberation of Palestine (DFLP), and the PFLP in several roundups in the occupied territories. According to the Government of Israel, Israeli authorities interrogate approximately 3,000 persons a year on suspicion of involvement in, or support for, terrorism.

Because of stepped-up border security by Israeli, Egyptian, and Jordanian forces, there were only seven guerrilla infiltration attempts from Lebanon, Jordan, and Egypt in 1992, as compared to more than 20 in 1991. Two of the attempts in 1992 were seaborne operations, including an attempt near Eilat in May in which one Israeli was killed. The infiltrators were linked to Fatah, the PIJ, and the DFLP. In most cases, the infiltrators failed to penetrate the Israeli border, and the precise intended targets were not clear. Nonetheless, Israeli communities along the border with Lebanon, as well as IDF and Army of South Lebanon units deployed in the security zone, remained vulnerable to paramilitary attacks from Syrian- and Iranian-backed militants based in southern Lebanon. Without apparent regard for the nature of the target, Hizballah fired rocket volleys into Israel and the security zone several times in 1992.

Israeli personnel and facilities were the targets of two terrorist attacks outside Israel in 1992, both in the aftermath of the killing of Sheikh Abbas Musawi. In March, suspected Hizballah members detonated a car bomb in front of the Israeli Embassy in Buenos Aires. Twenty-nine people were killed, more than 240 were wounded, and the building was destroyed. Also in March, a security officer at the Israeli Embassy in Ankara was killed by a bomb placed beneath his car; Iranian-backed Turkish fundamentalists are the leading suspects in the attack.

In 1992, Israel conducted no significant prosecutions of international terrorists, and it neither carried out nor requested any extraditions for terrorism. Israel's highest court upheld the deportation to Lebanon of Palestinian fundamentalists alleged to support terrorism. On 2 December, a bill to repeal the provision of the 1948 Prevention of Terrorism Ordinance that forbids contact with groups defined by Israel as terrorist passed a first reading in the Israeli parliament.

Intra-Palestinian violence in the occupied territories—mostly between Fatah and HAMAS—increased overall during 1992. The number of incidents rose in Gaza and declined somewhat in the West Bank. Nearly 200 Palestinians were killed by other Arabs in the occupied territories in 1992, as compared with some 140 in 1991.

Israeli authorities believe Jewish extremists were responsible for several anti-Palestinian and anti-US incidents in 1992. The Hashmona'im organization attempted to shoot at the house of the Mayor of Bethlehem in February. Members of the Kach party tried to assault Palestinian negotiator Faisal Husseini in a Jerusalem courtroom in May and may have been responsible for a grenade attack on a Jerusalem market in November. In addition, Jewish extremists attacked Palestinians in Jerusalem and the occupied territories many times in 1992. Israeli security and police increased their surveillance of Kach and other extreme right factions such as Hashmona'im and Gideon's Sword.

Jordan

The principal terrorism-related events in Jordan in 1992 were the December assassination of an Iraqi nuclear scientist on the streets of Amman and the conviction and subsequent royal pardon of two Jordanian legislators for involvement with a subversive Muslim group, Shabab al-Nafer al-Islami

(Vanguard of the Islamic Youth). During the trial of the two in October, prosecutors alleged that the Vanguard planned to attack the US, British, and French Embassies in Amman and conduct cross-border raids into the West Bank. Jordanian authorities also charged that the Vanguard received funding from Iran via the Popular Front for the Liberation of Palestine-General Command (PFLP-GC). In mid-November, a state security court convicted the legislators on several counts of criminal antiregime activity and sentenced them to 20 years at hard labor. A few days later, King Hussein granted a general pardon to prisoners convicted of political crimes in Jordan, and the two were released.

Jordanian security and police closely monitor secular and Islamic extremists inside the country and detain individuals suspected of involvement in violent acts aimed at destabilizing the government or its relations with neighboring states. Besides the crackdown on the Vanguard, Jordanian police in late November closed a PFLP-GC office in Amman and arrested several group members on charges of subversive activity. Islamic militants suspected of instigating violence have also been targeted for special scrutiny by Jordanian authorities. Security services cracked down on the fundamentalist Muhammad's Army in 1991, and no successor group of the same stature emerged in 1992. In addition, Jordan has tightened security along its border with Israel and last year interdicted several armed infiltration operations claimed by, or attributed to, factions of Arafat's Fatah or the Palestine Islamic Jihad (PIJ).

Jordan continues to recognize the "State of Palestine." It hosts a Palestinian "embassy" as well as offices of Fatah and such PLO "rejectionists" as the Popular Front for the Liberation of Palestine and the Democratic Front for the Liberation of Palestine. HAMAS—the Islamic Resistance Movement in the occupied territories—has an office in Amman. In addition, some extremist Palestinian groups with a history of anti-Western terrorist activity—including the PFLP-GC, Abu Abbas's faction of the Palestine Liberation Front, and some elements of the PIJ—maintain a presence in Jordan.

Kuwait

There were several minor terrorist incidents in Kuwait in 1992. On 26 June, a bomb blast at the residence of the Dean of Kuwait University's medical faculty killed the dean's gardener. In July, Kuwaiti police arrested a group of so-called freelance criminals and charged them with responsibility for the bombing. A trial date for the suspects has not been set. On 9 and 11 December, bombs exploded in a suburb of Kuwait City, causing damage to a video store and three nearby shops, but not injuries. No one claimed responsibility for the blast, although video shops in Kuwait have been targets of Islamic extremists.

Kuwait maintained its firm antiterrorist policy through 1992. Regarding Pan Am Flight 103, Kuwait complied with UN Security Council Resolution 748—which mandated a "significant reduction" in Libya's diplomatic presence—by expelling two Libyan diplomats during the summer. Kuwait also rejected Tripoli's request to reopen the Libyan Arab Airlines office.

Lebanon

In 1992 the number of international terrorist incidents in Lebanon dropped to a total of six as compared to 32 in 1991. The attacks resulted in two people killed and 10 wounded. Late in 1992, one Nepalese soldier—attached to the United Nations Interim Force (UNIFIL)—and one Israeli boy were killed in Hizballah rocket attacks on UN positions and Northern Israel. Ten other people were wounded in 1992 terrorist operations that included car bombings, shootings, and rocket attacks.

During 1992, Lebanon's central government continued to extend its authority beyond the Beirut and Tripoli areas to parts of the Syrian-controlled Bekaa Valley. In late July, the Lebanese Armed Forces, apparently with Syrian approval, reclaimed the Haykh Abdallah Barracks, a military training facility occupied by Iranian Revolutionary Guards and Hizballah fighters since 1982; late in the year, government authority was also extended into Beirut's southern suburbs. The Lebanese Government, however, has not taken steps necessary to disarm Hizballah or to expand its authority into areas of southern Lebanon controlled by Hizballah or the Israeli-backed southern Lebanon Army (SLA). Syria continues to maintain a sizable military presence in northern and eastern Lebanon, and Israel continues to occupy a self-declared security zone in the south.

An Israeli Defense Forces helicopter unit ambushed a Hizballah convoy in southern Lebanon on 16 February, killing the group's leader, Abbas Musawi, his wife, and six-year-old son. On 17 March, Islamic Jihad—a covername for Hizballah—publicly claimed responsibility for car bombing Israel's Embassy in Argentina in retaliation for the killing of Musawi. The attack killed 29 persons and injured more than 240 others. Islamic Jihad released a videotape of the Embassy taken before the bombing to authenticate its claim to have conducted Hizballah's first attack outside Lebanon since 1988.

In 1992, Iran, Iraq, Syria, and Libya continued to provide varying degrees of financial, military, and logistic support to terrorist groups based in Lebanon. In addition to the radical Shia group, Hizballah—which was legally recognized as a political party during the year and won eight of 128 seats in Lebanese parliamentary elections in August and September—several radical Palestinian groups have training facilities in Lebanon. These include the Popular Front for the Liberation of Palestine-General Command (PFLP-GC), the Palestine Islamic Jihad (PIJ), and the Abu Nidal organization (ANO). Several non-Palestinian groups—such as Turkey's Kurdistan Workers Party (PKK) and Revolutionary Left (Dev Sol)—also maintain facilities in Lebanon. Most of these groups are based in the Bekaa Valley.

The detention of Western hostages in Lebanon came to an end in 1992 with the release in June of two German relief workers who were abducted in 1989. The Freedom Strugglers—probably a covername for Iranian-backed Hizballah—

announced on 15 June that the Germans would be released because of Iranian and Syrian efforts to "resolve the issue" of Mohammed and Abbas Hammadi, Hizballah terrorists imprisoned in Germany. The fate of several Israeli military personnel missing in Lebanon remains unknown.

Saudi Arabia

No terrorist attacks or legal prosecutions related to terrorism took place in Saudi Arabia in 1992, and Sunni and Shia extremists who oppose the Saudi monarchy do not now pose a significant terrorist threat. The annual pilgrimage to Mecca —the hajj—passed relatively peacefully in 1992. Nonetheless, the government continues to be concerned about the possibility of terrorist acts against Saudi interests inside the Kingdom, particularly about attacks sponsored by Iraq or Iran. Outside Saudi Arabia, the Saudi Ambassador to Yemen was held hostage inside his Embassy in Sanaa for 18 hours in April by a Yemeni citizen. The Saudi and Yemeni Governments cooperated closely to resolve the incident, which ended when a Yemeni security officer overwhelmed the terrorist.

The Saudi Government has cooperated against terrorism in several areas. The Saudis, for example, refused to give landing clearances to an Ethiopian relief plane that was hijacked in Djibouti in July. Saudi Arabia has not resumed financial aid to the Palestine Liberation Organization (PLO) since the end of the Gulf war, although the Saudi Government provides the PLO with the proceeds of a tax on the income of Palestinians living in the kingdom. Some private Saudis probably provide funds to the PLO, HAMAS, and other Palestinian and fundamental groups throughout the region. The same is true regarding private Saudi support for other groups, including elements in Somalia and Sudan. Riyadh decries acts of terrorism committed in the name of the Palestine cause, but it nonetheless considers the cause to be legitimate as a movement of national liberation and as resistance to Israeli military occupation.

There has not been any reduction, however, in the small Libyan diplomatic presence in Saudi Arabia, as mandated in the UN resolutions imposing sanctions against Libya. Libya has six diplomats in Saudi Arabia, four in Riyadh, and two in Jeddah. Saudi Arabia is represented in Libya by one Second Secretary.

Tunisia

There were no terrorist attacks or incidents in Tunisia in 1992. The Tunisian Government has consistently claimed that Tunisian Islamic extremists, particularly members of the an-Nahda party, have used, or plotted to use, terrorist methods and that they are supported and financed by foreign governments, especially Iran and Sudan. At the end of August 1992. Tunisian military courts, after public trials in which there were allegations of serious irregularities, pronounced verdicts against 279 alleged an-Nahda supporters accused in 1991 of plotting to assassinate Tunisian Government leaders and overthrow the government. The courts sentenced 265 defendants to prison terms ranging from one year to life; 14 were acquitted. Party leader Rachid Ghannouchi—who is seeking political asylum in United Kingdom—was sentenced to life imprisonment in absentia. Tunisia has joined the Governments of Egypt and Algeria in calling on Iran and Sudan to stop supporting Islamic radicals across the Maghreb.

The Tunisian Government maintained a strong antiterrorism policy in 1992. Tunis condemned the August 1992 airport bombing in Algiers, as well as terrorist attacks against Western tourists in Egypt. The government continues to enforce the UN sanctions severing airlinks to Libya in connection with the bombings of Pan Am Flight 103 and UTA Flight 772, although Tunisia had not complied with the UN requirement to reduce significantly the Libyan diplomatic presence in Tunis.

Tunisia continues to serve as the location of the headquarters of the Palestine Liberation Organization (PLO). The Tunisian Government abides by the 1982 PLO–Tunisian agreement that allowed the PLO to establish itself in Tunisia and restricts access to Tunisia to include only those Palestinians it identifies as nationalists rather than terrorists. Tunis provides no training sites, training assistance, or support to terrorist organizations.

Yemen

A series of assassinations and bombings by unknown perpetrators took place in Yemen in 1992. On 26 April, the Yemeni Justice Minister was wounded by an unknown gunman while being driven in his car in Sanaa. The Minister subsequently recovered from his wounds. On 14 June, the brother of Yemeni Prime Minister Haydar Abu Bakr al-'Attas was shot and killed by unknown assailants in the city of Al Mukalla. On 20 June, an advisor to the Minister of Defense was shot and killed in Sanaa, apparently in an altercation with Yemeni security forces. In August and September, there was a series of bomb blasts at the homes or offices of leading Yemeni political figures in Sanaa.

Foreign interests have also been the targets of bombing attacks. On 23 September, a minor bomb explosion occurred behind the US Embassy. On 29 October, a bomb was detonated outside the wall of the German Embassy, and, on 9 November, another small bomb exploded just outside the perimeter wall of the US Embassy in Sanaa. There were no reported injuries in any of these bombings, and property damage in all cases appeared to be slight. Finally, there were two explosions in Aden on 29 December, one at a hotel and one at a hotel parking lot, which killed one person and injured several others. Although there were no US casualties, the explosion in the parking lot was near a hotel that billeted US military personnel involved in the airlift for Operation Rescue in Somalia. US personnel stationed in Aden were withdrawn from Yemen on 31 December.

Little information is available on what organizations or individuals were responsible for these incidents. In press reports, Yemeni authorities have accused the Yemeni Islamic Jihad members of the hotel bombing and other attacks.

Known Islamic Jihad members were arrested at the end of the year.

A Yemeni citizen held the Saudi Ambassador to Yemen hostage inside the Saudi Embassy in Sanaa for 18 hours on 19 and 20 April. The kidnapper reportedly demanded a $1 million ransom. The situation was resolved when a Yemeni security official overpowered the extremist and freed the Ambassador. A Yemeni court in October sentenced the kidnapper to three years in prison. The kidnapper apparently was acting on his own and was not part of a larger group or organization.

Yemeni officials frequently have announced their commitment to cutting ties to terrorist groups. Sanaa reportedly is narrowing criteria and tightening procedures for issuing passports to non-Yemenis, including Palestinians. A few terrorist groups, however, continue to maintain a presence in Yemeni territory, probably with the assistance of Yemeni officials from the former People's Democratic Republic of Yemen (PDRY) regime.

Patterns of Global Terrorism: 1993

The Year in Review

There were 427 international terrorist attacks in 1993, an increase from the 364 incidents recorded in 1992. The main reason for the increase was an accelerated terrorism campaign perpetrated by the Kurdistan Workers Party (PKK) against Turkish interests. Most of the group's 150 attacks took place on only two days, 24 June and 4 November, and were staged throughout Western Europe. Had it not been for these two days of coordinated attacks, the level of terrorism would have continued the downward trend of recent years.

Anti-US attacks fell to 88 last year from the 142 recorded in 1992. Approximately 21 percent of the international terrorist attacks last year were directed at US targets.[1]

The one international terrorist "spectacular" was the 26 February bombing of the World Trade Center (WTC) in New York City. This massive explosion left a 30 × 30-meter (100 × 100-foot) opening in the underground parking garage, scattered debris throughout an adjacent subway station, and filled all 110 floors of the north tower with smoke. The effects of the blast and the ensuing fire and smoke caused six deaths and 1,000 injuries. The six dead, all Americans, were John DiGiovanni of Valley Stream, New York; Robert Kirkpatrick of Suffern, New York; Steve Knapp of New York City; Monica Smith of Seaford, New York; William Macko of Bayonne, New Jersey; and Wilfredo Mercado of Brooklyn, New York.

---

[1] We have not included in our terrorism data base the 25 January 1993 shooting outside CIA Headquarters in Langley, Virginia, in which two CIA employees were killed and three others wounded. Mir Aimal Kansi, who is being sought in connection with the attack and is still at large, is not known to be affiliated with a terrorist group or to be an agent of a foreign government.

The WTC bombing is considered an act of international terrorism because of the political motivations that spurred the attack and because most of the suspects who have been arrested are foreign nationals. However, the FBI has not found evidence that a foreign government was responsible for the bombing. Some of the suspects arrested in the case are closely linked to others arrested in July in a thwarted plot to blow up selected targets in New York City, including the United Nations building and the Holland and Lincoln Tunnels. Umar Abd al-Rahman, the Muslim cleric from Egypt who resided in New Jersey, and several of his followers were indicted in connection with this plot and were charged with conspiracy. The case went to trial in September 1993, and four suspects were convicted in March 1994.

The WTC bombing was the only terrorist attack in 1993 that produced American fatalities. Two Americans, Jill Papineau and Raymond Matthew Chico, were wounded when a bomb exploded in a cafe in Cairo, Egypt, on the same day as the WTC bombing. Three people were killed, and 16 others were wounded in the cafe bombing. Western Europe had more international terrorist incidents in 1993—180 attacks —than any other region, primarily because of the two waves of PKK violence. The Middle East had the next highest number—101—followed by Latin America with 97. Iran remains the world's most active and most dangerous state sponsor of terrorism, through its own state agents and the radical groups it supports. Iraq also continues to sponsor terrorism. Iraq planned to assassinate former President George Bush during his visit to Kuwait in April, and its agents were responsible for numerous attacks on international humanitarian and relief personnel in Iraq. Last year 109 people were killed in terrorist attacks, and 1,393 were wounded, the highest casualty total in five years.

African Overview

Civil wars and ethnic conflict continue to ravage Sub-Saharan Africa (Somalia, Sudan, Angola, and Liberia), and the threat of international terrorism against US and other Western interests in the region continues. In August, the United States placed Sudan on the list of state sponsors of terrorism. This decision was made on the basis of convincing evidence from multiple sources that Sudan provides assistance to international terrorist groups.

Iran continues its active involvement in limited areas of Africa, particularly in Sudan and where expatriate Shia populations reside. Iranian-sponsored Hizballah continues to attempt to develop its presence in Sudan, Senegal, Cote d'Ivoire, Sierra Leone, Benin, and Nigeria. As Iran is the world's most active state sponsor of terrorism, this trend is disturbing and bears close monitoring. Libya's support for subversion has long been a problem throughout the continent and remains so. Some African countries have been the venue for terrorist activity in the past. Although there have been no dramatic terrorist attacks in the region since the 1989 bombing of UTA Flight 772, the threat remains.

Angola

Three terrorist incidents occurred in Angola in 1993. In February, insurgents of the Renovada faction of the Front for the Liberation of the Enclave of Cabinda (FLEC) kidnapped an officer of the United Nations Angola Verification Mission and released him unharmed three weeks later. During the same month, one person was injured when a bomb detonated next to the UN office in Luanda; no group claimed responsibility. In May, militants of the FLEC and—according to the government—the National Union for the Total Liberation of Angola (UNITA) jointly attacked the Cabinda Gulf Oil Company, owned by Chevron International of America, and took a number of Portuguese workers hostage. FLEC, which is seeking independence for the Enclave of Cabinda, has previously targeted Western oil companies with commercial ties to the Angolan Government.

Ghana

Ghanaian authorities in February detained Omar Mohammed Ali Rezaq, a Palestinian who participated in the 1985 hijacking of an Egyptair flight in which 60 passengers died in Malta, including one American and one Ghanaian. In July, US authorities took custody of Rezaq in Nigeria after the Government of Ghana deported him. He was then transported to the United States to stand trial on charges of aircraft piracy and aiding and abetting the 1985 hijacking. The Government of Ghana prosecuted four persons for bombings that occurred in Ghana after the 1992 election.

Nigeria

On 25 October, four members of the Nigerian Movement for the Advancement of Democracy (MAD) hijacked a Nigerian Airways plane and diverted it to Niamey, Niger. The Nigerian Government refused to refuel the aircraft, and police forces stormed the plane, freed the hostages, and captured the hijackers. During the rescue operation, one crew member was killed. The four hijackers, who intended to force the plane to Frankfurt, had demanded the resignation of Nigeria's Interim National Government, the prosecution of former President Ibrahim Babangida on corruption charges, and the opening of proscribed newspapers.

On 15 July, the Government of Nigeria cooperated in the FBI's apprehension of terrorist hijacker Mohammed Ali Rezaq in Lagos. Rezaq was returned to the United States to stand trial on charges of air piracy for the 1985 hijacking of an Egyptair flight in which 60 people died in Malta.

Asian Overview

South Asia posed serious terrorism concerns in 1993. Continuing ethnic tensions in Sri Lanka resulted in several large battles between the Army and Tamil rebels. The country also suffered the loss by assassination of President Premadasa, who was killed on 1 May, and opposition party leader Lalith Athulathmudali, who was killed one week earlier. In India, tensions subsided in Punjab but increased dramatically in Kashmir, where separatist militants continued attacks on military and civilian targets. In Pakistan, 16 persons died in bomb blasts in Hyderabad and Latifbad on 24 January. Pakistan and India have exchanged charges that the other side is aiding perpetrators of violent acts. In the border region with Afghanistan, there were assaults on members of UN and nongovernmental organizations. In Afghanistan, none of the warring factions in the titular government has gained control over the territory. An increasing number of reports state that militant groups, many of them "Arab mujahedin" asked by the Pakistani Government to leave Pakistan, are acquiring training and safehaven in Afghanistan.

In East Asia, violence continues in the Philippines, and some Americans were kidnapped, but there were no terrorist attacks by the Communist New Peoples Army against US interests in 1993. In Japan, the Chukaku-ha (Middle Core Faction) reduced its level of attacks, and the Japanese Red Army remained dormant.

Afghanistan

Afghanistan is still suffering from internecine battles among the former mujahedin factions. The rampant violence occasionally spills over into attacks on foreigners, particularly in the eastern provinces that border Pakistan. On 23 January, for example, militants attempted to ambush a UN vehicle near Jalalabad, and on 1 February four UN officials were killed when two UN vehicles were ambushed near Jalalabad. Similar violence occurs occasionally on the border of Pakistan where there are large concentrations of Afghan refugees.

Afghanistan's eastern and northern provinces are sites for mujahedin camps in which Muslim militants from around the world receive paramilitary training. Members of Egyptian, Algerian, and Kashmiri militant organizations have been trained in these camps, as have members of many other Middle Eastern and Asian groups. Beginning in early 1993, Pakistan started to expel Arab militants affiliated with various mujahedin groups and nongovernment aid organizations who were residing in its North-West Frontier Province. Many of these Arabs apparently have crossed into Afghanistan, and Islamabad is still working to control the Arab militants who remain in Pakistan.

India

India continues to suffer from ethnic, religious, and separatist violence. Terrorism and attacks on police and military targets have been conducted by Kashmiri militants and Sikh extremists, as well as several separatist organizations in northeast India. The level of violence was particularly high in Kashmir, where the militants' fight against Army and paramilitary forces has been ongoing since late 1989. In Punjab, however, Sikh groups have been decimated by Indian counterinsurgency efforts since mid-1992, and the level of violence has receded significantly. Indian forces have been particularly effective against the Sikh militant leadership, and all major Sikh groups have lost leaders during the past 18 months. The Punjab is not completely quiet. In January, the government foiled a Sikh plot to bomb government buildings during Republic Day celebrations, and, in September, Sikhs killed eight persons in New Delhi in a failed attempt to assassinate the Sikh head of the ruling Congress Party's youth wing. There are credible reports of support by the Government of Pakistan for Kashmiri militants and some reports of support for Sikh separatists.

Japan

No international terrorist groups based outside Japan conducted attacks there during 1993, and domestic extremist groups were less active than in recent years. Chukaku-ha, the most dangerous and active Japanese leftist group, was distracted by internal politics in the spring and is believed to have committed only nine attacks that resulted in minimal damage and no injuries. The group listed "crushing the Tokyo G-7 Summit" as a key 1993 combat objective, but it failed to attack the summit directly, although it launched four homemade rockets that landed in isolated areas of the US Army Base at Zama, outside Tokyo, on the first day of the summit. Other domestic leftist groups were even less active and were responsible for only a few bombings. The Japanese Red Army (JRA) remained dormant. Right-wing groups were responsible for a series of four fire-bombings at Japanese corporate leaders' homes in February.

On 7 December, a Tokyo District Court sentenced leading JRA member Osamu Maruoka to life imprisonment for his role in hijacking two Japan Airlines flights in 1973 and 1977.

Pakistan

As a result of continued instability in Afghanistan, Pakistan's northwest border region continues to witness violence against UN staff personnel, members of nongovernmental organizations, and figures within the Afghan refugee community. On 25 January, a handgrenade was thrown into the residential compound of the Director of Western Nongovernment Organization (NGO). On 4 February, a vehicle attempted to run down a UN employee on a residential street in Peshawar, the capital of the North-West Frontier Province. On 11 March, a grenade attack damaged a UN vehicle traveling on the main road through Peshawar. On 27 December, a prominent Afghan figure associated with moderate politics was murdered in a vehicle ambush on the North-West Frontier Province's main highway. Throughout the year, poster and media campaigns and intimidation efforts continued against Afghans and foreign NGO workers, threatening death to those who supported, even indirectly, rival Afghan parties. Human rights activists and Afghan intellectuals residing in Pakistan continue to report receiving direct threats. Since spring, Pakistan has moved to identify and expel illegal Arab residents who came to Pakistan to fight with mujahedin organizations or assist Afghan relief groups.

Pakistan also has suffered from violence arising from the country's endemic ethnic and criminal problems. On 12 January, a bomb exploded in a settlement of Biharis during a resettlement of Biharis from Bangladesh to Pakistan. On 24 January, 16 persons died in bomb blasts in the cities of Hyderabad and Latifbad. Government measures against drug traffickers also occasionally resulted in violence.

The Government of Pakistan acknowledges that it continues to give moral, political, and diplomatic support to Kashmiri militants but denies allegations of other assistance. However, there were credible reports in 1993 of official Pakistani support to Kashmiri militants who undertook attacks of terrorism in Indian-controlled Kashmir. Some support came from private organizations such as the Jamaat-i-Islami. There were also reports of support to Sikh militants engaged in terrorism in northern India.

Pakistan was the site of Iranian-sponsored terrorism. On 6 June, an Iranian oppositionist was shot and killed in Karachi, apparently by Iran's intelligence service.

Philippines

The southern Philippines is experiencing a disturbing pattern of violence against foreigners that may presage a trend beyond the familiar pattern of largely criminal activity by splinter insurgent groups. Missionaries and other religious workers have been targets for kidnappers in the south as evidenced by the abductions of several American religious workers in 1992 and 1993. Three Spanish religious workers were also abducted during this same period. Most recently, American Charles Walton was kidnapped in November 1993 by the radical Islamic Abu Sayuf Group (ASG). He was held three weeks before being released on 7 December. The ASG threatened to attack foreign missionaries as well as tourists in the Muslim-dominated areas of Mindanao.

Sectarian violence intensified in Mindanao by yearend when a cathedral and three mosques were attacked. The church bombing, believed to have been perpetrated by Muslim extremists, killed at least six persons and injured more than 150 others and may have been intended to disrupt ongoing peace negotiations between the government and Muslim rebels. Attacks against three local mosques were conducted late at night, and six people sustained minor injuries. On 13 December, Muslim extremists in Buluan, Maguindanao, stopped a bus and executed nine passengers after identifying them as Christians.

There were no terrorist attacks by the Communist New Peoples Army (NPA) against US interests in 1993. The Communist insurgency has declined dramatically over the past several years because of military losses, declining recruitment, and internal factionalism. The NPA has also been weakened by measures taken by President Ramos to end the 24-year-old insurgency, including the legalization of the Communist Party of the Philippines and the release of most imprisoned Communist detainees. The government continues to seek a reconciliation with the Communists and Muslim rebels in the south.

Sri Lanka

Sri Lanka continues to be the scene of separatist violence by the Liberation Tigers of Tamil Eelam (LTTE), which seeks to create a separate state called Tamil Eelam in northern and eastern Sri Lanka. In 1993, the LTTE fought several large battles with the Sri Lankan Army in the Tamil majority northern area of the island and in the ethnically mixed eastern region. The LTTE maintains effective control over the north and is seeking to drive Sinhalese and Muslim villagers out of eastern Sri Lanka. LTTE units are well led and equipped. Sri Lanka's Army chief resigned in December following the Army's defeat in November at Pooneryn, the biggest battle of the more than 10-year-old insurgency. The LTTE continued to stage suicide attacks against leading Sri Lankan officials. On 1 May, a suicide bomber killed former Sri Lankan President Premadasa and dozens of bystanders in Colombo. Opposition party leader Athulathmudali was assassinated the week before by an unidentified lone gunman who may have been an LTTE member. Athulathmudali had been Sri Lanka's most senior security official and a ruthless opponent of the LTTE. Some years before, when still a member of the ruling party, he served as Minister of Defense.

European Overview

International terrorism in Europe increased in 1993, primarily because of attacks by the Kurdistan Workers Party (PKK) on Turkish targets throughout Western Europe. No Americans died in any attacks during the year, although one American was kidnapped and eventually released by the PKK in Turkey. The Provisional Irish Republican Army (PIRA) and Loyalist paramilitaries continued their violent activity in the United Kingdom, mostly against domestic targets in Northern Ireland. In Spain, the Basque Fatherland and Liberty (ETA) continued its attacks as well. Elsewhere, leftwing groups such as Germany's Red Army Faction (RAF) and Italy's Red Brigades showed renewed signs of activity; the RAF undertook its first terrorist operation in two years.

Eastern Europe

Anarchist and skinhead groups in Eastern Europe, particularly in Poland and the Czech Republic, have engaged in violent demonstrations and clashes but have not engaged in acts of terrorism. In December, Polish anarchists held pro-PKK demonstrations at the German Consulate in Krakow. Antiforeigner violence by skinheads continues to be a problem in most East European countries.

France

On 9 November, the French Government responded to the killing of two French citizens and the kidnapping of three French Consular officers in Algeria by ordering the roundup of suspected Algerian Muslim extremists. In addition, in reaction to PKK activities in France, on 18 November police throughout France rounded up more than 100 alleged PKK members, including the suspected leader and deputy of the group in France; 24 of those arrested have been charged with conspiracy to commit terrorism. On 30 November, the French Cabinet voted to ban two groups—the Kurdistan Committee and the Federation of Kurdistan Cultural Associations and Patriotic Workers—which were front organizations for the PKK. On 9 December, French police rounded up a number of Tunisian Islamic extremists, including Saleh Karkar, a founder of Tunisia's banned An-Nahda Party. Despite an extradition request from Switzerland, on 30 December, France released two Iranian suspects in the assassination of an Iranian opposition leader in Geneva in 1990. The French Government explained its action by stating that it took this step in pursuit of French national interest. Finally, the two suspects accused of murdering former Iranian Prime Minister Shahpur Bakhtiar remain in prison awaiting trial in 1994.

Germany

The radical leftist German Red Army Faction (RAF) undertook its first terrorist operation in two years by blowing up an empty prison complex with at least 400 pounds of explosives on 27 March. On 27 June, German police arrested RAF commando-level member Birgit Hogefeld. RAF terrorist Wolfgang Grams died during the operation. Three separate German commissions refuted charges that the police had "executed" Grams, judging instead that he had committed suicide. Following the decline of Communism, the group has turned its attention to domestic issues and has said its primary targets will be the German justice system and officials involved in German and European unification. The RAF has not attacked US interests since strafing the US Embassy in February 1991.

German rightwing extremists were somewhat less active than in 1992 but continued to pose a threat to foreigners. In October, neo-Nazi hooligans attacked US Olympic athletes at a bar in Oberhof in eastern Germany. Two perpetrators were convicted for their roles in the incident. German authorities have cracked down on rightwing groups, banning six and monitoring many others. Two arsonists responsible for the deaths of three Turks received maximum sentences.

German authorities returned Hizballah member Abbas Ali Hammadi to Lebanon on 6 August in accordance with the German penal practice of releasing and deporting foreign convicts after they have served half their sentence. Abbas Hammadi was given a 13-year sentence for plotting to kidnap two West Germans in the hope of forcing the release of his brother, Mohammed Hammadi, who is serving a life sentence in Germany for hijacking and for murdering US Navy diver Robert Stethem.

German authorities responded to a violent wave of PKK attacks on 4 November by searching Kurdish offices and residences and confiscating PKK material. The government also banned the PKK and 35 associated Kurdish organizations on 26 November.

Greece

The new socialist government, which was elected in October, asked Parliament to strike down the so-called antiterrorism law passed by the previous conservative government in 1990. The Parliament repealed the law in December. The law had broadened police powers to wiretap, open mail, and freeze and confiscate assets; allowed authorities to hold suspects without specifying charges if disclosure would harm an investigation; and provided for jail terms and fines for publishing terrorist communiques. The trial of suspected terrorist Georgios Balafas, who was arrested in December 1992 and charged with maintaining a safehouse with explosives, had been scheduled for November but was postponed by the new government.

The Greek Revolutionary Organization 17 November did not target US interests this year or the previous year, but it remains a threat to US citizens.

Italy

Italian leftists claiming ties to the "Red Brigades for the Construction of the Combatant Communist Party" appeared to be attempting to revive the Red Brigades terrorist group. On 2 September, three individuals in a stolen car fired seven shots, and one of them threw a grenade at the US Airbase in Aviano; there were no injuries. Aviano is the staging base for US aircraft enforcing the no-fly zone over Bosnia. Callers saying they represented the Red Brigades phoned three Italian newspapers on 4 September to claim responsibility for the attack. In late October, Italian police arrested nine individuals connected with the attack, including the three who were directly involved. Police have identified two of those three as Red Brigades members. The Red Brigades had not conducted an attack since 1988 and had been largely inactive since Italian and French police arrested many of the group's members in 1989.

Red Brigades founder Renato Curcio, who had been in jail since 1976, was allowed to enter a work release program in April.

Spain

Spanish and French authorities continued to arrest key members of Basque Fatherland and Liberty (ETA). Among those apprehended this year were the group's main gunsmith and the suspected leader of ETA'S Barcelona cell, who was Spain's most wanted terrorist. French police also uncovered an underground arms workshop and firing range belonging to the group.

Despite these losses, ETA continued to attack Spanish security officials and Spanish and French commercial interests throughout the year. The most spectacular of these attacks were two car bombs in Madrid on 21 June that killed seven persons and injured 22 others, and two car bombs in Barcelona on 29 October. During the summer, ETA set off several smaller bombs at resort hotels along the Costa del Sol and at four locations in Barcelona, including a building that had been part of the Olympic Village.

Turkey

The Kurdistan Workers Party (PKK), which continues to lead a growing insurgency, posed the dominant terrorist threat in Turkey. Ending a unilateral cease-fire in May, the group began a terrorist campaign against the Turkish tourism industry, as well as attacks against Turkish security forces—including the massacre of 30 unarmed recruits. The PKK bombed hotels, restaurants, and tourist sites and planted grenades on Mediterranean beaches. In an effort to generate publicity, the PKK kidnapped 19 Western tourists, including one American, traveling in eastern Turkey; all were released unharmed.

The PKK staged two waves of attacks on dozens of Turkish diplomatic and commercial facilities in several European countries last year. The first round on 24 June consisted mostly of vandalism and demonstrations. They occupied the Turkish Consulate in Munich for a day, and Turkish Embassy officials killed a Kurdish demonstrator, who was storming the Embassy in Bern, Switzerland. On 4 November, the PKK firebombed many of its targets, killing a Turkish man in Wiesbaden, Germany. After the November attacks, police officials in Germany swept through Kurdish offices and apartments, confiscating PKK-related materials, while French police arrested more than 20 Kurds, including the two alleged PKK leaders in France. The German Interior Minister banned the PKK and 35 associated organizations on 26 November, and France banned the PKK and the Kurdistan Committee on 29 November.

The leftist terrorist group Dev Sol is still recuperating from severe factionalism and extensive Turkish police operations against it. During the past two years, the Turkish National Police has hammered at the group, killing a number of operatives, arresting dozens more, and eliminating safehouses and weapons caches. In the winter of 1992, a faction of Dev Sol members broke away from the main group, protesting a lack of leadership, financial mismanagement, and apparent security breaches. The original group is slowly establishing dominance over the breakaway faction in Turkey and in Europe. Despite the turmoil, the group assassinated several Turkish officials earlier in the fall, and it continues to target American interests.

United Kingdom

Sectarian violence accounted for the vast majority of terrorism in the United Kingdom (Great Britain and Northern Ireland) in 1993, and Loyalist paramilitaries again caused more deaths than the Provisional Irish Republican Army (PIRA). PIRA nonetheless remains the most active and lethal terrorist group in Western Europe. In March, it exploded two bombs at midday in a crowded shopping district in Warrington, killing two children. In April, the group detonated its largest bomb ever—a truck bomb with approximately 1 ton of explosives in the heart of London's financial district. The blast killed a reporter, injured more than 40 people, and resulted in damage estimated between $450 million and $1.5 billion. PIRA also conducted several bombings in Belfast that prompted revenge attacks by Loyalist paramilitaries. Altogether, Republican and Loyalist attacks in Northern Ireland resulted in 84 deaths. Continued violence during a period when PIRA was discussing the possibility of peace talks with the British Government suggests the group may be divided on the issue. The joint declaration issued in December by the British and Irish Prime Ministers offered constitutional parties and Sinn Fein, the political wing of PIRA, a part in negotiations in exchange for a permanent end to terrorist activities.

Former Yugoslavia

Ethnic conflict and endemic violence continued to plague many parts of the former Yugoslavia. Within this context, it was often difficult to separate terrorism from other forms of violence. Nevertheless, small-scale terrorism by unidentified attackers continues to pose a threat to foreign interests in the former Yugoslavia. In March, a grenade was thrown at the US Embassy in Belgrade, and a similar attack was made on the Bulgarian Embassy in June. Several Serb leaders, including Radovan Karadzic, leader of the Bosnian Serbs, and paramilitary leader Vojislav Seselj, have made numerous public threats to conduct terrorism against Western interests if the West intervenes in the war in Bosnia. Bosnian Vice President Ejup Ganic warned in June that Bosnians living in Europe were likely to resort to terrorism if the West did not come to Bosnia's aid, and outside terrorist groups are reportedly providing support to the Bosnian Muslims. In August, Croatian authorities confiscated weapons, explosives, and false documents from a "terrorist" network that had been aiding Bosnia. Hizballah and Iran have provided training to the Bosnian Muslim army.

Former Soviet Union

Separatist and internal power struggles have spawned domestic violence and could lead to acts of international terrorism. Domestic terrorism is common in the Trans-Caucasus and the North Caucasus region of Russia. In August, for example, unknown assassins in the North Caucasus killed Russian Special Envoy Polyanichko. Russian extremist groups have threatened to use terrorism against the government of President Boris Yel'tsin. In September, the Union of Soviet Stalinists threatened to assassinate members of the Stanislav Terekhov—charged with attacking the CIS military headquarters—was released by the police. There were many hijackings within the former Soviet Union, some with international repercussions. In February, a flight from Perm was hijacked to Tallinn and then Stockholm, where Swedish officials succeeded in getting the hijackers to surrender. In September, Iranian dissidents hijacked an Aeroflot Baku-to-Perm flight. Ukrainian authorities refueled the plane, provided it with a navigator, and allowed it to continue to Norway.

Latin American Overview

Latin America continued to have one of the highest levels of international terrorist activity of any region in the world, but the rate has declined by over 30 percent since 1992. Government counterterrorism successes in Peru and Chile and continued disaffection with militant leftist ideologies throughout the region account, in part, for the lower numbers. Even so, the bombing of the US Embassy in Peru in July and of two American fast-food franchises in Chile in September—as well as continued anti-Western terrorism in other Latin American countries—are reminders that US personnel and facilities in the region remain vulnerable.

As in previous years, most terrorist attacks in Latin America were directed against domestic targets: government institutions and personnel, economic infrastructure, and security forces. The violence claimed several international victims, however, and the tendency for guerrilla groups to turn increasingly to crime has led to an abundance of kidnappings-for-profit throughout the region. Many of the targets of such schemes have been wealthy businessmen or diplomats. In Colombia, a German businessman was killed in a botched kidnap attempt in September, and the body of an Italian honorary consul, kidnapped in the summer, was found in November.

Violence continues to be most disruptive in Peru and Colombia, where guerrillas and narcotraffickers are often linked. Counternarcotics operations in countries such as Bolivia, Colombia, and Peru risk coming under fire as subversive groups seek to protect the revenue netted from their narcotics operations. In addition, US and other foreign companies involved in exploring and developing Latin America's natural resources have often been targeted for attack. Foreign-owned oil pipelines in Colombia again were targeted this year. Terrorist attacks against foreign religious missions and aid workers also continue to be a problem; churches were bombed in Bolivia, Chile, and Peru, and three missionaries were kidnapped in Panama.

In May, Nicaraguan authorities uncovered a large arms cache belonging to a faction of El Salvador's Farabundo Marti National Liberation Front (FMLN) guerrillas in an auto repair shop in Managua. The cache contained ammunition and several types of weapons—including surface-to-air missiles—and documents, some of which pertained to an international kidnapping ring operated by leftists in the 1980s. The investigation revealed that the Managua repair shop was owned by a Spaniard—who is still at large—with connections to Spain's ETA terrorist group. The Nicaraguan Government invited Interpol and eight interested countries, including the United States, to form an international commission to share information on the case. Individuals connected to the current Nicaraguan Government are not known to be involved in or aware of the arms caches or related terrorist activities.

Chile

Terrorist organizations in Chile were seriously eroded over the past year as a result of government counterterrorism successes and the continued strength of its democratic institutions. Some old-line leftwing groups remain active, but the number of attacks dropped dramatically this year, and many of these represented criminal efforts by rogue elements to stay afloat financially. Chilean terrorists planted bombs at several Mormon churches, two McDonald's restaurants, and a Kentucky Fried Chicken restaurant. The Dissident Faction of the Manuel Rodriguez Patriotic Front (FPMR/D) and the Lautaro Youth Movement (MJL) may have been responsible for these, as well as the vast majority of domestic terrorist attacks in the past year. The 20th anniversary of the military coup that toppled President Allende in 1973 sparked some terrorist violence in mid-September; 11 bombings in a two-day period injured 55 Chileans.

The Chilean Government arrested dozens of members of the remaining terrorist organizations in 1993. Various elements of the Lautaro group were captured, including Delfin Diaz Quezada, the organization's second in command; the group's logistic chief; and the number-two commander of Lautaro's elite squad, the Lautaro Rebel Forces. Chilean police were also successful in their fight against the FPMR/D in 1993, capturing its military chief, Mauricio Hernandez Norambuena. Norambuena is believed to be behind several anti-US attacks in 1990 and 1991, which seriously injured an American diplomat and included a LAW rocket assault against the Marine Guard Detachment.

In November, a verdict was rendered in one of the country's most contentious and longstanding terrorism cases. The intelligence officers accused of ordering the assassination of former Chilean Foreign Minister Orlando Letelier and his aide Ronni Moffitt in Washington in 1976 were found guilty. Gen. Manuel Contreras and Col. Pedro Espinoza were sentenced to seven and six years in prison, respectively, although both are appealing the case to the Chilean Supreme Court.

Colombia

Colombia continued to be one of the most violent countries in the region in 1993, with numerous bombings against civilian targets attributed to insurgent and drug-related terrorism. Insurgents continued to attack foreign-owned oil pipelines on a regular basis, raising the number of international terrorist incidents in Colombia significantly above those of its neighbors.

Colombia's two major insurgent groups continued to demonstrate their capacity for violence. In the fall, the Army of National Liberation (ELN) and the Revolutionary Armed Forces of Colombia (FARC) waged a month long offensive they dubbed Black September against government targets, including ambushes on security forces in the countryside and stepped-up attacks on government targets in Bogota. Shopping centers, buses, and tourist hotels were targeted by guerrillas and narcotraffickers, sustaining the threat that foreigners could be injured in a bomb blast. Colombian guerrillas conducted cross-border attacks and kidnappings into neighboring countries.

The 17-month hunt for Medellin narcotics kingpin Pablo Escobar ended with his death on 2 December in a shootout with a unit of the Government of Colombia's Special Security Task Force.

The fate of three US missionaries kidnapped in March remains unknown. They were taken from their New Tribes Mission (NTM) camp near the Colombian border in Panama, but officials have speculated that the captors may have been Colombian. The kidnappers originally demanded a $5 million ransom but have since reduced the amount. A message recorded during the Christmas holidays included all three men and satisfied NTM that they are alive.

Ecuador

A group calling itself Puka Inti, an indigenous term meaning Red Sun, gained attention in Ecuador by bombing several government buildings over the past year. Formed largely from dissident members of the defunct Ecuadorian AVC guerrilla organization, Puka Inti probably has fewer than 100 members, and there is no evidence of public support for the group. Puka Inti was responsible for scattered minor bombings in 1993. Ecuador had been nearly free from terrorist acts during the past two years.

Peru

Peru's two insurgent groups, the Maoist Sendero Luminoso (SL) and the smaller, Marxist, Tupac Amaru Revolutionary Movement (MRTA) suffered setbacks in the face of ongoing government counterterrorism operations.

SL—badly stung by continued government successes against it—retains a much larger number of committed combatants than MRTA and is more difficult to dismantle. The group was caught off guard in the fall when the Peruvian Government publicized three letters written by imprisoned SL leader Abimael Guzman requesting peace talks. Guzman read the letters aloud in videotapes shown on national television. Guzman's hyperbolic praise for the Fujimori government in the second letter raised doubts about his intentions, and the videos did not halt the violence.

SL was disrupted but not dismantled by the setbacks in 1993 and continues to wage easy-to-plan attacks on vulnerable targets, including businesses and the tourist industry. Indeed, terrorist attacks in Lima proliferated during the year, as SL's damaged military capabilities led it to focus on less-well-protected civilian targets. In May, SL bombed the Chilean Embassy to protest talks between Santiago and Lima designed to resolve a border dispute; no one was injured. Two Swiss tourists were tortured and killed in early July. Also in July, the group set off a large car bomb in front of the US Embassy on the eve of Peruvian Independence Day celebrations.

An Embassy guard was injured by shrapnel, and the building suffered considerable damage. In November, presumed SL terrorists tossed a satchel bomb in front of the US-Peruvian Binational Center, breaking several windows but causing no injuries.

Attacks by SL in 1993 were plentiful but much less lethal than in previous years and appeared to require fewer skilled operatives and less coordination. The group continued to lash out violently to show that neither Guzman's arrest nor his "peace" letters have deterred them.

The government was more successful against MRTA, which was crippled by arrests, defections, and in-fighting. In mid-November, MRTA bombed an appliance store belonging to a Japanese-Peruvian entrepreneur the group had kidnapped earlier in the year. Some dedicated members of MRTA remain at large and are likely to continue trying to demonstrate the group's viability. The organization's actions over the past year, however, reinforced the view that it is nearly defunct.

Middle Eastern Overview

In 1993, about 100 international terrorist attacks occurred in the Middle East, up from 79 in 1992. The increase is a result of Iraqi attacks against UN and other humanitarian efforts in northern Iraq and escalated terrorist activity in Egypt. Ongoing, low-level attacks in Lebanon continued, along with violence generated by opposition to the Declaration of Principles (DOP) reached between the Israelis and the Palestinians.

Iran's involvement in and sponsorship of terrorist activity continued to pose significant threats in the Middle East, Europe, Africa, Latin America, and Asia. Tehran continued to hunt down and murder Iranian dissidents, with assassinations in Turkey, Italy, and Pakistan. Iranian involvement is also suspected in the murder of secular Turkish journalist Ugur Mumcu and the attempted murder of Istanbul Jewish businessman Jak Kamhi. Hizballah, with which Iran is closely associated, was responsible for rocket attacks into northern Israel that killed and injured civilians. The Iranian Government called for violence to derail the DOP and supported violence by several rejectionist groups. Egypt, Algeria, and Tunisia have accused Iran—and Sudan—of supporting local militant Islamist elements to undermine their governments. Iran also seeks to expand its influence in Latin America and Africa.

Iraq's capability to support international terrorism remains hampered by continued sanctions and the regime's international isolation, but Baghdad retains a limited capability to mount external operations, principally in neighboring countries. The prime example of this capability was the attempted assassination in Kuwait of former President Bush in April, which drew a retaliatory military response from the United States on 26 June. Baghdad also mounted numerous terrorist operations within Iraq against UN and other humanitarian relief operations. Moreover, Iraq continued to provide its traditional support and safehaven to terrorist Palestinians such as Abu Abbas and elements of the Abu Nidal organization (ANO).

There has been no direct evidence of Syrian Government involvement in terrorist acts since 1986, but Damascus continues to provide support and safehaven to Arab and non-Arab terrorist organizations in Syria and in parts of Lebanon where the Syrian Army is deployed. Syria's relationship with the PKK came under increasing scrutiny in 1993.

In response to ongoing Libyan defiance of the demands of the international community to cease all support for international terrorism, the UN Security Council adopted Resolution 883, which imposed additional sanctions for refusing to hand over for trial terrorists accused of bombing Pan Am Flight 103 and UTA Flight 772. The Qaddafi regime has made partial and largely cosmetic moves to close some terrorist facilities since the initial imposition of sanctions, but it still provides support and safehaven to such notorious terrorists as Abu Nidal. Although the case is still unresolved, most observers suspect an official Libyan hand in the December disappearance of Libyan dissident Mansour Kikhia from Cairo.

Domestic terrorism in Egypt continued to escalate during the year. The number of radical Islamic groups appeared to increase, and they continued their attacks against Egyptian security and civilian officials, local Christians, and tourist targets. Unsuccessful assassination attempts were made against the Minister of Information, the Minister of the Interior, and the Prime Minister. Indiscriminate bombings in Cairo from February through July killed 22 Egyptians and wounded over 100 others. Among the most serious tourists incidents was a December incident in which eight Austrian tourists and eight Egyptians were wounded when their bus was attacked in Old Cairo. American citizens were victims of other attacks: on 26 February, two Americans were among the injured when unknown perpetrators bombed Cairo's Wadi al-Nil cafe. The Egyptian Government has maintained that Iran and Sudan provided support to the organizations responsible for most of the attacks.

In North Africa, Tunisia and Morocco remained generally free of political violence. In Algeria, however, the situation continued to deteriorate as radical elements, most thought to be associated with the Armed Islamic Group, expanded their range of targets from security officials to secular intellectuals and, beginning in September, foreigners. The worst attack occurred in December when 12 Croatian and Bosnian expatriates died after having their throats slit at their work compound in Tamezquida.

After the signing of the Israeli-Palestinian DOP in September, proaccord elements of the PLO, including Fatah, appeared to cease all anti-Israeli operations except in one unauthorized incident. Rejectionist Palestinian groups, however, sought to derail the agreement with violence and terrorism. The Izz al-Din al-Qassam Forces arm of the Islamic Resistance Movement (HAMAS) and the Palestinian Islamic Jihad (PIJ) have led the violent opposition to the peace efforts, with civilians serving as frequent targets. HAMAS also added suicide car bombs to its arsenal. Jewish extremist settlers opposed to the DOP mounted several violent attacks during the year.

In Yemen, there were several attacks by unknown assailants on foreign interests. A small rocket hit the US Embassy in January, and a bomb exploded outside the British Embassy in March. Several foreigners were kidnapped by tribal elements during the year, prompted by economic or tribal motivations. Six members of the Yemeni Islamic Jihad, who were awaiting trial for the bombing of two hotels in Aden in 1992, escaped from prison in July. Several reports noted that private Islamic sources were financing the training of radicals in camps in remote areas of Yemen.

Algeria

The security situation in Algeria continued to deteriorate with a marked increase in attacks by Islamist extremists against the Algerian intelligentsia, economic and infrastructure targets, and foreigners. Extremists continued to focus most of their violent campaign on official Algerian and military targets throughout the year. The fundamentalist Islamic Salvation Front (FIS), which was banned in March 1992, reemerged as an underground movement but splintered into several factions. The official FIS leadership remains imprisoned in Algeria, and several other leaders went into exile following the regime crackdown on the movement. FIS factions abroad and within the country appear to be competing for influence over the movement. In addition, militant offshoots of the FIS and other extremist groups operate throughout Algeria, confusing responsibility for each attack.

By the fall, a few loosely organized militant factions had emerged, including the Armed Islamic Group (AIG), which is not affiliated with the FIS. The AIG claimed responsibility for killing two French surveyors in September and for the late October kidnapping of three French Consulate employees, two of whom were rescued by Algerian security services and one of whom was released by her captors on 31 October. The kidnappers warned foreigners that they had one month to leave the country. In early December, the campaign against foreigners resumed with attacks on a Spaniard, an Italian, a Russian, a Frenchmen, and a Briton. In the most heinous terrorist act in Algeria during the year, 12 Croatian and Bosnian workers were murdered in Tamezquida on 14 December.

Despite strict antiterrorist laws, three special antiterrorist courts, and 26 executions of convicted "terrorists," the government was unable to stem the violence. Nearly 400 death sentences were issued last year, and the military conducted sweeps of urban areas, deployed military units in Algiers, and extended curfews beyond urban areas, but, by the end of the year, extremist groups continued their attacks on official and infrastructure targets throughout the country.

Egypt

Islamic extremists continued to target the tourist industry, particularly in upper Egypt, throughout the year. Two foreigners were killed, and more than 18 others were injured in sporadic bombings of public places and attacks on tour buses. Four more foreigners were killed by a lone, apparently deranged gunman in a shooting at a Cairo hotel in October. Indiscriminate bombings from February through July were responsible for the deaths of 22 Egyptian civilians and the wounding of over 100 others. Most of the attacks on or near tour buses and Nile cruise ships resulted in few injuries and little damage. Nonetheless, Egypt's tourism industry suffered; figures estimate Cairo's earnings have dropped as much as 50 percent since attacks against tourist sites began in October 1992.

Most attacks were focused on government and security officials, the police, and Egyptian secularist Muslims. The Islamic Group (IG), which seeks the violent overthrow of the Egyptian Government, claimed responsibility for most of the terrorist attacks. Shaykh Umar Abd al Rahman, the so-called spiritual leader of the IG, was arrested in the United States on charges related to the conspiracy to attack various New York City institutions including the United Nations. IG members in Egypt threatened Americans there and abroad if their leader were harmed.

Another group or faction of extremists emerged in 1993, sometimes calling itself the New Jihad. This group claimed responsibility for some high profile attacks, including the attempted assassination of the Interior Minister in August and the assassination attempt on Prime Minister Sedky in November.

The Egyptian Government responded to increased domestic terrorism by detaining or arresting thousands of suspected terrorists and using military courts to try hundreds of them, convicting some and acquitting others. Some of the convicted received death sentences that were carried out.

In addition, Cairo called for more international coordination to combat terrorism and asked for the expulsion of many suspected Egyptian terrorists from Pakistan, Afghanistan, the Gulf states, and some European countries, among others. Cairo also asked for the extradition of Shaykh Umar Abd al-Rahman from the United States. The Egyptian Government believes Iran and Sudan support terrorism in Egypt. Cairo criticized Tehran for its role and expressed concern over alleged terrorist training bases in Sudan.

In March, Cairo handed over Egyptian citizen Mahmoud Abu Halima, a suspect in the World Trade Center bombing, to US officials. Cairo continued to attempt to mediate international efforts to bring Libya into compliance with UN Security Council resolutions stemming from Libya's role in the Pan Am Flight 103 and UTA Flight 772 bombings.

Israel and the Occupied Territories

Violence and terrorist acts instigated by Palestinians continued in 1993. Attacks on Israeli soldiers and civilians in Israel and the occupied territories left approximately 65 Israelis dead and 390 others wounded. Approximately 14 Palestinians were killed by Israeli civilians.

Intra-Palestinian violence in the occupied territories declined during the year; approximately 83 Palestinians were killed by other Palestinians as compared to nearly 200 in 1992. The decline is largely the result of a tacit cease-fire between the previous year's primary combatants, Fatah and HAMAS, and a decline in killings of alleged collaborators. Several prominent Fatah leaders in Gaza were assassinated late in the year, apparently by fellow Palestinians.

Before the 13 September signing of the Israeli-Palestinian DOP, Arafat's Fatah faction of the PLO, HAMAS, and the PIJ claimed responsibility for the majority of terrorist and violent actions. On 9 September, in letters to Israeli Prime Minister Rabin and Norwegian Foreign Minister Holst, PLO Chairman Arafat committed the PLO to cease all violence and terrorism. Between 9 September and 31 December, PLO factions loyal to Arafat complied with this commitment except for one, possibly two, instances. Members of Fatah were responsible for the 29 October murder of an Israeli settler, and an alleged member of the Fatah Hawks, a PLO-affiliated group in the Gaza Strip, claimed responsibility for the 31 December murder of two Israelis. In both cases, the responsible individuals apparently acted independently.

The level of violence in Israel and the occupied territories initially declined following the signing of the DOP; however, opposition groups determined to defeat the agreement contributed to an increase in the number of violent incidents and terrorist attacks over the last three months of the year. Since the DOP was signed, Palestinian attacks have resulted in the deaths of approximately 17 Israelis—10 civilians and 7 military personnel. Two groups under the PLO umbrella, the Popular Front for the Liberation of Palestine (PFLP), and the Democratic Front for the Liberation of Palestine (DFLP)-Hawatmeh faction suspended their participation in the PLO to protest the agreement, and they continued their campaign of violence. The PFLP claimed responsibility for the mid-October murder of two Israeli hikers and also for a failed seaborne raid on northern Israel.

Non-PLO groups that oppose the DOP, such as HAMAS and the PIJ, have been responsible for the majority of violent incidents since 13 September. HAMAS's underground armed wing, known as the Izz al-Din al Qassam Brigades, increased its violent operations in an attempt to disrupt implementation of the DOP. HAMAS has claimed at least 13 postagreement attacks, including several directed at civilians. The group mounted several suicide car-bomb attacks in late 1993, including the 4 October ramming of an explosives-laden vehicle into an Israeli bus that wounded 30 persons.

Israel conducted no significant prosecutions of international terrorists during the year; however, it authorized the extradition to the United States of two US citizens wanted for terrorist activities. Israeli security forces killed two senior members of the Izz al-Din al Qassam Brigades in late November. On 31 March, the Israeli Government, responding to a string of terrorist attacks, instituted a strict ban on Palestinian entry into Israel, which effectively curtailed Palestinian attacks in Israel proper. The ban was gradually eased to allow 52,000 Palestinians to work in Israel. Israel allowed nearly 400 HAMAS supporters that were expelled to Lebanon in December 1992 to return to the occupied territories in 1993. Half of the deportees returned in September, and the remainder—with the exception of 18 who decided to remain in Lebanon to avoid arrest—returned in December.

As a result of intensive border security by Israeli, Egyptian, and Jordanian forces, only one successful infiltration attempt into Israel occurred in 1993. On 29 December, three members believed to be of the non-PLO Abu Musa group infiltrated northern Israel from Lebanon. The three were killed by the Israeli Defense Forces; no Israelis were hurt or killed. Rocket attacks into northern Israel from southern Lebanon, however, increased dramatically in the first half of the year. Israel responded by launching a major air and artillery offensive—which it termed "Operation Accountability "against Lebanese Hizballah and Palestinian rejectionist positions in Lebanon. There were no more rocket attacks from Lebanon into Israel for the rest of the year.

Jewish extremist groups mounted several violent attacks in 1993. Kahane Chai reacted to Arafat's official visit to Paris by exploding two bombs near the French Embassy in Tel Aviv on 24 October; no one was injured. Kahane Chai also threatened to attack other French interests in the region. A settler, affiliated with the militant Kach group, claimed responsibility for an 8 November drive-by shooting that wounded two Palestinians in the West Bank. Israeli settlers opposed to the DOP rioted after the murder of Israeli settler Haim Mizrahi by randomly assaulting Palestinians and destroying property. One Palestinian was killed, and 18 others were wounded.

Jordan

In February, Jordanian border police arrested two men, allegedly members of the PIJ, who were smuggling weapons into Jordan. The suspects said they were ordered to attack Americans on organized bus tours. In April, Jordanian security forces uncovered an alleged plot to assassinate King Hussein at a military academy graduation ceremony in June. The suspects, all members of the outlawed Islamic Liberation Party, were put on trial. In November, three gunmen with reported links to the New York-based Egyptian cleric Shaykh Umar Abd al-Rahman attacked a Jordanian Army outpost near the West Bank border. All three assailants were killed.

Jordanian security and police closely monitor secular and Islamic extremists inside the country and detain individuals suspected of involvement in violent acts aimed at destabilizing the government or undermining its relations with neighboring states. Jordan maintains tight security along its border with Israel and last year interdicted several armed infiltration operations attributed to Palestinian factions.

Jordan continues to host PLO rejectionist groups such as the Popular and Democratic Fronts for the Liberation of Palestine. HAMAS also has an office in Amman. In addition, some extremist Palestinian groups with a history of anti-Western terrorist activity—including the Popular Front for the Liberation of Palestine-General Command (PFLP-GC), and some factions of the PIJ—maintain a presence in Jordan.

Kuwait

The Iraqi plot to assassinate former President Bush and to explode several bombs in Kuwait City in April was one of the year's most brazen attempts at terrorism. Eleven Iraqis and three Kuwaitis are on trial for the plot. They smuggled into Kuwait two vehicles, one loaded with 180 pounds of explosives, and a collection of time bombs, grenades, and pistols. The sophisticated remote-controlled firing device, as well as the blasting cap, wiring, and integrated circuitry of the car bomb matched devices that were already linked to Iraq. Kuwaiti authorities have identified some of the Iraqi suspects as employees of the Iraqi Intelligence Service.

Several minor terrorist incidents occurred in Kuwait last year, separate from the Iraqi plot. In March, a series of bombs exploded in music and video shops, one of which exploded near the Holiday Inn. Although no arrests or claims of responsibility were made for the attacks, local radical Muslim extremists have been blamed.

In June, a Kuwaiti court sentenced to death 10 members of the Arab Liberation Front, a Palestinian terrorist group based in Baghdad, for their collaboration with Iraq during the occupation of Kuwait.

Lebanon

The security situation in Lebanon has improved, and the Lebanese Government exercises authority over significant areas of the country. The Syrian military controls some areas, particularly in the Bekaa Valley along the border with Syria, and Israel occupies a self-declared security zone in the south. In the Bekaa Valley, parts of the south, and a few other areas of the country, however, terrorist groups continue to move about freely—notably Iranian-backed Hizballah. The Lebanese Government has not taken steps to disarm Hizballah or to expand its authority into areas of southern Lebanon controlled by the group; however, it deployed a small unit of the Lebanese Armed Forces into the region. Hizballah released the last of the Western hostages it held in 1992; it still holds many South Lebanese Army members that were taken prisoner during fighting in the south. The fate of several Israeli military personnel missing in Lebanon remains unknown.

Hizballah and Palestinian groups have launched attacks on northern Israel from southern Lebanon. Hizballah launched rockets into Israel throughout the year, reaching a crescendo with dozens of rockets launched daily at the end of July. Four Israeli civilians were killed in two of the attacks in July and August. The Israeli military responded with a major counterattack in southern Lebanon dubbed Operation Accountability.

There are still diverse elements in Lebanon willing to resort to terrorism. In January, a man with explosives strapped to his waist and several sticks of dynamite in his luggage was arrested as he was about to board a Middle East Airlines flight to Cyprus. In February, a bomb was placed in front of the Kuwait Airways office, and a bomb was thrown into the Kuwaiti Embassy compound the following month. Two bombs were discovered in June near the Danish Embassy in Beirut. The same month, two members of the radical Sunni "Islamic Grouping" were killed, and another was wounded while attempting to plant a bomb near a monastery in northern Lebanon. The intended target was a bus carrying Christians attending an international ecumenical conference. The government is prosecuting five members of the group. In August, a bomb was discovered near a building that houses Kuwait Airways. Iraqi agents or their surrogates were probably responsible for all three of the attempted bombings of Kuwaiti interests in Lebanon. In December, Kataiv (Phalange) Party headquarters in Beirut was blown up, killing several people. Factional feuding among Palestinians led to several assassinations of Palestinian leaders in Lebanon.

Iran, Iraq, and Syria continued to provide varying degrees of financial, military, and logistic support to terrorist groups based in Lebanon. Syria, in particular, maintains a considerable influence over Lebanese internal affairs and has not supported Lebanese Government attempts to control the radical Shia group, Hizballah. Hizballah, which now has eight members in Parliament, has been allowed to retain its well-armed militia and terrorist capabilities. In addition, several radical Palestinian groups have training facilities in Lebanon, including the PFLP-GC, the PIJ, and the ANO. Several non-Arab groups—such as Turkey's PKK, the Revolutionary Left (Dev Sol), and the Japanese Red Army (JRA)—also maintain facilities in Lebanon, most of which are in the Bekaa Valley.

The Lebanese Government has taken only minimal steps toward prosecuting terrorists responsible for the wave of hijackings, bombings, and abductions that swept through Lebanon during its civil war. During the last year, a military court sentenced one man to death, but later reduced the sentence to 10 years with hard labor, for car-bombing the American University in Beirut in 1991.

Saudi Arabia

No terrorist attacks or prosecutions related to terrorism occurred in Saudi Arabia in 1993. The annual pilgrimage to Mecca—the hajj—passed relatively peacefully. Nonetheless, the government continues to be concerned about the possibility of terrorist attacks sponsored by Iraq, Iran, or Muslim extremists from other countries.

Some private Saudi citizens probably provide private funds to HAMAS and other radical Palestinian groups throughout the region, as well as to extremist elements in Somalia, Sudan, and Yemen. Saudi benefactors also sponsor paramilitary training for radical Muslims from many countries in camps in Afghanistan, Yemen, and Sudan.

Yemen

There were several attacks on foreign interests in Yemen by unknown assailants in 1993. In January, a small rocket narrowly missed the US Embassy, and, in March, a small bomb exploded outside the British Embassy but did no damage.

Perpetrators of similar attacks on the US and German Embassies in late 1992 and 1993 have not been apprehended.

It became relatively common practice for Yemeni tribal members to take hostages briefly, including several foreigners, to settle tribal disputes or extort funds. Two foreigners were abducted in separate incidents in January in tribal disputes with Yemeni authorities. In April, six foreign oil workers were kidnapped and threatened with death to force a French oil company to hire more locals at a drilling site. In May, two US oil men were abducted to prevent the government from carrying out a death sentence imposed on a fellow tribesman. In November, a US diplomat was seized by gunmen and held hostage by tribal leaders seeking several concessions from the government.

Six religious extremists, members of the Yemeni Islamic Jihad awaiting trial for bombing two hotels in Aden at the end of 1992, escaped from prison in July. Paramilitary training is reportedly being conducted in parts of Yemen under weak government control and funded in large part by private donations gathered from other parts of the Islamic world.

Patterns of Global Terrorism: 1994

The Year in Review

There were 321 international terrorist attacks during 1994, a 25-percent decrease from the 431 recorded the previous year and the lowest annual total in 23 years. Sixty-six were anti-US attacks, down from 88 in 1993.

A powerful bomb destroyed a Jewish cultural center in Buenos Aires in July, killing nearly 100 persons and wounding more than 200 others. The bombing could well be the work of Hizballah, which claimed responsibility for an almost identical bombing of the Israeli Embassy in Buenos Aires in 1992.

A serious hijacking occurred on 24 December in Algiers when terrorists from the Armed Islamic Group took over an Air France jet, murdered three passengers, and flew the plane with 170 hostages to Marseille. The assault ended two days later with a remarkably successful rescue operation by French commandos that resulted in the deaths of all four hijackers and no other fatalities.

There were numerous deadly attacks by the Islamic extremist group HAMAS against Israelis. In April a bomb in Fula that exploded near a commuter bus killed eight persons and wounded 50, mostly children who were waiting to ride the bus back from school. In October a suicide bomber detonated a device inside a public bus in the heart of Tel Aviv's business and shopping district, killing 22 Israeli passengers plus the perpetrator and wounding at least 48. Also in October, two HAMAS gunmen armed with assault rifles and grenades attacked civilians in a popular restaurant district in the center of Jerusalem, killing two Israeli citizens and wounding 13 persons, including two Americans.

On 9 October, Israeli Army Corporal Nachshon Wachsman, while hitchhiking in central Israel, was kidnapped by HAMAS terrorists. They demanded the release of HAMAS spiritual leader Sheikh Yassin and 200 Palestinian prisoners from Israeli jails and released a videotape of Wachsman in captivity asking that Israel comply with the demand. Israeli forces located Wachsman in a West Bank house, which they stormed in an effort to free him, but his captors killed him as the raid began. One Israeli soldier and three kidnappers were also killed.

A member of the Jewish extremist group Kach attacked Palestinian worshippers at Hebron's al-Ibrahimi Mosque in February, killing 29 and wounding more than 200. The Israeli Cabinet subsequently outlawed Kach and the affiliated group Kahane Chai, declaring them to be terrorist organizations.

Four Americans were killed in terrorist attacks during 1994. Corporal Nachshon Wachsman, mentioned previously, held dual Israeli and American citizenship. Three other Americans died in an apparent suicide bombing of a Panamanian commuter aircraft in July that killed all 21 persons aboard. Four Americans were wounded as a result of HAMAS attacks in Israel during the year, and another—an American priest—was wounded after he was kidnapped by terrorists in the Philippines.

Worldwide casualties numbered 314 persons dead and 663 wounded.

There were no confirmed acts of terrorism—either international or domestic—committed in the United States during 1994. In January, explosive devices were found outside two New York City office buildings. Both buildings housed Jewish-American organizations that actively support the Middle East peace process. These suspected terrorist incidents remain under investigation by the FBI.

On 24 May, four men convicted in the February 1993 bombing of the World Trade Center in New York City were each sentenced to 240 years in prison. The judge arrived at this figure by calculating the life expectancy of each of the six persons killed in the attack and adding mandatory prison terms for assault on a federal officer. Two other suspects in the bombing remained at large at the end of the year.

The trial of 12 defendants accused of plotting to blow up several landmarks in New York City began in 1995.

In October, a judge in St. Louis, Missouri, sentenced three members of the Abu Nidal organization (ANO) to prison sentences of 21 months for plotting acts of terrorism within the United States. The three had pled guilty to Federal racketeering charges that included allegations they smuggled money and information, bought weapons, recruited members, illegally obtained passports, and obstructed investigations.

African Overview

Civil wars and ethnic conflict continue to rage in Sub-Saharan Africa (for example, Somalia, Sudan, Angola, and Liberia), and several acts of international terrorism took place in Africa in 1994. The rightwing South African rejectionist Afrikaner Resistance Movement detonated a car bomb in Johannesburg in protest of South Africa's first multiracial elections. Togolese oppositionists may have been responsible for a grenade attack on a French-owned restaurant that wounded five French and two Beninese citizens.

Sudan turned over the international terrorist Carlos to France in August, but insisted that action did not represent a change in Sudanese policy and would not affect other terrorists harbored in Sudan.

Angola

In January, rival factions of the Front for the Liberation of the Enclave of Cabinda (FLEC) claimed responsibility for a mortar attack on the Chevron administrative facility in Malongo. FLEC has targeted Western oil companies in the past in hopes of reducing government revenues. In late November, FLEC-Renovada claimed credit for kidnapping three Polish citizens employed by an Italian forestry company.

Sierra Leone

On 7 November the rebel group Revolutionary United Front (RUF) kidnapped two British engineers working for the Voluntary Service Organization. The group also captured four relief workers who were subsequently released.

South Africa

There were a number of serious incidents of domestic political violence in the runup to South Africa's first multiracial election in April 1994. There was also one act of international terrorism on 27 April when members of the rightwing Afrikaner Resistance Movement (AWB) detonated a car bomb at the Jan Smuts Airport in Johannesburg. The bomb injured 16, including two Russian diplomats and a pilot for Swiss Air.

Togo

There were a number of incidents of domestic political violence in Togo in 1994 and one act of international terrorism. Togolese oppositionists, retaliating for what they believe is French support for President Eyadama, were probably responsible for a grenade attack on a French-owned restaurant that wounded five French citizens and two Beninese.

Uganda

In 1994 the Lord's Resistance Army (LRA), an insurgent group operating in northern Uganda, carried out a number of attacks against foreign relief organizations, accusing them of collaborating with the Museveni government. On 23 June, for example, the LRA ambushed a World Food Program convoy belonging to the Catholic Relief Services.

Asian Overview

Ethnic tensions continued to pose serious terrorism concerns in South Asia in 1994. The Sri Lankan separatist group Liberation Tigers of Tamil Eelam (LTTE) is widely believed to have been behind an October suicide bombing attack that killed a leading presidential candidate and 56 other people. Pakistan continued to provide support to some of the insurgents fighting in Indian-controlled Kashmir. Targeting of foreigners by Kashmiri militants resulted in several high-profile kidnappings in 1994, including the abduction of British and American hostages in October and the abduction of British hikers near Srinigar, Kashmir, in June. Pakistan continued to claim that India supported separatists in Sindh Province.

Instability in Afghanistan occasionally spilled over into Pakistan. Afghan mujahedin kidnapped 81 Pakistanis on a schoolbus in Peshawar in February. Pakistani soldiers stormed the bus and killed the three Afghan gunmen. More than 20 camps in Afghanistan that once trained mujahedin to fight the Soviets are now being used to train militant Arabs, Kashmiris, Tajiks, and Muslims for new areas of conflict. Several hundred veterans of the Afghan war have been implicated in the violence that has wracked Algeria and Egypt during the last several years. Many of the supporters of the blind Egyptian cleric Sheikh Omar Abdul Rahman, several of whom were convicted of the bombing of the World Trade Center, fought with or actively supported the Afghan mujahedin.

There were no attacks against US facilities in the Philippines in 1994. Muslim extremist guerrillas—probably from the Abu Sayyaf Group (ASG)—kidnapped an American priest in July. He was rescued by Philippine Marines and members of another Muslim group. On 11 December a Philippine Airlines 747 en route from Manila to Tokyo was bombed, killing one person and injuring at least 10. Khmer Rouge insurgents posed a growing threat to travelers in Cambodia. Over the course of the year, the group kidnapped and killed at least six Westerners. An American was freed in May after one and one-half months in captivity. In Thailand, in March, police discovered a truck loaded with explosives in downtown Bangkok near the Israeli Embassy, which was probably the target of an attack that was aborted when the truck became involved in an accident, causing the driver to flee. One Iranian has been put on trial in the incident.

Afghanistan

Afghanistan, which lacks a functioning government, remains a training ground for Islamic militants committed to overthrowing regimes that maintain strong ties to Western governments. More than 20 camps in Afghanistan that once trained mujahedin to fight the Soviets are now being used to train militant Arabs, Kashmiris, Tajiks, and others for new areas of conflict. Most of these facilities—located south and east of Kabul—are overseen by the nominal Afghan Prime Minister, Gulbuddin Hikmatyar, or by one of his domestic rivals—Abdul Rasul Sayyaf, the leader of a small militant Afghan Wahhabi party, who is backed by several affluent foreign benefactors. Training in these camps focuses on tactics and techniques for conducting terrorist and insurgent operations, such as instruction on the use of sophisticated weapons, improvised explosives, boobytraps, and timing devices for bombs. The camps allow militants from throughout the world to train together, meet with new benefactors, and help foster relationships between otherwise disparate extremist groups.

Although only a few thousand veterans of the Afghan Jihad, along with a few hundred newly trained militants, are actively engaged in insurgent or terrorist activity worldwide, they are often responsible for raising the level of sophistication and destructiveness of extremist operations. Several hundred veterans of the Afghan war have been implicated in the violence that has wracked Algeria and Egypt during the last several years. Two of the leading Algerian extremists, Kamreddine Kherbane and Boudjemma Bounoua, participated in the Afghan Jihad. Many of the supporters of the blind Egyptian cleric, Sheikh Omar Abdul Rahman, several of whom were convicted of the bombing of the World Trade Center, fought with or actively supported the Afghan mujahedin. Many Islamists active in Egypt's two most violent extremist groups— al-Gama'a al-Islamiyya and al-Jihad—received training in Afghanistan.

The current Afghan regime—deeply embroiled in its own struggle for survival—has been unable to control or eliminate the training of extremists on its territory or terrorist use of the camps as safehavens. Some local Afghan leaders have taken some steps against the militants, but their efforts are limited by bickering, greed, and the militants' military and financial strength.

Cambodia

Diminished by defections and a declining support base, the Khmer Rouge increasingly turned toward banditry and terror in 1994. Khmer Rouge radio commentaries on several occasions threatened physical harm to Americans and other foreign nationals living in Cambodia. Travelers in some areas outside Phnom Penh, particularly remote rural districts, faced security threats from the Khmer Rouge and from bandits. An American was taken hostage and held by Khmer Rouge elements for one and one half months but was eventually released unharmed. Many other civilians, however, were killed by the Khmer Rouge in 1994. The victims were mainly ordinary Cambodian villagers, but foreigners, including Thais, Vietnamese, and six Western tourists (three from Britain, two from Australia, and one from France), were killed by the Khmer Rouge in 1994.

India

India continues to face significant security problems as a result of insurgencies in Kashmir and the northeast. Targeting of foreigners by Kashmiri militants resulted in several high-profile kidnappings in 1994, including the abduction of British and American hostages in October and the abduction of British hikers near Srinagar, Kashmir, in June. There are credible reports of support by the Government of Pakistan for Kashmiri militants. The Government of India has been largely successful in controlling the Sikh separatist movement in Punjab State, and Sikh militants now only rarely stage attacks in India.

The Indian Government proceeded with the investigation and trial of suspects in the series of blasts that struck Bombay on 12 March 1993. On 5 August 1994, the government arrested a key suspect in the case, Yaqub Memon. The Memon family allegedly perpetrated the Bombay attack. The Government of India has claimed that Memon was carrying documents that incriminated Pakistan.

Pakistan

Pakistan continues to experience occasional violence as a result of instability in Afghanistan. Much of this violence occurs in Pakistan's northwest border region. On 20 February, Afghan mujahedin kidnapped 81 Pakistanis on a schoolbus in Peshawar. The hijackers ordered the busdriver to proceed to Prime Minister Benazir Bhutto's residence in Islamabad. Following extensive negotiations, Pakistani soldiers stormed the bus and killed the three Afghan gunmen. Some regions of Pakistan also suffer from heavy sectarian, political, and criminal violence, particularly Sindh Province and its capital, Karachi, and the Pakistani tribal area bordering Afghanistan.

Pakistan recognizes the problems posed by Afghan mujahedin and sympathetic Arabs in the Pakistani regions that border Afghanistan. In 1994, Islamabad refused to extend the visas of many Arabs who had fought in the Afghan war and who had taken refuge in Pakistan's tribal areas and the North-West Frontier Province. Pakistan also closed several nongovernmental organizations it suspected were being used as cover agencies for Islamic militants from the Middle East. Pakistan concluded an extradition treaty with Egypt in late 1994 with the express purpose of extraditing "Arab mujahedin" operating in Peshawar.

The Government of Pakistan acknowledges that it continues to give moral, political, and diplomatic support to Kashmiri militants but denies allegations of other assistance. There were credible reports in 1994, however, of official Pakistani support to Kashmiri militants. Some support came from private organizations such as the Jamaat-i-Islami, Pakistan's largest Islamic party. Pakistan condemned the kidnappings in June and October 1994 of foreign tourists by Kashmiri militants in India. Pakistan has claimed that India provides support for separatists in Sindh Province.

Philippines

There were no attacks against official US facilities in the Philippines in 1994, but Muslim extremist guerrillas— probably from the Abu Sayyaf Group (ASG)—kidnapped an American priest, Clarence William Bertelsman, on 31 July. He was held for several hours before being rescued by Philippine Marines and members of the largest Muslim separatist group, the Moro National Liberation Front (MNLF). On 11 December a Philippine Airlines 747 en route from Manila to Tokyo was bombed, killing one person and injuring at least 10 others, mostly Japanese citizens. The Philippine Government has been trying to reach a negotiated settlement to both Communist and Muslim insurgencies and currently observes a cease-fire with the MNLF as talks continue.

Sri Lanka

The separatist group Liberation Tigers of Tamil Eelam (LTTE) continued to plague the government in 1994, with insurgency and terrorism directed against senior Sri Lankan political and military leaders in the countryside and in Colombo as well. Despite the beginning of peace negotiations between the government and the LTTE, the Tigers continued to pose a significant terrorist threat. The Tigers are widely believed to be behind an October suicide bombing attack that killed a leading presidential candidate and 56 other people.

The LTTE has refrained from targeting Western tourists out of fear that foreign governments would crack down on Tamil expatriates involved in fundraising activities abroad. However, in April 1994 the Ellalan Force, an LTTE front group, claimed credit for bombing several major tourist hotels in Colombo. The blasts, which caused only minor damage and two injuries, probably were intended to damage Colombo's tourist industry rather than to harm Westerners. The Ellalan Force also claimed in August to have poisoned tea—Sri Lanka's primary export—with arsenic, although none was ever found. Threatening Sri Lanka's two leading economic activities demonstrates the Tigers' interest in economic terrorism. The Tigers possess the infrastructure to make good on most of their recent threats should the current peace talks with the government fail.

Thailand

Thai police discovered a truck loaded with an ammonium nitrate mixture and about 6 pounds of plastic explosives in downtown Bangkok on 17 March. The driver abandoned the truck after hitting another vehicle near the Israeli Embassy, which was probably the intended target. The Thai Government is prosecuting one Iranian in connection with the attempted bombing but concluded it does not have enough evidence to charge two other suspects. In southern Thailand, Muslim separatists, such as the Pattani United Liberation Front, continued to engage in low-level violence against the government.

European Overview

Terrorism in Europe declined somewhat in 1994, in part because of a cease-fire in Northern Ireland declared by the Provisional Irish Republican Army (PIRA) on 1 September, and by the Loyalist paramilitary groups in early October. In the eastern Mediterranean region, the Greek leftist group 17 November continued to target foreign businesses and diplomats, as well as Greek Government figures, and the Turkish separatist Kurdistan Workers' Party (PKK) attacked tourist sites in western Turkish resort areas on the Aegean Sea. In Spain, the Basque Fatherland and Liberty group (ETA) continued lethal attacks against Spanish police and military targets. A Bosnian Muslim protesting the three-year-old conflict in the former Yugoslavia hijacked a domestic SAS flight in Norway; there were no casualties. Ethnic tensions in regions of the former Soviet Union have spawned acts of terrorism in the Caucasus and the Baltic republics. In September there was an attempted bombing of an airliner in Georgia. In November there was a hijacking of a Russian airliner to Estonia, which ended peacefully. In Lithuania, there were two bombings of a rail line connecting the Russian enclave of Kaliningrad with the Russian republic. Violence in this region has not, for the most part, been directed at foreigners.

Albania

On 10 April several gunmen crossed into Albania from Greece and stormed a border guard facility, killing two persons and seriously wounding three others before returning across the Greek border. A group calling itself the "Northern Epirus Liberation Front" (MAVI) claimed responsibility for the incident. It accused the Albanian Government of violating the rights of the ethnic Greek minority in Albania and berated Athens for not doing enough to support the minority. MAVI also issued a pamphlet last fall announcing the commencement of an "armed struggle" against Tirana and demanding, inter alia, the cessation of the alleged "colonization" of "Northern Epirus"—the Greek name for southern Albania, which has a large ethnic Greek population—by Albanians from the north. MAVI was the name of an ethnic Greek resistance group in Albania during World War II that operated first against the invading Italians and then against the Communists. Press reports state that the group was disbanded in the 1940s, although responsibility for the 1984 bombing of the Albanian Embassy in Athens was claimed in its name.

Azerbaijan

Several Armenian intelligence officers are being held in Moscow, accused of complicity in a series of bombings against the Baku Metro, as well as Azerbaijani trains in Russia and Azerbaijan that killed 45 persons and wounded at least 130. The Azerbaijani Supreme Court sentenced an ethnic Russian involved in the crimes to eight years in prison for engaging in intelligence work against Azerbaijan and committing acts of sabotage on its territory.

The Baltics

Anti-Russian sentiment may have been the catalyst for explosions and bomb threats in the Baltics last year. On 28

February, when Latvian and Russian delegations resumed talks on the withdrawal of Russian troops from Latvia, a minor blast caused by an estimated one-half kilogram of TNT damaged a power pylon near Skrunda. When Latvian and Russian officials initialed agreements on 15 March allowing Russia to retain its radar station for another five and a half years, Latvian police discovered and disarmed a timer-controlled device armed with 12 kilograms of TNT at the base of another pylon. In November, a powerful explosion destroyed a railroad bridge in Lithuania on the main railway line for international trains traveling between Moscow and the Russian exclave of Kaliningrad. The incident may have been connected to a controversy surrounding negotiations over an agreement to allow Russian military trains to transit Lithuania to Kaliningrad.

France

France scored a number of successes against international terrorists in 1994. In August, the Sudanese Government handed over notorious terrorist Illych Ramirez Sanchez, a.k.a. "Carlos," previously convicted in absentia in France for the murder of two French intelligence officers. He will probably be retried on this charge and possibly others after French officials complete their investigations. In September, French officials also arrested Dursun Karatas, leader of the Turkish leftwing group Dev Sol, for entering France using a false passport. (He has since apparently escaped.) Karatas is under investigation for complicity in attacks against French interests in Turkey during the Gulf war.

French authorities made a number of sweeps against foreign Islamic extremists, seizing arms and false documents. They arrested or expelled a number of North Africans believed to have links to extremist organizations. In November, for example, French police detained 80 persons tied to Algeria's Armed Islamic Group. French police also arrested several members of the Basque terrorist organization ETA, including the group's second-highest ranking member, in three separate incidents during the year.

In December, a French court convicted two Iranians of involvement in the murder of former Iranian Prime Minister Bakhtiar in 1991. A third defendant, an Iranian Embassy employee, was acquitted.

On 26 December, France's National Gendarmerie Action Group stormed an Air France plane hijacked from Algiers to Marseille, killing the four hijackers and rescuing 170 passengers and crew.

Germany

The Red Army Faction (RAF) remained deeply divided between those who opted for political means and those who wanted to engage in violence. German courts granted early release to two RAF members: Irmgard Moeller, who served 22 years of a life sentence for a car bomb attack that killed three US soldiers in 1972, and Ingrid Jakobsmeier, who served two-thirds of her sentence for participating in attacks against the US military in 1981. German authorities believe the two pose no further terrorist threat. Another RAF member, Birgit Hogefeld, went on trial in November for her part in a number of attacks, including a bombing at a US airbase in Frankfurt in 1985 that killed a US soldier.

Several smaller leftwing factions resumed operations. After a six-year hiatus, the Revolutionary Cells (RZ) reappeared with an arson attack on the Frankfurt subway system protesting higher fares and "racist" practices among ticket controllers. Red Zora, the feminist branch of the RZ, also reemerged and set fire to trucks belonging to a company that supplied groceries to refugee facilities on the premise that the firm was "making money off refugees." Unidentified leftwing terrorists, probably on the RAF periphery, bombed offices of the ruling political parties in two cities in September.

Rightwing extremist attacks continued to decline last year. There were still more than 1,000 reported attacks—down from about 2,200 in 1993—but arson and mob attacks against refugee homes virtually ceased, and assaults on individual foreigners occurred less frequently. The most significant incident took place on 12 May, when at least 50 youths chased five foreigners through the streets of Magdeburg. However, during 1994, the number of anti-Semitic attacks increased; rightwing extremists threw firebombs at a synagogue in Luebeck and desecrated Jewish cemeteries elsewhere.

Greece

Greece was the venue for a large number of international terrorist attacks in 1994. The most deadly attack was the 4 July assassination of the acting Deputy Chief of Mission of the Turkish Embassy, claimed by the Revolutionary Organization 17 November. Events in the Balkans probably sparked a number of other attacks against Western interests in Greece in April, including an unsuccessful mortar attack against the British aircraft carrier Ark Royal in Piraeus claimed by 17 November. Attacks also were made against American, Dutch, French, and German commercial and diplomatic targets. The Revolutionary People's Struggle (ELA) claimed two bombing attempts against the office of the UN High Commissioner for Refugee Affairs.

In July, three improvised bombs exploded on the Island of Rhodes, injuring one foreign tourist and a Greek citizen. No group has claimed responsibility.

Greek authorities made little progress in 1994 against terrorist groups, in part due to ambivalent government attitudes toward counterterrorism. Greece still lacks a new antiterrorism law to replace legislation repealed in December 1993 by the incoming PASOK government. In addition, suspected terrorist Georgios Balafas was acquitted on 25 July of murder, armed robbery, and other charges. He still faces trial in two other cases—weapons and narcotics charges—but was released in September on "humanitarian" grounds after a reported hunger strike. While in the prison hospital, he was visited by the then Minister of Transportation and Communications as a "gesture of support."

Italy

Leftwing groups modeled on the largely defunct Red Brigades carried out several small-scale attacks, including the bombing of the NATO Defense College in Rome on 10 January. The attack was claimed by the Combatant Communist Nuclei for the Construction of the Combatant Communist Party.

In September, four members of the Red Brigades for the Construction of the Communist Combatant Party, another neo-Red Brigades group, were convicted of involvement in the attack on the NATO base in Aviano in September 1993.

Russia

Separatist and internal power struggles, particularly in the North Caucasus region of Russia, continued to spawn domestic violence and terrorism. In July, four gunmen from the separatist Chechnya region hijacked a bus carrying more than 40 passengers. The incident ended tragically when four hostages were killed as Russian police stormed the hijackers' getaway helicopter. There were also a number of airplane hijackings, including one in the Chechnya region in which the hijacker blew himself up after releasing several passengers and watching the others escape.

Spain

Spanish authorities scored several successes against the separatist group Basque Fatherland and Liberty (ETA), including the disruption of the "Comando Vizcaya" subunit in November. One ETA member was killed and two arrested after a failed assassination attempt against a Spanish soldier. Continuing close cooperation between Spanish and French police resulted in a September raid on an ETA explosives factory in France and the arrest of five ETA members in November, including the group's number-two figure.

ETA carried out one act of international terrorism in 1994 with the attempted assassination of the Spanish military attache in Rome. Domestic attacks by ETA fell off at the end of the year, but the group retains its lethal capabilities.

Turkey

International terrorism has become an important part of the Kurdistan Workers' Party (PKK) campaign to establish a breakaway state in southeast Turkey and presents a potentially serious threat to US interests. PKK attacks against tourists in Turkey last year were particularly violent, although the overall number of terrorist attacks was significantly lower than in 1993. Three attacks on tourist sites in Istanbul in May killed two foreign tourists—the first to be killed by the PKK—and injured several others. In June, the PKK was also responsible for several small bombs that exploded in two Turkish resort towns on the Mediterranean coast, killing a British woman and injuring at least 10 other tourists. In the latest in a series of kidnappings of foreign travelers, the PKK abducted two Finnish tourists on 8 August and released them unharmed three weeks later. The PKK also attacked government and commercial targets in major Turkish cities, presenting an incidental risk to foreign visitors, as well as Turks. PKK terrorist attacks on Turkish citizens, including ethnic Kurds, continued unabated.

The PKK continued to expand its activities in Western Europe, where its members clashed with police frequently throughout the year. For the first time, the PKK also directly targeted Western interests in Europe. It blocked highways in Germany with burning tires in March and conducted demonstrations in a number of German cities, some of which turned into violent confrontations with the police. After German police killed a Kurdish youth in Hannover, the PKK organized protests and sit-ins at the German Embassy in Athens and a German Consulate in Denmark. The PKK also mounted demonstrations in several West European countries after British immigration authorities detained Kani Yilmaz, the senior PKK leader in Europe, in October. The PKK also opened offices of its political wing (ERNK) in Italy and Greece.

The Marxist/Leninist terrorist group Dev Sol (Devrimci Sol), or Revolutionary Left, remained a threat to US interests and personnel in Turkey, despite a series of setbacks the group has suffered over the last two years. Dev Sol's two factions were largely inactive last year as they continued to battle each other and as the Turkish police arrested numerous operatives. Some members of the group sprang into action after French authorities arrested Dursun Karatas, the head of the major Dev Sol faction, on 9 September as he tried to enter France from Italy on falsified documents. Over the next several weeks, Dev Sol supporters protested in Austria, Belgium, and the Netherlands demanding Karatas' release. Dev Sol operatives in Turkey assassinated former Justice Minister Mehmet Topac on 29 September in Ankara and also killed a policeman in Istanbul.

Several groups of loosely organized Turkish Islamic extremists, who advocate an Islamic government for Turkey, attacked targets associated with the Turkish secular state. They claimed attacks under a variety of names, such as Islamic Jihad, the Islamic Movement Organization, and the Islamic Great Eastern Raiders Front. The Islamic extremists also pursue a strong anti-Western agenda. In May 1994, Islamic terrorists claimed responsibility for bombing the Ankara branch of the Freemason organization. In September, a Turkish political scientist known for his secular writings escaped death when a car bomb planted by Islamic extremists failed to explode.

United Kingdom

The Provisional Irish Republican Army (PIRA) announced a "complete cessation of military operations" beginning on 1 September. Other Republican splinter groups in Northern Ireland also ceased attacks after that date, although most have not formally agreed to a cease-fire. PIRA's leadership denied authorizing the use of firearms in a robbery on 10 November carried out by a lower-level unit in Newry that resulted in the death of a postal worker. The Combined Military Loyalist Command, an umbrella group comprising three loyalist paramilitary groups, announced its own cease-fire beginning 14 October.

Both Loyalists and Republicans carried out a number of international and domestic terrorist attacks before the ceasefire. Loyalists carried out several attacks in the Republic of Ireland, including a lethal attack in May on a Dublin pub during a Sinn Fein fundraiser. In March three separate attacks by PIRA on Heathrow International Airport in London failed when the mortar rounds used did not detonate.

On 26 July, a bomb contained in a car exploded outside the Israeli Chancery in London at approximately noon causing substantial structural damage and injuring 14 persons. The car carrying the explosives was driven by a woman described as in her fifties and "Middle Eastern" in appearance. On 27 July, shortly after midnight, another bomb contained in a car exploded in north London outside Balfour House, a Jewish fundraising organization. This bomb caused some structural damage to the building but resulted in limited casualties, primarily because of the time it was detonated. Five passers-by were injured by the blast.

On 26 October, British authorities arrested Faysal Dunlayici, a.k.a. Kani Yilmaz, a high-ranking leader of the PKK based in Europe. The arrest sparked protests from PKK supporters in the United Kingdom, and Germany and Turkey have requested his extradition.

Former Yugoslavia

Ethnic conflict and endemic violence plagued the former Yugoslavia for a third year, although in 1994 the fighting was largely restricted to Bosnia and Herzegovina. Meanwhile, a Bosnian Muslim, claiming that he wanted to focus world attention on the plight of his kinsmen, hijacked an SAS airliner during a domestic flight in Norway on 3 November. He surrendered peacefully to Norwegian authorities after landing in Oslo. This was the first such incident on behalf of one of the warring factions of the former Yugoslavia.

Latin American Overview

Latin America continued to have a high level of international terrorist activity, although the number of attacks decreased by 40 percent from the previous year to 58 attacks.

In July, an attack on the Argentine-Israeli Mutual Association (AMIA) in Buenos Aires killed nearly 100 persons and injured more than 200. The leading suspect in this incident is Hizballah. Twenty-one persons, of whom 12 were Jewish, were killed when a Panamanian commuter aircraft was bombed in July, apparently by a suicide bomber. These attacks raised concerns about the reported presence of members of Hizballah in Latin America, especially in the triborder area where Brazilian, Argentine, and Paraguayan territories meet.

Colombia continued to suffer the highest incidence of terrorist violence in the region. Guerrillas attacked the democratic process by attempting to sabotage Colombia's 1994 presidential, congressional, and departmental elections. Rebel organizations also targeted petroleum companies and infiltrated trade unions, particularly in the banana and petroleum industries, intimidating rank-and-file union members. US business interests and Mormon missionaries were attacked by guerrillas, and nine US citizens were being held hostage by guerrillas at the end of the year. Six of these were US missionaries. Kidnapping continued as a major source of income for the Colombian guerrillas.

Guerrillas in the region continued to attack national interests causing damage to local economies particularly in Colombia, Peru, and Guatemala. In the Andean Region, the connection between guerrilla groups and narcotraffickers remained strong. Guerrillas forced coca and amapola cultivators to pay protection money and attacked government efforts to reduce production.

Terrorist violence decreased in Peru during the year. The Sendero Luminoso (Shining Path) assassinated 150 persons, down from 516 the previous year when its leader was imprisoned. Various Peruvian terrorist groups suffered setbacks due to arrests, casualties, and defections under the government's amnesty program. Government actions in Chile also resulted in a decline of terrorist violence.

In reaction to the terrorist violence in the region, the heads of state of the Western Hemisphere nations adopted a plan of action against terrorism at the December Summit of the Americas. The plan called for cooperation among nations in combating terrorism and for the prosecution of terrorists while protecting human rights. The nations of the hemisphere also agreed to convene a special OAS conference on the prevention of terrorism and reaffirmed the importance of extradition treaties in combating terrorism.

Argentina

Argentina suffered the worst terrorist attack perpetrated in Latin America during 1994. On 18 July, a suicide bomber detonated a vehicle loaded with explosives in front of the AMIA. The powerful bombing killed nearly 100 people, many of whom were crushed by the collapsing building. The bombing of Argentina's main Jewish center was operationally similar to the 1992 bombing directed against the Israeli Embassy in Buenos Aires, which left 29 persons dead and destroyed the building. The Islamic Jihad organization, an arm of the Lebanese Hizballah, claimed responsibility for the 1992 bombing. According to media reports, an organization using the name Ansar Allah, or Followers of God, issued a statement expressing support for the 1994 operation. The Argentine Government dedicated substantial resources to investigate the bombing, but the crime remained unsolved at yearend.

Chile

Politically motivated violence in Chile declined dramatically in 1994 as Chilean security forces reined in the nation's terrorist groups. In June, the government all but eliminated the

Lautaro terrorist organization by capturing its founder and leader, Guillermo Ossandon, one of the most wanted outlaws in Chile. A second round of arrests was made against second-tier Lautaro leaders in August. Two prominent members of the Manuel Rodriguez Patriotic Front (FPMR) voluntarily returned from exile to Chile and were arrested by police. One of them, Sergio Buschman—wanted for his role in directing a multiton shipment of Cuban-supplied weapons into Chile in 1986—had escaped from a Chilean prison in 1987 and lived several years in Nicaragua.

Colombia

Colombia's two main guerrilla groups—the Revolutionary Armed Forces of Colombia (FARC) and the National Liberation Army (ELN)—intensified political violence during 1994, particularly preceding presidential, congressional, and municipal elections. In part to intimidate politicians and government officials, the insurgents conducted dozens of bombings, kidnappings of candidates, and assassinations of local officials and members of the security forces. In July, the FARC assassinated an Army general, the highest ranking Army casualty in two decades.

While the vast majority of the violence in the nation was directed against local targets, Colombia was the location of 41 international terrorist attacks in 1994, the highest in the region. Oil pipelines owned jointly by the Government of Colombia and Western companies continued to be bombed by the rebels, but at a slower pace than in 1993. US interests sustained several terrorist attacks during the year, more than in any other Latin American country. For instance, suspected ELN rebels bombed a Coca-Cola plant in January, and FARC and ELN guerrillas attacked at least five Mormon churches during the year. The rebels also conducted a series of kidnappings of US citizens; the FARC is suspected of kidnapping at least five US citizens in 1994. At yearend, both rebel groups held hostage as many as nine Americans, six of whom are US missionaries. This appears to be the largest number of Americans held in Colombia at any one time.

In 1994 there were 1,378 reported kidnappings, a 35-percent increase from 1993. This figure, however, is considered low because many families deal with the kidnappers directly without reporting the crime. It is estimated that 50 percent of these recorded instances were by guerrillas who rely on the ransom payments to finance their activities.

In November, after only a few months in office, President Ernesto Samper announced his administration's willingness to negotiate with the nation's violent guerrilla organizations, emphasizing that the insurgents need to demonstrate a genuine desire for reaching a negotiated settlement. Unlike his predecessor, the President did not condition negotiations on a rebel cease-fire. While both the FARC and ELN have characterized the government's proposal as positive, government officials cautioned against expectations that negotiations would begin soon.

The government is also exposing further links between the guerrillas and narcotraffickers. Various guerrilla fronts, particularly in southeastern Colombia, provide security and other services for different narcotics trafficking organizations.

Ecuador

The only significant act of domestic terrorism in 1994 was the dynamiting of a power transmission tower in May by a group known as the Red Sun, which led to the rapid apprehension of the group's leadership. The group was disbanded following the arrest of its leaders.

Guatemala

Despite on-again/off-again peace talks, Guatemala's 34-year-old insurgency continues. There are three major armed guerrilla groups—the FAR (Revolutionary Armed Forces), the ORPA (Revolutionary Organization of the People in Arms), and the EGP (Guerrilla Army of the Poor). These groups, along with the Communist PGT (Guatemalan Workers' Party), are allied in the URNG (Guatemalan National Revolutionary Union).

Panama

On 19 July a bomb aboard a commuter plane flying between Colon and Panama City detonated, killing all 21 persons aboard, including three American citizens. Twelve of the passengers were Jews. According to media reports, an organization using the name Ansar Allah, or Followers of God, issued a statement expressing support for the bombing, which appeared to be a suicide operation by a person with a Middle Eastern name. Panama has made no arrests in connection with the bombing, but it is cooperating closely with a US law enforcement investigation.

At yearend, Panamanian authorities had outstanding arrest warrants for two of the three individuals sought for questioning in connection with the 1992 murder of US Army Corporal Zak Hernandez. On 23 September, Panamanian President Ernesto Perez Balladares granted amnesties to 216 individuals, including six former Panamanian Defense Force personnel linked to the 1989 kidnapping, torture, and murder of American citizen Raymond Dragseth during Operation Just Cause.

Peru

Political violence and the number of international terrorist incidents in Peru declined in 1994. Both of Peru's terrorist organizations—Sendero Luminoso (Shining Path) and the Tupac Amaru Revolutionary Movement (MRTA)—suffered serious reversals during the year, including numerous arrests, casualties, and defections under the government's amnesty program for terrorists, which was phased out in November. The MRTA, the smaller of the two groups, was hit hard by the government's counterterrorism effort and is virtually defunct.

Two years after the capture of Abimael Guzman, Sendero Luminoso's founder and leader, the Maoist terrorist group is struggling, attempting to rebuild and resolve its leadership problems. Guzman's 1993 peace offer continued to divide the organization between Sendero militants in favor of continuing the armed struggle and those preferring to adhere to their jailed leader's proposal. Consequently, recruitment of new cadres has been hindered. Moreover, during the past two years Sendero's financial lifeline—the narcotics industry in the coca-rich Upper Huallaga Valley (UHV)—was disrupted, largely because of a coca plant fungus in UHV and a more active government counternarcotics policy.

The Fujimori government continued to maintain its momentum against Sendero in 1994. Peruvian police detained two Sendero Central Committee members operating in Lima, weakening the group's urban infrastructure and a planned terrorism campaign to commemorate a revered Sendero anniversary in June. The arrests further exacerbated logistic and financial problems in the organization. One of the detainees, Moises Limaco, was one of the most senior Sendero leaders reportedly responsible for coordinating logistics and personnel.

Despite these setbacks, Sendero proved it can still inflict serious damage. During 1994, Sendero murdered more than 150 Peruvians, down from 516 in 1993. In February, suspected Sendero militants detonated an 80-kilogram car bomb against the Air Force headquarters building in central Lima, killing two persons. In October, the group destroyed six electrical towers, cutting off power temporarily in nearly all of Lima, much of the Peruvian coast, and part of the Sierra highlands.

Uruguay

Three suspected members of the Basque separatist movement ETA were extradited to Spain in August by the Uruguayan Supreme Court. President Luis Alberto Lacalle's refusal to grant political asylum for the three prompted death threats against Uruguayan diplomats in Spain. Riots outside the hospital where the hunger strikers were held on the day of their extradition resulted in one death, 90 injuries, and 28 arrests.

Middle Eastern Overview

Terrorist violence in the Middle East continued at a high level in 1994. Extremist Muslim groups, such as the Islamic Resistance Movement (HAMAS) and Palestinian Islamic Jihad (PIJ), demonstrated an increasingly deadly and sophisticated capability to mount terrorist attacks aimed at destroying the Middle East peace process. In Algeria, a brutal internal conflict escalated, posing new threats to the foreign community and the safety of civil aviation.

In Israel and the occupied territories, the peace process came under sustained attack by militants determined to derail the negotiations between the Palestinian Authority (PA) and the Government of Israel. Both HAMAS and the PIJ increased their activities within Israel, in the process demonstrating an improved ability to mount more sophisticated and deadly attacks. In the worst such incident during the year, the military wing of HAMAS, the Izz el-Din al-Qassam Brigades, claimed responsibility for the 19 October suicide bombing of a commuter bus in the heart of downtown Tel Aviv that killed 22 Israelis. PIJ also claimed numerous attacks on Israelis, including the 11 November suicide bombing at Netzarim junction in Gaza that killed three Israeli soldiers. The Chairman of the PA, Yasir Arafat, condemned these attacks and took some steps to counter anti-Israeli terrorism. PA security cooperation with Israeli authorities was generally close, as demonstrated by the substantial assistance provided by Palestinian security authorities to Israel during the hunt for a kidnapped Israeli Army corporal in October. Nevertheless, Israeli officials called for a more effective crackdown by the PA on Palestinian terrorist elements. Violent Jewish opposition to the peace process also occurred; in March, the Israeli Government banned the extremist Kach and Kahane Chai groups as terrorist organizations after a Kach member murdered 29 Palestinian worshippers in a Hebron mosque in February.

The security situation in Algeria continued to deteriorate as the Armed Islamic Group (AIG) stepped up attacks against the Algerian regime and civilians. Foreigners resident in Algeria were key targets as well; 63 were killed during 1994 by AIG forces. A French Consulate employee was slain in January, and in August an attempt was made to explode a car bomb at a French diplomatic housing compound. The AIG employed an ominous new tactic in December, when AIG militants hijacked an Air France jet at Algiers airport, killing a French Embassy cook and a Vietnamese diplomat in the process. Efforts by the major Islamist and non-Islamist opposition parties to establish a political dialogue with the regime were unsuccessful, increasing the likelihood of intensified political violence.

In Egypt, the security services scored numerous successes against militants seeking to overthrow the government and establish an Islamic state. Intensified counterterrorism efforts, improved police work, and the death of an important Islamic Group (IG) leader in a police raid in April helped disrupt IG activities and stem the tide of antiforeigner attacks, which killed five tourists in 1994. IG threats against the UN-sponsored International Conference on Population and Development did not result in any security incidents, most likely due to the efforts of Egyptian security authorities and a still disorganized IG. The IG does, however, retain the capacity to attack foreign targets and disrupt the tourism industry, as evidenced by shooting assaults in September and October that killed three foreigners and three Egyptians.

Jordanian authorities continued in 1994 to maintain a tight grip on the internal security situation. Dozens of individuals were arrested in terrorism-related cases during the year, including 20 persons suspected of involvement in a series of bombings and other planned terrorist incidents. Jordan and Israel signed a full treaty of peace on 26 October 1994. Under the terms of the treaty, Jordan and Israel are committed to cooperation in combating terrorism of all kinds. However, HAMAS and other Palestinian extremists continue to maintain a presence in Amman.

Security conditions in Lebanon improved during 1994 as the government continued to take steps to extend its authority and reestablish the rule of law. In January, the government promptly arrested and prosecuted persons associated with the ANO and who assassinated a Jordanian diplomat. In April a prominent Iraqi expatriate oppositionist residing in Beirut was assassinated. The Government of Lebanon stated that it had firm evidence linking the killing to the Government of Iraq, arrested two Iraqi diplomats in connection with the incident, and broke diplomatic relations with Iraq. In March, the government banned armed demonstrations after a public celebration by the militant organization Hizballah. The government also put on trial former Lebanese Forces warlord Samir Ja'ja on charges of domestic terrorism and announced that the investigation into the 1983 bombings of the US and French peacekeepers' barracks would be "revived." However, significant threats to the safety of foreigners remained. Hizballah publicly threatened American interests and continued to operate with impunity in areas of Lebanon not controlled by the central government, including the south, the Biq'a [Bekaa] Valley, and Beirut's southern suburbs. Numerous Palestinian groups with a history of terrorist violence maintain a presence in Lebanon; these include the Popular Front for the Liberation of Palestine-General Command and the ANO.

Moroccan authorities, alarmed by an attack on a hotel in Marrakech in August that killed two Spanish tourists, sought evidence that the incident was linked to other assaults in the country. Allegations surfaced that these attacks were politically related to the crisis in Algeria. Criminal motivations, however, are another strong possibility, and the August attack was not followed by other such incidents as of the end of the year.

Algeria

The overall security situation deteriorated even further in 1994 as violence intensified throughout the country, affecting Algerians from all walks of life. Although Islamic extremists remained highly fractionalized, most of the violence was focused against regime and military targets. The extremist AIG waged a bloody war against Algerian civilians. The AIG also targeted foreigners, with 63 killed in 1994.

The influence of the Islamic Salvation Front (FIS) over the extremist elements appeared to slip even further in 1994 as most of the group's leaders remained in prison. In September the government released into house arrest FIS president Abassi Madani and vice president Ali Belhadj. The overall level of violence on all sides nonetheless increased.

The extremist AIG instead intensified its attacks against Algerian civilians, including journalists, unveiled women and girls, the intelligentsia, and anyone it accused of "cooperating" with the regime. The group often used tactics such as beheading and throat-slitting. Attacks against foreigners also increased markedly since the AIG began its antiforeigner campaign in September 1993. On 15 January a French Consulate employee was murdered; the campaign against French residents in Algeria reached a peak with the 3 August attack on a French diplomat housing compound where extremists attempted to detonate a car laden with explosives.

Other examples of attacks against foreigners included the 8 May murders of two French priests, the 11 July attack against five foreigners on their way to work at a state-owned oil site, the one-week hostage holding of the Omani and Yemeni Ambassadors, and the 18 October execution of two Schlumberger employees at a Sonatrach oil site. The AIG's attacks against foreigners grew more sophisticated throughout 1994, and the group's operations demonstrated a significant level of coordination in some cases. While the AIG was responsible for most of the attacks against foreigners in 1994, there are many extremist cells operating in Algeria that do not fall under a central authority that may also be responsible for such attacks.

On 24 December, members of the AIG hijacked an Air France flight in Algeria. The plane arrived in Marseille, France, on 26 December. A French antiterrorist unit stormed the plane, ending the 54-hour siege in which three hostages were killed by the terrorists. All four terrorists were killed during the rescue.

Despite the Algerian regime's "carrot and stick" approach, the security situation at the end of 1994 remained grim. Efforts by the major Islamist and non-Islamist opposition parties to establish a political dialogue with the regime were unsuccessful; at no point during these efforts did the military halt its campaign against the Islamists. President Zeroual announced in November 1994 that presidential elections would take place by the end of 1995 but left open the question of who would be allowed to participate. The major opposition parties denounced the election proposal. Continued bloodshed appeared to be the most likely scenario for the beginning of 1995.

Egypt

The pace of attacks by Islamic extremists on tourist sites in Egypt fell off somewhat during 1994. Five foreign tourists were killed in separate attacks, and more than 20 Egyptian civilians were killed in various attacks throughout Egypt in 1994. Egypt's tourism industry, which had suffered greatly from the sustained 1993 campaign of attacks against tourist sites, began to recover somewhat in 1994 as the Egyptian Government made some successful gains in stemming the attacks.

Most attacks against Egyptian official and civilian targets, and against foreign tourists, were claimed by the extremist Islamic Group (IG). The IG seeks the violent overthrow of the Egyptian Government and began attacking tourist targets in 1992. The IG considers Sheikh Omar Abdel Rahman its "spiritual" leader; at yearend, he awaited trial in the United States on charges related to the conspiracy to attack various New York City landmarks and the United Nations.

In February, the IG initiated a limited bombing campaign against Western banks in the Cairo area. Over two months, seven banks were bombed, and an additional four bombs planted at other banks were defused. Injuries were limited, and only one of the banks suffered major damage. Nonetheless, the bank bombing campaign represented an extension of the IG's antiforeigner attacks, and it coincided with another IG campaign of attacks against trains in Assiut, upper Egypt. Eight tourists were injured in February in a series of shooting attacks against trains running in that province. The bank bombings ended in March with the arrests of the alleged perpetrators.

In April, Egypt stepped up its counterterrorism efforts, focusing particularly on the Cairo area. An important IG leader was killed during a police raid, which appeared to disrupt the organization of the group. There was a significant drop in the number of violent incidents from April through August throughout Egypt, but particularly in Cairo. This was accomplished by more effective police work, enhanced security in the troubled Assiut Province, and perhaps a dropoff in recruitment levels of extremists.

In August, the IG attacked a tourist bus in upper Egypt, killing one Spanish tourist and warning foreigners not to come to Egypt for the International Conference on Population and Development (ICPD). The UN-sponsored ICPD was held in September in Cairo; no incidents occurred in Cairo during the conference, probably due in part to greatly enhanced security and a still disorganized IG.

The IG continued to pose a limited threat to foreigners in Egypt at the close of 1994, as a September shooting attack on a market street in the Red Sea resort area of Hurghada resulted in the death of one German tourist and two Egyptians. In the fall, the IG appeared to shift the venue of its attacks to the upper Egyptian Provinces of Minya and Qena. An October attack on a minibus traveling in upper Egypt, which led to the death of a British tourist, demonstrated that the IG retained the capability to inflict injuries and damage the tourism industry.

Israel and the Occupied Territories

Terrorist attacks and violence instigated by Palestinians continued at a high level in 1994. Seventy-three Israeli soldiers and civilians were killed and more than 100 wounded in 1994, up slightly from 1993. There was a significant increase in the number of Israelis killed inside Israel—as compared with only 14 in 1993.

The Islamic Resistance Movement (HAMAS) killed roughly 55 Israelis and wounded more than 150 in 1994 as part of a terror campaign to derail the peace process. HAMAS's armed wing, the Izz el-Din al-Qassam, claimed responsibility for the April bombings of buses in Afula and Hadera, which together killed 14 Israelis and wounded nearly 75. In October, al-Qassam launched three high-profile attacks on Israelis: the 9 October shooting of people on the streets of Jerusalem, which left two dead; the kidnapping of Israel Defense Force Corporal Nachshon Wachsman, which resulted in the killing of Wachsman and one other Israeli soldier; and the bombing of a commuter bus in Tel Aviv, which killed 22. HAMAS spokesmen announced that these attacks were part of the group's policy of jihad against the "Israeli occupation of all of Palestine" and retaliation for the Hebron Massacre.

Other Palestinian groups that reject the Gaza-Jericho accord and the peace process also attacked Israelis. Palestinian Islamic Jihad (PIJ)–Shiqaqi faction claimed responsibility for a suicide bomber who attacked an Israeli patrol in Gaza in November killing three Israeli soldiers. PIJ claimed at least 18 other attacks on Israelis, including a shooting on a commuter bus stop on 7 April that killed two in Ashdod, south of Tel Aviv. The Democratic Front for the Liberation of Palestine and the Popular Front for the Liberation of Palestine claimed responsibility for several attacks on Israeli settlers and soldiers.

Yasir Arafat, Chairman of the Palestinian Authority (PA). tried to rein in Palestinian violence against Israel in 1994. The PA police force took some steps to curtail anti-Israeli attacks, including several mass detentions and a strong effort to find where Corporal Wachsman was detained by HAMAS. Arafat and other senior PA officials condemned acts of terrorism by HAMAS and the PIJ, but did not do so when individuals associated with the Fatah Hawks, nominally aligned with Arafat's Fatah organization, were responsible for a few attacks in early 1994. Israeli officials urged the PA to take tougher measures against terrorists.

Intra-Palestinian violence has increased since the implementation of the Gaza-Jericho accord began on 4 May. On 18 November, 13 Palestinians were killed and more than 150 wounded when Palestinian Police clashed with HAMAS and PIJ supporters who were planning to demonstrate in Gaza. This incident followed several protests by weapons-bearing Islamists in the weeks following the HAMAS kidnapping of Corporal Wachsman and the PA's mass roundup of HAMAS supporters. In 1994, Fatah Hawks and HAMAS killed at least 20 Palestinians whom the extremists labeled as collaborators.

The Israeli Cabinet outlawed the Jewish extremist groups Kach and Kahane Chai in March, declaring them to be terrorist organizations after Baruch Goldstein, who was a Kach member, attacked Palestinian worshippers at Hebron's al-Ibrahimi Mosque in February, killing 29 persons and wounding more than 200. Neither Kach nor Kahane Chai assisted or directed Goldstein in his attack, but both organizations vocally supported him. The leading figures of these groups were arrested and held in Israeli prisons on charges of calling for attacks on Palestinians and Israeli Government officials. In September, Shin Bet arrested 11 Jewish extremists who were planning terrorist attacks against Palestinians.

Israel's intense border security appeared effectively to prevent infiltrations from Syria, Lebanon, and Jordan. In March, a team of four DFLP terrorists was intercepted by Israel Defense Force troops. Katyusha rocket attacks from southern Lebanon into northern Israel by Hizballah and Palestinian rejectionist groups decreased in 1994, and no Israelis were killed in the attacks. Hizballah guerrillas, often in response to Israeli attacks on a Lebanese village, fired Katyusha rockets on four occasions from January to July 1994 and launched several Katyushas in October hours before the signing of the Jordanian-Israeli peace accord attended by President Clinton.

Jordan

Jordanian security and police closely monitor extremists inside the country and detain individuals suspected of involvement in violent acts aimed at destabilizing the government or undermining its relations with neighboring states. Jordan maintains tight security along its border with Israel and has interdicted individuals attempting to infiltrate into Israel. On 26 October 1994 Jordan and Israel signed a full treaty of peace that commits the two parties to cooperation in a variety of areas, including combating terrorism. In 1994 two new international border crossing points were established between Jordan and Israel.

Jordanian authorities arrested dozens of people in terrorism-related cases during 1994. On 20 February, authorities arrested 30 persons in Amman, including 15 suspected members of the ANO. The arrests reportedly occurred in connection with the assassination of a Jordanian diplomat in January in Beirut by the ANO. In 1994, 25 Islamists (referred to as the "Arab Afghans") were arrested and tried for planning to overthrow the government, assassinate prominent Jordanians, and attack public and private institutions. The State Security Court handed down verdicts on 21 December and sentenced 11 defendants to death, sentenced seven to various prison terms with hard labor, and acquitted the remaining defendants of all charges. Two individuals were also arrested for stabbing tourists in downtown Amman on 27 February, two days after the massacre of Palestinian worshippers on the West Bank by a Jewish extremist.

A variety of Palestinian rejectionist groups have offices in Jordan, including the PFLP, PFLP-GC, DFLP, PIJ, and HAMAS. In April, King Hussein announced that HAMAS was an "illegal" organization in Jordan. After the King's announcement, HAMAS spokespersons in Jordan were more circumspect in their statements and often issued statements from other locations.

Lebanon

The security situation in Lebanon continued to improve during 1994 as Beirut endeavored to reestablish its authority and rebuild the country in the wake of the devastating 16-year civil war. Although the Lebanese Government has made some moves to limit the autonomy of individuals and powerful groups—specifically Hizballah—there are still considerable areas of relative lawlessness throughout Lebanon. Beirut and its environs are safer for some non-Lebanese now than as recently as a year ago, but the Bekaa Valley and other Hizballah strongholds are considerably more dangerous than the capital, especially for Westerners, who are still subject to attacks. In June, for example, a German citizen was the victim of an apparent kidnapping attempt perpetrated by Hizballah in Ba'labakk. The would-be victim's assailants fled after passers-by noticed the commotion. There is credible evidence that Hizballah continues its surveillance of Americans; Hizballah also continues to issue public threats against American interests.

Hizballah has yet to be disarmed, but Beirut is making efforts to restrict activities by the group that challenge the government's authority. For example, the government banned armed demonstrations after Hizballah's celebration of Martyr's Day in the Bekaa Valley in March and issued arrest warrants for participants who were brandishing weapons during the march. In February when Hizballah, without reference to the state authority, tried and executed a teenager in Ba'labakk accused of murder, prominent members of Parliament publicly admonished the group and said such acts by nongovernmental organizations should not be tolerated. However, neither the judiciary nor law enforcement agencies made any effort to interfere in or investigate the affair.

The Lebanese Government took judicial steps during 1994 to signal that violence is not an acceptable means for achieving domestic political change. In January, the government promptly arrested and prosecuted persons associated with the ANO and who assassinated a Jordanian diplomat.

On 12 April, a prominent Iraqi expatriate oppositionist residing in Beirut was assassinated. The Government of Lebanon stated that it had firm evidence linking the killing to the Government of Iraq and arrested two Iraqi diplomats in connection with the incident. Lebanon subsequently broke diplomatic relations with Iraq.

In July a Lebanese criminal court refused to convict two defendants in the 1976 killings of the US Ambassador, Francis Meloy, and the economic counselor, Robert Waring. The Lebanese Court of Cassation agreed to order a retrial after intervention by the government's prosecutor general. The trial is set to begin in March 1995.

Lebanese authorities arrested Lebanese Forces Leader Samir Ja'ja on charges of domestic terrorism—including the bombing of a Maronite church in Zuk in February that killed 11 persons and wounded 59. His trial was ongoing as of the end of the year. In November, the government suggested it would "revive" the investigation into the 1983 bombings of the US and French Marine barracks. Although viewed by some as a message to Hizballah of government intention to reassert authority, the government has not yet followed its announcement with concrete action. In December the government accepted an invitation from the US Government to send an official delegation to Washington to discuss means to improve the security situation in Lebanon.

Morocco

On 24 August two Spanish tourists were killed when gunmen opened fire at the Atlas Asni hotel in Marrakech during an apparent robbery attempt. After initial investigations, Moroccan officials linked the hotel attack to other assaults throughout Morocco, including the attempted robberies of a bank and a McDonald's restaurant in 1993. Nine suspects were arrested, and Moroccan authorities claimed to have discovered an arms cache hidden by the group.

There have been allegations that Islamic extremists related to the Algerian militant movement were behind the Marrakech incident. But some Moroccan officials have also claimed that members of the Algerian security services were behind the attack, hoping to foment instability in Morocco to take the international focus off the Algerian crisis. The real motives of the attackers remain unclear, and the incident could easily have been an ordinary criminal attack. As of 31 December, the Marrakech attack was not followed by similar incidents in Morocco.

Patterns of Global Terrorism: 1995

The Year in Review

In most countries, the level of international terrorism in 1995 continued the downward trend of recent years, and there were fewer terrorist acts that caused deaths last year than in the previous year. However, the total number of international terrorist acts rose in 1995 from 322 to 440, largely because of a major increase in nonlethal terrorist attacks against property in Germany and in Turkey by the Kurdistan Workers' Party (PKK). (The PKK also committed lethal acts of terrorism.) The decline in lethal acts of international terrorism was not matched by a reduction in domestic terrorism or other forms of political violence that continued at a high level.

International terrorist attacks against US interests rose to 99 in 1995 from 66 in 1994, and the number of US citizens killed rose from four to 12. The total number of fatalities from international terrorism worldwide declined from 314 in 1994 to 165 in 1995, but the number of persons wounded increased by a factor of ten—to 6,291 persons; 5,500 were injured in a gas attack in the Tokyo subway system in March.

Significant acts of international terrorism during the year were:

- Two US employees of the US Consulate in Karachi, Jacqueline Keys Van Landingham and Gary C. Durell, were killed on 8 March when their shuttle bus came under armed attack. A third employee, Mark McCloy, was injured.
- On 20 March members of the Japanese cult Aum Shinrikyo placed containers of the deadly chemical nerve agent sarin on five trains of the Tokyo subway system during the morning rush hour. The cultists then punctured the containers, releasing poisonous gas into the trains and subway stations. The attack killed 12 persons, but despite the extreme toxicity of sarin, 5,500 escaped with injuries, including two US citizens. The attack was the first major use of chemical weapons by terrorists.
- Two US missionaries, Steve Welsh and Timothy Van Dyke, were killed by the Revolutionary Armed Forces of Colombia (FARC) during a confrontation with a Colombian Army patrol on 19 June. The guerrillas kidnapped the two New Tribes Mission members in January 1994 initially to force the withdrawal of US military personnel engaged in military assistance projects in Colombia. FARC later changed this demand to a monetary ransom. Four other US citizens still were held hostage by guerrillas in Colombia as of the end of 1995.
- On 26 June gunmen attempted to assassinate Egyptian President Hosni Mubarak during his visit to Ethiopia. The attempt was foiled by Ethiopian counterterrorist forces and Egyptian security forces. Al-Gama'at al-Islamiyya (Islamic Group or IG) claimed responsibility, and the suspects are believed to have fled to Sudan.
- Terrorists bombed the Riyadh headquarters of the Office of the Program Manager/Saudi Arabian National Guard on 13 November, killing seven people, including five US citizens, and seriously injuring 42 others.

Western Europe experienced more international terrorist attacks during 1995 than any other region. However, most of the 272 incidents that occurred there were the low-level PKK arson attacks mentioned above. There were only 11 attacks in Western Europe that were lethal, that is, that resulted in the death of one or more victims.

In Israel, Prime Minister Yitzhak Rabin was assassinated by a Jewish Israeli extremist in November, and Palestinian terrorists continued a series of massive suicide bombings and shootings in Israel, killing 47.

A high level of terrorism continued in Algeria by the Armed Islamic Group (GIA), and terrorists probably associated with the GIA launched a series of bombings or attempted bombings in France.

There was no known international involvement in the 19 April bombing of a federal building in Oklahoma City, which killed 168 people and wounded more than 500.

Twelve US citizens were killed in international terrorist attacks last year. In addition to the two US Consulate employees killed in Karachi, the two missionaries killed in Colombia, and the five citizens killed in Riyadh, a US tourist was murdered in Cambodia by the Khmer Rouge, a US citizen was killed in a suicide attack on an Israeli bus in Gaza, and another died in a similar attack on a bus in Jerusalem. Forty-eight US citizens were wounded during all of 1995.

Various foreign governments cooperated with the United States in 1995 in arresting and transferring to US custody major international terrorist suspects wanted for alleged violation of US counterterrorism laws. Ramzi Ahmed Yousef, who is under indictment as a key figure in the bombing in 1993 of the World Trade Center in New York City, was arrested and extradited to the United States by Pakistan in February. In August, Eyad Mahmoud Ismail Najim, a suspected accomplice of Yousef's in the New York bombing, was rendered to the United States by Jordan. In April, Abdul Hakim Murad was arrested and handed over to US custody by the Philippines for suspected involvement with Yousef in a plot to blow up US aircraft over Asia, and Wali Khan Amin Shah—another suspected coconspirator in this plot—was rendered to the United States by another foreign government in December.

On 1 October, Shaykh Umar Abd al-Rahman and nine codefendants were convicted in Manhattan federal court of conspiring to bomb the United Nations, the FBI building in New York, the Lincoln and Holland tunnels, and other New York landmarks, and for the terrorist bombing in 1993 of the World Trade Center. Abd al-Rahman, known as the "Blind Shaykh," also was found guilty of plotting to murder Egyptian President Hosni Mubarak, and defendant El Sayyid Nosair also was convicted of "murder in aid of racketeering" in relation to the death of Rabbi Meir Kahane in 1990. Trial evidence showed that Abd al-Rahman was the leader of an organization whose aim was to wage a self-styled "holy war" of terror against the United States because he considered it an enemy of Islam. Abd al-Rahman and Nosair were sentenced to life in prison; the others received prison terms ranging from 25 to 57 years.

Senior HAMAS official Musa Abu Marzuq, who is suspected of involvement in terrorist activities in Israel, was detained in New York on 25 July as he tried to enter the United States—where he had lived previously as a legal permanent resident—after immigration officials found his name on a watchlist of suspected terrorists. Israel has requested his extradition. At year's end, that request was pending before US courts.

Africa Overview

Ten international terrorist attacks occurred in Africa last year, down from 24 during 1994. Ethiopia was the scene of an attempted assassination of visiting Egyptian President Hosni Mubarak by members of an Egyptian terrorist group. Other attacks—primarily kidnappings—occurred in Angola, Chad, Sierra Leone, and Somalia.

Angola

The United Nations Angola Verification Mission (UNAVEM) was attacked by unknown perpetrators on 11 November. Two handgrenades were thrown into the UNAVEM III campsite in Cabinda city, seriously injuring one Bangladeshi police observer and damaging the facility.

Chad

On 18 March, an American UN worker, a Malian, and two Chadians were kidnapped in the city of Mao by the Movement for Democracy and Development, an armed Chadian opposition group. The US citizen was released on 27 March.

Ethiopia

Ethiopian counterterrorist forces foiled an assassination attempt against visiting Egyptian President Hosni Mubarak on 26 June. Mubarak had just arrived in Addis Ababa to attend the Organization of African Unity (OAU) summit when several members of the Egyptian extremist al-Gama'at al-Islamiyya (also known as the Islamic Group, or IG) attacked his motorcade. Ethiopian forces killed five of the attackers and captured three others. Ethiopia and Egypt have charged the Government of Sudan with complicity in the attack and harboring suspects and pursued the matter in both the OAU and the United Nations.

On 26 February, unknown assailants threw two grenades into the USAID compound in Addis Ababa, damaging the facility's windows and three vehicles. No one was injured.

Sierra Leone

The Revolutionary United Front (RUF) took several foreigners hostage in the first half of 1995 in an apparent attempt to force foreigners out of the country. On 5 January, a Swiss national working for a French-owned lumber firm was taken hostage. On 18 January, two Britons, a German, a Swede, and a dual Swiss/Australian,—all employed by the Swiss-owned Sierra Leone Ore and Metal Company (Sieromco)—were kidnapped. On 25 January, six Italian nuns and one Brazilian nun were taken hostage. The seven nuns were released on 21 March, and the others were released on 20 April. On 23 May, three Lebanese businessmen were abducted.

Somalia

On 30 April, a foreign businessman was kidnapped and killed near the southern port city of Chisimayu, probably by radical Islamic extremists as a political statement against the presence of foreigners.

Asia Overview

The most serious terrorist attack in Asia in 1995 was the nerve gas attack on the Tokyo subway system in March carried out by the religious cult Aum Shinrikyo. The attack—the first large-scale use of chemical agents by terrorists—apparently was meant to destabilize Japan and pave the way for the cult to seize control of the nation. The attack killed 12, injured thousands, and damaged Japan's sense of security. Japanese authorities have since arrested the leaders of Aum Shinrikyo and suppressed the organization. The Khmer Rouge murdered a US tourist in Cambodia in January, the only terrorist-related death of a US citizen in East Asia last year.

The East Asia/Pacific region was also the locale of a plot, discovered by the Philippine Government, by Ramzi Ahmed Yousef and his accomplices to assassinate the Pope and plant bombs on US airliners flying over the Pacific.

In the South Asia region, the continued presence of Islamic militant training camps in Afghanistan contributed to terrorist incidents in Europe, Africa, the Middle East, East Asia, and South Asia. Camps are supported by nearly all Afghan factions, and the nominal Rabbani government does not exercise control or authority over much of Afghanistan. The Rabbani regime has been accused by the Government of Pakistan of sponsoring a spate of bombings and assassinations in the Peshawar area in late October and early November.

A group of Kashmiri and non-Kashmiri terrorists kidnapped six Westerners in Indian-held Kashmir in July, demanding the release of militants belonging to the Harakat ul-Ansar (HUA), a militant group based in Pakistan. One hostage was killed and another escaped. Other Kashmiri groups claimed responsibility for bombings at Republic Day celebrations in Kashmir in January and at the office of the BBC correspondent in Kashmir in September. Credible reports continue to indicate official Pakistani support for militant groups fighting in Kashmir, including some groups that engage in terrorism, such as the HUA. The Sikh terrorist group, Babbar Khalsa, assassinated the Punjab Chief Minister in August.

Two US Consulate employees were assassinated in Karachi in March. The Egyptian Embassy in Islamabad was destroyed by a bomb in November, and three Egyptian groups claimed responsibility. In February, Pakistan extradited Ramzi Yousef, alleged mastermind of the World Trade Center bombing, to the United States.

Afghanistan

Afghanistan, which lacks an effective or recognized central government, remained a training ground for Islamic militants and terrorists in 1995. Nearly all of the factions competing for political power, including the nominal government in Kabul led by Burhanuddin Rabbani, are involved to some extent in harboring or facilitating camps that have trained terrorists from many nations who have been active in worldwide terrorist activity. Terrorists who trained in camps in Afghanistan perpetrated attacks in Europe, Africa, the Middle East, East Asia, and South Asia, including the World Trade Center bombing in 1993, the attempted assassination of Egyptian President Hosni Mubarak in Ethiopia in June, bombings in France by Algerian militants, and the Manila-based plot to attack Western interests. Ramzi Ahmed Yousef, suspected of involvement in this plot as well as the World Trade Center bombing in 1993, is linked to Afghan training. The group that claimed responsibility for the bombing in November of the Egyptian Embassy in Islamabad, Pakistan, also has extensive ties to the Afghan network.

Individuals who trained in Afghanistan in 1995 were involved in wars or insurgencies in Kashmir, Tajikistan, Bosnia, Chechnya, and the Philippines. In Tajikistan, the government claimed in May to have arrested a group of Afghan-trained Tajiks who were responsible for attacking a bus carrying Russian border guards in Dushanbe in February. Manila claims that veterans of Afghan camps are working with Philippine opposition groups that attacked and destroyed a village in April.

The Rabbani regime in Kabul has done little to curb the training of foreign militants. Indeed, one regime backer, Abd al-Rasul Sayyaf, continues to harbor and train potential terrorists in his camps in Afghanistan and Pakistan; the Government of Pakistan raided his facilities near Peshawar in November after the bombing of the Egyptian Embassy in Islamabad. The Rabbani regime did arrest foreign militants from camps run by other factions. Many remain in jail in Kabul, but some have been released.

Kabul has been accused by Islamabad of sponsoring a spate of bombings in the Peshawar area in late October and early November. Pakistani authorities claim to have arrested one Afghan in connection with the first bombing incident. The Taliban, an Afghan opposition movement that Kabul has accused Islamabad of supporting, forced a privately chartered Russian-flagged transport aircraft from Tatarstan to land on 3 August, and the seven-man crew was still held hostage in Qandahar at year's end. The Taliban has claimed that the crew members are prisoners of war, since the aircraft was carrying munitions for the Kabul regime. The group has demanded that, in exchange for the crew, Russia cease its aid to Kabul and provide information on thousands of Afghans who the Taliban claim have been missing since the Afghan-Soviet war.

Cambodia

The Khmer Rouge (KR) continued to decline in strength, relying on rural banditry and terror to support its policy of undermining the duly elected government. The KR threat was strongest in the north and west, particularly along the Thai border. However, in this region there is no official US presence and only a small number of US citizens or other Westerners, who work mostly with the UN and NGOs. Nevertheless, on 15 January a group of bandits, believed to have included Khmer Rouge, killed a US citizen, Susan Ginsburg Hadden, wounded her husband, and killed her Cambodian guide while the victims were touring temple areas near Angkor Wat. Several people were tried and sentenced to 15- to-20-year prison terms in connection with the killings. The government also followed up on past KR atrocities; six Khmer Rouge were sentenced to 15-year terms (five in absentia) for the murders of two Britons and an Australian in April 1994.

India

India continues to face significant security problems as a result of insurgencies in Kashmir and the northeast. A group of Kashmiri and non-Kashmiri terrorists kidnapped six Westerners—two US citizens, two Britons, a German, and a Norwegian—hiking near Srinagar, Kashmir, in July. The Norwegian hostage was beheaded, one US citizen escaped, and the others—still held captive at year's end—have been threatened with execution if India does not release several prisoners belonging to the Harakat ul-Ansar (HUA), a militant group headquartered in Pakistan.

Bombings claimed by Kashmiri groups occurred throughout the year, including explosions in a stadium in Kashmir during Republic Day festivities on 26 January. The targets were primarily Indian Government officials. military offices, and infrastructure facilities, but most of those killed and wounded were civilians. Kashmiri terrorists also targeted journalists in Srinagar. An AFP correspondent in Srinagar was killed on 7 September by a package bomb intended for the BBC correspondent. There are credible reports of official Pakistani support for militants fighting in Kashmir, including for the groups that claimed responsibility for the bombings.

In October, India signed an intelligence-sharing agreement with Egypt to combat international terrorism and organized crime.

The Government of India has been largely successful in controlling the Sikh separatist movement in Punjab State, but Sikh groups committed several acts of terrorism in India in 1995. The Babbar Khalsa group assassinated the Punjab Chief Minister outside his offices in Chandigarh on 31 August. Another Sikh group, the Khalistan Liberation Force, claimed responsibility for the bombing of three civilian targets in New Delhi and Panjpit on 26 September. Indian authorities suspect that the same Sikh group is responsible for a bombing in New Delhi on 21 November, which was claimed by both Sikh and Kashmiri groups. India claims that Pakistan harbors and supports Sikh militant groups. Pakistan claims that India supports a Pakistani separatist group in Sindh Province, which Islamabad claims has carried out terrorist attacks in Karachi.

Japan

In 1995, Japan suffered the world's first large-scale terrorist chemical gas attack when a Japanese religious cult, Aum Shinrikyo or Aum Supreme Truth, attacked the Tokyo subway system on 20 March. Five subway trains were simultaneously attacked, killing 12 persons and sending about 5,500 to area hospitals for treatment of symptoms of chemical poisoning from sarin gas. Foreigners, including two US citizens, one Swiss, one Irishman, and two Australians, were among those who sought treatment for chemical exposure. After an investigation, the Japanese police also charged the Aum for the sarin gas attack on June 1994 in Matsumoto that killed seven and injured about 500. Most of the suspected perpetrators of the gas attack and most of the group's leaders—including its founder Shoko Asahara—have been arrested and are awaiting trial.

On 15 November, an unknown perpetrator placed explosives on a powerline pylon, causing minor damage but no injury or power outage to a US military housing complex near Tokyo, five days before President Clinton was scheduled to visit the city.

Pakistan

Two US employees of the US Consulate in Karachi were killed by unknown gunmen on 8 March. On 19 November, the Egyptian Embassy in Islamabad was destroyed by a car bomb, for which three Egyptian militant opposition groups claimed responsibility. Pakistan continues to experience terrorist-related violence as a result of domestic conflicts and instability in Afghanistan. Pakistan claimed that the current Afghan regime was behind a spate of bombings and assassinations in the Peshawar area in October and November. Pakistan claims that India provides support for separatists in Sindh Province, especially in Karachi, where terrorism and other violence resulted in over 100 deaths each month during 1995.

Pakistan took steps in 1995 to curb the activities of Afghan *mujahedin* and sympathetic Arabs and Pakistanis in the Pakistani regions that border Afghanistan. In February, Pakistan arrested and extradited to the United States Ramzi Ahmed Yousef, suspected of masterminding the World Trade Center bombing in 1993 and a plot against US airlines in East Asia in 1995. Pakistan's discovery through subsequent investigations that Yousef had plotted to assassinate Prime Minister Bhutto led to arrests of his associates throughout Pakistan. Islamabad also undertook a partial crackdown in several Pakistani cities on nongovernmental organizations suspected of aiding militant organizations and terrorists. Under an extradition treaty with Egypt signed in late 1994, Pakistan returned to Egypt several suspected terrorists before the Egyptian Embassy bombing. As a result of this bombing, Pakistan rounded up suspects and their associates in several Pakistani cities, including a refugee camp in Pakistan run by Afghan leader Abd al-Rasul Sayyaf.

The Government of Pakistan acknowledges that it continues to give moral, political, and diplomatic support to Kashmiri militants but denies allegations of other assistance. There continued to be credible reports in 1995, however, of official Pakistani support to militants fighting in Kashmir, including Pakistani, Afghan, and Arab nationals, some of whom engage in terrorism. One Pakistan-backed group, Harakat ul-Ansar (HUA), is believed to be linked to Al-Faran, the group that claimed responsibility for the kidnapping in July in Kashmir of two US citizens, two Britons, a German, and a Norwegian. One US citizen escaped. The Norwegian was later beheaded, and at year's end the other hostages were still being held. In October there were reports that HUA was involved in an arms-smuggling ring with Pakistani military officers accused of plotting to overthrow the Bhutto government. Other Pakistan-backed groups claimed responsibility for numerous bombings in Kashmir, including one against foreign journalists.

Philippines

The Philippine Government continued its efforts to negotiate a settlement with the Moro National Liberation Front (MNLF); its cease-fire with the group mostly was observed while the talks continued. Other Islamists and leftist groups, however, continued to use terrorism to achieve their aims.

On 6 January, Philippine police in Manila discovered a plot by foreign Islamic extremists to place bombs on US airliners flying over the Pacific. They [the same group of extremists] also made plans to assassinate the Pope, who was about to visit the Philippines, and to attack foreign embassies. The plots were directed by Ramzi Ahmed Yousef, the alleged mastermind of the World Trade Center bombing in New York City in February 1993. Yousef escaped but was later arrested in Pakistan and extradited to the United States. Abdul Hakim Murad, another suspected conspirator, was arrested by Philippine officials and handed over to the United States.

On 26 March the leftist Alex Boncayao Brigade (ABB) hurled a grenade at the Singapore Airlines offices in Manila, damaging an armored car in the parking lot of an adjacent bank. The group claimed the attack was to show its displeasure with Singapore's decision to execute a Philippine maid who had pleaded guilty to murder

In December threats from the Abu Sayyaf Group led Philippine authorities to arrest 30 Filipinos and foreigners allegedly engaged in plans to carry out terrorist attacks in Manila. In response to Abu Sayyaf and ABB activities, the Philippine Government urged passage of legislation designed to facilitate police counterterrorist operations. Public opposition to the legislation, however, makes quick passage unlikely.

Also in December, the ABB carried out three ambushes, resulting in the death of a prominent Philippine-Chinese industrialist, his driver, and a small boy. ABB claimed the attacks were in response to labor violations at factories owned by the murdered industrialist and others. President Ramos called the attacks "a declaration of war" and ordered police to high alert, resulting in the arrest of a number of ABB operatives.

Sri Lanka

The separatist group Liberation Egers of Tamil Eelam (LTTE) continued to plague the government in 1995, with insurgency and terrorism directed against senior Sri Lankan political and military leaders, economic infrastructure-related facilities, and civilians. The LTTE withdrew from government-initiated peace talks in April and renewed its attacks. The government then launched the largest offensive of the 12-year war. Although the LTTE suffered heavy casualties, and at least temporarily lost its main base on the Jaffna Peninsula, it continued to pose a serious terrorist threat. In October, in their first attack on Sri Lanka's economic infrastructure in several years, the Tigers attacked oil and natural gas storage facilities in the Colombo suburbs and significantly reduced Sri Lanka's oil storage capability. The Tigers also conducted or planned suicide bombings against Indian Prime Minister Rao, Sri Lankan Army headquarters, other senior military and government officials, and government offices in Colombo.

The LTTE has refrained from targeting Western tourists possibly out of fear that foreign governments would crack down on Tamil expatriates involved in fundraising activities abroad. In July, however, the Ellalan Force, an LTTE front group, exploded bombs in Colombo's zoological gardens, in a park, and on a beach frequented by tourists; there were no casualties. They intended to damage the tourist trade rather than to harm foreigners. These attacks followed a threat by the Ellalan Force to carry out bomb strikes in Colombo unless the government agreed to investigate the military's alleged use of civilians as human shields.

Europe and Eurasia Overview

The number of lethal terrorist incidents in Europe declined from 46 in 1994 to 11 in 1995, although the total number of incidents rose from 88 to 272. In Eurasia, however, the total number dropped from 11 in 1994 to five in 1995. Most of the terrorist incidents that occurred in Europe and Eurasia were acts of arson or vandalism against Turkish-owned businesses largely in Germany. These acts are widely believed to be the work of the Kurdistan Workers' Party (PKK); several European nations permit the PKK to operate known front companies within their borders.

Islamic extremists upset with French Government policy toward the conflict in Algeria are suspected of being responsible for terrorist bombings in France during 1995 that left eight dead and 160 wounded. The bombers targeted subways, markets, and other public places to achieve a maximum effect. Islamic extremists also probably conducted a car bombing in front of police headquarters in Rijeka, Croatia, which killed the driver of the car. The Egyptian al-Gama'at al-Islamiyya (Islamic Group or IG) claimed responsibility.

Radical nationalism and xenophobia provoked a campaign of letter bombs directed at foreigners in Austria and in Germany, where neo-Nazi violence against foreigners continued. The terrorist group Basque Fatherland and Liberty (ETA) continued its campaign of murder and intimidation in Spain, including an attack on Partido Popular leader Jose Maria Aznar, and Spanish police in August foiled a plot to assassinate King Juan Carlos. In Greece the indigenous leftist Revolutionary Organization 17 November and other domestic terrorist groups continued to threaten US and Turkish diplomats and to target Greek business interests.

In Turkey, the PKK continued to engage in terrorism with the goal of creating a separate state. In addition, Marxist terrorist groups and Islamist radicals conducted terrorist attacks aimed at official Turkish interests and progovernment figures. The Marxist Revolutionary People's Liberation Party/Front, known by the Turkish initials DHKP/C—the successor to the group formerly known as Dev Sol—apparently continued to target US interests. The PKK also continued to attack sites frequented by US and other tourists but at a level sharply reduced from its height in 1993.

Austria

Attacks on foreigners that began in 1993 continued in 1995, killing four and injuring another 11 persons, including two in neighboring Germany. In June a third series of letter bombs linked to neo-Nazi elements included two that were mailed from Austria to an Austrian-born black TV commentator in Munich and to the mayor of Luebeck, injuring colleagues of the intended victims. The letters carried the logo of the Bajuwarian Liberation Front (also known as the Bavarian Liberation Army), an obscure rightwing group that had claimed responsibility for a number of attacks in Austria. In December another round of bombings was timed to try to embarrass Austrian authorities. Two of four letter bombs in a public mailbox exploded as the trial of two rightwing suspects in the bombings of December 1993 was wrapping up. (They were acquitted.)

On 20 September a leftwing group called the Red Daughters of Rage firebombed a German pharmaceutical firm in Vienna that was hosting US visitors and flying a US flag. The group claimed the firm was affiliated with a US genetic company that they alleged was involved in forced sterilization in developing countries. A leftwing group calling itself the Cell for Internationalism claimed responsibility for a similar firebombing the next day against the American International School. The same group claimed it was also involved in a firebombing on 20 December against an American Express office in Salzburg.

In February, Austrian officials released suspected Abu Nidal terrorist Bahij Younis from a Vienna prison, where he had served 13 years for complicity in the murder in 1981 of the president of the Austro-Israeli Society Nittel in Vienna. Younis is also believed to have masterminded the attack against a synagogue in Vienna in 1981. In March, Austria extradited to Belgium Rajeh Heshan Mohamed Baghdad, a PLO terrorist sentenced to life in 1982 for his role in a murder and terrorist attack in 1981.

Croatia

A car bomb detonated outside police headquarters in Rijeka on 20 October, injuring 29 bystanders and killing the driver of the car. The Egyptian organization Al-Gama'at al-Islamiyya (also known as the Islamic Group or IG) claimed responsibility for the bombing. The car bomb was detonated to press Croatian authorities into releasing IG spokesman Tala'at Fuad Kassem, who had been detained by Croatian police in Zagreb on 12 September. After the bombing, Croatian authorities said Kassem was no longer in the country.

France

A series of terrorist incidents in France in 1995 appeared to be the work of Algerian extremists. In July a cofounder of the Algerian opposition group Islamic Salvation Front (FIS), Abdelbaki Sahraoui, was murdered in Paris. Suspicion focused on another Algerian opposition group, the Armed Islamic Group (GIA), which had earlier put Sahraoui on a "death list" for his supposed conciliatory posture toward the Algerian Government.

A blast on 25 July in a Paris metro station kicked off a campaign of eight bombings or attempted bombings in France. Eight people were killed and 160 wounded in the attacks, which were staged in train stations, markets, and other public places to maximize civilian casualties. Although there were various claims of responsibility for the blasts, suspicions centered on the violent Islamic opposition to the Algerian Government. Some commentators argued that the GIA wanted to punish the Government of France for its supposed support for the Algerian Government, others claimed that the bombings were in retribution for the killing of four Algerian hijackers of an Air France Airbus in December 1994.

French police achieved a breakthrough in September when they traced fingerprints found on an unexploded bomb —discovered on high-speed train tracks near Lyon—to a French citizen of Algerian descent, Khaled Kelkal. The police killed Kelkal in a shootout later that month. In November fingerprints found on another unexploded device and other information led police to arrest several more people of North African descent, two of whom were formally charged with involvement in the bombings. There were no additional terrorist blasts in 1995 following these arrests. The French judiciary may reveal more about its understanding of the structure behind the crimes when the judicial cases against the accused come to trial.

In August assailants threw a molotov cocktail at a Turkish sporting and cultural association in Paris, injuring six and causing minor damage. The Kurdistan Workers' Party (PKK) probably is responsible.

Georgia

On 29 August unidentified assailants attempted to assassinate President Eduard Schevardnadze by detonating a car bomb near his motorcade as it left the presidential compound in T'bilisi. Schevardnadze suffered minor injuries, but four of his bodyguards were injured, one seriously.

Six armed men detonated a small bomb in front of the residence of the Russian Ambassador to Georgia on 9 April, shattering windows and causing minor damage to nearby houses. The Algeti Wolves claimed responsibility for that attack and for an armed assault two hours later on Russian troops in the city, citing Russian involvement in Chechnya as the reason for both attacks. There were no injuries.

Germany

Authorities continued to pursue and prosecute Red Army Faction (RAF) members. In September, a German court sentenced RAF member Sieglinde Hofmann to life imprisonment for assisting in five murders and three attempted murders, including the bomb attack in 1979 in Belgium on then-NATO Commander Alexander Haig. In October, Johannes Weinrich, a former RAF member and alleged deputy to international terrorist Illych Ramirez Sanchez (Carlos), was indicted in Berlin for transporting explosives into Germany that were later used to bomb the French cultural center; Weinrich had been extradited to Germany from Yemen. Germany released several former RAF terrorists who had served from 11 to 20 years of their sentences.

Although German officials say the RAF has largely disintegrated, they worry about successor organizations that have assumed the RAF's ideological mantle. The emerging Anti-Imperialist Cells (AIZ), for example, mounted several bombing attacks against German interests in 1995. Among far-right groups, German authorities noted an increasing tendency to link up with neo-Nazi groups abroad, especially through the use of electronic communication networks.

The number of arson attacks with proven or probable connections to foreign extremist groups were more than five times those carried out in 1994, largely because of two waves of attacks in March-April and July-August by the Kurdistan

Workers' Party (PKK). In more than 200 attacks on Turkish establishments—some of which may have been "copycat" attacks perpetrated by antiforeigner Germans rather than the PKK—two foreigners died and several others were injured. Although Germany banned the PKK and several associated Kurdish organizations in 1993, new PKK front organizations appear frequently in Germany, thus presenting a continuing problem for the government.

Attacks against US interests were rare, although US-owned Chrysler dealerships were targeted to protest the scheduled execution in the United States of convicted murderer Mumia Abu Jamal. In Kassel, vandals smashed car and showroom windows, and, elsewhere, the Anti-Imperialistic Group Liberty for Mumia Abu Jamal claimed responsibility for firebombing a vehicle parked outside a dealership.

In November a group calling itself Anti-Imperialist Freedom Connection for Benjamin claimed responsibility for setting fire to and destroying a vehicle belonging to a German-Spanish automobile joint venture; the claim letter protested the deportation trial of Benjamin Ramos-Vega, a member of the Basque Fatherland and Liberty (ETA) terrorist group.

Greece

Greek leftist and anarchist groups in 1995 again conducted numerous terrorist attacks against public and private Greek and foreign targets. The Revolutionary Organization 17 November, for example, fired two rockets at a MEGA TV station facility in March, causing extensive damage but no casualties. Greek terrorist groups also conducted several operations against foreign interests, including the August bombings of the American Express and Citibank offices in Athens.

Greece had some counterterrorist successes in 1995, including the successful conviction of Georgios Balafas, a suspected 17 November terrorist sentenced to 10 years in prison for stockpiling weapons. Greek counterterrorist efforts, however, could benefit from the passage of tougher, more comprehensive counterterrorist regulations. Since 1975 no one has been convicted of any of 17 November's terrorist attacks, including the murder of four US officials and a Greek employee of the US Embassy. While official statements indicate the government's resolve to confront Greece's domestic terrorist problem, frequent turnover of key personnel involved in the fight against terrorism—three public order ministers in the past year—hampers these efforts.

Greek authorities continued in 1995 to deny public Turkish charges that the anti-Turkish Kurdistan Workers' Party (PKK) conducts operational terrorist training and receives assistance in Greece. As is the case in certain other European countries, however, Greece permits the PKK to operate a known front organization in Athens. In May it also allowed the successor group to Dev Sol, another anti-Turkish and anti-US terrorist group, to open an office in Athens under its new name, the Revolutionary People's Liberation Party/Front (DHKP/C).

Italy

In the culmination of what journalists said was a two-year investigation, Milan police arrested 11 persons on 26 June at Milan's Islamic Center and made additional arrests a few days later. Police officials told the press that the group provided support for an international network of Islamic terrorist organizations, including the Egyptian al-Gama'at al-Islamiyya (Islamic Group or IG). A police spokesman also said the arrestees maintained contact with the "Blind Shaykh," Umar Abd al-Rahman, who was convicted in October for conspiring to commit terrorism in the United States. Charges against the accused include conspiracy, extortion, armed robbery, falsifying documents, and arms smuggling.

On the basis of a French warrant, Italian police arrested former Red Army Faction member Margo Froehlich in October. A German national, she was wanted for complicity in a Paris attack in 1982 carried out by international terrorist Illych Ramirez Sanchez (Carlos) that killed one person and injured 63.

Russia

On the afternoon of 13 September, a rocket-propelled grenade hit the sixth floor of the US Embassy in Moscow. The grenade penetrated the wall and exploded inside, causing some damage to office equipment but no casualties. No group claimed responsibility.

In December 1995, Russia participated in a first-of-its-kind counterterrorism ministerial conference that was called by the heads of the G-7 nations plus Russia at their June summit in Halifax.

Spain

In 1995, Basque Fatherland and Liberty (ETA) terrorists conducted attacks on Spanish rail lines and stations, banks, police officers, and political figures—including the assassination of the Partido Popular mayoral candidate in San Sebastian and the attempted assassination of the leading contender for the prime ministership. In addition, ETA targeted French interests in Spain in 1995. In February a suspected ETA bomb exploded at a French-owned bank. Following a joint Spanish-French operation that thwarted a plot to assassinate King Juan Carlos while he vacationed in Majorca last August, suspected ETA members or supporters tossed molotov cocktails at a Citroen car dealership in Navarre, destroying five vehicles. In mid-December suspected ETA members detonated a car bomb in Madrid, one of the worst attacks in years that claimed at least six lives and wounded 15 others.

Turkey

Turkey continued its vigorous pursuit of several violent leftist and Islamic extremist groups, especially the Kurdistan Workers' Party (PKK), responsible for terrorism in Turkey.

The PKK launched hundreds of attacks in 1995 in Turkey, including indiscriminate bombings in areas frequented by Turkish and foreign civilians, as part of its campaign to establish a breakaway state in southeastern Turkey. For example, the group set off a bomb outside a cafe/grocery store in Izmir on 17 September, killing five and wounding 29. The PKK also continued—albeit with less success—its three-year-old attempt to drive foreign tourists away from Turkey by attacking tourist sites. In August two US citizens were injured by shrapnel in a bombing of Istanbul's popular Taksim Square. Moreover, the PKK continued to expand its activities in Western Europe, especially in Germany, where its members frequently attacked ethnic Turks and Turkish commercial establishments.

A successor to the Marxist/Leninist Devrimci Sol (Dev Sol)—known as the Revolutionary People's Liberation Party/Front (DHKP/C)—and several Islamic extremist groups were active in 1995. Dev Sol has been responsible for several anti-US attacks since 1990, and the DHKP/C continues to target US citizens. In July the group took over a restaurant in Istanbul, holding several civilians—including three US tourists—hostage. All of the hostages eventually were released unharmed. Loosely organized Islamic extremist groups, such as the Islamic Movement Organization and IBDA-C, continued to launch attacks against targets associated with Turkish official facilities and functions. They may have been responsible for the attempted assassination in June of a prominent Jewish community leader in Ankara.

Ukraine

On 24 May, an explosive device detonated near the Austrian Airlines office in the Odessa airport in southern Ukraine. Austrian Airlines is the only Western airline that flies out of Odessa. Press reports said the device consisted of about six pounds of plastic explosive. There were no injuries. No group claimed responsibility for the attack, which may not have been politically motivated.

United Kingdom

The cease-fires begun in the autumn of 1994, led by the Provisional Irish Republican Army (PIRA) and followed by other Republican splinter groups and the three major Loyalist paramilitaries, still held at year's end. Nevertheless, sporadic incidents of politically motivated killings, arson, attempted bombings, punishment beatings, and abductions were reported. No progress was made on the decommissioning of weapons, and paramilitaries were combat ready. In November, Irish and British police forces intercepted a van loaded with hundreds of pounds of explosives in Ireland near the border with Northern Ireland. Authorities believe a Republican fringe group known as the Irish National Liberation Army (INLA) was intending to attack British security forces in Northern Ireland. A subsequent police sweep of the area discovered another cache of explosives and bombmaking equipment at a farm a few miles from the first operation.

In January an unidentified assailant shot and killed a Sikh newspaper editor. The victim may have been killed because of his support for an independent Sikh state in India. No one claimed responsibility.

A British court ruled on 25 July to extradite Kani Yilmaz, European chief of the Kurdistan Workers' Party (PKK), to Germany, where he faces charges of conspiracy to commit arson. The ruling sparked a large crowd of PKK supporters to battle London police, pelting them with bottles, bricks, and road signs, injuring more than a dozen police officers and an unknown number of others. The United Kingdom permits the PKK to operate a known front organization within its borders.

Latin America Overview

International terrorist activity rose in Latin America mostly due to the high number of attacks against international entities in Colombia. In 1995 the number of attacks in that country increased by 85 percent to 76 attacks. In all of Latin America, however, a total of eight international terrorist attacks last year were lethal.

Guerrillas continued to target the democratic process in Colombia through intimidation and violence. The Revolutionary Armed Forces of Colombia (FARC) held at least four US citizens hostage at the end of the year. The group killed two US missionaries in June after kidnapping them in 1994. Ransoms continued to provide guerrillas with significant income, making up for a decrease in protection payments from coca growers, who had lower production as a result of the government's eradication program. Government efforts to negotiate a peaceful settlement were met with increased guerrilla violence.

There were no international terrorist incidents reported in Argentina during 1995. The investigation into the bombing in 1994 of the Argentine Jewish Mutual Association remains unsolved. The Government of Argentina organized and hosted a regional counterterrorist conference in August in an effort to encourage cooperation in countering the international terrorist threat.

Peru successfully continued to counter its terrorist organizations, significantly lowering the level of violence in the country. While Peru's terrorist organizations, Sendero Luminoso (Shining Path or SL) and the Tupac Amaru Revolutionary Movement (MRTA) have significantly declined in strength, they still have the capacity to inflict damage against international targets. At year's end, the Government of Peru was planning to host an Organization of American States (OAS) conference on terrorism in 1996, which will focus on promoting cooperation among Western Hemisphere nations in combating terrorism while protecting human rights.

Argentina

Throughout 1995 the Argentine Government continued its investigation of the bombing in July 1994 of the Jewish community center building (AMIA) that killed nearly 100 persons. In September, Investigating Judge Juan Jose Galeano filed additional charges against detained suspect Carlos Telleldin, accusing him of criminal conspiracy relating to the stolen-car ring that allegedly provided the van used in the attack on the AMIA. The police detained other suspects in December to review their possible roles in the bombing attack.

The investigation into the bombing in March 1992 of the Israeli Embassy failed to develop any new leads. Paraguay extradited seven suspected terrorists to Argentina, where they were released after questioning. The Argentine Supreme Court now has responsibility for the case. The Iranian-backed Lebanese Hizballah remains the key suspect in both the 1992 and 1994 attacks.

One of Argentina's most wanted fugitives, Enrique Gorriaran Merlo, was detained on 28 October in Mexico and expelled shortly thereafter to Buenos Aires to stand trial. Gorriaran was involved in the kidnapping of the general manager of an Exxon refinery and managed the negotiations for the captive's release after a ransom was paid. Gorriaran was also an organizer of an attack on a military base in 1989 that left nearly 40 dead. He had been a leader of Argentina's People's Revolutionary Army (ERP), a largely leftist urban terrorist group that operated in the 1970s, and he personally took responsibility for the assassination of former Nicaraguan dictator Anastasio Somoza in Paraguay in 1980. If convicted of the several charges, Gorriaran faces life imprisonment.

Argentina took a leading role in regional cooperation against international counterterrorism in 1995. Buenos Aires hosted a regional counterterrorist conference in August to improve cooperation among its neighbors—Brazil, Chile, Paraguay, and Uruguay, as well as the United States and Canada. The Government of Argentina also is pressing for greater cooperation with Brazil and Paraguay to improve border controls in the "triborder" area, where their three frontiers meet. Argentina will introduce a new machine-readable passport in early 1996.

Colombia

Colombia continued to be wracked by violence in 1995, suffering numerous terrorist bombings, murders, and kidnappings for ransom. Drug traffickers, leftist insurgents, paramilitary squads, and common criminals committed scores of crimes with impunity, killing their targets as well as many innocent bystanders. Although most of the politically motivated violence was directed at local targets, Colombia recorded 76 international terrorist incidents during 1995, the highest number in Latin America and nearly twice the 41 such incidents in 1994.

The nation's two main guerrilla groups—the Revolutionary Armed Forces of Colombia (FARC) and the National Liberation Army (ELN)—intensified political violence during the year, ignoring offers for peace talks with the government. Rebel attacks against oil pipelines owned jointly by the Government of Colombia and Western companies escalated, accounting for most of the international incidents in Colombia in 1995.

Kidnapping for ransom continued to be a profitable business in Colombia; leftist guerrillas conducted approximately half of all abductions in the country, increasing their war chests by several million dollars. Colombians were the primary victims, but many foreign nationals also were abducted. At year's end, FARC rebels held at least four US citizens, three of whom were detained in 1993 and one in 1994. In August presumed FARC guerrillas released one US citizen kidnapped near Cali in 1994. Another US citizen, kidnapped in January, was released in April.

Kidnappings of foreigners sometimes have ended with the murder of the hostage. A British citizen kidnapped by guerrillas in June was found dead in August near Bogota. The guerrillas also kidnapped and subsequently released a UK Embassy employee. In June, FARC guerrillas murdered two US missionaries, held since January 1994, during a chance encounter with a Colombian army patrol. Police have issued arrest warrants for eight guerrillas suspected of kidnapping the two missionaries.

Despite President Samper's willingness to negotiate with the nation's guerrilla organizations, FARC and ELN insurgents did not demonstrate a sincere desire to pursue a negotiated settlement in 1995. Instead, they continued to attack government forces and other targets. On the anniversary of President Samper's inauguration in August, FARC rebels attacked a police counternarcotics base in Miraflores (in Guaviare Department), killing six and wounding 29 police officers. Unknown assailants, possibly guerrillas, bombed a sculpture in a crowded Medellin square, which left 28 persons dead and injured more than 175. FARC guerrillas operating in areas of heavy coca cultivation often fired on—and in one case shot down—government aircraft engaged in US-supported drug eradication efforts.

Twice during 1995, President Samper declared a "state of internal commotion," invoking exceptional measures because of increased violence nationwide and the assassination on 2 November of Conservative Party patriarch Alvaro Gomez Hurtado. On that date, President Samper announced that he was empowering the military, governors of the 32 departments (states), and all mayors to authorize the evacuation of civilians from municipalities to combat illegal armed groups, including the guerrilla organizations operating in Colombia.

Guatemala

Guatemala's 35-year-old insurgency continues at a low level, as talks toward a negotiated settlement progress. The three major armed guerrilla groups—the Revolutionary Armed Forces (FAR), the Revolutionary Organization of the People in Arms (ORPA), and the Guerrilla Army of the Poor (EGP)—are allied in the Guatemalan National Revolutionary Union (URNG). along with the Communist Guatemalan Workers' Party (PGT).

In April a bomb was detonated outside the Presidential

Palace during a visit by UN Secretary General Boutros Boutros-Ghali. Evidence points to guerrilla involvement, but no group claimed responsibility. In May presumed guerrillas fired on a US Embassy antinarcotics helicopter on a training flight over Palin. The aircraft sustained minor damage.

Panama

The bombing in July 1994 of a commuter airliner that killed all 21 persons aboard, including three US citizens, remained under investigation in 1995. Panama has made no arrests but continues to cooperate closely with US authorities.

Progress was made in two other terrorist cases. Pedro Miguel Gonzalez, one of the suspects in the murder in 1992 of US Army Corporal Zak Hernandez, turned himself over to Panamanian authorities in January 1995; his case had not yet gone to trial by the end of the year. Two others sought in connection with the murder of the US serviceman remained at large. Juan Barria, who confessed to having murdered a US citizen and a US Embassy employee during Operation Just Cause in 1989, was convicted after a jury trial on 19 November.

Peru

Peruvian Government security forces in 1995 continued to reduce the activities of Peru's terrorist organizations—Sendero Luminoso (Shining Path or SL) and the Tupac Amaru Revolutionary Movement (MRTA). Numerous detentions, casualties, and defections further weakened the two groups, and continued arrests of several terrorist leaders kept the level of violence by these groups low compared to previous years. Most of the violence in 1995 took place in rural areas, particularly the coca-rich Upper Huallaga Valley. Violence in Lima and other cities declined. In Lima there were two car bombings, the lowest number in years.

Police arrests helped disrupt Sendero's terrorist plans for the national elections in April 1995. In a major coordinated operation, counterterrorist police arrested approximately 20 members of Sendero Luminoso in the cities of Lima, Callao, Huancayo, and Arequipa. Among those captured was Sendero Central Committee member, and number-two leader of Sendero militants still at large, Margi Clavo Peralta. Clavo later publicly announced her support for peace talks with the government, which jailed Sendero leader and founder Abimael Guzman first advocated in 1993.

Three years after the capture of SL chieftain Guzman, the Maoist terrorist group is struggling, attempting to rebuild and resolve its leadership problems. Sendero Luminoso has become less active, its operations smaller and less sophisticated. While SL's capability to target international targets has diminished, it retains the capability to cause considerable harm, and its "anti-imperialist" animus has not changed. In May the group detonated a car bomb in front of a luxury Lima hotel, killing four and injuring several dozen persons. In July, Sendero terrorists killed a Peruvian employee of a US mining company after seeking by name a US geologist who had left the site a few days earlier.

On 1 December the number-two leader of MRTA still at large, Miguel Rincon, surrendered to police after a fire-fight that followed a raid of an MRTA safehouse. The police arrested more than a dozen other MRTA members and uncovered weapons and explosives in the residence. The police effort inflicted a severe blow to the weakened terrorist organization, disrupting its plans to conduct attacks.

Middle East Overview

The deadliest terrorist attack against US interests in the Middle East since the 1983 bombing of the Marine barracks in Beirut took place on 13 November in Riyadh, Saudi Arabia. A vehicle bomb badly damaged the headquarters of the Office of the Program Manager/Saudi Arabian National Guard (OPM/SANG), a military training mission. Seven persons, including five US citizens, were killed and 42 were wounded. Several shadowy groups, including the "Islamic Movement for Change," claimed responsibility for the incident. Saudi Arabian authorities are aggressively investigating the incident in close cooperation with the Federal Bureau of Investigation.

Fatalities from extremist violence in Egypt rose slightly above 1994 totals. Nevertheless, Egyptian authorities continued a successful crackdown against extremists, arresting some important leaders and confining violence to upper Egypt. In November, Al-Gama'at Islamiyya (the Islamic Group or IG) renewed efforts to target Egypt's tourist industry. In two shooting attacks against trains traveling through Qina and Al Minya Governorates in upper Egypt, two Europeans and 10 Egyptians were wounded.

For the first time, Egyptian extremists extended their campaign of violence outside Egypt's borders. The IG claimed responsibility for an assassination attempt against Egyptian President Hosni Mubarak in Ethiopia in June, and in November the Egyptian Embassy in Islamabad, Pakistan, was bombed, killing 16 and wounding 60. Both the IG and the Jihad Group claimed responsibility for this attack.

In Algeria widespread terrorism continued the trend of recent years. Armed insurgents turned increasingly to the use of indiscriminate bombings in their offensive against the government, deemphasizing their reliance on military-style attacks on Algerian security units. While attacks against foreigners in Algeria decreased overall, Islamic militants expanded their offensive to include targets overseas and US targets in Algeria. In November, Islamic militants set fire to a US Embassy warehouse; this was consistent with threats against foreign—including US—interests in Algeria issued by the Armed Islamic Group (GIA). The same group is suspected of responsibility for the murder in Paris in July of a prominent activist from the Islamic Salvation Front—another Algerian Islamist opposition group—as well as a bombing campaign in Paris that killed eight persons and wounded scores.

Elsewhere in North Africa, incidents of terrorist violence were low. Tunisian authorities maintained effective control of the internal security situation and, in particular, closely followed the activities of the Tunisian Islamic Front, which claimed responsibility for the murders of four policemen and has warned all foreigners to leave Tunisia. In Morocco, an Egyptian detonated a bomb in the consular section of the Russian Embassy, evidently to protest Russian policy in Chechnya. Islamic extremists continued efforts to smuggle weapons through Morocco into Algeria to support extremists there.

In Israel and the occupied territories/Palestinian autonomous areas, incidents of political violence and terrorism continued to plague the Palestinian-Israeli peace process. On 4 November, a Jewish Israeli extremist assassinated Prime Minister Yitzhak Rabin at a propeace rally in Tel Aviv. In subsequent statements the assassin said he acted to protest Rabin's peace process policies.

The overall number of anti-Israeli attacks declined to 33 in 1995 from 79 in 1994 due to a change in the nature of attacks, that is, less frequent but more lethal suicide bombings. Casualty figures thus remained high, with 45 Israeli soldiers and civilians killed, two US civilians killed, and nearly 280 persons wounded in 1995, compared to 55 persons killed and more than 150 wounded in the previous year. The Islamic Resistance Movement (HAMAS) and the Palestine Islamic Jihad (PIJ) claimed responsibility for most of these attacks, including several devastating suicide bombings. Chairman Yasir Arafat's Palestinian Authority (PA) launched a campaign to crack down on Islamic militants while at the same time initiating political dialogue with HAMAS to bring it into the political process. HAMAS announced a temporary suspension of military activities in August while engaging in talks with the PA; there were no major HAMAS attacks against Israelis through the end of 1995.

Lebanon witnessed small improvements in the internal security situation during the year, including in Beirut. Despite government efforts to extend its control, however, many parts of the country remained outside the central government's authority. The terrorist organization Hizballah has yet to be disarmed and still operates freely in several areas of the country, particularly the south. Incidents of internal political violence continued to trouble many parts of the country.

Algeria

The security situation in Algeria did not improve substantially in 1995. Accurate casualty figures are difficult to acquire, but as many as 50,000 Algerians—militants, security personnel, and civilians—have died as a result of the nearly four-year-old insurgency. Islamic extremists slowed their attacks against foreign nationals inside Algeria in 1995, but suspicions centered on the Algerian Armed Islamic Group (GIA) for a series of terrorist attacks in France in July, September, and October.

Last year extremists carried out their first attack against a US target in Algeria since Islamic militants began targeting foreigners in 1993. On 9 November, Islamic extremists set fire to a warehouse belonging to the US Embassy. The militants threatened the life of the Algerian security guard because he was working for the United States, and they specifically demanded to know whether there were any US citizens present. The GIA probably carried out the attacks. The group had threatened to strike US and other foreign targets in Algeria, and the modus operandi of the attack was consistent with past GIA operations against foreign facilities.

The GIA was responsible for the deaths of 31 foreigners in Algeria in 1995, compared to at least 64 in 1994. Most of the foreigners killed were "soft targets," such as teachers and nuns. From July to October a terrorist bombing campaign in France began against civilian targets, killing eight persons and wounding 160. Suspicion centered on the GIA as a protest of French support for Algiers. Suspicion also focused on the GIA for the death of FIS leader Abdelbaki Sahraoui in Paris in July; the group earlier had published Sahraoui's name in a list of FIS members marked for death due to their conciliatory posture toward negotiating with the Algerian regime.

Algerian militants changed their tactics slightly in 1995, relying more heavily on the use of homemade bombs—especially car bombs—and decreasing their reliance on more traditional military-style attacks on Algerian security units. The GIA claimed responsibility for the suicide car bombing of a police headquarters in downtown Algiers in January that killed more than 40 persons. Insurgents stepped up attacks on infrastructure targets this year, disabling bridges and electric power facilities throughout the country. In May, GIA commandos attacked foreign workers along a newly constructed gas pipeline, killing five. The GIA continued its attacks against civilian targets, killing women for refusing to wear the *hidjab*, intellectuals, and others it perceived as "cooperating" with the regime and "spreading Western influence." Over 25 journalists were killed in 1995, making Algeria the most dangerous place in the world for practitioners of this profession.

Violence in Algeria slowed significantly in the weeks before the presidential election on 16 November, primarily because of extraordinary measures employed by the security services. As these security measures were relaxed, however, Algeria's fragmented Islamic movement continued to attack foreigners; two Latvian sailors were shot within two weeks after the elections.

Egypt

Fatalities from Islamic extremist violence rose slightly in 1995, with the number of victims—including noncombatants and police—and extremists killed increasing from 286 in 1994 to 375 in 1995. Violence primarily was confined to provinces in upper Egypt; there were no attacks in Cairo or urban areas further north.

Al-Gama'at al-Islamiyya (Islamic Group or IG) continued to be the most active Islamic extremist organization in Egypt in 1995. All attacks occurred in upper Egypt, with much of the violence shifting from Asyu't—the previous center of conflict—to Al Minya Governorate, specifically around Mallawi. Some attacks also occurred in Qina Governorate. Police and security elements were the focus of many attacks. The IG also is believed to have been the culprit in the deaths of at least 28

Coptic Christians and at least 20 Muslims alleged to be police informants. In November, the IG also resumed its efforts to damage Egypt's tourist industry, claiming responsibility for two shooting attacks that month against trains traveling through Qina and Al Minya Governorates to tourist sites in upper Egypt. Two Europeans and 10 Egyptians were wounded in the attacks. The IG claims of responsibility were accompanied by warnings for all foreign tourists to leave the country.

Egypt has stepped up its counterterrorist campaign, preventing Islamic extremists from carrying out attacks in Cairo and other urban areas to the north. A police sweep in Al Minya in September resulted in the arrest of a key leader of the IG's military wing, who had been sought since the assassination of President Anwar Sadat in 1981.

During 1995, Egyptian Islamic extremist groups took their campaign of violence outside Egypt for the first time. The IG claimed responsibility for an assassination attempt against Egyptian President Hosni Mubarak in Ethiopia on 26 June. The IG also took responsibility for a car bombing in Rijeka, Croatia, in October that injured 29 Croatian nationals and killed the car's driver. The IG accused the Croatian Government of having arrested a visiting Gama'at member who had been living in Denmark. Both the IG and the Jihad Group claimed responsibility for the bombing on 19 November of the Egyptian Embassy in Islamabad, Pakistan. Sixteen persons were killed in the attack and another 60 were injured. The previously unknown International Justice Group also took responsibility for the bombing in Pakistan, as well as for the shooting death of an Egyptian diplomat in Geneva on 13 November.

Israel and the Occupied Territories/Palestinian Autonomous Areas

Yigal Amir, a Jewish extremist associated with the little-known "Fighting Jewish Organization" (EYAL), assassinated Prime Minister Yitzhak Rabin at a propeace rally in Tel Aviv on 4 November. Amir claimed to have acted alone, but Israeli security forces charged several other alleged conspirators. Israel also stepped up its investigations of EYAL and other extremist groups that may have had a hand in the murder. Kach and Kahane Chai—which Israel outlawed as terrorist groups after the Hebron massacre in February 1994—remained active in 1995, though they maintained lower profiles.

The overall number of anti-Israeli attacks instigated by Palestinians declined to 33 in 1995 from 79 in 1994 due to a change in the nature of attacks, that is, to less frequent but more lethal suicide bombings. Casualty figures remained high, with 45 Israeli soldiers and civilians and two US citizens killed and nearly 280 persons wounded in 1995, compared to 55 persons killed and more than 150 wounded the previous year. The increased lethality of the attacks was due mainly to Palestinian extremist groups' increased use of suicide bombings, which killed 39 and wounded 252.

The Islamic Resistance Movement (HAMAS) conducted five major anti-Israeli attacks in 1995 as part of its campaign to derail the peace process. The group claimed responsibility for three devastating suicide bombings, including the bombing on 21 August of a bus in Jerusalem's Ramat Eshkol neighborhood that resulted in the death of a US citizen, Joan Davenny, and three Israelis, and the wounding of more than 100 civilians. Following that operation, HAMAS temporarily suspended its military activities and entered into talks with the Palestinian Authority (PA), in which HAMAS discussed the possibility of ending anti-Israeli attacks and participating in the Palestinian elections on 20 January 1996. There were no major HAMAS attacks against Israelis from the August suicide bus bombing through the end of 1995.

Other Palestinian groups that reject the peace process also attacked Israelis. The Palestine Islamic Jihad (PIJ)-Shaqaqi Faction claimed responsibility for five suicide bombings that killed a total of 29 persons and wounded 107. One bus bombing on 9 April killed a US citizen, Alisa Flatow, and seven Israelis and wounded 41 other persons. Although the group suffered a strong blow when its leader, Fathi Shaqaqi, was assassinated in Malta on 26 October, it remained capable of striking at Israeli targets. On 2 November, the PIJ carried out two suicide bomb attacks against Israeli targets in Gaza to retaliate for Shaqaqi's murder, which the group believes Israel sponsored. No Israelis were killed in the attacks. The Democratic Front for the Liberation of Palestine (DFLP) and the Popular Front for the Liberation of Palestine (PFLP) also claimed responsibility for several attacks against Israelis that occurred outside Palestinian Authority (PA) held areas in the West Bank.

The PA increased its effort to rein in Palestinian violence against Israelis in 1995. The PA security apparatus stepped up its campaign to register and confiscate weapons, thwart terrorist plots, and convict Palestinians responsible for anti-Israeli acts. The PA thwarted a PIJ attack planned for 10 June. In August, the Palestinian Police Force arrested a HAMAS terrorist who was preparing a bomb to be set off in Israel. Arafat and other senior PA officials regularly condemned acts of terrorism as they occurred, especially the Rabin assassination.

Israel's vigilant border security appeared to effectively prevent infiltrations from Syria, Lebanon, and Jordan. Israeli troops on 12 August, for instance, captured a heavily armed guerrilla attempting to infiltrate into Israel from Jordan. Hizballah and Palestinian rejectionist groups continued to launch occasional—nine times in 1995—Katyusha rocket salvos into northern Israel from southern Lebanon. The most serious rocket attacks occurred in November, when militants in Lebanon fired 30 to 40 Katyushas into northern Israel over a two-day period, wounding six Israeli civilians.

Jordan

Jordanian security and police closely monitor secular and Islamic extremists inside the country, detaining individuals suspected of involvement in violent acts aimed at destabilizing the government or its relations with other states. Jordanian authorities detained dozens of persons in terrorist-related cases in 1995, including six members of the Islamic Renewal

Movement planning to attack foreign interests and two individuals suspected of shooting a French diplomat in February. In late July, Jordan arrested a suspect in the World Trade Center bombing, pursuant to a request from the United States, and rendered him to US law enforcement authorities in early August.

Jordan's peace treaty with Israel—signed on 26 October 1994—commits the two parties to cooperate against terrorism. Amman maintains tight security along its border with Israel and has stopped individuals attempting to infiltrate into the West Bank.

Several Palestinian rejectionist groups maintain a closely watched presence in Jordan, including the Palestine Islamic Jihad (PIJ), Democratic Front for the Liberation of Palestine (DFLP), Popular Front for the Liberation of Palestine (PFLP), Popular Front for the Liberation of Palestine–General Command (PFLP-GC), and the Islamic Resistance Movement (HAMAS) The government in April warned HAMAS spokesman Ibrahim Ghawsha. a Jordanian citizen, not to issue statements supportive of anti-Israeli violence, as this was in violation of Jordanian law. Under that law, Jordan expelled two senior HAMAS leaders in May for making inflammatory statements against Israel. The two did not hold Jordanian citizenship.

Lebanon

There was incremental improvement in the Lebanese security environment in 1995 as the Lebanese Government struggled to expand its authority throughout the country. The situation in the Beirut metropolitan area is somewhat improved but remains dangerous. Large sections of Lebanon, however, remain effectively beyond the central government's control. There is a risk to Westerners, in particular, in uncontrolled areas such as in the south and the Al Biqa' (Bekaa Valley). An unknown number of Lebanese civilians were killed, injured, or displaced in the fighting in southern Lebanon this year.

While the government has limited the activities of many violent individuals and groups in Lebanon, the terrorist organization Hizballah has yet to be disarmed and continues to operate as a separate polity within the country For example, Hizballah has announced that it will operate a separate judicial system based on Islamic jurisprudence within areas under its direct control

Hizballah's animosity toward the United States continues. In its public rhetoric, the group routinely denounces the United States. In March, Hizballah leader Fadlallah stated that Hizballah "continue(s) to oppose US policy everywhere." Hizballah also continues to make public statements condemning the Middle East peace process.

Militia personnel in February kidnapped two individuals and held them for four days before releasing them. Thousands of people seized during the Lebanese Civil War remain unaccounted for.

Ahmad al-Assad'ad, the son of former Lebanese Parliament speaker Kamel al-Assad'ad, apparently escaped injury on 3 July when handgrenades were thrown at him during a rally in Nabatiyah in southern Lebanon.

In August gunmen shot and killed Shaykh Nizar al-Halbi, the chairman of the Sunni fundamentalist group "Islamic Charitable Projects Association," as he left his home in a West Beirut neighborhood. A group calling itself the "Usama Kassass Organization" claimed responsibility. Two suspects subsequently were arrested.

A car bombing in Jibshit killed a local Hizballah security official in November. No one has claimed responsibility for the attack.

In December, Lebanese security forces reportedly broke up a terrorist ring operating in northern Lebanon. This ring was planning to begin a violent campaign of assassinations and bombings that month.

There were developments in several terrorism trials. In May, the Judicial Council trying Lebanese Forces Leader Samir Ja'ja on charges of domestic terrorism—for the bombing in February 1994 of a Maronite Church in Zuq Mikha'il that killed 11 and wounded 59—issued an indefinite continuance (Sine Die) that suspended the trial. A second defendant, Lebanese Forces Deputy Commander Fu'ad Malik, was granted bail on 17 May for medical reasons. Ja'ja remains imprisoned for the assassination of Dany Chamoun, a political rival, in 1990.

In June, Lebanon's Permanent Military Court sentenced (in absentia) two defendants to death for the Beirut car bombing in December 1994 that killed Hizballah member Fu'ad Mughniyah and two others. Two other defendants received prison sentences.

By the end of the year, following a number of postponements, a Lebanese court was set to proceed with the trial of three members of the Popular Front for the Liberation of Palestine (PFLP) for the murders in 1976 of US Ambassador to Lebanon Francis E. Meloy and US diplomat Robert O. Waring.

Several Palestinian groups that use terrorism to express their opposition to the Middle East peace process maintain an active presence in Lebanon. These include the Islamic Resistance Movement (HAMAS), the Abu Nidal organization (ANO), the Palestine Islamic Jihad (PIJ), and the Popular Front for the Liberation of Palestine–General Command (PFLP-GC). These organizations conduct terrorist training in southern Lebanon.

Morocco

There were few terrorist-related incidents in Morocco in 1995. The first terrorist attack against a foreign diplomat in Morocco since 1985 occurred on 28 February, however, when an Egyptian citizen detonated a bomb strapped to his body at the consular department of the Russian Embassy. Although Moroccan officials initially suspected that the bomber had ties to Islamic militants, subsequent investigations led Moroccan officials to believe that the man was acting alone, and that the attack was carried out to demonstrate his solidarity with the Chechen people.

Islamic extremists in Morocco continued their efforts to smuggle weapons into Algeria to support Islamic opposition elements there. In mid-October, Moroccan authorities arrested 16 persons in the eastern province of Oujda whom the Moroccans alleged were transporting weapons to Algeria's Islamic Salvation Front. Four of those arrested were Algerians, strengthening the government claims that the arms were intended for Algerian insurgents.

Saudi Arabia

On 13 November, a car bomb exploded outside the Riyadh headquarters of the Office of the Program Manager/Saudi Arabian National Guard (OPM/SANG). Seven persons died in the blast, five of whom were US citizens, and 42 were injured. At least three groups claimed responsibility for the attack, including the Islamic Movement for Change, the Tigers of the Gulf, and the Combatant Partisans of God. The Saudi Government is aggressively investigating this attack with the assistance of the Federal Bureau of Investigation.

Tunisia

Tunis maintained effective control of the security situation in 1995, paying special attention to Islamic dissidents, but did not prosecute any individuals for specific acts of terrorism. In May the extremist Tunisian Islamic Front (FIT) issued a warning that all foreigners in Tunisia should leave, but it did not follow up with any concrete threats or attacks. The group also claimed responsibility for a number of operations in Tunisia, including the murders of four policemen. Tunisian authorities have not confirmed or denied the claims.

There are allegations that the FIT is working in conjunction with the Algerian Armed Islamic Group (GIA), and that its members may be training in GIA camps. Several Tunisians were taken into custody in 1995 for alleged involvement with the GIA network in Europe. The FIT claimed responsibility for an attack in February against a Tunisian border post on the Tunisia-Algeria border in which seven border guards were killed, but some officials blame the GIA—possibly in conjunction with the FIT—for the attack. As of 31 December, there were no similar incidents.

Patterns of Global Terrorism 1996

The Year in Review

During 1996 there were 296 acts of international terrorism, the lowest annual total in 25 years and 144 fewer than in 1995. In contrast, the total number of casualties was one of the highest ever recorded: 311 persons killed and 2,652 wounded. A single bombing in Sri Lanka killed 90 persons and wounded more than 1,400 others.

Two-thirds of the attacks were bombings or firebombings. Only about one-sixth of the total number (45) resulted in fatalities. Approximately one-fourth (73) were anti-US attacks, and most of those were low-intensity bombings of oil pipelines in Colombia owned jointly by the Government of Colombia and Western companies but seen as US targets by Colombian terrorists.

Approximately one in four attacks (76) recorded last year were part of an ongoing terrorist campaign being waged by the Kurdistan Workers' Party (PKK) in Germany. Most of these attacks were minor bombings that produced no casualties and caused little damage. The level of PKK attacks during 1996 was significantly lower than in previous years.

Among the significant attacks during the year:

- On 25 June a large fuel truck exploded outside the US military's Khubar Towers housing facility near Dhahran, Saudi Arabia, killing 19 US citizens and wounding some 500 persons.
- On 17 December terrorists belonging to Peru's Tupac Amaru Revolutionary Movement (MRTA) took over the Japanese Ambassador's residence in Lima during a diplomatic reception, taking some 500 persons hostage, including eight US officials who were released after five days. The group's primary demand was the release of convicted MRTA terrorists from prison. At year's end, 81 hostages remained in captivity, and attempts to resolve the siege peacefully were ongoing.
- There were several deadly bombings in Tel Aviv and Jerusalem by the Islamic Resistance Movement (HAMAS). On 25 February a suicide bomber blew up a bus in Jerusalem, killing 26 persons, including three US citizens, and injuring at least 80 others, including another three US citizens. On 3 March a suicide bomber detonated an explosive device on a bus in Jerusalem, killing 19 persons, including six Romanians, and injuring six others. On 4 March a suicide bomber detonated an explosive device outside Dizengoff Center, a large shopping mall in Tel Aviv, killing 20 persons and injuring 75 others, including two US citizens.
- The deadliest attack of the year occurred in Sri Lanka on 31 January, when terrorists belonging to the separatist Liberation Tigers of Tamil Eelam (LTTE) rammed an explosives-laden truck into the Central Bank in the heart of downtown Colombo, killing 90 persons and wounding more than 1,400 others. Among the wounded were two US citizens, six Japanese, and one Dutch national. The explosion caused major damage to the Central Bank building, an American Express office, the Intercontinental Hotel, and several other buildings.
- On 9 February a bomb detonated in a parking garage in the Docklands area of London, killing two persons and wounding more than 100 others, including two US citizens. The Irish Republican Army claimed responsibility for the attack.

Twenty-four US citizens died in international terrorist attacks last year, more than twice the number that died in

1995. Nineteen were killed in the 25 June truck bombing of the US military housing facility near Dhahran, Saudi Arabia. This was the highest number of US citizens killed in a single act of international terrorism since the 1988 bombing of Pan Am 103, in which 189 US citizens died. Five US citizens died in bus bombings and drive-by shootings in Tel Aviv and Jerusalem. Two hundred and fifty US citizens were wounded in acts of terrorism around the world last year, five times the number injured in 1995.

There were no international terrorist attacks in the United States during the year.

On 19 July a US district court in Washington, DC, convicted Omar Mohammed Ali Rezaq of air piracy in connection with the 1985 terrorist hijacking of Egypt Air Flight 648. The Athens-to-Cairo flight was diverted to Malta by Rezaq and two other hijackers. On the plane, Rezaq separated US and Israeli passengers from the others and shot them in the head at point blank range. One US citizen and one Israeli died; two US citizens and one Israeli survived their wounds. When Egyptian commandos stormed the plane, dozens more died. Rezaq, the sole surviving hijacker, was tried and convicted in Malta on various charges and sentenced to 25 years in prison, but he was released after serving only seven years. With cooperation from the Governments of Nigeria and Ghana, FBI agents arrested Rezaq in Nigeria in 1993 and brought him to the United States to be tried for air piracy. Rezaq, a member of the Abu Nidal organization, claimed at his trial that he had suffered from post-traumatic stress disorder and was therefore insane at the time he hijacked the airplane. He further claimed that, because of his insanity, he could not be held criminally liable for his conduct. The jury found Rezaq guilty and rejected his claim that he was insane at the time he committed the crime. In October Rezaq was sentenced to life imprisonment.

On 5 September Ramzi Ahmed Yousef, Abdul Hakim Murad, and Wali Khan Amin Shah were convicted of a terrorist conspiracy to plant bombs aboard a number of US passenger airliners operating in East Asia. Yousef also was found guilty of placing a bomb aboard a Philippine airliner bound for Tokyo in December 1995 that exploded in midair, killing one person and injuring several others. This bombing was intended as a "trial run" for the planned multiple attacks against US aircraft, which were to take place over two days. Yousef is awaiting trial on charges that he was involved in the bombing of the World Trade Center in 1993.

On 22 September an Asian country turned over to US custody suspected Japanese Red Army terrorist Tsutomu Shirosaki to stand trial for a 1986 mortar attack against the US Embassy in Jakarta, Indonesia.

Africa Overview

Eleven international terrorist attacks occurred in Africa during 1996, one more than during the previous year. Most took place in Ethiopia, where there were several deadly bombings and armed attacks.

Ethiopia

Addis Ababa was the site of two deadly hotel bombings in 1996. On 18 January an explosion in a hotel frequented by diplomats and foreign visitors killed four persons and injured at least 20 others, among them several foreigners. A bomb exploded in a second hotel on 5 August, killing two persons and injuring 17, including a Belgian citizen. Antigovernment groups are believed responsible for both attacks.

On 8 July gunmen shot and wounded the Ethiopian Transport and Communications Minister in Addis Ababa. An ethnic Somali Islamic extremist group, al-Ittihaad al-Islami, claimed responsibility for the shooting.

In October unidentified assailants shot three foreigners in a shopping area in the eastern city of Dire Dawa. A German was killed on 5 October, and on 16 October a French national and a Yemeni were killed. Although no claims of responsibility were made, local officials blamed Islamic extremists for the attacks.

Uganda

On 24 October gunmen attacked a Sudanese refugee camp in Uganda near the border with Sudan, killing 16 refugees and wounding five others. No one claimed responsibility for the attack.

Asia Overview

Although terrorism remains a concern in East Asia, national reconciliation efforts in Cambodia and the Philippines, and successful prosecutions in Japan, have helped reduce the terrorist profile in the region. Continuing defections by Khmer Rouge troops in Cambodia have reduced their numbers considerably, although the Khmer Rouge is still considered active and dangerous. Talks between the Philippine Government and a major insurgent group there have resulted in a peace agreement, although another major insurgent group has continued attacks in the southern Philippines, and terrorist groups continue to plague that nation. In February the Philippines hosted an international conference on counterterrorism at Baguio, which was attended by representatives of 20 nations, including the United States. The prosecution of a series of leaders of the Aum Shinrikyo cult in Japan, based primarily on the 1995 sarin nerve gas attack in the Tokyo subway, and the continued pursuit of Aum leaders still at large have dealt a heavy blow to that group. Terrorist activities by the Free Papua Movement (OPM) in Indonesia and by insurgent groups in a number of East Asian countries continue to pose a threat.

In South Asia, terrorist training camps located in Afghanistan remain open. The fate of the four Western hostages, who were kidnapped in July 1995 by Kashmiri militants believed to be associated with the Pakistan-based Harakat ul-Ansar (HUA), remains unknown. Reports from Kashmiri militant sources maintain that the hostages were killed in December 1995, although these reports have not been confirmed.

In Sri Lanka, the Liberation Tigers of Tamil Eelam (LTTE) continued to carry out extremely violent attacks in its ongoing campaign to cripple the economy and target government officials. A truck bomb destroyed the Central Bank, killing some 90 persons and wounding hundreds more. A commuter train was bombed, and a bus was ambushed, killing more than 80. The LTTE continued to assassinate political opponents, both civilian and military.

The Indian and Pakistani Governments each claim that the intelligence service of the other country sponsors bombings on its territory.

Afghanistan

Plagued by the absence of a cohesive central government and ongoing fighting among rival factions, Afghanistan remained a training ground for Islamic militants and terrorists in 1996. Ahmed Shah Masood, Gulbuddin Hekmatyar, and Abdul Rasul Sayyaf all maintained training and indoctrination facilities in Afghanistan, mainly for non-Afghans. They continue to provide logistic support and training facilities to Islamic extremists despite military losses in the past year. Individuals who trained in these camps were involved in insurgencies in Bosnia and Herzegovina, Chechnya, Tajikistan, Kashmir, the Philippines, and the Middle East in 1996.

The Taliban militia, which took over the capital city, Kabul, in September, has permitted Islamic extremists to continue to train in territories under its control even though they claimed to have closed the camps. The group confiscated camps belonging to rival factions and turned them over to groups such as the Pakistan-based Kashmiri terrorist group Harakat ul-Ansar.

Saudi-born extremist Usama Bin Ladin relocated to Afghanistan from Sudan in mid-1996 in an area controlled by the Taliban and remained there through the end of the year, establishing a new base of operations. In August, and again in November, Bin Ladin announced his intention to stage terrorist and guerrilla attacks against US personnel in Saudi Arabia in order to force the United States to leave the region.

Cambodia

Continuing defections throughout 1996 have greatly reduced the number of Khmer Rouge guerrillas. Defectors are in the process of being integrated into the Royal Cambodian Armed Forces. Nevertheless, Khmer Rouge hardliners conducted numerous violent attacks, primarily against Cambodian military forces, and were also responsible for the killings, kidnapping, and abduction for forced labor of civilians.

In March the Khmer Rouge kidnapped a British citizen who was involved in clearing mines. Rumors of his death have been denied by Khmer Rouge spokesmen. There has been occasional Khmer Rouge rhetoric suggesting that Westerners especially are being targeted for terrorist acts, but a terrorist campaign specifically directed at Westerners has not developed.

India

India continues to face security problems because of the insurgency in Kashmir and separatist movements elsewhere in the country. Numerous small bombings and assassination attempts against local politicians occurred throughout the year, but particularly during the fall, when the first legislative assembly elections since 1987 were held in Kashmir and the newly elected state government was installed. A militant group based in Pakistan calling itself the Jammu and Kashmir Islamic Front (JKIF) claimed responsibility for car bombings in New Delhi in January and May and a bus bombing in Rajasthan in May that killed at least 40 people. Kashmiri militants, believed to be associated with the Pakistan-based Harakat ul-Ansar (HUA), may have killed the four remaining Westerners—one US citizen, two Britons, and one German—whom they captured in July 1995 hiking near Srinagar, Kashmir, although their deaths have not been confirmed. Another US citizen managed to escape, but a Norwegian hostage was killed in 1995.

The Government of India has been largely successful in controlling the Sikh separatist movement in Punjab State, but Sikh groups claimed to have worked with the Kashmiri JKIF to bomb targets in New Delhi.

Other insurgent groups in the northeastern state of Assam and the southern state of Andhra Pradesh attacked security officials, rival political leaders, civilians, and infrastructure targets throughout 1996. Insurgents in Assam damaged oil pipelines for the first time in November. In Andhra Pradesh, the Naxalite People's War Group staged several attacks on police and local political leaders from September through November after a previous ban on the group was reimposed.

The Indian and Pakistani Governments each claim that the intelligence service of the other country sponsors bombings on its territory. There were reports that official Pakistani support to militants fighting in Kashmir, including the HUA, continued well into 1996. Pakistan alleged in a detailed press report that India sponsored a series of bombings in Pakistan's Punjab Province from late 1995 to mid-1996 in which at least 18 civilians were killed.

Japan

The prosecution of Aum Shinrikyo leader Shoko Asahara and other cult leaders continued in 1996. Several additional Aum Shinrikyo members who had been implicated in the 1995 sarin nerve gas attack in the Tokyo subway that killed 12 persons were arrested in Japan in 1996.

Five former cult officials have testified in court that Asahara instructed them to carry out the subway gas attack and other killings. In addition to the murder charge stemming from the gas attack, Asahara faces 16 other charges ranging from kidnapping and murder to illegal production of drugs and weapons.

Although no longer active in Japan as a terrorist group, Japanese Red Army members remain at large elsewhere around the world.

Pakistan

Terrorist-related violence continues in Pakistan as a result of domestic conflicts. Sectarian violence, including bombings, continued throughout the year in Sindh, Punjab, and in the North-West Frontier Provinces, resulting in about 175 deaths. Although the government has quelled much of the violence in Karachi, it has yet to produce a political settlement that would provide a lasting peace. The Pakistani Government has attributed most terrorist acts in Karachi either to the ethnically based Mohajir Quami Movement (MQM) or to the Shaheed Bhutto group of the Pakistan People's Party, which was led by former Prime Minister Benazir Bhutto's brother until his death in a clash with police on 20 September.

The Government of Pakistan acknowledges that it continues to provide moral, political, and diplomatic support to Kashmiri militants but denies allegations of other assistance. Reports continued in 1996, however, of official Pakistani support to militants fighting in Kashmir. One Pakistan-backed group, the Jammu and Kashmir Islamic Front (JKIF), claimed responsibility for three bombings in and near New Delhi in early 1996 that killed at least 40 persons. There also are reports that militants associated with the Harakat ul-Ansar (HUA) may have killed four Westerners kidnapped in Kashmir in July 1995.

Pakistan alleged in a detailed report in the press that India had sponsored a series of bombings in Pakistan's Punjab Province from late 1995 to mid-1996, in which at least 18 persons were killed. In July authorities arrested a Pakistani national who claimed that Indian intelligence agents recruited him and provided him with explosives for the bombings. In mid-November a court in Lahore sentenced one individual to death and another to life imprisonment for their involvement in the bombings.

Philippines

The Philippine Government scored a major triumph when it concluded a peace agreement with the Moro National Liberation Front, the largest Muslim rebel group, ending its 24-year insurgency. Negotiations with the second-largest insurgent group, the Moro Islamic Liberation Front (MILF), proceeded slowly, however, and clashes continued between MILF and government forces in the southern Philippines. The MILF and the smaller, extremist Abu Sayyaf Group are both fighting for a separate Islamic state in the southern Philippines. Earlier in the year, a wave of bombings in Mindanao was attributed to Muslim extremists; several of the attacks targeted Christian churches. For the most part, these attacks have been limited to the southern Philippines, but in February a grenade attack in the Makati business district of Manila wounded four persons and damaged the local headquarters of both Shell and Citibank. Police suspect the Abu Sayyaf Group. Other terrorist groups in the Philippines include the Alex Boncayao Brigade, which claimed responsibility for the assassination of a former provincial vice governor in June 1996, and the New People's Army. These three groups were believed to have been planning attacks during the APEC conference, held in Manila in November; a bomb was discovered and defused at Ninoy Aquino International Airport that week. No group claimed responsibility, and no arrests were made.

The successful prosecution in the United States of Ramzi Ahmed Yousef on charges of plotting to bomb US passenger jets in Asia and the Pacific was due largely to outstanding cooperation from the Philippine Government. At the same time, persons convicted of terrorist acts in the Philippines are among those eligible to apply for amnesty under a national reconciliation program set up for former rebels who committed crimes in pursuit of political objectives.

In February the Philippines hosted the Baguio Conference, an international conference on counterterrorism. The 20 nations represented there, including the United States, issued a communique expressing their collective commitment to combat terrorism in several important ways.

Sri Lanka

The separatist group Liberation Tigers of Tamil Eelam (LTTE) continued its campaign of violence in 1996, attacking economic and infrastructure targets and assassinating political opponents. The LTTE exploded a truck bomb near the Central Bank in Colombo on 31 January, killing some 90 persons; bombed a commuter train on 24 July, killing 70; and ambushed a bus in September, killing 11 civilians. The group staged a suicide bomb attack on the Minister of Housing in Jaffna in July. Although the minister survived, 25 persons were killed, including a Brigadier General.

The LTTE has refrained from targeting Western tourists, but a front group—the Ellalan Force—continued to send threatening letters to Western missions and the press.

Europe and Eurasia Overview

The total number of incidents in Europe in 1996 declined significantly from 272 in 1995 to 121 in 1996. Most of the terrorist acts in 1996 were nonlethal acts of arson or vandalism against Turkish-owned businesses in Germany. These acts are widely believed to be the work of the Kurdistan Workers' Party (PKK). The number of terrorist acts instigated by the PKK was down significantly in 1996.

In 1996 the Irish Republican Army (IRA) resumed a campaign of violence in Northern Ireland, United Kingdom, breaking a 17-month cease-fire. Loyalist paramilitary groups maintained their cease-fire but are considering a resumption of violence in response to IRA bombings.

Algerian extremists are believed responsible for France's most devastating terrorist attack during 1996, when a bombing on a Paris commuter train during rush hour on 3 December killed four persons and injured more than 80. Although no one claimed responsibility for the incident, similarities between this attack and several bombings claimed by the Algerian Armed Islamic Group (GIA) in 1995 lead authorities to suspect Algerian extremists.

France was also the scene of several assassinations during 1996. An Iranian who served as Deputy Education Minister under the Shah was shot to death near Paris on 28 May; he had published writings opposing the Islamic regime in Tehran. On 5 August unidentified assailants brutally murdered the local chief representatives of the Kurdistan Democratic Party and a delegate of the "Iraqi Kurdish Autonomous Government" in Paris. Local Kurd leaders blamed Iraqi or Iranian state agents for the crime. On 26 October suspected Liberation Tigers of Tamil Eelam (LTTE) gunmen shot and killed the LTTE's international treasurer and a companion in Paris.

France and Spain worked vigorously against the separatist Basque Fatherland and Liberty (ETA) group in 1996, arresting at least three dozen members and sympathizers and uncovering several weapons caches. Among those arrested was Juan "Isuntza" Aguirre Lete, who is accused of being the mastermind behind a plot to assassinate King Juan Carlos in Majorca in 1995.

Unidentified attackers threw Molotov cocktails at the Consulate of Serbia and Montenegro in Milan, Italy, in mid-April. The building suffered only minor damage, and there were no injuries.

The Greek Government made no headway in its pursuit of Greek terrorists. The indigenous leftist Revolutionary Organization 17 November and other domestic terrorist groups continued to threaten US interests and to target Greek business interests. In Turkey, the number of terrorist incidents committed by the Kurdistan Workers' party (PKK) decreased significantly due to the group's almost yearlong self-imposed unilateral cease-fire. After the cease-fire ended in the fall of 1996, the PKK stepped up attacks against military and civilian targets, using the tactic of suicide bombings. The Marxist Revolutionary People's Liberation Party/Front, known by the Turkish initials DHKP/C—the successor to the group formerly known as Devrimci Sol—perpetrated a spectacular terrorist act in January with the assassination of a prominent Turkish businessman.

In Eurasia, the total number of terrorist incidents increased from five in 1995 to 24 in 1996. In Bosnia, several small-scale terrorist incidents occurred; the prime targets were international and multinational organizations assisting in the country's postwar transition. Ethnic tensions in the countries of the former Soviet Union continued to produce terrorist acts in many of these. In Russia, the ongoing hostilities between the government and Chechen rebels resulted in the taking of hostages and other acts, and Tajikistan was also the site of acts of violence against noncombatants. Armenia, Azerbaijan, and Georgia also experienced ethnic-related terrorist activity.

Bosnia and Herzegovina

Several small-scale terrorist incidents occurred in Bosnia in 1996; the prime targets were international and multinational organizations assisting in the country's postwar transition. A grenade was tossed into an International Police Task Force (IPTF) vehicle in November; there were no injuries. In August security officials in Sarajevo, tipped off by a telephone warning, defused a bomb in a building housing offices of the Organization for Security and Cooperation in Europe (OSCE). A bomb exploded outside IPTF headquarters in Vlasenica in July, damaging three vehicles and breaking some 30 windows in nearby buildings. That same month an assailant threw a handgrenade at a vehicle belonging to a member of the local OSCE office in Banja Luka; the blast destroyed the car and damaged a nearby building. The perpetrators of all of these attacks remain unidentified, but disgruntled members of the former warring factions are suspected.

On 15 February, Implementation Force (IFOR) troops raided a joint Bosnian-Iranian intelligence training facility in Fojnica and detained 11 persons, including three Iranians. Searches of the camp revealed classrooms and an extensive armory. Evidence collected at the site—including booby-trapped children's toys—indicated that at least some of the training was in terrorist tactics.

Croatia

A Croatian court sentenced five Bosnians on 21 June to prison terms ranging from four months to two years following their conviction on charges of plotting to assassinate Bosnian rebel leader Fikret Abdic. The Bosnians, who were arrested on 4 April in a town on the Dalmatian coast, allegedly planned to kill Abdic as he drove along a coastal highway. The group reportedly possessed a variety of weapons—including at least one hand-held grenade launcher, grenades, and machineguns—and was to receive financial remuneration for the assassination. Croatian officials claimed that the Bosnians had made statements implicating local Bihac and federal Bosnian security authorities as the masterminds of the plot; Sarajevo vociferously denied the charges.

France

The most devastating terrorist attack in France during 1996 was a bombing on a Paris commuter train during rush hour on 3 December that killed four persons and injured more than 80, some of them seriously. The bomb, a gas canister filled with explosives and nails, was designed and timed to cause extensive casualties. Although no one claimed responsibility for the incident, similarities between this attack and several bombings tied to the Algerian Armed Islamic Group (GIA) in 1995 lead authorities to suspect that Algerian extremists were responsible.

Several assassinations took place in France during 1996. An Iranian who served as Deputy Education Minister under the Shah was shot to death at his apartment near Paris on 28 May. The victim, Reza Mazlouman, had political refugee status in France and reportedly was active in opposition movements against the Iranian regime. At France's request, German authorities arrested an Iranian national in Bonn two days later on suspicion of participating in the assassination; the Iranian was extradited to France in October. A second assailant escaped and is believed to be in Iran. On 5 August unidentified assailants brutally murdered Jaffar Hasso Guly, the local chief representative of the Kurdistan Democratic Party and a delegate of the "Iraqi Kurdish Autonomous Government," in his home in Paris. Local Kurd leaders blamed Iraqi or Iranian state agents for the crime.

Suspected Liberation Tigers of Tamil Eelam (LTTE) gunmen shot and killed Kandiah Perinbanathan, the LTTE's international treasurer, and a companion in Paris on 26 October. Sri Lankan authorities said the treasurer may have been killed for extorting funds from his assailants.

French authorities worked vigorously against the separatist Basque Fatherland and Liberty (ETA) group in 1996, arresting at least three dozen members and sympathizers—some of whom were later released—and uncovering several weapons caches. In a key arrest in November, French customs authorities nabbed Juan "Isuntza" Aguirre Lete as he tried to run a checkpoint set up at a tollbooth. Madrid has accused Isuntza of masterminding a plot to assassinate King Juan Carlos in Majorca in 1995. Joint French-Spanish operations in July and November resulted in the capture in France of several ETA members and supporters, including Daniel Derguy, believed to be ETA's chief French operative; Julian "Pototo" Achurra Egurola, the head of the group's logistics wing; and Juan "Karpov" Maria Insausti, who Spanish authorities say is ETA's chief recruiter and explosives trainer. French officials also arrested Maria Nagore Mugica, one of Spain's most wanted criminals, at Charles de Gaulle Airport in May. Nagore belonged to various ETA command cells—including the group's chief cell in Madrid—between 1990 and 1993 and is suspected of involvement in several bombings. A French court authorized her extradition to Spain in December.

Antiterrorist judge Jean-Louis Bruguiere announced in September the completion of his investigation into the 1989 bombing of UTA Flight 772 over Niger. Arrest warrants—including two issued in 1996—are outstanding for a total of six Libyan Government officials, including a brother-in-law of Libyan leader Mu'ammar Qadhafi, for their alleged participation in the bombing. Bruguiere traveled to Libya in July to interview numerous secret service officials. Tripoli allowed him to return to France with a replica of the boobytrapped suitcase used in the bombing, as well as timers and detonators believed similar to those used to set off the explosives.

Germany

German prosecutors put their star witness, exiled former Iranian President Abolhassan Bani Sadr, on the stand in the trial of five men—four Lebanese and an Iranian—accused of murdering four Iranian dissidents in a gangland-style shooting at the Mykonos restaurant in Berlin in 1992. Bani Sadr told the court in August that Iran's religious leader, Ayatollah Ali Khamenei, ordered the killings of the three exiled Iranian Kurdish leaders and their translator and that President Akbar Hashemi Rafsanjani signed the order. He also referred to a suspected former Iranian intelligence officer (so-called Witness C and later identified as Abolqasem Messbahi), who also was called to testify. Statements in the prosecution's summation in November, which implicated Iran's senior leadership for directing the Mykonos killings, led to demonstrations in front of the German Embassy in Tehran and threats against the prosecutors. In March prosecutors issued an arrest warrant against Iranian Intelligence Minister Ali Fallahiyan in connection with the killings. A Berlin state court has spent almost three years hearing evidence in the Mykonos case. (Guilty verdicts for four of the accused were announced in April 1997.)

Suspected Palestinian terrorist Yasser Shraydi was extradited from Lebanon to Germany in May to stand trial in connection with the La Belle discotheque bombing in Berlin in 1986. In October three other suspects in the case were arrested and are in German custody. Arrest warrants also were issued against four former Libyan diplomats and intelligence officers believed to have been involved in the bombing. German prosecutors, who have stated that this bombing was a case of state terrorism directed from Tripoli, hope to begin the trial in mid-1997.

The number of terrorist acts instigated by the Kurdistan Workers' Party (PKK) decreased significantly in 1996. Security Services Chief Klaus Gruenewald had visited PKK leader Abdullah Ocalan in August 1995 to demand the cessation of PKK violence on German soil. PKK-attributable violence in Germany continued at a negligible level until early March when, on the occasion of Kurdish New Year's Day, PKK-affiliated demonstrations in Dortmund and other cities turned violent and injured several German policemen. Ocalan blamed the incidents on the German police but, in view of negative German public reaction, later apologized and promised to halt further PKK incidents in Germany. Earlier in the year, Ocalan had threatened to use PKK suicide bombers in Germany and also issued death threats against Chancellor Kohl and Foreign Minister Kinkel, but he later retracted these statements. This reflects his dual strategy of threatening to carry out violence in Germany, on the one hand, and trying to operate within the parameters of German law, on the other.

The Red Army Faction (RAF) has not been active in Germany for the past several years, although German authorities continue to pursue and prosecute RAF members for crimes committed during the 1980s. Following two years of hearings, the German courts convicted RAF member Birgit Hogefeld in November of three counts of murder—including the 1985 murder of a US soldier and the subsequent bombing attack at the US Rhein-Main Airbase—and four counts of attempted murder. She was sentenced to life in prison. Christoph Seidler—who was alleged to be, but claims never to have been, a member of the RAF—the main suspect in the 1989 car-bomb killing of Deutsche Bank chief executive Alfred Herrhausen, turned himself in to German authorities in November but was later released and a longstanding arrest warrant lifted.

German authorities scored a coup with the arrest of two

suspected members of the shadowy leftist Anti-Imperialist Cell (AIZ) in February. The two men—Bernhard Falk and Michael Steinau—are awaiting trial. The AIZ had claimed responsibility for a series of bomb attacks on the homes of second-tier conservative politicians in 1995, the last occurring in December 1995. Because no further incidents have occurred since the February arrests, the German Government believes the AIZ is no longer a viable threat.

Greece

The Greek Government continues to make no headway in its pursuit of Greek terrorists, in particular, the Revolutionary Organization 17 November that is responsible for numerous attacks against US interests, including the murder of four US officials. On 15 February an antiarmor rocket was fired at the US Embassy in Athens, causing some property damage but no casualties. Circumstances of the attack suggest it was a 17 November operation. On 28 May the IBM building in Athens was bombed, resulting in substantial property damage but no casualties. An anonymous call later claimed responsibility on behalf of the "Nihilist Faction," which first surfaced earlier in the year with bomb attacks against the residence of a supreme court prosecutor and a shopping mall in downtown Athens.

The Greek Government also continues to tolerate the official presence in Athens of two Turkish terrorist groups—the National Liberation Front of Kurdistan, which is the political wing of the Kurdistan Workers' Party (PKK), and the Revolutionary People's Liberation Party/Front (DHKP/C), formerly Devrimci Sol, which is responsible for the murder of two US Government contractors in Turkey.

The Greek judicial system continues to be hampered by obstacles to the prosecution of terrorists. The latest pending piece of legislation authorizes judges to exclude the testimony of a defendant against a codefendant in a criminal proceeding —including terrorist cases—which would make it difficult to obtain convictions against members of terrorist groups.

Under the terms of another Greek law that allows for release after two-fifths of a sentence has been served, on 5 December the Greek Government released convicted terrorist Mohammed Rashid from prison and expelled him from Greece. Rashid had been in jail for his role in the 1982 bombing of a Pan Am aircraft in which a 15-year old Japanese citizen was killed. He was sentenced to 18 years in prison, which was subsequently reduced to 15 years. The United States deplored the early release of this convicted terrorist, calling the court ruling "incomprehensible."

The Greek Government, however, also demonstrated some willingness to extradite non-Greeks in two high-profile cases: after completing a five-year Greek prison sentence on various charges, Abdul Rahim Khaled was handed over to Italian authorities pursuant to his conviction in absentia in 1987 by an Italian court for his part in the Achille Lauro hijacking; and Andrea Haeusler, a German citizen, faced extradition to Germany on charges stemming from her alleged participation in the bombing of the La Belle discotheque in Berlin. (She was extradited in January 1997.)

Italy

Unidentified attackers threw Molotov cocktails at the Consulate of Serbia and Montenegro in Milan on two successive nights in mid-April. The building suffered only minor damage, and there were no injuries. Following the second set of attacks, an anonymous caller telephoned the Milan police and reported the incident. Italian authorities also found traces of a poster saying "Free Bosnia" on the wall of the Consulate.

In a multicity operation on 7 November, Italian National Police officers arrested more than two dozen suspected members and supporters of the Algerian Armed Islamic Group (GIA) following a yearlong investigation. Authorities have charged the suspects, who include Algerians and other North Africans, with weapons trafficking, counterfeiting documents, and facilitating the illegal entry into Italy of Algerian terrorists. Police reported that some suspects were in possession of hardcopy and computer manuals regarding the preparation of explosives and the use of weapons.

Poland

On 24 April a group calling itself GN 95 detonated a bomb at a Shell gas station in Warsaw, killing a policeman who was preparing to defuse the device. GN 95 later justified the explosion by stating its opposition to the expansion of foreign investments into Poland. The group demanded $2 million from the Royal Dutch Shell Group.

Russia

Russia has sought to combat terrorism in a number of ways both overseas and at home. Moscow participated in a G-7/P-8 ministerial conference on counterterrorism in Paris in July and in a follow-up conference in October. Russian security authorities also conducted exercises of their counterterrorist components. The Russian prosecution of three Armenians for involvement in four bombings of Moscow-Baku passenger trains in 1993 and 1994 led to convictions and jail sentences.

The Russians have not made any headway, however, in their investigation of a series of bombs placed in public transportation vehicles in Moscow and elsewhere in the country, or of a bombing that leveled a nine-story apartment building in Kaspiysk, killing more than 50.

Several other terrorist acts took place in Russia during 1996. In January a Chechen group took as hostages up to 200 noncombatants in Pervomayskoye. On 7 August in St. Petersburg, a gunman shot and wounded Finnish Deputy Consul General Olli Perkheyentupa outside a hotel; no one claimed responsibility. In Vladivostok, a South Korean official was murdered on 1 October; Seoul suspects that North Korean agents were involved. On 17 December six Westerners who worked for the International Committee of the Red

Cross were murdered in Novyy Atagi. In late December authorities arrested several suspects, but released them without charging them.

Spain

The separatist Basque Fatherland and Liberty (ETA) organization conducted its biggest campaign against Spanish tourist sites in years—a total of 14 bombings or attempted bombings in July and August. In the most devastating attack, 35 persons—including approximately two dozen British tourists—were injured on 20 July when a bomb exploded in a waiting room at an airport near the coastal city of Tarragona. Authorities also believe that ETA, which occasionally targets French businesses in Spain, was responsible for a package bomb that exploded in a Citroen car dealership near Zaragoza in July, injuring the owner and his son. In March police defused a car bomb placed in front of a French-owned store in Madrid following a telephone warning from a caller claiming to represent the Basque extremist group. ETA also continued to attack Spanish military, police, and economic targets throughout 1996.

The Aznar government, which came to power in May, has vowed to work diligently to neutralize ETA and has put special emphasis on strengthening cooperation with other states—particularly France—in this effort. In May press reports indicated that France planned to assign a police attache to its Embassy in Madrid to coordinate daily cooperation with Spain. Moreover, Madrid and Paris signed an agreement in June that allowed for the establishment of four joint police stations—three on the French side of the border. Meanwhile, Spain persuaded France to help reform a European extradition treaty in the European Union to allow "simple membership in an armed band" to be sufficient cause for extradition.

Spanish authorities extradited Achille Lauro hijacker Majed Yousef al-Molqi to Italy in early December. They had captured al-Molqi on 22 March in southern Spain after he failed to return to an Italian prison in February following a 12-day furlough for good behavior. In 1986 an Italian court sentenced al-Molqi, a Palestinian affiliated with the Abu Abbas faction of the Palestine Liberation Front, to 30 years in prison for killing Leon Klinghoffer, a wheelchair-bound US citizen, during the hijacking of the Italian luxury ship in 1985.

Madrid struck a blow against the Algerian Armed Islamic Group's (GIA) infrastructure in Spain with the arrest of suspected GIA member Farid Rezgui on 14 June. Rezgui reportedly had some 30 sets of false Italian, French, Spanish, and Algerian identification documents in his possession, presumably for use by GIA members to facilitate their movements in Europe. Authorities reportedly also found magazines published by GIA and other Islamic extremist groups, as well as video and audiocassette tapes of speeches by Islamic leaders, including Shaykh Umar Abd al-Rahman, the spiritual leader of the Egyptian extremist al-Gama'at al-Islamiyya.

Tajikistan

Unidentified assailants conducted attacks against Russian servicemen stationed in Tajikistan, as well as their dependents. On 4 June several gunmen shot and killed two Russian servicemen's wives while the victims were visiting a cemetery in Dushanbe. No one claimed responsibility. On 15 August a remote-controlled explosive device with 2.5 pounds of TNT destroyed a Russian military truck. One serviceman was killed and one was wounded. On 20 November gunmen shot at two Russian servicemen getting off a bus in a Dushanbe neighborhood. Both servicemen were seriously wounded. Two days later assailants ambushed a bus of Russian border guards in Dushanbe using grenade launchers and handgrenades, killing the bus driver and injuring several border guards. On 20 December members of an armed independent gang kidnapped UN and other officials and demanded that several of their supporters be returned to them. The hostages were subsequently released.

Turkey

The number of terrorist incidents committed by the Kurdistan Workers' Party (PKK) in Turkey in 1996 declined significantly due to the group's unilateral cease-fire from December 1995 until the fall of 1996. Nonetheless, the PKK was responsible for sporadic terrorist attacks during the cease-fire period, most notably, the 30 June suicide bombing against a Turkish military parade in Tunceli. The attack killed nine security forces personnel and wounded another 35. The suicide bombing marked the first time the PKK had used this tactic even though PKK leader Abdullah Ocalan had threatened earlier in the year to use suicide bombings against Turkey's Western cities in an effort to drive away tourists.

Since the end of the cease-fire the PKK has stepped up its attacks against military and civilian targets in southeastern Turkey. The most noteworthy incidents include two more suicide bombings—in Adana and Sivas—in late October that killed two civilians in addition to eight security forces personnel. The suicide bombing in Sivas is of note because the city, well outside of the southeast, is in an area that the Turkish Government previously considered to be relatively secure. In two other incidents four schoolteachers were murdered outside of Diyarbakir in October and three tourists—including a US citizen—were kidnapped outside of Bingol in September. The US citizen and his Polish traveling companion were later released unharmed. There is no word on the status of the third hostage, reportedly an Iranian. The killing of schoolteachers and kidnapping of foreigners are traditional PKK terrorist acts but had not been seen in almost two years.

The number of violent PKK activities in Western Europe also was down in 1996, particularly after German Security Services Chief Klaus Gruenewald visited Ocalan in late 1995 to demand the cessation of PKK-instigated violence in Germany. PKK violence continued at a negligible level until early March when a PKK-affiliated demonstration in Bonn turned violent, injuring several German policemen. Ocalan later apologized for the incident and promised to suspend further PKK incidents on German soil.

The Marxist-Leninist Revolutionary People's Liberation Party/Front (DHKP/C)—the successor group to Devrimci Sol—pulled off a spectacular terrorist act in January with the high-profile assassination of prominent Turkish businessman Ozdemir Sabanci in his high-security office building in Istanbul. Previously, DHKP/C had managed only a few low-level assassinations against unprotected Turkish targets. The group also conducted several drive-by shootings of policemen in Istanbul. Although the drive-by shootings are not characteristic of DHKP/C's usually intensive surveillance and planning, its successful murder of Sabanci suggests that it is acquiring greater capabilities and that it could once again become a real threat.

United Kingdom

In 1996 the Irish Republican Army (IRA) resumed a campaign of violence in Northern Ireland and the United Kingdom, breaking a 17-month cease-fire. The Continuity Army Council (CAC)—also known as the Irish Continuity Army—a hardline Republican movement formed in 1994 to protest the IRA's cease-fire announcement in August of that year, also resumed its campaign of violence. Loyalist paramilitary groups maintained their cease-fire but remained combat ready and were considering a resumption of violence in response to the IRA bombings.

The IRA broke its cease-fire on 9 February, detonating more than 1,000 pounds of a homemade explosive mixture in a flatbed truck under a platform of London's Docklands light railway. The bomb killed two, injured more than 100, and caused extensive damage to five blocks of office buildings. On 18 February an IRA terrorist lost his life when a bomb he was carrying exploded prematurely in a bus in London. Nine persons were injured and the bus was destroyed. On 9 March a small improvised explosive device detonated inside a trash bin at the entrance to a London cemetery near a British Defense Ministry building. No one was injured. The IRA claimed responsibility for the bomb three days later.

On 24 April coded calls led police to a bomb containing about 30 pounds of plastic explosive under London's Hammersmith bridge. Police were evacuating the area when the two detonators exploded but failed to set off the plastic explosive charges; bomb squads disarmed the devices. The next night the IRA claimed responsibility for the bomb, calling its failure to explode "unfortunate."

A large fertilizer-based car bomb exploded near a shopping center in Manchester on 15 June, injuring more than 200 persons and causing an estimated $300 million in structural damage. The explosion coincided with a celebration in London marking the queen's official birthday.

IRA terrorists attacked a British army barracks in Osnabruck, Germany, on 28 June, with three mortar rounds launched from a truck-mounted rocket launcher. One of the shells hit the barracks, causing considerable damage but no injuries. The other two shells did not explode and were disarmed. The IRA also claimed credit for two vehicle bombs, each comprising about 800 pounds of homemade explosives, that exploded on the grounds of the British Army headquarters in Lisburn, Northern Ireland, on 7 October. The two blasts killed one serviceman and injured 31. Dual bombings are an IRA signature; the second bomb, placed in the path of victims fleeing from the first bomb, exploded about 10 minutes later.

The CAC claimed responsibility for a car bomb that exploded on 14 July at a hotel in Enniskillen, Northern Ireland. About 40 people were injured in the blast. In similar incidents, on 29 September and 22 November, the CAC planted car bombs loaded with homemade explosives in Belfast and Londonderry, respectively. Following warning calls, army explosives experts found the vehicles and detonated them in controlled explosions.

Ulster peace talks have seen little progress. Sinn Fein, the political wing of the IRA, is barred from the talks until the IRA accedes to an unconditional cease-fire. The decommissioning of Republican and Loyalist weapons is also a major sticking point to the talks.

Latin America Overview

Terrorists from the Tupac Amaru Revolutionary Movement (MRTA) took over the Japanese Ambassador's residence in Lima, Peru, during a diplomatic reception on 17 December. More than 500 persons were taken captive, including eight US officials, numerous foreign ambassadors, prominent Peruvians including the Foreign and Agriculture Ministers, six supreme court justices, high-ranking members of the police and military, as well as members of the Peruvian and international business community. Most hostages were freed in the first several days after the attack, including all of the US officials. At the end of the year efforts to resolve the crisis peacefully were under way.

Peru hosted the Inter-American Specialized Conference on Terrorism in Lima in April. Sponsored by the Organization of American States, the conference, which reflected heightened inter-American cooperation against terrorism, adopted the Declaration and Plan of Action, which strongly endorsed the characterization of terrorist acts, regardless of motivation, as common crimes rather than political offenses.

Colombian guerrillas continued in 1996 to foment violence directed at that country's infrastructure and armed forces. Efforts by the Colombian Government to negotiate a peace agreement were spurned by the guerrillas. There was a high level of domestic political violence, but international terrorist incidents declined, from 76 in 1995 to 66 in 1996. The guerrillas continued to use kidnapping for ransom as a major source of income. At year's end, guerrillas held four US citizens hostage.

In Mexico, the Popular Revolutionary Army (EPR) carried out a series of small-scale attacks, killing 17 persons including several civilians, and the Zapatista National Liberation Army (EZLN) signed an agreement on indigenous peoples' rights with the government.

Investigations into three major acts of international terrorism in Latin America—the 1992 bombing attack against the Israeli Embassy in Buenos Aires, the 1994 bombing of a Jewish community center building in Buenos Aires, and the 1994 bombing of a commuter airliner in Panama—continued without significant progress.

The Government of Guatemala and the Guatemalan National Revolutionary Unity (URNG) ended their 36-year armed conflict, the hemisphere's longest running, with a final peace accord signed 29 December.

Argentina

During 1996 the Argentine Government continued its investigation into the bombing in 1994 of the Argentine Jewish Mutual Association (AMIA) in which 86 persons were killed and about 300 were injured. In July the investigating judge ordered the arrest of one former and three current police officers from Buenos Aires Province. On the basis of leads developed after the 1995 arrest of Carlos Telleldin, accused of involvement in illegally obtaining the van used in the bombing, these officers were charged with possession of that van and were accused of being part of a police extortion ring that received the van as part of a down payment on an extortion debt owed by Telleldin. The policemen, however, have not been charged with complicity in the AMIA attack. The Argentine Government throughout the year reaffirmed its commitment to resolve this case and established a special congressional commission to follow and assist the court's investigation.

The Supreme Court's investigation into the March 1992 bombing of the Israeli Embassy in Buenos Aires failed to develop new leads. Interior Minister Carlos Corach on 27 November increased from $2 million to $3 million the reward offered to develop new leads in the investigations of the 1992 and 1994 bombings.

The Interior Minister negotiated and began implementing border security measures with Brazil and Paraguay to help address the growing security concerns in the "triborder" area where the frontiers of Paraguay, Argentina, and Brazil meet. Argentina adopted a machine-readable passport as part of its program to control the improper use of its passports.

Colombia

Colombia continued to grapple with widespread violence in 1996, suffering numerous terrorist bombings, murders, kidnappings, and narcotics-related violence. Drug traffickers, leftist insurgents, paramilitary squads, and common criminals committed with impunity scores of violent crimes. Although most of the politically motivated violence was directed at domestic targets, Colombia recorded 66 international terrorist incidents during 1996, a drop from 76 such incidents in 1995. The most frequent targets of international terrorist attacks were the nation's oil pipelines, which are operated in partnership with foreign oil companies.

The nation's two main leftist insurgent groups—the Revolutionary Armed Forces of Colombia (FARC) and the National Liberation Army (ELN)—showed little interest in pursuing serious peace talks with the government, preferring to press their violent agenda.

Throughout the year ECOPETROL, the national oil company, was forced to shut down production repeatedly due to ELN attacks. Foreign oil company employees were kidnapped and held for ransom as part of the guerrillas' continuing war of terror against the Colombian oil industry. ELN carried out 45 attacks against the oil pipeline, justifying its actions by claiming the government is giving away its precious oil reserves to foreigners.

The ELN and FARC staged numerous attacks against police and military installations throughout the year. In a 15 April attack on an army patrol in Narino Department, guerrillas killed 31 soldiers. In a countrywide offensive conducted in late August and early September, the ELN and FARC launched a major offensive in reprisal for the government's efforts to eradicate coca. At least 150 persons were killed in the attacks, including an unknown number of civilians. On 30 August the FARC overran a Colombian Army base in Putumayo Department, killing 27 soldiers and taking prisoner more than 60 others. By year's end the soldiers had not been released. A guerrilla attack in Guaviare Department on 6 September left 22 soldiers dead.

Narcoterrorists are suspected of placing a 173-kg car bomb on 5 November outside a Cali business owned by the family of a senator who advocated reinstating extradition of Colombians to the United States. Although the bomb did not explode, flyers found at the scene threatened US citizens and businesses as well as Colombian supporters of extraditing Colombian nationals.

Colombian guerrillas earn millions of dollars from ransom payments each year. Nearly three dozen foreigners were kidnapped by guerrillas during the year. In one major kidnapping, members of a group with possible terrorist links abducted Juan Carlos Gaviria, brother of former Colombian president and current Organization of American States General Secretary Cesar Gaviria. At the request of Cesar Gaviria and the Colombian Government, Cuba in June agreed to admit nine of the terrorists in exchange for the safe release of Juan Carlos Gaviria.

The United States issued arrest warrants against 12 members of the FARC for the murders of two New Tribes Missionaries, Steven Welsh and Timothy Van Dyke, who were killed while being held hostage by the FARC in June 1995. Four other US citizens remained hostage in Colombia at year's end: three missionaries from the New Tribes Mission who were abducted in 1993, and a US geologist who was kidnapped in early December. (The geologist was killed in February 1997.) Two other US hostages were released in May and June.

Some individual fronts of the FARC, and to a lesser extent the ELN, have symbiotic links with narcotraffickers, especially to the east of the Cordillera Oriental. In some instances, guerrillas have been known to provide security for coca fields, processing facilities, and clandestine shipping facilities. Drug-related activities—along with kidnapping for ransom, extortion, and robbing banks—help generate needed revenues to finance the groups' terrorist activities.

Guatemala

Guatemala's 36-year insurgency, the oldest in the hemisphere, formally came to an end 29 December with the signing of a final peace accord between the Guatemalan Government and the Guatemalan National Revolutionary Unity (URNG) guerrillas. The URNG is an umbrella organization formed in 1982 when four separate guerrilla/terrorist groups joined together: the Revolutionary Organization of the Armed People (ORPA), the Guerrilla Army of the Poor (EGP), the Rebel Armed Forces (FAR), and factions of the Guatemalan Labor (Communist) Party (PGT).

President Alvaro Arzu, who took office in January, assigned top priority to achieving a final peace accord in 1996. Negotiations resumed in an atmosphere of mutual confidence, and both sides suspended offensive military actions in March. Major agreements on economic and military issues were signed in May and September, although negotiations were temporarily suspended in October following the URNG's kidnapping of the 86-year-old handicapped wife of a prominent businessman. The victim was released unharmed in exchange for the release of a high-ranking guerrilla commander. The commander of ORPA accepted responsibility for the kidnapping and resigned from the URNG leadership, enabling negotiations to resume.

Despite the ongoing negotiations and the March suspension of hostilities, which held for the remainder of the year, isolated incidents by renegade URNG elements, or by common criminals claiming to be URNG, were reported. Several terrorist bombings by unknown perpetrators occurred; at least two persons died, and several were injured in the bombings. Several explosive devices were accompanied by URNG leaflets.

As part of the peace accords, URNG guerrillas will demobilize in the first half of 1997, under verification of UN military observers. Ex-URNG members will then form a legal political party.

Mexico

The self-proclaimed Popular Revolutionary Army (EPR) unveiled itself in the southwestern Guerrero State on 28 June during a ceremony marking the anniversary of a state police massacre of local peasants. The EPR has conducted small-scale attacks in several states, mostly against Mexican military and police outposts, public buildings, and power stations. The group has killed at least 17 persons, including several civilians. The Zedillo government has characterized the EPR as a terrorist group.

The Zapatista National Liberation Army (EZLN) launched no violent attacks in 1996. On 16 February EZLN representatives signed an agreement in southeastern Chiapas with the Mexican Government on the rights of indigenous people and made a commitment to negotiate a political settlement.

During 1996 Mexico moved to facilitate the extradition of suspected ETA terrorists by implementing its amended extradition treaty with Spain.

Panama

Panamanian authorities have made no arrests in connection with the bombing in July 1994 of a commuter airliner that killed all 21 persons aboard, including three US citizens. Panamanian officials continue to cooperate closely with the United States in the ongoing investigation.

In the 1992 murder case of US Army Corp. Zak Hernandez, suspect Pedro Miguel Gonzalez remains in custody. The case has been before a Panamanian Magistrate for over a year, awaiting a decision on whether to proceed to trial. The two other suspects remain at large.

Elements of the Revolutionary Armed Forces of Colombia (FARC) maintain a presence along the Panama-Colombia border and often cross over to Panama's Darien Province to hide from the Colombian Army and to obtain supplies.

Peru

The Peruvian Government's largely successful campaign against terrorism suffered a setback with the takeover of the Japanese Ambassador's residence in Lima on 17 December. In this attack, Tupac Amaru Revolutionary Movement (MRTA) terrorists captured more than 500 hostages, including eight US officials, numerous foreign ambassadors, prominent Peruvians, including the Foreign and Agriculture Ministers, six supreme court justices, and high-ranking members of the police and military, as well as members of the Peruvian and international business community. The heavily armed terrorists boobytrapped and mined the Japanese Ambassador's residence. Most hostages were freed in the first several days after the attack, including all of the US officials. At the end of the year, 81 hostages were still being held.

The MRTA's main demand was the release by the Peruvian Government of imprisoned MRTA members in Peru, a demand that stalled attempts to resolve the hostage situation. The crisis was exacerbated when an Uruguayan court denied extradition requests from Peru and Bolivia and released two MRTA members detained in Uruguay. The MRTA hostage takers in Lima released, almost simultaneously, the Uruguayan Ambassador from captivity. At year's end, efforts to resolve the crisis peacefully were under way.

The Government of Peru hosted the Inter-American Specialized Conference on Terrorism, sponsored by the Organization of American States, in Lima in April. This conference adopted the Declaration and Plan of Action, which strongly endorsed the characterization of terrorist acts, regardless of motivation, as common crimes rather than political offenses.

Sendero Luminoso was significantly weakened when its

founder Abimael Guzman was arrested in 1992, but it continued to carry out bombings and assassinations in 1996 against domestic targets. As in the previous year, in 1996 most terrorist violence took place in the Upper Huallaga and Apurimac Valleys, but even there Army-sponsored self-defense militias helped counter the terrorists. There were two international terrorist incidents in Peru in 1996: a car bombing of a Shell oil warehouse on 16 May and the MRTA hostage seizure in December.

Throughout 1996 Peruvian security forces captured several important terrorist suspects, including Elizabeth Cardenas, a.k.a. Comrade Aurora, a senior Sendero Luminoso leader who was arrested in December. In another blow against international terrorism, the Peruvian police in May arrested Yoshimura Kazue, a leading member of the Japanese Red Army wanted for her role in the 1974 seizure of the French Embassy in The Hague. She was subsequently deported to Japan. On 11 January Miguel Rincon, MRTA's second-highest ranking leader, was sentenced to life imprisonment.

Middle East Overview

Spectacular and horrific bombings in Dhahran, Tel Aviv, and Jerusalem dominated terrorist incidents in the Middle East in 1996, and nearly doubled the number of terrorist casualties to 837 from 445 in 1995. The truck bombing of the residential building occupied by US military personnel participating in the Joint Task Force/Southwest Asia near Dhahran, Saudi Arabia, on 25 June killed 19 US citizens and wounded over 500 persons. Several groups claimed responsibility, and the Federal Bureau of Investigation and Saudi Government continue their investigations into the incident.

In Tel Aviv and Jerusalem, suicide bombs in February and March killed 65 persons, including three US citizens. The radical Islamic Resistance Movement (HAMAS) was responsible for three of the bombings, and HAMAS and the Palestine Islamic Jihad (PIJ) both claimed responsibility for a fourth. In December the Popular Front for the Liberation of Palestine claimed responsibility for the shooting of an Israeli woman and her son. Israeli extremists were responsible for several attacks in 1996 that resulted in the deaths of at least two Palestinians.

Following the February and March bombings, 29 world leaders from the Middle East, Europe, North America, and Asia met in March and held the "Summit of the Peacemakers" in Sharm ash Shaykh, Egypt. They pledged to support the Middle East peace process and to take practical steps to expand regional cooperation against terrorism.

The Palestinian Authority continued its efforts—in cooperation with Israeli authorities—to combat the threat posed by terrorist groups such as HAMAS and the PIJ and to root out those who plan and carry out these attacks.

The Egyptian Government cracked down on extremist violence and significantly reduced terrorist incidents at the country's popular tourist sites where attacks had occurred during the previous two years. Fatalities from security incidents in Egypt decreased in 1996. However, extremist violence in upper Egypt and some outlying areas continued. In Cairo, 18 tourists were shot and killed by members of al-Gama'at al-Islamiyya (Islamic Group or IG). Also, the men responsible for carrying out the assassination attempt against President Mubarak in June 1995 remain at large.

In Algeria, political violence and random killings continued on a large scale around the country, causing major loss of life. Car bombs targeting Algerian municipalities, a press center, schools, and cafes were set off regularly. Indiscriminate killing of civilians at false highway checkpoints or in outlying towns were almost daily occurrences. Terrorists often targeted the families of members of government security services.

The Armed Islamic Group (GIA) kidnapped and subsequently killed seven French monks when its demands for the release of GIA members were not fulfilled. Otherwise, attacks against foreigners in Algeria decreased in 1996. Algerian extremists are believed to be behind a deadly bombing of a Paris commuter train in which four persons died and some 80 other passengers were wounded. Elsewhere in North Africa, there were few terrorist incidents.

In Lebanon, the security situation improved as the government continued its efforts to expand the rule of law to more of the country. Lebanese courts are increasingly active in prosecuting terrorists. One was convicted of terrorist attacks on Kuwaiti interests in Beirut in the early 1990s, and two others for the car-bombing death of the brother of a senior Hizballah official. A military appeals court upheld the conviction of the murderer of a French military attache killed in 1986, and another court extradited to Germany a man accused in the 1986 bombing of the La Belle discotheque in Berlin. A Lebanese court upheld the conviction for kidnapping of two men involved in the 1976 kidnapping and murder of two US diplomats—but then released the two under a Lebanese amnesty law. Terrorist groups, especially Hizballah, continued to operate with relative impunity in large areas of Lebanon, particularly the Al Biqa' (Bekaa Valley), southern Lebanon, and Beirut's southern suburbs.

Algeria

The internal security situation in Algeria has improved since 1994, but the incidence of domestic terrorism, which is among the world's worst, remained high. At least 60,000 Algerians—Islamic militants, civilians, and security personnel—have been killed since the insurgency began in 1992.

Government security forces made substantial progress against the Islamic Salvation Army (AIS)—the reported military wing of the Islamic Salvation Front—that primarily attacks government-related targets. The government was less successful against the Armed Islamic Group (GIA), the most radical of the insurgent groups, which continued terrorist operations against a broad spectrum of Algerian civilian targets in 1996, including women, children, and journalists.

The GIA continued to target foreigners in 1996 and killed at least nine, a sharp decline from the 31 foreigners the group killed in 1995. The total number of foreigners killed by the GIA since 1992 exceeds 110. Most were "soft" targets, including a former Bulgarian attache, who was found beheaded in a forest in mid-November. Although no claims were made for his murder, Algiers blamed the GIA for his death. In August the GIA claimed responsibility for the murder of the French Bishop of Oran, who was killed by a bomb placed outside his residence.

Earlier in 1996 the GIA kidnapped and later beheaded seven French monks from their monastery near Medea. The GIA issued a communique claiming that the monks had been killed because Paris had refused to negotiate with the insurgent group. Algerian extremists are suspected in an explosion in a Paris subway on 3 December that killed four and wounded more than 80. The bomb used in that attack was similar to those used by the GIA in its bombing campaign in France in 1995.

The Algerian Government prosecuted numerous cases of persons charged with committing terrorist acts or supporting terrorist groups in 1996. In July, for example, four men accused of committing murder on behalf of terrorist groups were sentenced to death. Algiers also continued its limited clemency program. Members of militant groups who had surrendered to the authorities for committing murders received 20-year prison sentences instead of the death penalty; those found guilty of membership in terrorist groups received shorter-than-normal prison sentences. President Liamine Zeroual told the Algerian press that, as a result of this program, nearly 2,000 Algerians had surrendered to authorities by September.

Bahrain

The security situation in Bahrain deteriorated somewhat early in the year but showed signs of improvement at year's end. Antiregime unrest was generally limited, with a few notable exceptions. In the worst incident, seven South Asians were killed in a 14 March arson attack on a restaurant. On 1 July three Bahrainis were convicted and sentenced to death, and five others received lengthy prison sentences for this incident. There were several other attacks, including some using small bombs and incendiary devices. Most of the unrest has consisted of burning tires, exploding propane gas cylinders, and acts of vandalism. Security forces, in return, have conducted a crackdown, killing more than 20 Bahrainis and arresting more than 2,000 since the unrest began in November 1994. At the end of 1996 the scope and intensity of the unrest diminished, though this may be temporary.

Only two incidents directly involved US citizens. On 28 August a US student rented a car that had an improvised incendiary device in the gas tank. The device failed to operate. On 16 September a US citizen's car, parked in front of a luxury hotel in downtown Manama, was firebombed. In neither case, however, does it appear the US citizens were targeted because of their nationality.

Manama in June publicly announced the discovery of an active Bahraini Hizballah cell that was recruited, trained, and supported by Iran. Diplomatic relations between Bahrain and Iran have been strained since the announcement. Bahrain retaliated by recalling its ambassador from Tehran and by restricting commercial services and air transportation between the two countries.

Egypt

Islamic extremist violence fell in 1996. The number of fatalities—including noncombatants (105), police (59), and extremists (38) killed—fell sharply from 375 in 1995 to 202. Most incidents continued to occur in the provinces of upper Egypt. In spite of improved security, however, al-Gama'at al-Islamiyya (Islamic Group or IG) succeeded in conducting a shooting attack against foreign tourists at a Cairo hotel in April. Although this hotel attack generated the largest casualty count from a single incident in Egypt's modern history, the total number of deaths from extremist violence dropped sharply in 1996 after increasing steadily during the previous four years.

The IG continued its pattern of hit-and-run attacks in upper Egypt against police and suspected police informers and its robberies of jewelry stores to finance its operations. Minya Governorate ranked highest in terrorist incidents—which included the IG's killing of a high-ranking police official in April—but attacks also occurred in Asyut Governorate. The IG's shooting attack in April outside the Europa Hotel in Cairo that killed 18 Greek tourists waiting to board a bus disrupted the previous year's lull in incidents in Cairo and northern urban areas. The IG said it had intended to kill Israeli tourists to avenge Israeli strikes earlier that month against Hizballah forces in southern Lebanon. The smaller group al-Jihad also condemned Israeli action and threatened to hit "American and Israeli targets everywhere." Al-Jihad did not claim responsibility for any attacks in Egypt during 1996.

Although the IG carried out no attacks outside Egypt in 1996, a senior IG leader who said he was speaking from Afghanistan publicly threatened in April to kidnap US citizens in retaliation for the sentencing to life in prison by the United States of Shaykh Umar Abd al-Rahman, the IG's spiritual leader, in January. The shaykh was convicted in October 1995 for planning to carry out several terrorist conspiracies in the United States.

The Egyptian Government hosted the Summit of Peacemakers in March at Sharm ash Shaykh to discuss terrorism and the peace process. President Clinton joined President Mubarak, then Prime Minister Peres, King Hussein, Chairman Arafat, and other heads of state and government at the meeting.

Israel and the Occupied Territories/ Palestinian Autonomous Areas

Terrorism continued to have a major impact in Israel and the occupied territories in 1996. Palestinian extremists opposed to peace with Israel conducted four massive suicide bombings in Tel Aviv and Jerusalem early in the year, which killed 65 civilians. The overall number of anti-Israeli terrorist attacks instigated by Palestinians declined to 14 in 1996 from 33 in 1995.

On 25 February a suicide bomber blew up a commuter bus in Jerusalem, killing 26, including three US citizens, and injuring 80 others, including another three US citizens. The Islamic Resistance Movement (HAMAS) claimed responsibility for the bombing. (HAMAS also claimed responsibility for a second bombing on the same day in Ashqelon, killing two persons, in an act of domestic terrorism.) On 3 March a suicide bomber detonated a bomb on a bus in Jerusalem, killing 19 and injuring six others. This bomb was wrapped with ball bearings and other metal fragments to increase casualties. A HAMAS spokesman claimed responsibility and said the attack was in response to Israel's rejection of a conditional cease-fire offered by HAMAS. On 4 March a suicide bomber detonated a bomb outside the Dizengoff Center, Tel Aviv's largest shopping mall, killing 20 and wounding 75 others, including two US citizens and children celebrating the Jewish Purim holiday. HAMAS and the PIJ both claimed responsibility for this bombing.

Other Palestinian groups that reject the peace process also launched anti-Israeli attacks in 1996, including the Popular Front for the Liberation of Palestine (PFLP) and Abu Musa's Fatah-Intifada. Unidentified gunmen, presumably Palestinian rejectionists, conducted another cross-border attack from Lebanon in March, killing 2 soldiers and wounding 9 others. On 11 December gunmen from the PFLP attacked a car carrying Israeli settlers near the settlement of Bet El north of Ram Allah in the West Bank, killing a woman and her 12-year-old son. The PFLP claimed responsibility and threatened other attacks on settlers. Palestinian Authority (PA) courts later convicted three PFLP members for the attack.

Israeli extremists also committed terrorist acts in 1996. On 4 February an unidentified Israeli reportedly fired on a group of Palestinian students on the main Nabulus-Ram Allah road, wounding a 16-year-old boy. On 1 October a Palestinian man died after being shot near Bet Shemesh. On 21 October an Israeli reportedly shot and killed a Palestinian man near the West Bank village of Sinjil.

The United States and Israel increased cooperation against terrorism in 1996. In April President Clinton and then Prime Minister Peres agreed to form the US-Israel Joint Counterterrorism Group, which held its first meeting in Washington in November. In response to the President's request, the US Congress voted to give Israel a grant of $100 million for the purchase of equipment to fight terrorism.

The Palestinian Authority, which is responsible for security in the Gaza Strip and most West Bank towns, continued in 1996 its effort to rein in Palestinian violence aimed at undermining the peace process. The PA security apparatus prevented several planned terrorist attacks and arrested Palestinians suspected of involvement in terrorist operations, including one who admitted his involvement in the murder of a dual US-Israeli citizen on 13 May. Chairman Arafat and other senior PA officials regularly condemned acts of terrorism.

Jordan

Jordan and Israel continued implementation of their peace treaty—signed on 26 October 1994—which commits the two parties to cooperate against terrorism. Amman maintains tight security along its border with the West Bank and has interdicted individuals attempting to infiltrate into the West Bank.

Jordanian security and police closely monitor secular and Islamic extremists inside the country and detain individuals suspected of involvement in violent acts aimed at destabilizing the government or its relations with other states. Jordanian authorities detained dozens of people in terrorism-related cases in 1996, including several individuals who reportedly infiltrated into Jordan from Syria with plans to attack Jordanian officials and Israeli tourists. After King Hussein raised the issue of possible Syrian complicity with President Asad in July, Damascus arrested some of the infiltrators' supporters in Syria.

Several Palestinian rejectionist groups maintain a closely watched presence in Jordan, including the Abu Nidal organization (ANO), the Palestine Islamic Jihad (PIJ), the Democratic Front for the Liberation of Palestine (DFLP), the Popular Front for the Liberation of Palestine (PFLP), and the Islamic Resistance Movement (HAMAS). Following the February 1996 suicide bombings in Israel, Jordanian security forces detained dozens of HAMAS members, including an alleged politburo official, and in May once again warned HAMAS spokesman Ibrahim Ghawsha, a Jordanian citizen, not to issue statements supporting anti-Israeli violence.

Kuwait

US military and diplomatic facilities and personnel came under increasing threat in 1996. International terrorist financier Usama Bin Ladin publicly threatened US interests in the Gulf, including Kuwait, in September and again in December. US and Western establishments received numerous telephoned and faxed bomb threats during the year.

Kuwaiti Hizballah, a Kuwaiti Shia organization that may have links to Iran, in 1996 allegedly assisted a Bahraini opposition group by smuggling weapons into Manama. Kuwaiti Hizballah may also have been engaged in activities directed against the US military presence in Kuwait.

Lebanon

Lebanon's security environment continued to improve in 1996 as the country worked to rebuild its infrastructure and institutions. However, parts of southern Lebanon and the Bekaa Valley, and portions of Beirut's southern suburbs—including areas surrounding Lebanon's main airport—remain effectively beyond the government's control. In these areas, a variety of terrorist groups, including Hizballah, the Islamic Resistance Movement (HAMAS), the Abu Nidal organization (ANO), the Palestine Islamic Jihad (PIJ), and the Popular Front for the Liberation of Palestine–General Command (PFLP-GC), continued to operate with relative impunity, conducting terrorist training and other operational activities.

Although no anti-US attacks occurred in Lebanon in 1996, the official US presence there remains under threat. Hizballah's animosity toward the United States has not abated, and the group continues to monitor the US Embassy and its personnel. Group leaders routinely denounce US policies and condemn the Middle East peace process.

Lebanon pursued several high-profile court cases against suspected terrorists in 1996:

- In October Mohammed Hilal, a former official of a Palestinian terrorist group, was convicted (in absentia) of throwing a handgrenade at the Kuwaiti Embassy in Beirut in March 1993 and of attempting to bomb the offices of Kuwait Airways in August 1993. The court sentenced him to life at hard labor and determined that he had acted on the orders of the Iraqi Government.
- Two men were tried in connection with the 1994 car-bombing death of Fuad Mughniyah, brother of senior Hizballah security official Imad Mughniyah. Both were found guilty. One was sentenced to 10 years' hard labor, the other to death. The death sentence was carried out 21 September.
- In October a military appeals court confirmed the life sentence of Hussein Tlays. Tlays had been found guilty previously of the 1986 assassination of a French military attache on the orders of a Hizballah official.
- The Lebanese courts also extradited a Palestinian, Yasser Shraydi, to Germany for trial in connection with the La Belle discotheque bombing in Berlin in 1986, in which three US servicemen and one Turkish woman were killed.

The Lebanese Government pursued through several appeals the case of the 1976 kidnapping and murder of US Ambassador Francis E. Meloy and Economic Counselor Robert O. Waring. In March the civil courts found the two accused guilty of the kidnappings but not the murders. Although the murder of diplomats is not covered by Lebanon's 1991 amnesty law, the law did apply to the kidnappings. Consequently, one of the accused was freed; the other continues to be held for unrelated crimes.

Morocco

There were few terrorist-related incidents in Morocco in 1996. In July the Russian Embassy in Rabat received a letter from a group calling itself "The Dar al-Islam Western Front" threatening to attack specific Russians in Morocco, but no such attacks followed. On 18 June a prominent Moroccan Jew was the victim of an assassination attempt in Casablanca. It was unclear, however, whether the attempt was the result of a personal vendetta or terrorist activity. Later that month, the US Consulate and another prominent Moroccan Jew, both in Casablanca, received threatening phone calls that future attacks would take place against the Jewish community. The Government of Morocco has demonstrated a readiness to respond to terrorist threats and has investigated such incidents thoroughly.

Saudi Arabia

On 22 April Saudi authorities televised the confessions of four Sunni Saudi nationals who admitted to planning and conducting the bombing of the Office of the Program Manager/Saudi Arabian National Guard (OPM/SANG) headquarters building in Riyadh in November 1995. They said their disillusionment with the way the regime practiced Islam and Islamic law motivated them to carry out the attack. Three were veterans of the conflicts in Afghanistan, Bosnia, and Chechnya. The four were executed on 31 May in accordance with Saudi law.

On 25 June a large fuel truck containing explosives detonated outside the US military's Khubar Towers housing facility near Dhahran, killing 19 American citizens and wounding some 500 persons. Khubar Towers housed US Air Force personnel and other Western military personnel assigned to duty in Saudi Arabia's Eastern Province as part of the Joint Task Force/Southwest Asia, which enforces the no-fly zone over southern Iraq. Several groups, both Shia and Sunni, purportedly claimed responsibility for the bombing, including: the "Brigades of the Martyr Abdallah al-Hudhaifi," "Hizballah al-Khalij," and the "Islamic Movement for Change." Saudi and US authorities are still investigating the incident.

Tunisia

There were no reported acts of terrorism in Tunisia in 1996, but the Government of Tunisia remains publicly committed to taking necessary actions to counter terrorist threats, particularly from religious extremists. Tunis continued throughout the year to prosecute individuals belonging to the illegal an-Nahda group, which it considers a terrorist organization, but did not blame an-Nahda for any specific terrorist attacks this year. In October the Tunisian Government arrested two individuals suspected of involvement in the assassination of Belgian Vice Premier Andre Cools in 1991. The investigation is expected to continue in 1997.

Yemen

In 1996 the Government of Yemen deported Abu Nidal organization (ANO) members residing in the country. Yemen also signed extradition agreements with the Governments of Egypt and Saudi Arabia. According to press reports, in October the Yemenis turned over to the Saudi Government several Saudi suspects. Furthermore, an Ethiopian national who hijacked an airliner to Yemen in April was arrested and jailed. He has not yet been tried.

Yemen, however, remained a base for some terrorist elements. The Yemeni Government has been unable to exercise full control over its territory, and terrorists have committed kidnappings and attacks on foreign interests in remote areas of the country. There were several attacks of this type in 1996:

- In January tribesmen in al Ma'rib Governorate kidnapped 17 elderly French tourists in order to pressure authorities into releasing a member of the tribe. The tourists were released unharmed three days later.
- In June an unidentified assailant threw an explosive device from a passing car into a vacant lot 30 meters from a US Embassy officer's residence near the office of the Canadian Occidental oil company. The company has been accused of polluting Yemeni natural resources.
- A French diplomat was kidnapped by tribesmen in the al Ma'rib Governorate in late October and was released unharmed in early November.

Moreover, Yemeni border security measures are lax and Yemeni passports are easily obtained by terrorist groups. The ruling government coalition also includes both tribal and Islamic elements which have facilitated the entry and documentation of foreign extremists.

Patterns of Global Terrorism 1997

The Year in Review

During 1997 there were 304 acts of international terrorism, eight more than occurred during 1996, but one of the lowest annual totals recorded since 1971. The number of casualties remained large but did not approach the high levels recorded during 1996. In 1997, 221 persons died and 693 were wounded in international terrorist attacks as compared to 314 dead and 2,912 wounded in 1996. Seven US citizens died and 21 were wounded in 1997, as compared with 23 dead and 510 wounded the previous year.

Approximately one-third of the attacks were against US targets, and most of those consisted of low-level bombings of multinational oil pipelines in Colombia. Terrorists there regard the pipelines as a US target.

The predominant type of attack during 1997 was bombing; the foremost target was business related.

The following were among the more significant attacks during the year:

- The deadliest terrorist attack ever committed in Egypt occurred on 17 November when six gunmen entered the Hatsheput Temple in Luxor and for 30 minutes methodically shot and knifed tourists trapped inside the Temple's alcoves. Fifty-eight foreign tourists were murdered, along with three Egyptian police officers and one Egyptian tour guide. The gunmen then commandeered an empty tour bus and fled the scene, but Egyptian security forces pursued them and all six were killed.
- On 18 September terrorists launched a grenade attack on a tour bus parked in front of the Egyptian National Antiquities Museum in Cairo. Nine German tourists and their Egyptian busdriver were killed, and eight others were wounded.
- On 12 November four US citizens, employees of Union Texas Petroleum, and their Pakistani driver were shot and killed when the vehicle in which they were riding was attacked 1 mile from the US Consulate in Karachi.
- The Government of Iran conducted at least 13 assassinations in 1997, the majority of which were carried out in northern Iraq.
- On 30 July two suicide bombers attacked a market in Jerusalem. Sixteen persons—including a US citizen—were killed, and 178 were wounded.
- On 4 September three suicide bombers attacked a pedestrian mall in central Jerusalem, killing seven persons—including a 14-year-old US citizen—and injuring nearly 200 persons.
- Frank Pescatore, a US geologist and mining consultant working in Colombia, was kidnapped by the Revolutionary Armed Forces of Colombia in December 1996 and later killed by his captors; his body was discovered 23 February 1997.
- On 30 March unknown assailants threw four grenades into a political demonstration in Phnom Penh, killing 19 persons and wounding more than 100 others. Among the injured were a US citizen from the International Republican Institute, a Chinese journalist from the Xinhua News Agency, and opposition leader Sam Rainsy, who led some 200 supporters of his Khmer Nations Party in the demonstration against the governing Cambodian People's Party.
- In April, in Bosnia and Herzegovina, police discovered and defused 23 landmines under a bridge that was part of Pope John Paul II's motorcade route in Sarajevo, several hours before the Pope's arrival.
- On 30 July, in Colombia, National Liberation Army terrorists bombed the Cano Limon-Covenas oil pipeline in Norte Santander. They had wrapped sticks of dynamite around the pipes of the pump, which caused a major oil spill on detonation. Pumping operations were suspended for more than a week, resulting in several million dollars in lost revenue.

In a notable counterterrorism achievement, Peruvian security forces staged on 22 April a raid on the Japanese Ambassador's residence in Lima where members of the Tupac Amaru Revolutionary Movement (MRTA) were holding 72 hostages for four months. All but one of the hostages were freed; after being shot during the rescue, that one suffered a heart attack and subsequently died. All the MRTA hostage takers were killed. The United States strongly supported the Government of Peru's steadfast refusal to make any concessions to the terrorists holding the hostages during the four-month ordeal.

Terrorists were brought to trial in various countries throughout the year:

- In April a judgment by a court in Berlin found that the highest levels of Iran's political leadership followed a deliberate policy of murdering political opponents who lived outside the country. The court found four defendants

guilty in the 1992 murders of four Iranian Kurdish opposition figures in Berlin's Mykonos restaurant. Three of the four convicted were members of the Lebanese Hizballah organization; the fourth was an Iranian national. The court made clear that other participants in the murders had escaped to Iran, where one of them was given a Mercedes for his role in the operation. In March 1996 a German court had issued an arrest warrant for former Iranian Minister of Intelligence and Security Ali Fallahian in this case.
- On 18 November the trial of five defendants suspected in the 1986 La Belle discotheque bombing opened in Berlin. Two US soldiers, Sgt. Kenneth Ford and Sgt. James Goins, were killed in the attack along with a Turkish citizen, and some 200 other persons were wounded, including 64 US citizens. The United States believes the attack was sponsored by Libya. The trial is expected to last two years.
- The notorious terrorist Illich Ramirez Sanchez, known as "Carlos the Jackal," was convicted in December by a French court for the 1975 murders of two French investigators and a Lebanese national. Although Ramirez had proclaimed during the trial that "There is no law for me," the court sentenced him to life in prison.

Several notable trials of international terrorist suspects in the United States also took place during the year:

- On 12 November a federal jury in Manhattan convicted Ramzi Ahmed Yousef of directing and helping to carry out the World Trade Center bombing in 1993. Eyad Mahmoud Ismail Najim, who drove the truck that carried the bomb, was also found guilty. Yousef was extradited to the United States from Pakistan in February 1995; Najim was arrested in Jordan in August of that year pursuant to an extradition request from the United States, and he was returned to the United States. (In January 1998 Yousef was sentenced to 240 years in solitary confinement for his role in the World Trade Center bombing. He also received an additional sentence of life imprisonment for his previous conviction in a terrorist conspiracy to plant bombs aboard US passenger airliners operating in East Asia.)
- In June 1997 US authorities arrested Mir Aimal Kansi, the suspected gunman in the attack on 25 January 1993 outside Central Intelligence Agency (CIA) Headquarters that killed two CIA employees and wounded three others. Kansi was apprehended abroad, remanded into US custody, and transported to the United States to stand trial. In November a jury in Fairfax, Virginia, found Kansi guilty of the capital murder of Frank A. Darling, the first degree murder of Lansing H. Bennett, and the malicious wounding of Nicholas Starr, Calvin R. Morgan, and Stephen E. Williams, as well as five firearms charges. (In January 1998, Kansi was sentenced to death.)
- A member of the Japanese Red Army terrorist organization, Tsutomu Shirosaki, was turned over to US authorities in 1996 in an Asian country and brought to the United States to stand trial for the improvised mortar attacks against the US Embassy in Jakarta, Indonesia, on 14 May 1986. The projectiles landed on the roof and in a courtyard but failed to explode. In November a US federal court in Washington, DC, found Shirosaki guilty of all charges, including attempted murder of US Embassy personnel and attempting to harm a US Embassy. (In February 1998 Shirosaki was sentenced to a 30-year prison term.)

There were 13 international terrorist incidents in the United States during the year, 12 involving letter bombs:

- In January a total of 12 letter bombs with Alexandria, Egypt, postmarks were discovered in holiday greeting cards mailed to the United States. On two separate days during January, nine letter bombs were discovered in the Washington, DC, and United Nations offices of the Saudi-owned *al-Hayat* newspaper. In addition, three letter bomb devices were sent to the federal prison in Fort Leavenworth Kansas. None of the letter bombs detonated, and there were no public claims of responsibility. A similar device mailed to the *al-Hayat* office in London on 13 January did explode, injuring two persons. Subsequently, three more devices were found. The incidents are under investigation by the FBI.
- On 23 February a Palestinian gunman entered the observation deck at the Empire State building in New York City and opened fire on tourists, killing a Danish man and wounding visitors from the United States, Argentina, Switzerland, and France before turning the gun on himself. A note carried by the gunman indicated that this was a punishment attack against the "enemies of Palestine."

Africa Overview

Ongoing civil war and ethnic violence in some regions of Africa continued to overshadow individual incidents of terrorism. During 1997, 11 international terrorist incidents occurred in Africa, the same number as the previous year. The methods used in the incidents were varied, and the targets included aid workers, UN personnel on humanitarian missions in war-torn countries, and expatriate workers.

Angola

On 8 February separatists from the Cabinda Liberation Front-Cabindan Armed Forces (FLEC-FAC) kidnapped a Malaysian citizen and a Filipino forest engineer in Cabinda. The group charged the two with spying for the Angolan Government and said they would be punished according to revolutionary law, either by expulsion or death. FLEC-FAC also issued an ultimatum to Western companies to leave the Cabinda enclave or become targets in the guerrilla struggle for independence.

Ethiopia

On 10 February two unidentified men tossed grenades into the Belaneh Hotel in Harer, wounding three Britons, one German, one Dutch national, and one French citizen. The attackers also killed a security officer at the hotel and wounded one other person. No group claimed responsibility for the attack.

In the Bale Zone of southern Oromiya, 10 armed men on 28 March stopped a private vehicle occupied by a Danish nurse from the Danish Ethiopian Mission and kidnapped her. The nurse's body was found on 3 April.

Nigeria

On 13 December angry villagers and employees of Western Geophysical, a US-owned oil exploration company, kidnapped one US citizen, one Australian, two Britons, and at least nine Nigerian employees of the firm. The victims were held hostage on a barge off the coast of Nigeria. All hostages were released unharmed by 18 December.

On 22 March armed members of the Ijaw community, protesting the redrawing of regional government boundaries, occupied Shell Oil buildings in the Niger Delta and held hostage 127 Nigerian employees of the Anglo-Dutch-owned Shell Oil Company. The protesters released 18 hostages on 25 March and the remaining 109 on 27 March. Three of the hostages were injured.

Rwanda

On 18 January armed Hutu militants attacked the Medicos del Mundo compound in Ruhengeri, killing three Spanish aid workers and injuring one US citizen aid worker.

On 2 February an unidentified gunman entered a church in Ruhengeri Prefecture and killed a Canadian priest as he served communion. No one claimed responsibility for the attack.

On 4 February suspected Hutu militants in Cyangugu Prefecture killed five members of the UN Human Rights Field Operation in Rwanda. The attackers used firearms, grenades, and machetes to kill one Briton, one Cambodian, and three Rwandans.

Somalia

On 21 November in Elayo village in the self-declared Republic of Somaliland, some 20 unidentified gunmen kidnapped five UN and European aid workers. The hostages—one Briton, one Canadian, two Kenyans, and one Indian—were released unharmed on 24 November.

South Africa

On 5 January a bomb exploded at a mosque in Rustenburg, injuring a Sudanese citizen and one South African. The Boere Aanvals Troepe claimed responsibility for the attack.

Uganda

On 31 October unknown assailants hurled two handgrenades into a tourist hostel in Kampala, injuring one South African, one Briton, and one unidentified foreign tourist.

Asia Overview

Incidents of terrorism in East Asia increased in 1997. Continuing defections from the Khmer Rouge to Cambodian forces reduced the threat from the terrorist group, but guerrillas in the Cambodian provinces have been responsible for deadly attacks on foreigners. The unstable political situation in Cambodia has led to marked political violence, and the most significant act of terrorism there was a grenade attack on an opposition political rally in March, which left 19 persons dead and injured more than 100, including a US citizen. In October, the Secretary of State designated the Khmer Rouge as a foreign terrorist organization pursuant to the Antiterrorism and Effective Death Penalty Act of 1996.

In the Philippines, implementation of a peace agreement with insurgent groups has reduced fighting with government forces, but former members of these insurgent groups and members of Philippine terrorist organizations continued attacks. Foreigners number among their victims. In October, the Secretary of State designated one of these terrorist organizations, the Abu Sayyaf Group, as a foreign terrorist organization pursuant to the Antiterrorism and Effective Death Penalty Act of 1996. In China and Indonesia, separatist violence not targeted against foreigners but having the potential to claim foreigners as collateral victims continued.

In Japan, the trial of the leader of Aum Shinrikyo, the group responsible for the sarin gas attack on the Tokyo subway system in 1995 continued. A government panel decided not to invoke an Anti-Subversive Law to ban Aum Shinrikyo, concluding that the group poses no future threat, although the group continued to operate and to recruit new members. In October, the Secretary of State designated Aum Shinrikyo as a foreign terrorist organization pursuant to the Antiterrorism and Effective Death Penalty Act of 1996.

In South Asia, many of the factions involved in the Afghanistan civil war—including large numbers of Egyptians, Algerians, Palestinians, and Saudis—continued to provide haven to terrorists by facilitating the operation of training camps in areas under their control. The factions remain engaged in a struggle for political and military supremacy over the country.

Efforts to ascertain the fate of the four Western hostages kidnapped in July 1995 in Kashmir by affiliates of the Harakat ul-Ansar (HUA) continued through 1997. There is no evidence to corroborate claims by multiple Kashmiri militant sources that the hostages were killed in December 1995. In October, the HUA was designated a foreign terrorist organization pursuant to the Antiterrorism and Effective Death Penalty Act of 1996.

In Pakistan, deadly incidents of sectarian violence, particularly in Sindh and Punjab Provinces, continued throughout 1997. In November, four US employees of Union Texas Petroleum and their Pakistani driver were murdered in Karachi when the vehicle in which they were riding was attacked 1 mile from the US Consulate in Karachi. In addition, five Iranian Air Force technicians were killed in September in Rawalpindi.

There continue to be credible reports of official Pakistani support for Kashmiri militant groups that engage in terrorism, such as the HUA.

In Sri Lanka, the Liberation Tigers of Tamil Eelam (LTTE) showed no signs of abandoning their campaign to cripple the Sri Lankan economy and target government officials. The group retains its ability to strike in the heart of Colombo, as demonstrated by an October bomb attack on the World Trade Center in the financial district that was reminiscent of the January 1996 truck bomb attack that destroyed the Central Bank. The LTTE was designated a foreign terrorist organization in October pursuant to the Antiterrorism and Effective Death Penalty Act of 1996.

Afghanistan

Islamic extremists from around the world—including large numbers of Egyptians, Algerians, Palestinians, and Saudis—continued to use Afghanistan as a training ground and home base from which to operate in 1997. The Taliban, as well as many of the other combatants in the Afghan civil war, facilitated the operation of training and indoctrination facilities for non-Afghans in the territories they controlled. Several Afghani factions also provided logistic support, free passage, and sometimes passports to the members of various terrorist organizations. These individuals, in turn, were involved in fighting in Bosnia and Herzegovina, Chechnya, Tajikistan, Kashmir, the Philippines, and parts of the Middle East.

Saudi-born terrorist financier Usama Bin Ladin relocated from Jalalabad to the Taliban's capital of Qandahar in early 1997 and established a new base of operations. He continued to incite violence against the United States, particularly against US forces in Saudi Arabia. Bin Ladin called on Muslims to retaliate against the US prosecutor in the Mir Aimal Kansi trial for disparaging comments he made about Pakistanis and praised the Pakistan-based Kashmiri group HUA in the wake of its formal designation as a foreign terrorist organization by the United States. According to the Pakistani press, following Kansi's rendition to the United States, Bin Ladin warned the United States that, if it attempted his capture, he would "teach them a lesson similar to the lesson they were taught in Somalia."

Burma

The explosion in April of a parcel bomb at the house of a senior official in Burma's military-led government was the most significant terrorist event in Burma in 1997. The blast killed the adult daughter of Lieutenant-General Tin Oo, Secretary Number Two of the ruling State Law and Order Restoration Council. No group or individual claimed responsibility for the attack, but the Government of Burma attributes the act to Burmese antigovernment activists in Japan; the package bore Japanese stamps and postmarks. The Burmese expatriate and student community in Japan denies any involvement in the incident.

Cambodia

Continued defections from the Khmer Rouge to the government and the split of the group into pro- and anti-Pol Pot factions have greatly reduced the threat it poses. Nevertheless, the hardliners based in the Khmer Rouge stronghold at Anlong Veng regularly launched guerrilla-style attacks on government troops in several provinces from July onward. Guerrillas are also suspected in two deadly attacks against ethnic Vietnamese civilians in Cambodia, but they have denied playing a role in the disappearance of two Filipino and two Malaysian employees of a logging company in December 1997.

The most significant terrorist incident in Cambodia in 1997 was the grenade attack on an opposition political rally on 30 March. Nineteen persons were killed in the attack, and more than 100 were injured, including one US citizen. Those responsible for the attack have not yet been apprehended.

Reacting to political violence throughout July, Second Prime Minister Hun Sen announced an eight-point program in August designed to improve the security situation in Cambodia. The new measures include government crackdowns on illegal roadblocks and weapons and a ban on tinted windows intended to discourage kidnapping and arms smuggling.

The fate of British mineclearing expert Christopher Howes, allegedly kidnapped by the Khmer Rouge in March 1996, remained unresolved in 1997. Unconfirmed reporting suggested Howes was with forces loyal to Pol Pot, and some Cambodian officials expressed fears publicly that he had been killed. In May, Khmer Rouge leader Khieu Samphan denied any knowledge of Howes' whereabouts.

China

There were no incidents of international terrorism in China in 1997, but Uygur separatists continued a campaign of violence. The Uygurs are a Chinese Muslim ethnic minority group concentrated in the Xinjiang Autonomous Region in far western China. In February, Uygur separatists conducted a series of bus bombings in Urumqi that killed nine persons and wounded 74. Uygur rioting earlier in the month in the city of Yining caused as many as 200 deaths. Uygur exiles in Turkey claimed responsibility for a small pipe bomb that exploded on a bus in Beijing in March and which killed three persons and injured eight. In August, Uygur separatists were blamed for killing five persons, including two policemen. The Chinese Government executed several individuals involved in both the rioting and bombings. Beijing claims that support for the Uygurs is coming from neighboring countries, an accusation these countries deny.

India

Security problems persist in India as a result of insurgencies in Kashmir and in the northeast. The violence also has spread to New Delhi; there were more than 25 bombings in the city in 1997—mainly in the marketplaces and buses of old Delhi—that left 10 persons dead and more than 200 injured. These attacks appeared to be aimed at spreading terror among the public rather than causing casualties. Nearly 100 bombings with similar characteristics took place elsewhere in the country in 1997, most with no claims of responsibility. Although foreigners were not the likely targets of these attacks, foreign tourists were injured in a train bombing outside Delhi in October.

The Indian and Pakistani Governments each claim that the intelligence service of the other country sponsors bombings on its territory. The Government of Pakistan acknowledges that it continues to provide moral, political, and diplomatic support to Kashmiri militants but denies allegations of other assistance. Reports continued in 1997, however, of official Pakistani support to militants fighting in Kashmir.

Indonesia

Separatist groups in East Timor apparently continued to target non-combatants and were involved in several bombmaking activities in 1997. In Irian Jaya, an attack allegedly by the separatist Free Papua Organization against a road surveying crew in April left two civilians dead.

Japan

The trials of Aum Shinrikyo leader Shoko Asahara and other members of the sect continued in 1997. Prosecutors reduced the number of victims listed in the indictments against Asahara to speed up the proceedings, which entered their second year. In addition to the murder charges stemming from the March 1995 sarin nerve gas attack on the Tokyo subway system, Asahara faces 16 other charges ranging from kidnapping and murder to illegal production of drugs and weapons. Nine former Aum members pleaded guilty or received sentences from 22 months to 17 years for crimes they committed on behalf of Asahara; one Aum member was acquitted of forcibly confining other cult members.

Despite the legal proceedings against Asahara and other members, what remained of Aum following the arrests of 1996 continued to exist, operate, and even recruit new members in Japan in 1997. In January a government panel decided not to invoke the Anti-Subversive Law against Aum Shinrikyo, which would have outlawed the sect. The panel ruled that Aum posed no future threat to Japanese society because it was financially bankrupt and most of its followers wanted by the police had been arrested.

Several members of the Japanese Red Army (JRA) were arrested in 1997. Five members were convicted in Lebanon on various charges related to forgery and illegal residency and sentenced to three years in prison. Another member, Jun Nishikawa, was captured in Bolivia and deported to Japan where he was indicted for his role in the 1977 hijacking of a Japanese Airlines flight.

Tsutomu Shirosaki was captured in 1996 and brought to the United States to stand trial for offenses arising from a rocket attack against the US Embassy in Jakarta, Indonesia, in 1986. He was convicted in Washington, DC, of assault with the intent to kill, attempted first degree murder of internationally protected persons, attempted destruction of buildings and property in the special maritime and territorial jurisdiction of the United States, and the committing of a violent attack on the official premises of internationally protected persons. (In February 1998 he was sentenced to 30 years in prison.)

Seven hardcore JRA members remain at large.

Pakistan

In November four US employees of Union Texas Petroleum and their Pakistani driver were murdered in Karachi when the vehicle in which they were traveling was attacked 1 mile from the US Consulate in Karachi. Shortly after the incident, two separate claims of responsibility for the killings were made: the Aimal Khufia Action Committee—a previously unknown group—and the Islami Inqilabi Mahaz, a Lahore-based group of Afghan veterans. Both groups cited as the motive for the attack the conviction of Mir Aimal Kansi, a Pakistani national who was tried in the United States in November for the murder of two CIA employees and the wounding of three others outside CIA Headquarters in 1993. Kansi was found guilty and sentenced to death.

Deadly incidents of sectarian violence, particularly in Punjab Province, surged in 1997. According to press reports, 200 people died during the year. In addition, five Iranian Air Force technicians were killed in September in Rawalpindi. Lashkar i-Jhangvi, a violent offshoot of the anti-Shiite Sunni group Sipah i Shahaba Pakistan, claimed responsibility. The Iranian Government-controlled press holds Pakistan responsible for failing to stop the attack and accused the United States of conspiring in the murders.

The United States designated the HUA a foreign terrorist organization in October. This group is responsible for the still unresolved July 1995 kidnapping of six Westerners in Kashmir; one of the six, a US citizen, managed to escape, but a Norwegian hostage was killed in August 1995.

Ramzi Ahmed Yousef, who was extradited from Pakistan to the United States in 1995, was convicted in New York in November for his role in the 1993 World Trade Center bombing in New York City.

Philippines

The Philippine Government began implementing terms of a peace agreement signed with the Moro National Liberation Front (MNLF) in 1996 and continued efforts to negotiate a peace agreement with the Moro Islamic Liberation Front (MILF). The government began the process of integrating former MNLF rebels into the Philippine military. A cease-fire with the MILF reduced the fighting that peaked in the first half of 1997, but the two sides failed to agree on a more comprehensive arrangement. The MILF and the smaller Abu Sayyaf Group continue to fight for a separate Islamic state in the southern Philippines.

Muslim rebels in the southern Philippines conducted several attacks against foreigners in 1997. A Japanese businessman and three Filipino boys were kidnapped in June by members of the Abu Sayyaf Group. A rescue operation by the Philippine military freed the Japanese hostage. A German businessman was abducted in September by former members of the MNLF and was released in December only after his family agreed to pay the kidnappers some $100,000 in ransom. In separate incidents in October and November, former MNLF members abducted priests—one Irish and one Belgian—and demanded payment of funds owed them under a government rehabilitation program. The captives were released after the government agreed to expedite disbursal of the funds.

The government had mixed results in its efforts against communist rebels in 1997. Philippine police captured some key communist personnel. The government again suspended negotiations with the political arm of the communist New People's Army (NPA) in late 1997 following an upsurge in small-scale attacks by the NPA on police and government units. In May communist guerrillas ambushed a vehicle owned by a subcontractor of a major US firm, killing two Filipino employees. In December, New People's Army rebels ambushed two army detachments and abducted 21 paramilitary troops in Davao City in Mindanao. The government pledged to revisit the issue of a dialogue with the communists if acceptable circumstances could be met. Another communist rebel group, the Alex Boncayao Brigade, is not participating in peace talks with the government.

In September a previously unknown group calling itself the Filipino Soldiers for the Nation claimed responsibility for grenade attacks at bus terminals in Manila and Bulcalan City that killed six persons and wounded 65. Press reports indicated the group claimed to favor a constitutionally prohibited second term for President Ramos. The Ramos government strongly condemned the attacks and blamed them on unknown provocateurs.

The Philippine Government continued its strong support for international cooperation against terrorism and actively sought to build a multilateral approach to counterterrorism in regional and other forums. The government cooperated in providing additional personnel to protect likely targets and to identify, investigate, and act against likely terrorists. The government quickly responded when a US company experienced what appeared to be an NPA attack on one of its subcontractors in Quezon, and officials at the Cabinet level met with company executives to discuss what could be done to improve security.

Sri Lanka

The Liberation Tigers of Tamil Eelam continued its terrorist activities in 1997, attacking government troops, economic infrastructure targets, and assassinating political opponents. The LTTE's most spectacular terrorist attack in 1997 was a truck bombing directed at the newly opened Colombo World Trade Center on 15 October. The explosion injured more than 100 persons, including many foreigners, and caused significant collateral damage to nearby buildings. Eighteen persons—including LTTE suicide bombers, hotel security guards, and Sri Lankan security forces—died in the explosion and aftermath. Two of the terrorists were shot by Sri Lankan authorities as they tried to escape, and another three killed themselves to avoid capture. One of the bombers lobbed a grenade into a monastery yard as he fled the scene, killing one monk.

In two separate incidents in June in the Tricomalee area, the LTTE assassinated two legislators and nine other civilians.

Also, during the summer months, naval elements of the LTTE conducted several attacks on commercial shipping, including numerous foreign vessels. In July LTTE rebels abducted the crew of an empty passenger ferry and set fire to the vessel. The captain and a crewmember—both Indonesian—were released after three days. Also in July, the LTTE stormed a North Korean cargo ship after it delivered a shipment of food and other goods for civilians on the Jaffna Peninsula, killing one of the vessel's 38 North Korean crewmembers in the process. The Tigers freed its North Korean captives five days later and eventually returned the vessel. Sri Lankan authorities charged the LTTE with the July hijacking of a shipment of more than 32,000 mortar rounds bound for the Sri Lankan military. In September the LTTE used rocket-propelled grenades to attack a Panamanian-flagged Chinese-owned merchant ship chartered by a US chemical company to load minerals for export. As many as 20 persons, including five Chinese crewmembers, were reported killed, wounded, or missing from the attack.

In August a group calling itself the Internet Black Tigers (IBT) claimed responsibility for e-mail harassment of several Sri Lankan missions around the world. The group claimed in Internet postings to be an elite department of the LTTE specializing in "suicide e-mail bombings" with the goal of countering Sri Lankan Government propaganda disseminated electronically. The IBT stated that the attacks were only warnings.

The Sri Lankan Government strongly supports international efforts to address the problem of terrorism. (It was the first to sign the International Convention for the Suppression of Terrorist Bombings in January 1998.) Colombo was quick to condemn terrorist attacks in other countries and raised terrorism issues in several international venues, including the UN General Assembly and the Commonwealth heads of government meeting in Edinburgh.

No confirmed cases of LTTE or other terrorist groups targeting US citizens in Sri Lanka occurred in 1997. The LTTE was among the 30 groups designated as foreign terrorist organizations by the United States on 8 October.

Thailand

An appeals court in Thailand upheld the conviction and death sentence passed on an Iranian convicted of a 1994 plot to bomb the Israeli Embassy in Bangkok. The defendant, Hossein Dastgiri, has appealed to the Supreme Court.

Muslim separatist groups in southern Thailand carried out a series of bombings and other violent attacks in 1997. Bomb attacks in October killed seven persons, and a bombing of a Chinese religious festival in December killed three and wounded 15. Government authorities credited separatist groups with assassinating 11 policemen in a two-month period and blowing up a railroad in May.

Vietnam

A Vietnamese court sentenced two persons to death and three others to life in prison for carrying out a grenade attack on the waterfront in Ho Chi Minh City in 1994, in which 20 persons, including 10 foreigners, were injured. The five were part of the "Vietnam Front for Regime Restoration," an antigovernment exile group based in the United States.

Europe and Eurasia Overview

The number of terrorist incidents in Western Europe remained low during 1997. Terrorist acts by the Kurdistan Workers' Party (PKK) declined in Germany as PKK leader Ocalan attempted to get out from under Germany's tough sanctions on terrorist organizations.

Spain and France continued to cooperate in bringing to justice members of the Basque Fatherland and Liberty (ETA) terrorist organization, while Spanish authorities have offered to negotiate with Basque groups that foreswear violence. Spanish authorities arrested, tried, and jailed the leadership of the ETA's political wing, the Herri Batasuna.

Although no major terrorist acts took place in France, security forces maintained a high public visibility as a precaution against repeats of the deadly 1996 bombing of a commuter train in Paris.

In Germany, acts of terrorist violence attributable to the PKK declined, although the PKK remains actively engaged in criminal activities, principally extortion and aggravated assault. A judgment by a court in Berlin in April in the so-called Mykonos trial found that the highest levels of Iran's political leadership followed a deliberate policy of murdering political opponents who lived outside the country. In March 1996 a German court had issued an arrest warrant for former Iranian Minister of Intelligence and Security Ali Fallahian in this case.

In the United Kingdom, the Irish Republican Army (IRA) announced another cease-fire, thereby making it possible for Sinn Fein to join the multiparty talks on Northern Ireland's future. Recalcitrant elements on both the Republican and Loyalist sides, however, showed their determination to continue the armed struggle over whether Northern Ireland should remain part of the United Kingdom or be united with the Republic of Ireland. At the end of the year, Republican prisoners in Belfast's Maze prison shot a rival prisoner, Loyalist terrorist leader Billy "King Rat" Wright. Within a day Wright's followers shot and killed a former IRA member in County Tyrone, and several other killings of Catholics followed.

Greek Government efforts during 1997 to crack down on indigenous terrorism continue to yield few successes. There has been no known progress in bringing members of the 17 November terrorist organization to justice. A major suspect in the 1986 bombing of the La Belle discotheque was extradited to Germany, however. An Italian Red Brigades terrorist who had been living freely in Greece for 12 years was arrested and entered into extradition proceedings. (A Greek court released him in early 1998).

In eastern Turkey, authorities and security forces remain locked in a war of attrition with the terrorist group PKK. There are also signs that the DHKP/C (formerly the Dev Sol terrorist organization) may be resurfacing and targeting Turkish Government figures and US military and commercial interests.

There were numerous attacks targeted against the international presence in Bosnia and Herzegovina, most consisting of small-scale bombings. Terrorist acts and threats have been triggered by dissatisfaction over the international community's handling of voter registration procedures, the return of refugees, and the apprehension of suspected war criminals.

In Russia, although the armed conflict between Federal forces and Chechen separatists has been resolved, there were numerous incidents of kidnapping and other acts. In Tajikistan, violence claimed the lives of Russian servicemen and a French humanitarian aid worker. Azerbaijan and Georgia also saw continued ethnic-related terrorist violence.

Austria

In October, Austrian police arrested a man suspected of a xenophobic letter bomb campaign since 1993 that has claimed the lives of four members of the Roma (gypsy) minority in Burgenland Province and injured 15 persons in Austria and Germany. The ongoing investigation convinced Austrian authorities that the suspect acted on his own and invented the name Bavarian Liberation Army, which was used in claims of responsibility for most of the bombings.

In June an Austrian investigative judge interrogated international terrorist Illich Ramirez Sanchez, alias "Carlos the Jackal," who is incarcerated in Paris. The terrorist is believed to have masterminded the terrorist attack on the OPEC Headquarters in Vienna in 1975.

Belgium

On 20 June unidentified individuals detonated a bomb at the Turkish Embassy in Brussels. An anonymous caller claimed the attack in the name of the "Gourken Yanikian Military Unite," a covername used by the Armenian Secret Army for the Liberation of Armenia (ASALA) terrorist organization during the 1980s. ASALA had not conducted terrorist attacks in several years, however, and it is unclear whether the attack was carried out by ASALA, individual Armenians with no terrorist affiliation, or another terrorist group—such as the Kurdistan Workers' Party—using Yanikian as a covername.

Bosnia and Herzegovina

Numerous attacks occurred against the international presence in Bosnia and Herzegovina during 1997. Most of these attacks consisted of small-scale bombings that resulted in material damage and few casualties. However, during the visit of Pope John Paul II to Bosnia and Herzegovina in April, an unidentified assailant planted over 23 remote-controlled landmines underneath a bridge that was part of the Pope's motorcade route. Acting on a report from a witness claiming to have seen a suspicious person near the bridge, police discovered and defused the mines a few hours before the Pope's arrival. No group claimed responsibility for the attempted attack.

Following the apprehension of two indicted Bosnian Serb war criminals in Prijedor by the Stabilization Force (SFOR) troops on 10 July, unidentified assailants mounted over 20 improvised bombings against facilities and individuals belonging to the Organization for Security and Cooperation in Europe, the International Police Task Force, and SFOR. In December unknown attackers threw a handgrenade at a Dutch SFOR compound the day after a Dutch SFOR unit apprehended two indicted Bosnian Croat war criminals near Vitez. Other small-scale bombings against the international community presence in Bosnia and Herzegovina occurred to protest the handling of local elections and voter registration procedures and the return of refugees and displaced persons to their prewar homes.

In November, Bosnian security services began an operation to apprehend former *mujahedin*—foreign Islamic fighters who served in the Bosnian Army during the war—suspected of involvement in a variety of criminal activities, including the murders of several Bosnian Croats and bombings of Croat houses and churches. By yearend, roughly 20 Arab and Bosnian Muslims had been arrested by Bosnian authorities.

Denmark

On 18 January, Danish police arrested several neo-Nazis in connection with the mailing of several letter bombs to targets in the United Kingdom. The bombs, which were mailed from Sweden, were intercepted by Swedish police and safely detonated. The remains of the bombs were provided to Danish police as evidence on 20 January. In September a Danish court sentenced three of the neo-Nazis in connection with this case.

France

French authorities continue to maintain a state of high alert in the aftermath of a wave of terrorist bombings by Algerian Islamic extremists during 1995 and 1996. The French mounted extensive security operations to protect Algeria's 17 consulates in France during the Algerian legislative elections in June, in which an estimated 2 million Algerians resident in France were eligible to vote. On 28 February a bomb exploded outside the American dormitory at Cite Universitaire near Paris. No one was injured in the incident, and no group has claimed responsibility for the attack.

(On 29 January 1998 antiterrorism magistrate Jean-Louis Brugiere officially completed his investigation into the 1989 downing of UTA flight 772. French prosecutors are examining his report in advance of a future trial, in absentia, of the Libyan intelligence agents believed to be responsible for the attack.)

The trial of notorious international terrorist Illich Ramirez Sanchez, alias "Carlos the Jackal," began in mid-December. Later that month, Ramirez was convicted by a French court for the 1975 murders of two French investigators and a Lebanese national.

Factions of the National Front for the Liberation of Corsica (FLNC) continued to carry out a campaign of low-level bombings, primarily directed against symbolic targets, such as banks and police stations. The vast majority of these bombings took place on Corsica, but several attacks were mounted on the French mainland.

French authorities continued to cooperate closely with their Spanish counterparts during 1997 to track down Basque Fatherland and Liberty (ETA) terrorists operating or seeking refuge in France. French authorities arrested more than 140 suspected ETA members and supporters, tried over 60 of these individuals, and extradited 23 ETA terrorists to Spain, including two of the group's key leaders. In May the French Basque group Ipparratarek claimed responsibility for bombing a fast-food restaurant in Saint Jean de Luz, causing extensive material damage but no injuries.

Georgia

The trial of Jaba Ioselliani, former head of the Georgian Mkhedrioni paramilitary organization, began on 1 December. He and 14 others are accused of conspiring against Georgian President Eduard Shevardnadze, culminating in an assassination attempt against the President in August 1995. The Georgian Government continues to seek the extradition of Igor Giorgadze, former head of the Georgian Security Ministry, from Russia for his alleged involvement in the plot against Shevardnadze.

Germany

PKK leader Abdullah Ocalan, in an ongoing effort to encourage the German Government to lift its four-year-old ban on his organization, reiterated his 1996 public promise to forbid PKK-instigated acts of violence on German soil. Indeed, acts of terrorist violence attributable to the PKK in Germany for the year declined significantly and PKK demonstrations were peaceful. The PKK actively engaged, however, in criminal activities, principally extortion, recruitment, and aggravated assault. (In January 1998 the German Federal prosecutor announced that the PKK would no longer be considered a terrorist organization. However, the German Interior Minister stated that the PKK remains a banned criminal organization in Germany and that German authorities will continue to work on PKK prosecutions.)

German prosecutors indicted the former PKK European spokesman, Kani Yilmaz (a.k.a. Faisal Dunlayiei), charging him with being one of the leaders of a terrorist organization and indirectly participating in two series of arson attacks on Turkish establishments in Germany in June and November 1993. (In February 1998 he was convicted and sentenced to seven and a half years. He was released on parole, however, because he had already served more than half of his sentence in pretrial detention in the United Kingdom and Germany.)

An important terrorism trial in Berlin concluded in April 1997. The Mykonos trial involved five defendants—an Iranian and four Lebanese—suspected in the 1992 killing of Iranian Kurdish dissidents, one of whom was then Secretary General of the Kurdish Democratic Party of Iran (KDPI), in Berlin's Mykonos restaurant. A German judge found the Iranian and three of the Lebanese guilty of the murders. Two defendants, Kazem Darabi and Abbas Rhayel, were sentenced to life in prison. Two others, Youssef Amin and Muhammad Atris, received sentences of 11 years and five years and three months, respectively. The fifth defendant, Ataollah Ayad, was acquitted. The court stated that the Government of Iran had followed a deliberate policy of liquidating the regime's opponents who lived outside Iran, including the opposition KDPI. The judge further stated that the Mykonos murders had been approved at the most senior levels of the Iranian Government by an extra-legal committee whose members included the Minister of Intelligence and Security, the Foreign Minister, the President, and the Supreme Leader. In March 1996 a German court had issued an arrest warrant in this case for Ali Fallahian, the former Iranian Minister of Intelligence and Security.

Germany in November 1997 began the trial of five defendants in the 1986 La Belle discotheque bombing in Berlin, which killed three persons, including two US servicemen, and wounded more than 200, many of them seriously. Both Italy and Greece arrested suspects in the case during 1997 and extradited them to Germany for trial. In his opening remarks, the German prosecutor said the bombing was "definitely an act of assassination commissioned by the Libyan state." German authorities have issued warrants for four Libyan officials for their role in the case. The four are believed to be in Libya.

Greece

Greek Government efforts during 1997 to crack down on indigenous terrorism yielded few successes. Revolutionary Organization 17 November claimed responsibility for its 22nd assassination; previous victims include five US Government employees. On 28 May, Greek shipping tycoon Constantine Peratikos was shot to death in broad daylight on an Athens street. The group issued a manifesto claiming that Peratikos was targeted because he allegedly misused a large government bailout and threatened to close down his shipyard, which would have forced the layoff of 2,000 employees. No member of 17 November has ever been arrested.

Greece's numerous leftist and anarchist groups stepped up the tempo of attacks in 1997, predominantly with Molotov cocktail attacks and low-level bombings against property. Some of the leftist groups—in particular, the Fighting (or Militant) Guerrilla Formation (FGF)—recently have attempted to assassinate Greek officials with improvised explosive devices. For example, the FGF attempted to bomb the home of a former Greek Government counterterrorism adviser in February—the bomb was discovered and dismantled—and also claimed responsibility for a bomb that exploded at the Minister of Development's parliamentary constituency office. No arrests have been made in these cases.

On 1 December, the Athens Court of Appeals overturned a 10-year prison sentence and acquitted suspected terrorist George Balafas of aggravated weapons possession and related indictments, including accessory to murder. Balafas is suspected of having links—if not direct involvement—with the Revolutionary People's Struggle (ELA), one of the country's more deadly terrorist groups.

Kurdish nationalist groups—including the terrorist PKK—enjoy widespread sympathy and some support among the Greek public. In April, 157 members of the Greek Parliament signed a petition calling for PKK leader Abdullah Ocalan to be officially invited to Greece.

The Greek Government extradited German citizen Andrea Haeusler to Germany in January for her alleged participation in the 1986 bombing of the La Belle discotheque in Berlin. In November, Greek police arrested former Italian Red Brigade member Enrico Bianco in western Greece and initiated procedures for his extradition to Italy, where he had been convicted in absentia. (A Greek court denied the extradition request in January 1998 and Bianco was released.)

Italy

Several incidents in Italy during 1997 involved domestic anarchists, although none of these resulted in casualties. A leftist group called Revolutionary Action claimed responsibility for a bombing on 25 April outside Milan's city hall. In May a hand-grenade was found in a store located near the Uffizi Gallery in Florence. The gallery had been the target of an anarchist bombing in 1993. In November, five days before local elections, a bomb was discovered before it detonated outside the Palace of Justice in Rome, site of Italy's highest court. The investigation is ongoing, but authorities suspect local anarchists were responsible.

In January several unarmed persons broke into the Peruvian Consulate in Padua and defaced the building with graffiti. Although the Peruvian MRTA claimed responsibility for the incident, Italian police believe Italian supporters of MRTA probably were responsible.

Eight members of a domestic separatist group took over the bell tower in Venice's main square, Piazza San Marco, on 9 May. The suspects were arrested and tried in July on charges of kidnapping for subversive purposes and unauthorized possession of weapons; all eight were found guilty and received sentences ranging from four years and nine months house arrest to six years in prison.

Italian authorities scored notable successes against foreign terrorists during 1997. In June a court in Turin sentenced five members of the Algerian Armed Islamic Group (GIA) to prison terms of one to three years on charges of forgery and membership in a criminal organization. In August, Italian police arrested Libyan citizen Eter Abulgassem Musbah, a suspect in the 1986 bombing of the La Belle discotheque in Berlin. Abulgassem was promptly extradited to Germany to stand trial for the La Belle bombing. In September, Italian authorities in Bologna arrested 14 foreign nationals suspected of belonging to the GIA. Nine of the suspects were later released due to lack of evidence.

Russia

In Russia, although the armed conflict between Federal forces and Chechen separatists was resolved, there were numerous incidents of kidnapping. Most of these involved ransom demands, although political motives cannot be excluded. Insurgents have been aided with equipment and training by *mujahedin* with extensive links to Middle Eastern and Southwest Asian terrorists. According to the Organization for Security and Cooperation in Europe, at yearend 71 hostages remained in captivity, including 15 foreign nationals, five of whom are journalists and 10 are NGO representatives.

Spain

Despite numerous Spanish counterterrorism successes and increased international cooperation with France and Latin American countries, the Basque Fatherland and Liberty (ETA) terrorist group continued its campaign of murder, bombings, kidnappings, and street violence. ETA killed 13 persons last year, as compared to five during 1996. ETA's primary targets remained members of the Spanish security forces and judicial and prison officials, but the group also stepped up attacks against local politicians belonging to the ruling Popular Party. ETA's kidnapping and murder of a Popular Party town councilor in July provoked widespread international condemnation and anti-ETA demonstrations involving millions of people throughout Spain.

The Spanish Government has energetically and successfully sought extradition from countries in which ETA fugitives reside. Spanish-French cooperation during 1997 led to the arrest in France of more than 140 persons directly or indirectly connected with ETA, including several of the group's key leaders. Some 60 ETA activists went to trial in France during the past year, and Spanish authorities negotiated the extradition to Spain of 23 terrorists. Spain also has sought extraditions from Latin American countries, successfully gaining extradition of ETA fugitives from the Dominican Republic and Mexico during 1997.

The Spanish Government moved for the first time in 1997 to prosecute ETA's legal political wing, the Herri Batasuna (HB) political party, on charges of criminal collaboration with a terrorist organization. The charges stemmed from HB's dissemination during the 1996 national election campaign of a video containing footage of ETA terrorists advocating violence. On 1 December sentences of seven years in prison and fines of about $3,500 were announced for all 23 members of HB's executive committee.

The leftwing terrorist group First of October Antifascist Resistance Group (GRAPO) remained inactive during 1997, even though some of the group's leaders were released from prison.

Spanish authorities moved forcefully against foreign terrorists in their country, breaking up a ring of the Algerian GIA operating in Valencia in April.

Sweden

In an effort to undermine Sweden's bid to host the summer Olympic Games in the year 2000, "We Who Built Sweden," a previously unknown group, exploded several bombs at Swedish sports stadiums.

Tajikistan

Security for the international community in Tajikistan deteriorated as militant followers of renegade Tajik warlords Rezvon and Bahrom Sodirov resorted again to kidnapping employees of international organizations, a precedent the group established in December 1996. In an incident that began on 4 February, armed militants affiliated with Bahrom Sodirov took UN and International Committee of the Red Cross (ICRC) personnel, Russian journalists, and the Tajik Security Minister hostage. Russian and Tajik negotiators conceded to Bahrom's demands for safe transport of his brother Rezvon Sodirov and his followers from Afghanistan to a camp outside Dushanbe, as well as for weapons and ammunition, and all the hostages were subsequently released. Authorities captured Bahrom following this incident. On 18 November, Rezvon Sodirov masterminded the kidnapping of two French humanitarian aid workers and demanded Bahrom's release from prison. The incident ended violently by month's end; one hostage was either released or escaped on 29 November, but the other hostage was fatally wounded on 30 November during a shootout between the kidnappers and government forces in a government rescue attempt. Reports of Rezvon Sodirov's death in the shootout have not been confirmed.

Unidentified assailants continued sporadic attacks against Russian servicemen in Tajikistan. On 18 February terrorists, probably followers of Rahmon "Hitler" Sanginov, assassinated two ethnic Russian, off-duty US Embassy guards. The assassinations were consistent with a surge in attacks against Russians in Tajikistan; authorities concluded that the victims' affiliation with the US Embassy was not a factor in the attacks.

Turkey

The Turkish Communist Laborers' Party/Leninist (TKEP/L) placed two improvised explosive devices against the wall of the US Consulate in Istanbul on 5 October. The police removed the devices before detonation, but the event marked the first time that the TKEP/L targeted a US Government facility. Ensuing police sweeps reportedly wrapped up the group's leader and most of its senior cadre members.

The virulently anti-US Revolutionary People's Liberation Party/Front (DHKP/C)—formerly known as Dev Sol—conducted three significant attacks during the year: all were light antiarmor weapon (LAW) rocket attacks against Turkish security facilities in Istanbul. The three attacks were flawed in execution: on 16 June the rocket fired at the Turkish National Police (TNP) headquarters missed and struck a wall; the LAW rocket launched against the Harbiye Officers' Club on 14 July hit the wall of the building but caused only minimal damage; and on 16 September the DHKP/C fired another rocket at the TNP headquarters, which glanced off a wall and broke apart. The TNP's counterterrorism operations against the DHKP/C may be forcing the group to use less experienced cadre members and standoff weapons—such as LAW rockets—rather then the group's preferred close-in handgun assassinations.

The Turkish Islamic fundamentalist group, Vasat, claimed responsibility for throwing a grenade at a book fair in Gaziantep on 14 September, killing one person and injuring 24. The attack was the most egregious by Turkey's increasingly violent Islamic terrorist groups, which include Turkish Hizballah and the Islamic Great Eastern Raiders/Front (IBDA/C). The latter is suspected of masterminding the 2 December bombing of the Ecumenical Patriarchate Cathedral in Istanbul.

PKK activities in Turkey were lower in 1997 than during the previous year, in part due to Turkish military operations into northern Iraq to disrupt the PKK's infrastructure for infiltrating its members into Turkey. PKK leader Abdullah Ocalan, residing in Syria, once again publicly threatened to target Turkey's tourist sites with bombs in an attempt to disrupt the country's vital tourist industry, but these attacks did not materialize.

United Kingdom

In 1997 the IRA continued a campaign of violence begun in February 1996 against Northern Irish police and UK military and economic targets in Northern Ireland and elsewhere in the United Kingdom. July, however, brought an IRA cessation of hostilities—its second cease-fire in three years—in an effort to secure a place for Sinn Fein, its political wing, in the Ulster peace talks. The IRA cease-fire prompted an increase in activity among Republican and Loyalist splinter terrorist groups opposed to the peace process. The Continuity Army Council (CAC)—also known as the Continuity Irish Republican Army—and the Irish National Liberation Army (INLA) increased their attacks to protest the talks. The Loyalist Volunteer Force (LVF)—a new group in 1997—attacked both Republican activists and Catholic civilians with no paramilitary affiliations.

The IRA increased the frequency of its attacks during the first months of 1997 in anticipation of British elections on 1 May. By 30 April the group had conducted 29 attacks, as compared with 11 in all of 1996. IRA targets included economic and infrastructure targets on the UK mainland, and their attacks caused massive disruption while avoiding civilian casualties:

- Two IRA bombs damaged railway lines in Wilmslow, England, on 26 March.
- IRA bomb warnings closed the M1, M5, and M6 highways, which connect London and points north, on 3 April. Police found and detonated two bombs, one of which contained up to one and a half pounds of Semtex explosive, and several hoax devices.
- IRA bomb threats on 21 April snarled British transportation, with police temporarily closing 17 rail and subway stations: London's Gatwick, Heathrow, Luton, and Stanstead airports; Trafalgar Square; and the eastern dock of the Port of Dover.

The landslide victory of the British Labor Party headed by Tony Blair in the 1 May election led to preliminary talks with Sinn Fein and ultimately to an IRA announcement on 19 July of a cessation of hostilities to take effect the following day. In early September, Sinn Fein leaders agreed to the so-called Mitchell principles of nonviolence—six statements drafted by George Mitchell, currently chairman of the Northern Ireland multiparty talks, that commit all parties to renouncing the use of violence, disarming paramilitary groups, and abiding by a peaceful resolution of the Northern Ireland conflict. Sinn Fein thus secured the party's seat in the Ulster peace talks. In response, hardline IRA members called an extraordinary conference to discuss the IRA's future strategy. The conference delegates reaffirmed Sinn Fein's current peace strategy, but some 20 IRA members resigned from the group in protest. Days later a dozen members of Sinn Fein from Dundalk, Ireland, walked out of a meeting protesting the party's adherence to the Mitchell principles. Since then, most of these dissidents have returned to the fold. However, Bernadette Sands, sister of deceased IRA icon Bobby Sands, reportedly established the "Thirty-Two County Sovereignty Committee" to oppose Sinn Fein's political negotiation and the IRA cease-fire.

In October the US Secretary of State did not include the IRA among 30 groups that she officially designated as foreign terrorist organizations under recently passed antiterrorism legislation. The Secretary took note of the 19 July announcement by the IRA of an unequivocal cease-fire. She also noted the subsequent decision by the British Government that the cease-fire was "genuine in word and deed," permitting Sinn Fein to join inclusive, all-party talks in Belfast. The Department stated that, under these circumstances, the Secretary would continue to review the IRA and that any resumption of violence by the group would have a direct impact on her review.

Following the IRA cease-fire, Republican splinter terrorist groups increased their attacks, seeking to replace the IRA as the dominant Republican terrorist group. On 16 September the CAC exploded a car bomb in Markethill, Northern Ireland—a predominantly Protestant village—causing extensive damage to a police station, a cattle market, and commercial and private premises. The CAC also claimed responsibility for a 30 October bomb attack, which caused minor damage to a British Government office in Londonderry, Northern Ireland. On 19 November a CAC bomb exploded outside Belfast City Hall, causing minor damage.

Gunmen from the INLA murdered a Northern Irish police trainee in Belfast on 9 May. The INLA also carried out several attacks against Northern Irish police and British troops in July during three days of heavy rioting in Belfast over controversial Loyalist parades, injuring five police officers and two Protestant teenagers.

The extremist LVF emerged in February 1997 as a rump of the mainstream Ulster Volunteer Force (UVF), which is maintaining the cease-fire. The LVF is comprised of UVF radicals and other Protestant criminals. It is notorious for its attacks against Republican activists and Northern Irish Catholic civilians with no political or paramilitary affiliations. The LVF claimed responsibility for firebombing Northern Irish tourist information offices on 9 March to protest cross-border arrangements with Ireland. On 12 May LVF terrorists abducted and murdered a veteran member of the Gaelic Athletic Association, a Catholic sports club. The LVF exploded a small bomb in Dundalk, Ireland, on 25 May. Authorities suspect LVF terrorists in the murder of an 18-year-old Catholic girl in Antrim, Northern Ireland. The girl was shot four times in the head, apparently because she had a Protestant boyfriend. In August unidentified gunmen attacked the homes of two prison guards; although the LVF did not claim responsibility, authorities suspect that the attacks were connected to simultaneous LVF prisoner riots. On 6 August, following a public demand that Catholics stay out of Protestant neighborhoods, LVF members attacked a Catholic taxi driver with Molotov cocktails in Armagh, Northern Ireland. The LVF planted three hoax devices in Dundalk, Ireland, and one small but viable bomb at a Dundalk shopping center on 17 November; bomb experts defused the device. Authorities charged the LVF with the murder of a Catholic man in front of St. Enda's Gaelic Athletic Club in Belfast on 5 December.

On 27 December, INLA members imprisoned in Northern Ireland's Maze Prison assassinated fellow inmate Billy "King Rat" Wright, leader of the LVF. Wright was serving an eight-year sentence in the Maze prison. The INLA gunmen smuggled weapons into the prison and shot him five times at close range. Wright's assassination drew an immediate response from his LVF colleagues. That same evening LVF members hijacked buses and set them on fire in Portadown, Northern Ireland. On 28 December three LVF gunmen opened fire on a hotel frequented by Catholics, killing one person and wounding three, including a teenager.

At the end of 1997 the Ulster peace process included parties from both Unionist and Republican camps, including Sinn Fein. Pressure is building for the parties to reach some agreement before the deadline for a settlement in May 1998. (In January 1998, Sinn Fein was banned from the talks until 9 March 1998 because of murders attributed to the IRA.)

Latin America Overview

Audiences around the world watched with anxiety, then relief, on 22 April as Peruvian military forces stormed the residence of the Japanese Ambassador in Lima, bringing to an end the hostage taking by the Tupac Amaru Revolutionary Movement (MRTA), which began in December 1996. Although there was widespread regret over the loss of life of one hostage, two Peruvian soldiers, and all 14 of the MRTA terrorists, most observers agreed that decisive action by the Peruvian Government was needed in order to resolve a prolonged and increasingly intractable standoff.

With the resolution of the MRTA crisis, terrorist activity in Peru remained at low levels compared to previous years. According to Peruvian Government statistics, terrorist incidents by the Sendero Luminoso and MRTA declined to less than a fourth of what they had been in the peak years of violence almost a decade ago. Peruvian authorities, nonetheless, remained vigilant against a possible regrouping and resurgence of the two groups.

Colombia's principal terrorist groups, the Revolutionary Armed Forces of Colombia (FARC) and the National Liberation Army (ELN), stepped up their campaigns of kidnapping, extortion, and violent attacks against government, political, and private interests. Colombian authorities faced increased challenges stemming from greater FARC and ELN involvement in narcotics trafficking and tensions with neighboring countries caused by terrorist groups' incursions across Colombia's borders. The two groups carried out a campaign of murder and intimidation in an effort to disrupt the October municipal elections.

US interests continued to be affected by Colombian terrorists, with four US citizens still held hostage at the end of 1997. US companies suffered severe economic damages due to terrorist attacks against oil pipelines.

The United States was deeply disappointed with the manner in which defendants in Panama were acquitted in October of murdering US serviceman Zak Hernandez. US authorities believe that Gerardo Gonzalez, president of Panama's legislative assembly and father of one of the defendants, manipulated the outcome through threats to witnesses and intimidation of the lead investigator in the case.

In Argentina moderate progress was made in the investigation of the Buenos Aires bombings of the Argentine-Israeli Mutual Association in 1994 and the Israeli Embassy in 1992. Several arrests were made, and additional personnel were assigned to the inquiries. In December, Argentina hosted an International Congress on Terrorism, which featured presentations given by representatives of eight countries active in the fight against terrorism.

Mercosur (the Southern Cone common market) Interior and Justice Ministers signed agreements on a number of initiatives to fight crime in the Southern Cone region, with particular emphasis being given to the need to cooperate in preventing terrorist activity.

Argentina

The Argentine Government in 1997 continued its investigations into two devastating bombings against Jewish and Israeli targets in Buenos Aires: the bombing in July 1994 of the Argentine-Israeli Mutual Association (AMIA) building that killed 86 persons and injured hundreds more; and the attack on the Israeli Embassy in Buenos Aires in March 1992, in which 29 persons died. Neither probe resulted in any breakthroughs during the course of the year, but the Argentine Government devoted additional resources to the investigations and some new information has been generated. In August the Argentine Supreme Court appointed a special investigator to oversee the 1992 bombing case, and Interior Minister Carlos Corach created a new 80-man counterterrorist unit within the Argentine Federal Police to assist in the investigations. The Iranian-backed Lebanese Hizballah remains the primary suspect in both bombings.

Argentina continued to take a leading role in promoting counterterrorism cooperation in the region in 1997. Interior Minister Corach pushed vigorously for stronger border controls and increased cooperation between local law enforcement services in the "triborder" region, where the boundaries of Argentina, Brazil, and Paraguay meet.

Chile

Chilean authorities pursued investigative leads throughout 1997 in an effort to locate and apprehend four terrorists from the dissident wing of the Manuel Rodriguez Patriotic Front (FPMR) who escaped from a maximum-security prison in Santiago on 30 December 1996. In September, one of the escapees, Patricio Ortiz Montenegro, was detained in Switzerland, where he remains in custody pending the outcome of a request for political asylum. Chilean investigators are exploring the possibility that the other three escapees are in Cuba, where other FPMR members have sought refuge in the past. The prosecutor responsible for the case has asked the Cuban Government to provide information on the whereabouts of the three fugitives, a request that Chilean President Eduardo Frei repeated in November during face-to-face talks with Cuban President Fidel Castro at the Ibero-American summit in Venezuela. Havana has not formally responded to Chile's request.

Colombia

Continued violence in Colombia accounted for the bulk of international terrorist incidents in Latin America during 1997. There were 107 such incidents last year, mostly oil pipeline bombings. Fueled by revenues from kidnapping, extortion, and ties to narcotraffickers, the country's two major terrorist groups, the FARC and the ELN, carried out numerous armed attacks and bombings targeting both civilians and security forces. The groups' activities often spilled over into neighboring Panama and Venezuela. In an effort to disrupt municipal elections in October, the terrorists further intensified their activities by threatening, kidnapping, and murdering candidates and local officeholders. ELN terrorists also kidnapped two election observers from the Organization of American States (OAS) in October and held them hostage for nine days. Rightwing paramilitary groups responded with their own campaign of violence and committed several assassinations and massacres targeting the terrorists and their alleged sympathizers.

Terrorists frequently directed attacks against foreign oil and mining companies operating in the Colombian countryside, both to disrupt the country's economy and to protest what they see as foreign exploitation of Colombia's resources. The violence hit the oil sector the hardest. Terrorists sabotaged oil pipelines owned jointly by the Colombian Government and Western companies some 90 times in 1997, causing extensive ecological damage and forcing Occidental Petroleum to suspend production temporarily in August.

Colombian terrorists continued to rely on ransoms from the kidnapping of foreigners and wealthy Colombians as a major source of funds for their insurgent activities, resulting in a heightened threat to US citizens. Since 1980 at least 85 US citizens have been kidnapped in Colombia, most by the country's terrorist groups. The terrorists were still holding four US citizens hostage at yearend: three missionaries abducted by the FARC in 1993 and a geologist kidnapped by the ELN in February 1997. Two other US citizens kidnapped earlier in the year obtained their release in November. Frank Pescatore, a US geologist and mining consultant, was kidnapped by the FARC in December 1996 and later killed by his captors; his body was discovered 23 February 1997.

Opponents of extradition legislation that was before the Colombian congress in 1997 repeatedly turned to terrorist tactics to generate pressure for their cause. Individuals identifying themselves as members of the "Extraditables," a narcotrafficker-sponsored group whose terrorist attacks in the late 1980s and early 1990s forced Bogota to ban the extradition of Colombians to the United States, sent written death threats to several Colombian newspapers and foreign journalists in April. In September police defused a 550-pound car bomb outside the offices of a newspaper in Medellin, an incident that was later claimed on behalf of the Extraditables. Police have been unable to verify the authenticity of the claims.

Panama

The trial in October of three Panamanians charged with the 1992 murder of US serviceman Zak Hernandez ended with the acquittal of all of the defendants, including Pedro Miguel Gonzalez, whose father is the head of Panama's ruling Democratic Revolutionary Party and president of the country's legislature. The United States expressed its deep disappointment with the results of the trial, citing reports of judicial manipulation, threats to prosecution witnesses, and judicial retaliation against the lead investigator in the case, who was convicted of evidence tampering in a trial also rife with irregularities. The US cases against Gonzalez and one other suspect remain open.

Panamanian authorities have made no arrests in connection with the bombing in July 1994 of a commuter airline that killed all 21 persons aboard, including three US citizens. Panamanian officials continue to cooperate closely with the United States in the ongoing investigation.

Peru

The first four months of 1997 were marred by the hostage situation at the Japanese Ambassador's residence in Lima. Fourteen terrorists from the MRTA, including the group's top operational leader, Nestor Cerpa Cartolini, seized the residence on 17 December 1996, taking hundreds of hostages, including foreign ambassadors, Peruvian cabinet ministers and security chiefs, and eight US officials. At the beginning of the year, the terrorists still held 81 hostages, most of whom were prominent Peruvian or Japanese citizens.

In February, Peruvian officials and MRTA leaders initiated talks to resolve the crisis, but the terrorists' insistence that the Peruvian Government release imprisoned MRTA members blocked the way to a peaceful outcome. On 22 April, after weeks of stalled talks and a MRTA refusal to allow medical personnel to visit the hostages, Peruvian military forces stormed the residence and successfully rescued all but one of the 72 remaining hostages. Two Peruvian soldiers and all 14 of the MRTA terrorists died in the assault.

The MRTA's activity dropped off dramatically after the rescue operation, but its larger and more violent counterpart, Sendero Luminoso, remained active in Lima and in some parts of the countryside. Sendero still has not recovered from the arrest of its founder, Abimael Guzman, in 1992, however, and its recent attacks have been less ambitious than those it mounted in the early 1990s. In August, Sendero kidnapped 30 employees of a French oil company in Junin Department and released them after two days in exchange for food, clothing, and other supplies. The group also car-bombed a police station in Lima in May, injuring eight policemen and more than a dozen civilians; later in the year, it set off several smaller bombs in Lima, which caused no injuries. Peruvian authorities continue to pursue aggressively members of both of the country's terrorist groups and have tightened security measures in Lima substantially since the hostage crisis.

Middle East Overview

The Middle East witnessed some of the world's most horrific acts of terrorism in 1997.

In November, the Egyptian Islamic extremist group al-Gama'at al-Islamiyya (Islamic Group or IG) demonstrated that it was still capable of carrying out devastating acts of terrorism by staging a brutal attack that left 58 tourists and four Egyptians dead. The attack, which occurred at Hatshepsut's Temple in Luxor, took place in spite of the Egyptian Government's crackdown on extremist groups that resulted in a dramatic decrease in terrorist incidents and calls from some imprisoned al-Gama'at leaders for a truce. Fatalities from security incidents in upper Egypt remained low.

In Algeria, political violence and random killings soared toward the end of the year, as Armed Islamic Group (GIA) members stormed villages and towns, some no more than a few dozen kilometers from Algiers. Killing of civilians at highway checkpoints and in outlying towns continued on a regular basis. The Government of Algeria publicly blamed Iran for providing support to Islamist militants. Elsewhere in North Africa, Morocco and Tunisia remain vigilant against the spillover of Algerian political violence into their countries. Security incidents in those two countries continued to be low to non-existent.

Suicide bombers from the Islamic Resistance Movement (HAMAS) set off bombs in crowded public places in Tel Aviv and Jerusalem three times in 1997:

- On 21 March a HAMAS satchel bomb exploded at the Apropo Cafe in Tel Aviv, killing three persons and injuring 48, including a six-month-old child.
- On 30 July two HAMAS suicide bombers blew themselves up in Jerusalem's Mahane Yehuda market, killing 16 persons, including a US citizen, and wounding 178.
- On 4 September three suicide bombers attacked Jerusalem's Ben Yehuda pedestrian mall, killing at least five persons—in addition to the suicide bombers—including a 14-year-old girl who was a US citizen, and injuring at least 181, including seven other US citizens.

The Palestinian Authority (PA) continued its efforts in cooperation with Israeli authorities to counter the threat posed by Palestinian terrorist groups and succeeded in 1997 in thwarting several planned terrorist attacks. At the same time, more effort is needed by the PA to enhance its bilateral cooperation with Israel and its unilateral fight against terrorism.

In Lebanon, the security situation improved incrementally as the government continued its efforts to expand its authority over more of the country. Despite these efforts, large areas of the Bekaa Valley, the southern suburbs of Beirut, and south Lebanon remain outside the effective control of the government. Terrorist groups, especially Hizballah and the Popular Front for the Liberation of Palestine-General Command (PFLP-GC), used these areas in 1997 to stage attacks and engage in terrorist training.

In Saudi Arabia, the investigation to identify those responsible for the June 1996 bombing of the Khubar Towers US Air Force residential compound continued without reaching a conclusion. The bombing killed 19 US servicemen.

Algeria

The Government of Algeria does not face a significant threat to its stability from Islamic extremists, but the country's domestic terrorist problem remained among the world's worst in 1997. At least 70,000 Algerians—Islamic militants, civilians, and security personnel—have been killed since Algerian militants began their campaign to topple the government in 1992.

The government made some progress against the Islamic Salvation Army (AIS)—the military wing of the Islamic Salvation Front (FIS) that primarily attacked government-related targets—which, together with the FIS, called for a cease-fire on 1 October. The government was less successful against the GIA, the most radical of the insurgent groups, although its efforts appear to have forced the group to operate in a smaller geographic area. GIA terrorist operations continued, nonetheless, against a broad spectrum of Algerian civilians in 1997, including women and children. The worst incident of 1997 occurred on 31 December when more than 400 civilians were killed in Relizane, approximately 150 miles southwest of the capital. This act of violence was also the single worst massacre since the GIA began its reign of terror in 1992.

Seven foreigners were killed in acts of terrorist violence in Algeria in 1997, bringing the total number of foreigners killed by the GIA in Algeria since 1992 to 133. The group did not claim responsibility for these killings, nor did it issue an official communique announcing a resurgence of its violent campaign against foreigners. It remains unclear whether the foreigners were being specifically targeted or whether those killed were incidental victims of violence.

The Algerian Government prosecuted cases of persons charged with committing terrorist acts or supporting terrorist groups in 1997. In July an Algerian court convicted a former lawyer for the FIS of belonging to an armed group, and in December an Algerian court jailed 17 GIA members for setting fire to an Algerian oilfield.

Bahrain

Bahrain continued to be plagued by arson attacks and other minor security incidents throughout 1997, most perpetrated by domestic dissidents. The most serious incident was an arson attack on a commercial establishment on 13 June that resulted in the death of four South Asian expatriates. One day later an abandoned vehicle detonated outside the passport directorate of Bahrain's Interior Ministry; the explosion caused no injuries.

Bahraini courts in March convicted and sentenced to jail 36 individuals for being members of Bahraini Hizballah, an Iranian-backed organization that sought the overthrow of the island's government. The jail sentences range from five to 15 years. Some Bahraini Hizballah members reportedly underwent terrorist training in camps in Iran and Lebanon.

In November the government convicted in absentia eight individuals for orchestrating and funding from abroad a campaign aimed at disrupting the security of Bahrain. Several of the defendants were charged with sending to Bahrain propaganda inciting violence and destruction, which led to damage to public property, such as electricity and water installations. In addition to jail sentences, six of the defendants (along with others previously convicted) were ordered to pay compensation totaling over $15 million for damage to public property.

Egypt

Reversing a trend since 1995 of decreasing death tolls, the number of fatalities from terrorist incidents in Egypt rose in 1997 due to a heightened level of attacks during the latter half of the year by al-Gama'at. The group claimed responsibility for a brutal attack at a pharaonic temple site in Luxor on 17 November that killed 58 foreign tourists and four Egyptians—the most lethal attack by the group. The six al-Gama'at perpetrators were killed in a shootout by police during their escape effort. Al-Gama'at claimed it intended to take hostages in the attack in exchange for the release of Shaykh Umar Abd al-Rahman, serving a life prison term in the United States after being convicted in 1995 for several terrorist conspiracies. The claim was belied, however, by surviving eyewitnesses who reported the perpetrators took their time to execute systematically victims trapped inside the temple.

The group also continued to launch attacks against police, police informants, and Coptic Christians in southern Egypt.

Foreign tourists also were attacked in September by two Egyptian gunmen who professed support for the Egyptian al-Jihad but who were not found to be linked to an established group. Nine Germans and their Egyptian busdriver were killed in the attack outside the National Museum in Cairo. One of the gunmen was an escaped mental hospital inmate who previously had killed four foreign nationals, including a US citizen, in an attack at a restaurant in the Semiramis Intercontinental hotel in Cairo in October 1993.

Following the attack in Luxor, Egyptian officials intensified security at tourist sites in Cairo and southern Egypt. Nevertheless, the attack and subsequent decline in tourism caused severe economic losses to the country. As part of its effort to thwart extremists, the Egyptian Government also published on the Internet's Worldwide Web a list of names and photographs of 14 Egyptians sought for their suspected role in terrorist activities by al-Gama'at and the smaller Egyptian al-Jihad/Vanguards of Conquest. All of the individuals are believed to be living in various countries outside Egypt. External leaders of al-Gama'at and al-Jihad publicly rejected a call for a cease-fire in July by leaders of the two groups imprisoned in Cairo and vowed to continue their attacks against the Egyptian Government.

Israel and the Occupied Territories/ Palestinian Autonomous Areas

Israel continued in 1997 to face terrorist attacks by Palestinian groups opposed to the peace process. HAMAS launched three deadly suicide bombings over the year: a 21 March bombing in a Tel Aviv cafe, killing three Israelis and wounding 48; a 30 July dual suicide bombing in a crowded Jerusalem market, which killed 16—including one US citizen—and wounded 178; and a 4 September triple suicide bombing at a popular Jerusalem pedestrian mall, which killed four Israelis and one US citizen, and wounded nearly 200. For its part, Israel imposed strict closures in the West Bank and Gaza Strip, carried out wide-scale arrests, and on 25 September launched a failed attempt to assassinate HAMAS official Khalid Mishal in Jordan. The Israeli agents were captured by Jordanian security officials and returned to Israel after the Israeli Government released HAMAS founder Shaykh Yassin and others from prison.

Numerous other serious but less spectacular attacks against Israel and its citizens also occurred, including the 20 November murder of an Israeli student in Jerusalem's Old City carried out by unknown assailants. In addition, Israeli border forces stopped several attempted terrorist infiltrations from Lebanon and Jordan, including a 4 March border crossing attempt from Lebanon in which two Israeli soldiers were killed.

Palestinians also suffered from terrorist attacks by Israelis during the year, including a 1 January incident in Hebron where an off-duty Israeli soldier fired into a crowded market, wounding seven persons.

The PA, which is responsible for security in Gaza and most major West Bank cities, continued to act against Palestinian perpetrators of violence against Israel in 1997. The PA's security apparatus preempted several anti-Israeli attacks over the year, including several planned suicide bombings, and detained hundreds of individuals for their alleged roles in terrorist operations. In July, for instance, the PA uncovered a HAMAS West Bank safehouse where the group was preparing bombs for attacks and arrested several HAMAS members affiliated with the site. The PA also closed down 17 HAMAS social and charitable institutions that were alleged to have channeled money to the group's terrorist wing.

At the same time, more effort is needed by the PA to enhance its bilateral cooperation with Israel and its unilateral fight against terrorism.

Jordan

Despite an active counterterrorism campaign, Jordan in 1997 continued to suffer from terrorism. A 22 September drive-by shooting of two Israeli Embassy security guards in Amman remains unsolved. In other violence, a Jordanian soldier on 13 March murdered seven Israeli schoolchildren visiting a peace park. The soldier, who was captured at the scene, was sentenced in July to life in prison.

Amman continued to maintain tight security along its border with Israel and to interdict individuals attempting to infiltrate into the West Bank. Jordanian security and police also continued to monitor secular and Islamic extremists inside the country and to detain individuals suspected of involvement in violent acts aimed at destabilizing the government or its relations with other states. Jordan, in early September, for instance, detained HAMAS spokesman Ibrahim Ghawsha, a Jordanian citizen, for issuing statements promoting anti-Israeli violence. In addition to HAMAS, several Palestinian rejectionist groups—such as the Palestine Islamic Jihad (PIJ), Abu Nidal organization (ANO), and the Popular and Democratic Fronts for the Liberation of Palestine (PFLP and DFLP) —maintain a closely watched presence in Jordan.

Lebanon

Lebanon's security environment continued to improve incrementally in 1997 as the country worked to rebuild its infrastructure and institutions. US Secretary of State Albright subsequently allowed restrictions on the use of US passports for travel to Lebanon, in place since 1987, to expire in July. Nevertheless, Lebanese Government control remains incomplete in parts of the Bekaa Valley and portions of Beirut's southern suburbs, including areas near Lebanon's main airport. There is no effective Lebanese Government presence in much of southern Lebanon, where guerrilla groups are engaged in fighting in the so-called security zone controlled by Israel and its surrogate militia.

In these areas, a variety of terrorist groups continued to operate with relative impunity, conducting terrorist training and other operational activities. These groups include Hizballah, HAMAS, the ANO, the PIJ, and the PFLP-GC.

There were no anti-US attacks in Lebanon in 1997; it is unclear if a small bombing against the American University of Beirut on 27 October was politically motivated. US interests in the country, however, remained under threat. Hizballah's animosity toward the United States has not abated, and the group continued to monitor the US Embassy and its personnel. Hizballah leaders routinely denounced US policies and condemned the Middle East Peace Process, of which the United States is a primary sponsor.

Incidents such as the still unsolved 28 October explosion at a major Beirut bus station further illustrate the potential dangers to US civilians traveling in Lebanon.

In the spring Lebanese authorities arrested five members of the Japanese Red Army residing in Lebanon. In July a Lebanese court convicted all five of using false documents and residing illegally in Lebanon and sentenced them to prison terms. The five remain in custody.

Morocco

There were no terrorist-related incidents in Morocco in 1997. The Government of Morocco has demonstrated a readiness to respond to terrorist threats and has investigated such incidents thoroughly. The Moroccan Government has worked actively to suppress Islamic unrest within its own borders, fearing a spillover of violence from neighboring Algeria. An Algerian Islamic Salvation Front (FIS) member considered to be one of the group's main donors was arrested in eastern Morocco in October.

Saudi Arabia

There has been no solution to the question of responsibility for the June 1996 bombing of the Khubar Towers housing facility near Dhahran, Saudi Arabia. In that incident, a large truck bomb killed 19 US citizens and wounded more than 500 others. Although the Saudi authorities have arrested and detained several persons in connection with the incident, legal proceedings have not reached a conclusion.

In March, a Saudi national named Hani al-Sayegh was arrested by Canadian authorities. Papers submitted to the Canadian court alleged al-Sayegh had participated in the Khubar Towers bombing as a member of Saudi Hizballah, and he was deported to the United States. Once he was in this country, however, al-Sayegh reneged on an agreement with US prosecutors, under the terms of which he would have pled guilty to a charge of conspiracy unrelated to the Khubar Towers attack, in return for providing information about those responsible for the bombing. US authorities were unable to marshal sufficient evidence to prosecute him for any crime. Prosecutors turned him over to US immigration authorities. He was ruled excludable, although a number of legal issues remain to be decided. Saudi authorities have requested that al-Sayegh be returned to Saudi Arabia in connection with their own Khubar investigation.

The United States continued to receive reports of threats against US military and civilian personnel and facilities in Saudi Arabia, including bomb threats, but there were no further terrorist incidents in the Kingdom.

In March 1997 renegade Saudi terrorist financier Usama Bin Ladin publicly threatened to attack US forces in Saudi Arabia to force a US withdrawal from the region. Local South Asian press reports indicated that he continued to make statements threatening Western interests throughout the year; however, in midyear statements to Western media, Bin Ladin evaded the question of his responsibility for previously claimed anti-US attacks in Somalia and Yemen.

Tunisia

There were no reported acts of terrorism in Tunisia in 1997, and the Government of Tunisia remains publicly committed to taking the necessary actions to counter terrorist threats, particularly from religious extremists. Tunisia plays an active role in combating terrorism by hosting conferences aimed at intensifying inter-Arab cooperation in the struggle against terrorism, such as the Council of Arab Ministers held in Tunis in January. Ministers agreed to take steps to cooperate in extradition, information exchange, and other measures. The Tunisian Government also actively condemns acts of Islamic terrorism throughout the world, such as the attack on tourists in Luxor, Egypt, in November.

Yemen

Sanaa took major steps during 1997 to improve control of its borders, territory, and travel documents. It continued to deport foreign nationals residing illegally, including Islamic extremists identified as posing a security risk to Yemen and several other Arab countries. The Interior Ministry issued new, reportedly tamper-resistant passports and began to computerize port-of-entry information. Nonetheless, lax implementation of security measures and poor central government control over remote areas continued to make Yemen an attractive safehaven for terrorists. Moreover, HAMAS and the PIJ maintain offices in Yemen.

A series of bombings in Aden in July, October, and November caused material damage but no injuries. No group claimed responsibility. The Yemeni Government blamed the attacks on Yemeni opposition elements that had been trained by foreign extremists and supported from abroad. A principal suspect confessed in court he was recruited and paid by Saudi intelligence, but this could not be independently verified.

Yemeni tribesmen kidnapped about 40 foreign nationals, including two US citizens, and held them for periods ranging up to one month. Yemeni Government officials frequently asserted that foreign powers instigated some kidnappings, but no corroborating evidence was provided. All were treated well and released unharmed, but one Italian was injured when resisting a kidnap attempt in August. The motivation for the kidnappings generally appeared to be tribal grievances against the central government. The government did not prosecute any of the kidnappers.

Patterns of Global Terrorism 1998

The Year in Review

There were 273 international terrorist attacks during 1998, a drop from the 304 attacks we recorded the previous year and the lowest annual total since 1971. The total number of persons killed or wounded in terrorist attacks, however, was the highest on record: 741 persons died, and 5,952 persons suffered injuries.

Most of these casualties resulted from the devastating bombings in August of the US Embassies in Nairobi, Kenya and Dar es Salaam, Tanzania. In Nairobi, where the US Embassy was located in a congested downtown area, 291 persons were killed in the attack, and about 5,000 were wounded. In Dar es Salaam, 10 persons were killed and 77 were wounded.

- About 40 percent of the attacks in 1998—111—were directed against US targets. The majority of these—77—were bombings of a multinational oil pipeline in Colombia, which terrorists regard as a US target.
- Twelve US citizens died in terrorist attacks last year, all in the Nairobi bombing. Each was an Embassy employee or dependent:
    —Marine Sgt. Jesse N. Aliganga, Marine Security Guard detachment
    —Julian L. Bartley, Sr., Consul General
    —Julian L. Bartley, Jr., son of the Consul General

—Jean Rose Dalizu, Defense Attache's Office

—Molly Huckaby Hardy, Administrative Office

—Army Sgt. Kenneth Ray Hobson, II, Defense Attache's Office

—Prabhi Kavaler, General Services Office

—Arlene Kirk, Military Assistance Office

—Mary Louise Martin, Centers for Disease Control and Prevention

—Air Force Senior Master Sgt. Sherry Lynn Olds, Military Assistance Office

—Michelle O'Connor, General Services Office

—Uttamlal Thomas Shah, Political Section

- Eleven other US citizens were wounded in terrorist attacks last year, including six in Nairobi and one in Dar es Salaam.
- Three-fifths—166—of the total attacks were bombings. The foremost type of target was business related.

There were no acts of international terrorism in the United States in 1998. There were successful efforts to bring international terrorist suspects to justice, however, in several important cases:

- On 4 November indictments were returned before the US District Court for the Southern District of New York in connection with the two US Embassy bombings in Africa. Charged in the indictment were: Usama Bin Ladin, his military commander Muhammad Atef, and al-Qaida members Wadih El Hage, Fazul Abdullah Mohammed, Mohammed Sadeek Odeh, and Mohamed Rashed Daoud al-Owhali. Two of these suspects, Odeh and al-Owhali, were turned over to US authorities in Kenya and brought to the United States to stand trial. Another suspect, Mamdouh Mahmud Salim, was arrested in Germany in September and extradited to the United States in December. On 16 December five others were indicted for their role in the Dar es Salaam Embassy bombing: Mustafa Mohammed Fadhil, Khalfan Khamis Mohamed, Ahmed Khalfan Ghailani, Fahid Mohommed Ally Msalam, and Sheikh Ahmed Salim Swedan.
- In June, Mohammed Rashid was turned over to US authorities overseas and brought to the United States to stand trial on charges of planting a bomb in 1982 on a Pan Am flight from Tokyo to Honolulu that detonated, killing one passenger and wounding 15 others. Rashid had served part of a prison term in Greece in connection with the bombing until that country released him from prison early and expelled him in December 1996, in a move the United States called "incomprehensible." The nine-count US indictment against Rashid charges him with murder, sabotage, bombing, and other crimes in connection with the Pan Am explosion.
- Three additional persons convicted in the bombing of the World Trade Center in 1993 were sentenced last year. Eyad Mahmoud Ismail Najim, who drove the explosive-laden van into the World Trade Center, was sentenced to 240 years in prison and ordered to pay $10 million in restitution and a $250,000 fine. Mohammad Abouhalima, who was convicted as an accessory for driving his brother to the Kennedy International Airport knowing he had participated in the bombing, was sentenced to eight years in prison. Ibrahim Ahmad Suleiman received a 10-month sentence on two counts of perjury for lying to the grand jury investigating the bombing.
- In May, Abdul Hakim Murad was sentenced to life in prison without parole for his role in the failed conspiracy in January 1995 to blow up a dozen US airliners over the Pacific Ocean. Murad received an additional 60-year sentence for his role and was fined $250,000. Ramzi Ahmed Yousef, who was convicted previously in this conspiracy and for his role in the World Trade Center bombing in 1993, is serving a life prison term.

Africa Overview

The murderous and near-simultaneous bombing attacks on the US Embassies in Nairobi, Kenya and Dar es Salaam, Tanzania on 7 August 1998 caused more casualties than any other terrorist attack during the year. In Nairobi, where the US Embassy was located in a congested downtown area, the attack killed 291 persons and wounded about 5,000. The bombing in Dar es Salaam killed 10 persons and wounded 77.

These attacks clarified more than ever that terrorism is a global phenomenon. In the months since the bombings, evidence has emerged of terrorist networks involved in potential anti-US activity in a number of African nations.

In addition, state sponsors of terrorism, particularly Libya, are increasing significantly their activities in Sub-Saharan Africa.

Angola

In late April, National Union for the Total Independence of Angola (UNITA) guerrillas kidnapped two Portuguese citizens from the commune of Ebangano. The two have not been found.

UNITA rebels fired on a United Nations Mission to Angola (MONUA) vehicle near Calandula on 19 May. The attack killed an Angolan official working for MONUA and wounded two foreigners.

On 23 March and 22 April, separatists from the Cabinda Liberation Front-Cabindan Armed Forces (FLEC-FAC) kidnapped three Portuguese citizens working for Mota & Company, a Portuguese construction firm. FLEC-FAC claimed it took the workers hostage to force Portugal to pressure the Angolan Government to leave Cabinda.

On 9 November more than 100 suspected UNITA rebels overran the Canadian-owned Yetwene diamond mine in eastern Angola, killing eight individuals—including two British nationals, one Portuguese, and five Angolans—and wounding at least 22 persons. The gunmen took four workers hostage: a South African, a British national, and two Filipinos.

Central African Republic

A small bomb detonated on 27 November outside the walls of the French Embassy, causing only minor damage.

Chad

On 3 February armed rebels of the Union of Democratic forces kidnapped four French citizens in Manda National Park. The four were released unharmed five days later. On 22 March a group calling itself the National Front for the Renewal of Chad took six French and two Italian nationals hostage in the Tibesti region. Chadian forces freed all but one hostage within hours. The militants announced they would not release the last hostage until all French troops and Western oil firms left Chad. Five days later Chadian security forces freed the last hostage.

Democratic Republic of Congo

On 12 August gunmen seized a tour group sightseeing along a nature trail in the Ruwenzori Range of western Congo. The tourists—one Canadian, two Swedes, and three New Zealanders—were abducted after they crossed from Uganda into the Congo. A previously unknown group, the People in Action for the Liberation of Rwanda, claimed responsibility for the abduction. Local authorities believe the gunmen are former Rwandan soldiers who fled to Congo after the former regime was forced from power in 1994. Two New Zealanders escaped one week later, and the Canadian was released on 19 August. The other victims still are missing.

Ethiopia

On 25 February rebels of the Ogaden National Liberation Front took an Austrian national hostage as she traveled from Gode to Denan. She was released in mid-April after the rebels determined that she "was not a spy for the Ethiopian Government."

An Islamic group based in Somalia, al-Ittihad al-Islami, claimed responsibility for kidnapping six International Committee of the Red Cross workers in the eastern Ogaden region of Ethiopia on 25 June. Al-Ittihad said the abducted workers—one Swiss national and five ethnic Somalis—were spies. The six were released unharmed on 10 July even though al-Ittihad found them "guilty of conducting business outside of their duties."

Kenya

On 7 August a car bomb exploded behind the US Embassy, killing 291 persons and wounding about 5,000. The majority of the casualties were Kenyan citizens. Twelve US citizens died, and six were injured in the attack. A group calling itself the "Islamic Army for the Liberation of the Holy Places" immediately claimed responsibility for the attacks in Nairobi and a near-simultaneous explosion in Dar es Salaam, Tanzania. US officials believe the group is a cover name used by Usama Bin Ladin's al-Qaida organization. Indictments were returned in the US District Court for the Southern District of New York charging Usama Bin Ladin and 11 other individuals for these and other terrorist acts against US citizens. At yearend, four of the indicted—Wadih El Hage, Mohamed Rashed Daoud al-Owhali, Mamdouh Mahmud Salim, and Mohammed Sadeeck Odeh—were being held in New York, while Khalid al-Fawwaz remained in the United Kingdom pending extradition to the United States. The other suspects remain at large. The Government of Kenya cooperated closely with the United States in the criminal investigation of the bombing. On 20 August, President Clinton amended Executive Order 12947 to add Usama Bin Ladin and his key associates to the list of terrorists, thus blocking their US assets—including property and bank accounts—and prohibiting all US financial transactions with them.

Nigeria

On 11 November a mob of angry youths abducted eight Shell Oil workers in Bayelsa. The hostages included three US citizens, one British citizen, one Croatian, one Italian, one South African, and one Nigerian. The youths demanded jobs and economic development projects for their community. After talks with the oil firm, all eight hostages were released unharmed on 18 November.

Sierra Leone

Revolutionary United Front (RUF) militants commanded by S.A.F. Musa kidnapped an Italian Catholic missionary from his residence in Kamalo on 15 November. In exchange for the hostage's release, Musa demanded medical supplies, a satellite phone, and contact with his family, who are being detained by regional peacekeeping forces in the capital. At yearend, talks between the RUF and the government were at a standstill.

South Africa

An explosion on 25 August in the entrance of the US-franchised Planet Hollywood restaurant in Cape Town killed one person and injured at least two dozen others, including nine British citizens. Muslims Against Global Opression (MAGO), a front organization for the Islamic radical groups People Against Gangsterism and Drugs (PAGAD) and Qibla, initially claimed responsibility but then denied involvement. Local authorities believe that PAGAD members masterminded the attack in retaliation for the US bombings of terrorism-related targets in Sudan and Afghanistan.

PAGAD, a vigilante group that first appeared in August 1996, conducted a series of violent attacks against criminal elements and moderate Muslim leaders in Cape Town last year. Though police are investigating PAGAD members aggressively, none has been convicted for these crimes.

Somalia

On 15 April militant Somali clansmen took nine foreign nationals hostage after their aircraft landed at a north Mogadishu airstrip. The hostages included one US citizen, a German, a Belgian, a Frenchman, a Norwegian, and two Swiss. The two pilots, a South African and a Kenyan, also were held. The clansmen demanded $100,000 ransom. The kidnappers released the hostages unharmed on 24 April without receiving any ransom, however, after the international community pressured the kidnappers' leaders.

Tanzania

Terrorists associated with Usama Bin Ladin's al-Qaida organization detonated an extremely large truck bomb outside the US Embassy in Dar es Salaam on 7 August, just as another truck bomb exploded outside the US Embassy in Nairobi. The blast killed 10 Tanzanians, including seven local Embassy employees, and injured 77 persons, including one US citizen. Tanzanian authorities cooperated closely with the United States in the criminal investigation of the bombing.

Uganda

Unidentified assailants on 4 April detonated bombs at two downtown Kampala restaurants, the Nile Grill and the outdoor cafe at the Speke Hotel, killing five persons—including Swedish and Rwandan nationals—and wounding six others. The Ugandan Government suspects that Islamic militants of the Allied Democratic Forces are responsible.

On 8 July a United Nations World Food Program worker was killed when rebels of the Uganda National Rescue Front II fired a rocket-propelled grenade at his truck while he was driving in northwestern Uganda.

Rebels of the Lord's Resistance Army attacked a civilian convoy traveling along a major corridor in the north on 27 November, killing seven persons and wounding 28 others.

Asia Overview

The overall number of terrorist incidents in East Asia decreased in 1998. Individual countries still suffered terrorist attacks and endured continued terrorist group activities, however.

In Cambodia, the last remnants of the weakened Khmer Rouge (KR) virtually disbanded in 1998, and two of the group's top three leaders came out of hiding to surrender. Earlier in the year, KR elements committed two acts of international terrorism that caused 12 deaths. The US Secretary of State has designated the KR a foreign terrorist organization pursuant to the Antiterrorism and Effective Death Penalty Act of 1996.

In Japan, the Aum Shinrikyo religious cult, accused of attacking the Tokyo subway system with sarin gas in March 1995, increased its membership and business activity in 1998. Prosecution of cult leaders continues at a sluggish pace. In June a Lebanese court rejected appeals by five imprisoned Japanese Red Army members; Japan has asked that they be deported to Japan upon completion of their three-year jail terms. Both groups are designated foreign terrorist organizations pursuant to the Antiterrorism and Effective Death Penalty Act of 1996.

The Philippines experienced violent attacks in the southern province of Mindanao from rebels in the Moro Islamic Liberation Army (MILF), the New Peoples Army (NPA), and the Abu Sayyaf Group (ASG). The government began negotiations with the MILF that showed little progress in 1998. The ASG experienced a major setback in December when its leader was killed during a government ambush. Other incidents, including attacks on rural police posts around the country and kidnappings of foreign nationals, occurred in 1998.

In Thailand, a strong military offensive against Muslim separatists of the New Pattani United Liberation Organization (New PULO)—in cooperation with Malaysia—helped restore calm in the south, which had experienced a wave of bombings in January. The Thai Supreme Court overturned the conviction of Hossein Dastgiri, an Iranian charged in 1994 with plotting to bomb the Israeli Embassy in Bangkok.

In South Asia, the Taliban has made Afghanistan a safehaven for international terrorists, particularly Usama Bin Ladin. The United States made it clear to the Taliban on numerous occasions that it must stop harboring such terrorists. Despite US engagement of the Taliban in an ongoing dialogue, its leaders have refused to expel Bin Ladin to a country where he can be brought to justice.

In 1998 the United States continued its efforts to ascertain the fate of the four Western hostages—including one US citizen—kidnapped in India's Kashmir in 1995 by affiliates of the Harakat-ul-Ansar (HUA). Despite ongoing cooperative efforts between US and Indian law enforcement authorities, we have been unable to determine their whereabouts. The HUA was designated a foreign terrorist organization in 1997 pursuant to the Antiterrorism and Effective Death Penalty Act of 1996.

In Pakistan, sectarian violence continues to affect lives and property. In Karachi and elsewhere in the Sindh and Punjab Provinces, clashes between rival ethnic and religious groups reached dangerously high levels. As in previous years, there were continuing credible reports of official Pakistani support for Kashmiri militant groups that engage in terrorism.

In Sri Lanka, the government continues to battle the Liberation Tigers of Tamil Eelam (LTTE). Designated a foreign terrorist organization in 1997 pursuant to the Antiterrorism and Effective Death Penalty Act of 1996, the LTTE has continued its attempts to gain a Tamil homeland through a campaign of violence, intimidation, and assassination. By targeting municipal officials and civilian infrastructure and conducting random attacks, the LTTE seeks to force the government to meet to its demands. The Government of Sri Lanka is pursuing a two-track policy of fighting the Tigers and building support for its ambitious package of political reforms aimed at addressing many of the Tamil minority's grievances. Recent military setbacks may push the government toward negotiations, but the LTTE has shown no willingness to move in this direction.

Afghanistan

Islamic extremists from around the world—including large numbers of Egyptians, Algerians, Palestinians, and Saudis—in 1998 continued to use Afghanistan as a training ground and a base of operations for their worldwide terrorist activities. The Taliban, which controls most of the territory in Afghanistan, facilitated the operation of training and indoctrination facilities for non-Afghans and provided logistical support and sometimes passports to members of various terrorist organizations. Throughout 1998 the Taliban continued to host Usama Bin Ladin, who was indicted in November for the bombings in August of two US Embassies in East Africa.

Cambodia

Weakened by defections and internal discord, the last remnants of the Khmer Rouge virtually disbanded in 1998 following 30 years of civil war and terror. The KR suffered significant losses in 1998, including the death of leader Pol Pot in April. During crackdowns in August, the government arrested Nuon Paet, a former KR fugitive suspected of ordering the execution of three European tourists after holding them hostage for two months in 1994. By late December the last main fighting unit of the KR had surrendered, including two of the group's top three leaders: Khieu Samphan and Nuon Chea.

Before fragmenting, Khmer Rouge elements committed two acts of international terrorism in 1998. In January, KR militants reportedly placed a handgrenade near the Vietnamese military attache's office in Phnom Penh. In April, KR forces murdered 12 Vietnamese nationals at a fishing village near Tonle Sap lake.

India

Security problems persisted in India in 1998 because of ongoing insurgencies in Kashmir and the northeast. Kashmiri militant groups stepped up attacks against civilian targets in India's Kashmir and shifted their tactics from bombings to targeted killings, including the massacres of Kashmiri villagers. In April the massacres spilled over to Udhampur district, where 28 villagers died in two simultaneous attacks. Elsewhere in India, election-related violence at the beginning of 1998 claimed more than 150 lives. In an effort to disrupt a Bharatiya Janata Party rally on 14 February, Islamic militants in Coimbatore conducted a series of bombings that killed 50 and wounded more than 200.

The Indian and Pakistani Governments each claim that the intelligence service of the other country sponsors bombings on its territory. The Government of Pakistan acknowledges that it continues to provide moral, political, and diplomatic support to Kashmiri militants but denies allegations of other assistance. Reports continued in 1998, however, of official Pakistani support to militants fighting in Kashmir.

Japan

Three years after the sarin nerve gas attack on the Tokyo subway system in March 1995, the prosecution of high-level Aum Shinrikyo religious cult leaders—including cult founder Shoko Asahara—continues. Press reports indicate that, if it maintains its current sluggish pace, the trial could take 30 years to complete. Japanese security officials reported a rise in Aum Shinrikyo membership and business activity in 1998, despite a severe police crackdown on the group following the sarin attack. The United States designated Aum Shinrikyo a foreign terrorist organization in 1997 pursuant to the Antiterrorism and Effective Death Penalty Act of 1996.

On 3 June the highest criminal court in Lebanon rejected an appeal made by five convicted Japanese Red Army members and endorsed their three-year prison sentence for forgery and illegal residency. Tokyo has asked that they be deported to Japan upon completion of their jail terms.

Pakistan

Sectarian and political violence surged in Pakistan in 1998 as Sunni and Shia extremists conducted attacks against each other, primarily in Punjab Province, and as rival wings of an ethnic party feuded in Karachi. The heightened political violence prompted the imposition of Governor's rule in Sindh Province in October. According to press reports, more than 900 persons were killed in Karachi from January to September, the majority by acts of domestic terrorism.

In the wake of US missile strikes on terrorist training camps in Afghanistan, several Pakistani-based Kashmiri militant groups vowed revenge for casualties their groups suffered. At a press conference held in Islamabad in November, former Harakat ul-Ansar and current Harakat ul-Mujahidin (HUM) leader Fazlur Rehman Khalil reportedly vowed: "We will kill one hundred Americans for one Muslim." Other Kashmiri and domestic Pakistani sectarian groups also threatened to target US interests. The leader of the Lashkar-i-Taiba declared a jihad against the United States, and the leader of the Lashkar-i-Jhangvi vowed publicly to kill US citizens and offered his support to Bin Ladin.

Pakistani officials stated publicly that, while the Government of Pakistan provides diplomatic, political, and moral support for "freedom fighters" in Kashmir, it is firmly against terrorism and provides no training or materiel support for Kashmiri militants. Kashmiri militant groups continued to operate in Pakistan, however, raising funds and recruiting new cadre. These activities created a fertile ground for the operations of militant and terrorist groups in Pakistan, including the HUA and its successor organization, the HUM.

Philippines

The new government of President Joseph Estrada continued the previous administration's attempts to reach a peaceful settlement with rebels of the Moro Islamic Liberation Front. In August the two sides pledged to begin substantive talks in September. By yearend, however, little progress had been made toward ending the conflict, and both sides continued to engage in low-level violence. The Communist New People's Army also was active in 1998, conducting a series of attacks on rural police posts throughout the country.

Clashes between government forces and various insurgent groups were particularly violent in the southern province of Mindanao. In this remote region the Philippine Armed Forces sporadically engaged militants of the MILF and the smaller, more extremist Abu Sayyaf Group. These periodic military sweeps appear to have weakened both groups. The ASG, in particular, suffered a major setback in late December when government security forces killed its leader during an ambush.

Islamic insurgents were responsible for several international terrorist incidents in the Philippines in 1998. In early September, suspected MILF and ASG militants conducted a rash of kidnappings of foreign nationals, including three Hong Kong businessmen and an Italian priest. Two months later, one group of rebels freed the Italian after 100 MILF fighters surrounded the rebels' jungle hideout and forced his release.

Sri Lanka

The Liberation Tigers of Tamil Eelam conducted significant levels of terrorist activity in 1998. The LTTE attacked government troops, bombed economic and infrastructure targets, and assassinated political opponents. An LTTE suicide vehicle bombing at the Temple of the Tooth in Kandy in January 1998 killed the three suicide bombers and 13 civilians—including three children—and injured 23. The LTTE's deadliest terrorist act in 1998 was a vehicle bomb explosion in the Maradana district of Colombo in March that killed 36 persons—including five schoolchildren—and wounded more than 250.

The LTTE assassinated several political and military officials in 1998. In May a suicide bomber killed a senior Sri Lankan Army commander, Brigadier Larry Wijeratne. Three days after that attack, armed gunmen assassinated newly elected Jaffna Mayor S. Yogeswaran—a widow of an LTTE-assassinated Tamil politician—in an attack claimed by the Sangilian Force, a suspected LTTE front group. In July an LTTE mine explosion killed Tamil parliamentarian S. Shanmuganathan, his son, and three bodyguards. In September an LTTE bomb planted in a Jaffna government building killed new Jaffna Mayor P. Sivapalan and 11 others.

During the year, the LTTE conducted numerous attacks on infrastructure and commercial shipping. In the first half of 1998 the LTTE bombed several telecommunications and power facilities in Sri Lanka. In August the LTTE stormed a Dubai-owned cargo ship, the Princess Kash, which was carrying food, concrete, and general supplies to the Jaffna Peninsula. The Tigers took hostage the 21 crewmembers—including 16 Indians—but released the Indians five days later.

"Operation Sure Victory," the Sri Lankan military's ground offensive aimed at reopening and securing a ground supply route through LTTE-held territory in northern Sri Lanka, continued through 1998. The offensive ended in December about 40 kilometers short of its goal. The Sri Lankan military immediately initiated a new offensive in the same area.

The Sri Lankan Government strongly supported international efforts to address the problem of terrorism in 1998. Colombo was quick to condemn terrorist attacks in other countries and has raised terrorism issues in several international venues, including the UN General Assembly in New York and the UN High Commission for Refugees in Geneva. Sri Lanka was the first country to sign the International Convention for the Suppression of Terrorist Bombings at the United Nations in January.

There were no confirmed cases of LTTE or other terrorist groups targeting US interests or citizens in Sri Lanka in 1998. Nonetheless, the Sri Lankan Government was quick to cooperate with US requests to enhance security for US personnel and facilities and cooperated fully with US officials investigating possible violations of US law by international terrorist organizations. Sri Lankan security forces received training in explosive incident countermeasures, vital installation security, and post-blast investigation under the US Anti-Terrorism Assistance Program.

Thailand

On February 18 the Thai Supreme Court overturned the conviction of Iranian Hossein Dastgiri, who had been prosecuted for a plot in 1994 to bomb the Israeli Embassy in Bangkok. The court ruled that conflicting eyewitness testimony failed to demonstrate beyond a reasonable doubt that Dastgiri was the driver of the bomb-laden truck. In southern Thailand, Muslim separatists of the New Pattani United Liberation Organization conducted a series of bombings in January. Thai authorities launched a military counteroffensive in mid-January that netted several PULO militants. These arrests, combined with unprecedented assistance from Malaysia, where PULO militants had traditionally found refuge, helped to restore calm in the south.

Eurasia Overview

In Russia, several prominent local officials were killed and some US and Russian citizens were kidnapped in Chechnya and the North Caucasus region. At least some of the killings appeared politically motivated, including the assassination of Russian State Duma deputy Galina Starovoytova and Shadid Bargishev, head of the Chechen antikidnapping squad. Some Chechen insurgents have links to terrorist Usama Bin Ladin.

Georgian President Eduard Shevardnadze survived an assassination attempt by supporters of a former president in 1998. The arrest of some of his attackers provoked further incidents and led to Russian cooperation in the arrest and extradition of an individual alleged to have conspired in planning the attack. The breakaway region of Abkhazia witnessed the abduction of four UN military observers in July and the ambush and wounding of UN observers in September.

The Kazakhstan Government averted a potential threat to the US Embassy in Almaty by arresting and expelling three Iranian Government agents for illegal activities. Four members of a United Nations mission of observers to Tajikistan were killed while on patrol 150 kilometers outside of Dushanbe. Of the various terrorist incidents that occurred in Tajikistan in 1998, this was of greatest concern to the international community.

Armenia

On 1 April local US Embassy guards discovered and safely disarmed a handgrenade outside the US Ambassador's residence. There was no claim of responsibility.

Georgia

Supporters of deceased former Georgian President Zviad Gamsakhurdia, known as "Zviadists," and ethnic Chechen mercenaries attempted to assassinate Georgian President Eduard Shevardnadze on 9 February. The assailants launched a well-organized attack against Shevardnadze's motorcade late in the evening using rocket-propelled grenades and automatic weapons. Shevardnadze survived the attack—the second against him in three years—but it almost succeeded. Two officers of Shevardnadze's protective service and one of the attackers, an ethnic Chechen, died in the ensuing gunfight. The government arrested 11 of the assailants within days of the attack.

Subsequently, some 15 of Shevardnadze's assailants kidnapped four United Nations observers from their compound in Zugdidi, western Georgia, to ensure the assailants' escape and their colleagues' release. The hostages escaped or were released following a dialogue between the Shevardnadze government and former members of Gamsakhurdia's faction. Some of the hostage takers surrendered, but Gocha Esebua, the Zviadist leader of the assassination team, escaped. According to press reports, Georgian police killed Esebua in a shootout on 31 March after they tracked him to a house in western Georgia.

Georgian officials also apprehended former Gamsakhurdia government Finance Minister Guram Absandze, the alleged mastermind of the assassination attempt. Russian security authorities detained Absandze in Smolensk, Russia, on 16 March and extradited him to Georgia three days later, where he was formally arrested.

Violence in Georgia's breakaway region of Abkhazia accounted for several incidents that involved foreign personnel. In July four UN military observers were taken hostage. On 21 September three UN military observers and their Abkhaz driver were wounded in Sukhumi during an ambush on a clearly marked UN vehicle, according to press reporting. Two of the injured were military observers from Bangladesh, and the third victim was a UN employee from Nigeria.

Kazakhstan

During 1998 the United States and Kazakhstan cooperated to avert potential security threats to the US Embassy in Almaty. In February, Committee for National Security (KNB) authorities arrested—and subsequently expelled—three Iranian Ministry of Intelligence and Security agents for illegal activities. The Government of Kazakhstan did not publicize details of the Iranian agents' activities or prosecute them before their expulsion, however. The US Government and the Government of Kazakhstan signed a joint statement on combating terrorism in November.

Kyrgyzstan

According to press reports, Kyrgyzstani security authorities alleged that Islamic extremists, vaguely identified as "Wahhabis," conducted two bombings in 1998 in Osh, Kyrgyzstan's second-largest city located in the Fergana Valley. On 30 May an explosion occurred in a public minibus, killing two persons and wounding 10, while an explosion in an apartment the next day killed two persons. The motive behind the explosions was unclear because of insufficient information. Nonetheless, Wahhabism, a fundamentalist Sunni Islamic sect originating in Saudi Arabia, never has been widespread in Kyrgyzstan.

Russia

The assassination on 20 November of noted reformist and Russian State Duma deputy Galina Starovoytova by unidentified assailants—possibly a politically motivated contract killing—highlights both the terrorist tactics used by domestic antagonists to influence Russian politics and Moscow's inability to curb this violence. Chechen militants assassinated Shadid Bargishev, head of the Chechen antikidnapping squad, on 25 October in reaction to widely publicized antikidnapping operations in Chechnya's capital, Groznyy. No one claimed responsibility for an explosive device that detonated under Chechen President Aslan Maskhadov's car in June. Maskhadov escaped without injury, but four others were killed in the attack.

At least three US citizens were kidnapped in Russia for financial gain in 1998. On 18 March unknown assailants abducted two US missionaries in Saratov, Russia, took their money and bank cards, and released them on 22 March. No ransom appears to have been paid. On 11 November in Makhachkala, Dagestan, unidentified assailants kidnapped US citizen Herbert Gregg, a member of a nondenominational Protestant organization based in Illinois. Russian authorities continue to investigate the incident.

Numerous abductions occurred in Russia's North Caucasus region during 1998. Most involved ransom demands, although political motives cannot be excluded. Some Chechen groups in 1998 used kidnapping to raise money, and hostages could be sold and resold among various Chechen kidnapping groups, according to Russian officials. Several foreigners and hundreds of Russian civilians and soldiers kidnapped in the region still are missing. On 20 January, Vincent Cochetel, a French citizen who led the United Nations Human Rights Commission's North Caucasus office, was abducted. He finally was released on 12 December. Four British employees of Granger Telecom were kidnapped in early October and on 8 December were found murdered. On 1 May, Valentin Vlasov, President Boris Yeltsin's representative to Chechnya, was kidnapped by unknown assailants. He was released on 13 November.

Mujahidin with extensive links to Middle Eastern and Southwest Asian terrorists aided Chechen insurgents with equipment and training. The insurgents were led by Habib Abdul Rahman, alias Ibn al-Khattab, an Arab *mujahidin* commander with links to Usama Bin Ladin. Khattab's forces launched attacks against Russian military targets, but their activities in Russia were localized in the North Caucasus region.

Tajikistan

Security for the international community in Tajikistan did not improve significantly in 1998, as a number of criminal and terrorist incidents—including bombings, assaults, and murders—took place. The most serious incident occurred on 20 July when attackers shot and killed four members of the United Nations mission of observers to Tajikistan while on patrol some 150 kilometers east of Dushanbe. Tajikistani authorities later arrested three former Tajikistani opposition members, who initially confessed to the killings but later recanted.

In September the US State Department ordered the suspension of Embassy operations in Dushanbe. The decision was made because of threats to US facilities worldwide following the US Embassy bombings on 7 August in East Africa, turmoil in Tajikistan, and the Embassy's limited ability to secure the safety of US and foreign personnel in the facility.

Europe Overview

The number of terrorist incidents declined in Europe in 1998, in large part because of increased vigilance by security forces and the recognition by some terrorist groups that longstanding political and ethnic controversies should be addressed in negotiations. Terrorism in Spain was attributable almost entirely to the Basque Fatherland and Liberty (ETA) group. In Turkey, most incidents were related to the Kurdistan Workers' Party (PKK). In Greece, a variety of anarchist and terrorist groups continued to operate with virtual impunity. The deadliest terrorist act occurred in Omagh, Northern Ireland, when a splinter Irish Republican Army (IRA) group exploded a 500-pound car bomb that killed 29 persons, including children.

In Northern Ireland, the Catholic and Protestant communities made a major commitment to end the violence by signing the Good Friday Accord. Under the leadership of the British and Irish Governments, both communities and the political parties that represent them agreed to compromises that are to create new, local governmental institutions for resolving conflicts and turn away from terrorism as an accepted political instrument. In support of the peace process, most paramilitary terrorist groups on both nationalist and loyalist sides agreed to a cease-fire. The issue of "decommissioning" the IRA's weaponry and bombs continued to complicate the process, however.

In Spain, the terrorist ETA declared a cease-fire on 16 September to provoke negotiations with the central government. Public outrage throughout Spain over the ETA assassinations of several local Spanish officials earlier in 1998 and the government's infiltration and dismantling of several ETA "commandos" in recent years prompted the group's cease-fire. Strong French legal pressure also eroded the ETA's support base in neighboring French provinces.

The Turkish Government's threat to act against PKK safehavens in neighboring Syria led Damascus to expel PKK leader Abdullah Ocalan, who for years had been directing PKK terrorist activities from his villa there. Ocalan's departure and subsequent flight to seek a new safehaven left the PKK in some disarray, although its members conducted several deadly suicide bombings in Turkey after his departure from Syria.

The Greek Government's counterterrorist efforts remained ineffective. The Revolutionary Organization 17 November group struck six times in early 1998, and several other groups claimed responsibility for bombings in various locations in Greece. The Greek Government has not arrested a single 17 November member in the 23 years since the group killed its first victim, a US Embassy employee; the group subsequently eliminated 22 other persons.

In Germany, the remnants of the Red Army Faction (RAF) announced the dissolution of their organization, once among the world's deadliest. The declaration suggested that the remaining members realized their terrorist group had lost its purpose.

Albania

Albania took an active stance against international terrorism in 1998 by launching a campaign of arrests and investigations against suspected Egyptian Islamic Jihad (EIJ) terrorists operating in the capital, Tirana. In late June, Albanian security forces captured four Egyptian extremists and rendered them immediately to Egypt. Despite public EIJ threats, Albanian police continued to pursue the group. In October security forces raided an EIJ safehouse, killing one suspected terrorist.

While these examples demonstrate the government's commitment to fight terrorism, Albania's poor internal security provides an environment conducive to terrorist activity.

Belgium

Belgian police arrested 10 suspected Armed Islamic Group (GIA) members in March during raids in Brussels. Police seized false documents, detonators, and some small caliber weapons. During a follow-up raid, police uncovered explosives in a GIA supporter's home. The arrests were part of a joint security operation with France, Britain, Sweden, and Italy before the World Cup soccer match in Paris.

In April, Belgium prosecuted three suspected GIA members for the grenade attack in December 1995 on two police officers in Bastogne. Two suspects, Kamel Saddeddine and Youssef El Majda, were convicted and sentenced to five years in prison. The other, Ah El Madja, also was convicted and sentenced to serve three years.

France

French authorities initiated a large-scale security effort across Europe before France hosted the World Cup soccer match last summer. In late May police apprehended about 100 suspected Algerian GIA members during simultaneous operations in France, Germany, Italy, Belgium, and Switzerland. Antiterrorism magistrate Jean-Louis Bruguiere described the coordinated effort as a "preventive" measure to protect the games.

In 1998, French authorities brought numerous terrorists to justice for past acts of violence. In September, French prosecutors began a mass trial of 138 Algerian terrorists for a wave of bombings committed in 1995 and 1996. Controversy marred the two-month trial, however, and more than 50 politicians signed a petition denouncing the proceedings as unfair and racist. Those convicted received sentences ranging from four months to 10 years.

In late November, France prosecuted eight suspected members of Algeria's Islamic Salvation Front (FIS) on charges of smuggling arms to terrorists. The suspects allegedly belong to a network headed by FIS leader Djamel Lounici, currently under house arrest in Italy pending trial. A French court already has sentenced Lounici in absentia to five years in prison for arms smuggling in another case concerning Morocco.

Germany

The Red Army Faction announced its "self-dissolution" in April, following more than two decades of struggle against the German Government. Meanwhile, German courts continued to adjudicate cases against RAF members for terrorist acts committed in the 1980s.

German police took an active stance against terrorism in 1998. Acting on a request from the United States, they detained Salim Mamdouh Mahmud, an associate of Usama Bin Ladin, in September and extradited him to the United States in December. In the weeks before the World Cup soccer match, they worked closely with the French to disrupt Algerian terrorist networks in Germany.

On the judicial front, the trial of five suspected terrorists continued for their part in the La Belle discotheque bombing in 1986 in Berlin. Controversy has plagued the trial from the start, and at the current pace a verdict is not expected before the year 2000.

The German Government showed less resolve in November when PKK leader Abdullah Ocalan arrived unannounced in Rome. Germany withdrew its longstanding international arrest warrant for the Kurdish terrorist leader after PKK militants threatened riots and violence in German cities if Ocalan were prosecuted there. The German action effectively precluded Ocalan's extradition from Italy.

Greece

The majority of the international terrorist incidents committed in Europe in 1998 occurred in Greece. Most of these attacks were firebombings that numerous leftist and anarchist groups conducted against businesses and Greek Government offices. The government made arrests in connection with only one attack.

Greece's most deadly terrorist group, the Revolutionary Organization 17 November, claimed responsibility for six attacks against US or US-related businesses in Athens between February and April, including a rocket attack on a Citibank office. As in the past, Greek efforts failed to achieve any tangible success against 17 November terrorists. To augment their counterterrorism capability, Greek officials met in September with FBI Director Louis Freeh. The discussions improved Greek cooperation with US law enforcement agencies.

In January an Athens appeals court denied Italy's petition to extradite Enrico Bianco, a former Red Brigades member whom Greek police arrested in November 1997 and subsequently freed. Bianco continues to live freely in Greece.

Greek relations with Turkey remained tense as numerous members of the Greek Parliament continued to court PKK members. In April some Greek parliamentarians attended a reception hosted by the PKK's political wing, the ERNK. At the reception a self-proclaimed PKK representative announced plans to open an office in Athens under the PKK's rubric. Greek officials interceded to prevent the opening.

In November, 109 Greek parliamentarians—mostly from the governing PASOK party—signed a letter reiterating a standing invitation to PKK leader Abdullah Ocalan to visit Greece. The Greek Government distanced itself from the invitation, saying Ocalan was not welcome. In November, Ocalan arrived in Rome at the beginning of what became an odyssey to gain asylum in Europe. (After his capture in Nairobi in February 1999, it became known that Ocalan had transited Greece at least twice during his travels with the knowledge and assistance of highly placed Greek officials. At one point, Ocalan remained in Greece for several days. Senior Greek officials took responsibility for providing Ocalan with haven in the Greek Embassy residence in Kenya in February 1999.)

Italy

On 12 November, PKK leader Abdullah Ocalan arrived unexpectedly in Rome and requested political asylum. He initially was detained there on an international warrant issued by Germany. Italy declined to act on a Turkish extradition request, citing Turkey's long-unused capital punishment statute, which prohibits extradition to countries with capital punishment. Italy also declined to exercise its option under international law to prosecute Ocalan. After Bonn withdrew the warrant, the Italians told Ocalan he was free to leave. After trying unsuccessfully to find a country willing to take him, Italian officials said he no longer was welcome in Italy. Ocalan eventually left for Russia, with the apparent assistance of Italian officials, beginning an odyssey that culminated in his seizure in Kenya in February 1999.

In October police arrested five Islamic terrorists in Turin for weapons violations and reported links to Usama Bin Ladin. The next month police arrested suspected GIA terrorist Rahid Fetter in Milan on charges of forgery, counterfeiting, and membership in a subversive organization. The Italians accused Fetter of providing shelter, funds, and false identification papers to GIA militants.

Latvia

A series of bomb attacks in the Latvian capital, Riga, targeted Russian and Jewish interests in 1998. On 2 April a bomb exploded in the courtyard of the main Jewish synagogue in Riga's historic Old Town. The blast caused extensive damage to the main entrance and a swastika-adorned Latvian flag was found on the scene, according to press reporting. On 5 April a mine exploded in a park across the street from the Russian Embassy in Riga. The explosion did not damage the Embassy, but it shattered the windows of four Embassy vehicles. These incidents, which occurred late at night, caused no casualities. There were no claims of responsibility, but authorities suspect members of Eduard Limonov's Russian National Bolshevist Party, a Russian ultranational group. On 19 October, Israeli officials discovered a mail bomb during a routine check of packages mailed to the Israeli Embassy in Riga. Latvian authorities safely destroyed the device.

Spain

The terrorist group Basque Fatherland and Liberty announced a unilateral and unconditional cease-fire on 16 September. At yearend the cease-fire was holding. ETA has not renounced terrorism and continued to engage in terrorist activity before the cease-fire. In 1998, the ETA killed six persons, compared with 13 in 1997. On 3 November, President Aznar called for direct talks with ETA to make the cease-fire permanent, but the two sides appear to have differing agendas for the talks. The government is offering some measures of relief for 530 ETA prisoners in Spanish jails and an estimated 1,000 exiles, while ETA wants to include political issues of sovereignty and self-determination.

The Spanish Government energetically and successfully has sought extradition of ETA fugitives from some countries, including France and several Latin American nations. A Spanish request for extradition from the United States of accused ETA terrorist Ramon Aldasoro was delayed in 1998, but on 4 February 1999 the US Court of Appeals for the Eleventh Circuit in Atlanta paved the way for Aldasoro's extradition.

In addition to ongoing police and law enforcement action to break up ETA commandos and arrest their members, the Spanish Government in 1998 undertook a series of measures designed to debilitate ETA's financial infrastructure. These measures included attempts to limit ETA's fundraising capabilities, shut down businesses with ETA involvement, and locate ETA's financial assets. In July the government shut down the pro-ETA newspaper Egin.

The leftwing terrorist First of October Anti-Fascist Resistance Group (GRAPO) reemerged in 1998 after a three-year hiatus. The government discounts GRAPO's operational capability, but the organization claimed responsibility for a number of bombings and sent extortion letters to businessmen.

Turkey

Turkey achieved some notable successes in its battle against terrorism in 1998, especially against the PKK, its foremost terrorist group. Turkey continued its vigorous campaign against the PKK in southeastern Turkey and northern Iraq. Turkey's large-scale military offensives appear to have affected greatly the PKK's ability to operate in Turkey. In March, Turkish military commandos captured Semdin Sakik, the PKK's second in command, in northern Iraq and bought him to Turkey. Turkish security forces launched a series of successful military campaigns in late spring and early fall that hampered PKK activity in southeast Turkey. In October, Turkey applied intense pressure on the Syrian Government to discourage Syrian support for the PKK. As a result, Syria forced PKK leader Ocalan to leave. Ocalan fled to Russia and then on to Italy where he requested political asylum. Italy subsequently refused to extradite Ocalan to Turkey and Ocalan left Italy. (Turkey scored a major coup against PKK terrorism in February 1999, when Turkish officials tracked down Ocalan in Nairobi, captured him, and brought him back to Turkey to stand trial.)

During 1998 the PKK continued to conduct acts of violence against military and civilian targets. On 10 April, PKK terrorists on a motorcycle threw a bomb into a park near the Blue Mosque in Istanbul. The explosion injured two Indians, a New Zealander, and four Turkish citizens. The PKK also continued its campaign of kidnappings in southeast Turkey. In early June, PKK terrorists kidnapped a German tourist and a Turkish truckdriver at a roadblock in Karakose. The German tourist was found unharmed the next morning near the kidnapping site, but the truckdriver still is missing. Immediately after Ocalan's arrest in Italy, the PKK conducted three suicide bombings in southeastern Turkey, which killed three persons and injured dozens of Turkish citizens, despite Ocalan's public renunciation of terrorism.

Several extreme leftist and other groups were active in Turkey in 1998. Leftist groups operating in Turkey include the Revolutionary People's Liberation Party/Front, Turkish Workers' and Peasants' Liberation Army, Turkish Peoples' Liberation Army, and the Turkish Peoples' Liberation Front. Fundamentalist Islamic organizations operating in Turkey include the so-called "Turkish Hizballah," the Islamic Movement Organization, and the Islamic Great Eastern Raiders Front. Effective Turkish security measures appear to have reduced the threat from these fringe groups over the years. For example, on 31 December, Turkish police arrested the head of the Islamic Great Eastern Raiders Front, Salih Mirzabeyoglou, in Istanbul.

United Kingdom

In April feuding Catholic and Protestant parties signed the landmark Good Friday Accord. This historic agreement outlined a comprehensive power-sharing arrangement between both communities in a multiparty administration of Northern Ireland. For the first time, the Irish Republican Army's political wing, Sinn Fein, was allowed to join the new administration, as long as its leaders remained committed to "exclusively peaceful means." Both sides hotly debated the meaning of this and other provisions in the accord following the signing. The most contentious issue was whether the IRA would abandon its weapons and bombs. Notwithstanding the IRA's commitment to uphold its cease-fire, several splinter groups continued to engage in terrorist activity.

As the debates wore on over the summer, Ireland suffered its worst single terrorist act. On 15 August terrorists from one of the splinter groups, the self-styled Real IRA, exploded a 500-pound car bomb outside a courthouse in downtown Omagh, killing 29 persons and injuring more than 330 others. This attack followed another terrorist bombing by the Real IRA in Banbridge on 1 August, which injured 35 persons and damaged approximately 200 homes.

By November the accord appeared on the verge of collapse as neither side could come to agreement on key issues. Both sides worked vigorously to jump-start negotiations by Christmas so that the new government could take power by February 1999. Only one paramilitary group—one of Northern Ireland's most vicious, the Loyalist Volunteer Force—willingly has surrendered a cache of weapons. Both sides viewed the group's disarmament as a sign that a breakthrough in the stalled peace accord was possible. The IRA continued to resist what it labels a "surrender" of its arms, however, while in its view the conditions that caused the conflict remain unresolved.

The United Kingdom continued to cooperate closely with the United States on counterterrorism issues in 1998. In September, British authorities arrested Khalid al-Fawwaz, a Saudi national, who is wanted by the United States for conspiring to murder US citizens between January 1993 and September 1998. Al-Fawwaz remains in British custody pending his extradition to the United States.

Latin America Overview

Colombia's principal insurgent groups, the Revolutionary Armed Forces of Colombia (FARC) and the National Liberation Army (ELN), stepped up attacks against security forces and civilians in 1998, despite a budding peace process with the Colombian Government. They continued to conduct kidnapping, bombing, and extortion campaigns against civilians and commercial interests.

Bogota pursued peace negotiations while guerrillas launched a concerted offensive against police and military bases throughout the country. By yearend, the government had completed the demilitarization of five municipalities as an incentive for talks, which began in January 1999.

In March, FARC commanders announced they would target US military personnel assisting Colombian security forces, but insurgent attacks—including intensified operations against police and military bases—did not harm US forces. Colombian terrorists continued to target private US interests, however. Guerrillas kidnapped US citizens in Colombia and northern Ecuador, and the FARC refused to account for the whereabouts of three missionaries it kidnapped in January 1993. Guerrillas also continued to bomb US commercial interests, such as oil pipelines and small businesses.

Arrests in Peru contributed to the steady decline in Sendero Luminoso (SL) and Tupac Amaru Revolutionary Movement (MRTA) terrorist capabilities. Peruvian officials arrested two of the four original members of SL's Central Emergency Committee, which comprises the SL's top leaders. The SL failed uncharacteristically to commemorate Peru's Independence Day in July with even a low-level attack or to disrupt municipal elections in October. The MRTA did not launch a terrorist attack in 1998, continuing a trend of relative inactivity since the hostage crisis at the Japanese Ambassador's residence in Lima ended in April 1997.

Switzerland denied Chile's request for the extradition of a terrorist from the dissident wing of the Manuel Rodriguez Patriotic Front, who escaped from a maximum security prison in Santiago in December 1996.

In the triborder area, Argentina, Brazil, and Paraguay consolidated efforts to stem the illicit activities of individuals linked to Islamic terrorist groups. The three countries consulted closely on enforcement efforts and actively promoted regional counterterrorist cooperation.

The Government of Argentina hosted an Organization of American States conference on terrorism and gained the participants' commitment to form a regional commission on counterterrorist initiatives.

Argentina

Investigations continued into the two devastating bombings against Jewish and Israeli targets in Buenos Aires: the attack in March 1992 against the Israeli Embassy in Buenos Aires, in which 29 persons died, and the bombing in July 1994 of the Argentine Israeli Mutual Association (AMIA) building that killed 86 persons and injured hundreds more. Islamic Jihad, Hizballah's terrorist arm, claimed responsibility for the attack in 1992. No clear claim for the AMIA bombing has been made, although the two attacks had many similarities. At yearend, Argentine authorities questioned two possible key informants in the attacks.

The Iranian Government expelled the Argentine commercial attache from Tehran in early 1998 in response to growing criticism in Argentina about a possible official Iranian role in the attacks. The Argentine Government responded by asking Tehran to reduce the number of diplomats in its mission in Buenos Aires to one, the number of official Argentines left in Iran. The judge responsible for the AMIA investigation interviewed Iranian defectors in Western Europe and the United States who claimed to have knowledge about the bombing. He also charged an Argentine citizen with providing the stolen vehicle used in the bombing. Several former Buenos Aires provincial police officials remain in custody for their role in supplying the vehicle.

In August, Argentine authorities arrested two SL members living in Argentina. At yearend, they were awaiting extradition to Peru.

Argentina, Brazil, and Paraguay cooperated actively in the triborder region against terrorism and continued their work to counter criminal activities of individuals linked to Islamic terrorist groups. In March the three countries signed a plan to improve security in the triborder area and created a commission to oversee implementation of the plan.

In late November, Argentina hosted the second Inter-American Specialized Conference on Terrorism in Mar del Plata. Conference participants agreed to recommend that the Organization of American States' General Assembly form an Inter-American Committee on Terrorism to coordinate regional cooperation against terrorism.

Chile

The Swiss Government denied Chile's extradition request for Patricio Ortiz Montenegro, a member of the Manuel Rodriguez Patriotic Front dissident wing who escaped from prison in Santiago on 30 December 1996, because it was concerned that Chile would not safeguard Ortiz's physical and psychological well-being. Chilean authorities continued to pursue the whereabouts of the three other terrorists who escaped with Ortiz.

Colombia

The incipient peace process in Colombia did not inhibit the guerrillas' use of terrorist tactics. The FARC and ELN continued to fund their insurgencies by protecting narcotics traffickers, conducting kidnap-for-ransom operations, and extorting money from oil and mining companies operating in the Colombian countryside.

Colombian insurgents began an offensive against security forces in the summer and retained their military momentum at yearend. The Colombian Government demilitarized five municipalities to meet FARC conditions for peace negotiations, and in mid-December the FARC leader agreed to meet Colombia's President on 7 January 1999 to set the agenda for talks.

FARC commanders announced in March that they would target US military personnel assisting Colombian security forces. The guerrillas did not act on these threats, and their heightened attacks against Colombian police and military bases did not target or incidentally kill or injure US forces.

Colombian terrorists continued to target private US interests, kidnapping seven US citizens in 1998. The FARC abducted four US birdwatchers in March at a FARC roadblock; one escaped and the terrorists released the three others in April. Also in March, the FARC kidnapped one retired US oil worker and released him in September. ELN terrorists in September released one US citizen held since February 1997. The ELN kidnapped two other US citizens in northern Ecuador in October; one hostage escaped, and the kidnappers released the other in late November. The FARC has not accounted for the whereabouts of three missionaries it kidnapped in January 1993.

Terrorists also continued to bomb US commercial interests, such as oil pipelines and small businesses, raising costs to US companies operating in Colombia. There were 77 pipeline bombings during the year. In October the ELN bombed Colombia's central oil pipeline—used by US companies—causing a massive explosion that killed 71 persons, including 28 children. An ELN commander subsequently announced that, despite the unanticipated death toll, the guerrillas would continue to target the nation's oil infrastructure to prevent the foreign "looting" of Colombia's wealth.

Panama

Alleged terrorist Pedro Miguel Gonzalez won the Democratic Revolutionary Party (PRD) candidacy for a seat in the National Assembly. Gonzalez, whose father heads the ruling PRD, was acquitted of the murder in 1992 of US serviceman Zak Hernandez in a Panamanian trial characterized by irregularities and political manipulation. The US case against Gonzalez and one other suspect remains open, and the US Embassy in Panama continues to raise the issue with senior Panamanian authorities.

Panamanian authorities made no arrests in connection with the bombing in 1994 of a commuter airline that killed 21 persons, including three US citizens. US law enforcement agencies continued to investigate the case actively but still had not determined whether the bombing was politically motivated or tied to drug traffickers.

Peru

Peruvian law enforcement and judicial authorities continued to arrest and prosecute members of the SL and MRTA terrorist groups. In 1998 they arrested Pedro Quinteros Ayylon and Jenny Maria Rodriguez Neyra, two of the four original members of SL's 25-person Central Emergency Committee who still were at large. The Peruvian Government also captured Andres Remigio Huarnan Ore, leader of the MRTA military detachment in the Chanchanmayo Valley, and most of that unit's members.

Peru extradited Peruvian citizen Cecilia Nunez Chipana, a Sendero Luminoso militant, from Venezuela. The Peruvian

Government also requested the extradition from Argentina of Peruvian nationals Julio Cesar Mera Collazo and Maria del Rosano Silva, two SL members accused of murder. At yearend the extradition request was pending in Buenos Aires.

Both groups failed to launch a significant terrorist operation in Lima in 1998 and generally limited their activities to low-level attacks and propaganda campaigns in rural areas. The SL continued to attack police stations and other government targets in the Peruvian countryside and in August conducted a particularly brutal attack in Sapasoa, killing the mayor and three of his supporters at a rally. The SL did not commemorate Peru's Independence Day or disrupt municipal elections in October with its characteristic terrorist violence. The MRTA had not engaged in major terrorist activities since the end of the hostage crisis at the Japanese Ambassador's residence in Lima in April 1997.

Middle East Overview

Middle Eastern terrorist groups and their state sponsors continued to plan, train for, and conduct terrorist acts in 1998, although their actions cumulatively were less lethal than in 1997. The lower level of fatalities resulted from more effective counterterrorist measures by various governments and from the absence in 1998 of the kinds of major incidents that had killed dozens the previous year, such as the attack on Luxor temple in Egypt and a series of HAMAS suicide bombings in public places in Israel. The most dramatic terrorist acts attributed to Middle Eastern terrorists in 1998 actually occurred in Africa, where Usama Bin Ladin's multinational al-Qaida network bombed the US Embassies in Nairobi and Dar es Salaam.

In Egypt, government security forces scored some successes in reducing violence by Islamist opponents, particularly the al-Gama'at al-Islamiyya, which had conducted the lethal attack on tourists at Luxor in 1997. Judicial proceedings brought convictions against many terrorists. Deaths from terrorism-related incidents in 1998 fell to 47, fewer than one-third the number in 1997. Nonetheless, there was troubling evidence of a growing collaboration in other countries between Egyptian extremists—from both the Gama' and the Egyptian al-Jihad—and Usama Bin Ladin.

The Algerian Government also made progress in combating domestic terrorism in 1998, undertaking aggressive counterinsurgency operations against the Armed Islamic Group (GIA) that slowed the GIA's campaign of indiscriminate violence against civilians. As the GIA's bloody tactics drew increasing criticism both inside and outside Algeria, other militants joined the unilateral cease-fire that the Islamic Salvation Army had declared in late 1997.

Palestinian groups opposed to the peace process mounted terrorist attacks in Israel, the West Bank, and Gaza. HAMAS conducted car bombings, shootings, and grenade attacks—injuring dozens of civilians—while two terrorists belonging to the Palestine Islamic Jihad (PIJ) launched a suicide bombing at a Jerusalem market. Both Israel and the Palestinian Authority conducted raids and arrests that undercut the extremists' ability to inflict as many fatalities as in previous years.

Security conditions in Lebanon improved in 1998, but the lack of complete government control in parts of Beirut, portions of the Bekaa Valley, and the so-called Israeli security zone in southern Lebanon enabled numerous terrorist groups to operate with relative impunity. Hizballah, HAMAS, the PIJ, and the Popular Front for the Liberation of Palestine-General Command (PFLP-GC) used camps in Lebanon for training and operational planning. The conflict in southern Lebanon between Lebanese armed groups and Israel and its local allies continued unabated.

In Yemen, foreign and indigenous extremists in 1998 conducted several bombings and numerous kidnappings, including the abduction and subsequent release of more than 60 foreign nationals. A group calling itself the Islamic Army of Aden claimed responsibility for the seizure of 16 Western tourists. The terrorists killed four of the hostages when Yemeni Government security forces tried to free them.

Iran, Syria, Libya, and Iraq all persisted in their direct and indirect state sponsorship of terrorism. In most cases, this support included providing assistance, training, or safehaven to terrorist groups opposed to the Middle East peace process. In some cases, particularly Iran and Iraq, it also included targeting dissidents and opponents of these authoritarian regimes for assassination or harassment.

Algeria

The Government of Algeria in 1998 made progress in combating domestic terrorism, which has claimed approximately 75,000 lives since Islamic extremists began their violent campaign to overthrow the government in 1992. The government intensified its counterinsurgency operations against the Armed Islamic Group, and several militant groups in 1998 joined the unilateral cease-fire declared by the Islamic Salvation Army (AIS)—the armed wing of the Islamic Salvation Front (FIS)—in October 1997. The GIA also suffered a number of setbacks to its networks in Europe. No foreign nationals were killed in acts of terrorism in Algeria during the year.

The GIA continued to conduct terrorist operations in Algeria in 1998, targeting a broad spectrum of Algerian civilians. The worst incident of 1998 occurred on 11 January during the holy month of Ramadan, when GIA extremists massacred numerous civilians in Sidi Hamed. Official estimates put the death toll at more than 100 civilians; press accounts reported the death toll even higher. Other smaller civilian massacres and acts of violence also continued throughout the year.

The seemingly indiscriminate and horrific violence against civilians—including women and children—was condemned widely in domestic and international circles and eroded Islamist support for the group abroad. The GIA's campaign of attacking civilians also exacerbated internal divisions: dissident GIA leader Hassan Hattab in May publicly criticized GIA faction leader Antar Zouabri for his attacks on civilians and in September formally separated from the GIA. Hattab created a new element, the Salafi Group for Call and Combat, aimed primarily at attacking security force elements. Despite the split from Zouabri, Hattab's faction continued to commit violence in Algeria throughout 1998. Hattab claimed responsibility for assassinating the popular Berber singer Matoub Lounes in June, an act that further alienated the Algerian public.

Bahrain

Minor security incidents continued to plague Bahrain in 1998. Bahraini security forces in November arrested several Bahraini and Lebanese citizens, seizing weapons and explosives, in connection with a plot to attack public facilities and other installations in Bahrain. Bahraini Prime Minister Shaykh Khalifa claimed the operation was planned in Lebanon, where members of the group reportedly had received military training. Some of those arrested allegedly also confessed to conducting arson attacks.

Bahrain continued in 1998 to seek the extradition of eight individuals—including five in the United Kingdom—who were convicted in absentia in November 1997 for orchestrating and funding from abroad a campaign aimed at disrupting Bahraini security.

Egypt

The number of deaths in 1998 from terrorist-related incidents fell to 47, fewer than one-third of the tally for 1997 and the lowest since 1992. Egyptian security forces increased security and counterterrorist operations against Egyptian extremists, particularly al-Gama'at al-Islamiyya, following its attack in November 1997 at Luxor that killed 58 foreign tourists and four Egyptians. Trials of Egyptian extremists responsible for various terrorist acts were held throughout the year, resulting in several convictions. The improving security situation led tourism to increase in 1998. Egypt also hosted in October an Interpol conference that promoted international cooperation in the fight against terrorism. Egypt also worked closely with other Arab countries in counterterrorism efforts, pursuant to an agreement reached among Arab interior ministers earlier in the year.

Despite the intensified security and counterterrorist actions following the Luxor incident, Egyptian extremists—particularly al-Jihad—continued to levy threats against Egypt and the United States for the arrests and extradition in 1998 of their cadre from Albania, Azerbaijan, South Africa, Italy, and the United Kingdom. Both al-Jihad and al-Gama'at al-Islamiyya signed terrorist sponsor Usama Bin Ladin's *fatwa* in February that called for attacks against US civilians, although al-Gama'at publicly denied that it is a member of Bin Ladin's World Islamic Front for the Jihad Against the Jews and Crusaders. Al-Gama'at leaders imprisoned in Egypt followed the lead of imprisoned Shaykh Umar Abd al-Rahman, issuing a public statement in early November that called for the cessation of operations in Egypt and urged al-Gama'at to create a "peaceful front." Gama'at leaders abroad endorsed the idea but emphasized they would continue to target US interests and support the jihad.

Israel, the West Bank, and Gaza Strip

Violence and terrorism by Palestinian groups opposed to the peace process continued in 1998, albeit at a reduced level as compared with the previous two years. HAMAS alone launched more than a dozen attacks over the year. Among the more notable were grenade attacks in Hebron in September that injured 25 persons and in Beersheva in October that injured more than 50. A HAMAS car bomb in the Gaza Strip in late October killed one Israeli soldier and injured several schoolchildren. The PIJ attempted a car bombing in November in Jerusalem that killed only the two militants.

Other serious attacks against Israel and its citizens also occurred, including the shooting deaths of two settlers on guard duty in early August and the assassination of a prominent rabbi in Hebron later that month. Small bomb explosions in Tel Aviv in August and in Jerusalem in September wounded a total of 13 Israelis.

For its part, Israel continued vigorous counterterrorist operations, including numerous arrests and seizures of weapons and explosives. In one of the most significant actions of the year, Israeli forces on 10 September raided a farmhouse near Hebron, killing two leading HAMAS terrorists, Adil and Imad Awadallah.

The Palestinian Authority (PA), which is responsible for security in Gaza and most major West Bank cities, continued to act against Palestinian perpetrators of anti-Israeli violence. The PA's security apparatus preempted several attacks over the year, including a planned HAMAS double-suicide bombing staged from the Gaza Strip in late September. The PA launched several large-scale arrest campaigns targeting individuals with ties to terrorist organizations and detained several leading HAMAS and PIJ political figures. In one of the more significant operations of the year, the PA in late September uncovered a HAMAS bomb lab filled with hundreds of kilograms of explosives. At the same time, more PA effort is needed to enhance its bilateral cooperation with Israel and its unilateral fight against terrorism.

In late October, the PA and Israel signed the Wye River Memorandum, which includes a number of provisions for increased security cooperation.

Jordan

There were no major international terrorist attacks in Jordan in 1998, but several low-level incidents kept security forces focused on combating the terrorist threat. In February, amid rising tensions over Iraqi weapons inspections, the British Embassy in Amman was the target of a firebomb attack that caused no damage. Between mid-March and early May, the Reform and Defiance Movement—a small, mostly indigenous radical Islamic group—conducted a string of small bombings in Amman targeting Jordanian security forces, the Modern American School, and a major hotel. These attacks caused minor property damage.

Amman continued to maintain tight security along its borders and to interdict and prosecute individuals caught smuggling weapons and explosives, primarily intended for Palestinian rejectionist groups in the West Bank. In September, Amman convicted two Jordanians of possession of illegal explosives with the intent to commit terrorist acts and sentenced them to 15 years in prison with hard labor. The two reportedly had planned to attack Israelis in Israel or the West Bank. In October the state prosecutor referred to the security court the case of six men accused of possessing and selling of explosives to support terrorist aims.

Jordan permitted and monitored the limited presence of several Palestinian rejectionist groups, including HAMAS, the PIJ, the Democratic Front for the Liberation of Palestine, Popular Front for the Liberation of Palestine (PFLP), and the Popular Front for the Liberation of the Palestine-General Command. The Jordanian Government allowed the HAMAS Political Bureau to maintain a small information office in Amman as well as personal offices for senior HAMAS members who live in Jordan, several of whom are Jordanian citizens. In 1998, Jordan did not permit known members of the group's military wing to reside or operate in country, however. In November, Jordan issued a public warning to HAMAS and other rejectionist groups that it would not tolerate acts that "impede implementation" of the Wye River Memorandum.

Jordan continued to cooperate with other regional states concerning terrorist threats to the region and in April signed the multilateral Arab Anti-Terrorism Agreement. King Hussein publicly voiced support for the US-UK initiative in the Pan Am 103 case.

Lebanon

Security conditions in Lebanon continued to improve in 1998, but lack of complete government control in several areas of the country—including portions of the Bekaa Valley and Beirut's southern suburbs—and easy access to arms and explosives throughout much of the country contributed to an environment with the potential for acts of violence. The Lebanese Government did not exert full control over militia groups engaged in fighting in and near the so-called security zone occupied by Israel and its proxy militia, the Army of South Lebanon.

In these areas, a variety of terrorist groups continued to operate with relative impunity, conducting terrorist training and other operational activities. These groups include Hizballah, HAMAS, the Abu Nidal organization (ANO), the PIJ and the PFLP-GC. Hizballah presents the most potent threat to US personnel and facilities in Lebanon by an organized group. Although Hizballah has not attacked US interests in Lebanon since 1991, its animosity toward the United States has not abated, and the group continued to monitor the US Embassy and its personnel in Beirut. Hizballah leaders routinely denounced US policies in the region and sharply condemned the Wye River Memorandum between Israel and the Palestinian Authority.

One anti-US attack occurred in Lebanon in 1998. On 21 June four rocket-propelled grenades were fired at the US Embassy in Beirut from some 700 meters away, falling only a short distance from their launch site and causing no damage. The grenades were launched from a crudely manufactured firing device, suggesting that the attack was not conducted by an organized group. Lebanese authorities responded swiftly to the incident, but as of 31 December investigators had not determined who had conducted the attack and there were no claims of responsibility. The reason for the attack is unclear, but its occurrence two days after Lebanese Prime Minister Hariri had visited Washington suggested it was intended as a sign of displeasure with US-Lebanese relations or was an attempt to embarrass Hariri.

Lebanese citizens also were the targets of random bombings in 1998. Car bombs targeted Amal and PIJ leaders in south Lebanon in October, a resident of Sidon in July, and a Sunni mayoral candidate in west Beirut in May. Although no one was killed, these incidents illustrate the potential danger from random political violence in Lebanon.

The Lebanese Government continued to support publicly international counterterrorist initiatives, and its judiciary system made limited progress in prosecuting terrorist court cases. In early June the Lebanese Supreme Court rejected a defense appeal for a retrial of five Japanese Red Army members and endorsed the three-year prison sentence handed down last year.

Saudi Arabia

There were several reported threats against US interests in Saudi Arabia in 1998 but no terrorist incidents. The US Embassy in Riyadh and Consulates in Jiddah and Dhahran closed for a few days in early October after receiving information that a terrorist attack was being planned against the Embassy.

Terrorist Usama Bin Ladin, whose Saudi citizenship was revoked in 1994, continued publicly to threaten US interests in Saudi Arabia in 1998. In a press conference in Afghanistan in May, Bin Ladin declared a holy war against US forces in the Arabian Peninsula, many of whom are stationed in Saudi Arabia. The declaration followed a communiqué in February in which Bin Ladin and other terrorists called for attacks on US and allied civilians and military interests worldwide.

The investigation into the bombing in June 1996 of the Khubar Towers housing facility near Dhahran, Saudi Arabia, continued in 1998, but it has not been resolved. In that incident, a large truck bomb killed 19 US citizens and wounded more than 500 others. The Saudi Government has requested that the United States extradite Hani al-Sayegh—a Saudi national arrested by the Canadians and deported to the United States in 1997—so they may question him about his alleged role in the bombing. At the end of 1998 a decision on al-Sayegh's extradition case was pending with the US Immigration and Naturalization Service. In November, Saudi Interior Minister Prince Nayif stated publicly that Bin Ladin was not responsible for the Khubar Towers bombing or the bombing in November 1995 of the Office of the Program Manager-Saudi Arabia National Guard (OPM/SANG) facility in Riyadh, which killed seven persons. Nayif allowed that individuals motivated by Bin Ladin could have conducted the attacks, however.

Tunisia

There were no terrorist incidents reported in Tunisia in 1998. The Government of Tunisia remains publicly committed to countering terrorist threats, particularly from Islamic extremists. The government continued publicly to express its opposition to international terrorism, strongly condemning the terrorist attacks in August against the US Embassies in Nairobi and Dar es Salaam. Tunis also remains concerned about Algeria's violence spilling over into Tunisia and employs strict domestic security controls to counter this threat.

Tunisia continued to participate in regional counterterrorism efforts. In January the government hosted a meeting of Arab League interior ministers at which an agreement was reached to enhance inter-Arab counterterrorism cooperation. Tunisia agreed to extradite convicted terrorists, improve information exchanges, and strengthen control on the infiltration and travel of suspected terrorists in Arab countries.

The government continued to prosecute individuals for membership in the outlawed An-Nahda movement, which it considers a terrorist organization, although there were no reports of terrorist attacks by the group in 1998. On 2 June a Tunisian court found two Tunisian nationals guilty of assassinating Belgian Vice Premier Andre Cools in Liege in 1991 and sentenced them to 20-year prison terms.

Yemen

A series of bombings in 1998 in Sanaa and southern Yemen caused numerous casualties and some property damage. A bombing in April at a mosque near Sanaa killed two persons and injured 27 others, including two US citizens. In response to the bombings, Yemeni authorities in August announced the arrest of several Yemeni oppositionists, alleging they were working for "foreign parties." Interior Minister Arab also blamed "foreign groups" for a bombing in September at a market in Aden that caused two deaths and 27 injuries. In August the United States warned US citizens in Yemen of a threat to US interests there, days after terrorists bombed the US Embassies in Kenya and Tanzania. Three persons were killed and several were injured in November when a car bomb exploded near the German Embassy in Sanaa.

Yemeni tribesmen kidnapped and released more than 60 foreign nationals in l998, more than three times the number abducted in 1997. The Islamic Army of Aden—a little known Islamic group that has issued anti-US threats—claimed responsibility for the kidnapping in late December of 16 Western tourists, including two US citizens. Four of the tourists died, and two others—including one US citizen—were wounded during a Yemeni Government rescue attempt that liberated the remaining hostages. Following the incident, the group issued a statement calling for the lifting of sanctions against Iraq. In addition, gunmen in December shot and wounded a US citizen working on a Dutch agricultural development project while they were attempting to hijack his car. The Yemeni Government issued a decree in August implementing severe punishment—including execution—for kidnappers and stepped up enforcement of the law on unlicensed weapons in major cities.

Continuing efforts begun in 1997, the Yemeni Government took further steps to rein in foreign extremists. Sanaa increased its security cooperation with other Arab countries and reportedly forced several foreign extremists to leave Yemen. The government also instituted the requirement that Algerian, British, Egyptian, Libyan, Sudanese, and Tunisian nationals seeking entry into Yemen travel directly from their home counties. Nevertheless, the government's inability to control many remote areas continued to make the country a safehaven for terrorist groups.

Patterns of Global Terrorism 1999

The Year in Review

The number of persons killed or wounded in international terrorist attacks during 1999 fell sharply because of the absence of any attack causing mass casualties. In 1999, 233 persons were killed and 706 were wounded, as compared with 741 persons killed and 5,952 wounded in 1998.

The number of terrorist attacks rose, however. During 1999, 392 international terrorist attacks occurred, up 43 percent from the 274 attacks recorded the previous year. The number of attacks increased in every region of the world except in the Middle East, where six fewer attacks occurred. There are several reasons for the increase:

- In Europe individuals mounted dozens of attacks to protest the NATO bombing campaign in Serbia and the Turkish authorities' capture of Kurdish Workers' Party (PKK) terrorist leader Abdullah Ocalan.
- In addition, radical youth gangs in Nigeria abducted and held for ransom more than three dozen foreign oil workers. The gangs held most of the hostages for a few days before releasing them unharmed.

Terrorists targeted US interests in 169 attacks in 1999, an increase of 52 percent from 1998. The increase was concentrated in four countries: Colombia, Greece, Nigeria, and Yemen.

- In Colombia the number of attacks against US targets, including bombings of commercial interests and an oil pipeline, rose to 91 in 1999.

- In Greece anti-NATO attacks frequently targeted US interests.
- In Nigeria and Yemen, US citizens were among the foreign nationals abducted.

Five US citizens died in these attacks:

- The Revolutionary Armed Forces of Colombia (FARC) kidnapped three US citizens working with the U'Wa Indians in Northeastern Colombia on 25 February. Their bodies were found on 4 March and were identified as Terence Freitas, Ingrid Washinawatok, and Lahe'ena'e Gay.
- A group of Rwandan Hutu rebels from the Interahamwe in the Bwindi Impenetrable National Park in Uganda kidnapped and then killed two US citizens, Susan Miller and Robert Haubner, on 1 March.

In 186 incidents in 1999, bombings remained the predominant type of terrorist attack. Since 1968, when the United States Government began keeping such statistics, more than 7,000 terrorist bombings have occurred worldwide.

Law Enforcement

The United States brought the rule of law to bear against international terrorists in several ongoing cases throughout the year:

- On 19 May the US District Court in the Southern District of New York unsealed an indictment against Ali Mohammed, charging him with conspiracy to kill US nationals overseas. Ali, suspected of being a member of Usama Bin Ladin's al-Qaida terrorist organization, had been arrested in the United States in September 1998 after testifying before a grand jury concerning the US Embassy bombings in East Africa.
- Authorities apprehended Khalfan Khamis Mohamed in South Africa on 5 October, after a joint investigation by the Department of State's Diplomatic Security Bureau, the Federal Bureau of Investigation (FBI), and South African law enforcement authorities. US officials brought him to New York to face charges in connection with the bombing of the US Embassy in Dar Es Salaam, Tanzania, on 7 August 1998.
- Three additional suspects in the Tanzanian and Kenyan US Embassy bombings currently are in custody in the United Kingdom, pending extradition to the United States: Khalid Al-Fawwaz, Adel Mohammed Abdul Almagid Bary, and Ibrahim Hussein Abdelhadi Eidarous. Eight other suspects, including Usama Bin Ladin, remain at large. The FBI added Bin Ladin to its Ten Most Wanted Fugitives list in June. The Department of State's Rewards for Justice program pays up to $5 million for information that leads to the arrest or conviction of these and other terrorist suspects.
- On 15 October, Siddig Ibrahim Siddig Ali was sentenced to 11 years in prison for his role in a plot to bomb New York City landmarks and to assassinate Egyptian President Hosni Mubarak in 1993. Siddig Ali was arrested in June 1993 on conspiracy charges and pleaded guilty in February 1995 to all charges against him. His cooperation with authorities helped prosecutors convict Shaykh Umar Abd al-Rahman and nine others for their roles in the bombing conspiracy.
- In September the US Justice Department informed Hani al-Sayegh, a Saudi Arabian citizen, that he would be removed from the United States and sent to Saudi Arabia. Authorities expelled him from the United States to Saudi Arabia on 11 October, where he remains in custody. He faces charges there in connection with the attack in June 1996 on US forces in Khubar, Saudi Arabia, that killed 19 US citizens and wounded more than 500 others. Al-Sayegh was paroled into the United States from Canada in June 1997. After he failed to abide by an initial plea agreement with the Justice Department concerning a separate case, the State Department terminated his parole in October 1997 and placed him in removal proceedings.

African Overview

Africa in 1999 witnessed no massive terrorist attacks as devastating as the bombings one year earlier of the US Embassies in Kenya and Tanzania, although evidence continued to emerge of terrorist activity and networks—both indigenous and foreign—on the continent. Terrorist organizations such as al-Qaida, the Palestinian Islamic Jihad, the Gama'at al-Islamiyya, and Hizballah posed a threat to US targets and interests throughout Africa and elsewhere. In the region's most deadly attack, Rwandan Hutu rebels murdered two US citizens and a number of tourists in March.

Angola

Insecurity continued to plague Angola in 1999. Angola's main guerrilla faction, the National Union for the Total Independence of Angola (UNITA), committed several acts of international terrorism as a tactic in its decades-old insurrection. In January, UNITA guerrillas ambushed a vehicle, killing one British national, one Brazilian, and two Angolan security guards. On 10 February, UNITA rebels reportedly kidnapped two Portuguese and two Spanish nationals. The next day, UNITA rebels attacked the scout vehicle for a convoy of diamond mine vehicles, killing three Angolan security guards and wounding five others. Five Angolan citizens were killed on 14 April when unidentified assailants attacked a Save the Children vehicle in Salina. UNITA's bloodiest terrorist assault was the ambush of a German humanitarian convoy near Bocoio on 6 July. Guerrilla forces killed at least 15 persons and injured 25 others.

In addition to assaults on isolated vehicle convoys, UNITA attacked three civilian aircraft in 1999. On 13 May, UNITA rebels claimed they had shot down a privately owned plane and abducted three Russian crewmembers. UNITA again claimed responsibility for shooting down a private aircraft on 30 June. One of the five Russian crewmembers died when the aircraft crash landed near Capenda-Camulemba. Three weeks later, UNITA rebels fired mortars at an International Committee for the Red Cross aircraft parked at Huambo airport but caused no injuries or damage.

Cabinda Liberation Front separatists are believed responsible for the kidnapping in mid-March of one Angolan, two French, and two Portuguese oil workers in the northern enclave of Cabinda. In past years the separatists have taken hostages to earn ransom and to pressure the Angolan Government to relinquish control over the region.

Ethiopia

Ogaden National Liberation Front rebels on 3 April kidnapped a French aid worker, two Ethiopian staff workers, and four Somalis. The next day, the group's "political secretary" announced the French hostage had been "pardoned" and was to be released to French diplomats.

Liberia

Two major kidnapping incidents occurred in Liberia in 1999. On 21 April unidentified assailants crossed the border from Guinea and laid siege to the town of Voinjama, kidnapping the visiting Dutch Ambassador, a Norwegian diplomat, a European Union representative, and 17 aid workers. The attackers, whom eyewitnesses said belonged to the United Liberation Movement for Democracy in Liberia, released all hostages later the same day. In August an armed gang kidnapped four British nationals, one Norwegian citizen, and one Italian national. The gang released them unharmed two days later.

Nigeria

Ethnic violence flared in Nigeria during the year as bloody feuds broke out among various indigenous groups battling for access to and control of limited local resources. Poverty-stricken Nigerians across the nation, particularly in the oil-producing southern regions, demanded a larger share of the nation's oil wealth. Radical ethnic Ijaw youth resorted to violence against oil firms as a means of expressing their grievances. The gangs abducted more than three dozen foreign oil workers, including 16 British nationals and four US citizens. The militant youths demanded ransoms from the victims' employers as well as compensation from the government on behalf of their village, ethnic group, or larger community. In most cases the youths held the hostages for only a few days before releasing them unharmed.

Sierra Leone

Security problems in Sierra Leone spiked during the first half of 1999 as insurgent forces mounted a last-gasp offensive on the capital in January. Revolutionary United Front (RUF) rebels took captive several foreign missionaries during the RUF's siege of Freetown. The failure of this offensive and a general sense of battle fatigue led guerrilla forces to sign a peace and ceasefire agreement in July, and Sierra Leone remained relatively calm for the remainder of the year. Violent flareups occurred sporadically, however, as the government tried to regain control of the countryside.

The most significant of the post-cease-fire incidents was the kidnapping of more than three dozen foreign nationals at a rebel demobilization and prisoner exchange ceremony. On 4 August members of an Armed Forces Revolutionary Council (AFRC) faction kidnapped 10 United Nations military observers, 14 regional peacekeepers, and eight civilians. Among the hostages were 14 Nigerian soldiers, seven British nationals, three Zambians, and two US citizens. The AFRC militants demanded the release of their leader, Johnny Paul Koromah, and humanitarian aid. After Koromah assured them that he was not imprisoned in the capital, the AFRC militants released most of hostages the next day and the rest on 10 August.

South Africa

Islamist militants associated with Qibla and People Against Gangsterism and Drugs (PAGAD) continued to conduct bombings and other acts of domestic terror in Cape Town. Only two of the attacks affected foreign interests, when unidentified youths on 8 and 10 January firebombed Kentucky Fried Chicken restaurants in Cape Town, causing major damage but no injuries.

Uganda

On 14 February a pipe bomb exploded inside a crowded bar, killing five persons and injuring 35 others. One Ethiopian and four Ugandans died in the blast. Among the injured were two Swiss nationals, one Pakistani, one US citizen, and 27 Ugandans. Ugandan authorities blamed the bombing and a number of other terrorist incidents in the capital on Islamist militants associated with the Allied Democratic Forces based along the border with the Democratic Republic of Congo.

Rwandan Hutu rebels attacked three tourist camps in the Bwindi National Forest on 1 March, kidnapping 14 tourists, including three US citizens, six British nationals, three New Zealanders, one Australian, and one Canadian. The rebels killed two US citizens, four British nationals, and two New Zealanders before releasing the others the next day. One month later, on 3 April, suspected Rwandan Hutu rebels based in the Democratic Republic of Congo again crossed over into Uganda and attacked a village in Kisoro, killing three persons.

Zambia

At least 16 bombs exploded across Lusaka on 28 February. One bomb exploded inside the Angolan Embassy, killing one person and causing major damage. Other bombs detonated near major water pipes, around powerlines, and in parks and residential districts, injuring two persons. There were no claims of responsibility.

South Asia Overview

In 1999 the locus of terrorism directed against the United States continued to shift from the Middle East to South Asia. The Taliban continued to provide safehaven for international terrorists, particularly Usama Bin Ladin and his network, in the portions of Afghanistan they controlled. Despite the serious and ongoing dialogue between the Taliban and the United States, Taliban leadership has refused to comply with a unanimously adopted UNSC resolution demanding that they turn Bin Ladin over to a country where he can be brought to justice.

The United States made repeated requests to Islamabad to end support for elements harboring and training terrorists in Afghanistan and urged the Government of Pakistan to close certain Pakistani religious schools that serve as conduits for terrorism. Credible reports also continued to indicate official Pakistani support for Kashmiri militant groups, such as the Harakat ul-Mujahidin (HUM), that engaged in terrorism.

In Sri Lanka the government continued its protracted conflict with the Liberation Tigers of Tamil Eelam (LTTE).

Afghanistan

Islamist extremists from around the world—including North America; Europe; Africa; the Middle East; and Central, South, and Southeast Asia—continued to use Afghanistan as a training ground and base of operations for their worldwide terrorist activities in 1999. The Taliban, which controlled most Afghan territory, permitted the operation of training and indoctrination facilities for non-Afghans and provided logistic support to members of various terrorist organizations and *mujahidin,* including those waging *jihads* in Chechnya, Lebanon, Kosovo, Kashmir, and elsewhere.

Throughout the year, the Taliban continued to host Usama Bin Ladin—indicted in November 1998 for the bombings of two US Embassies in East Africa—despite US and UN sanctions, a unanimously adopted United [Nations] Security Council resolution, and other international pressure to deliver him to stand trial in the United States or a third country. The United States repeatedly made clear to the Taliban that they will be held responsible for any terrorist acts undertaken by Bin Ladin while he is in their territory.

In early December, Jordanian authorities arrested members of a cell linked to Bin Ladin's al-Qaida organization—some of whom had undergone explosives and weapons training in Afghanistan—who were planning terrorist operations against Western tourists visiting holy sites in Jordan over the millennium holiday.

On 25 December the Taliban permitted hijacked Indian Airlines flight 814 to land at Qandahar airport after refusing it permission to land the previous day. The hijacking ended on 31 December when the Indian Government released from prison three individuals linked to Kashmiri militant groups in return for the release of the passengers aboard the aircraft. The hijackers, who had murdered one of the Indian passengers during the course of the incident, were allowed to go free. The Taliban stated that the hijackers, who reportedly are Kashmiri militants, would leave Afghanistan even if they were unable to obtain political asylum from another country. Their whereabouts remained unknown at yearend.

India

Security problems persisted in India in 1999 from ongoing insurgencies in Kashmir and the northeast. Kashmiri militant groups continued to attack Indian Government, military, and civilian targets in India-held Kashmir and elsewhere in the country. The militants probably bombed a passenger train traveling from Kashmir to New Delhi on 12 November, killing 13 persons and wounding 50. Militant groups operating in Kashmir also mounted a grenade attack against a wedding in Srinagar, Kashmir's summer capital, which wounded at least 20 wedding participants. In the northeast, Nagaland's Chief Minister escaped injury on 29 November when a local extremist group attacked his convoy. The attack killed two of his guards and injured several others.

The Indian Government took a number of steps against terrorism at home and abroad. In August the Indian cabinet ratified the international convention for the suppression of terrorist bombings. New Delhi also introduced a convention on the suppression of terrorism at the UN General Assembly meeting. Indian law enforcement authorities continued to cooperate with US officials to ascertain the fate of four Western hostages—including one US citizen— kidnapped in 1995 in Indian Kashmir, although the hostages' whereabouts remained unknown. New Delhi announced in November 1999 the establishment of a US-India Counterterrorism Working Group, which aimed to enhance efforts to counter international terrorism worldwide.

Pakistan

Pakistan is one of only three countries that maintains formal diplomatic relations with—and one of several that supported—Afghanistan's Taliban, which permitted many known terrorists to reside and operate in its territory. The United States repeatedly has asked Islamabad to end support to elements that conduct terrorist training in Afghanistan, to interdict travel of militants to and from camps in Afghanistan, to prevent militant groups from acquiring weapons, and to block financial and logistic support to camps in Afghanistan. In addition, the United States has urged Islamabad to close certain madrasses, or "religious" schools, that actually serve as conduits for terrorism.

Credible reports continued to indicate official Pakistani support for Kashmiri militant groups that engage in terrorism, such as the Harakat ul-Mujahidin (HUM). The hijackers of the Air India flight reportedly belong to one of these militant groups. One of the HUM leaders, Maulana Masood Azhar, was freed from an Indian prison in exchange for the hostages on the aircraft in the Air India hijacking in December and has since returned to Pakistan.

Kashmiri extremist groups continued to operate in Pakistan, raising funds and recruiting new cadre. The groups were responsible for numerous terrorist attacks in 1999 against civilian targets in India-held Kashmir and elsewhere in India. Pakistani officials from both Prime Minister Nawaz Sharif's government and, after his removal by the military, General Pervez Musharraf's regime publicly stated that Pakistan provided diplomatic, political, and moral support for "freedom fighters" in Kashmir—including the terrorist group Harakat ul-Mujahidin—but denied providing the militants training or materiel.

On 12 November, shortly after the United Nations authorized sanctions against the Taliban, but before the sanctions were implemented, unidentified terrorists launched a coordinated rocket attack against the US Embassy, the American center, and possibly UN offices in Islamabad. The attacks caused no fatalities but injured a guard and damaged US facilities.

Sectarian and political violence remained a problem in 1999 as Sunni and Shia extremists conducted attacks against each other, primarily in Punjab Province, and as rival wings of an ethnic party feuded in Karachi. Pakistan experienced a particularly strong wave of such attacks across the country in August and September. Domestic violence dropped significantly after the military coup on 12 October.

In the wake of US diplomatic intervention to end the Kargil conflict that broke out in April between Pakistan and India, several Pakistani and Kashmiri extremist groups stridently denounced US interference and activities. Jamiat-e-Ulema Islami leaders, for example, reacted to US diplomacy in the region by harshly and publicly berating US efforts to bring wanted terrorist Usama Bin Ladin, who is based in Afghanistan, to justice for his role in the 1998 US Embassy bombings in Nairobi and Dar es Salaam. The imposition of US sanctions on 14 November against Afghanistan's Taliban for its continued support for Bin Ladin drew a similar response.

Sri Lanka

The separatist group Liberation Tigers of Tamil Eelam (LTTE), which the United States has designated a Foreign Terrorist Organization, maintained a high level of violence in 1999, conducting numerous attacks on government, police, civilian, and military targets. President Chandrika Kumaratunga narrowly escaped an LTTE assassination attempt in December. The group's suicide bombers assassinated moderate Tamil politician Dr. Neelan Tiruchelvam in July and killed 34 bystanders at election rallies in December. LTTE gunmen murdered a Tamil Member of Parliament from Jaffna representing the Eelam People's Democratic Party and the leader of a Tamil military unit supporting the Sri Lankan Army.

Over the year, LTTE attacks against police officers killed 50 and wounded 77. Bombings of buses, trains, and bus terminals in March, April, and September killed four persons and injured more than 80, and Sri Lankan authorities attributed several bombings of telecommunications and power facilities to the LTTE. In July an LTTE suicide diver bombed a civilian passenger ferry while it was in Trincomalee port, and the group's Sea Tigers naval wing attacked a Chinese vessel that had come too close to the Sri Lankan coastline. The LTTE allegedly massacred more than 50 civilians in September, apparently retaliating against a Sri Lankan Air Force bombing that killed 21 Tamil civilians. The LTTE is suspected in the shooting death in Jaffna of a regional military commander for the progovernment People's Liberation Organization of Tamil Eelam (PLOTE) and may be responsible for bombings at a PLOTE office and a camp in Vavuniya that killed three and injured seven.

LTTE activity against the Sri Lankan Government centered on the continuing war in the north. The Sri Lankan military's offensive to open and secure a ground supply route through LTTE-held territory suffered a major defeat when the LTTE fought a series of intense battles in early November and regained control of nearly all land the government had captured in the past two years. The battles resulted in thousands of casualties on both sides.

There were no confirmed cases of LTTE or other terrorist groups targeting US citizens or businesses in Sri Lanka in 1999. Nonetheless, the Sri Lankan Government was quick to cooperate with US requests to enhance security for US personnel and facilities and cooperated fully with US officials investigating possible violations of US law by international terrorist organizations. Battlefield requirements forced Sri Lankan security forces to cancel their participation in a senior crisis management seminar under the Department of State's Anti-Terrorism Assistance Program in 1999.

East Asia Overview

The scorecard for terrorism in East Asian nations in 1999 was mixed, with some countries enjoying significant improvements and others suffering an upswing of attacks. The most positive development occurred in Cambodia, where the Khmer Rouge's once-deadly threat all but ended with the group's dissolution as a viable terrorist organization.

Political disagreements frequently were the inspiration for terrorist acts in East Asia. In Indonesia the overwhelming East Timor vote in favor of independence provoked violent reprisals by militias on that island as well as in Jakarta. In addition, a US-owned oil company's facilities were targeted in Aceh, Sumatra.

Japan's Aum Shinrikyo, which was redesignated a Foreign Terrorist Organization (FTO) in October, admitted to and apologized for its sarin attack on Tokyo's subway in 1995. Facing increasing public pressure, the Japanese Government instituted legal restrictions on the group. In response, the Aum announced plans to suspend its public activities as of 1 October. The Government of Japan also continued to seek the extradition of Japanese Red Army (JRA) members from Lebanon and Thailand.

Several groups in the Philippines engaged in or threatened violent acts. The Communist Party of the Philippines New People's Army (CPP/NPA) broke off peace talks in June in retaliation for the government's Visiting Forces Agreement with the United States that provides for joint military training exercises. While the CPP/NPA only threatened to attack US forces, it targeted Philippine security forces in numerous incidents. Both the separatist group Moro Islamic Liberation Front (MILF), as well as the redesignated FTO Abu Sayyaf Group (ASG), were blamed for various attacks and kidnappings for ransom.

In Thailand five prodemocracy students staged a takeover on 1 October of the Burmese Embassy in Bangkok, holding 32 persons hostage, including one US citizen. The incident ended without violence.

Cambodia

The Khmer Rouge (KR) insurgency ended in 1999 following a series of defections, military defeats, and the capture of group leader Ta Mok in March. The KR did not conduct international terrorism in 1999, and the US Government removed it from the list of designated Foreign Terrorist Organizations. Former KR members, however, still posed an isolated threat in remote areas of the country. Suspected ex-KR soldiers, for example, attacked a hill tribe in northeastern Cambodia in July in an apparent criminal incident.

The Cambodian Government worked on drafting a law for the United Nations to assist in establishing a court to try former KR members who were senior leaders of the regime responsible for the deaths of up to 2 million persons in Cambodia during the 1975-79 period. A former KR official warned in September, however, that unrest would resurface if the Cambodian Government put the KR on trial.

Indonesia

The ballot results on 30 August favoring East Timor's independence sparked prointegration militias—armed East Timorese favoring unity with Indonesia—to mount a violent campaign throughout September against proindependence supporters. A number of militia members accused the United Nations of manipulating the ballot results, leading some militia units to seek foreign targets in the province. Incidents included the serious wounding of a US police officer working for the UN Assistance Mission to East Timor, an attack against the Australian Ambassador's vehicle, and an assault against the Australian Consulate in Dili, East Timor's capital. Militiamen also allegedly killed a Dutch *Financial Times* reporter in a Dili suburb on 21 September after his motorcycle driver tried to flee six armed men. In a separate incident the same day, prointegrationists ambushed a British journalist and a US citizen photographer in Bacau, east of Dili, but Australian troops later rescued the two.

A prointegration militia leader told former Indonesian Armed Forces Commander General Wiranto in early September that he would have no regrets about killing nongovernmental organization or UN persons who supported the proindependence side. Militia threats and attacks against foreigners, however, dropped dramatically after late September, when the situation began to stabilize.

Indonesian nationalists, mostly in Jakarta, responded to the referendum and the subsequent deployment of the International Force for East Timor with protests and low-level violence against perceived interference in their country's internal affairs. In late September the Australian Embassy in Jakarta was the target of almost daily demonstrations that included petrol bombs and stone throwing. Gunmen fired shots at the Australian Embassy on three separate occasions in apparent anger over Canberra's role in the international peacekeeping mission. In addition, unidentified assailants threw Molotov cocktails at the Australian International School in Jakarta on 4 October, but no injuries resulted. As of 25 October, pursuant to a UN Security Council resolution, the United Nations Transitional Administration in East Timor assumed all legislative and executive authority in East Timor and responsibility for the administration of justice.

Separatist violence flared in other parts of the country, particularly in Aceh, Sumatra, where the Free Aceh Movement and its sympathizers clashed with Indonesian security forces throughout the year. The separatists, demanding a referendum on Aceh independence, primarily attacked Indonesian targets, but US interests in the province suffered collateral damage. Unidentified assailants, for example, fired at a Mobil Oil bus and burned a Mobil-operated community health clinic on two separate occasions in late September. Free Papua Movement separatists located in Irian Jaya did not attack foreign interests but conducted some violent protests and low-level attacks against Indonesian targets in 1999.

Several small-scale bombings of undetermined motivation also occurred in Indonesia during the year, including the attack against the National Istiqlal Mosque in Jakarta that injured six persons on 19 April. In addition, unidentified assailants conducted other bombings that injured several Indonesians in Jakarta's city center following the presidential election in October.

Japan

Aum Shinrikyo, the Japanese cult that conducted the sarin attack on the Tokyo subway system in March 1995, continued efforts to rebuild itself in 1999. The group's recruitment, training, fundraising—especially a computer business that generated more than $50 million—and property acquisition, however, provoked numerous police raids and an extensive public backlash that included protests and citizen-led efforts to monitor and barricade Aum facilities.

In an effort to alleviate public pressure and criticism, Aum leaders in late September announced the group would suspend its public activities for an indeterminate period beginning 1 October. The cult openly pledged to close its branch offices, discontinue public gatherings, cease distribution of propaganda, shut down most of its Internet Web site, and halt property purchases beyond that required to provide adequate housing for existing members. The cult also said it would stop using the name "Aum Shinrikyo." On 1 December, Aum leaders admitted the cult conducted the sarin attack and other crimes—which they had denied previously—and apologized publicly for the acts. The cult made its first compensation payment to victims' families in late December.

Japanese courts sentenced one Aum member to death and another to life in prison for the subway attack, while trials for other members involved in the attack remain ongoing. The prosecution of cult founder Shoko Asahara continued at a sluggish pace, and a verdict remained years away. Japanese authorities remained concerned over the release in late December of popular former cult spokesman Fumihiro Joyu—who served a three-and-a-half-year jail sentence for perjury—and his expected return to the cult as a senior leader. The Japanese parliament in December passed legislation strengthening government authority to crack down on groups resembling the Aum and allowing the government to confiscate funds from the group to compensate victims. The Public Security Investigation Agency stated that it would again seek to outlaw the Aum under the Anti-Subversive Activities Law. Separately, the Japanese Government continued to seek the extradition of members of the Japanese Red Army (JRA) from Lebanon and Thailand.

Philippines

The Communist Party of the Philippines New People's Army (CPP/NPA) broke off peace talks with the Philippine Government in June after the ratification of the US-Philippine Visiting Forces Agreement (VFA), which provides a legal framework for joint military training exercises between Philippine and US armed forces. The CPP/NPA continued to oppose a US military presence in the country and claimed that the VFA violates the nation's sovereignty. Communist insurgents did not target US interests during the year, but a Communist member told the press in May that guerrillas would target US troops taking part in the joint exercises. Press reporting in September alleged CPP/NPA plans to target US Embassy personnel at an unspecified time.

The CPP/NPA continued to target Philippine security forces in 1999. The organization conducted several ambushes and abductions against Philippine military and police elements in rural areas throughout the country. The CPP/NPA released most of its hostages unharmed by late April but still was holding Philippine Army Major Noel Buan and Philippine Police Official Abelardo Martin at yearend.

The Alex Boncayao Brigade (ABB)—a breakaway CPP/NPA faction—claimed responsibility for a rifle grenade attack on 2 December against Shell Oil's headquarters in Manila that injured a security guard. The attack apparently protested an increase in oil prices.

Islamist extremists also remained active in the southern Philippines, engaging in sporadic clashes with Philippine Armed Forces and conducting low-level attacks and abductions against civilian targets. The groups did not attack US interests in 1999, however. The Abu Sayyaf Group (ASG)—redesignated in 1999 as a Foreign Terrorist Organization—in June abducted two Belgians and held them captive for five days before releasing them unharmed without ransom. The ASG still was working to fill a leadership void resulting from the death of Abdurajak Abubakar Janjalani, who was killed in a clash with the Philippine Army on 18 December 1998.

The Philippine Government and the Moro Islamic Liberation Front (MILF), the largest Philippine Islamist separatist group, marked the opening of peace talks on 25 October. Nonetheless, both sides continued to engage in low-level clashes. MILF chief Hashim Salamat told the press in February that the group had received from Usama Bin Ladin funds that it used to build mosques, health centers, and schools in depressed Muslim communities.

Distinguishing between political and criminal motivation for many of the terrorist-related activities in the Philippines was difficult, most notably in the numerous cases of kidnapping for ransom in the south. Both Communist and Islamist insurgents sought to extort funds from businesses or other organizations in their operating areas, often conducting reprisal operations if money was not paid. Philippine police officials, for example, said that three separate bomb attacks in August against a bus company in the southern Philippines may have been the work of extortionists rather than terrorists.

Thailand

Five prodemocracy students armed with AK-47s and grenades seized the Burmese Embassy in Bangkok and held 32 hostages on 1 October. The hostages included 20 individuals applying for visas, one of whom was a US citizen. The terrorists demanded that the Burmese Government release all political prisoners in Burma and recognize the results of a national election held in 1990. No injuries occurred, and the situation was resolved the next day after the Thai Deputy Foreign Minister offered himself as a hostage in exchange for the safety of the hostages inside the Burmese Embassy. The five terrorists and the Deputy Foreign Minister were taken by helicopter to a remote jungle area on the Thai-Burmese border. The Burmese fled into the jungle. (At least one and perhaps three of the five were shot to death by Thai security forces on 25 January 2000 after participating in the seizure of a Thai provincial hospital.)

Some low-level bombings and hoax bomb threats also occurred in Thailand during the year, although no US interests suffered damage. Most of the incidents were directed against Thai interests, including the bombing of the Democratic Party headquarters in Bangkok on 14 January. Thai authorities suspect that a bomb found and defused at the construction site of a new post office in the south on 15 April was planted by members of the separatist New Pattani United Liberation Organization to avenge government operations against the group.

Eurasia Overview

Five gunmen attacked Armenia's Parliament in October, killing eight members, including the Prime Minister and National Assembly Speaker. Later in the year a grenade was thrown at the Russian Embassy, damaging several cars but causing no injuries.

A major Central Asian regional crisis erupted in Kyrgyzstan when members of the Islamic Movement of Uzbekistan (IMU) twice crossed the border from Tajikistan and took hostages. Among the several dozen hostages taken in the second incident were four Japanese geologists, who eventually were released after several nations intervened; ransom was rumored to have been paid.

Russian cities, including Moscow, were subjected to several bomb attacks, which killed and injured hundreds of persons. Police accused the attackers of belonging to Chechen and Dagestan insurgent groups with ties to Usama Bin Ladin and foreign *mujahidin* but presented no evidence linking Chechen separatists to the bombings. The attacks prompted Russia to send military forces into Chechnya to eliminate "foreign terrorists." Neighboring Caucasus states within the Russian Federation as well as surrounding countries feared Russia's military campaign in Chechnya would increase radicalization of Islamic internal populations and encourage violence and the spread of instability throughout the region. The Russian campaign into Chechnya also raised fears in Azerbaijan and Georgia, as well as Russia, that the Chechen insurgents increasingly would use those countries for financial and logistic support.

Uzbekistan experienced several major attacks by IMU insurgents seeking to overthrow the government. In February five coordinated car bombs exploded, killing 16 persons, in what the government labeled an attempt on the President's life. In September the IMU declared a *jihad* against the Uzbekistani Government. In November the IMU was blamed for a violent encounter outside the capital city of Tashkent that killed 10 Uzbekistani Government officials and 15 insurgents.

Armenia

On 27 October five Armenian gunmen opened fire on a Parliament session, killing eight government leaders, including Prime Minister Vazgen Sarkisyan and National Assembly Speaker Karen Demirchyan. The gunmen claimed they were protesting the responsibility of government officials for dire social and economic conditions in Armenia since the collapse of the Soviet Union in 1991. The gunmen later surrendered to authorities and at yearend were being detained with 10 other Armenians accused of complicity. An investigation of the incident was ongoing.

Russian facilities in Armenia also came under attack. On 25 November a grenade was thrown into the Russian Embassy compound in Yerevan, causing no injuries but damaging several cars.

Azerbaijan

Although Azerbaijan did not face a serious threat from international terrorism, it served as a logistic hub for international *mujahidin* with ties to terrorist groups, some of whom supported the Chechen insurgency in Russia. Azerbaijan increased its border controls with Russia when the Chechen conflict reignited during the year to prevent foreign *mujahidin* from operating within its borders.

Georgia

On 13 October terrorists kidnapped seven UN observers near Abkhazia and demanded a significant ransom for their release. Georgian officials secured the victims' freedom within two days, however, without acceding to the kidnappers' demands.

Georgia also faced spillover violence from the Chechen conflict and, like Azerbaijan, contended with international *mujahidin* seeking to use Georgia as a conduit for financial and logistic assistance to the Chechen fighters. Russia pressured the Georgian Government to introduce stronger border controls to stop the flow of men and arms. Russian officials also alleged that armed Chechen fighters entered Georgia with refugees to hide until a possible Chechen counterattack against Russia in the spring of 2000.

Violence again colored Georgian domestic politics, especially attacks against senior leaders. Although no attacks were conducted against the President this year, Georgian security officials disrupted an alleged coup plot in May, and other prominent officials were the victims or targets of political and criminal violence.

Kyrgyzstan

International terrorism shocked Kyrgyzstan for the first time in August when armed Islamic Movement of Uzbekistan (IMU) militants twice crossed into Kyrgyzstan and instigated a two-and-one-half-month hostage crisis. From 6 to 13 August, IMU militants from Tajikistan held four Kyrgyzstanis hostage in southern Kyrgyzstan before they released them without incident and retreated to Tajikistan. The militants returned in a larger force on 22 August and seized 13 hostages, including four Japanese geologists, their interpreter, a Kyrgyzstani Interior Ministry general, and several Kyrgyzstani soldiers. IMU militants continued to arrive in subsequent weeks, numbering as many as 1,000 at the incursion's peak.

The IMU's implicit goal was to infiltrate Uzbekistan and destabilize the government. The militants first demanded safe passage to Uzbekistan; additional demands called for money and a prisoner exchange. Uzbekistan refused to allow them to enter, leaving Kyrgyzstan's ill-prepared security forces to combat the terrorists with Uzbekistani military assistance, Russian logistic support, and negotiation assistance from other governments. The militants' guerrilla tactics enabled them to maintain their position in difficult mountainous terrain, frustrating the Kyrgyzstani military's attempts to dislodge them. Observers speculated that only the approach of winter forced the militants to retreat into Tajikistan, where negotiators were able to facilitate an agreement between the IMU and Kyrgyzstani representatives.

On 25 October the militants finally released all hostages

except a Kyrgystani soldier they had executed. Kyrgyzstan released an IMU prisoner, but Kyrgyzstani and Japanese officials denied Japanese press reports that they paid a monetary ransom for the hostages' release. Although an agreement stipulated that all IMU militants would leave Tajikistani territory after the hostage crisis, some IMU militants may have remained in the region. Central Asian officials and most external observers feared that a similar IMU incursion into Kyrgyzstan or Uzbekistan could occur in the spring, either from bases in Tajikistan or from terrorist camps in Afghanistan.

Russia

In the fall a series of bombings in Russian cities claimed hundreds of victims and raised concern about terrorism in the Russian Federation. On 4 September a truck bomb exploded in front of an apartment complex at a Russian military base in Buynaksk, Dagestan, killing 62 persons and wounding 174. Authorities discovered a second bomb on the base the same day and disarmed it before it caused further casualties. On 8 and 13 September powerful explosions demolished two Moscow apartment buildings, killing more than 200 persons and wounding 200 others. The two Moscow incidents were similar, with explosive materials placed in rented facilities on the ground floor of each building and detonated by timing devices in the early morning. The string of bomb attacks continued when a car bomb exploded in the southern Russian city of Volgodonsk on 16 September, killing 17 persons and wounding more than 500 others.

A caller to Russian authorities claimed responsibility for the Moscow bombings on behalf of the previously unknown "Dagestan Liberation Army," but no claims were made for the incidents in Buynaksk and Volgodonsk. Russian police suspected insurgent groups from Chechnya and Dagestan conducted the bombings at the behest of Chechen rebel leader Shamil Basayev and the *mujahidin* leader known as Ibn al-Khattab, although Russian authorities did not release evidence to confirm their suspicions. Russian authorities arrested eight individuals and issued warrants for nine others believed to be hiding in Chechnya but presented no evidence linking Chechen separatists to the bombings.

In response to the apartment building bombings and to an armed incursion by Basayev and Khattab into Dagestan from Chechnya, Russian troops entered Chechnya in October in a campaign to eliminate "foreign terrorists" from the North Caucasus. The forces fighting the Russian army were mostly ethnic Chechens and supporters from other regions of Russia. They received some support from foreign *mujahidin* with extensive links to Middle Eastern, South Asian, and Central Asian Islamist extremists, as well as to Usama Bin Ladin. At yearend, Chechen militant activity had been localized in the North Caucasus region, but Russia and Chechnya's neighboring states feared increased radicalization of Islamist populations would encourage violence and spread instability elsewhere in Russia and beyond.

There were few violent political acts against the United States in Russia during the year. Anti-NATO sentiment during the Kosovo campaign sparked an attack on the US Embassy in Moscow in late March when a protester unsuccessfully attempted to launch a rocket-propelled grenade (RPG) at the facility. The perpetrator sprayed the front of the building with machinegun fire after he failed to launch the RPG. At yearend no progress had been made in identifying or apprehending the assailant.

Tajikistan

Security for the international community in Tajikistan did not improve in 1999. The US Embassy in Dushanbe suspended operations in September 1998 because of the Tajikistani Government's limited ability to protect the safety of US and foreign personnel there. US personnel were moved to Almaty, although they travel regularly to Dushanbe.

The IMU's use of Tajikistan as a staging ground for its incursion into Kyrgyzstan was the most significant international terrorist activity in Tajikistan in 1999. The IMU militants entered Kyrgyzstan from bases in Tajikistan and returned to the area with their Japanese and Central Asian hostages when they fled Kyrgyzstan in late September and October. As part of the agreement that resolved the incident, the Uzbekistani militants left Tajikistan, although some IMU fighters may have remained in some regions of the country.

Uzbekistan

On 16 February five coordinated car bombs targeted at Uzbekistani Government facilities exploded within a two-hour period in downtown Tashkent, killing 16 persons and wounding more than 100 others. Such an attack was unprecedented in a former Soviet republic. Uzbekistani officials feared the attacks were aimed at assassinating President Islom Karimov and suspected the IMU, some of whose members had opposed the Karimov regime for many years. By summer the government had arrested or questioned hundreds of suspects about their possible involvement in the bombings. Ultimately the government condemned 11 suspects to death and sentenced more than 120 others to prison terms.

The IMU threat to Uzbekistan continued, however, with the group's incursion into Kyrgyzstan in August. Although the IMU militants did not attack Uzbekistani soil or personnel at the time, they tried to achieve a foothold in Uzbekistan for future IMU action. The militants in Kyrgyzstan also publicly declared *jihad* against the Uzbekistani Government on 3 September.

In November a group of Uzbekistani forest rangers encountered a group of IMU members in a mountainous region approximately 80 kilometers east of Tashkent. Initially reported to be bandits, the IMU militants killed four foresters and three Ministry of Internal Affairs (MVD) police. An extensive MVD search-and-destroy operation resulted in the death of 15 suspected insurgents and three additional MVD special forces officers. During a press conference, the Minister of the Interior identified some of the insurgents as IMU members who had taken hostages in Kyrgyzstan in August.

Europe Overview

Europe experienced fewer terrorist incidents and casualties in 1999 than in the previous year. Strong police and intelligence efforts—particularly in France, Belgium, Germany, Turkey, and Spain—reduced the threat from Armed Islamic Group (GIA), Revolutionary People's Liberation Party/Front (DHKP-C), Kurdistan Workers' Party (PKK), and Basque Fatherland and Liberty (ETA) terrorists in those countries. Nonetheless, some European governments avoided their treaty obligations by neglecting to bring PKK terrorist leader Abdullah Ocalan to justice during his three-month stay in Italy. Greece's performance against terrorists of all stripes continued to be feeble, and senior government officials gave Ocalan sanctuary and support. There were signs of a possible resurgence of leftwing and anarchist terrorism in Italy, where a group claiming to be the Red Brigades took responsibility for the assassination of Italian labor leader Massimo D'Antono in May.

In the United Kingdom, the Good Friday accords effectively prolonged the de facto peace while the various parties continued to seek a resolution through negotiations. The Irish Republican Army's refusal to abandon its caches of arms remained the principal stumbling block. Some breakaway terrorist factions—both Loyalist and Republican—attempted to undermine the process through low-level bombings and other terrorist activity.

Turkey moved aggressively against the deadly DHKP-C, which attempted a rocket attack in June against the US Consulate General in Istanbul. Following Abdullah Ocalan's conviction on capital offenses, PKK terrorist acts dropped sharply. The decrease possibly reflected a second-tier leadership decision to heed Ocalan's request to refrain from conducting terrorist activity.

Albania

Despite Albania's counterterrorist efforts and commitment to fight terrorism, a lack of resources, porous borders, and high crime rates continued to provide an environment conducive to terrorist activity. After senior US officials canceled a visit to Albania in June because of terrorist threats, Albanian authorities arrested and expelled two Syrians and an Iraqi suspected of terrorist activities. The men had been arrested in February and charged with falsifying official documents but were released after serving a prison sentence.

In October, Albanian authorities expelled two other individuals with suspected ties to terrorists, who officially were in the region to provide humanitarian assistance to refugees. Albanian authorities suspected the two had connections to Usama Bin Ladin and denied them permission to return to Albania.

Austria

As with many west European countries, Austria suffered a Kurdish backlash in the aftermath of the arrest of PKK leader Abdullah Ocalan in Kenya on 16 February. Kurdish demonstrators almost immediately occupied the Greek and Kenyan Embassies in Vienna, vacating the facilities peacefully the following day. Kurds also held largely peaceful protest rallies in front of the US chancery and at numerous other locations across the country. PKK followers subsequently refrained from violence, focusing instead on rebuilding strained relations with the Austrian Government and lobbying for Ankara to spare Ocalan's life. In addition to the PKK, the Kurdish National Liberation Front—a PKK front organization—continued to operate an office in Vienna.

In the fight against domestic terrorism, an Austrian court in March sentenced Styrian-born Franz Fuchs to life imprisonment for carrying out a deadly letter-bomb campaign from 1993 to 1997 that killed four members of the Roma minority in Burgenland Province and injured 15 persons in Austria and Germany. Jurors unanimously found that Fuchs was the sole member of the fictitious "Bajuvarian Liberation Army" on whose behalf Fuchs had claimed to act.

In a shootout in Vienna in mid-September, Austrian police killed suspected German Red Army Faction (RAF) terrorist Horst Ludwig-Mayer. Authorities arrested his accomplice, Andrea Klump, and on 23 December extradited her to Germany to face charges in connection with membership in the outlawed RAF, possible complicity in an attack against the chairman of the Deutsche Bank, and involvement in an attack against a NATO installation in Spain in 1988.

Belgium

In September, Belgian police raided a safehouse in Knokke belonging to the Turkish terrorist group DHKP/C and arrested six individuals believed to be involved in planning and support activities. During the operation officials seized false documents, detonators, small-caliber weapons, and ammunition. All six detainees filed appeals, and, at yearend, Belgian authorities released two of them. The Turkish Government requested the extradition of one group member, Fehriye Erdal, for participating in the murder in 1996 of a Turkish industrialist.

A claim made in the name of the GIA in July threatened to create a "blood bath" in Belgium "within 20 days" if Belgian authorities did not release imprisoned group members. Brussels took the threat seriously but showed resolve in not meeting any of GIA's demands, and no terrorist acts followed the missed deadline. In addition, a Belgian court in October convicted Farid Melouk—a French citizen of Algerian origin previously convicted in absentia by a French court as an accessory in the Paris metro bombings in 1995—for attempted murder, criminal association, sedition, and forgery and sentenced him to imprisonment for nine years. In the same month, Belgium convicted a second GIA member, Ibrahim Azaouaj, for criminal association and sentenced him to two years in prison.

France

France continued its aggressive efforts to detain and prosecute persons suspected of supporting Algerian terrorists or terrorist networks in France. Paris requested the extradition of several suspected Algerian terrorists from the United Kingdom, but the requests remained outstanding at yearend. In addition, the French Government's nationwide "Vigi-Pirate" plan —launched in 1998 to prevent a repeat of the Paris metro attacks by Algerian terrorists—remained in effect. Under the plan, military personnel reinforced police security in Paris and other major cities, particularly at strategic sites such as metro and train stations and during holiday periods. Vigi-Pirate also increased border controls and expanded identity checks countrywide.

French officials in January and February arrested David Courtailler and Ahmed Laidouni, who had received training at a camp affiliated with Usama Bin Ladin in Afghanistan. Laidouni, who also was charged in connection with the "Roubaix" GIA Faction, and Courtailler remained imprisoned in France, and a French magistrate was investigating their cases, although there is no known evidence that they were planning a terrorist act.

Prime Minister Lionel Jospin vowed to increase France's already close and successful cooperation with Spain to track down ETA terrorists taking refuge in or launching attacks from France. French officials arrested some of ETA's most experienced cadre and seized several large weapons and explosives caches. Nonetheless, in September, ETA militants stole large quantities of explosives from an armory in Brittany, some of which were later seized from ETA terrorists in Spain. In late October, French officials arrested ETA terrorist Belen Gonzalez-Penalva, believed to be involved in the car-bomb attack on 9 September 1985 against Spanish security officials that also killed a US citizen. Gonzalez's capture followed a celebrated arrest earlier in September in southwest France of ETA members who may have been operating with Breton separatists. At yearend several senior ETA Basque leaders were on trial in Paris.

On the judicial front, a special court in Paris in March tried and convicted in absentia six Libyan terrorists for their involvement in the bombing in 1989 of UTA flight 772 over Niger and sentenced them to life imprisonment. The court assessed Libya 211 million French francs to compensate the victims' families. By midyear, Libya had transferred the payment to the French Government. France filed lookout notices for the six convicted terrorists with INTERPOL. A French court also allowed an investigating magistrate to file a civil suit on behalf of the victims' families against Libyan leader Muammar Qadhafi for his alleged complicity in the UTA affair.

Germany

German officials saw no signs of renewed leftwing terrorism in 1999. The Red Army Faction (RAF) officially disbanded in March 1998, and authorities uncovered no renewed RAF activity. Several former RAF members still were wanted by German authorities, who assessed that the terrorists were willing to use violence to avoid capture. In mid-September, Austrian police in Vienna killed suspected German RAF terrorist Horst Ludwig-Mayer and arrested his accomplice Andrea Klump. Klump was extradited to Germany for membership in the outlawed RAF, possible complicity in an attack on the Deutsche Bank chairman, and involvement in an attack against a NATO installation in Spain in 1988.

Officials have no evidence of organized, politically motivated rightwing terrorist activity in Germany, but rightwing "skinheads" continued to attack foreigners in 1999. The government stepped up efforts to combat xenophobic violence, including trying some skinheads at the federal level and initiating a program called the "German Forum to Prevent Criminality" to deal with the social causes of violence. Some German states also set up antiterrorist police units that successfully reduced attacks by skinheads.

German police took an active stance against terrorism in 1999. On 19 October a special German commando unit apprehended the hijacker of an Egypt Air flight after the plane landed in Hamburg. The perpetrator, who requested political asylum in Germany, was slated to be tried in German courts. Officials had no reason to believe the hijacker was linked to any terrorist organizations.

Germany showed far less resolve when it refused to seek extradition of PKK terrorist leader Abdullah Ocalan following his detention in Italy in November 1998 on a German INTERPOL warrant. The German Government refused to act because it feared that a trial in Germany would cause widespread street violence, posing an unacceptable threat to Germany's domestic security. This and other factors eventually led the Italians to release Ocalan, whose subsequent flight to Russia and Greece culminated in his capture in Kenya in February. News of Ocalan's capture produced violent Kurdish protests throughout Germany, including demonstrations against US diplomatic facilities and the storming of Greek, Kenyan, and Israeli diplomatic missions. In Berlin, Israeli security personnel shot to death four protesters who had stormed the Israeli Consulate General.

On the judicial front, the trial of five suspects charged in the bombing in 1986 against Labelle Discotheque in Berlin, which killed two US servicemen and one Turkish citizen, progressed slowly in 1999. The trial may take several more years to reach a conclusion.

On 1 September a German court convicted two members of the leftwing terrorist group "Anti-Imperialist Cell" and sentenced them to lengthy jail terms for their ties to a series of bombings in 1995 against several German politicians' residences.

Greece

Greece remained one of the weakest links in Europe's efforts against terrorism. Greece led Europe in the number of anti-US terrorist attacks in 1999 and ranked second worldwide only to Colombia. Greek terrorists committed 20 acts of violence against US Government and private interests in

Greece and dramatically increased their attacks against Greek and third-country targets. The absence of strong public government leadership and initiatives to improve police capabilities and morale contributed to the lack of breakthroughs against terrorists. Popular opinion makers generally downplayed terrorism as a threat to public order, even as terrorists continued to act with virtual impunity.

In attempting to help PKK terrorist leader Abdullah Ocalan find safehaven, senior government officials facilitated Ocalan's transit through Greece and provided temporary refuge in the Greek Ambassador's residence in Nairobi. The Foreign Minister, the Minister of Public Order, the Minister of Interior, and the intelligence chief subsequently resigned for their roles in these actions. After Ocalan's rendition to Turkey, the Greek Government extended political asylum to two of Ocalan's associates. In March the terrorist group Revolutionary Organization 17 November issued a communique blaming the Greek Government, among others, for Ocalan's arrest and challenging the US Government to apprehend them.

NATO action against Serbia precipitated several months of violent anti-US and anti-NATO actions in Greece. From March to May, Western interests suffered some 40 attacks. In early April a woman attempting to firebomb the US Consulate in Thessaloniki was caught by an alert Consulate guard, but Greek authorities released the woman after a few days' detention with a nominal fine. The incident was the only arrest by Greek authorities for a terrorist act committed in 1999. Later in the month, Greek police defused a bomb outside the Fulbright Foundation in Thessaloniki. On 27 April a bomb exploded at the Intercontinental Hotel in Athens, killing one Greek citizen and injuring another; a terrorist group known as Revolutionary Nuclei claimed responsibility. Numerous bomb and other threats against the US Embassy, Consulate, and the American Community School proved to be hoaxes. In response to these incidents, the US Government issued a public announcement in April advising US citizens and travelers of the security conditions in Greece.

Although it never claimed responsibility, 17 November is suspected of conducting seven rocket attacks and bombings against US, Greek, and third-country interests from March through May. The targets included two offices of the governing PASOK party; American, British, and French banks; and the Dutch Ambassador's residence. A rocket attack in May on the German Ambassador's residence yielded excellent forensic evidence, but the Greek police did not follow up aggressively and made no arrests.

Numerous other terrorist attacks during the year involved the use of improvised explosive or incendiary devices or drive-by shootings from motorcycles. President Clinton's visit to Greece in November precipitated violent and widespread anti-US demonstrations and attacks against US, Greek, and third-country targets.

Greece and the United States signed a Mutual Legal Assistance Treaty and, at yearend, nearly had completed a police cooperation agreement. Newly appointed Minister of Public Order Chrysochoidis met in July with US Coordinator for Counterterrorism, Ambassador Michael Sheehan, to discuss improving counterterrorist cooperation. In an October visit to Washington, Chrysochoidis outlined plans to modernize the Greek counterterrorist police. By yearend these promised reforms had not yet yielded results. Greek counterterrorist cooperation with the United States and other Western nations will require substantially greater attention and commitment if Greece is to achieve success.

On 23 December, Greek narcotics police arrested Avraam Lesperoglou, a suspect in six murders and one attempted murder from the 1980s, after he arrived at Athens airport under a false name. Lesperoglou was sentenced to three and one half years on misdemeanor charges relating to his false documents and illegal entry; a trial was pending on the more serious charges. Lesperoglou was believed to be linked to Revolutionary People's Struggle and possibly other terrorist groups.

Italy

The major domestic terrorist act in 1999 was the murder in May of Massimo D'Antona, an adviser to Italy's Labor Minister, by individuals who claimed to be from the Red Brigades, despite the leftist group's dormancy since 1988. Prime Minister D'Alema subsequently said Italy had let down its guard on domestic terrorism in the mistaken belief that homegrown terrorist groups no longer posed a danger. He added that Rome was now working hard to identify and neutralize the group that killed D'Antona.

In spite of that attack, Italy achieved some success against domestic terrorism during the year. Italian law enforcement and judicial officials arrested and sentenced several individuals tied to terrorist groups, while magistrates requested that many more cases be opened in the year 2000. A notable success for Italian security was a raid against the instigators of the demonstration on 13 May at the US Consulate in Florence protesting NATO airstrikes in Kosovo. The instigators included several members of the Red Brigades, *Lotta Continua* (The Continuous Struggle), and the Cobas Union.

The Italian Government dealt ineptly in the matter of PKK terrorist leader Ocalan, who arrived in Rome in November 1998 and requested political asylum. Italian authorities detained him on an international arrest warrant Germany had issued but declined a Turkish extradition request because Italy's Constitution prohibits extradition to countries that permit capital punishment. The Italian Government sought unsuccessfully to find a European trial venue while declining to invoke the 1977 European counterterrorist convention to prosecute Ocalan in Italy. Unable to find a third country willing to take the PKK leader, the government simply told Ocalan he no longer was welcome in Italy.

Ocalan eventually left for Russia with the apparent assistance of Italian officials, beginning an odyssey that culminated in his capture by Turkish security forces in Kenya in February. Following Ocalan's arrest, PKK and other Kurdish sympathizers held demonstrations—some violent—in several Italian cities, including the Greek consulate in Milan. Since

February, however, PKK followers were nonviolent and focused on rebuilding strained relations with the Italian Government and lobbying for Ankara to spare Ocalan's life.

The NATO bombing campaign against Serbia produced leftwing anger and some anti-US violence. The leftist Anti-imperialist Territorial Nuclei, which formed in 1995 and was believed to be allied with former Red Brigades members, held several anti-NATO, anti-US demonstrations. Militant leftists conducted some low-level violence against US interests, such as vandalizing the US airbase at Aviano, and issued public threats to US businesses located in Italy.

Spain

The terrorist group ETA ended its 14-month-old unilateral cease-fire on 27 November, and members of the group conducted low-level attacks in December. Spanish security authorities intercepted two vans loaded with explosives and reportedly headed for Madrid, detaining one driver. ETA and Spanish Government representatives met in Switzerland in May but could not find common ground. The ETA had hoped to use the talks to make progress toward its goal of Basque self-determination and eventual independence, while Madrid pushed for the ETA to declare a permanent end to terrorism and renewed its offer for relief for the group's prisoners and exiles.

The Spanish Government energetically combated the ETA even as it sought a dialogue with the terrorist group. Spanish law enforcement officials, working closely with counterparts in France and other countries where ETA fugitives reside, arrested several of the group's most experienced leaders and cadre and shut down one of its last known commando cells. Spanish and French security forces also confiscated large amounts of explosives, weapons, logistics, and targeting information. Moreover, in late October, French authorities arrested terrorist Belen Gonzalez-Penalva, believed to be involved in the car-bomb attack in 1985 against Spanish security officials that also killed a US citizen. Madrid's request for extradition of accused ETA terrorist Ramon Aldasoro from the United States was delayed by court appeals in 1998. Aldasoro finally was extradited to Spain in late December 1999.

Spain's other domestic terrorist group, the First of October Anti-Fascist Resistance Group (GRAPO), remained largely inactive in 1999, mounting only a few symbolic attacks against property. The last major case involving GRAPO, the kidnapping of a Zaragoza businessman in July 1995, remained unsolved.

Switzerland

On 29 January, Swiss authorities arrested Red Brigades activist Marcello Ghiringhelli and a Swiss accomplice on suspected violations of the war materiels law. Police seized several weapons and rounds of ammunition. The trial started in La Chaux-de-Fonds in December. Italy requested the extradition of Ghiringhelli, who had been sentenced to life imprisonment in Italy.

Switzerland also was caught in the Kurdish backlash in the aftermath of Ocalan's apprehension in Kenya on 16 February. That day about 70 Kurds stormed the Greek Consulate in Zurich, taking hostage a policeman and the building's owner. The same day, 30 to 100 Kurds occupied the Greek Embassy in Bern while another 200 protesters gathered outside. The occupiers carried canisters of gasoline and threatened to immolate themselves but did not follow through. Both incidents ended peacefully.

On 19 February several Kurds took two persons hostage at the Free Democratic Party Headquarters in Bern but released them unharmed a few hours later. The Swiss Government prosecuted the hostage takers in Bern and Zurich but took no further action against the Kurdish protesters in the Greek Embassy because the Greek Embassy did not press charges for trespassing or property damage. On 20 February, PKK sympathizers carried out several arson attacks against Turkish-owned businesses and torched two trucks from Turkey in Basel. At yearend, police investigations were pending. Since February, however, PKK followers were nonviolent, focusing instead on rebuilding strained relations with the Swiss Government and lobbying Ankara to spare Ocalan's life.

Ocalan's arrest, as well as the conflict in Kosovo, gave rise to several demonstrations in front of the US Embassy in Bern. The Swiss Government took no action to ban the events because the protests were organized lawfully, although not always conducted as the organizers had promised. Bern, however, called up approximately 500 Swiss militia from March to November to guard the US and UN missions and other embassies considered to be potential terrorist targets.

Turkey

Turkish authorities struck a significant blow against Kurdistan Workers' Party (PKK) terrorism in mid-February when PKK Chairman Abdullah Ocalan was apprehended after he left his safehaven in the Greek Ambassador's residence in Nairobi, Kenya. The Turkish State Security Court tried Ocalan in Turkey in late June and sentenced him to death for treason, a decision the Supreme Court of Appeals upheld in a ruling issued on 25 November. The government took no further action on the sentence in 1999, although Turkish law requires that all death sentences be ratified by Parliament and endorsed by the President. Ocalan's lawyers requested the European Court of Human Rights (ECHR) review the case. The ECHR asked Turkey to delay a decision on whether Ocalan should be executed until the Court completed its review.

Meanwhile, Ocalan launched a "peace offensive" in early August, requesting a dialogue with Ankara and calling on PKK militants to end the armed struggle against Turkey and withdraw from Turkish territory. The PKK's political wing quickly expressed support for the move, and press reports indicated that several hundred militants had left Turkey by October. In December, Turkish General Staff Chief Kivrikoglu said that 500 to 550 PKK militants remained in Turkey.

Although the PKK exodus to neighboring Iran, Iraq, and Syria is an annual event, it usually starts later in the fall, suggesting that the withdrawal in 1999 was tied to Ocalan's announcement. In addition, two groups of about eight PKK members each turned themselves in to Turkish authorities in October and November as a gesture of goodwill and as a means of testing a new Turkish repentance law.

The leftwing Revolutionary People's Liberation Party/Front (DHKP/C) fell victim to numerous Turkish counterterrorist operations in 1999. Turkish police killed two DHKP/C members in a shootout on 4 June as the terrorists prepared unsuccessfully to fire a light antitank weapon at the US Consulate in Istanbul from a nearby construction site. Authorities also arrested some 160 DHKP/C members and supporters in Turkey and confiscated numerous weapons, ammunition, bombs, and bombmaking materials over the course of the year, dealing a harsh blow to the organization.

Turkish authorities continued to arrest and try Islamist terrorists vigorously in 1999. Nonetheless, militants from the two major groups—Turkish Hizballah, a Kurdish group not affiliated with Lebanese Hizballah, and the Islamic Great Eastern Raiders-Front—managed to conduct low-level attacks.

Meanwhile, there were at least two attempted bombings against Russian interests in Turkey during 1999. On 10 December authorities discovered a bomb outside a building housing the offices of the Russian airline Aero-flot in Istanbul. The bomb weighed approximately 14 kilograms, was concealed in a suitcase, and was similar to a bomb found on the grounds of the Russian Consulate in Istanbul in mid-November. Turkish officials suspect that Chechen sympathizers were responsible.

United Kingdom

The United Kingdom continued its aggressive efforts against domestic and international terrorism in 1999. In December the Blair Government introduced new national antiterrorist legislation meant to replace laws that had been developed to combat terrorism in Northern Ireland. The bill, which is expected to become law by midsummer 2000, would extend most provisions of earlier laws to all forms of international and domestic terrorism. The police would have authority to arrest, detain, confiscate evidence, and seize cash suspected of being used to fund terrorist activities and designated terrorist organizations. The legislation includes provisions for proscribing membership in terrorist groups.

The United Kingdom continued its close cooperation with the United States to bring terrorists to justice. In 1999 the British Government detained numerous individuals suspected of conducting anti-US violence and whom the United States sought to extradite. At yearend, the United Kingdom was holding three of the 15 individuals indicted in the Southern District of New York on charges connected with the bombings in 1998 of the US Embassies in Nairobi and Dar Es Salaam.

In April the Libyan Government handed over the two Libyans charged with the bombing in 1988 of Pan Am flight 103 over Lockerbie, Scotland, after a joint US-UK initiative enabled a Scottish court to sit in the Netherlands to try the accused. Scottish authorities intend to charge the two Libyans with murder, breach of the UK aviation security act, and conspiracy. The trial was set to begin in May 2000.

In the immediate aftermath of the arrest in February of PKK leader Abdullah Ocalan in Kenya, PKK members and supporters staged violent demonstrations in London, and militants occupied the Greek Embassy for two days. British officials subsequently arrested 79 individuals and suspended the broadcast license for Med-TV, a Kurdish satellite television station tied to the PKK. Following subsequent broadcasts that were deemed inflammatory, authorities revoked Med-TV's license. Since February, PKK followers were peaceful, focusing instead on rebuilding strained relations with the British Government and lobbying for Ankara to spare Ocalan's life.

Washington's ties to London and Dublin played a key role in facilitating historic political developments in the Northern Ireland peace process that resulted in a significant decline in terrorist activity. Following a year of intense negotiations and a review of the entire peace process by former US Senator George Mitchell, Britain devolved power to Ulster, and Ireland gave up its constitutional claim to Northern Ireland; the Catholic and Protestant parties agreed to govern Ulster together in a joint Executive, which held its inaugural meeting on 13 December. Much of the contention between the parties was, and remains, about how to address the implementation of the Good Friday Agreement, including the issue of decommissioning paramilitary weapons.

Republican and Loyalist paramilitary splinter groups, including the Continuity IRA, the Real IRA, the Red Hand Defenders, and the Orange Volunteers, continued terrorist activities during the year. These included punishment attacks on civilians as well as actions against police, military, and security personnel. Among the most heinous attacks was the car-bombing murder on 15 March of Rosemary Nelson, a prominent lawyer and human rights campaigner. Although it is widely assumed that hardline loyalist paramilitaries were responsible, no charges were filed in the case. The British Government said that a scaling back or normalization of the security presence in Northern Ireland will be linked to a reduction of the security threat there.

Latin America Overview

Although much of Latin America continued to be free from terrorist attacks, Colombia, Peru, and the triborder region experienced terrorist activity. In Colombia, insurgent and paramilitary terrorist groups continued to pose a significant threat to the country's national security and to the security of innocent civilians caught up in the conflict. Despite the beginnings of a slow and sometimes unsure peace process, Colombia's two largest guerrilla groups, the Revolutionary Armed Forces of Colombia (FARC) and the National Liberation Army (ELN), failed to moderate their terrorist attacks. The ELN carried out several high-profile kidnappings, including the hijacking in April of an aircraft carrying 46 persons and the kidnapping in May of a church congregation that resulted in 160 hostages. The FARC increased its attacks on Colombian security officials and attempted to use kidnapped soldiers and police officers as bargaining chips in negotiations. The FARC also kidnapped and killed three US nongovernmental organization workers in March and outraged international public opinion by refusing to turn over the perpetrators to the proper judicial authorities. The FARC continued refusing to account for the three New Tribes Missionaries it kidnapped in 1993.

Over the year, US concern grew over the involvement of the FARC, the ELN, and paramilitary groups in protecting narcotics trafficking. Estimates of the profits to terrorist groups from their involvement in narcotics ranged into the hundreds of millions of dollars. During 1999 the Colombian Army trained, equipped, and fielded its first counternarcotics battalion, designed to support national police efforts to break terrorist links to narcotics production.

In a development in the investigation of the bombing in 1992 of the Israeli Embassy, the Supreme Court of Argentina released in May a report identifying the cause as a car bomb and issued an international arrest warrant for Hizballah terrorist leader Imad Mughniyah. Argentine authorities similarly brought charges against all suspects being held in connection with the bombing of the Argentine-Israeli Community Center (AMIA) in 1994.

Peru's determination to combat terrorism diminished the capabilities of both the Sendero Luminoso (SL) and the Tupac Amaru Revolutionary Movement (MRTA). Peruvian authorities arrested and prosecuted several of the few remaining active SL members in 1999, including Principal Regional Committee leader Oscar Alberto Ramirez Durand. Nonetheless, the SL continued to attack government targets in the Peruvian countryside. A particularly deadly skirmish occurred in November, leaving five soldiers and six guerrilla fighters dead. The MRTA has not conducted a major terrorist operation since the end of the hostage crisis at the Japanese Ambassador's residence in Lima in April 1997.

Argentina, Brazil, and Paraguay consolidated efforts to stem the illicit activities of individuals linked to Islamist terrorist groups in the triborder region and cooperated in promoting regional counterterrorist efforts. Argentina led efforts to create the Inter-American Committee on Counterterrorism within the Organization of American States (OAS).

Argentina

Investigations continued into the bombing of the Israeli Embassy in 1992 and the terrorist attack against the Argentine-Israeli Community Center (AMIA) in 1994, both in Buenos Aires. In May the Argentine Supreme Court released a report concluding that the attack on the Israeli Embassy was a car bomb and issued an international arrest warrant for Hizballah terrorist leader Imad Mughniyah. The investigating judge in the AMIA case determined in February that there was insufficient evidence to continue holding an Iranian woman for possible complicity in the bombing. In July, Argentine authorities brought charges against all suspects then held in connection with the bombing, but at yearend the trials had yet to begin.

The Argentine Government was one of the primary motivators in the creation of the Inter-American Committee on Counterterrorism within the Organization of American States.

Colombia

The nascent and slow-moving peace process did not prompt Colombia's two largest guerrilla groups, the FARC and the ELN, or their paramilitary opponents to reduce their terrorist activity. Bogota's exclusion of the ELN in talks it began with the FARC was a factor in the ELN's series of spectacular hijackings and kidnappings—including the Avianca hijacking in April that netted 41 hostages, including one US citizen, and the Cali church kidnapping in May that took 160 hostages. With these acts the ELN sought to demonstrate its continued viability and induce President Andres Pastrana to include it in the peace process as an equal. For its part, the FARC escalated insurgent violence targeting security officials to demonstrate its power and strengthen its negotiating position.

Colombian insurgent groups and paramilitaries continued to fund their activities by protecting narcotics traffickers. Estimates of the profits to terrorist groups from their involvement in narcotics ranged into the hundreds of millions of dollars. In 1999 the Colombian Army trained, equipped, and fielded its first counternarcotics battalion, designed to support national police efforts to break terrorist links to narcotics production.

The FARC and ELN also generated income by kidnapping Colombians and foreigners for ransom and extorting money from businesses and individuals in the Colombian countryside. In addition, both insurgent groups attacked the nation's energy infrastructure—including US commercial interests—by bombing oil pipelines and destroying the electric power grid. US citizens who fell victim to guerrilla terrorism, including three Indian rights workers the FARC kidnapped in Colombia and murdered in Venezuela in March, were targeted because of wealth or opportunity rather than their nationality. The whereabouts of the three New Tribes missionaries kidnapped by the FARC in 1993 remain unknown.

In December, President Pastrana extended the FARC's demilitarized zone (DMZ) through 7 June 2000. Reports of FARC abuses inside the DMZ continued to reduce the FARC's popularity. Colombia's peace commissioner asserted that Bogota would not enter official peace talks or a "National Convention" with the ELN until all remaining hostages were released.

Peru

In 1999 the Peruvian judicial system continued to prosecute vigorously persons accused of committing acts of international and domestic terrorism. Peruvian authorities arrested and prosecuted several of the few remaining active SL members in 1999, including Principal Regional Committee leader Oscar Alberto Ramirez Durand (a.k.a. Feliciano). Feliciano had headed the decimated group since the capture in 1992 of its founder and leader Abimael Guzman, and his arrest dealt a mortal blow to one of the region's most violent rebel groups.

Peru's tough antiterrorist legislation and improved military intelligence diminished the capabilities of both the SL and the MRTA. Both groups failed to launch a significant terrorist operation in Lima in 1999 and generally limited their activities to low-level attacks and propaganda in the rural areas. The SL continued to attack government targets in the Peruvian countryside. Deadly clashes between the SL and the military continued in the central and southern regions as soldiers pursued two columns of approximately 60 to 80 rebels, led by "Comrade Alipio," through the southern jungle region. A particularly deadly skirmish occurred in November, leaving five soldiers and six guerrilla fighters dead. The MRTA has not conducted a major terrorist operation since the end of the hostage crisis at the Japanese Ambassador's residence in Lima in April 1997.

The Government of Peru requested the extradition of SL member and suspected terrorist Cecilia Nunez Chipana from Venezuela. The Government of Uruguay informed Peru that MRTA member Luis Alberto Samaniego, whom Uruguay refused to extradite in 1996, had disappeared.

Triborder Region: Argentina, Brazil, and Paraguay

In 1999 the Governments of Argentina, Brazil, and Paraguay consolidated efforts to stem the illicit activities of individuals linked to Islamist terrorist groups in the triborder region and continued to cooperate actively in promoting regional counterterrorist efforts. Despite some success, however, the triborder remained the focal point for Islamist extremism in Latin America.

Middle East Overview

Middle Eastern terrorist groups and their state sponsors continued to plan, train for, and carry out acts of terrorism in 1999 at a level comparable to that of the previous year. Casualties remained relatively low, partly as result of counterterrorist measures by various governments, improved international cooperation, and the absence of major incidents that might have caused high numbers of fatalities. Nonetheless, certain terrorist groups remained active and continued to try to mount lethal attacks. These included Usama Bin Ladin's multinational al-Qaida organization as well as The Islamic Resistance Movement (HAMAS) and Palestinian Islamic Jihad (PIJ), both of which receive support from Iran.

In Egypt, for the first time in years, there were no terrorism-related deaths, due in large measure to successful counterterrorist efforts by the Egyptian Government and a cease-fire declared by the Gama'at al-Islamiyya, Egypt's largest terrorist group. Egyptian authorities released more than 2,000 Gama'at prisoners during the year but continued to arrest and convict other active Gama'at terrorists as well as Egyptian Islamic Jihad (EIJ) members. The EIJ continued to threaten Egyptian and US interests despite the eruption of internal schisms that wracked the group during the year.

The Algerian Government also made progress in combating domestic terrorism during the year, undertaking aggressive counterinsurgency operations against the Armed Islamic Group (GIA), weakening the GIA's campaign of indiscriminate violence against civilians. The pace of killings slowed, but suspected GIA militants still carried out massacres, the worst of which left 27 dead in a village in Bechar in August. The Islamic Salvation Army maintained its cease-fire throughout the year.

Palestinians and Israeli Arabs opposed to the peace process mounted small-scale terrorist attacks in Israel, the West Bank, and Gaza, injuring a small number of civilians. Several failed bombing attempts were traced to HAMAS and the PIJ. Both Israel and the Palestinian Authority (PA) scored successes in their efforts to disrupt these groups' operations; Israeli officials publicly credited the PA with preventing a bombing in Tel Aviv in March.

Jordanian authorities in December arrested a group of terrorists associated with Usama Bin Ladin's al-Qaida organization reportedly planning to attack US and Israeli targets in connection with millennium events. Jordan also closed the Amman offices of the HAMAS political bureau in August, arrested a number of HAMAS activists, and expelled several group leaders.

Overall security conditions in Lebanon continued to improve in 1999, despite several local terrorist incidents that included the assassination of four judges in Sidon in June. The lack of effective government control in parts of Beirut, the Bekaa Valley, and southern Lebanon enabled numerous terrorist groups to operate with impunity, as they had in previous years. Hizballah, HAMAS, the PIJ, the Popular Front for the Liberation of Palestine–General Command (PFLP–GC), and other Palestinian groups used camps in Lebanon for training and operational planning. Hizballah continued to fire rockets from southern Lebanon at civilian centers in Israel. The Lebanese Government remained unresponsive to US requests for cooperation in bringing to justice terrorists responsible for attacks on US citizens in the 1980s.

Iran, Syria, and Iraq all persisted in their direct or indirect state sponsorship of terrorism. In most cases, the support included providing assistance, training, or safehaven to terrorist groups opposed to the Middle East peace process. In some cases, particularly Iran, it also included targeting regime dissidents and opponents for assassination or harassment. Libyan support for terrorism has declined significantly in recent years, but Libya continued to have residual contacts and relationships with terrorist organizations.

Algeria

The Government of Algeria in 1999 made significant progress in combating domestic terrorism, which President Abdelaziz Bouteflika said has claimed approximately 100,000 lives since Islamist extremists began their brutal campaign to overthrow the secular regime in 1992. As a result, terrorist attacks—especially against civilians—decreased significantly. Increased factionalization within the ranks of Antar Zouabri's Armed Islamic Group (GIA) and Hassan Hattab's dissident faction, the Salafi Group for Call and Combat (GSPC), contributed further to the reduction in terrorist activity. Bouteflika, who in April replaced President Liamine Zeroual, initiated an amnesty plan under the Law on Civil Concord that is intended to expand the ceasefire with the Islamic Salvation Army that took effect in October 1997. At yearend the government was attempting to convince the GSPC to surrender, but dissidents within the GSPC and the GIA—which denounced the reconciliation plan and vowed to continue fighting—were attempting to thwart those efforts.

No foreign nationals were killed in Algeria during the year. Although the tempo of violence in Algeria decreased noticeably in 1999, the killings continued. The worst terrorist incident occurred on 17 August when suspected GIA extremists massacred 27 civilians in Bechar near the Moroccan border. In November a senior official of the banned Islamic Salvation Front, Abdelkader Hachani, was assassinated. Other massacres and acts of violence continued throughout the year.

Egypt

No terrorist-related deaths were reported in Egypt in 1999. In early September, a lone assailant attacked President Hosni Mubarak during a campaign rally in Port Said. Mubarak was wounded slightly, but it is unclear whether the attack had links to terrorism. The absence of international terrorist incidents in 1999 is attributable in part to the unilateral cease-fire that Egypt's largest terrorist group, al-Gama'at al-Islamiyya, issued in March and in part to successful Egyptian counterterrorist efforts. Al-Gama'at's incarcerated spiritual leader, Shaykh Umar Abd al-Rahman, initiated the cease-fire, which senior Gama'at leaders imprisoned in Egypt later endorsed. Al-Gama'at's external leaders also endorsed the cease-fire in an attempt to negotiate with the Egyptian Government for the release of their jailed comrades. Although Cairo said publicly it would not negotiate with al-Gama'at, it released more than 2,000 Gama'at prisoners during the year. The Egyptian Government continued to arrest other Gama'at members in Egypt, and security officials in September disrupted a Gama'at cell outside Cairo, resulting in the death of Farid Kidwani, the group's operational leader in Egypt.

The Egyptian Government tried and convicted more than 100 Egyptian extremists in April, including Egyptian Islamic Jihad (EIJ) members responsible for planning an attack against the US Embassy in Albania in August 1998. A faction of the EIJ closely allied to Usama Bin Ladin's organization continued to levy threats against the United States.

Gama'at leader Rifa'i Taha Musa—who is closely associated with Bin Ladin—broke ranks with other Gama'at leaders, threatening anti-US action in October and warning in late November of another attack similar to the one at Luxor in November 1997 that killed 58 foreign tourists. International counterterrorist cooperation remained a key foreign policy priority for the Egyptian Government in 1999.

Israel, the West Bank, and the Gaza Strip

Violence and terrorism by Palestinian groups opposed to the peace process continued in 1999. Throughout the year, HAMAS and the PIJ were responsible for numerous small-scale attacks, such as shootings and stabbings, although the number of incidents continued to decline from previous years. Among the more notable attacks were two failed bombing attempts in Haifa and Tiberias on 5 September carried out by Israeli Arabs working on behalf of HAMAS's military wing. The bombs—intended for Israeli buses—exploded prematurely, killing three of the perpetrators and injuring two Israelis.

Other terrorist incidents included a shooting in early August in Hebron that injured two Israeli settlers; a double murder of a young Israeli couple hiking near Megiddo in late August; and several explosions of homemade pipe bombs in Netanya in August, November, and December, one of which injured more than 30 Israelis. In mid-August a West Bank Palestinian, who was reported to have been inspired by literature on HAMAS, rammed his car into a group of hitchhiking Israeli soldiers, injuring at least 11. In late October a shooting attack on a bus near the Tarqumiya junction wounded five Israelis.

Israel continued vigorous counterterrorist operations, including numerous arrests and seizures of weapons and explosives. In early May, Israeli officials uncovered a plan to smuggle several wanted Palestinians—who were carrying paraphernalia for manufacturing bombs—from Gaza into Israel. In mid-August, Israeli authorities apprehended seven members of a PIJ cell near Janin who admitted to perpetrating four attacks on Israelis dating back to 1998. Israeli authorities also captured a four-man PIJ squad in late August as the men tried to infiltrate into Israel to carry out a suicide mission. In mid-December an undercover unit of the Israeli Defense Force killed two HAMAS members—one of whom was a leader of the group's military wing—in a shootout near Hebron. Authorities detained three other HAMAS militants in the incident.

The Palestinian Authority (PA), which was responsible for security in Gaza and most major West Bank cities, continued to act against Palestinian perpetrators of violence against Israel. The PA's security forces preempted several terrorist attacks over the year, including the arrests in mid-May of two close associates of a senior HAMAS military leader and, in early June, of 10 HAMAS members who planned to carry out anti-Israeli bombings. Israeli Prime Minister Ehud Barak and other senior officials publicly acknowledged the continuing improvement in Israeli-PA security cooperation. Israeli security officials publicly credited the Palestinian security services for foiling a terrorist bombing in Tel Aviv in March and for preventing at least two attacks against Israeli civilians in October. The PA also sought more actively to develop leads about HAMAS and PIJ activity and acted—in some cases—in cooperation with Israel to disrupt the groups' activities. While the PA's counterterrorist campaign showed improvement, it continued to face challenges from the resilient terrorist infrastructure of groups opposed to the peace process.

In early September the PA and Israel signed a follow-on accord to the Wye agreement at Sharm el-Sheikh, which reaffirmed a number of provisions regarding security cooperation.

Jordan

There were no major international terrorist attacks in Jordan in 1999. Jordan continued its strong counterterrorist stand, highlighted by the arrests in December of several extremists reportedly planning terrorist attacks against US and Israeli tourists during millennium celebrations in Jordan, its crackdown on HAMAS in August, and its quick response to various security incidents in the latter part of the year.

In early December, Jordanian authorities arrested a group of Jordanians, an Iraqi, and an Algerian with ties to Bin Ladin's al-Qaida organization who reportedly were planning to carry out terrorist operations against US and Israeli tourists visiting Jordan over the new year. The Jordanians in mid-December took custody of Khalil al-Deek, a dual US-Jordanian citizen arrested in Pakistan, who allegedly had links to the arrested group. Some group members had undergone explosives and weapons training in Afghanistan, according to Jordanian authorities.

In late August, Jordanian authorities closed the HAMAS Political Bureau offices in Amman, detained 21 HAMAS members, and issued arrest warrants for the group's senior Jordan-based leaders, three of whom were in Iran at the time. Jordanian officials arrested two of the HAMAS officials—Jordanian citizens Khalid Mishal and Ibrahim Ghawsha—upon their return to Amman in September and refused entry to a third—Musa Abu Marzuq, who holds Yemeni citizenship. Jordanian authorities in November expelled Mishal, Ghawsha, and two other members to Qatar; released the remaining detainees; and announced that the HAMAS offices would remain closed permanently. Charges against the HAMAS officials included possession of weapons and explosives for use in illegal acts—crimes that can carry the death penalty.

Several low-level incidents kept security forces focused on combating threats to the Kingdom. Police in Ma'an detained approximately 60 suspects in connection with the firebombings on 25 October of cars belonging to professors at al-Hussein University and Ma'an Community College and a machinegun attack two days later on a female student residence at al-Hussein University.

Leaflets distributed by a group calling itself the "Islamic Awakening Youths" charged that the professors were masons and that the female students fraternized with men. The assailants appeared to have ties to the outlawed al-Tahrir movement, which was the target of a government crackdown in 1998.

In late November, Jordanian authorities arrested a 22-year-old Jordanian of Palestinian descent who had pointed a fake gun at the Israeli Embassy in Amman. An Embassy guard shot the suspect in the hand, wounding him slightly. Authorities released him after it was determined that he had not committed any crime, had a history of mental problems, and was not affiliated with any terrorist group.

The Jordanian State Security Court in April sentenced members of the outlawed "Reform and Defiance Movement"—a small, mostly indigenous radical Islamist group—for conducting a string of small bombings in Amman between mid-March and early May 1998 targeting Jordanian security forces, the Modern American School, and a major hotel. The attacks caused minor property damage but no casualties. The individuals were convicted of membership in an illegal terrorist organization, possession of illegal arms and explosives, and conspiracy to commit terrorist acts. Three were convicted in absentia and sentenced to life imprisonment with hard labor, while another received a 15-year prison sentence. Three others were acquitted. Meanwhile, no ruling was issued against six members of the Takfir wa al-Hijra (Apostasy and Migration) group, whose case was referred to the courts in October 1998. The six had been arrested for possession and sale of explosives with the intent to conduct terrorist attacks.

Amman continued to maintain tight security along its borders to thwart any attempts to smuggle weapons and explosives via Jordan to Palestinian rejectionist groups in the West Bank. Jordan permitted the limited presence—and monitored closely the activities—of several Palestinian rejectionist groups, including the PIJ, the Democratic Front for the Liberation of Palestine (DFLP), the Popular Front for the Liberation of Palestine (PFLP), and the Popular Front for the Liberation of Palestine–General Command (PFLP–GC). Amman allowed HAMAS members to reside in Jordan but banned them from engaging in activities on behalf of the group.

The Jordanian Government was outspoken in its support for the Middle East peace process and made it clear it would not tolerate efforts to undermine the negotiations from its territory. Senior government officials, including King Abdallah, condemned major terrorist incidents in the region, including attacks by Palestinian rejectionist groups against Israeli targets. In October, Jordan hosted a meeting between leaders of the DFLP and Israeli Knesset members to discuss the possible entry of DFLP members into the Palestinian-controlled areas.

Jordan continued to cooperate with other regional states and the United States concerning terrorist threats to the region. In August the government refused to grant a request by a lower house of Parliament committee to pardon Ahmed

Daqamseh, a Jordanian soldier who killed six Israeli schoolgirls in 1997, and 11 Jordanian "Arab Afghans" serving life sentences for their conviction in 1995 for plotting against the state.

Lebanon

Security conditions in Lebanon continued to improve in 1999 despite a series of terrorist-related activities. The government's continued lack of control in parts of the country, however—including portions of the Bekaa Valley, Beirut's southern suburbs, Palestinian refugee camps, and south Lebanon—and easy access to arms and explosives throughout much of the country contributed to an environment with the potential for acts of violence. The Lebanese Government did not exert full control over militia groups engaged in fighting in and near the so-called security zone occupied by Israel and its proxy militia, the Army of South Lebanon.

A variety of terrorist groups continued to operate with relative impunity in those areas, conducting terrorist training and other operational activities. The groups include Hizballah, HAMAS, the PIJ, the PFLP–GC, the Abu Nidal organization (ANO), Asbat al-Ansar, and several local Sunni extremist organizations. Hizballah represents the most potent threat to US interests in Lebanon by an organized group. Although Hizballah has not attacked US targets in Lebanon since 1991, its animosity toward the United States has not abated, and the group continued to monitor the US Embassy and its personnel in the country. Hizballah leaders routinely denounced US policies in the region and continued to condemn the peace process.

Lebanon suffered several terrorist attacks in 1999 involving local actors and victims. On 8 September, for example, a bomb exploded at the Customs Department office in Sidon, causing no injuries. Unidentified gunmen on 8 June shot and killed four judges at a courthouse in Sidon. Although Lebanese authorities had not apprehended the assailants, they believed the Palestinian extremist group Asbat al-Ansar was responsible. Moreover, a previously unknown group, the Liberation Army of Veneration, on 28 June issued a communiqué containing a death threat to the US Ambassador in Lebanon. Local authorities speculated that the Asbat al-Ansar was behind the threat.

The Lebanese Government continued to support international counterterrorist initiatives. It agreed in principle to examine a Japanese request to take custody of five Japanese Red Army members whose jail sentences in Lebanon end in March 2000. The Lebanese Government, however, did not act on repeated US requests to turn over Lebanese terrorists involved in the hijacking in 1985 of TWA flight 847 and in the abduction, torture, and—in some cases—murders of US hostages from 1984 to 1991.

Saudi Arabia

Several threats against US military and civilian personnel and facilities in Saudi Arabia were reported in 1999, but there were no terrorist incidents. Terrorist Usama Bin Ladin, based in Afghanistan, continued publicly to threaten US interests in Saudi Arabia during the year.

The Saudi Arabian Government, at all levels, continued to reaffirm its commitment to combating terrorism. Saudi Crown Prince Abdallah stated publicly that terrorist actions are un-Islamic and called for a "concerted international effort" to eradicate terrorism. The Saudi Minister of Defense indicated during a visit to Washington that he was determined to work with the United States to defeat terrorism. The Saudis urged the Taliban to expel Bin Ladin from Afghanistan so that he may be brought to justice in another country.

The Government of Saudi Arabia continued to investigate the bombing in June 1996 of the Khubar Towers housing facility near Dhahran and to cooperate with the United States in its investigation of the incident. Saudi authorities arrested and detained several persons in connection with the attack but reached no conclusion in the investigation. The Saudi Government stated that it still was looking for three Saudi suspects linked to the bombing who authorities believed were outside the Kingdom. The United States expelled Saudi national Hani al-Sayegh to Saudi Arabia on 11 October. He faces charges there for his alleged role in the bombing. Al-Sayegh originally was detained in Canada in March 1997, and documents submitted to the Canadian court alleged al-Sayegh, as a member of the Saudi Hizballah, had participated in the Khubar Towers bombing.

Yemen

Yemen expanded security cooperation with other Arab countries in 1999 and signed a number of international antiterrorist conventions. The government introduced incremental measures to better control its borders, territory, and travel documents and initiated specialized training for a newly established counterterrorist unit within the Ministry of Interior. Nonetheless, lax and inefficient enforcement of security procedures and the government's inability to exercise authority over remote areas of the country continued to make the country a safehaven for terrorist groups. HAMAS and the PIJ had official representatives in Yemen, and sympathizers or members of other international terrorist groups—including the Egyptian Islamic Jihad, al-Gama'at al-Islamiyya, Libyan opposition groups, and the Algerian Armed Islamic Group—also resided in the country.

Yemeni courts convicted the four surviving terrorists involved in the kidnapping in December 1998 of Western tourists in Mudiyah following a lengthy trial and appeals process. The 16 Western tourists held captive in that incident included two US citizens. Four of the tourists died, and two others—including one US citizen—were wounded during a Yemeni Government rescue attempt that liberated the remaining hostages. The leader of the Islamic Army of Aden, Zein al-Abidine al-Midhar, admitted to all charges against him in the incident and was executed by firing squad on 17 October. The three other defendants each received 20-year prison sentences. In a separate case, a Yemeni court in August convicted

10 terrorists—eight Britons and two Algerians—of conspiring to commit terrorist acts, including attacks targeting US citizens.

Kidnappings of foreigners by well-armed and independent tribesmen continued to be fairly common in Yemen. The tribesmen's grievances were more often with the Yemeni Government than with Western governments. Tribesmen kidnapped and released fewer than 30 foreign nationals during the year, a significant decline from the number abducted the previous year. On 17 January, two US Embassy employees escaped a kidnap attempt; later the same day, tribesmen kidnapped six Europeans, who overheard their captors saying they wanted "to kidnap an American." In October, tribesmen kidnapped three US citizens and released them unharmed in less than two days. In an effort to contain the kidnapping of foreigners, the Yemeni Government in October announced the creation of a special court and prosecutor to try suspects charged under a law, promulgated in August 1998, that imposes severe punishment for convicted kidnappers and saboteurs.

North America Overview

International terrorist attacks in North America are relatively rare. In 1999 the United States and Canada cooperated in investigating a noteworthy incident involving the smuggling of explosives from Canada into Washington State.

Canada

In mid-December, US authorities arrested Ahmed Ressam, an Algerian national, as he entered the United States from Canada at Port Angeles, Washington. The vehicle he was driving was carrying explosives and detonating devices. The Government of Canada cooperated closely in the follow-up investigation into Ressam's activities and associates in Canada. Some Algerians arrested in connection with this case apparently are "Afghan alumni," who trained with the *mujahidin* in Afghanistan and are linked to Usama Bin Ladin. Canada has a longstanding cooperative relationship with the United States on counterterrorist matters, and the two countries meet regularly to discuss ways to enhance this cooperation and improve border security.

While a potentially serious incident was avoided with Ressam's arrest, at yearend both Canada and the United States remained concerned about the possibility of a heightened threat of terrorism in North America, and the two countries were exploring new mechanisms for exchanging information on individuals with links to terrorism.

Terrorism in the New Millennium

Overview of Terrorism in the New Millennium

Anna Sabasteanski

Worldwide Terrorist Attacks, 2000–2004

2000	423 attacks
2001	346 attacks
2002	199 attacks
2003	208 attacks
2004	651 attacks

The year 2000 saw another increase in international terrorist attacks, from 392 to 423. The number of casualties also increased, and the trend toward attacking U.S. interests continued. Bombings against a multinational oil pipeline in Colombia accounted for 152 of the attacks that year. However, the most notable attack was al-Qaeda's suicide boat attack on the USS *Cole* in the port of Aden, in Yemen. Seventeen sailors were killed in that attack.

Although the new millennium opened well, with one potential attack—a millennium bomb threat against the United States—stopped at the border, any sense of complacency was shattered with the attacks of September 11, 2001. *Patterns of Global Terrorism 2001* described the event:

> The worst international terrorist attack ever—involving four separate but coordinated aircraft hijackings—occurred in the United States on September 11, 2001. The 19 hijackers belonged to the al-Qaida terrorist network. According to investigators and records of cellular phone calls made by passengers aboard the planes, the hijackers used knives and boxcutters to kill or wound passengers and the pilots, and then commandeer the aircraft, which the hijackers used to destroy preselected targets.
>
> - Five terrorists hijacked American Airlines flight 11, which departed Boston for Los Angeles at 7:45 a.m. An hour later it was deliberately piloted into the North Tower of the World Trade Center in New York City.
> - Five terrorists hijacked United Airlines flight 175, which departed Boston for Los Angeles at 7:58 a.m. At 9:05 the plane crashed into the South Tower of the World Trade Center. Both towers collapsed shortly thereafter, killing approximately 3000 persons, including hundreds of firefighters and rescue personnel who were helping to evacuate the buildings.
> - Four terrorists hijacked United Airlines flight 93, which departed Newark for San Francisco at 8:01 a.m. At 10:10 the plane crashed in Stony Creek Township, Pennsylvania killing all 45 persons on board. The intended target of this hijacked plane is not known, but it is believed that passengers overpowered the terrorists, thus preventing the aircraft from being used as a missile.
> - Five terrorists hijacked American Airlines flight 77, which departed Washington Dulles Airport for Los Angeles at 8:10 a.m. At 9:39 the plane was flown directly into the Pentagon in Arlington, Virginia, near Washington D.C. A total of 189 persons were killed, including all who were onboard the plane.

The 2001 report contained the standard detail but added extensive coverage of U.S. programs and policies and international cooperation with U.S. efforts. The report was just over 200 pages long. Although the September 11 attack led to the highest death toll from terrorism ever recorded (a final estimate, as of October 2003, set the number at 2,752 deaths in New York City, 185 at the Pentagon, and 40 in Pennsylvania, not including the hijackers), the number of attacks fell from 423 in 2000 to 346 in 2001. Of those, 51 percent (178) were bombings against Colombia's multinational oil pipeline.

Following the September 11 disaster, there were several investigations into the events and government's failure to identify and intervene in such a large-scale plot. The Congressional Research Service's (CRS) report, *Proposals for Intelligence Reorganization, 1949–2004* (which appears in this section) summarizes the contemporary initiatives as well as those that followed World War II. Another CRS report, *Terrorism: Key Recommendations of the 9/11 Commission and Recent Major Commissions and Inquiries*, which appears later in this section, provides some additional information.

In 2002 the number of international terrorist attacks dropped by 44 percent, to 199, and casualties were also far fewer. The most notorious incident was the kidnapping and beheading of journalist Daniel Pearl. The worst attack was the bombing of a nightclub in Bali, Indonesia, on 12 October, which killed more than two hundred people from two dozen countries.

In 2003 the data used in *Patterns* was provided for the first time by the new Terrorist Threat Integration Center (TTIC), which had been established based on recommendations from the 9/11 Commission and other commissions and inquiries. The TTIC data indicated another fall in the number of international terrorist attacks, to 190. It quickly became apparent that this was incorrect and for the first time ever, the report had to be corrected. The new number, 208, showed a small increase. (See Office of Inspector General's report.)

In 2004 the State Department transferred responsibility for statistical reporting to the new National Counterterrorism Center (NCTC) and changed the report to focus only on congressionally mandated items. With the change in focus came a change in name: *Patterns of Global Terrorism* became *Country Reports on Terrorism*. To explain the reasoning behind this change, we have included the transcript of a State Department briefing, testimony submitted for House hearings on the report, and a report on the NCTC.

Patterns of Global Terrorism 2000

The Year in Review

There were 423 international terrorist attacks in 2000, an increase of 8 percent from the 392 attacks recorded during 1999. The main reason for the increase was an upsurge in the number of bombings of a multinational oil pipeline in Colombia by two terrorist groups there. The pipeline was bombed 152 times, producing in the Latin American region the largest increase in terrorist attacks from the previous year, from 121 to 193. Western Europe saw the largest decrease—from 85 to 30—owing to fewer attacks in Germany, Greece, and Italy as well as to the absence of any attacks in Turkey.

The number of casualties caused by terrorists also increased in 2000. During the year, 405 persons were killed and 791 were wounded, up from the 1999 totals of 233 dead and 706 wounded.

The number of anti-US attacks rose from 169 in 1999 to 200 in 2000, a result of the increase in bombing attacks against the oil pipeline in Colombia, which is viewed by the terrorists as a US target.

Nineteen US citizens were killed in acts of international terrorism in 2000. Seventeen were sailors who died in the attack against the USS Cole on 12 October in the Yemeni port of Aden. They were:

    Kenneth Eugene Clodfelter
    Richard Costelow
    Lakeina Monique Francis
    Timothy Lee Gauna
    Cherone Louis Gunn
    James Rodrick McDaniels
    Mark Ian Nieto
    Ronald Scott Owens
    Lakiba Nicole Palmer
    Joshua Langdon Parlett
    Patrick Howard Roy
    Kevin Shawn Rux
    Ronchester Mananga Santiago
    Timothy Lamont Saunders
    Gary Graham Swenchonis
    Andrew Triplett
    Craig Bryan Wibberley

Two other US citizens were murdered in terrorist attacks during the year:

- Carlos Caceres was one of three aid workers murdered when a militia-led mob in Atambua, West Timor, attacked a United Nations High Commissioner for Refugees aid office on 6 September.
- Kurt Erich Schork was one of two journalists killed when rebels in Sierra Leone shot down a UN helicopter on 25 May.

In December new indictments were issued in connection with the bombings in 1998 at two US embassies in East Africa. A federal grand jury in New York charged five men—Saif Al Adel, Muhsin Musa Matwalli Atwah, Ahmed Mohamed Hamed Ali, Anas Al Liby, and Abdullah Ahmed Abdullah—in connection with the bombing attacks in Nairobi and Dar es Salaam, bringing to 22 the total number of persons charged. At the end of 2000, one suspect had pled guilty to conspiring in the attacks, five were in custody in New York awaiting trial, three were in the United Kingdom pending extradition to the United States, and 13 were fugitives, including Usama Bin Ladin.

A trial began in January 2001 in federal court in the Southern District of New York of four suspects in connection with the bombings at the US embassies in Kenya and Tanzania. Three of the four were extradited to the United States in 1999 to stand trial; the fourth was arrested in this country. The trial is expected to last through 2001.

A trial of two Libyans accused of bombing Pan Am flight 103 in 1988 began in the Netherlands on 3 May 2000. A Scottish court presided over the trial and issued its verdict on 31 January 2001. It found Abdel Basset al-Megrahi guilty of the charge of murdering 259 passengers and crew as well as 11 residents of Lockerbie, Scotland, "while acting in furtherance of the purposes of . . . Libyan Intelligence Services." Concerning the other defendant, Al-Amin Kalifa Fahima, the court concluded it had insufficient evidence to satisfy the high standard of "proof beyond reasonable doubt" that is necessary in criminal cases. The verdict of the court represents a victory for the international effort to hold terrorists accountable for their crimes.

Africa Overview

Africa in 2000 witnessed an increase in the number of terrorist attacks against foreigners or foreign interests—part of a growing trend in which the number of international terrorist incidents on the continent has risen steadily each year since 1995. Most attacks stemmed from internal civil unrest and spillover from regional wars as African rebel movements and opposition groups employed terrorism to further their political, social, or economic objectives. International terrorist organizations, including al-Qaida, Lebanese Hizballah, and Egyptian terrorist groups, continued to operate in Africa during 2000 and to pose a threat to US interests there.

Angola

Angola continued to be plagued by the protracted civil war between the National Union for the Total Independence of Angola (UNITA) and the Angolan Government. Several international terrorist attacks originating in this conflict occurred in 2000, while throughout the year members of the separatist group the Front for the Liberation of the Enclave of Cabinda (FLEC) took hostage several foreigners in Cabinda Province.

Unidentified militants, suspected of being UNITA rebels, ambushed a vehicle near Soyo on 25 January and killed a Portuguese citizen. During May, UNITA rebels attacked two World Food Program convoys in northern Angola, killing one person and causing significant property damage. On 18 and 19 August, suspected UNITA fighters attacked two diamond mines in northeast Angola, killing nine South Africans and abducting seven Angolans.

The group's most significant incident for the year occurred on 24 May, when FLEC rebels kidnapped three Portuguese construction workers and one Angolan in Cabinda Province.

Guinea

Spillover from fighting in Sierra Leone resulted in several international terrorist acts in Guinea during 2000. Revolutionary United Front (RUF) rebels crossed the border into Guinea from Sierra Leone on 7 September and kidnapped two foreign Catholic priests who escaped their captors in early December. On 17 September suspected RUF rebels from Sierra Leone attacked and killed a Togolese United Nations High Commissioner for Refugees staff employee and kidnapped an Ivorian secretary.

Namibia

During 2000 violence from the Angolan civil war spilled over into Namibia after Angolan Government troops were invited into border areas where Angolan National Union for the Total Independence of Angola (UNITA) rebels had been active for 20 years. Clashes in the border area killed nine individuals, including several foreigners. Three French children were killed on 3 January in the Caprivi region of Namibia when their vehicle was attacked by uniformed armed men of unknown affiliation. The local police commissioner blamed UNITA rebels for the attack, but a UNITA spokesman denied any responsibility. In other attacks on vehicles, gunmen of unknown affiliation also wounded two French citizens, two Danish aid workers, and a Scottish citizen.

Niger

In January, a suspected threat from Algerian terrorists forced organizers to cancel the Niger stage of the Paris-Dakar Road Rally. Race officials bypassed Niger and airlifted competitors to Libya after receiving information that Islamic extremists based in Niger were planning a terrorist attack. No terrorist attacks occurred on the 11,000-kilometer race through Senegal, Burkina Faso, Mali, Libya, and Egypt.

Nigeria

In 2000, impoverished ethnic groups in the southern oil-producing region of Nigeria continued to kidnap local and foreign oil workers in an effort to acquire a greater share of Nigeria's oil wealth. (Abductions in the oil region are common, and hostages are rarely harmed.) Some 300 persons, including 54 foreigners, were abducted between April and July. The most serious kidnapping incident occurred on 31 July when armed youths attacked two oil drilling rigs and took 165 hostages, including seven US citizens and five Britons. All hostages were released unharmed on 4 August.

Sierra Leone

Sierra Leone's warring factions carried out more high-profile terrorist attacks against foreign interests in 2000 than in 1999, killing and kidnapping United Nations Assistance Mission in Sierra Leone (UNAMSIL) peacekeepers, foreign journalists, and humanitarian aid workers.

The most violent attacks occurred in May when Revolutionary United Front (RUF) rebels resorted to terrorism in an effort to force out UN peacekeepers who had arrived to replace a regional peacekeeping force. In those attacks, RUF militiamen killed five UN peacekeepers and kidnapped some 500 others—most of whom were later released. The RUF also is believed responsible for shooting down a UN helicopter and killing two foreign journalists—including one US citizen—in May. Armed militants kidnapped two British aid workers on 9 May and released them a month later.

Sporadic terrorist attacks continued from June until August, resulting in the deaths of four more peacekeepers and the kidnapping of at least 30 additional UN troops. RUF fighters were responsible for most of the attacks.

Somalia

According to the US Embassy in Nairobi, Kenya, unidentified Somali gunmen on 30 March opened fire on a UN aircraft departing the port city of Kismaayo in southern Somalia. No group claimed responsibility for the attack, which resulted in no injuries and only minor damage to the aircraft. The UN responded by temporarily suspending humanitarian operations in Kismaayo.

South Africa

Cape Town continued to experience a series of bombings and other acts of urban terrorism in 2000. Nine bombings resulted in some 30 injuries. Five of the nine attacks were car-bombings that targeted South African authorities, public places, and restaurants and nightclubs with Western associations. According to US Embassy reporting, the spate of bombings in 2000—the latest of several urban terrorism episodes that Cape Town has experienced since 1998—was distinguished by larger bombs triggered by more sophisticated remote detonation devices.

South African authorities suspect that People Against Gangsterism and Drugs (PAGAD)—South Africa's most militant Muslim organization—was responsible for most of the bombings. According to press reports, anonymous calls to news reporters demanding the release of PAGAD cadre preceded four of the bombings. One unidentified individual called a local radio station before a bombing on 29 August and gave precise details of the timing and location of the attack. In raids in November, police arrested several suspects affiliated with PAGAD and confiscated several pipe bombs. There were no bombings or incidents after the arrests.

Uganda

The Sudanese-backed Lord's Resistance Army (LRA) in northern Uganda and the Sudanese- and Congolese-supported Allied Democratic Forces (ADF) in Western Uganda continued their insurgent campaigns to undermine the Ugandan Government in 2000—resulting in several terrorist attacks against foreign nationals. Suspected LRA rebels kidnapped two Italian missionaries on 4 March and released them unharmed several hours later. In October, LRA militants shot and killed another Italian priest as he drove to his church.

Government counterterrorist efforts initiated in 1999 helped prevent any major bombings during 2000 in the capital, Kampala. Islamist militants associated with the ADF are believed responsible for a series of deadly bombings and other urban terrorist incidents that occurred from 1997 to 1999.

South Asia Overview

In 2000, South Asia remained a focal point for terrorism directed against the United States, further confirming the trend of terrorism shifting from the Middle East to South Asia. The Taliban continued to provide safehaven for international terrorists, particularly Usama Bin Ladin and his network, in the portions of Afghanistan it controlled.

The Government of Pakistan increased its support to the Taliban and continued its support to militant groups active in Indian-held Kashmir, such as the Harakat ul-Mujahidin (HUM), some of which engaged in terrorism. In Sri Lanka the government continued its 17-year conflict with the Liberation Tigers of Tamil Eelam (LTTE), which engaged in several terrorist acts against government and civilian targets during the year.

Afghanistan

Islamic extremists from around the world—including North America, Europe, Africa, the Middle East, and Central, South, and Southeast Asia—continued to use Afghanistan as a training ground and base of operations for their worldwide terrorist activities in 2000. The Taliban, which controlled most Afghan territory, permitted the operation of training and indoctrination facilities for non-Afghans and provided logistics support to members of various terrorist organizations and *mujahidin,* including those waging *jihads* (holy wars) in Central Asia, Chechnya, and Kashmir.

Throughout 2000 the Taliban continued to host Usama Bin Ladin despite UN sanctions and international pressure to hand him over to stand trial in the United States or a third country. In a serious and ongoing dialogue with the Taliban, the United States repeatedly made clear to the Taliban that it would be held responsible for any terrorist attacks undertaken by Bin Ladin while he is in its territory.

In October, a terrorist bomb attack against the USS Cole in Aden Harbor, Yemen, killed 17 US sailors and injured scores of others. Although no definitive link has been made to Bin Ladin's organization, Yemeni authorities have determined that some suspects in custody and at large are veterans of Afghan training camps.

In August, Bangladeshi authorities uncovered a bomb plot to assassinate Prime Minister Sheikh Hasina at a public rally. Bangladeshi police maintained that Islamic terrorists trained in Afghanistan planted the bomb.

India

Security problems associated with various insurgencies, particularly in Kashmir, persisted through 2000 in India. Massacres of civilians in Kashmir during March and August were attributed to Lashkar-e-Tayyiba (LT) and other militant groups. India also faced continued violence associated with several separatist movements based in the northeast of the country.

The Indian Government continued cooperative efforts with the United States against terrorism. During the year, the US-India Joint Counterterrorism Working Group—founded in November 1999—met twice and agreed to increased cooperation on mutual counterterrorism interests. New Delhi continued to cooperate with US officials to ascertain the fate of four Western hostages—including one US citizen—kidnapped in Indian-held Kashmir in 1995, although the hostages' whereabouts remained unknown.

Pakistan

Pakistan's military government, headed by Gen. Pervez Musharraf, continued previous Pakistani Government support of the Kashmir insurgency, and Kashmiri militant groups continued to operate in Pakistan, raising funds and recruiting new cadre. Several of these groups were responsible for attacks against civilians in Indian-held Kashmir, and the largest of the groups, the Lashkar-e-Tayyiba, claimed responsibility for a suicide car-bomb attack against an Indian garrison in Srinagar in April.

In addition, the Harakat ul-Mujahidin (HUM), a designated Foreign Terrorist Organization, continues to be active in Pakistan without discouragement by the Government of Pakistan. Members of the group were associated with the hijacking in December 1999 of an Air India flight that resulted in the release from an Indian jail of former HUM leader Maulana Masood Azhar. Azhar since has founded his own Kashmiri militant group, Jaish-e-Mohammed, and publicly has threatened the United States.

The United States remains concerned about reports of continued Pakistani support for the Taliban's military operations in Afghanistan. Credible reporting indicates that Pakistan is providing the Taliban with materiel, fuel, funding, technical assistance, and military advisers. Pakistan has not prevented large numbers of Pakistani nationals from moving into Afghanistan to fight for the Taliban. Islamabad also failed to take effective steps to curb the activities of certain madrassas, or religious schools, that serve as recruiting grounds for terrorism. Pakistan publicly and privately said it intends to comply fully with UNSCR 1333, which imposes an arms embargo on the Taliban.

The attack on the USS Cole in Yemen in October prompted fears of US retaliatory strikes against Bin Ladin's organization and targets in Afghanistan if the investigation pointed in that direction. Pakistani religious party leaders and militant groups threatened US citizens and facilities if such an action were to occur, much as they did after the US attacks on training camps in Afghanistan in August 1998 and following the US diplomatic intervention in the Kargil conflict between Pakistan and India in 1999. The Government of Pakistan generally has cooperated with US requests to enhance security for US facilities and personnel.

Sri Lanka

The separatist group the Liberation Tigers of Tamil Eelam (LTTE)—redesignated as a Foreign Terrorist Organization in 1999—remained violent in 2000, engaging in several terrorist acts against government and civilian targets. LTTE attacks, including those involving suicide bombers, killed more than 100 persons, including Minister of Industrial Development Goonaratne, and wounded dozens. Two US citizens and a British national were apparent incidental victims of the group in October, when an LTTE suicide bomber cornered by the police detonated his bomb near the Town Hall in Colombo. The LTTE continued to strike civilian shipping in Sri Lanka, conducting a naval suicide bombing of a merchant vessel and hijacking a Russian ship.

The war in the north between the Tigers and the Sri Lankan Government continued, although by year's end the government had re-taken 70 percent of the Jaffna Peninsula. The Government of Norway initiated efforts to broker peace between the two parties and may have contributed to an LTTE decision to announce unilaterally a cease-fire in December.

Several terrorist acts have been attributed to other domestic Sri Lankan groups. Suspected Sinhalese extremists protesting Norway's peace efforts used small improvised explosive devices to attack the Norwegian-run charity Save the Children as well as the Norwegian Embassy. Sinhalese extremists also are suspected of assassinating pro-LTTE politician G. G. Kumar Ponnambalam, Jr., in January.

East Asia Overview

Japan continued to make progress in its counterterrorist efforts. Legal restrictions instituted in 1999 began to take effect on the Aum. Four Aum Shinrikyo members who had personally placed the sarin on the subway in 1995 were sentenced to death. Tokyo also made substantial progress in its efforts to return several Japanese Red Army (JRA) members to Japan. The Government of Japan indicted four JRA members who were forcibly returned after being deported from Lebanon. Tokyo also took two others into custody: Yoshimi Tanaka, a fugitive JRA member involved in hijacking a Japanese airliner in 1970, who was extradited from Thailand, and Fusako Shigenobu, a JRA founder and leader, who had been on the run for 30 years and was arrested in Japan in November.

Several nations in East Asia experienced terrorist violence in 2000. Burmese dissidents took over a provincial hospital in Thailand; authorities stormed the hospital, killed the hostage takers, and freed the hostages unharmed. In Indonesia, there was a sharp increase in international and domestic terrorism, including several bombings, two of which targeted official foreign interests. Pro-Jakarta militia units continued attacks on UN personnel in East Timor. In one incident in September, three aid workers, including one US citizen, were killed.

Small-scale violence in Cambodia, Laos, and Vietnam occurred in 2000, some connected to antigovernment groups, allegedly with support from foreign nationals. Several small-scale bombings occurred in the Laotian capital, some of which targeted tourist destinations and injured foreign nationals. An attack on 24 November in downtown Phnom Penh, Cambodia, resulted in deaths and injuries. The US Government released a statement on 19 December that "deplores and condemns" alleged US national or permanent resident support, encouragement, or participation in violent antigovernment activities in several foreign countries with which the United States is at peace, specifically Vietnam, Cambodia, and Laos.

In the Philippines, the Abu Sayyaf Group (ASG) abducted 21 persons, including 10 foreign tourists, from a Malaysian resort in April, the first time the group conducted operations outside the southern Philippines. ASG members later abducted several foreign journalists, three Malaysians, and one US citizen in the southern Philippines. (The US citizen and one Filipino remained captive at year's end.) After breaking off peace talks in Manila in April, the Moro Islamic Liberation Front (MILF) mounted several terrorist attacks in the southern Philippines against Philippine security and civilian targets. Philippine officials also suspect MILF operatives conducted bombings in Manila, including two at popular shopping malls in May. Other groups, including the Communist Party of the Philippines New People's Army, and the Alex Boncayao Brigade, mounted attacks in the archipelago.

Burma

In January, 10 armed Burmese dissidents—linked to the takeover in 1999 of the Burmese Embassy in Bangkok—took over the Ratchaburi provincial hospital in Thailand. Thai security forces stormed the hospital and freed the victims. All the hostage takers were killed, and no hostages were injured during the assault. Separately, Burma sentenced to death one terrorist involved in the 1999 Embassy seizure.

Indonesia

Indonesia experienced a sharp rise in international and domestic terrorism during the year, as weakening central government control and a difficult transition to democracy provided fertile ground for terrorist activities. Several bombings occurred in 2000, two of which targeted official foreign interests. Unidentified assailants detonated a car bomb in front of the Philippine Ambassador's residence in central Jakarta as the Ambassador was entering the compound on 1 August. The explosion killed two Indonesians, seriously injured three other persons—including the Ambassador—and slightly injured 18 bystanders, including one Filipino and two Bulgarians. Unidentified perpetrators also conducted a grenade attack against the Malaysian Embassy on 27 August, but no injuries resulted.

Six other bombings from July to November targeted domestic interests in the capital. The most destructive occurred on 13 September when a car bomb in the Jakarta stock exchange's underground parking garage killed 10 Indonesians. Other targets included the Attorney General's office, the Jakarta Governor's residence, a Jakarta hotel, a local nongovernmental organization, as well as the Ministry of Agriculture, which was used as the courtroom venue for former President Soeharto's corruption trial. Multiple bombings also occurred in major cities in North Sumatra, Riau, and East Java.

Indonesian officials made little progress in apprehending and prosecuting those responsible for the bombings. The Indonesian National Police arrested 34 persons suspected of involvement in the Malaysian Embassy and the stock-exchange bombings, but a lack of evidence forced the release of all suspects in mid-October. The police claim the Free Aceh Movement (GAM)—a group seeking an independent state in northern Sumatra—conducted both attacks and planned another against the US Embassy to "create chaos" in Jakarta. The evidence made public as of December, however, does not support elements of this theory. Nevertheless, the GAM or Achenese separatists did conduct sporadic attacks on ExxonMobil oil facilities in Aceh early in the year. The group's primary target was Indonesian security elements, some of which continued to guard ExxonMobil facilities.

Indonesian nationalists and some radical Islamist groups occasionally carried out violent protests outside US diplomatic facilities in response to perceived US interference in domestic affairs and support for Israel. One demonstration culminated in a mob attack against the US Consulate in Surabaya on 15 September, and another involved the Islamist militant Front Pembela Islam (Islamic Defenders' Front) threatening US citizens in the country. Other Islamist extremists in October searched for US citizens in a central Javanese city, warning them to leave the country.

Militiamen attacked a UNHCR aid office in Atambua, West Timor, on 6 September, killing three aid workers, including one US citizen. Suspected militia members also killed two UN peacekeepers—a New Zealander and a Nepalese national—during the year.

Japan

Aum Shinrikyo, which conducted the sarin nerve agent attack in the Tokyo subway system in 1995, remained under active government surveillance. The Aum now is required by law to report regularly on its membership, residences, and other holdings. The Tokyo district court in 1999 and 2000 sentenced to death four of the five senior cultists who actually placed the sarin on the subway. (The fifth culprit, Ikuo Hayashi, showed a repentant and cooperative attitude and, in 1998, received a less severe life sentence.) The prosecution of cult leader Shoko Asahara continued, with four drug-related charges dropped in October in an effort to expedite a verdict. Aum leadership took further steps to improve the cult's image following up its public apology and admission of responsibility for the subway attack with an agreement to pay $40 million damage to attack victims, rejection of cult founder Asahara as a religious prophet, a pledge to remove teachings advocating murder from the cult's religious doctrine, and a change of its name to Aleph.

Separately, four Japanese Red Army (JRA) members were returned to Japan in March after being deported from Lebanon. They later were indicted on charges of attempted murder and forgery of official documents. Japanese officials continued to seek the extradition of a fifth colleague, Kozo Okamoto, who was granted political asylum by Lebanon because he had participated in operations against Israel. In June, the Japanese Government successfully extradited Yoshimi Tanaka—one of the fugitive members of the JRA involved in hijacking a Japanese Airlines plane to North Korea in 1970—from Thailand. During a preliminary hearing before the Tokyo district court in July, Tanaka publicly apologized and submitted a signed report admitting to hijacking and assault charges. His trial began on 16 December.

In November, Osaka police successfully tracked down and arrested Fusako Shigenobu, a founder and leader of the JRA, who had been on the run for 30 years. Prosecutors have charged her with suspicion of conspiracy related to JRA's seizure of the French Embassy in The Hague in 1974, as well as attempted murder, and passport fraud. Police later seized two supporters who allegedly helped her evade detection while in Japan. Only a handful of JRA members remain at large.

Japan has yet to sign the International Convention for the Suppression of Terrorist Financing.

Laos

Several small-scale bombings of undetermined origin occurred in Vientiane during 2000, some of which targeted tourist destinations and injured foreign nationals. Unidentified assailants threw an explosive device at a restaurant on 30 March, injuring 10 tourists from Britain, Germany, and Denmark. Bombings also occurred at Vientiane's morning market in May—injuring four Thai nationals—and the central post office in July, where two foreign tourists narrowly escaped injury. Unidentified perpetrators also detonated explosives at the Vientiane bus station, the domestic airport terminal, and a national monument. Authorities discovered other bombs planted at the morning market, a foreign embassy, and in a hotel outside Vientiane and rendered them safe.

Press reporting during the year indicated that political dissidents conducted some of the attacks in the capital, although the suspected groups denied involvement.

Malaysia

Malaysia experienced two incidents of international terrorism in 2000, both perpetrated by the Philippine-based Abu Sayyaf Group (ASG). The ASG abducted 21 persons, including 10 foreign tourists, from the Sipadan diving resort in eastern Malaysia on 23 April. A suspected ASG faction also kidnapped three Malaysians from a resort on Pandanan Island in eastern Malaysia on 10 September. The group released most of the hostages from both incidents but continued to hold one Filipino abducted from Sipadan as of the end of the year.

A Malaysian Islamist sect known as Al-Ma'unah targeted domestic security forces for the first time in July. Members of the group raided two military armories in Perak state, about 175 miles north of Kuala Lumpur, and took four locals hostage. Sect members killed two of the hostages—a Malaysian police officer and soldier—before surrendering on 6 July. Malaysian authorities arrested and detained several dozen members following the incident and suspect that 29 of those held also launched attacks against a Hindu temple, a brewery, and an electrical power tower.

Philippines

Islamist separatist groups in the Philippines increased attacks against foreign and domestic targets in 2000. The Abu Sayyaf Group (ASG)—designated one of 29 Foreign Terrorist Organizations by the US Government—conducted operations outside the southern Philippines for the first time when it abducted 21 persons—including 10 foreign tourists—from a Malaysian resort in April. In a series of subsequent, separate incidents, ASG group members abducted several foreign journalists, three Malaysians, and one US citizen in the southern Philippines. Although obtaining ransom money was a primary goal, the hostage takers issued several disparate political demands ranging from releasing international terrorists jailed in the United States to establishing an independent Islamic state. The group released most of the hostages by October allegedly for ransoms totaling several million dollars, while Philippine Government assaults on ASG positions paved the way for some other hostages to escape. The ASG, however, continued to hold the US citizen and a Filipino captive at year's end.

Manila made some legal progress against ASG kidnapping activities in 2000 when a regional trial court sentenced three group members to life in prison for abducting Dr. Nilo Barandino and 10 members of his household in 1992. The Philippine Government also filed charges against ASG members involved in multiple kidnapping cases, although the suspects remained at large.

The Moro Islamic Liberation Front (MILF)—the largest remaining Philippine Islamist separatist group—broke off stalled peace talks with Manila in late April. After the military launched an offensive capturing several MILF strongholds and attacking rebel checkpoints near Camp Abubakar—the MILF headquarters in the southern Philippines—the MILF mounted several terrorist attacks in the southern Philippines against Philippine security and civilian targets. In July, Philippine Armed Forces captured Camp Abubakar, and the MILF responded by declaring a "holy war" against Manila and continuing attacks against civilian and government targets in the southern Philippines. Philippine law enforcement officials also have accused MILF operatives of responsibility for several bombings in Manila, including two at popular shopping malls in May and five at different locations in Manila on 30 December. Police arrested 26 suspected MILF members in connection with the May bombings and still held them at year's end.

Communist rebels also remained active in 2000, occasionally targeting businesses and engaging in sporadic clashes with Philippine security forces. Press reporting indicates that early in the year the Communist Party of the Philippines New People's Army (CPP/NPA) attacked a South Korean construction company and in March issued an order to target foreign businesses "whose operations hurt the country's economy and environment." The Alex Boncayao Brigade (ABB)—a breakaway CPP/NPA faction—strafed Shell Oil offices in the central Philippines in March. The group warned of more attacks against oil companies, including US-owned Caltex, to protest rising oil prices.

Distinguishing between political and criminal motivation for many of the terrorist-related activities in the Philippines continued to be difficult, most notably in the numerous cases of kidnapping for ransom in the southern Philippines. Both Islamist and Communist insurgents sought to extort funds from businesses in their operating areas, occasionally conducting reprisal operations if money was not paid.

Thailand

In January 2000, 10 armed Burmese dissidents—linked to the takeover in 1999 of the Burmese Embassy in Bangkok—took over the Ratchaburi provincial hospital. Thai security forces stormed the hospital and freed the victims. Although no hostages were injured during the assault, all the hostage takers were killed. Separately, Burma sentenced to death one terrorist involved in the 1999 Embassy takeover.

Authorities responded with military force and legal action to separatist activity in the south. In February, security forces dealt a severe blow to the New Pattani United Liberation Organization—a Muslim separatist group—when they killed its leader Saarli Taloh-Meyaw. Authorities claim that he was responsible for 90 percent of the terrorist activities in Narathiwat, a southern Thai province.

In April, police arrested the deputy leader of the outlawed Barisan Revolusi Nasional (BRN)—a Southern separatist group—in Pattani. The case was still pending before the court at year's end.

Authorities suspect Muslim separatists conducted several small-scale attacks on public schools, a government-run clinic, and a police station in the south.

In June, a Thai criminal court ordered extradited to Japan Yoshimi Tanaka—a member of the radical Japanese Red Army Faction, wanted for the hijacking in 1970 of a Japan Airlines plane. His trial in Tokyo began in mid-December.

Thai officials again publicly pledged to halt the use of Thailand as a logistics base by the Sri Lankan group the Liberation Tigers of Tamil Eelam (LTTE). The pledges, which echoed reassurances made by Bangkok in previous years, followed the discovery in June of a partially completed submersible at a shipyard in Phuket, Thailand, owned by an LTTE-sympathizer, as well as an unclassified paper by Canadian intelligence published in December that outlined the Tigers' use of front companies to procure weapons via Thailand.

Eurasia Overview

No major terrorist attacks occurred in Eurasia in 2000, but counterterrorist efforts, often in conjunction with counterinsurgency efforts, continued in the states of the former Soviet Union.

Russia, China, and the United States were all involved in regional efforts to combat terrorism. In 2000, members of the Commonwealth of Independent States (CIS) discussed establishing a CIS-wide counterterrorism center in Bishkek, although past efforts have been unsuccessful. The heads of the CIS states security services put forward Gen. Boris Mylnikov, former First Deputy Director of the Russian Federal Security Service (FSB) Department for Protecting the Constitutional Order and Combating Terrorism, to lead the potential CIS Counterterrorism Center, and on 1 December the CIS heads of state agreed on funding for the organization, half of which will be provided by Russia. The center began operations in December 2000 and reportedly has been tasked by the CIS to maintain a database of information on terrorism.

The Shanghai Forum—Kyrgyzstan, Kazakhstan, Tajikistan, Russia, and China—met in July and discussed cooperation among the five states as well as with Uzbekistan against terrorism, insurgency, and Islamic extremism. The Forum supported a proposal to establish a regional counterterrorism center in Bishkek, although no progress had been made in implementing this decision by year's end.

All five Central Asian states participated in the Central Asian Counterterrorism Conference in June sponsored by the US Department of State. Other participants included representatives from Russia, Egypt, and Spain. The United Kingdom, Turkey, China, and the Organization for Security and Cooperation in Europe (OSCE) sent observers.

Several Central Asian states also concluded counterterrorism agreements in 2000. Uzbekistan in early May signed an agreement with India that included an extradition treaty and mutual assistance in criminal investigations with an eye toward counterterrorist operations. In June, Kazkahstan and Kyrgyzstan separately reached bilateral agreements with China to cooperate on counterterrorist matters. In October and November, Uzbekistan also signed agreements on counterterrorism cooperation with Turkey, China, and Italy.

Azerbaijan

Azerbaijan took strong steps to curb the international logistics networks that support the fighters in Chechnya, to include closing international Islamic relief organizations believed to assist militants in Chechnya, strengthening border controls with Russia, and arresting and extraditing suspected *mujahidin* supporters. There has been good cooperation on counterterrorism cases between the Government of Azerbaijan and US law enforcement. In mid-September, Azerbaijani police arrested seven Dagestani men under suspicion of working with the *mujahidin* and extradited them to Russia. The government has cooperated closely and effectively with the United States on antiterrorism issues, and a program of antiterrorism assistance has been initiated. Azerbaijan intends to join the CIS Counterterrorism Center.

Azerbaijan and Russia signed a border agreement extension in early June to limit the flow of arms and militants across the borders.

In early October, the Supreme Court in Baku found 13 members of Jayshullah, an indigenous terrorist group who may have had plans to attack the US Embassy, guilty of committing terrorist actions. The court sentenced them to prison terms ranging from eight years to life.

Georgia

Georgia faced the potential for spillover violence from the Chechen conflict and contended with international *mujahidin* seeking to use Georgian territory as a conduit for financial and logistic support to the *mujahidin* in Chechnya. Russia continued to pressure Georgia for stronger border controls.

With international assistance, Georgia has steadily increased its border control presence on its northern border and invited monitors from the Organization for Security and Cooperation in Europe (OSCE). The OSCE has not recorded any movement of *mujahidin* across the Georgian border with Chechnya, although some evidence suggests that, despite these efforts, neither Russian nor Georgian border guards have been able to seal the border entirely from individuals and small groups passing to and from Chechnya.

Russia alleged that there are *mujahidin* in the Pankisi Gorge in northern Georgia. Georgia moved more Interior Ministry units into the region. Hostage taking for ransom by criminal gangs continued to be a problem in some parts of Georgia. Five persons were kidnapped in the Abkhazia region, including two unarmed UN military observers and an international NGO employee, in early June, then released without payment of ransom. Two International Red Cross staff employees were taken hostage on 4 August in the Pankisi Gorge and released one week later under the condition that their kidnappers would not face criminal charges.

Kazakhstan

In Almaty in September, Kazakhstani police killed four suspected Uighur separatist militants who were sought in connection with the murders of two policemen and a leader of the Uighur community in Kyrgyzstan.

Kyrgyzstan

The only clear instances of international terrorism in Central Asia this year occurred in Kyrgyzstan as the Islamic Movement of Uzbekistan's (IMU) insurgent efforts continued. Four US citizen mountain climbers were taken hostage by IMU militants operating in southern Kyrgyzstan in early August and held captive for several days before they escaped unharmed. IMU militants also took six German, three Russian, one Ukrainian, and two Uzbek mountaineers hostage, but later freed them.

Russia

Russian authorities continued to search for suspects in the four deadly apartment bombings that took place in August and September 1999. The trial of the six Dagestani men accused of conducting the bombing in Buinaksk, which killed 62 persons, began in December. There still are no suspects in custody for the bombings of two buildings in Moscow or a building in Volgodonsk. In November, Polish authorities arrested two Russian organized crime members, whom they suspect are connected to the August bombing in Moscow's Pushkin Square, which killed eight persons.

Tajikistan

Several incidents of domestic terrorism occurred in Tajikistan in 2000. A small car bomb, planted on a vehicle belonging to the European Community Humanitarian Organization (ECHO), exploded on 16 July in Dushanbe and injured several children. In addition, in October an unoccupied car belonging to the Chairman of the Democratic Party, Mahmadruzi Iskandarov, was bombed. Bombings and other violence marred Tajikistani Parliamentary elections in February, which concluded the Tajikistani Peace Process ending a five-year civil war. On 1 October and 31 December four churches were bombed. Several deaths and numerous casualties resulted from the bombing in October. There is no evidence that any of the attacks, either on the churches or during the elections, involved international interests. While the Tajikistani Government does not support the Islamic Movement of Uzbekistan (IMU), it has been unable to prevent it from transiting its territory.

Uzbekistan

The Islamic Movement of Uzbekistan (IMU) infiltrated fighters into mountainous areas of Surkhandar'inskaya Oblast [in] southern Uzbekistan during the spring and summer of 2000. Uzbekistani military forces discovered the fighters and drove them back into Tajikistan. Tohir Yuldashev and Juma Khodjiev (a.k.a. Juma Namangani), the leaders of the IMU, were tried in absentia together with 10 other persons accused of terrorism or anticonstitutional activity. All defendants were convicted at a trial that failed to conform to international standards for the protection of the human rights of the defendants. The court sentenced Yuldashev and Khodjiev to death and the remaining defendants to prison terms. On 25 September, the United States designated the IMU a Foreign Terrorist Organization, citing both its armed incursions into Uzbekistan and neighboring Kyrgyzstan and its taking of foreign hostages, including US citizens.

Europe Overview

Western Europe had the largest decline in the number of international terrorist incidents of any region in 2000. Several European states moved to strengthen and codify antiterrorism legislation, and many signed the International Convention for the Suppression of Terrorist Financing, which was opened for signature on 10 January 2000. There were notable examples of counterterrorism cooperation among several countries, such as the US-UK-Greek collaboration on the British Defense Attache's assassination in Athens, Spanish-French cooperation against the Basque terrorist group Basque Fatherland and Liberty (ETA), and Italy and Spain's agreement to create common judicial space. Greece undertook a series of more stringent counterterrorism measures in the wake of the murder of the UK Defense Attache by the terrorist group 17 November, but Athens still has not made any arrests in connection with any of the group's 21 murders over the past quarter century. France and Turkey both made impressive strides in combating terrorism through aggressively pursuing the perpetrators and their terrorist groups.

In Southeastern Europe, groups of ethnic Albanians have

conducted armed attacks against government forces in southern Serbia and in Macedonia since 1999. One group in southern Serbia calls itself the Liberation Army of Presevo, Medvedja, and Bujanovac (PMBLA). One group in Macedonia calls itself the National Liberation Army (NLA). Both groups include members who fought with the Kosovo Liberation Army (KLA) in 1998-99 and have used their wartime connections to obtain funding and weapons from Kosovo and elsewhere. The PMBLA has, on occasion, harassed and detained civilians traveling through areas it controls. Both the PMBLA and the NLA have fired indiscriminately upon civilian centers. (In the same region, ethnic Albanian assailants carried out a terrorist attack against a bus in Kosovo on 16 February 2001, killing at least seven civilians and wounding 43 others.)

Austria

In keeping with Austria's constructive security relationship with the United States, the Interior Minister discussed closer cooperation in countering crime and terrorism during a visit to Washington in August. Vienna also enacted an expanded police-powers bill enabling authorities to collect and analyze information more effectively.

On 26 February, Austrian letter bomber Franz Fuchs committed suicide in his prison cell where he had been serving a life sentence for masterminding a series of letter-bomb campaigns in Austria and Germany between 1993 and 1997.

Authorities held Halimeh Nimr, a suspected member of the terrorist Abu Nidal organization (ANO), in custody from January to May. In September, she failed to appear in court to be tried on charges of attempting to withdraw some $8 million from a bank account controlled by the ANO, which subsequently threatened to target Austrian interests if the funds were not released to the group.

In 2000, citing the statute of limitations, France declined an Austrian Government request that Illich Ramirez Sanchez, a.k.a. Carlos the Jackal, be extradited to face criminal charges for a terrorist attack on the Vienna headquarters of OPEC in 1975.

The Austrian Government continued to allow the political front of the Kurdistan Workers' Party (PKK) to maintain its offices in Vienna, which have been open since 1995. Authorities estimate some 400 PKK militants and 4,000 sympathizers reside in Austria.

Belgium

The Interior Ministers of Belgium and Spain met in Brussels in June to discuss Belgium's refusal to extradite Basque Fatherland and Liberty (ETA) members suspected of terrorist acts. The Belgian minister pledged that his government would no longer refuse Spanish extradition requests.

In 2000, Belgium did reject Turkey's request for the extradition of suspected Turkish terrorist Fehriye Erdal to prosecute her for her alleged role in the 1996 handgun murder of a prominent Turkish industrialist and two associates in Istanbul. Erdal, arrested in Belgium in 1999, is allegedly a member of the Turkish Revolutionary People's Liberation Party/Front (DHKP/C) terrorist group. Belgian authorities denied Turkey's request on the grounds she could receive the death penalty if tried in Turkey. Belgium also declined to prosecute her under the 1977 European Convention on the Suppression of Terrorism, noting that it covers only terrorist acts using bombs or automatic weapons. After Brussels denied Ms. Erdal's political asylum request, she went on a hunger strike and subsequently was released from prison and placed under house arrest. She may be tried later on charges arising from criminal activities in Belgium.

In February, authorities paroled two members of the "Cellules Communistes Combattantes" after they had served 14 years of their life sentences for involvement in a series of bomb attacks against US, NATO, and Belgian interests in 1984 and 1985. One attack resulted in the deaths of two firemen in Brussels.

Belgium has yet to sign the International Convention for the Suppression of Terrorist Financing.

France

During 2000, France maintained its traditional tough stance against terrorism. On the legal front, Paris was the first to sign the International Convention for the Suppression of Terrorist Financing, which was a French initiative. The French Government's nationwide "Vigi-Pirate" plan—which uses military forces to reinforce police security in Paris and other major cities to prevent a repeat of the Paris metro attacks by Algerian terrorists—remained in effect. Vigi-Pirate increased security at metro and train stations, enhanced border controls, and expanded identity checks countrywide.

In January, the Basque Fatherland and Liberty (ETA) relaunched its assassination and bombing campaign in Spain, and French police responded aggressively by interdicting cross-border operations, arresting group members, and shutting down logistics and supply cells in France. At year's end, ETA had killed 23 persons and wounded scores more.

On the judicial front, French courts tried and convicted numerous ETA terrorists. In January, Javier Arizkuren Ruiz, alias Kantauri, a former ETA military operations chief, was sentenced to eight years' imprisonment. A Paris appeals court in September reportedly authorized Ruiz's extradition to Spain to stand trial for an attempt to kill King Juan Carlos in 1995. Twelve other ETA militants received lengthy jail sentences. The court sent Daniel Derguy, believed to be the ETA chief in France, to prison for 10 years. In October, 10 senior French and Spanish ETA members were convicted of criminal conspiracy in connection with a terrorist organization. Ignacio Gracia Arregui, alias Inaki de Renteria, reportedly a top ETA leader, was sentenced in December to five years in jail. Others convicted received prison sentences of five to 10 years. France often has extradited convicted ETA terrorists to Spain when they have completed their prison sentences.

In October, a French judge ruled in favor of a suit charging Libyan leader Muammar Qadhafi with "complicity to murder" in the bomb attack in 1989 against a UTA airliner over the Niger desert that killed 170 persons.

In November, French courts also convicted seven Spanish citizens of membership in First of October Anti-Fascist Resistance Group (GRAPO), a Spanish leftist terrorist group. In raids during the year, police officials seized bombmaking paraphernalia, false identity documents, and large amounts of cash.

French courts convicted a number of Algerian nationals on terrorist-related charges. Amar Bouakaze, an Algerian, was convicted in June for criminal conspiracy in connection with a terrorist organization. Evidence linked Bouakaze to Ahmed Ressam, a suspected terrorist being held in the United States. Another Algerian national was convicted of an attack that derailed a train in France in June, leaving two persons dead.

The Breton Resistance Army (ARB) claimed responsibility for a bomb attack in April that damaged a McDonald's restaurant at Pornic, but the group denied involvement in another attack the same month against a McDonald's restaurant near Dinan that killed a French employee. French police arrested four members of the Breton nationalist group Emgann (Combat) on charges of involvement in the Dinan bombing.

Six proindependence Corsican groups joined in proclaiming a cease-fire in late 1999, but bomb attacks against government offices on the island continued intermittently in 2000. One such Corsican group claimed responsibility for a failed attack in Paris in June. In October, Corsican separatists placed a car bomb in front of the police station in Marseilles. The device was not built to detonate but to serve as a warning for a possible future attack and to highlight the group's capabilities. Also in October, French courts sentenced 10 Corsican nationalists to four years' imprisonment for an attack that damaged an estate complex on Corsica in 1994.

France's counterterrorism efforts have been less robust on the diplomatic front where it has blocked concerted action by the G-8 aimed at Iranian-sponsored terrorism in the Middle East. Also, France's presidency of the EU yielded little practical US-EU counterterrorism cooperation.

Germany

Extreme rightwing violence against foreign nationals in Germany increased in 2000 and became a major political issue. Interior ministers from the German states met in November to address the problem and recommended the federal authorities adopt control measures, including establishing databases to track rightwing and leftwing extremists.

German officials detected no revival of organized extreme leftwing terrorist activity in 2000. Authorities sought several former members of the Red Army Faction (RAF), which was dissolved in 1998, and continued to prosecute former RAF members in court. Johannes Weinreich, a former RAF member and lieutenant to Carlos the Jackal, was convicted in January of committing murder and attempted murder during an attack in 1983 on a French cultural center in then-West Berlin. In November, RAF member Andrea Klump went on trial on charges of participation in a failed attack on the NATO base at Rota, Spain, in 1988. In December, Foreign Minister Joschka Fischer testified at the trial of former acquaintance Hans-Joachim Klein, who was charged with three murders in connection with the 1975 attack in Vienna on petroleum ministers from OPEC states by "Carlos"-led terrorists.

The courts convicted Metin Kaplan, leader of the violent Turkish Islamist group Kalifatstaat, and sentenced him to four years in prison for publicly calling for the death of a rival. The trial of five defendants accused of the 1986 Libyan-sponsored bombing against the Labelle Discotheque, which killed two US servicemen, continued to progress slowly. The 1993 ban on the Kurdistan Workers' Party (PKK) and its affiliates remained in effect. The PKK ceased to conduct violent demonstrations in 2000, following the seizure of the group's leader Ocalan.

Germany continued to cooperate multilaterally and bilaterally—notably with the United States—to combat terrorism. In 2000, German authorities arrested and extradited to the United States a suspect in the bombings in 1998 of the US embassies in East Africa.

Greece

The Greek Government undertook some meaningful steps to combat terrorism—especially in the wake of the Revolutionary Organization 17 November's (17 November) murder of UK Defense Attache Saunders in Athens—including efforts to persuade a historically skeptical public of the damage inflicted by terrorism on Greece's interests and international reputation. The government strengthened the police counterterrorism unit, implemented a multimillion-dollar reward program, and began drafting legislation to provide a legal basis for more vigorous counterterrorism efforts. Greek, British, and US experts cooperated closely in the still ongoing investigation of the Saunders murder. Nonetheless, despite these and other promising initiatives, as well as closer Greek-US cooperation, Athens resolved no outstanding terrorist incident and arrested no terrorist suspects in 2000.

In June, two motorcyclists shot and killed British Defense Attache Stephen Saunders in Athens' rush hour traffic. Revolutionary Organization 17 November, a violent far-left nationalist group, claimed the murder as revenge against NATO's military action in 1999 against Serbia. The group simultaneously claimed responsibility for attacks it had mounted in 1999 on the German and Dutch ambassadors' residences, on three Western banks, and on offices of the governing PASOK party. In a follow-up communique released in December, 17 November defended itself against mounting public criticism by trying to appeal to populist, pro-Serb sentiments and also by urging Greeks not to cooperate with the government's counterterrorism efforts.

The Saunders murder and Greek preparations for the 2004 Olympics contributed to a political and public opinion climate more supportive of effective counterterrorism measures. The Prime Minister, his cabinet colleagues, and opposition leaders denounced the murder of Saunders and spoke out against terrorism in general. The Greek media provided extensive coverage of Heather Saunders' eloquent public statements in the aftermath of her husband's murder. The public widely observed a national moment of silence for all victims of terrorism, and Orthodox Archbishop Christodoulos held an unprecedented memorial service for all Greek and foreign victims of terrorism in Greece.

The police sought to involve the public in the Saunders investigation and encouraged witnesses to come forward. Minister of Public Order (MPO) Khrisokhoidhis led the government's efforts, which included increasing the reward for information on terrorist attacks to $2.5 million. The police also opened toll-free hotlines to enable informants to pass tips anonymously. Although failure to cordon off the Saunders crime scene initially hampered the investigation, the Greek police subsequently worked effectively with British investigators to pursue a small number of useful leads. At year's end, the British Defense Attache's murder remained unsolved.

In the spring, Revolutionary Nuclei, another far-left, nationalist terrorist group, bombed buildings belonging to two Greek construction companies linked to the Greek Government, military, and NATO. Police safely removed a bomb the group had left outside the Peiraiefs (Piraeus) office of a former PASOK minister. On 12 November, the group mounted three separate but nearly simultaneous attacks against a British bank, a US bank, and the studio and home of the Greek sculptor whose statue of Gen. George C. Marshall is displayed at the US Embassy.

Throughout the year, a host of anarchist groups claimed responsibility for an average of two arson or bomb attacks per week on offices, shops, and vehicles, almost always in Athens; many of the targeted vehicles belonged to foreign diplomats, foreign companies, Greek officials, and Greek public-sector executives. The two most prolific groups, Black Star and Anarchist Faction, together carried out 31 attacks in 2000. No fatalities or arrests resulted from these attacks.

Suspected terrorist Avraam Lesperoglou, already imprisoned since December 1999 for passport fraud and draftdodging, was convicted in October of attempting to murder a policeman and sentenced to 17 years. Lesperoglou, who is suspected of being linked to Revolutionary People's Struggle (ELA) and possibly other groups, still awaits trial on several terrorism-related murder charges.

In late November, a Justice Ministry expert committee began drafting legislation on terrorism and organized crime for presentation to Parliament. The controversial legislation is expected to provide for greater admissability of evidence from undercover police operations, use of DNA evidence, adjudication by all-judge panels of certain classes of terrorist cases, and protection of witnesses. The Greek Government has indicated the legislation will be consistent with EU standards and international norms.

In 2000, Greece and the United States ratified a mutual legal assistance treaty and signed a police cooperation memorandum to enhance bilateral cooperation on law enforcement, including terrorism. During the year, MPO Khrisokhoidhis met with cabinet-level officials in the United States and in the United Kingdom and signed a bilateral counterterrorism agreement in London. By year's end, Greece had signed all 12 and ratified all but two of the UN counterterrorism conventions.

Italy

Italy's counterterrorism efforts in 2000 focused primarily on the assassination in 1999 of Labor Ministry Adviser Massimo d'Antona by individuals who claimed to be from the extreme leftist Red Brigades-Combatant Communist Party (BR-PCC). Leaks from the investigation, however, complicated the arrest and interrogation of several suspects. One much-publicized suspect was released because of lack of evidence but remains under investigation. Later in the year, the Revolutionary Proletarian Nucleus, a leftist-anarchist group, issued a communique claiming responsibility for placing a bomb at the Milan office of the Italian Confederation of Free Trade Unions in July.

In February, Interior Minister Bianco warned of a possible resurgence of rightwing terrorism, and the Italian Government subsequently dissolved the neofascist organization Fronte Nazionale (National Front) and in October confiscated its assets. Bianco maintained, however, that leftwing and anarchist violence, exemplified by the BR-PCC and the Territorial Anti-Imperialist Nuclei (NTA), posed the greater threat. A spinoff group of the NTA—an anti-US, anti-NATO group—was behind several low-level bombing and incendiary attacks on Aviano Airbase in 1999.

In October authorities in Naples issued arrest warrants for 11 members of Al-Takfir w'al Hijra, a North African Muslim extremist group. Seven were apprehended in Naples, France, and Algeria, but four eluded arrest. Officials noted that members of the group, also active in Milan and other cities, engaged primarily in forging travel documents and raising funds from expatriate Muslims.

In January, the government expelled to his native country illegal immigrant and Algerian national Yamin Rachek, husband of Italian-Canadian dual national Lucia Garofolo who was arrested in December for carrying explosives from Canada into the United States. In June, the government pardoned Turkish national Ali Agca for his attack on the Pope in 1981 and extradited him to his native Turkey.

In late 2000, Italy and Spain signed an agreement to create a common judicial space between them, eliminating extradition procedures in the case of serious felonies, including terrorist activities.

Spain

Spain was wracked by domestic terrorism in 2000. After abandoning its cease-fire in late 1999, the terrorist group Basque Fatherland and Liberty (ETA) began a countrywide bombing and assassination campaign, killing 23 and wounding scores more by year's end. ETA traditionally targets police, military personnel, and politicians, as well as journalists and businessmen. As 2000 progressed, however, the group appeared to become increasingly indiscriminate in its attacks, targeting, for example, intersections and shopping areas.

The public responded with huge demonstrations in major cities, demanding an end to the violence. Also in 2000, the Spanish and French Basque youth groups united and continued their campaign of street violence and arson. Spanish authorities diligently prosecuted ETA members on terrorism and criminal charges, and the Aznar government reiterated its determination to eliminate terrorism and not negotiate over independence for the constitutionally autonomous Basque provinces. After difficult discussions over the role of moderate Basques represented by the Basque Nationalist Party (PNV), the governing and opposition Socialist parties signed a common anti-ETA pact at year's end.

The First of October Anti-Fascist Resistance Group (GRAPO), quiescent in recent years, stepped up its activity in 2000. In November, the group murdered a Spanish policeman following the arrest of seven GRAPO leaders in Paris, killed two security guards during a botched armed robbery attempt of a security van in May, and carried out several bombings that damaged property but caused no injuries. In November, the Spanish Interior Minister stated that arrests of GRAPO operatives in France had effectively dismantled the leadership and operational command of the group.

In June, Spain's Interior Minister Jaime Mayor Oreja visited Washington in keeping with the active, high-level dialogue on terrorism between the United States and Spain. Spain also played an important role in the Central Asian Counterterrorism Conference sponsored by the US Department of State held in Washington in June. A Spanish court convicted Ramon Aldasoro, whom the United States extradited to Spain in December 1999, for his participation in the bombing of a police barracks in 1988.

Spanish and French interior ministries cooperated closely in combating terrorism, including arresting numerous ETA members and raiding logistics and support cells. France regularly delivered detained ETA terrorists, including several senior leaders, into Spanish custody. Spain also secured a pledge from Mexico to deny safehaven to ETA members. Spain welcomed the condemnation of ETA in November by all Ibero-American presidents—except Cuba's Castro, whose refusal harmed bilateral relations.

Spain has urged the European Union to adopt more vigorous measures against terrorism, including creating a common judicial space. Spain and Italy signed such an agreement.

Turkey

Combating terrorism remained a top Turkish domestic and foreign policy priority as ethnic, Islamist, leftist, and transnational terrorist groups continued to threaten Turkey. In 2000, previous Turkish successes in fighting these groups were consolidated, producing a dramatically lowered incidence of terrorist activity. The Turkish Government remained in the forefront of cooperative international counterterrorism efforts and worked closely with Washington on combating groups that target US personnel and facilities.

At the direction of its imprisoned leader, Abdullah Ocalan, the Kurdistan Workers' Party (PKK), which long had sought to achieve an independent Kurdish state through violence, asserted that it now seeks, through a political campaign, only guarantees of Kurdish political, economic, social, and cultural rights in a democratic Turkey. The government did not respond to the PKK's declared change in tactics and goals. Prime Minister Ecevit warned that his government would reconsider its decision not to press for the death sentence against Ocalan if the PKK renewed its violence while the European Court of Human Rights reviewed his trial. The Court took up Ocalan's appeal in November.

Meanwhile, the number of violent clashes between PKK and government forces in Turkey declined significantly with 45 confrontations in the first 11 months of 2000, according to the Turkish General Staff, compared with thousands in previous years. Turkish forces mounted vigorous operations against the few hundred PKK guerrillas in southeastern Turkey and the several thousand who had withdrawn to northern Iraq, enlisting the aid of Iraqi Kurdish groups that have fought sporadically with the PKK over the last several years. Turkish officials and newspapers noted that Syria observed its commitment made in 1998 to abjure support to the PKK. In contrast, Iran allegedly continued to provide at least a safehaven to armed PKK militants.

Turkish security forces continued their effective campaign against the extreme-left terrorist group Revolutionary People's Liberation Party/Front (DHKP/C, formerly Dev Sol). The group was able to mount only a few attacks. In August, the police arrested seven suspected DHKP/C terrorists that allegedly planned to attack the airbase at Incirlik, from which a joint US-British-Turkish force maintains "Operation Northern Watch" over the no-fly zone in Iraq. Several European countries, including Belgium, have declined Turkish requests to extradite PKK, DHKP/C, and other terrorists, citing Turkey's retention of the death penalty and the political motivation of the suspects' crimes.

The DHKP/C, joined by small extreme leftist factions, staged repeated violent uprisings in prisons to protest the government's efforts to transfer prisoners from overcrowded older prisons—in which terrorist and criminal groups effectively controlled entire wards—to newer prisons with cells for two or three prisoners. In December, the outlawed terrorist group Turkish Communist Party/Marxist-Leninist showed its opposition to the transfer program by killing two policemen. "Operation Return to Life," undertaken in December by security forces to gain control of the prison wards, left about 30 prisoners dead, some by their own hand.

The police and the judiciary dealt heavy blows to domestic Islamist terrorist groups in 2000, including the Turkish Hizballah, a domestic terrorist group of mostly Kurdish Sunni Islamists with no known ties to Lebanese Hizballah. Turkish officials and media assert that Turkish Hizballah has received limited Iranian support. Turkish Hizballah's adherents are anti-Western but primarily target Kurds who are viewed as insufficiently Islamic or unwilling to meet the group's extortion demands. They have not targeted US citizens. Through October, 723 police operations, mostly in predominantly Kurdish southeastern Turkey, netted more than

2,700 Turkish Hizballah suspects, approximately 1,700 of whom were arrested. The trial of 15 Turkish Hizballah suspects accused of 156 murders began in July in Diyarbakir.

Turkish authorities arrested members of the Jerusalem Warriors, a small ethnic Turkish Sunni Islamist group with tenuous links to the Turkish Hizballah. Turkish officials and media reported that they had received direction, training, and support from Iran. In August, 17 Warriors went on trial for involvement in 22 murders, including assassinations of several prominent Turkish secularist intellectuals. Four have been accused of killing USAF Sgt. Victor Marvick in a car-bombing in 1991.

United Kingdom

The United Kingdom enacted two far-reaching counterterrorism laws and continued its close cooperation with the United States and other nations in the fight against terrorism. As in previous years, UK authorities focused primarily on the threat posed by dissident Republican and Loyalist terrorist groups in Northern Ireland, while continuing their efforts to combat transnational Islamist terrorists settled in or transiting the United Kingdom.

The Terrorism Act, enacted in July and effective February 2001, replaces temporary and emergency laws that dealt with Northern Ireland-related terrorism. It broadens the definition of domestic and transnational terrorism throughout the United Kingdom to cover violent acts and threats against individuals and property—including electronic systems—intended to influence the government or promote political, religious, or ideological causes. The Act authorizes the government to ban groups involved in domestic or transnational terrorism and to use special arrest powers to prosecute their members or supporters. The Regulation of Investigatory Powers Act, effective July 2000, created a statutory basis for intercepting communications and for covert surveillance.

London continued to work vigorously to combat Northern Ireland-related terrorism, but British press reports indicated that terrorist killings in the north increased from seven in 1999 to 18 in 2000. The dissident Real Irish Republican Army (RIRA) is credited in press reports to have been responsible for attacks in Northern Ireland as well as in central London. The most spectacular incident involved a rocket attack in September that caused minor damage to the headquarters of Britain's foreign intelligence service, MI6, in central London. UK officials continued to prosecute dissidents suspected in previous attacks. Authorities repeatedly urged witnesses to come forward with evidence relating to RIRA's 1998 bombing in Omagh, which left 29 dead, and to the murder in 1999 of Republican defense lawyer Rosemary Nelson by Loyalist Red Hand Defenders.

Making the most of close US ties to the United Kingdom and Ireland, Washington continued its efforts to encourage normalization of political, law enforcement, and security arrangements in Northern Ireland as called for in the Good Friday Agreement. President Clinton's December visit demonstrated US support for achieving lasting peace in the troubled region.

London and Washington worked together to bring to justice suspects in the bombing of two US embassies in East Africa in 1998 and in the Pan Am 103 bombing over Lockerbie, Scotland, in 1988. UK courts found Khaled al-Fawwaz, Ibrahim Hussein Abd al-Hadi Eidarous, and Abel Muhammad Abd al-Majid—indicted in the United States for involvement in the embassy attacks—extraditable to the United States. The three men are appealing the decision. In April, Manchester police, responding to a US request, searched two residences of associates of Usama Bin Ladin and his al-Qaida terrorist network. In May, a Scottish court sitting in the Netherlands commenced the trial of two Libyans accused of murder, conspiracy, and breach of the UK Aviation Security Act in perpetrating the Pan Am 103 bombing. All charges but murder were later dropped. (In January 2001, one of the Libyans was found guilty of murder in connection with that attack. The judges found that he acted "in furtherance of the purposes of... Libyan Intelligence Services." Concerning the other defendant, Al-Amin Kalifa Fahima, the court concluded that the Crown failed to present sufficient evidence to satisfy the high standard of "proof beyond reasonable doubt" that is necessary in criminal cases.)

British authorities assisted Greek officials in investigating the assassination in June of Britain's Defense Attache in Athens by the terrorist group 17 November. London continues to investigate the murder of British and US citizens in Yemen in 1998 and a bomb incident in its Embassy in Sanaa in 2000, the day after the bombing of the USS Cole.

Latin America Overview

Latin America witnessed an increase in terrorist attacks from the previous year, from 121 to 193. In Colombia, leftist guerilla groups abducted hostages and attacked civil infrastructure, while rightwing paramilitary groups abducted congressional representatives, killed political candidates, and massacred civilians in an attempt to thwart the guerilas. In Ecuador, organized criminal elements with possible links to terrorists and terrorist groups abducted 10 oil workers and also claimed responsibility for oil pipeline bombings that killed seven civilians. Extremist religious groups continued to pose a terrorist concern in the triborder area of Argentina, Brazil, and Paraguay. Terrorist incidents continued a downward trend in Peru despite a deteriorating political situation and the abrupt resignation of hardline President Fujimori.

Colombia

Despite ongoing peace talks, Colombia's two largest guerrilla groups, the Revolutionary Armed Forces of Colombia (FARC) and the National Liberation Army (ELN), continued to conduct international terrorist acts, including kidnapping private US and foreign citizens and extorting money from businesses and individuals in the Colombian countryside.

A significant development during the year involved a series of FARC attacks on interests of US coal firm Drummond, Inc., in Colombia, which publicly refused to pay the group millions of dollars annually in extortion under the terms of FARC Law 002, a tax on entities valued at more than $1 million. As a result of FARC actions, Drummond did not bid on a state-owned coal company, potentially costing Bogota tens of millions of dollars in lost privatization revenue. Colombia's second-largest crude oil pipeline, the Cano Limon, was attacked 152 times in 2000—a record—which the army blames mostly on the ELN. The attacks forced Occidental Petroleum to halt exports through most of August and September.

In October, the Colombian police rescued a five-year-old US citizen who had been held six months by individuals connected with the FARC.

The FARC and the ELN continued to reach out to government and nongovernment groups throughout the world and especially in Europe and Latin America through international representatives and attendance at regional conferences and meetings, such as the Sao Paulo Forum. The FARC also continued to target security forces and other symbols of government authority to demonstrate its power and to strengthen its negotiating position. President Pastrana in December extended the FARC's demilitarized zone to 31 January 2001 and pledged to place government controls over the zone. The FARC—which said it would not return to the table until Bogota reined in the rightwing paramilitaries—unilaterally froze peace talks in November.

Meanwhile, rightwing paramilitary groups continued to grow and expanded their reach in 2000, most notably in southern Colombia's prime coca growing areas. The groups, in addition to massacring civilians in their attempts to erode FARC and ELN areas of influence, also abducted seven national congressional representatives in December, demanding negotiations with the government.

Ecuador

On 12 October, organized criminal elements with possible links to terrorists and terrorist groups abducted 10 aviation company employees and oil workers (five US citizens, two French, one Chilean, one Argentine, and one New Zealander) in the northern canton of Sucumbios. In December, the kidnappers also claimed responsibility for multiple bomb attacks on the Trans-Ecuadorian Oil pipeline, one of which killed seven Ecuadorian bystanders. At year's end, the terrorists were demanding $80 million in ransom for eight hostages (two escaped), and the situation had not been resolved. The exact identity of the terrorists remained uncertain. (The group executed one of their hostages, a US citizen, in January 2001. Following extended negotiations with representatives of the oil companies that employed the hostages, the remaining captives were released on 1 March 2001. The United States has pledged to bring those responsible to justice.)

Peru

There were no international acts of terrorism in Peru in 2000, but the Peruvian judicial system continued to prosecute vigorously individuals accused of committing domestic terrorist acts. Of the 314 persons Peruvian authorities arrested for involvement in significant acts of terrorism, 30 were sentenced to life imprisonment and 25 were sentenced to 20 to 30 years. Lima requested the extradition from Bolivia of suspected terrorist Justino Soto Vargas. La Paz granted the request, but at year's end Soto's asylum status remained unchanged, impeding his extradition.

In April, government authorities captured Shining Path (SL) commander Jose Arcela Chiroque (a.k.a. Ormeno) and as of late November 2000 continued large-scale efforts to apprehend SL leaders Macario Ala (a.k.a. Artemio) and "Comrade Alipio." Government operations targeted pockets of terrorist activity in the Upper Huallaga River Valley and the Apurimac/Ene River Valley, where SL columns continued to conduct periodic attacks.

The Peruvian Government continued to oppose strongly support to terrorists, but investigations continued into allegations that a small group of Peruvian military officers sold a substantial quantity of small arms to the Revolutionary Armed Forces of Colombia. Lima remained receptive to US Government-sponsored antiterrorism training and cooperated fully to prevent terrorist attacks by providing valuable information, including access to law enforcement files, records, and databases concerning domestic terrorist groups.

Triborder (Argentina, Brazil, and Paraguay)

In 2000, the triborder region of South America—where the borders of Argentina, Brazil, and Paraguay meet—remained a focal point for Islamic extremism in Latin America, but no acts of international terrorism occurred in any of the three countries. The Governments of Argentina, Brazil, and Paraguay continued efforts to stem criminal activities of individuals linked to international Islamic terrorist groups, but limited resources, porous borders, and corruption remained obstacles.

Paraguayan authorities in February arrested Ali Khalil Mehri, a Lebanese businessman having financial links to Hizballah, for violating intellectual property rights laws and aiding a criminal enterprise involved in distributing CDs espousing Hizballah's extremist ideals. He fled the country in June after faulty judicial procedures allowed his release. In November, Paraguayan authorities arrested Salah Abdul Karim Yassine, a Palestinian who allegedly threatened to bomb the US and Israeli Embassies in Asuncion, and charged him with possession of false documents and entering the country illegally. Yassine remained in prison at year's end. Paraguayan counternarcotics police in October also arrested an individual believed to be representing the FARC for possible involvement in a guns-for-cocaine ring between Paraguay and the Colombian terrorist group. Despite these successes, an ineffective judicial system and pervasive corruption, which facilitate criminal activity supporting terrorist groups, hampered counterterrorism efforts in Paraguay.

Argentina continued investigations into the bombings of the Israeli Embassy in 1992 and the Argentine-Israeli Community Center (AMIA) in 1994, both in Buenos Aires. In early February, the magistrate in the AMIA case presented his conclusions, which included charges of complicity against numerous former police officials and local civilians and a determination that a car bomb loaded with 300 kilograms of explosives was used to execute the attack. In May, INTERPOL agents also arrested a Paraguayan businessman for suspected links to the AMIA bombing. Trials were set to begin in early 2001.

Middle East Overview

Middle Eastern terrorist groups and their state sponsors continued to plan, train for, and carry out acts of terrorism throughout 2000. The last few months of the year brought a significant increase in the overall level of political violence and terrorism in the region, especially in Israel and the occupied territories. Much of the late-year increase in violence was driven by a breakdown in negotiations and counterterrorism cooperation between Israel and the Palestinian Authority. The breakdown sparked a cycle of violence between Israelis and Palestinians that continued to spiral at the end of the year.

Israeli-Palestinian violence also prompted widespread anger at Israel, as well as the United States, throughout the Middle East, demonstrated in part by numerous, occasionally violent protests against US interests in several Middle Eastern countries. Palestinian terrorist groups, with the assistance of Iran and the Lebanese Hizballah, took advantage of Palestinian and regional anger to escalate their terrorist attacks against Israeli targets.

Other terrorists also keyed on Israeli-Palestinian difficulties to increase their rhetorical and operational activities against Israel and the United States. Usama Bin Ladin's al-Qaida organization, the Egyptian Islamic Jihad, and other terrorist groups that focus on US and Israeli targets escalated their efforts to conduct and promote terrorism in the Middle East. Several disrupted plans to attack US and Israeli targets in the Middle East purportedly were intended to demonstrate anger over Israel's sometimes disproportionate use of force to contain protests and perceptions that the United States "allowed" Israel to act.

Al-Qaida and its affiliates especially used their ability to provide money and training as leverage to establish ties to and build the terrorist capabilities of a variety of small Middle Eastern terrorist groups such as the Lebanese Asbat al-Ansar.

The most significant act of anti-US terrorism in the region in 2000—the bombing of the USS Cole in Yemen on 12 October—was not driven by events in the Levant. Although the joint US-Yemeni investigation into the savage bombing—which killed 17 US sailors and wounded 39 others—continued through the end of 2000, initial indications suggested the attack may have originated in Taliban-controlled Afghanistan, where al-Qaida, the Egyptian Islamic Jihad, and other terrorist groups are based and some of the alleged USS Cole attackers received training. The Yemeni Government, as much a victim of the attack as the United States, was working closely with the US Government to bring to justice those responsible for the act.

Many other Middle Eastern governments also increased their efforts to counter the threat from regional and Afghanistan-based terrorists, including the provision of enhanced security for high-risk US Government targets. The Government of Kuwait, for instance, cooperated with regional counterparts in November to disrupt a suspected international terrorist cell. Kuwait arrested 13 individuals and recovered a large quantity of explosives and weapons. The cell reportedly was planning to attack both Kuwaiti officials and US targets in Kuwait and the region.

Algeria

President Bouteflika's Law on Civil Concord in 2000 initially contributed to a decrease in violence against civilians inside Algeria. Nonetheless, two main armed groups continued to reject the government's amnesty program for terrorists, and it is estimated that domestic terrorism kills between 100 to 300 persons each month. Antar Zouabri's Armed Islamic Group (GIA) actively targeted civilians, although such tactics caused his group to lose popular support. In contrast, Hassan Hattab's splinter faction—the Salafi Group for Call and Combat (GSPC)—stated it would limit attacks on civilians, enabling it to co-opt Zouabri's supporters and eclipse the GIA as the most effective terrorist group operating inside Algeria.

Although at year's end the GSPC had not staged an anti-Western terrorist attack, various security services in January suspected Algerian extremists associated with the GSPC of planning to disrupt the Paris-Dakar Road Rally, leading organizers to reroute the race.

No foreign nationals were killed in Algeria during 2000, although in May GSPC troops crossed into Tunisia and attacked an outpost, killing three border guards. The GSPC frequently used false roadblocks to rob passengers of money. In one incident on 3 May, 19 persons were killed and 26 injured when militants sprayed a bus with bullets after the driver refused to stop.

Egypt

No terrorist attacks in Egypt or by Egyptian groups were reported in 2000. The Egyptian Government continued to regard terrorism as its most serious threat. Cairo tried and convicted numerous terrorists in 2000, including 14 al-Gama'a al-Islamiyya members, in connection with attempts to reactivate al-Gama'a in Egypt. Two Egyptian Islamic Jihad members, who were convicted in 1999 for planning an attack against the US Embassy in August 1998, were executed in

February. Security forces attacked a terrorist hideout in Aswan in late October, killing two al-Gama'a members, including the group's military leader in charge of armed operations in Qina, Suhaj, and Luxor.

International counterterrorism cooperation remained a key foreign policy priority for the Egyptian Government throughout the year. In September, at the UN General Assembly Millennium Summit, Egypt signed the International Convention for the Suppression of Terrorist Financing.

The Egyptian Government worked closely with the United States on a broad range of counterterrorism issues in 2000. It cooperated with US authorities after the bombing in October of the USS Cole in Yemen, conducting a security survey of the Suez Canal and recommending measures to protect ships from possible terrorist attacks while transiting the canal. Egypt also played an important role in sharing its expertise at the Central Asian Counterterrorism Conference sponsored by the US Department of State and held in Washington in June.

In 2000, Egyptian security forces and government agencies continued to place a high priority on protecting US citizens and facilities in Egypt from terrorist attacks. The Egyptian Government increased security for the US Embassy and other official facilities in light of disturbances in Israel and the Palestinian territories and related threats against US interests.

Israel, the West Bank, and the Gaza Strip

Terrorism by Palestinian extremist groups opposed to the peace process increased in late 2000 against the backdrop of violent Palestinian-Israeli clashes. The Palestine Islamic Jihad (PIJ) and Islamic Resistance Movement (HAMAS) claimed responsibility for several attacks during the crisis, ending a period of more than two years without a large-scale successful terrorist operation. Both groups publicly threatened more anti-Israeli attacks to avenge Palestinian casualties.

In an operation almost certainly timed to mark the anniversary of the death of PIJ founder Fathi Shaqaqi in 1995, on 26 October a PIJ operative on a bicycle detonated an explosive device near a Jewish settlement in Gaza, killing himself and injuring an Israeli soldier. The PIJ also claimed responsibility for a car bomb that exploded near a Jerusalem market on 2 November, killing two Israeli civilians—including the daughter of Israeli National Religious Party leader Yitzhak Levy—and wounding nine. The bomb—which was concealed in a parked car—reportedly was remotely detonated; the perpetrators escaped. On 28 December, PIJ operatives detonated explosive charges near the Sufa crossing in Gaza, injuring four Israeli explosives-disposal experts, two of whom later died. The PIJ claimed the attack in honor of a PIJ member killed by Israeli forces earlier that month and promised further revenge attacks.

The PIJ stepped up its rhetoric condemning Israeli-Palestinian peace talks at Camp David and Israel for its role in clashes with the Palestinians and vowed to continue attacks against Israel. Before the crisis, PIJ leader Shallah had issued threats against US interests in response to speculation during the summer that Washington was considering moving the US Embassy from Tel Aviv to Jerusalem.

HAMAS also claimed responsibility for several attacks during the unrest, including the bombing of an Israeli bus on 22 November in downtown Hadera that killed two Israeli civilians and wounded more than 20. Resembling the car-bombing on 2 November, the bomb apparently also was hidden in a parked car and detonated as the bus passed; at year's end no suspects had been arrested for the attack. The group also took responsibility for launching an explosives-laden craft against an Israeli naval patrol boat off the Gaza coast on 7 November. The operative died in the explosion, according to a HAMAS statement, but the Israeli boat suffered no damage. A suicide bomber killed himself and injured three Israeli soldiers at a cafe in Moshav Mehola on 22 December; HAMAS's military wing claimed responsibility four days later.

In addition, other groups or individuals may have carried out terrorist attacks during the year. Three little-known groups—Palestinian Hizballah, Umar al-Mukhtar Forces, and the Martyrs of al-Aqsa—claimed responsibility for the bombing of an Israeli settler school bus in Gaza on 20 November that killed two Israelis. The al-Aqsa group also claimed responsibility for killing prominent Jewish extremist Binyamin Kahane, himself the leader of a terrorist organization, and his wife on 31 December. Kahane's death prompted heightened concern among Israeli security services that Jewish extremists would extend their violent attacks against Palestinian civilians to include "spectacular" operations, including against the Haram al-Sharif/Temple Mount. A group calling itself Salah al-Din Battalions claimed responsibility for bombing a bus in Tel Aviv on 28 December, injuring 13 persons. Israeli authorities accused Palestinian Authority (PA) security officials of facilitating the attack. The Salah al-Din Battalions reportedly also carried out a shooting attack in mid-November that killed at least one Israeli soldier.

In late summer, Israeli authorities arrested Nabil Awkil, a militant they suspect has links to HAMAS and Usama Bin Ladin. Israeli officials claim that Awkil underwent terrorist training in Bin Ladin-affiliated camps in Afghanistan before returning to the West Bank and Gaza to establish terrorist cells.

Earlier in the year, PA and Israeli security forces disrupted HAMAS networks that were planning several large-scale anti-Israeli attacks. On 10 February a botched bombing plot in Nabulus led to the discovery of a HAMAS explosives lab, several caches, and a multicell network in the West Bank. The network was preparing major terrorist operations designed to inflict mass casualties, including the bombing of a high-rise building in Jerusalem. The Israelis linked those arrested to a series of pipe-bomb attacks in Hadera in 1999. In March, an Israeli raid on a HAMAS hideout in the predominantly Israeli-Arab town of Et Taiyiba uncovered an extensive HAMAS network with ties to Gaza that was planning multiple terrorist attacks in Israel. The cell planned to carry out four-to-five simultaneous suicide bombings against Israeli targets, including bus stops and hitchhiking stations inside Israel frequented by Israeli soldiers. The PA discovered additional explosives in a Gaza kindergarten and arrested a bodyguard of HAMAS leader Shaykh Yasin on suspicion of having links to the Et Taiyiba cell. Israeli authorities arrested a Jewish settler and indicted an Israeli Arab for allegedly assisting the cell.

Israeli and PA security officials took additional measures, often coordinated, to further disrupt HAMAS terrorist planning. PA police in mid-March, following up on the Et Taiyiba raid, uncovered a HAMAS explosives lab in Tulkarm. Separate Israeli and PA operations disrupted HAMAS cells in Janin later that month. The PA also disrupted in mid-July another HAMAS explosives lab in Nabulus and made at least a dozen arrests. The PA inflicted additional damage on HAMAS's military wing with the arrest of two key leaders in 2000. In May, PA security forces arrested Gaza military wing leader Muhammad al-Dayf. In November, Dayf escaped from PA custody. West Bank military wing leader Mahmud al-Shuli (a.k.a. Abu Hanud) surrendered to PA security officials in August after a firefight with IDF soldiers in his hometown of 'Asirah ash Shamaliyah near the West Bank town of Nabulus. Three IDF soldiers were killed by friendly fire in the incident. At year's end Abu Hanud remained in Palestinian custody, serving a 12-year sentence handed down by a PA security court.

During the unrest HAMAS issued numerous statements calling for Palestinians to fight the Israelis with all means available and threatened to continue attacks to avenge Palestinian casualties. The group also vowed revenge for the killing of several HAMAS operatives during the unrest at year's end, including Ibrahim 'Awda, who was killed on 23 November in Nabulus. HAMAS issued public statements accusing the Israelis of assassinating 'Awda, who reportedly died when the headrest in the car he was driving exploded, although the Israelis claim he died transporting an explosive device. HAMAS vowed revenge for the killing of activist Abbas Othman Ewaywi, who was gunned down by Israeli security forces in front of a shop in Hebron on 13 December.

Despite demonstrated Palestinian efforts to uproot terrorist infrastructure earlier in the year, Israeli officials publicly expressed their dissatisfaction with PA counter-terrorism efforts during the crisis. The Israelis also accused PA security officials and Fatah members of facilitating and taking part in shooting and bombing attacks against Israeli targets, including the bus bombing in Tel Aviv on 28 December. The Israelis charged that the release of several prisoners during the crisis had facilitated terrorist planning by the groups and that Palestinian security officials had not been responsive to their calls for more decisive measures against the violence.

Israeli officials publicly expressed well-founded concern that Iran supported Palestinian rejectionist efforts to disrupt the Middle East peace process. The Israelis also stated Palestinian rejectionists increasingly were influenced by Lebanese Hizballah. Public statements by HAMAS, the PIJ, and other Palestinian rejectionist officials since the Israeli withdrawal from southern Lebanon in May lauded Hizballah's actions and called for emulating Hizballah's victory in the territories.

Jordan

Jordan remained vigilant against terrorism in 2000. On 18 September, the State Security Court convicted several Sunni extremists, some in absentia, for plotting terrorist attacks against US and Israeli targets during the millennium celebrations in late 1999. The accused allegedly acted on behalf of Usama Bin Ladin. The three-member military tribunal sentenced eight defendants to death but immediately commuted two of the sentences to life imprisonment at hard labor, citing family reasons. Six others, including a minor, were acquitted, while the remaining 14 received prison sentences ranging from seven-and-a-half to 15 years. Lawyers for 10 of the convicted men have appealed the verdicts.

On 9 December the State Security Court indicted Ra'id Hijazi, a US-Jordanian dual national who had been sentenced to death in absentia in January for having had a role in the millenial plot. He had been recently remanded by Syria. Khalil Deek, another US-Jordanian dual citizen, was brought to Jordan from Pakistan in December 1999 to face charges in the plot but at year's end had yet to be tried. Jordanian authorities were handling his case separately from the other suspects.

Two Israeli diplomats in Jordan were targets of shooting attacks in the latter part of the year. An unidentified gunman shot at Israeli Vice Consul Yoram Havivian outside his home in Amman on 19 November. On 5 December, an unidentified gunman wounded another Israeli diplomat, Shlomo Ratzabi, as he, his wife, and bodyguard left a grocery store in Amman. Both diplomats suffered minor injuries and returned to Israel soon after the attacks. By year's end, Jordanian authorities had detained several suspects and were continuing their investigation. Two previously unknown groups, the Movement for the Struggle of the Jordanian Islamic Resistance and the Holy Warriors of Ahmad Daqamseh, claimed responsibility for the attacks, which coincided with rising public sympathy in Jordan for Palestinians in ongoing violence with Israel. (Ahmad Daqamseh is a Jordanian soldier currently serving a life sentence for killing six Israeli schoolgirls in 1997.)

Jordan continued to ban all HAMAS activity, and the Supreme Court upheld the expulsion of four Political Bureau leaders. Jordan's Prime Minister reiterated the government's conditions for their return at a meeting with HAMAS leaders during the Organization of the Islamic Conference summit in Doha in November. The conditions reportedly included a renunciation of their HAMAS affiliation. In December, lawyers for the group announced their intention to appeal once again to Jordan's Supreme Court to contest the deportation. Jordan refused to permit HAMAS military wing members to reside or operate in the country but allowed other lower-level HAMAS members to remain in Jordan provided they did not conduct activities on the group's behalf.

Several low-level incidents kept security forces focused on

combating threats to Jordan. Police in the southern city of Ma'an in January detained 15 suspects in connection with two shooting attacks against a female dormitory at Al-Hussein University. Four women were injured slightly in one attack. Police sources reported that the suspects were affiliated with a group called the Islamic Renewal and Reform Organization. Before the attacks, leaflets denouncing coeducation and calling for women to wear veils were distributed on campus.

The Government of Jordan also regularly interdicted the smuggling across Jordan's borders of weapons and explosives, which, in many cases, may have been destined for Palestinian rejectionist groups in the West Bank and Gaza. The government prosecuted individuals suspected of such activity.

In March, the government expelled eight Libyans it suspected of having terrorist links, and in September it refused entry to the leader of Israel's Islamic Movement, Shaykh Ra'id Salah. The Israelis publicly claimed that followers of Shaykh Salah have links to HAMAS and were involved in plans to conduct terrorist operations against Israeli interests earlier in the year.

Jordanian security forces coordinated closely with the US Embassy on security matters and acted quickly to bolster security at US Government facilities in response to other threats, including one against the US Embassy in June 2000.

Kuwait

In November the Government of Kuwait disrupted a suspected international terrorist cell. Working with regional counterparts, Kuwaiti security services arrested 13 individuals and recovered a large quantity of explosives and weapons. The terrorist cell reportedly was planning to attack both Kuwaiti officials and US targets in Kuwait and the region.

Lebanon

Throughout the year, the Lebanese Government's continued lack of control in portions of the country—including parts of the Bekaa Valley, Beirut's southern suburbs, Palestinian refugee camps, and the southern border area—as well as easy access to arms and explosives, contributed to an environment with a high potential for acts of violence and terrorism.

A variety of terrorist groups—including Hizballah, Usama Bin Ladin's (UBL) al-Qaida network, HAMAS, the PIJ, the PFLP-GC, 'Asbat al-Ansar, and several local Sunni extremist organizations—continued to operate with varying degrees of impunity, conducting training and other operational activities. Hizballah continued to pose the most potent threat to US interests in Lebanon. Although Hizballah has not attacked US targets in Lebanon since 1991, it continued to pose a significant terrorist threat to US interests globally from its base in Lebanon. Hizballah voiced its support for terrorist actions by Palestinian rejectionist groups in Israel and the occupied territories. While the Lebanese Government expressed support for "resistance" activities along its southern border, it has only limited influence over Hizballah and the Palestinian rejectionists.

UBL's al-Qaida network maintained a presence in Lebanon. Although the Lebanese Government actively monitored and arrested UBL-affiliated operatives, it did not control the Palestinian refugee camps where the operatives conducted terrorist training and anti-US indoctrination.

In the fall, Hizballah kidnapped an Israeli noncombatant whom it may have lured to Lebanon on a false pretense. Hizballah has been using hostages, including captured IDF soldiers, as bargaining chips to win the release of Lebanese prisoners in Israel.

In January, Lebanese security forces clashed in the north with a Sunni extremist movement that had ambushed and killed four Lebanese soldiers. The group had ties to UBL operatives. The same month, Asbat al-Ansar launched a grenade attack against the Russian Embassy. In October, the Sunni extremist group, Takfir wa Hijra, claimed responsibility for a grenade attack against a Christian Member of Parliament's residence, though there are indications others may have been behind this attack.

The Lebanese Government continued to support some international counterterrorist initiatives and moved against UBL-affiliated operatives in 2000. In February, Lebanese authorities arrested members of a UBL cell in Lebanon. In March, the government fulfilled a Japanese Government request and deported four Japanese Red Army (JRA) members after it had refused to do so for years. It allowed one JRA member to remain in Lebanon. It did not act, however, on repeated US requests to turn over Lebanese terrorists involved in the hijacking in 1985 of TWA flight 847 and in the abduction, torture, and—in some cases—murders of US hostages from 1984 to 1991.

Saudi Arabia

Several threats against US military and civilian personnel and facilities in Saudi Arabia were reported in 2000, but there were no confirmed terrorist incidents. At year's end Saudi authorities were investigating a shooting by a lone gunman who opened fire on British and US nationals near the town of Khamis Mushayt in early August 2000. The gunman fired more than 100 rounds on a Royal Saudi Air Force checkpoint, killing one Saudi and wounding two other Saudi guards. The gunman was wounded in the exchange of fire.

Terrorist Usama Bin Ladin, whose Saudi citizenship was revoked in 1994, continued to publicly threaten US interests in Saudi Arabia during the year. In a videotaped statement released in September, Bin Ladin once again publicly threatened US interests.

The Government of Saudi Arabia continued to investigate the bombing in June 1996 of the Khubar Towers housing facility near Dhahran that killed 19 US military personnel and wounded some 500 US and Saudi personnel. The Government of Saudi Arabia publicly stated that it still was looking for three Saudi suspects whom it wanted for questioning in connection with the bombing and whom authorities believed to be currently outside Saudi Arabia. The Saudis continued to hold in detention a number of Saudi citizens linked to the attack, including Hani al-Sayegh, whom the United States expelled to Saudi Arabia in 1999.

The Government of Saudi Arabia reaffirmed its commitment to combating terrorism. It required nongovernmental organizations and private voluntary agencies to obtain government authorization before soliciting contributions for domestic or international causes. It was not clear that these regulations were enforced consistently; however, allegations continued to surface that some international terrorist organization representatives solicited and collected funds from private citizens in Saudi Arabia.

Yemen

On 12 October a boat carrying explosives was detonated next to the USS Cole, killing 17 US Navy members and injuring another 39. The US destroyer, en route to the Persian Gulf, was making a prearranged fuel stop in the Yemeni port of Aden when the attack occurred. At least three groups reportedly claimed responsibility for the attack, including the Islamic Army of Aden, Muhammad's Army, and a previously unknown group called the Islamic Deterrence Force.

The Yemeni Government strongly condemned the attack on the USS Cole and actively engaged in investigative efforts to find the perpetrators. On 29 November, Yemen and the United States signed a memorandum of agreement delineating guidelines for joint investigation to further facilitate cooperation between the two governments. The Yemeni Government's ability to conduct international terrorism investigations was enhanced by joint investigative efforts undertaken pursuant to these guidelines.

Several terrorist organizations maintained a presence in Yemen. HAMAS and the Palestinian Islamic Jihad continued to be recognized as legal organizations and maintained offices in Yemen but did not engage in terrorist activities there. Other international terrorist groups that have an illegal presence in Yemen included the Egyptian Islamic Jihad, al-Gama'a al-Islamiyya, Libyan opposition groups, the Algerian Armed Islamic Group, and al-Qaida. Press reports indicated indigenous groups such as the Islamic Army of Aden remained active in Yemen.

The Government of Yemen did not provide direct or indirect support to terrorists, but its inability to control fully its borders, territory, or its own travel documents did little to discourage the terrorist presence in Yemen. Improved cooperation with Saudi Arabia as a result of the Yemeni-Saudi border treaty, concluded in June, promised to reduce illegal border crossings and trafficking in weapons and explosives, although border clashes continued after the agreement's ratification. The government attempted to resolve some of its passport problems in 2000 by requiring proof of nationality when submitting an application, although terrorists continued to have access to forged Yemeni identity documents.

Patterns of Global Terrorism 2001

September 11

The worst international terrorist attack ever—involving four separate but coordinated aircraft hijackings—occurred in the United States on September 11, 2001. The 19 hijackers belonged to the al-Qaida terrorist network. According to investigators and records of cellular phone calls made by passengers aboard the planes, the hijackers used knives and boxcutters to kill or wound passengers and the pilots, and then commandeer the aircraft, which the hijackers used to destroy preselected targets.

- Five terrorists hijacked American Airlines flight 11, which departed Boston for Los Angeles at 7:45 a.m. An hour later it was deliberately piloted into the North Tower of the World Trade Center in New York City.
- Five terrorists hijacked United Airlines flight 175, which departed Boston for Los Angeles at 7:58 a.m. At 9:05 the plane crashed into the South Tower of the World Trade Center. Both towers collapsed shortly thereafter, killing approximately 3000 persons, including hundreds of firefighters and rescue personnel who were helping to evacuate the buildings.
- Four terrorists hijacked United Airlines flight 93, which departed Newark for San Francisco at 8:01 a.m. At 10:10 the plane crashed in Stony Creek Township, Pennsylvania killing all 45 persons on board. The intended target of this hijack[ed] plane is not known, but it is believed that passengers overpowered the terrorists, thus preventing the aircraft from being used as a missile.
- Five terrorists hijacked American Airlines flight 77, which departed Washington Dulles Airport for Los Angeles at 8:10 a.m. At 9:39 the plane was flown directly into the Pentagon in Arlington, Virginia, near Washington, D.C. A total of 189 persons were killed, including all who were onboard the plane.

More than 3000 persons were killed in these four attacks. Citizens of 78 countries perished at the World Trade Center site. "Freedom and democracy are under attack," said President Bush the following day. Leaders from around the world called the events of September 11 an attack on civilization itself.

The coordinated attack was an act of war against the United States. President Bush said in a 20 September 2001 address to a joint session of Congress: "Our war on terror begins with al-Qaida, but it does not end there. It will not end until every terrorist group of global reach has been found, stopped, and defeated."

Virtually every nation condemned the attack and joined the US-led Coalition to fight terror on several fronts: diplomatic, economic, intelligence, law enforcement, and military. Operation Enduring Freedom, the military component of the

Coalition, began on 7 October. The first targets were the al-Qaida training camps and military installations of the Taliban regime in Afghanistan. Islamic extremists from around the world—including North America, Europe, Africa, the Middle East, and Central, South, and Southeast Asia—had used Afghanistan as a training ground and base of operations for worldwide terrorist activities.

Within months, the Taliban was driven from power, and nearly 1000 al-Qaida operatives were arrested in over 60 countries.

At year's end, the war continued to be waged on all fronts and was certain to last well into the future.

Review of Terrorism in 2001

Despite the horrific events of September 11, the number of international terrorist attacks in 2001 declined to 346, down from 426 the previous year. One hundred seventy-eight of the attacks were bombings against a multinational oil pipeline in Colombia—constituting 51 percent of the year's total number of attacks. In the year 2000, there were 152 pipeline bombings in Colombia, which accounted for 40 percent of the total.

A total of 3,547 persons were killed in international terrorist attacks in 2001, the highest annual death toll from terrorism ever recorded. Ninety percent of the fatalities occurred in the September 11 attacks. In 2000, 409 persons died in terrorist attacks. The number of persons wounded in terrorist attacks in 2001 was 1080, up from 796 wounded the previous year. Violence in the Middle East and South Asia also accounted for the increase in casualty totals for 2001.

In addition to the US citizens killed and injured on September 11, eight other US citizens were killed and 15 were wounded in acts of terrorism last year.

- Ronald Sander, one of the five American oil workers kidnapped in Ecuador in October 2000, was killed by his captors—an armed gang led by former members of a Colombian terrorist group.
- On 9 May, two teenagers were stoned to death in Wadi Haritun cave near Teqoa (Israeli settlement) in the West Bank. Yaakov Nathan Mandell was one of the youths killed. A claim of responsibility for this attack was made in the name of "Palestinian Hizballah."
- Guillermo Sobero, one of three US citizens in a group of 20 persons kidnapped on 27 May from a resort on Palawan Island in the southern Philippines by the Abu Sayyaf Group, was subsequently murdered by his captors.
- On 29 May in the West Bank, militants fired on a passing vehicle, killing two persons, including US citizen Sara Blaustein. Two other US citizens were injured in the ambush. The Al-Aqsa Martyrs Brigade claimed responsibility.
- On 9 August in Jerusalem, a suicide bomber walked into a busy downtown restaurant and detonated a 10-pound bomb that he was wearing, killing 15 persons and wounding 130 others. Among the fatalities were US citizens Judith Greenbaum and Malka Roth. Four other US citizens were injured in the explosion. HAMAS claimed responsibility for the attack.
- On 6 October in al-Khobar, Saudi Arabia, a terrorist threw a parcel bomb into a busy shopping area, killing Michael Jerrald Martin, Jr., and wounding five other persons, among them two US citizens.
- On 4 November, Shoshana Ben Yashai was killed in a shooting attack in east Jerusalem near French Hill. The assailant was also killed in the attack, which was claimed by Palestine Islamic Jihad.

Africa Overview

There was nearly universal condemnation of the September 11 attacks on the United States among Sub-Saharan African governments. These governments also pledged their support to the war against terrorism. In addition to bilateral cooperation with the United States and the global Coalition, multilateral organizations such as the Organization for African Unity and the Southern African Development Community have committed themselves to fighting terrorism. The shock produced by the September 11 attacks and renewed international cooperation to combat global terrorism is producing a new readiness on the part of African leaders to address the problems of international terrorism. Africa's increased cooperation may help counter the persistent threat and use of terrorism as an instrument of violence and coercion against civilians. Most terrorist attacks in Africa stem from internal civil unrest and spillover from regional wars as African rebel movements and opposition groups employ terrorist tactics in pursuit of their political, social, or economic goals. Countries where insurgent groups have indiscriminately employed terrorist tactics and attacked civilians include the Democratic Republic of the Congo, Liberia and Sierra Leone. International terrorist organizations with Islamic ties, including al-Qaida and Lebanese Hizballah, have a presence in Africa and continue to exploit Africa's permissive operating environment —porous borders, conflict, lax financial systems, and the wide availability of weapons—to expand and strengthen their networks. Further, these groups are able to flourish in "failed states" or those with weak governments that are unable to monitor the activities of terrorists and their supporters within their borders. Press reports also indicate that terrorists may be using the illicit trade in conflict diamonds both to launder money and to finance their operations.

[*Eds. Note*: Sudan, one of the seven state sponsors of terrorism, is discussed in Part 1 in the section on "State Sponsorship of Terrorism."]

Angola

Angola made strides in combating terrorism since the September 11 terrorist attacks on the United States. In late November, the National Assembly passed a resolution calling for Angola to participate in regional and international efforts to combat terrorism, to include sharing intelligence, technical expertise, and financial information, and cooperating on legal issues. President dos Santos publicly backed US military actions and supports the Organization for African Unity resolutions against terrorism.

For more than two decades, Angola has been plagued by the protracted civil war between the National Union for the Total Independence of Angola (UNITA) and the Angolan Government. UNITA is believed to have been responsible for several brutal attacks on civilian targets in 2001. Unidentified militants—suspected of being UNITA rebels—ambushed a train killing 256 persons and injuring 161 others in August. Later that month, armed men fired a missile at a passing bus, killing approximately 55 and wounding 10. UNITA rebels are also suspected of attacking a farm in May, killing one person, wounding one, and kidnapping 50 others.

During 2001, violence from the Angolan civil war again spilled over into neighboring Namibia. The Angolan Government, operating on the invitation of the Namibian Government, pursued UNITA rebels into Namibia. Border clashes resulted in several attacks. In May, rebels attacked a village killing one person and wounding one other. Earlier in the year, armed men entered a village, abducting eight persons who were taken to Angola and held hostage.

(On 4 April, 2002, shortly after the death of Jonas Savimbi, UNITA leaders signed a cease-fire agreement with the Government of Angola.)

Djibouti

Djibouti pledged early, strong, and consistent support for the US-led Coalition in the global war on terrorism. Djibouti also hosts Coalition forces from France, Germany, the United Kingdom, and the United States. Djibouti closed financial networks suspected of funneling funds for terrorist operations that operated there and issued a Djiboutian executive order that commits the country to cooperate fully with US counterterrorist financial measures.

Ethiopia

Ethiopia has been another strong supporter of the campaign against terror. The Ethiopian response was immediate and vocal following the September 11 attacks. Ethiopia also has shut down terrorist financial networks operating in its territory. Ethiopia continues to cooperate in examining potential terrorist activity in the region, including in Somalia.

Kenya

Kenya already had suffered from an al-Qaida attack on the US Embassy in Nairobi in August 1998. Kenya remained a key ally in the region, implementing new measures to impose asset freezes and other financial controls, offering to cooperate with the United States to combat terrorism, and leading the current regional effort toward national reconciliation in Somalia. Kenya is a party to 10 of the 11 antiterrorism conventions and is a signatory to the newest, the 1999 UN Convention for the Suppression of the Financing of Terrorism.

Nigeria

Nigeria has strongly supported US antiterrorism efforts around the world as well as the military action in Afghanistan. Nigeria led diplomatic efforts in the UN and the Economic Community of West African State (ECOWAS) and in the battle against terrorism. The Nigerian Government has drafted legislation—the Anti-Terrorism, Economic and Financial Crimes Commission Act—that contains explicit criminal sanctions against terrorism and its financing. The Government of Nigeria is committed to preventing its territory—home to Africa's largest Muslim population—from becoming a safehaven for Islamic extremists.

Senegal

Senegal has been a leader in the African response to the attacks of September 11, with President Abdoulaye Wade's proposed African Pact Against Terrorism. President Wade stressed this issue with many of the continent's leaders during a two-day conference in Dakar in October 2001 and is energizing countries to join the fight via the Organization of African Unity/African Union. The Senegal Central Bank and regional banks based in Dakar have modified regulations to restrict terrorist funding. Senegal has also created a regional counterterrorism intelligence center, using assets of its security and intelligence services along with assistance from the United States. Senegal plans to ratify all remaining UN conventions against terrorism in the near future.

Somalia

Somalia, a nation with no central government, represents a potential breeding ground as well as safehaven for terrorist networks. Civil war, clan conflict, and poverty have combined to turn Somalia into a "failed state," with no one group currently able to govern the entire country, poor or nonexistent law enforcement, and an inability to monitor the financial sector. Some major factions within Somalia have pledged to fight terrorism. However one indigenous group, al-Ittihad al-Islami (AIAI), is dedicated to creating an Islamic state in Somalia, has carried out terrorist acts in Ethiopia, and may have some ties to al-Qaida. AIAI remains active in several parts of Somalia.

In July, gunmen in Mogadishu attacked a World Food Program convoy, killing six persons and wounding several others. In March, extremists attacked a Medecins Sans Frontieres medical charity facility, killing 11 persons, wounding 40, and taking nine hostages. The hostages were later released.

The need for cooperation among Somalia's neighbors in the Horn of Africa is obvious, given the long borders shared with Somalia by Djibouti, Ethiopia, and Kenya. These countries have—individually and, in cooperation with the United States—taken steps to close their ports of entry to potential terrorists, deny use of their banking systems to transfer terrorist-linked assets, and to bring about the peaceful reconciliation and long-term stability that will remove the "failed-state" conditions currently found in Somalia.

South Africa

South Africa expressed its unreserved condemnation for the 11 September terrorist attacks on the United States. The Government has offered its support for US-led diplomatic efforts to fight terrorism. South Africa also supports the Organization for African Unity's counterterrorism resolution. South Africa continued to experience some incidents of urban terrorism in 2001.

Uganda

President Yoweri Museveni publicly condemned the 11 September attacks and called upon the world to act together against terrorism. Two insurgent groups—the Lord's Resistance Army (LRA) in Northern Uganda and the Allied Democratic Forces in Western Uganda—continued military operations aimed at undermining the Kampala government in 2001—resulting in several terrorist attacks that injured foreign nationals. In June, three bombs exploded simultaneously in public areas in Kampala killing one and wounding 19 persons. Suspected LRA rebels ambushed a Catholic Relief Services vehicle in September, killing five persons and wounding two others.

South Asia Overview

In 2001, South Asia remained a central point for terrorism directed against the United States and its friends and allies around the world. Throughout the region, Foreign Terrorist Organizations (FTOs) committed several significant acts of murder, kidnapping and destruction, including the vicious 13 December attack on India's Parliament. The September 11 attacks focused global attention on terrorist activities emanating from Afghanistan, which became the first military battleground of the war on terrorism. Coalition military objectives in Afghanistan were clear: 1) destroy al-Qaida and its terrorist infrastructure in Afghanistan; 2) remove the Taliban from power; and 3) restore a broadly representative government in Afghanistan. All countries in South Asia have strongly supported the Coalition effort against terrorism. The challenge from here is to turn that support into concrete action that will, over time, significantly weaken the threat posed by terrorists in and from the region.

Some clear and important signs of fresh thinking are already apparent. After September 11, Pakistan's President, Gen. Pervez Musharraf, made significant changes to Pakistan's policy and has rendered unprecedented levels of cooperation to support the war on terrorism. Pakistan not only broke its previously close ties with the Taliban regime but also allowed the US military to use bases within the country for military operations in Afghanistan. Pakistan sealed its border with Afghanistan to help prevent the escape of fugitives and continues to work closely with the United States to identify and detain fugitives. Musharraf also has taken important steps against domestic extremists, detaining more than 2,000 including Jaish-e-Mohammed leader Maulana Masood Azhar.

In Sri Lanka, there are fragile indications of a possible peaceful settlement to the decades-old conflict between the Sri Lankan Government and the Liberation Tigers of Tamil Eelam (LTTE). In 2001, the LTTE was responsible for the devastating attack on the colocated international and military airports north of Colombo. In December, however, the LTTE and the Government of Sri Lanka established a cease-fire brokered by Norway. The United States continues to support the Norwegian Government's facilitation effort and its focus on helping to bring about a negotiated settlement of the conflict. Despite the possibility of positive change, the US will continue to maintain the LTTE on its Foreign Terrorist Organization List until the group no longer poses a terrorist threat.

Afghanistan

After years of ignoring calls from the international community to put an end to terrorist activities within its borders, the Taliban, which controlled most Afghan territory, became the first military target of the US-led coalition against terrorism. During the first three quarters of 2001, Islamic extremists from around the world—including North America, Europe, Africa, the Middle East, and Central, South, and Southeast Asia—used Afghanistan as a training ground and base of operations for their worldwide terrorist activities. Senior al-Qaida leaders were based in Afghanistan, including Usama Bin Ladin, wanted for his role in the September 11 terrorist attacks in New York, Washington, and Pennsylvania as well as for his role in the 1998 US Embassy bombings in Kenya and Tanzania. The al-Qaida leadership took advantage of its safehaven in Afghanistan to recruit and train terrorists, to manage worldwide fundraising for its terrorist activity, to plan terrorist operations, and to conduct violent anti-American and antidemocratic agitation to provoke extremists in other countries to attack US interests and those of other countries. This was punctuated by the horrendous attacks on the United States in September. The attacks brought a forceful military response from the US and the international Coalition. Our war against the Taliban and al-Qaida has been very successful, and Afghans now serve side-by-side with US and other Coalition forces in military operations to eliminate the remnants of Taliban and al-Qaida fighters in the country.

In a UN-sponsored process in Bonn, Germany, Afghans representing various factions agreed to a framework that would help Afghanistan end its tragic conflict and promote national reconciliation, lasting peace, and stability. Included in the text of the Bonn agreement that established Afghanistan's Interim Authority was a promise by the international community to help rebuild Afghanistan as part of the fight against terrorism.

In turn, in January 2002 the international community

pledged $4.5 billion in assistance to the people of Afghanistan to help them recover from the ravages of Taliban rule.

India

India was itself a target of terrorism throughout the year but unstintingly endorsed the US military response to the September 11 attack and offered to provide the US with logistic support and staging areas. To address internal threats, the Indian cabinet approved in October an ordinance granting sweeping powers to security forces to suppress terrorism. Since then, at least 25 groups have been put on the Indian Government's list of "terrorist organizations" and declared "unlawful." The Union Home Ministry asked all other ministries to create a centralized point for sorting Government mail after a powder-laced letter was discovered in late October at the office of the Home Minister. The Ministry also deployed additional security forces to guard important installations following a suicide attack in October on an Indian Air Force base in the Kashmir Valley. The security posture was significantly upgraded, including large-scale mobilization of Indian Armed Forces, following the attack in December on India's Parliament.

Security problems associated with various insurgencies, particularly in Kashmir, persisted through 2001 in India. On 1 October, 31 persons were killed and at least 60 others were injured when militants detonated a bomb at the main entrance of the Jammu and Kashmir legislative assembly building in Srinagar. The Kashmiri terrorist group Jaish e-Mohammed claimed responsibility for the attack. On 13 December an armed group attacked India's Parliament in New Delhi. The incident resulted in the death of 13 terrorists and security personnel. India has blamed FTOs Lashkar-e-Tayyiba and Jaish e-Mohammed for the attack and demanded that the Government of Pakistan deal immediately with terrorist groups operating from Pakistan or Pakistan-controlled territory. India also faced continued violence associated with several separatist movements based in the northeast. (On 22 January 2002, armed gunmen fired on a group of police outside the American Center in Kolkata, (Calcutta), killing four and wounding at least nine. The investigation of this attack is ongoing. Although no US citizens were injured, Indian police have indicated that the American Center was deliberately chosen. One US contract guard was injured in the assault.)

The Indian Government continued cooperative bilateral efforts with the United States against terrorism, including extensive cooperation between US and Indian law-enforcement agencies. The US-India Counterterrorism Joint Working Group—founded in November 1999—met in June 2001 in Washington and January 2002 in New Delhi and included contacts between interagency partners from both governments. The group agreed to pursue even closer cooperation on shared counterterrorism goals and will reconvene in Washington in summer 2002.

Nepal

Nepal was an early and strong supporter of the Coalition against global terrorism and of military operations at the onset of Operation Enduring Freedom, agreeing to allow access to their airports and airspace.

Like India, Nepal was more a target of terrorism—primarily from indigenous Maoist revolutionaries—than a base for terrorism against the United States. The indigenous Maoist insurgency now controls at least five districts, has a significant presence in at least 17 others, and at least some presence in nearly all the remaining 53 districts. Until recently, the Government used the police to address the increase in Maoist activity, but elements of the Nepalese Army were being deployed in July 2001.

Prime Minister Sher Bahadur Deuba came to power in July pledging to resolve the conflict through a negotiated peace. The Government and the Maoists agreed to a cease-fire and held three rounds of talks, during which Deuba announced plans for significant social reform that addressed some of the Maoists' economic and social concerns. The Maoists ultimately walked away from the talks and the cease-fire, and on 23 November launched simultaneous nationwide terrorist attacks. The Government declared a state of emergency. In mid-2001, the Maoists began expanding their operations with attacks on officials and commercial enterprises. Prospects for negotiations in the near future are very dim.

The Maoists often have used terrorist tactics in their campaign against the Government, including targeting unarmed civilians. Of particular concern is the increase in the number of attacks against international relief organizations and US targets. (For example, terrorists burned the CARE International building when they attacked the town of Mangalsen 16-17 February 2002.) Before that attack, on 15 December, a US Embassy local employee was murdered. Nepalese police and US officials are still investigating the December killing. So far, no motive for the attack has been established and no suspects have been identified.

(A small bomb exploded at the Coca-Cola factory in Bharatpur, southwest of Kathmandu, the evening of 29 January 2002. The bomb caused only slight damage, and there were no injuries.) A similar device was set off at the Coca-Cola bottling plant in Kathmandu in late November. No US citizens are employed at either Coca-Cola plant.

Pakistan

After September 11, Pakistan pledged and provided full support for the Coalition effort in the war on terrorism. Pakistan has afforded the United States unprecedented levels of cooperation by allowing the US military to use bases within the country. Pakistan also worked closely with the United States to identify and detain extremists and to seal the border between Pakistan and Afghanistan. (In February 2002, the United States and Pakistan agreed to institutionalize counterterrorism exchanges as a component of a newly created, wide-ranging Law Enforcement Joint Working Group.)

As of November, Islamabad had frozen over $300,000 in terrorist-related assets in several banks. In December President Pervez Musharraf announced to the Government a proposal to bring Pakistan's madrassas (religious schools)—

some of which have served as breeding grounds for extremists —into the mainstream educational system. Pakistan also began sweeping police reforms, upgraded its immigration control system, and began work on new anti-terrorist finance laws.

In December, Musharraf cracked down on "anti-Pakistan" extremists and, by January 2002, Pakistani authorities had arrested more than 2,000 including leaders of the Lashkar-e-Tayyiba (LT), and Jaish-e-Mohammed (JEM), both designated as Foreign Terrorist Organizations—as well as the Jamiat Ulema-I-Islami (JUI), a religious party with ties to the Taliban and Kashmiri militant groups. Pakistani support for Kashmiri militant groups designated as Foreign Terrorist Organizations waned after September 11. Questions remain, however, whether Musharraf's "get tough" policy with local militants and his stated pledge to oppose terrorism anywhere will be fully implemented and sustained.

Sri Lanka

Sri Lanka declared support for US-led military action in Afghanistan following the September 11 attacks and welcomed US resolve to root out terrorism wherever it exists. On 1 October the Government of Sri Lanka issued a statement of support and ordered that all financial institutions notify the Central Bank of transactions by named terrorists. The Government has issued a freeze order on certain terrorist assets and has promulgated regulations to meet requirements under UNSCR 1373. Colombo has taken measures since September to strengthen domestic security such as posting extra security forces at sites that may be particularly vulnerable to attack and acceding to the Convention on Plastic Explosives —a weapon favored by domestic terrorists.

In early 2001 the Liberation Tigers of Tamil Eelam (LTTE) continued its unilateral cease-fire, begun in late 2000. In April it broke the cease-fire and resumed a high level of violence against government, police, civilian, and military targets. On 24 July the LTTE carried out a large-scale attack at the colocated military and international airports north of Colombo, causing severe damage to aircraft and installations. An LTTE attack in November killed 14 policemen and wounded 18 others, including four civilians. Also in November, LTTE members were implicated in the assassination of an opposition politician who had planned to run in December's parliamentary elections. There were no confirmed cases of LTTE or other terrorist groups targeting US citizens or businesses in Sri Lanka in 2001.

On 24 December, the LTTE began a one-month cease-fire. Shortly thereafter, the newly elected Sri Lankan Government reciprocated and announced its own unilateral cease-fire. (In 2002, both parties renewed the cease-fire monthly and continued to work with the Norwegian Government in moving the peace process forward. On 21 February 2002, both sides agreed to a formal cease-fire accord. There have been no significant incidents of violence attributed to the LTTE since the December 2001 cease-fire. On 21 January the LTTE repatriated 10 prisoners it had been holding—seven civilians it had captured in 1998 and three military officers held since 1993. It is unknown how many other captives the LTTE continues to hold hostage.)

The United States continues strongly to support Norway's facilitation effort and is helping to bring about a negotiated settlement of the conflict. Agreement by both sides for direct discussions is a hopeful sign. Nonetheless, given the ruthless and violent history of the LTTE (including acts within the past year), and its failure to renounce terrorism as a political tool, the United States maintains the LTTE on its Foreign Terrorist Organization List.

East Asia Overview

In the wake of the September 11 events, East Asian nations were universal in their condemnation of the attacks, with most providing substantial direct support to the war on terrorism and making significant progress in building indigenous counterterrorism capabilities. Shutting down and apprehending al-Qaida-linked terrorists cells were achievements that drew headlines, but perhaps just as importantly, several states and independent law-enforcement jurisdictions (Hong Kong, for example) strengthened their financial regulatory and legal frameworks to cut off terrorist groups from their resource base and further restrict the activities of terrorists still at large.

The Government of Japan fully committed itself to the global Coalition against terrorism including providing support for the campaign in Afghanistan. Japan was also active in the G-8 Counterterrorism Experts' Group, participating in developing an international counterterrorism strategy to address such concerns as terrorist financing, the drug trade, and mutual legal assistance.

For the first time in history, Australia invoked the ANZUS treaty to provide general military support to the United States. Australia was quick to sign the UN Convention for the Suppression of Terrorist Financing, less than seven weeks after September 11. Australia prepared new counterterrorism legislation, implemented UN resolutions against terrorism, and took steps to freeze assets listed in US Executive Order 13224. It has contributed $11.5 million to Afghan relief and has committed troops and equipment to fight in Operation Enduring Freedom (OEF).

New Zealand sent troops to Afghanistan in support of OEF and fully supports UN resolutions and the US executive order on terrorist financing. New Zealand has new regulations and legislation to implement those resolutions and deployed a C-130 aircraft to Afghanistan for humanitarian relief operations.

The Philippines, under President Macapagal-Arroyo's leadership, has emerged as one of our staunchest Asian allies in the war on terrorism. Macapagal-Arroyo was the first ASEAN leader to voice support for the United States in the wake of the September 11 terrorist attacks. She immediately offered the US broad overflight clearances; use of military bases, including Clark and Subic, for transit, staging, and maintenance of US assets used in Operation Enduring Freedom; enhanced intelligence cooperation; logistics support, including medical personnel, medical supplies, and medicines;

and Philippine troops for an international operation, dependent on Philippine congressional approval. Macapagal-Arroyo also spearheaded efforts to forge an ASEAN regional counterterrorism approach.

South Korea has given unconditional support to the US war on terrorism and pledged "all necessary cooperation and assistance as a close US ally in the spirit of the Republic of Korea-United States Mutual Defense Treaty." To that end, South Korea contributed air and sea transport craft and a medical unit in support of the military action in Afghanistan. It also has provided humanitarian relief and reconstruction funds to help rebuild that country. South Korea also has strengthened its domestic legislation and institutions to combat financial support for terrorism, including the creation of a financial intelligence unit. It also has made an important diplomatic contribution as President of the United Nations General Assembly during this critical period.

China, which also has been a victim of terrorism, provided valuable diplomatic support to our efforts against terrorism, both at the United Nations and in the South and Central Asian regions, including financial and material support for the Afghan Interim Authority. Beijing has agreed to all our requests for assistance, and we have established a counterterrorism dialogue at both senior and operational levels.

At year's end, however, much remained to be done. Trafficking in drugs, persons, and weapons, as well as organized crime and official corruption, remain as serious problems and potential avenues of operation for terrorists to exploit.

Southeast Asian terrorist organizations with cells linked to al-Qaida were uncovered late in the year by Singapore and Malaysia. The groups' activities, movements, and connections crossed the region, and plans to conduct major attacks were discovered. Singapore detained 13 Jemaah Islamiah members in December, disrupting a plot to bomb the US and other Embassies, and other targets in Singapore. Malaysia arrested dozens of terrorist suspects in 2001, and investigations, broadening across the region at the end of the year, revealed the outline of a large international terrorist network. The multinational nature of the Jemaah Islamiah network illustrated for most countries in East Asia the crucial need for effective regional counterterrorism mechanisms. In a move that bodes well for the region's efforts, the ASEAN Regional Forum undertook an extensive counterterrorism agenda.

Several East Asian nations suffered terrorist violence in 2001, mostly related to domestic political disputes. The Abu Sayyaf Group (ASG) in the Philippines repeated the type of kidnappings endemic to the Philippines in 2000. On 27 May, the ASG kidnapped three US citizens and 17 others from a resort in the southern Philippines. Among many others, one US citizen was brutally murdered, and two US citizens and one Filipino remained hostages at year's end. Indonesia, China, and Thailand also suffered a number of bombings throughout the year, many believed by authorities to be the work of Islamic extremists in those countries; few arrests have been made, however.

[*Eds. Note*: North Korea, one of the seven state sponsors of terrorism, is discussed in Part 1 in the section on "State Sponsorship of Terrorism."]

Burma

Burma issued a letter to the United Nations on 30 November outlining its commitment to counterterrorism. The Government stated its opposition to terrorism and declared government officials would not allow the country to be used as a safehaven or a location for the planning and execution of terrorist acts. The letter also indicated the country had signed the UN Convention for the Suppression of Financing of Terrorism on 12 November, and the Government provided banks and financial institutions with the names of all terrorists and terrorist organizations listed under UN Security Council Resolution 1333. The letter declared that the Government of Burma would cooperate in criminal investigations of terrorism and bring terrorists to justice "in accordance with the laws of the land." Burma had signed six of the 12 counterterrorism conventions and was considering signing the other six. Drug trafficking and related organized crime are additional challenges in Burma that present terrorists with opportunities to exploit.

China

Chinese officials strongly condemned the September 11 attacks and announced China would strengthen cooperation with the international community in fighting terrorism on the basis of the UN Charter and international law. China voted in support of both UN Security Council resolutions after the attack. Its vote for Resolution 1368 marked the first time it has voted in favor of authorizing the international use of force. China also has taken a constructive approach to terrorism problems in South and Central Asia, publicly supporting the Coalition campaign in Afghanistan and using its influence with Pakistan to urge support for multinational efforts against the Taliban and al-Qaida. China and the United States began a counterterrorism dialogue in late-September, which was followed by further discussions during Ambassador Taylor's trip in December to Beijing. The September 11 attacks added urgency to discussions held in Washington, DC, Beijing, and Hong Kong. The results have been encouraging and concrete; the Government of China has approved establishment of an FBI Legal Attache in Beijing and agreed to create US-China counterterrorism working groups on financing and law enforcement.

In the wake of the attacks, Chinese authorities undertook a number of measures to improve China's counterterrorism posture and domestic security. These included increasing its vigilance in Xinjiang, western China, where Uighur separatist groups have conducted violent attacks in recent years, to include increasing the readiness levels of its military and police units in the region. China also bolstered Chinese regular army units near the borders with Afghanistan and Pakistan to block terrorists fleeing from Afghanistan and strengthening overall domestic preparedness. At the request of the United

States, China conducted a search within Chinese banks for evidence to attack terrorist financing mechanisms.

A number of bombing attacks—some of which were probably separatist-related—occurred in China in 2001. Bomb attacks are among the most common violent crimes in China due to the scarcity of firearms and the wide availability of explosives for construction projects.

China has expressed concern that Islamic extremists operating in and around the Xinjiang-Uighur Autonomous Region who are opposed to Chinese rule received training, equipment, and inspiration from al-Qaida, the Taliban, and other extremists in Afghanistan and elsewhere. Several press reports claimed that Uighurs trained and fought with Islamic groups in the former Soviet Union, including Chechnya.

Two groups in particular are cause for concern: the East Turkestan Islamic Party (ETIP) and the East Turkestan Liberation Organization (or Sharki Turkestan Azatlik Tashkilati, known by the acronym SHAT). ETIP was founded in the early 1980s with the goal of establishing an independent state of Eastern Turkestan and advocates armed struggle. SHAT's members have reportedly been involved in various bomb plots and shootouts.

Uighurs were found fighting with al-Qaida in Afghanistan. We are aware of credible reports that some Uighurs who were trained by al-Qaida have returned to China.

Previous Chinese crackdowns on ethnic Uighurs and others in Xinjiang raised concerns about possible human-rights abuses. The United States has made clear that a counterterrorism campaign cannot serve as a substitute for addressing legitimate social and economic aspirations.

Indonesia

Immediately after the September 11th attacks, President Megawati expressed public support for a global war on terrorism and promised to implement UN counterterrorism resolutions. The Indonesian Government, however, said it opposed unilateral US military action in Afghanistan. The Government has since taken limited action in support of international antiterrorist efforts. It made some effort to bring its legal and regulatory counterterrorism regime up to international standards. Although often slow to acknowledge terrorism problems at home, Indonesia also has taken some steps against terrorist operations within its borders. Police interviewed Abu Bakar Baasyir, leader of the Majelis Mujahadeen Indonesia, about his possible connections to Jemaah Islamiah or Kumpulan Mujahidin Malaysia (KMM). Police arrested a Malaysian in August when he was wounded in an attempt to detonate a bomb at a Jakarta shopping mall. Two Malaysians were arrested in Indonesia thus far in conjunction with the bombing of the Atrium shopping mall. In addition, Indonesia has issued blocking orders on some of the terrorists as required under UN Security Council Resolution 1333, and bank compliance with freezing and reporting requirements is pending. At the end of the year the United States remained concerned that terrorists related to al-Qaida, Jemaah Islamiyah, and KMM were operating in Indonesia.

Radical Indonesian Islamic groups threatened to attack the US Embassy and violently expel US citizens and foreigners from the country in response to the US-led campaign in Afghanistan. A strong Indonesian police presence prevented militant demonstrators from attacking the compound in October. One of the most vocal of the Indonesian groups, Front Pembela Islam (Islamic Defenders Front), had previously threatened US citizens in the country.

Press accounts reported over 30 major bombing incidents throughout the archipelago, including blasts in June and December at the US-owned ExxonMobil facility in Aceh Region. Unidentified gunmen also kidnapped and assassinated several prominent Indonesians during the year, including a Papuan independence activist and a leading Acehnese academic. Officials made little progress in apprehending and prosecuting those responsible for the bombings in 2001, having arrested only five persons. Laskar Jihad, Indonesia's largest radical group, remained a concern at year's end as a continuing source of domestic instability.

Communal violence between Christians and Muslims in the Provinces of Maluku and Central Sulawesi continued in 2001. Several villages were razed in Sulawesi in November and December, leading to a major security response from the Indonesian military.

(Indonesia and Australia signed a Memorandum of Understanding on counterterrorism cooperation in early 2002, preparing the way for concrete actions against the spread of terrorism in Southeast Asia.)

Japan

Japan acted with unprecedented speed in responding to the September terrorist attacks in the United States. Prime Minister Koizumi led an aggressive campaign that resulted in new legislation allowing Japan's Self Defense Forces to provide substantial rear area support for the campaign in Afghanistan. The Government has frozen suspected terrorist assets and maintains a watch list that contains nearly 300 groups and individuals. The Government has signed all 12 terrorism-related international conventions and is moving quickly with legislation to approve the sole treaty Japan has not ratified, the International Convention for the Suppression of the Financing of Terrorism.

Laos

The Laotian Government has stated it condemns all forms of terrorism and supports the global war on terrorism. The Bank of Laos has issued orders to freeze terrorist assets and instructed banks to locate and seize such assets. Laos, however, has been slow to ratify international conventions against terrorism. Public and Government commentary on the US–led war on terrorism has been overwhelmingly supportive.

Malaysia

Malaysian Prime Minister Mahathir condemned the September 11 attacks as unjustified and made a first-ever visit to the

US Embassy to sign the condolence book and express solidarity with the United States in the fight against international terrorism. The Malaysian Government cooperated with international law-enforcement and intelligence efforts, made strides in implementing financial counterterrorism measures, aggressively pursued domestic counterterrorism before and after September 11, and increased security surrounding the US Embassy and diplomatic residences. The Government in October expressed strong reservations about US military action in Afghanistan.

Malaysia suffered no incidents of international terrorism in 2001, although Malaysian police authorities made a series of arrests of persons associated with regional Islamic extremist groups with al-Qaida links. Between May and December close to 30 members of the domestic Kumpulan Mujahidin Malaysia (KMM) group and an extremist wing of KMM were arrested for activities deemed threatening to Malaysia's national security. KMM detainees were being held on a wide range of charges, to include planning to wage a *jihad*, possessing weaponry, carrying out bombings and robberies, murdering a former state assemblyman, and planning attacks on foreigners, including US citizens. Several of the arrested militants reportedly underwent military training in Afghanistan, and several key leaders of the KMM are also deeply involved in Jemaah Islamiah. Jemaah Islamiah is alleged to have ties not only to the KMM, but to Islamic extremist organizations in Indonesia, Singapore, and the Philippines; Malaysian police also have been investigating whether Jemaah Islamiah has connections to September 11 terrorist suspect Zacharias Moussaoui.

Nineteen members of the Malaysian Islamist sect al-Ma'unah, who were detained in July 2000 following the group's raid on two military armories in northern Malaysia, were found guilty of treason in their bid to overthrow the Government and establish an Islamic state. Sixteen members received life sentences while the remaining three were sentenced to death. Ten other members had pleaded guilty earlier to a reduced charge of preparing to wage war against the king and were sentenced to 10 years in prison, although the sentences of two were reduced to seven years on appeal. An additional 15 al-Ma'unah members remained in detention under the Internal Security Act.

Philippines

Philippine President Macapagal-Arroyo has been Southeast Asia's staunchest supporter of the international counterterrorism effort, offering medical assistance for Coalition forces, blanket overflight clearance, and landing rights for US aircraft involved in Operation Enduring Freedom. After marathon sessions, the Philippine Congress passed the Anti-Money-laundering Act of 2001 on 29 September. This legislation overcame vocal opposition and passed quickly as the Philippine Congress took steps to support the international effort to freeze terrorist assets throughout the world. In addition, the Philippine military, with US training and assistance, in October intensified its offensive against the terrorist Abu Sayyaf Group (ASG)—which has been involved in high-profile kidnappings for many years.

Small radical groups in the Philippines continued attacks against foreign and domestic targets in 2001. The ASG, designated a Foreign Terrorist Organization by the US Government in 1997 and redesignated in 1999 and 2001, kidnapped three US citizens and 17 Filipinos in May from a resort on Palawan Island in the southern Philippines. Of the original 20 hostages kidnapped, 15 escaped or were ransomed; three hostages (including Guillermo Sobero, a US citizen) were murdered; and two US citizens remained captive at year's end. The "Pentagon Gang" kidnap-for-ransom group, which is responsible for the kidnap and/or murder of Chinese, Italian, and Filipino nationals in 2001, was added to the US Terrorism Exclusion List (TEL) in December.

Peace talks with the Communist Party of the Philippines/New People's Army (CPP/NPA) began in April but broke down in June after the NPA, the military wing of the CPP, claimed responsibility for the assassination on 12 June of a Philippine congressman from Cagayan. The Alex Boncayao Brigade (ABB)—a breakaway CPP/NPA faction—engaged in intermittent fighting with Philippine security forces during the year.

Distinguishing between political and criminal motivation for many of the terrorist-related activities in the Philippines continued to be problematic, most notably in the numerous cases of kidnapping for ransom in the southern Philippines. Both Islamist separatists and Communist insurgents sought to extort funds from businesses in their operating areas, occasionally conducting reprisal operations if money was not paid.

Singapore

Singapore Prime Minister Goh strongly condemned the September 11 attacks on New York City and Washington, unequivocally affirming support for US antiterrorism efforts. Singapore was supportive of war efforts in Afghanistan for humanitarian relief. More broadly, the Government quickly passed omnibus legislation intended to enable it to comply with mandatory UN Security Council Resolutions and was instrumental in uncovering and disrupting international terrorists operating in Southeast Asia.

Singapore did not experience any incidents of domestic or international terrorism in 2001, but police officials in December disrupted an al-Qaida-linked extremist organization called Jemaah Islamiyah whose members were plotting to attack US, British, Australian, and Israeli interests in Singapore. Thirteen individuals were detained, and investigations were continuing at the end of 2001.

As a regional transportation, shipping, and financial hub, Singapore plays a crucial role in international efforts against terrorism. Efforts were continuing at year's end to make improvements to security in all of these areas, including, in particular, the collection of detailed data on all cargoes passing through Singapore's port.

Taiwan

Taiwan President Chen committed publicly on several occasions, including soon after the September 11 attacks, that Taiwan would "fully support the spirit and determination of the antiterrorist campaign, as well as any effective, substantive measures that may be adopted." Taiwan announced that it would fully abide by the 12 UN counterterrorism conventions, even though it is not a member of the United Nations. Taiwan strengthened laws on money laundering and criminal-case-procedure law in the aftermath of September 11.

Thailand

Prime Minister Thaksin condemned the September 11 terrorist attacks and said his country would stand by the United States in the international Coalition to combat terrorism. The Government pledged cooperation on counterterrorism between US and Thai agencies, committed to signing all the UN counterterrorism conventions, and offered to participate in the reconstruction of Afghanistan. Thailand took several concrete actions in support of the war on terrorism. Thai financial authorities began investigating financial transactions covered under UN resolutions to freeze al-Qaida and Taliban assets. In an effort to prevent terrorism and crime, immigration officials in December announced initiatives to expand the list of countries whose citizens are required to obtain visas before they arrive in Thailand. Thailand also offered to dispatch one construction battalion and five medical teams to serve in UN-mandated operations in Afghanistan. In Thailand, police stepped up security around US and Western-owned buildings immediately following the September 11 attacks.

Thai authorities suspect Muslim organized crime groups from the predominately Muslim provinces in southern Thailand were responsible for several small-scale attacks in 2001, including three bombings in early April that killed a child and wounded dozens of persons, an unexploded truck bomb that was found next to a hotel in southern Thailand in November, and, in December, a series of coordinated attacks on police checkpoints in southern Thailand that killed five police officers and a defense volunteer.

On 19 June, authorities averted an attempted bombing at the Vietnamese Embassy in Bangkok when they found and disarmed two explosive devices that had failed to detonate. Three ethnic Vietnamese males were taken into custody. One was charged with illegal possession of explosives and conspiracy to cause an explosion in connection with the incident. The others were released after police determined there was insufficient evidence to link them to the crime.

In central Bangkok in early December, a rocket-propelled grenade was fired at a multistory building housing a ticketing office of the Israeli airline El Al, although police doubted the Israeli carrier was the intended target. There were no casualties.

Eurasia Overview

No major terrorist attacks occurred in Eurasia in 2001. The region, however, which has suffered for years from Afghanistan-based extremism, provided integral support to the international Coalition against terrorism. States in the region provided overflight and temporary basing rights, shared law-enforcement and intelligence information, and moved aggressively to identify, monitor, and apprehend al-Qaida members and other terrorists. In the immediate aftermath of September 11, governments also took swift action to enhance security at US embassies and other key facilities against terrorist attacks. Countries in the region also took diplomatic and political steps to contribute to the international struggle against terrorism, such as becoming party to the 12 United Nations conventions against terrorism. The signatories to the Commonwealth of Independent States (CIS) Collective Security Treaty (CST) called for increased security along the borders of the member states, tighter passport and visa controls, increased involvement of law-enforcement agencies, and the reinforcement of military units. In addition, the CST Security Council planned to strengthen the year-old CIS antiterrorist center.

Enhancing regional counterterrorism cooperation has been a critical priority for the United States. Toward that end, the US Department of State Office of the Coordinator for Counterterrorism held the second annual Central Asia Counterterrorism Conference in Istanbul in June. Counterterrorism officials from four Central Asian countries, as well as Russia, Canada, Egypt, Turkey, and the United Kingdom, explored topics such as human rights, the rule of law, and combating terrorist financing. Throughout the conference, and in other bilateral and multilateral fora, the United States has consistently stressed that effective counterterrorism is impossible without respect for human rights and that the rule of law is a formidable and essential weapon in the fight against al-Qaida and other international terrorist organizations. A policy exercise held on the last day of the conference helped reinforce key tenets of effective counterterrorism policy and operations, including the need for sustained, high-level official attention, regional cooperation, and the importance of contingency planning for terrorist incident management and response. (The next Conference is planned for 24–26 June 2002, in Ankara.)

In December, Kyrgyzstan hosted the Organization for Security and Cooperation in Europe (OSCE) Bishkek International Conference on Enhancing Security in Central Asia: Strengthening Efforts to Counter Terrorism. The Conference was attended by over 300 high-level participants from over 60 countries and organizations. The Conference concluded that the countries of Central Asia play a critical role in preventing terrorism; enhanced regional cooperation is needed; and terrorism cannot be combated through law enforcement only—social and economic roots of discord also must be addressed and rule of law strengthened. Delegations endorsed a program of action that emphasizes the need for increased coordination and interagency cooperation as well as the need to take steps to prevent illegal activities of persons, groups, or organizations that instigate terrorist acts.

Countries within the region have been taking steps to enhance their common efforts against international terrorism. Fears of an influx of Afghan fighters and refugees as a result of the fighting in Afghanistan spurred cooperative efforts to tighten border security and to combat extremist organizations. The Islamic Movement of Uzbekistan (IMU), a group on the US FTO list that seeks to overthrow the Uzbek Government and create an Islamic state, continued to be a concern. Unlike 1999 and 2000, an anticipated large-scale IMU offensive failed to materialize in 2001, most likely because of better host-government military preparedness and the IMU's participation in the Taliban's summer offensive against the Northern Alliance. There were, however, incidents against local security forces that never were definitively linked to the group. IMU members fought alongside the Taliban in Afghanistan in 2000 and 2001. A large number of IMU fighters, reportedly including their military leader Namangani, were killed at the Kondoz battle in November 2001. The United States and regional governments also continued to monitor the Hizb ut-Tahrir, a radical Islamic political movement that advocates the practice of pure Islamic doctrine and the establishment of an Islamic caliphate in Central Asia. Despite regional governments' claims, the United States has not found clear links between Hizb ut-Tahrir and terrorist activities. The Eurasian countries also recognized the growing links between terrorism and other criminal enterprises and have taken steps to break the nexus among terrorism, organized crime, trafficking in persons and drugs, and other illicit activities.

Five years after it began meeting as a body to discuss border disputes with China, the Shanghai Forum—Kazakhstan, Kyrgyzstan, Tajikistan, Russia, and China—admitted Uzbekistan as a sixth member in June, renamed itself the Shanghai Cooperation Organization (SCO), and continued its focus on regional security. Earlier in the year the group laid the groundwork for a counterterrorist center in the Kyrgyzstani capital of Bishkek. Members also signed an agreement at their June summit to cooperate against "terrorism, ethnic separatism, and religious extremism."

Three Central Asian states—Kazakhstan, Kyrgyzstan, and Tajikistan—along with Russia, Belarus, and Armenia, agreed at a CIS collective-security summit in May to create a rapid-reaction force to respond to regional threats, including terrorism and Islamic extremism. The headquarters of the force is to be based in Bishkek. Each of the three Central Asian states and Russia agreed to train a battalion that, if requested by a member state, would deploy to meet regional threats. The security chiefs of these states also met in Dushanbe in October to discuss strengthening border security.

Several Central Asian states concluded counterterrorism or border security agreements in 2001. Kyrgyzstan and Tajikistan agreed to speed up the exchange of information between their frontier forces, and Kazakhstan signed an agreement with Turkmenistan on border security in July. Continuing past cooperation, in December, Kyrgyzstan and Russia signed an agreement to exchange counterterrorism information. In the summer, the Kyrgyzstani parliament refused to ratify a border accord with Uzbekistan against international terrorism, citing, among other reasons, Uzbekistan's decision unilaterally to mine its border with Kyrgyzstan in the fall of 2000. The Uzbek mines on the undemarcated Kyrgyzstani border have been blamed for at least two dozen civilian deaths. The Uzbeks also unilaterally have mined the undemarcated border with Tajikistan, resulting in deaths as well.

Azerbaijan

Azerbaijan and the United States have a good record of cooperation on counterterrorism issues that predates the September 11 attacks. Azerbaijan assisted in the investigation of the 1998 East Africa Embassy bombings and has cooperated with the US Embassy in Baku against terrorist threats to the mission. In the wake of the September 11 attacks, the Government of Azerbaijan expressed unqualified support for the United States and offered "whatever means necessary" to the US-led antiterrorism coalition. To date, Azerbaijan has granted blanket overflight clearance, offered the use of bases, and engaged in information sharing and law-enforcement cooperation.

Azerbaijan also has provided strong political support to the United States. In a ceremony at the US Ambassador's residence on 11 December, President Aliyev reiterated his intention to support all measures taken by the United States in the fight against international terrorism. In early October, the parliament voted to ratify the UN Convention on the Suppression of the Financing of Terrorism, bringing to eight the number of international counterterrorism conventions to which Azerbaijan is a party.

While Azerbaijan previously had been a route for international *mujahidin* with ties to terrorist organizations seeking to move men, money, and materiel throughout the Caucasus, Baku stepped up its efforts to curb the international logistics networks supporting the *mujahidin* in Chechnya, and has effectively reduced their presence and hampered their activities. Azerbaijan has taken steps to combat terrorist financing. It has made a concerted effort to identify possible terrorist-related funding by distributing lists of suspected terrorist groups and individuals to local banks. In August, Azerbaijani law enforcement arrested six members of the Hizb ut-Tahrir terrorist group who were put on trial in early 2002. Members of Jayshullah, an indigenous terrorist group, who were arrested in 1999 and tried in 2000, remain in prison. In December 2001, Azerbaijani authorities revoked the registration of the local branch of the Kuwait Society for the Revival of the Islamic Heritage, an Islamic nongovernmental organization (NGO) suspected of supporting terrorist groups. After the September 11 attacks, Azerbaijan increased patrols along its southern land and maritime borders with Iran and detained several persons crossing the border illegally. It has deported at least six persons with suspected ties to terrorists, including three to Saudi Arabia and three to Egypt. The Department of Aviation Security increased security at Baku's Bina Airport and has implemented International Civil Aviation Organization recommendations on aviation security.

Georgia

The Georgian Government condemned the September 11 terrorist attacks and supports the international Coalition's fight against terrorism. Immediately following the attacks, the Georgian border guard troops along the border with Russia went on high alert to monitor the passage of potential terrorists in the area. In early October, Tbilisi offered the United States the use of its airfields and airspace.

Georgia continued to face spillover violence from the Chechen conflict, including a short period of fighting in the separatist region of Abkhazia and bombings by aircraft from Russian territory on Georgia under the guise of antiterrorist operations. Like Azerbaijan, Georgia also contended with international *mujahidin* using Georgia as a conduit for financial and logistic support for the *mujahidin* and Chechen fighters. The Georgian Government has not been able to establish effective control over the eastern part of the country. In early October, Georgian authorities extradited 13 Chechen guerrillas to Russia, moving closer to cooperation with Russia. President Shevardnadze in November promised to cooperate with Russia in apprehending Chechen separatist fighters and foreign *mujahidin* in the Pankisi Gorge—a region in northern Georgia that Russian authorities accuse Georgia of allowing Chechen terrorists to use as a safehaven—if Moscow furnishes Tbilisi with concrete information on their whereabouts and alleged wrongdoing. The United States has provided training and other assistance to help Georgian authorities implement tighter counterterrorism controls in problem areas.

Kidnappings continued to be a problem in Georgia. Two Spanish businessmen who were kidnapped on 30 November 2000 and held near the Pankisi Gorge were released on 8 December 2001. A Japanese journalist was taken hostage in the Pankisi Gorge in August and released on 9 December.

Kazakhstan

President Nazarbayev allied Kazakhstan with the United States after September 11 and backed the US-led Coalition. Permission was given for overflights, increased intelligence sharing, and for Coalition aircraft to be based in the country. Nazarbayev said publicly that Kazakhstan is "ready to fulfill its obligations stemming from UN resolutions and agreements with the United States" in the Coalition against terrorism. Kazakhstan also declared its intent to ratify international conventions on terrorism, with priority given to the Convention for the Suppression of the Financing of Terrorism, and has taken steps to block the assets of terrorists.

Kazakhstan stepped up security on its southern borders during 2001 in response to Islamic extremist incursions into neighboring states. The Government set up a special military district to help cover the sparsely populated southern flank of the country. It continued efforts to prevent the spread of Islamic militant groups, including actions such as detaining individuals for distributing leaflets for the Islamic militant group, Hizb ut-Tahrir, calling for the violent overthrow of the Kazakhstan Government.

Kyrgyzstan

Kyrgyzstan offered a wide range of assistance in the fight against terrorism, including the use of Kyrgyzstani facilities for humanitarian support and combat operations. In December, the Kyrgyzstani parliament ratified a Status of Forces Agreement which allows basing US military forces at Manas International Airport in Bishkek. Kyrgyzstan also hosted in Bishkek in December an Organization for Security and Cooperation in Europe (OSCE) conference on enhancing security and stability in Central Asia that was attended by some 60 countries and organizations. Kyrgyzstan has also taken steps to block the assets of terrorists.

Kyrgyzstan experienced several Islamic Movement of Uzbekistan (IMU) incursions in 1999 and 2000. As a result, it created the Southern Group of Forces comprising approximately six thousand troops from various components of the armed forces that deploy in the southern Batken Oblasty to defend against renewed IMU incursions. In May, a military court handed down death sentences against two foreign nationals for taking part in IMU activity in 2000. One defendant was convicted of kidnapping in connection with militants who took four US mountain climbers hostage in Kyrgyzstan.

Russia

Following the terrorist crimes of September 11, counterterrorism cooperation between the United States and Russia grew to unprecedented and invaluable levels in multiple areas—political, economic, law enforcement, intelligence, and military. Areas of common interest ranged from sharing financial intelligence to identifying and blocking terrorist assets to agreements on overflights by US military aircraft involved in Operation Enduring Freedom (OEF). The Russians offered search-and-rescue assistance in support of the OEF efforts in Afghanistan. Both countries have underscored the value of their extensive exchange of counterterrorism information and their enhanced ability to collect and exploit threat information. A mutual interest in fighting criminal activities that support or facilitate terrorism resulted in better-coordinated approaches to border control, counternarcotics efforts, and immigration controls in Central Asia.

Much of the collaboration was through multilateral fora —such as the UN, the Organization for Security and Cooperation in Europe (OSCE) and the Group of Eight (G-8)— and international efforts as part of the Coalition against terrorism with global reach. The United States-Russia Working Group on Afghanistan was the central bilateral forum for addressing terrorism and terrorism-related issues, including terrorist financing, chemical, biological, radiological, and nuclear (CBRN) terrorism, and the nexus between terrorism, drug trafficking, and other criminal activity.

On 24 September, President Putin publicly laid out a broad program of cooperation with, and support for, US counterterrorism efforts. In early October, Russian Defense Minister Ivanov stated that Russia supports any efforts designed to end international terrorism. In mid-October, the Justice Ministry amended terrorism laws to include penalties for legal entities that finance terrorist activity.

Russia was the site of a number of terrorist events in 2001, many connected to the ongoing insurgency and instability in Chechnya. The current conflict, which began in late summer 1999, has been characterized by widespread destruction, displacement of hundreds of thousands of civilians, and accusations of human-rights abuses by Russian servicemen and various rebel factions. One rebel faction, which consists of both Chechen and foreign—predominantly Arabic—*mujahidin* fighters, is connected to international Islamic terrorists and has used terrorist methods. Russian forces continue to conduct operations against Chechen fighters but also draw heavy criticism from human-rights groups over credible reports of human-rights violations. On 9 January, US aid worker Kenneth Gluck was kidnapped while traveling in Chechnya; he was released on 6 February. The kidnapping was attributed to an Arab *mujahidin* commander. Chechen guerrilla leader Shamil Basayev, however, accepted overall responsibility and apologized, saying it was a "misunderstanding."

Russia also has experienced numerous other kidnappings, bombings, and assassinations, which may be attributed to either terrorists or criminals. On 5 February a bomb exploded in Moscow's Byelorusskaya metro station wounding nine persons. On 15 March three Chechen men armed with knives commandeered a Russian charter flight soon after it departed Istanbul for Moscow, demanding that the pilots divert the plane to an Islamic country. Saudi special forces stormed the plane upon its arrival in the country, arresting two of the hijackers, while the third hijacker, one crewmember, and one passenger were killed during the rescue. On 24 March three car bombs exploded in Stavropol, one in a busy market and two in front of police stations, killing at least 20 persons and wounding almost 100. In December, a Russian court sentenced five persons to prison terms ranging from nine to 15 years for involvement in two apartment bombings in 1999 in Moscow that killed more than 200 persons.

Tajikistan

Tajikistan, which strongly opposed the Taliban since it took power, expressed its support without reservations for Coalition actions in Afghanistan and continues to offer tangible assistance to operations in the area. Security along the Afghan border was reinforced after September 11. President Rahmonov and all sides of his government, including the opposition, offered full support at all levels in the fight against terrorism and invited US forces to use Tajik airbases for offensive operations against Afghanistan. More broadly, Tajikistan has made a commitment to cooperate with the United States on a range of related issues, including the proliferation of CBRN, illicit trafficking in weapons and drugs, and preventing the funding of terrorist activities.

Incidents of domestic terrorism continued in 2001, including armed clashes, murders of government officials, and hostage taking. The United States issued a travel warning for Tajikistan in May. Three senior Tajik officials were murdered during the year, including the Deputy Minister of Internal Affairs and the Minister of Culture. In April, an armed group seized several policemen in eastern Tajikistan attempting to negotiate the release of their group members from prison; three policemen were found dead several days later. In June, armed men at a roadblock kidnapped 15 persons, including a US citizen and two German nationals belonging to a German nongovernmental organization for three days. The kidnappers were lower-level former combatants in the Tajik civil war who were not included in the 1997 Peace Accord. After the hostages were released, due to pressure by the former opposition now serving in government, Government troops launched a military operation, which killed at least sixty of the combatants and the group's leader.

The Supreme Court in Tajikistan sentenced two Madesh students to death in May for bombing a Korean Protestant church in Dushanbe in October 2000; nine persons died, and more than 30 were injured in the attack. While the Church asked that these sentences be commuted, the students were executed in 2001. The Court also sentenced several members of the Islamic political group, Hizb ut-Tahrir, to prison terms. More than 100 members of the group were arrested in 2001.

Uzbekistan

Uzbekistan, which already worked closely with the United States on security and counterterrorism programs before September 11, has played an important role in supporting the Coalition against terrorism. In October, the United States and Uzbekistan signed an agreement to cooperate in the fight against international terrorism by allowing the United States to use Uzbek airspace and an air base for humanitarian purposes. In December, to facilitate the flow of humanitarian aid into northern Afghanistan, Uzbekistan reopened the Friendship Bridge, which had been closed for several years. Tashkent has issued blocking orders on terrorist assets, signed the UN Convention on the Suppression of the Financing of Terrorism, and says that it is a "full-fledged" party to all UN antiterrorism conventions.

Uzbekistan experienced no significant terrorist incidents in 2001 but continued actively to pursue and detain suspected Islamic extremists. The Islamic Movement of Uzbekistan (IMU) participated in combat against US-allied Northern Alliance forces during the early stages of the war against terrorism, particularly in the area of Kunduz. Although the IMU suffered significant losses during this campaign, there is information that the IMU may still maintain a capability to infiltrate into Uzbekistan for possible attacks. Uzbekistan continued to confront increased Hizb ut-Tahrir activity. In October, the group distributed leaflets claiming that the United States and Britain have declared war on Islam and urged Muslims to resist Uzbekistan's support for the US-led Coalition.

Europe Overview

In the wake of the September 11 terrorist attacks in the United States, European nations responded in dramatic fashion, offering immediate assistance to manage the crisis and working overtime to help build and sustain the international Coalition against terrorism. Working together bilaterally and multilaterally, the United States and its friends and allies in Europe demonstrated the positive impact of coordinated action. Sustaining this close cooperation and unity of purpose will be a strong element of a successful campaign over the long haul.

Many European countries acted quickly to share law-enforcement and intelligence information, conduct investigations into the attacks, and strengthen laws to aid the fight against terrorism. The UK, France, Italy, and other European allies partnered with the US in military operations to root out the Taliban and al-Qaida from Afghanistan. Belgium, the holder of the six-month rotating EU presidency on September 11, immediately focused its agenda on the fight against terrorism. Spain not only continued to weaken the Basque terrorist group, Basque Fatherland and Liberty (ETA), but captured leaders and members of an al-Qaida cell in Spain, and has moved to make counterterrorism a central item on the agenda of its six-month presidency of the EU which began in January 2002. Al-Qaida-related arrests were similarly carried out in Belgium, Bosnia, France, Germany, Italy, and the UK.

During the year it held the rotating presidency of the Group of Eight (G-8), Italy's guidance of joint activities of the Lyon Group law-enforcement experts and the Counterterrorism Experts Group (Roma Group) resulted in substantial progress on an Action Plan for combating terrorism. France provided outstanding political, diplomatic, and military support to the global counterterrorism campaign. The French have helped invigorate measures to bolster the UN's ability to contribute to measures against terrorism and to enhance regional counterterrorism cooperation within Europe. Greece offered noteworthy support for the antiterrorism Coalition. However, it remains troubling that there have been no successful arrests and prosecutions of members of the 17 November terrorist group. Germany's response to the September 11 attacks was superb, with important contributions to key diplomatic, law-enforcement, and military efforts. German police moved swiftly to investigate leads related to the attacks, identified al-Qaida members, made arrests, and issued warrants. Turkey provided invaluable logistic and basing support to the campaign in Afghanistan as well as its full diplomatic and political support. Although Turkey's effective campaign against the PKK, DHKP/C, and Turkish Hizballah dealt setbacks to those groups, they still remain capable of lethal attacks.

The European multilateral response to the September 11 attacks through the European Union (EU) and NATO was immediate, forceful, and unprecedented. The EU showed itself to be a strong partner in sustaining the global Coalition and in fostering international political cooperation against terrorism. On the day of the attacks, the EU (under Belgium's presidency) voiced its solidarity with the United States. EU member states provided strong support for our efforts at the UN to adopt strong counterterrorism resolutions and for our diplomatic efforts around the world to get third countries to stand up against terrorism. Thereafter, the Council of the European Union adopted an Action Plan to identify areas—such as police and judicial cooperation, humanitarian assistance, transportation security, and economic and finance policy—that could make a contribution to fighting terrorism. In addition, the Council adopted a "common position," a framework regulation, and an implementing decision that significantly strengthened its legal and administrative ability and that of EU member states to take action against terrorists and their supporters—including freezing their assets. The EU strengthened its capacity to stanch the flow of terrorist financing by approving a regulation that enables it to freeze terrorist assets on an EU-wide basis without waiting for a UN resolution. The United States signed the US-Europol Agreement in December to facilitate cooperation between our law-enforcement authorities. The EU reached agreement on a European arrest warrant, which will greatly facilitate extradition within member states. Under the Belgian presidency, the EU also agreed on a regulation to freeze assets of persons and entities associated with terrorism; the measure was approved in December by the European Parliament. The EU also reached agreement on a common definition of terrorism and on a common list of terrorist groups and committed to coordinated initiatives to combat terrorism, including the intent to adopt quickly a directive preventing money laundering in the financial system and expanding procedures for freezing assets—to include proceeds from terrorism-related crimes. The EU is continuing to work internally and with the US and other countries to improve our ability to take common actions against terrorism.

For its part, NATO invoked Article V of the NATO charter for the first time, bringing the full weight of the organization to bear to provide for self defense against terrorism. NATO forces have played a key role in the effort to end Afghanistan's role as a safehaven and in providing direct military support in securing the United States from additional terrorist attacks.

Two of the newest NATO members, the Czech Republic and Hungary, made immediate offers of humanitarian and military assistance after the September 11 attacks. Amidst offers to "backfill" American and British troops in the Balkans, the Czech Republic deployed the 9th NBC (nuclear/biological/chemical) company to participate in Operation Enduring Freedom in Kuwait and loaned NATO, for its use, a TU-154 transport plane. Hungary offered a military medical unit and is providing antiterrorism training to other countries in the region. Both countries pledged significant humanitarian assistance to Afghanistan at the Tokyo donors' conference.

The 10 Vilnius Group countries (Albania, Bulgaria, Croatia, Estonia, Latvia, Lithuania, Macedonia, Romania, Slovakia, Slovenia) collectively and individually joined in condemning the September 11 attacks. These countries have actively supported the international Coalition against terrorism, offering military and diplomatic assistance and, in some cases, providing logistic support. They have undertaken numerous antiterrorism measures, ranging from strengthening border security to investigating suspect financial transactions.

In Southeastern Europe, groups of ethnic Albanians have conducted armed attacks against government forces in southern Serbia and Macedonia since 1999. Ethnic Albanian extremists of the so-called National Liberation Army (NLA or UCK) launched an armed insurgency in Macedonia in February. The NLA, which announced its disbandment in July, received funding and weapons not only from Macedonian sources, but also from Kosovo and elsewhere. The NLA and a group that operated in southern Serbia called the Liberation Army of Presevo, Medvedja, and Bujanovac (PMBLA or UCPMB) had strong ties with Kosovar political organizations, including the Popular Movement of Kosovo and the National Movement for the Liberation of Kosovo. Both NLA and UCPMB killed civilians and government security-force members and harassed and detained civilians in areas they controlled. Other ethnic Albanian extremist groups also espouse and threaten violence against state institutions in Macedonia and the region, including the so-called Albanian National Army (ANA or AKSH) and the National Committee for the Liberation and Protection of Albanian Lands (KKCMTSH).

Albania

Albania continued to be an active partner in the fight against international terrorism in the wake of September 11, pledging "any and all assistance" to US efforts. Government and political leaders quickly condemned the attacks. The Government also pledged NATO access to air and seaports for units participating in Operation Enduring Freedom, as well as commando troops. In addition, the parliamentary Assembly called upon all banks in Albania to locate the accounts of individuals suspected of possessing terrorist ties and to prevent fund withdrawal or transfer. The Albanian courts already have frozen the assets of one suspected al-Qaida supporter. The Ministry of Finance is working to strengthen its anti-money laundering legislation.

Various Middle Eastern-based nongovernmental organizations (NGOs) that have been identified as supporting terrorist activities continued to maintain a presence in Albania. Some of the NGOs continued to provide assistance to Islamic extremists throughout the region, to include procuring false documents and facilitating terrorist travel. In early October, however, the Albanian Government simultaneously raided the Tirana headquarters of four Islamic-based NGOs believed to be involved in international Islamic extremism, detained and interrogated their principal officers, then deported them, together with their families, into the custody of police authorities from their home countries. From late October through December, Albanian authorities conducted three additional raids: two on Islamic-based NGOs suspected of supporting extremist activity, and the third on the Tirana headquarters of an Albanian business owned by a suspected al-Qaida supporter watchlisted by the US Department of the Treasury. The Albanian Government detained and interrogated those organizations' principal officers.

Albania continues to cooperate closely with US counterterrorism efforts on a number of levels. Grossly insufficient border security, corruption, organized crime, and institutional weaknesses, however, combine to make Albanian territory an attractive target for exploitation by terrorist and Islamic extremist groups.

Belgium

Belgian Government reaction to the tragedy of September 11 was swift and supportive. Prime Minister Verhofstadt publicly condemned the attacks on September 11 and again on 12 September before the European Parliament. During Belgium's six-month term of the rotating EU presidency in the second half of 2001, the EU made significant progress in combating terrorism. Belgium immediately thrust counterterrorism to the top of its agenda for EU reform efforts in the wake of the attacks. Belgium helped to obtain key EU-wide agreement on a European arrest warrant, which will greatly facilitate extradition within member states. As a NATO ally, Belgium contributed a navy frigate in the Mediterranean and backfill for Operation Enduring Freedom and provided aircraft for humanitarian assistance to Afghanistan.

The Belgians cooperated on many levels with US counterterrorism efforts, from information sharing to policymaking. Belgian authorities arrested on 13 September Tunisian national, Nizar Trabelsi and Moroccan Tabdelkrim El Hadouti, (brother of Said El Hadouti who was charged in Morocco with helping to provide false documents to the Massoud suicide bombers) for involvement in an alleged plot against the US Embassy in Paris. Police also seized from Trabelsi's apartment a sub-machinegun, ammunition, and chemical formulas for making explosive devices.

Terrorists, however, have found it relatively easy to exploit Belgium's liberal asylum laws, open land borders, and investigative, prosecutorial, or procedural weaknesses in order to use the country as an operational staging area for international terrorist attacks. The forgery of Belgian passports and theft of Belgian passports from Belgian Government offices have facilitated terrorists' ability to travel. For example, the two suicide-assassins of Northern Alliance leader Ahmad Shah Massoud in Afghanistan on 9 September had traveled as journalists under false names on Belgian passports stolen from consulates in France and the Netherlands. The Belgian Government instituted a new passport with state-of-the-art anti-fraud features in March 2001.

In December, Belgian authorities arrested Tarek Maaroufi, a Tunisian-born Belgian national, on charges of involvement in trafficking of forged Belgian passports. Maaroufi was charged with forgery, criminal association, and recruiting for a foreign army or armed force. Belgian authorities suspect the forged passports are linked to those used by the two suicide-assassins of Northern Alliance leader Massoud. Italian authorities also sought Maaroufi for his ties to known al-Qaida cells. Belgian authorities also opened an investigation into the activities of Richard Reid, the accused "shoe bomber" who on 2 December was overpowered on board American Airlines Flight 63. Reid stayed at a hotel in Brussels from 5–16 December and frequented local cybercafes.

Belgium is beginning to add legislative and judicial tools that will increase its ability to respond to terrorist threats. The Belgian Government assisted in the investigation of several cases of international terrorism, both among European states and with the United States. Belgian cabinet ministers agreed in November on a draft bill aimed at facilitating wiretaps, the use of informants, and other expanded investigative techniques.

Belgium fully implemented all UNSC resolutions requiring freezing of Taliban-related assets.

Bosnia and Herzegovina

After September 11, Bosnian Government authorities pledged to put all possible resources toward the fight against international terrorism. As Bosnia has been a transit point for Islamic extremists, the State border service enacted a variety of measures to control the borders more effectively, including the introduction of a new landing-card document travelers are required to complete upon arrival at the airport.

Following the attacks on September 11, Ministry of the Interior authorities arrested several individuals suspected of involvement in terrorist activity, including an associate of Bin Ladin lieutenant Abu Zubaydah and five Algerian nationals suspected of being Algerian Armed Islamic Group (GIA) operatives; Sabir Lahmar, one of the detained GIA operatives, had made threats against SFOR and US interests in the past.

Even before the September 11 attacks, the Bosnian Government was engaged actively in measures to combat terrorism. In April, authorities arrested Sa'id Atmani, a suspected GIA associate who roomed with Ahmed Ressam while he was in Canada, and extradited him to France in July, where he was wanted on an INTERPOL warrant. In July, Bosnian Government authorities arrested two members of the Egyptian group al-Gama'a al-Islamiyya—Imad al-Misri and al-Sharif Hassan Sa'ad. Both men were extradited to Egypt in October.

Various NGOs that have been identified as supporting terrorist activities, however, maintained a presence in Bosnia. The NGOs, which came to the region during the 1992–1995 Bosnian war, continued to provide assistance to Islamic extremists throughout Bosnia, to include procuring false documents and facilitating terrorist travel. The Government has taken some significant steps to freeze assets and monitor activities of some of the NGOs, but their ability to carry out efforts to combat these organizations has been weakened by some residual support for those in the Islamic world that supported Bosnia wartime efforts.

Following September 11, Bosnian banking authorities have worked diligently to identify and freeze suspected terrorist assets in the financial sector.

France

France has provided substantial diplomatic, political, and other support to the war against terrorism. French officials expressed their determination to eradicate the "perverse illness" of terrorism and offered military and logistics contributions. Following the attacks on the United States, France played an important role in crafting a UN response to terrorism and joined other NATO allies in invoking Article 5, the mutual-defense clause of the NATO treaty. Paris quickly granted three-month blanket overflight clearances for US aircraft and offered air, naval, and ground assets that were integrated into Operation Enduring Freedom. At year's end, the French had also committed ground troops as part of the international peacekeeping force in Afghanistan.

During 2001, French law-enforcement officers tracked, arrested, and prosecuted individuals who they suspected had ties to al-Qaida and other extremist groups. In April, a Paris court sentenced Fateh Kamel to eight years in prison for running an underground terrorist logistics network linked to al-Qaida. French authorities established clear links between Kamel and Ahmed Ressam, who had plotted to attack the Los Angeles Airport in December 1999. On 10 September, a French magistrate opened a formal investigation into an alleged plot by an al-Qaida-linked group to target US interests in France and placed its alleged ringleader, Djamel Beghal, who was extradited from the United Arab Emirates on 1 October, in investigative detention.

In November, the French Parliament passed the "everyday security" bill, which allows for expanded police searches and telephone and Internet monitoring, along with enhanced measures to disrupt terrorist finances. Finance Minister Fabius responded rapidly to US requests related to Executive Order 13224 to freeze Taliban and al-Qaida finances. As of December, France had frozen $4 million in Taliban assets. Fabius also established a new interagency unit, designated FINTER, to provide a focal point within the Ministry for efforts to block the financing of terrorism. On an international level, the French were among the principal advocates for creating the UN Security Council's counterterrorism committee, and they cooperated with US officials in G-8 counterterrorism meetings.

Regionally, Paris continued working with Madrid to crack down on the terrorist group Basque Fatherland and Liberty (ETA). In late 2001, the number of confrontations between French officers and the Basque group increased notably, resulting in the wounding of several policemen. French authorities also discovered that major ETA training activities were taking place within France. In an unprecedented decision in September, French magistrates refused residency to 17 Spanish Basque residents who had links to ETA and gave them one month to leave French territory. Moreover, French officials arrested several ETA members in September, including

Asier Oyarzabal, the suspected head of ETA's logistics apparatus.

Pro-independence Corsican groups continued to attack Government offices on the island. The murder of nationalist leader Francois Santoni in August and the ongoing debate with the mainland over the island's autonomy heightened tensions and increased the threat of continued violence. French officers arrested Rene Agonstini in September for complicity in murder and kidnapping.

Germany

Immediately following the September 11 attacks, Chancellor Schroeder pledged "unreserved solidarity" with the United States, initiated a sweeping criminal investigation in close cooperation with US law enforcement, and moved to prepare the German public and his Government to adopt antiterrorism legislation that included closing legal loopholes and increasing the monitoring of suspected terrorist groups.

On 16 November the Bundestag approved German military participation in Operation Enduring Freedom (OEF). German soldiers are currently serving in OEF and the International Security Assistance Force in Afghanistan, and Germany has taken a leading role in efforts to train and equip a new Afghan police force.

Soon after the attack, German police conducted raids on several apartments in Hamburg where the September 11 hijackers and associates once resided. Numerous law-enforcement actions followed.

On 10 October, German police arrested a Libyan, Lased Ben Henin, near his Munich home in coordinated raids that also included the arrest of two Tunisians in Italy. Ben Henin is suspected of links to al-Qaida's terrorist network and was extradited to Italy on 23 November.

On 18 October, German authorities issued an international arrest warrant for Zakariya Essabar, Said Bahaji, and Ramzi Omar who allegedly belonged to a Hamburg terrorist cell that included three of the September 11 hijackers.

On 28 November, German police arrested Mounir El Motassadeq, a 27-year old Moroccan, at his Hamburg apartment on charges he controlled an account used to bankroll several of the September 11 hijackers and had "intensive contacts" with the terrorist cell. The Federal Prosecutor's Office stated that El Motassadeq had close contact over a period of years with several members of the Hamburg cell, including the suspected ringleader, Mohamed Atta. He had power of attorney over hijacker Marwan al-Shehhi's bank account, according to the statement.

On 12 December, Germany banned a network of radical Islamic groups centered on the Cologne-based Kaplan organization. Police conducted 200 house searches in seven different German states in connection with the ban and seized the headquarters of the Kaplan group, which authorities had previously characterized as antidemocratic and anti-Semitic. The ban also covers the Kaplan-associated foundation, "Servants of Islam" and 19 other subsidiary groups with a total of approximately 1,100 members. The leader of the group, Metin Kaplan, who is serving a jail term for calling for the murder of a rival religious leader, is widely known in Germany as the "Caliph of Cologne."

Germany increased funding for the security services by some $1.5 billion and announced the creation of 2,320 new positions in various agencies to combat terrorism. Government authorities are using advanced technology to uncover potential terrorists, including so-called "sleepers" and terrorist-support personnel in Germany.

After four years of testimony and deliberations, a German court convicted four of five suspects in the 1986 bombing of the Labelle Discotheque in Berlin, in which two US servicemen died. One defendant was convicted of murder while three others were convicted as accessories to murder and sentenced to prison terms of 12–14 years each. A fifth suspect was acquitted for lack of evidence. The court's verdict also made clear Libyan Government involvement in planning and facilitating the attack. The prosecution has appealed the verdict to seek longer sentences, while the defense has appealed as well; the appeal process could take up to two years.

Greece

The Greek Government, after September 11, joined its EU partners in setting up interdiction mechanisms in support of the war on terrorism, to include greater security at points of entry, information sharing with the United States and its Coalition allies, and the monitoring of suspected terrorist financial assets. The Greek Parliament took meaningful steps toward demonstrating its commitment to combating terrorism by passing a comprehensive anti-organized-crime-and-terrorism bill. Among its key provisions, the legislation mandates magistrate trials (eliminating citizen jurors, who have in the past been vulnerable to personal threats), sanctions police undercover operations, authorizes the use of DNA as court evidence, and permits electronic surveillance beyond traditional wiretaps.

Greek and US authorities maintained good cooperation investigating past terrorist attacks on US citizens. Nevertheless, the Greek Government has not yet arrested or convicted those terrorists responsible for attacks conducted by Revolutionary Organization 17 November (17N) or Revolutionary Nuclei (RN) over the past two decades.

A series of court rulings that effectively reduced the sentences of suspected Greek terrorists or overturned guilty verdicts in high-profile terrorist-related cases represented a setback on one counterterrorism front.

Anti-State Struggle terrorist and longtime criminal fugitive Avraam Lesperoglou had been found guilty of several charges, including involvement in the attempted murder of a Greek police officer, for which he received a 17-year sentence. In April, the verdict was overturned on appeal. By October, charges regarding Lesperoglou's association with Anti-State Struggle similarly were dropped after prosecution witnesses failed to appear in court or recanted previous testimony identifying him at the scene of the crime. Following these developments, there were allegations of witness intimidation. In

November, Lesperoglou was cleared of all charges and set free.

In another prominent case, self-confessed Urban Anarchist guerrilla Nikos Maziotis had his 15-year sentence reduced to fewer than 5 years. Afterwards, the trial judge ruled that he agreed with the unrepentant Maziotis' contention that "the placement of an explosive device at a Greek Government ministry was a political statement and not an act of terrorism."

The courts imposed only token penalties on a young woman caught in the act of placing a gas-canister bomb in front of the US Consulate General in Thessaloniki in 1999 and delayed until 2003 a prosecutor's request to retry the case.

Anti-US terrorist attacks in Greece declined significantly from a high of 20 in 1999 to only three in 2001. Greece's most lethal terrorist group, Revolutionary Organization 17 November did not claim any attacks in 2001, nor did Greece's other prominent terrorist group, Revolutionary Nuclei. Anarchist groups appeared more active in employing terrorist tactics, however, seizing upon antiglobalization and antiwar themes. The three low-level incendiary attacks on US interests in Greece in 2001 consisted of one unclaimed attack against a US fast-food chain and two others against US-plated vehicles by the group Black Star. Other lesser-known groups attacked numerous domestic targets while the "Revolutionary Violence Group" attacked Thai and Israeli official interests.

Greek officials began planning for security for the 2004 Summer Olympic Games in Athens and continued to work with key countries having extensive security and/or Olympics experience through a series of consultative conferences and symposiums, to include several meetings of the seven-nation Olympic Security Advisory Group—Australia, France, Germany, Israel, Spain, United Kingdom, and United States.

Italy

Italy stepped up its counterterrorism efforts following the September 11 attacks and has vigorously supported the United States diplomatically and politically. Taking a prominent role in the international Coalition against al-Qaida, Italy declared its support for the US-led war and offered to contribute military forces, including naval, air and ground units. Italy also enhanced its law-enforcement capabilities, recently passing a series of antiterrorism laws enumerating new criminal offenses for terrorist acts and providing new and expanded police powers.

In the weeks following the attacks, Italian law-enforcement officials intensified their efforts to track and arrest individuals they suspect have ties to al-Qaida and other extremist groups. On 10 October they arrested several extremists connected to Essid Sami Ben Khemais—the Tunisian Combatant Group leader arrested by the Italians in April for plotting to bomb the US Embassy in Rome. In mid and late November, Italian officials raided the Islamic Cultural Institute in Milan and arrested Islamic extremists having possible ties to al-Qaida. Italy also cooperated in stemming the flow of finances linked to terrorism. The Financial Security Committee, comprising senior officials of various ministries, including Finance, Foreign Affairs, and Justice, and representatives from law-enforcement agencies, was created in October to identify and block the funding of terrorist activity.

During the year Italy also concentrated on dismantling not only indigenous terrorist groups that in the past attacked Italian and US interests, but also groups suspected of international terrorist affiliations operating within and outside Italy's borders. In April, the Revolutionary Proletarian Initiative Nuclei (NIPR) bombed the Institute of International Affairs in Rome. The Anti-Imperialist Territorial Nuclei (NTA) claimed to have attacked the tribunal courthouse building in Venice in August and the Central European Initiative (INCE) office in Trieste in September 2000. Both groups are leftist-anarchist entities that promote anti-US/anti-NATO rhetoric and espouse the ideals of the Red Brigades of the 1970s and 1980s.

Italy's vigorous leadership of the Group of Eight (G-8) Counterterrorism Expert's Group resulted in significant progress on a 25-point plan to guide the G-8's contribution to the global counterterrorism campaign. The Action Plan has fostered greater counterterrorism coordination among the foreign affairs and law-enforcement agencies of G-8 members. Italy's work with other European countries to combat terrorism as well as extensive cooperation among Italy, the United States, and several European countries—including Spain, France, Germany, Britain, and Belgium—led to the arrests on 10 October. Moreover, Rome worked with Madrid to improve bilateral efforts against terrorism, agreeing in early November at a summit in Granada to create a joint investigative team to fight terrorism and conduct joint patrols on long-distance trains to prevent illegal immigration.

Poland

Stressing solidarity as a NATO ally, Poland has taken a leadership role in expanding counterterrorism cooperation with key regional and international partners. In November, President Kwasniewski hosted the Warsaw Conference on Combating Terrorism. The Conference resulted in an action plan and a declaration that identified areas for regional cooperation and called for nations in the region to enhance their abilities to contribute to the global war on terrorism. Poland strongly supported the campaign against the Taliban and al-Qaida in Afghanistan, and the US Central Command has accepted Poland's offer of specialized units. The Government of Poland has also taken significant steps to bolster its own internal capabilities to combat terrorist activities and the movement of terrorist funds. Poland's excellent border controls, high level of airport security, and its close cooperation on law-enforcement issues have discouraged potential terrorist movements through Poland.

Spain

The September 11 attacks in the United States triggered unqualified support from Madrid in the global fight against terrorism. Spain, which has waged a 30-year battle against the Basque Fatherland and Liberty (ETA) terrorist group, champions mutual assistance as a strategy to deny safehaven to terrorists and welcomes the global focus to help defeat all forms of terrorism. Immediately after the attacks, President Aznar announced that his Government will stand "shoulder to shoulder" with the United States in fighting terrorism; he has directed all relevant agencies to work closely with US law-enforcement counterparts. Spanish police broke up two al-Qaida-affiliated cells, arresting six members in late September and eight in November. Spain also offered military aid to Coalition efforts in Afghanistan. Madrid plans to use its leadership of the European Union—in the first half of 2002—to promote continued EU support for counterterrorism cooperation.

During his trip to Spain in June, President Bush declared that the United States stands "side by side with the government of Spain and will not yield in the face of terrorism."

Madrid's top counterterrorism priority beyond supporting the global Coalition against terrorism remained combating ETA, which maintained its violent strategy throughout 2001, despite a Basque regional election that demonstrated diminishing popular support for the group's political wing. The group made good on its threats to target Spain's tourist areas during its summer campaign with a series of attacks that caused mainly property damage: a car bomb at Madrid's Barajas International Airport damaged scores of cars, while a bomb attack at a popular tourist resort near Barcelona slightly injured about 10 persons. It also continued to attack traditional targets—politicians, military personnel, journalists, and police. A bomb in Catalonia in March killed one police officer, while another bomb in Madrid in June fatally injured a Spanish general. An ETA commando headquartered in the Basque region is suspected of killing a Basque police officer in July. According to official Spanish Government data, ETA terrorists killed 15 persons in 2001, most of whom were members of either the military or security services.

Madrid scored a variety of successes against ETA during the year, dismantling a dozen important terrorist cells and disrupting some of the group's logistics bases. In October, the Spanish National Police dismantled an ETA cell in the Basque region that, in addition to organizing smaller commando cells, was planning to launch attacks. Two of those arrested were linked to the assassination of a senior Basque Socialist politician in February 2000. Spanish police in early December arrested several members of a cell suspected in several car bombings during the year, including the attack at Madrid's airport. They confiscated more than 100 pounds of explosives and a variety of false documentation.

Spain continued to forge bilateral agreements with states that can help it defeat ETA terrorism. In January, Madrid signed a joint political declaration with the United States, which included an explicit commitment to work jointly against ETA. Spain also concluded important agreements with France and Mexico, two key partners in the effort to deny potential sanctuaries to ETA members. During his visit to Mexico in July, President Aznar signed an agreement with Mexico that boosted intelligence sharing, security, and judicial cooperation on terrorism. In early October, Paris and Madrid signed a new bilateral agreement that eases extraditions of ETA suspects and improves antiterrorism cooperation. Under the agreement, a former ETA leader—charged in an attempted assassination of King Juan Carlos in 1995—was temporarily extradited to Spain to stand trial. Following his trial, he will be returned to France to complete a 10-year sentence there before being sent back to Spain to serve any additional time meted out by the Spanish court.

Turkey

The Turkish Government, long a staunch counterterrorism ally, fully supported the campaign against terrorism. Turkey provided basing and overflight rights and has sent troops to Afghanistan to train the local military and participate in the International Security Assistance Force. At home, Turkish security authorities dealt heavy blows to the country's two most active terrorist organizations, the DHKP/C and Turkish Hizballah—a Kurdish Islamic (Sunni) extremist organization unrelated to Lebanese Hizballah. Police arrested more than 100 members and supporters of the DHKP/C and several hundred members and supporters of Turkish Hizballah and raided numerous safe houses, recovering large caches of weapons, computers and other technical equipment, and miscellaneous documents.

Despite these setbacks, the DHKP/C retained a lethal capability and, for the first time in its history, conducted suicide bombings. On 3 January, a DHKP/C operative walked into a police regional headquarters in Istanbul and detonated a bomb strapped to his body, killing himself and a policeman, and injuring seven others. A second DHKP/C suicide bomber attacked a police booth in a public square in Istanbul on 10 September, killing two policemen, mortally wounding an Australian tourist, and injuring more than 20.

Turkish Hizballah conducted its first attack against official Turkish interests with the assassination on 24 January of Diyarbakir Police Chief Gaffar Okkan and five policemen—revealing a greater sophistication than the group had shown in previous attacks. According to press reports, four teams consisting of as many as 20 operatives ambushed Okkan's motorcade as he departed the Diyarbakir Governor's office. Authorities recovered approximately 460 bullet casings at the scene. Hizballah operatives also ambushed three police officers in Istanbul on 14 October, killing two and wounding the other.

Chechen separatists and sympathizers also used Turkey as a staging ground for terrorist attacks. On 22 April, 13 pro-Chechen gunmen—led by Muhammed Tokcan, an ethnic-Chechen Turkish national who served fewer than four years in prison for hijacking a Russian ferry from Turkey in 1996—took over a prominent Istanbul hotel, holding hostage for 12 hours approximately 150 guests, including 37 US citizens. The gunmen, who eventually surrendered peacefully, claimed that they wanted to focus world attention on Russia's activities in Chechnya. Turkey's court system has been relatively lenient with pro-Chechen terrorists. The state court addressing the hotel incident did not indict Tokcan's group under the country's stringent antiterrorism laws but instead charged the militants with less serious crimes, including weapons possession and deprivation of liberty.

Separately, three Chechens hijacked a Russian charter jet carrying 175 passengers, mostly Russian nationals, from Istanbul to Moscow on 15 March. Fuel limitations forced the plane to land in Medina, Saudi Arabia. Saudi authorities negotiated with the hijackers overnight before special forces stormed the plane and captured two of the separatists. The third hijacker, one crewmember, and one passenger were killed during the rescue.

The PKK continued to pursue its "peace initiative"—launched by imprisoned PKK Chairman Abdullah Ocalan in August 1999—concentrating largely on its public relations efforts in Western Europe. The leadership announced early in the year the inauguration of a second phase of its peace initiative, called *serhildan* (uprising)—the term usually connotes violent activity, but the PKK uses it to refer to civil disobedience—in which PKK members in Europe openly declare their identity as Kurds and their involvement in the group, sign petitions, and hold demonstrations in an effort to push for improved rights for the Kurdish minority in Turkey. The PKK began conducting *serhildan* activities in Turkey toward the end of the year; authorities arrested some PKK members who participated.

United Kingdom

The United Kingdom has been Washington's closest partner in the post-September 11 international Coalition against terrorism. The UK stepped forward to share the military burden of the battle against al-Qaida and the Taliban in Afghanistan. More than 4,000 British personnel were assigned to Operation Veritas, the UK contribution to the US-led Operation Enduring Freedom, which began on 7 October. Significant UK naval, air, ground, and special forces participated in operations against the Taliban and al-Qaida. London is leading the International Security Assistance Force to help the new Afghan Interim Authority provide security and stability in Kabul.

At home, the British detained 10 individuals with suspected foreign terrorist links and intensified surveillance of other individuals based on information indicating links to terrorist activities. At year's end, the UK had detained and was assisting in extraditing to the US four individuals charged with terrorist acts in the United States or against US citizens. Consistent with the UK's Terrorism Act of 2000, which widened the definition of terrorism to include international as well as domestic activities, the Government in February 2001 added 21 international terrorist organizations—including al-Qaida—to its list of proscribed organizations. Parliament in mid-December passed the Anti-Terrorism, Security, and Crime Act, providing authorities with additional tools in the battle against terrorism. The new legislation gives the Government legal authority to detain for six-month renewable terms foreign terrorist suspects who cannot be deported under UK law. It also provides for tightened airport security, allows security services full access to lists of air and ferry passengers, tightens asylum rules, and criminalizes the act of assisting foreign groups to acquire weapons of mass destruction.

The United Kingdom has been working with the United States and the UN to disrupt the cash supply of suspected terrorist groups. As of late 2001, UK authorities had frozen more than 70 million pounds ($100,000,000) of suspected terrorist assets. A proposed antiterrorism bill would require financial institutions to report suspicious transactions or face legal penalties.

In ongoing efforts to end domestic terrorism, the UK and other parties to the Northern Ireland peace process made progress toward fulfilling terms of the Good Friday Agreement. In October, the Irish Republican Army (IRA) put an undisclosed amount of weapons and ammunition "beyond use." Dissident Republican splinter groups—the Real IRA (RIRA) and the Continuity IRA (CIRA)—denounced the move, and called on disgruntled IRA members to join RIRA and CIRA. Statistics indicated that the number of terrorist killings in the North remained consistent, with 18 deaths in 2000 and 17 in 2001. UK authorities believe that RIRA is responsible for an intensified bombing campaign during the year on the mainland, with bombs exploding outside the BBC's London headquarters (March); in North London (April); in West London (August); and in Birmingham (November). Moreover, the year saw an upswing in Loyalist paramilitary violence, primarily in the form of pipe-bomb attacks on Catholic homes in North Belfast. In addition, for 12 weeks during the autumn, Protestants residing near a Catholic school in North Belfast held highly publicized protests that were sometimes marred by violence.

The United States continued to lend support to the Northern Ireland peace process, with President Bush stating in March that Washington stands ready to help London and Dublin ". . . in any way the governments would find useful." In March, the USG designated the RIRA as a Foreign Terrorist Organizations; and following September 11, the US Government included CIRA, the Orange Volunteers and the Red Hand Defenders on the Terrorist Exclusion List (TEL)—a move that means their members are barred from entering the United States. Later in the year, the Government of Colombia detained three individuals with IRA links based on suspicion they had been training rebels from the Revolutionary Armed Forces of Colombia (FARC), a Marxist guerrilla group involved in drugs and on the US list of Foreign Terrorist Organizations. US officials made clear Washington's displeasure about possible IRA/FARC connections, stating that the United States will have no tolerance for any ongoing or future cooperation between these organizations.

Yugoslavia/Kosovo

The Government of the Federal Republic of Yugoslavia announced its support for international efforts to combat terrorism immediately after the September 11 attacks. Belgrade, already a party to six of the UN antiterrorism conventions, by year's end signed the convention on funding of terrorism and reportedly intended to sign four more in the near future. In addition, the Government of Yugoslavia planned to take steps to implement financial sanctions against groups involved in terrorist-related activity. Yugoslav officials arrested and detained several suspect Arabs in November and December, including 32 Afghanis transiting Serbia in late October.

The UN and NATO, the international civil and security presence exercising authority in Kosovo, have firmly supported international efforts to combat terrorism. The UN promulgated new regulations that will make it easier to identify and apprehend suspected terrorists and has worked to improve Kosovo's border security. NATO has increased its own border-interdiction efforts and its monitoring of organizations with potential links to terrorism. Kosovar political leaders expressed their strong support for the fight against global terrorism.

Various NGOs identified as supporting terrorist activities maintained a presence in Kosovo. The NGOs, largely staffed by a small number of foreign Islamic extremists and a few dozen local radicals, do not enjoy wide support among Kosovo's moderate Muslim population. In December, NATO Troops conducted raids against the Global Relief Foundation, an NGO in Kosovo with alleged links to terrorist organizations.

Latin America Overview

The countries of Latin America (with the exception of Cuba) joined as one in condemning the attacks of September 11 when the Organization of American States became the first international organization to express outrage at the "attack on all the democratic and free states of the world" and to voice solidarity with the United States. Ten days later, the OAS Foreign Ministers called for a series of strong measures to combat terrorism, and those members that are party to the Inter-American Treaty of Reciprocal Assistance took the unprecedented step of invoking the principle of mutual assistance—an agreement by which an attack on any state party to the treaty is considered an attack on them all.

Kidnapping remained one of the most pernicious problems in the region. Nineteen US citizens were kidnapped in Latin America in 2001, including five each in Colombia and Haiti, and four in Mexico. Elite counterterrorism units in Colombia arrested 50 persons in connection with the abduction in October 2000 of five US oil workers in Ecuador and the subsequent murder in January 2001 of US hostage Ron Sander.

September 11 brought renewed attention to the activities of the Lebanese-based terrorist organization Hizballah, as well as other terrorist groups, in the triborder area of Argentina, Brazil, and Paraguay, where terrorists raise millions of dollars annually via criminal enterprises. There is evidence of the presence of Hizballah members or sympathizers in other areas of Latin America as well: in northern Chile, especially around Iquique; in Maicao, Colombia near the border with Venezuela; on Margarita Island in Venezuela; and in Panama's Colon Free Trade Zone. Allegations of Usama Bin Ladin or al-Qaida support cells in Latin America were investigated by US and local intelligence and law-enforcement organizations, but at year's end they remained uncorroborated.

On 10 September, Secretary of State Powell officially designated the Colombian paramilitary organization United Self-Defense Forces (AUC) as a Foreign Terrorist Organization (FTO) due in part to their explosive growth—the AUC swelled to an estimated 9,000 fighters in 2001—and reliance on terrorist tactics. Colombia's largest terrorist organization, the 16,000-member Revolutionary Armed Forces of Colombia (FARC), unleashed such a wave of violence and terror in 2001 and early 2002 that Colombian President Andres Pastrana decided, in February 2002, to terminate the peace talks that had been a cornerstone of his presidency and to reassert government control over the FARC's demilitarized zone, or *despeje*.

Three members of the Irish Republican Army—alleged explosives experts helping the FARC prepare for an urban terror campaign—were arrested as they departed the *despeje* in August. Allegations of similar support by the terrorist group Basque Fatherland and Liberty, or ETA, to the FARC were reported by Colombian media. Ecuador is viewed by many analysts as a strategic point in the international weapons transshipment routes for arms, ammunition, and explosives destined for Colombian terrorist groups.

In Peru, the Shining Path showed signs of making a comeback as a terrorist organization, albeit with a greater focus on narcotics than on ideological insurgency. The MRTA, largely wiped out in the late 1990s, did not take any terrorist actions in 2001.

[*Eds. Note*: Cuba, one of the seven state sponsors of terrorism, is discussed in Part 1 in the section on "State Sponsorship of Terrorism."]

Bolivia

Although no acts of international terrorism took place in Bolivia in 2001, there were numerous incidents of domestic terrorism, capped by the car-bomb explosion on 21 December near the entrance to the Bolivian National Police Department district office in Santa Cruz. The attack killed one and caused numerous injuries; nearby buildings, including one that houses US Drug Enforcement Agency offices, also sustained collateral damage. Bolivian officials suspect the bombing may have been related to recent police successes against a captured group of robbery suspects, including some Peruvians, apparently led by a former Bolivian police official.

Most other incidents were thought to be perpetrated by illegal coca growers ("cocaleros"), including using snipers against security forces and boobytrapping areas where eradication efforts take place principally in the Chapare area of Cochabamba Department.

In the months following September 11, Bolivia became a party to all 12 UN and the one OAS counterterrorism conventions. In addition, Bolivia issued blocking orders on terrorist assets.

Chile

Two apparently terrorist-related incidents occurred in Chile during 2001. In late September, the US Embassy received a functional letter bomb that local police successfully destroyed in a controlled demolition. The second incident involved an anthrax-tainted letter received at a Santiago doctor's office; the anthrax strain, however, did not match that found in US cases, and it was possible that this incident was perpetrated locally.

In the letter-bomb case, two Chilean suspects, Lenin Guardia and Humbero Lopez Candia, were taken into custody, charged with obstruction of justice and possession of illegal weapons, and manufacturing and sending the bomb, respectively. Although they both face 20-year prison sentences upon conviction under Chile's antiterrorism law, it appeared that the US Embassy was a high-profile target of opportunity for persons acting out of personal and selfish motivations.

The Chilean Government also opened an investigation into the activities in the northern port city of Iquique of Lebanese businessman Assad Ahmed Mohamed Barakat—the same Barakat wanted by Paraguayan authorities and who, at year's end, continued to reside in Brazil. In Iquique, authorities suspect Barakat, along with his Lebanese partner, established two businesses as cover operations to transfer potentially millions of dollars to Hizballah.

Chile also began taking concrete steps to improve its own counterterrorism capabilities and to comply with its international treaty obligations. Aside from becoming party to all 12 UN counterterrorism conventions, the steps include proposals for new money-laundering laws to target terrorist financing, special counterterrorism investigative units, and a new national intelligence agency.

Chile—working with Brazil and Argentina—has led efforts to coordinate hemispheric support for the United States in the aftermath of September 11 in its capacity as the 2001 head (Secretary pro Tempore) of the Rio Group. The efforts included convening the OAS Permanent Council and OAS foreign ministers in the week following the attacks, the historic invocation of the Rio Treaty, and taking part in a special session of the OAS Inter-American Committee Against Terrorism.

Colombia

An increased international awareness of terrorism did nothing to stop or even slow the pace of terrorist actions by Colombia's three terrorist organizations—the Revolutionary Armed Forces of Colombia (FARC), National Liberation Army (ELN), and United Self-Defense Forces of Colombia (AUC)—in 2001. Some 3,500 murders were attributed to these groups.

On 10 September, Secretary of State Colin Powell announced the designation of the AUC as a Foreign Terrorist Organization, citing the AUC's explosive growth—to an estimated 9,000 fighters by year's end—and their increasing reliance on terrorist methods such as the use of massacres to purposefully displace segments of the population, as primary reasons for the designation. With this addition, all three of Colombia's major illegal armed groups have now been designated by the United States as Foreign Terrorist Organizations (the FARC and ELN were designated in 1997). Colombian estimates for 2001 suggested that the AUC was accountable for some 43 percent of Colombia's internally displaced persons, mostly rural peasants, while the FARC and ELN were responsible for some 35 percent.

In 2001, as in years past, there were more kidnappings in Colombia than in any other country in the world, and the financial transfer from victims to terrorists by way of ransom payments and extortion fees continued to cripple the Colombian economy. The FARC and ELN were purportedly responsible in 2001 for approximately 80 percent of the more than 2,800 kidnappings of Colombian and foreign nationals—including some whose governments or agencies (the UN, for example) were helping mediate the ongoing civil conflict. Since 1980, the FARC has murdered at least ten US citizens, and three New Tribes Missionaries abducted by the FARC in 1993 remain unaccounted for.

The FARC and the AUC continued their deadly practice of massacring one another's alleged supporters, especially in areas where they were competing for narcotics-trafficking corridors or prime coca-growing terrain. The FARC and ELN struggled with one another for dominance in the bombing of the Cano-Limon-Covenas oil pipe-line—combining for an unprecedented 178 attacks which had a devastating ecological and economic impact—with the larger FARC (an estimated 16,000 fighters vs. under 5,000 for the ELN) beginning to gain the upper hand by year's end.

As in past years, the on-again, off-again peace talks between Bogotá and the FARC or the ELN did not lead to substantive breakthroughs with either group. (As of press time, President Pastrana had broken off talks with the FARC following the group's 2 February 2002 hijacking of Aires Flight 1891, the abduction of Colombian Senator Jorge Gechen, as well as the separate abduction of presidential candidate Ingrid Betancourt; the Colombian military also had reasserted control over the FARC's demilitarized zone, or *despeje*.) Talks with the ELN were ongoing. For its part, the AUC continued to press, without success, for political recognition by the Government of Colombia.

Throughout 2001, Colombia's government acted against all three terrorist groups through direct military action as well as through legal and judicial means. The Prosecutor General successfully prosecuted many FARC, ELN, and AUC members on domestic terrorism charges. Bogotá also pursued insurgent and paramilitary sources of financing with some success, capturing in a short period in late 2001, for example, four FARC finance chiefs. In May, raids on high-ranking AUC residences in Monteria netted key evidence regarding that group's financial backers. On a more disturbing note, the Government alleged links between these groups and other terrorist organizations outside Colombia. The capture in August of three Irish Republican Army members who have been charged with sharing their expertise and providing training on explosives in the FARC's demilitarized zone is perhaps the most notable example.

The Colombian Government has been very supportive of US antiterrorist efforts in international fora, particularly the United Nations and the Organization of American States (OAS). Colombia was one of the region's leaders in the effort to impose sanctions against the Taliban in the United Nations before the events of September 11, and it continues to cooperate in enforcing UNSC and UNGA antiterrorist resolutions, including Resolutions 1267, 1333, and 1368. Colombia also signed the UN Convention on the Suppression of the Financing of Terrorism. In the OAS, Colombia continued to be an active member of the Inter-American Committee Against Terrorism and was selected to chair the subcommittee that deals with monitoring and interdicting terrorist financial flows. Colombia also planned to broaden its capability to combat terrorism within its borders by means of a three-part strategy unveiled in late October. The main components include strengthening the public security forces, modernizing the penitentiary system, and expanding and improving civil and criminal investigation mechanisms. Also included are provisions for the seizure and forfeiture of terrorist assets, reduction of bank secrecy rights, and measures to insulate municipal and departmental finances from corruption. At year's end, the implementation of this strategy was awaiting passage of additional legislation.

Ecuador

The kidnapping on 12 October 2000 of a group of eight oil workers (including five US citizens) by an armed band played out well into 2001. On 31 January, the hostage takers executed US hostage Ron Sander. The remaining seven hostages, including the four surviving US citizens, were released in March, following payment of a multi-million-dollar ransom. In June, Colombian police arrested more than 50 Colombian and Ecuadorian criminal and ex-guerrilla suspects, including the group's leaders, connected to the case. At year's end, five of the suspects were awaiting extradition to the United States.

Beyond the murder of Ron Sander, there were no significant acts of terrorism in Ecuador in 2001, although unidentified individuals or groups perpetrated some low-level bombings. Two McDonald's restaurants were firebombed in April. Over a four-day period in mid-November, four pamphlet bombs containing anti-US propaganda were detonated in downtown Quito.

As did most Latin American nations in the wake of the September 11 attacks in the United States, Ecuador voiced its strong support for US, OAS, and UN antiterrorism declarations and initiatives put forth in various international fora, including UNSCR 1373, as well as for Coalition actions in Afghanistan. Ecuador, however, neither improved control over its porous borders nor cracked down on illegal emigration/immigration. Quito's weak financial controls and widespread document fraud remained issues of concern, as did Ecuador's reputation as a strategic corridor for arms, ammunition, and explosives destined for Colombian terrorist groups.

Peru

Although there were no international acts of terrorism in Peru in 2001, the number of domestic terrorist acts (130 by year's end) increased markedly and eclipsed the number perpetrated in the previous three years. Most incidents occurred in remote areas of Peru associated with narcotics trafficking. Sendero Luminoso (SL) was the most active terrorist group—in fact, the level of SL-related activity and its aggressive posture appeared to be on the rise through 2001. The Tupac Amaru Revolutionary Movement, although active politically, was not known to have committed any terrorist acts in 2001. US citizen Lori Berenson received a civilian re-trial and was once again convicted for terrorism based on her involvement with the Tupac Amaru Revolutionary Front, or MRTA. (The conviction and sentence were upheld by the Peruvian Supreme Court 18 February 2002.) Peruvian police also were investigating a series of attacks against Lima's electric power companies' infrastructure throughout the fall.

In a notable case in late November, Peruvian police thwarted a possible SL terrorist attack against a likely US target—possibly the US Embassy—when it arrested two Lima SL cell members. At the time of his arrest, one cell member possessed paper scraps with route diagrams and addresses of several US-affiliated facilities in Lima. Although they were still investigating the incident at year's end, Peruvian officials suspected that the SL had planned a car-bomb attack against US interests to coincide with the 3 December birthday of jailed SL founder Abimael Guzman. (Car bombings were a regular component of SL's modus operandi during the 1980s and early 1990s.)

Peru continued to pursue a number of individuals accused of committing terrorist acts in 2001, and notable captures included several key SL members. Among these were the arrests in October of Ruller Mazoombite (a.k.a. Camarada Cayo), chief of the protection team for SL leader Macario Ala (a.k.a. Artemio), and Evoricio Ascencios (a.k.a. Camarada Canale), the logistics chief of the Huallaga Regional Committee. By the end of November, some 259 suspected terrorists had been arrested.

Since September 11, Lima has been a regional leader in strongly supporting antiterrorism initiatives through the drafting and passage of key legislation (some still pending at year's end) against money laundering as well as adopting an even more active stance against terrorism in general. In late September, Peru introduced a draft Inter-American Convention against Terrorism at the OAS and, in October, assumed the chair of the Border Controls Working Group of the OAS Inter-American Committee Against Terrorism. Peru has remained very receptive to antiterrorism training opportunities and has participated in the US State Department Antiterrorism Training Assistance program since 1986. Peru has yet to issue blocking orders on terrorist assets, however.

Triborder (Argentina, Brazil, Paraguay)

South America's triborder area (TBA)—where the borders of Argentina, Brazil, and Paraguay converge and which hosts a large Arab population—took on a new prominence in the wake of the September 11 attacks in the United States. Although arms and drug trafficking, contraband smuggling, document and currency fraud, money laundering, and pirated goods have long been associated with this region, it also has been characterized as a hub for Hizballah and HAMAS activities, particularly for logistic and financial purposes. At year's end, press reports of al-Qaida operatives in the TBA had been disproved or remained uncorroborated by intelligence and law-enforcement officials.

All three governments, especially Paraguay, took steps to rein in the individuals most strongly suspected of materially aiding terrorist groups—most prominently Hizballah—and continued to monitor the area as well as hold outstanding arrest warrants for those not yet captured. Security officials from each country, as well as a contingent from Uruguay, continued to coordinate closely on sharing information. The four nations also were trying to improve very limited joint operations in the fight against terrorism. The governments also condemned the September 11 attacks and generally stood in strong support of US counterterrorism efforts.

Argentina suffered no acts of terrorism in 2001. The oral trial for alleged Argentine accomplices to the terrorist attack in 1994 on the Argentine-Israeli Community Center (AMIA) began in late September. Twenty suspects are being tried—of whom 15 are former police officers, and include a one-time Buenos Aires police captain—and are accused of supplying the stolen vehicle that carried the car bomb. The trial is expected to last through much of 2002.

Argentine authorities also continued to investigate the bombing in 1992 of the Israeli Embassy in Buenos Aires and to seek those directly responsible for the AMIA attack. A team of FBI investigators—at Argentina's request—visited the country in June to work jointly with the legal and judicial officials involved in the AMIA bombing to review the investigation. Despite the elapsed time since the attacks, the public trial of the accessories now underway has led some to expect that new information relating to one or both of these terrorist acts will come to light.

In Brazil, one incident occurred during 2001 that could be characterized as a terrorist incident—an after-hours bombing of a McDonald's restaurant in Rio de Janeiro in October. The incident resulted in property damage but no injuries, and while Brazilian police suspect antiglobalization extremists perpetrated the attack, no arrests were made.

Following the September 11 attacks, Brasilia initiated and led a successful campaign to invoke the Inter-American Treaty of Reciprocal Assistance (the Rio Treaty) in support of the United States. Brazil also played host to a conference in November on regional counterterrorism initiatives and participated in several other regional meetings on counterterrorist cooperation. Brazil raided several clandestine telephone centers from which calls to numerous Middle Eastern countries had been traced. Brazilian officials were still investigating possible links to terrorist activities.

Since September 11, Paraguay has been an active and prominent partner in the war on terror. It has, inter alia, arrested some 23 individuals suspected of Hizballah/HAMAS fundraising, initiated a ministerial-level dialogue with regional governments, cracked down on visa and passport fraud, and hosted, in late December, a successful regional counterterrorism seminar that included a keynote speech by the United States Coordinator for Counterterrorism.

Paraguayan officials raided a variety of businesses and detained numerous suspects believed to have materially aided either Hizballah or HAMAS, primarily in the triborder city of Ciudad del Este or in Encarnación. Prominent among the raids were the arrests on 3 October of Mazen Ali Saleh and Saleh Mahmoud Fayad (on criminal association/tax evasion charges) and the arrest on 8 November of Sobhi Mahmoud Fayad (on criminal association and related charges); all three are linked to Hizballah. In addition, the businesses that were raided revealed extensive ties to Hizballah—in particular, records showed the transfers of millions of dollars to Hizballah operatives, "charities," and entities worldwide. Several other TBA personalities, including Assad Barakat and Ali Hassan Abdallah, are considered fugitives. Barakat, who is considered Hizballah's principal TBA leader, lives in Foz do Iguazu, but owns a business ("Casa Apollo") in Ciudad del Este; Paraguay has sought an INTERPOL warrant for his arrest.

Among the others arrested were some 17 ethnic Arabs (mostly Lebanese) on charges of possessing false documents; Paraguayan officials suspect some have links to HAMAS. Three Paraguayans—an attorney, a consular officer, and an Interior Ministry employee—also were arrested in connection with fraudulently issuing immigration documents to the 17 individuals.

Asunción, through its money-laundering unit, also identified 46 individuals who transferred funds in a suspicious manner from accounts held by Middle Eastern customers or to Middle East organizations.

Despite the apparent successes, Paraguayan counterterrorist enforcement continued to be impeded by a lack of specific criminal legislation against terrorist activities, although such a bill was introduced before the legislature. Until its passage, Paraguay must rely on charges such as criminal association, tax evasion, money laundering, or possession of false documents to hold suspects. Pervasive corruption also continued to be a problem for Paraguay, and some suspected terrorists were able to co-opt law-enforcement or judicial officials.

Uruguay

Uruguay suffered no acts of international terrorism in 2001. Before September 11, Montevideo had been involved in an effort to create a permanent working group on terrorism with neighboring countries. Since September 11, Uruguay has actively supported various regional counterterrorism conventions and initiatives, paying particular attention to the tri-border area as well as to its shared border with Brazil.

Egypt has asked Uruguay to extradite a suspected terrorist in a case that came before Uruguay's courts in 2001. The defendant, al-Said Hassan Mokhles, is a member of the Gama'a al-Islamiyya (Islamic Group, IG)—a group with ties to al-Qa'ida. Although the Court of Appeals granted his extradition, Mokhles has appealed his case to the Uruguayan Supreme Court. Mokhles was imprisoned, charged with document fraud, as his suspected IG activities took place before he arrived in Uruguay; there is no reported IG cell presence in Uruguay.

Venezuela

Following the events of September 11, Venezuela joined the rest of the OAS in condemning the attacks, and Venezuelan officials worked closely with US officials to track down terrorist assets in Venezuela's financial system. Venezuela condemned terrorism but opposed using force to combat it.

It was widely reported in the press that Venezuela maintained contact with the FARC and ELN and may have helped them obtain arms and ammunition; the press reports also included turning a blind eye to occasional cross-border insurgency and extortion by FARC and ELN operatives of Venezuelan ranchers.

In December 2001, Venezuela extradited Colombian national (and accused ELN member) Jose Maria Ballestas, wanted as a suspect for his role in the hijacking of an Avianca aircraft in Colombia in April 1999.

Middle East Overview

Middle East terrorism witnessed two major developments this year. On the one hand, terrorist groups and their state sponsors continued their terrorist activities and planning throughout 2001. Most notable among these groups was Usama Bin Ladin's al-Qaida, which perpetrated in the United States the most significant act of anti-US terrorism. On the other, however, most Middle Eastern countries—including some with which the United States has political difficulties—showed an unprecedented degree of cooperation with the Coalition's campaign against terrorism in the aftermath of the September 11 attacks. Some of our Middle Eastern allies thwarted terrorist incidents targeted against US interests and citizens, disrupted terrorist cells, and enhanced their counterterrorism relations with the United States. A number provided tangible support for Operation Enduring Freedom, including personnel, basing, and overflight privileges. Most Middle East governments froze al-Qaida financial assets pursuant to UNSCR 1373. Notably, all Middle Eastern countries with an American diplomatic presence were responsive to US requests for enhanced security for personnel and facilities during periods of heightened alert.

The Government of Yemen, for example, launched a military campaign against al-Qaida and suspected al-Qaida members within its territory. Jordan maintained extreme vigilance in monitoring suspected terrorists and put a number on trial. Qatar, as head of the Organization of the Islamic Conference (OIC), coordinated an official OIC communiqué supportive of action by the international Coalition. Egypt used its regional clout to build consensus for the Coalition. The United Arab Emirates broke off diplomatic relations with the Taliban 11 days after the attack and took significant antiterrorism financing measures. And Algeria continued its aggressive campaign against domestic terrorism and bolstered its security cooperation with the US Government.

Middle Eastern governments that still lack peace agreements with Israel, most notably Syria and Lebanon, cooperated with the US Government and its partners in investigating al-Qaida and some other organizations, but they refused to recognize Hizballah, HAMAS, the Palestine Islamic Jihad and other Palestinian rejectionist groups for what they are—terrorists. They and other Arab/Muslim countries held the view that violent activities by these groups constitute legitimate resistance. They sometimes even condone Palestinian suicide bombings and other attacks against civilian targets within Israel, the West Bank, and Gaza Strip.

The Gulf countries of Bahrain, Kuwait, Oman, Qatar, Saudi Arabia, and the United Arab Emirates played strong roles in the international Coalition against terrorism. In addition to condemning the September 11 attacks publicly, these governments took positive steps to halt the flow of terrorism financing and, in some cases, authorized basing and/ or overflight provisions. In several cases, they did so despite popular disquiet over their governments' military support for Operation Enduring Freedom. As in other Arab countries, US interests were often subject to terrorist threats. The Gulf governments as a whole were extremely responsive in providing appropriate and effective security measures.

[*Eds. Note*: Iran, Iraq, Libya, and Syria, which are among the seven state sponsors of terrorism, are discussed in Part 1 in the section on "State Sponsorship of Terrorism."]

Algeria

President Bouteflika, who met twice in 2001 with President Bush, publicly pledged his Government's full cooperation with the Coalition's campaign. As part of this cooperation, the Government of Algeria strengthened its information sharing with the United States and worked actively with European and other governments to eliminate terrorist support networks linked to Algerian groups, most of which are located in Europe.

Algeria itself has been ravaged by terrorism since the early 1990s. Since 1999, Algerian extremists operating abroad also have stepped-up their anti-US activities, a development that has contributed to a closer, mutually beneficial counterterrorism relationship between our two countries. For example, in April, Algerian authorities announced the arrest of international fugitive Abdelmajid Dahoumane, as he tried to re-enter the country. Dahoumane is an accomplice of Ahmed Ressam, who is awaiting sentencing for planning a thwarted attack on the Los Angeles International Airport in December 1999.

Terrorism within Algeria remained a serious problem in 2001, although its magnitude decreased as Government forces continued to improve their ability to combat it. There were fewer massacres and false roadside checkpoints set up by militants. Most violence occurred in areas outside the capital. The worst single incident of terrorist violence occurred on 1 February when Islamic extremists massacred 26 persons near Berrouaghia in Medea Province.

Militants continued their attacks in the Algiers area on occasion, despite improved measures by the Government to secure the capital. Also, for the first time since 1997, Salafist Group for Call and Combat (GSPC) forces in early 2001 killed foreign nationals—four Russian scientists and one French/Algerian woman—although press reports suggest that the victims were not targeted based upon their nationalities.

The GSPC—the largest, most active terrorist organization operating inside Algeria—maintained the capability to conduct operations. It collaborated with smugglers and Islamists in the south who supplied insurgents with weapons and communications equipment in northern strongholds.

(In a shootout in early 2002, Algerian Government security forces killed Antar Zouabri, head of the Algerian terrorist organization Armed Islamic Group, which has been responsible for most of the civilian massacres over the past decade.)

Bahrain

There were no terrorist incidents in Bahrain in 2001. Amir Shaykh Hamad bin Isa Al-Khalifa used his country's 2001 presidency of the Gulf Cooperation Council (GCC) to advocate, consistently, a proactive GCC position against terrorism. In addition, the Bahrain Monetary Authority implemented UNSCR 1373 and quickly took action to freeze terrorist assets.

Egypt

The Egyptian and US Governments continued to work closely together on a broad range of counterterrorism issues in 2001. The relationship was further strengthened in the wake of the September 11 attacks. Key Egyptian Government and religious officials condemned the attacks; President Mubarak was the first Arab leader to support the US military campaign in Afghanistan publicly. Egypt also supported efforts to cut off the flow of terrorism financing by strengthening banking regulations, including preparing a money-laundering bill for this purpose. The Government of Egypt renewed its appeals to foreign governments to extradite or return Egyptian fugitives.

Other actions taken by the Government of Egypt to support US counterterrorism efforts following the September 11 attacks included continuing to place a high priority on protecting US citizens and facilities in Egypt from attack; strengthening security for US forces transiting the Suez Canal; implementing aviation security directives; agreeing to participate in the voluntary Advanced Passenger Information System; and granting extensive overflight and Canal transit clearances.

Egypt itself has been for many years a victim of terrorism, although it has abated. No terrorism-related deaths were reported in Egypt in 2001, but the Egyptian Government continued to regard terrorism and extremist activity as an urgent challenge. The Egyptian Government indicted nearly 300 Egyptians and foreigners on terrorism-related charges. They will be tried by a military tribunal. Other terrorists' detentions were extended. Of those arrested, 87 were members of a group Egyptian authorities dubbed "al-Wa'ad" (The Promise). They were accused of planning to assassinate key Egyptian figures and blow up strategic targets; at the time of the arrests, authorities reportedly discovered arms caches and bomb-making materials. Those arrested included 170 al-Gama'a al-Islamiyya (IG) members, accused of killing police and civilians. They also were accused of targeting tourists and robbing banks between 1994 and 1998. Egypt's principal terrorist organizations, the Egyptian Islamic Jihad (EIJ) and the IG, suffered setbacks following September 11. International members of both groups and some suspects were returned to Egypt from abroad for trial. The Government renewed its appeals to foreign governments to extradite or return other Egyptian fugitives. In early 2001, IG leader Rifa'i Ahmad Taha Musa published a book in which he attempted to justify terrorist attacks that result in mass civilian casualties. He disappeared several months thereafter, and his whereabouts at the time of this report's publication remained unknown.

Israel, the West Bank, and Gaza Strip

Traditionally, Israel has been one of the United States' staunchest supporters in fighting terrorism. September 11 reinforced US-Israeli security cooperation in this area. There is no known al-Qaida presence in the West Bank and Gaza Strip, and Palestinian Authority Chairman Arafat forcefully denounced the September 11 attacks. Even HAMAS publicly distanced itself from Usama Bin Ladin.

Israeli-Palestinian violence escalated in 2001, and terrorist activity increased in scale and lethality. Israel responded to terrorist attacks with military strikes against PA facilities, targeted killings of suspected terrorists, and tightened security measures, including roadblocks and closures of Palestinian towns and villages.

HAMAS conducted several suicide bombings inside Israeli cities from March to June, culminating in the attack outside a Tel Aviv nightclub on 1 June that killed 22 Israeli teenagers and injured at least 65 others. On 9 August, HAMAS mounted a suicide attack in a Jerusalem pizzeria, killing 15 persons and wounding more than 60 others.

Attacks by the Palestine Islamic Jihad (PIJ) against Israel were similar to those of HAMAS. They included car bombings, shooting attacks, and suicide bombings. In general, PIJ operations were significantly less lethal than those of HAMAS. The PIJ claimed several shootings during the year, including an attack on 4 November in which a PIJ member ambushed an Israeli bus carrying schoolchildren in the French Hill section of East Jerusalem. The attack killed two children, including one dual US-Israeli national, and wounded at least 35 other persons.

The Popular Front for the Liberation of Palestine (PFLP) raised its profile in 2001. It carried out car bombings in Jerusalem, few of which caused serious injury. The PFLP, however, assassinated Israeli cabinet minister Rehav'am Ze'evi in an East Jerusalem hotel on 17 October, purportedly in retaliation for Israel's killing of its leader, Abu Ali Mustafa.

Members of the Tanzim, which is made up of small and loosely organized cells of militants drawn from the street-level membership of Fatah, conducted attacks against Israeli targets in the West Bank over the course of the year. In mid-March, Israel arrested several Tanzim members who confessed to participating in at least 25 shootings over a five-month period. Some Tanzim militants also were active in al-Aqsa Martyrs Brigade, which claimed responsibility for numerous attacks in the West Bank—mainly shootings and roadside bombings against settlers and Israeli soldiers. Al-Aqsa Martyrs Brigade also claimed credit for at least one mortar attack.

Other secular Palestinian entities carried out terrorist attacks in 2001. Israel announced in the fall that it had detained 15 members of a terrorist squad linked to the Iraq-based Palestine Liberation Front. In early May, the Damascus-based Popular Front for the Liberation of Palestine-General Command (PFLP-GC) tried to smuggle weapons into Gaza aboard the *Santorini*. Apparently unaffiliated Palestinians also committed acts of political violence. For example, on 14 February, a Palestinian from Gaza, employed by Israel's Egged civilian bus company and with no known links to any terrorist organization, drove his bus into a group of Israeli soldiers at a bus stop killing eight and wounding 21 persons.

Israeli Arabs, constituting nearly one-fifth of Israel's population, appeared to have played a limited role in the violence in 2001. On 9 September, Israeli Arab Muhammad Hubayshi conducted a suicide attack at a train station in Nahariyah. HAMAS claimed credit for the attack. Israeli Arabs generally refrained from aiding and abetting terrorists from the West Bank and Gaza, however. At year's end, Israel indicted four Israeli Arabs linked to rejectionist groups, although they were uninvolved in terrorist operations or planning.

Jewish extremists attacked Palestinian civilians and their properties in the West Bank and Gaza Strip in 2001. The attacks claimed the lives of Palestinian civilians and destroyed Palestinian farmlands, homes, businesses, and automobiles. In April, six Israeli policemen were wounded when settlers blew up a Palestinian shop. In late November, Israel's Shin Bet security service assessed that five Palestinians were killed and fourteen wounded in attacks that were likely staged by Israeli settlers in the West Bank. Investigations into many of these attacks produced inconclusive results, leading to several arrests but no formal charges.

During 2001, Israeli military forces killed more than two dozen suspected terrorists affiliated with HAMAS, the PIJ, Fatah, or the PFLP. An unspecified number of Palestinian civilians also were killed in the strikes.

Unlike the pre-*intifadah* era, when Israeli-PA security cooperation was generally effective, PA counterterrorism activities remained sporadic throughout the year. Israel's destruction of the PA's security infrastructure contributed to the ineffectiveness of the PA. Significantly reduced Israeli-PA security cooperation and a lax security environment allowed HAMAS and other groups to rebuild terrorist infrastructure in the Palestinian territories.

PA security services did thwart some attacks aimed at Israelis. They also discovered and confiscated some caches of weapons and explosives. But violence continued throughout the West Bank and Gaza Strip, resulting in almost 200 Israelis and over 500 Palestinians killed in 2001.

Early in December, the White House called upon Arafat to take "meaningful, long-term and enduring action against terrorists operating out of Palestinian territory." On 16 December, Arafat issued a public statement urging adherence to his call for a cease-fire. This was followed by PA arrests of dozens of HAMAS and PIJ activists, although the conditions of their arrest and the military role that some of them may have played remain unclear. The PA also closed some social services centers run by HAMAS and the PIJ. In December, and under pressure from the PA, HAMAS announced that it would halt suicide attacks within Israel. It retained the option of continuing operations against Israel inside the West Bank and Gaza Strip, however. The top PIJ leadership inside and outside the West Bank and Gaza Strip did not endorse Arafat's call for a cease-fire agreement.

(In January 2002, Israeli forces boarded the vessel Karine-A in the Red Sea and uncovered nearly 50 tons of Iranian arms, including Katyusha missiles, apparently bound for militants in the West Bank and Gaza Strip.)

Jordan

Jordanian officials strongly condemned the September 11 attacks and responded favorably to US requests for assistance. King Abdullah served as an influential and moderating force in the region and stressed in multilateral venues the need to combat terrorism cooperatively. Jordan strengthened its counterterrorism laws, defining terrorism more broadly, specifying punishment for terrorist offenses, and facilitating the seizure of terrorist finances. Moreover, the Government of Jordan continued its vigilant counterterrorism posture in 2001, facing threats that included possible retribution for the late-1999 interdiction of an al-Qaida-linked terrorist plot and efforts to exploit Jordanian territory for attacks against Israel.

In late April, Jordanian authorities publicly released details of the arrest on 29 January of 13 militants who allegedly had planned to attack unspecified Israeli and Western targets in the country. The 13 were referred to a state security court for trial on four counts: membership in an illegal organization, conspiracy to carry out terrorist acts, possession of explosives without a license and for illegal purposes, and preparing an explosive device without a license. Some cell members possessed homemade explosives at the time they were detained.

On 3 December, a state security court sentenced Sabri al-Banna, head of the Abu Nidal terrorist organization (ANO), to death in absentia. Al-Banna, also known as Abu Nidal, was charged with the assassination in 1994 of a Jordanian diplomat in Lebanon. Four ANO members were also sentenced to death. (One was arrested in Jordan upon his arrival from Libya in early January 2002 and three still remain at large.)

Jordanian prosecutors requested the death penalty in the trial of dual US-Jordanian national Ra'ed Hijazi, who had been implicated in the Bin Ladin-linked Millennium plot in late 1999. Hijazi allegedly confessed to planning terrorist attacks in Jordan and to undergoing military training in al-Qaida camps inside Afghanistan. (In 2000, Hijazi had been convicted in absentia and sentenced to death along with five others. Hijazi's death sentence was commuted to life imprisonment on 11 February 2002 by the State Security Court.)

The Jordanian authorities foiled numerous attempts by militants to infiltrate Israel from Jordan during the year. In June, Jordanian security officials arrested four Jordanians and charged them with planning to transfer a cache of arms into the West Bank and Gaza Strip. Jordanian authorities also retrieved various types of weapons—including explosives—allegedly concealed along the Jordanian-Iraqi border after having been smuggled from Lebanon. By the end of 2001, at least two suspected terrorists associated with this plot were still at large in Lebanon and the West Bank.

Jordan retained its tight restrictions and close monitoring of HAMAS and other Palestinian rejectionist groups in its territory. For example, the Jordanian Government settled a two-week long standoff involving Ibrahim Ghawsha, a deported HAMAS leader, who flew back to Amman without warning. Jordan permitted his return only after he had agreed not to be a spokesman or conduct political work on behalf of HAMAS.

On 7 August, an Israeli businessman was shot dead outside his Amman apartment. The motive for the attack remained unclear, although two groups—Nobles of Jordan and Holy Warriors for Ahmad Daqamseh—claimed responsibility. (Ahmad Daqamseh is a Jordanian soldier currently serving a life sentence for killing six Israeli schoolgirls in 1997.)

As of early December, a Jordanian court was investigating the activities of an Iraqi truck driver who allegedly smuggled weapons into Jordan the previous month. The suspect insisted he was paid by an unidentified Iraqi to transport the weapons to Jordan only. Upon further questioning, however, the driver admitted that at least 13 machineguns were destined for the West Bank and Gaza Strip.

Kuwait

Kuwait supported the Coalition against terrorism through public statements and a variety of practical measures. Crown Prince Saad, in an October speech opening the National Assembly, identified counterterrorism as the Government's top priority. Kuwait has ratified or signed all 12 UN counterterrorism conventions. On the financial front, it ordered all international monetary transfers to be sent through its Central Bank, instructed all financial institutions to freeze and seize assets of those designated in Executive Order 13224, and ordered the shutdown of all unlicensed charities by 2002. In December, the Government pledged to cooperate with US experts in investigating suspected cases of terrorism financing. The Government created a higher council to oversee Islamic charities and directed clerics not to use their positions to incite political conflict. Kuwait responded positively and quickly to all Coalition requests for support of Operation Enduring Freedom. It also took the initiative to deliver multiple shipments of humanitarian aid to Afghan refugees during Operation Enduring Freedom. It raised over $8 million in direct donations for the refugees and granted over $250 million in aid to Pakistan during 2001. There were no terrorist incidents in Kuwait in 2001.

Lebanon

The president of Lebanon as well as other senior Lebanese officials consistently condemned the September 11 attacks and offered to help the US Government in its efforts to arrest individuals with ties to al-Qaida and freeze the assets of suspected Sunni extremists. In October, Lebanese security forces arrested two 'Asbat al-Ansar members who allegedly had been planning to attack the Embassies of the United States and the United Kingdom, as well as other unspecified Arab targets in Beirut. 'Asbat al-Ansar, which operates mainly from 'Ayn al Hilwah camp, has been outlawed and its leader, Abu Muhjin, sentenced to death in absentia by Lebanese courts.

The Lebanese Government, however, condones Hizballah's actions against Israel, arguing that they are "resistance activities." Several terrorist organizations continued to operate or maintain a presence in Lebanon, including Hizballah, the Islamic Resistance Movement (HAMAS), the Palestine Islamic Jihad, the Popular Front for the Liberation of Palestine-General Command, 'Asbat al-Ansar, and several local Sunni extremist organizations.

The Lebanese Government failed to hand over to US authorities three senior Hizballah operatives, including Imad Mugniyah, after the men were placed on the FBI's list of most wanted terrorists in 2001 for their role in the 1985 hijacking of TWA flight 847. Lebanese law prohibits the extradition of Lebanese nationals, but the Government has not taken adequate steps to pursue the cases in Lebanese courts, claims the individuals are not in Lebanon, and that it does not know their whereabouts.

Since the Lebanese Government deems organizations that target Israel to be legitimate, Hizballah, HAMAS, the Palestine Islamic Jihad, and other Palestinian terrorist organizations were recognized as legal organizations and were allowed to maintain offices in Beirut. The Government refused to freeze the assets of Hizballah or close down the offices of rejectionist Palestinian organizations. It also continued to reject the US Government's position that Hizballah has a global reach, asserting it to be a local, indigenous organization integral to Lebanese society and politics. The Government of Lebanon informed the United States and the UN that it opposed terrorism and was working to control it. The United States and Lebanon did not agree on a definition of terrorism, however. The Lebanese Government, like other Arab countries, has called for a UN-sponsored conference to define and address the underlying causes of terrorism.

Security conditions in most of Lebanon remained stable in 2001, despite inadequate government control over several areas of the country, including Beirut's southern suburbs, the Beka'a Valley, the southern border area, and Palestinian refugee camps. The continuing inability of Lebanon to exert such control created a permissive environment for the smuggling of small arms and explosives as well as training activities by terrorist organizations. Hizballah has not attacked US interests in Lebanon since 1991, but it continued to maintain the capability to target US personnel and facilities there and abroad. During 2001, Hizballah provided training to HAMAS and the Palestine Islamic Jihad at training facilities in the Beka'a Valley. In addition, Hizballah reportedly increased the export of weaponry into the West Bank and Gaza Strip for use by these groups against Israeli targets.

There were no attacks on US interests in Lebanon in 2001, but there were random acts of political violence/hate crimes. In May, unknown gunmen assassinated a senior commander of Yasir Arafat's Fatah organization in the 'Ayn al Hulwah Palestinian refugee camp near Sidon, an area outside Lebanese Government control. In September, another Fatah official escaped an assassination attempt near his home in Sidon. In September and October, two churches were attacked, resulting in property damage but no loss of life. In October, a mosque in the predominantly Christian town of Batroun was slightly damaged by arson.

Morocco

King Mohammed VI unambiguously condemned the September 11 attacks and offered the international Coalition his country's full cooperation in the war against terrorism. On 24 September the Government of Morocco signed the UN Convention for the Suppression of the Financing of Terrorism and is complying fully with UNSCR resolutions that seek to eliminate terrorist financing.

Domestically, the Moroccan Government's record of vigilance against terrorist activity and intolerance for the perpetrators of terrorism remained uninterrupted in 2001. While no reported terrorist activity took place inside Morocco, King Mohammed reiterated his outright condemnation of those who conduct or espouse terrorism.

Oman

The Government of Oman was very responsive to requests from the Coalition. It proactively responded to US requests related to terrorism financing Executive Order 13224 to ensure that there were no accounts available to any listed terrorist entity or individual. The Government of Oman has signed nine of the 12 UN counterterrorism conventions. There were no terrorist incidents in Oman in 2001.

Qatar

Qatar provided important and substantial support for the Coalition. As Chair of the Organization of the Islamic Conference (OIC), Qatar immediately issued public statements condemning the September 11 attacks and disassociating them from Islam. As host of an emergency OIC Ministerial on 16 October, the Government of Qatar helped draft a final communiqué supportive of action by the international Coalition against terror. Qatari law-enforcement authorities worked closely with US counterparts to detain and investigate terrorist suspects. The Qatar Central Bank instructed all financial institutions to freeze and seize the terrorist assets of those designated in Executive Order 13224.

Saudi Arabia

After September 11 and the realization that 15 of 19 of the attackers were Saudi citizens, the Saudi Government reaffirmed its commitment to combat terrorism and responded positively to requests for concrete action in support of Coalition efforts against al-Qaida and the Taliban. The King, Crown Prince, Government-appointed religious leaders, and official news media publicly and consistently condemned terrorism and refuted the few ideological and religious justifications made by some clerics.

In October, the Saudi Government announced it would implement UNSCR 1373, which called for, among other things, the freezing of terrorist related funds. The Saudi Government has ratified six of 12 UN conventions relating to terrorism and signed an additional three, including the UN Convention for the Suppression of the Financing of Terrorism. The remaining three conventions are under consideration. The Saudi Government also pressed nongovernmental organizations and private agencies to implement existing Saudi laws that govern the soliciting of contributions for domestic or international humanitarian causes.

These laws were not scrupulously enforced in the past, and some representatives of international terrorist organizations solicited and collected funds from private citizens and businesses in Saudi Arabia. In December, Saudi authorities agreed to cooperate with US investigators in suspected cases of terrorism financing.

Several threats against US civilian and military personnel and facilities in Saudi Arabia were reported in 2001, but none materialized. By year's end, Saudi authorities had finished an investigation into a series of bombings in Riyadh and the Eastern Province (Ash-Sharqiyah) and determined that the bombings were criminal rather than political in motivation. In October an apparent suicide bombing in al-Khubar killed one US citizen and injured another. The Saudi investigation since revealed that the bomber was a Palestinian, acting alone, for unverified motives relating to the Palestinian *intifadah.*

There was only one significant act of international terrorism in Saudi Arabia in 2001—the hijacking of a Turkish plane en route to Russia in March, perpetrated to protest Russian actions in Chechnya. Saudi forces stormed the plane, rescuing most of the passengers. The Saudi Government denied requests from Russia and Turkey to extradite the hijackers.

The Government of Saudi Arabia continued to investigate the June 1996 bombing of the Khubar Towers housing facility near Dhahran that killed 19 US military personnel and wounded some 500 US and Saudi personnel. The Saudi Government continued to hold in detention a number of Saudi citizens linked to the attack, including Hani al-Sayegh, extradited by the United States in 1999.

Tunisia

The September 11 attacks strengthened the Tunisian Government's active posture against terrorism in 2001. The only Arab nation represented on the United Nations Security Council in 2001, Tunisia supported Security Council Resolutions 1368 and 1373. These cooperative international measures matched the Tunisian Government's concrete stand against terrorism within its borders. Most Tunisians oppose Islamist movements because they do not want the violence of neighboring Algeria repeated in Tunisia.

There were no reported acts of terrorism in Tunisia in 2001, yet the Government continued to bring judicial, law-enforcement, and military resources to bear against terrorist suspects. On 29 November a military court convicted a Tunisian, extradited from Italy, on charges of training members of a terrorist cell in Italy. On the military front, the Government of Tunisia, in concert with the Government of Algeria, took steps to protect its borders from what it considered a potentially destabilizing influx of extremists. The efforts culminated in the signing in November of a military cooperation agreement with Algeria aimed at strengthening border guard units to better control terrorist movements and the illegal trafficking of arms, drugs, and contraband materials.

United Arab Emirates

Formerly one of three countries to recognize the Taliban regime in Afghanistan, the UAE cut diplomatic relations 11 days after the attacks on the United States. During his December National Day address, President Zayid promised to "fight and uproot terrorism." This posture was underscored by significant actions taken on the law-enforcement, diplomatic, and humanitarian fronts. The UAE took major steps to curb terrorist funding: the country's Central Bank ordered all financial institutions—from banks and investment firms to moneychangers—to freeze and seize the accounts of almost 150 groups and individuals linked to terrorism, including the Al-Barakat group based in Dubai. The UAE also adopted the Gulf Coordination Council's most comprehensive criminal law prohibiting money laundering. The UAE continued to investigate Marwan Al-Shihi and Fayiz Bani-Hamed, UAE nationals linked to the September 11 attacks. In July, the UAE arrested Djamel Beghal in Dubai and extradited him to France where he was placed under formal investigation after being linked to a planned attack on the US Embassy and American cultural center in Paris. Finally, the UAE contributed $265 million in aid to Pakistan and the UAE Red Crescent Society joined with Dubai Crown Prince Muhammad bin Rashid Al-Maktums's Foundation and Sharjah Charity International in contributing over $20 million for the establishment of five refugee camps/humanitarian centers along the Afghan-Pakistan border and supplied medicine, clothing, and blankets for needy Afghans.

Yemen

Yemen immediately condemned the terrorist attacks of September 11. The Yemeni Government also publicly condemned terrorism "in all its forms and sources," expressing support for the international fight against terror. Moreover, the Yemeni Government took practical steps to enhance its intelligence and military cooperation with the United States. During his official visit to Washington in November, President Salih underscored Yemen's determination to function as an active partner in counterterrorism with the United States. Senior US officials welcomed President Salih's commitment but made clear that any counterterrorism cooperation will be judged by its results.

The United States and Yemen continued their joint investigation of the attack in October 2000 on the USS Cole. Cooperation was productive, particularly in the aftermath of September 11, and established important linkages between the East Africa US Embassy bombings, the USS Cole bombing, and the September 11 attacks. The Yemeni Government's assistance in providing investigators with key documents, allowing evidence to be processed in the United States, and facilitating access to suspects made the discoveries possible.

In 2001, the Yemeni Government arrested suspected terrorists and pledged to neutralize key al-Qaida nodes in Yemen. Increased pressure from security services forced some terrorists to relocate. Yemen has enhanced previously lax security at its borders, tightened its visa procedures, and prevented the travel to Afghanistan of potential terrorists. Authorities carefully monitored travelers returning from abroad and cracked down on foreigners who were residing in the country illegally or were suspected of engaging in terrorist activities. On the education front, the Government began integrating formerly autonomous private religious schools—some of which were propagating extremism—into the national educational system, and has tightened requirements for visiting foreign students. The Yemeni Government asked a large number of foreign students from Arab or Islamic backgrounds to leave the country.

Several terrorist organizations maintained a presence in Yemen. HAMAS and the Palestine Islamic Jihad continued to maintain offices in Yemen legally. Other international terrorist groups with members operating illegally in Yemen included the al-Qaida, the Egyptian Islamic Jihad, al-Gama'a al-Islamiyya, Libyan opposition groups, and the Algerian Armed Islamic Group. An indigenous terrorist group, the Islamic Army of Aden, remained active in the country.

North American Overview

Canada

In the immediate wake of the 9/11 terrorist attacks, Canada played an immensely helpful role by accepting the bulk of civil aviation traffic bound for the United States that was diverted when US airspace was ordered closed. Canada provided support for all stranded passengers. Media in the United States and elsewhere erroneously reported that some of the 19 hijackers responsible for crashing the four US commercial airliners had come to the United States via Canada; these allegations were proven false by subsequent investigation.

Overall anti-terrorism cooperation with Canada is excellent, and stands as a model of how the US and another nation can work together on terrorism issues. The relationship is exemplified by the US-Canadian Bilateral Consultative Group on Counterterrorism Cooperation, or BCG, which meets annually to review international terrorist trends and to plan ways to intensify joint counterterrorist efforts. BCG subgroups meet continually to carry out specific projects and exercises. Established in 1988, the BCG builds on a long history of mutual cooperation and complements numerous other bilateral fora that address law enforcement and immigration issues. All of these bilateral mechanisms have continued to grow and improve, especially in the wake of two significant arrests: the December 1999 arrest in Washington State of Usama Bin Ladin associate Ahmed Res-sam, and the March 1998 arrest in Canada of Saudi national Hani Al-Sayegh in connection with the Khubar Towers bombing. Under the US-Canada Terrorist Interdiction Program, or TIP, Canada records about one "hit" of known or suspected terrorists per week from the State Department's Visa Lookout List.

Excellent law enforcement cooperation between the US and Canada is essential to protecting our citizens from crime and maintaining the massive flow of legitimate cross-border traffic. Day-to-day cooperation between law enforcement agencies is close and continuous. Seven US law enforcement agencies have officers posted to Ottawa and other Canadian cities. The Attorney General and Canadian Solicitor General conduct policy coordination at the US-Canada Cross-Border Crime Forum, established during the Prime Minister's 1997 visit to Washington. (The Forum met most recently March 6, 2002 in Washington.) Other cooperative mechanisms include groups led by the immigration and customs services known as Border Vision and the Shared Border Accord, extradition and mutual legal assistance treaties, and an information-sharing agreement between the US Drug Enforcement Administration and the Royal Canadian Mounted Police.

Mexico

Mexican President Fox immediately expressed his support and condolence to President Bush after the 9/11 attacks and sent a team of earthquake response specialists to New York City to assist in the search for victims. Mexico also has expressed firm support for US military action and joined the consensus agreement behind Organization of American States resolutions voicing solidarity with the United States, invoking collective security, and invoking the Rio Treaty. Mexico also played a leading and successful role within the Organization of American States in negotiations for a new Convention on Terrorism.

On the security front, Mexico has taken many steps to enhance border security cooperation. Mexico implemented additional screening requirements for visa applicants from more than 50 countries. In addition, Mexico is implementing a photo-digitized passport-security system to tighten border controls and reduce fraud. The Mexican Secretary of Defense and Energy Secretary tightened security for petroleum and gas facilities and assigned a Navy task force to protect the offshore gas and oil infrastructure. Additionally, there are several points in the US-Mexico Border Partnership Action Plan related to homeland security issues, including those on Infrastructure protection, harmonization of entry port operations, precleared travelers, advanced passenger information, deterrence of alien smuggling, visa policy consultations, compatible databases and electronic exchange of information, screening third-country nationals, public/private-sector cooperation, secure in-transit shipments Mexico also has taken steps on the financial front. The Government of Mexico is working to ensure that domestic legislation and regulation are compliant with United Nations Security Council Resolutions. On several occasions, the National Bank Commission identified and reported suspicious financial transactions. In addition, the Treasury Secretary secured a bank account and several cash transactions linked to an identified terrorist. Furthermore, the Government of Mexico adopted new measures to counter terrorist financing, including increased monitoring of financial movements, exchange of information on unusual movements of capital, and more effective measures to combat money laundering.

As with Canada, there were erroneous media allegations that the September 11 hijackers used Mexico to enter the United States.

Patterns of Global Terrorism 2002

The Year in Review

International terrorists conducted 199 attacks in 2002, a significant drop (44%) from the 355 attacks recorded during 2001. A total of 725 persons were killed in last year's attacks, far fewer than the 3,295 persons killed the previous year, which included the thousands of fatalities resulting from the September 11 attacks in New York, Washington, and Pennsylvania.

A total of 2,013 persons were wounded by terrorists in 2002, down from the 2,283 persons wounded the year before.

The number of anti-US attacks was 77, down 65% from the previous year's total of 219. The main reason for the decrease was the sharp drop in oil pipeline bombings in Colombia (41 last year, compared to 178 in 2001).

Thirty US citizens were killed in terrorist attacks last year:

- On 15 January, terrorists in Bayt Sahur, West Bank, attacked a vehicle carrying two persons, killing one and wounding the other. The individual killed, Avi Boaz, held dual US-Israeli citizenship. The Al-Aqsa Martyrs Brigade claimed responsibility.
- On 23 January, Daniel Pearl, the Wall Street Journal's South Asia bureau chief was kidnapped in Karachi, Pakistan. On 21 February, it was learned that he had been murdered.
- On 31 January, two hikers on the slopes of the Pinatubo volcano in the Philippines were attacked by militants. One of the hikers, US citizen Brian Thomas Smith, was killed.
- On 16 February, a suicide bomber detonated a device at a pizzeria in Karnei Shomron in the West Bank, killing four persons and wounding 27 others. Two US citizens—Keren Shatsky, and Rachel Donna Thaler—were among the dead. The Popular Front for the Liberation of Palestine claimed responsibility.
- On 14 March, two US citizens—Jaime Raul and Jorge Alberto Orjuela—were murdered in Cali, Colombia, by motorcycle-riding gunmen.
- On 17 March, grenades were thrown into a Protestant church in Islamabad, Pakistan, killing five persons including two US citizens, Barbara Green and Kristen Wormsley.
- On 27 March, a HAMAS homicide bomber entered the crowded restaurant of a hotel in Netanya, Israel, and detonated a bomb, killing 22 persons, including one US citizen, Hannah Rogen.
- On 7 June, US citizen Martin Burnham, who along with his wife, Gracia, had been held hostage for more than a year in the Philippines by the Abu Sayyaf Group, was killed as Philippine military units on a rescue mission engaged the terrorists in a firefight. Gracia Burnham was wounded.
- On 31 July, a bomb planted by HAMAS terrorists exploded at Hebrew University in Jerusalem, killing nine persons and wounding 87 others. Among the dead were five US citizens—Benjamin Blutstein, Marla Bennett, Diane Leslie Carter, Janis Ruth Coulter, and David Gritz.
- On 8 October, in Failaka Island, Kuwait, gunmen attacked US soldiers conducting a live-fire exercise killing one Marine, Lance Cpl. Antonio J. Sledd.
- The worst terrorist attack since September 11 occurred on 12 October at a resort in Bali, Indonesia, when a car bomb exploded in a busy tourist area filled with nightclubs, cafes, and bars. The attack killed over 200 persons from two-dozen nations. Seven US citizens died—Deborah Lea Snodgrass, Karri Casner, Jacob Young, Steven Webster, George "Joe" Milligan, Megan Heffernan, and Robert McCormick.
- One US citizen—Sandy Alan Booker—died in the Moscow theater attack on 23 October as Russian commandos attempted to rescue 800 hostages held for three days by Chechen terrorists.
- On 28 October, a gunman in Amman, Jordan, shot and killed Laurence Foley, a senior administrator of the US Agency for International Development, as he was leaving his home for work.
- On 21 November in Sidon, Lebanon, an office manager/nurse at a church-run health facility, GUS citizen Bonnie Denise Witherall, was killed by a gunman.
- Three US citizens—Kathleen Gariety, William Koehn, and Martha Myers—were murdered on G30 December by a gunman who stormed a Baptist missionary hospital in Yemen and opened fire.

Africa Overview

The simultaneous attacks against a commercial airliner and a hotel in Mombasa, Kenya, in November that killed 12 Kenyans and three Israeli tourists provide dramatic and tragic evidence that sub-Saharan Africa continues to suffer from terrorism, from both indigenous, insurgent groups that use terrorist tactics and international terrorist groups.

The commitment and support of Kenya, Djibouti, and Ethiopia have been vital in the successful pursuit of US counterterrorism efforts in the Horn of Africa and Arabian Peninsula. The desire to cooperate in this global effort against terrorism has extended from Sudan to South Africa and from The Gambia to a number of groups in Somalia.

In 2002, Sub-Saharan African governments almost universally maintained their commitment to fight global terrorism through both unilateral and multilateral efforts.

To this end, in September 2002 the African Union (AU) held a counterterrorism conference in Algiers. (Note: the Organization of African Unity (OAU) became the African Union in 2002.) The September meeting also produced a plan of action to implement the 1999 OAU Convention on Preventing and Combating Terrorism and agreed to establish an African Terrorism Study and Research Center to be based in Algeria. The AU strongly supports UN Security Council Resolution (UNSCR) 1373, which, among other stipulations, requires states to prevent and suppress the financing of terrorist acts. The AU also strongly supports UN Security Council Resolution 1269, which reaffirms that the suppression of acts of international terrorism, including those in which states are involved, is an essential contribution to maintaining international peace and security. The 16 members of the Economic Community of West African States (ECOWAS) met in September to consider the establishment of a regional criminal investigation and intelligence bureau that would give special attention to terrorism, as well as to illicit drug trafficking, money laundering, illicit arms running, and counterfeiting.

The United States engaged African countries in a number of ways to enhance their counterterrorism capabilities. One, the Pan Sahel Initiative (PSI), is a US Department of State program designed to assist Mali, Niger, Chad, and Mauritania in protecting their borders, tracking movement of persons, combating terrorism, and enhancing regional stability. The PSI will assist these countries in countering known terrorist operations and border incursions as well as the trafficking of persons and illicit materials. Along with US training and material support will be a program to bring military and civilian officials from the four countries together to encourage greater cooperation on counterterrorism and border issues within and among the governments of the region. It also includes training and assistance to improve critical skills for police and security forces, strengthen airport security, and tighten immigration and customs procedures.

A number of African countries have moved to become parties to the 12 international conventions and protocols relating to terrorism, as UNSCR 1373 calls on states to do. African countries that are parties to all 12 of the conventions and protocols include Botswana, Mali, and Ghana. Many African governments have taken positive steps to combat terrorist financing by freezing assets of individuals and entities designated by the United States pursuant to Executive Order 13224. Many African governments also have taken steps to freeze the assets of persons and entities included on the UNSCR 1267 Sanctions Committee's consolidated list as having links to Usama Bin Ladin and members of al-Qaida and the Taliban, whose assets UN-member states are required to freeze pursuant to Chapter VII of the UN Charter.

Despite attempts to enhance counterterrorism efforts since 11 September 2001, conditions that make many countries in Africa desirable locations for terrorists still persist. These include a shortage of financial and technical resources, areas of instability and prolonged violence, corruption, weak judicial and financial regulatory systems, and porous borders and unregulated coastlines facilitating the movement of persons and illicit goods.

[*Eds. Note*: Sudan, one of the seven state sponsors of terrorism, is discussed in Part 1 in the section on "State Sponsorship of Terrorism."]

Angola

In April, following the death of Jonas Savimbi, Angola ended its 27-year civil conflict with the National Union for the Total Independence of Angola (UNITA), an organization responsible for numerous brutal attacks on civilians. Separatists in Cabinda Province continued their guerrilla campaigns against the Government. In May, there was a grenade attack on a convoy of US oil workers in Cabinda. Although no one claimed responsibility, the attackers were likely Cabindan separatists. The Government has cooperated in increasing security for private oil companies in Cabinda.

Angola is a party to three of the 12 international conventions and protocols relating to terrorism.

Djibouti

Djibouti, a critical frontline state in the global war on terrorism and a member of the Arab League, has taken a strong stand against international terrorist organizations and individuals. Djibouti hosts Coalition forces from five countries and the only US military base in Sub-Saharan Africa. The Government has closed down terrorist-linked financial institutions and shared security information on possible terrorist activity in the region. The counterterrorism committee under President Guelleh moved to enhance coordination and action on information concerning terrorist organizations.

In October, the United States established the Combined Joint Task Force–Horn of Africa (CJTF–HOA). Based in Djibouti, CJTF–HOA coordinates Coalition counterterrorism operations in six East African countries and Yemen.

Djibouti is a party to three of the 12 international conventions and protocols relating to terrorism.

Ethiopia

Ethiopia has been consistently helpful in its cooperation in the global war on terrorism. Significant counterterrorism activities included political, financial, media, military, and law-enforcement actions. The Ethiopian Central Bank has been prompt in complying with US requests for name checks and asset freezes as part of the effort to curb terrorist financing. To counter the threat from the Somalia-based Al-Ittihad al-Islami (AIAI), Ethiopia has undertaken increased military efforts to control its lengthy border with Somalia. The Ethiopian Government believes the Oromo Liberation Front (OLF), an indigenous group, was responsible for a June attack on a railway station in Dire Dawa and a September bombing of an Addis Ababa hotel. The OLF denied responsibility for the hotel bombing.

Ethiopia is a party to four of the 12 international conventions and protocols relating to terrorism.

Kenya

Kenya was hit once again by terrorist attacks on 28 November 2002, when terrorists fired missiles at an Israeli airliner carrying over 200 passengers and drove a car bomb into a hotel popular with Israeli tourists in the coastal city of Mombasa. The missiles barely missed the plane, but 12 Kenyans and three Israelis were murdered by two suicide bombers in the hotel attack. Al-Qaida claimed responsibility for the simultaneous attacks. If true, it represents the second al-Qaida attack on Kenyan soil since the car-bomb explosion at the US Embassy in Nairobi on 7 August 1998, which killed 291 and wounded over 5,000 persons. While Kenya continued to be a key partner and lend high-level support in the global war on terrorism, its counterterrorism capacity continued to be limited by inadequate training and resources. There has been ongoing law-enforcement cooperation and sharing of information between the United States and Kenya concerning suspected terrorists. Kenya also participates in the US Terrorist Interdiction Program and is a party to 11 of the 12 international counterterrorism conventions and protocols.

Mali

Mali has taken active steps to combat terrorism and has been responsive on terrorist financing issues. In May, the National Assembly ratified the remaining six international counterterrorism conventions, making Mali a party to all 12. The Malian Government has been receptive to the idea of strengthening its borders, and it held discussions in October 2002 with a US delegation concerning the Pan Sahel Initiative. Mali has a border-security agreement with Niger, Algeria, and Mauritania, although a lack of resources hampers its effectiveness.

Nigeria

Nigeria remained committed to the global war against terrorism and has continued diplomatic efforts in both global and regional fora concerning counterterrorism issues. At a White House ceremony in March, the Nigerian ambassador renewed Nigeria's solidarity with the US-led antiterror Coalition. Nigeria has been helping to monitor threats to US citizens living in Nigeria and has cooperated with the United States on tracking and freezing terrorists' assets. Nigeria's relatively large and complex banking sector, combined with widespread corruption, makes combating terrorism financing more difficult, however. There are growing concerns about the rise of radical Islam in Nigeria, home of Africa's largest Muslim population.

Nigeria is a party to four of the 12 international conventions and protocols relating to terrorism.

Rwanda

Rwanda is a party to eight of the 12 international counterterrorism conventions and protocols, and the government has continued to give full support to US-led efforts to combat terrorism. The Government has been responsive to US requests to eradicate terrorism financing; has begun to track radical Islamist groups; and has increased surveillance of airports, border controls, and hotel registrations in an effort to identify terrorists. Rwanda established an intergovernmental counterterrorism committee and has an antiterrorism section in its police intelligence unit. During 2002, the Government aggressively pursued the Army for the Liberation of Rwanda (ALIR), an armed rebel force composed of former Rwandan Army soldiers and supporters of the previous government that orchestrated the 1994 genocide. The group, which operates in Rwanda and in the Democratic Republic of the Congo, employs terrorist tactics. In 1999, ALIR was responsible for the kidnapping and murder of nine persons, including two US tourists in Bwindi Park. The Rwandan National Police have several suspects in custody and have been very supportive of the ongoing FBI investigation into the murders of the US citizens. In March 2003, the Rwandan Government transferred custody of three of the suspected perpetrators of these murders to the United States. ALIR remained operational, although at a lower level than in 1999.

Somalia

Somalia's lack of a functioning central government; protracted state of instability and violence; and long coastline, porous borders, and proximity to the Arabian Peninsula makes it a potential location for international terrorists seeking a transit or launching point to conduct operations elsewhere. Regional efforts to bring about a national reconciliation and establish peace and stability in Somalia are ongoing. The US Government does not have official relations with any entity in Somalia. Although the ability of Somali entities to carry out counterterrorism activities is constrained, some have taken limited actions in this direction. The Somali-based al-Ittihad al-Islami (AIAI) has committed terrorist acts in the past, primarily in Ethiopia. AIAI was originally formed in the early 1990s with a goal of creating an Islamic state in Somalia. In recent years, AIAI has become factionalized, and its membership is difficult to define. Certain extremist factions may continue to pose a regional terrorist threat. Somalia is not a party to any of the 12 international conventions and protocols relating to terrorism.

South Africa

South Africa has taken a number of actions in 2002 in support of the global war on terrorism. President Mbeki has voiced his opinion several times that "no circumstances whatsoever can ever justify resorting to terrorism." South Africa enacted legislation establishing a financial intelligence unit, which targets money laundering. A draft antiterrorism law was approved by the cabinet and informally submitted to the Parliament. South Africa provided support to the United States by extraditing a member of the Symbionese Liberation Army. There were two acts of domestic terrorism in South Africa in 2002. A series of bombings in Soweto in late October killed one and wounded another, and in mid-November, a pipe bomb exploded at the serious violent crimes police unit in Cape Town, but no injuries occurred. A previously unknown right-wing extremist group, "Warriors of the Boer Nation," claimed responsibility for the Soweto attack. Police were searching for the culprits in the Cape Town case, although People Against Gangsterism and Drugs (PAGAD) is suspected. The activities of PAGAD remained severely curtailed in 2002 by a broadly successful law-enforcement and prosecutorial effort against leading members of the organization. South Africa is a party to five of the 12 international conventions and protocols relating to terrorism.

Tanzania

Tanzania has been a supportive partner in the global Coalition against terrorism. The Tanzanian Government has cooperated with the United States to bring to justice those responsible for the 1998 bombing of the US Embassy in Dar es Salaam. In 2001, for example, a Tanzanian national—extradited from South Africa to the United States to stand trial for his role in the Embassy bombing—was convicted and sentenced to life in prison. The US and Tanzanian Governments cooperated on a number of bilateral programs to combat terrorism in 2002, including civil aviation security, anti-money-laundering initiatives, border control, and police training. Tanzania also worked through multilateral organizations, such as the World Bank and the United Nations, to enhance its counterterrorism efforts. New legislation was approved by Tanzania's Parliament in November that criminalizes support for terrorist groups operating in Tanzania or overseas. Tanzania is a party to seven of the 12 international conventions and protocols relating to terrorism.

Uganda

Uganda continued its firm stance against local and international terrorism in 2002. Uganda is a party to four of the 12 international conventions and protocols relating to terrorism, and in 2002 it worked to complete the process required to become a party to all 12. In May, the government enacted the 2002 Suppression of Terrorism Act, which imposes a mandatory death penalty for terrorists and potential death penalty for their sponsors and supporters. The Act's list of terrorist organizations includes al-Qaida, the Lord's Resistance Army (LRA), and the Allied Democratic Front (ADF). There were many attacks against civilian targets in northern Uganda by the LRA during 2002, resulting in hundreds of deaths. In March, Uganda launched a major military offensive to destroy the LRA in southern Sudan and northern Uganda. The Ugandan military continued its successful operations against the ADF, resulting in a decrease in ADF activities in western Uganda.

South Asia Overview

In 2002, South Asia remained a central battle-ground in the global war on terrorism. The liberation of Afghanistan from the Taliban regime eliminated al-Qaida's principal base and sanctuary, but remnant cells continued to present a danger throughout Afghanistan. Fleeing terrorists also caused trouble in Pakistan and other states through which they transited. All countries in the South Asia region have strongly supported the Coalition effort against terrorism by al-Qaida and the remnants of the Taliban, and the establishment of the new Transitional Authority in Afghanistan has fostered significant improvements in regional security. Further efforts and continued long-term international assistance will be needed to sustain progress, however.

Pakistan remained a key ally in the antiterrorism effort, offering support to US operations in Afghanistan, implementing close law-enforcement cooperation, and cracking down on domestic extremists. Extremist violence in Kashmir, meanwhile, fueled by infiltration from Pakistan across the Line of Control, threatened to become a flashpoint for a wider India-Pakistan conflict during most of the year.

The cease-fire in Sri Lanka between the Liberation Tigers of Tamil Eelam and the Sri Lankan Government held throughout 2002, and the two sides began direct talks, facilitated by Norway, aimed at ending the country's long civil war and its attendant terrorism. At the same time, the Maoist insurgency in Nepal continued to be a bloody conflict characterized by the use of terrorist tactics. (The Government of Nepal and the Maoists adopted a cease-fire in January 2003.)

Afghanistan

In 2002, the Afghan people, supported by a US-led international Coalition, decisively defeated the brutal Taliban regime, which had provided sanctuary to terrorists and extremists from around the world—including North America, Europe, Africa, the Middle East, and Asia. The extremists had used Afghanistan as a training ground and base of operations for worldwide terrorism. Senior al-Qaida leaders, including Usama Bin Ladin—wanted by the United States for his role in the September 11 attacks as well as the US Embassy bombings in Kenya and Tanzania in 1998—had been based in Afghanistan, protected by the illegitimate Taliban regime.

In July 2002, representatives from all Afghan regions, factions, and ethnic groups met in an emergency "Loya Jirga," to elect Hamid Karzai as the President of the Traditional Islamic State of Afghanistan (TISA), which replaced the Afghan Interim Administration established by the December 2001 Bonn Agreement.

The new Afghan Government has pledged its support for the war on terrorism. Al-Qaida, which despite its setbacks still regards Afghanistan as a key battlefield in its war against the United States, will continue its armed opposition to the US presence, however. Al-Qaida has pockets of fighters throughout Afghanistan and probably several more in the neighboring tribal areas of Pakistan. To ensure that former Taliban and al-Qaida holdouts do not reemerge as a significant threat, the TISA must consolidate its support among the country's rival ethnic and regional factions.

Afghans have already passed several milestones on the road toward building a government in accordance with the Bonn Agreement, and the most critical steps—such as demobilizing rival militias, building a stable Afghan army, drafting a constitution, holding democratic elections, and creating a legal system—were underway at the end of the year.

Afghanistan is a party to three of the 12 international conventions and protocols relating to terrorism.

India

New Delhi continued to support the global Coalition against terrorism in 2002 while engaging in its own efforts to address internal and external threats. The Government of India enacted the Prevention of Terrorism Act to provide the central and state governments with additional law-enforcement tools in the war on terrorism. An anti-money-laundering bill was passed by Parliament in 2002 and signed into law in January 2003. Once implemented, it will establish a financial intelligence unit to monitor suspected terrorist transactions. In May, India and the United States launched the Indo-US Cyber Security Forum to safeguard critical infrastructures from cyber attack. The US-India Counterterrorism Joint Working Group met twice during 2002.

Like the United States, India faces a significant terrorist threat. Its primary source is the activity of militants opposed to continued Indian rule over the disputed province of Kashmir. In December 2001, terrorists staged a dramatic attack on the Indian Parliament. In January 2003, armed gunmen opened fire on police outside the American Center in Calcutta, killing four Indian policemen assigned to protect the building. The Government of India asserts that Lashkar-e-Tayyiba (LT) was behind a series of high-profile attacks. Among them were the May assault on an army base in Jammu that killed 36, an attack in July in Kashmir that killed 27 civilians, and two attacks on the Ragunath temple in Jammu in which at least 19 were killed. India also accused the LT of masterminding the 26 September attack at the Akshardham temple in Gujarat, which killed 31 persons. The United States has designated Lashkar-e Tayyiba a Foreign Terrorist Organization and has designated it pursuant to Executive Order 13224.

In 2002, India became a party to the 1979 Convention on the Physical Protection of Nuclear Material, making it a party to 11 of the 12 international conventions and protocols relating to terrorism.

Nepal

The Nepalese Government in 2002 strongly supported US counterterrorism activities and was responsive to multilateral efforts to police international terrorism. Nepal is party to five of the 12 international conventions and protocols relating to terrorism. Nepal's primary focus, however, remained the seven-year Maoist insurgency, which had claimed nearly 7,000 lives by the end of 2002.

The Maoist insurgency poses a continuing threat to US citizens and property in Nepal. Repeated anti-US rhetoric and actions suggest the Maoists view Western support for Kathmandu as a key obstacle to their goal of establishing a doctrinaire communist dictatorship. Furthermore, the Maoists have forged cooperative links with extremist groups across South Asia. In 2002, Maoists claimed responsibility for assassinating two US Embassy guards. In a press statement, they threatened foreign missions, including the US Embassy, to discourage foreign governments from supporting the Government of Nepal. Maoists, targeting US symbols, also bombed locally operated Coca-Cola bottling plants in November 2001 and in January and April 2002. In May, Maoists destroyed a Pepsi Cola truck and its contents.

Limited government finances, weak border controls, and poor security infrastructure have made Nepal a convenient logistics and transit point for some outside militants and international terrorists. The country also possesses a number of relatively soft targets that make it a potentially attractive site for terrorist operations. Security remains weak at many public facilities, including the Kathmandu International Airport, but the United States and others are actively working with the Government to improve security. The Nepalese Department of Immigration has made recent improvements in its watch list capability.

Pakistan

In 2002, Pakistan remained a vital partner in the global Coalition against terrorism, playing a key role in the diplomatic, law-enforcement, and military fight to eliminate al-Qaida. Pakistan granted logistic support and overflight rights to support Operation Enduring Freedom, consulted extensively with the United States and the United Nations on ways to combat terrorist financing, and drafted anti-money-laundering legislation. In January, the Government of Pakistan arrested and transferred to US custody nearly 500 suspected al-Qaida and Taliban terrorists, detained hundreds of extremists, and banned five extremist organizations: Lashkar-e-Tayyiba (LT), Jaish-e-Mohammed (JEM), Sipah-e-Sahaba Pakistan (SSP), Tehrik-i-Jafria Pakistan (TJP), and Tehrik-i-Nifaz-i-Shariat-i Mohammadi (TNSM). The United States has designated LT and JEM as Foreign Terrorist Organizations and also has designated them pursuant to Executive Order 13224.

In 2002, Pakistan became a party to the 1997 International Convention for the Suppression of Terrorist Bombings, making it a party to 10 of the 12 international conventions and protocols relating to terrorism.

Anti-US and anti-Western attacks in Pakistan increased in 2002 over the previous year, primarily due to opposition to the US-led Coalition in the war against terrorism. Significant attacks included the kidnapping and murder of US journalist Daniel Pearl; a grenade attack in March on an Islamabad church that killed five—among them two US citizens; a bus bombing in Karachi in May that killed 14, including 11 French naval engineers; and the bombing in June of the US Consulate in Karachi that killed 12 Pakistanis. In response, police have implemented enhanced security measures at diplomatic facilities, churches, and other sensitive sites. The Government of Pakistan has arrested, tried, and convicted those involved in the Daniel Pearl murder.

US-Pakistan joint counterterrorism efforts have been extensive. They include cooperative efforts in border security, criminal investigations, as well as several long-term training projects. In 2002, the United States and Pakistan established the Working Group on Counterterrorism and Law-Enforcement Cooperation. The meetings provide a forum for discussing ongoing US-Pakistani efforts, as well as a means for improving capabilities and cooperation. Islamabad has facilitated the transfer of over 400 captured alleged terrorists to

US custody, and Pakistan remained ranked third in the world (behind the United States and Switzerland) in seizing terrorist assets. Abuse of the informal money-transfer system known as *hawala* remained a serious problem throughout the region, however.

Sri Lanka

The positive developments in Sri Lanka that began in 2001 continued in 2002. Historically, the Liberation Tigers of Tamil Eelam (LTTE) has been one of the world's deadliest terror groups—it pioneered the use of suicide vests and has committed far more suicide-bomb attacks than any other terrorist organization. The cease-fire between the LTTE and the Government, established in December 2001, was formalized in February 2002. Formal peace negotiations began in September 2002 and were continuing into 2003.

The LTTE has publicly accepted the concept of internal autonomy within a federal Sri Lankan state, conceding its longstanding demand for a separate Tamil Eelam state. Its recent public statements give reason to hope that it intends to transform itself from a terrorist organization into a legitimate political entity.

The LTTE, however, has not renounced terrorism; it continues to smuggle in weaponry; and it continues forcible recruitment, including the recruitment of children into its ranks. It is too early to tell whether the Sri Lankan peace process will ultimately bear fruit or whether the LTTE will actually reform itself. Although guarded optimism surrounds the peace process, the United States will continue to designate the LTTE as a Foreign Terrorist Organization until it unequivocally renounces terrorism in both word and deed.

Sri Lanka is a party to 10 of the 12 international conventions and protocols relating to terrorism.

East Asia Overview

In 2002, the deadliest terrorist attack since the September 11, 2001 attacks in the United States occurred in the East Asia region—the bombings in Bali, Indonesia. Although East Asian nations had lent substantial support to the war on terrorism, made progress in arresting and interdicting terrorists, and built and improved their counterterrorism capabilities, many nations redoubled such efforts after the 12 October Bali attack. High-profile arrests continued alongside less visible efforts to improve legal and regulatory regimes to restrict the flows of terrorist money, manpower, and materiel through banks, borders, and brokers in the region.

The Philippines continued its strong support for the war on terrorism in 2002. The Philippines and United States cooperated closely to resolve a hostage crisis involving US citizens in the Philippines and to step up efforts to bring to justice the Abu Sayyaf Group (ASG) terrorists responsible for the kidnapping. The United States brought indictments against and offered rewards for five ASG leaders and trained and assisted Philippine forces in going after the ASG. The United States also added the Communist Party of the Philippines/New People's Army (CPP/NPA) to its list of Foreign Terrorist Organizations, and it added CPP/NPA and CPP leader Jose Maria Sison to the list of entities and individuals designated under Executive Order 13224. The Philippines sentenced terrorism suspect Agus Dwikarna to 10 years on explosives charges and continued to consult and cooperate with other regional nations on counterterrorism issues.

Indonesia made great strides in bringing perpetrators of the Bali bombings to justice and exposing the scale and deadliness of the terrorist group Jemaah Islamiya (JI), believed to be responsible for the bombings. The Indonesian police cooperated closely with other regional partners in the Bali investigation and widened the investigation beyond the Bali attacks to look at JI in general, often through cooperation with other nations in the region. Indonesia arrested Abu Bakar Bashir, spiritual leader of JI, on several charges, including attempting to assassinate the President of Indonesia and charges related to a string of bombings in December 2000. The United States continued to work closely with Indonesia to improve its counterterrorism capabilities through training and assistance programs, and in supporting the country's legal and regulatory regimes.

Japan was fully committed to the war on terrorism in 2002 and continued to provide robust assistance to Operation Enduring Freedom, major assistance to rebuild Afghanistan, and other aid to East Asian countries to enhance their counterterrorism capabilities. Japan was an active participant in G-8, EU, ASEAN Regional Forum (ARF), and UN efforts to coordinate counterterrorism activities, and it was a regional leader in adhering to international standards for implementing an effective counterterrorism regime.

Australia was hit hard by the Bali bombings, losing 85 citizens. The tragedy strengthened Australia's already firm resolve to lend robust support to the war on terrorism, including support for the Bali investigation. Australia provided combat forces to Operation Enduring Freedom and was very active in regional cooperation. Australia implemented broad reforms of its legal and regulatory counterterrorism mechanisms, and it undertook significant bureaucratic reorganization to enhance its counterterrorism capabilities at home and abroad.

Malaysia and Singapore continued to make arrests of JI suspects, disrupting their operations and ability to function. Malaysia approved the concept of a regional counterterrorism center and continued to develop it through the end of the year. The Philippines, Indonesia, and Malaysia signed an agreement on counterterrorism cooperation, which was later joined by Thailand and Cambodia. Several other nations in the region signed similar cooperative agreements, and cooperation between governments—in particular law-enforcement and intelligence agencies—increased in 2002, making possible additional successes in interdicting or arresting terrorists in the region.

Thailand was also a staunch ally in the war on terror and continued to cooperate closely with the United States and its neighbors on counterterrorism, intelligence, and law enforcement. In 2002, US access to Thai bases and airspace continued to be critical for rapid force projection into the Operation Enduring Freedom theater. Thailand contributed to the UN Afghanistan Reconstruction Fund and agreed to send military engineers to participate in Afghan reconstruction.

Terrorist organizations in the region, however, demonstrated their flexibility and resilience in the face of more effective antiterrorist efforts by East Asian nations. Terrorists shifted their targets and patterns of operation, and much work remains to be done so that the region's counterterrorism regimes can deal effectively with the threat that terrorists continue to pose to East Asian nations—and their partners and allies. Trafficking in drugs, persons, and weapons, for example, as well as organized crime, official corruption, and some inadequacies in legal and regulatory regimes persist as weaknesses that can be exploited by terrorists.

While regional nations did much to expose, arrest, and disrupt JI in 2002, the organization continues to function, and many of its leaders remain at large. JI and other terrorist groups continue to pose significant threats to the region, and only through increasing collaboration and cooperation can those threats be met.

The hard-won lesson of recent years is that such cooperation and communication are perhaps the most important weapons in the counterterrorism arsenal. Through such cooperation, nations can strengthen the security, law-enforcement, intelligence, and financial institutions that constitute the frontline in the war against global terrorism.

[*Eds. Note*: North Korea, one of the seven state sponsors of terrorism, is discussed in Part 1 in the section on "State Sponsorship of Terrorism."]

Australia

Canberra strengthened its already close working relationship with its international counterparts in the global war on terrorism in 2002. The Australian Defence Force maintained its substantial contribution to Operation Enduring Freedom, including deploying a Special Air Services contingent in Afghanistan, aerial tankers in Kyrgyzstan, and P-3 patrol aircraft in the Persian Gulf region, while two Australian warships participated in the multinational interception force in the Arabian Gulf. The Australian Government strongly condemned all acts of international terrorism during the year, particularly the 12 October Bali bombings, in which 85 Australians died. Australia was instrumental in providing assistance to the Government of Indonesia in the aftermath of the attack.

Canberra signed bilateral counterterrorism memoranda of understanding with Indonesia, Malaysia, and Thailand in 2002, and it is negotiating such a memorandum with the Philippines. Canberra is a party to 11 of the 12 international conventions and protocols relating to terrorism. The Government also enacted laws that create new definitions for terrorism; provide stronger penalties for carrying out, abetting, or financing terrorist acts; and enhance Australian Customs' powers to enforce border security. Federal and state leaders formalized a new intergovernmental agreement on Australia's national counterterrorism arrangements in October. The agreement provides a new and strong framework for cooperation between jurisdictions and creates a national counterterrorism committee to recommend additional federal-state measures to upgrade security. Several states strengthened their own antiterrorism laws as well.

Australia sought to block assets of all individuals and entities included on the UN Security Council Resolution 1267 Sanctions Committee's consolidated list of persons and entities associated with Usama Bin Ladin, members of al-Qaida, and members of the Taliban. It also sought to block assets of individuals and entities designated by the United States pursuant to Executive Order 13224. The Government also proscribed six organizations, including al-Qaida and Jemaah Islamiya (JI), under antiterrorism legislation enacted in June 2002. The legislation allows prosecution of members of such organizations or persons who provide financial or logistic support to them.

Australian law-enforcement and intelligence organizations actively investigated possible links between foreign terrorist organizations and individuals and organizations in Australia. In the wake of the bombings in Bali, the Australian Federal Police conducted a joint investigation of the attack with the Indonesian National Police. The Australian Security Intelligence Organization and State Police conducted raids on several houses of persons in Perth and Sydney who were suspected of having links to JI.

In November, Australian authorities in Perth charged an Australian citizen with conspiracy in connection with an alleged plan to bomb the Israeli Embassy in Canberra and the Israeli Consulate in Sydney. The same month, the Parliament enacted a law creating a crime of extraterritorial murder, manslaughter, or intentional harm to Australians, retroactive to 1 October 2002. The law gives Australia jurisdiction to prosecute those responsible for attacks on Australians overseas, such as the perpetrators of the Bali bombings.

Burma

Rangoon has taken a solid stance against international terrorism. It is party to five of the 12 international conventions and protocols relating to terrorism and has enacted an anti-money-laundering law that could help block terrorism assets. Burmese authorities frequently make public statements supportive of international counterterrorism efforts, and they also have expressed their willingness to cooperate in sharing information on counterterrorism issues.

There were no incidents of international terrorism in Burma during 2002. Several Burmese embassies abroad received letters containing blasting caps and electric batteries, although none exploded. The military government is currently involved in several low-intensity conflicts with ethnic insurgent groups. At least one group is alleged to have ties to South Asian extremist (possibly terrorist) elements.

China

The People's Republic of China continued to cooperate with the United States in the war on terrorism. Chinese officials regularly denounced terrorism, both in public statements and in international fora, and China regularly participated in UN Security Council discussions on terrorism and served as a permanent member of the UN Counterterrorism Committee established under UN Security Council Resolution (UNSCR) 1373. In 2002, China was well represented at international meetings, including the Munich Conference on Security Policy and the Southeast Asia Counterterrorism Conference held in Honolulu. During the 2002 Asian Pacific Economic Cooperation meeting, Beijing again articulated its counterterrorism stance and joined in statements denouncing terrorism.

Beijing continued to undertake measures to improve its counterterrorism posture and domestic security, including careful monitoring of its borders with Afghanistan and Pakistan and some efforts toward disrupting the financial links of terrorist groups. China made some progress in 2002 in strengthening financial-monitoring mechanisms, including prompting China's financial institutions to search for and freeze assets of designated terrorist entities.

Beijing regularly holds expert-level consultations with the United States on the financial aspects of terrorism, conducts semiannual counterterrorism consultations, and shares information through law-enforcement channels concerning persons possibly involved in terrorist activities. Beijing treats individuals and entities designated under US Executive Order 13224 on the same basis as it treats individuals and entities identified by the UNSCR 1267 Sanctions Committee, whose assets UN member states are required to freeze pursuant to Chapter VII of the UN Charter.

In 2002, there were no acts of terrorism committed in China against US citizens or interests, but there were several reports of bombings in various parts of China. It is unclear whether the attacks were politically motivated acts, terrorism, or criminal attacks.

China continued to express concern that Islamic extremists operating in and around the Xinjiang-Uighur Autonomous Region received training, equipment, and inspiration from al-Qaida, the Taliban, and other extremists in Afghanistan. Several press reports claimed that Uighurs trained and fought with Islamic groups in the former Soviet Union, including Chechnya. Uighurs were found fighting with al-Qaida in Afghanistan, and some Uighurs who were trained by al-Qaida have returned to China. Previous Chinese crackdowns on ethnic Uighurs and others in Xinjiang raised concerns about possible human rights abuses. For example, while the United States designated the East Turkestan Islamic Movement as a terrorist organization under Executive Order 13224 in 2002, it continued to emphasize to the Chinese that the war on terrorism must not be used as a substitute for addressing legitimate social and economic aspirations.

China is a party to nine of the 12 international conventions and protocols relating to terrorism.

Indonesia

In the wake of the Bali bombing on 12 October, the Indonesian Government stepped up internal investigations against international terrorist groups, although it had provided limited support for the global Coalition against terrorism before this event. Indonesia participated in a number of regional and international fora focused on terrorism and supported declarations on joint action against terrorism, including the declarations issued at the US-sponsored Southeast Asian Counter-Terrorism Conference, the ASEAN Summit, and a regional conference on combating terrorist financing. Internal administrative and legal weaknesses, however, hampered indigenous counterterrorism efforts.

Jakarta's response to the 12 October terrorist attacks in Bali represented a major and multifaceted counterterrorism effort. Jakarta undertook a number of significant actions, including the quick adoption of antiterrorism decrees (PERPU), the introduction into the legislature of a counterterrorism bill, and an aggressive investigation into the Bali attacks in particular. Jakarta, with international assistance, has taken action against Jemaah Islamiya (JI), an organization now designated by the United States pursuant to Executive Order 13224 and included on the UNSCR 1267 Sanctions Committee's consolidated list of organizations and individuals, whose assets UN member states are required to freeze. Indonesia supported this designation. Authorities detained JI spiritual leader Abu Bakar Bashir and arrested members of the JI cell believed responsible for the Bali bombings, including JI leaders Imam Samudra and Ali Ghufron, a.k.a. Mukhlas.

The 12 October Bali terrorist bombings, which killed some 200 persons and maimed hundreds more, has been clearly attributed to the al-Qaida–linked terrorist organization Jemaah Islamiya. The attack in Bali's crowded Kuta tourist district was initiated with a possible suicide bombing inside a tourist bar that funneled panicking victims into the street, exposing the crowd to the full blast of a large car bomb parked next to a neighboring club.

A smaller, nearly simultaneous bombing occurred about 300 yards from the US Consular office in Bali. Those arrested have indicated that the consular agency was the target. Hours before the Bali bombings, a small explosion had occurred at the Philippine Consulate in Sulawesi, which damaged the compound gates and blew out several windows. No casualties were reported in either bombing. Other bombings in 2002 in Indonesia included a botched grenade attack on a US diplomatic residence in Jakarta in September and the bombing on 4 December of a US-based/owned fast-food franchise and a car dealership in Makassar.

In 2002, Indonesia did not discover or freeze any terrorist assets. Indonesia's weak rule of law and poorly regulated financial system have produced roadblocks in uncovering terrorist assets, notwithstanding its willingness to freeze terrorist assets, consistent with the requirements of UNSCR 1373, as well as UNSCRs 1267, 1390, and 1455.

Indonesia is a party to four of the 12 international conventions and protocols relating to terrorism.

Japan

Tokyo has stood firm with the United States in combating terrorism. Tokyo twice renewed its Basic Plan, authorizing Japan's Self-Defense Forces to provide logistic support for

Operation Enduring Freedom, including refueling US and UK vessels and deploying an Aegis antimissile-equipped destroyer in the Indian Ocean, as well as transporting heavy equipment into Afghanistan.

Japan is party to all 12 international conventions and protocols relating to terrorism. At the request of the United States, it has blocked the assets of individuals and entities designated by the United States under Executive Order 13224.

Japan continued to participate actively in international fora designed to strengthen counterterrorism measures and took a leadership role in rebuilding Afghanistan. While hosting the January Afghanistan Reconstruction Conference, Tokyo announced a $500-million aid package for Afghanistan. In March, Tokyo hosted the Asia Counterterrorism Conference. Tokyo is coordinating with the United States on efforts to build a homeland security capacity within Asia, and it has invited officials from Asia to receive training in areas of homeland defense, including immigration control, aviation security, customs cooperation, export control, police and law enforcement, and terrorist financing.

In 2002, Japan had no incidents of international terrorism and continued to prosecute the alleged perpetrators of earlier terrorism acts. The Tokyo District Court sentenced two Aum Shinrikyo (Aum) members to death for the sarin gas attack on the Tokyo subway in 1995. Trials were still underway for four other members, and a ruling in the trial of Aum leader Matsumoto was expected in early 2003.

Laos

The Government of Laos has continued to provide strong support for the global war on terrorism. The Government became a party to four international conventions and protocols relating to terrorism in July 2002, in addition to the three to which it was already a party.

Laos joined other Association of Southeast Asian Nations (ASEAN) countries in taking strong positions against terrorism and, with other ASEAN nations, became a participant in the United States-ASEAN Joint Declaration for Cooperation on Counterterrorism, which was signed in August 2002.

Responding to requests by the United States and its obligations pursuant to UNSCR 1373, as well as UNSCRs 1267, 1390, and 1455, Laos has continued efforts to identify assets of terrorists and sponsors of terrorism. The Bank of Laos has issued orders blocking assets of organizations and individuals named in lists provided by the United States. The Bank, however, had yet to take steps to report on Government compliance with UNSCR 1373 or to freeze the assets of individuals and entities associated with Usama Bin Ladin, members of al-Qaida, and members of the Taliban included on the UNSCR 1267 Sanctions Committee's consolidated list. Pursuant to Chapter VII of the UN Charter, UN member states are required to block the assets of persons and individuals on that list.

Laos has no distinct counterterrorism laws; acts of terrorism fall under Laotian criminal law. The Ministry of Foreign Affairs, Ministry of Justice, and the National Assembly are currently discussing amendments to its criminal law to identify acts of terrorism as crimes and to strengthen the penalties for those crimes. The Laotian Government has increased security at all public events, and it has tightened airport and immigration security.

Malaysia

During 2002, the Malaysian Government continued to cooperate with international law-enforcement and intelligence efforts in the global war on terrorism and aggressively pursued domestic counterterrorism measures within its borders.

Malaysia suffered no incidents of international or domestic terrorism in 2002, although Malaysian police authorities continued their investigations of the regional terrorist organization Jemaah Islamiya (JI) and domestic Kumpulan Mujahidin Malaysia group, resulting in about 40 arrests of individuals suspected of involvement in either group. In late 2001, Malaysian authorities arrested Philippine national Nur Misuari, former Moro National Liberation Front (MNLF) leader and ex-governor of the Autonomous Region of Muslim Mindanao, for illegal entry and transferred him to the Philippines in January 2002. On 19 November 2001, Misuari had declared war on the Arroyo government, and armed MNLF guerrillas loyal to him attacked an army headquarters in Jolo, Sulu, that left over 100 persons dead and scores wounded. At year's end, Misuari's trial on rebellion charges was ongoing.

Kuala Lumpur sought to freeze assets of entities on the UNSCR 1267 Sanctions Committee's consolidated list, although it has not located terrorist assets to date. Kuala Lumpur requires financial institutions to file suspicious transaction reports on all names of individuals and entities designated under US Executive Order 13224, but it was not yet a party to the 1999 International Convention for the Suppression of the Financing of Terrorism. Malaysia is a party to three of the 12 international conventions and protocols relating to terrorism.

The Malaysian Government passed legislation in 2002 that will allow the negotiation of mutual legal-assistance treaties with other countries. In addition, Malaysia, the Philippines, and Indonesia signed a counterterrorism agreement on 7 May—later joined by Thailand and Cambodia—that establishes a framework for cooperation and interoperability of the three nations' procedures for handling border and security incidents. Twenty specific projects are detailed in the agreement, to include such measures as setting up hotlines, sharing airline passenger lists, and conducting joint training.

In May, Malaysia signed a joint counterterrorism declaration of cooperation with the United States, and in November the Malaysian cabinet approved establishment of a Malaysian-based regional counterterrorism training center in Kuala Lumpur.

Malaysia joined several ASEAN members in October 2002 in successfully requesting that the UNSCR 1267 Sanctions Committee include JI on its consolidated list of individuals and entities associated with Usama Bin Ladin, the members of al-Qaida, and the members of the Taliban.

New Zealand

New Zealand has contributed to Operation Enduring Freedom. It originally deployed one squadron of Special Forces to Afghanistan. New Zealand is reaffirming its commitment by deploying a frigate and a P-3 Orion to join the Coalition task force in the region. A C-130 Hercules transport aircraft will also become available from mid-2003.

New Zealand has supported regional efforts among other Pacific Island countries to adopt counterterrorism measures and coordinate their regional counterterrorism activities with the United States and Australia. It has a number of ongoing programs in the areas of police, customs, immigration, and judicial training/aid.

New Zealand is also a party to 10 of the 12 international conventions and protocols relating to international terrorism. Most recently, the Government announced a US $12.5 million package of new intelligence, police, customs, and immigration measures to enhance its counterterrorism capability.

Philippines

The Philippines in 2002 continued to work closely with international counterparts in the global war on terrorism and made significant progress in counterterrorism legislation, legal action against suspected terrorists, and hostage-rescue efforts. The Philippines has signed, but not ratified, the International Convention for the Suppression of Terrorism Financing. The Philippines is a party to six out of the 12 international conventions and protocols relating to terrorism. The Philippines, Malaysia, and Indonesia also signed a counterterrorism agreement on 7 May that establishes a framework for cooperation and interoperability of the three nations' procedures for handling border and security incidents. The agreement, which Thailand and Cambodia have now joined, enumerates 20 different projects.

The Philippines passed anti-money-laundering legislation in September 2001 and adopted related regulations in March 2002. The law criminalized money laundering, called for the establishment of a system of covered-transaction reporting, and created the Anti-Money-Laundering Council (AMLC). The 2001 legislation was insufficient to get the Philippines removed from the Organization of Economic Cooperation and Development's Financial Action Task Force (FATF) list of Non-Cooperating Countries and Territories. Based on FATF recommendations, however, the AMLC prepared a new draft bill that seeks to eliminate weaknesses in the existing legislation by lowering the reporting threshold, eliminating the requirement of a court order to freeze accounts, and revising bank-secrecy provisions. The Philippine Congress had not approved it by the end of the year, however.

On 19 November, as a result of an investigation by the US Embassy's Customs Attache Office, the Philippine Court of Appeals moved to block the assets in bank accounts suspected of being owned or controlled by key Abu Sayyaf Group (ASG) members or their family members.

In January 2002, Nur Misuari, former Moro National Liberation Front leader and ex-governor of the Autonomous Region of Muslim Mindanao, and an aide were transferred from Malaysia back to the Philippines where they have been detained. In late 2001, Malaysian authorities had arrested Misuari after he and his aides had fled the Philippines following an uprising in November 2001 that claimed the lives of 113 persons. The Philippine Government filed sedition and rebellion charges against Misuari, based on allegations that he instigated the attacks, and at year's end his trial was ongoing.

The Philippines made a series of arrests of suspected extremists and terrorists in 2002. On 15 January, Philippine National Police and Bureau of Immigration agents arrested Indonesian citizen Fathur Rahman Al-Ghozi, a.k.a. Abu Saad or Sammi Sali Jamin, in Manila on charges of forging travel documents. Al-Ghozi is a member of the regional terrorist organization, Jemaah Islamiya (JI), which has a close connection to some elements of the Moro Islamic Liberation Front (MILF), the largest Islamic extremist group in the Philippines. Members of the JI used a MILF base for training in the past. The JI operated its own training facility at an MILF camp, although its current status is unclear. Based on information supplied by Al-Ghozi, police and military intelligence agents raided two houses in General Santos City. They arrested three brothers and seized TNT, detonators, rolls of detonating cord, and M-16 rifles. Al-Ghozi pled guilty to possession of explosives and was sentenced to a 10–12 year jail term and fined. He still faces charges of illegal possession of assault rifles.

Philippine authorities in March arrested three other Indonesian citizens—Agus Dwikarna, Abdul Jamal Balfas, and Tamsil Linrung—in Manila and charged them with unlawful possession of explosive materials. Balfas and Linrung were later handed over to Indonesian authorities. On 12 July, Dwikarna was convicted by a Philippine regional trial court and sentenced to ten years imprisonment.

In 2002, the US Department of Justice issued several terrorist-related indictments against Philippine nationals, and other indictments are pending. On 23 July, the US Deputy Attorney General announced an indictment charging five ASG leaders with taking US citizens hostage, hostage taking resulting in death, and conspiracy resulting in death. This action mirrors an indictment in February 2002 that previously had been kept sealed for fear of endangering the lives of ASG-held hostages.

The Armed Forces of the Philippines (AFP) has undertaken other initiatives to rescue ASG-held hostages. During the first half of 2002, the AFP launched an operation to locate and rescue hostages held by the ASG, including US citizens Gracia and Martin Burnham. On 7 June, AFP forces rescued Mrs. Burnham, but tragically, Mr. Burnham and Philippine nurse Deborah Yap were killed during the operation. Two weeks later, Philippine special warfare troops fired at a vessel carrying ASG leader Aldam Tilao, a.k.a. Abu Sabaya, responsible for taking the hostages. Sabaya's body was never found, but there is strong evidence that he is dead. Four other ASG members were captured during the incident.

In August 2002, the AFP launched Operation End Game, which is aimed at rescuing three Indonesians, four Filipino Jehovah's Witness members, and one remaining hostage taken in 2000 and still held by the ASG. The operation is also geared to locating and destroying ASG subgroups operating in Jolo and Basilan.

In other activities targeting the ASG, beginning in January 2002, the US military provided a broad range of training to the AFP to improve its ability to fight the ASG. During the training program, 10 US servicemen were killed in an accident when an MH-47 Chinook helicopter crashed into the Sulu Sea. On 2 October, one US serviceman was killed and another wounded in a bombing that targeted US personnel. The ASG is believed to be responsible for the attack.

In May, the US Government launched a Rewards for Justice campaign targeting ASG leaders. Under the program, the US Government offered to pay up to $5 million for information leading to the arrest or conviction of the following ASG terrorists: Amir Khadafi Abubakar Janjalani, a.k.a. Abu Mukhtar; Jainal Antel Sali, Jr., a.k.a. Abu Solaiman; Aldam Tilao, a.k.a. Abu Sabaya (presumed dead); Isnilon Totoni Hapilon, a.k.a. Abu Musab; and Hamsiraji Sali, a.k.a. Jose Ramirez.

The Philippine Government publicly welcomed the US Government's designation in August 2002 of the Communist Party of the Philippines/New People's Army (CPP/NPA), as a Foreign Terrorist Organization. The US Government also designated CPP/NPA and its founder Jose Maria Sison pursuant to Executive Order 13224. Authorities in The Netherlands, where Sison is living in self-exile, subsequently froze assets in his bank accounts there and cut off his social benefits. In October, Philippine Foreign Secretary Ople urged the European Union to place a similar designation on a faction of the CPP, the National Democratic Front (NDF). The Philippines continued to campaign for inclusion of all Communist factions, the CPP, NPA, and NDF, on the Sanctions Committee's consolidated list of individuals and entities associated with Usama Bin Ladin, the members of al-Qaida, and those of the Taliban, whose assets UN member states are required to freeze pursuant to Chapter VII of the UN Charter.

Throughout 2002, the Communist People's Party/New People's Army/New Democratic Front (CPP/NPA/NDF) continued sporadic attacks against Government and commercial sites as well as against public officials and private citizens. In September, the Communist New People's Army (NPA) claimed responsibility for assassinating a mayor, attacking a police station (and killing the police chief), and blowing up a mobile telecommunications-transmission station. The violence in September prompted the AFP to launch a new counterinsurgency drive against NPA fighters. A coordinated campaign by military forces, police units, and civilian volunteers—called Gordian Knot—was aimed at overrunning CPP/NPA/NDF strongholds and capturing terrorist suspects. Nevertheless, the Macapagal-Arroyo administration at the end of 2002 remained open to a negotiated peace settlement with the CPP/NPA/NDF.

Singapore

In 2002, Singapore continued to work closely with international counterparts in the global war on terrorism. In addition to multilateral activities, Singapore continued its cooperation with the United States on import controls and also took domestic legislative and judicial initiatives.

In October, Singapore joined over 40 countries in requesting that the UNSCR 1267 Sanctions Committee add the Jemaah Islamiya (JI) to its consolidated list of individuals and entities associated with Usama Bin Ladin, the members of al-Qaida, and the Taliban. The same month, Singapore joined the Asia Pacific Economic Cooperation Summit's counterterrorism declaration. In July, the United States and the ASEAN signed a nonbinding joint declaration for cooperation on counterterrorism. As an ASEAN member, Singapore is a participant in the declaration. In addition, Singapore became a party to the 1999 International Convention for the Suppression of Terrorism Financing in December 2002 and passed legislation that would enable it to become a party to the Convention on the Marking of Plastic Explosives. (In January 2003, Singapore became a party to that Convention. Singapore is now a party to six of the 12 international conventions and protocols relating to terrorism.)

In September, Singapore signed a declaration outlining its participation as a pilot port in the US Container Security Initiative; implementation was continuing at the end of the year. The Singapore Parliament also passed legislation effective 1 January 2003 establishing a new strategic trade-controls framework. The framework establishes controls over items exported from or transshipped/transiting through Singapore that are related to weapons of mass destruction but places the burden of reporting on shippers.

There were no incidents of international or domestic terrorism in Singapore in 2002, but authorities continued their investigation of the local JI network, a regional terrorist organization that has ties to al-Qaida. Since December 2001, Singapore authorities have detained 36 individuals for suspected involvement in the JI. Thirty-one of those individuals were placed under renewable two-year detention orders. Singapore authorities have publicly provided details of the allegations against those arrested, including publishing in January 2003 a white paper on terrorism. The documents indicate that 11 of the detainees were reported to have received training at al-Qaida camps in Afghanistan. Those arrested reportedly were involved in plots to attack Singaporean official and civilian targets as well as citizens of the United States, the United Kingdom, Australia, and Israel in Singapore.

Taiwan

Taiwan has supported the global war on terrorism and taken steps to improve its counterterrorism laws and regulations. After the September 11, 2001 attacks, Taiwan was quick to implement fully all increased security requirements requested by the US Transportation Security Administration and to increase security for the American Institute on Taiwan. In May 2002, Taiwan Minister of Economic Affairs Lin Yi-Fu said during the Asia Pacific Economic Cooperation conference in Puerto Vallarta, Mexico, that Taiwan fully supports the ongoing global war on terrorism. In October, President Chen Shui-Bian condemned the terrorist bombing in Bali and said that Taiwan would offer assistance to Indonesia.

Although Taiwan currently has no antiterrorism laws, the Taiwan Executive Yuan in October ordered the Ministry of Justice to draft a special antiterrorism law. The new law, if enacted, would simplify the process of freezing financial accounts and enhance the use of compulsory measures such as a prosecutor's power to search, detain, and summon suspects and witnesses. At the end of the year, the draft of the antiterrorism law had undergone an extensive interagency review process coordinated by the Executive Yuan and awaited consideration by the Legislative Yuan.

(In January 2003, the Legislative Yuan passed an enhanced anti-money-laundering law, which lowers the threshold of amounts required to report, raises the penalties for noncompliance, and allows the Government to seize suspicious bank accounts.) Even before the passage of this legislation, the Ministries of Finance and Justice had followed up on requests by the United States to check suspicious bank accounts in Taiwan.

Thailand

Thailand continued to cooperate closely with the United States on counterterrorism, intelligence, and law-enforcement matters, and the Government enhanced its counterterrorism cooperation with its neighbors. During the year, Thailand indicated its intent to join the Container Security Initiative and began active negotiations with US Customs. In 2002, Thailand began discussions with the United States on the possible introduction of a border-security system called the Terrorist Interdiction Program. Regionally, Thailand joined a counterterrorism agreement—initially signed by Malaysia, the Philippines, and Indonesia—that establishes a framework for cooperation and inter-operability of procedures for handling border and security incidents. Thailand also signed a bilateral counterterrorism cooperation agreement with Australia. It signed an ASEAN-sponsored Declaration of Cooperation with the United States on counterterrorism and joined the Asia Pacific Economic Cooperation Conference counterterrorism declaration. It reaffirmed its commitment to accede to the remaining seven of 12 UN antiterrorism conventions.

On terrorism finance, Thailand established an interagency financial crimes group to coordinate CT finance policy. It submitted CT finance revisions to its Anti-Money-Laundering Act and the penal code to Parliament in the fall, where they were awaiting adoption at the end of the year. Thailand has been a strong supporter of US and other efforts to designate terrorists and terrorist entities at the UN Sanctions Committee. Thailand is a party to four of the 12 international conventions and protocols relating to terrorism.

Thailand served as host to four US-Thai bilateral military exercises with significant counterterrorism components, providing valuable training to US forces and reinforcing Thai capabilities to respond to potential terrorist incidents in Thailand. In 2002, there were no incidents of terrorism in Thailand.

Eurasia Overview

Central Asia, which for years had suffered from Afghanistan-based extremism, saw no significant terrorist activity in 2002. The operations of the Islamic Movement of Uzbekistan (IMU), a group on the US Foreign Terrorist Organization list that seeks to overthrow the Uzbekistani Government and create an Islamic state, were seriously disrupted when some of its leaders and many of its members were killed in Afghanistan fighting with the Taliban against Coalition forces. Russia, however, continued to be the target of terrorist attacks in 2002, most of which were carried out by extremists fighting in Chechnya. The most significant was the 23 October takeover of the Dubrovka Theater in Moscow, where some 40 extremists held 800 theatergoers hostage and threatened to blow up the theater.

States in the region continued to provide overflight and temporary basing rights; share law-enforcement and intelligence information; and identify, monitor, and apprehend al-Qaida members and other terrorists. Countries in the region also took diplomatic and political steps to contribute to the international struggle against terrorism, such as becoming party to some or all of the 12 United Nations international conventions and protocols relating to terrorism.

Enhancing regional counterterrorism cooperation has been a priority for the United States. Toward that end, the US Department of State's Coordinator for Counterterrorism hosted the Fourth Annual Counterterrorism Conference for Central Asia and the Caucasus in Ankara in June 2002. Counterterrorism officials from Central Asia and the Caucasus, as well as observers from Russia, Turkey, Afghanistan, China, the European Union, and the Organization for Security and Cooperation in Europe (OSCE), discussed issues related to human rights, the rule of law, and combating terrorist financing. Throughout the conference, and in other bilateral and multilateral fora, the United States stressed that effective counterterrorism is impossible without respect for human rights, and that the rule of law is a formidable and essential weapon in the fight against al-Qaida and other international terrorist organizations. A policy exercise held on the last day of the conference helped reinforce key tenets of effective counterterrorism policy and operations.

The United States continues to work with the OSCE and other regional organizations to strengthen policing capability, encourage improved regional cooperation, and combat terrorist financing. The OSCE held a meeting on terrorist-financing issues in Prague in May, which addressed the 40 Financial Action Task Force (FATF) recommendations on money laundering and how to strengthen states' capabilities to implement these standards. Following the conference, OSCE participating states adopted a US proposal committing each state to complete the FATF self-assessment exercise by 1 September 2002, and virtually all of them did so by that date. In cooperation with the UN Office of Drug Control and Crime Prevention, the OSCE is conducting training seminars in Central Asia on money-laundering and terrorist-financing issues to strengthen states' abilities to prevent terrorist organizations from obtaining access to funds. The United States was the major contributor to this project.

The European Union (EU) has also been deeply involved with both Russia and the OSCE in an effort to enhance counterterrorism cooperation throughout the region. At the November 2002 Summit, the EU and Russia reached agreement on a far-reaching framework for the fight against terrorism through more intensified cooperation. The framework sets out the shared values and commitments in the fight against terrorism and identifies a series of specific areas for future EU-Russia cooperation. EU-OSCE cooperation also has advanced through close contact between the Personal Representative on Counter Terrorism of the OSCE and the Chairman of the OSCE. The objective is to maximize the abilities of both organizations to counter terrorism in the region, especially in Central Asia.

In August, the United States designated the terrorist group East Turkistan Islamic Movement under Executive Order 13224 on terrorist financing. The organization had been involved in several terrorist acts in eastern China, and some of its members had been caught trying to carry out an attack against US Embassies in Central Asia.

Azerbaijan

In 2002, Azerbaijan continued to be a staunch supporter of the United States in the war against terrorism. Since September 11, 2001, Azerbaijan has added to an already strong record of cooperation with the United States, rendering dozens of foreign citizens with suspected ties to terrorists. Azerbaijan's border guards have increased their patrols of the southern border with Iran, and the aviation department has increased security at Baku's Bina Airport as well as implemented recommendations of the international civil aviation organization on aviation security.

While Azerbaijan had previously been a route for international mujahidin with ties to terrorist organizations seeking to move men, money, and materiel throughout the Caucasus, Baku stepped up its interdiction efforts in 2002 and has had some success in suppressing these activities. Azerbaijan has taken steps to combat terrorist-related funding by distributing lists of suspected terrorist groups and individuals to local banks. In November, a platoon of Azerbaijani soldiers joined the Turkish peacekeeping contingent in Afghanistan.

On 25 January, President Bush waived section 907 of the Freedom Support Act for 2002, thereby lifting restrictions on US assistance to the Government of Azerbaijan. The waiver cleared the way for the United States to deepen its cooperation with Azerbaijan in fighting terrorism and in impeding the movement of terrorists into the South Caucasus. The waiver also provided a foundation to deepen security cooperation with Azerbaijan on a common antiterrorist agenda.

Azerbaijan has also provided strong political support to the United States and to the global Coalition against terrorism. In May, President Aliyev instructed his government to implement UN Security Council Resolutions (UNSCR) 1368, 1373, and 1377. The Government also approved changes to the criminal code that increased the maximum penalty for acts of terrorism from 15 years to life imprisonment and added a provision making the financing of terrorist activities a crime. In October, Baku hosted a US-sponsored seminar on money laundering and financial crimes, including terrorist financing. The United States is working with the Government of Azerbaijan to develop a plan to combat financial crimes.

In April, the Justice Ministry revoked the registrations of two Islamic charities—the Kuwait Fund for the Sick and the Qatar Humanitarian Organization—for activities against Azerbaijan's national interests. In November, Azerbaijan froze the bank accounts of locally registered Benevolence International Foundation (BIF) pursuant to UNSCR 1373. The Justice Ministry subsequently revoked BIF's registration.

In April, the Government sentenced six members of Hizb ut-Tahrir, an extremist political movement that wants to establish a borderless, theocratic caliphate throughout the entire Muslim world, to up to seven years in prison for attempted terrorist activities. In May, Azerbaijan convicted seven Azerbaijani citizens who had received military and other training in Georgia's Pankisi Gorge and who had intended to fight in Chechnya. Four received suspended sentences, and the others were sentenced to four to five years in prison. Members of Jayshullah, an indigenous terrorist group, who were arrested in 2000 and tried in 2001 for planning an attack against the US Embassy, remained in prison.

Azerbaijan is a party to eight of the 12 international conventions and protocols relating to terrorism.

Georgia

Georgian officials, including the President, issued repeated statements condemning terrorism throughout 2002 and supported the United States and global Coalition against terrorism in international fora, in word and deed.

The United States has encouraged Georgia and Russia to work together to promote border security within their respective territories and to find negotiated, political solutions to their many disagreements. The presence in Georgia's Pankisi Gorge of third-country international terrorists with links to al-Qaida and significant numbers of Chechen fighters, nevertheless, accounted for the most significant Georgian counterterrorism issue of 2002.

In 2002, the United States strongly urged Georgia to regain control of the Pankisi Gorge where third country terrorists with links to al-Qaida had established themselves. These extremists threatened Georgia's security and stability, as well as Russia's.

Georgia has deployed troops from the Ministries of State Security and Interior into the Pankisi Gorge to establish checkpoints and root out Chechen fighters and criminal and international terrorist elements. The efforts signal Georgia's commitment to restoring Georgian authority in the Pankisi Gorge and dealing seriously with international terrorists linked to al-Qaida.

The United States assisted Georgia in addressing this

internal-security problem through assistance and cooperative programs, including the four-phase Georgia Train and Equip Program (GTEP). The program is intended to help the Government of Georgia eliminate terrorists, secure its borders, reassert central control over its territory, and deny use of its territory to foreign militants and international terrorists. Headquarters and staff training began in late May 2002 with 120 students receiving classroom instruction. In early June, additional staff training for the Land Forces Command began and ended with a successful command-post exercise. By September, US trainers had begun conducting unit-level tactical military training of Georgia's Ministry of Defense and other security forces to strengthen Georgia's ability to fight terrorism, control its borders, and increase internal security. In December, the first Georgian battalion completed GTEP training.

In July, Georgia extradited Adam Dekkushev to Russia for his suspected involvement in the bombing of apartment buildings in Moscow and Volgodonsk in 1999, blasts that resulted in approximately 300 deaths and for which no one has yet been convicted. A second suspect in the same bombings, Russian citizen Yusef Krymshamkhalov, was extradited to Russia in December. In October, Georgia extradited five individuals accused of terrorism and/or terrorist-related activities to the Russian Federation. They were among 13 Chechen fighters captured by Georgian authorities along the Russian-Georgian border in August. Georgia determined that two of those captured were Georgian nationals whom it will not extradite to Russia. Of the remaining six, three have pending Georgian court appeals on their extradition to Russia. Before extraditing the other three, Georgia has requested further documentation from Russia.

In 2002, Georgia became a party to the 1999 International Convention for the Suppression of the Financing of Terrorism. Georgia is now a party to six of the 12 international conventions and protocols relating to terrorism.

Kazakhstan

The Government of Kazakhstan continued to be outspoken and supportive in the fight against terrorism. In 2002, President Nazarbayev and senior Government officials have consistently spoken out against terrorism and have taken concrete action to support the international Coalition against terrorism.

In July, the Government signed an agreement to use Almaty Airport as an alternative airfield for Operation Enduring Freedom (OEF). Kazakhstan has allowed more than 800 US overflights in support of OEF since December 2001.

When the US Embassy has requested increased protection, the Government of Kazakhstan has repeatedly deployed rapid-reaction antiterrorist teams and elite police units to respond to changing security circumstances at US Government facilities. It has also continued to be responsive to requests to increase security at major oil facilities with US private investment.

In 2002, Kazakhstan became a party to the International Convention for the Suppression of Terrorism Bombings; Kazakhstan is now a party to 11 of the 12 international terrorism conventions and protocols relating to terrorism. The 1979 Convention on the Physical Protection of Nuclear Material is in the process of being ratified, undergoing the second round of interagency review. On 27 February, after approval by the Parliament, President Nazarbayev signed into law the two remaining conventions—the Convention for the Suppression of Unlawful Acts against the Safety of Maritime Navigation and the Protocol for the Suppression of Unlawful Acts against the Safety of Fixed Platforms Located on the Continental Shelf.

Kazakhstan has also strengthened its antiterrorism legislation. In February, the Government adopted tougher penalties and more precise definitions of terrorist acts. In October, the National Bank issued orders to freeze the assets belonging to an individual identified on the Executive Order 13224 terrorist asset-freeze list who had held shares in a local bank.

Kyrgyz Republic

Since September 11, 2001, President Akayev has repeatedly demonstrated his strong support for the war against terrorism. Following the September 11 events, the Kyrgyz Government immediately offered assistance and allowed US and Coalition combat and support aircraft to operate from Ganci airbase, located at Manas International Airport in Bishkek.

(On 3 January 2003, the Legislative Assembly [lower house of Parliament] ratified the International Convention Against Terrorist Financing and forwarded it to the People's Representative Assembly [upper house of Parliament] for ratification. The International Relations Committee of the People's Representative Assembly recommended the Convention for ratification. The next People's Representative Assembly session was to begin on 1 March 2003, and ratification was to have been on its agenda.) The Kyrgyz Republic is a party to six of the 12 international conventions and protocols relating to terrorism.

The Kyrgyz Republic is a member of the Shanghai Cooperation Organization, launched in June 2001 and grouping China, Kazakhstan, Kyrgyzstan, Russia, Tajikistan, and Uzbekistan. President Akayev has also announced his country's support for China's stand against the terrorist forces of the East Turkestan Independence Movement (ETIM), which the United States has designated pursuant to Executive Order 13224. The ETIM was responsible for planning and executing a series of terrorist acts within and outside China.

The Kyrgyz Government has been working toward creating a new Drug Control Agency that is designed to stifle cross-border shipments of drugs and arms related to terrorism.

Several thousand members of Hizb ut-Tahrir, an extremist political movement that wants to establish a borderless, theocratic caliphate throughout the entire Muslim world, are present in Kyrgyzstan, Tajikistan, and Uzbekistan. Hizb ut-Tahrir pamphlets, filled with anti-US propaganda, have been distributed throughout the southern region of the country and even appeared in Bishkek. There is no evidence to date that Hizb ut-Tahrir has committed any terrorist acts, but the group is clearly sympathetic to Islamist extremist objectives.

Russia

The past year saw a continuation of the US-Russian counterterrorism cooperation that emerged following the attacks of September 11, 2001.

At the Presidential Summit in Moscow in May 2002, Presidents Bush and Putin agreed to expand the scope of the United States-Russia Working Group on Afghanistan, co-chaired by Deputy Secretary of State Richard Armitage and Russian First Deputy Foreign Minister Vyacheslav Trubnikov. It is now known as the US-Russia Working Group on Counterterrorism. This interagency working group met for the first time under its expanded mandate on 26 July 2002 in Annapolis, Maryland, and again in Moscow on 22–23 January 2003.

But even as the United States and Russia cooperated in the global war on terrorism on all fronts in 2002, Russia faced terrorist acts that struck at the heart of its national security.

Russia continued to be subject to a number of terrorist events in 2002, many connected to the ongoing insurgency and instability in Chechnya. The continuing conflict, which began in late summer 1999, has been characterized by widespread destruction, displacement of hundreds of thousands of civilians, and human rights abuses by Russian servicemen and various rebel factions. At least three rebel factions, which consist of both Chechen and foreign—predominantly Arabic—mujahidin fighters, are connected to international Islamic terrorists and have used terrorist methods. (They have been designated, in 2003, as terrorist organizations for asset freeze under Executive Order 13224.) Russian forces have continued to conduct operations against Chechen fighters but also draw heavy criticism over credible reports of human rights violations.

Extremist groups and individuals seeking to create an independent Islamic state in the north Caucasus were responsible for dozens of terrorist attacks in 2002. Russian citizens were the victims of frequent attacks with command-detonated mines, including one that killed 36 persons, 12 of them children, and wounded over 100 others attending a Memorial Day parade in Kaspiisk, Dagestan.

But Russia's most serious terrorist event of 2002 occurred on 23 October when more than 40 armed militants took hostage 800 Moscow theatergoers to demand an immediate end to all Russian security operations in Chechnya. More than 120 of the hostages—including one US citizen (and a US Legal Permanent Resident)—died from a narcotic gas used during the rescue operation.

The terrorists, who included several female suicide bombers wearing explosive "suicide" vests, placed several mines throughout the theater and threatened to begin killing the hostages unless their demands were met. The leader of the attack was identified by the Chechen mujahidin news agency Kavkaz Tsentr, and later by Russian news agencies, as Movsar Barayev, commander of the Special Purpose Islamic Regiment (SPIR) of the Chechen State Defense Committee (Majlis al-Shura). On 24 October, the Arabic news agency Al-Jazirah identified the group as the previously unknown "Sabotage and Military Surveillance Group of the 'Riyadh al-Salikhin' Martyrs" (a.k.a. the Riyadus-Salikhin Reconnaissance and Sabotage Battalion of Chechen Martyrs). A group member said in a recorded statement, "Our demands are stopping the war and withdrawal of Russian forces. We are implementing the operation by order of the military commander of the Chechen Republic." These two groups—Special Purpose Islamic Regiment and Sabotage and Military Surveillance Group of the 'Riyadh al-Salikhin' Martyrs—were among the three that the US Government designated as terrorist groups for asset freeze.

On 24 October, the Government of Russia immediately drafted and introduced UNSCR 1440 condemning the Moscow hostage taking as a terrorist act and urging all states, in accordance with their obligations under UNSCR 1373 (2001), to cooperate with Russian authorities in finding and bringing to justice the perpetrators, organizers, and sponsors of this terrorist attack. The resolution was unanimously adopted the same day.

On 1 November, Chechen rebel commander Shamil Basayev, in a letter to Kavkaz-Tsentr, publicly claimed full responsibility for organizing the attack. Basayev said that the Riyadus-Salikhin Reconnaissance and Sabotage Battalion of Chechen Martyrs (RSMB) had been under his direct command and that Chechen President Maskhadov had no prior knowledge of the event. Basayev then publicly resigned his positions as Amir of the Council (Majlis) of Muslims of Chechnya and Dagestan and as the Military Commander of the Islamist International Brigade, saying he would henceforth devote himself completely to the RSMB.

Less than one month later, however, Basayev was once again commanding mujahidin units in Chechnya, according to President Maskhadov's official news agency, and warned that all "military, industrial, and strategic facilities on Russian territory, to whomever they belong" were legitimate targets for attack. Usama Bin Ladin also acknowledged the Moscow hostage takers in a November 2002 audiotape message, saying to the Russians, "If you were distressed by the killing of your nationals in Moscow, remember ours in Chechnya."

Throughout 2002, Russia continued to take important steps toward strengthening its participation in the global war on terrorism, particularly by ratifying the International Convention for the Suppression of the Financing of Terrorism. By the end of the year, Russia was a party to 11 of the 12 international conventions and protocols relating to terrorism. Before 2002, Russia had signed but not ratified the Convention on the Marking of Plastic Explosives for the Purpose of Detection. Russian officials were optimistic that official ratification of the 1991 Convention on the Marking of Plastic Explosives for the Purpose of Detection would soon occur.

The Government of Russia enacted domestic legislation and executive orders to enable its fight against terrorism in 2002. On 11 January, President Putin signed a decree entitled

"On Measures to Implement the UN Security Council Resolution No. 1373 of September 28, 2001" that introduced criminal liability for anyone intentionally providing or collecting assets for terrorist use as well as instructions to relevant agencies on how to seize terrorist assets.

On 11 October, Russia was removed from the Financial Action Task Force's (FATF) list of Non-Cooperating Countries and Territories, in part due to the establishment of a Russian financial intelligence unit, the Financial Monitoring Committee. A functioning financial intelligence unit is central to Russia's ability to cooperate internationally to combat money laundering, to its participation in the Egmont Group and FATF, and to track and freeze terrorist assets.

Although the Russia Federation maintains diplomatic relations with the seven states presently on the US Government's State Sponsors of Terrorism list, the Russian Government firmly opposes state-sponsored terrorism and supports international initiatives to combat it. The Government of Russia maintains that its relationships with such states serve as a positive influence that has—or may have—moderated or diminished the support these governments provide for terrorism.

In February, the Federal Security Service hosted an antiterrorism conference in St. Petersburg. They invited representatives from the law-enforcement and intelligence agencies of approximately 40 countries, including the United States.

At the United Nations, Russia circulated a draft General Assembly resolution calling for enhanced cooperation among all components of the UN system in the fight against terrorism. The resolution also noted the interconnection between terrorism, transnational organized crime, and drug trafficking. Russia is using its seat at the new NATO-Russia Council to emphasize counterterrorism cooperation. In December, Russia hosted a NATO-Russia conference on the Role of the Military in Combating Terrorism. At the most recent Asia-Pacific Economic Cooperation (APEC) summit, held at the same time of the Moscow hostage crisis in October, President Putin's representative, Prime Minister Mikhail Kasyanov, said that the Moscow crisis compelled "the countries that were to some extent reluctant to join in this coalition to more actively participate in combating all signs of terrorism." The APEC summit generated a very strong statement against terrorism, including a decision to monitor the misuse of the Islamic alternative remittance *hawala* system.

In a much publicized statement on 11 September, President Putin asserted what he claimed was Russia's international right to take unilateral military action against Chechen fighters and other terrorists in Georgia's Pankisi Gorge (near the border with Russia) if Georgia did not carry out more active measures against the fighters. He followed his statement with a letter to President Bush, which he copied to the United Nations and world leaders. From 29 July to the end of 2002 there were at least five instances of Russian cross-border aerial bombardment of Georgian territory. During an attack on 23 August—witnessed by OSCE border monitors and confirmed through independent means—Russian bombs claimed the life of a Georgian civilian and wounded seven others.

The US Government has stated its unequivocal opposition to any unilateral military action by Russia inside Georgia and repeated its strong support for Georgia's sovereignty and territorial integrity. It has urged Georgia to address the security problems arising from the presence of Chechen and third-country extremists with connections to al-Qaida in the Pankisi Gorge. The United States has encouraged Georgia and Russia to work together to promote regional security within their respective territories and to find negotiated, political solutions to their many disagreements.

Tajikistan

The Government of Tajikistan continued to cooperate fully with US antiterrorism efforts throughout 2002.

In March, the Government submitted its report on counterterrorism efforts to the UN Security Council Committee created under UNSCR 1373.

Throughout the year, moreover, the government consistently supported antiterrorist efforts in the United Nations and the OSCE. It was also a signatory to the Shanghai Cooperation Organization's June statement and its antiterrorism clauses.

Tajikistan continues to be extremely supportive of and cooperative in the global effort to end terrorism. During 2002, Dushanbe became a party to two international antiterrorist conventions—the 1979 International Convention against the Taking of Hostages (6 May 2002) and the 1997 Convention for the Suppression of Terrorist Bombings (29 July 2002). The Government of Tajikistan is now party to eight of the 12 international conventions and protocols against terrorism. Dushanbe has indicated its willingness to become a party to the Convention on the Marking of Plastic Explosives. (It should be noted that Tajikistan is a landlocked country, and the remaining two conventions relate to maritime navigation and offshore platforms.)

Tajikistan conducted several significant antiterrorist operations during 2002, including the arrests of a number of suspected terrorists. Additionally, in October and November, Government security forces conducted a large counterterrorist operation in the central portion of the country. The Government had announced in November 2001 its agreement to the basing of US and Coalition troops and aircraft in Tajikistan, and throughout 2002, US and Coalition aircraft were permitted to carry out refueling operations at Dushanbe International Airport. The Ministry of Defense detailed four liaison officers to US Central Command Headquarters in connection with Operation Enduring Freedom.

Tajikistani security authorities, moreover, have stepped up border security and pledged to prevent escape attempts into Tajikistan by Taliban and al-Qaida members. The Government has been open to participating in US Government-supplied antiterrorism training and assistance. The Ministries of Foreign Affairs and Finance have also cooperated with

Washington's attempts to trace and freeze terrorist assets and have worked to tighten their financial controls.

Throughout 2002, Dushanbe continued its investigations into a number of incidents of domestic and international terrorism that had occurred in Tajikistan in 2001. In August, the Government announced the formation of a special investigation and prosecution unit to look into the assassinations of a number of high-ranking officials in 2001 and previous years. The effort included the killings of the First Deputy Minister of the Interior, the State Advisor to the President on International Affairs, and the Minister of Culture—as well as the Independence Day suicide bombing (which injured one other person) in September 2001 and the murder of two members of the Baha'i faith in Dushanbe in late 2001. According to public statements by the Deputy State Procurator-General (head of the special unit), arrests were made in several of the cases. The investigations continued. Convictions were obtained in some of the cases, including the murders of the First Deputy Minister of the Interior and the Minister of Culture; in both cases, those convicted received the death penalty.

On 3 November 2002, the Government announced the extradition of 12 members of the Islamic Movement of Uzbekistan, which the United States has designated a Foreign Terrorist Organization and also has designated pursuant to Executive Order 13224, to Uzbekistan for prosecution. The Tajikistani Ministry of Security captured the suspects during a security sweep, according to a public statement. While the United States currently does not have an extradition treaty with Tajikistan, Dushanbe has officially declared that multilateral instruments such as international conventions against terrorism or the UN Convention Against Transnational Organized Crime, when it enters into force internationally, could form a basis for extradition under Tajikistani law. In particular, the Government announced in September that those arrested in the investigation of the murders of two adherents of the Baha'i faith were found to have links to Iranian-backed terrorist groups.

There were no prosecutions during the year of cases relating directly to terrorism, although several participants in the 1998 coup attempt led by Col. Mahmud Khudoberdiev were convicted on charges that included terrorism. The charges stemmed from their association with Khudoberdiev rather than from involvement in terrorist acts.

Ukraine

The Government of Ukraine supported US antiterrorism efforts throughout 2002. Since the beginning of operations in Afghanistan, Ukraine has allowed more than 5,000 overflights for aircraft participating in Operation Enduring Freedom and provided airlift assets for some Coalition forces participating in the operation. The Government also provided, at Washington's request, light weapons and kits to equip the equivalent of a brigade's worth of Afghan National Army troops. Ukraine has become party to all 12 of the United Nations conventions against terrorism, and it also has adopted legislation bringing it into legal conformity with the Financial Action Task Force (FATF) standards. The Government of Ukraine has agreed to install US Government-funded nuclear portal monitors at 20 border crossings, airports, and ports to detect the transit of nuclear material and is working with us to implement technical upgrades for nuclear plant security. We are also working closely with the Ukrainians to implement a program to upgrade security at institutes whose biological agents could be used to produce weapons. The Ukrainian Rada (parliament) recently passed legislation tightening Ukraine's export-control laws to protect against the proliferation of weapons to rogue states.

President Kuchma has repeatedly made public statements supporting US Government efforts against terrorism. Ukrainian citizens were among the victims of the seizure of the Dubrovka Theater in Moscow on 23 October by 40 armed Chechen extremists. Three Ukrainian citizens were killed in the incident.

Uzbekistan

The Government of Uzbekistan continued its unprecedented support of Coalition efforts in the war on terrorism during 2002. It has continued to make public statements condemning terrorist acts, and it has allowed basing of Coalition forces at Karshi-Khanabad and Termez and overflight by Coalition forces. The Ministry of Defense detailed five liaison officers to US Central Command Headquarters in connection with Operation Enduring Freedom. Tashkent agreed to all US requests to freeze assets of groups linked to terrorism financing.

Uzbekistan has continued to be extremely supportive of and cooperative in the global effort to end terrorism. The Government has continued to participate in US-led initiatives such as the Department of State's Antiterrorism Assistance Program, border-security and law-enforcement projects funded by the Department's Bureau for International Narcotics and Law Enforcement Affairs, US Customs export-control and border-security programs, and the Defense Department's programs on threat reduction and weapons of mass destruction.

Several thousand members of Hizb ut-Tahrir, an extremist political movement that wants to establish a borderless, theocratic caliphate throughout the entire Muslim world, are present in Uzbekistan. Hizb ut-Tahrir pamphlets, full of anti-US propaganda, have been distributed throughout the country. There is no evidence to date that Hizb ut-Tahrir has committed any terrorist acts, but the group is clearly sympathetic to Islamist extremist objectives.

The Government of Uzbekistan continues to go to extraordinary lengths to ensure security, especially during significant national holidays, against terrorist acts. Uzbekistan maintains relatively tight security on its borders and is working with the US Government to upgrade its capabilities to detect items of concern related to the spread of weapons of mass destruction. Although no incidents were reported in

2002, Uzbek border guards have detected radioactive shipments on the border in previous years.

Tashkent remains vigilant against potential actions by the Islamic Movement of Uzbekistan, despite the loss of its charismatic leader Juma Namangani and their former sanctuary with the Taliban in Afghanistan. Uzbekistan also plays an active role in the counterterrorism agenda of the Shanghai Cooperation Organization, the Organization for Cooperation and Security in Europe, and the United Nations.

Uzbekistan is a party to all 12 international conventions and protocols relating to terrorism.

Europe Overview

European nations continued to work in close partnership with the United States in the global counterterrorism campaign. In addition to sharing intelligence information and working with the United States on investigations of terrorist groups, European countries forged closer cooperative links with their neighbors. As a result, European authorities arrested a significant number of terrorists, disrupted planning for terrorist attacks, and intercepted funds destined for terrorist organizations.

The United Kingdom continued its close partnership with the United States, redoubling its counterterrorism efforts around the world. UK authorities detained several extremists in the United Kingdom on terrorism-related charges. The United Kingdom aggressively moved to freeze the assets of organizations and persons with terrorist links and to proscribe terrorist groups. The United Kingdom provided significant counterterrorism assistance and training to a number of countries and worked with other countries to investigate the Bali bombings in October 2002.

Italy continued its exemplary work against terrorism, disrupting suspected terrorist cells and capturing al-Qaida suspects in Milan and elsewhere who were providing support to terrorist operations and planning attacks. An Italian court sentenced members of the Tunisian Combatant Group to prison terms, marking the first conviction of al-Qaida associates in Europe since 11 September 2001. Members of the New Red Brigades, an offshoot of the once-powerful entity that disrupted Italian life in the 1970s, are suspected of the murder of an adviser to the Italian Government. Other terrorist groups also carried out several small-scale attacks.

Spain's vigorous investigation of extremist groups resulted in the detention of a significant number of terrorist suspects, including two individuals believed to be financiers for the al-Qaida network. Spanish police, working with French counterparts, also continued to score substantial successes against the Basque Fatherland and Liberty (ETA) terrorist organization, arresting two of the group's senior leaders. Spanish and French authorities dealt a strong blow against the First of October Antifascist Resistance Group (GRAPO) when they conducted a joint investigation that resulted in the arrest of over 20 GRAPO suspects. French investigators probed terrorist attacks that killed at least 20 French citizens in Tunisia, Pakistan, and Indonesia.

Cooperation among European law-enforcement authorities was a feature of many successes during the past year. For example, in addition to joint efforts between France and Spain against ETA and GRAPO, France, Belgium, the United Kingdom, and others were involved in investigations of "shoe bomber" Richard Reid.

Officials in Germany continued their extensive investigation of extremists associated with the al-Qaida Hamburg cell that supported the September 11 hijackers. Germany also placed several high-profile terrorists on trial, including a member of the Hamburg cell and four North Africans accused of plotting to attack the Strasbourg Christmas market in 2000. Twenty German citizens fell victim to terrorist attacks in Djerba, Tunisia, and in Bali, Indonesia.

Turkey arrested a number of individuals with ties to al-Qaida and continued to fight dangerous domestic terrorist groups. For the first time, Greece arrested members of Revolutionary Organization 17 November, marking significant progress against a domestic terrorism problem. The arrests appeared to have begun the unraveling and dismantling of one of Europe's oldest terrorist groups.

The countries of southeast Europe have actively supported the international Coalition against terrorism. Albania and Bulgaria have extended blanket landing and overflight clearances. Along with Croatia, they have also contributed troops to the International Security Assistance Force in Afghanistan and weapons and ammunition to the Afghan National Army. Albania and Bosnia and Herzegovina have shut down nongovernmental organizations with links to terrorist networks and frozen terrorist assets, and the Bosnian Government arrested and transferred to US control several terrorist suspects accused of planning an attack against the US Embassy in Sarajevo.

Denmark also made noteworthy contributions to the war on terrorism. On the economic front under its European Union (EU) Presidency leadership, in forging a workable EU Clearinghouse they froze assets of terrorist groups, even those not taken to the UN Security Council Resolution (UNSCR) 1267 Sanctions Committee. On the military front, they continued their commitment to Operation Enduring Freedom through the Danish-Norwegian-Dutch F-16 contingent at Manas Airbase.

Heads of State and government met at the Prague Summit in November to endorse NATO's commitment to develop capabilities to meet new challenges such as terrorism and weapons of mass destruction.

Albania

Despite its limited resources, Albania has provided considerable support on counterterrorism. Albania supported US and international counterterrorist initiatives by extending blanket landing and overflight clearances for Operation Enduring Freedom; providing commando troops to the International Security Assistance Force in Afghanistan and weapons to the Afghan National Army; and adopting legislation to coordinate the counterterrorism efforts of its police, military, intelligence service, and Ministries of Finance and Foreign Affairs. Albania also joined international efforts to fight terrorism by signing agreements with Germany to repatriate illegal immigrants and with Romania to combat terrorism, drug trafficking, and organized crime. Albania had some success in implementing measures at its major ports to combat illegal trafficking.

Tirana took measures to freeze terrorist assets and shut down nongovernmental organizations suspected of international extremist activity and detained or expelled individuals suspected of having links to terrorism. Albania also provided ongoing close cooperation to the United States in sharing information and investigating terrorist-related groups and activities. Institutional weaknesses, corruption, organized crime, and difficult terrain continued to hamper Albania's ability to carry out counterterrorism initiatives, however. Efforts to strengthen Albania's money-laundering legislation in May did not clarify or increase the scope of the laws in 2002, but Parliament expects to pass improved legislation, including specific terrorist-financing provisions, in 2003.

The aftershocks of the Chechen hostage crisis at the Moscow Theater in Russia reached Albania. At the Russian Government's request, Albania denied entry to Chechen delegates who tried to attend the Transnational Radical Party Congress, which supports Chechen independence. Although a previously unknown Islamic terrorist group, "Allah's Martyrs," threatened to disrupt the Congress, the Government stepped up security measures, and the Congress concluded peacefully.

Albania is a party to 11 of the 12 UN international conventions and protocols relating to terrorism.

Belgium

The Belgian Government has cooperated with US counterterrorism efforts on several levels. Brussels was timely and proactive in sharing information with the United States regarding terrorist threats to US citizens or facilities. Belgium's Financial Intelligence Unit provided the US Financial Crimes Enforcement Unit with information on individuals and entities with suspected ties to terrorist groups. The Belgian General Intelligence and Security Service also cooperated closely with US authorities.

Belgian authorities are continuing their investigations of several individuals arrested in 2001 who are of interest to the United States. Authorities are examining Richard Reid's activities and associates in Belgium, particularly in light of Reid's stay at a Brussels hotel shortly before he attempted to ignite his shoe bomb while on American Airlines Flight 63 in December 2001. Nizar Trabelsi, a Tunisian national arrested by Belgian authorities in September 2001 for his involvement with a plot to bomb the US Embassy in Paris, claimed in June 2002 that his plan was to attack Kleine Brogel airbase in Belgium. Authorities have nearly completed the investigation of Tarek Maaroufi—a Tunisian-born Belgian national arrested in December 2001 for allegedly providing forged passports to the two assassins of Northern Alliance leader Ahmad Shah Massoud.

Belgian authorities have been working on several initiatives to improve the country's counterterrorism capabilities. In May 2002, the Government created the Office of the Federal Prosecutor, which has the potential of becoming a centralized point of contact for counterterrorism cooperation with other countries. Before the September 11 attacks, Belgium had established an Anti-Terrorism Unit (ATU) within the federal police to centralize domestic investigations of terrorism-related activity. While the ATU was not given formal jurisdiction over terrorism-related cases, it works closely with local police.

Parliament passed legislation expanding the range of investigative measures available to police and was to consider a draft bill that would enhance the Government's ability to combat terrorism. The bill defines and outlaws membership in, or support for, a terrorist organization. Additional pieces of legislation aimed at enhancing the capabilities of the intelligence service to track terrorist suspects and increasing the access of counterterrorism officials to information gathered by independent investigative magistrates were also being drafted.

Belgium is a party to six of the 12 international conventions and protocols relating to terrorism. Belgium has frozen the assets of individuals and entities included on the UNSCR 1267 Sanctions Committee's consolidated list of individuals as being associated with Usama Bin Ladin, members of al-Qaida, and members of the Taliban. Nonetheless, because the Government lacks the legal authority to do so, Belgium has not fulfilled the broader obligations of UNSCR 1373, which requires nations to freeze the financial assets of terrorists.

Bosnia and Herzegovina

The Government of Bosnia and Herzegovina (BiH) has taken a strong stance against terrorism and condemned acts of international terrorism. Bosnia is a party to seven of the 12 international conventions and protocols relating to terrorism and has initiated procedures to ratify four additional ones.

In early 2002, BiH authorities arrested and transferred to US control several individuals suspected of planning an attack on the US Embassy in Sarajevo. In October, Stabilization Force (SFOR) detained an individual linked to al-Qaida for conducting surveillance of SFOR personnel and facilities and for possessing a rocket-propelled grenade launcher. (The suspect was turned over to Bosnian Federation authorities in late January 2003, who released him on bail. The Federation Government filed charges against him for illegal weapons possession in February 2003.)

In accordance with UNSCRs 1267 and 1373, the Government also froze the assets and prohibited future transactions of several Islamic nongovernmental organizations (NGOs), including the Benevolence International Foundation (BIF), Al-Haramain Islamic Foundation, and the Global Relief Fund, which have direct links to al-Qaida and Usama Bin Ladin. Documents seized from the offices of the BIF link its leader directly to Usama Bin Ladin. Bosnian cooperation with US law enforcement, including the testimony of BiH officials, supported successful prosecution of the BIF leader in US Federal Court.

The Government has continued to investigate the role of six former Bosnian Federation officials suspected of operating a terrorist-training camp in BiH with Iran in the mid-1990s. Criticism by nationalist Bosnian Muslim politicians, particularly in the run up to October's general elections, appears to have made some officials hesitant to pursue this case and other high-profile counterterrorism actions, however. The formation of nationalist governments at the state, entity, and cantonal levels may adversely affect future cooperation in the fight against terrorism.

The Bosnian Government introduced measures to address some of the administrative and legal challenges it faces in combating terrorism. The Government strengthened its border and financial controls, created a unified Federation intelligence service, and created Bosnia's first national identity card. (The High Representative's imposition of a new state-level criminal code and criminal procedure code in January 2003 reinforced the criminal justice system, including specific provisions aimed at terrorism.) Several additional pieces of antiterrorism legislation remain pending before parliament, however. As of October 2002, the State Border System had assumed coverage over 100 percent of Bosnia's borders and all operating international airports. Since introducing tighter immigration controls, authorities have reduced illegal immigration via Sarajevo Airport by an estimated 90 percent. The State Information and Protection Agency, whose mission includes combating terrorism, illegal trafficking, organized crime, and smuggling of weapons of mass destruction, thus far has been ineffective because it lacks authority and resources.

France

France has provided outstanding military, judicial, and law-enforcement support to the war against terrorism. France made a significant military contribution to Operation Enduring Freedom, including some 4,200 military personnel supporting operations in Afghanistan. The Charles de Gaulle carrier battle group flew more than 2,000 air reconnaissance, strike, and electronic warfare missions over Afghanistan. France provided close air support to US and Coalition forces during Operation Anaconda.

French investigators cooperated in a joint investigation with the FBI of Richard Reid, the would-be "shoe bomber." In the 30-day period after Reid's arrest in December 2001, the FBI and the Paris Criminal Brigade maintained often twice-daily contact with US authorities and provided information that proved critical to building the criminal case against Reid. French authorities have continued aggressively to pursue leads related to the Reid case.

The French Government reached a compromise agreement with the United States to provide evidence gathered in the Zacarias Moussaoui case, despite domestic criticism.

The French judiciary continued to pursue domestic terrorism cases vigorously. A French court in October convicted and sentenced two Islamist terrorists to life in prison for their roles in a series of bombings of the Paris subway in 1995 that killed eight persons and wounded more than 200. In October, the Justice Ministry decided to add a fifth investigative magistrate to its specialized team of antiterrorist judges.

In November, French authorities arrested Slimane Khalfaoui, who is likely associated with the Meliani cell, a group of five individuals arrested in December 2000 and April 2001 for allegedly planning to attack the cathedral square in Strasbourg, France. Khalfaoui also is suspected of ties to Ahmad Ressam—the Algerian arrested in December 1999 at the US-Canadian border in an alleged plot to bomb Los Angeles International Airport—and Rabah Kadri, an Islamic radical arrested in the United Kingdom for a plot to attack the London subway.

France continued to cooperate with Spain in dismantling Basque Fatherland and Liberty (ETA), the Basque terrorist organization. In November, both countries signed a protocol granting Spanish counterterrorism officials enhanced access to French information obtained from arrested ETA members. In September, two principal ETA leaders, Juan Antonio Olarra and Ainhoa Mugica Goni, were arrested in a joint operation in Bordeaux. Olarra was linked to at least nine murders.

In October, France requested that the UNSCR 1267 Sanctions Committee add two North African terrorist groups operating in France—the Tunisian Combatant Group and the Moroccan Islamic Combatant Group—to its consolidated list of individuals and entities associated with Usama Bin Ladin, al-Qaida, and the Taliban. The United States subsequently blocked the groups' assets under Executive Order 13224. Despite its generally cooperative stance against terrorism, France opposes listing Hizballah as a terrorist organization. France designates terrorist groups in concert with the EU. The EU has designated the "terrorist wing" of HAMAS but not the group as a whole, citing its political and social role in Lebanon.

France has become a party to 11 of the 12 international conventions and protocols relating to terrorism.

Terrorists attacked French interests or citizens several times in 2002. In April, two French citizens were killed in a suicide attack against a synagogue on the Tunisian island of Djerba. In May, a suicide bomber exploded a vehicle alongside a bus in Karachi, killing 14 persons, including 11 French engineers. Terrorists also attacked the Limburg, a French supertanker, off the coast of Yemen in October. The attack resulted in one casualty and caused an oil spill of 90,000 barrels into the Gulf of Aden. Four French nationals were killed and seven wounded in the bombing of a Bali nightclub in October. The Corsican National Liberation Front claimed responsibility for a string of nonlethal bombings in Paris and Marseilles in early May. There were multiple, nonlethal, unclaimed bombings on Corsica in November.

Germany

Germany is an active and critically important participant in the global Coalition against terrorism. The country's efforts have made a valuable contribution to fighting terrorists inside and outside of German territory.

Several German citizens were killed in terrorist attacks in 2002. In April, 14 German tourists died in a suicide attack against a synagogue on the Tunisian island of Djerba. Six German citizens were killed in the bombing of a Bali nightclub in October.

During 2002, Germany played an important role in both Operation Enduring Freedom (OEF) and the UN's International Security Assistance Force (ISAF) in Afghanistan. Germany's contribution to OEF included 100 special-forces soldiers; 50 troops manning nuclear, biological, and chemical detection units in Kuwait; and approximately 1,800 personnel in a naval task force off the Horn of Africa. Germany reinforced ISAF's capabilities with approximately 1,300 troops, and German troop levels will increase to approximately 2,500 in connection with the undertaking by Germany and the Netherlands in December to assume leadership of ISAF in February 2003.

Germany has taken a lead role in Afghanistan's reconstruction through humanitarian and development assistance. German personnel helped train and equip a new Afghan police force, and Germany contributed 10 million Euros to the force.

German law-enforcement officials arrested several suspected terrorists. In October, authorities arrested Abdelghani Mzoudi for allegedly supporting the al-Qaida cell in Hamburg involved in the September 11, 2001 attacks. Mounir el Motassadeq, a Moroccan national who was arrested in November 2001 for his alleged membership in the Hamburg cell, went on trial, and it was continuing at year's end. (El Motassadeq was convicted early in 2003.) Five reported members of the al-Qaida–linked al-Tawhid organization were arrested in April and were awaiting indictment. German police thwarted a possible terrorist attack when they arrested a Turkish male and an American female suspected of attempting to bomb the US military base in Heidelberg.

In April, a trial opened in Frankfurt against four Algerians and a Moroccan accused of planning an attack on the Strasbourg Christmas market in December 2000. Some of the defendants claim that their intention was to bomb an empty Jewish synagogue but not kill anyone.

After lengthy negotiations, Germany agreed in November to provide the US Government with evidence in the US trial of French national Zacarias Moussaoui, who was arrested in August 2001 and is suspected of involvement with the September 11 hijackings.

Germany continued to take action against Caliphate State —a radical Turkish Islamic group based in Cologne—which was outlawed in December 2001. In September 2002, German authorities banned another 16 groups linked to Caliphate State and raided the homes and offices of suspected affiliates.

Germany has adopted antiterrorism reforms that should further its ability to fight terrorism. The reforms include bolstering the ability of intelligence officials and police to identify and pursue suspected terrorists, screening visa applicants for terrorists, improving border security, and allowing armed air marshals on German aircraft. Germany broadened its legal code to permit prosecutions of terrorists based outside of the country. Germany also modified its law on associations to remove the "religious privilege" clause, which had allowed extremist organizations to operate freely as religious organizations. The Government has used its new legislation, particularly the strengthened law on associations, to ban violence-prone extremist organizations.

Strong data-privacy protections and high evidentiary standards mean that terrorist investigations may take several months before arrests can be made, although administrative measures under the law of associations can be used to hamper the activities of extremist groups. Strong German opposition to the US death penalty has complicated efforts to forge a Mutual Legal Assistance Treaty with the United States, but negotiations are continuing.

Germany is a party to 10 of the 12 international conventions and protocols relating to terrorism.

Germany has frozen 30 bank accounts associated with terrorist groups valued at about $95,000.

In 2002, Germany was chosen to chair the international Financial Action Task Force, which coordinates multilateral efforts on countering terrorist financing and money laundering.

Greece

Greece made significant progress in 2002 combating domestic terrorism. For the first time, Greek authorities arrested suspected members of Revolutionary Organization 17 November (17 November), a group regarded as one of Europe's deadliest and most enduring in its nearly three decades of operations. Eighteen suspects were put on trial. The Government seized assets belonging to suspected 17 November members and blocked accounts belonging to other indigenous European terrorist organizations. Police also have been seeking evidence that will allow them to arrest members of Greece's other domestic terrorist groups, including Revolutionary Nuclei, its predecessor Revolutionary Peoples' Struggle, and 1 May. Despite the high-profile arrests, other leftist groups and anarchists conducted low-level attacks and demonstrations in Athens and Thessaloniki. The number of anti-US terrorist attacks—all nonlethal—rose from 2001's low of three to seven.

The Greek Government's record against transnational terrorist groups is mixed. It provided engineering troops to the International Security Assistance Force in Afghanistan, stationed a frigate in the Arabian Sea, and deployed two cargo aircraft to Pakistan to support the global Coalition against terrorism. The Government also ordered all banks and credit institutions to search for and block accounts belonging to Usama Bin Ladin, the al-Qaida network, and officials of the former Taliban regime.

Greece is a party to 10 of the 12 international conventions and protocols relating to terrorism.

The Government continued its security preparations for the 2004 Olympics and views the Games as an opportunity to increase international counterterrorism cooperation. To comply with EU counterterrorism regulations, Greece was expected to pass counterterrorism legislation mandating minimum sentences for terrorists and extending the statute of limitations for terrorist-related homicides from 20 to 30 years, in early 2003. Greece also pledged counterterrorism cooperation with its neighbors Romania and Bulgaria.

Hungary

Hungary has been fully supportive of the war against terrorism and US initiatives against al-Qaida and other terrorist organizations both within its borders and abroad. Throughout 2002, Hungary maintained consistent political support for the war on terror, actively promoting the US position in NATO and the UN, and giving high-level endorsement to our policies.

In support of Operation Enduring Freedom, Hungary developed a package of excess weapons, ammunition, and equipment to be donated to help with our Georgia Train and Equip Program and the Afghan National Army training project. The total amount for Afghanistan was 437 tons, valued at $3.7 million. The Georgia program was 8 tons, valued at $25,000. Also in 2002, Hungary offered a military medical unit as part of the International Security Assistance Force peacekeeping force, which was to deploy in early March to Afghanistan.

The Government has affirmed the previous government's commitment to contribute $1 million in humanitarian aid to Afghanistan, $300,000 of which was sent in December 2001 and the remainder of which will be delivered in 2003. Also in 2002, Hungary ratified the last of the international conventions and protocols relating to terrorism; it is now a party to all 12. In addition to a December 2001 law on money laundering and terrorist financing which brought it into full compliance with EU and Financial Action Task Force norms, Hungary has developed additional legislation which would go well beyond that of most countries in reporting requirements for financial transactions. This legislation is currently before the Hungarian Parliament.

Cooperation with US and regional officials on export and border controls also continues to be outstanding. In several cases, Hungarian officials have proactively pursued and developed leads and provided extensive cooperation to US officers that have stopped the transshipment of hazardous goods. Hungary is actively improving its technical ability to track and control dangerous materials, and its imminent accession into the EU is accelerating this process. Finally, Hungary has been active in mentoring its neighbors to the south and east and in 2002 offered four training courses or programs on counterterrorism and export controls for Balkan neighbors.

Italy

Italy has been an active partner in the war against terror, providing its only carrier battle group—more than 13 percent of its naval forces—to support combat operations in the North Arabian Sea for use in Operation Enduring Freedom (OEF). The "De La Penne" group (a destroyer and a frigate) relieved the carrier battle group on 15 March 2002. In addition to the 350 Italian troops serving as part of the International Security and Assistance Force in Afghanistan, the Italian Parliament agreed in October to send some 1,000 soldiers to support OEF and deployed troops shortly thereafter. The Italian Air Force has been flying sorties out of Manas Airbase, and Italian engineers helped repair a runway at Bagram Airfield.

Italian police arrested several suspected terrorists and disrupted potential attacks against the United States and its allies. In May, Italian police in Milan arrested five individuals who were suspected of providing funds to al-Qaida. In October, Italian authorities arrested four Tunisians for document forgery; they may have also been planning to conduct a terrorist attack in Europe, possibly in France.

Italy prosecuted several al-Qaida–affiliated individuals, putting on trial three North Africans suspected of providing logistics support to the group. In February, a judge in Milan sentenced four members of the Tunisian Combatant Group to up to five years in jail for providing false documentation and planning to acquire and transport arms and other illegal goods. Italian authorities also suspect the group was planning a terrorist attack against the US Embassy in Rome. This was the first time al-Qaida associates were convicted in Europe since September 11, 2001.

In August, working with the US Treasury Department, Italian authorities froze the assets of 25 individuals and organizations designated by the United States under Executive Order 13224. Eleven were individuals connected to the Salafist Group for Call and Combat, while 14 were organizations linked to two known al-Qaida–linked financiers, Ahmed Idris Nasreddin and Youssef Nada.

A variety of leftwing terrorist groups carried out attacks in Italy. In March, the recently resurgent Red Brigades–Communist Combatant Party (BR–PCC) was accused of assassinating Marco Biagi, an advisor to the Italian Labor Ministry. Several other groups, including the Anti-Imperialist Territorial Nuclei, the 20 July Brigades, and the Proletarian Nuclei for Communism, claimed responsibility for numerous small-scale attacks throughout Italy.

Italy is a party to 10 of the 12 international conventions and protocols relating to terrorism.

Lithuania

Lithuania took several steps to combat terrorism. Although there are no known al-Qaida operatives in Lithuania, the Government has worked effectively to arrest and deport a small number of individuals associated with HAMAS and Hizballah. The Government also monitored and reported to the United States on the transfer of $100,000 to a suspected terrorist via a Lithuanian bank. Lithuania has deployed limited personnel in support of Operation Enduring Freedom and the International Security Assistance Force in Afghanistan.

To improve its overall counterterrorist efforts, the Government adopted the National Counter-Terrorism Program, which identified deficiencies, goals, and deadlines and established the Interagency Coordination Commission Against Terrorism. It also increased security along its border with Belarus, at the Vilnius airport, and at the Ignalina Nuclear Power Plant. As a result of increased scrutiny at the country's border-control points, Lithuanian Border Guards apprehended more than 1,000 persons—mostly Lithuanians—sought by police, none with established terrorist connections.

The Lithuanian Government has emphasized working with European Union and North Atlantic Treaty Organization partners, as well as other countries. In April, Lithuania cosponsored with the United States an international conference on terrorist challenges, and in October the Ministry of Defense signed an agreement with the US Defense Department on the prevention of proliferation of weapons of mass destruction. Vilnius has bilateral agreements with Belarus, Germany, Hungary, and Kazakhstan to cooperate in the fight against terrorism. During visits to Azerbaijan, Armenia, and Georgia in April, Lithuania's Foreign Minister and his counterparts discussed joint antiterrorism efforts.

Lithuania is a party to 10 of the 12 major UN antiterrorism conventions and protocols.

The Netherlands

The Netherlands supported the global Coalition against terrorism with leadership, personnel, and materiel, including the deployment of more than 200 ground troops to Afghanistan. (In 2003, it took over joint command of the International Security Assistance Force with Germany.)

The Dutch implemented two agreements with the United States to increase border security. The Netherlands became the first country to agree to host a US Customs team; it will deploy under the Global Container Security Initiative at Rotterdam, one of Europe's busiest ports. The Government also agreed to allow US immigration officers at Amsterdam's Schiphol Airport to work on joint anticrime and counterterrorism operations. The Netherlands' Prime Minister stated that the United States and his country stand "shoulder to shoulder" in the struggle for global security.

In April and August, Dutch authorities arrested approximately two-dozen extremists—10 of whom remain in custody—who are accused of supporting terrorists and recruiting combatants for jihad. Authorities are also investigating their possible links with the assassins of Afghan opposition leader Ahmad Shad Massoud, who was killed in 2001 by al-Qaida members. In September, police arrested Ansar al-Islam's leader, Mullah Krekar. (In January 2003, the Dutch Justice Minister unexpectedly released and deported Krekar to Norway despite a pending Jordanian request for extradition.) In February 2002, a Dutch court, citing insufficient evidence, ordered the release of a man suspected of involvement in an al-Qaida plot to blow up the US Embassy in Paris.

The Dutch have taken a leading role, particularly in the European Union, to establish financial protocols to combat terrorism. They also donated $400,000 to the International Monetary Fund to provide assistance to countries that lack the wherewithal to implement some of these measures immediately.

The Government has proposed changes to Dutch law that will make it easier to prosecute supporters of terrorist groups. Under Dutch law, terrorist organizations are not illegal entities. The new legislation will criminalize the provision of information, money, and material assistance to terrorist organizations. The Netherlands is a party to all 12 UN antiterrorism conventions and protocols.

The Dutch have taken steps to freeze the assets of individuals and groups included on the UNSCR 1267 Sanctions Committee's consolidated list, most notably the New People's Army and the leader of its political wing, Jose Maria Sison. Nevertheless, the political wings of other terrorist groups, such as KADEK (formerly the PKK) and the Revolutionary People's Liberation Party/Front (DHKP/C), are allowed to operate as long as they do not commit terrorist acts or other crimes in The Netherlands.

Spain

Spain has offered strong, multifaceted support in the global war against terrorism. In May, the Spanish Government approved a contribution of 1,200 troops to the International Security and Assistance Force. As part of Operation Enduring Freedom, Spain participated in several humanitarian transport missions and contributed three C-130 Hercules planes and 70 soldiers to an airborne detachment. From January to October, a Spanish medical detachment served at the Bagram Air Base near Kabul. Spain also is heading a naval task force off the Horn of Africa to disrupt terrorist movements in the region.

In 2002, Spain arrested several individuals with possible links to al-Qaida. In July, Spanish authorities arrested three individuals of Syrian origin because of their alleged al-Qaida links. One of the detainees made suspicious video recordings while on a trip to the United States in 1997, including a videotape of the World Trade Center. The three individuals were released on bail because of weak evidence in the case. In April, Spanish police arrested two suspected al-Qaida financiers—Mohammed Galeb Kalaje Zouaydi, a naturalized Spanish citizen of Syrian descent, and Ahmed Brahim, an Algerian. In January, police arrested Najib Chaib Mohamed, a Moroccan national, for his alleged involvement in a suspected al-Qaida recruiting and logistics cell headed by Imad Eddin Barakat Yarkas, whom Spanish authorities had apprehended in November 2001.

Spain made progress in its decades-old campaign to eliminate domestic terrorist groups, including the Basque Fatherland and Liberty (ETA) organization—a radical Basque terrorist group. In November, Spain and France signed a protocol granting Spanish counterterrorism officials enhanced access to French information obtained from arrested ETA members. In September, Spanish and French police arrested two principal ETA leaders, Juan Antonio Olarra and Ainhoa Mugica Goni, in a joint operation with French authorities in Bordeaux. Olarra is linked to at least nine murders. The Spanish Parliament passed a law that provides a strong mechanism for the possible de-legalization of Batasuna, ETA's political wing. A case against Batasuna was before the Spanish Supreme Court at year's end. In a separate case in August, a judge ordered a provisional ban on Batasuna's activities, froze the group's financial assets, and closed their offices. ETA's attacks, nonetheless, had killed five Spanish citizens by year's end, down from 15 in 2001 and 23 in 2000.

Thirty-two ETA members and ETA-related organizations, such as Askatasuna [a.k.a. Batasuna], were included in Executive Order 13224, which blocks the assets of terrorists.

Spanish and French authorities made joint advances against the domestic terrorist group First of October Anti-Fascist Resistance Group (GRAPO). A series of arrests in July and November resulted in the capture of 22 suspected GRAPO members.

Spain is a party to all 12 international conventions and protocols relating to terrorism.

Turkey

The Turkish Government, long a staunch counterterrorism ally, continued to provide strong support in the campaign against terrorism. Turkey was quick to provide military assistance to Operation Enduring Freedom. Former Prime Minister Ecevit backed a parliamentary resolution permitting the Government to send Turkish troops abroad and to allow foreign troops to be stationed on Turkish soil. Turkey offered to provide a 90-man special-operations unit in Afghanistan. In June, Turkey took the leadership of the United Nation's International Security Assistance Force and contributed 1,400 soldiers to the peacekeeping force.

Turkish authorities have arrested several suspected terrorists who may be linked to al-Qaida. In August, authorities arrested Mevlut Kar, a Turkish citizen suspected of being an Islamic terrorist, at the Ankara airport. In April, Turkish authorities arrested four individuals associated with al-Qaida in Bursa.

Three members of the Union of Imams, a Jordanian group with links to al-Qaida, were arrested in February in Van. The individuals were suspected of planning a bombing attack in Israel. Subsequently, Turkish police arrested Ahmet Abdullah, a courier from northern Iraq, for providing assistance to the Union of Imams.

The Government of Turkey continued to take steps against domestic terrorist groups. Turkish authorities arrested several members from the Revolutionary People's Liberation Party/Front (DHKP/C)—a virulently anti-US group that killed two US defense contractors and wounded a US Air Force officer during the Gulf war. Although the group did not conduct any attacks in 2002, Turkish officials have expressed displeasure that the group's leadership is ensconced in Western Europe. The European Union included the DHKP/C on its terrorism list in May.

Turkish arrests also weakened Turkish Hizballah, a Kurdish Islamic (Sunni) extremist group that is unrelated to Lebanese Hizballah. In December, authorities arrested Ali Aslan Isik, reportedly one of the group's top leaders. The group's last attack in October 2001 killed two Turkish police officers in Istanbul.

In April, the Kurdistan Workers' Party (PKK) changed its name to the Kurdistan Freedom and Democracy Congress (KADEK) and declared its commitment to political versus armed tactics to advance Kurdish rights in Turkey. In October, a Turkish court commuted Abdullah Ocalan's, the group's imprisoned leader, death sentence to a life term. KADEK maintains that it has continued to abide by its self-declared peace initiative throughout 2002, but it continues to arm an estimated 8,000 trained fighters in and around Turkey.

Turkey is a party to all 12 international conventions and protocols relating to terrorism.

United Kingdom

The United Kingdom, which has taken important political, financial, and law-enforcement steps to advance international counterterrorist efforts, remains one of the United States' staunchest allies. At its peak, the British contribution to Operation Enduring Freedom included more than 4,500 personnel as well as aircraft, ships, and submarines. In March, it deployed a 1,700-strong force to Afghanistan to combat al-Qaida and initially led the International Security Assistance Force. It also participated in Coalition counterterrorism operations outside Afghanistan, including maritime patrols in the Arabian Sea. London has unfrozen assets linked to al-Qaida and the Taliban totaling $100 million and made them available to the legitimate Afghan Government.

The United Kingdom is a party to all 12 international conventions and protocols relating to terrorism and chairs the UN's Counter Terrorism Committee. The United Kingdom actively campaigned in the European Union, G-8, North Atlantic Treaty Organization, and United Nations for coordinated counterterrorism efforts and routinely lobbied UN members to become parties to the 12 antiterrorism conventions and protocols.

The United Kingdom launched aggressive efforts to disrupt and prosecute terrorists. Since December 2001, the Government has detained 15 foreign nationals under its Anti-Terrorism, Crime and Security Act, which allows extended detention of non-British nationals suspected of being international terrorists but who cannot be removed from the country immediately. The Government defeated a legal challenge to the antiterrorism law on appeal after the Special Immigration Appeals Commission ruled the law discriminatory and unlawful. Several other terror suspects also have been arrested and charged with terrorism-related offenses. In February authorities arrested Shaykh Abdullah Ibrahim el-Faisal on charges of inciting racial hatred for remarks he made calling for the murder of nonbelievers, Jews, Americans, and Hindus. He was charged with crimes under the Public Order Act and the Offences Against the Person Act.

The United Kingdom froze the assets of more than 100 organizations and 200 individuals with links to terrorism. In October, the Government proscribed four terrorist groups associated with al-Qaida—Jemaah Islamiya, the Abu Sayyaf Group, the Islamic Movement of Uzbekistan, and Asbat al-Ansar—bringing to 25 the total number of groups banned under the Terrorism Act of 2000. The United Kingdom has not frozen the assets belonging to political or humanitarian wings of terrorist groups HAMAS and Hizballah, owing to Britain's definition of terrorist organizations.

The United Kingdom was assisting in extraditing four individuals charged with terrorist acts in the United States or against US citizens, including an Algerian suspected of involvement in the 2000 "Millennium Conspiracy." The US request to extradite three men for their involvement in the 1998 US Embassy bombings in East Africa is pending an appeal to the European Court of Human Rights. British courts denied one US extradition request—an Algerian pilot suspected of training the September 11 hijackers, citing insufficient evidence. In November, the Government introduced legislation to streamline the lengthy extradition process. The United States and United Kingdom are also in the process of negotiating a new extradition treaty.

Training and financial assistance have been in the forefront of the UK's bilateral counterterrorism relationships. The United Kingdom trained security personnel in bomb disposal and hostage-negotiating techniques, assisted law-enforcement and regulatory authorities in terrorist-finance investigations, and, through its capacity-building programs, helped countries draft counterterrorism legislation.

The United Kingdom's intelligence and security agencies significantly deepened their bilateral counterterrorist relationships. It established major counterterrorism-assistance programs in South and Southeast Asia and worked with Indonesia, Australia, and the United States to investigate the October bombings in Bali. The British Government in November introduced a new bill on international crime cooperation that would allow police from EU member states to operate independently in Britain under specific circumstances and permit British police to track suspicious individuals across most UK borders, except its border with Ireland. The British police have worked closely with the Greek police to investigate the assassination in June 2000 of the British military attache in Athens and in the wider hunt for members of the 17 November terrorist group.

The Government took steps against domestic terrorism as well. Security officials disrupted numerous planned terrorist attacks, although in August the Real IRA (RIRA) killed a construction worker at a British Army base. In October, RIRA threatened additional violence. The investigation into the 1998 Omagh bombing linked to the RIRA continues, and British authorities also prepared for the trial of two suspected RIRA members connected with a series of car bombings in England in 2001. Sectarian violence—in large part fueled by loyalist paramilitaries—continued throughout the year and served as the backdrop to the decision by the British Government to suspend the Northern Ireland Assembly in October.

Middle East Overview

Terrorism remained a fundamental feature of the Middle East political landscape in 2002. Terrorist groups and their state sponsors continued terrorist activities and planning throughout 2002. Usama Bin Ladin's al-Qaida continued to be active in the region. Additionally, HAMAS, the Palestine Islamic Jihad (PIJ), Hizballah, and other groups opposed to a comprehensive Middle East peace maintained their attacks on civilians. Most Middle Eastern countries—including some that sponsor terrorist groups and with which the United States has differences—showed significant cooperation with the US-led campaign against terrorism, however.

In many nations, Middle Eastern allies of the United States thwarted terrorist incidents targeted against US interests and citizens, disrupted terrorist planning and operations, and enhanced their counterterrorism relations with the United States. Many have continued to provide tangible support for Operation Enduring Freedom, including personnel, basing, and overflight privileges. Most Middle East governments froze al-Qaida financial assets pursuant to UN Security Council Resolutions 1373, 1267, 1390 and 1455. Notably, all Middle Eastern countries with an American diplomatic and/or military presence were responsive to US requests for enhanced security for personnel and facilities during periods of heightened alert. The Government of Saudi Arabia, for example, has begun enhanced direct cooperation and coordination with the United States to counter terrorist financing and operations.

The Government of Yemen has continued a broad counterterrorism campaign against al-Qaida and suspected al-Qaida members within its territory with several notable successes and provided excellent cooperation with the United States. Jordan and Kuwait continued to counter suspected terrorists and provided superb security support to US facilities in the wake of the assassination of US diplomat Laurence Foley in Amman and the fatal shootings of US servicemen in Kuwait. The United Arab Emirates continued to buttress ongoing counterterrorism efforts in the Gulf.

Egypt's solid record of counterterrorism cooperation included efforts at brokering a cease-fire among Palestinian rejectionist groups that would halt terrorist violence in Israel and the Occupied Territories. The Governments of Algeria, Tunisia, and Morocco all actively supported the global campaign against terrorism.

Syria cooperated with the US Government and its partners in investigating al-Qaida and some other organizations. Damascus has continued, however, to support Hizballah, HAMAS, the PIJ, and other Palestinian rejectionist groups that conduct terrorist operations in the region. The Syrians have continued to assert that the activities of these groups constitute legitimate resistance. They sometimes even condone Palestinian suicide bombings and other attacks against civilian targets within Israel, the West Bank, and Gaza Strip.

The Gulf countries of Bahrain, Kuwait, Oman, Qatar, Saudi Arabia, and the United Arab Emirates played strong roles in the international Coalition against terrorism. These governments have continued to implement positive steps to halt the flow of terrorism financing and provide other assistance in the war on terrorism. In many instances, they did so despite popular disquiet over their governments' military support for Operation Enduring Freedom and other counterterrorism activities. As in many other countries, US interests were often subject to terrorist threats. The Gulf governments as a whole were extremely responsive in providing appropriate and effective security measures.

Maghreb governments likewise gave strong support by searching for terrorist financing, providing increased security to US interests, and thwarting actual terrorist plots. For example, Morocco arrested and prosecuted Saudis and Moroccans who allegedly were planning to attack NATO ships in the Straits of Gibraltar and also developed comprehensive antiterrorism legislation.

[Eds. Note: Iran, Iraq, Libya, and Syria, which have been designated as state sponsors of terrorism, are discussed in Part 1 in the section on "State Sponsorship of Terrorism."]

Algeria

President Bouteflika has publicly pledged his Government's full cooperation in the war against terror. As part of its effort, the Government of Algeria strengthened its information sharing with the United States and worked with European and other governments to eliminate terrorist-support networks linked to Algerian groups, most of which are in Europe. In 2002, Algeria hosted an international conference on crime and counterterrorism that was attended by almost 20 international delegations. The Government also hosted the Africa Union Summit on terrorism.

The Algerian Government enacted new laws combating violent extremism, most significantly a presidential decree allowing Government institutions to monitor accounts in private banks and creating a unit in the Ministry of Finance to fight money laundering. On the security front, Algerian authorities in late November announced that they had eliminated an al-Qaida operative who had been working with the country's domestic extremist groups.

Algeria is a party to 10 of the 12 international conventions and protocols relating to terrorism.

Algeria itself has been ravaged by terrorism since the early 1990s. Terrorism within the country remained a serious problem in 2002, although the level of violence has declined markedly over the past decade as Government forces have steadily reduced the areas in which militants operate. Most violence occurred in areas outside the capital, although militants on occasion still attempt attacks in the Algiers region.

The Salafist Group for Call and Combat—the largest, most active terrorist organization operating in the country—maintained the capability to conduct operations. It collaborated with smugglers and Islamists in the south who supplied insurgents with weapons and communications equipment for attacks in the north.

Bahrain

Bahrain, which hosts the US Naval Forces Central/ Fifth Fleet Headquarters and provides basing and extensive overflight clearances for a multitude of US military aircraft, has been essential to the continued success of Operation Enduring Freedom (OEF). Bahraini military assets have participated in OEF Coalition naval operations including terrorist interdiction efforts, and Bahrain offered a medical unit for OEF duty. The King, Crown Prince, and other senior Bahrani ministers have been outspoken public proponents of the war on terrorism. The Government of Bahrain cooperated closely and effectively on criminal investigations related to the campaign against terrorism. In September, for instance, Bahraini authorities were essential in the transfer to US custody of Mukhtar al-Bakri, a US citizen suspected of terrorist activity.

Equally important, the Bahrain Monetary Authority quickly implemented UN Security Council Resolutions (UNSCR) 1267, 1390, and 1455, as well as 1373, ordering financial institutions to identify and freeze accounts of organizations associated with members of al-Qaida, Usama Bin Ladin, and members of the Taliban that the UNSCR 1267 Sanctions Committee has included on its consolidated list. To date, seven accounts have been identified and frozen. Bahrain has developed financial regulations to ensure that charitable contributions are not channeled to financing terrorists. The Government of Bahrain has been extraordinarily responsive to US Government requests for additional security measures in recent years and continued to give the highest priority to the protection of US lives and property in Bahrain.

Bahrain is a party to five of the 12 international conventions and protocols relating to terrorism.

Egypt

The Egyptian and US Governments continued their close cooperation on a broad range of counterterrorism issues in 2002. The relationship deepened in 2002 as the countries coordinated closely on law enforcement issues and the freezing of assets, consistent with the requirements of UNSCRs 1373, 1267, 1390 and 1455. Egypt also cooperated with the United States in freezing the assets of individuals and organizations designated by the United States pursuant to Executive Order 13224. In law enforcement, the Egyptian Government deepened its information-sharing relationship in terrorist-related investigations. The Government provided immediate information, for example, in the investigation of the shootings on 4 July at Los Angeles airport, which involved an Egyptian national. Its response was critical in determining that the shooting was an individual act, not part of a terrorist conspiracy. The Egyptian Government also provided the name and full identification (numerical identifiers and photo) of a terrorist believed to be in the United States.

The Government of Egypt has continued to be committed to searching and freezing terrorist funds in Egyptian banks. In 2002, the Egyptian parliament passed an anti-money laundering law that strengthens banking regulations and permits the Government more latitude in its campaign to staunch the flow of terrorist funds. The Egyptian Government, both secular and clerical, continued to make public statements supportive of US efforts and indicative of its commitment to the worldwide campaign against terrorism.

In addition to combating global terrorism, Cairo continued to place a high priority on the protection of US citizens and facilities in Egypt. It increased security for US citizens and facilities and for US forces, both stationed in Egypt and transiting the country to the Gulf, by air or through the Suez Canal. Egypt has strengthened its airport security, agreed to stricter aviation-security measures, and granted extensive overflight and canal transit clearances.

Egypt was for many years itself a victim of terrorism. President Mubarak first called for an international conference to combat terrorism in 1986. With US assistance and training, Egypt has effectively combated the internal terrorist/extremist threat. There were no acts of terrorism in Egypt in 2002, either against US citizens, Egyptians, or other nationals. The Government continued a "zero tolerance" policy toward suspected terrorists and extremists.

During 2002, the Government prosecuted 94 members (seven of whom were tried in absentia) of a group dubbed "al-Wa'ad" (the Promise), accused of having supplied arms and financial support to Chechen rebels and HAMAS. On 9 September, the military tribunal sentenced 51 defendants to terms ranging from two to 15 years while acquitting 43. On 20 October, the Government brought 26 members of the Islamic Liberation Party to trial in the supreme state security court. The defendants, who include three Britons, stand accused of joining a banned group, attempting to recruit members for that group, and spreading extremist ideology. The group was banned in Egypt in 1974, following an attempt to overthrow the Government and establish an Islamic caliphate.

The United States deported a member of the Egyptian Islamic Jihad in 2002 for trial in connection with the assassination of President Anwar Sadat. Several other members of Egyptian terrorist organizations were returned to Egypt from abroad. During the summer, the Egyptian Government announced plans to release from prison a large group of al-Gama'a al-Islamiyya (IG) leaders and members, sentenced in the early 1980s. In 1997, the group's leadership in prison declared a cease-fire and halt to all armed operations and acts of violence. In 1999, IG leadership abroad declared their support for the initiative. This year, the IG leadership in prison in Egypt published four pamphlets on the religious basis and legitimacy for ending all violence and armed operations. In the fall, the Government began releasing IG members and leaders who they believe have transformed their ideology and religious beliefs while in prison.

Egypt is a party to nine of the 12 international conventions and protocols relating to terrorism.

Israel, the West Bank, and Gaza Strip

Israel maintained staunch support for US-led counterterrorist operations as terrorist activity in Israel, the West Bank, and Gaza Strip continued at a heightened level in 2002. HAMAS, the Palestine Islamic Jihad (PIJ), and the al-Aqsa Martyrs Brigades, all of which the United States has designated as Foreign Terrorist Organizations and has designated pursuant to Executive Order 13224, were responsible for most of the attacks, which included suicide bombings, shootings, and mortar firings against civilian and military targets. Terrorists killed more than 370 persons—including at least 10 US citizens—compared to fewer than 200 persons killed in 2001.

Israel is a party to eight of the 12 international conventions and protocols relating to terrorism.

Israeli authorities arrested individuals claiming allegiance to al-Qaida, although the group does not appear to have an operational presence in Israel, the West Bank, and the Gaza Strip. Palestinian terrorist groups in these areas publicly distanced themselves from Usama Bin Ladin and appear focused on attacking Israel, versus joining in a fight against the West.

Israel responded to Palestinian terrorism with large-scale military operations. Israeli forces launched incursions into the West Bank and the Gaza Strip, conducted targeted killings of suspected Palestinian terrorists, destroyed the homes of families of suicide bombers, and imposed closures and curfews in Palestinian areas. Israel expelled two family members of Palestinian terrorists from the West Bank to the Gaza Strip in September. Two of Israeli's most extensive operations—Defensive Shield, launched in March, and Determined Path, launched in June—reduced the frequency of Palestinian attacks; continuing attacks, however, show the groups remained potent.

HAMAS was particularly active, carrying out over 50 attacks, including shootings, suicide bombings, and standoff mortar-and-rocket attacks against civilian and military targets. The group was responsible for the most deadly Palestinian terrorist attack of the year—the suicide bombing of a Passover gathering at a Netanya hotel that killed 29 Israelis, including one dual US-Israeli citizen. HAMAS's bombing of a cafeteria on the Hebrew University campus, which killed nine, including five US citizens, demonstrated its willingness to stage operations in areas frequented by Westerners, including US citizens.

The PIJ increased its number of lethal attacks in 2002, staging a car bombing in June that killed 17 Israelis near Megiddo. It carried out similar attacks in or near Afula, Haifa, and Hadera. PIJ terrorists conducted deadly shooting attacks in 2002 as well, including a two-stage ambush in Hebron in late November that killed at least 12 persons, including several security personnel who responded to the initial attack. Syrian officials declined to act on a US request in November to close the PIJ's offices in Damascus.

In March, the US Department of State officially designated the al-Aqsa Martyrs Brigades (al-Aqsa), which emerged in 2000, as a Foreign Terrorist Organization (FTO), and designated it pursuant to Executive Order 13224. Al-Aqsa–linked attacks have killed at least five US citizens. The group conducted numerous shooting attacks and suicide bombings in 2002, some of which employed new techniques. On 27 January, an al-Aqsa suicide bombing that killed one person and injured 50 used a female suicide bomber for the first time. The group claimed responsibility for a shooting attack that killed six Israelis waiting to vote in the Israeli Likud party elections in November. Documents seized by the Israelis and information gleaned from the interrogation of arrested al-Aqsa members indicate that Palestinian Authority (PA) and Fatah members, including Chairman Yasir Arafat, made payments to al-Aqsa members known to have been involved in violence against Israelis.

Payments by Iraq to the families of Palestinian "martyrs" in 2002 were intended to encourage attacks against Israeli targets and garner more support for Iraq among Palestinians. In October, the West Bank leader of the Iraqi-backed Arab Liberation Front admitted under Israeli interrogation to having overseen the transfer and distribution of up to $15 million in Iraqi money to martyrs' families, confirming Palestinian and other press accounts of such transfers.

Jewish extremists raised their profile in 2002. Several Jewish extremists, some with ties to Kach, a designated FTO, were arrested in April and May for plotting to blow up a Palestinian school for girls or a Palestinian hospital in Jerusalem. Jewish extremists were also arrested for inciting a violent clash between Israeli settlers and Israeli security forces in October; extremists also attacked and injured Palestinian agricultural workers, and some US citizens were also the victims in these attacks.

The Palestinian Authority's efforts to thwart terrorist operations were minimal in 2002. Israeli military operations in the West Bank and Gaza Strip degraded a PA security apparatus that was already hobbled by corruption, infighting, and poor leadership. Some personnel in the security services, including several senior officers, have continued to assist terrorist operations. Incidents such as the seizure in January of the Karine-A, a ship carrying weapons that Iran planned to deliver to the PA, further called into question the PA's ability and desire to help prevent terrorist operations. President Bush expressed "disappointment" in Arafat, indicating the intercepted shipment would encourage terrorism. In June, President Bush called for a new Palestinian leadership "not compromised by terror."

Jordan

The Jordanian Government continued to strongly support global counterterrorist efforts while remaining vigilant against the threat of terrorism at home. Jordan was highly responsive to the security needs of US citizens in country and played a critical role in thwarting attempts to exploit Jordanian territory for attacks in Israel.

Jordan aggressively pursued suspected terrorists and successfully prosecuted and convicted many involved in plots against US or Israeli interests. Jordanian authorities, in mid-January 2003, convicted 10 Jordanians of weapons charges but acquitted them of participating in a plot to target US interests in Jordan. Jordan is working closely with US officials to investigate the murder in late October of USAID officer Laurence Foley. In December, Jordanian authorities arrested two men, a Libyan and a Jordanian, who later admitted to carrying out the assassination after receiving money from al-Qaida leader Abu Musab al-Zarqawi. The two have been charged with the murder and remain in Jordanian custody awaiting trial.

Suspected terrorists continued attempts to exploit Jordanian territory to transit weapons to and from groups in neighboring states, or to use Jordanian territory to facilitate terrorist attacks. Jordanian authorities have successfully intercepted such transiting weapons and personnel on virtually all of its borders. In June, Jordan rendered to Lebanese security authorities three Lebanese Hizballah members arrested after allegedly trying to smuggle weapons destined for the West Bank into Jordan. Jordanian authorities in June also reportedly arrested three Jordanian youths suspected of planning to infiltrate into Israel to conduct terrorist attacks. In July, four Syrians were sentenced to prison terms for illegally possessing explosives they intended to transport to the West Bank. In October, Jordan's State Security Court sentenced four individuals to prison terms ranging from five to eight years after convicting them of possessing and attempting to transport machineguns and missiles into the West Bank.

In May, Jordan's State Security Court indicted six unnamed suspects in connection with a bombing in late February of a Jordanian counterterrorism official's vehicle, killing two passersby.

Jordan is a party to seven of the 12 international conventions and protocols relating to terrorism.

Kuwait

Kuwait has continued to support and cooperate with all actions and requests for assistance in the war on terrorism, particularly in the aftermath of the 8 October attack on Failaka Island in which one US Marine was killed and another wounded, and the attack on 21 November that took place on a Kuwaiti highway in which two US soldiers were wounded. These were the only confirmed terrorist incidents among the Gulf Cooperation Council (GCC) nations in 2002. The attacks strengthened the Government's concerns about the activities of extremists within Kuwait. In the immediate aftermath of the October incident, the Government of Kuwait rapidly located and arrested individuals involved (the two shooters were killed during the attack) and continued to respond favorably to all US Government requests in connection with the ongoing investigation and other security threats. Kuwaiti authorities completed their investigations of the 26 persons suspected of involvement in the attack. Twenty-one were released, and five were referred to the public prosecutor. Trials had begun by year's end. A policeman suspected of carrying out the November shooting was arrested immediately after the attack and remains in Kuwaiti custody.

Cooperation has been strong in the area of terrorist financing as well. Following a review of Kuwaiti laws by the Financial Services Assessment Team, the United States is preparing a technical-assistance program for Kuwait. The Government remains eager to receive formal proposals for training and has indicated a willingness to support such efforts. The Government of Kuwait also established a new entity within the Ministry of Social Affairs and Labor to monitor Islamic charities.

Kuwait is a party to seven of the 12 international conventions and protocols relating to terrorism.

Lebanon

Despite its counterterrorism efforts in 2002, Lebanon experienced an increase in terrorist attacks by Sunni extremist and terrorist groups. Explosions at several US-franchise restaurants and a spike of cross-border attacks into Israel in March and April indicated worsening security conditions. Large demonstrations at the US Embassy during April against US policy in the Middle East highlighted rising public anger. The murder of a US missionary in Sidon on 21 November may not have been entirely politically motivated, but it clearly demonstrated the danger US citizens face in Lebanon. Prime Minister Hariri condemned the murder, and Lebanese law-enforcement officials launched a full investigation of the crime.

In 2002, the Lebanese Government demonstrated greater efforts against Sunni terrorist groups such as Asbat al-Ansar, which was outlawed. The United States has designated Asbat al-Ansar a Foreign Terrorist Organization and has designated it pursuant to Executive Order 13224. A July confrontation at the Ayn al-Hilwah Palestinian refugee camp—the center of Asbat's activities—resulted in the surrender of a Sunni extremist who had fled into the camp after killing three Lebanese military personnel in Sidon. The Lebanese Armed Forces, however, did not itself enter the camp, and Palestinian refugee camps, much of the Beka'a Valley, southern Beirut, and the southern border area remain effectively outside the Government's control. In October, the judiciary arrested three men (two Lebanese and one Saudi) and indicted 18 others *in absentia* on charges of preparing to carry out terrorist attacks and forging documents and passports. The detainees, because of their al-Qaida connections, will be tried in a military tribunal.

Lebanese efforts against Sunni extremists, including al-Qaida, stand in contrast to its continuing unwillingness to condemn as terrorists several organizations that maintain a presence in Lebanon: Hizballah, the Palestine Islamic Jihad (PIJ), the Popular Front for the Liberation of Palestine-General Command (PFLP-GC), the Abu Nidal organization (ANO), and the Islamic Resistance Movement (HAMAS). The Lebanese Government has long considered these organizations that target Israel to be legitimate resistance groups and has permitted them to establish offices in Beirut. The Government refused to freeze the assets of Hizballah or close down the offices of rejectionist Palestinian organizations. It also continued to reject the US Government's position that Hizballah has a global reach, instead concentrating on its political wing and asserting it to be a local, indigenous organization integral to Lebanese society and politics. Syrian and Iranian support for Hizballah activities in the south, as well as training and assistance to Palestinian rejectionist groups in Lebanon, help permit terrorist elements to flourish. On 12 March, infiltrators from Lebanon killed six Israelis in Shelomi, Israel, and Hizballah-Palestinian rejectionist groups carried out several cross-border attacks—including firing Katyusha rockets—into Israel.

The Lebanese Government acknowledges the UN list of terrorist groups designated pursuant to UN Security Council Resolutions 1267 and 1390. It does not, however, acknowledge the terrorist groups designated only by the US Government and will take no action against these groups. Constitutional provisions prohibit the extradition of any Lebanese national to a third country. Lebanese authorities maintain that the Government's provision of amnesty to Lebanese involved in acts of violence during the civil war prevents them from prosecuting many cases of interest to the United States, including the 1985 hijacking of TWA 847 and the murder associated with it, and the abduction, torture, and murder of US hostages from 1984 to 1991. US courts have brought indictments against Hizballah operatives responsible for a number of those crimes, and some of these defendants remain prominent in the organization.

The Lebanese Government has insisted that Imad Mugniyah—wanted in connection with the TWA hijacking and other terrorist acts, and placed on the FBI's list of most-wanted terrorists in 2001—is no longer present in Lebanon. The Government's legal system has also failed to hold a hearing on the prosecutor's appeal in the case of Tawfiz Muhammad Farroukh, who, despite the evidence against him, had been found not guilty of murder for his role in the killings of US Ambassador Francis Meloy and two others in 1976.

The Financial Action Task Force recognized Lebanon's amendments to its penal code and administrative efforts against money laundering in June when it dropped Lebanon from the list of countries deemed uncooperative. The Government of Lebanon also offered cooperation with the US Government on the investigation of September 11 hijacker Ziad Jarah, a Lebanese national.

Lebanon is a party to 10 of the 12 international conventions and protocols relating to terrorism.

Morocco

The Moroccan Government has been quite helpful in the war on terror. King Muhammad VI has unambiguously condemned those who espouse or conduct terrorism and has worked to keep Rabat firmly on the side of the United States against extremists. Morocco is a party to 10 of the 12 international conventions and protocols relating to terrorism.

Domestically, the Moroccan Government's solid record of vigilance against terrorist activity and intolerance for the perpetrators of terrorism remained uninterrupted in 2002. In order to fight terrorism better, the Government began to draft new, stronger laws in the financial and law-enforcement sectors. In addition, Moroccan authorities in 2002 detained several individuals suspected of belonging to an al-Qaida cell. Moroccan authorities say the individuals—some Saudi, some Moroccan—were involved in a plot to attack Western shipping interests in the Straits of Gibraltar. The Moroccan Government put the suspected terrorists on trial.

Oman

Oman continued to provide public and private statements of support for the war on terrorism in 2002 and has been responsive to all Coalition requests for military and/or civilian support. Omani financial authorities have worked closely with the Coalition to prevent financing of terrorism and have shown keen interest in pursuing cases of particular interest to US law enforcement. In 2002, Oman became a party to the 1991 Convention on the Marking of Plastic Explosives for the Purpose of Detection, making it a party to nine of 12 antiterrorism treaties. It is reviewing the three remaining conventions. There were no incidents of terrorist activity in Oman in 2002.

Qatar

Qatar's support for the United States after the attacks of September 11, 2001 continued throughout 2002. Qatar provides substantial ongoing support for Operation Enduring Freedom. It publicly and repeatedly condemned terrorism, most recently on the occasion of the attack in Bali. The Government took steps to improve border security and has supported US and international efforts to combat terrorist financing. It independently strengthened laws and regulations to prevent money laundering. Both in coordination with the United States and at its own initiative, Qatari law-enforcement authorities detained and investigated individuals suspected of supporting terrorist networks. The Government of Qatar also provided additional security for US installations in response to threat warnings, as requested.

Qatar is a party to five of the 12 international conventions and protocols relating to terrorism.

Saudi Arabia

Saudi Arabia over the past year has continued to provide support for the war on terror. Riyadh has supported Operation Enduring Freedom, has contributed to the stabilization of the situation in Afghanistan through significant donations and has worked as one of the co-chairs of the Afghanistan Reconstruction Steering Committee, and has worked to enhance security at US installations to match the heightened threat level throughout the Arabian Peninsula. Many within the Government of Saudi Arabia view the events of September 11 as a direct attack against the Kingdom and US-Saudi relations.

Riyadh has expanded its cooperation in the war on terror in some areas, such as sharing threat information and details of ongoing investigations. As a first step in dealing with terrorism financing, the Saudi Government has undertaken a review of its charitable organizations and measures to regulate their operations better, including the adoption of new financial-control mechanisms. In September, the Saudi Interior Minister announced the establishment of the Saudi Higher Authority for Religion and Charity Work to ensure that humanitarian assistance was channeled to appropriate persons and purposes. In October, the Crown Prince brought together the heads of Saudi Arabia's major charities and called for greater responsibility and transparency in their work. The Government is currently in the process of implementing these reforms. It is too soon to tell whether these reforms are preventing terrorists from exploiting these funds.

There were no major successful terrorist attacks in the Kingdom in 2002. Saudi authorities arrested a Sudanese and five Saudis for firing a missile at a US military aircraft taking off from a Saudi airbase, and they continued to investigate the incident. Riyadh was investigating a string of recent car bombings in the Kingdom but maintained that no firm ties to terrorism had been established. In late June, a British national died in a car-bomb explosion in Riyadh. Nine days later, Saudi police removed an explosive device from the car of a US resident in Riyadh. In September, a German national died in another similar car explosion in Riyadh. In addition to investigations of recent incidents, Saudi authorities continued to investigate past terrorist attacks, including the 1996 bombing of the Khubar Towers in which 19 US servicemen died.

Saudi Arabia is a party to six of the 12 international conventions and protocols relating to terrorism.

Tunisia

The Tunisian Government has supported the international Coalition against terrorism and has responded to requests from the US Government for assistance in blocking financial assets and providing information on extremists. In October, the United States blocked the assets of the Tunisian Combatant Group under Executive Order 13224, at the same time France proposed adding the group to the UN Security Council Resolution 1267 Sanctions Committee's consolidated list. Tunisian President Zine el-Abidine Ben Ali has forcefully condemned terrorist activities and reiterated his country's determination to combat violence and extremism. Tunisia is now a full party to 11 of the 12 existing UN antiterrorism conventions; it has yet to accede to the Convention on the Physical Protection of Nuclear Material agreed to in October 1979.

The Tunisian Government's active stance against terrorism was reinforced by the bombing attack against the El-Ghriba synagogue on the Tunisian island of Djerba on 11 April, which claimed more than 20 lives. In the wake of this attack, the Tunisian Government continued to bring judicial, law-enforcement, and military resources to bear against terrorist suspects. Tunisian authorities have detained an individual in connection with the attack; the suspect is awaiting trial. Earlier in 2002, Tunisian authorities convicted 34 persons—31 *in absentia*—of belonging to Al-Jamaa wal Sunnah, a terrorist organization linked to al-Qaida. The Government says the accused were involved in recruiting European-based Tunisians to fight in Chechnya, Bosnia, and Afghanistan. The Tunisian Government also continued to play a role in countering threats in the region. After signing a 2001 agreement with the Algerian Government to strengthen border security, Tunisia continued to respond quickly to counter possible border incursions from Islamic militants in Algeria.

Tunisia is a party to 10 of the 12 international conventions and protocols relating to terrorism.

United Arab Emirates

In 2002, the United Arab Emirates continued to provide considerable assistance and cooperation in the war on terrorism. In November, UAE authorities arrested and subsequently turned over to US authorities Abdul Raheem Al-Nashiri, the head of al-Qaida operations in the Arabian Gulf and the mastermind of the October 2000 attack on the USS Cole in Aden, Yemen. UAE authorities, in the course of their investigation into Al-Nashiri's activities, discovered that he had been planning terrorist operations against major economic targets in the UAE that would have resulted in massive civilian casualties.

In suppressing terrorist financing, the UAE played a critical role in the continuing investigation into the September 11 attacks and provided literally thousands of pages of financial documents pertaining to the movement of terrorist funds. The UAE has created a stronger legal and regulatory framework to deter abuse of UAE financial markets through the passage in January of a comprehensive law criminalizing money laundering, including terrorist money laundering and tightened reporting requirements and oversight. Cooperation across the board—from the financial realm through to security and intelligence—has been strong and sustained.

The UAE in 2002 indicated its commitment to ratifying the international conventions and protocols relating to terrorism to which it is not yet a party and is working toward that goal. (In early 2003, the UAE became a party to the 1973 Convention on the Prevention and Punishment of Crimes against Internationally Protected Persons, including Diplomatic Agents.) The UAE is now a party to six of the 12 international conventions and protocols relating to terrorism. The Government is in the process of drafting domestic legislation to bring the UAE's counterterrorism legislation fully into compliance with the relevant UN Security Council resolutions. In June 2002, the United States sponsored the UAE's financial-intelligence unit (FIU) for membership in the prestigious Egmont Group, an informal association founded in 1995 to provide support for the FIUs of different nations. The UAE thus became the first Middle Eastern country to join this organization.

The UAE in May hosted a groundbreaking international conference to draw attention to the need for concerted action on the hawala informal money-transfer system—a remittance system handling billions of dollars annually but whose informal nature and lack of reporting requirements renders it vulnerable to abuse by terrorists. In November, the UAE began implementing over-sight regulations for the local hawala market.

Yemen

The Government of Yemen has continued a broad counterterrorism campaign against al-Qaida and cooperated with the United States in eliminating Abu Ali al-Harithi, al-Qaida's senior leader in Yemen, as cited by President Bush in his State of the Union Address. The Yemeni Government continued to express public support for the international fight against terror throughout 2002. During the year, Yemen enhanced intelligence, military, and law-enforcement cooperation with the United States and, during Vice President Cheney's visit to Sanaa in March, President Salih underscored Yemen's determination to be an active counterterrorism partner. Senior US officials acknowledged that their Yemeni counterparts face challenges in the counterterrorism arena and welcomed President Salih's commitment but made clear that any counterterrorism cooperation will be judged on its continuing results.

There was very close and productive law-enforcement cooperation between Yemeni and US law-enforcement authorities throughout the year. In cooperation with the US Government, Yemen has been actively preparing trials for the majority of those accused of the 12 October 2000 attack on the USS Cole. In addition, Yemeni counterparts cooperated with US law-enforcement elements in several investigations, including that of an explosion in an al-Qaida safehouse in Sanaa on 9 August, analysis of evidence after a raid on 21 September by Yemeni security forces of another al-Qaida location in a northern suburb of Sanaa, joint investigation with Yemeni and French law-enforcement agents of the terrorist attack on 6 October against the French oil tanker Limburg near the Yemeni port of Mukalla, and investigation of suspected al-Qaida involvement in a shooting on 3 November at a Yemen Hunt helicopter shortly after takeoff from Sanaa airport.

As in 2001, the Yemeni Government arrested suspected terrorists and pledged to neutralize key al-Qaida nodes in the country. Political will against terrorism has also been augmented by President Salih's public campaign against terrorism that includes speeches, meetings with local political leaders, and articles in national newspapers. Since September 11, 2001, Yemen has enhanced previously lax security at its borders, tightened its visa procedures, installed the Terrorist Interdiction Program at most border crossings, and prevented potential terrorists from traveling to Afghanistan. Authorities have continued to carefully monitor travelers returning from abroad and have cracked down on foreigners who were residing in the country illegally or were suspected of engaging in terrorist activities. The Government integrated formerly autonomous private religious schools—many of which were propagating extremism—into the national educational system and tightened requirements for visiting foreign students.

Numerous threats against US personnel and facilities in Yemen were reported in 2002. Yemeni security services, however, provided extensive security protection for official US diplomatic and business interests in the country. The Yemeni Government's attitude has been that an attack against US interests would also be an attack against Yemen's interests.

Several terrorist organizations maintained a presence in Yemen throughout 2002. HAMAS and the Palestine Islamic Jihad continued to be recognized as legal organizations and maintained offices in Yemen but did not engage in terrorist activities there. Other international terrorist groups that had an illegal presence in Yemen included the Egyptian Islamic Jihad, al-Gama'a al-Islamiyya, and al-Qaida. Similarly, members of indigenous terrorist groups such as the Aden Abuyan Islamic Army may continue to be active in Yemen.

Yemen is a party to eight of the 12 international terrorist conventions and protocols relating to terrorism.

Western Hemisphere Overview

When compared to other regions of the world, the Western Hemisphere generally does not attract attention as a "hot zone" in the war on terror. Terrorism in the region was not born on 11 September 2001, however; Latin American countries have struggled with domestic sources of terrorism for decades. International terrorist groups, moreover, have not hesitated to make Latin America a battleground to advance their causes elsewhere. The bombings of the Israeli Embassy in Buenos Aires in 1992 and the Argentine-Jewish Cultural Center in 1994 are two well-known examples. More recent international terrorist attacks in Bali, Indonesia, and Mombasa, Kenya, in 2002 demonstrate that no region of the world —and no type of target—is beyond the reach or strategic interest of international terrorist organizations.

Recognizing this threat and the impact of terrorism on their economic and social development, the vast majority of countries across the Americas and the Caribbean have given strong support to the international Coalition against terrorism. In June, at the OAS General Assembly in Barbados, member states adopted and opened for signature the Inter-American Convention Against Terrorism—a direct response to the 11 September 2001 terrorist attacks on the United States and the first international treaty against terrorism adopted since the attacks. The Convention, a binding legal instrument which is consistent with, and builds upon, previous UN conventions and protocols relating to terrorism and UN Security Council Resolution 1373, will improve regional cooperation in the fight against terrorism through exchanges of information, experience and training, technical cooperation, and mutual legal assistance. The Convention will enter into force when six states have deposited their instruments of ratification. All OAS member states but one have signed (Dominica is the exception); Canada became the first state to ratify in late 2002. President Bush transmitted the Convention to the Senate for its advice and consent to ratification in November.

Spurred by the Convention and the September 11 attacks, many countries in the Hemisphere have sought to shore up legislative tools to outlaw terrorism, discourage terrorist financing, and make their territory as unattractive as possible to terrorists fleeing from other regions who might seek safehaven in the hemisphere. A number of countries, however, remain engaged in deep internal debate over the scope of new antiterrorism bills that would grant governments broader powers necessary to prosecute the war on terror. An ongoing OAS Legislative Action Against Terrorism project with Central American parliaments, for example, is aimed specifically at helping legislatures draft antiterrorism legislation and ratify the Inter-American Convention Against Terrorism.

The Western Hemisphere has created a model regional counterterrorism institution in its Inter-American Committee Against Terrorism (known by its Spanish acronym CICTE). CICTE is a body of the OAS that was created in 1998. Since 11 September 2001, it has been reinvigorated as an effective coordinating body for OAS member states on all counterterrorism issues—but with a primary focus on information sharing, training, and strengthening of financial and border controls. Under US chairmanship and Argentine vice-chairmanship, CICTE established a full-time Secretariat in 2002 that is funded by voluntary donations from OAS member states.

(At its Third Regular Session in El Salvador in early 2003, CICTE member states adopted a strong "Declaration of San Salvador Against Terrorism" and made recommendations on counterterrorism initiatives for adoption by the Special Conference on Hemispheric Security, to be held May 2003. The declaration and recommendations both call for increased cooperation to prevent and combat terrorism and recognize the emerging threats posed to the Hemisphere by international terrorist groups and attacks on cyber security.)

The OAS in 2002 also played an important role in the investigation of an illicit diversion in late 2001 of more than 3,000 AK-47 rifles and ammunition from Nicaraguan police and army stocks to the United Self-Defense Forces of Colombia (AUC), which the United States has designated as a Foreign Terrorist Organization and has designated pursuant to Executive Order 13224 on terrorist financing. (The OAS-commissioned report, released in January 2003, contained a detailed analysis of the case along with a series of recommendations for improving the existing inter-American, arms-control regime. The Government of Nicaragua quickly expressed its intention to follow up on the report and to strengthen its arms-controls and export procedures.)

Domestic terrorist groups have continued to ravage Colombia and, to a lesser extent, Peru. The Colombian Government in February under former President Pastrana cut off long-running peace talks with the Revolutionary Armed Forces of Colombia (FARC), which the United States has designated a Foreign Terrorist Organization, after a series of provocative actions, including kidnapping of a Colombian senator. The FARC intensified its campaign throughout the year and steadily moved its attacks from the countryside to the cities. On 7 August, new Colombian President Alvaro Uribe was inaugurated amid an errant FARC mortar attack that killed 21 residents of a poor Bogota neighborhood. Some elements of the AUC disbanded and reconstituted themselves in an effort to seek political legitimacy, but their ties to narcotrafficking and human rights abuses persist. In December, the AUC declared a unilateral cease-fire and sought peace negotiations with the Government. The National Liberation Army—like the FARC—continued to pursue its favorite terrorist methods of kidnapping and infrastructure bombing. All three organizations are linked to narcotrafficking.

In Peru, a resilient Shining Path is suspected of carrying out the 20 March car bombing at a shopping center across from the US Embassy, two days before a state visit by President Bush. Ten Peruvians died in the attack, including security personnel protecting the Embassy.

At year's end, there was no confirmed, credible information of an established al-Qaida presence in Latin America. Terrorist fundraising continued to be a concern throughout the region, however. Activities of suspected Hizballah and HAMAS financiers in the Triborder area (Argentina, Brazil, and Paraguay) led those three countries to take determined and cooperative action during 2002 to investigate and disrupt illicit financial activities. Argentina, Brazil, and Paraguay also invited the United States to join a new "Three Plus One" counterterrorism consultative and cooperation mechanism to analyze and combat any terrorist-related threats in the Triborder. The mechanism is an excellent example of terrorism prevention and regional foresight.

Canada and Mexico worked closely with the United States to secure their common borders and to implement the comprehensive bilateral border accords (signed in December 2001 and March 2002, respectively). The accords aim to ensure national border security while facilitating the free and rapid flow of legitimate travel and commerce.

[*Eds. Note*: Cuba, which has been designated as a state sponsor of terrorism, is discussed in Part 1 in the section on "State Sponsorship of Terrorism."]

Bolivia

The Bolivian Government demonstrated its commitment to combating terrorism in 2002. Since the September 11 attacks, Bolivia has become a party to nine international conventions and protocols relating to terrorism, making it a party to all 12. On 3 June, Bolivia signed the new Inter-American Convention Against Terrorism, although it has not yet ratified the treaty. Throughout the year, Bolivia's financial investigations unit cooperated with the US Embassy in sharing information about possible terrorist-linked financial transactions and preventing the abuse of Bolivian financial institutions by terrorists.

Bolivia's new government—inaugurated on 6 August 2002—has maintained its predecessor's policy of forcibly eradicating illegal coca plants. This policy ensures that Bolivia does not revert to its former status as a key source of coca for cocaine and, through this connection, bolster the terrorist organizations that thrive on the drug trade.

There were no significant acts of terrorism in Bolivia in 2002. Illegal coca growers (*cocaleros*) are thought to be responsible for the deaths of five military and police in 2002, although no individuals have been charged with the crimes. Legal proceedings continued against the alleged perpetrators of a car-bomb explosion near the regional headquarters of the Bolivian National Police in Santa Cruz in December 2001. Some of the alleged perpetrators in custody are former members of the Bolivian national police, and the bombing itself appeared to have been related to local criminal activity.

Chile

The Chilean Government is a consistent and active supporter of US counterterrorism efforts and has taken an active interest in the activities of Islamic extremists connected to the Triborder area of Argentina, Brazil, and Paraguay. In addition, the Chilean Government is working to enact new counterterrorism legislation and strengthen current laws. Chile is a party to 11 of the 12 international conventions and protocols relating to terrorism. The Chilean Senate is considering a bill to create a new Financial Intelligence Unit and criminalize money laundering for arms trafficking and terrorist financing. Chilean officials have sought advice from the US Embassy on how to improve the money-laundering bill and have participated in training courses to improve financial investigations.

The Chilean Government also has contracted an independent consulting firm to author a study on how US law-enforcement agencies have implemented new counterterrorism legislation. Although the Chilean Government has cooperated in efforts to eliminate terrorist financing, it is limited in its ability to investigate and prosecute suspect individuals. Currently, Chilean money-laundering legislation does not cover terrorist activity, so efforts to freeze terrorist funds are hindered by a lack of legal authority.

There were no acts of international terrorism in Chile in 2002, but there were significant developments in three counterterrorism investigations begun in 2001. In late September 2001, the US Embassy had received a letter bomb that local police successfully destroyed in a controlled demolition, and a Santiago doctor's office received an anthrax-tainted letter. The Chilean Government also opened an investigation into the activities in the northern port city of Iquique of Brazil-based Lebanese businessman Assad Ahmad Barakat—suspected of opening two businesses as cover to move money clandestinely to Lebanese Hizballah.

In September 2002, a Chilean judge sentenced two individuals—Lenin Guardia and Humberto Lopez—to 10 years and 300 days in prison for sending the letter bomb to the US Embassy and another to a prominent Chilean attorney. The motivation of Guardia, the professed ringleader, was to create fear in order to generate business for his security-consulting firm.

Another Chilean judge, with the assistance of the FBI, determined the anthrax letter sent in November 2001 to Dr. Antonio Bafi Pacheco was not related to the anthrax cases in the United States and was contaminated locally. This investigation continues.

The investigation into Assad Ahmad Barakat's business in Chile has not led to new information. Barakat was arrested in Brazil in June 2002, and the Brazilian Supreme Court ordered his extradition to Paraguay in December. His lawyers have applied for refugee status in Brazil, and Barakat will remain in detention in Brazil while his refugee case is considered. Barakat no longer has significant holdings in Chile, and his partners in Saleh Trading Limited, located in the northern duty-free port of Iquique, severed ties with him in 2002. Assad and his brother still own an import-export business in Iquique, but according to the Chilean Government, it has not been active.

In August and September, Chilean authorities discovered several small arms caches throughout Santiago and other cities as well as the remnants of explosive material at two communications transmission towers outside Santiago. The weapons and explosives are believed to belong to the largely defunct terrorist group Manual Rodriguez Patriotic Front (FPMR). Law-enforcement agents believe the weapons were smuggled into Chile in the 1980s, at the height of FPMR's activity, but some view the caches as evidence of an FPMR comeback.

Chile continues to lead other South American nations in its implementation of aviation security. The Government has implemented FAA security regulations ahead of schedule, including the installation of reinforced cockpit doors and the transfer of responsibility for inspecting unaccompanied baggage to the Government.

Colombia

Colombia's three terrorist organizations—the Revolutionary Armed Forces of Colombia (FARC), National Liberation Army (ELN), and United Self-Defense Forces of Colombia (AUC)—were responsible for some 3,500 murders in 2002. By February, President Pastrana had broken off three-year-old peace talks—a cornerstone of his presidency—with Colombia's largest terrorist organization, the 16,000-member FARC. That month, the group's abduction of a Colombian Senator during an airliner hijacking proved to be the incident that led to the collapse of the discussions. In addition to ending the dialogue, Pastrana also terminated the group's *despeje*, or demilitarized zone, where the FARC had been allowed to exist without government interference during the deliberations.

The inauguration of President Alvaro Uribe on 7 August 2002 set the stage for an intensified war on domestic terrorism. The FARC carried out errant mortar attacks on a military facility and the Presidential Palace—with heads of state and high-level representatives from many nations in attendance—resulting in the deaths of 21 residents of a poor Bogota neighborhood near the Palace. President Uribe has proposed pension and labor reforms and has imposed a government austerity program, as well as a one-time "wealth tax," to improve Bogota's fiscal ability to prosecute its war on terrorism. Bogota's goal is to increase government defense spending from 3.2 percent of gross domestic product to more than five percent. Colombia is party to four of the 12 international conventions and protocols relating to terrorism.

In 2002, as in years past, Colombia endured more kidnappings (roughly 3,000) than any other country in the world. Ransom payments and extortion fees demanded by the primary perpetrators of kidnapping—the FARC and ELN—continued to hobble the Colombian economy and limit investor confidence. Since 1980, the FARC has murdered at least 10 US citizens, and three New Tribes Missionaries abducted by the FARC in 1993 remain unaccounted for.

Throughout 2002, Colombia was highly cooperative in blocking terrorist assets. Bogota created the Financial Information and Analysis Unit, similar in function to the US Financial Crimes Enforcement Unit. Bogota also has been very responsive to US requests for extradition. As of 6 December, Colombia had extradited 29 Colombian citizens to the United States during 2002, with 26 additional cases pending. Of the six FARC members indicted for the capture and killing in 1999 of three US peace activists, one has been apprehended. Three other FARC members not included in the original indictment were arrested in November 2002 in connection with the murders. The FARC and the AUC continued their practice of massacring one another's alleged supporters, especially in areas where they were competing for narcotics-trafficking corridors and prime coca-growing terrain. FARC and ELN attacks on oil pipelines and other infrastructure vital to the Colombian economy continued as well, although at a reduced level.

As in past years, the on-again, off-again peace talks between Bogota and the ELN did not lead to substantive breakthroughs. The AUC disbanded itself and subsequently reorganized during 2002. It continued to press for political recognition by the Colombian Government and, as of 1 December, began a unilateral cease-fire that included most of the elements that fall under the AUC's umbrella.

Ecuador

Although Ecuador has generally supported US counterterrorism initiatives, the Government's weak financial controls, inadequately trained security personnel, and widespread document fraud limit its counterterrorism efforts. Quito signed the Inter-American Convention Against Terrorism but has not yet ratified it. Ecuador is party to seven of the 12 international conventions and protocols relating to terrorism.

Ecuadorian security forces worked to reduce the smuggling of arms destined for Colombian terrorist groups and limited travel at a key border crossing to daytime hours. Nevertheless, armed violence on the Colombian side of the border contributed to increased lawlessness in Ecuador's northern provinces.

In the autumn there were two bombings in Guayaquil, possibly related to Ecuador's presidential elections, while thousands of protesters traveled to Quito for the Free Trade Area of the Americas Ministerial in October. Several police and demonstrators were shot in the protests and the police dispersed tear gas.

Peru

Major actions taken by the Peruvian Government during 2002 against terrorism included attempts to strengthen its counterterrorism laws. In June, Lima passed a law that facilitates prosecution for money laundering related to terrorism and mandates the establishment of a financial intelligence unit (FIU). Implementing regulations for the FIU were issued on 31 October, but Lima has provided only token funding for 2003. The Congressional Defense Committee has been reviewing a draft antiterrorism law designed to strengthen law-enforcement agencies, simplify judicial procedures in terrorism cases, increase prison sentences for terrorists, and ensure that Peruvian antiterrorism legislation conforms to international norms. The executive branch also has proposed a draft law that would change the formula for reducing sentences of terrorists from one day off for two days of good behavior to one day off for five days of good behavior.

Peru has aggressively prosecuted terrorist suspects. The Peruvian National Police reported that 199 suspected terrorists were arrested between January and mid-November. These cases and those involving common crimes, however, can remain in the judicial system for years before being resolved. Some 67 percent of inmates held in prisons have not been sentenced. In January, President Toledo directly addressed the issue of long imprisonment for individuals wrongfully held by publicly apologizing to them. A total of 760 persons have been pardoned and released since 1996 after it was determined that they had been accused unjustly of terrorism. Another 1,664 cases are pending review.

In the most significant terrorist act in Peru in 2002, Sendero Luminoso (SL), or Shining Path, is suspected of being responsible for the bombing on 20 March across the street from the US Embassy that killed 10 persons. Peruvian authorities have so far arrested eight suspected SL members for alleged complicity in the bombing. They were being held pending charges, which could take up to one year. SL's involvement in the illegal narcotics business in Peru is noticeably growing, providing the terrorists with a greater source of funding with which to conduct operations. SL is believed to have conducted 119 terrorist acts in 2002 including roadblocks, harassment of security forces, and raids of towns and villages.

Peru is a party to all 12 of the conventions and protocols relating to terrorism.

Triborder Area (Argentina, Brazil, and Paraguay)

The Triborder area (TBA)—where Argentina, Brazil, and Paraguay converge—has long been characterized as a regional hub for Hizballah and HAMAS fundraising activities, but it is also used for arms and drug trafficking, contraband smuggling, document and currency fraud, money laundering, and the manufacture and movement of pirated goods. Although there were numerous media reports in 2002 of an al-Qaida presence in the TBA, these reports remained uncorroborated by intelligence and law-enforcement officials.

In December, a high-level interagency delegation from the United States attended a special meeting in Buenos Aires of the Tripartite Commission of the Triple Frontier, a security mechanism established by the three TBA countries in 1998. This "Three Plus One" meeting (the three TBA countries plus the United States) is intended to serve as a continuing forum of counterterrorism cooperation and prevention among all four countries. At the conclusion of the December talks, the four countries agreed to establish a permanent working group to examine specific counterterrorism issues affecting the four countries. The first issue the working group will tackle in 2003 is that of terrorist fundraising on behalf of Hizballah and HAMAS. Experts from the "Three Plus One" countries will share available information on the problem, draw conclusions, and cooperate to reinforce existing countermeasures.

Host of the December meeting on the Triborder area and a past target of international terrorism, the Government of **Argentina** demonstrated its continuing strong support for the global war on terrorism throughout 2002. Argentina cooperated closely in all significant international counterterrorism efforts within the United Nations and the Organization of American States (OAS), where it was vice-chair of the Inter-American Committee Against Terrorism; the United States was chair. The Argentine Government was instrumental in promoting improved coordination with its neighbors (Brazil, Paraguay, Uruguay, Bolivia, and Chile) in strengthening security and countering terrorist-support networks in the Triborder area. The Government of Argentina has been particularly cooperative in responding to requests related to blocking the financial assets of terrorists. Argentina is a party to eight of the 12 conventions and protocols relating to terrorism.

In 2002, Argentina reiterated its offer—initially made shortly after the September 11 attacks—of material support for UN-mandated Coalition peacekeeping operations in Afghanistan or elsewhere, if needed.

Although there were no acts of international terrorism in Argentina in 2002, investigations into the 1992 bombing of the Israeli Embassy and the 1994 bombing of the Argentina-Israeli Community Center (AMIA) continued. The trials of 20 suspects in the AMIA bombing—of whom 15 are former police officers—were expected to continue well into 2003.

Since 11 September 2001, Argentina has made no significant progress in enacting new antiterrorism laws that would facilitate the investigation and prosecution of terrorists—largely because past abuses by military regimes have limited the degree to which the public will accept an enhancement of the Government's police powers. In January, the Government created a new office within the Foreign Ministry to coordinate action and policy on international counterterrorism issues, however. In October, Argentina also established a new Financial Intelligence Unit to investigate money laundering and terrorist finance-related crimes.

The Government of **Brazil** extended practical, effective support to US counterterrorism efforts in 2002. Authorities have been cooperative, following up on leads provided by the US Government on terrorist suspects.

A Sao Paulo judge sentenced three Chileans, two Colombians, and one Argentine to 16 years in prison for kidnapping a Brazilian advertising executive. A well-known terrorist and former high-ranking member of the largely defunct Manuel Rodriquez Patriotic Front (Chile), Mauricio Hernandez Norambuena, was among those sentenced.

The Brazilian Federal Police in 2002 arrested individuals with alleged ties to terrorist groups. In April, police arrested Egyptian Mohammed Ali Aboul-Ezz al-Mahdi Ibrahim Soliman (a.k.a. Suleiman), in the Triborder city of Foz do Iguazu. Soliman was arrested on the basis of an Egyptian Government extradition request for his alleged involvement in the 1997 al-Gama'a al-Islamiyya (Islamic Group, IG) attack on tourists in Luxor, Egypt, but the Brazilian Supreme Court released him on 11 September due to insufficient evidence to extradite. On 14 September, another IG suspect, Hesham al-Tarabili was arrested in Brazil at Egypt's request in connection with the Luxor attack.

In another case, authorities in June arrested Assad Ahmad Barakat as a result of an extradition request from Paraguay on charges of tax evasion and criminal association. Barakat is a naturalized Paraguayan of Lebanese origin who had lived in the Triborder area for approximately seven years and had become notorious for allegedly moving millions of dollars to Lebanese Hizballah. The Brazilian Supreme Court on 19 December approved the extradition request. At year's end, Barakat was still in Brazilian custody and applying for refugee status in Brazil.

In January, former President Fernando Cardoso proposed a revision of Brazil's antiterrorism laws that would define terrorism more precisely and impose stricter punishment for those involved in terrorist acts. Brazil became a party to the International Convention for the Suppression of Terrorist Bombings in 2002, making it party to nine of the 12 international conventions and protocols relating to terrorism. Legislation also was pending to allow wiretaps for court-approved investigations and to become a party to the 1999 International Convention for the Suppression of the Financing of Terrorism. At year's end, neither piece of legislation had yet been submitted for Congressional approval. The Brazilian Government is willing and able to monitor financial operations domestically.

Paraguay continued to be an active partner in the war on terror in 2002. Paraguayan authorities have taken numerous steps to disrupt illicit networks that supply substantial funds to Middle East terrorist groups. Authorities carried out two raids on suspected financial terror cells and pursued the extradition from Brazil of local Lebanese Hizballah leader Assad Ahmad Barakat.

Paraguay became a party to the Montreal Protocol in 2002, making it now a party to six of the 12 international conventions and protocols relating to terrorism. Paraguay has diligently responded to requests to block the assets of individuals or organizations designated by the United States, included on the UN Security Council Resolution 1267 Sanctions Committee's consolidated list, or designated by the European Union as terrorists or affiliates.

During 2002, the United States provided technical assistance to help the Government of Paraguay assess vulnerabilities in its financial system and to plan appropriate policy remedies.

Paraguayan authorities arrested Hizballah fundraiser Sobhi Fayad—an associate of Barakat—after he violated the terms of his conditional release from detention while awaiting trial. Because Paraguay's antiterrorism legislation still has not been passed—due to concerns of possible abuses of the law by authorities—Fayad had been imprisoned for nearly 10 months on charges of tax evasion and criminal association. He subsequently was convicted and sentenced to six-and-a-half years in prison.

During the year, authorities took legal action against persons and organizations in the Triborder area involved in illicit activities in an attempt to disrupt the ability of sympathizers to raise funds for terrorists. For example, Paraguay's counterterrorism Secretariat (SEPRINTE) on 27 June arrested suspected Sunni extremist Ali Nizar Dahroug, nephew of former Triborder shopkeeper and suspected al-Qaida associate Muhammad Dahroug Dahroug. Police seized counterfeit goods and receipts documenting wire transfers of large sums of money to persons in the United States and the Middle East, some payable to Muhammad Dahroug Dahroug in Lebanon.

On 25 July, SEPRINTE raided the Ciudad del Este office and apartment of alleged money launderer Fajkumar Naraindas Sabnani, who is allegedly connected to Hizballah. Police found letters detailing the sale of military assault rifles and other military weapons, receipts for large wire transfers, and what appeared to be bomb-making materials. Although police arrested three employees of Sabnani, he remained in Hong Kong.

Officials also have increased security at Asuncion airport. In November, immigration officials detained a self-proclaimed supporter of Usama Bin Ladin en route to the United States, and airline agents prevented three persons claiming to be from Taiwan bearing false passports and US visas from boarding an aircraft bound for the United States.

The Paraguayan Congress rejected antiterrorism legislation that would have defined terrorism and established criminal penalties for activities related to terrorism. Many legislators fear that a corrupt government could use the new law to target political opposition.

Uruguay

Uruguay did not experience any acts of international terrorism in 2002. The Uruguayan Government has been supportive of the global Coalition's war against terrorism and routinely condemns acts of international terrorism. Uruguay is a party to eight of the 12 international conventions and protocols relating to terrorism. Although Uruguay does not have the financial or military resources to play a direct role in the war on terrorism, it provides troops to international peacekeeping missions in Africa and the Middle East. Uruguay has seconded staff to the secretariat of the OAS Inter-American Committee Against Terrorism (CICTE) and, following its offer to host CICTE in 2004, was elected Vice Chair in early 2003.

Uruguayan authorities routinely share information and cooperate on counterterrorism efforts with their counterparts —Argentina, Brazil, and Paraguay. Since the Islamic extremist activity is centered on Uruguay's northern border with Brazil, the two countries have worked together closely.

In 2002, Uruguayan law-enforcement authorities assisted with international investigations to monitor the movements and activities of suspected terrorists, and the Parliament is currently drafting new terrorism laws that will further facilitate domestic and international counterterrorism efforts. The Uruguayan Government readily cooperates with US Government requests to investigate individuals or financial transactions linked to terrorism.

Egypt has asked Uruguay to extradite suspected al-Gama'a al-Islamiyya (Islamic Group, IG) terrorist al-Said Hassan Mokhles, wanted in connection with the 1997 attack on tourists in Luxor, Egypt. He has been held in Uruguay since early 1999 on charges of document fraud, but Uruguay and Egypt have been unable to agree on the terms for extradition, in part, because Egypt has not guaranteed in writing that Mokhles will not be subject to the death penalty.

Venezuela

While the Venezuelan Government expressed sympathy in the months following the 11 September 2001 attacks, Caracas made it clear that it opposed the use of force in Afghanistan and has sent mixed signals during the war on terrorism. Venezuela signed the OAS Inter-American Convention Against Terrorism in June 2002, but has not yet ratified the treaty. Venezuela is a party to four of the 12 international conventions and protocols relating to terrorism.

Nevertheless, Venezuelan laws do not support the efficient investigation of terrorist organization financing or activities; the United States during 2002 provided technical assistance to help the Government of Venezuela assess vulnerabilities in its financial system and to plan appropriate policy remedies. The political crisis at the end of the year, however, had pushed all unrelated issues to the backburner. While Venezuela did extradite two members of the terrorist organization Basque Fatherland and Liberty to Spain, reports abounded that the Revolutionary Armed Forces of Colombia (FARC) and the Colombian National Liberation Army were using the border area between Venezuela and Colombia for cross-border incursions and as an unchallenged safehaven for the guerrillas. Additionally, unconfirmed reports persist that elements of the Venezuelan Government may have provided material support to the FARC, particularly weapons.

Canada

At the end of 2001, the Canadian Parliament passed into law an antiterrorism act that toughens penalties for terrorists and terrorist supporters and provides new investigative tools for Canadian law-enforcement and national-security agencies. It also makes terrorist fundraising illegal and allows officials to freeze the assets of suspected terrorists, but it cannot be applied retroactively to activities before the law was passed. In July 2002, Canadian officials published a list of banned terrorist organizations pursuant to the antiterrorism act, which consisted of al-Qaida and six of its known affiliate groups. Addendums to the list in late November and mid-December added nine more groups, including HAMAS and Hizballah, and Canadian officials expect the list to grow further as they examine and evaluate more organizations.

The Government of Canada has been a helpful and strong supporter of the United States in the fight against international terrorism. Despite some differences in approach, overall antiterrorism cooperation with Canada remains excellent and is a model for bilateral cooperation on counterterrorism issues. Seven US law-enforcement agencies have officers posted to Ottawa and other Canadian cities. Canadian law-enforcement personnel, in turn, are assigned to the United States.

Some US law-enforcement officers have expressed concern that Canadian privacy laws, as well as funding levels for law enforcement, inhibit a fuller and more timely exchange of information and response to requests for assistance. Also, Canadian laws and regulations intended to protect Canadian citizens and landed immigrants from Government intrusion sometimes limit the depth of investigations.

The US Attorney General and Canadian Solicitor General conduct policy coordination at the US-Canada Cross-Border Crime Forum, established during the Prime Minister's 1997 visit to Washington. (The Forum met most recently in Calgary in July 2002.) Under the US-Canada Terrorist Interdiction Program, or TIP, Canada records about one "hit" of known or suspected terrorists per week from the State Department's Visa Lookout List.

Additionally, Canada and the United States will hold a new round of talks under the auspices of the Bilateral Consultative Group on Counterterrorism Cooperation, or BCG. This bilateral group is tasked with reviewing international terrorist trends and planning ways to intensify joint counterterrorist efforts. It last met in June 2001 and was expected to meet in mid-2003. Other cooperative mechanisms include groups led by the immigration and customs services known as Border Vision and the Shared Border Accord, extradition and mutual legal-assistance treaties, and an information-sharing agreement between the US Drug Enforcement Administration and the Royal Canadian Mounted Police. In 2002, Canada cooperated with the United States in implementing most provisions of the Smart Border Action Plan. This plan and its bilateral implementation have become a model for securing national frontiers while ensuring the free and rapid flow of legitimate travel and commerce.

Canada has continued to be a strong supporter of international efforts to combat terrorism. Besides signing and ratifying the International Convention for the Suppression of Terrorist Financing and implementing UN Security Council Resolution 1373, Canada is active in the G-7, G-8, and G-20 and promotes the Financial Action Task Force on Money Laundering's Special Recommendations on Terrorist Financing and other international efforts to counter terrorist financing.

Continued in Volume 2, page 536.